P9-DGB-703

SHERLOCK HOLMES

THE NOVELS

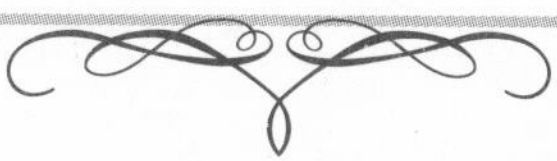

OTHER ANNOTATED BOOKS FROM W. W. NORTON & COMPANY

The Annotated Alice
by Lewis Carroll, edited with an introduction
and notes by Martin Gardner

The Annotated Wizard of Oz
by L. Frank Baum, edited with an introduction
and notes by Michael Patrick Hearn

The Annotated Huckleberry Finn
by Mark Twain, edited with an introduction
and notes by Michael Patrick Hearn

The Annotated Christmas Carol
by Charles Dickens, edited with an introduction
and notes by Michael Patrick Hearn

The Annotated Classic Fairy Tales
Translated and edited with an introduction
and notes by Maria Tatar

The Annotated Brothers Grimm
Translated and edited with a preface
and notes by Maria Tatar

The New Annotated Sherlock Holmes, Volumes I and II,
by Sir Arthur Conan Doyle, with an introduction by John le Carré, edited
with a foreword and notes by Leslie S. Klinger

The Annotated Uncle Tom's Cabin
by Harriet Beecher Stowe, edited with an
introduction and notes by Henry Louis Gates Jr.
and Hollis Robbins
(forthcoming)

ALSO BY LESLIE S. KLINGER

The Life and Times of Mr. Sherlock Holmes, John H. Watson, M.D., Sir Arthur Conan Doyle, and Other Notable Personages

"The Date Being?"—A Compendium of Chronological Data (with Andrew Jay Peck)

The Adventure of the Wooden Box

THE SHERLOCK HOLMES REFERENCE LIBRARY:

Adventures of Sherlock Holmes

Memoirs of Sherlock Holmes

A Study in Scarlet

The Hound of the Basekervilles

Return of Sherlock Holmes

The Sign of Four

The Valley of Fear

His Last Bow (forthcoming)

Case-Book of Sherlock Holmes (forthcoming)

Leslie S. Klinger is the editor of the *Sherlock Holmes Reference Library*, a nine-volume scholarly edition of the Sherlock Holmes stories published by Gasogene Press. The *Reference Library* quotes extensively from published Sherlockian criticism and provides detailed reviews of the scholarly literature.

Sherlock Holmes.
Unpublished drawing by Sidney Paget. Reprinted with the permission of Constantine Rossakis, BSI, and Sotheby's

W. W. NORTON & COMPANY
New York London

SHERLOCK HOLMES

THE NOVELS

A STUDY IN SCARLET
THE SIGN OF FOUR
THE HOUND OF THE BASKERVILLES
THE VALLEY OF FEAR

SIR ARTHUR CONAN DOYLE

Edited with annotations by LESLIE S. KLINGER

With additional research by JANET BYRNE and PATRICIA J. CHUI

This book is published by arrangement with Wessex Press, LLC.

Illustrations by Frederic Dorr Steele reproduced with permission of the Eastern Press.

Grateful acknowledgment to the Estate of Dame Jean Conan Doyle for permission to publish *The Case-Book of Sherlock Holmes* by Sir Arthur Conan Doyle, protected by copyright in the United States of America.

Printed in the United States of America
First Edition

Manufacturing by Courier Westford
Book design by JAM Design
Production manager: Julia Druskin

Library of Congress Cataloging-in-Publication Data

Doyle, Arthur Conan, Sir, 1859–1930.
The new annotated Sherlock Holmes / by Sir Arthur Conan Doyle ; edited, with a foreword and notes by Leslie S. Klinger ; introduction by John le Carré ; with additional research by Patricia J. Chui.
p. cm.
Includes bibliographical references.
ISBN 0-393-05916-2 (v. 1 and v. 2)
1. Holmes, Sherlock (Fictitious character)—Fiction. 2. Watson, John H. (Fictitious character)—Fiction. 3. Private investigators—England—Fiction. 4. Detective and mystery stories, English. I. Klinger, Leslie. II. Title.
PR4621.K55 2005
823'.8—dc22
2004007890

ISBN 0-393-05800-X

W. W. Norton & Company, Inc., 500 Fifth Avenue, New York, N.Y. 10110
www.wwnorton.com

W. W. Norton & Company Ltd., Castle House, 75/76 Wells Street, London W1T 3QT

1 2 3 4 5 6 7 8 9 0

To Sir Arthur Conan Doyle

"Steel true, blade straight"

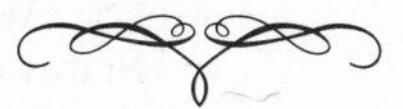

Contents

PREFACE

In 1968, when I was supposed to be engrossed in law school studies, I received a gift of William S. Baring-Gould's *The Annotated Sherlock Holmes*, published the previous year. This magical pair of volumes entranced me and led me back to the stories that I had enjoyed when I was young(er) and had subsequently forgotten. More importantly, the books introduced me to the idea of Sherlockian scholarship, the "game" of treating the stories as biography, not fiction. In later years, as I avidly collected things Sherlockian, I dreamed that someday I, too, would produce an annotated version of the Canon.

Baring-Gould's *Annotated Sherlock Holmes* remained in print for more than twenty-five years and became the cornerstone of every Sherlock Holmes library. Yet it had its idiosyncrasies, with the stories arranged in the controversial chronological order created by Baring-Gould and with footnotes that embraced, in many cases, Baring-Gould's questionable theories regarding the life of Holmes. Furthermore, there were occasional errors that were never corrected because, sadly, Baring-Gould did not live to see publication of his greatest work. While the *Oxford Sherlock Holmes*, published in 1993, presented the stories in nine volumes (as they were originally published in book form), the scholarly notes largely ignored Sherlockian scholarship, concentrating more traditionally on analysis of Doyle's sources.

I set out to create for the first time an annotated set that reflected the spectrum of views on Sherlockian controversies, rather than the editor's own theories. In addition, this work brings current Baring-Gould's long-outdated survey of the literature, including references to hundreds of works published subsequently. In recognition that many of the events recorded in the stories took place in England over 100 to 150 years ago, it also includes extensive background information on the Victorian age, its history, culture, and vocabulary. For the serious scholar of the Sherlockian Canon, there is an extensive bibliography at the end of this volume. A chronological table, summarising the key dates in the lives of Holmes, Watson, and Conan Doyle, and major world events, is also set forth at the end of the volume. I have avoided "lawyerly" citations of the works consulted, but full citations may be found in the nine volumes of my *Sherlock Holmes Reference Library*, published by Gasogene Books.

Thirty-eight years have passed since publication of Baring-Gould's monumental work, and the world of Sherlock Holmes has grown much larger. This edition was created with the assistance of new resources that now exist for the serious student—Ronald L. DeWaal's *Universal Sherlock Holmes*, Jack Tracy's *Encyclopaedia Sherlockiana*, Steve Clarkson's *Canonical Compendium*, and scores of other handbooks, reference works, indexes, and collections, many in computerised format. It also reflects the aid of a new tool—the Internet, which makes immense quantities of minute information accessible to the student.

This is not a work for the serious student of Arthur Conan Doyle. While Doylean scholarship is vitally important, the reader of these volumes will not find reference to the literary sources of the stories or to biographical incidents in the life of Sir Arthur that may be reflected in the Canon. Here I perpetuate the gentle fiction that Holmes and Watson really lived and that (except as noted) Dr. John H. Watson wrote the stories about Sherlock Holmes, even though he graciously allowed them to be published under the byline of his colleague and literary agent Sir Arthur Conan Doyle.

To keep this work from approaching the length of a telephone book, it is published in three volumes: The first two volumes consist of the fifty-six short stories which appeared from 1887 to 1927 (Vol. I containing the stories collected in the volumes called *Adventures of Sherlock Holmes* and *Memoirs of Sherlock Holmes*, Vol. II containing the stories collected under the titles of *Return of Sherlock Holmes*, *His Last Bow*, and *Case-Book of Sherlock Holmes*); the third volume presents the four novels *A Study in Scarlet*, *The Sign of Four*, *The Hound of the Baskervilles*, and *The Valley of Fear*. To avoid constant cross-reference to other volumes, and reflecting its separate publication, this volume repeats the relevant parts of notes that appear in the first two volumes. All in all, here is the complete record of the career of Mr. Sherlock Holmes. For the first-time reader of these tales, my best advice is to plunge immediately into the stories, skipping the introduction. Whether this is your first reading or your fifty-first reading of the Canon, I wish you joy in the experience, and I hope that you find that this edition enriches it.

SHERLOCK HOLMES

THE NOVELS

1 *A Study in Scarlet* was published in *Beeton's Christmas Annual* for 1887, alongside two plays: *Food for Powder*, by R. André, and *The Four-Leaved Shamrock*, by C. J. Hamilton. The first book edition of *A Study in Scarlet* was published by Ward, Lock & Co. in July 1888; the first American edition was published in 1890 by J. B. Lippincott Company. The 1893 edition published by Ward, Lock & Bowden Limited (the successors to the original publisher) added a "Publishers' Note to this Edition," as follows: "As it is in 'A Study in Scarlet' that Mr. Sherlock Holmes is first introduced to the public, and his methods of work described, it occurred to the publishers of the volume that a paper on 'Sherlock Holmes,' which Dr. Doyle's old master, Dr. Joseph Bell, the original of Sherlock Holmes, contributed recently to *The Bookman*, would greatly interest readers who did not see it when it appeared in that publication.

"Dr. Bell's 'intuitive powers' in dealing

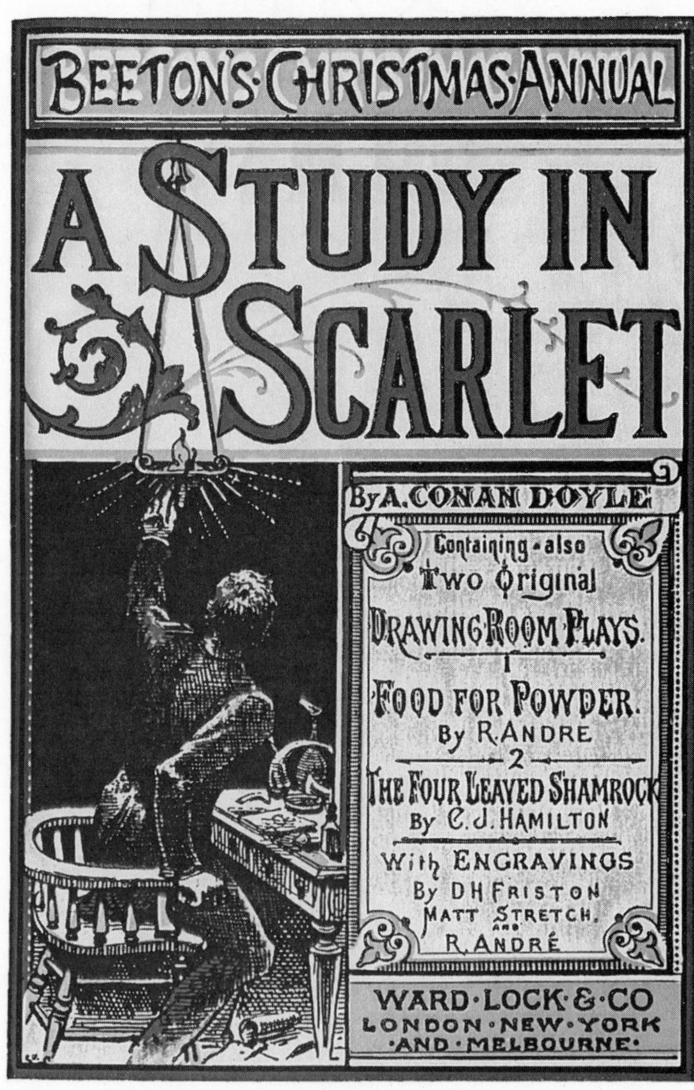

Beeton's Christmas Annual (1887).
Artist unknown

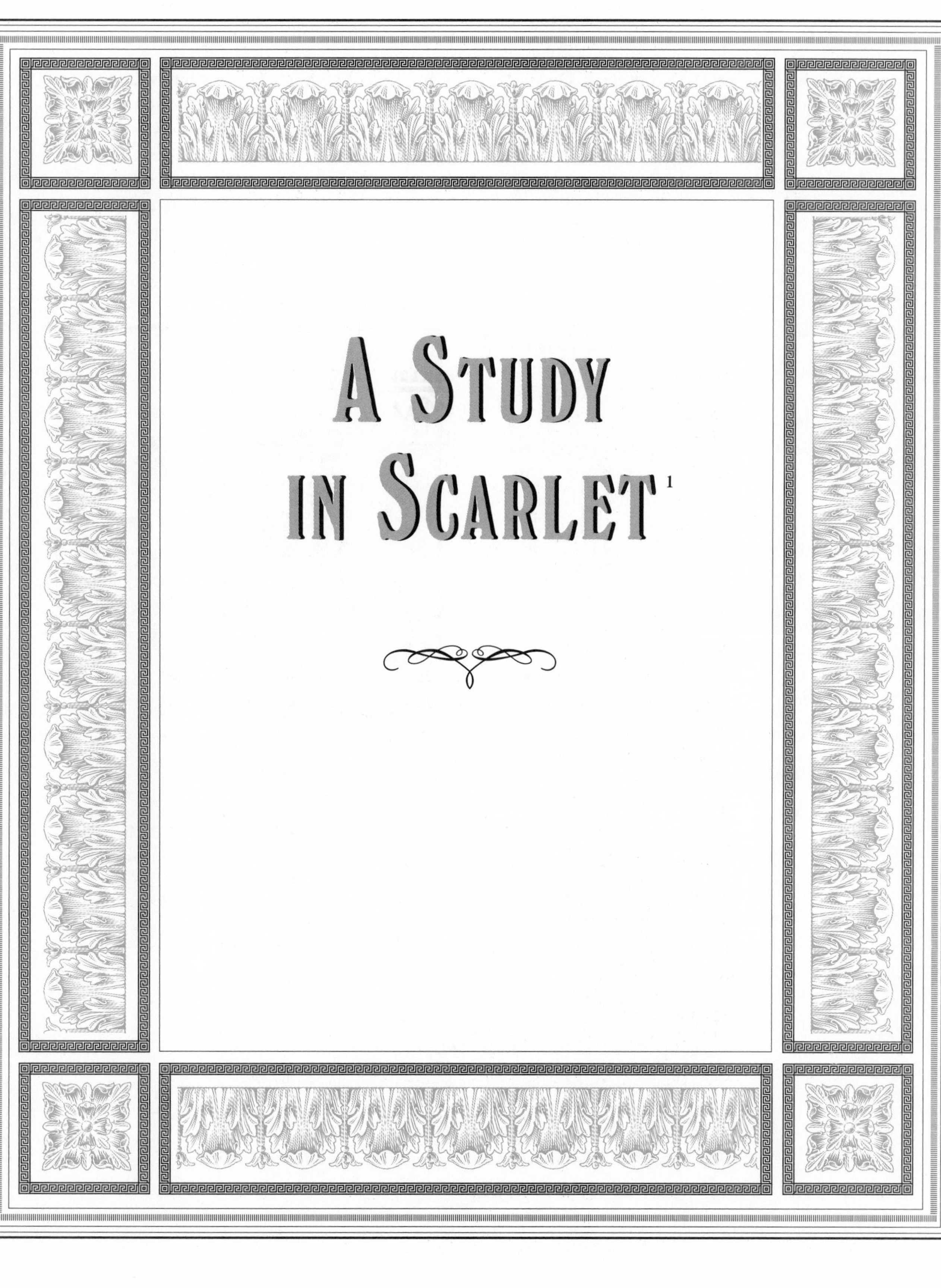

A Study in Scarlet[1]

with his patients were, so his pupil, Dr. Doyle, tells us in the pages of *The Strand Magazine*, 'simply marvellous.' Case No. 1 would step up.

> "I see," said Mr. Bell, "you're suffering from drink. You even carry a flask in the inside breast pocket of your coat."
>
> Another case would come forward.
>
> "Cobbler, I see." Then he would turn to the students, and point out to them that the inside of the knee of the man's trousers was worn. That was where the man had rested the lapstone—a peculiarity only found in cobblers.
>
> All this impressed me very much. He was continually before me—his sharp, piercing eyes, eagle nose, and striking features. There he would sit in in his chair with fingers together—he was very dextrous with his hands—and just look at the man or woman before him. He was most kind and painstaking with the students—a real good friend—and when I took my degree and went to Africa the remarkable individuality and discriminating tact of my old master made a deep and lasting impression on me, though I had not the faintest idea that it would one day lead me to forsake medicine for story-writing.

"That it did lead Dr. Doyle 'to forsake medicine for story-writing,' and with what result, every one knows. And as Mr. Sherlock Holmes has now become a household word and almost a public institution, the publishers of 'A Study in Scarlet' hope that the following paper, in which some particulars of Dr. Doyle's early education and training, and of the circumstances which led him to form the habit of making careful observations, will prove of interest to his many readers. Their cordial thanks are due to Dr. Doyle, Dr. Bell, and to the editor and proprietors of *The Bookman* for courteously consenting to the reproduction of the paper." (Dr. Bell's paper is reproduced as an *Appendix* to this tale.)

A Study in Scarlet.
(London: Ward Lock & Co., 1888)

A Study in Scarlet

Scholars and casual Sherlockians alike have come to regard A Study in Scarlet *(1887) as a fascinating book of Genesis, as it marked the very first public appearance of Sherlock Holmes. Here, after a brief glimpse of Watson's life before Baker Street, we are witness to a momentous occasion: the initial meeting between Sherlock Holmes and his "Boswell," Dr. John H. Watson, in a hospital laboratory. ("I've found it! I've found it," are Holmes's first words, appropriately enough.) The two men decide to share lodgings, and Watson discovers that his new roommate has an unorthodox occupation, as the world's sole consulting detective. Soon enough, the unsuspecting doctor finds himself involved in a dark tale of revenge and murder. Central to Watson's account of Holmes's brilliant detection is a "flashback"-type narrative, penned by an unknown author, of the Mormons in Utah under the leadership of Brigham Young. Arresting and lively, the account nonetheless reflects Victorian England's distorted views of the Mormons and their history in the American West.*

When one compares this picture of the youthful Holmes (he was only twenty-seven when he met Watson) to the balance of the Canon, it is apparent that the Master's character changed little over the years of his remarkable career. His secretiveness, his bohemian habits, and his low opinion of the official police are all on display here; and while Holmes's drug use is only hinted at, his other vices and virtues are quickly revealed to the reader (although Watson's early assessments of Holmes's "limits" are soon disproved). The author of A Study in Scarlet *may have earned little commercial reward from the book's early publication, but the stage was set for what would later become the most successful series of stories ever published.*

PART I

(Being a reprint from the reminiscences of John H.[2] Watson, M.D., late of the Army Medical Department[3])[4]

CHAPTER I

MR. SHERLOCK HOLMES

IN THE YEAR 1878 I took my degree of Doctor of Medicine[5] of the University of London,[6] and proceeded to Netley[7] to go through the course prescribed for surgeons in the Army.[8] Having completed my studies there, I was duly attached to the Fifth Northumberland Fusiliers[9] as Assistant Surgeon. The regiment was stationed in India at the time, and before I could join it, the second Afghan war[10] had broken out. On landing at Bombay, I learned that my corps had advanced through the passes, and was already deep in the enemy's country. I followed, however, with many other officers who were in the same situation as myself, and succeeded in reaching Candahar[11] in safety, where I found my regiment, and at once entered upon my new duties.

The campaign brought honours and promotion to many, but for me it had nothing but misfortune and disaster. I was removed from my brigade and attached to the Berkshires,[12] with whom I served at the fatal battle of Maiwand.[13] There I was struck on the shoulder[14] by a Jezail[15] bullet, which shattered the bone and grazed the subclavian artery. I should have

2 Watson's middle initial appears in the Sherlock Holmes Canon only three times: at the foot of the sketch plan illustrating "The Priory School" (in the *Strand Magazine* for February 1904); on the lid of the tin box at Cox's Bank ("Thor Bridge"); and here. Dorothy L. Sayers, in her classic article "Dr. Watson's Christian Name," argues that the "H" stands for "Hamish," a Scotch equivalent to "James" (see "Man with the Twisted Lip" for an instance in which Watson's wife refers to him as "James"). Several other scholars propose "Henry," owing primarily to high contemporary regard for John Henry Newman (1801–1890), the cardinal who helped found the Oxford movement by attempting to incorporate Roman Catholic practices into the Church of England. Still others, for varied but ultimately unconvincing reasons, propose "Hampton," "Harrington," "Hector," "Horatio," "Hubert," "Huffham," and even "Holmes."

Only fragments of the manuscript of *A Study in Scarlet* are extant, consisting of one page of notes for the story and a four-line excerpt from a notebook, reproduced here. The page of notes reveals that Dr. Watson originally considered using the pseudonyms Sherrinford Holmes and Ormond Sacker (the latter for himself). Whether the names he eventually used are the parties' *real* names is a subject beyond the scope of this work. See this editor's "What Do We Really Know About Sherlock Holmes and John H. Watson?"

3 Army surgeon-majors and surgeons were attached to regiments and corps, or served as executive officers in the hospitals. Every battalion in India had one surgeon-major and two surgeons. An appointment as a surgeon brought a starting rank as a lieutenant; six years' full-pay service qualified the practitioner as a captain. There is no mention in the Canon of Watson's rank, but his title would have been Acting Surgeon (the Assistant Surgeon title was abolished in 1872) and his pay grade that of a lieutenant.

Windsor Magazine Christmas Number (1895). Artist unknown

10

'A tangled skein—' A Study in scarlet.
The terrified woman rushing up to the cabman. The two going in search of a policeman. John Reeves had been 7 years in the force, John Reeves went back with them.

Notes for *A Study in Scarlet.*

4 Edgar W. Smith proposes, in "A Bibliographical Note," that Watson's "reminiscences" were originally published privately in 1885 or so; and that in addition to the material reprinted as *A Study in Scarlet*, they covered "an assortment of the doctor's earlier writings." These may have included Watson's experiences with women "extending over many nations and three separate continents" (*The Sign of Four*) and further details of his experiences in India. "There was much he had to say," Smith concludes, ". . . being the man he was."

Bliss Austin concurs with the notion that Watson's reminiscences were printed prior to their inclusion in *A Study in Scarlet.* He goes on to argue that they served as the basis for Watson's meeting Arthur Conan Doyle, who was to serve a pivotal role in the doctor's literary career. In his autobiography *Memories and Adventures*, Austin points out, Conan Doyle may well have been thinking of Watson when he wrote, "My pleasant recollection of those days from 1880 to 1893 lay in my first introduction, as a more or less rising author, to the literary life of London." Among the authors he noted meeting were "Rudyard Kipling, James Stephen Phillips, Watson . . . and a whole list of others."

Yet not everyone agrees that "reprint" necessarily signifies a previous printing. John Ball, for one, concludes, in "The Second Collaboration," that the reminiscences were never published at all but that this statement was Conan Doyle's way of recognising Watson's co-authorship of the work (Conan Doyle, Ball deduces, wrote "The Country of the Saints"—see note 241, below).

5 In order to receive his M.D., Watson would have first had to acquire membership in the Royal College of Surgeons and a licence from the Royal College of Physicians, according to Michael Harrison's *The London of Sherlock Holmes*. The latter two qualifications were essential for Watson to open his own medical practice; the M.D. degree, however, indicates that Watson continued his education past the normal medical degree, the M.B. (equivalent to the American M.D.), in pursuit of his interests. In *Sherlock Holmes and Dr. Watson: A Medical Digression*, Maurice Campbell surmises that Watson received his Bachelor of Medicine (M.B., B.S.—a prerequisite for the M.D. degree) in 1876 from St. Bartholomew's Hospital Medical College (see note 28, below). Robert S. Katz, M.D., in "Doctor Watson—A Physician of Mediocre Qualifications?," points out that the British M.D. degree is conditioned on presentation of a thesis of outstanding merit and concludes that Watson wrote his thesis on neuropathology, a remarkable achievement in light of the fledgling nature of the field in 1878.

6 When London's first university college was founded in Bloomsbury in 1828, its mission was—at least in part—to make higher education available to non-Anglicans, who were at that time barred from attending Oxford and Cambridge. "It was a true London institution," writes Peter Ackroyd in *London: The Biography*, "its founders comprising radicals, Dissenters, Jews and utilitarians." (Historian Roy Porter reports that critics scorned it as "that godless institution in Gower Street.") The college's educational philosophy, too, differed fundamentally from that of Oxford and Cambridge: the goal of what became known as University College was to produce practising doctors and engineers, not scholars and theologians. A second London college, King's College, was founded in 1829 by members of the Anglican church; and in 1836, the University of London was formed as an administrative entity designed to examine and confer degrees upon students from both institutions. That jurisdiction was broadened by the Supplemental Charter of 1849, which allowed students from anywhere in the British Empire to earn degrees from the University of London. In 1878—the year Watson earned his degree—the university became the first in the United Kingdom to grant degrees to women, and in fact had been educating women at its London School of Medicine for Women since 1874. The university did not begin offering its own courses until 1900. There is no indication of where Watson actually studied.

Watson's course of study likely followed along lines similar to those pursued by Dr. Arthur Conan Doyle, when he studied at the University of Edinburgh from 1876 to 1881. In his *Memories and Adventures*, Conan Doyle

"The London University Building, Burlington Gardens," by Pennethorne.
Graphic (1870)

describes his course of study as "one long weary grind at botany, chemistry, anatomy, physiology and a whole list of compulsory subjects, many of which have a very indirect bearing upon the art of curing. The whole system of teaching, as I look back upon it, seems far too oblique and not nearly practical enough for the purpose in view." Students learned surgery by observing operations from seats in tiers encircling an operating table. Basic laboratory techniques were also studied, and the fortunate had the benefit of instructors like Dr. Joseph Bell, who could teach the art of diagnosis (see note 1, above). Conan Doyle took employment during his school years as a medical assistant (which required no qualifications), both for the money and the practical experience.

Conan Doyle's living experience, however, may have been markedly different from Watson's. Conan Doyle found the University of Edinburgh to be "more practical than most other colleges," he wrote, "since there is none of the atmosphere of an enlarged public school, as is the case in English Universities, but the student lives a free man in his own rooms with no restrictions of any sort." Where Watson lived during these years is unknown.

7 The Royal Victoria Military Hospital at Netley (now the site of the Royal Victoria Country Park) was opened in 1863 thanks largely to the efforts of Florence Nightingale, whose experiences in the Crimean War inspired her to fight for better medical treatment for wounded soldiers. Lytton Strachey, in his seminal *Emininent Victorians*, recounts that Nightingale frequently butted heads in this mission with Fox Maule Ramsay, Lord Panmure (known as "the Bison"), the secretary of state for war from 1855 to 1858 and a man, according to Strachey, who was conservative and ambivalent about making any major changes in the established medical order. Lord Panmure supervised construction of the new hospital while Nightingale was out of the country, and she returned to find the plans unacceptable—outdated and adhering to notions of hospital care that she had hoped to reform. Despite her personal appeal to Lord Palmerston, Lord Panmure stood his ground, and construction proceeded apace; "and so," Strachey writes, "the chief military hospital in England was triumphantly completed on unsanitary principles, with unventilated rooms, and with all the patients' windows facing northeast."

8 The prescribed course at Netley consisted of six months' study of military surgery, military medicine, hygiene, and pathology. Two sessions or courses were given each year, one beginning in April, the other in October, for candidates who passed an entrance examination. Elliot Kimball, in *Dr. John H. Watson at Netley*, establishes that Watson took the course beginning in October 1879 and terminating in March 1880, having spent the time between June 1878 and October 1879 travelling on the Continent for personal reasons.

9 Created in 1674, the 5th Regiment of Foot—also known as the Fifth Foot, the Fighting Fifth, and the Old and Bold Fifth—became the 5th (Northumberland) Regiment of Fusiliers in 1836, its members serving in the Indian Mutiny and the Second Afghan War. The regiment was renamed as the Northumberland Fusiliers in 1881.

10 The Second Afghan War (1878–1880) was one of three conflicts in which Britain tried to exert control over Afghanistan, a region considered extremely valuable for its northern proximity to India. Further complicating matters was the concern that Russia was gaining greater influence in central Asia, thus posing a threat to British imperialism there. It was an anxiety held most deeply by the viceroy of India, Edward Robert Bulwer-Lytton, future

1st Earl of Lytton (a diplomat and sometime poet whose father, Edward George Earle Bulwer-Lytton, 1st Baron of Lytton, penned the famous "It was a dark and stormy night," the first words of the opening sentence of his 1830 novel *Paul Clifford*). When the emir of Afghanistan, Sher Ali, received a Russian diplomatic mission in Kabul and refused to do likewise for the British, Lytton interpreted the emir's actions as hostile and called for military maneuvers. "The usual British invasion," writes Simon Schama in *A History of Britain*, "was followed by the equally time-honoured local uprising and wholesale slaughter of the British mission, which as usual required a second, punitive campaign—in this case punitive for the British in the losses of both men and money." Victory was achieved and certain areas of Afghanistan ceded to Britain, but the war's heavy cost (including the murder of a British envoy at Kabul) helped turn public opinion against the government's increasingly jingoistic tendencies.

The charge at Maiwand.

11 Also spelled Kandahar or Qandahar, the city was established as the capital of Afghanistan in 1747. It was occupied by the British during the First Afghan War (1839–1842) and from 1879 to 1881.

12 The Berkshires, officially Princess Charlotte of Wales's (Berkshire) Regiment, was formed in 1881 from the former 49th and 66th Infantry Regiments. The 66th Foot, as it was known, fought at Maiwand, but by the time Watson wrote up his account (and perhaps by the time he was retired) the Regiment had been incorporated into the Berkshires, and Watson uses the then-current name here.

13 The village of Maiwand, fifty miles from Kandahar, was the scene of a horrific battle that took place on July 27, 1880. The conflict began after Ayub Khan, the governor of Herat and a son of Sher Ali, advanced upon Kandahar with a contingent of 25,000 men. His intent was to displace Sher Ali's nephew, Abdur-Rahman Khan, now installed as the British-approved emir. General George Burrows and the 66th Infantry Regiment set out to intercept Ayub with the understanding that aid would come from some 6,000 Afghan tribesmen who had been armed by the British. But when the

"There I was struck on the shoulder by a bullet."
Geo. Hutchinson, *A Study in Scarlet* (London: Ward, Lock Bowden, and Co., 1891)

tribesmen defected to join Ayub, the general was left with 2,500 British soldiers to face a force of 25,000 Afghans. "When the enemy cavalry cleared the front," wrote Captain Mosley Mayne, of the 3rd Cavalry, "we were able to see indistinctly masses and masses of men. Due to the haze it was only when they moved about that we could distinguish them as men and not a dense forest." Burrows's forces were routed, and Ayub occupied Maiwand until Sir Frederick Roberts arrived from Kabul with a force of 10,000 to retake the area. Walter Richards, historian of the British Army in India, writes, "There is no grimmer story in all the war annals of the country; no names shine in her honour-roll with more brilliant lustre than do those of the officers and men of the 66th who died in that wild day of terror and ruin on the fatal ridge of Maiwand."

14 Watson's report here of a wounded shoulder contradicts his testimony—in *The Sign of Four* and elsewhere—of a wounded leg. In "The Noble Bachelor," for example, Watson mentions that "the Jezail bullet which I had brought back in one of my limbs" forces him to sit with his legs propped up on a chair, and in *The Sign of Four*, he describes himself as seated "nursing my wounded leg. I had had a jezail bullet through it some time before." W. B. Hepburn, in "The Jezail Bullet," reaches the logical conclusion that Watson was wounded twice, but many other scholars ingeniously attempt to explain how two wounds could have been caused by one bullet only. Alvin Rodin and Jack Key, in *Medical Casebook of Doctor Arthur Conan Doyle*, suggest that Watson may have been bent over a patient when shot, with the bullet passing through Watson's shoulder *and* leg. Similarly, Peter Brain proposes that Watson was shot from below while squatting over a cliff to answer a call of nature. Others hypothesise that a single bullet may have ricocheted off the bone, grazed the artery, left the body at an

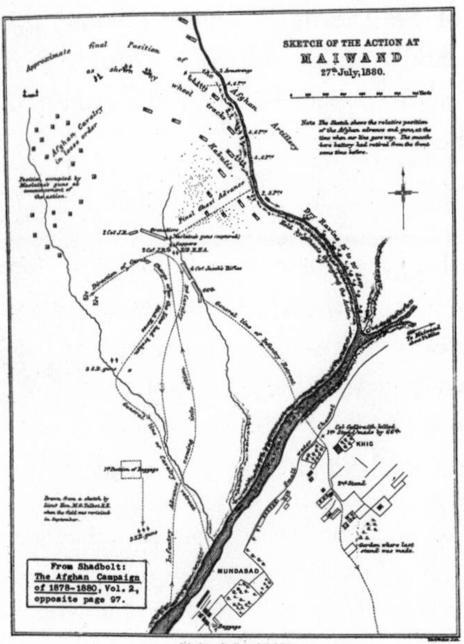

Sketch of the action at Maiwand on July 27, 1880.

acute angle, and then entered the leg, while several physician-scholars point out that the bullet may have passed along the subclavian artery and lodged in a place remote from the entry wound. Julian Wolff, however, concludes that Watson deliberately misrepresented the site of the wound so as to avoid mentioning the actual, embarrassing site: his groin.

15 Although the original text is "Jezail," the correct form of the word is "jezail," not capitalised, referring not to an Afghan tribe but to a type of gun. Whether this is a printer's error or the author's is unclear. According to George

Jezail rifle.
Courtesy of Richard D. Lesh, BSI, and the Maiwand Jezails, a scion society of the BSI.

fallen into the hands of the murderous Ghazis[16] had it not been for the devotion and courage shown by Murray,[17] my orderly, who threw me across a pack-horse, and succeeded in bringing me safely to the British lines.

Worn with pain, and weak from the prolonged hardships which I had undergone, I was removed, with a great train of wounded sufferers, to the base hospital at Peshawur. Here I rallied, and had already improved so far as to be able to walk about the wards, and even to bask a little upon the verandah, when I was struck down by enteric fever,[18] that curse of our Indian possessions. For months my life was despaired of, and when at last I came to myself and became convalescent, I was so weak and emaciated that a medical board determined that not a day should be lost in sending me back to England. I was despatched, accordingly, in the troopship *Orontes*, and landed a

"I should have fallen into the hands of the murderous ghazis had it not been for the devotion and courage shown by Murray, my orderly."
Richard Gutschmidt, *Späte Rache* (Stuttgart: Robert Lutz Verlag, 1902)

Clifford Whitworth (*An Anglo-Indian Dictionary: A Glossary of Indian Terms Used in English and of Such English or Other Non-Indian Terms as Have Obtained Special Meaning in India*), "juzail (Pashto, corrupt form)" is a "large heavy rifle, with an iron forked rest, used by Afghâns; it carries generally an ounce ball, which is put into the barrel naked." The ball must be "hammered a good deal to get it home." Philip Weller, in "On Jezails and Things Afghan," describes the word as "a rather loose, generic term, similar in nature to the word 'musket,' in that it could be applied to lots of different sorts of weapons, with one of the only common features being the muzzle-loading aspect." It may be derived from the Arabic word for "big": *jazil* and, in the plural, *jaza'il*; the person armed with a *jezail* is a *jaza'ilchi*. In *Eighteen Years in the Khyber* (1900), the Anglo-Indian soldier and administrator Colonel Sir Robert Warburton (1842–1899) speaks of soldiers called *Jezailchies*. And, in Rudyard Kipling's 1900 poem "The Last Suttee," "All night the cressets glimmered pale / On Ulwar sabre and Tonk jezail."

16 "Ghazi" was an honorific applied to veteran Muslim warriors, particularly for those who had fought successfully against infidels. They were reputed to use torture and painful methods of execution—hence Watson's description of them as "murderous."

17 Stephen M. Black contends that Watson was killed, not wounded, at Maiwand, and that "Murray" (whom he identifies as Pvt. Henry Murrell, Serial #1555, Rifleman, 66th Berkshires) took his identity. Murrell's guilt for this masquerade, Black argues, induced all of the errors of dates, places, and names rampant throughout the Canon, including his absentmindedness about his own wound.

18 Probably what is now termed typhoid fever, which Watson could have contracted by

The Prince Consort, Albert of Saxe-Coburg.
Oscar G. Reylander (*ca.* 1860)

ingesting food or water contaminated with the bacterium *Salmonella typhi*. Food may be contaminated by flies (who pick up the bacterium from human waste), by infected persons who may have handled the food, or by polluted water that has been used for cleaning. Typhoid fever unfortunately remains a common disease worldwide, with an estimated 10 percent fatality rate, and claimed the lives of many famous victims during the nineteenth century and early twentieth century, including Rudyard Kipling, Wilbur Wright, Franz Schubert, and Albert of Saxe-Coburg-Gotha, Victoria's consort (although later diagnosticians suggest Albert may have actually died from stomach cancer).

It was not until 1907, with the identification of the infamous "Typhoid Mary" Mallon, a cook in a private home, as the source of an outbreak of typhoid fever, that American health officials realised that a healthy person, with no symptoms of the disease, could be a deadly carrier. Initially confined to a government-controlled island in the Bronx's East River, after a legal struggle, Mallon won

month later on Portsmouth jetty, with my health irretrievably ruined, but with permission from a paternal government to spend the next nine months in attempting to improve it.

I had neither kith nor kin in England,[19] and was therefore as free as air—or as free as an income of eleven shillings and sixpence[20] a day will permit a man to be. Under such circumstances, I naturally gravitated to London, that great cesspool into which all the loungers and idlers of the Empire are irresistibly drained. There I stayed for some time at a private hotel[21] in the Strand,[22] leading a comfortless, meaningless existence, and spending such money as I had, considerably more freely than I ought. So alarming did the state of my finances become, that I soon realized that I must either leave the metropolis and rusticate somewhere in the country, or that I must make a complete alteration in my style of living.[23] Choosing the latter alternative, I began by making up my mind to leave the hotel, and to take up my quarters in some less pretentious and less expensive domicile.

On the very day that I had come to this conclusion,[24] I was standing at the Criterion Bar,[25] when someone tapped me on the shoulder, and turning round I recognized young Stamford,[26] who had been a dresser[27] under me at Bart's.[28] The sight of a friendly face in the great wilderness of London is a

Criterion Bar, interior (*ca.* 1881).

her release, agreeing to give up her occupation and report to health officials regularly. She proceeded to vanish for five years. When an epidemic of typhus broke out in a Manhattan maternity hospital, Mallon was discovered working there as a cook under a false name. She was again confined to the island facility, where she remained until her death twenty-three years later. The infection of forty-seven people, three of whom died, is attributed to Mallon. At the time of Mallon's first arrest, there was at least one other known carrier in New York, Tony Labella, who had caused more cases of typhoid (120) and deaths (seven) than Mallon. Labella fled to New Jersey and was no more cooperative than Mallon.

Watson's symptoms would have included fever, coughing, loss of appetite, diarrhea or constipation, possible intestinal haemorrhaging, and a skin rash of rose-coloured spots. A vaccine was not available until 1898, too late to aid Watson. A British soldier's risk of dying from a disease such as typhoid was often greater than his risk of dying in battle.

19 Where *were* Watson's "kith and kin"? Watson's father, J. Watson, had been dead "many years" by 1888, and his elder brother had died of drink shortly before the events recorded in *The Sign of Four* (see text accompanying note 32 to that novel, below). There are numerous suggestions of Watson's family home, including Hampshire, Berkshire, Northumberland, Ireland, Scotland, Australia, and even America. In "Watson: Treason in the Blood," Hartley R. Nathan and Clifford S. Goldfarb present evidence that Watson may have descended from two of the leaders of the 1816 Regency Rebellion, James Watson and his son James (Jemmy) Watson, who subsequently fled to America. Our Dr. Watson was in fact also named James, point out the authors (see "The Man with the Twisted Lip"), but evidently changed his name to John to avoid the stigma of identification with his grandfather and great-grandfather. This thesis explains Watson's lack of British family and suggests an American origin. In contrast, in "Art in Whose Blood?," this editor proposes a relationship with Scottish portrait painter John Watson Gordon (real name: John Watson).

20 This would have been worth about U.S. $2.87 in 1878, or about £29 (U.S. $45) in today's purchasing power. Eleven shillings and sixpence would have been barely enough to support Watson in London, where lodgings at a boardinghouse might have cost 7*s*. per day, although less expensive locations might have run as little as 30*s*. to 40*s*. per week. Several scholars suggest that Watson may have been receiving support from his family during this time, although his father and brother had little enough later (see *The Sign of Four*, text accompanying note 32).

21 *Baedeker*, in 1896, lists numerous "quiet and comfortable" hotels in the streets leading from the Strand to the Thames. For example, the Arundel Hotel, at No. 19 Arundel St., on the Embankment, charged from 6*s*. per day for "room, attendance, and breakfast," with dinner an additional 3*s*.

22 So named because it originally skirted the bank of the river Thames, the Strand was the great artery of traffic between the City and the West End. It contained many newspaper offices and theatres and has Canonical associations as the home of "Simpson's" restaurant, a favourite of Holmes ("The Dying Detective" and "The Illustrious Client"), and the namesake of the *Strand Magazine*, headquartered near the corner of the Strand and Southampton Street, as fancifully depicted on its cover.

23 John Ball expresses the view that Arthur Conan Doyle and Watson met at this time, for both were in similar circumstances, seeking gainful employment as doctors. Whether they met in the offices of a physician's supplier, at a lecture, or at a library, "a friendship and a collaboration was formed which was to enrich the world. For, great as was the association between Dr. Watson and Sherlock Holmes, of nearly equal importance to posterity was the second collaboration between Dr. Watson and the other physician who was also destined for immortal fame, Dr. Arthur Conan Doyle."

24 The novelist and Sherlockian scholar Christopher Morley, founder of the Baker Street Irregulars, in an unpublished letter to Edgar Smith, then editor of the *Baker Street Journal*, proposes January 1, 1881, as the day of Watson's fateful decision—"a day when Watson would naturally be making resolutions for a more frugal life." The holiday also explains, suggests Morley, why the laboratory to which Stamford led Watson was all but deserted.

25 The Criterion, more formally the American Bar at the Criterion, near Piccadilly Circus, was an establishment that Michael Harrison deems (in *The London of Sherlock Holmes*) "one of London's then more expensive bars." It was also, according to James E. Holroyd, a gathering place for horse-racing aficionados—thus, a likely haunt for Watson, whom Holmes, in "Shoscombe Old Place," affectionately referred to as his "Handy Guide to the Turf." Today the Bar is gone, but the Criterion *Brasserie* has returned to its former architectural glory, and a plaque at the *Brasserie* commemorates the meeting of Stamford and Watson.

26 J. N. Williamson, in "The Sad Case of Young Stamford," argues that "young Stamford" had criminal tendencies known to Holmes, which explains why Stamford declined the opportunity to room with Holmes. Young Stamford is the same person, according to Williamson, as Archie Stamford, the forger mentioned in passing in "The Solitary Cyclist." This same young man, in Williamson's theory, pops up again as "Archie," an associate of the villainous John Clay in "The Red-Headed League." Williamson posits that he was captured and apparently turned to lawful means of employment; Holmes sends to "Stamford" in the *Strand* text of *The Hound of the Baskervilles* to obtain an Ordnance map (although the latter is demonstrably a slip of the pen for "Stanford's," the well-known map establishment). Taking an altogether different tack is H.E.B. Curjel, who, in "Young Doctor Stamford of Barts," postulates that Stamford is a member of the teaching staff in the anatomy department of Barts—whereas Cal Wood, in "Stamford: A Closer Look," takes the somewhat far-fetched view that Stamford was Holmes's roommate.

27 A surgeon's assistant.

28 St. Bartholomew's Hospital Medical College, known popularly as "Barts" or "Bart's," was founded in 1123 by—legend has it—Rahere, a jester at Henry I's court. Having taken ill in Rome, Rahere prayed on the banks of the Tiber, on the island of St. Bartholomew, that he might recover in time to die on his native soil. St. Bartholomew appeared to him in a vision, commanding him to return to London and build a church and hospital in his name. By 1896, the hospital had grown to 678 beds, treating some 6,500 in-patients and 16,000 out-patients annually. Among the instructors at its famous medical school (which was opened in 1843) was William Harvey (1578–1657), who both determined the role of the heart in the circulation of blood and demonstrated how blood flowed in a continuous cycle.

A hansom cab outside the Albert Hall (1900).
Victorian and Edwardian London

pleasant thing indeed to a lonely man. In old days Stamford had never been a particular crony of mine, but now I hailed him with enthusiasm, and he, in his turn, appeared to be delighted to see me. In the exuberance of my joy, I asked him to lunch with me at the Holborn,[29] and we started off together in a hansom.

"Whatever have you been doing with yourself, Watson?" he asked in undisguised wonder, as we rattled through the crowded London streets. "You are as thin as a lath and as brown as a nut."[30]

I gave him a short sketch of my adventures, and had hardly concluded it by the time that we reached our destination.

"Poor devil!" he said, commiseratingly, after he had listened to my misfortunes. "What are you up to now?"

"Looking for lodgings," I answered. "Trying to solve the problem as to whether it is possible to get comfortable rooms at a reasonable price."

"That's a strange thing," remarked my companion; "you are the second man to-day that has used that expression to me."

"And who was the first?" I asked.

"A fellow who is working at the chemical laboratory up at the hospital. He was bemoaning himself this morning because he

29 An 1880 advertisement for the Holborn Restaurant described it as "one of the sights and one of the comforts of London," combining the "attractions of the chief Parisian establishments with the quiet and order essential to English custom." William H. Gill, in "Some Notable Sherlockian Buildings," takes a less benign view, describing the restaurant architecturally as "Victorian classicism at its worst."

The Holborn was known as a favoured establishment of the Prince of Wales, which may well have impressed the young Watson and Stamford. Lieut. Col. Newnham-Davis captured something of the Holborn's scale in his *Dinners and Diners: Where and How to Dine in London* (1899), in which he and his dining companion "wanted something a little more elaborate than a grill-room would give us, and more amusing company than we were likely to find at the smaller dining places we knew

Holborn Restaurant (*ca.* 1900).

THE HOLBORN RESTAURANT

Bill of Fare

FOR THE GRILL ROOM.

Thursday Evening July 17th, 1884.

	s.	d.
SOUPS.		
Thick or Clear Turtle	2	6
Mulligatawny	1	0
Consomme with Italian Paste		10
FISH.		
Boiled Salmon and Lobster Sauce	1	6
Eels Matelotte	1	0
Whitebait	1	0
ENTREES		
Calf's Head and Piquant Sauce	1	3
Pigeon and Peas	1	3
Haricot Ox Tail	1	0
POULTRY.		
Half Duckling	2	0
Half Roast Spring Chicken and Ham	2	0
Pigeon	1	6
ROAST GAME.		
Virginia Quail	1	3

Menu from the Holborn Restaurant, 1884.

of." During dinner in "the many-coloured marble hall, with its marble staircase springing from either side," Newnham-Davis and his companion listen to "a good band, but much too loud" and dine on beef and brussels sprouts, chicken and ham; when they refuse dessert, the waiter expresses concern "that something must be the matter with us, for most people at the Holborn eat their dinner steadily through." Chapter 16 of the same book recounts Newnham-Davis's dining experience at the American Bar at the Criterion, a "very good place for an undress dinner."

30 Ian McQueen expresses doubt that Watson's tan, if in fact acquired, would have survived his journey from Afghanistan to London. See note 81, below.

could not get someone to go halves with him in some nice rooms which he had found, and which were too much for his purse."

"By Jove!" I cried, "if he really wants someone to share the rooms and the expense, I am the very man for him. I should prefer having a partner to being alone."

Young Stamford looked rather strangely at me over his wine-glass.[31] "You don't know Sherlock Holmes yet," he said; "perhaps you would not care for him as a constant companion."

"Why, what is there against him?"

"Oh, I didn't say there was anything against him. He is a little queer in his ideas—an enthusiast in some branches of science. As far as I know he is a decent fellow enough."

"A medical student, I suppose?" said I.

"No—I have no idea what he intends to go in for. I believe he is well up in anatomy,[32] and he is a first-class chemist; but, as far as I know, he has never taken out any systematic medical classes. His studies are very desultory and eccentric, but he has amassed a lot of out-of-the-way knowledge which would astonish his professors."

"Did you never ask him what he was going in for?" I asked.

"No; he is not a man that it is easy to draw out, though he can be communicative enough when the fancy seizes him."

"I should like to meet him," I said. "If I am to lodge with anyone, I should prefer a man of studious and quiet habits. I am not strong enough yet to stand much noise or excitement. I had enough of both in Afghanistan to last me for the remainder of my natural existence. How could I meet this friend of yours?"

"He is sure to be at the laboratory," returned my companion. "He either avoids the place for weeks, or else he works there from morning to night. If you like, we shall drive round together after luncheon."

"Certainly," I answered, and the conversation drifted away into other channels.

As we made our way to the hospital after leaving the Holborn, Stamford gave me a few more particulars about the gentleman whom I proposed to take as a fellow-lodger.

"You mustn't blame me if you don't get on with him," he said; "I know nothing more of him than I have learned from meeting him occasionally in the laboratory. You proposed this arrangement, so you must not hold me responsible."

"If we don't get on it will be easy to part company," I answered. "It seems to me, Stamford," I added, looking hard at my companion, "that you have some reason for washing your hands of the matter. Is this fellow's temper so formidable, or what is it? Don't be mealy-mouthed about it."

"It is not easy to express the inexpressible," he answered with a laugh. "Holmes is a little too scientific for my tastes—it approaches to cold-bloodedness. I could imagine his giving a friend a little pinch of the latest vegetable alkaloid,[33] not out of malevolence, you understand, but simply out of a spirit of inquiry in order to have an accurate idea of the effects. To do him justice, I think that he would take it himself with the same readiness. He appears to have a passion for definite and exact knowledge."

"Very right too."

"Yes, but it may be pushed to excess. When it comes to beating the subjects in the dissecting-rooms with a stick,[34] it is certainly taking rather a bizarre shape."

"Beating the subjects!"

"Yes, to verify how far bruises may be produced after death. I saw him at it with my own eyes."

"And yet you say he is not a medical student?"

"No. Heaven knows what the objects of his studies are. But

St. Bartholomew's Hospital: the West Entrance.
Queen's London (1897)

31 S. C. Roberts, in *Dr. Watson*, wonders whether Stamford's strange look and hesitation meant that he foresaw his impending destiny as "one of the great liaison-officers of literary history"—comparable, in Roberts's view, to Tom Davies, who introduced Boswell to Dr. Samuel Johnson. The analogy is apt in light of Holmes's own characterisation of Watson as "my Boswell" ("A Scandal in Bohemia").

32 Watson comes to develop a slightly more sceptical view of Holmes's faculties, as in listing Holmes's "limits" he will soon deem Holmes's knowledge of anatomy "[a]ccurate, but unsystematic."

33 Alkaloids, which occur naturally in plants, are known for their powerful physiological effects on humans and animals. (Morphine, strychnine, quinine, nicotine, cocaine, and curare are but a few examples.) The first alkaloid to be isolated and crystallized was morphine, extracted from the poppy plant in 1805–1806. By 1878, Holmes may have been able to experiment with various isolated alkaloids, which tend to be odourless and bitter in taste; but at the same time, not much was yet known definitively about their properties.

Alkaloids appear throughout the Canon: morphine in "The Man with the Twisted Lip," cocaine in "A Scandal in Bohemia," and quinine in *The Sign of Four*; the alkaloid tubocurarine, a muscle relaxant, is the active ingredient in curare, the South American poison that plays a significant role in both *The Sign of Four* and "The Sussex Vampire." Of course, nicotine, which originates in the tobacco plant, is ubiquitous in the smoke-filled rooms of Baker Street and elsewhere. Stamford's shrewd observation here remarkably foreshadows Holmes's experimentation on Watson and himself in "The Devil's Foot," although whether *Radix pedis diaboli* is an alkaloid is unsettled.

Pathological Laboratory, St. Bartholomew's Hospital (*ca.* 1881).

here we are, and you must form your own impressions about him." As he spoke, we turned down a narrow lane and passed through a small side-door, which opened into a wing of the great hospital. It was familiar ground to me, and I needed no guiding as we ascended the bleak stone staircase and made our way down the long corridor with its vista of whitewashed wall and dun-coloured doors. Near the farther end a low arched passage branched away from it and led to the chemical laboratory.

This was a lofty chamber, lined and littered with countless bottles. Broad, low tables were scattered about, which bristled with retorts, test-tubes, and little Bunsen lamps,[35] with their blue flickering flames. There was only one student in the room,[36] who was bending over a distant table absorbed in his work. At the sound of our steps he glanced round and sprang to his feet with a cry of pleasure. "I've found it! I've found it," he shouted to my companion, running towards us with a test-tube in his hand. "I have found a re-agent which is precipitated by haemoglobin, and by nothing else." Had he discovered a gold mine, greater delight could not have shone upon his features.

"Dr. Watson, Mr. Sherlock Holmes," said Stamford, introducing us.

"How are you?" he said cordially, gripping my hand with a

34 Holmes's fondness for experimentation on corpses was not limited to human cadavers; in "Black Peter," Watson records that Holmes tested the sticking-power of harpoons on the carcasses of pigs at the shop of Allardyce the butcher.

35 Named after Robert Wilhelm Bunsen, the German chemist who introduced (but did not invent) it in 1855, the Bunsen burner combines a hollow metal tube with a valve at the base that allows for regulation of the supply of air. Flammable gas and air together are forced upward through the tube and then lit to produce a hot flame. The principles behind the Bunsen burner paved the way for the invention of the gas-stove burner and the gas furnace.

36 In "Some Observations on Sherlock Holmes and Dr. Watson at Bart's," Adrian Griffith notes that in the memoirs of Sir Norman Moore, Moore recounts that he and an unnamed other student were private students of Augustus Matthiessen, who lectured in chemistry at Bart's from 1870 onward. In 1869, Matthiessen, an employee of Friedrich Bayer & Co.—then a manufacturer of textile dyes—removed two atoms of hydrogen and one of oxygen from morphine to derive the subsidiary alkaloid apomorphine. Its primary function was to induce vomiting, and Bayer marketed it as a purgative similar to castor oil. It was later touted as a treatment for Parkinson's disease and a "cure" for homosexuality, and today it is sold as a sexual-enhancement drug for both men and women. Griffith suggests that Holmes was the unnamed student of Matthiessen. Considering Matthiessen's work on alkaloids, Holmes's interest in the subject may well have started at Bart's, and Moore's recollections of Matthiessen's career suggest to Griffith that Holmes and Matthiessen may have even collaborated on the occasional project.

strength for which I should hardly have given him credit. "You have been in Afghanistan, I perceive."

"How on earth did you know that?" I asked in astonishment.

"Never mind," said he, chuckling to himself. "The question now is about haemoglobin. No doubt you see the significance of this discovery of mine?"

"It is interesting, chemically, no doubt," I answered, "but practically—"

"Why, man, it is the most practical medico-legal discovery for years. Don't you see that it gives us an infallible test for blood stains? Come over here now!" He seized me by the coat-sleeve in his eagerness, and drew me over to the table at which he had been working. "Let us have some fresh blood," he said, digging a long bodkin[37] into his finger, and drawing off the resulting drop of blood in a chemical pipette. "Now, I add this small quantity of blood to a litre of water. You perceive that the

37 An instrument for piercing holes.

"'I've found it! I've found it!' he shouted."
Geo. Hutchinson, *A Study in Scarlet* (London: Ward, Lock Bowden, and Co., 1891)

38 If Holmes's discovery were valid, argues Remsen Ten Eyck Schenck, in "Baker Street Fables," it would be universally used today. The fact that it is not leads Schenck to label "unfounded" the notion that only hæmoglobin caused the agent to react. "Presumably," Schenck continues, "[Holmes] discovered on further study that a similar result was obtained with other common substances, or else that it was not due to hæmoglobin at all, but rather to some other ingredient present in the blood, but not peculiar to it." Holmes was even wrong about the concentration of his blood solution: Schenck estimates that the ratio of a "drop" of blood to a litre of water would have actually been about one part blood to 30,000 parts water, rather than the "one in a million" proportion Holmes cites shortly (although a "drop" is an imprecise unit, the smallest unit used in medicine is a "minim," .06 of a millilitre, which would produce a ratio of 1 to 60,000). The detective "no doubt soon bitterly regretted that he had even mentioned his test, even to Watson," Schenck concludes, "and this could well explain why it was never again referred to."

But Leon S. Holstein, in "7. Knowledge of Chemistry—Profound" disagrees, suggesting that the test was an early version of the present-day hæmochromogen test, which is used to identify bloodstains. When blood is present, hæmochromogen crystals turn pinkish, which is perhaps, as Holstein surmises, a shade not that far removed from the "dull mahogany colour" that Holmes observes.

Christine L. Huber, in "The Sherlock Holmes Blood Test: The Solution to a Century-Old Mystery," identifies the test as one "rediscovered" in the 1930s, when it was "discovered" that hæmoglobin A is denatured by sodium hydroxide ("white crystals") and then precipitated with saturated ammonium sulfate (a "transparent fluid"). "[T]he Holmes Test . . . has been in almost daily use in hospitals and research laboratories, as a part

" 'I've found it! I've found it,' he shouted to my companion."
Richard Gutschmidt, *Späte Rache* (Stuttgart: Robert Lutz Verlag, 1902)

resulting mixture has the appearance of pure water. The proportion of blood cannot be more than one in a million. I have no doubt, however, that we shall be able to obtain the characteristic reaction." As he spoke, he threw into the vessel a few white crystals, and then added some drops of a transparent fluid. In an instant the contents assumed a dull mahogany colour, and a brownish dust was precipitated to the bottom of the glass jar.[38]

"Ha! ha!" he cried, clapping his hands, and looking as delighted as a child with a new toy. "What do you think of that?"

"It seems to be a very delicate test," I remarked.

"Beautiful! beautiful! The old guaiacum test[39] was very clumsy and uncertain. So is the microscopic examination for blood corpuscles. The latter is valueless if the stains are a few hours old. Now, this appears to act as well whether the blood is old or new. Had this test been invented, there are hundreds of men now walking the earth who would long ago have paid the penalty of their crimes."

"Indeed!" I murmured.

"Criminal cases are continually hinging upon that one point. A man is suspected of a crime months perhaps after it has been committed. His linen or clothes are examined, and brownish stains discovered upon them. Are they blood stains, or mud stains, or rust stains, or fruit stains, or what are they? That is a question which has puzzled many an expert, and why? Because there was no reliable test. Now we have the Sherlock Holmes test, and there will no longer be any difficulty."[40]

His eyes fairly glittered as he spoke, and he put his hand over his heart and bowed as if to some applauding crowd conjured up by his imagination.

"You are to be congratulated," I remarked, considerably surprised at his enthusiasm.

"There was the case of Von Bischoff at Frankfort last year. He would certainly have been hung had this test been in existence. Then there was Mason of Bradford, and the notorious Muller,[41] and Lefevre of Montpellier, and Samson of New Orleans. I could name a score of cases in which it would have been decisive."[42]

"You seem to be a walking calendar of crime," said Stamford with a laugh. "You might start a paper on those lines. Call it the 'Police News of the Past.' "

"Very interesting reading it might be made, too," remarked Sherlock Holmes, sticking a small piece of plaster over the prick on his finger. "I have to be careful," he continued, turning to me with a smile, "for I dabble with poisons a good deal." He held out his hand as he spoke, and I noticed that it was all mottled over with similar pieces of plaster, and discoloured with strong acids.

"We came here on business," said Stamford, sitting down on a high three-legged stool, and pushing another one in my direction with his foot. "My friend here wants to take diggings; and as you were complaining that you could get no one to go halves with you, I thought that I had better bring you together."

Sherlock Holmes seemed delighted at the idea of sharing his rooms with me. "I have my eye on a suite in Baker Street,"[43]

of the electrophoretic process, since its rediscovery," she claims. "How it was lost in the first place and why Holmes never received acknowledgment for it remains a mystery."

39 In another test for hæmoglobin (and consequently for the presence of blood), the greenish-brown resin of the guaiacum tree, or lignum vitae, was mixed with alcohol; this substance was added to the liquid being tested and then shaken with a few drops of hydrogen peroxide in ether. The presence of hæmoglobin would turn the mixture bright blue. The test was first reported in 1861 in a modified form by J. Van Deen.

R. Austin Freeman describes this test in *The Shadow of the Wolf* (1925), an account of the great medico-legal detective Dr. John Evelyn Thorndyke—whose cases, like those of Holmes, were written up in several other books, from *The Red Thumb Mark* (1907) to *The Jacob Street Mystery* (1942). After pouring some tincture of guaiacum on a questionable stain, Thorndyke watches as the liquid spreads outward, then adds the ether and allows the two liquids to mix. "Gradually the ether spread towards the stain," Freeman writes, "and, first at one point and then at another, approached and finally crossed the wavy grey line; and at each point the same change occurred: first the faint grey line turned into a strong blue line, and then the colour extended to the enclosed space until the entire area of the stain stood out in a conspicuous blue patch. 'You understand the meaning of this,' said Thorndyke. 'This is a bloodstain.' "

P. M. Stone asserts, in "The Other Friendship: A Speculation," that Holmes and Thorndyke actually met and exchanged views at some point. "[I]t is not unlikely," comments Edgar Smith in his introduction to the essay, "that Sherlock Holmes . . . was inclined to seek variety—and shall we say relief?—in intellectual converse on the higher plane with someone whose capacities and inclinations were just a little closer to his own."

There were in fact eleven original tests for haemoglobin developed between 1800 and 1881, and numerous variations were proposed. The tests, several of which remain in modern use, are summarised in Raymond J. McGowan's "Sherlock Holmes and Forensic Chemistry."

40 Michael Harrison surmises that Holmes offered his test to the British police, who snubbed him. It is no wonder, then, Harrison suggests, that Holmes, "nursing an unconquerable prejudice against the British police system, preferred to go his own highly individual way."

41 D. Martin Dakin notes that "Muller" cannot have been "the Franz Müller who was the first railway murderer (1864) since he *was* convicted and that not by bloodstains, but by his absentmindedly going off with his victim's hat!"

42 Owen Dudley Edwards observes, "Holmes is evidently shooting off these names at great speed with the obsessiveness of a devotee determined to bombard his audience with proofs of their own ignorance in a field he intends to evangelize."

43 The provenance of the "Baker" in "Baker Street" is somewhat unclear. According to Hector Bolitho and Derek Peel's *Without the City Wall: An Adventure in London Street-names North of the River*, most of the streets in the western part of the Marylebone district were named after members of the family of William Henry Portman (of Orchard Portman in Somerset), who inherited the land in the mid-1700s. Baker Street was, for some reason, an exception to this rule. Some scholars believe that the street was named after Sir Edward Baker, a neighbour and friend of Mr. Portman's in Dorset. Bolitho and Peel, however, claim that a William Baker leased a number of acres near Portman Square from Mr. Portman for the purposes of development, and that it was after this Baker that the street was named.

Baker Street, *ca.* 1895.
Round London (1896)

he said, "which would suit us down to the ground. You don't mind the smell of strong tobacco, I hope?"[44]

"I always smoke 'ship's' myself,"[45] I answered.

"That's good enough. I generally have chemicals about, and occasionally do experiments. Would that annoy you?"

"By no means."

"Let me see—what are my other shortcomings? I get in the dumps at times, and don't open my mouth for days on end. You must not think I am sulky when I do that. Just let me alone, and I'll soon be right. What have you to confess now? It's just as well for two fellows to know the worst of one another before they begin to live together."

I laughed at this cross-examination. "I keep a bull pup,"[46] I said, "and I object to rows because my nerves are shaken, and I get up at all sorts of ungodly hours, and I am extremely lazy. I have another set of vices when I'm well,[47] but those are the principal ones at present."

44 Ian McQueen remarks, "The pair must rank as two of the most famous smokers of their time. [This] exchange of details about their smoking habits forms the very first swapped confidence between them . . ."

45 Was Watson referring to ship's tobacco, or did he favor some particular brand? Sherry Keen, in "Ship's or 'ship's?': That is the Question," notes that both *A Dictionary of Slang and Unconventional English*, by Eric Partridge, and *Soldier and Sailor, Words and Phrases*, by Fraser and Gibbons, refer to "ship's" as a "naval cocoa tobacco." Yet Jack Tracy's *Encyclopedia Sherlockiana* unhesitatingly identifies "Ship's" as "*Schippers Tabak Special*, a strong tobacco blend manufactured in the Netherlands and much favoured by sailors." William Baring-Gould suggests that Watson took up "Ship's" on board the *Orontes*. But remember that Watson, in returning to England, was in a much weakened state, nearly an invalid; and on that basis, W. E. Edwards surmises that he learned the habit on his voyage *to* India. In any event, concludes Baring-Gould, the tobacco was a "passing fancy," for in "The Crooked Man," Watson has returned to smoking "the Arcadia mixture of [his] bachelor days."

46 The bull pup is never again mentioned in the Canon, and a variety of explanations have been offered for its mysterious disappearance. Robert S. Morgan, in "The Puzzle of the Bull Pup," suggests that the dog met with a fatal accident shortly after Watson's move, resulting in a shock to Watson's nervous system and a permanent injury to his memory. Thomas Tully's theory, in "Bull Pup," is that Watson was only keeping the dog temporarily. More ingeniously, Carol P. Woods, in "A Curtailed Report on a Dogged Investigation," speculates that Watson misidentified his pet as a dog when it was, in fact, a ferret. After Holmes called him on this error, an embarrassed Watson never mentioned the animal again. But Watson's new roommate might have been responsible for getting rid of the animal. William Baring-Gould reasonably points out, "We must remember that Holmes in his college days had been bitten in the ankle by a bull terrier (Victor Trevor's) and Watson's bull pup may have found the same target irresistible. 'Watson, that dog must go!' "

Several scholars doubt the very existence of the dog. L. S. Holstein, for example, does not believe that a "private hotel in the Strand" would have allowed Watson to keep a dog. W. E. Edwards, among others, takes the phrase "bull pup" to refer to a short-barrelled pistol (similar to the model referred to as a "bulldog") rather than "a domestic pet impossible in Afghanistan, illegal on the *Orontes*, inappropriate for a private hotel, and invisible in Baker Street." Similar identifications are made by George Fletcher (who believes the reference is to a military rifle) and J. R. Stockler and R. N. Brodie (a military revolver). Others point to Jacques Barzun, who writes, in *Simple & Direct: A Rhetoric for Writers*, without citing a source, that the phrase referred to a person with a hot temper. From this, scholars postulate that Watson fabricated the existence of the dog to warn Holmes to watch his step (Bruce Kennedy, "What Bull Pup?"). Perhaps most interesting is Arthur M. Axelrad's suggestion, in "Dr. Watson's Bull Pup: A Psycholinguistic Solution," that "I keep a bull pup" was a "psycholinguistic" distortion under stress of "I keep a full cup" (that is, "I am an immoderate drinker").

47 Baring-Gould suggests that this may refer to Watson's experience of women—extending "over many nations and three separate continents" (see *The Sign of Four*, note 38, and text accompanying)—or his propensity for gambling (see, for example, "Shoscombe Old Place").

48 In "The Mazarin Stone," an unnamed narrator declares that "Holmes seldom laughed, but he got as near it as his old friend Watson

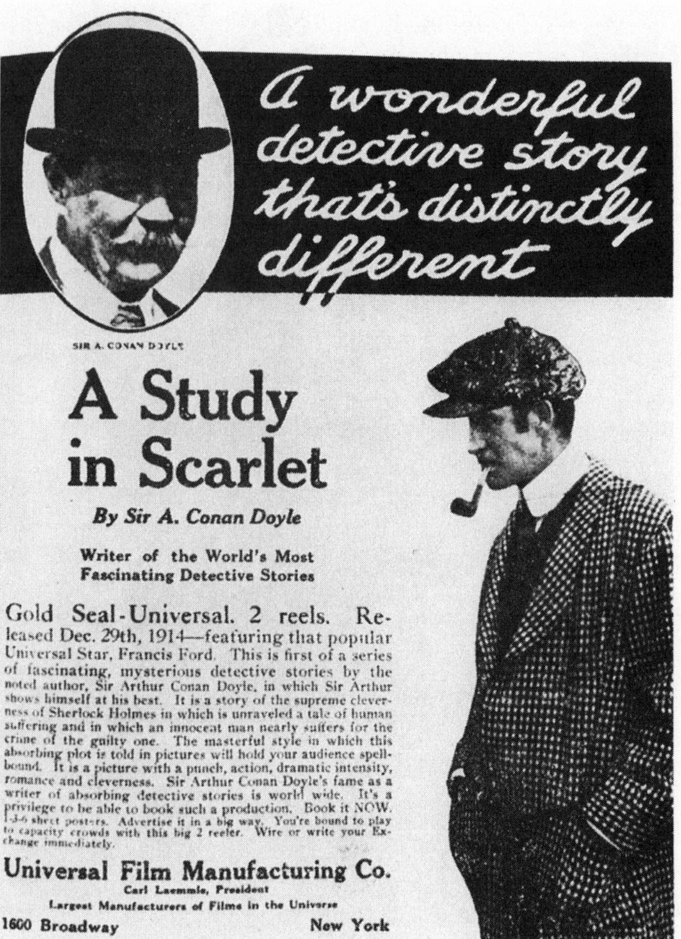

Poster for *A Study in Scarlet*.
(United States: Gold Seal/Universal Film Mfg. Co., 1914)

"Do you include violin-playing in your category of rows?" he asked, anxiously.

"It depends on the player," I answered. "A well-played violin is a treat for the gods—a badly-played one—"

"Oh, that's all right," he cried, with a merry laugh.[48] "I think we may consider the thing as settled—that is, if the rooms are agreeable to you."

"When shall we see them?"

"Call for me here at noon to-morrow, and we'll go together and settle everything," he answered.

"All right—noon exactly," said I, shaking his hand.

We left him working among his chemicals, and we walked together towards my hotel.

"By the way," I asked suddenly, stopping and turning upon Stamford, "how the deuce did he know that I had come from Afghanistan?"

My companion smiled an enigmatical smile. "That's just his little peculiarity," he said. "A good many people have wanted to know how he finds things out."

"Oh! a mystery is it?" I cried, rubbing my hands. "This is very piquant. I am much obliged to you for bringing us together. " 'The proper study of mankind is man,'[49] you know."

"You must study him, then," Stamford said, as he bade me good-bye. "You'll find him a knotty problem, though. I'll wager he learns more about you than you about him. Good-bye."

"Good-bye," I answered, and strolled on to my hotel, considerably interested in my new acquaintance.

could remember." Clearly, that statement is disproved here. A. G. Cooper, in "Holmesian Humour," claims to have counted 292 examples of the Master's laughter, while Charles E. Lauterbach and Edward S. Lauterbach, in "The Man Who Seldom Laughed," compiled the following table:

Frequency Table Showing the Number and Kind of Responses Sherlock Holmes Made to Humorous Situations and Comments in His 60 Recorded Adventures	
Smile	103
Laugh	65
Joke	58
Chuckle	31
Humor	10
Amusement	9
Cheer	7
Delight	7
Twinkle	7
Miscellaneous	19
Total	316

49 Watson quotes here from *An Essay on Man* by Alexander Pope (1688–1744): "Know then thyself, presume not God to scan; / The proper study of Mankind is Man."

CHAPTER II

The Science of Deduction

WE MET NEXT day as he had arranged, and inspected the rooms at No. 221B,[50] Baker Street, of which he had spoken at our meeting. They consisted of a couple of comfortable bedrooms and a single large airy sitting-room, cheerfully furnished, and illuminated by two broad windows.[51] So desirable in every way were the apartments, and so moderate did the terms seem[52] when divided between us, that the bargain was concluded upon the spot, and we at once entered into possession. That very evening I moved my things round from the hotel, and on the following morning Sherlock Holmes followed me with several boxes and portmanteaus. For a day or two we were busily employed in unpacking and laying out our property to the best advantage. That done, we gradually began to settle down and to accommodate ourselves to our new surroundings.

Holmes was certainly not a difficult man to live with. He was quiet in his ways, and his habits were regular. It was rare for him to be up after ten at night, and he had invariably breakfasted and gone out before I rose in the morning.[53] Sometimes he spent his day at the chemical laboratory, sometimes in the dissecting-rooms, and occasionally in long walks, which

50 Many U.S. editions omit the "B."

51 See this editor's "Layout of a 'Most Desirable Residence' " for a discussion of the room arrangement and furnishings.

52 After researching reasonable rents of the time, Michael Harrison estimates, in *In the Footsteps of Sherlock Holmes*, that Holmes and Watson likely paid an "all-in" rent of between £3 and £4 a week. This would have included laundry and food but probably did not cover gas, which "may explain the references, frequent throughout Watson's writings, to the oil-lamps at 221B."

53 In Chapter I, Watson advised Holmes that he got up "at all sorts of ungodly hours." But in "The Speckled Band," Holmes is described by Watson as "a late riser as a rule," and Watson describes himself as "regular in my habits." A similar depiction crops up in

Dustjacket, "Photoplay Edition," *A Study in Scarlet.*
(New York: A. L. Burt Co., *ca.* 1940)

appeared to take him into the lowest portions of the City.[54] Nothing could exceed his energy when the working fit was upon him; but now and again a reaction would seize him, and for days on end he would lie upon the sofa in the sitting-room, hardly uttering a word or moving a muscle from morning to night. On these occasions I have noticed such a dreamy, vacant expression in his eyes, that I might have suspected him of being addicted to the use of some narcotic, had not the temperance and cleanliness of his whole life forbidden such a notion.[55]

As the weeks went by, my interest in him and my curiosity as to his aims in life, gradually deepened and increased. His very person and appearance were such as to strike the attention of the most casual observer. In height he was rather over six feet, and so excessively lean that he seemed to be considerably taller. His eyes were sharp and piercing, save during those intervals of torpor to which I have alluded; and his thin, hawk-

The Hound of the Baskervilles (see note 2 and accompanying text), with Watson recounting that Holmes "was usually very late in the mornings." At the very least, Holmes's habits seem variable; "The Engineer's Thumb" finds Watson expecting to encounter Holmes at breakfast soon after 7:00 A.M. The only consistent pattern suggested is that Watson must have regularly arisen *very* late, as confirmed by his late breakfast in "The Boscombe Valley Mystery."

54 William Baring-Gould gathers that these "long walks" must have been case-related, as Holmes was "a man who seldom took exercise for exercise's sake" ("The Yellow Face").

The term "low," W. E. Edwards explains, "was a characteristic Victorian epithet to express contempt. There was a good deal of class hatred in the term 'lower-class,' its polite version being 'working-class.' " In the Victorian era, industrialisation saw a rapid expansion of the "middle class": shopkeepers, merchants, clerks, teachers, doctors, and lawyers; or, in other words, those who employed servants yet did not belong to the aristocracy. Those in this new middle class (whose members would have counted Holmes and Watson), who aspired to upward mobility and yet were desperate not to slip backward in status, sought to distance themselves from the working class of street vendors, miners, servants, ironworkers, and most factory workers. In 1909, the English politician C.F.G. Masterman astutely remarked that "The Rich despise the Working People, the Middle Classes fear them."

55 In fact, it is later evident to Dr. Watson that Holmes is a regular user of cocaine (a seven-per-cent solution), and he undertakes to wean him from the drug. His use of cocaine is explicitly mentioned in "The Five Orange Pips," "A Scandal in Bohemia," *The Sign of Four,* "The Man with the Twisted Lip," and

"The Yellow Face," and in *The Sign of Four*, Watson implies that Holmes has also been taking morphine. In "A Scandal in Bohemia," Watson describes Holmes as alternating between the "drowsiness" of the drug and "the fierce energy of his own keen nature." In "The Five Orange Pips," Watson accused Holmes of being a "self-posioner," and in *The Sign of Four*, Holmes admitted that the influence of the drug "is physically a bad one." He defended his use on the basis that "I find it, however, so transcendently stimulating and clarifying to the mind that its secondary action is a matter of small moment."

William S. Baring-Gould believes that the detective first sought solace in the drug following his nervous collapse in "The Reigate Squires," which probably occurred in April 1887. In that story, Watson notes Holmes's "strain caused by his immense exertions in the spring of '87" (in an unrecounted case involving the mysterious Netherlands-Sumatra Company) and describes arriving at his sickroom to find the detective exhausted, bored, and "a prey to the blackest depression." But Dr. Charles Goodman concludes that Holmes first took to cocaine neither from weakness nor from boredom but from toothache, as a chronic sufferer from pyorrhea.

In "The Missing Three-Quarter," generally accepted as occurring in 1896 or 1897, Watson describes his efforts to rehabilitate Holmes: "For years I had gradually weaned him from that drug mania which had threatened once to check his remarkable career. Now I knew that under ordinary conditions he no longer craved for this artificial stimulus; but I was well aware that the fiend was not dead, but sleeping; and I have known that the sleep was a light one and the waking near when in periods of idleness I have seen the drawn look upon Holmes's ascetic face, and the brooding of his deep-set and inscrutable eyes."

Not all scholars accept the notion that Holmes used recreational drugs. Dr. George F.

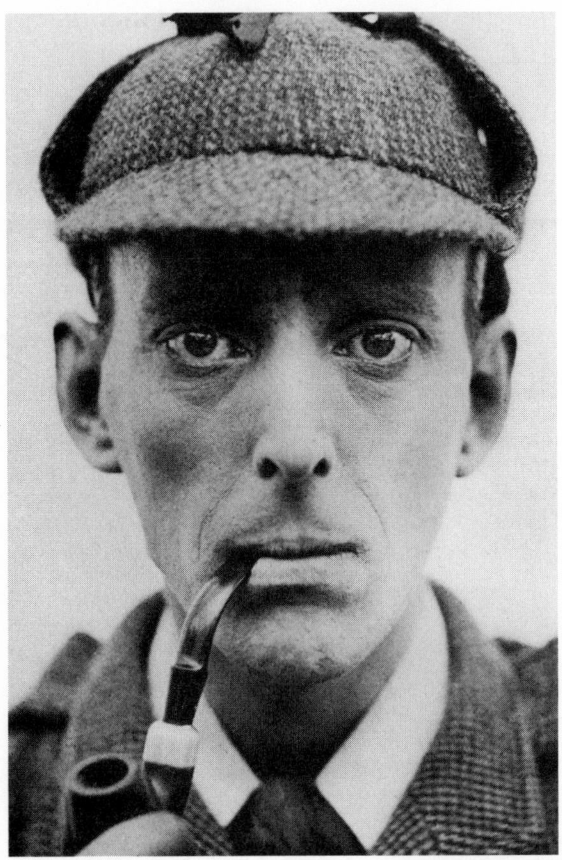

James Bragington as Sherlock Holmes, in *A Study in Scarlet.*
(Great Britain: Samuelson Film Mfg. Co. Ltd., 1914)

like nose gave his whole expression an air of alertness and decision. His chin, too, had the prominence and squareness which mark the man of determination.[56] His hands were invariably blotted with ink and stained with chemicals, yet he was possessed of extraordinary delicacy of touch, as I frequently had occasion to observe when I watched him manipulating his fragile philosophical instruments.[57]

The reader may set me down as a hopeless busybody, when I confess how much this man stimulated my curiosity, and how often I endeavoured to break through the reticence which he showed on all that concerned himself. Before pronouncing judgment, however, be it remembered how objectless was my life, and how little there was to engage my attention. My

McCleary arrives at the conclusion that despite Watson's statement in *The Sign of Four* that he had witnessed Holmes inject himself three times daily "for many months," in fact, Holmes was never a drug addict but was deliberately deceiving Watson. He bases this conclusion on the "evidence" of Holmes's skill with makeup and disguise and his personality traits (that is, that Holmes does not fit the "profile" of the common drug user), concluding that Holmes was playing a joke on Watson and that whatever he did inject was not cocaine. Interesting as this theory is, McCleary offers no motivation for this cruel joke. Michael Harrison, on the other hand, asserts that Watson's descriptions of Holmes—his restlessness, ability to work for days without adequate sleep, and even without rest at all, abrupt changes of mood, and abrupt collapses into somnolence—"are the unmistakable evidence of heavy and prolonged indulgence in some powerful narcotic."

A more moderate view, shared by Dr. Eugene F. Carey ("Holmes, Watson and Cocaine") and Edgar W. Smith ("Up from the Needle"), is that Holmes was, in Carey's words, a "judicious user." Smith concludes that "he was never a slave to the vice in the clinical sense of the term, for . . . he was always able to cast off the spell, and to find inspiration in the exhilaration of the chase."

56 Despite Watson's description of Holmes as "excessively lean" and possessed of a "hawk-like" nose, Richard Asher believes that Holmes was, with the exception of his heavily tobacco-stained teeth, "enormously attractive to women." He was, Asher asserts, "a man endowed with all those gifts mental, physical and social which should have made him a success with women." He buttresses this conclusion by noting Holmes's effect on Mary Morstan (*The Sign of Four*), Irene Adler ("A Scandal in Bohemia"), Mrs. Neville St. Clair ("The Man with the Twisted Lip"), Violet Hunter ("The Copper Beeches"), and of course Agatha the housemaid ("Charles Augustus Milverton"), all of whom, Asher asserts, were tangibly drawn to Holmes.

The earliest known illustration of Holmes (reproduced on page 63) belies this picture of Holmes as physically attractive, although there is no evidence that the illustration was drawn from life. The drawings of Charles Doyle, father of Arthur Conan Doyle, who must have met Holmes, depict him even less handsomely (as may be seen on pages 56, 87 and 99), although the low point of Holmesian portraiture must be the Charles Kerr illustration for *The Sign of Four* reproduced on page 270. Not until Sidney Paget took up his pen and began to illustrate the *Adventures* was Holmes depicted in a way that may be viewed as attractive. Unfortunately, it is well known that Paget used his brother Walter as his model; Holmes himself was in Tibet and points east.

57 An archaic term for scientific instruments.

health forbade me from venturing out unless the weather was exceptionally genial, and I had no friends who would call upon me and break the monotony of my daily existence. Under these circumstances, I eagerly hailed the little mystery which hung around my companion, and spent much of my time in endeavouring to unravel it.

He was not studying medicine. He had himself, in reply to a question, confirmed Stamford's opinion upon that point. Neither did he appear to have pursued any course of reading which might fit him for a degree in science or any other recognised portal which would give him an entrance into the learned world.[58] Yet his zeal for certain studies was remarkable, and within eccentric limits his knowledge was so extraordinarily ample and minute that his observations have fairly astounded me. Surely no man would work so hard or attain such precise information unless he had some definite end in view. Desultory readers are seldom remarkable for the exactness of their learning. No man burdens his mind with small matters unless he has some very good reason for doing so.

His ignorance was as remarkable as his knowledge. Of contemporary literature, philosophy and politics he appeared to know next to nothing. Upon my quoting Thomas Carlyle, he inquired in the naivest way who he might be and what he had done.[59] My surprise reached a climax, however, when I found incidentally that he was ignorant of the Copernican Theory[60] and of the composition of the Solar System. That any civilized human being in this nineteenth century should not be aware that the earth travelled round the sun appeared to be to me such an extraordinary fact that I could hardly realize it.[61]

"You appear to be astonished," he said, smiling at my expression of surprise. "Now that I do know it I shall do my best to forget it."

"To forget it!"

"You see," he explained, "I consider that a man's brain originally is like a little empty attic, and you have to stock it with such furniture as you choose. A fool takes in all the lumber of every sort that he comes across, so that the knowledge which might be useful to him gets crowded out, or at best is jumbled up with a lot of other things so that he has a difficulty in laying his hands upon it. Now the skilful workman is very careful indeed as to what he takes into his brain-attic. He will have

58 Although there is no mention in the Canon of Holmes obtaining a degree, it is clear that he *participated* in the "learned world" and contributed a number of scholarly monographs to various fields. Most scholars agree that Holmes attended one of the great universities, either Oxford or Cambridge, although a few suggest that he attended both, and several scholars propose a supplemental course at London University. The intricacies of the arguments, depending heavily on the culture of each of the schools, are well beyond the scope of this work. Notwithstanding his partiality, Nicholas Utechin, long editor of the *Sherlock Holmes Journal*, published by the Sherlock Holmes Society of London, has produced a fine work entitled *Sherlock Holmes at Oxford*, which affords an excellent summary of the arguments.

59 Thomas Carlyle (1795–1881) was a British historian and essayist, born in Scotland and heavily influenced by German writers such as Goethe. Carlyle, who taught mathematics and studied law, sharply criticized hypocrisy and materialism, and Holmes might have admired his firm belief that heroic leaders were integral to the shaping and altering of world events. Writing in a strange, almost violent style comprising unusual words and phrases, frenetic rhythms, and German-influenced expressions, Carlyle published several major works, including the three-volume *The French Revolution* (1837), the public lecture *On Heroes, Hero-Worship, and the Heroic in History* (1841), and the biography *History of Friedrich II of Prussia, Called Frederick the Great* (1858–1865). He also wrote biographies of Friedrich von Schiller, Oliver Cromwell, and John Sterling.

Despite Watson's statement here, few scholars believe that the knowledgeable Holmes was actually unaware of Carlyle's work. In *My Dear Holmes*, Gavin Brend suggests that Holmes may have pleaded ignorance of Carlyle in an attempt to get Watson to leave him alone. Brend writes that "probably it was at a time when Holmes wanted to give his whole attention to a case, as yet unsolved, and simply could not be bothered to be drawn into a discussion about Carlyle or anything else." Christopher Morley proposes that Holmes's inquiry was made on the date of Carlyle's death: February 5, 1881. Holmes's pretence of ignorance of Carlyle is not long maintained (see note 115, below). In *The Sign of Four*, Holmes remarks on Watson's reading of Carlyle with no suggestion that he has not himself read Carlyle's work.

60 The Copernican theory (or system), established by Polish astronomer Nicholas Copernicus, held that the sun remained in a fixed position and that the planets revolved around it; in addition, Copernicus proposed that the Earth rotated on its own axis once every day. His depiction of the heavens represented a slight but significant deviation from the Ptolemaic system, which placed the Earth, not the sun, at the centre of the universe. Although Copernicus wrote up his theory between 1508 and 1514, it was published, as *De revolutionibus orbium coelestium libri VI* (*Six Books Concerning the Revolutions of the Heavenly Orbs)*, only in 1543, the year of his death. It was a theory that not only gave rise to the work of Descartes, Galileo, Kepler, and Newton but also had far-reaching implications for the rise of modern science—the Earth would henceforth no longer be considered the center of the cosmos but merely one planet among many.

61 This, opines William Baring-Gould, would appear to be another situation in which Holmes is doing some "leg-pulling." The detective's knowledge of astronomy is clear from references in "The Musgrave Ritual" (Holmes speaks of "allowance for personal equation, as the astronomers have dubbed it"), "The Bruce-Partington Plans," (Mycroft's visit to 221B is likened to "a planet leaving its orbit"), and "The Greek Interpreter" (Holmes chats about "the causes of the change in the obliquity of the ecliptic").

nothing but the tools which may help him in doing his work, but of these he has a large assortment, and all in the most perfect order. It is a mistake to think that that little room has elastic walls and can distend to any extent. Depend upon it there comes a time when for every addition of knowledge you forget something that you knew before. It is of the highest importance, therefore, not to have useless facts elbowing out the useful ones."[62]

"But the Solar System!" I protested.

"What the deuce is it to me?" he interrupted impatiently; "you say that we go round the sun. If we went round the moon it would not make a pennyworth of difference to me or to my work."

I was on the point of asking him what that work might be, but something in his manner showed me that the question would be an unwelcome one. I pondered over our short conversation, however, and endeavoured to draw my deductions from it. He said that he would acquire no knowledge which did not bear upon his object. Therefore all the knowledge which he possessed was such as would be useful to him. I enumerated in my own mind all the various points upon which he had shown me that he was exceptionally well-informed. I even took a pencil and jotted them down. I could not help smiling at the document when I had completed it. It ran in this way:

Sherlock Holmes—his limits[63]

1. Knowledge of Literature.—Nil.
2. " " Philosophy.—Nil.[64]
3. " " Astronomy.—Nil.
4. " " Politics.—Feeble.[65]
5. " " Botany.—Variable. Well up in belladonna, opium, and poisons generally. Knows nothing of practical gardening.
6. " " Geology.—Practical, but limited. Tells at a glance different soils from each other. After walks has shown me splashes upon his trousers, and told me by their colour and consistence in what part of London he had received them.
7. " " Chemistry.—Profound.
8. " " Anatomy.—Accurate, but unsystematic.

62 In "The Lion's Mane," Holmes appears to contradict this statement by proudly proclaiming that "I am an omnivorous reader with a strangely retentive memory for trifles."

63 "A list of Watson's own points might, at this juncture, have been headed by the specification: 1. Knowledge of Sherlock Holmes.—Nil," says Edgar W. Smith.

64 In the preface to *His Last Bow*, Watson reports that Holmes, in retirement, divides his time "between philosophy and agriculture." That this is not an interest developed late in life is evident from Holmes's reading of books such as Winwood Reade's *The Martyrdom of Man*, which (in *The Sign of Four*) Holmes termed "one of the most remarkable [books] ever penned." Therefore, we must conclude that this is another misperception of Watson's.

65 H. W. Bell believes that Watson may underestimate Holmes's knowledge of international politics, well displayed in such cases as "The Naval Treaty" and "The Second Stain." Likewise, S. C. Roberts emphasises Holmes's staunch belief in democracy and progress by noting Holmes's description, in "The Naval Treaty," of board-schools (England's first taxpayer-supported schools, dedicated to educating the poor) as "Light-houses, my boy! Beacons of the future! Capsules with hundreds of bright little seeds in each, out of which will spring the wiser, better England of the future." "It would be difficult," Roberts observes, "to find a more concise expression of the confident aspirations of late Victorian liberalism."

Siding with Watson's "feeble" assessment is T. S. Blakeney, who reminds us that in "The Bruce-Partington Plans," Holmes's interest was not particularly aroused by "the news of a revolution, of a possible war, and of an impending change of Government." Blakeney holds that Holmes, "who had so close a

9. " " Sensational Literature.—Immense. He appears to know every detail of every horror perpetrated in the century.[66]
10. Plays the violin well.
11. Is an expert singlestick player,[67] boxer, and swordsman.
12. Has a good practical knowledge of British law.[68]

When I had got so far in my list I threw it into the fire in despair. "If I can only find what the fellow is driving at by reconciling all these accomplishments, and discovering a calling which needs them all," I said to myself, "I may as well give up the attempt at once."

I see that I have alluded above to his powers upon the violin. These were very remarkable, but as eccentric as all his other accomplishments. That he could play pieces, and difficult pieces, I knew well, because at my request he has played me some of Mendelssohn's *Lieder*,[69] and other favourites.

"Leaning back in his armchair of an evening, he would close his eyes and scrape carelessly at the fiddle which was thrown across his knee."
Richard Gutschmidt, *Späte Rache* (Stuttgart: Robert Lutz Verlag, 1902)

grip on realities," would hardly be interested in the petty squabbles of politicians, nor, in Blakeney's view, "could so strong an individualist have anything but contempt for the equalitarian ideals of much modern sociological theory."

66 Throughout his career, Holmes refers frequently to classic stories of crime. In *The Valley of Fear*, he compares Professor Moriarty to Jonathan Wild, a notorious fence who sold stolen goods back to their owners and was hanged at Tyburn in 1725. In "The Illustrious Client," he alludes to "Wainwright," who may have been either Thomas Griffiths Wainewright, the art critic who allegedly poisoned his uncle, mother-in-law, and sister-in-law; or Henry Wainwright, a brush manufacturer who killed his mistress and was caught attempting to dispose of her body parts. As book-dealer Madeleine B. Stern observes, while Holmes likely owned various editions of *The Newgate Calendar*—a series of wildly popular books containing accounts of prisoners who had been incarcerated at Newgate—his "immense" knowledge of crimes seems to draw heavily on "his own commonplace books in which, from time to time, he placed his cuttings on crime, pasted extracts, and made out his ever-useful indexes."

67 The singlestick was a slender piece of wood, resembling a cane and used in fencing. One end, thicker than the other, was encased in a basket guard, which protected the user's hand. Singlesticks were invented in the sixteenth century as a means of practising swordplay, but in the eighteenth century, singlesticking became a sport in its own right. The instrument was used much like a sabre in that one player would strike his opponent with its edge, rather than sticking him with the point. Thomas Hughes gives a marvellous and graphic description of the sport in *Tom Brown's Schooldays* (1857): "The old gamester going into action only takes off his hat and coat, and arms himself with a stick; he then loops the fingers of his left hand in a handkerchief or strap, which he fastens round his left leg. . . . Then he advances his right hand above and in front of his head, holding his stick across, so that its point projects an inch or two over his left elbow; and thus his whole head is completely guarded, and he faces his man armed in like manner; and they stand some three feet apart, often nearer, and feint, and strike, and return at one another's heads, until one cries 'hold,' or blood flows."

There is no express instance of Holmes actually using the singlestick, although he wields a hunting crop in a similar manner in "The Speckled Band," and in "The Illustrious Client" he reminds Watson that he is "a bit of a single-stick expert" and speaks of taking blows from men armed with sticks "on his guard" (perhaps meaning his walking-stick).

68 Albert P. Blaustein, in "Sherlock Holmes as a Lawyer," maintains that Holmes *was* a lawyer. Not only does he talk like a lawyer (see, for example, "The Noble Bachelor," where he reports that the maid Alice "deposes" that she went to her room), he acts like one in "The Boscombe Valley Mystery," when he prepares objections for trial and submits them to McCarthy's defense counsel. He points also to Holmes's legally punctilious behaviour in "The Six Napoleons" in obtaining title to the sixth bust. Fletcher Pratt concurs, in "Very Little Murder," adding that "when the record of Mr. Holmes's cases is examined, we find that in every single case where an actual crime has been committed . . . he obtained legal proof full enough to satisfy any jury; witness evidence plus circumstantial evidence, and in many cases . . . a confession in addition."

Such a view is not universally shared. Attorney Andrew G. Fusco, in "The Case Against Mr. Holmes," argues in great detail that

"He would close his eyes and scrape carelessly at the fiddle."
Geo. Hutchinson, *A Study in Scarlet* (London: Ward, Lock Bowden, and Co., 1891)

When left to himself, however, he would seldom produce any music or attempt any recognised air. Leaning back in his armchair of an evening, he would close his eyes and scrape carelessly at the fiddle which was thrown across his knee. Sometimes the chords were sonorous and melancholy. Occasionally they were fantastic and cheerful.[70] Clearly they reflected the thoughts which possessed him, but whether the music aided those thoughts, or whether the playing was simply the result of a whim or fancy was more than I could determine. I might have rebelled against these exasperating solos had it not been that he usually terminated them by playing in quick succession a whole series of my favourite airs as a slight compensation for the trial upon my patience.[71]

During the first week or so we had no callers, and I had begun to think that my companion was as friendless a man as I was myself. Presently, however, I found that he had many

Holmes had no special legal knowledge or training. He points out that Holmes's use of legal terminology is often improper technically. In "The Boscombe Valley Mystery," he may have done nothing more than present the facts of the case to defense counsel, which readily produced objections to be raised at trial. His diligent search for legal proofs of guilt may be nothing more than the product of his compulsive personality. Furthermore, there is no evidence of Holmes receiving any formal legal education. In short, Fusco concludes, Holmes had nothing more than a "good practical knowledge of British law," as would be expected of a detective who frequently dealt with the law and the police.

69 Felix Mendelssohn (1809–1847) completed the first volume of *Lieder ohne Wortes* (*Songs Without Words*), a book of music for the pianoforte, in 1830. There were eight volumes in all, the last of which was finished in 1845. Several scholars speculate that because Holmes played the violin and not the pianoforte, he must have been working out simple melodies for the unmusical Watson, not tackling full transcriptions of the pieces.

70 In the essay "Sherlock Holmes and Music," Harvey Officer, composer of the *Baker Street Suite* for violin and piano, challenges Watson's recollection by attesting that Holmes could have played neither "sonorous and melancholy" chords nor "fantastic and cheerful" ones while playing a violin "thrown across his knee." "Chords on a violin," Officer explains, "are not natural to the instrument. They can only be played when the violin is held strongly in its accustomed position, and even then they are not the violin's most expressive sounds. It is preeminently the instrument of melody, not of harmony."

But William Braid White, a musicology expert, considers that a seated Holmes may have "placed the tail piece of the violin against his middle, holding his left arm under it and the fingers of that arm on the fingerboard in the usual way. This would bring the violin to a position nearly at right angles to his body as he sat in the chair, leaving his right arm and hand free to use the bow, and the left arm and hand, as before remarked, equally free for the fingerboard." When Holmes produced these chords, White concludes, he was reminding himself of, and perhaps practising, the famous "Chaconne" (at any rate, the introductory parts of it) from Johann Sebastian Bach's *D Minor Sonata* for violin, which, he apparently believes, any listener would characterise as "fantastic and cheerful."

Rolfe Boswell, among others, points out that Watson never says that Holmes placed a *violin* across his knee, but rather a *fiddle*. This could well have been the medieval fiddle, which was flat and oval and had five strings; or any bowed, stringed instrument in the violin family, all of which are termed in the vernacular "fiddles." Boswell favors the latter interpretation, arguing that Holmes's instrument of choice was the viola.

71 Emanuel Berg takes Watson's wording here (a *series* as compensation for the *trial* upon his *patience*) to indicate that the "series

Scene from a production of Gilbert and Sullivan's *Patience* (*ca.* 1881).

"I found that he had many acquaintances."
C. Coulston, *Sherlock Holmes Series* (New York and London: Harper & Bros., 1904)

acquaintances, and those in the most different classes of society. There was one little sallow rat-faced, dark-eyed fellow, who was introduced to me as Mr. Lestrade,[72] and who came three or four times in a single week. One morning a young girl called, fashionably dressed, and stayed for half an hour or more. The same afternoon brought a gray-headed, seedy visitor, looking like a Jew pedlar, who appeared to me to be much excited, and who was closely followed by a slip-shod elderly woman. On another occasion an old white-haired gentleman had an interview with my companion; and on another a railway porter in his velveteen uniform.[73] When any of these nondescript individuals put in an appearance, Sherlock Holmes used to beg for the use of the sitting-room, and I would retire to my bed-room. He always apologised to me for putting me to this inconvenience. "I have to use this room as a place of business," he said, "and these people are my clients." Again I had an opportunity of asking him a point blank question, and again my delicacy prevented me from forcing another man to confide in me. I imagined at the time that he had some strong reason for not alluding to it, but he soon dispelled the idea by coming round to the subject of his own accord.

It was upon the 4th of March, as I have good reason to remember, that I rose somewhat earlier than usual, and found

of favourite airs" were the work of William Schwenk Gilbert (1836–1911) and Sir Arthur Seymour Sullivan (1842–1900), the lyricist and composer of our most enduring comic operas. Watson's preference, according to Berg, would have been for those works between *Trial by Jury* (March 25, 1875) and *Patience* (April 23, 1881), a period of productivity that included *H.M.S. Pinafore* (1878) and *The Pirates of Penzance* (1879). Guy Warrack suggests that Mendelssohn's *Auf Flügeln des Gesanges* might well have been another of Watson's favourites.

72 G. Lestrade, as he signs a letter in "The Cardboard Box," a policeman assigned to Scotland Yard, appears in fourteen of Watson's published accounts. While Holmes upheld a friendly attitude toward Lestrade and his brethren, he disdained their methods. Holmes called Lestrade the best of the professionals (*The Hound of the Baskervilles*), the "pick of a bad lot" (*A Study in Scarlet*), lacking in imagination ("The Norwood Builder"), and normally out of his depth (*The Sign of Four*).

Lestrade frequently patronised Holmes's methods yet evidently bore a secret respect for Holmes. At the conclusion of "The Six Napoleons," Lestrade, congratulating Holmes on his successful investigation, remarks, "We're not jealous of you at Scotland Yard. No, sir, we are very proud of you, and if you come down to-morrow there's not a man, from the oldest inspector to the youngest constable, who wouldn't be glad to shake you by the hand." L. S. Holstein, who has conducted a thorough analysis of Lestrade's career, places him at around forty at the time of the affair reported in *A Study in Scarlet*; and Lestrade continues to interact with Holmes as late as "The Three Garridebs" (1902). From this, Holstein concludes that Lestrade was born sometime between 1844 and 1846, making him ten or twelve years older than Holmes. Aside from the mention of Lestrade's first ini-

that Sherlock Holmes had not yet finished his breakfast. The landlady[74] had become so accustomed to my late habits that my place had not been laid nor my coffee prepared. With the unreasonable petulance of mankind I rang the bell and gave a curt intimation that I was ready. Then I picked up a magazine[75] from the table and attempted to while away the time with it, while my companion munched silently at his toast. One of the articles had a pencil mark at the heading, and I naturally began to run my eye through it.

Its somewhat ambitious title was "The Book of Life," and it attempted to show how much an observant man might learn by an accurate and systematic examination of all that came in his way. It struck me as being a remarkable mixture of shrewdness and of absurdity. The reasoning was close and intense, but the deductions appeared to me to be far-fetched and exaggerated. The writer claimed by a momentary expression, a twitch of a muscle or a glance of an eye, to fathom a man's inmost thoughts. Deceit, according to him, was an impossibility in the case of one trained to observation and analysis. His conclusions were as infallible as so many propositions of Euclid.[76] So startling would his results appear to the uninitiated that until they learned the processes by which

"There was a little sallow rat-faced, dark-eyed fellow,"
Geo Hutchinson, *A Study in Scarlet*, (London: Ward Lock Bowden, and Co., 1891)

"Gray-headed, seedy visitor."
Geo. Hutchinson, *A Study in Scarlet* (London: Ward, Lock Bowden, and Co., 1891)

tial, there are no indications of what the detective's first name might be; nor is there any clear consensus among scholars on the pronunciation of "Lestrade."

73 R. K. Leavitt observes, in "Nummi in Arca or The Fiscal Holmes," that these clients were Holmes's daily fare, not the more profitable Reginald Musgraves. "Holmes very soon outgrew his dependence upon [such clients], though he continued (be it said to his credit) to interest himself in such cases all through his years of affluence."

74 Despite a lack of concrete evidence either here or elsewhere in the story, William S. Baring-Gould declares that this is "the famous Mrs. Hudson," Holmes's faithful landlady, who is mentioned by that name throughout the rest of the Canon. Baring-Gould and other scholars further assert that the landlady's first name is Martha. They make this claim based on the text of "The Lion's Mane," in which the retired Holmes refers to "my old housekeeper," who tends to him in Sussex Downs, and "His Last Bow," in which Holmes speaks of a "dear old ruddy-faced woman" who is "Martha, the only servant I have left." William Hyder, in "The Martha Myth," disputes these assumptions, concluding on the basis of Watson's descriptions that Mrs. Hudson, Holmes's Sussex housekeeper, and Martha are in fact three separate women.

As to Mrs. Hudson, little is known about her personal life. Vincent Starrett speculates, in "The Singular Adventures of Martha Hudson," that she was a young widow who took up housekeeping after her marriage ended for reasons unknown. "But," Starrett laments, "no whisper of her life before that day in 1881, when Holmes first called upon her, has ever been revealed. The notion persists that she had been unhappy; she kept so very still about it all." D. Martin Dakin finds it curious that in all of the *Strand Magazine* illustrations of the Canon (many drawn from life, some believe), there is no depiction of Mrs. Hudson.

75 Edgar W. Smith speculates, in *Baker Street Inventory*, that that magazine was the March 1881 issue of the popular literary journal *Cornhill Magazine* (1860–1975). Specialising in the serialisation of novels, the magazine, whose first editor was William Makepeace Thackeray, published the work of George Eliot, Thomas Hardy, Anthony Trollope, Elizabeth Gaskell, and Wilkie Collins. Arthur Conan Doyle was also a frequent contributor. Tage La Cour suggests that a scientific magazine would be a more likely source for an article on deductive reasoning.

76 Euclid, in Greek Eucleides (fl. *ca.* 300 B.C., Alexandria), is best known for his thirteen-book *Elements*, which laid out the principles of geometry and other mathematics. The first six books cover elementary plane geometry, the continuing bane of many a modern high school student. See *The Sign of Four*, note 16.

"An old white-haired gentleman had an interview with my companion."
Geo. Hutchinson, *A Study in Scarlet* (London: Ward, Lock Bowden, and Co., 1891)

he had arrived at them they might well consider him as a necromancer.

"From a drop of water," said the writer, "a logician could infer the possibility of an Atlantic or a Niagara without having seen or heard of one or the other. So all life is a great chain, the nature of which is known whenever we are shown a single link of it. Like all other arts, the Science of Deduction and Analysis is one which can only be acquired by long and patient study, nor is life long enough to allow any mortal to attain the highest possible perfection in it. Before turning to those moral and mental aspects of the matter which present the greatest difficulties, let the inquirer begin by mastering more elementary problems. Let him, on meeting a fellow-mortal, learn at a glance to distinguish the history of the man, and the trade or profession to which he belongs. Puerile as such an exercise may seem, it sharpens the faculties of observation, and teaches one where to look and what to look for. By a man's finger nails, by his coat-sleeve, by his boot, by his trouser knees, by the callosities of his forefinger and thumb, by his expression, by his shirt cuffs—by each of these things a man's calling is plainly revealed. That all united should fail to enlighten the competent inquirer in any case is almost inconceivable."

"What ineffable twaddle!" I cried, slapping the magazine down on the table, "I never read such rubbish in my life."

"What is it?" asked Sherlock Holmes.

"Why, this article," I said, pointing at it with my egg spoon as I sat down to my breakfast. "I see that you have read it since you have marked it. I don't deny that it is smartly written. It irritates me though. It is evidently the theory of some armchair lounger who evolves all these neat little paradoxes in the seclusion of his own study. It is not practical. I should like to see him clapped down in a third class carriage[77] on the Underground,[78] and asked to give the trades of all his fellow-travellers. I would lay a thousand to one against him."[79]

"You would lose your money," Sherlock Holmes remarked calmly. "As for the article, I wrote it myself."

"You!"

"Yes, I have a turn both for observation and for deduction. The theories which I have expressed there, and which appear to you to be so chimerical, are really extremely practical—so practical that I depend upon them for my bread and cheese."

"And how?" I asked involuntarily.

"Well, I have a trade of my own. I suppose I am the only one in the world. I'm a consulting detective, if you can understand what that is. Here in London we have lots of Government detectives and lots of private ones. When these fellows are at fault they come to me, and I manage to put them on the right scent. They lay all the evidence before me, and I am generally able, by the help of my knowledge of the history of crime, to set them straight. There is a strong family resemblance about misdeeds, and if you have all the details of a thousand at your finger ends, it is odd if you can't unravel the thousand and first. Lestrade is a well-known detective. He got himself into a fog recently over a forgery case, and that was what brought him here."

"And these other people?"

"They are mostly sent on by private inquiry agencies. They are all people who are in trouble about something, and want a

77 Originally, third-class carriages in the British railway system had no roofs or seats, and passengers—largely the poor and working class—were left unprotected from the elements, flying sparks, or pollution. Later, the 1844 Railway Act mandated that all third-class carriages be covered. Thomas Hardy, in his story "The Fiddler of the Reels" (1893), describes those early days of transportation by noting that "the unfortunate occupants of these vehicles were, on the train drawing up at the London terminus, found to be in a pitiable condition from their long journey; blue-faced, stiff-necked, sneezing, rain-beaten, chilled to the marrow, many of the men being hatless; in fact, they resembled people who had been out all night in an open boat on a rough sea, rather than inland excursionists for pleasure."

Although third-class accommodations had improved considerably by the time of the events in *A Study in Scarlet*, they were still far from luxurious, and a professional such as Watson may have attached some stigma to travelling in such a fashion. In "The Retired Colourman," Josiah Amberley's insistence on travelling third class leads Watson to label him a "miser."

78 The "Underground Railways," more properly the Metropolitan and Metropolitan District, and City and South London Railways, irrevocably changed the fabric of everyday life in London, carrying over 110 million passengers per year by 1896, according to *Baedeker*. First opened in 1860, the trains for the most part ran through tunnels or cuttings between high walls. London was the first city to adopt underground railways. The railway figures prominently in "The Bruce-Partington Plans," but the only recorded instance of Holmes or Watson actually travelling by Underground occurs in "The Red-Headed League," when the pair journey to Aldersgate.

Christopher Morley points out the timeli-

little enlightening. I listen to their story, they listen to my comments, and then I pocket my fee."[80]

"But do you mean to say," I said, "that without leaving your room you can unravel some knot which other men can make nothing of, although they have seen every detail for themselves?"

"Quite so. I have a kind of intuition that way. Now and again a case turns up which is a little more complex. Then I have to bustle about and see things with my own eyes. You see I have a lot of special knowledge which I apply to the problem, and which facilitates matters wonderfully. Those rules of deduction laid down in that article which aroused your scorn, are invaluable to me in practical work. Observation with me is second nature. You appeared to be surprised when I told you, on our first meeting, that you had come from Afghanistan."

"You were told, no doubt."

"Nothing of the sort. I *knew* you came from Afghanistan. From long habit the train of thoughts ran so swiftly through my mind, that I arrived at the conclusion without being conscious of intermediate steps. There were such steps, however. The train of reasoning ran, 'Here is a gentleman of a medical type, but with the air of a military man. Clearly an army doctor, then. He has just come from the tropics, for his face is dark,[81] and that is not the natural tint of his skin, for his wrists are fair. He has undergone hardship and sickness, as his haggard face says clearly. His left arm has been injured. He holds it in a stiff and unnatural manner. Where in the tropics could an English army doctor have seen much hardship and got his arm wounded? Clearly in Afghanistan.'[82] The whole train of thought did not occupy a second. I then remarked that you came from Afghanistan, and you were astonished."

"It is simple enough as you explain it," I said, smiling. "You remind me of Edgar Allan Poe's Dupin.[83] I had no idea that such individuals did exist outside of stories."

Sherlock Holmes rose and lit his pipe. "No doubt you think that you are complimenting me in comparing me to Dupin," he observed. "Now, in my opinion, Dupin was a very inferior fellow.[84] That trick of his of breaking in on his friends' thoughts with an apropos remark after a quarter of an hour's silence is really very showy and superficial. He had some ana-

ness of Watson's mention of the Underground here; the nearby Baker Street station, first opened in 1863, was then undergoing expansion.

79 William S. Baring-Gould calls this an early sign of Watson's predilection for gambling, to which he refers many years later in "The Dancing Men" and "Shoscombe Old Place." In the latter story, when Holmes asks Watson whether he knows anything about horse racing, the doctor replies, "I ought to. I pay for it with about half my wound pension."

80 Holmes's fees varied widely during his career. For a detailed discussion of Holmes's income at this time in his career and later, see this editor's "On Sherlock Holmes's Money."

81 Ian McQueen is dubious that Watson would have had sufficient time to acquire a marked degree of facial tanning. Instead, McQueen suggests, Watson, "revelling in his rôle as the old campaigner," may have exaggerated, "partly for understandable reasons of vanity, partly with the object of enabling Holmes to display his remarkable deductive capacity. It may be that Holmes was not so quick with his inference about Afghanistan as Watson would have the reader believe."

82 This is not as foregone a conclusion as Holmes pretends it to be; Samuel F. Howard notes that on the basis of the limited data reported by Watson, Holmes might well have concluded that Watson was returning from South Africa, where the Zulu campaign (1879–1880) was just concluding. Furthermore, as several commentators note, Afghanistan is not in the "tropics" in any normal sense of the word. "Either Holmes had other data that he did not explain to Watson (or Watson did not pass on to us)," Howard writes in "More About Maiwand," "or he was lytical genius, no doubt; but he was by no means such a phenomenon as Poe appeared to imagine."

"Have you read Gaboriau's works?" I asked. "Does Lecoq come up to your idea of a detective?"[85]

Sherlock Holmes sniffed sardonically. "Lecoq was a miserable bungler," he said, in an angry voice; "he had only one thing to recommend him, and that was his energy. That book made me positively ill. The question was how to identify an unknown prisoner. I could have done it in twenty-four hours. Lecoq took six months or so. It might be made a text-book for detectives to teach them what to avoid."[86]

I felt rather indignant at having two characters whom I had admired treated in this cavalier style. I walked over to the window and stood looking out into the busy street. "This fellow may be very clever," I said to myself, "but he is certainly very conceited."

"There are no crimes and no criminals in these days,"[87] he said, querulously. "What is the use of having brains in our profession? I know well that I have it in me to make my name famous. No man lives or has ever lived who has brought the same amount of study and of natural talent to the detection of crime which I have done. And what is the result? There is no crime to detect, or, at most, some bungling villainy with a motive so transparent that even a Scotland Yard[88] official can see through it."

I was still annoyed at his bumptious style of conversation. I thought it best to change the topic.

"I wonder what that fellow is looking for?" I asked, pointing to a stalwart, plainly dressed individual who was walking slowly down the other side of the street, looking anxiously at the numbers. He had a large blue envelope in his hand, and was evidently the bearer of a message.

"You mean the retired sergeant of Marines," said Sherlock Holmes.

"Brag and bounce!" thought I to myself. "He knows that I cannot verify his guess."

The thought had hardly passed through my mind when the man whom we were watching caught sight of the number on our door, and ran rapidly across the roadway. We heard a loud knock, a deep voice below, and heavy steps ascending the stair.

guilty of sheer guesswork. I prefer to believe he observed some other detail in Watson's appearance that he did not bother to repeat to Watson when, months later, he explained his methods to him."

83 The Chevalier Auguste Dupin, whose adventures are recorded in Edgar Allan Poe's "The Murders in the Rue Morgue" (1841), "Mystery of Marie Roget" (1842), and "Purloined Letter" (1844), was of "illustrious parentage" but lived in poverty in a small back library at No. 33 Rue Dunot, Faubourg-St. Germain. An anonymous chronicler reports that Dupin preferred to sit behind closed shutters, lit only by "a couple of tapers which, strongly perfumed, threw out only the ghastliest and feeblest of rays." He would emerge from his rooms, "when the fit was upon him," to wander through Paris and experience "the infinity of mental excitement" resulting from his observation of Parisian life. A heavy smoker who favored a meerschaum pipe, Dupin was disdainful of the Paris police and had contempt for their methods.

"The Murders in the Rue Morgue," the story of a mother-daughter murder that baffles police, is widely considered the first modern detective story. It was published in *Graham's Magazine* (of which Poe was the editor). Steinbrunner and Penzler's *Encyclopedia of Mystery and Detection* calls Dupin "the model for virtually every cerebral crime solver who followed."

84 Arthur Conan Doyle disagreed with Holmes, assessing Poe's hero-detective in a preface to the twelve-volume Author's Edition of Poe's works: "Edgar Allan Poe . . . was the father of the detective tale, and covered its limits so completely that I fail to see how his followers can find any fresh ground which they can confidently call their own. . . . On this narrow path [of creating a "hero" character] the writer must walk and he sees the footmarks of Poe always in front of him. He is happy if he ever finds the means of breaking away and striking out on some little side-track of his own."

Holmes's dismissive description of Dupin may belie a more deep-seated impulse. "There was always just a touch of professional jealousy in Holmes's character," writes Vincent Starrett, "—entirely natural, no doubt—that even Watson could not gloss away." Yet in "The Cardboard Box," Holmes takes quite a different tone, evidently referring to Dupin when he speaks favourably of the "close reasoner" in Poe's "sketches." Morris Rosenblum is one scholar who presumes that Watson must have been perplexed by this about-face; but Marshall Shaw Dickman believes he has found the reason for it: In "On Matters Surrounding the Case of the Purloined Letter," Dickman relates his discovery of a manuscript suggesting that Dupin's activities after "The Purloined Letter" resulted in the birth of Holmes's mother. This would make Dupin Holmes's grandfather. Could Holmes have seen the manuscript?

85 M. Lecoq, whose adventures are reported in a series of books by Emile Gaboriau, was a criminal-turned-detective for the Paris *Surêté*, or security police. The early career of Lecoq closely resembles that of the headline-making François Eugène Vidocq (1775–1857), who joined the *Surêté* as a police spy after serving prison time for a variety of petty crimes. Vidocq became chief of detectives, leaving the force in 1827 and returning in 1832—only to be dismissed that same year for allegedly orchestrating a robbery with the intention of "solving" it. Vidocq's memoirs were published in four volumes in 1828 and 1829. Partly fictional and probably ghost-written, they were widely read.

Monsieur Lecoq (Gaboriau never revealed his first name) was born around 1844 to "respectable" parents but turned to crime after his father's financial ruin. Just when his life seemed headed down the wrong path, he consulted an astronomer, who told him, "When one has your disposition, and is poor, one may either become a famous thief or a great detective. Choose." He chose the latter and became an expert at the use of disguise, developing useful tests to determine when a bed had been last used and when the hands of a clock had been set back. His adventures are recounted in *L'Affair Lerouge* (1866) (U.S. title *The Widow Lerouge*, 1873), *Le Dossier No. 113* (1867) (U.S. title *File No. 113*, 1875), *Monsieur Lecoq* (1869), *Le Crime de Orcival* (1867) (U.S. title *The Mystery of Orcival*, 1871), *Les Enclaves de Paris* (1868) (U.S. title *The Slaves of Paris*, 1882), and the posthumously published long story *Le Petit Vieux des Batignolles* (1876) (U.S. title *The Little Old Man of Batignolles*, 1880). In his first case, *L'Affaire Lerouge*, Lecoq plays only a small part; the principal detection is by Père Tabaret, known as Tir-au-clair, an amateur detective who tutors Lecoq.

86 The book that Holmes so scorns is likely *Monsieur Lecoq*, in which Lecoq releases a prisoner and follows him for an extended period to determine his identity. In the judgement of historians and scholars, there is little in Lecoq's career to justify Holmes's verdict of "a miserable bungler," although Lecoq's mentor Père Tabaret himself described Lecoq in this case as committing "a great many blunders" and complained that he had squandered three or four opportunities to solve the case.

87 Holmes similarly laments a dearth of nefariousness in *The Sign of Four* (which probably took place in 1888): "Crime is commonplace, existence is commonplace, and no qualities save those that are commonplace have any function on earth." The high point of his career was clearly his extended struggle with Professor Moriarty, which was not to commence until 1890 or so (in "The Final

Problem," Moriarty says that Holmes first "crossed his path" in January 1891, but that could not have been Holmes's first knowledge of Moriarty). When that investigation was over, however, Holmes returned to relative boredom, causing him to sigh in "Wisteria Lodge" (1894 or 1895): "Life is commonplace, the papers are sterile; audacity and romance seem to have passed forever from the criminal world." T. S. Blakeney comments, "We clearly see from these observations that the artist [in Holmes] has outstripped the social worker. . . . More than once we catch a wistful tone in his reference to the dear departed Professor Moriarty—see *The Norwood Builder* and the tinge of hope that inspired his suggestion (*The Missing Three-Quarter*) that Dr. Leslie Armstrong might fill the gap left by the professor's death."

Self-portrait of artist George Hutchinson.
Beeton's Christmas Annual, 1892

88 Scotland Yard, originally a specific location, became the colloquial name for the detectives of the London Metropolitan Police. The first headquarters of the Metropolitan Police were the back premises of 4 Whitehall Place. The location had been the site of a residence owned by the kings of Scotland before the Union and used and occupied by them and/or their ambassadors when in London, and was known as "Scotland." The courtyard was later used by Sir Christopher Wren and known as "Scotland Yard." The residence backed on to Great Scotland Yard, the name of which was said to have been derived from the Scott family's ownership during the Middle Ages. In either case, by 1887, the police headquarters embraced numbers 3, 4, 5, 21, and 22 Whitehall Place, numbers 8 and 9 Great Scotland Yard, numbers 1, 2, and 3 Palace Place, and various stables and outbuildings. In 1890, the headquarters moved to premises on the Victoria Embankment designed by Richard Norman Shaw, which became known as "New Scotland Yard" and was presumably well known to Holmes. In 1967, because of the need for a larger and more modern headquarters, a further move took place to the present site at Broadway, S.W.1, also known as "New Scotland Yard."

89 The Royal Marines, the amphibious infantry of Britain's Royal Navy, was formed in 1664 via an Order-in-Council calling for the recruitment of 1,200 soldiers who would fight on land and at sea. These men were initially known as the Duke of York and Albany's Maritime Regiment of Foot, or the Admiral's Regiment. In 1855, a separate artillery division was formed, and the naval infantry itself was given the name Royal Marines, Light Infantry (altered to the Royal Marine Light Infantry in 1862). The two divisions merged in 1923.

HRH Prince Edward (very briefly) and the English authors Evelyn Waugh, John Fowles, and John Gardner (author of several novels about Professor Moriarty) served in the Royal Marines.

" 'For Mr. Sherlock Holmes,' he said."
Richard Gutschmidt, *Späte Rache* (Stuttgart: Robert Lutz Verlag, 1902)

"For Mr. Sherlock Holmes," he said, stepping into the room and handing my friend the letter.

Here was an opportunity of taking the conceit out of him. He little thought of this when he made that random shot. "May I ask, my lad," I said, in the blandest voice, "what your trade may be?"

"Commissionaire, sir," he said, gruffly. "Uniform away for repairs."

"And you were?" I asked, with a slightly malicious glance at my companion.

"A sergeant, sir, Royal Marine Light Infantry,[89] sir. No answer? Right, sir."

He clicked his heels together, raised his hand in salute, and was gone.

CHAPTER III

The Lauriston Garden Mystery

I CONFESS THAT I was considerably startled by this fresh proof of the practical nature of my companion's theories. My respect for his powers of analysis increased wondrously. There still remained some lurking suspicion in my mind, however, that the whole thing was a pre-arranged episode, intended to dazzle me, though what earthly object he could have in taking me in was past my comprehension. When I looked at him he had finished reading the note, and his eyes had assumed the vacant, lack-lustre expression which showed mental abstraction.

"How in the world did you deduce that?" I asked.

"Deduce what?" said he, petulantly.

"Why, that he was a retired sergeant of Marines."

"I have no time for trifles," he answered, brusquely; then with a smile, "Excuse my rudeness. You broke the thread of my thoughts; but perhaps it is as well. So you actually were not able to see that that man was a sergeant of Marines?"

"No, indeed."

"It was easier to know it than to explain why I knew it. If you were asked to prove that two and two made four, you might find some difficulty, and yet you are quite sure of the

Poster for *A Study in Scarlet* (United States: World Wide, 1933), starring Reginald Owen as Sherlock Holmes.

fact. Even across the street I could see a great blue anchor tattooed on the back of the fellow's hand. That smacked of the sea. He had a military carriage, however, and regulation side whiskers. There we have the marine. He was a man with some amount of self-importance and a certain air of command. You must have observed the way in which he held his head and swung his cane. A steady, respectable, middle-aged man, too, on the face of him—all facts which led me to believe that he had been a sergeant."

"Wonderful!" I ejaculated.

"Commonplace," said Holmes, though I thought from his expression that he was pleased at my evident surprise and admiration. "I said just now that there were no criminals. It appears that I am wrong—look at this!" He threw me over the note which the commissionaire had brought.

"Why," I cried, as I cast my eye over it, "this is terrible!"

"It does seem to be a little out of the common," he remarked, calmly. "Would you mind reading it to me aloud?"[90]

This is the letter which I read to him—

MY DEAR MR. SHERLOCK HOLMES—,

There has been a bad business during the night at 3, Lauriston Gardens, off the Brixton Road. Our man on the beat saw a light there about two in the morning, and as the house was an empty one, suspected that something was amiss. He found the door open, and in the front room, which is bare of furniture, discovered the body of a gentleman, well dressed, and having cards in his pocket bearing the name of "Enoch J. Drebber, Cleveland, Ohio, U.S.A." There had been no robbery, nor is there any evidence as to how the man met his death. There are marks of blood in the room, but there is no wound upon his person. We are at a loss as to how he came into the empty house; indeed, the whole affair is a puzzler. If you can come round to the house any time before twelve, you will find me there. I have left everything *in statu quo*[91] until I hear from you.[92] If you are unable to come I shall give you fuller details, and would esteem it a great kindness if you would favour me with your opinion.

Yours faithfully—,
TOBIAS GREGSON.

"Gregson[93] is the smartest of the Scotland Yarders," my friend remarked; "he and Lestrade are the pick of a bad lot. They are both quick and energetic, but conventional—shockingly so. They have their knives into one another, too. They are as jealous as a pair of professional beauties. There will be some fun over this case if they are both put upon the scent."[94]

I was amazed at the calm way in which he rippled on. "Surely there is not a moment to be lost," I cried; "shall I go and order you a cab?"[95]

"I'm not sure about whether I shall go. I am the most incurably lazy devil that ever stood in shoe leather—that is, when the fit is on me, for I can be spry enough at times."

90 Jerry Neal Williamson, in " 'And Especially Your Eyes,' " uses this scene to argue that Holmes was farsighted. Here, he points out, there is evidence of Holmes's uncanny "long vision": while he was able to spot the tattoo on the back of the marine's hand, he cannot read the note to his satisfaction without enlisting Watson's help. But there are numerous conflicting statements about Holmes's vision throughout the Canon, as Richard L. Vaught, M.D., notes in "Now See Here, Holmes!" For example, Holmes has no trouble reading a "little brown-backed volume" (see text accompanying note 150, below), which was undoubtedly printed with very small type. Trevor H. Hall, in "The Late Sherlock Holmes," proposes that Holmes developed amblyopia (a lazy eye) from his excessive tobacco use and eventually faced total blindness. Dr. Vaught concludes that Holmes was nearsighted in one eye and farsighted in the other, and he coins a new term, "antimetropia," for this condition. (The medical term for farsightedness is hyperopia; for nearsightedness, myopia.)

91 The Latin phrase literally means "in the state in which," or in its former state.

92 Mystery writer John Ball, Jr., in "Early Days in Baker Street," sees in this and Lestrade's later question "What do you think of it, sir?" remarkable deference to a "civilian" not part of the Yard. In Ball's view, through the offices of Mycroft Holmes, Sherlock Holmes became a private agent in Her Majesty's Government, "probably with the classification of Queen's Messenger, a unique and highly restricted office. Queen's (or King's) Messengers may go anywhere in the British Empire on official business, and have extraordinary authority in the field."

R. K. Leavitt takes the contrary view, expressed in "Nummi in Arca or The Fiscal Holmes," that Holmes had been hired privately by the inspectors from the Yard, to enhance their professional reputations.

93 Although Gregson appears or is mentioned in five cases (the others are *The Sign of Four*, "The Greek Interpreter," "Wisteria Lodge," and "The Red Circle"), this is the only case in which he is truly involved.

94 This is the only recorded case in which Scotland Yard's two leading inspectors, Gregson and Lestrade, work together. Gavin Brend wonders whether a bit of intercontinental rivalry might have led to their teaming up. Perhaps, he writes, the officials at Scotland Yard "wished to impress their Transatlantic brethren by demonstrating that they were quite capable of discovering the murderer of Enoch J. Drebber of Cleveland, Ohio." But the ranks of Gregson and Lestrade are never actually mentioned by Watson, and Bernard Davies suggests that the two were mere detective-sergeants at the time—making their pairing far less momentous.

95 William S. Baring-Gould points out that the nearest cab-rank was at the corner of Dorset Street, only a block away.

96 John Ball, Jr., who argues that Holmes was a "Queen's Messenger" (see note 92 above), discounts this remark as being a mere cover for his official status. The detective, he reminds us, "is certainly not the first confidential agent in history to deny the true source of his employment."

Headquarters of the Metropolitan Police in Great Scotland Yard, Charing Cross (*ca.* 1881)

"Why, it is just such a chance as you have been longing for."

"My dear fellow, what does it matter to me? Supposing I unravel the whole matter, you may be sure that Gregson, Lestrade, and Co. will pocket all the credit. That comes of being an unofficial personage."[96]

"But he begs you to help him."

"Yes. He knows that I am his superior, and acknowledges it to me; but he would cut his tongue out before he would own it to any third person. However, we may as well go and have a look. I shall work it out on my own hook. I may have a laugh at them, if I have nothing else. Come on!"

He hustled on his overcoat, and bustled about in a way that showed that an energetic fit had superseded the apathetic one.

"Get your hat," he said.

"You wish me to come?"

"Yes, if you have nothing better to do." A minute later we were both in a hansom, driving furiously for the Brixton Road.

It was a foggy, cloudy morning,

Victorian policeman.

"He hustled on his overcoat."
Geo. Hutchinson, *A Study in Scarlet* (London: Ward, Lock Bowden, and Co., 1891)

and a dun-coloured veil hung over the house-tops, looking like the reflection of the mud-coloured streets beneath. My companion was in the best of spirits, and prattled away about Cremona fiddles, and the difference between a Stradivarius[97] and an Amati.[98] As for myself, I was silent, for the dull weather and the melancholy business upon which we were engaged, depressed my spirits.

"You don't seem to give much thought to the matter in hand," I said at last, interrupting Holmes's musical disquisition.

"No data yet," he answered. "It is a capital mistake to theorize before you have all the evidence. It biases the judgment."[99]

"You will have your data soon," I remarked, pointing with my finger; "this is the Brixton Road, and that is the house, if I am not very much mistaken."

"So it is. Stop, driver, stop!" We were still a hundred yards or so from it, but he insisted upon our alighting, and we finished our journey upon foot.

97 The violins made by Antonio Stradivari (1644–1737) at his workshop in Cremona, Italy, have long been prized for their perfect design and pure tone. While apprenticing with Nicolò Amati in 1666 (see below), Stradivari began making improvements upon Amati's model and creating violins with the Latin inscription *Antonius Stradivarius Cremonensis Faciebat Anno* [date] imprinted on them. (It should be noted that such a label may or may not indicate authenticity.) Stradivari's best work was done after 1700; the instruments he produced during that period set the standard by which modern violins are designed and judged. A fitting description is found in *The Lost Stradivarius* (1895), by John Meade Falkner, in which a Stradivarius discovered in an old cupboard is described as possessing "a light-red colour, with a varnish of peculiar lustre and softness. The neck seemed rather longer than ordinary, and the scroll was remarkably bold and free." Approximately 650 of Stradivari's more than 1,100 violins, cellos, harps, guitars, mandolins, and violas survive today.

Professor Joseph Nagyvary, a Stradivarius expert, described the "Stradivari sound" in *Scientific American* as "very lively. It flickers, it constantly trembles, it moves like candlelight." There is disagreement over how Stradivari was able to produce an instrument with such a superior tone: some believe the Alpine spruce he used was particularly dense, whereas others speculate that he treated the wood with a special varnish that affected the sound. Still others, of course, credit the violin-maker, in particular his grasp of geometry as it relates to design, rather than his materials.

Holmes himself was the proud owner of one of these rare instruments. In "The Cardboard Box," Holmes recounts to Watson "with great exultation how he had purchased his own Stradivarius, which was worth at least five hundred guineas, at a Jew broker's in Tottenham Court Road for fifty-five shillings."

98 The Amati family of violin-makers lived in Cremona in the sixteenth and seventeenth centuries. The head of the family and founder of the "Cremona school" was Andrea Amati (*ca.* 1520–1578), whose flat, shallow design, later modified to perfection by Stradivari, provided the basic model for the modern violin. Nicolò Amati, Andrea's grandson, was perhaps the family's most famous violin-maker; a master craftsman, he counted among his students Stradivari and Andrea Guarneri (*ca.* 1626–1698), and his graceful, dulcet-toned violins represented the height of the Amati line. Nicolò's son, Girolamo (1649–1740), continued in the family business, but his violins are thought to be somewhat inferior in quality to those of his father and great-grandfather.

Some of the alterations that Stradivari made to the original Cremona model were to fashion the current violin bridge, as well as to make the body of the violin even shallower and hence more resonant. There were changes also in the thickness of the wood, the type of varnish used, and various other minor but ultimately significant details such that, according to the *Encyclopædia Britannica* (9th Edition), "the majority of violins since made, whether by good or bad makers, are copies of Stradivari."

Guy Warrack, in *Sherlock Holmes and Music*, notes that Holmes omits to mention the third great family of Cremona violin-makers, the Guarneris. "Possibly," Warrack writes, "Holmes was true enough to his principle [expressed earlier to Watson, of not having 'useless facts elbowing out the useful ones'] to shun knowledge of Guarneri violins in order to leave more room for knowledge of Stradivaris."

99 This theme is oft repeated in the Canon. Holmes makes almost the identical remark in "A Scandal in Bohemia," and in other tales formulates the dictate as follows: "It is an error to argue in front of your data. You find yourself insensibly twisting them round to fit your theories" ("Wisteria Lodge"); "We approached the case with an absolutely blank mind, which is always an advantage" ("The Cardboard Box"); "One forms provisional theories and waits for time or fuller knowledge to explode them. A bad habit . . ." ("The Sussex Vampire"); "I make a point of never having any prejudices and of following docilely wherever fact may lead me" ("The Reigate Squires").

"These abundant references to the topic," remarks T. S. Blakeney, "show how keenly Holmes appreciated the liability to form one's suspicions on insufficient evidence. He was not, however, entirely immune from the tendency himself, for both in *The Sign of Four* [where he misjudged the hiding place of the *Aurora*] and *The Missing Three-Quarter* [when he suspected Dr. Leslie Armstrong of villainy] he had to reform his theories, and in *The Yellow Face* his conclusions were definitely wrong."

Number 3, Lauriston Gardens wore an ill-omened and minatory look. It was one of four which stood back some little way from the street, two being occupied and two empty.[100] The latter looked out with three tiers of vacant melancholy windows, which were blank and dreary, save that here and there a "To Let" card had developed like a cataract upon the bleared panes. A small garden sprinkled over with a scattered eruption of sickly plants separated each of these houses from the street, and was traversed by a narrow pathway, yellowish in colour, and consisting apparently of a mixture of clay and of gravel. The whole place was very sloppy from the rain which had fallen through the night. The garden was bounded by a three-foot brick wall with a fringe of wood rails upon the top, and against this wall was leaning a stalwart police constable, surrounded by a small knot of loafers, who craned their necks and strained their eyes in the vain hope of catching some glimpse of the proceedings within.

I had imagined that Sherlock Holmes would at once have hurried into the house and plunged into a study of the mystery. Nothing appeared to be further from his intention. With an air of nonchalance which, under the circumstances, seemed to me to border upon affectation, he lounged up and down the pavement, and gazed vacantly at the ground, the sky, the opposite houses and the line of railings. Having finished his scrutiny, he proceeded slowly down the path, or rather down the fringe of grass which flanked the path, keeping his eyes riveted upon the ground. Twice he stopped, and once I saw him smile, and heard him utter an exclamation of satisfaction. There were many marks of footsteps upon the wet clayey soil; but since the police had been coming and going over it, I was unable to see how my companion could hope to learn anything from it. Still I had had such extraordinary evidence of the quickness of his perceptive faculties, that I had no doubt that he could see a great deal which was hidden from me.

At the door of the house we were met by a tall, white-faced, flaxen-haired man, with a notebook in his hand, who rushed forward and wrung my companion's hand with effusion. "It is indeed kind of you to come," he said, "I have had everything left untouched."

"Except that!" my friend answered, pointing at the pathway. "If a herd of buffaloes[101] had passed along there could not be

100 Where exactly was "Number 3, Lauriston Gardens"?

Both H. W. Bell ("Three Identifications: Lauriston Gardens, Upper Swandam Lane, Saxe-Coburg Square") and Michael Harrison take the view that the row of four houses was on Brixton Road, yet set back some distance from the pavement. "And in fact," Bell writes, "there is no such group of four houses in any of the streets intersecting the Road." Bell does locate a single group of four on Brixton Road, numbered from 314 to 320, which, he claims, correspond perfectly to Watson's description. "Since Watson specified No. 3, we may suppose that No. 318, the third in the row, was the scene of the death of Enoch J. Drebber."

Michael Harrison comes to a similar conclusion as to the street—that is, that the house was on Brixton Road and not an adjoining street—but (seemingly unaware of Bell's work) selects a group of five as fitting Watson's description, namely numbers 152 to 160.

Bernard Davies, making an extended analysis in "The Book of Genesis," rejects the suggestions of both Bell and Harrison. Watson's later description of a central hallway with doors "to the left and to the right," Davies notes, would be appropriate only for a double-fronted house: one with two reception areas. No. 318 Brixton (Bell's choice), by contrast, was a semi-detached single-fronted house, with just one reception area. Similarly, Harrison's candidate is discarded not only for being single-fronted but also for lacking front gardens. Davies identifies the group of houses at Nos. 329–335 Brixton Road, on the east side, between Villa Road and St. John's Road (now St. John's Crescent), as "Lauriston Gardens." A 1962 photograph of the location is reproduced on page 54.

Colin Prestige takes a different approach, in "South London Adventures," latching on to the house's proximity to the White Hart Tavern (see note 133, below) as a telling clue.

No. 3, Lauriston Gardens?
Photographed by Bernard Davies (1962)

Given that the tavern was situated at the junction of Loughborough Road and Lilford Road, Prestige decides that "the area known as Myatt's Fields immediately stands out as being the most probable location [for the house]." He argues that No. 3, Lauriston Gardens was one of the houses along the northern stretch of Knatchbull Road, on a direct route from the White Hart to Holland Grove.

Note the curious title of this chapter, taken from the *Beeton's* text. The "Garden" became plural in later book editions.

101 According to William S. Baring-Gould, Christopher Morley seized on this expression (used again in "The Boscombe Valley Mystery") as an important indication that Holmes had been in America before 1881. Morley pursues this theme at length in "Was Sherlock Holmes an American?" He points to numerous indications of Holmes's fondness for America and Americans, including his choice of disguise (in "His Last Bow") as an Irish-American, his lack of knowledge of rugby (an institution of British schooling; "The Missing Three-Quarter"), and his famous remark "It is always a joy to meet an American."

Franklin Delano Roosevelt took this thesis even further in letters to the Baker Street Irregulars (of which he was a secret honorary

a greater mess. No doubt, however, you had drawn your own conclusions, Gregson, before you permitted this."

"I have had so much to do inside the house," the detective said evasively. "My colleague, Mr. Lestrade, is here. I had relied upon him to look after this."

Holmes glanced at me and raised his eyebrows sardonically. "With two such men as yourself and Lestrade upon the ground, there will not be much for a third party to find out," he said.

Gregson rubbed his hands in a self-satisfied way. "I think we have done all that can be done," he answered; "it's a queer case though, and I knew your taste for such things."

"You did not come here in a cab?"[102] asked Sherlock Holmes.

"No, sir."

"Nor Lestrade?"

"No, sir."

"Then let us go and look at the room." With which inconsequent remark he strode on into the house, followed by Gregson, whose features expressed his astonishment.

A short passage, bare planked and dusty, led to the kitchen and offices.[103] Two doors opened out of it to the left and to the right. One of these had obviously been closed for many weeks. The other belonged to the dining-room, which was the apartment in which the mysterious affair had occurred. Holmes walked in, and I followed him with that subdued feeling at my heart which the presence of death inspires.

It was a large square room, looking all the larger from the absence of all furniture. A vulgar flaring paper adorned the walls, but it was blotched in places with mildew, and here and there great strips had become detached and hung down, exposing the yellow plaster beneath. Opposite the door was a showy fireplace, surmounted by a mantelpiece of imitation white marble. On one corner of this was stuck the stump of a red wax candle. The solitary window was so dirty that the light was hazy and uncertain, giving a dull gray tinge to everything, which was intensified by the thick layer of dust which coated the whole apartment.

All these details I observed afterwards. At present my attention was centred upon the single grim motionless figure which lay stretched upon the boards, with vacant sightless eyes star-

"My attention was centred upon the single grim motionless figure which lay stretched upon the boards."
Richard Gutschmidt, *Späte Rache* (Stuttgart: Robert Lutz Verlag, 1902)

ing up at the discoloured ceiling. It was that of a man about forty-three or forty-four years of age, middle-sized, broad shouldered, with crisp curling black hair, and a short stubbly beard. He was dressed in a heavy broadcloth frock coat and waistcoat, with light-coloured trousers, and immaculate collar and cuffs. A top hat, well brushed and trim, was placed upon the floor beside him. His hands were clenched and his arms thrown abroad, while his lower limbs were interlocked as though his death struggle had been a grievous one. On his rigid face there stood an expression of horror, and, as it seemed to me, of hatred, such as I have never seen upon human features. This malignant and terrible contortion, combined with the low forehead, blunt nose, and prognathous jaw gave the dead man a singularly simious and ape-like appearance, which was increased by his writhing, unnatural posture. I have seen death in many forms, but never has it appeared to me in a more fear-

member), eventually published in *A Baker Street Folio: Letters about Sherlock Holmes from Franklin Delano Roosevelt* (1945), edited by Edgar W. Smith. The President declared in a letter dated December 18, 1944: "On further study I am inclined to revise my former estimate that Holmes was a foundling. Actually he was born an American and was brought up by his father or a foster father in the underground world, thus learning all the tricks of the trade in the highly developed American art of crime. At an early age he felt the urge to do something for mankind. He was too well known in top circles in this country and, therefore, chose to operate in England. His attributes were primarily American, not English. I feel that further study of this postulant will bring good results to history."

102 In pursuit of the continuing mystery of the house's location, Owen Dudley Edwards calls this "a nice clue" and proposes that the inspectors must have taken a public conveyance to the local police station, where they interviewed the local man and then walked to 3 Lauriston Gardens.

103 D. S. Friesland, in a letter to the *Baker Street Journal*, points out that "offices" in this context meant "the parts of a house, or buildings attached to a house, specially devoted to household work or service; the kitchen and rooms connected with it, as pantry, scullery, cellars, laundry, and the like."

104 This modern-sounding slang was clearly in use in the nineteenth century. John Camden Hotten's *Slang Dictionary* (1865) defines it as "a term applied to anything young, small, or insignificant; CHICKEN STAKES; 'she's no CHICKEN,' said of an old maid." It is unclear as to when the saying was altered to specify the fowl as a "spring chicken."

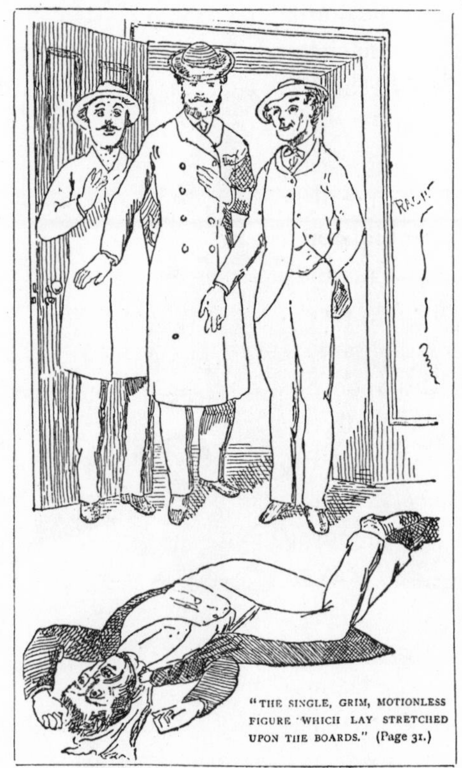

"The single, grim, motionless figure which lay stretched upon the boards."
Charles Doyle, *A Study in Scarlet* (London and New York: Ward, Lock & Co., 1888)

some aspect than in that dark grimy apartment, which looked out upon one of the main arteries of suburban London.

Lestrade, lean and ferret-like as ever, was standing by the doorway, and greeted my companion and myself.

"This case will make a stir, sir," he remarked. "It beats anything I have seen, and I am no chicken."[104]

"There is no clue?" said Gregson.

"None at all," chimed in Lestrade.

Sherlock Holmes approached the body, and, kneeling down, examined it intently. "You are sure that there is no wound?" he asked, pointing to numerous gouts and splashes of blood which lay all round.

"Positive!" cried both detectives.

"Then, of course, this blood belongs to a second individual—presumably the murderer, if murder has been committed. It reminds me of the circumstances attendant on the death of Van Jansen, in Utrecht,[105] in the year '34. Do you remember the case, Gregson?"

"No, sir."

"Read it up—you really should. There is nothing new under the sun.[106] It has all been done before."

As he spoke, his nimble fingers were flying here, there, and everywhere, feeling, pressing, unbuttoning, examining, while his eyes wore the same far-away expression which I have already remarked upon. So swiftly was the examination made, that one would hardly have guessed the minuteness with which it was conducted. Finally, he sniffed the dead man's lips, and then glanced at the soles of his patent leather boots.

"He has not been moved at all?" he asked.

"No more than was necessary for the purposes of our examination."

"You can take him to the mortuary now," he said. "There is nothing more to be learned."

Gregson had a stretcher and four men at hand. At his call they entered the room, and the stranger was lifted and carried out. As they raised him, a ring tinkled down and rolled across the floor. Lestrade grabbed it up and stared at it with mystified eyes.

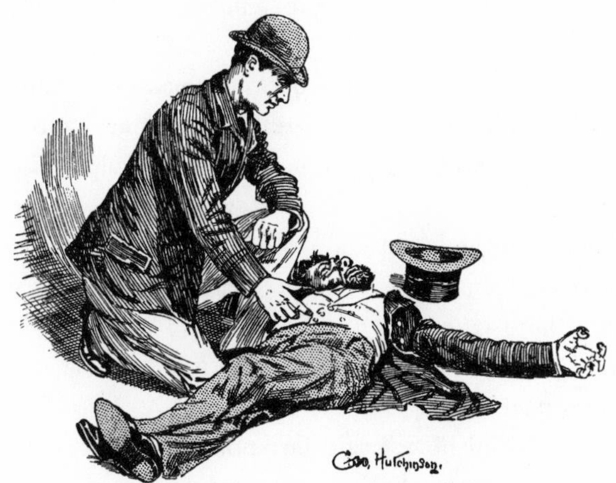

"Sherlock Holmes approached the body, and, kneeling down examined it intently."
Geo. Hutchinson, *A Study in Scarlet* (London: Ward, Lock Bowden, and Co., 1891)

105 Utrecht, in the Netherlands, was the site of a series of peace treaties signed from 1713 to 1714. Under the Peace of Utrecht, France and Spain came to terms with a number of European powers to conclude the War of Spanish Succession. Holmes's interest in Utrecht would have likely been more natural than political, as the province was a center for bee-keeping, with a bee-market held nearby in Veenendaal.

Curiously, for over two hundred years, Utrecht was the headquarters of Jansenism, a Roman Catholic movement founded by the theologian Cornelis Jansen (1585–1638). Jansenists claimed to be disciples of St. Augustine and opposed the Jesuits in many theological respects. Yet there is no known connection between the sect and the "Van Jansen" that Holmes mentions. "Jansen" (the Dutch equivalent of Johnson) is, in fact, a common name in Holland.

106 Ecclesiastes, 1:9: "The thing that hath been, it is that which shall be; and that which is done is that which shall be done: and there is no new thing under the sun." Holmes's expression of philosophy here clearly has a practical bent and motivates his study of criminal history. "As a rule," he explains in "The Red-Headed League," "when I have heard some slight indication of the course of events, I am able to guide myself by the thousands of other similar cases which occur to my memory."

107 Paul Phillip Barraud was the founder of a seventeenth-century watchmaking dynasty that lasted into the twentieth century; his firm's early watches and clocks were marked "Barraud, London." After about 1840, the firm traded as Barraud & Lund and had premises at 49, Cornhill, E.C. Owen Dudley Edwards comments that possession of such a prestigious gold timepiece is surely indicative of its owner's "self-indulgence and profligacy."

108 A watch-chain made up of heavy links, named after Albert, prince consort of Queen Victoria. Albert, himself viewed as stolid and pompous by the masses, was not very popular but nonetheless set the style of male society. Pawnbroker Jabez Wilson ("The Red-Headed League") and "Hosmer Angel," Mary Sutherland's supposed fiancé ("A Case of Identity"), also wore gold Albert chains, and those two men would seem to share with Enoch J. Drebber a vulgar ostentation.

109 Freemasons (the shorthand term for Free and Accepted Masons) were members of a secret society, the origin of which, by tradition, has been traced back to the Knights Templar, the old Roman empire, the pharaohs, Hiram of Tyre, the Temple of Solomon, or even to the times of the Tower of Babel and the Ark of Noah. The masons of England date back to 926 A.D., although modern freemasonry arose in the eighteenth century.

According to D. A. Redmond, in "The Masons and the Mormons," by the time of *A Study in Scarlet* there was significant hostility between adherents of American freemasonry and those of Mormonism. Redmond quotes the "Proceedings of the Most Worshipful Grand Lodge of the State of Kansas, 29th Annual Communication" (Emporia, 1885) as stating that freemasonry, "in a territory over which barbarism prevails, will if continued, be the principle [*sic*] means on which reliance can be placed to dispel the baleful shadow

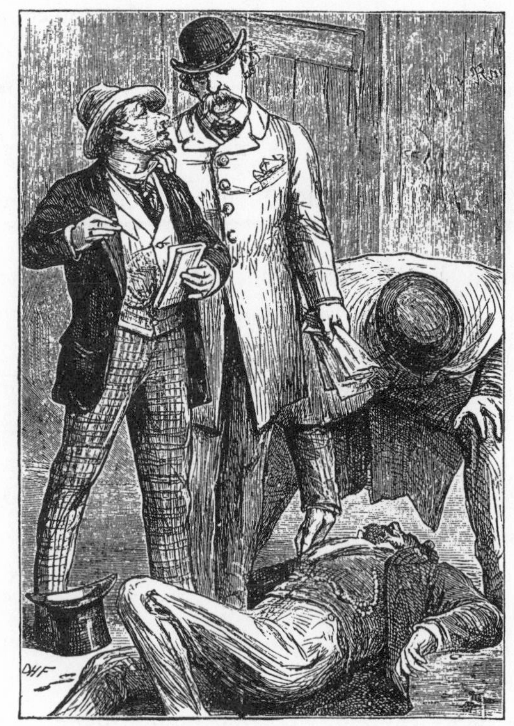

"As he spoke, his nimble fingers were flying here, there, and everywhere."
D. H. Friston, *Beeton's Christmas Annual*, 1887

"There's been a woman here," he cried. "It's a woman's wedding-ring."

He held it out, as he spoke, upon the palm of his hand. We all gathered round him and gazed at it. There could be no doubt that that circlet of plain gold had once adorned the finger of a bride.

"This complicates matters," said Gregson. "Heaven knows, they were complicated enough before."

"You're sure it doesn't simplify them?" observed Holmes. "There's nothing to be learned by staring at it. What did you find in his pockets?"

"We have it all here," said Gregson, pointing to a litter of objects upon one of the bottom steps of the stairs. "A gold watch, No. 97163, by Barraud, of London.[107] Gold Albert chain,[108] very heavy and solid. Gold ring, with masonic[109] device. Gold pin—bull-dog's head, with rubies as eyes. Russian leather card-case, with cards of Enoch J. Drebber of Cleve-

The American Exchange (1895).

land, corresponding with the E. J. D. upon the linen. No purse, but loose money to the extent of seven pounds thirteen. Pocket edition of Boccaccio's 'Decameron,'[110] with name of Joseph Stangerson upon the fly-leaf. Two letters—one addressed to E. J. Drebber and one to Joseph Stangerson."

"At what address?"

"American Exchange,[111] Strand—to be left till called for. They are both from the Guion Steamship Company,[112] and refer to the sailing of their boats from Liverpool. It is clear that this unfortunate man was about to return to New York."

"Have you made any inquiries as to this man Stangerson?"

"I did it at once, sir," said Gregson. "I have had advertisements sent to all the newspapers, and one of my men has gone to the American Exchange, but he has not returned yet."

"Have you sent to Cleveland?"

"We telegraphed this morning."

"How did you word your inquiries?"

"We simply detailed the circumstances, and said that we should be glad of any information which could help us."

"You did not ask for particulars on any point which appeared to you to be crucial?"

"I asked about Stangerson."

cast by Mormonism and root out this latest form of tyranny, based on stolid, deplorable ignorance and gross uncleanness." Redmond speculates that Drebber wore the insignia "as a cover, to lend respectability and possibly to provide an entrée to genuine lodges in his travels."

Jabez Wilson was a Freemason ("The Red-Headed League"), as were John Hector McFarlane ("The Norwood Builder") and Holmes's "hated rival," detective Barker ("The Retired Colourman"). Cecil A. Ryder, Jr., in "A Study in Masonry," concludes that Holmes and Watson were also members. Arthur Conan Doyle joined the Phoenix Lodge of the Masons in 1887, and Ryder suggests that it was there that Dr. Doyle met Dr. Watson, leading to the publication of *A Study in Scarlet.*

110 The masterpiece of Giovanni Boccaccio (1313–1375), Italian poet and scholar, consists of 100 stories, told over the course of ten days by seven women and three men who have fled plague-ravaged Florence in 1348. (*Decameron* means "Ten Days' Work.") At the end of each day, the story-teller sings a song meant for dancing. Boccaccio's theme was the way of life of the bourgeoisie. By focussing on human limitations and moral values, he depicted man overcoming his misfortunes by accepting the consequences of his own actions. This was a startling departure from most literature of the Middle Ages, which tended to look to the divine to explain and respond to the complications of human life.

While Boccaccio's work is hailed as the first great example of Italian prose, its Victorian reputation lay in no insignificant part as a source of "dirty" stories. For example, several Victorian editions omitted the tenth story of the third day, "Alibech Puts the Devil Back into Hell," as indecent, and the Comstock laws in America made it illegal for decades to mail copies of the work. Owen Dudley Edwards suggests that the edition carried by

Drebber was the selection published in 1884 by George Routledge & Sons, with an introduction by Henry Morley, in "Morley's Universal Library."

111 More properly, Gillig's United States Exchange at 9 Strand, which also had a reading room with American newspapers.

112 James Montgomery, in "A Hearty Sea-Story," reproduces several advertisements of the Guion Shipping Line: " 'The provisions supplied,' says a card, 'are abundant and excellent in quality, and are served and cooked by the company's stewards.' 'Bear in mind,' says another, 'that the Guion Line has not lost a single English, Welsh, Scotch or Irish passenger for the last 25 years.' " Presumably Mr. Drebber of Cleveland felt that the same safety record would hold for an American.

The Guion Line.

"Nothing else? Is there no circumstance on which this whole case appears to hinge? Will you not telegraph again?"

"I have said all I have to say," said Gregson, in an offended voice.

Sherlock Holmes chuckled to himself, and appeared to be about to make some remark, when Lestrade, who had been in the front room while we were holding this conversation in the hall, reappeared upon the scene, rubbing his hands in a pompous and self-satisfied manner.

"Mr. Gregson," he said, "I have just made a discovery of the highest importance, and one which would have been overlooked had I not made a careful examination of the walls."

The little man's eyes sparkled as he spoke, and he was evidently in a state of suppressed exultation at having scored a point against his colleague.

"Come here," he said, bustling back into the room, the atmosphere of which felt clearer since the removal of its ghastly inmate. "Now, stand there!"

He struck a match on his boot and held it up against the wall.

"Look at that!" he said, triumphantly.

I have remarked that the paper had fallen away in parts. In this particular corner of the room a large piece had peeled off, leaving a yellow square of coarse plastering. Across this bare space there was scrawled in blood-red letters a single word—

RACHE.

"What do you think of that?" cried the detective, with the air of a showman exhibiting his show. "This was overlooked because it was in the darkest corner of the room, and no one thought of looking there. The murderer has written it with his or her own blood. See this smear where it has trickled down the wall! That disposes of the idea of suicide anyhow. Why was that corner chosen to write it on? I will tell you. See that candle on the mantelpiece. It was lit at the time, and if it was lit this corner would be the brightest instead of the darkest portion of the wall."

"And what does it mean now that you *have* found it?" asked Gregson in a depreciatory voice.

"Mean? Why, it means that the writer was going to put the female name Rachel, but was disturbed before he or she had time to finish. You mark my words, when this case comes to be cleared up you will find that a woman named Rachel has some-

"He struck a match on his boot and held it up against the wall."
Geo. Hutchinson, *A Study in Scarlet* (London: Ward, Lock Bowden, and Co., 1891)

thing to do with it. It's all very well for you to laugh, Mr. Sherlock Holmes. You may be very smart and clever, but the old hound is the best, when all is said and done."

"I really beg your pardon!" said my companion, who had ruffled the little man's temper by bursting into an explosion of laughter. "You certainly have the credit of being the first of us to find this out and, as you say, it bears every mark of having been written by the other participant in last night's mystery. I have not had time to examine this room yet,[113] but with your permission I shall do so now."

As he spoke, he whipped a tape measure and a large round magnifying glass[114] from his pocket. With these two implements he trotted noiselessly about the room, sometimes stopping, occasionally kneeling, and once lying flat upon his face. So engrossed was he with his occupation that he appeared to have forgotten our presence, for he chattered away to himself

113 James Cole, in "The Curious Incident of Holmes's Doing Little in the Daytime," is critical of Holmes for failing to examine the murder scene before leaving the room but chalks it up to Holmes's inexperience with cases other than those of the "armchair" variety. If Lestrade had not made his discovery of the writing, Cole wonders, would Holmes have even troubled to investigate the room?

114 In "Sherlock's Murder Bag," J. N. Williamson counts sixteen stories in which Holmes is reported as using the lens. Michael Harrison, in *The World of Sherlock Holmes*, wonders why a man of Holmes's young age (twenty-seven, by most accounts) "should need a glass to see anything? . . . [I]f a *large* piece of wallpaper had peeled away, then an equally *large* 'yellow square of coarse plastering' must have been left. And, not improbably, the word *Rache* was written in 'blood-red' characters not small." He concludes that Holmes's use of "the sort of high-powered single lens with which shaky old men read newspapers in public libraries" is an indication of his markedly precocious presybyopia (usually age-related blurring of near objects). For other theories about Holmes's vision, see note 90, above.

" 'Look at that!' he said, triumphantly."
Richard Gutschmidt, *Späte Rache* (Stuttgart: Robert Lutz Verlag, 1902)

under his breath the whole time, keeping up a running fire of exclamations, groans, whistles, and little cries suggestive of encouragement and of hope. As I watched him I was irresistibly reminded of a pure-blooded, well-trained foxhound as it dashes backward and forward through the covert, whining in its eagerness, until it comes across the lost scent. For twenty minutes or more he continued his researches, measuring with the most exact care the distance between marks which were entirely invisible to me, and occasionally applying his tape to the walls in an equally incomprehensible manner. In one place he gathered up very carefully a little pile of grey dust from the floor, and packed it away in an envelope. Finally, he examined with his glass the word upon the wall, going over every letter of it with the most minute exactness. This done, he appeared to be satisfied, for he replaced his tape and his glass in his pocket.

"They say that genius is an infinite capacity for taking

pains,"[115] he remarked with a smile. "It's a very bad definition, but it does apply to detective work."

Gregson and Lestrade had watched the manœuvres of their amateur companion with considerable curiosity and some contempt. They evidently failed to appreciate the fact, which I had begun to realize, that Sherlock Holmes's smallest actions were all directed towards some definite and practical end.

"What do you think of it sir?" they both asked.

"It would be robbing you of the credit of the case if I was to presume to help you," remarked my friend. "You are doing so well now that it would be a pity for anyone to interfere." There was a world of sarcasm in his voice as he spoke. "If you will let me know how your investigations go," he continued, "I shall be happy to give you any help I can. In the meantime I should like to speak to the constable who found the body. Can you give me his name and address?"

Lestrade glanced at his notebook. "John Rance," he said.

"He examined with the glass the word upon the wall, going over every letter of it with the most minute exactness."
D. H. Friston, *Beeton's Christmas Annual*, 1887

115 William S. Baring-Gould reminds us that this sentiment may be attributed to Thomas Carlyle, who wrote, in *Life of Frederick the Great*, "Genius . . . which is the transcendent capacity for taking trouble first of all." Of course, Holmes has earlier inquired "in the naivest way who [Carlyle] might be and what he had done." His quoting the historian here seems to prove that his earlier ignorance was merely an act.

"He is off duty now. You will find him at 46, Audley Court, Kennington Park Gate."[116]

Holmes took a note of the address.

"Come along, Doctor," he said: "we shall go and look him up. I'll tell you one thing which may help you in the case," he continued, turning to the two detectives. "There has been murder done,[117] and the murderer was a man. He was more than six feet high, was in the prime of life, had small feet for his height, wore coarse square-toed boots and smoked a Trichinopoly[118] cigar. He came here with his victim in a four-wheeled cab, which was drawn by a horse with three old shoes and one new one on his off fore leg.[119] In all probability the murderer had a florid face, and the finger-nails of his right hand were remarkably long. These are only a few indications, but they may assist you."

Lestrade and Gregson glanced at each other with an incredulous smile.

"If this man was murdered, how was it done?" asked the former.

"Poison," said Sherlock Holmes curtly, and strode off. "One other thing, Lestrade," he added, turning round at the door: " 'Rache' is the German for 'revenge'; so don't lose your time looking for Miss Rachel."[120]

With which Parthian shot[121] he walked away, leaving the two rivals open-mouthed behind him.

116 There is no Kennington Park Gate in London. Kennington *Park* is located at the intersection of Kennington Park Road and Camberwell New Road, and an Audley *Square* does exist, though far removed from Kennington. Bernard Davies identifies "Audley Court" as Aulton Place, the combined name given to Aulton Passage and Grove Place in 1893.

117 There are 65 murder victims and 57 murderers mentioned in the Canon, comprehensively listed in Kelvin Jones's *The Sherlock Holmes Murder File.*

118 The city and district of Trichinopoly, located near Tiruchirapali, in southern India, was a well-known source of tobacco.

119 The horse's right side; the left side, on which the rider mounts, is known as "near."

120 Jay Finley Christ disputes whether any of the evidence adduced by Holmes to this point is helpful, pointing out that none of it conclusively incriminates the criminal.

121 The Parthians, an ancient Persian race, legendarily had the habit of turning around in the saddle to discharge an arrow at a pursuer—hence, a parting shot.

CHAPTER IV

WHAT JOHN RANCE HAD TO TELL

It was one o'clock when we left No. 3, Lauriston Gardens. Sherlock Holmes led me to the nearest telegraph office,[122] whence he dispatched a long telegram.[123] He then hailed a cab, and ordered the driver to take us to the address given us by Lestrade.

"There is nothing like first hand evidence," he remarked; "as a matter of fact, my mind is entirely made up upon the case, but still we may as well learn all that is to be learned."[124]

"You amaze me, Holmes," said I. "Surely you are not as sure as you pretend to be of all those particulars which you gave."

"There's no room for a mistake," he answered. "The very first thing which I observed on arriving there was that a cab had made two ruts with its wheels close to the curb. Now, up to last night we have had no rain for a week, so that those wheels which left such a deep impression must have been there during the night. There were the marks of the horse's hoofs, too, the outline of one of which was far more clearly cut than that of the other three, showing that that was a new shoe. Since the cab was there after the rain began, and was not there at any time during the morning—I have Gregson's word for that—it

122 To support his identification of No. 318, Brixton Road, as "No. 3, Lauriston Gardens" (see note 100, above), H. W. Bell observes that as late as 1896, there was a post office—from which one could send telegrams—located some sixty yards up the road from No. 318.

123 In "The Devil's Foot," Watson said of Holmes: "[H]e was never known to write where a telegram would serve." By the end of the nineteenth century—despite the invention of the telephone in 1876—sending telegrams was still an immensely popular way to communicate personal messages quickly. England's first electromagnetic telegraph, which used a battery, copper wires, and a magnetic needle to tap out messages, had been patented in 1837 by physicists Sir William Cooke and Charles Wheatstone. That year, the first practical telegraph was constructed in London with the purpose of enabling railway stations to relay simple emergency signals to each other. Meanwhile, in America, Samuel Morse had invented his own telegraph and alphabetic code (his first message, sent in 1844 on a wire between Washington and Baltimore, was "What hath God wrought!"). The Morse telegraph would eventually become the most commonly used in the world.

An important factor in the public's acceptance of the telegram as a powerful means of communication was the sensational 1845 Tawell murder case. Tawell was hunted for the murder of a woman near Windsor. When he was spotted at the Slough railway station boarding a train to London's Paddington Station, a telegram was dispatched to London officials with his description, and he was apprehended on his arrival. After his conviction and execution, the telegraph was dubbed "the wires that hanged Tawell" (described in Robert N. Brodie's " 'Take a Wire, Like a Good Fellow': The Telegraph in the Canon"). By 1869, 80,000 miles of telegraph wire had been erected throughout the United Kingdom. Designed along the low-cost lines of the postal system, an ordinary telegram from 1885 to 1915 cost 6*d.* for twelve words or less, plus 1/2*d.* for every excess word. As late as 1903, Holmes was sending his customary terse telegraphic messages to Watson: "Come at once if convenient—if inconvenient come all the same" ("The Creeping Man").

124 This statement ("it's always useful to obtain the facts, although I don't really need them") seems to fly in the face of Holmes's own careful doctrine respecting theorising in advance of the evidence, expressed earlier. It appears to be Holmes trying to impress his newfound colleague on their first case together.

125 J. B. Mackenzie provided a quick and valid counterpoint to Holmes's statement, arguing, in "Sherlock Holmes's Plots and

Dustjacket, *A Study in Scarlet.*
(London and Melbourne: Ward, Lock & Co., Ltd., *ca.* 1950)

follows that it must have been there during the night, and therefore, that it brought those two individuals to the house."

"That seems simple enough," said I; "but how about the other man's height?"

"Why, the height of a man, in nine cases out of ten, can be told from the length of his stride.[125] It is a simple calculation enough, though there is no use my boring you with figures. I had this fellow's stride both on the clay outside and on the dust within. Then I had a way of checking my calculation. When a man writes on a wall, his instinct leads him to write above the level of his own eyes. Now that writing was just over six feet from the ground. It was child's play."

"And his age?" I asked.

"Well, if a man can stride four and a half feet without the smallest effort, he can't be quite in the sere and yellow.[126] That was the breadth of a puddle on the garden walk which he had evidently walked across. Patent-leather boots had gone round, and Square-toes had hopped over. There is no mystery about it at all. I am simply applying to ordinary life a few of those precepts of observation and deduction which I advocated in that article. Is there anything else that puzzles you?"

"The finger-nails and the Trichinopoly," I suggested.

"The writing on the wall was done with a man's forefinger dipped in blood. My glass allowed me to observe that the plaster was slightly scratched in doing it, which would not have been the case if the man's nail had been trimmed. I gathered up some scattered ash from the floor. It was dark in colour and flaky—such an ash is only made by a Trichinopoly. I have made a special study of cigar ashes—in fact, I have written a monograph upon the subject.[127] I flatter myself that I can distinguish at a glance the ash of any known brand[128] either of cigar or of tobacco. It is just in such details that the skilled detective differs from the Gregson and Lestrade type."

"And the florid face?" I asked.

"Ah, that was a more daring shot, though I have no doubt that I was right. You must not ask me that at the present state of the affair."

I passed my hand over my brow. "My head is in a whirl,"[129] I remarked; "the more one thinks of it the more mysterious it grows. How came these two men—if there were two men—into an empty house? What has become of the cabman who drove them? How could one man compel another to take poison? Where did the blood come from? What was the object of the murderer, since robbery had no part in it? How came the woman's ring there? Above all, why should the second man write up the German word RACHE before decamping? I confess that I cannot see any possible way of reconciling all these facts."

My companion smiled approvingly.

"You sum up the difficulties of the situation succinctly and well," he said. "There is much that is still obscure, though I have quite made up my mind on the main facts. As to poor Lestrade's discovery, it was simply a blind intended to put the

Strategy" (1902), "[I]s not the length of a man's pace largely a matter of idiosyncrasy—something which is not, at any rate materially, dependent upon stature? Do not very many tall men take comparatively short steps, and a good number, of less inches, cover more ground with each? Have we not, besides, experience to testify that the upper and lower halves of the human body are often largely disproportioned?"

126 "Sere" is a term used to describe vegetation that has turned arid; "in the sere and yellow," then, recalls a withered tree in the late autumn—in other words, one that is old. Shakespeare's Macbeth calls upon the image when he mourns, "I have lived long enough. My way of life / Is fall'n into the sere, the yellow leaf." William S. Baring-Gould, in *Sherlock Holmes of Baker Street*, proposes, on the basis of Holmes's frequent quotation and paraphrasing of Shakespeare, that Holmes actually spent several post-University years on the stage, touring America with a Shakespeare company.

127 Holmes's study of tobacco was written sometime before 1881, when the events of *A Study in Scarlet* occurred. According to Madeleine B. Stern, the monograph would almost certainly have influenced Gaetano Casoria's 1882 book *Sulla Combustibilitá alcune Varietá de Tobacchi*, a detailed study of of the ash of various tobaccos. Watson did not give the exact name of Holmes's monograph until 1889, in *The Sign of Four*, where it is revealed to be *Upon the Distinction Between the Ashes of the Various Tobaccos: An Enumeration of 140 Forms of Cigar, Cigarette, and Pipe Tobacco, with Coloured Plates Illustrating the Difference in the Ash*. During that case, Holmes remarks that French detective François le Villard was translating the work into his native tongue.

In "The Writings of Mr. Sherlock Holmes," Walter Klinefelter notes that the monograph is the only one of Holmes's writings that he mentions more than once in the Canon. (He refers to it again in "The Boscombe Valley Mystery.") "Consequently," Klinefelter writes, "it may be inferred that he took more than a little pride in its authorship, probably considering it his most important contribution to what may be termed the minutiæ of scientific detection." This opinion was not shared by Arthur Conan Doyle, who found it "rather funny" when a Philadelphia tobacconist inquired of him where a copy could be obtained.

128 In 1951, the editors of *Sherlock Holmes: Catalogue of an Exhibition Held at Abbey House, Baker Street, London, May–September 1951*, stated that it was "not generally considered possible" to distinguish different types of tobacco ash. But Raymond J. McGowan, in "A Chemist's Evaluation of Sherlock Holmes's Monograph on Tobacco," undertook to determine the feasibility of Holmes's boast by performing a chemical analysis of the major types of tobacco, both for cigarettes and cigars. McGowan found that the source of tobacco ashes could indeed be determined from the concentration of manganese chloride and magnesium oxide present, and that as the concentration of the two chemicals increased, the colour of the resultant compound (magnesium permanganate) changed. Yet McGowan's conclusion was that the colour change, from light blue to dark blue, is largely visible only under a microscope. While McGowan seems to have proven Holmes's work, then (note that the monograph mentioned "coloured plates") the detective appears to have exaggerated his abilities here and simplified the technique, perhaps to impress Dr. Watson.

129 "But let us note," William S. Baring-Gould comments wryly, "that having said this, Watson immediately comes out with a string of seven quite apposite questions."

police upon a wrong track, by suggesting Socialism and secret societies.[130] It was not done by a German. The A, if you noticed, was printed somewhat after the German fashion. Now, a real German invariably prints in the Latin character, so that we may safely say that this was not written by one, but by a clumsy imitator who overdid his part. It was simply a ruse to divert inquiry into a wrong channel. I'm not going to tell you much more of the case, Doctor. You know a conjurer gets no credit when once he has explained his trick, and if I show you too much of my method of working, you will come to the conclusion that I am a very ordinary individual after all."

"I shall never do that," I answered; "you have brought detection as near an exact science as it ever will be brought in this world."

My companion flushed up with pleasure at my words, and the earnest way in which I uttered them. I had already observed that he was as sensitive to flattery on the score of his art as any girl could be of her beauty.

"I'll tell you one other thing," he said. "Patent-leather and Square-toes came in the same cab, and they walked down the pathway together as friendly as possible—arm-in-arm, in all probability. When they got inside they walked up and down the room—or rather, Patent-leathers stood still while Square-toes walked up and down. I could read all that in the dust; and I could read that as he walked he grew more and more excited. That is shown by the increased length of his strides. He was talking all the while, and working himself up, no doubt, into a fury. Then the tragedy occurred. I've told you all I know myself now, for the rest is mere surmise and conjecture. We have a good working basis, however, on which to start. We must hurry up, for I want to go to Hallé's concert[131] to hear Norman-Neruda[132] this afternoon."

This conversation had occurred while our cab had been threading its way through a long succession of dingy streets and dreary by-ways. In the dingiest and dreariest of them our driver suddenly came to a stand. "That's Audley Court in there," he said, pointing to a narrow slit in the line of dead-coloured brick. "You'll find me here when you come back."

Audley Court was not an attractive locality. The narrow passage led us into a quadrangle paved with flags and lined by sordid dwellings. We picked our way among groups of dirty

130 Socialism, which arose out of the social and economic injustices suffered by factory workers during the Industrial Revolution (1750–1850, roughly), was far slower to take hold in Britain than it was in Germany. Historian A. N. Wilson describes socialism as "a minor issue" for Britain during the late 1800s, in part because the rise of the middle class made late Victorians feel as though they were capable of their own self-betterment; they didn't need, as Wilson puts it, "ideas culled from foreigners with funny names."

Despite this prevailing attitude, there were in fact a number of British socialist organisations that, inspired by Karl Marx and Friedrich Engels's seminal *The Communist Manifesto* (1848), dedicated themselves to speaking out against poor working conditions and capitalism in general. One of these was the Social Democratic Federation (SDF), founded in 1881 by Henry Hyndman, an eccentric figure who, according to Wilson, "never abandoned his silk hat, frock-coat and silver-topped cane," and whose unsolicited visits to Marx were considered "a great bore." Influential artist, designer, and poet William Morris joined SDF in 1883, only to split off in 1884 to found the Socialist League.

Morris was a key figure in what became known as Bloody Sunday, a socialist demonstration that took place on November 13, 1887. Demanding the release of Irish Nationalist MP William O'Brien, some ten thousand marchers—among them Morris and the renowned orator Annie Besant—marched from various locations to Trafalgar Square, where some two thousand police and four hundred soldiers had gathered. Wilson quotes *The Times* as reporting that "the police, mounted and on foot, charged in among the people, striking indiscriminately in all directions and causing complete disorder in the ranks of the processionists. I witnessed several cases of injury to men who had been struck on the head or the face by the police. The blood, in most instances, was flowing freely from the wound and the spectacle was indeed a sickening one." Three people were killed and two hundred were injured.

The chaos of Bloody Sunday was hardly indicative of socialist activities as a whole, and in fact, the Christian Socialism movement, which leaned on the writings of Thomas Carlyle and Samuel Coleridge in linking the church to anti-capitalist ideals, experienced a spirited revival in the 1880s. But Bloody Sunday was no doubt instrumental in causing some to look negatively upon socialism and its adherents. Christopher Morley observes that "socialists were sometimes (and unfairly) associated in the public mind with other groups who believed in violent action as a protest against the inequalities of civilization." Robert Louis Stevenson's *More New Arabian Nights: The Dynamiter* (1885) is a satirical series of tales framed by a story of an incompetent bomber involved with Irish independence and illustrates the public linkage of social causes and violence.

Socialism attracted many free-thinking individuals, and Dr. Watson's colleague Arthur Conan Doyle, who was deeply involved in another great movement of free-thinkers, Spiritualism, crossed paths with many of them, including the founder of Owenite socialism, the philanthropist Robert Owen, and Theosophist Besant. Despite his reformist interests (for example, he presided over the Divorce Law Reform Union), Conan Doyle never appeared comfortable in one or another political party. Early in his Portsmouth years, he joined the Liberal-Unionist party; when he stood for Parliament in 1905, he ran as a Conservative-Unionist. He wrote to a newspaper during that campaign: "My attention has been called to a note in your issue of the 29th ult., in which surprise is expressed that a gentleman of Socialistic views, who is a Home Ruler, should address an audience on my behalf. I hope that the incident will emphasise the fact, which I have frequently asserted, that this election will, so far as I can make it so, not be a matter of Tory, Radical, or Socialist, but will be a contest between those who wish to improve the conditions of British trade and those who desire to leave them as they are. All other subjects are secondary to this, and all minor differences may be sunk in pursuit of the one main object." In *A Visit to Three Fronts* (1916), recounting his travels during the Great War, Conan Doyle wrote, "Socialism has never had an attraction for me, but I should be a Socialist to-morrow if I thought that to ease a tax on wealth these men should ever suffer for the time or health that they gave to the public cause."

131 Sir Charles Hallé (1819–1895) was a British pianist and conductor. Born in Germany, he studied in Darmstadt and in Paris, where he socialised with Frederic Chopin, Franz Liszt, and Hector Berlioz. After the revolution forced him to flee Paris, he settled in Manchester with his family and began to give pianoforte concerts, first out of his home and then, starting in 1861, at St. James's Hall in London. These Popular Concerts found great favor among the general public and were influential in promoting appreciation of Beethoven's pianoforte sonatas. Hallé also founded, in 1858, the highly regarded Hallé Orchestra in Manchester, which today is Britain's oldest professional symphony orchestra. In recognition of his many contributions to the popularising of fine music in England, Hallé was knighted by Queen Victoria in 1888.

132 Hallé's wife, Czech violinist Wilhelmina (Wilma) Norman-Neruda (1839–1911), was the greatest female violinist of her time, so respected that she was referred to as "the female Paganini." Her first marriage was to

"The door was decorated with a small slip of brass on which the name Rance was engraved."
Richard Gutschmidt, *Späte Rache* (Stuttgart: Robert Lutz Verlag, 1902)

Ludwig Norman, a Swedish conductor and composer. (Her father was the organist Josef Neruda.) In 1888, three years after Norman's death, she married Hallé, in whose Popular Concerts she had appeared for nearly twenty years. Queen Alexandra bestowed upon Norman-Neruda the honorary title of Violinist to the Queen in 1901.

Holmes may have had a particular interest in seeing Norman-Neruda play because, as Paul S. Clarkson points out, she—like Holmes—was the owner of a Stradivarius violin. Norman-Neruda's Stradivarius, known as the Ernst Violin, was once owned by the virtuoso Heinrich Ernst. In 1874, after Ernst's death, Queen Victoria's son Alfred, then Duke of Edinburgh, presented it to Norman-Neruda as a token of his esteem.

Note that in the original *Beeton's* text and many book texts, the name is not hyphenated.

children, and through lines of discoloured linen, until we came to Number 46, the door of which was decorated with a small slip of brass on which the name Rance was engraved. On inquiry we found that the constable was in bed, and we were shown into a little front parlour to await his coming.

He appeared presently, looking a little irritable at being disturbed in his slumbers. "I made my report at the office," he said.

Holmes took a half-sovereign from his pocket and played with it pensively. "We thought that we should like to hear it all from your own lips," he said.

"I shall be most happy to tell you anything I can," the constable answered, with his eyes upon the little golden disc.

"Just let us hear it all in your own way as it occurred."

Rance sat down on the horsehair sofa, and knitted his brows, as though determined not to omit anything in his narrative.

"I'll tell it ye from the beginning," he said. "My time is from

133 H. W. Bell identifies the tavern as the Old White Horse, located across from the post-office on the Brixton Road. (See notes 100 and 122, above.) But Colin Prestige, writing in 1957, declared that there was an actual White Hart tavern in the district near Myatt's Field (where he places Lauriston Gardens—see note 100, above), which lay at the corner of Lilford Road and Holland Road in Camberwell: "[A]lthough the present White Hart has only been in existence since 1938, it replaces an earlier 'pub' of the same name of considerable antiquity, which was on the same site until demolished for rebuilding in the 1930s."

134 Unlike Henrietta St. (see next note) and Audley Court, "Holland Grove" is a real street, two streets east of the Brixton Road and just south of Kennington Park.

135 There is a Henrietta Street in Cavendish Square and a Henrietta Street in Covent Garden; however, both are north of the Thames and a long way from the Brixton Road. This, then, is a fictitious location.

136 That is, fourpence (8¢) worth of gin, mixed with hot water and lemon.

"He appeared presently, looking a little irritable."
Geo. Hutchinson, *A Study in Scarlet* (London: Ward, Lock Bowden, and Co., 1891)

ten at night to six in the morning. At eleven there was a fight at the White Hart[133]; but bar that all was quiet enough on the beat. At one o'clock it began to rain, and I met Harry Murcher—him who has the Holland Grove[134] beat—and we stood together at the corner of Henrietta Street[135] a-talkin'. Presently—maybe about two or a little after—I thought I would take a look round and see that all was right down the Brixton Road. It was precious dirty and lonely. Not a soul did I meet all the way down, though a cab or two went past me. I was a-strollin' down, thinkin' between ourselves how uncommon handy a four of gin hot[136] would be, when suddenly the glint of a light caught my eye in the window of that same house. Now, I knew that them two houses in Lauriston Gardens was empty on account of him that owns them who won't have the drains seed to, though the very last tenant what lived in one of them died o' typhoid fever. I was knocked all in a heap, therefore, at seeing a light in the window, and I suspected as something was wrong. When I got to the door—"

"You stopped, and then walked back to the garden gate," my companion interrupted. "What did you do that for?"

Rance gave a violent jump, and stared at Sherlock Holmes with the utmost amazement upon his features.

"Why, that's true, sir," he said; "though how you come to know it, Heaven only knows. Ye see, when I got up to the door it was so still and so lonesome, that I thought I'd be none the worse for someone with me. I ain't afeared of anything on this side o' the grave; but I thought that maybe it was him that died o' the typhoid inspecting the drains what killed him. The thought gave me a kind o' turn, and I walked back to the gate to see if I could see Murcher's lantern,[137] but there wasn't no sign of him nor of anyone else."

"There was no one in the street?"

"Not a livin' soul, sir, nor as much as a dog. Then I pulled myself together and went back and pushed the door open. All was quiet inside, so I went into the room where the light was a-burnin'. There was a candle flickerin' on the mantelpiece—a red wax one—and by its light I saw—"

"Yes, I know all that you saw. You walked round the room several times, and you knelt down by the body, and then you walked through and tried the kitchen door, and then—"

John Rance sprang to his feet with a frightened face and suspicion in his eyes. "Where was you hid to see all that?"[138] he cried. "It seems to me that you knows a deal more than you should."

Holmes laughed and threw his card across the table to the constable. "Don't go arresting me for the murder," he said. "I am one of the hounds and not the wolf; Mr. Gregson or Mr. Lestrade will answer for that. Go on, though. What did you do next?"

Rance resumed his seat, without, however, losing his mystified expression. "I went back to the gate and sounded my whistle. That brought Murcher and two more to the spot."

Bull's-eye police lantern.

137 Police officers (as well as burglars) often made use of a "dark lantern," a modification of an ordinary gas or kerosene hand lantern that could be darkened while lit, by a sliding shield that covered the light without extinguishing the flame. In this way, it was the predecessor of the electric hand torch or flashlight.

138 Robert S. Morgan, eliminating the impossible—that Holmes was disguised as Drebber or the murderer—concludes Holmes did indeed obtain his facts by being "hid," disguised as the horse. "We know that Holmes was an expert at disguise," Morgan writes in *Spotlight on a Simple Case, or Wiggins, Who Was That Horse I Saw With You Last Night.* "If Holmes wanted to disguise himself as a horse he would be a horse."

139 Edwards takes this title to be a conflation of the American patriotic songs "Hail, Columbia!" and "The Star-Spangled Banner" and suggests that Rance's recollection reinforces Holmes's conclusion that the murderer was an American. Karen Murdock argues that the song was the American Civil War song "Pat Murphy of the Irish Brigade," which has as the last line of its first verse the phrase "America's bright starry banner," easily misremembered as "Columbia's star-spangled banner" or some such phrase.

"John Rance sprang to his feet with a frightened face."
Geo. Hutchinson, *A Study in Scarlet* (London: Ward, Lock Bowden, and Co., 1891)

"Was the street empty then?"

"Well, it was, as far as anybody that could be of any good goes."

"What do you mean?"

The constable's features broadened into a grin. "I've seen many a drunk chap in my time," he said, "but never anyone so cryin' drunk as that cove. He was at the gate when I came out, a-leanin' up agin the railings, and a-singin' at the pitch o' his lungs about Columbine's New-fangled Banner,[139] or some such stuff. He couldn't stand, far less help."

"What sort of a man was he?" asked Sherlock Holmes.

John Rance appeared to be somewhat irritated at this digression. "He was an uncommon drunk sort o' man," he said. "He'd ha' found hisself in the station if we hadn't been so took up."

"His face—his dress—didn't you notice them?" Holmes broke in impatiently.

"I should think I did notice them, seeing that I had to prop him up—me and Murcher between us. He was a long chap, with a red face, the lower part muffled round—"

"That will do," cried Holmes. "What became of him?"

"We'd enough to do without lookin' after him," the policeman said, in an aggrieved voice. "I'll wager he found his way home all right."

"How was he dressed?"

"A brown overcoat"

"Had he a whip in his hand?"

"A whip—no."

"He must have left it behind," muttered my companion. "You didn't happen to see or hear a cab after that?"

"No."

"There's a half-sovereign for you," my companion said, standing up and taking his hat. "I am afraid, Rance, that you will never rise in the force. That head of yours should be for use as well as ornament. You might have gained your sergeant's stripes last night. The man whom you held in your hands is the man who holds the clue of this mystery, and whom we are

" 'I've seen many a drunk chap in my time,' he said, 'but never anyone so cryin' drunk as that cove.' "
Richard Gutschmidt, *Späte Rache* (Stuttgart: Robert Lutz Verlag, 1902)

140 Controversial and bohemian American painter James Abbott McNeill Whistler (1834–1903), after a critic referred to his early work *The Woman in White* (1862) as "un symphonie du blanc," changed the title of that painting to *A Symphony in White No. 1: The White Girl* and frequently used titles with musical compositions and colours in them. His best-known works include *Nocturne in Green and Gold* (*ca.* 1874) and the famous portrait of his mother, *Arrangement in Grey and Black No. 1: The Artist's Mother* (1871–1872). Whistler painted another *Arrangement in Grey and Black No. 1*, this one of Thomas Carlyle (1873); his portrait of Miss Cicely Alexander was a *Harmony in Grey and Green* (*ca.* 1873). Whistler was constantly in the public eye, and Holmes's appreciation of contemporary artists is evident when he admires the work of the "modern Belgian masters" (see *The Hound of the Baskervilles*, note 78, below), and Whistler's later *Arrangement in Black: Portrait of Senor Pablo de Sarasate* (1884) was likely well known to Holmes in light of his fondness for the violinist. In formally affixing Holmes's throw-

Mr. James Abbott McNeill Whistler—A "Symphony."
"Spy," *Vanity Fair* (1887)

" 'He was an uncommon drunk sort of man.' "
Geo. Hutchinson, *A Study in Scarlet* (London: Ward, Lock Bowden, and Co., 1891)

seeking. There is no use of arguing about it now; I tell you that it is so. Come along, Doctor."

We started off for the cab together, leaving our informant incredulous, but obviously uncomfortable.

"The blundering fool," Holmes said, bitterly, as we drove back to our lodgings. "Just to think of his having such an incomparable bit of good luck, and not taking advantage of it."

"I am rather in the dark still. It is true that the description of this man tallies with your idea of the second party in this mystery. But why should he come back to the house after leaving it? That is not the way of criminals."

"The ring, man, the ring: that was what he came back for. If we have no other way of catching him, we can always bait our line with the ring. I shall have him, Doctor—I'll lay you two to one that I have him. I must thank you for it all. I might not have gone but for you, and so have missed the finest study I ever came across: a study in scarlet, eh? Why shouldn't we use a little art jargon.[140] There's the scarlet thread of murder running through the colourless skein of life, and our duty is to unravel it, and isolate it, and expose every inch of it. And now for lunch, and then for Norman-Neruda. Her attack and her bowing are splendid. What's that little thing of Chopin's she plays so magnificently: Tra-la-la-lira-lira-lay."[141]

Leaning back in the cab, this amateur bloodhound carolled away like a lark while I meditated upon the many-sidedness of the human mind.

away line to his first literary effort, Watson was setting the bar rather high; Morley deems the title "consciously highbrow."

141 Chopin never wrote any pieces for the solo violin, as Paul S. Clarkson and others are quick to report. After searching all reported concert programs and failing to find any record of a Chopin piece played by Norman-Neruda, Clarkson suggests that the date was June 4, 1880, and that Holmes heard Charles Hallé play Chopin's Nocturne in E (Op. 62, No. 2), as well as the composer's Barcarolle in F sharp (Op. 60). On that night, Norman-Neruda played one of her particular favourites, Handel's D major sonata; and Clarkson remarks that numerous passages of this, "the most beautiful of Handel's six violin sonatas," may have been mistakenly attributed, either by Holmes or Watson, to Chopin.

Clarkson's is an ingenious suggestion, but it is only one of many put forward. As Julian Wolff notes, in "Just What Was That Little Thing of Chopin's?," "great interest in this question is evidenced by the amount of research that has been done and the number of papers published." Wolff himself, Patrick Drazen tells us with some scorn, makes the "timid suggestion" that Holmes never actually said "Tra-la-la-lira-lira-lay" at all, but that Watson assigned him dialogue and, in doing so, misquoted Tennyson's "The Lady of Shalott" ("From the bank and from the river / He flash'd into the crystal mirror, / 'Tirra lirra,' by the river / Sang Sir Lancelot").

Among the attempts to ascertain which work Holmes might have meant:

1) *F minor Nocturne (Nocturne for piano, No. 15 in F minor)*, identified by Guy Warrack, *Sherlock Holmes and Music*, on what Warrack describes as "*prima facie* evidence." Warrack admits that it could hardly be described as a "little thing" but points out that Watson has

omitted one "la," unless Holmes was guilty of faulty phrasing.

2) *Etude in E major, Opus 10 (Etude in E major for Piano, Op. 10, No. 3)*, selected by the beloved Baker Street Irregular tenor James Montgomery, in his "Chopin in Baker Street." After "most exhaustive study," Montgomery concludes that this piece is almost the only one of Chopin's many operas that fits Holmes's rhythm flawlessly.

3) *Valse in E minor, No. 14 (Op. Posth.)*. Ernest Bloomfield Zeisler, in "Tra-la-la-lira-lira-lay," heard Bronislaw Hubermann play his own arrangement of this piece in a Vienna recital in 1929 and recognised the tune.

4) *Mazurka in E flat minor, Op. 6, No. 4*. Eric H. Thiman, Mus. D., asserts in a letter to the Editor of the *Sherlock Holmes Journal* that Zeisler's identification is in error. He points out that E minor is a more suitable key for a string player and that the piece he recommends is very short, extremely singable, and fits the rhythm exactly (unlike the Warrack suggestion).

5) *Study in A minor, Op. 25, No.11*. Winifred M. Christie, in "Some Reflections on That Little Thing of Chopin's," examines the previous suggestions of Warrack and Montgomery with care and, using the principle of exclusion, reduces the possibilities to Chopin's *Etudes*. Among these, she finds only one possible solution.

6) *Fourth Polonaise, in C minor*. William Smith, in "That Little Thing of Chopin's: The Laying of the Ghost," reviews in detail Christie's analysis and finds a number of flaws. Most importantly, he asserts that Holmes's phrase must be equated to the music on the basis of one syllable per note, with no distortion of the melody rhythmically or accentually. He analyses the complete piano works of Chopin using these principles.

7) *Polish Songs, "The Maiden's Wish."* Harold C. Schonberg, the eminent *New York Times* music critic, in an essay in that paper entitled "Tra-la-la-lira-lira-lay," considered that the piece should fit Holmes's happy mood and therefore rejects the minor-keyed pieces. The short piece he identifies was, in his estimation, "one of the most popular short pieces of the century, . . . makes a wonderful violin encore, and Norman-Neruda's arrangement . . . would have had an expert like Holmes in ecstasy."

This is not an exhaustive list of proposals, and some even assert that the piece was not Chopin at all. The ingenuity of those weighing in is indeed a testament to the "many-sidedness of the human mind."

CHAPTER V

Our Advertisement Brings a Visitor

Our morning's exertions had been too much for my weak health, and I was tired out in the afternoon. After Holmes's departure for the concert, I lay down upon the sofa and endeavoured to get a couple of hours' sleep. It was a useless attempt. My mind had been too much excited by all that had occurred, and the strangest fancies and surmises crowded into it. Every time that I closed my eyes I saw before me the distorted baboon-like countenance of the murdered man. So sinister was the impression which that face had produced upon me that I found it difficult to feel anything but gratitude for him who had removed its owner from the world. If ever human features bespoke vice of the most malignant type, they were certainly those of Enoch J. Drebber, of Cleveland. Still I recognized that justice must be done, and that the depravity of the victim was no condonement in the eyes of the law.

The more I thought of it the more extraordinary did my companion's hypothesis, that the man had been poisoned, appear. I remembered how he had sniffed his lips, and had no doubt that he had detected something which had given rise to the idea. Then, again, if not poison, what had caused this man's

Scene from *A Study in Scarlet* (Great Britain: Samuelson Film Mfg. Co. Ltd., 1914), starring James Bragington as Sherlock Holmes.

death, since there was neither wound nor marks of strangulation? But, on the other hand, whose blood was that which lay so thickly upon the floor? There were no signs of a struggle, nor had the victim any weapon with which he might have wounded an antagonist. As long as all these questions were unsolved, I felt that sleep would be no easy matter, either for Holmes or myself. His quiet self-confident manner convinced me that he had already formed a theory which explained all the facts, though what it was I could not for an instant conjecture.

He was very late in returning—so late, that I knew that the concert could not have detained him all the time. Dinner was on the table before he appeared.

"It was magnificent," he said, as he took his seat. "Do you remember what Darwin says about music? He claims that the power of producing and appreciating it existed among the human race long before the power of speech was arrived at.[142] Perhaps that is why we are so subtly influenced by it. There are vague memories in our souls of those misty centuries when the world was in its childhood."

"That's rather a broad idea," I remarked.

"One's ideas must be as broad as Nature if they are to inter-

142 The theory of Charles Robert Darwin, the great English naturalist (1809–1882), to which Holmes alludes is likely that expressed in *The Descent of Man, and Selection in Relation to Sex* (1871). Darwin writes:

> As we have every reason to suppose that articulate speech is one of the latest, as it is certainly the highest, of the arts acquired by man, and as the instinctive power of producing musical notes and rhythms is developed low down in the animal series, it would be altogether opposed to the principle of evolution, if we were to admit that man's musical capacity has been developed from the tones used in impassioned speech. We must suppose that the rhythms and cadences of oratory are derived from previously developed musical powers. We can thus understand how it is that music, dancing, song, and poetry are such very ancient arts. We may go even further than this, and . . . believe that musical sounds afforded one of the bases for the development of language.

pret Nature," he answered. "What's the matter? You're not looking quite yourself. This Brixton Road affair has upset you."

"To tell the truth, it has," I said. "I ought to be more case-hardened after my Afghan experiences. I saw my own comrades hacked to pieces at Maiwand without losing my nerve."

"I can understand. There is a mystery about this which stimulates the imagination; where there is no imagination there is no horror. Have you seen the evening paper?"[143]

"No."

"It gives a fairly good account of the affair. It does not mention the fact that when the man was raised up, a woman's wedding ring fell upon the floor.[144] It is just as well it does not."

"Why?"

"Look at this advertisement," he answered. "I had one sent to every paper this morning immediately after the affair."

He threw the paper across to me and I glanced at the place indicated. It was the first announcement in the "Found" column.[145] "In Brixton Road, this morning," it ran, "a plain gold wedding ring, found in the roadway between the 'White Hart' Tavern and Holland Grove. Apply Dr. Watson, 221B, Baker Street, between eight and nine this evening."

"Excuse my using your name," he said. "If I used my own, some of these dunderheads would recognize it, and want to meddle in the affair."

"That is all right," I answered. "But supposing anyone applies, I have no ring."

"Oh yes, you have," said he, handing me one. "This will do very well. It is almost a facsimile."

"And who do you expect will answer this advertisement?"

"Why, the man in the brown coat—our florid friend with the square toes. If he does not come himself he will send an accomplice."

"Would he not consider it as too dangerous?"

"Not at all. If my view of the case is correct, and I have every reason to believe that it is, this man would rather risk anything than lose the ring. According to my notion he dropped it while stooping over Drebber's body, and did not miss it at the time. After leaving the house he discovered his loss and hurried back, but found the police already in possession, owing to his own folly in leaving the candle burning. He had to pretend to be drunk in order to allay the suspicions which might have

143 Madeleine B. Stern proposes that Holmes obtained his papers from the news-vendor, James Ellis Hawkins, located at 36 Baker Street. While Holmes was not reported to be a registered regular reader of any particular newspaper, he always seemed to have *The Times* at hand; it is mentioned in seven different tales. In Holmes's London, newspapers were not distributed through the post but rather by news-vendors and the news-boys who worked for them. Many of the latter had regular customers who expected delivery of one or more papers at regular times, but this was an arrangement with the news-vendor and not the publisher. This business method continues today.

News-vendors, Ludgate Circus (1892).
Victorian and Edwardian London

144 Edwards calls Holmes's conclusion that the ring was accidentally dropped a speculation. "The ring might have been thrown on the body after it had been flourished before Drebber's eyes."

145 This is the first indication of Holmes's affection for the "agony columns" (personal advertisements) of the London newspapers. Holmes advertised again in *The Sign of Four* (for the *Aurora*), in "The Blue Carbuncle" (for Henry Baker), and in "The Naval Treaty" (for Joseph Harrison's cab-driver). Holmes characterised the columns as ". . . a chorus of groans, cries, and bleatings! What a rag-bag of singu-

been aroused by his appearance at the gate. Now put yourself in that man's place. On thinking the matter over, it must have occurred to him that it was possible that he had lost the ring in the road after leaving the house. What would he do, then? He would eagerly look out for the evening papers in the hope of seeing it among the articles found. His eye, of course, would light upon this. He would be overjoyed. Why should he fear a trap? There would be no reason in his eyes why the finding of the ring should be connected with the murder. He would come. He will come. You shall see him within an hour."

"And then?" I asked.

"Oh, you can leave me to deal with him then. Have you any arms?"

"I have my old service revolver[146] and a few cartridges."

"You had better clean it and load it. He will be a desperate man, and though I shall take him unawares, it is as well to be ready for anything."

I went to my bedroom and followed his advice. When I returned with the pistol the table had been cleared, and Holmes was engaged in his favourite occupation of scraping upon his violin.

"When I returned with the pistol."
Geo. Hutchinson, *A Study in Scarlet* (London: Ward, Lock Bowden, and Co., 1891)

lar happenings! But surely the most valuable hunting-ground that ever was given to a student of the unusual" ("The Red-Headed League").

146 In "The Speckled Band," Holmes appears to give more specifics of Watson's revolver when he says to him, "I should be very much obliged if you would slip your revolver into your pocket. An Eley's No. 2 is an excellent argument with gentlemen who can twist steel pokers into knots." But as Eley was a manufacturer of ammunition rather than actual weaponry, such a make of gun did not in fact exist. The editors of the *Catalogue of the 1951 Sherlock Holmes Exhibition* suggest that Holmes probably meant to refer to a .320-bore Webley's No. 2, a small "pocket pistol" that used Eley bullets. The *Catalogue* editors described the .320-bore Webley No. 2 as taking up little space but as being "adequate for dealing with the most determined criminal. It was the smallest really practicable weapon of its time."

Contrary to the view of the editors of the *Catalogue of the 1951 Sherlock Holmes Exhibition*, Charles A. Meyer argues that Watson's pistol was a Webley-Pryse revolver, also known at the Webley No. 4. Garry James, in "Shooting the Guns of Sherlock Holmes," on the basis of the "No. 2" reference, concludes that Watson's revolver is a Mark II Adams, which fired "No. 2" or "II" ammunition.

In "Firearms in the Canon: The Guns of Sherlock Holmes and John H. Watson," Dante M. Torrese persuasively argues that Watson's service revolver was an Adams No. 3 but that his *pocket* pistol was a Webley Metro-Police. William Ballew makes an excellent case for Watson owning only one gun, a Webley of the "Bull Dog" variety.

The multi-gun approach is also espoused by Daniel P. King, who concurs with William S. Baring-Gould's assessment that Watson's *service* revolver was an Adams .450-calibre

"The plot thickens," he said, as I entered; "I have just had an answer to my American telegram. My view of the case is the correct one."

"And that is—?" I asked eagerly.

"My fiddle would be the better for new strings," he remarked. "Put your pistol in your pocket. When the fellow comes, speak to him in an ordinary way. Leave the rest to me. Don't frighten him by looking at him too hard."

"It is eight o'clock now," I said, glancing at my watch.

"Yes. He will probably be here in a few minutes. Open the door slightly. That will do. Now put the key on the inside. Thank you! This is a queer old book I picked up at a stall yesterday[147]—*De jure inter Gentes*[148]—published in Latin at Liege in the Lowlands, in 1642. Charles's head was still firm on his shoulders[149] when this little brown-backed volume was struck off."

"Who is the printer?"

"Philippe de Croy, whoever he may have been.[150] On the fly-leaf, in very faded ink, is written *Ex libris Guliolmi Whyte.* I wonder who William Whyte was. Some pragmatical seventeenth century lawyer, I suppose. His writing has a legal twist about it.[151] Here comes our man, I think."

As he spoke there was a sharp ring at the bell. Sherlock Holmes rose softly and moved his chair in the direction of the door. We heard the servant pass along the hall, and the sharp click of the latch as she opened it.[152]

"Does Dr. Watson live here?" asked a clear but rather harsh voice. We could not hear the servant's reply, but the door closed, and someone began to ascend the stairs. The footfall was an uncertain and shuffling one. A look of surprise passed over the face of my companion as he listened to it. It came slowly along the passage, and there was a feeble tap at the door.

"Come in," I cried.

At my summons, instead of the man of violence whom we expected, a very old and wrinkled woman hobbled into the apartment. She appeared to be dazzled by the sudden blaze of light, and after dropping a curtsey, she stood blinking at us with her bleared eyes and fumbling in her pocket with nervous, shaky fingers. I glanced at my companion, and his face had assumed such a disconsolate expression that it was all I could do to keep my countenance.

centre-fire Model 1872 mark III, but by the time of "The Speckled Band" (1883), Watson was carrying a Webley's Solid-Frame Civilian Pocket Model. Later, in "Thor Bridge," Watson had switched to a more modern weapon, the W.P. (Webley Pocket) Hammerless Model 1898.

A similar view—of a varied armoury—is expressed by Harald Curjel, in "Some Further Thoughts on Canonical Weaponry," who identifies either the .450/455 Tranter Army pistol or the Adams Central Fire Breech-loading revolver as Watson's "service" revolver, the Webley "bulldog" as another weapon of Watson's, yet a third (unidentified) revolver in "Thor Bridge," and finally a different weapon altogether in "The Speckled Band," for the "Eley No. 2," Curjel contends, would fit none of these.

147 Several scholars—collectors themselves—not surprisingly conclude that Holmes was a devoted bibliophile. He chose to disguise himself as an elderly book-dealer in "The Empty House," and he exhibited an extraordinary knowledge of and interest in typefaces, palimpsests, and old books. Madeleine B. Stern devotes an entire pamphlet (*Sherlock Holmes: Rare-Book Collector*) to the subject of Holmes's collection, based on various Canonical references. Although Holmes here discloses to Watson a specific title in his collection, he must have been appalled to find the information published, and aside from mentioning an author or two, he never again revealed the holdings of his collection—like many a collector, seeking to avoid rival collectors and predatory dealers.

148 The Latin phrase means "law among nations," or international law. Morris Rosenblum, in "Some Latin Byways in the Canon," tentatively identifies the volume as either a pirated edition of Hugo Grotius's *De Jure Belli et Pacis*, first printed in Paris in 1625, or the continuation of Grotius's work, written by Samuel Pofendorf in 1672 and entitled *De Jure Naturae et Gentium*. Madeleine B. Stern contends that the "queer old book" was the *De Jure inter Gentes*, written by the English author Richard Zouche (1590–1661) and published anonymously. Zouche, a professor of civil law at Oxford, a justice on the Court of Admiralty, and a member of Parliament, is credited not only with helping to establish the foundations of international law but also with popularising the term *jure inter gentes*, replacing the previously used *jus gentium* ("law of nations"). His influential treatise on international law, *Juris et Judicii Fecialis, sive Juris inter gentes*, was published in 1650; but Stern explains that the same treatise appeared the following year, under the Leyden imprint, and without Zouche's name. "Holmes's copy," she marvels, "antedates even the so-called first edition of 1650, and hence is a find of extraordinary magnitude, one of the most desirable books in any legal collection." If Watson correctly recorded the bibliographic data, a true rarity vanished with the rest of Holmes's collection—perhaps burned in the fire that took place at 221 Baker Street during the "Great Hiatus" (mentioned in "The Empty House").

149 Charles I (1600–1649), king of Great Britain and Ireland from 1625 to 1649, was beheaded on January 30, 1649, having been tried and convicted of treason by his enemies in Parliament. Charles's relationship with Parliament had long been troubled, and he governed without a Parliament for eleven years, from 1629 to 1640. His power struggle with opposition leaders, among them Oliver Cromwell, plunged England into two civil wars, also known as the Puritan Revolution; his death helped precipitate the establishment of a republican commonwealth.

150 Peter Blau, in a letter to Donald Redmond, states that Philippe de Croy was a printer in Leiden who worked for the Elzevirs and printed Grotius's *Poemata Omnia* in 1645.

151 Madeleine B. Stern scoffs, "As if [Holmes] did not know that the copy had belonged to the English divine, William White, 1604–1678, who had fathered several interesting Latin works under the pseudonym of 'Gulielmus Phalerius.' "

152 It is unclear *whose* servant this is. There is no reference in the Canon to any servant employed by Holmes or Watson while in residence at Baker Street; therefore, we may conclude that this servant worked for the landlady of 221 Baker Street. A Baker Street "page" is referred to numerous times over the course of Holmes and Watson's tenancy, and a "maid" is mentioned in "The Five Orange Pips" and "The Bruce-Partington Plans" as well as later in *A Study in Scarlet* (see note 158, below).

"The duties of a general servant are *general*," advised *The Household Oracle*, edited by Alfred H. Miles and billed as "A Popular Referee on Subjects of Household Enquiry" (1897). "There is little or nothing that has to be done in the way of service in a house," Miles went on, "that may not under some circumstances become the duty of a general servant. A maid of all work, she is expected to be a Jack of all trades, and unlike the proverbial Jack to be proficient in all departments of her work." Miles gave the yearly wages of a general servant as anywhere from £10 to £18—the equivalent of £650 to £1,150, or U.S. $1,100 to $1,950, today.

"A very old and wrinkled woman hobbled into the apartment."
Richard Gutschmidt, *Späte Rache* (Stuttgart: Robert Lutz Verlag, 1902)

The old crone drew out an evening paper, and pointed at our advertisement. "It's this as has brought me, good gentlemen," she said, dropping another curtsey; "a gold wedding ring in the Brixton Road. It belongs to my girl Sally, as was married only this time twelvemonth, which her husband is steward aboard a Union boat,[153] and what he'd say if he come 'ome and found her without her ring is more than I can think, he being short enough at the best o' times, but more especially when he has

Astley's Circus (*ca.* 1850).

153 William S. Baring-Gould identifies this as a ship of the Union Steam Ship Company, which ran to South Africa. In 1900, the Union and Castle Packet Company lines merged to form the Union-Castle Line. The Line ceased its regular voyages in 1977, but a Centenary Voyage from Southampton to Cape Town and back was held in 1999–2000, lasting two months.

154 The modern circus, which originated sometime in the late eighteenth century, featured equestrian trick-riding performed in a single ring; but by the Victorian era, a visitor to the circus would also marvel at aerial displays, juggling, and trained animal acts—all, after 1873, taking place in two rings under a main tent.

The most successful British circus proprietors at the time were George Sanger (1827–1911) and his brother John (1816–1889), who formed a small travelling circus in 1853. By 1871, they were able to buy Astley's Amphitheatre and stage grand productions both there and at Agricultural Hall, all the while continuing to tour England. The self-styled "Lords" would parade their gilded wagons and eccentric performers through the streets of towns they visited; "Lord" George's wife, who danced with snakes in the lion's cage, would often ride in the lead wagon, dressed as Britannia with a lion at her feet. Each brother eventually produced his own travelling show, and the shows continued after their deaths, using the family name.

Another great circus proprietor was Frederick Charles Hengler (1820–1887). Hengler was the son of Henry, a famous circus performer, and pursued a career as a rope-dancer and horseman until he started his own troupe in 1848. Hengler saw that his prosperity lay not in performances in traditional tents but instead in permanent venues. His first establishment was the old Prince's Theatre in West Nile Street, Glasgow, which he bought in 1863; by 1875 Hengler's Circuses were established in Glasgow, Liverpool, Edinburgh, and London (the latter at 7 Argyll St., where it remained until the early twentieth century).

Numerous travelling circuses also appeared in London, at venues such as Cremorne Gardens (in Battersea) or the Olympia Hippodrome.

155 Why would the woman identify the ring as Sally's? It clearly was not the correct ring,

"The old crone drew out an evening paper and pointed at our advertisement."
Geo. Hutchinson, *A Study in Scarlet* (London: Ward, Lock Bowden, and Co., 1891)

the drink. If it please you, she went to the circus[154] last night along with—"

"Is that her ring?" I asked.

"The Lord be thanked!" cried the old woman; "Sally will be a glad woman this night. That's the ring."[155]

"And what may your address be?" I inquired, taking up a pencil.

"13, Duncan Street, Houndsditch. A weary way from here."

"The Brixton Road does not lie between any circus and Houndsditch," said Sherlock Holmes sharply.

The old woman faced round and looked keenly at him from her little red-rimmed eyes. "The gentleman asked me for *my* address," she said. "Sally lives in lodgings at 3, Mayfield Place, Peckham."[156]

"And your name is—?"

"My name is Sawyer—hers is Dennis, which Tom Dennis

married her—and a smart, clean lad, too, as long as he's at sea, and no steward in the company more thought of; but when on shore, what with the women and what with liquor shops—"

"Here is your ring, Mrs. Sawyer," I interrupted, in obedience to a sign from my companion; "it clearly belongs to your daughter, and I am glad to be able to restore it to the rightful owner."

With many mumbled blessings and protestations of gratitude the old crone packed it away in her pocket, and shuffled off down the stairs. Sherlock Holmes sprang to his feet the moment that she was gone and rushed into his room. He returned in a few seconds enveloped in an ulster and a cravat. "I'll follow her," he said, hurriedly; "she must be an accomplice, and will lead me to him. Wait up for me." The hall door had hardly slammed behind our visitor before Holmes had

"THE OLD WOMAN FACED ROUND AND LOOKED KEENLY AT HIM."—(Page 58.)

"The old woman faced round and looked keenly at him."
Charles Doyle, *A Study in Scarlet* (London and New York: Ward, Lock & Co., 1888)

and it would not profit the criminal to recover a substitute ring. Is it possible that the criminal failed to provide "Mrs. Sawyer" with a description of the ring?

156 Not surprisingly, there does not appear to be (or have been) a Mayfield Place in Peckham (formerly in the metropolitan borough of Camberwell, now in the Greater London borough of Southwark, not far east of the Brixton Road).

157 Henri Murger (1822–1861) was a French poet and novelist. His *Scènes de la vie de bohème* ("Scenes of Bohemian Life"), published from 1845 to 1849, was about the struggles and joys of a group of penniless artists and writers, one of whom, Rodolfe, was based on Murger himself. Puccini brought further fame to Murger's work by adapting it to his opera *La Bohème* (1896).

Christopher Morley doubts that Watson was much of a connoisseur of French literature and suggests, "Perhaps Watson was trying to improve his rather simple French by reading some of Holmes's books. . . . [*La Bohème*] was not produced until 1896 but when it came to Covent Garden I'm sure Holmes and Watson had seats in the stalls."

Similar aspersions on Watson's reading habits are cast by Benjamin Grosbayne, who writes, in "Sherlock Holmes—Musician," "Good old Watson, who tries to impress us with the not-so-sly implications . . . that he read wicked French books in the original so easily that he could skip about and . . . what a gay old dog he really is 'neath his respectable exterior."

158 This is the first mention of the "maid" as a part of the Hudson establishment at 221 Baker Street. The maid is only mentioned as such two other times, in "The Five Orange Pips" and "The Bruce-Partington Plans," where she is completely nondescript, although some have speculated that "Mrs. Turner" of "A Scandal in Bohemia" may have been the maid.

159 Some scholars believe Mrs. Hudson's "stately tread" signifies that she is heavy of bearing, or "corpulent," as Manly Wade Wellman puts it, in "The Great Man's Great Son: An Inquiry into the Most Private Life of Mr. Sherlock Holmes." Rushing to Mrs. Hudson's defence, Wellman reminds us that "stately, too, is the tread of many a queenly artist's model and showgirl."

"Her pursuer dogged her some little distance behind."
Geo. Hutchinson, *A Study in Scarlet* (London: Ward, Lock Bowden, and Co., 1891)

descended the stair. Looking through the window I could see her walking feebly along the other side, while her pursuer dogged her some little distance behind. "Either his whole theory is incorrect," I thought to myself, "or else he will be led now to the heart of the mystery." There was no need for him to ask me to wait up for him, for I felt that sleep was impossible until I heard the result of his adventure.

It was close upon nine when he set out. I had no idea how long he might be, but I sat stolidly puffing at my pipe and skipping over the pages of Henri Murger's *Vie de Bohème.*[157] Ten o'clock passed, and I heard the footsteps of the maid[158] as they pattered off to bed. Eleven, and the more stately tread[159] of the landlady passed my door, bound for the same destination. It was close upon twelve before I heard the sharp sound of his latch-key. The instant he entered I saw by his face that he had not been successful. Amusement and chagrin seemed to be struggling for the mastery, until the former suddenly carried the day, and he burst into a hearty laugh.

"I wouldn't have the Scotland Yarders know it for the

world," he cried, dropping into his chair; "I have chaffed them so much that they would never have let me hear the end of it. I can afford to laugh, because I know that I will be even with them in the long run."

"What is it then?" I asked.

"Oh, I don't mind telling a story against myself. That creature had gone a little way when she began to limp and show every sign of being footsore. Presently she came to a halt, and hailed a four-wheeler which was passing. I managed to be close to her so as to hear the address, but I need not have been so anxious, for she sang it out loud enough to be heard at the other side of the street, 'Drive to 13, Duncan Street, Houndsditch,' she cried. This begins to look genuine,[160] I thought, and having seen her safely inside, I perched myself behind. That's an art which every detective should be an expert at. Well, away we rattled, and never drew rein until we reached the street in question. I hopped off before we came to the door, and strolled down the street in an easy, lounging way. I saw the cab pull up. The driver jumped down, and I saw him open the door and stand expectantly. Nothing came out though. When I reached him he was groping about frantically in the empty cab, and giving vent to the finest assorted collection of oaths that ever I listened to. There was no sign or trace of his passenger, and I fear it will be some time before he gets his fare. On inquiring at Number 13 we found that the house belonged to a respectable paperhanger,[161] named Keswick, and that no one

Geo. Hutchinson, *A Study in Scarlet* (London: Ward, Lock Bowden, and Co., 1891)

160 By "genuine," Holmes must have meant merely that the woman had not concealed her address. This seems very naive of Holmes, but then the accomplice doesn't seem to act very logically—see note 155, above—and perhaps Holmes counted on her stupidity.

161 A person who hangs wallpaper.

of the name either of Sawyer or Dennis had ever been heard of there."

"You don't mean to say," I cried, in amazement, "that that tottering, feeble old woman was able to get out of the cab while it was in motion, without either you or the driver seeing her?"

"Old woman be damned!"[162] said Sherlock Holmes, sharply. "We were the old women to be so taken in. It must have been a young man, and an active one, too, besides being an incomparable actor. The get-up was inimitable.[163] He saw that he was followed, no doubt, and used this means of giving me the slip. It shows that the man we are after is not as lonely as I

"Still pondering over the strange problem."
W. H. Hyde, *Harper's Weekly*, 1899 (reused from "The Musgrave Ritual" and recaptioned, in *Sherlock Holmes Series*, Vol. I [New York: Harper & Bros., 1904])

162 "Although we will read of many other occasions on which Holmes cursed, swore, or raved, this is the one instance on record on which we are told what he said," observes William S. Baring-Gould.

163 Holmes himself is fond of donning a disguise in order to investigate a case (for example, as a seaman in *The Sign of Four* and as a "drunken-looking groom" and a clergyman in "A Scandal in Bohemia"), but given his familiarity with the technique, it is surprising that he does not have a better sense of when it is adopted by others. Nathan Bengis, in "Sherlock Stays After School," calls readers' attention to two instances in which Holmes was fooled by the disguise of another: here and in "A Scandal in Bohemia," in which Irene Adler is dressed as a "slim youth."

Who was "Mrs. Sawyer"? Jack Tracy argues, in " 'Old Woman Be Damned!' A Partial Identification of Jefferson Hope's Accomplice," that the accomplice must have been an employee of the true culprit, while Rick Lai, in "The Hansoms of John Clay," fingers the notorious John Clay of "The Red-Headed League." Steve Clarkson, in "Another Case of Identity," identifies the accomplice as none other than Irene Adler, the alluring figure from "Scandal in Bohemia" usually known simply as "*the* woman."

imagined he was, but has friends who are ready to risk something for him. Now, Doctor, you are looking done-up. Take my advice and turn in."

I was certainly feeling very weary, so I obeyed his injunction. I left Holmes seated in front of the smouldering fire, and long into the watches of the night I heard the low melancholy wailings of his violin,[164] and knew that he was still pondering over the strange problem which he had set himself to unravel.

164 On the basis of Watson's brief description, Benjamin Grosbayne ventures that Holmes may have been playing Johann Sebastian Bach's "Aria for the G String" or Nicolò Paganini's "Moses" variations. Or, Grosbayne continues, Holmes may have been improvising in the style of Paganini, a musician whom Holmes admired greatly. (In "The Cardboard Box," Watson recalls how a conversation about violins led Holmes to the subject of Paganini, "and we sat for an hour over a bottle of claret while he told me anecdote after anecdote of that extraordinary man.") So adept is Holmes at improvising upon his violin, in fact, that Grosbayne wonders whether the skill, "a characteristic of Hungarian and Gypsy performers rather than that of Englishmen, may yet be proved some day to stem from far more mixed ancestry than present research has thus far justified us to suppose."

CHAPTER VI

Tobias Gregson Shows What He Can Do

THE PAPERS NEXT day were full of the "Brixton Mystery," as they termed it. Each had a long account of the affair, and some had leaders[165] upon it in addition. There was some information in them which was new to me. I still retain in my scrap-book numerous clippings and extracts bearing upon the case. Here is a condensation of a few of them:—

The *Daily Telegraph*[166] remarked that in the history of crime there had seldom been a tragedy which presented stranger features. The German name of the victim, the absence of all other motive, and the sinister inscription on the wall, all pointed to its perpetration by political refugees and revolutionists. The Socialists had many branches in America, and the deceased had, no doubt, infringed their unwritten laws, and been tracked down by them.[167] After alluding airily to the Vehmgericht,[168] aqua tofana,[169] Carbonari,[170] the Marchioness de Brinvilliers,[171] the Darwinian theory, the principles of Malthus,[172] and the Ratcliff Highway murders,[173] the article concluded by admonishing the Government and advocating a closer watch over foreigners in England.

The *Standard* commented upon the fact that lawless out-

165 British term for editorials.

166 In the course of Watson's ensuing narration, he mentions three newspapers by name: the *Daily Telegraph*, the *Standard*, and the *Daily News*. Christopher Morley explains that the material referenced by Watson "is acute parody based on the style and predilections of each. The *Telegraph*, then edited by the flamboyant G. A. Sala, was a popular journal of lively tone. The *Standard* was Conservative and genteel. The *Daily News* was Liberal in sympathies."

The *Daily Telegraph* was originally founded by Colonel Sleigh on June 29, 1855, and printed for him by Joseph Moses Levy, owner of the *Sunday Times* (which was deliberately named after *The Times* but not connected to it otherwise). When Sleigh proved unable to pay his bills, Levy took over, lowering the price—the *Daily Telegraph* became the first "penny newspaper" in London—and appointing his son, Edward Levy-Lawson, and Thornton Leigh Hunt to serve as editors. The paper was relaunched on September 17, 1855. The reading public early embraced the *Daily Telegraph*'s colourful style, and within less than a year, Levy's newspaper was outselling not only *The Times* but also every other newspaper in England.

Founded in 1827, *The Standard* flourished into the 1880s but saw declining readership by the end of the nineteenth century. Journalist Cyril Arthur Pearson purchased *The Standard* in 1904 and turned it from a Conservative newspaper into a Liberal one, a move that did little to improve the newspaper's circulation.

The *Daily News* was founded by the novelist Charles Dickens, who saw the newspaper as an outlet for Liberal reform and published its first edition on January 21, 1846, declaring that it would advocate "principles of progress and improvement; of education, civil and religious liberty, and equal legislation." Dickens presided over the newspaper for seventeen issues before handing it off to John Forster.

167 Holmes has four cases involving organisations carrying out "vendettas," "The Five Orange Pips" (the KKK), "The Red Circle" (the "Red Circle," probably the Mafia, which is described as related to the "old Carbonari"), *The Valley of Fear* (the "Scowrers"), and "The Golden Pince-Nez" (Russian nihilists).

168 The Vehmgerichte, known in English as fehmic or vehmic courts, were criminal tribunals used in medieval Germany. Some of the proceedings were open to the public, but the arcane methods and severe punishments often meted out—accusations could be made by attaching a notice to a tree, failure to appear in court was punishable by death, and the two available verdicts were acquittal and hanging—lent the powerful Vehmgerichte a reputation of ruthless intimidation. According to the *Encyclopædia Britannica* (9th Ed.), "from the extent of their organization and the mystery which surrounded their proceedings, [the Vehmgerichte] inspired a feeling of dread in all who came within their jurisdiction."

169 An arsenic-based poison whose invention is attributed to a seventeenth-century Sicilian woman named Toffa or Tofana. Executed at Naples in 1709, she was said to have murdered more than 600 people. Brewer's *Dictionary of Phrase and Fable* called the poison "much used in Italy in the seventeenth century by young wives who wanted to get rid of their husbands," and there was wide speculation that Wolfgang Amadeus Mozart's death was caused by this substance.

170 The Carbonari (Italian for "Charcoal Burners") were members of a secret political society that was active in early nineteenth-century southern Italy and may have originated with the Freemasonry. These dissidents first began agitating for political freedom during the reign of Gioacchino Murat, Napoleon's brother-in-law and the king of Naples (1808–1815). In general, while the Carbonari tended to advocate Italian unification and some form of constitutional and representative government, a more precise agenda was never defined.

As with the Freemasonry and other secret societies, the Carbonari had their own ritual language, gestures, initiation ceremony, and hierarchy (in this case, made up of "apprentices" and "masters"). Their revolutionary fervour spread from Naples to like-minded areas such as Piedmont, the Papal States, Bologna, Parma, and Modena; and to other countries, including Spain and France. In 1831, the nationalist Risorgimento movement was formed and eventually subsumed most of the Carbonari.

171 Marie-Madeleine-Marguérite d'Aubray,

Marchioness de Brinvilliers (*ca.* 1630–1676), was a Frenchwoman who plotted with her lover to poison her father, her brothers, and her husband. In part, d'Aubray sought to control her family's fortunes and to end interference in her affair with J.-B. Godin de Sainte-Croix, a friend of her husband's. Sainte-Croix had his own motives, having been imprisoned at the Bastille by d'Aubray's father. After allegedly testing poisons on hospital patients, d'Aubray successfully murdered her father (in 1666) and her two brothers (in 1670), but her husband survived the attempt on his life. D'Aubray was arrested at Liège in 1676, and for her crimes was beheaded and burned.

In all, the notorious murderess was reputed to have killed fifty people, and she declared under interrogation, "Half the people of quality are involved in this sort of thing, and I could ruin them if I were to talk." Her trial set off a string of hysteria-driven investigations in which prominent members of the bourgeoisie, who often had done little more than purchase aphrodisiacs from fortune-tellers, were accused of being poisoners and practitioners of witchcraft.

Holmes and Watson may well have known d'Aubray from the popular romance entitled *The Marchioness of Brinvilliers, the Poisoner of the Seven*, written by Albert Smith and published in London in 1860. Arthur Conan Doyle turned to the story of the Marchioness in his tale "The Leather Funnel," published in the *Strand Magazine* in 1902.

172 The famed economist and sociologist Thomas Robert Malthus (1766–1834) was the father of modern population theory: the notion that population growth will always outrun the supply of natural resources, inevitably producing poverty and deprivation unless human reproduction can be curbed by war, famine, disease, or "moral restraint." In 1798, he published (anonymously) his great work, *An Essay on the Principle of Population as it affects the Future Improvement of Society, with remarks on the speculations of Mr. Godwin, M. Condorcet, and other writers.* It attracted immediate attention and was revised and expanded in 1803; the sixth and final version of Malthus's seminal work appeared in 1826.

173 Ratcliff Highway, located in the East End near the docks, became notorious early in the nineteenth century when it was the scene of a series of murders committed at the end of 1811. Thomas De Quincey, who wrote about the crimes in his *Murder Considered as One of the Fine Arts*, called the area one of "manifold ruffianism." Among the murders were those of the draper Mr. Marr, his wife, their infant child, and a boy who worked in the Marrs' shop. *The Complete Newgate Calender*, Volume V (1926), recounts that when a servant girl and a watchman rang the Marrs' bell and received no answer, a number of neighbours scaled the wall and entered the house; "and there was presented the most woeful scene that, perhaps, ever disgraced human nature: the bodies of Mr Marr and his shop-boy, the latter of whom appeared from evident marks to have

The Ratcliff Highway, Stepney (1896).
Victorian and Edwardian London

rages of the sort usually occurred under a Liberal Administration.[174] They arose from the unsettling of the minds of the masses, and the consequent weakening of all authority. The deceased was an American gentleman who had been residing for some weeks in the Metropolis. He had stayed at the boarding-house of Madame Charpentier, in Torquay Terrace, Camberwell.[175] He was accompanied in his travels by his private secretary, Mr. Joseph Stangerson. The two bade adieu to their landlady upon Tuesday, the 4th inst.,[176] and departed to Euston Station[177] with the avowed intention of catching the Liverpool express. They were afterwards seen together upon the platform. Nothing more is known of them until Mr. Drebber's body was, as recorded, discovered in an empty house in the Brixton Road, many miles from Euston. How he came there, or how he met his fate, are questions which are still involved in mystery. Nothing is known of the whereabouts of Stangerson. We are glad to learn that Mr. Lestrade and Mr. Gregson, of Scotland Yard, are both engaged upon the case, and it is confidently anticipated that these well-known officers will speedily throw light upon the matter.

The *Daily News* observed that there was no doubt as to the crime being a political one. The despotism and hatred of Liberalism which animated the Continental Governments had had the effect of driving to our shores a number of men who might have made excellent citizens were they not soured by the recollection of all that they had undergone. Among these men there was a stringent code of honour, any infringement of which was punished by death. Every effort should be made to find the secretary, Stangerson, and to ascertain some particulars of the habits of the deceased. A great step had been gained by the discovery of the address of the house at which he had boarded—a result which was entirely due to the acuteness and energy of Mr. Gregson of Scotland Yard.

Sherlock Holmes and I read these notices over together at breakfast, and they appeared to afford him considerable amusement.

"I told you that, whatever happened, Lestrade and Gregson would be sure to score."

"That depends on how it turns out."

"Oh, bless you, it doesn't matter in the least. If the man is caught, it will be *on account* of their exertions; if he escapes, it

struggled for life with the assassins, near each other; that of Mrs Marr in the passage; and the infant in its cradle—all dead, but yet warm and weltering in their blood." At final count, seven people were killed over the course of eight days. Although the murders were no doubt the work of more than one perpetrator, the only person arrested was a man named John Williams, who escaped trial by committing suicide in his cell at Coldbath Fields Prison.

As a result of the murders, the street acquired such sinister repute that its name was changed to St. George's Street. By 1895, when depicted in *The Queen's London*, it was reported that the street once regarded as unsavory and dangerous was "now . . . chiefly remarkable for the shops of dealers in wild beasts, birds, *etc.*"

174 Britain's Liberal party, which replaced the original Whig party of wealthy landowners and merchants, came to prominence under William Gladstone's first government in 1868. Liberals tended to advocate educational and electoral reform, free trade, and a loosening of the ties between church and state. While Gladstone was the steward of the Liberal party for more then twelve years and served four terms as prime minister, his ideas were not always greeted with popular enthusiasm—the critic John Ruskin told an audience of university students, "I hate all Liberalism as I do Beelzebub"—and Conservative opposition to his reforms, along with a poor foreign policy, drove the party from power in 1874. The Conservative Benjamin Disraeli was prime minister during the American events of *A Study in Scarlet*, but Gladstone resumed the office in 1880, and again in 1886. Ultimately, his insistence on Irish Home Rule (self-government) doomed his third ministry and caused many prominent Liberals to leave the party. After World War I, the Liberal party was nearly defunct, having lost considerable ground to the new Labour party.

175 Christopher Morley observes, "Camberwell, across the Thames in South London, was an unusual lodging place for well-to-do tourists—unless possibly they chose to be near the Crystal Palace, still very famous in those days." The composer Felix Mendelssohn, who had relatives in Camberwell, wrote "Camberwell Green" (later renamed "Spring Song") after staying there. The poet Robert Browning (1812–1889), whose reputation was eclipsed by that of his wife, fellow poet Elizabeth Barrett Browning (1806–1861), was born in Camberwell and lived there until he was twenty-eight. Bernard Davies identifies Torquay Terrace as Dover Terrace in Coldharbour Lane.

176 That is, on March 4 (*inst.* is an abbreviation of "instant" and in archaic usage meant a date in the current month). The date on which the pair departed was plainly March 3, inasmuch as Drebber's death occurred before 2:00 A.M. on March 4. "This inaccuracy," Christopher Morley suggests, "may of course be intended to satirize the inaccuracy of the Tory newspaper, but probably should be accepted as the first of Dr. Watson's many inconsistencies in chronology."

177 Euston Station was opened in 1837 as the terminus for the London-Birmingham Railway (later the London & Northern Western Railway). It was expanded several times, including in 1873, but was demolished and completely reconstructed in the 1960s. "This deliberate act of official vandalism," writes Holmesian scholar Roger Johnson, "led to a new appreciation of Victorian architecture. There is still a Euston Station, but Holmes and Watson would not recognise it."

will be *in spite* of their exertions. It's heads I win and tails you lose. Whatever they do, they will have followers. *Un sot trouve toujours un plus sot qui l'admire.*"[178]

"What on earth is this?" I cried, for at this moment there came the pattering of many steps in the hall and on the stairs, accompanied by audible expressions of disgust upon the part of our landlady.

"It's the Baker Street division of the detective police force," said my companion, gravely; and as he spoke there rushed into the room half a dozen of the dirtiest and most ragged street Arabs that ever I clapped eyes on.[179]

" 'Tention!" cried Holmes, in a sharp tone, and the six dirty little scoundrels stood in a line like so many disreputable statuettes. "In future you shall send up Wiggins alone to report, and the rest of you must wait in the street. Have you found it, Wiggins?"

" 'It's the Baker Street division of the detective police force.' "
Geo. Hutchinson, *A Study in Scarlet* (London: Ward, Lock Bowden, and Co., 1891)

178 The final line of Canto I of *L'Art Poétique* by Nicolas Boileau-Despréaux (1636–1711), which may be translated as, "A fool can always find a greater fool to admire him." Scholars point to Holmes's facility in the French language as part of his French heritage. In "The Greek Interpreter," Holmes alludes to "my grandmother, who was the sister of Vernet, the French artist." This artist, Holmes's great-uncle, was likely Émile Jean Horace Vernet (1789–1863), whose paintings decorate the Battle Gallery at Versailles.

179 A "street Arab" was a homeless child, or urchin, who wandered the city streets. E. Cobham Brewer's *Dictionary of Phrase and Fable* explains that they are "[s]o called because, like the Arabs, they are nomads or wanderers with no settled home." Jacob A. Riis's *How the Other Half Lives* (1890) attempts to paint a fuller picture, and he takes a somewhat romanticised look at what he deems a New York City "institution" when he writes, "Vagabond that he is, acknowledging no authority and owing no allegiance to anybody or anything, with his grimy fist raised against society whenever it tries to coerce him, [the street Arab] is as bright and sharp as the weasel, which, among all the predatory beasts, he most resembles."

Holmes's band of "street Arabs," led by the redoubtable Wiggins, is again put to use by the detective in *The Sign of Four* and in "The Crooked Man." It is in *The Sign of Four*, in fact, that Holmes refers to his foot soldiers as "the unofficial force—the Baker Street irregulars." The Baker Street Irregulars, of course, is the name taken by the prominent society of Sherlockian scholars, founded in 1934 by Christopher Morley.

Street Arabs (1888).
Jacob Riis, *How the Other Half Lives*
(New York: Charles Scribner's Sons, 1890)

"No, sir, we hain't," said one of the youths.

"I hardly expected you would. You must keep on until you do. Here are your wages." He handed each of them a shilling. "Now, off you go, and come back with a better report next time."

He waved his hand, and they scampered away downstairs like so many rats, and we heard their shrill voices next moment in the street.

"There's more work to be got out of one of those little beggars than out of a dozen of the force," Holmes remarked. "The mere sight of an official-looking person seals men's lips. These youngsters, however, go everywhere and hear everything. They are as sharp as needles, too; all they want is organisation."

"Is it on this Brixton case that you are employing them?" I asked.

"Yes; there is a point which I wish to ascertain. It is merely a

"'’Tention!' cried Holmes in a sharp tone."
Charles Doyle, *A Study in Scarlet* (London and New York: Ward, Lock & Co., 1888)

matter of time. Hullo! we are going to hear some news now with a vengeance! Here is Gregson coming down the road with beatitude written upon every feature of his face. Bound for us, I know. Yes, he is stopping. There he is!"

There was a violent peal at the bell, and in a few seconds the fair-haired detective came up the stairs, three steps at a time, and burst into our sitting-room.

"My dear fellow," he cried, wringing Holmes's unresponsive hand, "congratulate me! I have made the whole thing as clear as day."

A shade of anxiety seemed to me to cross my companion's expressive face.

"Do you mean that you are on the right track?" he asked,

"The right track! Why, sir, we have the man under lock and key."

"And his name is?"

" 'Have you found it, Wiggins?' "
Richard Gutschmidt, *Späte Rache* (Stuttgart: Robert Lutz Verlag, 1902)

"Arthur Charpentier, sub-lieutenant in Her Majesty's navy," cried Gregson, pompously, rubbing his fat hands and inflating his chest.

Sherlock Holmes gave a sigh of relief, and relaxed into a smile.

"Take a seat, and try one of these cigars," he said. "We are anxious to know how you managed it. Will you have some whisky and water?"

"I don't mind if I do," the detective answered. "The tremendous exertions which I have gone through during the last day or two have worn me out. Not so much bodily exertion, you understand, as the strain upon the mind. You will appreciate that, Mr. Sherlock Holmes, for we are both brain-workers."

"You do me too much honour," said Holmes, gravely. "Let us hear how you arrived at this most gratifying result."

The detective seated himself in the arm-chair, and puffed complacently at his cigar. Then suddenly he slapped his thigh in a paroxysm of amusement.

"Came up the stairs three steps at a time."
Geo. Hutchinson, *A Study in Scarlet* (London: Ward, Lock, Bowden, and Co., 1891)

"The fun of it is," he cried, "that that fool Lestrade, who thinks himself so smart, has gone off upon the wrong track altogether. He is after the secretary Stangerson, who had no more to do with the crime than the babe unborn.[180] I have no doubt that he has caught him by this time."

The idea tickled Gregson so much that he laughed until he choked.

"And how did you get your clue?"

"Ah, I'll tell you all about it. Of course, Dr. Watson, this is strictly between ourselves. The first difficulty which we had to contend with was the finding of this American's antecedents. Some people would have waited until their advertisements were answered, or until parties came forward and volunteered information. That is not Tobias Gregson's way of going to work. You remember the hat beside the dead man?"

"Yes," said Holmes; "by John Underwood and Sons, 129, Camberwell Road."

Gregson looked quite crest-fallen.

"I had no idea that you noticed that," he said. "Have you been there?"

"No."

180 Andrew G. Fusco, in "The Final Outrage of Enoch Drebber," argues that there *was* in fact a babe unborn—the child of Enoch Drebber, carried by Alice Charpentier as a result of Drebber's "advances"—and that Gregson knew about it.

"Ha!" cried Gregson, in a relieved voice; "you should never neglect a chance, however small it may seem."

"To a great mind, nothing is little,"[181] remarked Holmes, sententiously.

"Well, I went to Underwood, and asked him if he had sold a hat of that size and description. He looked over his books, and came on it at once. He had sent the hat to a Mr. Drebber, residing at Charpentier's Boarding Establishment, Torquay Terrace. Thus I got at his address."

"Smart—very smart!" murmured Sherlock Holmes.

"I next called upon Madame Charpentier," continued the detective. "I found her very pale and distressed. Her daughter was in the room, too—an uncommonly fine girl she is, too; she was looking red about the eyes and her lips trembled as I spoke to her. That didn't escape my notice. I began to smell a rat. You know the feeling, Mr. Sherlock Holmes, when you come upon the right scent—a kind of thrill in your nerves. 'Have you heard of the mysterious death of your late boarder Mr. Enoch J. Drebber, of Cleveland?' I asked.

A private hotel in London. Note the appeal of the advertisement to foreigners ("Ici on parle Francais. Mein spricht Deutsch").

181 Holmes makes similar statements during other cases, for example (as noted by T. S. Blakeney), "You know my method. It is founded upon the observance of trifles" ("The Boscombe Valley Mystery"); "It is of course a trifle, but there is nothing so important as trifles" ("The Man with the Twisted Lip"); and "I dare call nothing trivial when I reflect that some of my most classic cases have had the least promising commencement" ("The Six Napoleons"). Blakeney concludes that "Holmes has, as Watson remarked [in *The Sign of Four*], an extraordinary gift for minutiae, and he was already ready to be at any pains to elicit them."

"The mother nodded. She didn't seem able to get out a word. The daughter burst into tears. I felt more than ever that these people knew something of the matter.

" 'At what o'clock did Mr. Drebber leave your house for the train?' I asked.

" 'At eight o'clock,' she said, gulping in her throat to keep down her agitation. 'His secretary, Mr. Stangerson, said that there were two trains—one at 9:15 and one at 11. He was to catch the first.'

" 'And was that the last which you saw of him?'

"A terrible change came over the woman's face as I asked the question. Her features turned perfectly livid. It was some seconds before she could get out the single word 'Yes'—and when it did come it was in a husky, unnatural tone.

"There was silence for a moment, and then the daughter spoke in a calm, clear voice.

" 'No good can ever come of falsehood, mother,' she said. 'Let us be frank with this gentleman. We *did* see Mr. Drebber again.'

" 'God forgive you!' cried Madame Charpentier, throwing up her hands and sinking back in her chair. 'You have murdered your brother.'

" 'Arthur would rather that we spoke the truth,' the girl answered firmly.

" 'You had best tell me all about it now,' I said. 'Half-confidences are worse than none. Besides, you do not know how much we know of it.'

" 'On your head be it, Alice!' cried her mother; and then, turning to me, 'I will tell you all, sir. Do not imagine that my agitation on behalf of my son arises from any fear lest he should have had a hand in this terrible affair. He is utterly innocent of it. My dread is, however, that in your eyes and in the eyes of others he may appear to be compromised. That however is surely impossible. His high character, his profession, his antecedents would all forbid it.'

" 'Your best way is to make a clean breast of the facts,' I answered. 'Depend upon it, if your son is innocent he will be none the worse.'

" 'Perhaps, Alice, you had better leave us together,' she said, and her daughter withdrew. 'Now, sir,' she continued, 'I had no intention of telling you all this, but since my poor daughter has

" 'God forgive you!' cried Madame Charpentier, 'you have murdered your brother.' "
James Greig, *A Study in Scarlet* (London, Melbourne and Toronto: Ward, Lock & Co., Limited, n.d.)

disclosed it I have no alternative. Having once decided to speak, I will tell you all without omitting any particular.'

" 'It is your wisest course,' said I.

" 'Mr. Drebber has been with us nearly three weeks. He and his secretary, Mr. Stangerson, had been travelling on the Continent. I noticed a "Copenhagen" label upon each of their trunks, showing that that had been their last stopping place. Stangerson was a quiet reserved man, but his employer, I am sorry to say, was far otherwise. He was coarse in his habits and brutish in his ways. The very night of his arrival he became very much the worse for drink, and, indeed, after twelve o'clock in the day he could hardly ever be said to be sober. His manners towards the maid-servants were disgustingly free and familiar. Worst of all, he speedily assumed the same attitude towards my daughter, Alice, and spoke to her more than once in a way which, fortunately, she is too innocent to understand.

On one occasion he actually seized her in his arms and embraced her—an outrage which caused his own secretary to reproach him for his unmanly conduct.'

" 'But why did you stand all this?' I asked. 'I suppose that you can get rid of your boarders when you wish,'

"Mrs. Charpentier blushed at my pertinent question. 'Would to God that I had given him notice on the very day that he came,' she said. 'But it was a sore temptation. They were paying a pound a day each—fourteen pounds a week,[182] and this is the slack season. I am a widow, and my boy in the Navy has cost me much. I grudged to lose the money. I acted for the best. This last was too much, however, and I gave him notice to leave on account of it. That was the reason of his going.'

" 'Well?'

" 'My heart grew light when I saw him drive away. My son is on leave just now, but I did not tell him anything of all this, for his temper is violent, and he is passionately fond of his sister. When I closed the door behind them a load seemed to be lifted from my mind. Alas, in less than an hour there was a ring at the bell, and I learned that Mr. Drebber had returned. He was much excited, and evidently the worse for drink. He forced his way into the room, where I was sitting with my daughter, and made some incoherent remark about having missed his train. He then turned to Alice, and before my very face, proposed to her that she should fly with him. "You are of age," he said, "and there is no law to stop you. I have money enough and to spare. Never mind the old girl here, but come along with me now straight away. You shall live like a princess." Poor Alice was so frightened that she shrunk away from him, but he caught her by the wrist and endeavoured to draw her towards the door. I screamed, and at that moment my son Arthur came into the room. What happened then I do not know. I heard oaths and the confused sounds of a scuffle. I was too terrified to raise my head. When I did look up I saw Arthur standing in the doorway laughing, with a stick in his hand. "I don't think that fine fellow will trouble us again," he said. "I will just go after him and see what he does with himself." With those words he took his hat and started off down the street. The next morning we heard of Mr. Drebber's mysterious death.'

"This statement came from Mrs. Charpentier's lips with many gasps and pauses. At times she spoke so low that I could

182 Drebber may well have expected some form of special treatment, given that he was paying the Charpentiers well above the market rate (the modern equivalent of £715, or over $1,300, per week). *Baedeker* gives the top price for a boarding-house (Mrs. Phillips's, at Portland Place, in the fashionable West End) as £3 13*s*. 6*d*. per week.

" 'He caught her by the wrist and endeavoured to draw her toward the door.' "
Geo. Hutchinson, *A Study in Scarlet* (London: Ward, Lock Bowden, and Co., 1891)

hardly catch the words. I made shorthand notes[183] of all that she said, however, so that there should be no possibility of a mistake."

"It's quite exciting," said Sherlock Holmes, with a yawn. "What happened next?"

"When Mrs. Charpentier paused," the detective continued, "I saw that the whole case hung upon one point. Fixing her with my eye in a way which I always found effective with women, I asked her at what hour her son returned.

" 'I do not know,' she answered.

" 'Not know?'

" 'No; he has a latchkey, and he let himself in.'

" 'After you went to bed?'

" 'Yes.'

" 'When did you go to bed?'

183 Modern shorthand was invented in England by the educator Isaac Pitman (1813–1897) in 1837. Breaking new ground, his *Stenographic Sound-Hand* used phonetics, rather than normal spelling, to represent full words. Different degrees of shading indicated the various phonetic sounds. Toward the end of the nineteenth century, one report found that 97 percent of American writers used the Pitman system or some variation of it, owing largely to the institute that Pitman's brother, Benn Pitman, opened in Cincinnati in 1852. While it is considered perhaps the most rapid shorthand system—making it a preferred choice among many court reporters today—the Pitman method has been largely supplanted in the United States by Gregg Shorthand, a phonetics-based system that utilises curves instead of Pitman's shading. The Irish-born John Robert Gregg (1867–1948) introduced the system in his book *Light-Line Phonography* (1888) and brought it to the United States in 1893.

In 1881, the date of *A Study in Scarlet*, it seems likely that Gregson and Lestrade used the Pitman method, although many alternative systems did flourish. The *Encyclopædia Britannica* (9th Ed.) estimated that by 1886, no fewer than 483 distinct systems of English shorthand had been published ("and doubtless many more of them have been invented for private use").

" 'About eleven.'

" 'So your son was gone at least two hours?'

" 'Yes.'

" 'Possibly four or five?'

" 'Yes.'

" 'What was he doing during that time?'

" 'I do not know,' she answered, turning white to her very lips.

"Of course after that there was nothing more to be done. I found out where Lieutenant Charpentier was, took two officers with me, and arrested him. When I touched him on the shoulder and warned him to come quietly with us, he answered us as bold as brass, 'I suppose you are arresting me for being concerned in the death of that scoundrel Drebber,' he said. We had said nothing to him about it, so that his alluding to it had a most suspicious aspect."

"Very," said Holmes.

"He still carried the heavy stick which the mother described him as having with him when he followed Drebber. It was a stout oak cudgel."

"What is your theory, then?"

"Well, my theory is that he followed Drebber as far as the Brixton Road. When there, a fresh altercation arose between them, in the course of which Drebber received a blow from the stick, in the pit of the stomach perhaps, which killed him without leaving any mark. The night was so wet that no one was about, so Charpentier dragged the body of his victim into the empty house. As to the candle, and the blood, and the writing on the wall, and the ring, they may all be so many tricks to throw the police on to the wrong scent."

"Well done!" said Holmes in an encouraging voice. "Really, Gregson, you are getting along. We shall make something of you yet."

"I flatter myself that I have managed it rather neatly," the detective answered proudly. "The young man volunteered a statement, in which he said that after following Drebber some time, the latter perceived him, and took a cab in order to get away from him. On his way home he met an old shipmate, and took a long walk with him. On being asked where this old shipmate lived, he was unable to give any satisfactory reply. I think the whole case fits together uncommonly well. What amuses me is to think of Lestrade, who had started off upon the wrong scent. I am afraid he won't make much of it. Why, by Jove, here's the very man himself!"

It was indeed Lestrade, who had ascended the stairs while we were talking, and who now entered the room. The assurance and jauntiness which generally marked his demeanour and dress were, however, wanting. His face was disturbed and troubled, while his clothes were disarranged and untidy. He had evidently come with the intention of consulting with Sherlock Holmes, for on perceiving his colleague he appeared to be embarrassed and put out. He stood in the centre of the room, fumbling nervously with his hat and uncertain what to do. "This is a most extraordinary case," he said at last—"a most incomprehensible affair."

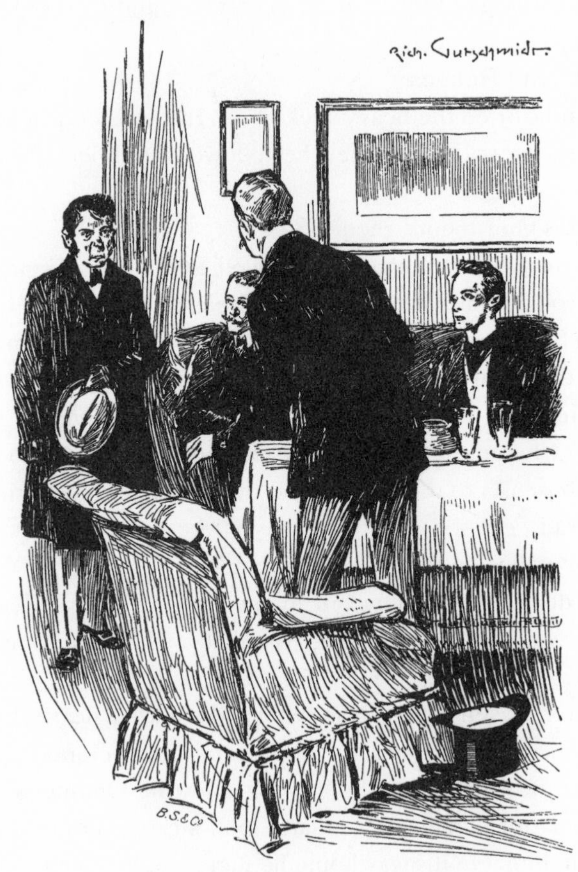

"Lestrade stood in the centre of the room, fumbling nervously with his hat and uncertain what to do."
Richard Gutschmidt, *Späte Rache* (Stuttgart: Robert Lutz Verlag, 1902)

"Ah, you find it so, Mr. Lestrade!" cried Gregson, triumphantly. "I thought you would come to that conclusion. Have you managed to find the Secretary, Mr. Joseph Stangerson?"

"The Secretary, Mr. Joseph Stangerson," said Lestrade, gravely "was murdered at Halliday's Private Hotel[184] about six o'clock this morning."

184 Bernard Davies identifies "Halliday's" as Emm's Private Hotel at No. 56 Drummond Street.

CHAPTER VII

Light in the Darkness

THE INTELLIGENCE WITH which Lestrade greeted us was so momentous and so unexpected that we were all three fairly dumfoundered.[185] Gregson sprang out of his chair and upset the remainder of his whisky and water. I stared in silence at Sherlock Holmes, whose lips were compressed and his brows drawn down over his eyes.

"Stangerson too!" he muttered. "The plot thickens."[186]

"It was quite thick enough before," grumbled Lestrade, taking a chair. "I seem to have dropped into a sort of council of war."

"Are you—are you sure of this piece of intelligence?" stammered Gregson.

"I have just come from his room," said Lestrade. "I was the first to discover what had occurred."

"We have been hearing Gregson's view of the matter," Holmes observed. "Would you mind letting us know what you have seen and done?"

"I have no objection," Lestrade answered, seating himself. "I freely confess that I was of the opinion that Stangerson was concerned in the death of Drebber. This fresh development

185 This is the Scottish spelling, used in the *Beeton's* and English book edition; in American editions, it is generally changed to the American version, "dumbfounded." *The Slang Dictionary* gives the meaning as "to perplex, to beat soundly till not able to speak."

186 Because it is the Master, we can perhaps forgive the repetition of this phrase from Chapter V, for it had not yet become a cliché.

has shown me that I was completely mistaken. Full of the one idea, I set myself to find out what had become of the Secretary. They had been seen together at Euston Station about half-past eight on the evening of the third. At two in the morning Drebber had been found in the Brixton Road. The question which confronted me was to find out how Stangerson had been employed between 8.30 and the time of the crime, and what had become of him afterwards. I telegraphed to Liverpool, giving a description of the man, and warning them to keep a watch upon the American boats. I then set to work calling upon all the hotels and lodging-houses in the vicinity of Euston. You see, I argued that if Drebber and his companion had become separated, the natural course for the latter would be to put up somewhere in the vicinity for the night, and then to hang about the station again next morning."

"They would be likely to agree on some meeting-place beforehand," remarked Holmes.

"So it proved. I spent the whole of yesterday evening in making inquiries entirely without avail. This morning I began very early, and at eight o'clock I reached Halliday's Private Hotel, in Little George Street. On my inquiry as to whether a Mr. Stangerson was living there, they at once answered me in the affirmative.

" 'No doubt you are the gentleman whom he was expecting,' they said. 'He has been waiting for a gentleman for two days.'

" 'Where is he now?' I asked.

" 'He is upstairs in bed. He wished to be called at nine.'

" 'I will go up and see him at once,' I said.

"It seemed to me that my sudden appearance might shake his nerves and lead him to say something unguarded. The Boots[187] volunteered to show me the room: it was on the second floor, and there was a small corridor leading up to it. The Boots pointed out the door to me, and was about to go downstairs again when I saw something that made me feel sickish, in spite of my twenty years' experience. From under the door there curled a little red ribbon of blood, which had meandered across the passage and formed a little pool along the skirting at the other side. I gave a cry, which brought the Boots back. He nearly fainted when he saw it. The door was locked on the inside, but we put our shoulders to it, and knocked it in. The window of the room was open, and beside the window, all hud-

187 The hotel servant whose job included boot-cleaning.

188 A set of stables grouped around an open yard or alley. "Sherlock Mews," known less interestingly as York Mews South in Watson's Day, is just off Baker Street.

"He nearly fainted when he saw it."
Geo. Hutchinson, *A Study in Scarlet* (London: Ward, Lock Bowden, and Co., 1891)

dled up, lay the body of a man in his nightdress. He was quite dead, and had been for some time, for his limbs were rigid and cold. When we turned him over, the Boots recognized him at once as being the same gentleman who had engaged the room under the name of Joseph Stangerson. The cause of death was a deep stab in the left side, which must have penetrated the heart. And now comes the strangest part of the affair. What do you suppose was above the murdered man?"

I felt a creeping of the flesh, and a presentiment of coming horror, even before Sherlock Holmes answered.

"The word RACHE, written in letters of blood," he said.

"That was it," said Lestrade, in an awestruck voice; and we were all silent for awhile.

There was something so methodical and so incomprehensible about the deeds of this unknown assassin, that it imparted a fresh ghastliness to his crimes. My nerves, which were steady enough on the field of battle, tingled as I thought of it.

"The man was seen," continued Lestrade. "A milk boy, passing on his way to the dairy, happened to walk down the lane which leads from the mews[188] at the back of the hotel. He noticed that a ladder, which usually lay there, was raised against one of the windows of the second floor, which was wide open. After passing, he looked back and saw a man descend the ladder. He came down so quietly and openly that the boy imagined him to be some carpenter or joiner at work in the hotel. He took no particular notice of him, beyond thinking in his own mind that it was early for him to be at work. He has an impression that the man was tall, had a reddish face, and was dressed in a long, brownish coat. He must have stayed in the room some little time after the murder, for we found blood-stained water in the basin, where he had washed his hands, and marks on the sheets where he had deliberately wiped his knife."

I glanced at Holmes on hearing the description of the murderer, which tallied so exactly with his own. There was, however, no trace of exultation or satisfaction upon his face.

"Did you find nothing in the room which could furnish a clue to the murderer?" he asked.

"Nothing. Stangerson had Drebber's purse in his pocket, but it seems that this was usual, as he did all the paying. There was eighty odd pounds in it, but nothing had been taken. Whatever the motives of these extraordinary crimes, robbery is certainly not one of them. There were no papers or memoranda in the murdered man's pocket, except a single telegram, dated from Cleveland about a month ago, and containing the words, 'J. H. is in Europe.'[189] There was no name appended to this message."

"And there was nothing else?" Holmes asked.

"Nothing of any importance. The man's novel, with which he had read himself to sleep was lying upon the bed, and his pipe was on a chair beside him. There was a glass of water on the table, and on the window-sill a small chip ointment box containing a couple of pills."

Sherlock Holmes sprang from his chair with an exclamation of delight.

"The last link," he cried, exultantly. "My case is complete."

The two detectives stared at him in amazement.

"I have now in my hands," my companion said, confidently, "all the threads which have formed such a tangle. There are, of course, details to be filled in, but I am as certain of all the main facts, from the time that Drebber parted from Stangerson at the station, up to the discovery of the body of the latter, as if I

189 Stangerson certainly did not need to refer to this telegram from time to time. Why, then, was it still in his possession at the time of his death, over a month after receipt? One assumes, by the way, that this refers to Jefferson Hope, whom Holmes later identifies as the object of Drebber's search, and not to "J. H." Watson. The latter suggestion is especially intriguing in light of Arthur Conan Doyle's play *Angels of Darkness*, which places Dr. Watson in San Francisco, where he meets Jefferson Hope, who, with his dying breath, urges Watson to marry Lucy Ferrier!

had seen them with my own eyes. I will give you a proof of my knowledge. Could you lay your hand upon those pills?"

"I have them," said Lestrade, producing a small white box; "I took them and the purse and the telegram, intending to have them put in a place of safety at the Police Station. It was the merest chance my taking these pills, for I am bound to say that I do not attach any importance to them."

"Give them here," said Holmes. "Now, Doctor," turning to me, "are those ordinary pills?"

They certainly were not. They were of a pearly grey colour, small, round, and almost transparent against the light. "From their lightness and transparency, I should imagine that they are soluble in water," I remarked.

"Precisely so," answered Holmes. "Now would you mind going down and fetching that poor little devil of a terrier which has been bad so long, and which the landlady wanted you to put out of its pain yesterday?"

I went downstairs and carried the dog upstairs in my arms. Its laboured breathing and glazing eye showed that it was not far from its end. Indeed, its snow-white muzzle proclaimed that it had already exceeded the usual term of canine existence. I placed it upon a cushion on the rug.

"I will now cut one of these pills in two," said Holmes, and drawing his penknife he suited the action to the word. "One half we return into the box for future purposes. The other half I will place in this wineglass, in which is a teaspoonful of water. You perceive that our friend, the Doctor, is right, and that it readily dissolves."

"This may be very interesting," said Lestrade, in the injured tone of one who suspects that he is being laughed at, "I cannot see, however, what it has to do with the death of Mr. Joseph Stangerson."

"Patience, my friend, patience! You will find in time that it has everything to do with it. I shall now add a little milk to make the mixture palatable, and on presenting it to the dog we find that he laps it up readily enough."

As he spoke he turned the contents of the wineglass into a saucer and placed it in front of the terrier, who speedily licked it dry. Sherlock Holmes's earnest demeanour had so far convinced us that we all sat in silence, watching the animal intently, and expecting some startling effect. None such

"The dog continued to lie stretched upon the cushion."
Richard Gutschmidt, *Späte Rache* (Stuttgart: Robert Lutz Verlag, 1902)

appeared, however. The dog continued to lie stretched upon the cushion, breathing in a laboured way, but apparently neither the better nor the worse for its draught.

Holmes had taken out his watch, and as minute followed minute without result, an expression of the utmost chagrin and disappointment appeared upon his features. He gnawed his lip, drummed his fingers upon the table, and showed every other symptom of acute impatience. So great was his emotion that I felt sincerely sorry for him, while the two detectives smiled derisively, by no means displeased at this check which he had met.

"It can't be a coincidence," he cried, at last springing from his chair and pacing wildly up and down the room; "it is impossible that it should be a mere coincidence. The very pills which I suspected in the case of Drebber are actually found after the death of Stangerson. And yet they are inert. What can it mean? Surely my whole chain of reasoning cannot have been

"The unfortunate creature's tongue seemed hardly to have been moistened in it before it gave a convulsive shiver in every limb, and lay as rigid and lifeless as if it had been struck by lightning."
Geo. Hutchinson, *A Study in Scarlet* (London: Ward, Lock Bowden, and Co., 1891)

false. It is impossible! And yet this wretched dog is none the worse. Ah, I have it! I have it!" With a perfect shriek of delight he rushed to the box, cut the other pill in two, dissolved it, added milk, and presented it to the terrier. The unfortunate creature's tongue seemed hardly to have been moistened in it before it gave a convulsive shiver in every limb, and lay as rigid and lifeless as if it had been struck by lightning.

Sherlock Holmes drew a long breath, and wiped the perspiration from his forehead. "I should have more faith," he said; "I ought to know by this time that when a fact appears to be opposed to a long train of deductions, it invariably proves to be capable of bearing some other interpretation.[190] Of the two pills in that box one was of the most deadly poison, and the other was entirely harmless. I ought to have known that before ever I saw the box at all."

This last statement appeared to me to be so startling, that I could hardly believe that he was in his sober senses. There was the dead dog, however, to prove that his conjecture had been correct. It seemed to me that the mists in my own mind were gradually clearing away, and I began to have a dim, vague perception of the truth.

"All this seems strange to you," continued Holmes, "because you failed at the beginning of the inquiry to grasp the importance of the single real clue which was presented to you. I had the good fortune to seize upon that, and everything which has occurred since then has served to confirm my original supposition, and, indeed, was the logical sequence of it. Hence things which have perplexed you and made the case more obscure, have served to enlighten me and to strengthen my conclusions. It is a mistake to confound strangeness with mystery. The most commonplace crime is often the most mysterious, because it presents no new or special features from which deductions may be drawn.[191] This murder would have been infinitely more difficult to unravel had the body of the victim been simply found lying in the roadway without any of those outré and sensational accompaniments which have rendered it remarkable. These strange details, far from making the case more difficult, have really had the effect of making it less so."

Mr. Gregson, who had listened to this address with considerable impatience, could contain himself no longer. "Look here, Mr. Sherlock Holmes," he said, "we are all ready to acknowledge that you are a smart man, and that you have your own methods of working. We want something more than mere theory and preaching now, though. It is a case of taking the man. I have made my case out, and it seems I was wrong. Young Charpentier could not have been engaged in this second affair. Lestrade went after his man, Stangerson, and it appears that he was wrong too. You have thrown out hints here, and hints there, and seem to know more than we do, but the time

190 This is a familiar theme for Holmes, who has expressed similar sentiments elsewhere: "One should always look for a possible alternative and provide against it. It is the first rule of criminal investigation" ("Black Peter"); "When you follow two separate trains of thought, you will find some point of intersection which should approximate to the truth" ("Lady Frances Carfax"); "One drawback of an active mind is that one can always conceive alternative explanations, which would make our scent a false one" ("Thor Bridge"). Holmes here discusses the essence of the scientific method: One attempts to formulate a general principle that explains disparate phenomena or data points but retains the flexibility to discard the principle when an unexpected phenomenon or data point occurs. At the point of abandoning the prior principle, the scientist attempts to formulate a *new* general principle that explains the previously explained phenomena as well as the unexplained. Historian Thomas S. Kuhn examined the approach in detail in his seminal *The Structure of Scientific Revolutions* (1962), calling the abandonment of the unworkable explanation a "paradigm shift."

191 Again, Holmes reveals another bit of his own personal dogma, articulated throughout the years: "Singularity is almost invariably a clue. The more featureless and commonplace a crime is, the more difficult it is to bring home" ("Boscombe Valley Mystery"); "The more bizarre a thing is the less mysterious it proves to be" ("Red-Headed League"). In the context of the scientific method, it is the *unusual* data point that tests the viability of a theory.

192 The *Encyclopædia Britannica* (9th Ed.) puts the population of the London Police District, "Greater London," at 4,764,312 in 1881.

has come when we feel that we have a right to ask you straight how much you do know of the business. Can you name the man who did it?"

"I cannot help feeling that Gregson is right, sir," remarked Lestrade. "We have both tried, and we have both failed. You have remarked more than once since I have been in the room that you had all the evidence which you require. Surely you will not withhold it any longer."

"Any delay in arresting the assassin," I observed, "might give him time to perpetrate some fresh atrocity."

Thus pressed by us all, Holmes showed signs of irresolution. He continued to walk up and down the room with his head sunk on his chest and his brows drawn down, as was his habit when lost in thought.

"There will be no more murders," he said at last, stopping abruptly and facing us. "You can put that consideration out of the question. You have asked me if I know the name of the assassin. I do. The mere knowing of his name is a small thing, however, compared with the power of laying our hands upon him. This I expect very shortly to do. I have good hopes of managing it through my own arrangements; but it is a thing which needs delicate handling, for we have a shrewd and desperate man to deal with, who is supported, as I have had occasion to prove, by another who is as clever as himself. As long as this man has no idea that anyone can have a clue there is some chance of securing him; but if he had the slightest suspicion, he would change his name, and vanish in an instant among the four million inhabitants of this great city.[192] Without meaning to hurt either of your feelings, I am bound to say that I consider these men to be more than a match for the official force, and that is why I have not asked your assistance. If I fail, I shall, of course, incur all the blame due to this omission; but that I am prepared for. At present I am ready to promise that the instant that I can communicate with you without endangering my own combinations, I shall do so."

Gregson and Lestrade seemed to be far from satisfied by this assurance, or by the depreciating allusion to the detective police. The former had flushed up to the roots of his flaxen hair, while the other's beady eyes glistened with curiosity and resentment. Neither of them had time to speak, however, before there was a tap at the door, and the spokesman of the street Arabs, young Wiggins, introduced his insignificant and unsavoury person.

"Please, sir," he said, touching his forelock, "I have the cab downstairs."

"Good boy," said Holmes, blandly. "Why don't you introduce this pattern at Scotland Yard?" he continued, taking a pair of steel handcuffs from a drawer, "See how beautifully the spring works. They fasten in an instant."[193]

"The old pattern is good enough," remarked Lestrade, "if we can only find the man to put them on."[194]

"Very good, very good," said Holmes, smiling. "The cabman may as well help me with my boxes. Just ask him to step up, Wiggins."

I was surprised to find my companion speaking as though he were about to set out on a journey, since he had not said any-

"Lestrade and Holmes sprang upon him like so many staghounds."
Geo. Hutchinson, *A Study in Scarlet* (London: Ward, Lock & Bowden, Limited, 1893)

193 In an 1894 article in the *Strand Magazine*, Inspector Maurice Moser, late of Scotland Yard, complained:

> English handcuffs . . . are heavy unwieldy, awkward machines, which at the best of times, and under the most favorable circumstances are extremely difficult of application. They weigh over a pound, and have to be unlocked with a key in a manner not greatly differing from the operation of winding up the average eight-day clock, and fastened on to the prisoner's wrists, how, the fates and good luck only know. This lengthy, difficult, and particularly disagreeable operation, with a prisoner struggling and fighting, is to a degree almost incredible. The prisoner practically has to be overpowered or to submit before he can be finally and certainly secured. . . . As the English handcuffs have only been formed for criminals who submitted quietly to necessity, it was considered expedient to find an instrument applicable to all cases. The perfected article comes from America . . . and, being lighter, less clumsy, and more easily concealed, finds general favour among the officers of Scotland Yard.

Handcuff design had taken a major step forward with W. V. Adams's 1862 patent of adjustable ratchets, which ensured a snug, secure fit for both thick- and thin-wristed captives. But Elliott Kimball, in "Origin and Evo-

American handcuffs, recommended by Inspector Maurice Moser of Scotland Yard.
Strand Magazine (1894)

lution of G. Lestrade—2. A Matter of Mancinism," informs us that automatically locking handcuffs of the kind Holmes displays here were not available prior to 1896, and Kimball concludes that the darbies in question were Holmes's own (and only) mechanical invention. But Kimball appears incorrect: There were, in fact, numerous varieties of automatically locking cuffs in use, and the principal problem facing the arresting officer was often *keeping* the cuffs from locking before the cuffs were placed on the prisoner. This was dealt with elegantly in 1882, when E. D. Bean patented his first handcuff featuring a unique release button to solve the problem of premature locking. In his patent application, dated September 1, 1882, Bean stated:

> It often occurs in the attempt of a policeman to arrest and manacle an offender that the handcuff becomes in the struggle accidentally closed and locked before the officer can succeed in placing it about his prisoner's wrist, and when this occurs it is a matter of time and difficulty to unlock the instrument, and more chance is afforded the offender to escape from the control of the officer. The object of this invention is to prevent accidental or premature locking of a handcuff by providing it with a lock containing an adjustable stop controlled by a readily accessible thumb-knob, by means of which the latch or bolt of the lock is restrained from engaging the hasp until such time as the officer shall release them by pressure upon such said thumb-piece.

Holmes's cuffs may have been an improvement on one of the dozens of designs then available.

194 Lestrade's somewhat dismissive statement may have been indicative of officers' ambivalence about using the restraints. Former Scotland Yard Inspector Maurice Moser, note 193, above, wrote in 1894, "My personal experience of handcuffs is small, because I dislike them, for in addition to their clumsiness, I know that when I have laid my hands upon my man, it will be difficult for him to escape. . . . Regarding handcuffs generally, in my opinion not one of the inventions I have mentioned now in use is sufficiently easy of application."

thing to me about it. There was a small portmanteau in the room, and this he pulled out and began to strap. He was busily engaged at it when the cabman entered the room.

"Just give me a help with this buckle, cabman," he said, kneeling over his task, and never turning his head.

The fellow came forward with a somewhat sullen, defiant air, and put down his hands to assist. At that instant there was a sharp click, the jangling of metal, and Sherlock Holmes sprang to his feet again.

"Gentlemen," he cried, with flashing eyes, "let me introduce you to Mr. Jefferson Hope, the murderer of Enoch Drebber and of Joseph Stangerson."

The whole thing occurred in a moment—so quickly that I had no time to realize it. I have a vivid recollection of that instant, of Holmes's triumphant expression and the ring of his voice, of the cabman's dazed, savage face, as he glared at the glittering handcuffs, which had appeared as if by magic upon his wrists. For a second or two we might have been a group of

"So powerful and so fierce was he that the four of us were shaken off again and again."
Richard Gutschmidt, *Späte Rache* (Stuttgart: Robert Lutz Verlag, 1902)

statues. Then, with an inarticulate roar of fury, the prisoner wrenched himself free from Holmes's grasp, and hurled himself through the window. Woodwork and glass gave way before him; but before he got quite through, Gregson, Lestrade, and Holmes sprang upon him like so many staghounds. He was dragged back into the room, and then commenced a terrific conflict. So powerful and so fierce was he, that the four of us were shaken off again and again. He appeared to have the convulsive strength of a man in an epileptic fit. His face and hands were terribly mangled by his passage through the glass, but loss of blood had no effect in diminishing his resistance. It was not until Lestrade succeeded in getting his hand inside his neckcloth and half-strangling him that we made him realize that his struggles were of no avail; and even then we felt no security until we had pinioned his feet as well as his hands. That done, we rose to our feet breathless and panting.

"We have his cab," said Sherlock Holmes. "It will serve to take him to Scotland Yard. And now, gentlemen," he continued, with a pleasant smile, "we have reached the end of our little mystery. You are very welcome to put any questions that you like to me now, and there is no danger that I will refuse to answer them."

PART II

The Country of the Saints[195]

CHAPTER I

On the Great Alkali Plain[196]

IN THE CENTRAL portion of the great North American Continent there lies an arid and repulsive desert, which for many a long year served as a barrier against the advance of civilization. From the Sierra Nevada to Nebraska, and from the Yellowstone River in the north to the Colorado upon the south, is a region of desolation and silence. Nor is Nature always in one mood throughout this grim district. It comprises snow-capped and lofty mountains, and dark and gloomy valleys. There are swift-flowing rivers which dash through jagged cañons; and there are enormous plains, which in winter are white with snow, and in summer are grey with the saline alkali dust. They all preserve, however, the common characteristics of barrenness, inhospitality, and misery.

There are no inhabitants of this land of despair. A band of Pawnees or of Blackfeet may occasionally traverse it in order to reach other hunting-grounds, but the hardiest of the braves are glad to lose sight of those awesome plains, and to find themselves once more upon their prairies. The coyote skulks among the scrub, the buzzard flaps heavily through the air, and the clumsy grizzly bear lumbers through the dark ravines, and

195 In Jack Tracy's definitive *Conan Doyle and the Latter-day Saints* (henceforth referred to as *Saints*), Tracy compares the descriptions in the chapters that follow with the realities of Mormon culture in Utah from 1846 to 1860. There is endless speculation about who might have written "Part II: The Country of the Saints," which is clearly not narrated (nor written) by Watson. Tracy, for his part, concludes that Arthur Conan Doyle was the author. See note 241, below.

196 While the Great Alkali Plain is an invented geographical name, Carey and Lee's *Atlas* of 1827 located the "Great American Desert" as an indefinite domain in the areas that became Colorado, Kansas, Nebraska, the Indian Territory, and Texas. Bradford's *Atlas* (1838) referenced a great desert that extended from the Arkansas Territory into Colorado and Wyoming, including South Dakota and parts of Nebraska and Kansas. Others estimated picks up such sustenance as it can amongst the rocks. These are the sole dwellers in the wilderness.

In the whole world there can be no more dreary view than that from the northern slope of the Sierra Blanco.[197] As far as the eye can reach stretches the great flat plain-land, all dusted over with patches of alkali, and intersected by clumps of the dwarfish chaparral bushes. On the extreme verge of the horizon lie a long chain of mountain peaks, with their rugged summits flecked with snow. In this great stretch of country there is no sign of life, nor of anything appertaining to life. There is no bird in the steel-blue heaven, no movement upon the dull, grey earth—above all, there is absolute silence. Listen as one may, there is no shadow of a sound in all that mighty wilderness; nothing but silence—complete and heart-subduing silence.

It has been said there is nothing appertaining to life upon the broad plain. That is hardly true. Looking down from the Sierra Blanco, one sees a pathway traced out across the desert, which winds away and is lost in the extreme distance. It is rutted with wheels and trodden down by the feet of many adventurers. Here and there there are scattered white objects which glisten in the sun, and stand out against the dull deposit of alkali. Approach, and examine them! They are bones: some large and coarse, others smaller and more delicate. The former have belonged to oxen, and the latter to men. For fifteen hundred miles one may trace this ghastly caravan route by these scattered remains of those who had fallen by the wayside.

Looking down on this very scene, there stood upon the fourth of May, eighteen hundred and forty-seven, a solitary traveller. His appearance was such that he might have been the very genius or demon of the region. An observer would have found it difficult to say whether he was nearer to forty or to sixty. His face was lean and haggard, and the brown parchment-like skin was drawn tightly over the projecting bones; his long, brown hair and beard were all flecked and dashed with white; his eyes were sunken in his head, and burned with an unnatural lustre; while the hand which grasped his rifle was hardly more fleshy than that of a skeleton. As he stood, he leaned upon his weapon for support, and yet his tall figure and the massive framework of his bones suggested a wiry and vigorous constitution. His gaunt face, however, and

that the desert comprised an area 500 miles wide, lying directly east of the Rocky Mountains and extending from the northern boundary of the United States to the Rio Grande. The section shown by the various geographies grew smaller every year, until, by 1912, one encyclopaedist could write, "The free library, the telegraph, telephone, rural mail delivery, and all the complexities of modern times have in reality crowded the Great American Desert off the map into the land of fancy from which it came" (*Kansas: a cyclopedia of state history, embracing events, institutions, industries, counties, cities, towns, prominent persons,* etc.). The remnants of what was once called the Great American Desert are now generally known as the Great Plains.

197 Jack Tracy's *Encyclopaedia Sherlockiana* identifies Sierra Blanca as the name of an isolated mountain peak in New Mexico and short range of mountains in Colorado, but concedes that neither is near the Mormons' historical trail to Utah. Wayne Melander, in "Sierra Blanco—Found(?)," carefully traces the path of the Mormons and identifies the peak in question as Oregon Buttes, near South Pass, Wyoming, chalking up the grammatically incorrect "Sierra Blanco" to the travellers' having misheard their guide.

his clothes, which hung so baggily over his shriveled limbs, proclaimed what it was that gave him that senile and decrepit appearance. The man was dying—dying from hunger and from thirst.

He had toiled painfully down the ravine, and on to this little elevation, in the vain hope of seeing some signs of water. Now the great salt plain stretched before his eyes, and the distant belt of savage mountains, without a sign anywhere of plant or tree, which might indicate the presence of moisture. In all that broad landscape there was no gleam of hope. North, and east, and west he looked with wild, questioning eyes, and then he realized that his wanderings had come to an end, and that there, on that barren crag, he was about to die. "Why not here, as well as in a feather bed, twenty years hence?" he muttered, as he seated himself in the shelter of a boulder.

Before sitting down, he had deposited upon the ground his useless rifle, and also a large bundle tied up in a grey shawl, which he had carried slung over his right shoulder. It appeared to be somewhat too heavy for his strength, for in lowering it, it

"Dying from hunger."
Geo. Hutchinson, *A Study in Scarlet* (London: Ward, Lock Bowden, and Co., 1891)

Scene from *A Study in Scarlet* (Great Britain: Samuelson Film Mfg. Co. Ltd., 1914), starring Winnifred Pearson as the young Lucy Ferrier and James LeFre as John Ferrier.

came down on the ground with some little violence. Instantly there broke from the grey parcel a little moaning cry, and from it there protruded a small, scared face, with very bright brown eyes, and two little speckled dimpled fists.

"You've hurt me!" said a childish voice, reproachfully.

"Have I, though?" the man answered penitently. "I didn't go for to do it." As he spoke he unwrapped the grey shawl and extricated a pretty little girl of about five years of age, whose dainty shoes and smart pink frock with its little linen apron, all bespoke a mother's care. The child was pale and wan, but her healthy arms and legs showed that she had suffered less than her companion.

"How is it now?" he answered anxiously, for she was still rubbing the towsy golden curls which covered the back of her head.

"Kiss it and make it well," she said, with perfect gravity, shoving the injured part up to him. "That's what mother used to do. Where's mother?"

"Mother's gone. I guess you'll see her before long."

"Gone, eh!" said the little girl. "Funny, she didn't say good-bye; she 'most always did if she was just goin' over to Auntie's for tea, and now she's been away three days. Say, it's awful dry, ain't it? Ain't there no water, nor nothing to eat?"

"No, there ain't nothing, dearie. You'll just need to be patient awhile, and then you'll be all right. Put your head up ag'in me like that, and then you'll feel bullier.[198] It ain't easy to talk when your lips is like leather, but I guess I'd best let you know how the cards lie. What's that you've got?"

"Pretty things! fine things!" cried the little girl enthusiastically, holding up two glittering fragments of mica. "When we goes back to home I'll give them to brother Bob."

"You'll see prettier things than them soon," said the man confidently. "You just wait a bit. I was going to tell you though—you remember when we left the river?"

"Oh, yes."

"Well, we reckoned we'd strike another river soon, d'ye see. But there was somethin' wrong; compasses, or map, or somethin', and it didn't turn up. Water ran out. Just except a little drop for the likes of you and—and—"

"And you couldn't wash yourself," interrupted his companion gravely, staring up at his grimy visage.

"No, nor drink. And Mr. Bender, he was the fust to go, and then Indian Pete, and then Mrs. McGregor, and then Johnny Hones, and then, dearie, your mother."

"Then mother's a deader too," cried the little girl, dropping her face in her pinafore and sobbing bitterly.

"Yes, they all went except you and me. Then I thought there was some chance of water in this direction, so I heaved you over my shoulder and we tramped it together. It don't seem as though we've improved matters. There's an almighty small chance for us now!"

"Do you mean that we are going to die too?" asked the child, checking her sobs, and raising her tear-stained face.

"I guess that's about the size of it."

"Why didn't you say so before?" she said, laughing gleefully. "You gave me such a fright. Why, of course, now as long as we die we'll be with mother again."

"Yes, you will, dearie."

"And you too. I'll tell her how awful good you've been. I'll bet she meets us at the door of Heaven with a big pitcher of water, and a lot of buckwheat cakes, hot, and toasted on both sides, like Bob and me was fond of. How long will it be first?"

"I don't know—not very long." The man's eyes were fixed upon the northern horizon. In the blue vault of the heaven

198 The *Slang Dictionary* (1865) states that "[t]his epithet is often applied in a commendable sense among the vulgar; thus—a good fellow or a good horse will be termed 'a BULLY fellow,' 'a BULLY horse;' and 'a BULLY woman' signifies a right, good, motherly old soul."

there had appeared three little specks which increased in size every moment, so rapidly did they approach. They speedily resolved themselves into three large brown birds, which circled over the heads of the two wanderers, and then settled upon some rocks which overlooked them. They were buzzards, the vultures of the West, whose coming is the forerunner of death.

"Cocks and hens," cried the little girl gleefully, pointing at their ill-omened forms, and clapping her hands to make them rise. "Say, did God make this country?"

"In course He did," said her companion, rather startled by this unexpected question.

"He made the country down in Illinois, and He made the Missouri," the little girl continued. "I guess somebody else made the country in these parts. It's not nearly so well done. They forgot the water and the trees."

"What would ye think of offering up prayer?" the man asked diffidently.

"It ain't night yet," she answered.

"It don't matter. It ain't quite regular, but He won't mind that, you bet. You say over them ones that you used to say every night in the wagon when we was on the Plains."

"Why don't you say some yourself?" the child asked, with wondering eyes.

"I disremember them," he answered. "I hain't said none since I was half the height o' that gun. I guess it's never too late. You say them out, and I'll stand by and come in on the choruses."

"Then you'll need to kneel down, and me too," she said, laying the shawl out for that purpose. "You've got to put your hands up like this. It makes you feel kind o' good."

It was a strange sight had there been anything but the buzzards to see it. Side by side on the narrow shawl knelt the two wanderers, the little prattling child and the reckless, hardened adventurer. Her chubby face and his haggard, angular visage were both turned up to the cloudless heaven in heartfelt entreaty to that dread Being with whom they were face to face, while the two voices—the one thin and clear, the other deep and harsh—united in the entreaty for mercy and forgiveness. The prayer finished, they resumed their seat in the shadow of the boulder until the child fell asleep, nestling upon the broad breast of her protector. He watched over her slumber for some

" 'You've got to put your hands up like this.
It makes you feel kind o' good.' "
Richard Gutschmidt, *Späte Rache* (Stuttgart: Robert Lutz Verlag, 1902)

time, but Nature proved to be too strong for him. For three days and three nights he had allowed himself neither rest nor repose. Slowly the eyelids drooped over the tired eyes, and the head sunk lower and lower upon the breast, until the man's grizzled beard was mixed with the gold tresses of his companion, and both slept the same deep and dreamless slumber.

Had the wanderer remained awake for another half hour a strange sight would have met his eyes. Far away on the extreme verge of the alkali plain there rose up a little spray of dust, very slight at first, and hardly to be distinguished from the mists of the distance, but gradually growing higher and broader until it formed a solid well-defined cloud. This cloud continued to increase in size until it became evident that it could only be raised by a great multitude of moving creatures. In more fertile spots the observer would have come to the conclusion that one of those great herds of bisons which graze upon the prairie land was approaching him. This was obviously impossible in these arid wilds. As the whirl of dust drew nearer to the solitary bluff upon which the two castaways were repos-

"Side by side on the narrow shawl knelt the two wanderers."
Geo. Hutchinson, *A Study in Scarlet* (London: Ward, Lock Bowden, and Co., 1891)

ing, the canvas-covered tilts of wagons and the figures of armed horsemen began to show up through the haze, and the apparition revealed itself as being a great caravan upon its journey for the West. But what a caravan! When the head of it had reached the base of the mountains, the rear was not yet visible on the horizon. Right across the enormous plain stretched the straggling array, wagons and carts, men on horseback, and men on foot. Innumerable women who staggered along under burdens, and children who toddled beside the wagons or peeped out from under the white coverings. This was evidently no ordinary party of immigrants, but rather some nomad people who had been compelled from stress of circumstances to seek themselves a new country. There rose through the clear air a confused clattering and rumbling from this great mass of humanity, with the creaking of wheels and the neighing of horses. Loud as it was, it was not sufficient to rouse the two tired wayfarers above them.

At the head of the column there rode a score or more of grave iron-faced men, clad in sombre homespun garments and armed with rifles. On reaching the base of the bluff they halted, and held a short council among themselves.

"The wells are to the right, my brothers," said one, a hard-lipped, clean-shaven man with grizzly hair.

"To the right of the Sierra Blanco—so we shall reach the Rio Grande," said another.

"Fear not for water," cried a third. "He who could draw it from the rocks will not now abandon His own chosen people."

"Amen! amen!" responded the whole party.

They were about to resume their journey when one of the youngest and keenest-eyed uttered an exclamation and pointed up at the rugged crag above them. From its summit there fluttered a little wisp of pink, showing up hard and bright against the grey rocks behind. At the sight there was a general reining up of horses and unslinging of guns, while fresh horsemen came galloping up to reinforce the vanguard. The word "Redskins" was on every lip.

"There can't be any number of Injuns here," said the elderly man who appeared to be in command. "We have passed the Pawnees, and there are no other tribes until we cross the great mountains."[199]

"Shall I go forward and see, Brother Stangerson?" asked one of the band.

"And I," "And I," cried a dozen voices.

"Leave your horses below and we will await you here," the

Scene from *A Study in Scarlet.*
(Great Britain: Samuelson Film Mfg. Co. Ltd., 1914)

199 The Pawnee, originally from Texas, settled in southern Nebraska's Platte River valley in the mid-sixteenth century. By the time *A Study in Scarlet* was published, the Great American Desert would be empty of Pawnee, as they had ceded their Nebraska lands to the government in 1875 and relocated to a reservation in Oklahoma. Had these travellers come across any members of the tribe, they would likely have encountered little to no resistance; relations between the Pawnee and white settlers were cordial, and some Pawnee even worked for the U.S. Army as frontier scouts.

Elder answered. In a moment the young fellows had dismounted, fastened their horses, and were ascending the precipitous slope which led up to the object which had excited their curiosity. They advanced rapidly and noiselessly, with the confidence and dexterity of practised scouts. The watchers from the plain below could see them flit from rock to rock until their figures stood out against the sky-line. The young man who had first given the alarm was leading them. Suddenly his followers saw him throw up his hands, as though overcome with astonishment, and on joining him they were affected in the same way by the sight which met their eyes.

On the little plateau which crowned the barren hill there stood a single giant boulder, and against this boulder there lay a tall man, long-bearded and hard-featured, but of an excessive thinness. His placid face and regular breathing showed that he was fast asleep. Beside him lay a little child, with her round white arms encircling his brown sinewy neck, and her golden-haired head resting upon the breast of his velveteen tunic. Her rosy lips were parted, showing the regular line of snow-white

"On the ledge of rock above this strange couple stood three solemn buzzards."
Charles Doyle, *A Study in Scarlet* (London and New York: Ward, Lock & Co., 1888)

teeth within, and a playful smile played over her infantile features. Her plump little white legs terminating in white socks and neat shoes with shining buckles, offered a strange contrast to the long shrivelled members of her companion. On the ledge of rock above this strange couple there stood three solemn buzzards, who, at the sight of the newcomers, uttered raucous screams of disappointment and flapped sullenly away.

The cries of the foul birds awoke the two sleepers, who stared about them in bewilderment. The man staggered to his feet and looked down upon the plain which had been so desolate when sleep had overtaken him, and which was now traversed by this enormous body of men and of beasts. His face assumed an expression of incredulity as he gazed, and he passed his bony hand over his eyes. "This is what they call delirium, I guess," he muttered. The child stood beside him, holding on to the skirt of his coat, and said nothing but looked all round her with the wondering questioning gaze of childhood.

The rescuing party were speedily able to convince the two castaways that their appearance was no delusion. One of them seized the little girl, and hoisted her upon his shoulder, while

"One of them seized the little girl, and hoisted her upon his shoulder."
Geo. Hutchinson, *A Study in Scarlet* (London: Ward, Lock Bowden, and Co., 1891)

200 Brigham Young's own record of the Mormons' journey to the Great Salt Lake Valley in 1847 mentions only 143 men, 3 women, and 2 children.

201 This is incorrectly given as "the Angel Merona" in the *Beeton's* and English book text. According to Joseph Smith (1805–1844), the founder of Mormonism, the angel Moroni appeared to him three times on the night of September 21, 1823, telling the fourteen-year-old boy that a divine gift was buried near his home in western New York. In 1827, Smith returned to the spot indicated, where the angel purportedly presented him with a stone box containing a volume of thin gold plates. (According to other accounts, Smith dug up the plates where the angel indicated.) Upon these plates was inscribed the history of a group of Hebrew people who had traveled to North America from Jerusalem six centuries before Christ. This sacred text had been abridged from earlier plates and written down by the prophet Mormon, 1,400 years before Smith received them. Moroni was Mormon's son. The contents of the gold plates, which subsequently disappeared, were translated by Smith from "reformed Egyptian" and published in 1830 as *The Book of Mormon.* (James Strang, who attempted to become Smith's successor but lost out to Brigham Young, also claimed that he had found buried metallic plates, but in Voree [Burlington], Wisconsin.)

"One of the rescue party seized the little girl and hoisted her upon his shoulder."
Richard Gutschmidt, *Späte Rache* (Stuttgart: Robert Lutz Verlag, 1902)

two others supported her gaunt companion, and assisted him towards the wagons.

"My name is John Ferrier," the wanderer explained; "me and that little un are all that's left o' twenty-one people. The rest is all dead o' thirst and hunger away down in the south."

"Is she your child?" asked someone.

"I guess she is now," the other cried, defiantly; "she's mine 'cause I saved her. No man will take her from me. She's Lucy Ferrier from this day on. Who are you, though?" he continued, glancing with curiosity at his stalwart sunburned rescuers; "there seems to be a powerful lot of ye."

"Nigh upon ten thousand,"[200] said one of the young men; "we are the persecuted children of God—the chosen of the Angel Moroni."[201]

"I never heard tell on him," said the wanderer. "He appears to have chosen a fair crowd of ye."

"Do not jest at that which is sacred," said the other, sternly. "We are of those who believe in those sacred writings, drawn in Egyptian letters on plates of beaten gold, which were handed unto the holy Joseph Smith[202] at Palmyra. We have come from Nauvoo,[203] in the state of Illinois, where we had founded our temple. We have come to seek a refuge from the violent man and from the godless, even though it be the heart of the desert."

The name of Nauvoo evidently recalled recollections to John Ferrier. "I see," he said, "you are the Mormons."

"We are the Mormons," answered his companions with one voice.

"And where are you going?"

"We do not know.[204] The hand of God is leading us under the person of our Prophet. You must come before him. He shall say what is to be done with you."

They had reached the base of the hill by this time, and were surrounded by crowds of the pilgrims—pale-faced, meek-looking women; strong laughing children; and anxious earnest-

"One of them seized the little girl, and hoisted her upon his shoulder."
W. M. R. Quick (possibly Quick was the engraver, the artist D. H. Friston), *Beeton's Christmas Annual*, 1887

202 Smith's family originally settled in Palmyra, New York, but moved four years later to Manchester, some six miles off. It was in Manchester that Smith had his visions of the angel Moroni. Further revelations proclaiming him "seer, translator, prophet, apostle of Jesus Christ, and elder of the church" led him to found his own church, officially known as the Church of Jesus Christ of Latter-day Saints, which held its first conference on April 6, 1830, in Fayette, New York. Smith and his followers sought to practice Christianity in its ancient, "true" form—that is, the religion as it once was before its various sects supposedly led it astray.

203 In 1831, Smith moved with his followers, now thirty in number, to Kirtland, Ohio, which was to be the seat of the New Jerusalem. A large temple was consecrated in Kirtland in 1836, and Smith's devoted missionaries began spreading his teachings to other U.S. states, as well as to England. (The ministry of Orson Hyde and Heber C. Kimball achieved great success among the labourers in Manchester, Liverpool, Birmingham, Leeds, and Glasgow, and in the mining districts of South Wales.) But in Kirtland and western Missouri, where Smith had established another community, suspicion toward the Mormons made their lives increasingly difficult. Not only were their beliefs unorthodox and their communal living difficult for outsiders to understand, but Smith and others also engaged in polygamy (see note 210, below). Continuing persecution of the Mormons included murder and the burning of property.

After Smith and other Mormon leaders were imprisoned awaiting trial for numerous charges, among them treason, 15,000 of Smith's followers left Missouri for Illinois in 1839 and settled near Commerce, in Hancock County. Smith escaped from prison and rejoined the sect there. Having obtained a charter from the government that gave them a substantial degree of autonomy, the Mormons founded the city of Nauvoo, with Smith as their mayor. Converts from all over the United States flocked to join them, and Nauvoo soon became the largest city in Illinois.

204 The Mormon exodus was indeed unplanned, at least in its inception. In February 1844, Smith, having become one of the most powerful figures in the West, declared his candidacy for presidency of the United States. Disaffected members of the church, unhappy with Smith's ambition and his encouragement of polygamy, used the occasion to attack the Mormon leader in their opposition newspaper, the *Expositor*. When Smith shut down the newspaper, violence erupted. Smith called out the Nauvoo militia to protect the city, and he and his brother, Hyrum, were arrested for treason and imprisoned in a Carthage jail. An angry mob broke into the prison and killed the two men on June 27, 1844.

Joseph Smith quickly became a martyr, and in the confusion following his death, Brigham Young (1801–1877), a senior member of the Council of the Twelve Apostles, became the president of the church. Upon the Illinois legislature's repeal of Nauvoo's charter in 1845, Brigham Young led the Mormons out of Illinois, traveling 1,100 miles (1,800 kilometers) across the wilderness to Utah in 1846–1847. Young and an advance party of some 170 settlers reached the Great Salt Lake Valley in July 1847, and there they founded Salt Lake City, the spiritual and theocratic home of Mormonism to this day.

205 In fact, Brigham Young was forty-five or forty-six at the time of the migration.

206 The "big head, big brain; big brain, great mind" principle, a subset of the Victorian science of phrenology, had a great many Victo-

eyed men. Many were the cries of astonishment and of commiseration which arose from them when they perceived the youth of one of the strangers and the destitution of the other. Their escort did not halt, however, but pushed on, followed by a great crowd of Mormons, until they reached a wagon, which was conspicuous for its great size and for the gaudiness and smartness of its appearance. Six horses were yoked to it, whereas the others were furnished with two, or, at most, four apiece. Beside the driver there sat a man who could not have been more than thirty years of age,[205] but whose massive head[206] and resolute expression marked him as a leader. He was reading a brown-backed volume, but as the crowd approached he laid it aside, and listened attentively to an account of the episode. Then he turned to the two castaways.

"If we take you with us," he said, in solemn words, "it can only be as believers in our own creed. We shall have no wolves in our fold. Better far that your bones should bleach in this wilderness than that you should prove to be that little speck of decay which in time corrupts the whole fruit. Will you come with us on these terms?"

"Guess I'll come with you on any terms," said Ferrier, with such emphasis that the grave Elders could not restrain a smile. The leader alone retained his stern, impressive expression.

"Take him, Brother Stangerson," he said, "give him food and drink, and the child likewise. Let it be your task also to teach him our holy creed. We have delayed long enough. Forward! On, on to Zion!"

"On, on to Zion!" cried the crowd of Mormons, and the words rippled down the long caravan, passing from mouth to mouth until they died away in a dull murmur in the far distance. With a cracking of whips and a creaking of wheels the great wagons got into motion, and soon the whole caravan was winding along once more. The Elder to whose care the two waifs had been committed, led them to his wagon, where a meal was already awaiting them.

"You shall remain here," he said. "In a few days you will have recovered from your fatigues. In the meantime, remember that now and for ever you are of our religion.[207] Brigham Young[208] has said it, and he has spoken with the voice of Joseph Smith, which is the voice of God."

rian followers. It was first espoused by the Viennese physician Franz Joseph Gall, who laid out his theory in an October 1, 1798, letter to Joseph von Retzer, explaining—his tongue, we might assume, at least partly in cheek—"A man like you possesses more than double the quantity of brain in a stupid bigot; and at least one-sixth more than the wisest or the most sagacious elephant." The thinking went that the larger the skull, the larger the brain beneath it, and the greater that brain's power. Gall and his successors further believed that personality traits such as self-esteem and wit, as well as a faculty for music or math, were determined by thirty-five "organs" comprising the brain. A person's characteristics could thus be discerned by observing which parts of his or her skull seemed relatively large or small.

Phrenology might have remained the province of scientific and intellectual debate had it not been for the American brothers Lorenzo and Orson Fowler, who founded the *American Phrenological Journal* in 1838 and began conducting "head readings," lectures, and courses in New York and England (Lorenzo opened the Fowler Institute in London in 1863). Older phrenologists regarded the avowedly practical Fowlers as hucksters, but the public took eagerly to this new "science"—with decidedly mixed results. The esteemed British journalist and abolitionist Harriet Martineau, in her 1877 *Autobiography*, expressed her reservations at the phenomenon by recounting how, after one phrenologist read the head of one Sydney Smith and proclaimed him a born naturalist, Mr. Smith, in wonderment, replied, "I don't know a fish from a bird"; and also how her own reading determined that she "could never accomplish any thing, through my remarkable deficiency in both physical and moral courage." Ambrose Bierce, in his satiric *The Devil's Dictionary* (1911; first published as *The Cynic's Word Book* in 1906), summed up his own scepticism by defining phrenology, in part, as "the science of picking the pocket through the scalp."

Madeleine Stern suggests, in *The Game's A Head*, that Holmes himself may well have studied with Lorenzo Fowler in London and points out many fields of interest common to the two scholars. Perhaps at the behest of Holmes, Arthur Conan Doyle had a phrenological analysis made by the Institute in 1896.

207 Tracy notes in *Saints*: "[The] suggestion that the Ferriers were forced to convert in order to be rescued is a patent misrepresentation of the Mormons' often demonstrated generosity toward their fellow travelers. . . . [I]t is a little known fact that not all the members of [the group of pilgrims] were Mormons at all. [See *Wilford Woodruff's Journal* for May 29, 1847, cited in B. H. Roberts, *A Comprehensive History of the Church of Jesus Christ of Latter-Day Saints* (Salt Lake City: Church of Jesus Christ of Latter-Day Saints, 6 vols., 1930).]"

208 In 1850, U.S. President Millard Fillmore created the Territory of Utah and appointed Brigham Young as governor. He was appointed to a second term in 1854, but friction between the Mormons and the federal judiciary led President James Buchanan to replace Young in 1857, at which time the U.S. Army was sent in to put down a rumoured "rebellion" and establish the authority of the federal government in Utah. Young never again held political office, but he continued to serve as president of the Mormon church until his death.

CHAPTER II

The Flower of Utah

209 In fact, by the end of 1830, the 200 to 500 converts whom Smith had attracted hailed from Pennsylvania, New York, and Ohio (Dean L. May, "A Demographic Portrait of the Mormons, 1830–1980," in *After 150 Years: The Later-day Saints in Sesquicentennial Perspective*, edited by Thomas G. Alexander and Jessie L. Embry [Provo, Utah: Charles Redd Center for Western Studies, 1983]).

This is not the place to commemorate the trials and privations endured by the immigrant Mormons before they came to their final haven. From the shores of the Mississippi to the western slopes of the Rocky Mountains they had struggled on with a constancy almost unparalleled in history. The savage man, and the savage beast, hunger, thirst, fatigue, and disease—every impediment which Nature could place in the way, had all been overcome with Anglo-Saxon[209] tenacity. Yet the long journey and the accumulated terrors had shaken the hearts of the stoutest among them. There was not one who did not sink upon his knees in heartfelt prayer when they saw the broad valley of Utah bathed in the sunlight beneath them, and learned from the lips of their leader that this was the promised land, and that these virgin acres were to be theirs for evermore.

Young speedily proved himself to be a skilful administrator as well as a resolute chief. Maps were drawn and charts prepared, in which the future city was sketched out. All around farms were apportioned and allotted in proportion to the standing of each individual. The tradesman was put to his trade and the artisan to his calling. In the town streets and squares sprang

Salt Lake City in 1850.
Samuel Manning, *American Pictures Drawn with Pen and Ink*, 1876

up, as if by magic. In the country there was draining and hedging, planting and clearing, until the next summer saw the whole country golden with the wheat crop. Everything prospered in the strange settlement. Above all, the great temple which they had erected in the centre of the city grew ever taller and larger. From the first blush of dawn until the closing of the twilight, the clatter of the hammer and the rasp of the saw were never absent from the monument which the immigrants erected to Him who had led them safe through many dangers.

The two castaways, John Ferrier and the little girl who had shared his fortunes and had been adopted as his daughter, accompanied the Mormons to the end of their great pilgrimage. Little Lucy Ferrier was borne along pleasantly enough in Elder Stangerson's wagon, a retreat which she shared with the Mormon's three wives[210] and with his son, a headstrong, forward boy of twelve. Having rallied, with the elasticity of childhood, from the shock caused by her mother's death, she soon became a pet with the women, and reconciled herself to this new life in her moving canvas-covered home. In the meantime Ferrier having recovered from his privations, distinguished himself as a useful guide and an indefatigable hunter. So rapidly did he gain the esteem of his new companions, that when they reached the end of their wanderings, it was unanimously agreed that he should be provided with as large and as fertile a tract of land as any of the settlers, with the exception of Young himself, and of Stangerson, Kemball,[211] Johnston,[212] and Drebber, who were the four principal Elders.

On the farm thus acquired John Ferrier built himself a substantial log-house, which received so many additions in succeeding years that it grew into a roomy villa. He was a man of

210 On July 12, 1843, Joseph Smith announced that he had received a divine revelation approving polygamy. (The more accurate term, in fact, is polygyny, in which a man marries multiple wives.) Known as the Law of Abraham, polygamy was accepted and encouraged within the church, though not publicly acknowledged until 1852. The practice was outlawed by the U.S. government in 1871, but it was not formally renounced by the church until 1890, as a condition of achieving statehood for Utah. Even after that, some fundamentalist groups in Utah and northern Arizona continued to enter into plural marriages, despite being excommunicated for doing so.

Brigham Young was just as fervent an advocate of polygamy as Joseph Smith was, if not more so. Young served as president when Mormon polygamy was out in the open. In the Mormons' *Journal of Discourses, Volume 11* (1866), Young is quoted as saying, "The only men who become Gods, even the Sons of God, are those who enter into polygamy. Others attain unto a glory and may even be permitted to come into the presence of the Father and the Son; but they cannot reign as kings in glory, because they had blessings offered unto them, and they refused to accept them." Public records show that upon his death in 1877, Brigham Young left his fortune of over $2 million to his seventeen wives and fifty-six children, though some sources put the number of wives at fifty-five.

211 That is, Heber C. Kimball (1801–1868), the prominent officer and missionary who accompanied Brigham Young to Utah, shortly thereafter becoming his first counsellor. The name is consistently misspelled in various editions.

212 Luke S. Johnson (1807–1861) was a member of the pioneer party who had little role in the Church thereafter.

a practical turn of mind, keen in his dealings and skilful with his hands. His iron constitution enabled him to work morning and evening at improving and tilling his lands. Hence it came about that his farm and all that belonged to him prospered exceedingly. In three years he was better off than his neighbours, in six he was well-to-do, in nine he was rich, and in twelve there were not half a dozen men in the whole of Salt Lake City who could compare with him. From the great inland sea to the distant Wasatch[213] Mountains there was no name better known than that of John Ferrier.

There was one way and only one in which he offended the susceptibilities of his co-religionists. No argument or persuasion could ever induce him to set up a female establishment after the manner of his companions. He never gave reasons for this persistent refusal, but contented himself by resolutely and inflexibly adhering to his determination. There were some who accused him of lukewarmness in his adopted religion, and others who put it down to greed of wealth and reluctance to incur expense. Others, again, spoke of some early love affair, and of a fair-haired girl who had pined away on the shores of the Atlantic. Whatever the reason, Ferrier remained strictly celibate. In every other respect he conformed to the religion of the young settlement, and gained the name of being an orthodox and straight-walking man.

Lucy Ferrier grew up within the log-house, and assisted her adopted father in all his undertakings. The keen air of the mountains and the balsamic odour of the pine trees took the place of nurse and mother to the young girl. As year succeeded to year she grew taller and stronger, her cheek more ruddy, and her step more elastic. Many a wayfarer upon the high road which ran by Ferrier's farm felt long-forgotten thoughts revive in his mind as he[214] watched her lithe girlish figure tripping through the wheatfields, or met her mounted upon her father's mustang, and managing it with all the ease and grace of a true child of the West. So the bud blossomed into a flower, and the year which saw her father the richest of the farmers left her as fair a specimen of American girlhood as could be found in the whole Pacific slope.

It was not the father, however, who first discovered that the child had developed into the woman. It seldom is in such cases. That mysterious change is too subtle and too gradual to

213 Incorrectly termed the "Wahsatch" Mountains in the *Beeton's* and English texts.

214 The phrase is "their minds as they" in the English book edition.

be measured by dates. Least of all does the maiden herself know it until the tone of a voice or the touch of a hand sets her heart thrilling within her, and she learns, with a mixture of pride and of fear, that a new and a larger nature has awoke within her. There are few who cannot recall that day and remember the one little incident which heralded the dawn of a new life. In the case of Lucy Ferrier the occasion was serious enough in itself, apart from its future influence on her destiny and that of many besides.

It was a warm June morning, and the Latter Day Saints were as busy as the bees whose hive they have chosen for their emblem. In the fields and in the streets rose the same hum of human industry. Down the dusty high roads defiled long streams of heavily-laden mules, all heading to the west, for the gold fever had broken out in California,[215] and the Overland Route lay through the City of the Elect. There, too, were droves of sheep and bullocks coming in from the outlying pasture lands, and trains of tired immigrants, men and horses equally weary of their interminable journey. Through all this motley assemblage, threading her way with the skill of an

"Down the dusty high road defiled long streams of heavily-laden mules."
Geo. Hutchinson, *A Study in Scarlet* (London: Ward, Lock Bowden, and Co., 1891)

215 "Gold fever" first broke out in 1848, when gold was discovered near Sacramento, California, at the unfinished sawmill of cattle rancher John Sutter. On January 24, Sutter's carpenter, James Marshall, discovered several pea-sized nuggets of gold at the construction site. He brought the pieces back to Sutter, and the two men decided to keep Marshall's find a secret. But it was not long before the secret was out, spread in part by Sam Brannan, a Mormon preacher and entrepreneur who ran through the streets of San Francisco holding up a bottle of gold dust and shouting, "Gold! Gold in the American River!" (Brannan, in fact, had no interest in the gold itself, but in selling the shovels that gold-seekers would need to purchase.) Potential prospectors streamed into California, and by the end of 1849 some 80,000 "forty-niners" had arrived seeking to make their fortunes.

Most of the gold near Sutter's Mill had run out by the middle of 1849, but the miners' dreams were slow to die, and further discoveries kept their hopes alive. In 1855, another frenzy erupted further south when gold was found along the upper Kern River, in Kern County; in 1858, the Fraser River gold rush in British Columbia saw disillusioned miners packing up their things and stampeding northward. But many of those who made the trip to Fraser River would come to regret it. By the early 1860s, the Fraser River rush and the succeeding Cariboo rush were over, and British Columbia lapsed into a recession. Apparently the Fraser River rush, which led prospectors to *leave* California, is what the text refers to as the "gold fever . . . in California."

accomplished rider, there galloped Lucy Ferrier, her fair face flushed with the exercise and her long chestnut hair floating out behind her. She had a commission from her father in the City, and was dashing in as she had done many a time before, with all the fearlessness of youth, thinking only of her task and how it was to be performed. The travel-stained adventurers gazed after her in astonishment, and even the unemotional Indians, journeying in with their pelties,[216] relaxed their accustomed stoicism as they marvelled at the beauty of the pale-faced maiden.

She had reached the outskirts of the city when she found the road blocked by a great drove of cattle, driven by a half-dozen wild-looking herdsmen from the plains. In her impatience she endeavoured to pass this obstacle by pushing her horse into what appeared to be a gap. Scarcely had she got fairly into it, however, before the beasts closed in behind her, and she found herself completely embedded in the moving stream of fierce-eyed, long-horned bullocks. Accustomed as she was to deal with cattle, she was not alarmed at her situation, but took advantage of every opportunity to urge her horse on in the hopes of pushing her way through the cavalcade. Unfortunately the horns of one of the creatures, either by accident or design, came in violent contact with the flank of the mustang, and excited it to madness. In an instant it reared up upon its hind legs with a snort of rage, and pranced and tossed in a way that would have unseated any but a most skilful rider. The situation was full of peril. Every plunge of the excited horse brought it against the horns again, and goaded it to fresh madness. It was all that the girl could do to keep herself in the saddle, yet a slip would mean a terrible death under the hoofs of the unwieldy and terrified animals. Unaccustomed to sudden emergencies, her head began to swim, and her grip upon the bridle to relax. Choked by the rising cloud of dust and by the steam from the struggling creatures, she might have abandoned her efforts in despair, but for a kindly voice at her elbow which assured her of assistance. At the same moment a sinewy brown hand caught the frightened horse by the curb,[217] and forcing a way through the drove, soon brought her to the outskirts.

"You're not hurt, I hope, miss," said her preserver, respectfully.

She looked up at his dark, fierce face, and laughed saucily.

216 The proper word is "peltry," meaning pelts, furs; especially, raw, undressed skins.

217 A bit that exerts severe pressure on a horse's jaws; also, the chain or strap attached to it.

"A sinewy brown hand caught the frightened horse by the curb."
Geo. Hutchinson, *A Study in Scarlet* (London: Ward, Lock Bowden, and Co., 1891)

"I'm awful frightened," she said, naively; "whoever would have thought that Poncho would have been so scared by a lot of cows?"

"Thank God you kept your seat," the other said, earnestly. He was a tall, savage-looking young fellow, mounted on a powerful roan horse, and clad in the rough dress of a hunter, with a long rifle slung over his shoulders. "I guess you are the daughter of John Ferrier," he remarked. "I saw you ride down from his house. When you see him, ask him if he remembers the Jefferson Hopes of St. Louis. If he's the same Ferrier, my father and he were pretty thick."

"Hadn't you better come and ask yourself?" she asked, demurely.

The young fellow seemed pleased at the suggestion, and his dark eyes sparkled with pleasure. "I'll do so," he said, "we've

"A sinewy brown hand caught the frightened horse by the curb."
Richard Gutschmidt, *Späte Rache* (Stuttgart: Robert Lutz Verlag, 1902)

been in the mountains for two months, and are not over and above in visiting condition. He must take us as he finds us."

"He has a good deal to thank you for, and so have I," she answered, "he's awful fond of me. If those cows had jumped on me he'd have never got over it."

"Neither would I," said her companion.

"You! Well, I don't see that it would make much matter to you, anyhow. You ain't even a friend of ours."

The young hunter's dark face grew so gloomy over this remark that Lucy Ferrier laughed aloud.

"There, I didn't mean that," she said; "of course, you are a friend now. You must come and see us. Now I must push along, or father won't trust me with his business any more. Good-bye!"

"Good-bye," he answered, raising his broad sombrero, and

bending over her little hand. She wheeled her mustang round, gave it a cut with her riding-whip, and darted away down the broad road in a rolling cloud of dust.

Young Jefferson Hope rode on with his companions, gloomy and taciturn. He and they had been among the Nevada Mountains prospecting for silver, and were returning to Salt Lake City in the hope of raising capital enough to work some lodes which they had discovered. He had been as keen as any of them upon the business until this sudden incident had drawn his thoughts into another channel. The sight of the fair young girl, as frank and wholesome as the Sierra breezes, had stirred his volcanic, untamed heart to its very depths. When she had vanished from his sight, he realized that a crisis had come in his life, and that neither silver speculations nor any other questions could ever be of such importance to him as this new and all-absorbing one. The love which had sprung up in his heart was not the sudden, changeable fancy of a boy, but rather the wild, fierce passion of a man of strong will and imperious temper. He had been accustomed to succeed in all that he undertook. He swore in his heart that he would not fail in this if human effort and human perseverance could render him successful.

He called on John Ferrier that night, and many times again, until his face was a familiar one at the farmhouse. John, cooped up in the valley, and absorbed in his work, had had little chance of learning the news of the outside world during the last twelve years. All this Jefferson Hope was able to tell him, and in a style which interested Lucy as well as her father. He had been a pioneer in California, and could narrate many a strange tale of fortunes made and fortunes lost in those wild, halcyon days. He had been a scout too, and a trapper, a silver explorer, and a ranchman. Wherever stirring adventures were to be had, Jefferson Hope had been there in search of them. He soon became a favourite with the old farmer, who spoke eloquently of his virtues. On such occasions, Lucy was silent, but her blushing cheek and her bright, happy eyes, showed only too clearly that her young heart was no longer her own. Her honest father may not have observed these symptoms, but they were assuredly not thrown away upon the man who had won her affections.

It was a summer evening when he came galloping down the

"One summer evening he came galloping down the road."
Geo. Hutchinson, *A Study in Scarlet* (London:
Ward, Lock Bowden, and Co., 1891)

road and pulled up at the gate. She was at the doorway, and came down to meet him. He threw the bridle over the fence and strode up the pathway.

"I am off, Lucy," he said, taking her two hands in his, and gazing tenderly down into her face; "I won't ask you to come with me now, but will you be ready to come when I am here again?"

"And when will that be?" she asked, blushing and laughing.

"A couple of months at the outside. I will come and claim you then, my darling. There's no one who can stand between us."

"And how about father?" she asked.

"He has given his consent, provided we get these mines working all right. I have no fear on that head."

"Oh, well; of course, if you and father have arranged it all, there's no more to be said," she whispered, with her cheek against his broad breast.

"Thank God!" he said, hoarsely, stooping and kissing her. "It is settled, then. The longer I stay, the harder it will be to go. They are waiting for me at the cañon. Good-bye, my own darling—good-bye. In two months you shall see me."

He tore himself from her as he spoke, and, flinging himself upon his horse, galloped furiously away, never even looking round, as though afraid that his resolution might fail him if he took one glance at what he was leaving. She stood at the gate, gazing after him until he vanished from her sight. Then she walked back into the house, the happiest girl in all Utah.

" 'It is settled, then. The longer I stay, the harder it will be to go.' "
Richard Gutschmidt, *Späte Rache* (Stuttgart: Robert Lutz Verlag, 1902)

CHAPTER III

John Ferrier Talks with the Prophet

THREE WEEKS HAD passed since Jefferson Hope and his comrades had departed from Salt Lake City. John Ferrier's heart was sore within him when he thought of the young man's return, and of the impending loss of his adopted child. Yet her bright and happy face reconciled him to the arrangement more than any argument could have done. He had always determined, deep down in his resolute heart, that nothing would ever induce him to allow his daughter to wed a Mormon. Such a marriage he regarded as no marriage at all, but as a shame and a disgrace. Whatever he might think of the Mormon doctrines, upon that one point he was inflexible. He had to seal his mouth on the subject, however, for to express a unorthodox opinion was a dangerous matter in those days in the Land of the Saints.

Yes, a dangerous matter—so dangerous that even the most saintly dared only whisper their religious opinions with bated breath, lest something which fell from their lips might be misconstrued, and bring down a swift retribution upon them. The victims of persecution had now turned persecutors on their own account, and persecutors of the most terrible description.

Not the Inquisition of Seville,[218] nor the German Vehmgericht[219] nor the secret societies of Italy,[220] were ever able to put a more formidable machinery in motion than that which cast a cloud over the state of Utah.

Its invisibility, and the mystery which was attached to it, made this organization doubly terrible. It appeared to be omniscient and omnipotent, and yet was neither seen nor heard. The man who held out against the Church vanished away, and none knew whither he had gone or what had befallen him. His wife and his children awaited him at home, but no father ever returned to tell them how he had fared at the hands of his secret judges. A rash word or a hasty act was followed by annihilation, and yet none knew what the nature might be of this terrible power which was suspended over them. No wonder that men went about in fear and trembling, and that even in the heart of the wilderness they dared not whisper the doubts which oppressed them.

At first this vague and terrible power was exercised only upon the recalcitrants who, having embraced the Mormon faith, wished afterwards to pervert or to abandon it. Soon, however, it took a wider range. The supply of adult women was

"Armed men, masked, stealthy and noiseless."
Geo. Hutchinson, *A Study in Scarlet* (London: Ward, Lock Bowden, and Co., 1891)

218 The Spanish Inquisition, a tribunal intended to pass judgement on accused heretics of the Roman Catholic Church, was established in 1478 by Ferdinand and Isabella. The pope at the time, Sixtus IV, had given the Spanish sovereigns his papal approval; but he soon came to regret that he had handed such far-reaching ecclesiastical powers over to the royal court, which did not have to report to Rome regarding its secret proceedings and use of torture. Defendants were not allowed counsel, and those who were condemned to execution had their property confiscated and distributed among the crown, the church, and the accusers. While the tribunal was originally set up to investigate Jews who had converted to the faith (*conversos*), in time it extended to converted Muslims, Protestants, and people accused of other crimes. In Spain alone, through 1809, over 340,000 individuals were killed by one means or another in the name of the Inquisition.

219 See note 168, above.

220 See note 170, above.

running short, and polygamy without a female population on which to draw was a barren doctrine indeed. Strange rumours began to be bandied about—rumours of murdered immigrants and rifled camps in regions where Indians had never been seen. Fresh women appeared in the harems of the Elders—women who pined and wept, and bore upon their faces the traces of an unextinguishable horror. Belated wanderers upon the mountains spoke of gangs of armed men, masked, stealthy, and noiseless, who flitted by them in the darkness. These tales and rumours took substance and shape, and were corroborated and re-corroborated, until they resolved themselves into a definite name. To this day, in the lonely ranches of the West, the name of the Danite[221] Band, or the Avenging Angels, is a sinister and an ill-omened one.[222]

Fuller knowledge of the organization which produced such terrible results served to increase rather than to lessen the horror which it inspired in the minds of men. None knew who belonged to this ruthless society. The names of the participators in the deeds of blood and violence done under the name of religion were kept profoundly secret. The very friend to whom you communicated your misgivings as to the Prophet and his mission might be one of those who would come forth at night with fire and sword to exact a terrible reparation. Hence every man feared his neighbour, and none spoke of the things which were nearest his heart.

One fine morning, John Ferrier was about to set out to his wheatfields, when he heard the click of the latch, and, looking through the window, saw a stout, sandy-haired, middle-aged[223] man coming up the pathway. His heart leapt to his mouth, for this was none other than the great Brigham Young himself. Full of trepidation—for he knew that such a visit boded him little good—Ferrier ran to the door to greet the Mormon chief. The latter, however, received his salutations coldly, and followed him with a stern face into the sitting-room.

"Brother Ferrier," he said, taking a seat, and eyeing the farmer keenly from under his light-coloured eyelashes, "the true believers have been good friends to you. We picked you up when you were starving in the desert, we shared our food with you, led you safe to the Chosen Valley, gave you a goodly share of land, and allowed you to wax rich under our protection. Is not this so?"

221 During the Mormons' period of settlement in Missouri, Smith's previously unquestioned leadership began to show cracks, as he was criticised both from outside the community and, quietly, within his own ranks. The 1888 *Encyclopædia Britannica* (9th Ed.) reported that "his gross profligacy had repelled many of his leading supporters and bred internal dissensions, while from the outside the brethren were harassed and threatened by the steadily growing hostility of the native Missourians."

Smith's most devoted followers rallied to his defence. The Danites, or Sons of Dan, were a secret society organised in Missouri in 1838 by Dr. Samson Avard, a recent convert to the church. (The original tribe of Dan was one of twelve groups of Israelites who would later become the Jewish people. Dan was the first-born son of Jacob.) While the organisation vowed vengeance against all who crossed the church, it also had larger ambitions. Its intent, according to the *Britannica*, was to support Smith "at all hazards, of upholding the authority of his revelation and decrees as superior to the laws of the land, and of helping him to get possession, first of the State, then of the United States, and ultimately of the world."

Smith himself had little desire to condone this form of "support." Upon learning of the Danites' existence, he disbanded the group and excommunicated Avard before any acts of vengeance could be carried out. "Nonetheless," Tracy writes in *Saints*, "the depredations of 'the Danite Band, or the Avenging Angels' were featured in anti-Mormon literature for another fifty years following its abolition." Tracy asserts that no evidence exists that the society ever engaged in any activities in Utah.

222 Michael Harrison, in *In the Footsteps of Sherlock Holmes*, explains that the mid-Victorian English impression of Mormons was as "white slavers," who stole English servant-

"It is so," answered John Ferrier.

"In return for all this we asked but one condition: that was, that you should embrace the true faith, and conform in every way to its usages. This you promised to do, and this, if common report says truly, you have neglected."

"And how have I neglected it?" asked Ferrier, throwing out his hands in expostulation. "Have I not given to the common fund? Have I not attended at the Temple? Have I not—?"

"Where are your wives?" asked Young, looking round him. "Call them in, that I may greet them."

"It is true that I have not married," Ferrier answered. "But women were few, and there were many who had better claims than I. I was not a lonely man: I had my daughter to attend to my wants."

"It is of that daughter that I would speak to you," said the leader of the Mormons. "She has grown to be the flower of Utah, and has found favour in the eyes of many who are high in the land."

John Ferrier groaned internally.

"There are stories of her which I would fain disbelieve—stories that she is sealed to some Gentile. This must be the gossip of idle tongues. What is the thirteenth rule in the code of the sainted Joseph Smith? 'Let every maiden of the true faith marry one of the elect; for if she wed a Gentile, she commits a grievous sin.' This being so, it is impossible that you, who profess the holy creed, should suffer your daughter to violate it."

John Ferrier made no answer, but he played nervously with his riding-whip.

"Upon this one point your whole faith shall be tested—so it has been decided in the Sacred Council of Four. The girl is young,[224] and we would not have her wed grey hairs, neither would we deprive her of all choice. We Elders have many heifers,[225] but our children must also be provided. Stangerson has a son, and Drebber has a son, and either of them would gladly welcome your daughter to their house. Let her choose between them. They are young and rich, and of the true faith. What say you to that?"

Ferrier remained silent for some little time with his brows knitted.

"You will give us time," he said at last. "My daughter is very young—she is scarce of an age to marry."

girls and spirited them away to Utah. "There were riots over the Mormons, especially when the servant girls [who compared] their lot below-stairs with the prospects offered of life in a state which has never known unemployment, . . . left voluntarily and in quite large numbers. . . . [W]hen Watson recorded the case of *A Study in Scarlet*, it must have confirmed a good many of the more traditional British in their view that there was nothing wickeder than a Mormon."

223 The events that follow reveal that the year was 1860, at which time Brigham Young was fifty-nine.

224 Lucy, who was five in 1847, was in fact eighteen years old in 1860.

225 The English and American book editions here include a footnote (probably added by Arthur Conan Doyle) that "Heber C. Kemball, in one of his sermons, alludes to his hundred wives under this endearing epithet."

226 In fact, the "Holy Four" was a literary device. Upon the death of Smith, the church voted to place supreme authority in the hands of the "Quorum of the Twelve" or the "Twelve Apostles," headed by Brigham Young.

"She shall have a month to choose," said Young, rising from his seat. "At the end of that time she shall give her answer."

He was passing through the door, when he turned, with flushed face and flashing eyes. "It were better for you, John Ferrier," he thundered, "that you and she were now lying blanched skeletons upon the Sierra Blanco, than that you should put your weak wills against the orders of the Holy Four!"[226]

With a threatening gesture of his hand, he turned from the door, and Ferrier heard his heavy steps scrunching along the shingly path.

He was still sitting with his elbows upon his knees, considering how he should broach the matter to his daughter, when a soft hand was laid upon his, and looking up, he saw her standing beside him. One glance at her pale, frightened face showed him that she had heard what had passed.

"I could not help it," she said, in answer to his look. "His voice rang through the house. "Oh, father, father, what shall we do?"

"Don't you scare yourself," he answered, drawing her to

"He was passing through the door when he turned with flushed face and flashing eyes."
Geo. Hutchinson, *A Study in Scarlet* (London: Ward, Lock Bowden, and Co., 1891)

" 'It were better for you, John Ferrier,' he thundered, 'that you and she were now lying blanched skeletons upon the Sierra Blanco, than that you should put your weak wills against the orders of the Holy Four!' "
Richard Gutschmidt, *Späte Rache* (Stuttgart: Robert Lutz Verlag, 1902)

him, and passing his broad, rough hand caressingly over her chestnut hair. "We'll fix it up somehow or another. You don't find your fancy kind o' lessening for this chap, do you?"

A sob and a squeeze of his hand was her only answer.

"No; of course not. I shouldn't care to hear you say you did. He's a likely lad, and he's a Christian, which is more than these folks here, in spite o' all their praying and preaching. There's a party starting for Nevada to-morrow, and I'll manage to send him a message letting him know the hole we are in. If I know anything o' that young man, he'll be back here with a speed that would whip electro-telegraphs."

Lucy laughed through her tears at her father's description.

"When he comes, he will advise us for the best. But it is for you that I am frightened, dear. One hears—one bears such dreadful stories about those who oppose the Prophet: something terrible always happens to them."

"But we haven't opposed him yet," her father answered. "It will be time to look out for squalls when we do. We have a clear month before us; at the end of that, I guess we had best shin out[227] of Utah."

227 In English slang, to clear off or run away. Jack Tracy, in his *Encyclopaedia Sherlockiana*, notes that the teller of this tale puts a distinctly English colloquialism in the mouth of the American John Ferrier.

"He was still sitting with his elbow upon his knee."
Geo. Hutchinson, *A Study in Scarlet* (London: Ward, Lock Bowden, and Co., 1891)

"Leave Utah!"

"That's about the size of it."

"But the farm?"

"We will raise as much as we can in money, and let the rest go. To tell the truth, Lucy, it isn't the first time I have thought of doing it. I don't care about knuckling under to any man, as these folk do to their darned Prophet. I'm a free-born American, and it's all new to me. Guess I'm too old to learn. If he comes browsing about this farm, he might chance to run up against a charge of buckshot travelling in the opposite direction."

"But they won't let us leave," his daughter objected.

"Wait till Jefferson comes, and we'll soon manage that. In the meantime, don't you fret yourself, my dearie, and don't get your eyes swelled up, else he'll be walking into me when he sees you. There's nothing to be afeared about, and there's no danger at all."

John Ferrier uttered these consoling remarks in a very confident tone, but she could not help observing that he paid unusual care to the fastening of the doors that night, and that he carefully cleaned and loaded the rusty old shotgun which hung upon the wall of his bedroom.

CHAPTER IV

A Flight for Life

On the morning which followed his interview with the Mormon Prophet, John Ferrier went in to Salt Lake City, and having found his acquaintance, who was bound for the Nevada Mountains, he entrusted him with his message to Jefferson Hope. In it he told the young man of the imminent danger which threatened them, and how necessary it was that he should return. Having done thus he felt easier in his mind, and returned home with a lighter heart.

As he approached his farm, he was surprised to see a horse hitched to each of the posts of the gate. Still more surprised was he on the entering to find two young men in possession of his sitting room. One, with a long pale face, was leaning back in the rocking-chair, with his feet cocked up upon the stove. The other, a bull-necked youth with coarse, bloated features, was standing in front of the window with his hands in his pockets whistling a popular hymn. Both of them nodded to Ferrier as he entered, and the one in the rocking-chair commenced the conversation.

"Maybe you don't know us," he said. "This here is the son of Elder Drebber, and I'm Joseph Stangerson, who travelled with you in the desert when the Lord stretched out His hand and gathered you into the true fold."

"As He will all the nations in His own good time," said the other in a nasal voice; "He grindeth slowly but exceeding small."

John Ferrier bowed coldly. He had guessed who his visitors were.

"We have come," continued Stangerson, "at the advice of our fathers to solicit the hand of your daughter for whichever of us may seem good to you and to her. As I have but four wives and Brother Drebber here has seven, it appears to me that my claim is the stronger one."

"Nay, nay, Brother Stangerson," cried the other; "the question is not how many wives we have, but how many we can keep. My father has now given over his mills to me, and I am the richer man."

"But my prospects are better," said the other, warmly. "When the Lord removes my father, I shall have his tanning yard and his leather factory. Then I am your elder, and am higher in the Church."

"It will be for the maiden to decide," rejoined young Drebber, smirking at his own reflection in the glass. "We will leave it all to her decision."

During this dialogue, John Ferrier had stood fuming in the doorway, hardly able to keep his riding-whip from the backs of his two visitors.

"Look here," he said at last, striding up to them, "when my daughter summons you, you can come, but until then I don't want to see your faces again."

The two young Mormons stared at him in amazement. In their eyes this competition between them for the maiden's hand was the highest of honours both to her and her father.

"There are two ways out of the room," cried Ferrier; "there is the door, and there is the window. Which do you care to use?"

His brown face looked so savage, and his gaunt hands so threatening, that his visitors sprang to their feet and beat a hurried retreat. The old farmer followed them to the door.

"Let me know when you have settled which it is to be," he said, sardonically.

"You shall smart for this!" Stangerson cried, white with rage.

" 'You shall smart for this!' Stangerson cried, white with rage."
Geo. Hutchinson, *A Study in Scarlet* (London: Ward, Lock Bowden, and Co., 1891)

"You have defied the Prophet and the Council of Four. You shall rue it to the end of your days."

"The hand of the Lord shall be heavy upon you," cried young Drebber; "He will arise and smite you!"

"Then I'll start the smiting," exclaimed Ferrier furiously, and would have rushed upstairs for his gun had not Lucy seized him by the arm and restrained him. Before he could escape from her, the clatter of horses' hoofs told him that they were beyond his reach.

"The young canting rascals!" he exclaimed, wiping the perspiration from his forehead; "I would sooner see you in your grave, my girl, than the wife of either of them."

"And so should I, father," she answered, with spirit; "but Jefferson will soon be here."

"Yes. It will not be long before he comes. The sooner the better, for we do not know what their next move may be."

It was, indeed, high time that someone capable of giving

advice and help should come to the aid of the sturdy old farmer and his adopted daughter. In the whole history of the settlement there had never been such a case of rank disobedience to the authority of the Elders. If minor errors were punished so sternly, what would be the fate of this arch rebel? Ferrier knew that his wealth and position would be of no avail to him. Others as well known and as rich as himself had been spirited away before now, and their goods given over to the Church. He was a brave man, but he trembled at the vague, shadowy terrors which hung over him. Any known danger he could face with a firm lip, but this suspense was unnerving. He concealed his fears from his daughter, however, and affected to make light of the whole matter, though she, with the keen eye of love, saw plainly that he was ill at ease.

He expected that he would receive some message or remonstrance from Young as to his conduct, and he was not mistaken, though it came in an unlooked-for manner. Upon rising next morning he found, to his surprise, a small square of paper pinned on to the coverlet of his bed just over his chest. On it was printed, in bold, straggling letters:—

> Twenty-nine days are given you for amendment, and then—

The dash was more fear-inspiring than any threat could have been. How this warning came into his room puzzled John Fer-

"A small square of paper pinned on to the coverlet of his bed."
Geo. Hutchinson, *A Study in Scarlet* (London: Ward, Lock Bowden, and Co., 1891)

IN THE CENTRE OF THE CEILING WAS SCRAWLED, WITH A BURNT STICK APPARENTLY, THE NUMBER 28.

"In the centre of the ceiling was scrawled,
with a burnt stick apparently, the number 28."
Charles Doyle, *A Study in Scarlet* (London and New York: Ward, Lock & Co., 1888)

rier sorely, for his servants slept in an outhouse, and the doors and windows had all been secured. He crumpled the paper up and said nothing to his daughter, but the incident struck a chill into his heart. The twenty-nine days were evidently the balance of the month which Young had promised. What strength or courage could avail against an enemy armed with such mysterious powers? The hand which fastened that pin might have struck him to the heart, and he could never have known who had slain him.

Still more shaken was he next morning. They had sat down to their breakfast, when Lucy with a cry of surprise pointed upwards. In the centre of the ceiling was scrawled, with a burned stick apparently, the number 28. To his daughter it was unintelligible, and he did not enlighten her. That night he sat up with his gun and kept watch and ward. He saw and he heard nothing, and yet in the morning a great 27 had been painted upon the outside of his door.

Thus day followed day; and as sure as morning came he found that his unseen enemies had kept their register, and had marked up in some conspicuous position how many days were still left to him out of the month of grace. Sometimes the fatal numbers appeared upon the walls, sometimes upon the floors, occasionally they were on small placards stuck upon the garden gate or the railings. With all his vigilance John Ferrier could not discover whence these daily warnings proceeded. A horror which was almost superstitious came upon him at the sight of them. He became haggard and restless, and his eyes had the troubled look of some hunted creature. He had but one hope in life now, and that was for the arrival of the young hunter from Nevada.

Twenty had changed to fifteen, and fifteen to ten, but there was no news of the absentee. One by one the numbers dwindled down, and still there came no sign of him. Whenever a horseman clattered down the road, or a driver shouted at his team, the old farmer hurried to the gate, thinking that help had arrived at last. At last, when he saw five give way to four and that again to three, he lost heart, and abandoned all hope of escape. Singlehanded, and with his limited knowledge of the mountains which surrounded the settlement, he knew that he was powerless. The more-frequented roads were strictly watched and guarded, and none could pass along them without an order from the Council. Turn which way he would, there appeared to be no avoiding the blow which hung over him. Yet the old man never wavered in his resolution to part with life itself before he consented to what he regarded as his daughter's dishonour.

He was sitting alone one evening pondering deeply over his troubles, and searching vainly for some way out of them. That morning had shown the figure 2 upon the wall of his house, and the next day would be the last of the allotted time. What was to happen then? All manner of vague and terrible fancies filled his imagination. And his daughter—what was to become of her after he was gone? Was there no escape from the invisible network which was drawn all round them? He sank his head upon the table and sobbed at the thought of his own impotence.

What was that? In the silence he heard a gentle scratching sound—low, but very distinct in the quiet of the night. It came from the door of the house. Ferrier crept into the hall and listened intently. There was a pause for a few moments, and then the low, insidious sound was repeated. Someone was evidently tapping very gently upon one of the panels of the door. Was it some midnight assassin who had come to carry out the murderous orders of the secret tribunal? Or was it some agent who was marking up that the last day of grace had arrived? John Ferrier felt that instant death would be better than the suspense which shook his nerves and chilled his heart. Springing forward, he drew the bolt and threw the door open.

Outside all was calm and quiet. The night was fine, and the stars were twinkling brightly overhead. The little front garden lay before the farmer's eyes bounded by the fence and gate, but neither there nor on the road was any human being to be seen. With a sigh of relief, Ferrier looked to right and to left, until happening to glance straight down at his own feet he saw to his astonishment a man lying flat upon his face upon the ground, with arms and legs all asprawl.

So unnerved was he at the sight that he leaned up against

"He saw to his astonishment a man lying flat upon his face upon the ground."
Richard Gutschmidt, *Späte Rache* (Stuttgart: Robert Lutz Verlag, 1902)

228 The phrase was a common expression for "food or drink."

the wall with his hand to his throat to stifle his inclination to call out. His first thought was that the prostrate figure was that of some wounded or dying man, but as he watched it he saw it writhe along the ground and into the hall with the rapidity and noiselessness of a serpent. Once within the house the man sprang to his feet, closed the door, and revealed to the astonished farmer the fierce face and resolute expression of Jefferson Hope.

"Good God!" gasped John Ferrier. "How you scared me! Whatever made you come in like that?"

"Give me food," the other said, hoarsely. "I have had no time for bit or sup[228] for eight-and-forty hours." He flung himself upon the cold meat and bread which were still lying upon the table from his host's supper, and devoured it voraciously. "Does Lucy bear up well?" he asked, when he had satisfied his hunger.

"Yes. She does not know the danger," her father answered.

"He saw to his astonishment a man lying flat upon his face."
Geo. Hutchinson, *A Study in Scarlet* (London: Ward, Lock Bowden, and Co., 1891)

"As he watched it he saw it writhe along the ground."
D. H. Friston, *Beeton's Christmas Annual*, 1887

"That is well. The house is watched on every side. That is why I crawled my way up to it. They may be darned sharp, but they're not quite sharp enough to catch a Washoe hunter."[229]

John Ferrier felt a different man now that he realized that he had a devoted ally. He seized the young man's leathery hand and wrung it cordially. "You're a man to be proud of," he said. "There are not many who would come to share our danger and our troubles."

"You've hit it there, pard," the young hunter answered. "I have a respect for you, but if you were alone in this business I'd think twice before I put my head into such a hornet's nest. It's Lucy that brings me here, and before harm comes on her I guess there will be one less o' the Hope family in Utah."

"What are we to do?"

"To-morrow is your last day, and unless you act to-night you are lost. I have a mule and two horses waiting in the Eagle Ravine. How much money have you?"

"Two thousand dollars in gold, and five in notes."[230]

229 The Washoe mountain range is part of the Virginia Mountains in northwestern Nevada. The name is shared by the Washoe tribe of the nearby Lake Tahoe area, but by "Washoe hunter," Hope is doubtless referring to himself.

230 A. Carson Simpson, in "A Very Treasury of Coin of Divers Realms," conjectures that Ferrier's "two thousand dollars in gold" consisted of "privately-issued gold pieces—really tokens—used at this time in the Far West; these are often referred to as 'pioneer' or 'territorial' gold." Simpson adds that the hoard may also have included tokens struck by the Mormons themselves. The latter were first issued in 1849.

"That will do. I have as much more to add to it. We must push for Carson City[231] through the mountains. You had best wake Lucy. It is as well that the servants do not sleep in the house."

While Ferrier was absent, preparing his daughter for the approaching journey, Jefferson Hope packed all the eatables that he could find into a small parcel, and filled a stoneware jar with water, for he knew by experience that the mountain wells were few and far between. He had hardly completed his arrangements before the farmer returned with his daughter all dressed and ready for a start. The greeting between the lovers was warm, but brief, for minutes were precious, and there was much to be done.

"We must make our start at once," said Jefferson Hope, speaking in a low but resolute voice, like one who realizes the greatness of the peril, but has steeled his heart to meet it. "The front and back entrances are watched, but with caution we may get away through the side window and across the fields. Once on the road we are only two miles from the Ravine where the horses are waiting. By daybreak we should be halfway through the mountains."

"What if we are stopped?" asked Ferrier.

Hope slapped the revolver butt which protruded from the front of his tunic. "If they are too many for us, we shall take two or three of them with us," he said with a sinister smile.

The lights inside the house had all been extinguished, and from the darkened window Ferrier peered over the fields which had been his own, and which he was now about to abandon for ever. He had long nerved himself to the sacrifice, however, and the thought of the honour and happiness of his daughter outweighed any regret at his ruined fortunes. All looked so peaceful and happy, the rustling trees and the broad silent stretch of grain-land, that it was difficult to realize that the spirit of murder lurked through it all. Yet the white face and set expression of the young hunter showed that in his approach to the house he had seen enough to satisfy him upon that head.

Ferrier carried the bag of gold and notes, Jefferson Hope had the scanty provisions and water, while Lucy had a small bundle containing a few of her more valued possessions. Opening the window very slowly and carefully, they waited until a dark

231 The city, named after explorer Kit Carson, was founded in 1858 and was made the capital of Nevada when the territory became a state in 1864. Although its official population in 1880 was only 4,229, Carson City represented the heart of silver-mining country at the time. The state's richest silver deposit was discovered in 1859 at the Comstock Lode, some fifteen miles away; copious amounts of silver were brought down to the Carson River, treated, and sold in town. To coin the silver, the federal government established a mint in Carson City.

Mark Twain, who lived and worked in and around Carson City in the late 1870s and early 1880s, reported on its sights in *Roughing It* (1891), calling Carson City "a 'wooden' town. . . . The main street consisted of four or five blocks of little white frame stores which were too high to sit down on, but not too high for various other purposes; in fact, hardly high enough. They were packed close together, side by side, as if room were scarce in that mighty plain."

cloud had somewhat obscured the night, and then one by one passed through into the little garden. With bated breath and crouching figures they stumbled across it, and gained the shelter of the hedge, which they skirted until they came to the gap which opened into the cornfields. They had just reached this point when the young man seized his two companions and dragged them down into the shadow, where they lay silent and trembling.

It was as well that his prairie training had given Jefferson Hope the ears of a lynx. He and his friends had hardly crouched down before the melancholy hooting of a mountain owl was heard within a few yards of them, which was immediately answered by another hoot at a small distance. At the same moment a vague shadowy figure emerged from the gap for which they had been making, and uttered the plaintive signal cry again, on which a second man appeared out of the obscurity.

"To-morrow at midnight," said the first, who appeared to be in authority. "When the Whip-poor-Will calls three times."

"It is well," returned the other. "Shall I tell Brother Drebber?"

"Pass it on to him, and from him to the others. Nine to seven!"

"Seven to five!" repeated the other; and the two figures flitted away in different directions. Their concluding words had evidently been some form of sign and countersign.[232] The instant that their footsteps had died away in the distance, Jefferson Hope sprang to his feet, and helping his companions through the gap, led the way across the fields at the top of his speed, supporting and half-carrying the girl when her strength appeared to fail her.

"Hurry on! hurry on!" he gasped from time to time. "We are through the line of sentinels. Everything depends on speed. Hurry on!"

Once on the high road they made rapid progress. Only once did they meet anyone, and then they managed to slip into a field, and so avoid recognition. Before reaching the town the hunter branched away into a rugged and narrow footpath which led to the mountains. Two dark jagged peaks loomed above them through the darkness, and the defile which led between them was the Eagle Cañon in which the horses were awaiting them. With unerring instinct Jefferson Hope picked

232 Ben Vizoskie, in "Who Wrote the American Chapters of *A Study in Scarlet*?," makes the ingenious suggestion that "seven to five" is a shorthanded reference to the *Book of Mormon*'s Book of Mosiah, Chapter 7, verse 25: "But wo[e] unto him that has the law given, yea, that has all the commandments of God, like unto us, and that transgresseth them and that wasteth the days of his probation, for awful is his state"—a phrase that seems truly apt in referring to John Ferrier. Vizoskie also claims that "nine to seven" refers to Chapter 9, verse 27, of the Book of Nephi: "For if this people had not fallen into transgression, the Lord would not have suffered that this great evil should come upon them," which might apply to the Mormon avengers. The full quotations would have been unwieldy as passwords, Vizoskie explains, and so the references instead were used. Years later, Hope could only remember the numbers and omitted the references to the Books.

In discussions with this editor, Vizoskie now amends his suggestion: The references were to the secret, *unpublished* version of the *Book of Mormon*, known only to the Elders and their agents. The *Book of Mormon* was not published with chapter and verse references until the 1879 edition devised by Orson Pratt. For a fascinating bibliographical history of this important work, see Thomas W. Mackay's "Mormon as Editor: A Study in Colophons, Headers, and Source Indicators."

233 In the *Beeton's* and English book editions, the sign and countersign are here given as "nine *from* seven" and "seven *from* five."

his way among the great boulders and along the bed of a dried-up watercourse, until he came to the retired corner, screened with rocks, where the faithful animals had been picketed. The girl was placed upon the mule, and old Ferrier upon one of the horses, with his money-bag, while Jefferson Hope led the other along the precipitous and dangerous path.

It was a bewildering route for anyone who was not accustomed to face Nature in her wildest moods. On the one side a great crag towered up a thousand feet or more, black, stern, and menacing, with long basaltic columns upon its rugged surface like the ribs of some petrified monster. On the other hand a wild chaos of boulders and debris made all advance impossible. Between the two ran the irregular track, so narrow in places that they had to travel in Indian file, and so rough that only practised riders could have traversed it at all. Yet, in spite of all dangers and difficulties, the hearts of the fugitives were light within them, for every step increased the distance between them and the terrible despotism from which they were flying.

They soon had a proof, however, that they were still within the jurisdiction of the Saints. They had reached the very wildest and most desolate portion of the pass when the girl gave a startled cry, and pointed upwards. On a rock which overlooked the track, showing out dark and plain against the sky, there stood a solitary sentinel. He saw them as soon as they perceived him, and his military challenge of "Who goes there?" rang through the silent ravine.

"Travellers for Nevada," said Jefferson Hope, with his hand upon the rifle which hung by his saddle.

They could see the lonely watcher fingering his gun, and peering down at them as if dissatisfied at their reply.

"By whose permission?" he asked.

"The Holy Four," answered Ferrier. His Mormon experiences had taught him that that was the highest authority to which he could refer.

"Nine to seven," cried the sentinel.

"Seven to five," returned Jefferson Hope promptly, remembering the countersign which he had heard in the garden.[233]

"Pass, and the Lord go with you," said the voice from above. Beyond his post the path broadened out, and the horses were able to break into a trot. Looking back, they could see the solitary watcher leaning upon his gun, and knew that they had passed the outlying post of the chosen people, and that freedom lay before them.

" 'Nine to seven,' cried the sentinel."
Richard Gutschmidt, *Späte Rache* (Stuttgart: Robert Lutz Verlag, 1902)

CHAPTER V

The Avenging Angels

All night their course lay through intricate defiles and over irregular and rock-strewn paths. More than once they lost their way, but Hope's intimate knowledge of the mountains enabled them to regain the track once more. When morning broke, a scene of marvellous though savage beauty lay before them. In every direction the great snow-capped peaks hemmed them in, peeping over each other's shoulders to the far horizon. So steep were the rocky banks on either side of them that the larch and the pine seemed to be suspended over their heads, and to need only a gust of wind to come hurtling down upon them. Nor was the fear entirely an illusion, for the barren valley was thickly strewn with trees and boulders which had fallen in a similar manner. Even as they passed, a great rock came thundering down with a hoarse rattle which woke the echoes in the silent gorges, and startled the weary horses into a gallop.

As the sun rose slowly above the eastern horizon, the caps of the great mountains lit up one after the other, like lamps at a festival, until they were all ruddy and glowing. The magnificent spectacle cheered the hearts of the three fugitives and gave them fresh energy. At a wild torrent which swept out of a ravine they called a halt and watered their horses, while they partook of a hasty breakfast. Lucy and her father would fain have rested longer, but Jefferson Hope was inexorable. "They will be upon our track by this time," he said. "Everything depends upon our speed. Once safe in Carson, we may rest for the remainder of our lives."

During the whole of that day they struggled on through the defiles, and by evening they calculated that they were more than thirty miles from their enemies. At night-time they chose the base of a beetling crag, where the rocks offered some protection from the chill wind, and there, huddled together for warmth, they enjoyed a few hours' sleep. Before daybreak, however, they were up and on their way once more. They had seen no signs of any pursuers, and Jefferson Hope began to think that they were fairly out of the reach of the terrible organization whose enmity they had incurred. He little knew how far that iron grasp could reach, or how soon it was to close upon them and crush them.

About the middle of the second day of their flight their scanty store of provisions began to run out. This gave the hunter little uneasiness, however, for there was game to be had among the mountains, and he had frequently before had to depend upon his rifle for the needs of life. Choosing a sheltered nook, be piled together a few dried branches and made a blazing fire, at which his companions might warm themselves, for they were now nearly five thousand feet above the sea level, and the air was bitter and keen. Having tethered the horses, and bade Lucy adieu, he threw his gun over his shoulder, and set out in search of whatever chance might throw in his way. Looking back he saw the old man and the young girl crouching over the blazing fire, while the three animals stood motionless in the back-ground. Then the intervening rocks hid them from his view.

He walked for a couple of miles through one ravine after another without success, though from the marks upon the bark of the trees, and other indications, he judged that there were numerous bears in the vicinity. At last, after two or three hours' fruitless search, he was thinking of turning back in despair, when casting his eyes upwards he saw a sight which sent a thrill of pleasure through his heart. On the edge of a jutting pinnacle, three or four hundred feet above him, there stood a creature somewhat resembling a sheep in appearance, but armed with a pair of gigantic horns. The big-horn—for so it is called—was acting, probably, as a guardian over a flock which were invisible to the hunter; but fortunately it was heading in the opposite direction, and had not perceived him. Lying on his face, he rested his rifle upon a rock, and took a long and steady aim before drawing the trigger. The animal sprang into the air, tottered for a moment upon the edge of the precipice, and then came crashing down into the valley beneath.

The creature was too unwieldy to lift, so the hunter contented himself with cutting away one haunch and part of the flank. With this trophy over his shoulder, he hastened to retrace his steps, for the evening was already drawing in. He had hardly started, however, before he realized the difficulty which faced him. In his eagerness he had wandered far past the ravines which were known to him, and it was no easy matter to pick out the path which he had taken. The valley in which he found himself divided and sub-divided into many gorges, which were so like each other that it was impossible to distinguish one from the other. He followed one for a mile or more until he came to a mountain torrent which he was sure that he had never seen before. Convinced that he had taken the wrong turn, he tried another, but with the same result. Night was coming on rapidly, and it was almost dark before he at last found himself in a defile which was familiar to him. Even then it was no easy matter to keep to the right track, for the moon had not yet risen,[234] and the high cliffs on either side made the obscurity more profound. Weighed down with his burden, and weary from his exertions, he stumbled along, keeping up his heart by the reflection that every step brought him nearer to Lucy, and that he carried with him enough to ensure them food for the remainder of their journey.

He had now come to the mouth of the very defile in which he had left them. Even in the darkness he could recognize the outline of the cliffs which bounded it. They must, he reflected, be awaiting him anxiously, for he had been absent nearly five hours. In the gladness of his heart he put his hands to his mouth and made the glen re-echo to a loud halloo as a signal that he was coming. He paused and listened for an answer.

234 Commenting on Dr. Watson's recurring difficulties with the moon, Jay Finley Christ writes, in "An Adventure in the Lower Criticism, Part II: Dr. Watson and the Moon," "When Hope returned to his camp, it was 'dark,' because 'the moon had not yet risen.' The moon had been full on August 1st; on the 4th the sun set at 7:41 and the moon rose at 8:21 P.M. Twilight ended officially at 9:00 P.M., according to the American Almanac. Perhaps it was dark in the canyons."

None came save his own cry, which clattered up the dreary silent ravines, and was borne back to his ears in countless repetitions. Again he shouted, even louder than before, and again no whisper came back from the friends whom he had left such a short time ago. A vague, nameless dread came over him, and he hurried onwards frantically, dropping the precious food in his agitation.

When he turned the corner, he came full in sight of the spot where the fire had been lit. There was still a glowing pile of wood ashes there, but it had evidently not been tended since his departure. The same dead silence still reigned all round. With his fears all changed to convictions, he hurried on. There was no living creature near the remains of the fire: animals, man, maiden, all were gone. It was only too clear that some sudden and terrible disaster had occurred during his absence—a disaster which had embraced them all, and yet had left no traces behind it.

Bewildered and stunned by this blow, Jefferson Hope felt his head spin round, and had to lean upon his rifle to save himself from falling. He was essentially a man of action, however, and speedily recovered from his temporary impotence. Seizing a half-consumed piece of wood from the smouldering fire, he blew it into a flame, and proceeded with its help to examine the little camp. The ground was all stamped down by the feet of horses, showing that a large party of mounted men had overtaken the fugitives, and the direction of their tracks proved that they had afterwards turned back to Salt Lake City. Had they carried back both of his companions with them? Jefferson Hope had almost persuaded himself that they must have done so, when his eye fell upon an object which made every nerve of his body tingle within him. A little way on one side of the camp was a low-lying heap of reddish soil, which had assuredly not been there before. There was no mistaking it for anything but a newly dug grave. As the young hunter approached it, he perceived that a stick had been planted on it, with a sheet of paper stuck in the cleft fork of it. The inscription upon the paper was brief, but to the point:

JOHN FERRIER,
Formerly of Salt Lake City,
Died August 4th, 1860.

"The inscription upon the paper was brief, but to the point."
Geo. Hutchinson, *A Study in Scarlet* (London: Ward, Lock Bowden, and Co., 1891)

The sturdy old man, whom he had left so short a time before, was gone, then, and this was all his epitaph. Jefferson Hope looked wildly round to see if there was a second grave, but there was no sign of one. Lucy had been carried back by their terrible pursuers to fulfil her original destiny, by becoming one of the harem of an Elder's son. As the young fellow realized the certainty of her fate, and his own powerlessness to prevent it, he wished that he, too, was lying with the old farmer in his last silent resting-place.

Again, however, his active spirit shook off the lethargy which springs from despair. If there was nothing else left to him, he could at least devote his life to revenge. With indomitable patience and perseverance, Jefferson Hope possessed also a power of sustained vindictiveness, which he may have learned from the Indians amongst whom he had lived. As he stood by the desolate fire, he felt that the only one thing which could assuage his grief would be thorough and complete retribution, brought by his own hand upon his enemies. His strong will and

" 'John Ferrier, formerly of Salt Lake City. Died August 4th, 1860.' "
Richard Gutschmidt, *Späte Rache* (Stuttgart: Robert Lutz Verlag, 1902)

untiring energy should, he determined, be devoted to that one end. With a grim, white face, he retraced his steps to where he had dropped the food, and having stirred up the smouldering fire, he cooked enough to last him for a few days. This he made up into a bundle, and, tired as he was, he set himself to walk back through the mountains upon the track of the Avenging Angels.

For five days he toiled footsore and weary through the defiles which he had already traversed on horseback. At night he flung himself down among the rocks, and snatched a few hours of sleep; but before daybreak he was always well on his way. On the sixth day, he reached the Eagle Cañon, from which they had commenced their ill-fated flight. Thence he could look down upon the home of the Saints. Worn and exhausted, he leaned upon his rifle and shook his gaunt hand fiercely at the silent widespread city beneath him. As he looked at it, he observed that there were flags in some of the principal streets, and other signs of festivity. He was still speculating as to what this might mean when he heard the clatter of horse's hoofs, and saw a mounted man riding towards him. As he approached, he recognized him as a Mormon named Cowper, to whom he had rendered services at different times. He therefore accosted him when he got up to him, with the object of finding out what Lucy Ferrier's fate had been.

"I am Jefferson Hope," he said. "You remember me."

The Mormon looked at him with undisguised astonishment—indeed, it was difficult to recognize in this tattered, unkempt wanderer, with ghastly white face and fierce, wild eyes, the spruce young hunter of former days. Having, however, at last satisfied himself as to his identity, the man's surprise changed to consternation.

"You are mad to come here," he cried. "It is as much as my own life is worth to be seen talking with you. There is a warrant against you from the Holy Four for assisting the Ferriers away."

"I don't fear them, or their warrant," Hope said, earnestly. "You must know something of this matter, Cowper. I conjure you by everything you hold dear to answer a few questions. We have always been friends. For God's sake, don't refuse to answer me."

"What is it?" the Mormon asked, uneasily. "Be quick. The very rocks have ears and the trees eyes."

"What has become of Lucy Ferrier?"

"She was married yesterday to young Drebber. Hold up, man, hold up, you have no life left in you."

"Don't mind me," said Hope faintly. He was white to the very lips, and had sunk down on the stone against which he had been leaning. "Married, you say?"

"Married yesterday—that's what those flags are for on the Endowment House.[235] There was some words between young Drebber and young Stangerson as to which was to have her. They'd both been in the party that followed them, and Stangerson had shot her father, which seemed to give him the best claim; but when they argued it out in council, Drebber's party was the stronger, so the Prophet gave her over to him. No one won't have her very long though, for I saw death in her face yesterday. She is more like a ghost than a woman. Are you off, then?"

"Yes, I am off," said Jefferson Hope, who had risen from his seat. His face might have been chiselled out of marble, so hard and set was its expression, while its eyes glowed with a baleful light.

235 Pronounced On-dew'ment, this was the name given to a former two-story building in Salt Lake City used by the Mormon Church for rituals of ordination, or endowment, into certain priestly orders. According to Tracy's *Encyclopaedia Sherlockiana*, "The sealing of husbands and wives in eternal marriage was a part of the ceremony, and all polygamous marriages were required to be performed here." However, there is no evidence that the flying of flags was a Mormon practice.

"Where are you going?"

"Never mind," he answered; and, slinging his weapon over his shoulder, strode off down the gorge and so away into the heart of the mountains to the haunts of the wild beasts. Amongst them all there was none so fierce and so dangerous as himself.

The prediction of the Mormon was only too well fulfilled. Whether it was the terrible death of her father or the effects of the hateful marriage into which she had been forced, poor Lucy never held up her head again, but pined away and died within a month. Her sottish husband, who had married her principally for the sake of John Ferrier's property, did not affect any great grief at his bereavement; but his other wives mourned over her, and sat up with her the night before the burial, as is the Mormon custom.[236] They were grouped round the bier in the early hours of the morning when, to their inexpressible fear and astonishment, the door was flung open, and a savage-looking, weather-beaten man in tattered garments strode into the room. Without a glance or a word to the cowering women, he walked up to the white silent figure which had once contained the pure soul of Lucy Ferrier. Stooping over her, he pressed his lips reverently to her cold forehead, and then, snatching up her hand, he took the wedding-ring from her finger. "She shall not be buried in that," he cried with a

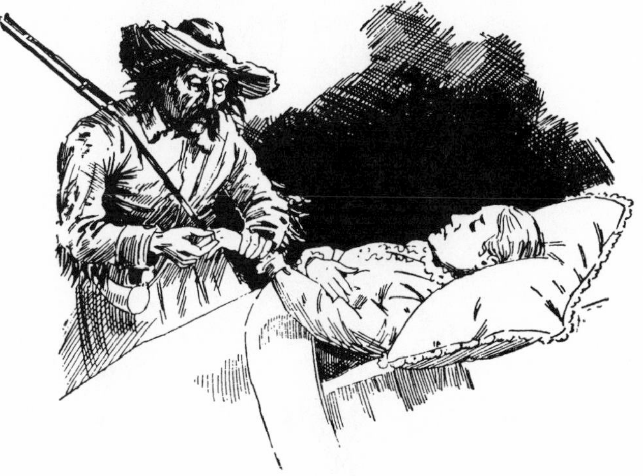

"Snatching up her hand, he took the wedding-ring from her finger."
Geo. Hutchinson, *A Study in Scarlet* (London:
Ward, Lock Bowden, and Co., 1891)

236 Again, there is no evidence of such a Mormon custom.

fierce snarl, and before an alarm could be raised sprang down the stairs and was gone. So strange and so brief was the episode that the watchers might have found it hard to believe it themselves or persuade other people of it, had it not been for the undeniable fact that the circlet of gold which marked her as having been a bride had disappeared.

For some months Jefferson Hope lingered among the mountains, leading a strange wild life, and nursing in his heart the fierce desire for vengeance which possessed him. Tales were told in the City of the weird figure which was seen prowling about the suburbs, and which haunted the lonely mountain gorges. Once a bullet whistled through Stangerson's window and flattened itself upon the wall within a foot of him. On another occasion, as Drebber passed under a cliff a great boulder crashed down on him, and he only escaped a terrible death by throwing himself upon his face. The two young Mormons were not long in discovering the reason of these attempts upon their lives, and led repeated expeditions into the mountains in the hope of capturing or killing their enemy, but always with-

"A great boulder crashed down on him."
Geo. Hutchinson, *A Study in Scarlet* (London: Ward, Lock Bowden, and Co., 1891)

out success. Then they adopted the precaution of never going out alone or after nightfall, and of having their houses guarded. After a time they were able to relax these measures, for nothing was either heard or seen of their opponent, and they hoped that time had cooled his vindictiveness.

Far from doing so, it had, if anything, augmented it. The hunter's mind was of a hard, unyielding nature, and the predominant idea of revenge had taken such complete possession of it that there was no room for any other emotion. He was, however, above all things, practical. He soon realized that even his iron constitution could not stand the incessant strain which he was putting upon it. Exposure and want of wholesome food were wearing him out. If he died like a dog among the mountains, what was to become of his revenge then? And yet such a death was sure to overtake him if he persisted. He felt that that was to play his enemy's game, so he reluctantly returned to the old Nevada mines, there to recruit his health and to amass money enough to allow him to pursue his object without privation.

His intention had been to be absent a year at the most, but a combination of unforeseen circumstances prevented his leaving the mines for nearly five.[237] At the end of that time, however, his memory of his wrongs and his craving for revenge were quite as keen as on that memorable night when he had stood by John Ferrier's grave. Disguised, and under an assumed name, he returned to Salt Lake City, careless what became of his own life, as long as he obtained what he knew to be justice. There he found evil tidings awaiting him. There had been a schism among the Chosen People a few months before, some of the younger members of the Church having rebelled against the authority of the Elders, and the result had been the secession of a certain number of the malcontents, who had left Utah and become Gentiles.[238] Among these had been Drebber and Stangerson; and no one knew whither they had gone. Rumour reported that Drebber had managed to convert a large part of his property into money, and that he had departed a wealthy man, while his companion, Stangerson, was comparatively poor. There was no clue at all, however, as to their whereabouts.

Many a man, however vindictive, would have abandoned all thought of revenge in the face of such a difficulty, but Jeffer-

237 That is, until about the middle to end of 1865. Jack Tracy, in *Saints*, suggests that the "unforeseen circumstances" were the events of the American Civil War.

238 No single group of "malcontents" fits this description, but there were at least two significant defections within this time frame, both based upon a mistrust of Brigham Young's authority. In 1861, members of the Morrisite movement—so named after Joseph Morris (1817–1862), who had received numerous revelations and claimed to be the seventh angel of the apocalypse—split from the church and moved to South Weber on the grounds that Morris was a true prophet, but Brigham Young was not. The following year, having detained some disgruntled members who were trying to leave the sect, Morris was instructed by Utah authorities to set his prisoners free. When Morris, believing himself and his followers to be above the law, refused, a posse of two hundred men arrived to bring him to Salt Lake City. In the siege that followed, Morris and a few others were killed. The rest of the Morrisites surrendered, and after a trial and a collective pardon, they scattered to surrounding states.

Another schism was instigated by the group that came to be known as The Reorganized Church of Latter-day Saints (now the Community of Christ). Its adherents were opposed to polygamy, which they claimed had been endorsed not by Joseph Smith but by Young. Choosing to remain in Nauvoo rather than following Young to Utah, they elected Joseph Smith's son, Joseph Smith III, as their president in 1860, and until 1996 each president thereafter was also a descendant of Smith's. In 1863–1864, The Reorganized Church of Jesus Christ of Latter-day Saints sent a mission to Utah and was able to convert some Mormons to the cause.

son Hope never faltered for a moment. With the small competence[239] he possessed, eked out by such employment as he could pick up, he travelled from town to town through the United States in quest of his enemies. Year passed into year, his black hair turned grizzled, but still he wandered on, a human bloodhound, with his mind wholly set upon the one object to which he had devoted his life. At last his perseverance was rewarded. It was but a glance of a face in a window, but that one glance told him that Cleveland in Ohio possessed the men whom he was in pursuit of. He returned to his miserable lodgings with his plan of vengeance all arranged. It chanced, however, that Drebber, looking from his window, had recognized the vagrant in the street, and had read murder in his eyes. He hurried before a justice of the peace, accompanied by Stangerson, who had become his private secretary, and represented to him that they were in danger of their lives from the jealousy and hatred of an old rival. That evening Jefferson Hope was taken into custody, and not being able to find sureties,[240] was detained for some weeks. When at last he was liberated, it was only to find that Drebber's house was deserted, and that he and his secretary had departed for Europe.

Again the avenger had been foiled, and again his concentrated hatred urged him to continue the pursuit. Funds were wanting, however, and for some time he had to return to work, saving every dollar for his approaching journey. At last, having collected enough to keep life in him, he departed for Europe, and tracked his enemies from city to city, working his way in any menial capacity, but never overtaking the fugitives. When he reached St. Petersburg, they had departed for Paris; and when he followed them there, he learned that they had just set off for Copenhagen. At the Danish capital he was again a few days late, for they had journeyed on to London, where he at last succeeded in running them to earth. As to what occurred there, we cannot do better than quote the old hunter's own account, as duly recorded in Dr. Watson's Journal, to which we are already under such obligations.[241]

239 Means for the necessities and conveniences of life; an allowance.

240 That is, persons who would post a bail bond or take responsibility for Hope.

241 Who wrote these words? It cannot have been Jefferson Hope, because when Lestrade later takes his statement, Hope explains his motives by saying merely: "It don't much matter to you why I hated these men . . ." And how could he have been acquainted with the earlier part of the story, from the desert rescue onward?

D. Martin Dakin concludes that it was Arthur Conan Doyle who added these sentences: "[U]nless Watson is deliberately adopting a temporary Caesarian detachment," Dakin explains, "this phrase must come from a third hand, which can scarcely be other than that of him who prepared Watson's narratives for publication, referred to by Sherlockians as the Literary Agent." This view is supported by Jack Tracy in *Saints*, and in the *Encyclopaedia Sherlockiana*, he describes Conan Doyle's authorship of the entire "Country of the Saints" section as "generally agreed." Charles A. Meyer, in "A Computer Analysis of Authorship in *A Study in Scarlet*," reaches the same conclusion.

But "generally agreed" appears to be an overstatement. Dakin himself asserts that Watson wrote the material based on Hope's narrative, which must have included a recounting of Ferrier's own history (Hope could not have retained a *written* history prepared by Ferrier, unless he coincidentally took it with him on his last hunting expedition before Ferrier's death). Dakin finds it strange, however, that Hope's verbal narrative would have preserved such exact detail. "Are we driven to the shocking suspicion that Watson, given an outline story, could not resist embroidering it with details form his own imagination?" He notes also that the style appears Watsonesque, rather than resembling the abrupt style of Hope recorded in Lestrade's notebook.

Peter Horrocks makes the case, in "Saints and Sinners: An Appraisal of 'The Country of the Saints,' " that Holmes and Conan Doyle wrote the interlude together. John L. Benton, in "Who Was Dr. Watson's 'Good Authority?,' " suggests that Holmes supplied the background information to Watson, while W. E. Edwards asserts, "The only possible answer would seem to be from the only confidant Hope is known to have had: his young actor friend whose performance as Mrs. Sawyer was so successful."

As to the "Journal" itself, Bernard Davies writes,

> [A]11 the evidence is against there being anything resembling a meticulous, day-by-day record in a slim leather-covered volume. Odd memos on the backs of old envelopes or betting-slips seem much more likely. The passage sounds like a piece of editorial flim-flam, intended, at best, as a sop to the feelings of the tyro author [Dr. Watson] who was going to considerable pains to impress [his readers with his sophistication] . . .

In short, Davies concludes, "The 'Journal' . . . is just as much a figment as the *Reminiscences*." (See note 4, above.)

CHAPTER VI

A Continuation of the Reminiscences of John H. Watson, M.D.

OUR PRISONER'S FURIOUS resistance did not apparently indicate any ferocity in his disposition towards ourselves, for on finding himself powerless, he smiled in an affable manner, and expressed his hopes that he had not hurt any of us in the scuffle. "I guess you're going to take me to the police-station," he remarked to Sherlock Holmes. "My cab's at the door. If you'll loose my legs I'll walk down to it. I'm not so light to lift as I used to be."

Gregson and Lestrade exchanged glances as if they thought this proposition rather a bold one; but Holmes at once took the prisoner at his word, and loosened the towel which we had bound round his ankles. He rose and stretched his legs, as though to assure himself that they were free once more. I remember that I thought to myself, as I eyed him, that I had seldom seen a more powerfully built man; and his dark sunburned face bore an expression of determination and energy which was as formidable as his personal strength.

"If there's a vacant place for a chief of the police, I reckon you are the man for it," he said, gazing with undisguised admiration at my fellow-lodger. "The way you kept on my trail was a caution."

"You had better come with me," said Holmes to the two detectives.

"I can drive you," said Lestrade.

"Good! and Gregson can come inside with me. You too, Doctor. You have taken an interest in the case, and may as well stick to us."

I assented gladly, and we all descended together. Our prisoner made no attempt at escape, but stepped calmly into the cab which had been his, and we followed him. Lestrade mounted the box, whipped up the horse, and brought us in a very short time to our destination. We were ushered into a small chamber where a police Inspector noted down our prisoner's name and the names of the men with whose murder he had been charged. The official was a white-faced unemotional man, who went through his duties in a dull, mechanical way. "The prisoner will be put before the magistrates in the course of the week," he said; "in the meantime, Mr. Jefferson Hope, have you anything that you wish to say? I must warn you that your words will be taken down, and may be used against you."

"I've got a good deal to say," our prisoner said slowly. "I want to tell you gentlemen all about it."

"Hadn't you better reserve that for your trial?" asked the Inspector.

"I may never be tried," he answered. "You needn't look startled. It isn't suicide I am thinking of. Are you a doctor?" He turned his fierce dark eyes upon me as he asked this last question.

"Yes; I am," I answered.

"Then put your hand here," he said, with a smile, motioning with his manacled wrists towards his chest.

I did so; and became at once conscious of an extraordinary throbbing and commotion which was going on inside. The walls of his chest seemed to thrill and quiver as a frail building would do inside when some powerful engine was at work. In the silence of the room I could hear a dull humming and buzzing noise[242] which proceeded from the same source.

"Why," I cried, "you have an aortic aneurism!"[243]

"That's what they call it," he said, placidly. "I went to a doctor last week about it, and he told me that it is bound to burst

242 Some scholars object to Watson's description of the sound, deeming it overly sensational, but Helen Simpson writes, in "Medical Career and Capacities of Dr. J. H. Watson" that "it must be remembered that Watson was speaking as a doctor, to whom the implications of any considerable variation from the normal heartbeat were at once apparent; [his] phrases therefore must not be taken as his impression of actual sounds, but of sounds whose significance as danger signals he could only convey by some exaggeration in speech."

243 An aortic aneurysm occurs when blood pressure upon the aorta, the main artery leading away from the heart, becomes weakened. The artery dilates or bulges at that weakened site, and while the condition is often asymptomatic, a sudden rupture may cause hæmorrhaging and death.

244 The causes of aortic aneurysms are varied (smoking and high cholesterol are frequent risk factors), but they can include syphilis and the congenital tissue disorder known as Marfan's syndrome. People afflicted with Marfan's syndrome are quite tall, with long limbs and fingers—Abraham Lincoln was thought by many to have suffered from the disease—and their arterial walls are abnormally weak. Alvin Rodin and Jack D. Key, in their fine *Medical Case Book of Arthur Conan Doyle*, note that Jefferson Hope is six feet tall, and they credit E. M. Cooperman for proposing, in "Marfan's Syndrome and Sherlock Holmes," that Hope suffered from the disorder. They also observe that Watson wrote *A Study in Scarlet* ten years before French paediatrician Antonin Bernard Jean Marfan identified the syndrome in 1896. D. A. Redmond, for one, in "Marfan's Syndrome and Sherlock Holmes," makes the case that Watson deserves recognition for diagnosing Marfan's syndrome before Marfan himself did.

Yet Rodin and Key also point out that an aneurysm caused by Marfan's syndrome does not produce the "humming and buzzing" described by Watson and generally kills off its victims within one year. Indeed, the diagnosis of syphilis is put forth by Helen Simpson and others, including H. R. Bates (in "Sherlock Holmes and Syphilis"), who suggests that Hope's lapse of memory leading to his capture was due to destruction of his nervous system by syphilitic infection.

Whatever the true cause of Hope's affliction, it seems clear that it was not brought about by "over-exposure and under-feeding among the Salt Lake Mountains," unless he was "over-exposed" there to a carrier of syphilis.

" 'I've got a good deal to say,' our prisoner said slowly."
Richard Gutschmidt, *Späte Rache* (Stuttgart: Robert Lutz Verlag, 1902)

before many days passed. It has been getting worse for years. I got it from over-exposure and under-feeding[244] among the Salt Lake Mountains. I've done my work now, and I don't care how soon I go, but I should like to leave some account of the business behind me. I don't want to be remembered as a common cut-throat."

The Inspector and the two detectives had a hurried discussion as to the advisability of allowing him to tell his story.

"Do you consider, Doctor, that there is immediate danger?" the former asked.

"Most certainly there is," I answered.

"In that case it is clearly our duty, in the interests of justice, to take his statement," said the Inspector. "You are at liberty, sir, to give your account, which I again warn you will be taken down."

"I'll sit down, with your leave," the prisoner said, suiting the action to the word. "This aneurism of mine makes me easily tired, and the tussle we had half an hour ago has not mended matters. I'm on the brink of the grave, and I am not likely to lie to you. Every word I say is the absolute truth, and how you use it is a matter of no consequence to me."

With these words, Jefferson Hope leaned back in his chair and began the following remarkable statement. He spoke in a calm and methodical manner, as though the events which he narrated were commonplace enough. I can vouch for the accuracy of the subjoined account, for I have had access to Lestrade's note-book, in which the prisoner's words were taken down exactly as they were uttered.

"It don't much matter to you why I hated these men," he said; "it's enough that they were guilty of the death of two human beings—a father and daughter—and that they had, therefore, forfeited their own lives. After the lapse of time that has passed since their crime, it was impossible for me to secure a conviction against them in any court. I knew of their guilt though, and I determined that I should be judge, jury, and executioner all rolled into one. You'd have done the same, if you have any manhood in you, if you had been in my place.

"That girl that I spoke of was to have married me twenty years ago.[245] She was forced into marrying that same Drebber, and broke her heart over it. I took the marriage ring from her dead finger, and I vowed that his dying eyes should rest upon that very ring, and that his last thoughts should be of the crime for which he was punished. I have carried it about with me, and have followed him and his accomplice over two continents until I caught them. They thought to tire me out, but they could not do it. If I die to-morrow, as is likely enough, I die knowing that my work in this world is done, and well done. They have perished, and by my hand. There is nothing left for me to hope for, or to desire.

"They were rich and I was poor, so that it was no easy matter for me to follow them. When I got to London my pocket was about empty, and I found that I must turn my hand to something for my living. Driving and riding are as natural to me as walking, so I applied at a cabowner's office, and soon got employment. I was to bring a certain sum a week to the owner, and whatever was over that I might keep for myself. There was seldom much over, but I managed to scrape along somehow.

245 That is, 1861; Hope's "engagement" took place in 1860, and Lucy's wedding to Drebber actually occurred in 1860.

246 Christopher Morley remarks, "To 'drop across' two travelers lodging in Camberwell would be (using New York as an illustration) like a Manhattan taxi driver finding two strangers in Flatbush."

The hardest job was to learn my way about, for I reckon that of all the mazes that ever were contrived, this city is the most confusing. I had a map beside me though, and when once I had spotted the principal hotels and stations, I got on pretty well.

"It was some time before I found out where my two gentlemen were living; but I inquired and inquired until at last I dropped across them. They were at a boarding-house at Camberwell,[246] over on the other side of the river. When once I found them out I knew that I had them at my mercy. I had grown my beard, and there was no chance of their recognizing me. I would dog them and follow them until I saw my opportunity. I was determined that they should not escape me again.

"They were very near doing it for all that. Go where they would about London, I was always at their heels. Sometimes I followed them on my cab, and sometimes on foot, but the former was the best, for then they could not get away from me. It was only early in the morning or late at night that I could earn anything, so that I began to get behindhand with my employer. I did not mind that, however, as long as I could lay my hand upon the men I wanted.

"They were very cunning, though. They must have thought that there was some chance of their being followed, for they would never go out alone, and never after nightfall. During two weeks I drove behind them every day, and never once saw them separate. Drebber himself was drunk half the time, but Stangerson was not to be caught napping. I watched them late and early, but never saw the ghost of a chance; but I was not discouraged, for something told me that the hour had almost come. My only fear was that this thing in my chest might burst a little too soon and leave my work undone.

"At last, one evening I was driving up and down Torquay Terrace, as the street was called in which they boarded, when I saw a cab drive up to their door. Presently some luggage was brought out, and after a time Drebber and Stangerson followed it, and drove off. I whipped up my horse and kept within sight of them, feeling very ill at ease, for I feared that they were going to shift their quarters. At Euston Station they got out, and I left a boy to hold my horse, and followed them on to the platform. I heard them ask for the Liverpool train, and the guard answer that one had just gone and there would not be another for some hours. Stangerson seemed to be put out at that, but Drebber was rather pleased than otherwise. I got so close to them in the bustle that I could hear every word that passed between them. Drebber said that he had a little business of his own to do, and that if the other would wait for him he would soon rejoin him. His companion remonstrated with him, and reminded him that they had resolved to stick together. Drebber answered that the matter was a delicate one, and that he must go alone. I could not catch what Stangerson said to that, but the other burst out swearing, and reminded him that he was nothing more than his paid servant, and that he must not presume to dictate to him. On that the Secretary gave it up as a bad job, and simply bargained with him that if he missed the last train he should rejoin him at Halliday's Private Hotel; to which Drebber answered that he would be back on the platform before eleven, and made his way out of the station.

"The moment for which I had waited so long had at last come. I had my enemies within my power. Together they could protect each other, but singly they were at my mercy. I did not act, however, with undue precipitation. My plans were already formed. There is no satisfaction in vengeance unless the offender has time to realize who it is that strikes him, and why retribution has come upon him. I had my plans arranged by which I should have the opportunity of making the man who had wronged me understand that his old sin had found him out. It chanced that some days before a gentleman who had been engaged in looking over some houses in the Brixton Road had dropped the key of one of them in my carriage.[247] It was claimed that same evening, and returned; but in the interval I had taken a moulding of it, and had a duplicate constructed. By means of this I had access to at least one spot in this great city where I could rely upon being free from interruption. How to get Drebber to that house was the difficult problem which I had now to solve.

"He walked down the road and went into one or two liquor shops, staying for nearly half-an-hour in the last of them. When he came out, he staggered in his walk, and was evidently pretty well on. There was a hansom just in front of me, and he hailed it. I followed it so close that the nose of my horse was within a yard of his driver the whole way. We rattled across Waterloo Bridge[248] and through miles of streets, until, to my astonish-

247 Edwards suggests that if Holmes had looked at the lock when he first viewed the crime scene, he would have observed that it had not been forced. This would have led him, Edwards believes, to question the "gentleman who had been engaged in looking over some houses in the Brixton Road," presumably a house-agent. This witness, in turn, would have reported that the key had been lost but returned by the cabman. In this way, Holmes might have quickly been introduced to the criminal. "We can all do it, when it has been done," Edwards concludes self-mockingly.

248 Built between 1811 and 1817 over the Thames, this bridge was known as the "Bridge of Sighs" for the numerous suicides leaping from its railings. Thomas Hood's 1844 poem, "The Bridge of Sighs," mourns "One more Unfortunate, / Weary of breath, / Rashly importunate, / Gone to her death!" It was originally named the Strand Bridge until changed in 1816 by an Act of Parliament.

ment, we found ourselves back in the Terrace in which he had boarded. I could not imagine what his intention was in returning there; but I went on and pulled up my cab a hundred yards or so from the house. He entered it, and his hansom drove away. Give me a glass of water, if you please. My mouth gets dry with the talking."[249]

I handed him the glass, and he drank it down.

"That's better," he said. "Well, I waited for a quarter of an hour, or more, when suddenly there came a noise like people struggling inside the house. Next moment the door was flung open and two men appeared, one of whom was Drebber, and the other was a young chap whom I had never seen before. This fellow had Drebber by the collar, and when they came to the head of the steps he gave him a shove and a kick which sent him half across the road. 'You hound!' he cried, shaking his stick at him; 'I'll teach you to insult an honest girl!' He was so hot that I think he would have thrashed Drebber with his cudgel, only that the cur staggered away down the road as fast as his legs would carry him. He ran as far as the corner, and then, seeing my cab, he hailed me and jumped in. 'Drive me to Halliday's Private Hotel,' said he.

"When I had him fairly inside my cab, my heart jumped so with joy that I feared lest at this last moment my aneurism might go wrong. I drove along slowly, weighing in my own mind what it was best to do. I might take him right out into the country, and there in some deserted lane have my last interview with him. I had almost decided upon this, when he solved the problem for me. The craze for drink had seized him again, and he ordered me to pull up outside a gin palace. He went in, leaving word that I should wait for him. There he remained until closing time, and when he came out he was so far gone that I knew the game was in my own hands.

"Don't imagine that I intended to kill him in cold blood. It would only have been rigid justice if I had done so, but I could not bring myself to do it. I had long determined that he should have a show for his life if he chose to take advantage of it. Among the many billets which I have filled in America during my wandering life, I was once janitor and sweeper-out of the laboratory at York College.[250] One day the professor was lecturing on poisons, and he showed his students some alkaloid,

249 Given Hope's Herculean efforts to escape, heavy loss of blood, and near-strangulation by Lestrade, it seems peculiar that his only physical affliction seems to be a dry mouth. Should he not at least have needed some time to get his wind back? "Indeed the only people short of breath," writes Vernon Pennell, in his "Resumé of the Medical Life of John H. Watson, Late of the Army Medical Department," "were his captors who 'rose to their feet breathless and panting.' As Watson pronounced him *in extremis* and likely to die at any moment, one wonders why the violent struggle had not already precipitated the aneurismal burst which took place later in the comparative quietude of the prison cell, the night after his capture."

250 Christopher Morley identifies "York College" as the old medical college of New York University. "There is a York College in Nebraska," he explains, "but it was not founded until 1890." Dave M. Hershey, in "The True York College," proposes York College of Pennsylvania, then known as the York Collegiate Institute.

as he called it, which he had extracted from some South American arrow poison,[251] and which was so powerful that the least grain meant instant death. I spotted the bottle in which this preparation was kept, and when they were all gone, I helped myself to a little of it. I was a fairly good dispenser, so I worked this alkaloid into small, soluble pills, and each pill I put in a box with a similar pill made without the poison. I determined at the time that when I had my chance my gentlemen should each have a draw out of one of these boxes, while I ate the pill that remained. It would be quite as deadly and a good deal less noisy than firing across a handkerchief. From that day I had always my pill boxes about with me, and the time had now come when I was to use them.

"It was nearer one than twelve, and a wild, bleak night, blowing hard and raining in torrents. Dismal as it was outside, I was glad within—so glad that I could have shouted out from pure exultation. If any of you gentlemen have ever pined for a thing, and longed for it during twenty long years, and then suddenly found it within your reach, you would understand my feelings. I lit a cigar, and puffed at it to steady my nerves, but my hands were trembling and my temples throbbing with excitement. As I drove, I could see old John Ferrier and sweet Lucy looking at me out of the darkness and smiling at me, just as plain as I see you all in this room. All the way they were ahead of me, one on each side of the horse until I pulled up at the house in the Brixton Road.

"There was not a soul to be seen, nor a sound to be heard, except the dripping of the rain. When I looked in at the window, I found Drebber all huddled together in a drunken sleep. I shook him by the arm, 'It's time to get out,' I said.

" 'All right, cabby,' said he.

"I suppose he thought we had come to the hotel that he had mentioned, for he got out without another word, and followed me down the garden. I had to walk beside him to keep him steady, for he was still a little top-heavy. When we came to the door, I opened it and led him into the front room. I give you my word that all the way, the father and the daughter were walking in front of us.

" 'It's infernally dark,' said he, stamping about.

" 'We'll soon have a light,' I said, striking a match and put-

251 Hope presumably thought that he was using curare, but as J. Raymond Hendrickson indicates in "De Re Pharmaca," none of the details of Drebber's appearance support the use of that poison. Instead, Hendrickson concludes that the poison responsible for Drebber's death was nicotine, which, in its pure form, is deadly (one account of a nicotine-suicide recounts how the victim who drank the poison died even before he hit the floor). F. A. Allen theorises that the poison was an alkaloid derived from the Erythrina flowering tropical plant; he writes in "Devilish Drugs, Part 1," "Let us suggest that an odorous and more potent alkaloid than . . . erythroidine, from the seeds of *E. corraloides* [*sic*], awaits discovery by the explorer." In "The Poisons of the Canon," however, George B. Koelle expresses his belief that Hope must have confused a "South American arrow poison" with a "South African ordeal poison"—physostigmine or eserine. "This is highly potent, readily absorbed when taken by mouth, and the victim remains conscious nearly to the time of death; all these facts are consistent with Hope's account and Holmes's deductions."

"Who am I?"
Geo. Hutchinson, *A Study in Scarlet* (London: Ward, Lock Bowden, and Co., 1891)

ting it to a wax candle which I had brought with me. 'Now, Enoch Drebber,' I continued, turning to him, and holding the light to my own face, 'who am I?'

"He gazed at me with bleared, drunken eyes for a moment, and then I saw a horror spring up in them, and convulse his whole features, which showed me that he knew me. He stag-

" 'He gazed at me with bleared, drunken eyes for a moment, and then I saw a horror spring up in them, and convulse his whole features, which showed me that he knew me.' "
Richard Gutschmidt, *Späte Rache* (Stuttgart: Robert Lutz Verlag, 1902)

"He staggered back . . . and I saw the perspiration break out on his brow."
James Greig, *A Study in Scarlet*, n.d.

gered back with a livid face, and I saw the perspiration break out upon his brow, while his teeth chattered in his head. At the sight I leaned my back against the door and laughed loud and long. I had always known that vengeance would be sweet, but I had never hoped for the contentment of soul which now possessed me.

" 'You dog!' I said; 'I have hunted you from Salt Lake City to St. Petersburg, and you have always escaped me. Now, at last your wanderings have come to an end, for either you or I shall never see to-morrow's sun rise.' He shrunk still farther away as I spoke, and I could see on his face that he thought I was mad. So I was for the time. The pulses in my temples beat like sledge-hammers, and I believe I would have had a fit of some sort if the blood had not gushed from my nose and relieved me.

" 'What do you think of Lucy Ferrier now?' I cried, locking the door, and shaking the key in his face. 'Punishment has been slow in coming, but it has overtaken you at last.' I saw his coward lips tremble as I spoke. He would have begged for his life, but he knew well that it was useless.

"Choose and eat. There is death in the one and life in the other."
Charles Doyle, *A Study in Scarlet* (London and New York: Ward, Lock & Co., 1888)

" 'Would you murder me?' he stammered.

" 'There is no murder,' I answered. 'Who talks of murdering a mad dog? What mercy had you upon my poor darling, when you dragged her from her slaughtered father, and bore her away to your accursed and shameless harem?'

" 'It was not I who killed her father,' he cried.

" 'But it was you who broke her innocent heart,' I shrieked, thrusting the box before him. 'Let the high God judge between us. Choose and eat. There is death in one and life in the other. I shall take what you leave. Let us see if there is justice upon the earth, or if we are ruled by chance.'

"He cowered away with wild cries and prayers for mercy, but I drew my knife and held it to his throat until he had obeyed me. Then I swallowed the other, and we stood facing one another in silence for a minute or more, waiting to see which

"He cowered away with wild cries and prayers for mercy."
Arthur Twidle, *A Study in Scarlet*, collected in *Works of A. Conan Doyle* (New York: D. Appleton and Co., 1903)

was to live and which was to die. Shall I ever forget the look which came over his face when the first warning pangs told him that the poison was in his system? I laughed as I saw it, and held Lucy's marriage ring in front of his eyes. It was but for a moment, for the action of the alkaloid is rapid. A spasm of pain contorted his features; he threw his hands out in front of him, staggered, and then, with a hoarse cry, fell heavily upon the floor. I turned him over with my foot, and placed my hand upon his heart. There was no movement. He was dead!

"The blood had been streaming from my nose, but I had taken no notice of it. I don't know what it was that put it into my head to write upon the wall with it. Perhaps it was some mischievous idea of setting the police upon a wrong track, for I felt light-hearted and cheerful. I remembered a German being found in New York with RACHE written up above him, and it was argued at the time in the newspapers that the secret societies must have done it. I guessed that what puzzled the New Yorkers would puzzle the Londoners, so I dipped my finger in my own blood and printed it on a convenient place on the wall. Then I walked down to my cab and found that there was nobody about, and that the night was still very wild. I had

"He cowered away with wild cries and prayers for mercy."
Geo. Hutchinson, *A Study in Scarlet* (London: Ward, Lock Bowden, and Co., 1891)

driven some distance, when I put my hand into the pocket in which I usually kept Lucy's ring, and found that it was not there. I was thunderstruck at this, for it was the only memento that I had of her.[252] Thinking that I might have dropped it when I stooped over Drebber's body, I drove back, and leaving my cab in a side street, I went boldly up to the house—for I was ready to dare anything rather than lose the ring. When I arrived there, I walked right into the arms of a police-officer who was coming out, and only managed to disarm his suspicions by pretending to be hopelessly drunk.

"That was how Enoch Drebber came to his end. All I had to do then was to do as much for Stangerson, and so pay off John Ferrier's debt. I knew that he was staying at Halliday's Private Hotel, and I hung about all day, but he never came out. I fancy that he suspected something when Drebber failed to put in an appearance. He was cunning, was Stangerson, and always on his guard. If he thought he could keep me off by staying indoors he was very much mistaken. I soon found out which

252 Hope's attachment to the ring seems somewhat misplaced, since it was a gift not from Lucy Ferrier to him but rather from Drebber to Lucy on their wedding day. (Remember that Hope obtained it by snatching it off the dead Lucy's finger.) "One could understand his keeping it," D. Martin Dakin muses,

> to flourish in Drebber's face when he taxed him with his crime, as indeed he did; but once that was done, why should he retain any sentimental regard (even at the risk of his own liberty) for the thing which, even if it was the only memento he had of Lucy, was the badge of her union with the hated enemy he had just killed? One would expect him to regard it with loathing; and to have left it with the body would have been more in accordance with his idea of revenge. His . . . was indeed a baffling mentality.

was the window of his bedroom, and early next morning I took advantage of some ladders which were lying in the lane behind the hotel, and so made my way into his room in the grey of the dawn. I woke him up and told him that the hour had come when he was to answer for the life he had taken so long before. I described Drebber's death to him, and I gave him the same choice of the poisoned pills. Instead of grasping at the chance of safety which that offered him, he sprang from his bed and flew at my throat. In self-defence I stabbed him to the heart. It would have been the same in any case, for Providence would never have allowed his guilty hand to pick out anything but the poison.

"I have little more to say, and it's as well, for I am about done up. I went on cabbing it for a day or so, intending to keep at it until I could save enough to take me back to America. I was standing in the yard[253] when a ragged youngster asked if there was a cabby there called Jefferson Hope, and said that his cab

"He sprang from his bed and flew at my throat."
Geo. Hutchinson, *A Study in Scarlet* (London: Ward, Lock Bowden, and Co., 1891)

253 The "yard" was the storage place for off-duty cabs, usually maintained by the cab-owner who leased out the vehicles to drivers for a share of the fares.

was wanted by a gentleman at 221B, Baker Street. I went round, suspecting no harm,[254] and the next thing I knew, this young man here had the bracelets on my wrists, and as neatly snackled[255] as ever I saw in my life. That's the whole of my story, gentlemen. You may consider me to be a murderer; but I hold that I am just as much an officer of justice as you are."

So thrilling had the man's narrative been, and his manner was so impressive that we had sat silent and absorbed. Even the professional detectives, *blasé* as they were in every detail of crime, appeared to be keenly interested in the man's story. When he finished, we sat for some minutes in a stillness which was only broken by the scratching of Lestrade's pencil as he gave the finishing touches to his shorthand account.

"There is only one point on which I should like a little more information," Sherlock Holmes said at last. "Who was your accomplice who came for the ring which I advertised?"

The prisoner winked at my friend jocosely. "I can tell my own secrets," he said, "but I don't get other people into trouble. I saw your advertisement, and I thought it might be a plant, or it might be the ring which I wanted. My friend volunteered to go and see.[256] I think you'll own he did it smartly."

"Not a doubt of that," said Holmes, heartily.

"Now, gentlemen," the Inspector remarked gravely, "the forms of the law must be complied with. On Thursday the prisoner will be brought before the magistrates, and your attendance will be required. Until then I will be responsible for him." He rang the bell as he spoke, and Jefferson Hope was led off by a couple of warders, while my friend and I made our way out of the Station and took a cab back to Baker Street.

254 It is this naïve statement that prompts C. B. H. Vaill ("A Study in Intellects") to nominate Hope as "Number One Dolt." "Since Hope had by this time completed his second murder," Vaill marvels, "it would be reasonable to suppose that his caution would be increased. But no; the fact that he was singled out of all the cabbies in London by name, and directed to call at the very address which had proven to be a trap only a short time before, did not arouse even that 'slightest suspicion' which Holmes feared."

Larry Van Gelder proposes that Hope's actions were motivated by a desire to commit suicide. Recognising Holmes's address, he deliberately allowed himself to be entrapped, hoping that his aneurysm would kill him. "This theory," Edgar W. Smith comments, "seems much more plausible, it must be admitted, than the incredible system of events in which Watson would have us believe."

255 Corrected to "shackled" in later texts, but the word seems an apt Watsonian *portmanteau*. "Snaffled" is defined in the *Slang Dictionary* as "arrested, 'pulled up,'—so termed from a kind of horse's bit, called a SNAFFLE." The *Oxford English Dictionary* accepts the word as meaning "to hold fast," of obscure origins, and cites this usage as its first appearance.

256 Hope was a stranger to London. Therefore, how could he know of Holmes or have a friend in London who would help him—and who, conveniently, was an expert female impersonator? Robert R. Pattrick believes he knows who the "friend" must have been: an employee of Holmes's future nemesis, Professor Moriarty, whom Hope hired for a healthy fee. Pattrick supposes that Holmes was aware of the mastermind's role in the affair, writing, in "Moriarty Was There": "The agent escaped, and Hope would not give evidence.

But the significance of the agent was not lost on Holmes." Only a few minutes earlier, Patrick points out, Holmes had warned Gregson and Lestrade: "We have a shrewd and desperate man to deal with, who is supported, as I have had occasion to prove, by another who is as clever as himself. . . . I am bound to say that I consider these men to be more than a match for the official force."

However, others suggest an accomplice already known to Hope: George R. Skornickel, Jr., in "Who Was the Mysterious Mrs. Sawyer?," makes a case for John Ferrier's "acquaintance who was bound for the Nevada mountains," while Brad Keefauver, in "The Hundred-Year-Old Mystery of Mrs. Sawyer Solved," reveals her to be Lucy Ferrier-Drebber.

CHAPTER VII

The Conclusion

WE HAD ALL been warned to appear before the magistrates upon the Thursday; but when the Thursday came there was no occasion for our testimony. A higher Judge had taken the matter in hand, and Jefferson Hope had been summoned before a tribunal where strict justice would be meted out to him. On the very night after his capture the aneurism burst, and he was found in the morning stretched upon the floor of the cell, with a placid smile upon his face, as though he had been able in his dying moments to look back upon a useful life, and on work well done.

"Gregson and Lestrade will be wild about his death," Holmes remarked, as we chatted it over next evening. "Where will their grand advertisement be now?"

"I don't see that they had very much to do with his capture," I answered.

"What you do in this world is a matter of no consequence," returned my companion, bitterly. "The question is, what can you make people believe that you have done? Never mind," he continued, more brightly, after a pause. "I would not have missed the investigation for anything. There has been no bet-

"A higher judge had taken the matter in hand."
Geo. Hutchinson, *A Study in Scarlet* (London: Ward, Lock Bowden, and Co., 1891)

ter case within my recollection. Simple as it was, there were several most instructive points about it."

"Simple!" I ejaculated.

"Well, really, it can hardly be described as otherwise," said Sherlock Holmes, smiling at my surprise. "The proof of its intrinsic simplicity is, that without any help save a few very ordinary deductions I was able to lay my hand upon the criminal within three days."

"That is true," said I.

"I have already explained to you that what is out of the common is usually a guide rather than a hindrance. In solving a problem of this sort, the grand thing is to be able to reason backwards. That is a very useful accomplishment and a very easy one, but people do not practise it much. In the every-day affairs of life it is more useful to reason forwards, and so the other comes to be neglected. There are fifty who can reason synthetically for one who can reason analytically."

"I confess," said I, "that I do not quite follow you."

"I hardly expected that you would. Let me see if I can make it clearer. Most people, if you describe a train of events to them, will tell you what the result would be. They can put those events together in their minds, and argue from them that something will come to pass. There are few people, however, who, if you told them a result, would be able to evolve from their own inner consciousness what the steps were which led up to that result. This power is what I mean when I talk of reasoning backwards, or analytically."

"I understand," said I.

"Now this was a case in which you were given the result and had to find everything else for yourself. Now let me endeavour to show you the different steps in my reasoning. To begin at the beginning. I approached the house, as you know, on foot, and with my mind entirely free from all impressions. I naturally began by examining the roadway, and there, as I have already explained to you, I saw clearly the marks of a cab, which, I ascertained by inquiry, must have been there during the night. I satisfied myself that it was a cab and not a private carriage by the narrow gauge of the wheels. The ordinary London growler is considerably less wide than a gentleman's brougham.[257]

"This was the first point gained. I then walked slowly down the garden path, which happened to be composed of a clay soil, peculiarly suitable for taking impressions. No doubt it appeared to you to be a mere trampled line of slush, but to my trained eyes every mark upon its surface had a meaning. There is no branch of detective science which is so important and so much neglected as the art of tracing footsteps.[258] Happily, I have always laid great stress upon it, and much practice has made it second nature to me. I saw the heavy footmarks of the constables, but I saw also the track of the two men who had first passed through the garden. It was easy to tell that they had been before the others, because in places their marks had been entirely obliterated by the others coming upon the top of them. In this way my second link was formed, which told me that the nocturnal visitors were two in number, one remarkable for his height (as I calculated from the length of his stride), and the other fashionably dressed, to judge from the small and elegant impression left by his boots.

"On entering the house this last inference was confirmed. My well-booted man lay before me. The tall one, then, had done the murder, if murder there was. There was no wound upon the dead man's person, but the agitated expression upon his face assured me that he had foreseen his fate before it came upon him. Men who die from heart disease, or any sudden nat-

257 The brougham was originally designed (*ca.* 1838) by Henry Peter Brougham, a future baron and former lord chancellor of England. A four-wheeled covered carriage, it was pulled by one horse and had an open driver's seat in the front.

A brougham.

258 So important did Holmes think this subject that he eventually wrote a monograph about it. In *The Sign of Four*, he speaks of his work entitled "Upon the tracing of footsteps, with some remarks upon the use of plaster of Paris as a preserver of impresses."

ural cause, never by any chance exhibit agitation upon their features. Having sniffed the dead man's lips, I detected a slightly sour smell,[259] and I came to the conclusion that he had had poison forced upon him. Again, I argued that it had been forced upon him from the hatred and fear expressed upon his face. By the method of exclusion, I had arrived at this result, for no other hypothesis would meet the facts. Do not imagine that it was a very unheard-of idea. The forcible administration of poison is by no means a new thing in criminal annals. The cases of Dolsky in Odessa, and of Leturier in Montpellier, will occur at once to any toxicologist.

"And now came the great question as to the reason why. Robbery had not been the object of the murder, for nothing was taken. Was it politics, then, or was it a woman? That was the question which confronted me. I was inclined from the first to the latter supposition. Political assassins are only too glad to do their work and to fly. This murder had, on the contrary, been done most deliberately, and the perpetrator had left his tracks all over the room, showing that he had been there all the time. It must have been a private wrong, and not a political one, which called for such a methodical revenge. When the inscription was discovered upon the wall, I was more inclined than ever to my opinion. The thing was too evidently a blind. When the ring was found, however, it settled the question. Clearly the murderer had used it to remind his victim of some dead or absent woman. It was at this point that I asked Gregson whether he had inquired in his telegram to Cleveland as to any particular point in Mr. Drebber's former career. He answered, you remember, in the negative.

"I then proceeded to make a careful examination of the room, which confirmed me in my opinion as to the murderer's height, and furnished me with the additional details as to the Trichinopoly cigar and the length of his nails. I had already come to the conclusion, since there were no signs of a struggle, that the blood which covered the floor had burst from the murderer's nose in his excitement. I could perceive that the track of blood coincided with the track of his feet, It is seldom that any man, unless he is very full-blooded, breaks out in this way through emotion, so I hazarded the opinion that the criminal was probably a robust and ruddy-faced man. Events proved that I had judged correctly.

259 A remarkable feat, taking into account the quantity of gin consumed by Drebber.

"Having left the house, I proceeded to do what Gregson had neglected. I telegraphed to the head of the police at Cleveland,[260] limiting my inquiry to the circumstances connected with the marriage of Enoch Drebber. The answer was conclusive. It told me that Drebber had already applied for the protection of the law against an old rival in love, named Jefferson Hope, and that this same Hope was at present in Europe. I knew now that I held the clue to the mystery in my hand, and all that remained was to secure the murderer.

"I had already determined in my own mind that the man who had walked into the house with Drebber was none other than the man who had driven the cab. The marks in the road showed me that the horse had wandered on in a way which would have been impossible had there been anyone in charge of it. Where, then, could the driver be, unless he were inside the house? Again, it is absurd to suppose that any sane man would carry out a deliberate crime under the very eyes, as it were, of a third person, who was sure to betray him. Lastly, supposing one man wished to dog another through London, what better means could he adopt than to turn cabdriver? All these considerations led me to the irresistible conclusion that Jefferson Hope was to be found among the jarveys[261] of the Metropolis.

"If he had been one, there was no reason to believe that he had ceased to be. On the contrary, from his point of view, any sudden change would be likely to draw attention to himself. He would, probably, for a time at least, continue to perform his duties. There was no reason to suppose that he was going under an assumed name. Why should he change his name in a country where no one knew his original one? I therefore organized my street Arab detective corps, and sent them systematically to every cab proprietor in London until they ferreted out the man that I wanted. How well they succeeded, and how quickly I took advantage of it, are still fresh in your recollection. The murder of Stangerson was an incident which was entirely unexpected, but which could hardly in any case have been prevented. Through it, as you know, I came into possession of the pills, the existence of which I had already surmised. You see, the whole thing is a chain of logical sequences without a break or flaw."

"It is wonderful!" I cried. "Your merits should be publicly

260 Ralph Mendelson, in "Hero Neglected, A True Account," identifies this person as Jacob W. Schmitt, the Cleveland superintendent of police from 1871 to 1893. While relatively unheralded in Watson's account, the efficient Schmitt deserves his own share of credit in the success of Holmes's career, at least according to Mendelson. "If Superintendent Schmitt had not acted promptly and furnished even more information than Holmes had requested," he observes, "Holmes would have been discredited in the eyes of Scotland Yard. Worse than that, he would have been discredited in the eyes of Dr. Watson. . . . And without the admiring Watson to bolster his career, Holmes would have remained the unknown consultant that he was when Watson first met him."

261 A jarvey was a driver of a hackney coach, or any carriage available for hire. Brewer's *Dictionary of Phrase and Fable* explains that the term is "[s]aid to be a contraction of Geoffrey; and the reason why this name was selected was because coachmen say to their horses gee-o, and Ge-o is a contraction of Geoffrey. Ballantine says, that one Jarvis, a noted hackney-coachman who was hanged, was the original Jarvey." Another suggested source is St. Gervais, whose symbol is a whip.

recognized. You should publish an account of the case. If you won't, I will for you."

"You may do what you like, Doctor," he answered. "See here!" he continued, handing a paper over to me, "look at this!"

It was the *Echo* for the day, and the paragraph to which he pointed was devoted to the case in question.

"The public," it said, "have lost a sensational treat through the sudden death of the man Hope, who was suspected of the murder of Mr. Enoch Drebber and of Mr. Joseph Stangerson. The details of the case will probably be never known now, though we are informed upon good authority, that the crime was the result of an old-standing and romantic feud, in which love and Mormonism bore a part. It seems that both the victims belonged, in their younger days, to the Latter Day Saints, and Hope, the deceased prisoner, hails also from Salt Lake City. If the case has had no other effect, it, at least, brings out in the most striking manner the efficiency of our detective

" 'You may do what you like, Doctor.' "
Geo. Hutchinson, *A Study in Scarlet* (London: Ward, Lock Bowden, and Co., 1891)

262 Holmes's habit of ending his early cases with a quotation or saying, here attributed to Watson, apes the reported cases of "that inferior fellow" M. Dupin. (See note 83, above.) Morris Rosenblum, in "Hafiz and Horace, Huxtable and Holmes," translates the quotation (from Horace's *First Satire*) as: "The people hiss at me but I applaud myself in my own home, as I gaze fondly at the coins in my strong-box."

Holmes exhibits a disdain of publicity in numerous cases. As he says in "The Problem of Thor Bridge": "It may surprise you to know that I prefer to work anonymously, and that it is the problem itself which attracts me." He later disparages Watson's accounts of his cases as ruining "what might have been an instructive and even classical series of demonstrations" ("The Abbey Grange"). Yet the growth of his practice likely occurred in large part because of Watson's publications. The subject of Holmes's ambivalence about publicity is considered in more detail in this editor's "What Do We Really Know About Sherlock Holmes and John H. Watson?"

" 'See here! Look at this!' "
Richard Gutschmidt, *Späte Rache*
(Stuttgart: Robert Lutz Verlag, 1902)

police force, and will serve as a lesson to all foreigners that they will do wisely to settle their feuds at home, and not to carry them on to British soil. It is an open secret that the credit of this smart capture belongs entirely to the well-known Scotland Yard officials, Messrs. Lestrade and Gregson. The man was apprehended, it appears, in the rooms of a certain Mr. Sherlock Holmes, who has himself, as an amateur, shown some talent in the detective line and who, with such instructors, may hope in time to attain to some degree of their skill. It is expected that a testimonial of some sort will be presented to the two officers as a fitting recognition of their services."

"Didn't I tell you so when we started?" cried Sherlock Holmes with a laugh. "That's the result of all our Study in Scarlet: to get them a testimonial!"

"Never mind," I answered, "I have all the facts in my journal, and the public shall know them. In the meantime you must make yourself contented by the consciousness of success, like the Roman miser—

Populus me sibilat, at mihi plaudo
Ipse domi simul ac nummos contemplar in arca.[262]

APPENDIX

"Mr. Sherlock Holmes"

By Dr. Joseph Bell[263]

It is not entirely a bad sign of this weary, worn-out century that in this, its last decade, even the petty street-bred people are beginning, as the nurses say, to take notice. An insatiable and generally prurient curiosity, as to the doings of the class immediately above us is pandered to by the society journals, and encouraged even by the daily newspapers. Such information is valueless intellectually, and tends to moral degradation; it exer-

Dr. A. Conan Doyle.

263 Dr. Bell's essay first appeared in *The Bookman* (London) for December 1892 under the title "The Adventures of Sherlock Holmes" and is reprinted in the 1893 Ward, Lock & Bowden Ltd. edition of *A Study in Scarlet.*

cises none of the senses, and pauperises the imagination. Celebrities at home, illustrated interviews, society scandal on all levels merely titillate the itching ear of the gossip. Memoirs, recollections, anecdotes of the Bar or of the Academy are much more interesting, and may be valuable as throwing sidelights on history, but still only amuse and help to kill the time of which we forget the value. But in the last few years there has been a distinct demand for books which, to a certain poor extent, encourage thought and stimulate observation. The whole "Gamekeeper at Home" series[264] and its imitations opened the eyes of town dwellers, who had forgotten or never known White of Selborne,[265] to the delightful sights and sounds that were the harvest of the open eye and ear. Something of the same interest is given to the "crowded city's horrible street" by the suggestions of crime and romance, of curiosity and its gratification, which we find written with more or less cleverness in the enormous mass of so-called detective literature under which the press groans. Every bookstall has its shilling shocker, and every magazine which aims at a circulation must have its mystery of robbery or murder. Most of these are poor enough stuff; complicated plots, which can be discounted in the first chapter, extraordinary coincidences, preternaturally gifted detectives, who make discoveries more or less useless by flashes of insight which no one else can understand, become wearisome in their sameness, and the interest, such as it is, centres only in the results and not in the methods. We may admire Lecocq [*sic*], but we do not see ourselves in his shoes. Dr. Conan Doyle has made a well-deserved success for his detective stories, and made the name of his hero beloved by the boys of this country by the marvellous cleverness of his method. He shows how easy it is, if only you can observe, to find out a great deal as to the works and ways of your innocent and unconscious friends, and, by an extension of the same method, to baffle the criminal and lay bare the manner of his crime. There is nothing new under the sun. Voltaire taught us the method of Zadig,[266] and every good teacher of medicine or surgery exemplifies every day in his teaching and practice the method and its results. The precise and intelligent recognition and appreciation of minor differences is the real essential factor in all successful medical diagnosis. Carried into ordinary life, granted the presence of an insatiable curiosity and fairly

264 John Richard Jeffries (1848–1887) was a naturalist, essayist, and novelist whose twenty books included numerous semi-mystical tales of nature. His entry in the *Encyclopædia Britannica* describes him as one whose "prophetic vision was unappreciated in his own Victorian age. . . . By combining detailed observation with a mystic apprehension of nature, he was a master both of a straightforward descriptive style and of a sensuous, poetic prose." Originally a reporter for the *North Wilts Herald*, Jeffries got perhaps his biggest break when the *Times* published his 4,000-word letter about the Wiltshire agricultural labourer. *The Gamekeeper at Home*, a nonfiction work containing his musings on country life and nature, was serialised in the *Pall Mall Gazette* in 1878 and published in book form in 1887. Despite being a prolific writer, Jeffries suffered from poor health, and he died of tuberculosis at the age of thirty-eight, as yet largely unrecognised in the literary world.

265 Gilbert White (1720–1793), of Selborne, England, was a naturalist, poet, and clergyman. He is best known for his great work *The Natural History and Antiquities of Selborne* (1789), a collection of letters written to his friends Thomas Pennant and Daines Barrington over the course of twenty years. *The Cambridge History of English and American Literature* (1907–1921) calls it "the solitary classic of natural history. It is not easy to give, in a few words, a reason for its remarkable success. It is, in fact, not so much a logically arranged and systematic book as an invaluable record of the life work of a simple and refined man who succeeded in picturing himself as well as what he saw."

266 Voltaire's short novel *Zadig Memnon* (1747) is generally thought to be one of the earliest examples of "Sherlockian" deduction. In the novel, Zadig is a young Babylonian who suffers Job-like privations in learning that acute senses, you have Sherlock Holmes as he astonishes his somewhat dense friend Watson; carried out in a specialised training, you have Sherlock Holmes the skilled detective.

Dr. Conan Doyle's education as a student of medicine taught him how to observe, and his practice, both as a general practitioner and a specialist, has been a splendid training for a man such as he is, gifted with eyes, memory, and imagination. Eyes and ears which can see and hear, memory to record at once and to recall at pleasure the impressions of the senses, and an imagination capable of weaving a theory or piecing together a broken chain or unravelling a tangled clue, such are implements of his trade to a successful diagnostician. If in addition the doctor is also a born story-teller, then it is a mere matter of choice whether he writes detective stories or keeps his strength for a great historical romance as is the "White Company."[267] Syme, one of the greatest teachers of surgical diagnosis that ever lived, had a favourite illustration which, as a tradition of his school, has made a mark on Dr. Conan Doyle's method, "Try to learn the features of a disease or injury as precisely as you know the features, the gait, the tricks of manner of your most intimate friend." Him, even in a crowd, you can recognise at once; it may be a crowd of men dressed alike, and each having his complement of eyes, nose, hair, and limbs; in every essential they resemble each other, only in trifles do they differ; and yet, by knowing these trifles well, you make your diagnosis or recognition with ease. So it is with disease of mind or body or morals. Racial peculiarities, hereditary tricks of manner, accent, occupation or the want of it, education, environment of all kinds, by their little trivial impressions gradually mould or curve the individual, and leave finger marks or chisel scores which the expert can recognise. The great broad characteristics which at a glance can be recognised as indicative of heart disease or consumption, chronic drunkenness or long-continued loss of blood, are the common property of the veriest tyro in medicine, while to masters of their art there are myriads of signs eloquent and instructive, but which need the educated eye to detect. A fair-sized and valuable book has lately been written on the one symptom, the pulse; to any one but a trained physician it seems as much an absurdity as is Sherlock Holmes' immortal treatise on the one hundred and fourteen varieties of tobacco ash. The greatest stride that has

good and evil are inexorably intertwined, and that happiness may come only after great suffering. Eventually, he becomes a king and a sage. What Bell means by the "method of Zadig" is his tendency to observe things closely and—rather like Holmes—draw conclusions from what he sees. When the king's horse and the queen's dog are stolen, Zadig is questioned, and, although he states that he has not seen the missing animals, he is able to describe them minutely. He is immediately arrested for the theft but released when the stolen animals are found. Zadig is then fined for having lied about seeing the animals. He defends himself, however, by explaining how he " 'observed the marks of a horse's shoes, all at equal distances. . . . This must be a horse, I said to myself, that gallops excellently. The dust on the trees in the road that was but seven feet wide was a little brushed off, at the distance of three feet and a half from the middle of the road. This horse, said I, has a tail three and a half feet long, which [was] whisked to the right and left . . .' " He also makes similar observations about the dog. Eventually he is refunded his fine, only to pay almost all of it to his lawyers. When a prisoner later escapes and Zadig observes him through a window, Zadig determines not to become involved but is fined for failing to report his evidence. " 'Great God!' said he to himself, 'what a misfortune it is to walk in a wood through which the queen's spaniel or the king's horse has passed! How dangerous to look out at a window! And how difficult to be happy in this life!' " (Translation by Tobias Smollett, 1749.) Fortunately, Holmes did not share Zadig's conclusions.

267 Conan Doyle's fine novel *The White Company* was published in 1891 (London: Smith, Elder & Co.). The tale of knights, fair ladies, war, chivalry, and honour is set in the reign of Edward III (1312–1377) and contains a wealth of historically accurate description.

been made of late years in preventive and diagnostic medicine consists in the recognition and differentiation by bacteriological research of those minute organisms which disseminate cholera and fever, tubercle and anthrax. The importance of the infinitely little is incalculable. Poison a well at Mecca with the cholera bacillus, and the holy water which the pilgrims carry off in their bottles will infect a continent, and the rags of the victims of the plague will terrify every seaport in Christendom.

Trained as he has been to notice and appreciate minute detail, Dr. Doyle saw how he could interest his intelligent readers by taking them into his confidence, and showing his mode of working. He created a shrewd, quick-sighted, inquisitive man, half doctor, half virtuoso, with plenty of spare time, a retentive memory, and perhaps with the best gift of all—the power of unloading the mind of all the burden of trying to remember unnecessary details. Holmes tells Watson: "A man should keep his little brain-attic stocked with all the furniture that he is likely to use, as the rest he can put away in the lumber-room of his library, where he can get it if he wants it."[268] But to him the petty results of environment, the sign-manuals of labour, the stains of trade, the incidents of travel, have living interest, as they tend to satisfy an insatiable, almost inhuman, because impersonal curiosity. He puts the man in the position of an amateur, and therefore irresponsible, detective, who is consulted in all sorts of cases, and then he lets us see how he works. He makes him explain to the good Watson the trivial, or apparently trivial, links in his chain of evidence. These are at once so obvious, when explained, and so easy, once you know them, that the ingenuous reader at once feels, and says to himself, I also could do this; life is not so dull after all; I will keep my eyes open, and find out things. The gold watch, with its scratched keyhole and pawnbrokers' marks, told such an easy tale about Watson's brother.[269] The dusty old billycock hat revealed that its master had taken to drinking some years ago, and had got his hair cut yesterday.[270] The tiny thorn-prick and fearsome footmark of the thing that was neither a child nor a monkey enabled Holmes to identify and capture the Andaman Islander.[271] Yet, after all, you say, there is nothing wonderful; we could all do the same.

The experienced physician and the trained surgeon every day, in their examinations of the humblest patient, have to go

268 "The Five Orange Pips." Holmes makes a similar remark in *A Study in Scarlet.*

269 *The Sign of Four*, in which Holmes deduces the existence of Watson's brother and his descent into alcoholism from scratches on Watson's newly acquired watch.

270 "The Blue Carbuncle." Here, in a *tour de force*, Holmes makes a series of deductions about the unfortunate Henry Baker from his lost hat, to be proved virtually one hundred percent correct when they later meet.

271 Bell refers here to the pygmy Tonga and his characteristic blow-gun (*The Sign of Four*).

through a similar process of reasoning, quick or slow according to the personal equations of each, almost automatic in the experienced man, laboured and often erratic in the tyro, yet requiring just the same simple requisites, senses to notice facts, and education and intelligence to apply them. Mere acuteness of the senses is not enough. Your Indian tracker will tell you that the footprint on the leaves was not a redskin's, but a paleface's, because it marked a shoeprint, but it needs an expert in shoe-leather to tell where that shoe was made. A sharp-eyed detective may notice the thumb-mark of a grimy or bloody hand on the velvet or the mirror, but it needs all the scientific knowledge of a Galton[272] to render the ridges and furrows of the stain visible and permanent, and then to identify by their sign-manual the suspected thief or murderer. Sherlock Holmes has acute senses, and the special education and information that make these valuable; and he can afford to let us into the secrets of his method. But in addition to the creation of his hero, Dr. Conan Doyle in this remarkable series of stories has proved himself a born story-teller. He has had the wit to devise excellent plots, interesting complications; he tells them in honest Saxon-English with directness and pith; and, above all his other merits, his stories are absolutely free from padding. He knows how delicious brevity is, how everything tends to be too long, and he has given us stories that we can read at a sitting between dinner and coffee, and we have not a chance to forget the beginning before we reach the end. The ordinary detective story, from Gaboriau[273] or Boisgobey[274] down to the latest shocker, really needs an effort of memory quite misplaced to keep the circumstances of the crimes and all the wrong scents of the various meddlers before the wearied reader. Dr. Doyle never gives you a chance to forget an incident or miss a point.

272 Francis Galton (1822–1911) was an anthropologist and the half-first cousin of Charles Darwin, and is widely credited with having fathered the science of fingerprinting. In 1892, after expanding upon the research of Sir William Herschel and Dr. Henry Faulds, he published the book *Finger Prints*, which not only determined that no two people's fingerprints were alike but also introduced a classification system that broke down the patterns of each print's loops, arches, and whorls. This system was developed further by Edward R. Henry, future commissioner of the London metropolitan police. Following the 1893 endorsement of the Troup Committee (named after the longtime civil servant and Home Office figure Edward Troup, a Scot who pioneered the practice of delegation of responsibility in the office), fingerprinting was successfully introduced in India in 1897, and in 1901 Scotland Yard established its own fingerprint bureau using the so-called Galton-Henry system (or Galton's Details), which remains the preferred classification system today. Galton was knighted in 1909.

For more on Galton, Herschel, and Faulds, see "Sherlock Holmes and Fingerprinting" in *The New Annotated Sherlock Holmes*, Volume II, page 860.

273 See note 85, above.

274 Fortuné du Boisgobey (1824–1891) was a French writer of fiction. Although largely forgotten today, his police stories enjoyed wide circulation, and many of them were translated into English. These included *Les Mystères du nouveau Paris* (1876), *Le Demi-Monde sous la Terreur* (1877), *Les Nuits de Constantinople* (1882), *Le Cri du sang* (1885), and *La Main froide* (1889). Boisgobey's 1878 novel *Le Vieillesse de Monsieur Lecoq* is, as its title indicates, about Gaboriau's detective-hero.

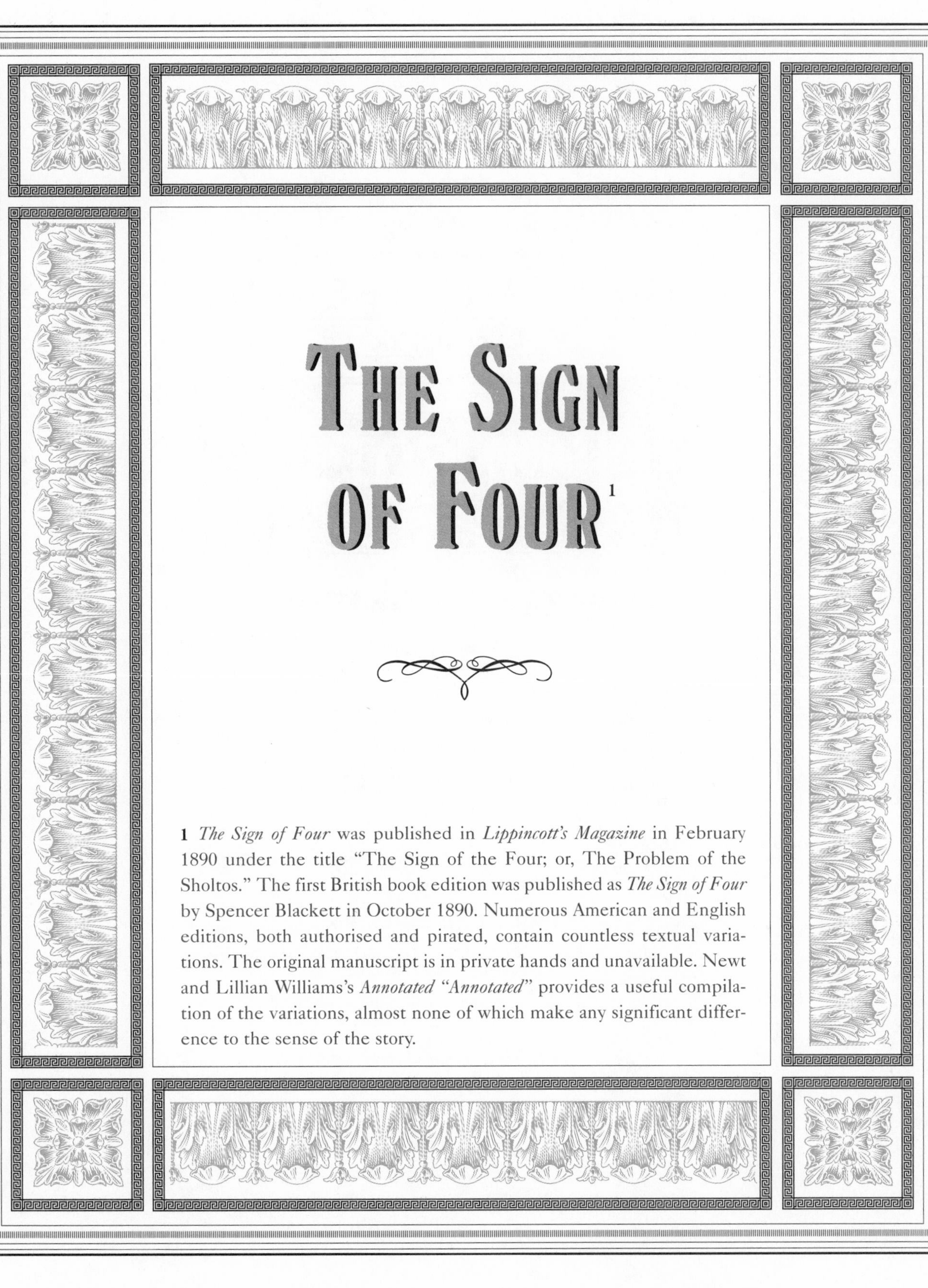

The Sign of Four[1]

1 *The Sign of Four* was published in *Lippincott's Magazine* in February 1890 under the title "The Sign of the Four; or, The Problem of the Sholtos." The first British book edition was published as *The Sign of Four* by Spencer Blackett in October 1890. Numerous American and English editions, both authorised and pirated, contain countless textual variations. The original manuscript is in private hands and unavailable. Newt and Lillian Williams's *Annotated "Annotated"* provides a useful compilation of the variations, almost none of which make any significant difference to the sense of the story.

This Number Contains a Complete Story,

THE SIGN OF THE FOUR

BY A. CONAN DOYLE.

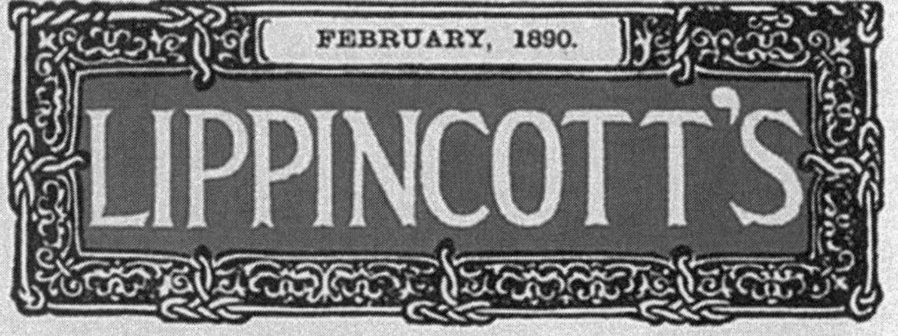

MONTHLY MAGAZINE.

CONTENTS.

PRICE ONE SHILLING.

London: WARD, LOCK AND CO., Salisbury Square, E.C.

Philadelphia: J. B. Lippincott Co.

The Sign of the Four.

(London: *Lippincott's Monthly Magazine*, February 1890)

The Sign of Four

No longer the newly minted consulting detective of A Study in Scarlet, *Holmes is at his most confident in* The Sign of Four *(1890), irresistibly drawn to the plight of his client, Mary Morstan, a beautiful woman plagued by a mysterious past. Holmes occupies centre-stage for virtually the full length of this supremely satisfying tale of detection, while Watson, not to be outpaced, comes into full flower as a human being in a case that sadly shows Holmes steeped in his drugs and ends with the breakup of the shared lodgings of the two men in Baker Street. Only seven years have passed since the events of* A Study in Scarlet, *but Holmes seems in the interim to have accumulated a lifetime's worth of experience, which he brings to bear on an adventure—rooted in the Indian Mutiny—that is packed with cinematic elements: occult figures of a pigmy and a wooden-legged man, a desperate hunt, a dependable dog, and a breathless chase down the Thames. The subject of English colonialism and its impact on the Victorian world is encapsulated during the final minutes of the novel in the back-story of murder, robbery, betrayal, and revenge related by Holmes's prey.*

CHAPTER I

The Science of Deduction[2]

SHERLOCK HOLMES TOOK his bottle from the corner of the mantelpiece, and his hypodermic syringe[3] from its neat morocco case. With his long, white, nervous fingers he adjusted the delicate needle and rolled back his left shirtcuff. For some little time his eyes rested thoughtfully upon the sinewy forearm and wrist, all dotted and scarred with innumerable puncture-marks. Finally, he thrust the sharp point home, pressed down the tiny piston, and sank back into the velvet-lined arm-chair with a long sigh of satisfaction.[4]

Three times a day for many months I had witnessed this performance, but custom had not reconciled my mind to it. On the contrary, from day to day I had become more irritable at the sight, and my conscience swelled nightly within me at the thought that I had lacked the courage to protest. Again and again I had registered a vow that I should deliver my soul upon the subject; but there was that in the cool, nonchalant air of my companion which made him the last man with whom one would care to take anything approaching to a liberty. His great powers, his masterly manner, and the experience which I had

2 Note that the chapter has the same title as Chapter II of *A Study in Scarlet*. Watson apparently felt compelled to reintroduce Holmes, inasmuch as this was only the second tale published about him (publication of the series of short stories known as the *Adventures* did not commence until 1891).

3 Dr. Kohki Naganuma, a doctor of economics and not medicine, notes, in "Sherlock Holmes and Cocaine," that Charles Gabriel Pravaz (1791–1853), a surgeon in Lyons, invented the hypodermic syringe in 1853 but that Carl Ludwig Schleich (1859–1922), of Berlin, was the first surgeon to use cocaine solution in hypodermic injection, and in sufficient dilution; this use occurred in 1891. Independently of Pravaz, the Scottish physician Alexander Wood (1817–1884) also developed a hypodermic syringe, which he used in 1855 to inject a patient with morphia. Naganuma

finds the evidence inconclusive that Holmes actually injected cocaine. But Dr. Julian Wolff (a medical doctor) replies, in "A Narcotic Monograph," that in fact the first use of cocaine by injection was in 1884, by the American Dr. William S. Halsted (1852–1922). This was "early enough so that it was no anachronism for Holmes to be taking cocaine injections when Watson said he was."

Jack Tracy and Jim Berkey, in *Subcutaneously, My Dear Watson*, write that at the time of *The Sign of Four*, "the hypodermic injection of morphia had been commonplace, among both physicians and addicts, for thirty years and more." However, Holmes was not injecting cocaine intravenously but, rather, subcutaneously (as physicians generally preferred) or intramuscularly (as most morphine users did). "There was a universal belief that intravenous injection put an undue strain on the system and was to be avoided . . ." However, in "Devilish Drugs, Part One," F. A. Allen, M.P.S., finds the mention of puncture marks in Holmes's *wrist* "sinister" and suggestive of intravenous injection.

4 Dr. Charles Goodman, in "The Dental Holmes," contends that Holmes's addiction stemmed from receiving cocaine for dental problems. In the 1880s, cocaine was a commonly used local anaesthetic. As late as 1897, *Warner's Pocket Medical Dictionary* listed cocaine as a "nerve stimulant and local anaesthetic."

5 Beaune is a French city, in the Burgundy region, about halfway between Dijon and Chalon-sur-Saône, which has given its name to the variety of local wine. A striking example of antiquity, Beaune is circular and has ramparts that date from the fifteenth century, and once it was a thriving textile centre—until, when the Edict of Nantes was revoked in 1685, the city's Protestant artisans were driven out. Today, there is a wine school and research facilities, and among the city's factories

"His eyes rested thoughtfully upon the sinewy forearm and wrist."
Richard Gutschmidt, *Das Zeichen der Vier* (Stuttgart: Robert Lutz Verlag, 1902)

had of his many extraordinary qualities, all made me diffident and backward in crossing him.

Yet upon that afternoon, whether it was the Beaune[5] which I had taken with my lunch or the additional exasperation produced by the extreme deliberation of his manner, I suddenly felt that I could hold out no longer.

"Which is it to-day," I asked, "morphine[6] or cocaine?"[7]

He raised his eyes languidly from the old black-letter volume[8] which he had opened.

"It is cocaine," he said, "a seven-per-cent solution.[9] Would you care to try it?"[10]

"No, indeed," I answered brusquely. "My constitution has not got over the Afghan campaign yet.[11] I cannot afford to throw any extra strain upon it."

He smiled at my vehemence. "Perhaps you are right, Watson," he said. "I suppose that its influence is physically a bad one. I find it, however, so transcendently stimulating and clarifying to the mind that its secondary action is a matter of small moment."

"But consider!" I said earnestly. "Count the cost! Your brain may, as you say, be roused and excited, but it is a pathological and morbid process, which involves increased tissue-change and businesses are those that produce wine-making equipment. "Beaune, like Pommard, used to be a convenient deception," writes Matt Kramer, in *Making Sense of Burgundy*. "For centuries, it has been the centre from which wine shippers ruled viticultural Burgundy almost as peremptorily as the Burgundian dukes previously ruled political Burgundy. . . . So, as with Pommard, Nuits-Saint-Georges, and Chambertin, wines of a certain style were baptized 'Beaune,' never mind where they came from or even whether they were composed exclusively of Pinot Noir."

Christopher Morley opines that Beaune is "[t]oo strong a drink for lunch, likely to cause either sleep or irritability." In fact, it is no more "potent" than any other non-fortified wine, and this editor wishes it to be known that he is available for experimentation on the suitability of the wine for lunch. In "Dr. Watson's Secret," Morley expresses the further view that Watson was fortifying himself because, unknown to Holmes, he had married Mary Morstan some months before and knew that she would be calling on Holmes as a client that very afternoon. Some American editors of the Canon, apparently fearing the lack of oenophiles among their readers, substitute the word "claret" for "Beaune."

6 William S. Baring-Gould, in *The Annotated Sherlock Holmes*, points out that this is the only occasion in the Canon on which there is even the suggestion that Holmes took morphine.

7 Bernard Davies, in "Doctor Watson's Deuteronomy: A Centenary Companion-piece," writes that Watson, who would have noticed Holmes going back and forth between states of hyperactivity and morphine-induced torpor, seems confused by the morphine-cocaine dichotomy. He points out that, in "A Scandal in Bohemia," Watson reports Holmes "alternating from week to week between cocaine and ambition, the drowsiness of the drug, and the fierce energy of his own keen nature." "Medical knowledge apart," Davies notes, "his own experience should have told him that drowsiness was the precise opposite of the effect of cocaine."

8 These were books printed in a typeface used by early printers; the term is probably meant here to suggest an antiquarian book. We see Holmes indulging in the same bibliophilia in "The Red-Headed League," where his "black-letter editions" are also mentioned. Holmes's book-collecting is discussed in more detail in *A Study in Scarlet*, note 147, above.

9 According to F. A. Allen, "The strength of *injectio cocainae hypodermica* became official in the [*British Pharmacopoeia*] in 1898 at ten per cent. May it not be presumed that, at least, Holmes was trying to 'cut down'?" Allen suggests that when Holmes weaned himself from the drug, he may have begun using heroin, which had been introduced from Germany about this time as a cure for the morphia habit, and not condemned until a *British Medical Journal* editorial in 1906. Tracy and Berkey point out that "[b]lack market 'street' cocaine today generally contains 5% to 30% of the drug, though it should be kept in mind that the intravenous administration common now is many times as effective as Holmes's subcutaneous method." Based on the dosage and the method of taking the drug, they judge Holmes's cocaine use to be "moderate and even therapeutic."

Nicholas Meyer's novel *The Seven-Per-Cent Solution* (1974), subsequently made into a very successful film starring Nicol Williamson as Holmes, Robert Duvall as Dr. Watson, and Alan Arkin as Sigmund Freud, records Holmes's cure of his addiction with Freud's aid. Freud helps Holmes understand that the villainous Moriarty was but a projection of Holmes's mind, based on Holmes's childhood discovery that his mother had committed and may at least leave a permanent weakness. You know, too, what a black reaction comes upon you.[12] Surely the game is hardly worth the candle. Why should you, for a mere passing pleasure, risk the loss of those great powers with which you have been endowed? Remember that I speak not only as one comrade to another, but as a medical man to one for whose constitution he is to some extent answerable."[13]

He did not seem offended. On the contrary, he put his finger-tips together, and leaned his elbows on the arms of his chair, like one who has a relish for conversation.

"My mind," he said, "rebels at stagnation. Give me problems, give me work, give me the most abstruse cryptogram or

" 'I abhor the dull routine of existence.' "
Frederic Dorr Steele, *Adventures of Sherlock Holmes*, Vol. I, 1950. The illustration indicates that it was "re-drawn by Mr. Steele for this edition." James Montgomery, in *A Study in Pictures*, identifies the original work as an illustration for "The Blanched Soldier," appearing in the *Louisville Courier-Journal* on January 30, 1927 (note the "26" next to the artist's signature), in which the seated figure undoubtedly represented Mr. James M. Dodd!

adultery with his tutor Professor Moriarty (portrayed by Laurence Olivier in the film).

10 Michael Harrison points out, in *In the Footsteps of Sherlock Holmes*, that Holmes's purchases of cocaine were strictly legal at the time and that the drug was likely available at his neighbourhood chemist's shop.

11 See *A Study in Scarlet*, Chapter 1, and especially notes 9 through 16 and accompanying text. Compare this comment, however, to Watson's exertion in connection with the six-mile search for Tonga, in Chapter VI, below.

12 Cocaine, an alkaloid occurring to the extent of about 1 percent in the leaves of *Erythroxylon coca*, cultivated in the Andes and known as *coca* or *cuca*, was little understood in the Victorian era. The *Encyclopædia Britannica* (9th Ed.), a bellwether of common knowledge, has nothing to say about the *injection* of coca leaves, although *chewing* coca leaves, "when [they are] fresh and good, and used in moderate quantity, increases nervous energy, removes drowsiness, enlivens the spirits, and enables the [user] to bear cold, wet, great bodily exertion, and even want of food, to a surprising degree, with apparent ease and impunity." By 1910, the *Encyclopædia Britannica* (11th Ed.) reported:

> The injection of coca leaves has a very remarkable effect upon the higher tracts of the nervous system—an effect curiously contrary to that produced by their chief ingredient upon the peripheral parts of the nervous apparatus. The mental power is, at any rate subjectively, enhanced in marked degrees. In the absence of extended experiments in psychological laboratories, such as have been conducted with alcohol, it is not possible to say whether the apparent enhancement of the intellect is an objectively demonstrable fact. The physi-

the most intricate analysis, and I am in my own proper atmosphere. I can dispense then with artificial stimulants. But I abhor the dull routine of existence. I crave for mental exaltation. That is why I have chosen my own particular profession, or rather created it, for I am the only one in the world."

"The only unofficial detective?" I said, raising my eyebrows.

"The only unofficial consulting detective," he answered. "I am the last and highest court of appeal in detection. When Gregson or Lestrade or Athelney Jones are out of their depths—which, by the way, is their normal state—the matter is laid before me. I examine the data, as an expert, and pronounce a specialist's opinion. I claim no credit in such cases. My name figures in no newspaper. The work itself, the pleasure of finding a field for my peculiar powers, is my highest reward. But you have yourself had some experience of my methods of work in the Jefferson Hope case."

"Yes, indeed," said I, cordially. "I was never so struck by anything in my life. I even embodied it in a small brochure, with the somewhat fantastic title of 'A Study in Scarlet.' "[14]

He shook his head sadly.

"I glanced over it," said he. "Honestly, I cannot congratulate you upon it. Detection is, or ought to be, an exact science and should be treated in the same cold and unemotional manner. You have attempted to tinge it with romanticism,[15] which produces much the same effect as if you worked a love-story or an elopement into the fifth proposition of Euclid."[16]

"But the romance was there," I remonstrated. "I could not tamper with the facts."

"Some facts should be suppressed, or, at least, a just sense of proportion should be observed in treating them. The only point in the case which deserved mention was the curious analytical reasoning from effects to causes, by which I succeeded in unravelling it."

I was annoyed at this criticism of a work which had been specially designed to please him. I confess, too, that I was irritated by the egotism which seemed to demand that every line of my pamphlet should be devoted to his own special doings. More than once during the years that I had lived with him in Baker Street I had observed that a small vanity underlay my companion's quiet and didactic manner. I made no remark, however, but sat nursing my wounded leg.[17] I had had a

cal power is unquestionably increased, such muscular exercises as are involved in ascending mountains being made much easier after the chewing of an ounce or so of these leaves. Excess in coca-chewing leads in many cases to great bodily wasting, mental failure, insomnia, weakness of the circulation and extreme dyspepsia.

Modern studies show that the effects of cocaine are short-lived, and that withdrawal from it produces a severe depressive reaction that the user often believes can be relieved only by further cocaine use.

13 That Holmes was a cocaine addict is questioned by W. H. Miller, in "The Habit of Sherlock Holmes." Miller cites the lack of descriptions of behaviour consistent with cocaine usage and the lack of any evidence of withdrawal symptoms. Holmes's remark he puts down to a joking rebuff of Watson's shockingly "cheeky" question, and Miller concludes that Holmes must have been injecting atropine—an alkaloid that affects the nervous system and that is used today as pre-anaesthesia—in connection with experiments with "vegetable alkaloids" (see *A Study in Scarlet*, note 33, above). However, D. M. Grilly, in "A Reply to Miller's 'The Habit of Sherlock Holmes,' " contends that Miller's conclusions are based on out-of-date research and that Watson's report of Holmes's symptoms "is accurate and consistent with what is presently known about cocaine." In particular, he argues that recent evidence suggests that cocaine is not necessarily addictive—that many may experience the mood elevation Holmes evidently sought without becoming compulsive users.

14 The first example of Watsonian self-promotion, a practice he shamelessly pursued throughout his writing career.

John Hall, in *Sidelights on Holmes*, defends 1887 as the date of the events recorded in *The*

Sign of Four and says that "by no stretch of the imagination could Holmes have glanced at anything other than a first draft of Watson's first story—and, indeed, Watson could not have claimed to have published it, unless it were an edition we know absolutely nothing about, copies of which have never come to light." If Hall is correct, then either Holmes did not make this statement (at least not at this time), or Watson's account of Holmes's remark is correct—in which case it would be necessary to move the events of *The Sign of Four* to 1888, with what Hall notes as that date's attendant problems. H. B. Williams, in "The Unknown Watson," backs 1887 as well, suggesting that it was the *original* publication of Watson's reminiscences (see *A Study in Scarlet*, note 2) that Watson refers to here as "a small brochure" and "my pamphlet," and that Watson was not referring to the *second* publication of *A Study in Scarlet*, in *Beeton's Christmas Annual* in late 1887.

However, most chronologists take this mention of a "small brochure" as a reference not to a draft or ur-*Study* but to the *Beeton's* publication of *A Study in Scarlet* and therefore date the events of *The Sign of Four* after 1887—see *Appendix*. This view is buttressed by Holmes's later remark that the criminal classes were coming to know him well, especially since Watson had taken to publishing "some" of his cases. Note, however (as Roger Johnson points out in private correspondence to this editor), that Watson does not claim to have *published* the tale, only to have *embodied* it "in a small brochure."

In either event, Watson's businesslike approach to his writing craft is first evidenced here. Although Watson had in desperation agreed in 1887 (at the apparent behest of Arthur Conan Doyle) to an outright sale of the British copyright to *A Study in Scarlet*, he presumably hoped to earn additional profits from the American market, and the first American publication of *The Sign of Four* (in *Lippincott's Magazine*, in February 1890) was almost immediately followed by publication of an edition of *A Study in Scarlet* (J. B. Lippincott, March 1890). See Donald A. Redmond's *Sherlock Holmes Among the Pirates* for a discussion of the numerous "pirated" American editions that followed as a result of the then-current American laws (which granted no copyright protection to a publication of a British author in the United States).

15 William S. Baring-Gould jokes, "It was probably the interlude with the Mormons that Holmes found tiresome."

16 Euclid's "fifth proposition" is: "If a straight line falling on two straight lines makes the interior angles on the same side less than two right angles, the two straight lines, if produced indefinitely, meet on that side on which are the angles less than the two right angles." "The Master here referred to the fifth proposition probably merely to illustrate his point," Ernest Bloomfield Zeisler writes, in "A Chronological *Study in Scarlet*," "for careful research has failed to reveal why any other proposition of Euclid would not have done as well." But Raymond Holly, in "Dubious and Questionable," points out that the fifth proposition is "the first proposition that refers to a naturally occurring pair—the base angles of an isosceles triangle" and implies that Holmes's remark here was a reference to his attitude toward love, expressed in the text accompanying note 277, below.

17 The subject of Watson's wounds is complex and intricate. A brief discussion may be found in *A Study in Scarlet*, note 14. See also note 146, below.

jezail[18] bullet through it some time before, and though it did not prevent me from walking, it ached wearily at every change of the weather.

"My practice has extended recently to the Continent," said Holmes after a while, filling up his old brier-root pipe. "I was consulted last week by François le Villard,[19] who, as you probably know, has come rather to the front lately in the French detective service. He has all the Celtic power of quick intuition, but he is deficient in the wide range of exact knowledge which is essential to the higher developments of his art. The case was concerned with a will and possessed some features of interest. I was able to refer him to two parallel cases, the one at Riga in 1857, and the other at St. Louis in 1871, which have suggested to him the true solution. Here is the letter which I had this morning acknowledging my assistance."

He tossed over, as he spoke, a crumpled sheet of foreign notepaper. I glanced my eyes down it, catching a profusion of notes of admiration, with stray *magnifiques*, *coup-de-maîtres*[20] and *tours-de-force*, all testifying to the ardent admiration of the Frenchman.

"He speaks as a pupil to his master," said I.

"Oh, he rates my assistance too highly," said Sherlock Holmes lightly. "He has considerable gifts himself. He possesses two out of the three qualities necessary for the ideal detective. He has the power of observation and that of deduction. He is only wanting in knowledge, and that may come in time. He is now translating my small works into French."

"Your works?"

"Oh, didn't you know?" he cried, laughing. "Yes, I have been guilty of several monographs. They are all upon technical subjects. Here, for example, is one 'Upon the Distinction between the Ashes of the Various Tobaccos.'[21] In it I enumerate a hundred and forty forms of cigar, cigarette, and pipe tobacco, with coloured plates[22] illustrating the difference in the ash. It is a point which is continually turning up in criminal trials, and which is sometimes of supreme importance as a clue. If you can say definitely, for example, that some murder had been done by a man who was smoking an Indian lunkah,[23] it obviously narrows your field of search. To the trained eye there is as much difference between the black ash of a Trichinop-

18 See *A Study in Scarlet*, note 15.

19 Madeline B. Stern, in *Sherlock Holmes: Rare Book Collector*, identifies him as the son of Francisque le Villard, who flourished about 1847 and wrote about the Paris theatre.

20 French: master strokes.

21 Holmes mentions his monograph on cigar ashes in *A Study in Scarlet*, but without disclosing its title. See *A Study in Scarlet*, note 127.

22 Poul Anderson (in "Art in the Blood") asserts that the meticulous Holmes must have been a fine draftsman and painter: "Surely he would not have entrusted the preparation of these plates to anyone else."

23 A strong Indian cigar that resembles a cheroot.

oly[24] and the white fluff of bird's-eye[25] as there is between a cabbage and a potato."

"You have an extraordinary genius for minutiae," I remarked.

"I appreciate their importance. Here is my monograph upon the tracing of footsteps, with some remarks upon the uses of plaster of Paris as a preserver of impresses.[26] Here, too, is a curious little work upon the influence of a trade upon the form of the hand,[27] with lithotypes of the hands of slaters, sailors, cork-cutters, compositors, weavers, and diamond-polishers.[28] That is a matter of great practical interest to the scientific detective—especially in cases of unclaimed bodies, or in discovering the antecedents of criminals. But I weary you with my hobby."[29]

"Not at all," I answered earnestly. "It is of the greatest interest to me, especially since I have had the opportunity of observing your practical application of it. But you spoke just now of observation and deduction. Surely the one to some extent implies the other."

"Why, hardly," he answered, leaning back luxuriously in his armchair and sending up thick blue wreaths from his pipe. "For example, observation shows me that you have been to the Wigmore Street Post-Office this morning, but deduction lets me know that when there you despatched a telegram."

"Right!" said I. "Right on both points! But I confess that I don't see how you arrived at it. It was a sudden impulse upon my part, and I have mentioned it to no one.

"It is simplicity itself," he remarked, chuckling at my surprise—"so absurdly simple that an explanation is superfluous; and yet it may serve to define the limits of observation and of deduction. Observation tells me that you have a little reddish mould adhering to your instep. Just opposite the Wigmore Street Office they have taken up the pavement and thrown up some earth, which lies in such a way that it is difficult to avoid treading in it in entering. The earth is of this peculiar reddish tint which is found, as far as I know, nowhere else in the neighbourhood. So much is observation. The rest is deduction."

"How, then, did you deduce the telegram?"

"Why, of course I knew that you had not written a letter, since I sat opposite to you all morning. I see also in your open desk there that you have a sheet of stamps and a thick bundle of postcards. What could you go into the post-office for, then,

24 See *A Study in Scarlet*, note 118.

25 A special cut of tobacco, resembling in appearance a bird's eye.

26 "There is no branch of detective science which is so important and so much neglected as the art of tracing footsteps," remarks Holmes in *A Study in Scarlet*, and numerous examples throughout the Canon demonstrate his expertise.

27 In "The Effects of Trades Upon Hands," Archibald Hart accuses Gilbert Forbes ("a transparent alias") of reprinting Holmes's work under the title "Some Observations on Occupational Markings," purportedly written by Forbes, in the *Police Journal* (London, October–November 1946; reprinted in the United States in the *Journal of Criminal Law and Criminology* [November–December 1947]). Remsen Ten Eyck Schenck notes a similar work, *Occupational Marks*, by Francesco Ronchese, M.D. (New York: Grune & Stratton, 1948).

In "A Case of Identity," "The Red-Headed League," "The Copper Beeches," and "The Solitary Cyclist," Holmes demonstrates his ability to observe the effects of various trades upon the hands. Dr. Joseph Bell (see Introduction, Volume I of this series, for a discussion of his relationship with Arthur Conan Doyle) preached the practical use of such knowledge in an introduction to a reprint of *A Study in Scarlet* in 1892. There, Bell expresses "how easy it is, if only you can observe, to find out a great deal as to the works and ways of your innocent and unconscious friends, and, by an extension of the same method, to baffle the criminal and lay bare the manner of his crime." In "The Adventure of the Copper Beeches," Holmes remarks, "Pshaw, my dear fellow, what do the public, the great unobservant public, who could hardly tell a weaver by his tooth or a compositor by his left thumb, care about the finer shades of analysis and deduction!"

28 Schenck notes, "The marks [of a slater—a roofer, in modern parlance] probably included the fingertips of the left hand worn smooth by handling the stone, as seen also in masons and bricklayers . . . , and calluses across the right palm from gripping the hammer. It is also reasonable that callosities of the knees would be prominent . . . , since roofing is done chiefly in a kneeling position."

Nothing specific would distinguish a sailor's hands from those of another person working hard outdoors. So reasons Schenck, who also points out that ship's chores are more varied than repetitive, and furthermore that the right and left hands are used equally.

Cork-cutters, who have largely vanished with the advent of modern machinery, would, Schenck speculates, have "calluses [that] were produced on the thumb and first two fingers of the left hand by grasping the cork, and similarly on the thumb and across the inside of all four fingers of the right by the handle of the knife." And, of the compositor, the "left thumb is often characterized by the formation of a callus on the tip, often with abrasion of the skin lower down, across the 'ball' of the digit," Schenck writes. "In setting type, the 'stick' is held in the left hand and the type placed in it with the right. As each piece of type is dropped into the stick, the left thumb slides it into position against the last addition, and then holds the accumulated mass snugly in a corner."

Schenck writes that it is not possible "to establish just what constituted for Holmes the unmistakable manual stigma of the weaver. A wide variety of calluses peculiar to the textile trades is described by [Francesco Ronchese], but these differ with the particular assignment of the worker at the machine—the doffer, the quiller, the hooker, the mule spinner, etc.—and none of them could have been created by hand-looming." He calls "highly likely" the possibility that the "marks to which Holmes referred were calluses on the right hand from handling the shuttle, and perhaps on the left from the heddles."

Clues to the hand of the diamond-polisher, according to Schenck, include the fact that "jewellery polishers have nails worn smooth and stained red by the rouge . . . , lens polishers show certain nails worn down from picking the glass from its pitch bed . . . , and those who polish metal jewellery wear calluses from holding the metal parts against the wheel." Diamonds, he points out, "are polished in a pitch bed at the end of a 'dop stick' . . . any or all of the three marks described might appear in a lapidary doing much hand work."

29 Bernard Davies doubts that a conversation covering this much ground could have been compressed into the number of minutes to which it appears to have been reduced here, and he also questions the convenience of Mary Morstan's appearing at the end of it. Indeed, in a chapter deliberately bearing the same title as one in *A Study in Scarlet*, it seems likely that Watson took literary licence here to boast to readers of Holmes's abilities.

but to send a wire?[30] Eliminate all other factors, and the one which remains must be the truth."[31]

"In this case it certainly is so," I replied after a little thought. "The thing, however, is, as you say, of the simplest. Would you think me impertinent if I were to put your theories to a more severe test?"

"On the contrary," he answered, "it would prevent me from taking a second dose of cocaine. I should be delighted to look into any problem which you might submit to me."

"I have heard you say it is difficult for a man to have any object in daily use without leaving the impress of his individuality upon it in such a way that a trained observer might read it. Now, I have here a watch which has recently come into my possession. Would you have the kindness to let me have an opinion upon the character or habits of the late owner?"

I handed him over the watch with some slight feeling of amusement in my heart, for the test was, as I thought, an impossible one, and I intended it as a lesson against the somewhat dogmatic tone which he occasionally assumed. He balanced the watch in his hand, gazed hard at the dial, opened the back, and examined the works, first with his naked eyes and then with a powerful convex lens. I could hardly keep from smiling at his crestfallen face when he finally snapped the case to and handed it back.

"He balanced the watch in his hand."
Richard Gutschmidt, *Das Zeichen der Vier* (Stuttgart: Robert Lutz Verlag, 1902)

30 Watson could just as easily have been in the Post Office for other reasons. According to Vernon Rendall ("The Limitations of Sherlock Holmes"), perhaps he was buying a money or postal order, getting package rates, or buying stamps.

But there is a much more serious problem here. In the original version of *The Sign of Four*, as it appeared in *Lippincott's Magazine*, the reference is to the Seymour Street Post Office. Putting aside the issues of other reasons for Watson's trip, Bernard Davies notes that Nos. 59–61 Seymour Street "was not a Post and Telegraph Office. You could purchase what you liked, but, though you begged on your knees, you could not send a telegram from there." Why, Davies wonders, did Watson not amend his error by inserting the name of a nearby telegraph office, such as the Baker Street Post Office or one on the way to the West End, at No. 43 Duke Street, one block from Portman Square? Instead Watson invented the Wigmore Street Post Office, which did not exist in 1890. "How this charade came to be inserted in the manuscript in the first place is a mystery. . . . The most charitable explanation is that [Watson] tried a bit too hard to be clever, by combining two quite separate incidents."

31 T. S. Blakeney identifies this as Holmes's "most famous maxim" (*Sherlock Holmes: Fact or Fiction?*). It appears twice in *The Sign of Four* and is repeated almost identically in "The Beryl Coronet," "The Bruce-Partington Plans," and "The Blanched Soldier."

"There are hardly any data," he remarked. "The watch has been recently cleaned, which robs me of my most suggestive facts."

"You are right," I answered. "It was cleaned before being sent to me."

In my heart I accused my companion of putting forward a most lame and impotent excuse to cover his failure. What data could he expect from an uncleaned watch?

"Though unsatisfactory, my research has not been entirely barren," he observed, staring up at the ceiling with dreamy, lack-lustre eyes. "Subject to your correction, I should judge that the watch belonged to your elder brother, who inherited it from your father."

"That you gather, no doubt, from the H. W. upon the back?"

"Quite so. The W. suggests your own name. The date of the watch is nearly fifty years back, and the initials are as old as the watch: so it was made for the last generation. Jewellery usually descends to the eldest son, and he is most likely to have the same name as the father.[32] Your father has, if I remember right, been dead many years. It has, therefore, been in the hands of your eldest brother."

"Right, so far," said I. "Anything else?"

"He was a man of untidy habits—very untidy and careless. He was left with good prospects, but he threw away his chances, lived for some time in poverty with occasional short intervals of prosperity, and finally, taking to drink, he died. That is all I can gather."

I sprang from my chair and limped impatiently about the room with considerable bitterness in my heart.

"This is unworthy of you, Holmes," I said, "I could not have believed that you would have descended to this. You have made inquiries into the history of my unhappy brother, and you now pretend to deduce this knowledge in some fanciful way. You cannot expect me to believe that you have read all this from his old watch! It is unkind and, to speak plainly, has a touch of charlatanism in it."

"My dear doctor," said he kindly, "pray accept my apologies. Viewing the matter as an abstract problem, I had forgotten how personal and painful a thing it might be to you. I assure you, however, that I never even knew that you had a brother until you handed me the watch."

32 This remark suggests that Holmes knew Watson's father's Christian name, which we do not.

"Then how in the name of all that is wonderful did you get these facts? They are absolutely correct in every particular."

"Ah, that is good luck. I could only say what was the balance of probability. I did not at all expect to be so accurate."

"But it was not mere guess-work?"

"No, no: I never guess. It is a shocking habit—destructive to the logical faculty. What seems strange to you is only so because you do not follow my train of thought or observe the small facts upon which large inferences may depend. For example, I began by stating that your brother was careless. When you observe the lower part of that watch-case you notice that it is not only dinted in two places, but it is cut and marked all over from the habit of keeping other hard objects, such as coins or keys, in the same pocket. Surely it is no great feat to assume that a man who treats a fifty-guinea watch[33] so cavalierly must be a careless man. Neither is it a very far-fetched inference that a man who inherits one article of such value is pretty well provided for in other respects."

I nodded, to show that I followed his reasoning.

"It is very customary for pawnbrokers in England, when they take a watch, to scratch the numbers of the ticket with a pin-point upon the inside of the case. It is more handy than a label, as there is no risk of the number being lost or transposed. There are no less than four such numbers visible to my lens on the inside of this case. Inference—that your brother was often at low water. Secondary inference—that he had occasional bursts of prosperity, or he could not have redeemed the pledge. Finally, I ask you to look at the inner plate, which contains the keyhole.[34] Look at the thousands of scratches all round the hole marks where the key has slipped. What sober man's key could have scored those grooves? But you will never see a drunkard's watch without them. He winds it at night, and he leaves these traces of his unsteady hand.[35] Where is the mystery in all this?"

"It is as clear as daylight," I answered. "I regret the injustice which I did you. I should have had more faith in your marvellous faculty. May I ask whether you have any professional inquiry on foot at present?"

"None. Hence the cocaine. I cannot live without brainwork. What else is there to live for? Stand at the window here. Was ever such a dreary, dismal, unprofitable world? See how the

33 The reader will recall that Watson's daily pension was 11*s.* 6*d.* The watch represents almost a full two years' pension.

34 Watches that could be wound without a key were a relatively recent invention (the patents for a crown winder were filed between 1845 and 1860), and Watson's father's watch may well have predated the introduction of practical keyless watches. An earlier invention was the so-called Breguet key, also referred to as the tipsy key, which could only be turned in one direction.

35 Holmes may be right that this feature always shows up on the watch of a drunkard, but it is faulty reasoning to say that the scratches prove that the owner is a drunkard. For example, the owner could suffer palsy or simply be careless, with little regard for possessions.

yellow fog swirls down the street and drifts across the dun-coloured houses. What could be more hopelessly prosaic and material? What is the use of having powers, Doctor, when one has no field upon which to exert them? Crime is commonplace, existence is commonplace, and no qualities save those which are commonplace have any function upon earth."

I had opened my mouth to reply to this tirade, when, with a crisp knock, our landlady entered, bearing a card upon the brass salver.

"A young lady for you, sir," she said, addressing my companion.[36]

"Miss Mary Morstan," he read. "Hum! I have no recollection of the name. Ask the young lady to step up, Mrs. Hudson. Don't go, Doctor. I should prefer that you remain."

36 Daniel L. Moriarty (no apparent relation) makes a compelling case, in "The Woman Who Beat Sherlock Holmes," that Mary Morstan came to Baker Street expressly to marry Holmes. It became quickly apparent to her that Holmes had deduced her game, and, although she was unprepared to find a second bachelor in residence, she quickly changed her target to Watson. Moriarty argues that she had no evil intent but merely sought to make her way in the world.

CHAPTER II

The Statement of the Case

Miss Morstan entered the room with a firm step and an outward composure of manner. She was a blonde young lady, small, dainty, well gloved,[37] and dressed in the most perfect taste. There was, however, a plainness and simplicity about her costume which bore with it a suggestion of limited means. The dress was a sombre grayish beige, untrimmed and unbraided, and she wore a small turban of the same dull hue, relieved only by a suspicion of white feather in the side. Her face had neither regularity of feature nor beauty of complexion, but her expression was sweet and amiable, and her large blue eyes were singularly spiritual and sympathetic. In an experience of women which extends over many nations and three separate continents,[38] I have never looked upon a face which gave a clearer promise of a refined and sensitive nature. I could not but observe that as she took the seat which Sherlock Holmes placed for her, her lip trembled, her hand quivered, and she showed every sign of intense inward agitation.

"I have come to you, Mr. Holmes," she said, "because you once enabled my employer, Mrs. Cecil Forrester,[39] to unravel

37 In an age when at least one popular British magazine, the *Wasp*, dealt almost exclusively with the art and science of the proper corset fit for young women (one did not purchase a corset alone but with the help of a professional corsetiere), correctly fitting gloves were essential. According to "The Corsetee's Creed," to be recited by the wearer, "I . . . shall . . . at all proper times endeavor to be correctly gloved, shod, and above all, corseted, whether at home or abroad." *Collier's Cyclopedia of Commercial and Social Information* advised, under "Etiquette for Ladies," "Never be seen in the street without gloves. Your gloves should fit to the last degree of perfection."

38 Which continents, and when was this experience obtained? "It is usually assumed that the three continents are Europe, Asia and Australia," remarks D. Martin Dakin, in *A*

Dustjacket, *The Sign of Four*.
(London: John Murray, 1924)

a little domestic complication.[40] She was much impressed by your kindness and skill."

"Mrs. Cecil Forrester," he repeated thoughtfully.[41] "I believe that I was of some slight service to her. The case, however, as I remember it, was a very simple one."

"She did not think so. But at least you cannot say the same of mine. I can hardly imagine anything more strange, more utterly inexplicable, than the situation in which I find myself."

Holmes rubbed his hands, and his eyes glistened. He leaned forward in his chair with an expression of extraordinary concentration upon his clear-cut, hawk-like features.

"State your case," said he, in brisk business tones.

I felt that my position was an embarrassing one.

"You will, I am sure, excuse me," I said, rising from my chair.[42]

Sherlock Holmes Commentary. Australia is apparently one, for Watson himself remarks about Ballarat later in *The Sign of Four*. However, this visit to Ballarat must have occurred in Watson's boyhood, for there are no gaps of sufficient length in his recorded adult life history for such a long trip, and therefore he may not have been old enough to have "experience of women." "His opportunities must have been equally limited in India," comments Dakin, "unless we think of the hospital nurses, and he was too ill for much dalliance with them."

Baring-Gould posits a stay in America, prior to Watson's relationship with Holmes, and Arthur Conan Doyle's play *Angels of Darkness*, first published in 2002, seems to bear this out. However, the fidelity of this record is dubious. See *Chronological Table*, note 2. Ian McQueen, in *Sherlock Holmes Detected: The Problems of the Long Stories*, expresses the view that Watson is to be taken at his word and suggests that the three "separate continents" do not include Australia: "His experience in Asia and Africa must necessarily have been exceedingly limited, but he probably had some spare time available for amorous excursions in such places as Bombay and Peshawar, as well as in Egypt, while on the way to join his regiment." McQueen points to Watson's remark upon first meeting Holmes (in *A Study in Scarlet*) that when he was well, "he had 'another set of vices,' and sexual encounters were probably not excluded."

But many commentators are quick to discard this statement as boasting by Watson. Dorothy Sayers, in *Unpopular Opinions*, asserts that Watson was simply not that sort of man. As Dakin puts it, "His demeanour throughout his relations with Mary Morstan, whether in romantic dreams of her, in confused conversation in the cab, or in childlike hand-holding in the dark, is not that of an accomplished cavalier but of a man . . . falling headlong in love for the first time." Similarly, Christopher Redmond, in his fascinating *In Bed with Sherlock Holmes*, observes that if Watson is telling the truth, his encounters were most likely casual rather than serious, "possibly a visit to a judiciously chosen prostitute rather than any dealings, let alone a romance, between equals. . . . [Watson's conduct] is not the behaviour of a roué. It is the behaviour of a young man . . . whose life as a medical student, a soldier, and a convalescent has kept him so busy that he has less, not more, experience of women than the average, and who has just fallen in love for the first time."

And yet, as Janet Byrne notes to this editor in private correspondence, "Isn't it intriguing, and suggestive, that at the beginning of Chapter XII, Watson says, "A very patient man was that inspector in the cab, for it was a weary time before I rejoined him"?—especially inasmuch as Chapter XI ends with Watson "[drawing Mary Morstan] to his side"?

39 Donald A. Redmond, in *Sherlock Holmes: A Study in Sources*, identifies her as Mary Anne Forester, widow of David Ochterloney Dyce Sombré and daughter of Edward Jervis, 2nd Viscount St. Vincent, who married George Cecil Weld, 3rd Baron Forester of Willey Park, on November 8, 1862. Mrs. For[r]ester died in 1895.

40 Robert Keith Leavitt suggests (in "Who Was Cecil Forrester?") that Mr. Cecil Forrester, Farintosh of "The Speckled Band," Woodhouse of "The Bruce-Partington Plans," and Colonel Upwood of *The Hound of the Baskervilles*, were all one and the same man—"former friend of Captain Morstan and probably of the none-too-scrupulous Major Sholto, sometime husband of Mary Morstan's employer, party hanger-on, card-sharp and all-too-dubious hero of the strange adventure of the politician, the lighthouse and the trained cormorant" (the latter referred to in "The Veiled Lodger").

And Ruth Douglass, in "The Camberwell Poisoner," advances the speculation that the "little domestic complication" in Mrs. Forrester's household was the Camberwell Poisoning mentioned in "The Five Orange Pips"; that the poisoner was Mrs. Forrester; that she escaped justice and used Mary first as bait (for Watson) and then as a tool (in order to obtain poison, through Mary, from Watson's medical cabinet). She finally killed Mary.

41 Rosemary Michaud, in "Another Case of Identity," proposes that the woman who came to see Holmes here was not Mary Morstan but rather the daughter of Mrs. Cecil Forrester. Holmes knew perfectly well who she was but, presented with a pearl, went along to find out what the case was about. Miss Morstan had died earlier, Michaud suggests, and the Forresters—swindlers by trade—decided to pursue the *Times* advertisement themselves. Holmes had no knowledge of how serious relations had become between "Miss Morstan" and Watson until too late and probably assumed that recovery of the treasure would put an end to "Miss Morstan's" interest in Watson. This thesis also explains the reference in "The Five Orange Pips" to Mary visiting her "mother" (see note 276, below).

An alternate but equally startling suggestion is made by Charles A. Meyer, in "The Remarkable Forrester Case." Meyer suggests that Mrs. Forrester and Holmes had an affair and that only after the passions had cooled for ten years was Mrs. Forrester comfortable in recommending that Mary Morstan consult Holmes. This explains, in Meyer's view, the otherwise "dull" behaviour of Miss Morstan in accepting for so many years the twin mysteries of her father's disappearance and the annual pearls.

42 Various chronologists point to this as an indication of a case early in the Partnership; compare, for example, "A Case of Identity" (pre-Return) or "The Norwood Builder" (post-Return), where Watson makes not the slightest move to excuse himself from the presence of either Mary Sutherland or John Hector McFarlane. "I cannot escape the impression," writes D. Martin Dakin, "that Watson was trying to put back into this story the conditions of a much earlier period before his co-operation was taken for granted. It all adds up to the conclusion that in 1890 he did not anticipate the publication of any Holmes stories but these two." Dakin proposes that this was the result of Holmes's censorship of Watson's publications. The censorship resulted in the postponement of publication of the cases collected as the *Adventures* and the *Memoirs* until Holmes's disappearance in 1891. (The last of the *Memoirs* appeared in 1893, before Holmes's return.) The cases that took place *after* Holmes's return in 1894 were not published until after Holmes's retirement in 1901 (the first appearing in 1903).

43 The dating of *The Sign of Four* is a vast and complex topic, with myriad implications for the dating of the remainder of the Canon. The conclusions of the major chronologists are summarised in the *Appendix*.

"Miss Morstan entered the room with a firm step."
Artist unknown, *Sherlock Holmes Series*, Vol. I
(New York & London: Harper & Bros., 1904)

To my surprise, the young lady held up her gloved hand to detain me.

"If your friend," she said, "would be good enough to stop, he might be of inestimable service to me."

I relapsed into my chair.

"Briefly," she continued, "the facts are these. My father was an officer in an Indian regiment, who sent me home when I was quite a child. My mother was dead, and I had no relative in England. I was placed, however, in a comfortable boarding establishment at Edinburgh, and there I remained until I was seventeen years of age. In the year 1878[43] my father, who was senior captain of his regiment, obtained twelve months' leave and came home. He telegraphed to me from London that he

" 'State your case,' said he in brisk business tones."
Richard Gutschmidt, *Das Zeichen der Vier* (Stuttgart: Robert Lutz Verlag, 1902)

had arrived all safe and directed me to come down at once, giving the Langham Hotel as his address. His message, as I remember, was full of kindness and love. On reaching London I drove to the Langham and was informed that Captain Morstan was staying there, but that he had gone out the night before and had not returned. I waited all day without news of

" 'If your friend,' she said, 'would be good enough to stay, he might be of inestimable service to me.' "
H. B. Eddy, Sunday *American*, April 21, 1912

him. That night, on the advice of the manager of the hotel, I communicated with the police, and next morning we advertised in all the papers. Our inquiries led to no result; and from that day to this no word has ever been heard of my unfortunate father. He came home with his heart full of hope to find some peace, some comfort, and instead—"

She put her hand to her throat, and a choking sob cut short the sentence.[44]

"The date?" asked Holmes, opening his note-book.

"He disappeared upon the 3rd of December, 1878—nearly ten years ago."

"His luggage?"

"Remained at the hotel. There was nothing in it to suggest a clue—some clothes, some books, and a considerable number of curiosities from the Andaman Islands.[45] He had been one of the officers in charge of the convict-guard there."

"Had he any friends in town?"

"Only one that we know of—Major Sholto, of his own regiment, the 34th Bombay Infantry.[46] The major had retired some little time before and lived at Upper Norwood.[47] We communicated with him, of course, but he did not even know that his brother officer was in England."

"A singular case," remarked Holmes.

"I have not yet described to you the most singular part. About six years ago—to be exact, upon the 4th of May, 1882—an advertisement appeared in the *Times* asking for the address of Miss Mary Morstan, and stating that it would be to her advantage to come forward. There was no name or address appended. I had at that time just entered the family of Mrs. Cecil Forrester in the capacity of governess.[48] By her advice I published my address in the advertisement column. The same day there arrived through the post a small cardboard box addressed to me, which I found to contain a very large lustrous pearl. No word of writing was enclosed. Since then every year upon the same date there has always appeared a similar box, containing a similar pearl, without any clue as to the sender. They have been pronounced by an expert to be of a rare variety and of considerable value. You can see for yourself that they are very handsome."

She opened a flat box as she spoke and showed me six of the finest pearls that I had ever seen.[49]

44 "This is rather excessive emotion to be exhibited by an Englishwoman of the upper classes when speaking of an event which occurred ten years before and of a person she has long believed dead," T. B. Hunt and H. W. Starr observe, in "What Happened to Mary Morstan?" "She is subject to similar collapses whenever Captain Morstan's death is mentioned. How else can this be explained save by the existence of a marked Oedipus complex?" Hunt and Starr conclude that Mary suffered mental illness and that Watson cared for her throughout her long decline into insanity and referred to this as his "sad bereavement" in "The Empty House."

45 Infamous as the site of one of the world's most sweeping colonial efforts to segregate rebels, the Andamans are a group of 204 islands in the Bay of Bengal, about 120 miles from Cape Negrais, Burma, and 340 miles from the northernmost point of Sumatra. The *Encyclopædia Britannica* (11th Ed.) comments, "The point of enduring interest as regards the Andamans is the penal system, the object of which is to turn the life-sentence and few long-sentence convicts, who alone are sent to the settlement, into honest, self-respecting men and women, by leading them along a continuous course of practice in self-help and self-restraint, and by offering them every inducement to take advantage of that practice." Opened in 1858 and run primarily by James Patterson Walker, a Scotsman who served as surgeon-general of Great Britain, the settlement developed as a response to the mutiny and rebellion against the East India Company of the previous year and was almost entirely for political prisoners. These numbered, at the settlement's opening, 773 Indian convicts, many of whom died shortly after arrival on the Andamans because they were forced to do manual labour in chains and fetters; additionally, 86 prisoners who escaped were hunted down, then hanged and buried in a mass grave, with their fetters still attached. By 1901, there were 11,947 convicts. The penal colony closed in 1947, the year of Indian independence.

46 "At the period of the Mutiny, when the events relating to Morstan and Sholto began, the regimental numbers of the Bombay Infantry of the Indian Army appear to have gone no higher than Thirty," Mrs. Crighton Sellars writes, in "Dr. Watson and the British Army." "Moreover, in the record of their achievements, a thick veil is drawn over the history of the Bombay Infantry during the Mutiny, a sure sign that they were not loyal." She concludes that Watson created a fictional regiment to save the actual company from embarrassment and suggests that Morstan and Sholto were assigned to the Bengal 38th Infantry, known as "The Agra Regiment."

47 Norwood is a large suburban district of London. In 1888, it was divided into Upper, Lower, and South Norwood, all consisting principally of villa residences and detached houses inhabited by the "better classes." There were also a number of large public institutions, including the Lambeth Workhouse Industrial Schools, the Westmoreland Society School, and the Jews Hospital & Orphan Asylum, this last on Knights Hill Road (see note 91, below).

48 Robert J. Bousquet, in "Mary Morstan: Clothed in Euphemism," makes the suggestion (humourously, one hopes) that Mary Morstan was employed as a "governess" in the sense of a *dominatrix* in the Forrester brothel.

49 William S. Baring-Gould argues for a date for the case of 1887, on the basis of the number of pearls (counting one for 1882 and five more for subsequent years). T. S. Blakeney suggests that there were *seven* pearls, but that Mary Morstan had the first pearl made up into a brooch or pendant, not expecting any more. Jay Finley Christ, in *Irregular Chronology of Sherlock Holmes of Baker Street*, agrees with the seven-pearl theory and proposes that Mary may have sold the first one.

Ernest Bloomfield Zeisler is inclined (in his careful *Baker Street Chronology*) to take Mary Morstan at her word: "Miss Morstan's account is detailed, precise and unhesitating. When she says 'About six years ago—to be exact, upon the 4th of May, 1882' she is precise. She has brought the six pearls she has received. She has brought the letter—in its envelope—received by her than morning. She has brought the 'half a dozen pieces of paper' with 'the pearl-box addresses.' There is nowhere the slightest suggestion that her account is not entirely reliable. On the contrary, the Master relies on it, and there is no reason for us not to rely on it." He therefore concludes that the case must be dated in 1887.

"Your statement is most interesting," said Sherlock Holmes. "Has anything else occurred to you?"

"Yes, and no later than to-day. That is why I have come to you. This morning I received this letter, which you will perhaps read for yourself."

"Thank you," said Holmes. "The envelope, too, please. Post-mark, London, S. W. Date, July 7.[50] Hum! Man's thumb-mark on corner—probably postman. Best quality paper. Envelopes at sixpence a packet. Particular man in his stationery. No address. 'Be at the third pillar from the left outside the Lyceum Theatre to-night at seven o'clock. If you are distrustful bring two friends. You are a wronged woman and shall have justice. Do not bring police. If you do, all will be in vain. Your unknown friend.' Well, really, this is a very pretty little mystery! What do you intend to do, Miss Morstan?"

"That is exactly what I want to ask you."

"Then we shall most certainly go—you and I and—yes, why Dr. Watson is the very man. Your correspondent says two friends. He and I have worked together before."

"But would he come?" she asked with something appealing in her voice and expression.

"I shall be proud and happy," said I, fervently, "if I can be of any service."

"You are both very kind," she answered. "I have led a retired life and have no friends whom I could appeal to. If I am here at six it will do, I suppose?"

"You must not be later," said Holmes. "There is one other point, however. Is this handwriting the same as that upon the pearl-box addresses?"

"I have them here," she answered, producing half a dozen pieces of paper.

"You are certainly a model client. You have the correct intuition. Let us see, now." He spread out the papers upon the table and gave little darting glances from one to the other. "They are disguised hands, except the letter," he said presently; "but there can be no question as to the authorship. See how the irrepressible Greek *e* will break out, and see the twirl of the final *s*. They are undoubtedly by the same person. I should not like to suggest false hopes, Miss Morstan, but is there any resemblance between this hand and that of your father?"

50 Arthur Conan Doyle wrote to J. M. Stoddart, editor of *Lippincott's Magazine*, on March 6, 1890: "By the way there is one very obvious mistake which must be corrected in book form—in the second chapter the letter is headed July 7th, and on almost the same page I [*sic*] talk of its being a September evening." (The letter is reproduced in Richard Lancelyn Green's *Uncollected Sherlock Holmes*). Where Doyle obtained this information is unknown, and Watson made no correction in subsequent texts evidently supervised by him.

"Nothing could be more unlike."

"I expected to hear you say so. We shall look out for you, then, at six. Pray allow me to keep the papers. I may look into the matter before then. It is only half-past three. *Au revoir*, then."

"*Au revoir*," said our visitor; and with a bright, kindly glance from one to the other of us, she replaced her pearl-box in her bosom and hurried away.

Standing at the window, I watched her walking briskly down the street until the grey turban and white feather were but a speck in the sombre crowd.

"What a very attractive woman!" I exclaimed, turning to my companion.

He had lit his pipe again and was leaning back with drooping eyelids. "Is she?" he said languidly; "I did not observe."[51]

"You really are an automaton—a calculating machine," I cried. "There is something positively inhuman in you at times."

He smiled gently.

"It is of the first importance," he said, "not to allow your judgment to be biased by personal qualities. A client is to me a mere unit, a factor in a problem. The emotional qualities are antagonistic to clear reasoning. I assure you that the most winning woman I ever knew was hanged for poisoning three little children for their insurance-money,[52] and the most repellent man of my acquaintance is a philanthropist who has spent nearly a quarter of a million upon the London poor."

"In this case, however—"

"I never make exceptions. An exception disproves the rule. Have you ever had occasion to study character in handwriting? What do you make of this fellow's scribble?"[53]

"It is legible and regular," I answered. "A man of business habits and some force of character."

Holmes shook his head.

"Look at his long letters," he said. "They hardly rise above the common herd. That *d* might be an *a*, and that *l* an *e*. Men of character always differentiate their long letters, however illegibly they may write. There is vacillation in his *k*'s and self-esteem in his capitals. I am going out now. I have some few references to make. Let me recommend this book—one of the most remarkable ever penned. It is Winwood Reade's *Martyrdom of Man*.[54] I shall be back in an hour."

51 "Is it possible that a man so observant that he would even notice the depth to which parsley had sunk into the butter on a hot day could fail to notice that Mary Morstan was attractive?" Dr. Richard Asher asks, in "Holmes and the Fair Sex." "No; Holmes was aware of her charms and on guard against them." Holmes intentionally suppressed any emotional feelings for Miss Morstan, he concludes, partly because he recognised Watson's growing feelings. See also the view of Daniel Moriarty, in note 36, above.

52 Asher suggests that this woman may have been Mrs. Morgan, "for a poisoner called Morgan occupied a place of honour in his index among other distinguished M's ('The Empty House')." Donald A. Redmond proposes Mary Ann Cotton (1832–1873), the British serial killer who is said to have used arsenic to fatally poison fourteen to twenty-one people, though she was tried—at the Durham Assizes in March 1873—for the murder of only one, her seven-year-old stepson Charles. Cotton's defence rested on the theory that Charles had ingested bits of his bedroom wallpaper, said to contain traces of arsenic. Pregnant with her seventh child when convicted, Cotton gave birth at Durham County Gaol. She was hanged in the jail yard by executioners Thomas Askern and William Calcraft.

53 The study of handwriting is an important plot device in several stories, most notably "The Reigate Squires," where Holmes makes twenty-seven deductions from the handwriting on a letter.

54 William Winwood Reade (1838–1875) was a traveller, an indifferent novelist, and, briefly, during the portion of the Ashanti War that was fought chiefly in present-day Ghana (1873), a *Times* correspondent. *Martyrdom of Man*, a religious treatment of history that skewered accepted opinion because of its non-religious orientation, was published in London in 1872 and, despite a uniformly hostile public reception (it was not reviewed favourably until 1906), achieved both mass readership and wide popularity among intellectuals such as H. G. Wells. The work remains in print today. Among Reade's other books were his *African Sketch Book*, a travelogue told in the form of a journal (addressed to "Dear Margaret"), and *The Outcast*, completed and published the year Reade died, in which the author—ill from the lingering effects of dysentery and fever contracted during the Ashanti campaign that culminated in the taking of Coomassie (now Kumasi), which he was the only civilian to witness—spoke in fictional form of the effects of persecution that comes from professing one's lack of religious belief. Some view this novel as a confession of belief on the part of Reade. Perhaps one of the most oft-quoted sentences from *Martyrdom of Man*: "Artistic genius is an expansion of monkey imitativeness."

I sat in the window with the volume in my hand, but my thoughts were far from the daring speculations of the writer. My mind ran upon our late visitor—her smiles, the deep rich tones of her voice, the strange mystery which overhung her life. If she were seventeen at the time of her father's disappearance she must be seven-and-twenty now—a sweet age, when youth has lost its self-consciousness and become a little sobered by experience. So I sat and mused until such dangerous thoughts came into my head that I hurried away to my desk and plunged furiously into the latest treatise upon pathology. What was I, an army surgeon with a weak leg and a weaker banking account, that I should dare to think of such things? She was a unit, a factor—nothing more. If my future were black, it was better surely to face it like a man than to attempt to brighten it by mere will-o'-the-wisps of the imagination.

CHAPTER III

In Quest of a Solution

It was half-past five before Holmes returned. He was bright, eager, and in excellent spirits, a mood which in his case alternated with fits of the blackest depression.

"There is no great mystery in this matter," he said, taking the cup of tea which I had poured out for him; "the facts appear to admit of only one explanation."

"What! you have solved it already?"

"Well, that would be too much to say. I have discovered a suggestive fact, that is all. It is, however, *very* suggestive. The details are still to be added. I have just found, on consulting the back files of the *Times*, that Major Sholto, of Upper Norwood, late of the 34th Bombay Infantry, died upon the 28th of April, 1882."

"I may be very obtuse, Holmes, but I fail to see what this suggests."

"No? You surprise me. Look at it in this way, then. Captain Morstan disappears. The only person in London whom he could have visited is Major Sholto. Major Sholto denies having heard that he was in London. Four years later Sholto dies. *Within a week of his death* Captain Morstan's daughter receives a

Dustjacket, *The Sign of Four.*
(London: George Newnes, Ltd., *ca.* 1920)

valuable present, which is repeated from year to year and now culminates in a letter which describes her as a wronged woman. What wrong can it refer to except this deprivation of her father? And why should the presents begin immediately after Sholto's death, unless it is that Sholto's heir knows something of the mystery and desires to make compensation? Have you any alternative theory which will meet the facts?"

"But what a strange compensation! And how strangely made! Why, too, should he write a letter now, rather than six years ago? Again, the letter speaks of giving her justice. What justice can she have? It is too much to suppose that her father is still alive. There is no other injustice in her case that you know of."

"There are difficulties; there are certainly difficulties," said Sherlock Holmes pensively; "but our expedition of to-night will solve them all. Ah, here is a four-wheeler, and Miss Morstan is inside. Are you all ready? Then we had better go down, for it is a little past the hour."

I picked up my hat and my heaviest stick, but I observed that Holmes took his revolver from his drawer and slipped it into his pocket. It was clear that he thought that our night's work might be a serious one.

Miss Morstan was muffled in a dark cloak, and her sensitive face was composed but pale. She must have been more than woman if she did not feel some uneasiness at the strange enterprise upon which we were embarking, yet her self-control was perfect, and she readily answered the few additional questions which Sherlock Holmes put to her.

"Major Sholto was a very particular friend of Papa's," she said. "His letters were full of allusions to the major. He and Papa were in command of the troops at the Andaman Islands, so they were thrown a great deal together. By the way, a curious paper was found in Papa's desk which no one could understand. I don't suppose that it is of the slightest importance, but I thought you might care to see it, so I brought it with me. It is here."

Holmes unfolded the paper carefully and smoothed it out upon his knee. He then very methodically examined it all over with his double lens.

"It is paper of native Indian manufacture," he remarked. "It has at some time been pinned to a board. The diagram upon it appears to be a plan of part of a large building with numerous halls, corridors, and passages. At one point is a small cross done in red ink, and above it is '3.37 from left,' in faded pencil-writing. In the left-hand corner is a curious hieroglyphic like four crosses in a line with their arms touching. Beside it is written, in very rough and coarse characters, 'The sign of the four—Jonathan Small, Mahomet Singh, Abdullah Khan, Dost Akbar.' No, I confess that I do not see how this bears upon the matter. Yet it is evidently a document of importance. It has been kept carefully in a pocket-book, for the one side is as clean as the other."

"It was in his pocket-book that we found it."[55]

"Preserve it carefully, then, Miss Morstan, for it may prove

55 Bernard Davies notes, in "Doctor Watson's Deuteronomy," that Captain Morstan left his pocket-book with the document safe at his hotel, rather than carrying it on his person. "The 'pocket-book' was popularised in Continental countries where the carrying of identity papers was mandatory. This no free-born Englishman could abide, and the habit of carrying pocket-books did not become widespread in Britain until banknotes came into general use after 1914." In popular culture, one of the more memorable uses of a man's pocket-book is in the 1915 novel *The Thirty-Nine Steps*, by John Buchan. (Alfred Hitchcock's 1935 classic *The 39 Steps*, while based on the novel, deviates from it in almost every important aspect.) The protagonist of the book is Richard Hannay, a Scot living in London. Hannay receives a visit from a stranger, Franklin P. Scudder, who reveals a political plot to Hannay and is then murdered, leaving behind a pocket-book containing a substitution cipher and various notes. Hannay, in disguise and carrying the dead man's pocket-book, goes into hiding, cracks the substitution cipher, and eventually helps safeguard Britain's military secrets as World War I looms.

H. B. Eddy, "The Sign of the Four."
San Francisco Call, October 10, 1907

to be of use to us. I begin to suspect that this matter may turn out to be much deeper and more subtle than I at first supposed, I must reconsider my ideas."

He leaned back in the cab, and I could see by his drawn brow and his vacant eye that he was thinking intently. Miss Morstan and I chatted in an undertone about our present expedition and its possible outcome, but our companion maintained his impenetrable reserve until the end of our journey.

It was a September evening and not yet seven o'clock, but the day had been a dreary one, and a dense drizzly fog lay low upon the great city. Mud-coloured clouds drooped sadly over the muddy streets. Down the Strand the lamps were but misty splotches of diffused light which threw a feeble circular glimmer upon the slimy pavement. The yellow glare from the shop-windows streamed out into the steamy, vaporous air and threw a murky, shifting radiance across the crowded thoroughfare. There was, to my mind, something eerie and ghost-like in the endless procession of faces which flitted across these narrow bars of light—sad faces and glad, haggard and merry. Like all humankind, they flitted from the gloom into the light, and so back into the gloom once more. I am not subject to impressions, but the dull, heavy evening, with the strange business upon which we were engaged, combined to make me nervous and depressed. I could see from Miss Morstan's manner that she was suffering from the same feeling. Holmes alone could rise superior to petty influences. He held his open notebook upon his knee, and from time to time he jotted down figures and memoranda in the light of his pocket-lantern.[56]

At the Lyceum Theatre the crowds[57] were already thick at the side-entrances.[58] In front a continuous stream of hansoms and four-wheelers were rattling up, discharging their cargoes of shirt-fronted men and be-shawled, be-diamonded women. We had hardly reached the third pillar, which was our rendezvous, before a small, dark, brisk man in the dress of a coachman accosted us.

"Are you the parties who come with Miss Morstan?" he asked.

"I am Miss Morstan, and these two gentlemen are my friends," said she.

He bent a pair of wonderfully penetrating and questioning eyes upon us.

"You will excuse me, miss," he said, with a certain dogged manner, "but I was to ask you to give me your word that neither of your companions is a police-officer."

"After the Play—Under the Lyceum Portico."
Graphic (1881)

56 This is a pocket-sized version of the "dark lantern" mentioned in a number of the stories (for example, "The Red-Headed League"). See *A Study in Scarlet*, note 137. Of course, the heat of the flame would deter keeping a lit pocket lantern in one's pocket.

57 A number of American editions and the Crowborough edition have the curious misprint "crows." According to the *Annotated "Annotated,"* "Peter Blau and Cameron Hollyer determined that the 'crows' appeared first in the *Crow*borough edition [of the Canon]. The Doubleday Memorial Edition in two volumes [the standard American text] was printed from the Crowborough plates. When new plates were made for the 1936 single-volume Doubleday edition the error was copied. These plates were used for the 1953 two-volume edition."

58 The Lyceum Theatre had a long association (1878–1903) with eminent actors Henry Irving (1838–1905) and Ellen Terry (1848–1928) and was managed by civil servant and drama critic Abraham "Bram" Stoker, the author of *Dracula* (1897). According to Christopher Morley, "They were probably playing Shakespeare at the time of this rendezvous, which would account for the crowd of devotees, though seven o'clock is surely too early for the carriage trade to be arriving." Morley also notes the "happy coincidence" that William Gillette's play *Sherlock Holmes* was performed at the Lyceum in 1901.

59 Kelvin I. Jones, in *The Carfax Syndrome*, observes that the physical characteristics of the driver match those of Bram Stoker and concludes that the meeting-place of the Lyceum was not randomly selected and that Holmes was involved in the affairs described in Stoker's *Dracula*. However, Barbara Belford, in *Bram Stoker: A Biography of the Author of Dracula*, describes Stoker as an undergraduate as six foot two inches in height and weighing 175 pounds—hardly "small."

"A small, brisk man in the dress of a coachman accosted us."
Frederic Dorr Steele, *Adventures of Sherlock Holmes*, Vol. I, 1950. The illustration indicates that it was "re-drawn by Mr. Steele for this edition." Andrew Malec, in a fine bit of detection, identifies the picture as first appearing as an illustration to Richard Harding Davis's *The Adventures of the Scarlet Car*, in *Collier's Weekly* for December 15, 1906 (although difficult to see, note the '06 next to the artist's signature). Note the flashlights and motoring garb, certainly anachronistic for 1888; also, one of the figures mentioned in the text is missing.

"I give you my word on that," she answered.

He gave a shrill whistle, on which a street Arab led across a four-wheeler and opened the door. The man who had addressed us mounted to the box, while we took our places inside. We had hardly done so before the driver[59] whipped up his horse, and we plunged away at a furious pace through the foggy streets.

The situation was a curious one. We were driving to an unknown place, on an unknown errand. Yet our invitation was either a complete hoax—which was an inconceivable hypothesis—or else we had good reason to think that important issues might hang upon our journey. Miss Morstan's demeanour was as resolute and collected as ever. I endeavoured to cheer and amuse her by reminiscences of my adventures in Afghanistan; but, to tell the truth, I was myself so excited at our situation, and so curious as to our destination, that my stories were slightly involved. To this day she declares that I told her one moving anecdote as to how a musket looked into my tent at the dead of night, and how I fired a double-barrelled tiger cub[60] at it. At first I had some idea as to the direction in which we were driving; but soon, what with our pace, the fog, and my own limited knowledge of London,[61] I lost my bearings and knew nothing save that we seemed to be going a very long way. Sherlock Holmes was never at fault, however,[62] and he muttered the names as the cab rattled through squares and in and out by tortuous by-streets.[63]

"Rochester Row,"[64] said he. "Now Vincent Square.[65] Now we come out on the Vauxhall Bridge Road.[66] We are making for the Surrey side[67] apparently. Yes, I thought so. Now we are on the bridge.[68] You can catch glimpses of the river."

We did indeed get a fleeting view of a stretch of the Thames, with the lamps shining upon the broad, silent water; but our cab dashed on and was soon involved in a labyrinth of streets upon the other side.

"Wandsworth Road,"[69] said my companion. "Priory Road.[70] Larkhall Lane.[71] Stockwell Place.[72] Robert Street.[73] Coldharbour Lane.[74] Our quest does not appear to take us to very fashionable regions."

We had indeed reached a questionable and forbidding neighbourhood. Long lines of dull brick houses were only relieved by the coarse glare and tawdry brilliancy of public-houses at the corner. Then came rows of two-storeyed villas, each with a fronting of miniature garden, and then again interminable lines of new, staring brick buildings—the monster tentacles which the giant city was throwing out into the country. At last the cab drew up at the third house in a new ter-

"... a small, dark, brisk man in the dress of a coachman ..."
Richard Gutschmidt, *Das Zeichen der Vier* (Stuttgart: Robert Lutz Verlag, 1902)

60 "The celebrated 'double-barrelled' tiger cub must, I think, have been a snow leopard," T. S. Blakeney writes, in "Thoughts on The Sign of the Four," pointing out that tigers do not inhabit either the Kandahar/Maiwand region or the Peshawar region, where Watson would have found one. The double-barrelled gun was invented in Italy in 1653 by Giuliano Bossi and was widely used in warfare. Napoleon commissioned a beautiful double-barrelled musket for his personal use.

61 This seems to be self-effacing nonsense; Watson had certainly lived in the great metropolis for at least seven years by the time of *The Sign of Four.*

62 "It is a hobby of mine to have an exact knowledge of London," Holmes says in "The Red-Headed League," and in "The Empty House," Watson writes: "Holmes's knowledge of the byways of London was extraordinary."

63 In "Was Holmes a Londoner?" Bernard Davies concludes that, in light of Holmes's use of obsolete street names (see, *e.g.*, notes 72 and 73, below), "Holmes's knowledge of this part of London, while of an extremely detailed kind, had not been brought up to date. . . . It was a knowledge born of an intimate acquaintance many years before, certainly long before he appears in his London rooms in *The Gloria Scott.*"

64 Rochester Row, leading to Horseferry Road, is about halfway along the Vauxhall Bridge Road on the east side. Nearby is Tothill Fields Prison, built in 1836, and the police court for this district, opened in 1846, is in the Row.

65 According to Augustus J. C. Hare, in his *Walks in London*, "The large open space called *Vincent Square* is used as a playground by the Westminster Scholars."

66 The Vauxhall Bridge Road connects Hyde Park Corner, Grosvenor Place, and the south of London and was originally conceived as part of a thoroughfare from Hyde Park Corner to Greenwich.

67 The Surrey Side, as the area south of the Thames was commonly known, housed over 750,000 people in 1896. *Baedeker* describes it as "a scene of great business life and bustle from Lambeth to Bermondsey, but its sights, institutions, and public buildings are few."

68 The Vauxhall Bridge, originally a nine-span structure called (at least during the initial phases of construction) Regent's Bridge, was completed in 1816 and substantially rebuilt from 1904 to 1906. Featuring sculpted bronze female figures by Frederick Pomeroy and Alfred Drury that apostrophise Agriculture, Engineering, and other arts and sciences, it was the first cast-iron bridge across the Thames, and the first to convey trams. Though not as spectacular as, for example, the 1817 Waterloo Bridge ("a colossal monument worthy of Sesostris and the Caesars"—M. Dupin), its history is venerable.

69 American editions of the Canon refer to "Wordsworth Road." Wandsworth Road is a major artery in South Lambeth. If one consults a map, it is evident that the party should not have turned on Wandsworth Road but instead travelled south on Lambeth Road. However, the reference to Priory Road (which changes its name before reaching Lambeth Road) makes it clear that, for whatever reason (traffic, perhaps), the driver proceeded slightly out of the way by driving south on Wandsworth Road and then "cut over" on Priory/Lansdowne Road.

70 Priory Road runs perpendicular to Wandsworth—east, until it becomes Lansdowne Road, connecting Wandsworth Road to Clapham Road.

71 Larkhall Lane is parallel to Wandsworth Road, off Lansdowne Road.

72 Stockwell Place is not a road but rather an *address*, a row of some dozen houses in Clapham Road, Stockwell, abolished in 1869 when the road was renumbered. Watson's faithful listing of the names Holmes rattled off, consisting, as it does, not only of streets but of this building, may confuse the casual reader into searching for a non-existent road. Or perhaps Holmes actually said "Stockwell Park Road," the continuation of Lansdowne Road after it crosses the Clapham Road. This entire area is called Stockwell. While this is a logical route to Cold Harbour Lane, it is not necessarily the shortest. However, only on this street would the party have passed Robert Street. A shorter route would have been to turn off Lansdowne Road onto Binfield Road, continuing on Stockwell Road, which, with its continuation named Canterbury Road, runs directly to Cold Harbour Lane. Again, the dictates of traffic may have suggested the alternate route.

73 Stockwell Park Road continues to Robsart Street, a left turn from the Park Road. William S. Baring-Gould notes that Robsart Street was the renamed version of the combination of Park and Robert Streets, effected in April 1880.

74 Cold Harbour Lane is an east-west road beginning at approximately the intersection of the Brixton Road and Effra Road, where it is the continuation of Clapham Park Street and Acre Lane. A quick glance at a map will show that the party would not have turned on the Robsart Road, only driven past it. It is the last cross-street along Stockwell Park Road before coming to the Brixton Road and only a race.[75] None of the other houses were inhabited, and that at which we stopped was as dark as its neighbours, save for a single glimmer in the kitchen-window. On our knocking, however, the door was instantly thrown open by a Hindoo servant, clad in a yellow turban, white loose-fitting clothes, and a yellow sash. There was something strangely incongruous in this Oriental figure framed in the commonplace doorway of a third-rate suburban dwelling-house.

"The *sahib*[76] awaits you," said he, and even as he spoke, there came a high, piping voice from some inner room.

"Show them in to me, *khitmutgar*,"[77] it said. "Show them straight in to me."

few blocks from the sharp left turn off the Brixton Road into Cold Harbour Lane. This is the vicinity of Brixton Station, and the neighbourhood, abutting Angell Town, is known, of course, as Brixton.

75 There is little to go on here to identify Thaddeus Sholto's "oasis," but several try: Robert R. Pattrick, in " 'The Oasis in the Howling Desert,' " nominates a location on Dorchester Drive. Humphrey Morton, in his entry in a photographic competition of the *Sherlock Holmes Journal*, selects No. 3, Milkwood Road. Percy Metcalfe ("Reflections on the Sign of Four or Oreamnosis Once Removed") proposes Dalberg Road, while Bernard Davies ("Dr. Watson's Deuteronomy") presents the two connected double houses on Gubyon Avenue just south of Woodquest Avenue. David L. Hammer, in *The Worth of the Game*, casts his vote for Davies's candidate.

76 According to the *Anglo-Indian Dictionary*, the word means "[a] lord, a master. The word is often affixed to titles expressive of rank, as Rájá Sáheb, Collector Sáheb. It is similarly affixed to proper names. It is also used by itself as a respectful appellation. Again, the word is often used as the peculiar designation of an English gentleman."

77 Hindustani: A servant or personal attendant.

CHAPTER IV

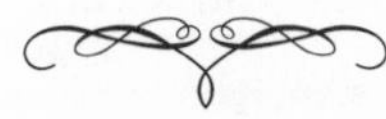

The Story of the Bald-Headed Man

78 "Rubbed" in various editions.

WE FOLLOWED THE Indian down a sordid and common passage, ill-lit and worse furnished, until he came to a door upon the right, which he threw open. A blaze of yellow light streamed out upon us, and in the centre of the glare there stood a small man with a very high head, a bristle of red hair all round the fringe of it, and a bald, shining scalp which shot out from among it like a mountain-peak from fir-trees. He writhed[78] his hands together as he stood, and his features were in a perpetual jerk—now smiling, now scowling, but never for an instant in repose. Nature had given him a pendulous lip, and a too visible line of yellow and irregular teeth, which he strove feebly to conceal by constantly passing his hand over the lower part of his face. In spite of his obtrusive baldness, he gave the impression of youth. In point of fact, he had just turned his thirtieth year.

"Your servant, Miss Morstan," he kept repeating, in a thin, high voice. "Your servant, gentlemen. Pray step into my little sanctum. A small place, miss, but furnished to my own liking. An oasis of art in the howling desert of South London."

We were all astonished by the appearance of the apartment

Dustjacket, *The Sign of Four.*
Sixpenny Series (London: George Newnes, Ltd., *ca.* 1920)

into which he invited us. In that sorry house it looked as out of place as a diamond of the first water in a setting of brass. The richest and glossiest of curtains and tapestries draped the walls, looped back here and there to expose some richly-mounted painting or Oriental vase. The carpet was of amber and black, so soft and so thick that the foot sank pleasantly into it, as into a bed of moss. Two great tiger-skins thrown athwart it increased the suggestion of Eastern luxury, as did a huge *hookah* which stood upon a mat in the corner. A lamp in the fashion of a silver dove was hung from an almost invisible golden wire in the centre of the room. As it burned it filled the air with a subtle and aromatic odour.[79]

"Mr. Thaddeus Sholto,"[80] said the little man, still jerking and smiling. "That is my name. You are Miss Morstan, of course. And these gentlemen—"

"This is Mr. Sherlock Holmes, and this Dr. Watson."

"A doctor, eh?" cried he, much excited. "Have you your stethoscope?[81] Might I ask you—would you have the kindness? I have grave doubts as to my mitral valve, if you would be so very good. The aortic I may rely upon, but I should value your opinion upon the mitral."[82]

I listened to his heart, as requested, but was unable to find anything amiss, save, indeed, that he was in an ecstasy of fear, for he shivered from head to foot.

"It appears to be normal," I said. "You have no cause for uneasiness."[83]

"You will excuse my anxiety, Miss Morstan," he remarked airily. "I am a great sufferer, and I have long had suspicions as to that valve. I am delighted to hear that they are unwarranted. Had your father, Miss Morstan, refrained from throwing a strain upon his heart, he might have been alive now."

I could have struck the man across the face, so hot was I at this callous and offhand reference to so delicate a matter. Miss Morstan sat down, and her face grew white to the lips.

"I knew in my heart that he was dead," said she.

"I can give you every information," said he; "and, what is more, I can do you justice; and I will, too, whatever Brother Bartholomew[84] may say. I am so glad to have your friends here not only as an escort to you but also as witnesses to what I am about to do and say. The three of us can show a bold front to Brother Bartholomew. But let us have no outsiders—no police or officials. We can settle everything satisfactorily among ourselves without any interference. Nothing would annoy Brother Bartholomew more than any publicity."

He sat down upon a low settee and blinked at us inquiringly with his weak, watery blue eyes.

"For my part," said Holmes, "whatever you may choose to say will go no further."

I nodded to show my agreement.

"That is well! That is well!" said he. "May I offer you a glass of Chianti, Miss Morstan? Or of Tokay?[85] I keep no other

79 Rodin and Key suggest that Sholto "may have smoked opium in [the] hookah to calm his nerves."

80 Randy Roberts, in "Dr. Watson's Warning," argues that Watson, in disguising the real identity of Thaddeus Sholto, deliberately caricatured Oscar Wilde in order to convey information to the eighth Marquess of Queensberry (John *Sholto* Douglas) about the relationship between Wilde and the Marquess's son Lord Alfred Douglas. While the idea is interesting, Roberts fails to answer why Watson should have *published* the warning, rather than merely conveying it in a private letter. The characteristics common to the two men are notable: the discoloured teeth, the thick sensual lips, the habit of covering their mouths when speaking (referred to by Hesketh Pearson in his biography *Oscar Wilde: His Life and Wit* [1949]), their tastes in decor and art (Wilde's are frequently mentioned in his private letters). On the other hand, Wilde was not small, bald-headed, or red-haired, and no one has suggested that Sholto *was* Oscar Wilde.

81 "It is surprising to learn that [Watson] carried his stethoscope around when he was not in practice, and at that time did not expect to be," comments D. Martin Dakin. "He was indeed a Boy Scout before his time, determined to Be Prepared for anything."

82 A heartbeat has two parts. The first is the distinctive sound of the closing of the mitral and tricuspid valves; the second is the equally specific, recognisable sound of the closing of the pulmonary and aortic semilunar valves. These sounds—sometimes rendered as "lub-dub"—are caused by the vibration of the walls of the heart and major vessels around the heart and can be heard with a stethoscope when the vibrations of the blood flow reach

wines.[86] Shall I open a flask? No? Well, then, I trust that you have no objection to tobacco-smoke, to the balsamic odour of the Eastern tobacco. I am a little nervous, and I find my hookah an invaluable sedative."

He applied a taper to the great bowl, and the smoke bubbled merrily through the rose-water. We sat all three in a semicircle, with our heads advanced and our chins upon our hands, while the strange, jerky little fellow, with his high, shining head, puffed uneasily in the centre.

"When I first determined to make this communication to you," said he, "I might have given you my address; but I feared that you might disregard my request and bring unpleasant people with you. I took the liberty, therefore, of making an appointment in such a way that my man Williams might be able to see you first. I have complete confidence in his discretion, and he had orders, if he were dissatisfied, to proceed no further in the matter. You will excuse these precautions, but I am a man of somewhat retiring, and I might even say refined, tastes, and there is nothing more unaesthetic than a policeman. I have a natural shrinking from all forms of rough materialism, I seldom come in contact with the rough crowd. I live, as you see, with some little atmosphere of elegance around me. I may call myself a patron of the arts. It is my weakness. The landscape is a genuine Corot,[87] and, though a connoisseur might

Souvenier de Mortefontaine.
Corot (Salon of 1864)

that portion of the chest wall in contact with the heart.

83 But Donald A. Redmond, in "The Oasis in the Howling Desert," concludes that Watson mis-diagnosed Sholto, because he failed to take into account the visible signs of Sholto's nervous agitation—his facial and manual gestures—suggesting aortic regurgitation.

84 D. Martin Dakin wonders at the biblical names bestowed on the disreputable Major Sholto's sons. "Perhaps it was the deceased Mrs. Sholto who was responsible."

85 Noel Coward, in his operetta *Bitter Sweet* (1929), set in nineteenth-century Austria and revolving around the elopement of a young woman with her music teacher, called it "Tokay, the golden sunshine of a summer day." The Hungarian wine is made from three varieties of white grape—Furmint, Hárslevelü, and Muskotály—with the first being predominant. "Tokaji alone on a label is almost certainly a fraud," according to wine expert André L. Simon. "[I]t should be followed by Aszu, Szamorodni or Essencia." The first and last are sweet; the middle, dry. Tokay is mentioned again in "His Last Bow," when Holmes and Watson share a bottle.

86 Cyrus Durgin points out, in "The Speckled Band," that Chianti, a dry table wine that stores poorly, and Tokay, a commonly fortified wine similar to brandy, are an unusual combination to be found in an Englishman's at-hand bar. "I suppose the only conclusion is that a person who would keep only Tokay and Chianti—two wines very different in every respect—would necessarily be an eccentric person. I think we are entitled to assume, from the evidence of the narrative, that Mr. Thaddeus Sholto was indeed peculiar."

87 Jean Baptiste Camille Corot (1796–1875),

perhaps throw a doubt upon that Salvator Rosa,[88] there cannot be the least question about the Bouguereau.[89] I am partial to the modern French school."[90]

"You will excuse me, Mr. Sholto," said Miss Morstan, "but I am here at your request to learn something which you desire to tell me. It is very late, and I should desire the interview to be as short as possible."

"At the best it must take some time," he answered; "for we shall certainly have to go to Norwood and see Brother Bartholomew. We shall all go and try if we can get the better of Brother Bartholomew. He is very angry with me for taking the course which has seemed right to me. I had quite high words with him last night. You cannot imagine what a terrible fellow he is when he is angry."

"If we are to go to Norwood, it would perhaps be as well to start at once," I ventured to remark.

He laughed until his ears were quite red.

"That would hardly do," he cried. "I don't know what he

Soldiers and Peasants in a Rocky Landscape.
Salvator Rosa (*ca.* 1650)

French landscape and figure painter. Forgeries of his work abound. Corot was a painter who never descended to ideological controversy, and in his personal habits he was unassuming and generous, providing for his contemporary Honoré Daumier (1808–1875), for instance, when the great political cartoonist and painter was near-destitute and had lost his sight. Oscar Wilde expressed his delight in the painter's works in a private letter.

88 A renowned painter of the Neapolitan School (1615–1673), Rosa was also a poet and satirist. In a private letter, Wilde expressed the hope that his play *The Duchess of Padua* would have a "Salvator Rosa" effect.

89 Adolphe William Bouguereau (1825–1905), a French painter whose works were most frequently of religious and mythological subjects. Christopher Morley remarks, "Mr. Sholto, as a man of refined tastes, would have been grieved to know that Bouguereau's *Nymphs and Faun* was for many years the most famous barroom painting in New York, at the old Hoffman House on Fifth Avenue."

90 Ben Wolf ("Zero Wolf Meets Sherlock Holmes") raises an eyebrow at Sholto's statement that he favours the modern school, "since Sholto's statement was made in the year 1888, 14 years after the Impressionists had shown in Paris. Thaddeus would seem to have permitted his subscription to the *Gazette des Beaux-Arts* to lapse some years earlier."

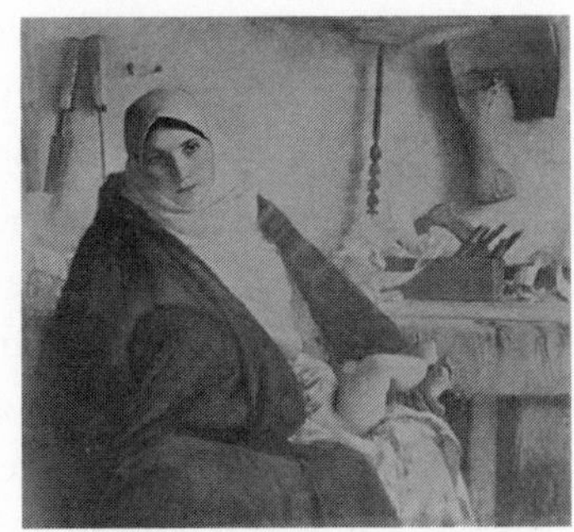

Madonna.
Bouguereau (1885)

would say if I brought you in that sudden way. No, I must prepare you by showing you how we all stand to each other. In the first place, I must tell you that there are several points in the story of which I am myself ignorant. I can only lay the facts before you as far as I know them myself.

"My father was, as you may have guessed, Major John Sholto, once of the Indian Army. He retired some eleven years ago and came to live at Pondicherry Lodge in Upper Norwood.[91] He had prospered in India and brought back with him a considerable sum of money, a large collection of valuable curiosities, and a staff of native servants. With these advantages he bought himself a house, and lived in great luxury. My twin-brother Bartholomew and I were the only children.

"I very well remember the sensation which was caused by the disappearance of Captain Morstan. We read the details in the papers, and knowing that he had been a friend of our father's we discussed the case freely in his presence. He used to join in our speculations as to what could have happened. Never for an instant did we suspect that he had the whole secret hidden in his own breast, that of all men he alone knew the fate of Arthur Morstan.[92]

"We did know, however, that some mystery, some positive danger, overhung our father. He was very fearful of going out alone, and he always employed two prize-fighters to act as porters at Pondicherry Lodge. Williams, who drove you to-night, was one of them. He was once light-weight champion of England. Our father would never tell us what it was he feared, but he had a most marked aversion to men with wooden legs.

91 David L. Hammer identifies the house as "Beaulieu Lodge" (pronounced Bewley), off Church Street, on the summit of South Norwood Hill. Percy Metcalfe suggests either Beaulieu or, more likely, in his view, Hazelwood, about a mile and a half from Knights Hill, while Bernard Davies builds a detailed case for Kilravock House, now Ross Road SE26, but formerly in Upper Norwood.

92 It is curious that Jonathan Small knew nothing of the fate of Captain Morstan and apparently cared nothing about it. He expresses his solidarity with the remaining three of the "Four" but seems to have little sympathy for the Captain, who was cheated by Sholto as badly as the others were and who seems to have acted fairly toward Small and the others.

On one occasion he actually fired his revolver at a wooden-legged man, who proved to be a harmless tradesman canvassing for orders.[93] We had to pay a large sum to hush the matter up. My brother and I used to think this a mere whim of my father's, but events have since led us to change our opinion.

"Early in 1882 my father received a letter from India which was a great shock to him.[94] He nearly fainted at the breakfast-table when he opened it, and from that day he sickened to his death. What was in the letter we could never discover, but I could see as he held it that it was short and written in a scrawling hand. He had suffered for years from an enlarged spleen, but he now became rapidly worse, and towards the end of April we were informed that he was beyond all hope, and that he wished to make a last communication to us.

"When we entered his room, he was propped up with pillows and breathing heavily.[95] He besought us to lock the door and to come upon either side of the bed. Then, grasping our hands he made a remarkable statement to us in a voice which was broken as much by emotion as by pain. I shall try and give it to you in his own very words.

" 'I have only one thing,' he said, 'which weighs upon my mind at this supreme moment. It is my treatment of poor Morstan's orphan. The cursed greed which has been my besetting sin through life has withheld from her the treasure, half at least of which should have been hers. And yet I have made no use of it myself, so blind and foolish a thing is avarice. The mere feeling of possession has been so dear to me that I could not bear to share it with another. See that chaplet tipped with pearls beside the quinine bottle. Even that I could not bear to part with, although I had got it out with the design of sending it to her. You, my sons, will give her a fair share of the Agra[96] treasure. But send her nothing—not even the chaplet—until I am gone. After all, men have been as bad as this and have recovered.[97]

" 'I will tell you how Morstan died,' he continued. 'He had suffered for years from a weak heart, but he concealed it from every one. I alone knew it. When in India, he and I, through a remarkable chain of circumstances, came into possession of a considerable treasure. I brought it over to England, and on the night of Morstan's arrival he came straight over here to claim his share. He walked over from the station and was admitted

93 The only other wooden-legged men who are named in the Canon are Josiah Amberley, the eponymous client in "The Retired Colourman," and Francis Prosper, suitor of the maid Lucy Parr in "The Beryl Coronet." Prosper is described as a "greengrocer," assuredly a tradesman, and Upper Norwood does lie adjacent to Streatham, the scene of "The Beryl Coronet." The suggestion of the identity of the "tradesman" was first made by Gavin Brend to T. S. Blakeney. (An unnamed wooden-legged news-vendor appears in "The Illustrious Client" and is depicted on the cover of the *Sherlock Holmes Journal* of the Sherlock Holmes Society of London.)

94 What was in this letter? We may deduce that the "great shock" that the letter contained must have been the news that Jonathan Small had escaped from his confinement in the Andamans. However, the letter surely cannot have been the news that Small had *just* escaped, for in 1882, "three or four years ago," according to Small (although this does not square with the other indications that the case took place in 1888), after "drift[ing] about the world" for some apparent time, Small travelled to London. Therefore, Small must have escaped shortly after Captain Morstan's death, in 1879 or 1880.

Who would have sent Sholto a letter containing such news, even if late? Presumably neither Sholto nor Morstan would have told any of their colleagues of their financial arrangement with Small. It is possible that the letter came from a colleague of Sholto's who had been posted to India and who merely wrote Sholto of various gossip concerning his old posting in the Andamans. Ian McQueen suggests that Small himself wrote this letter from India, just before his travel to London (see note 145, below.)

95 On the basis of the skimpy evidence, medical authorities suggest varying diagnoses, including orthopnea (difficulty breathing except when upright), heart failure due to hypertension, and pneumonia.

" 'I will tell you how Morstan died,' he continued."
Richard Gutschmidt, *Das Zeichen der Vier* (Stuttgart: Robert Lutz Verlag, 1902)

by my faithful old Lal Chowdar, who is now dead. Morstan and I had a difference of opinion as to the division of the treasure, and we came to heated words. Morstan had sprung out of his chair in a paroxysm of anger, when he suddenly pressed his hand to his side, his face turned a dusky hue, and he fell backwards, cutting his head against the corner of the treasure-chest. When I stooped over him I found, to my horror, that he was dead.

" 'For a long time I sat half distracted, wondering what I should do. My first impulse was, of course, to call for assistance; but I could not but recognize that there was every chance that I would be accused of his murder. His death at the moment of a quarrel, and the gash in his head, would be black against me. Again, an official inquiry could not be made without bringing out some facts about the treasure, which I was

96 Agra, capital (or "headquarters") of the Agra district of India and until 1648 the capital of India, is famous for the Agra fort, which features in Jonathan Small's narrative, and the Táj-Mahal, a splendid mausoleum built during the Mughal dynasty (mid-sixteenth to seventeenth centuries) by the Emperor Sháh Jahán (1592–1666) for the remains of his favourite wife, Mumtázá Mahal, who died delivering their fourteenth child. Shah Jahan himself, "King of the World," is also buried there, having lived out his last years as a prisoner in the Agra fort during the course of his four sons' internecine fight for the throne.

Agra Fort.

97 T. S. Blakeney notes that Sholto's conduct is reflective of the generally low standard of conduct of officers of the British and Indian Armies as reported in the Canon—see, for example, Colonel Sebastian Moran (of "The Empty House") or Colonel Valentine Walter ("The Bruce-Partington Plans"). Not only did Sholto gamble to the point of ruin, he assisted in the escape of four murderers, ultimately double-crossing them. "Even his regrets about Miss Morstan were lip-service only—he urged his sons to do nothing for her in his lifetime. He must have had a hardened conscience indeed!"

"I found to my horror that he was dead."
Charles A. Cox, *The Sign of the Four* (Chicago and New York: The Henneberry Company, n.d.)

particularly anxious to keep secret. He had told me that no soul upon earth knew where he had gone. There seemed to be no necessity why any soul ever should know.

" 'I was still pondering over the matter, when, looking up, I saw my servant, Lal Chowdar, in the doorway. He stole in and bolted the door behind him. "Do not fear, *sahib*," he said; "no one need know that you have killed him. Let us hide him away, and who is the wiser?" "I did not kill him," said I. Lal Chowdar shook his head and smiled. "I heard it all, *sahib*," said he; "I heard you quarrel, and I heard the blow. But my lips are sealed. All are asleep in the house. Let us put him away together." That was enough to decide me. If my own servant could not believe my innocence, how could I hope to make it good before twelve foolish tradesmen in a jury-box? Lal Chowdar and I disposed of the body that night, and within a few days the London papers were full of the mysterious disappearance of Captain Morstan. You will see from what I say that I can hardly be blamed in the matter. My fault lies in the fact that we concealed not only the body, but also the treasure, and that I have clung to Morstan's share as well as to my own. I wish you, therefore, to make restitution. Put your ears down to my mouth. The treasure is hidden in—'

"At this instant a horrible change came over his expression; his eyes stared wildly, his jaw dropped, and he yelled, in a voice which I can never forget, 'Keep him out! For Christ's sake keep him out!' We both stared round at the window behind us upon which his gaze was fixed. A face was looking in at us out of the darkness. We could see the whitening of the

"He yelled in a voice which I can never forget,
'Keep him out! For Christ's sake keep him out!' "
R. Courtois, *La Marque des Quatre* (Paris: Pierre Lafitte, 1923)

nose where it was pressed against the glass. It was a bearded, hairy face, with wild cruel eyes and an expression of concentrated malevolence. My brother and I rushed towards the window, but the man was gone. When we returned to my father his head had dropped and his pulse had ceased to beat.

"We searched the garden that night but found no sign of the intruder save that just under the window a single footmark was visible in the flower-bed. But for that one trace, we might have thought that our imaginations had conjured up that wild, fierce face. We soon, however, had another and a more striking proof that there were secret agencies at work all round us. The window of my father's room was found open in the morning, his cupboards and boxes had been rifled, and upon his chest was fixed a torn piece of paper, with the words 'The sign of the four' scrawled across it. What the phrase meant or who our secret visitor may have been, we never knew. As far as we can judge, none of my father's property had been actually stolen, though everything had been turned out. My brother and I naturally associated this peculiar incident with the fear which haunted my father during his life, but it is still a complete mystery to us."

The little man stopped to relight his hookah and puffed thoughtfully for a few moments. We had all sat absorbed, listening to his extraordinary narrative. At the short account of her father's death Miss Morstan had turned deadly white, and for a moment I feared that she was about to faint. She rallied, however, on drinking a glass of water which I quietly poured out for her from a Venetian carafe upon the side-table. Sherlock Holmes leaned back in his chair with an abstracted expression and the lids drawn low over his glittering eyes. As I glanced at him I could not but think how on that very day he had complained bitterly of the commonplaceness of life. Here at least was a problem which would tax his sagacity to the utmost. Mr. Thaddeus Sholto looked from one to the other of us with an obvious pride at the effect which his story had produced and then continued between the puffs of his overgrown pipe.

"My brother and I," said he, "were, as you may imagine, much excited as to the treasure which my father had spoken of. For weeks and for months we dug and delved in every part of the garden without discovering its whereabouts. It was maddening to think that the hiding-place was on his very lips at the moment that he died. We could judge the splendour of the missing riches by the chaplet which he had taken out. Over this chaplet my brother Bartholomew and I had some little discussion. The pearls were evidently of great value, and he was averse to part with them, for, between friends, my brother was himself a little inclined to my father's fault. He thought, too, that if we parted with the chaplet it might give rise to gossip and finally bring us into trouble. It was all that I could do to persuade him to let me find out Miss Morstan's address and send her a detached pearl at fixed intervals, so that at least she might never feel destitute."

"It was a kindly thought," said our companion earnestly; "it was extremely good of you."

The little man waved his hand deprecatingly.

"We were your trustees," he said; "that was the view which I took of it, though Brother Bartholomew could not altogether see it in that light. We had plenty of money ourselves. I desired no more. Besides, it would have been such bad taste to have treated a young lady in so scurvy a fashion. '*Le mauvais goût mène au crime.*'[98] The French have a very neat way of putting these things. Our difference of opinion on this subject went so far that I thought it best to set up rooms for myself; so I left Pondicherry Lodge, taking the old *khitmutgar* and Williams with me. Yesterday, however, I learned that an event of extreme importance has occurred. The treasure has been discovered. I instantly communicated with Miss Morstan, and it only remains for us to drive out to Norwood and demand our share. I explained my views last night to Brother Bartholomew, so we shall be expected, if not welcome, visitors."

Mr. Thaddeus Sholto ceased and sat twitching on his luxurious settee. We all remained silent, with our thoughts upon the new development which the mysterious business had taken. Holmes was the first to spring to his feet.

"You have done well, sir, from first to last," said he. "It is possible that we may be able to make you some small return by throwing some light upon that which is still dark to you. But, as Miss Morstan remarked just now, it is late, and we had best put the matter through without delay."

Our new acquaintance very deliberately coiled up the tube of his hookah and produced from behind a curtain a very long

98 "Bad taste leads to crime." William S. Baring-Gould observes that the expression was coined by Le Baron de Mareste but was immortalised by the writer Stendhal (Henri Beyle, 1783–1842).

befrogged[99] topcoat with astrakhan collar and cuffs. This he buttoned tightly up in spite of the extreme closeness of the night and finished his attire by putting on a rabbit-skin cap with hanging lappets[100] which covered the ears, so that no part of him was visible save his mobile and peaky[101] face.

"My health is somewhat fragile," he remarked as he led the way down the passage. "I am compelled to be a valetudinarian."[102]

Our cab was awaiting us outside, and our programme was evidently prearranged, for the driver started off at once at a rapid pace. Thaddeus Sholto talked incessantly in a voice which rose high above the rattle of the wheels.

"Bartholomew is a clever fellow," said he. "How do you think he found out where the treasure was? He had come to the conclusion that it was somewhere indoors, so he worked out all the cubic space of the house and made measurements everywhere so that not one inch should be unaccounted for. Among other things, he found that the height of the building was seventy-four feet, but on adding together the heights of all the separate rooms and making every allowance for the space between, which he ascertained by borings, he could not bring the total to more than seventy feet. There were four feet unaccounted for. These could only be at the top of the building. He knocked a hole, therefore, in the lath and plaster ceiling of the highest room, and there, sure enough, he came upon another little garret above it, which had been sealed up and was known to no one. In the centre stood the treasure-chest resting upon two rafters. He lowered it through the hole, and there it lies. He computes the value of the jewels at not less than half a million sterling."[103]

At the mention of this gigantic sum we all stared at one another open-eyed. Miss Morstan, could we secure her rights, would change from a needy governess to the richest heiress in England. Surely it was the place of a loyal friend to rejoice at such news; yet I am ashamed to say that selfishness took me by the soul and that my heart turned as heavy as lead within me. I stammered out some few halting words of congratulation and then sat downcast, with my head drooped, deaf to the babble of our new acquaintance. He was clearly a confirmed hypochondriac, and I was dreamily conscious that he was pouring forth interminable trains of symptoms, and imploring informa-

99 Buttoned with "frogs," loops (often braided) that pass over a bar-shaped button, knot, or decorative fastening.

100 Ear-flaps.

101 Having a pinched or emaciated look; more commonly "peaked" today.

102 A person with a weak constitution, or one who is sickly, and whose overriding concern is chronic invalidism.

103 About $2.5 million in American dollars, over £32 million, or over $60 million, in 2005 purchasing power.

tion as to the composition and action of innumerable quack nostrums, some of which he bore about in a leather case in his pocket. I trust that he may not remember any of the answers which I gave him that night. Holmes declares that he overheard me caution him against the great danger of taking more than two drops of castor-oil, while I recommended strychnine in large doses as a sedative.[104] However that may be, I was certainly relieved when our cab pulled up with a jerk and the coachman sprang down to open the door.

"This, Miss Morstan, is Pondicherry Lodge," said Mr. Thaddeus Sholto, as he handed her out.

104 Strychnine, derived from the dried seeds of the East Indian tree *Strychnos nux vomica*, is an alkaloid obtained in crystal form. Even a small dose of the drug (0.2 *mg/kg*) causes convulsions, muscle spasms, and death. "Watson could almost have been forgiven if he actually had given the injection to Thaddeus Sholto," remarks Dr. Maurice Campbell, "who must have been very trying in the cab on that journey."

CHAPTER V

The Tragedy of Pondicherry Lodge

IT WAS NEARLY eleven o'clock when we reached this final stage of our night's adventures. We had left the damp fog of the great city behind us, and the night was fairly fine. A warm wind blew from the westward, and heavy clouds moved slowly across the sky, with half a moon peeping occasionally through the rifts. It was clear enough to see for some distance, but Thaddeus Sholto took down one of the side-lamps from the carriage to give us a better light upon our way.

Pondicherry Lodge stood in its own grounds and was girt round with a very high stone wall topped with broken glass. A single narrow iron-clamped door formed the only means of entrance. On this our guide knocked with a peculiar postman-like rat-tat.[105]

"Who is there?" cried a gruff voice from within.

"It is I, McMurdo. You surely know my knock by this time."

There was a grumbling sound and a clanking and jarring of keys. The door swung heavily back, and a short, deep-chested man stood in the opening, with the yellow light of the lantern shining upon his protruded face and twinkling, distrustful eyes.

105 The postman's double knock is heard in *The Pickwick Papers* (1836–1837) and elsewhere in the works of Charles Dickens. Christopher Morley observes that this traditional knock was replaced later by the double ring of the bell—the basis of James M. Cain's hard-boiled first novel *The Postman Always Rings Twice* (1934). The novel was made, in 1946, into the brilliant *film noir* of the same name, starring John Garfield and Lana Turner, and, in 1981, remade into a vehicle for Jack Nicholson and Jessica Lange.

Dustjacket, *The Sign of Four.*
(New York: Grosset & Dunlap, 1932)

"That you, Mr. Thaddeus? But who are the others? I had no orders about them from the master."

"No, McMurdo? You surprise me! I told my brother last night that I should bring some friends."

"He hain't been out o' his room to-day, Mr. Thaddeus, and I have no orders. You know very well that I must stick to regulations. I can let you in, but your friends they must just stop where they are."

This was an unexpected obstacle. Thaddeus Sholto looked about him in a perplexed and helpless manner.

"This is too bad of you, McMurdo!" he said. "If I guarantee them, that is enough for you. There is the young lady, too. She cannot wait on the public road at this hour."

106 By the time of *The Sign of Four*, boxing was no longer illegal *per se* within the borders of London (although wagering on boxing was still banned), and the authorities turned a blind eye on matches conducted under the Queensberry Rules. In 1865, John Graham Chambers, a member of the Amateur Athletic Club, wrote rules for the conduct of matches that were adopted in 1867, under the patronage of John Sholto Douglas, the Marquess of Queensberry. Chambers intended the rules for amateur boxing matches, such as those conducted by the AAC, and they were first used for a tournament of such matches in 1872. The rules stressed short rounds, with rest periods, eliminated hugging or wrestling, required gloves to be worn, and provided for the match to end if a boxer was down and unable to arise on his own within ten seconds—in short, much like modern rules. Benefits for down-and-out boxers were a longstanding tradition of the sport. The milieu of boxing in the pre-Queensberry period is brought to life in Arthur Conan Doyle's *Rodney Stone* (1896) and George MacDonald Fraser's *Black Ajax* (1997).

107 "Four years back" would be 1883 or 1884, depending on the date assigned to the events of *The Sign of Four* (see *Chronological Table*). But T. S. Blakeney points out that McMurdo must have joined the Sholto household before Major Sholto's death in 1882, for brother Bartholomew had no need for a protector. "[McMurdo's] benefit night (presumably when he retired from the ring) would have been just prior to his being engaged by Major Sholto on the latter's retirement from the Army—about 1877."

108 "The right cross," H. T. Webster observes, "is indeed the characteristic Sunday punch of the tall rangy type of boxer, as the left hook is the main reliance of the short and stocky one. This punch, to the head or body,

"Our guide knocked with a peculiar postmanlike rat, tat."
Artist unknown, *The Sign of the Four* (New York and Boston: H. M. Caldwell Co., n.d.)

"Very sorry, Mr. Thaddeus," said the porter inexorably. "Folk may be friends o' yours, and yet no friends o' the master's. He pays me well to do my duty, and my duty I'll do. I don't know none o' your friends."

"Oh, yes, you do, McMurdo," cried Sherlock Holmes genially. "I don't think you can have forgotten me. Don't you remember that amateur who fought three rounds with you at Alison's rooms on the night of your benefit[106] four years back?"[107]

"Not Mr. Sherlock Holmes!" roared the prize-fighter. "God's truth! how could I have mistook you? If instead o' standin' there so quiet you had just stepped up and given me that cross-hit of yours under the jaw,[108] I'd ha' known you without a question. Ah, you're one that has wasted your gifts,

"A short, deep-chested man stood in the opening."
Richard Gutschmidt, *Das Zeichen der Vier* (Stuttgart: Robert Lutz Verlag, 1902)

is delivered straight from the shoulder but with a slight pivoting motion of the body which gives it something of the character of a hook. It is called a cross, because it must cross either over or under the opponent's left arm to land." Holmes used a left jab against Roaring Jack Woodley, the "slogging ruffian" of "The Solitary Cyclist," who, it will be remembered, had to be carried home in a cart after taking on Holmes. Webster concludes that Holmes fought in the classic style, standing up straight and using his extraordinary speed of foot to avoid infighting. He would have punished his opponents with straight lefts and then finished them off with his powerful right cross. While J. N. Williamson characterises Holmes as a welterweight or middleweight, Patrick J. Leonard, Sr., recounts his discovery of how Holmes fought heavyweight champion John L. Sullivan (1858–1918) to a draw on March 10, 1888.

you have! You might have aimed high, if you had joined the fancy."

"You see, Watson, if all else fails me, I have still one of the scientific professions open to me," said Holmes, laughing. "Our friend won't keep us out in the cold now, I am sure."

"In you come, sir, in you come—you and your friends," he answered. "Very sorry, Mr. Thaddeus, but orders are very strict. Had to be certain of your friends before I let them in."

Inside, a gravel path wound through desolate grounds to a huge clump of a house, square and prosaic, all plunged in shadow save where a moonbeam struck one corner and glimmered in a garret window. The vast size of the building, with its gloom and its deathly silence, struck a chill to the heart. Even Thaddeus Sholto seemed ill at ease, and the lantern quivered and rattled in his hand.

"I cannot understand it," he said. "There must be some mistake. I distinctly told Bartholomew that we should be here, and

The National Sporting Club, London.
Sketches from "Punch," by Phil May (1897)

yet there is no light in his window. I do not know what to make of it."

"Does he always guard the premises in this way?" asked Holmes.

"Yes; he has followed my father's custom. He was the favourite son, you know, and I sometimes think that my father may have told him more than he ever told me. That is Bartholomew's window up there where the moonshine strikes. It is quite bright, but there is no light from within, I think."

"None," said Holmes. "But I see the glint of a light in that little window beside the door."

"Ah, that is the housekeeper's room. That is where old Mrs. Bernstone sits. She can tell us all about it. But perhaps you would not mind waiting here for a minute or two, for if we all go in together, and she has had no word of our coming, she may be alarmed. But, hush! what is that?"

He held up the lantern, and his hand shook until the circles of light flickered and wavered all round us. Miss Morstan seized my wrist, and we all stood, with thumping hearts, straining our ears. From the great black house there sounded through the silent night the saddest and most pitiful of sounds—the shrill, broken whimpering of a frightened woman.

"It is Mrs. Bernstone," said Sholto. "She is the only woman in the house. Wait here. I shall be back in a moment."

He hurried for the door and knocked in his peculiar way. We could see a tall old woman admit him and sway with pleasure at the very sight of him.

"Oh, Mr. Thaddeus, sir, I am so glad you have come! I am so glad you have come, Mr. Thaddeus, sir!"

We heard her reiterated rejoicings until the door was closed and her voice died away into a muffled monotone.

Our guide had left us the lantern. Holmes swung it slowly round and peered keenly at the house and at the great rubbish-heaps which cumbered the grounds. Miss Morstan and I stood together, and her hand was in mine. A wondrous subtle thing is love, for here were we two, who had never seen each other before that day, between whom no word or even look of affection had ever passed, and yet now in an hour of trouble our hands instinctively sought for each other. I have marvelled at it since, but at the time it seemed the most natural thing that I should go out to her so, and, as she has often told me, there was in her also the instinct to turn to me for comfort and protection. So we stood hand-in-hand like two children, and there was peace in our hearts for all the dark things that surrounded us.

"What a strange place!" she said, looking round.

"It looks as though all the moles in England had been let loose in it. I have seen something of the sort on the side of a hill near Ballarat,[109] where the prospectors had been at work."

"And from the same cause," said Holmes. "These are the traces of the treasure-seekers. You must remember that they were six years looking for it. No wonder that the grounds look like a gravel-pit."

At that moment the door of the house burst open, and Thaddeus Sholto came running out, with his hands thrown forward and terror in his eyes.

"There is something amiss with Bartholomew!" he cried. "I am frightened! My nerves cannot stand it."

He was, indeed, half blubbering with fear, and his twitching, feeble face peeping out from the great astrakhan collar had the helpless, appealing expression of a terrified child.

"Come into the house," said Holmes in his crisp, firm way.

"Yes, do!" pleaded Thaddeus Sholto. "I really do not feel equal to giving directions."

109 Robert Hughes, in recounting the history of the Australian gold rush in 1851, terms Ballarat "the richest field of all." After the discovery of gold there by John Dunlop, an aged digger, Hughes writes, "The word ran back to Melbourne that gold was everywhere. . . . [B]y November 1851 . . . a cataract of gold was pouring from Ballarat." Within a few months, Hughes estimates, perhaps 50,000 people were on the diggings.

Did Watson actually visit Australia? John Hall suggests that Watson added the reference to Ballarat as a result of Holmes's mention of it as recorded in "The Boscombe Valley Mystery," during the events of which Watson may have been writing up his notes of the events of *The Sign of Four*. Hall and others conclude that Watson did not see the mines themselves but rather a sketch or photograph in a book. However, Christopher Redmond, in "Art in the Blood: Two Canonical Relatives. II. 'The History of My Unhappy Brother,' " suggests that Watson went to Australia between the time of the events of *A Study in Scarlet* and the events of *The Sign of Four* to look after his older brother. Both of these views are thoughtfully rejected by William Hyder ("Watson's Education and Medical Career"), who proposes that Watson spent at least part of his boyhood in Australia.

We all followed him into the housekeeper's room, which stood upon the left-hand side of the passage. The old woman was pacing up and down with a scared look and restless, picking fingers, but the sight of Miss Morstan appeared to have a soothing effect upon her.

"God bless your sweet, calm face!" she cried, with an hysterical sob. "It does me good to see you. Oh, but I have been sorely tried this day!"

Our companion patted her thin, work-worn hand and murmured some few words of kindly, womanly comfort which brought the colour back into the other's bloodless cheeks.

"Master has locked himself in and will not answer me," she explained. "All day I have waited to hear from him, for he often likes to be alone; but an hour ago I feared that something was amiss, so I went up and peeped through the keyhole. You must go up, Mr. Thaddeus—you must go up and look for yourself. I have seen Mr. Bartholomew Sholto in joy and in sorrow for ten long years, but I never saw him with such a face on him as that."

Sherlock Holmes took the lamp and led the way, for Thaddeus Sholto's teeth were chattering in his head. So shaken was he that I had to pass my hand under his arm as we went up the stairs, for his knees were trembling under him. Twice as we ascended, Holmes whipped his lens out of his pocket and carefully examined marks which appeared to me to be mere shapeless smudges of dust upon the coconut matting which served as a stair-carpet. He walked slowly from step to step, holding the lamp low, and shooting keen glances to right and left. Miss Morstan had remained behind with the frightened housekeeper.

The third flight of stairs ended in a straight passage of some length, with a great picture in Indian tapestry upon the right of it and three doors upon the left. Holmes advanced along it in the same slow and methodical way, while we kept close at his heels, with our long, black shadows streaming backward down the corridor. The third door was that which we were seeking. Holmes knocked without receiving any answer, and then tried to turn the handle and force it open. It was locked on the inside, however, and by a broad and powerful bolt, as we could see when we set our lamp up against it. The key being turned, however, the hole was not entirely closed. Sherlock Holmes bent down to it and instantly rose again with a sharp intaking of the breath.

"There is something devilish in this, Watson," said he, more moved than I had ever before seen him. "What do you make of it?"

I stooped to the hole and recoiled in horror. Moonlight was streaming into the room, and it was bright with a vague and shifty radiance. Looking straight at me and suspended, as it were, in the air, for all beneath was in shadow, there hung a face—the very face of our companion Thaddeus. There was the same high, shining head, the same circular bristle of red hair,[110] the same bloodless countenance. The features were set, however, in a horrible smile, a fixed and unnatural grin, which in that still and moonlit room was more jarring to the nerves than any scowl or contortion. So like was the face to that of our little friend that I looked round at him to make sure that he was indeed with us. Then I recalled to mind that he had mentioned to us that his brother and he were twins.

"This is terrible!" I said to Holmes. "What is to be done?"

"The door must come down," he answered, and springing against it, he put all his weight upon the lock.

It creaked and groaned but did not yield. Together we flung ourselves upon it once more, and this time it gave way with a sudden snap, and we found ourselves within Bartholomew Sholto's chamber.

It appeared to have been fitted up as a chemical laboratory. A double line of glass-stoppered bottles was drawn up upon the wall opposite the door, and the table was littered over with Bunsen burners, test-tubes, and retorts. In the corners stood carboys of acid in wicker baskets. One of these appeared to leak or to have been broken, for a stream of dark-coloured liquid had trickled out from it, and the air was heavy with a peculiarly pungent, tar-like odour. A set of steps stood at one side of the room in the midst of a litter of lath and plaster, and above them there was an opening in the ceiling large enough for a man to pass through. At the foot of the steps a long coil of rope was thrown carelessly together.

By the table, in a wooden armchair the master of the house was seated all in a heap, with his head sunk upon his left shoulder and that ghastly, inscrutable smile upon his face. He was stiff and cold and had clearly been dead many hours. It seemed

110 Jay Finley Christ finds this to be an "amazing" identification. "The reader is invited to try to distinguish red hair from brown or even from black, by the light of a half-moon, while the observer is peering through a partially stopped key-hole. Let him try it in the open, too, if he likes."

"In a wooden armchair the master of the house was seated all in a heap, with his head sunk upon his left shoulder and that ghastly, inscrutable smile upon his face."
Richard Gutschmidt, *Das Zeichen der Vier* (Stuttgart: Robert Lutz Verlag, 1902)

to me that not only his features but all his limbs were twisted and turned in the most fantastic fashion. By his hand upon the table there lay a peculiar instrument—a brown, close-grained stick, with a stone head like a hammer, rudely lashed on with coarse twine. Beside it was a torn sheet of note-paper with

"Not only his features, but all his limbs were twisted and turned in a most fantastic fashion."
H. B. Eddy, Sunday *American*, April 21, 1912

Death of Bartholomew Sholto.
F. H. Townsend, *The Sign of Four* (London: George Newnes, Ltd., 1903)

some words scrawled upon it. Holmes glanced at it and then handed it to me.

"You see," he said, with a significant raising of the eyebrows.

In the light of the lantern I read with a thrill of horror, "The sign of the four."

"In God's name, what does it all mean?" I asked.

"It means murder," said he, stooping over the dead man. "Ah! I expected it. Look here!"

He pointed to what looked like a long, dark thorn stuck in the skin just above the ear.

"It looks like a thorn," said I.

"It is a thorn. You may pick it out. But be careful, for it is poisoned."

I took it up between my finger and thumb. It came away from the skin so readily that hardly any mark was left behind. One tiny speck of blood showed where the puncture had been.

"This is all an insoluble mystery to me," said I. "It grows darker instead of clearer."

"On the contrary," he answered, "it clears every instant. I

" 'I read, with a thrill of horror, "The Sign of Four." ' "
Charles Kerr, *The Sign of Four* (London: Spencer Blackett, 1890)

only require a few missing links to have an entirely connected case."

We had almost forgotten our companion's presence since we entered the chamber. He was still standing in the doorway, the very picture of terror, wringing his hands and moaning to himself. Suddenly, however, he broke out into a sharp, querulous cry.

"The treasure is gone!" he said. "They have robbed him of the treasure! There is the hole through which we lowered it. I helped him to do it! I was the last person who saw him! I left him here last night, and I heard him lock the door as I came downstairs."

"What time was that?"

"It was ten o'clock. And now he is dead, and the police will be called in, and I shall be suspected of having had a hand in it. Oh, yes, I am sure I shall. But you don't think so, gentlemen? Surely, you don't think that it was I? Is it likely that I would have brought you here if it were I? Oh, dear! oh, dear! I know that I shall go mad!"

He jerked his arms and stamped his feet in a kind of convulsive frenzy.

"You have no reason for fear, Mr. Sholto," said Holmes kindly, putting his hand upon his shoulder; "take my advice and drive down to the station to report the matter to the police. Offer to assist them in every way. We shall wait here until your return."

The little man obeyed in a half-stupefied fashion, and we heard him stumbling down the stairs in the dark.

CHAPTER VI

Sherlock Holmes Gives a Demonstration

111 A "snib" is a lock.

"Now, Watson," said Holmes, rubbing his hands, "we have half an hour to ourselves. Let us make good use of it. My case is, as I have told you, almost complete; but we must not err on the side of over-confidence. Simple as the case seems now, there may be something deeper underlying it."

"Simple!" I ejaculated.

"Surely," said he with something of the air of a clinical professor expounding to his class. "Just sit in the corner there, that your footprints may not complicate matters. Now to work! In the first place, how did these folk come and how did they go? The door has not been opened since last night. How of the window?" He carried the lamp across to it, muttering his observations aloud the while but addressing them to himself rather than to me. "Window is snibbed[111] on the inner side. Framework is solid. No hinges at the side. Let us open it. No water-pipe near. Roof quite out of reach. Yet a man has mounted by the window. It rained a little last night. Here is the print of a foot in mould upon the sill. And here is a circular muddy mark, and here again upon the floor, and here again by the table. See here, Watson! This is really a very pretty demonstration."

The Sign of the Four.
(Chicago: M. A. Donohue & Co., n.d.)

I looked at the round, well-defined muddy discs.

"That is not a footmark," said I.

"It is something much more valuable to us. It is the impression of a wooden stump. You see here on the sill is the boot-mark, a heavy boot with a broad metal heel, and beside it is the mark of the timber-toe."

"It is the wooden-legged man."

"Quite so. But there has been someone else—a very able and efficient ally. Could you scale that wall, Doctor?"

I looked out of the open window. The moon still shone brightly on that angle of the house. We were a good sixty feet from the ground, and, look where I would, I could see no foothold, nor as much as a crevice in the brickwork.

"It is absolutely impossible," I answered.

"Without aid it is so. But suppose you had a friend up here who lowered you this good stout rope which I see in the corner, securing one end of it to this great hook in the wall. Then, I think, if you were an active man, you might swarm up, wooden leg and all. You would depart, of course, in the same fashion, and your ally would draw up the rope, untie it from the hook, shut the window, snib it on the inside, and get away in the way that he originally came. As a minor point, it may be noted," he continued, fingering the rope, "that our wooden-legged friend, though a fair climber, was not a professional sailor. His hands were far from horny. My lens discloses more than one blood-mark, especially towards the end of the rope, from which I gather that he slipped down with such velocity that he took the skin off his hands."

"This is all very well," said I; "but the thing becomes more unintelligible than ever. How about this mysterious ally? How came he into the room?"

"Yes, the ally!" repeated Holmes pensively. "There are features of interest about this ally. He lifts the case from the regions of the commonplace. I fancy that this ally breaks fresh ground in the annals of crime in this country—though parallel cases suggest themselves from India and, if my memory serves me, from Senegambia."[112]

"How came he, then?" I reiterated. "The door is locked; the window is inaccessible. Was it through the chimney?"

"The grate is much too small," he answered. "I had already considered that possibility."

"How, then?" I persisted.

"You will not apply my precept," he said, shaking his head. "How often have I said to you that when you have eliminated the impossible, whatever remains, *however improbable*, must be the truth? We know that he did not come through the door, the window, or the chimney. We also know that he could not have been concealed in the room, as there is no concealment possible. Whence, then, did he come?"

"He came through the hole in the roof!" I cried.

"Of course he did. He must have done so. If you will have the kindness to hold the lamp for me, we shall now extend our researches to the room above—the secret room in which the treasure was found."

112 Then a region of more than 10 million, located in west Africa between the Senegal and Gambia rivers, it was comprised of French Senegambia (the colony called Senegal), English Senegambia (the colony of Gambia and the islands of Los), Portuguese Senegambia, and various independent states. Today it encompasses Senegal and The Gambia, the latter an English-speaking Muslim country with a Catholic minority.

He mounted the steps, and, seizing a rafter with either hand, he swung himself up into the garret. Then, lying on his face, he reached down for the lamp and held it while I followed him.

The chamber in which we found ourselves was about ten feet one way and six the other. The floor was formed by the rafters, with thin lath and plaster between, so that in walking one had to step from beam to beam.[113] The roof ran up to an apex and was evidently the inner shell of the true roof of the house. There was no furniture of any sort, and the accumulated dust of years lay thick upon the floor.

"Here you are, you see," said Sherlock Holmes, putting his hand against the sloping wall. "This is a trapdoor which leads out on to the roof. I can press it back, and here is the roof itself, sloping at a gentle angle. This, then, is the way by which Number One entered. Let us see if we can find some other traces of his individuality?"

He held down the lamp to the floor, and as he did so I saw for the second time that night a startled, surprised look come

" 'Here you are, you see,' said Sherlock Holmes."
Artist unknown, *Sherlock Holmes Series*, Vol. I
(New York & London: Harper & Bros., 1904)

113 Donald A. Redmond, in "Stop Changing Your Mind, Watson!," points out the inconsistency of this description with the observation two paragraphs later that "[t]he floor was covered thickly with the prints of a naked foot."

"He held down the lamp to the floor."
Richard Gutschmidt, *Das Zeichen der Vier* (Stuttgart: Robert Lutz Verlag, 1902)

over his face. For myself, as I followed his gaze, my skin was cold under my clothes. The floor was covered thickly with the prints of a naked foot—clear, well-defined, perfectly formed, but scarce half the size of those of an ordinary man.

"Holmes," I said in a whisper, "a child has done this horrid thing."

He had recovered his self-possession in an instant.

"I was staggered for the moment," he said, "but the thing is quite natural. My memory failed me, or I should have been able to foretell it. There is nothing more to be learned here. Let us go down."

"What is your theory, then, as to those footmarks?" I asked, eagerly, when we had regained the lower room once more.

"My dear Watson, try a little analysis yourself," said he, with a touch of impatience. "You know my methods. Apply them, and it will be instructive to compare results."

"I cannot conceive anything which will cover the facts," I answered.

"It will be clear enough to you soon," he said, in an offhand way. "I think that there is nothing else of importance here, but I will look."

He whipped out his lens and a tape measure and hurried about the room on his knees, measuring, comparing, examining, with his long, thin nose only a few inches from the planks and his beady eyes gleaming and deep-set like those of a bird.[114] So swift, silent, and furtive were his movements, like those of a trained bloodhound picking out a scent, that I could not but think what a terrible criminal he would have made had he turned his energy and sagacity against the law instead of exerting them in its defence. As he hunted about, he kept muttering to himself, and finally he broke out into a loud crow of delight.

"We are certainly in luck," said he. "We ought to have very little trouble now. Number One has had the misfortune to tread in the creosote.[115] You can see the outline of the edge of

" 'Holmes,' I said, 'a child has done this horrid thing.' "
F. H. Townsend, *The Sign of Four* (London: George Newnes, Ltd., 1903)

114 Newt and Lillian Williams wonder: "What bird has 'deep-set' eyes?"

115 A distillation from wood tar then used to treat wood; also used in medicine, both in Victorian times and today, as an expectorant for chronic bronchitis. Railroad ties are treated with creosote, a source of the distinctive and not unpleasing smell at train tracks.

his small foot here at the side of this evil-smelling mess. The carboy has been cracked, you see, and the stuff has leaked out."

"What then?" I asked.

"Why, we have got him, that's all," said he.

"I know a dog that would follow that scent to the world's end. If a pack can track a trailed herring across a shire, how far can a specially-trained hound follow so pungent a smell as this? It sounds like a sum in the rule of three.[116] The answer should give us the—But hallo! here are the accredited representatives of the law."

Heavy steps and the clamour of loud voices were audible from below, and the hall door shut with a loud crash.

"Before they come," said Holmes, "just put your hand here on this poor fellow's arm, and here on his leg. What do you feel?"

"The muscles are as hard as a board," I answered.

"Quite so. They are in a state of extreme contraction, far exceeding the usual *rigor mortis*.[117] Coupled with this distortion of the face, this Hippocratic smile, or '*risus sardonicus*,'[118] as the old writers called it, what conclusion would it suggest to your mind?"

"Death from some powerful vegetable alkaloid,"[119] I answered, "some strychnine-like substance[120] which would produce tetanus."

"That was the idea which occurred to me the instant I saw the drawn muscles of the face. On getting into the room I at once looked for the means by which the poison had entered the system. As you saw, I discovered a thorn which had been driven or shot with no great force into the scalp. You observe that the part struck was that which would be turned towards the hole in the ceiling if the man were erect in his chair. Now examine this thorn."

I took it up gingerly and held it in the light of the lantern. It was long, sharp, and black, with a glazed look near the point as though some gummy substance had dried upon it. The blunt end had been trimmed and rounded off with a knife.

"Is that an English thorn?" he asked.

"No, it certainly is not."

"With all these data you should be able to draw some just

116 The "Rule of Three" is a name for the rule of fractions that if a/b=c/d, then a times d equals b times c, and if *three* of the values of a, b, c, and d are known, the fourth may be determined. For example, if 2/3=x/27, then x=2 times 27 (54) divided by 3, or 18, so that 2/3=18/27.

117 When the body's energy reserves are depleted, certain proteins in the muscles lose their extendability, and the muscles become stiff. This condition is commonly referred to as *rigor mortis*. The time a corpse requires to enter *rigor mortis* depends on how quickly the body chills (the process is slower at lower room temperatures) and the amount of stress the person experiences before death.

118 A facial expression caused by a spasm of the facial muscles, characterised by raised eyebrows and grinning distortion of the face (see note 120, below). It occurs frequently in cases of tetanus.

119 See *A Study in Scarlet*, note 33.

120 George B. Koelle suggests several possibilities, including strophanthin (a cardiac drug similar to digitalis) and two central nervous system stimulants, picrotoxin and strychnine. According to Koelle, strychnine itself is the most logical choice. He notes that it "would probably be rapidly absorbed from a wound. Following a series of violent convulsions, it produces death by tonic respiratory paralysis. One of its most striking features is the *risus sardonicus*, or sardonic grin, which may remain on the face of the victim." It is curious that Watson himself absent-mindedly prescribed strychnine to Thaddeus Sholto (see note 104, above).

inference. But here are the regulars, so the auxiliary forces may beat a retreat."

As he spoke, the steps which had been coming nearer sounded loudly on the passage, and a very stout, portly man in a grey suit strode heavily into the room. He was red-faced, burly, and plethoric, with a pair of very small, twinkling eyes, which looked keenly out from between swollen and puffy pouches. He was closely followed by an inspector in uniform and by the still palpitating Thaddeus Sholto.

"Here's a business!" he cried, in a muffled, husky voice. "Here's a pretty business! But who are all these? Why, the house seems to be as full as a rabbit-warren!"

"I think you must recollect me, Mr. Athelney Jones," said Holmes quietly.

"Why, of course I do!" he wheezed. "It's Mr. Sherlock Holmes, the theorist. Remember you! I'll never forget how you lectured us all on causes and inferences and effects in the Bishopgate[121] jewel case. It's true you set us on the right track; but you'll own now that it was more by good luck than good guidance."

"It was a piece of very simple reasoning."

"Oh, come, now, come! Never be ashamed to own up. But what is all this? Bad business! Bad business! Stern facts here—no room for theories. How lucky that I happened to be out at Norwood over another case! I was at the station when the message arrived. What d'you think the man died of?"

"Oh, this is hardly a case for me to theorize over," said Holmes dryly.

"No, no. Still, we can't deny that you hit the nail on the head sometimes. Dear me! Door locked, I understand. Jewels worth half a million missing. How was the window?"

"Fastened; but there are steps on the sill."

"Well, well, if it was fastened the steps could have nothing to do with the matter. That's common sense. Man might have died in a fit; but then the jewels are missing. Ha! I have a theory. These flashes come upon me at times. Just step outside, Sergeant,[122] and you, Mr. Sholto. Your friend can remain. What do you think of this, Holmes? Sholto was, on his own confession, with his brother last night. The brother died in a fit, on which Sholto walked off with the treasure? How's that?"

121 Bishopsgate Street, called "Bishopgate" Street in many older publications, is in Bethnal Green, and Bishopsgate Station is a station of the London Underground. In Holmes's time, it was actually bifurcated in common reference into "Bishopsgate Street Within" (the City) and "Bishopsgate Street Without" and was the main northern thoroughfare out of the City.

122 Donald A. Redmond points out that Watson's characterisation of the police officer as a "sergeant" is either in error or unexplained, for nine paragraphs earlier, Watson recounts how Jones arrived "followed by an inspector in uniform." Eight paragraphs later, Watson records Jones as referring to the "inspector," but in Chapter VII, the man is described by Watson as a "weary-looking police sergeant." There is no indication of the presence of two separate men.

123 Drawn from *Les Maximes* by François, Duc de La Rochefoucauld (1613–1680), this is translated as: "There are no fools so troublesome as those who have some wit." The saying appears in Benjamin Franklin's *Poor Richard's Almanack* for 1741 and 1745.

"On which the dead man very considerately got up and locked the door on the inside."

"Hum! There's a flaw there. Let us apply common sense to the matter. This Thaddeus Sholto *was* with his brother; there *was* a quarrel: so much we know. The brother is dead and the jewels are gone. So much also we know. No one saw the brother from the time Thaddeus left him. His bed had not been slept in. Thaddeus is evidently in a most disturbed state of mind. His appearance is—well, not attractive. You see that I am weaving my web round Thaddeus. The net begins to close upon him."

"You are not quite in possession of the facts yet," said Holmes. "This splinter of wood, which I have every reason to believe to be poisoned, was in the man's scalp where you still see the mark; this card, inscribed as you see it, was on the table, and beside it lay this rather curious stone-headed instrument. How does all that fit into your theory?"

"Confirms it in every respect," said the fat detective pompously. "House is full of Indian curiosities. Thaddeus brought this up, and if this splinter be poisonous, Thaddeus may as well have made murderous use of it as any other man. The card is some hocus-pocus—a blind, as like as not. The only question is, how did he depart? Ah, of course, here is a hole in the roof."

With great activity, considering his bulk, he sprang up the steps and squeezed through into the garret, and immediately afterwards we heard his exulting voice proclaiming that he had found the trap-door.

"He can find something," remarked Holmes, shrugging his shoulders; "he has occasional glimmerings of reason. *Il n'y a pas des sots si incommodes que ceux qui ont de l'esprit*!"[123]

"You see!" said Athelney Jones, reappearing down the steps again; "facts are better than theories, after all. My view of the case is confirmed. There is a trap-door communicating with the roof, and it is partly open."

"It was I who opened it."

"Oh, indeed! You did notice it, then?" He seemed a little crestfallen at the discovery. "Well, whoever noticed it, it shows how our gentleman got away. Inspector!"

"Yes, sir," from the passage.

"Ask Mr. Sholto to step this way.—Mr. Sholto, it is my duty

" 'Mr. Sholto, it is my duty to inform you that anything which you may say will be used against you.' "
Richard Gutschmidt, *Das Zeichen der Vier* (Stuttgart: Robert Lutz Verlag, 1902)

to inform you that anything which you may say will be used against you. I arrest you in the Queen's name as being concerned in the death of your brother."

"There, now! Didn't I tell you!" cried the poor little man, throwing out his hands and looking from one to the other of us.

"Don't trouble yourself about it, Mr. Sholto," said Holmes; "I think that I can engage to clear you of the charge."

"Don't promise too much, Mr. Theorist, don't promise too much!" snapped the detective. "You may find it a harder matter than you think."

"Not only will I clear him, Mr. Jones, but I will make you a free present of the name and description of one of the two people who were in this room last night. His name, I have every reason to believe, is Jonathan Small. He is a poorly educated man, small, active, with his right leg off, and wearing a wooden stump which is worn away upon the inner side. His left boot has a coarse, square-toed sole, with an iron band round the heel. He is a middle-aged man, much sunburned, and has been a convict. These few indications may be of some assistance to you, coupled with the fact that there is a good deal of skin missing from the palm of his hand. The other man—"

"Ah! the other man?" asked Athelney Jones in a sneering voice, but impressed none the less, as I could easily see, by the precision of the other's manner.

"Is a rather curious person," said Sherlock Holmes, turning upon his heel. "I hope before very long to be able to introduce you to the pair of them. A word with you, Watson."

He led me out to the head of the stair.

"This unexpected occurrence," he said, "has caused us rather to lose sight of the original purpose of our journey."

"I have just been thinking so," I answered; "it is not right that Miss Morstan should remain in this stricken house."

"No. You must escort her home. She lives with Mrs. Cecil Forrester, in Lower Camberwell,[124] so it is not very far. I will wait for you here if you will drive out again. Or perhaps you are too tired?"

"By no means. I don't think I could rest until I know more of this fantastic business. I have seen something of the rough side of life, but I give you my word that this quick succession of strange surprises to-night has shaken my nerve completely. I should like, however, to see the matter through with you, now that I have got so far."

"Your presence will be of great service to me," he answered. "We shall work the case out independently and leave this fellow Jones to exult over any mare's-nest which he may choose to construct. When you have dropped Miss Morstan, I wish you to go on to No. 3 Pinchin Lane, down near the water's edge at Lambeth.[125] The third house on the right-hand side is a bird-stuffer's; Sherman is the name. You will see a weasel holding a young rabbit in the window. Knock old Sherman up and tell him, with my compliments, that I want Toby[126] at once. You will bring Toby back in the cab with you."

"A dog, I suppose."

"Yes, a queer mongrel, with a most amazing power of scent. I would rather have Toby's help than that of the whole detective force of London."

"I shall bring him then," said I. "It is one now. I ought to be back before three if I can get a fresh horse."

"And I," said Holmes, "shall see what I can learn from Mrs. Bernstone and from the Indian servant, who, Mr. Thaddeus tells me, sleeps in the next garret.[127] Then I shall study the great Jones's methods and listen to his not too delicate sarcasms. '*Wir sind gewohnt das die Menschen verhöhnen was sie nicht verstehen.*'[128] Goethe is always pithy."

124 See *A Study in Scarlet*, note 175.

125 Situated at the foot of Westminster Bridge, Lambeth is described by Augustus J. C. Hare, writing in 1884, as "densely populated, and covered with a labyrinth of featureless streets and poverty-stricken courts."

126 For Victorian readers, observes Donald Girard Jewell, in *A Canonical Dog's Life*, the name Toby would instantly call to mind the live dog who appeared, with elaborate neck ruffle, in the Punch and Judy shows, and was trained "to bark or grab Punch's ample proboscis on cue." Traditionally a bull terrier, Toby sometimes took the form of a puppet or stuffed dog. According to an interview with an unnamed nineteenth-century London Punchman, conducted by Henry Mayhew, at one time three live singing dogs were featured simultaneously: ". . . a great hit it war. It made a surprising alteration in the exhibition, for till lately the performance was called Punch and Toby as well. . . . but we can't get three dogs to do it now. The mother of them dogs, ye see, was a singer, and had two pups what was singers too" ("The Domination of Fancy or Punch's Opera," in *London Labour and the London Poor*, 1851). The Punchman noted that the dogs also were trained to smoke pipes.

127 But, as Donald A. Redmond observes, Holmes apparently failed to do so—in Chapter VII he refers to the butler as "Lal Rao, whom we have not seen."

128 From Goethe's *Faust*, Part I (1808), this is translated by Bayard Taylor (in 1870–1871) as "We are used to see that Man despises what he never comprehends." Madeleine B. Stern proposes that Holmes owned a set of the works of Johann Wolfgang von Goethe (1749–1832), critic, journalist, painter, theatre manager, statesman, educationalist, natural philosopher, and perhaps the last European to emulate the great personalities of the Renaissance.

CHAPTER VII

The Episode of the Barrel

THE POLICE HAD brought a cab with them, and in this I escorted Miss Morstan back to her home. After the angelic fashion of women, she had borne trouble with a calm face as long as there was someone weaker than herself to support, and I had found her bright and placid by the side of the frightened housekeeper. In the cab, however, she first turned faint and then burst into a passion of weeping—so sorely had she been tried by the adventures of the night. She has told me since that she thought me cold and distant upon that journey. She little guessed the struggle within my breast, or the effort of self-restraint which held me back. My sympathies and my love went out to her, even as my hand had in the garden. I felt that years of the conventionalities of life could not teach me to know her sweet, brave nature as had this one day of strange experiences. Yet there were two thoughts which sealed the words of affection upon my lips. She was weak and helpless, shaken in mind and nerve. It was to take her at a disadvantage to obtrude love upon her at such a time. Worse still, she was rich. If Holmes's researches were successful, she would be an heiress. Was it fair, was it honourable, that a half-pay surgeon should take such advantage of an intimacy which chance had brought about? Might she not look upon me as a mere vulgar fortune-seeker? I could not bear to risk that such a thought should cross her mind. This Agra treasure intervened like an impassable barrier between us.

It was nearly two o'clock when we reached Mrs. Cecil Forrester's. The servants had retired hours ago, but Mrs. Forrester had been so interested by the strange message which Miss Morstan had received that she had sat up in the hope of her return. She opened the door herself, a middle-aged, graceful woman, and it gave me joy to see how tenderly her arm stole round the other's waist and how motherly was the voice in which she greeted her.[129] She was clearly no mere paid dependant but an honoured friend. I was introduced, and Mrs. Forrester earnestly begged me to step in and tell her our adventures. I explained, however, the importance of my errand and promised faithfully to call and report any progress which we might make with the case. As we drove away I stole a glance back, and I still seem to see that little group on the step—the two graceful, clinging figures, the half-opened door, the hall-light shining through stained glass,[130] the barometer, and the bright stair-rods.[131] It was soothing to catch even that

129 See note 41, above, for an interesting explanation of this relationship.

130 Although many Victorian middle-class residences contained stained-glass windows, once the perquisite of only the rich, Mrs. Forrester's suburban residence may have contained a "Patent Glacier Window," described by Alfred Miles, editor of *The Household Oracle* (*ca.* 1898), as having "the merit of approaching real stained glass in colour and appearance more nearly than anything previously introduced, and [being] at the same time easy to affix. . . . Of course it is merely an imitation and therefore not comparable with the real, but it may effectively hide ugly realities which are even more objectionable than artistic imitations."

131 Mercury wheel, stick, and marine barometers, beautiful glass-and-wood objects used to predict the weather and now prized as antiques, were often found in Victorian homes. Stair rods are usually brass rods at the foot of each riser, used to keep the carpeting in place.

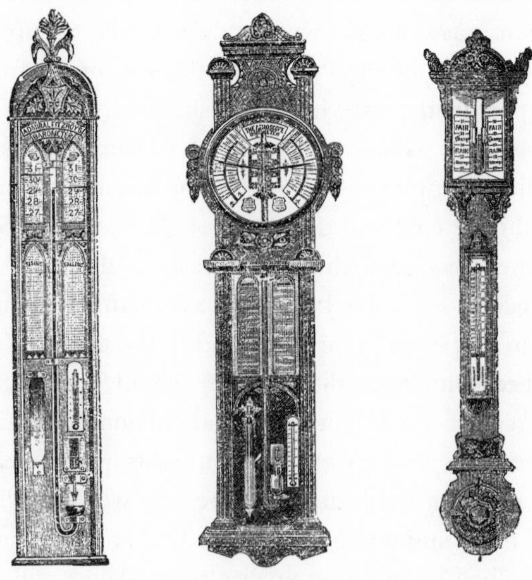

Barometers.

Victorian Shopping (Harrod's 1895 Catalogue)

passing glimpse of a tranquil English home in the midst of the wild, dark business which had absorbed us.

And the more I thought of what had happened, the wilder and darker it grew. I reviewed the whole extraordinary sequence of events as I rattled on through the silent, gas-lit streets. There was the original problem: that at least was pretty clear now. The death of Captain Morstan, the sending of the pearls, the advertisement, the letter—we had had light upon all those events. They had only led us, however, to a deeper and far more tragic mystery. The Indian treasure, the curious plan found among Morstan's baggage, the strange scene at Major Sholto's death, the rediscovery of the treasure immediately followed by the murder of the discoverer, the very singular accompaniments to the crime, the footsteps, the remarkable weapons, the words upon the card, corresponding with those upon Captain Morstan's chart—here was indeed a labyrinth in which a man less singularly endowed than my fellow-lodger might well despair of ever finding the clue.

Pinchin Lane was a row of shabby, two-storied brick houses in the lower quarter of Lambeth.[132] I had to knock for some time at No. 3 before I could make any impression. At last, however, there was the glint of a candle behind the blind, and a face looked out at the upper window.

"Go on, you drunken vagabond," said the face. "If you kick up any more row, I'll open the kennels and let out forty-three dogs upon you."

"If you'll let one out, it's just what I have come for," said I.

"Go on!" yelled the voice. "So help me gracious, I have a wiper in this bag, an' I'll drop it on your 'ead if you don't hook it!"[133]

"But I want a dog," I cried.

"I won't be argued with!" shouted Mr. Sherman. "Now stand clear; for when I say 'three,' down goes the wiper."

"Mr. Sherlock Holmes—" I began; but the words had a most magical effect, for the window instantly slammed down, and within a minute the door was unbarred and open. Mr. Sherman was a lanky, lean old man, with stooping shoulders, a stringy neck, and blue-tinted glasses.

"A friend of Mr. Sherlock[134] is always welcome," said he. "Step in, sir. Keep clear of the badger, for he bites. Ah, naughty, naughty; would you take a nip at the gentleman?"

132 No such street is to be found in London. Bernard Davies identifies the shop as that of John Hale, at 81 Prince's Road.

133 By a "wiper," Mr. Sherman means a "viper," a snake. Sherman's pronunciation echoes the cockney of Sam Weller in Dickens's *The Pickwick Papers*. The distinctive swapping of the "v" and "w" sounds were largely extinct by the 1880s, but the music hall singer Gus Elen popularised it in his songs through the 1920s. "Hook it" is translated as "get out of the way" or "be off about your business" by John Camden Hotten in *The Slang Dictionary* (1865).

134 Mr. Sherman, points out Bernard Davies, is the only person other than his brother, Mycroft, to refer to Holmes by his first name. "We can picture [Mr. Sherlock] now, a thin, eager youth helping the older man with the skinning, making impressions of bird and animal tracks in plaster of Paris, bursting with questions as to the poisonous effects of 'wipers,' not to mention 'swamp adders.' " Still, the familiarity does not extend to dropping the "Mr.," and Mr. Sherman's particular form of usage, and his tone, seem more servile than intimate.

This to a stoat which thrust its wicked head and red eyes between the bars of its cage. "Don't mind that, sir; it's only a slowworm.[135] It hain't got no fangs, so I gives it the run o' the room, for it keeps the beetles down. You must not mind my bein' just a little short wi' you at first, for I'm guyed at by the children, and there's many a one just comes down this lane to knock me up. What was it that Mr. Sherlock Holmes wanted, sir?"

"He wanted a dog of yours."

"Ah! that would be Toby."

"Yes, Toby was the name."

"Toby lives at No. 7 on the left here."

He moved slowly forward with his candle among the queer animal family which he had gathered round him. In the uncertain, shadowy light I could see dimly that there were glancing, glimmering eyes peeping down at us from every cranny and corner. Even the rafters above our heads were lined by solemn fowls, who lazily shifted their weight from one leg to the other as our voices disturbed their slumbers.[136]

" 'A friend of Mr. Sherlock is always welcome,' said he."
Richard Gutschmidt, *Das Zeichen der Vier* (Stuttgart: Robert Lutz Verlag, 1902)

Toby proved to be an ugly, long-haired, lop-eared creature, half spaniel and half lurcher,[137] brown and white in colour, with a very clumsy, waddling gait. It accepted, after some hesitation, a lump of sugar[138] which the old naturalist handed to me, and, having thus sealed an alliance, it followed me to the cab and made no difficulties about accompanying me. It had just struck three on the Palace clock[139] when I found myself back once more at Pondicherry Lodge. The ex-prize-fighter McMurdo had, I found, been arrested as an accessory, and both he and Mr. Sholto had been marched off to the station. Two constables guarded the narrow gate, but they allowed me to pass with the dog on my mentioning the detective's name.

135 Also called blindworm (*Anguis fragilis*), a legless, snakelike lizard of the family *Anguidae*, order Gymnophiona. It burrows in the grasses and open woodlands of Great Britain, Europe, and the Caucasus Mountains. The adult is about a foot long, but some specimens grow to almost two feet in length. The lizard eats snails and slugs and other soft animals, using pointed, fanglike teeth. Said to be blind, it has eyes that are so tiny as to be almost invisible.

136 Deborah Laubach, in her fascinating essay "A Study in Number Three," comments: "Watson, a total stranger, walks amidst the scrutiny of every animal in Pinchin Lane without an uproar; what was that the Master once said about a dog in the nighttime?"

137 Donald Girard Jewell describes the lurcher as originally a cross between a German shepherd and a greyhound. "Though almost a quarter shorter than a greyhound, the lurcher exhibited great speed and could run any rabbit out in the open or quickly cut the creature off from its burrow in a warren. Not only was it fast, however, the lurcher was also smart. It offered the added advantage of being able to hunt by both sight and scent." A type of dog rather than a breed, lurchers were favourites of poachers for their ability to hunt silently.

138 Stuart Palmer, in his "Notes on Certain Evidence of Caniphobia in Mr. Sherlock Holmes and His Associates," expresses shock that the old naturalist would allow Watson to feed sugar to a dog, with the resulting dental damage.

139 Which "Palace" clock is a matter of some contention. Christopher Morley identifies it as that of Lambeth Palace, but Humfrey Michell points out, in a letter to the *Baker Street Journal*, that it was impossible to hear the Lambeth Palace clock from Upper Nor-

Holmes was standing on the doorstep with his hands in his pockets, smoking his pipe.

"Ah, you have him there!" said he. "Good dog, then! Athelney Jones has gone. We have had an immense display of energy since you left. He has arrested not only friend Thaddeus but the gatekeeper, the housekeeper, and the Indian servant. We have the place to ourselves but for a sergeant upstairs. Leave the dog here and come up."

We tied Toby to the hall table and reascended the stairs. The room was as we had left it, save that a sheet had been draped over the central figure. A weary-looking police-sergeant reclined in the corner.

"Lend me your bull's-eye,[140] Sergeant," said my companion. "Now tie this bit of cord[141] round my neck, so as to hang it in front of me. Thank you. Now I must kick off my boots and stockings. Just you carry them down with you, Watson. I am going to do a little climbing. And dip my handkerchief into the creosote. That will do. Now come up into the garret with me for a moment."

We clambered up through the hole. Holmes turned his light once more upon the footsteps in the dust.

"I wish you particularly to notice these footmarks," he said. "Do you observe anything noteworthy about them?"

"They belong," I said, "to a child or a small woman."

"Apart from their size, though. Is there nothing else?"

"They appear to be much as other footmarks."

"Not at all. Look here! This is the print of a right foot in the dust. Now I make one with my naked foot beside it. What is the chief difference?"

"Your toes are all cramped together. The other print has each toe distinctly divided."

"Quite so. That is the point. Bear that in mind. Now, would you kindly step over to that flap-window and smell the edge of the wood-work? I shall stay over here, as I have this handkerchief in my hand."

I did as he directed and was instantly conscious of a strong tarry smell.

"That is where he put his foot in getting out. If *you* can trace him, I should think that Toby will have no difficulty. Now run downstairs, loose the dog, and look out for Blondin."[142]

By the time that I got out into the grounds Sherlock Holmes

wood. What Watson meant, Michell explains, was the *Crystal* Palace, which then stood nearby on Sydenham Hill. But Watson himself was in error, for there was no chiming clock at the Crystal Palace. "What he heard undoubtedly was the clock on the tower of the School for the Blind in Upper Norwood, which, for the benefit of those who could not see, struck the quarters, halves and hours in very resonant tones audible over a wide area."

Morley's and Michell's suggestions are well refuted in William P. Schweikert's "The Palace Clock," in which he argues that Watson heard Big Ben, the Westminster Palace clock. Schweikert points out that Arthur Conan Doyle lived in South Norwood and, knowing what clocks were audible in the neighbourhood, would have pointed out an error to Watson for correction in later editions. However, Bernard Davies, in a *coup-de-maître*, identifies the clock as the instrument in the belltower of All Saint's Church, Upper Norwood. The clock, manufactured by James Moore of Clerkenwell in 1840, was fitted to chime the hours. "It had apparently been doing this for forty-eight years before Watson's cab passed that way around three in the morning. . . . [S]ome way down South Norwood Hill and quite close to the house, Watson would have heard the clock strike three above him and only a short distance behind. Not being well acquainted with the Crystal Palace, his assumption was not such an odd one to make" (letter to this editor, April 30, 2000).

140 A lantern, that is, incorporating a fresnel or "bull's-eye" lense to intensify the light.

141 The magazine and early book editions of *The Sign of Four* all read "card" instead of "cord." Of course, a "card" would not be useful to suspend the bull's-eye lantern around Holmes's neck.

142 Charles Blondin (1824–1897) was the

stage name of Jean François Gravelet, the acrobat renowned for having crossed Niagara Falls on a tightrope. Orlando Park, in *Sherlock Holmes, Esq., and John H. Watson, M.D.: An Encyclopaedia of Their Affairs*, suggests the alternate possibility that this was the name of the constable on guard.

143 A bullet fired from a Martini-Henry rifle. Properly called the Peabody-Martini-Henry rifle, this self-cocking, hammerless gun, designed by Friedrich von Martini and Alexander Henry, was adopted in 1871 as the primary weapon of the British infantry and remained the mainstay of the forces until it and the older Snider-Enfield rifles were replaced by the Lee-Metford in the 1890s. Some Martini-Henrys remained in use with colonial forces well into the twentieth century.

Martini-Henry rifle.

144 "Holmes could not possibly have used those very words," points out Bernard Davies. At the time of this exchange, Holmes had no way of knowing the length of the trail. Perhaps Watson reconstructed this exchange from hindsight.

was on the roof, and I could see him like an enormous glow-worm crawling very slowly along the ridge. I lost sight of him behind a stack of chimneys, but he presently reappeared and then vanished once more upon the opposite side. When I made my way round there I found him seated at one of the corner eaves.

"That you, Watson?" he cried.

"Yes."

"This is the place. What is that black thing down there?"

"A water-barrel."

"Top on it?"

"Yes."

"No sign of a ladder?"

"No."

"Confound the fellow! It's a most breakneck place. I ought to be able to come down where he could climb up. The water-pipe feels pretty firm. Here goes, anyhow."

There was a scuffling of feet, and the lantern began to come steadily down the side of the wall. Then with a light spring he came on to the barrel, and from there to the earth.

"It was easy to follow him," he said, drawing on his stockings and boots. "Tiles were loosened the whole way along, and in his hurry he had dropped this. It confirms my diagnosis, as you doctors express it."

The object which he held up to me was a small pocket or pouch woven out of coloured grasses and with a few tawdry beads strung round it. In shape and size it was not unlike a cigarette-case. Inside were half-a-dozen spines of dark wood, sharp at one end and rounded at the other, like that which had struck Bartholomew Sholto.

"They are hellish things," said he. "Look out that you don't prick yourself. I'm delighted to have them, for the chances are that they are all he has. There is the less fear of you or me finding one in our skin before long. I would sooner face a Martini bullet,[143] myself. Are you game for a six-mile trudge, Watson?"[144]

"Certainly," I answered.

"Your leg will stand it?"

"Oh, yes."

"Here you are, doggy! Good old Toby! Smell it, Toby, smell it!" He pushed the creosote handkerchief under the dog's

"Pattered off upon the trail."
F. H. Townsend, *The Sign of Four* (London:
George Newnes, Ltd., 1903)

nose, while the creature stood with its fluffy legs separated, and with a most comical cock to its head, like a connoisseur sniffing the *bouquet* of a famous vintage. Holmes then threw the handkerchief to a distance, fastened a stout cord to the mongrel's collar, and led him to the foot of the water-barrel. The creature instantly broke into a succession of high, tremulous yelps and, with his nose on the ground and his tail in the air, pattered off upon the trail at a pace which strained his leash and kept us at the top of our speed.

The east had been gradually whitening, and we could now see some distance in the cold, grey light. The square, massive house, with its black, empty windows and high, bare walls, towered up, sad and forlorn, behind us. Our course led right across the grounds, in and out among the trenches and pits with which they were scarred and intersected. The whole place, with its scattered dirt-heaps and ill-grown shrubs, had a blighted, ill-omened look which harmonized with the black tragedy which hung over it.

On reaching the boundary wall Toby ran along, whining eagerly, underneath its shadow, and stopped finally in a corner screened by a young beech. Where the two walls joined, several bricks had been loosened, and the crevices left were worn down and rounded upon the lower side, as though they had frequently been used as a ladder. Holmes clambered up, and, taking the dog from me, he dropped it over upon the other side.

"There's the print of Wooden-leg's hand," he remarked, as I mounted up beside him. "You see the slight smudge of blood upon the white plaster. What a lucky thing it is that we have had no very heavy rain since yesterday! The scent will lie upon the road in spite of their eight-and-twenty hours' start."

I confess that I had my doubts myself when I reflected upon the great traffic which had passed along the London road in the interval. My fears were soon appeased, however. Toby never hesitated or swerved but waddled on in his peculiar rolling fashion. Clearly, the pungent smell of the creosote rose high above all other contending scents.

"Do not imagine," said Holmes, "that I depend for my success in this case upon the mere chance of one of these fellows having put his foot in the chemical. I have knowledge now which would enable me to trace them in many different ways. This, however, is the readiest, and, since fortune has put it into our hands, I should be culpable if I neglected it. It has, however, prevented the case from becoming the pretty little intellectual problem which it at one time promised to be. There might have been some credit to be gained out of it, but for this too palpable clue."

"There is credit, and to spare," said I. "I assure you, Holmes, that I marvel at the means by which you obtain your results in this case, even more than I did in the Jefferson Hope murder. The thing seems to me to be deeper and more inexplicable. How, for example, could you describe with such confidence the wooden-legged man?"

"Pshaw, my dear boy! it was simplicity itself. I don't wish to be theatrical. It is all patent and above-board. Two officers who are in command of a convict guard learn an important secret as to buried treasure. A map is drawn for them by an Englishman named Jonathan Small. You remember that we saw the name upon the chart in Captain Morstan's possession. He had signed it in behalf of himself and his associates—the sign of the four, as he somewhat dramatically called it. Aided by this chart, the officers—or one of them—gets the treasure and brings it to England, leaving, we will suppose, some condition under which he received it unfulfilled. Now, then, why did not Jonathan Small get the treasure himself? The answer is obvious. The chart is dated at a time when Morstan was brought into close association with convicts. Jonathan Small did not get the treasure because he and his associates were themselves convicts and could not get away."

"But this is mere speculation," said I.

"It is more than that. It is the only hypothesis which covers the facts. Let us see how it fits in with the sequel. Major Sholto remains at peace for some years, happy in the possession of his treasure. Then he receives a letter from India which gives him a great fright. What was that?"

"A letter to say that the men whom he had wronged had been set free."

"Or had escaped. That is much more likely, for he would have known what their term of imprisonment was. It would not have been a surprise to him.[145] What does he do then? He guards himself against a wooden-legged man—a white man, mark you, for he mistakes a white tradesman for him and actually fires a pistol at him. Now, only one white man's name is on the chart. The others are Hindoos or Mohammedans. There is no other white man. Therefore, we may say with confidence that the wooden-legged man is identical with Jonathan Small. Does the reasoning strike you as being faulty?"

"No: it is clear and concise."

"Well, now, let us put ourselves in the place of Jonathan Small. Let us look at it from his point of view. He comes to England with the double idea of regaining what he would consider to be his rights and of having his revenge upon the man who had wronged him. He found out where Sholto lived, and very possibly he established communications with someone inside the house. There is this butler, Lal Rao, whom we have not seen. Mrs. Bernstone gives him far from a good character. Small could not find out, however, where the treasure was hid,

145 Ian McQueen points out that this cannot be so. Small must have escaped from the Andamans even before Morstan left India. It is possible, McQueen suggests, that Morstan told Sholto of the escape, causing a more violent quarrel about the treasure than would have taken place if only the two British officers had been at liberty. McQueen concludes that the letter must have been written from India long after Small had gained his freedom and proposes that Small himself was its writer, posting it just before his departure for England. "The period from 'early in 1882' until 'the end of April' gave Small exactly the length of time he needed to reconnoitre his adversary's heavily defended position and plan his attack. How nearly he succeeded, and how wrong was Holmes's deduction about that letter."

for no one ever knew save the major and one faithful servant who had died. Suddenly, Small learns that the major is on his deathbed. In a frenzy lest the secret of the treasure die with him, he runs the gauntlet of the guards, makes his way to the dying man's window, and is only deterred from entering by the presence of his two sons. Mad with hate, however, against the dead man, he enters the room that night, searches his private papers in the hope of discovering some memorandum relating to the treasure, and finally leaves a memento of his visit in the short inscription upon the card. He had doubtless planned beforehand that, should he slay the major, he would leave some such record upon the body as a sign that it was not a common murder but, from the point of view of the four associates, something in the nature of an act of justice. Whimsical and bizarre conceits of this kind are common enough in the annals of crime and usually afford valuable indications as to the criminal. Do you follow all this?"

"Very clearly."

"Now, what could Jonathan Small do? He could only continue to keep a secret watch upon the efforts made to find the treasure. Possibly he leaves England and only comes back at intervals. Then comes the discovery of the garret, and he is instantly informed of it. We again trace the presence of some confederate in the household. Jonathan, with his wooden leg, is utterly unable to reach the lofty room of Bartholomew Sholto. He takes with him, however, a rather curious associate, who gets over this difficulty but dips his naked foot into creosote, whence come Toby, and a six-mile limp for a half-pay officer with a damaged *tendo Achillis*."[146]

"But it was the associate, and not Jonathan, who committed the crime."

"Quite so. And rather to Jonathan's disgust, to judge by the way he stamped about when he got into the room. He bore no grudge against Bartholomew Sholto and would have preferred if he could have been simply bound and gagged. He did not wish to put his head in a halter. There was no help for it, however: the savage instincts of his companion had broken out, and the poison had done its work: so Jonathan Small left his record, lowered the treasure-box to the ground, and followed it himself. That was the train of events as far as I can decipher them. Of course, as to his personal appearance, he must be middle-

146 George Cleve Haynes suggests that this is not the "wounded leg" referred to in Chapter I (see note 17, above, and text accompanying) but a different problem. Watson never refers to the injury to his Achilles' tendon as a war injury. Haynes notes that such tendon injuries usually result from strain or from a tear (or cut). Dr. Watson's damaged tendon, he concludes, was likely the result of some vigorous sporting activity (such as rugby, mentioned in "The Sussex Vampire" as a sport in which Watson formerly engaged). It was not a permanent injury, never again appearing in Watson's records.

aged and must be sunburned after serving his time in such an oven as the Andamans. His height is readily calculated from the length of his stride, and we know that he was bearded. His hairiness was the one point which impressed itself upon Thaddeus Sholto when he saw him at the window. I don't know that there is anything else."

"The associate?"

"Ah, well, there is no great mystery in that. But you will know all about it soon enough. How sweet the morning air is! See how that one little cloud floats like a pink feather from some gigantic flamingo.[147] Now the red rim of the sun pushes itself over the London cloud-bank. It shines on a good many folk, but on none, I dare bet, who are on a stranger errand than you and I. How small we feel, with our petty ambitions and strivings, in the presence of the great elemental forces of Nature! Are you well up in your Jean Paul?"[148]

"Fairly so. I worked back to him through Carlyle.[149]

"That was like following the brook to the parent lake. He makes one curious but profound remark. It is that the chief proof of man's real greatness lies in his perception of his own smallness. It argues, you see, a power of comparison and of appreciation which is in itself a proof of nobility. There is much food for thought in Richter. You have not a pistol, have you?"

"I have my stick."

"It is just possible that we may need something of the sort if we get to their lair. Jonathan I shall leave to you, but if the other turns nasty I shall shoot him dead."

He took out his revolver as he spoke, and, having loaded two of the chambers,[150] he put it back into the right-hand pocket of his jacket.

We had during this time been following the guidance of Toby down the half-rural villa-lined roads which lead to the metropolis. Now, however, we were beginning to come among continuous streets, where labourers and dockmen were already astir, and slatternly women were taking down shutters and brushing doorsteps. At the square-topped corner public-houses business was just beginning, and rough-looking men were emerging, rubbing their sleeves across their beards after their morning wet. Strange dogs sauntered up and stared wonderingly at us as we passed, but our inimitable Toby looked neither to the right nor to the left but trotted onward with his nose

147 This from the man who has the nerve to admonish Watson, in describing a "high sun-baked wall mottled with lichens and topped with moss" ("The Retired Colourman") to "cut out the poetry"?

148 Johann Paul Friedrich Richter (1763–1825), usually called Jean Paul, was a German humourist. Carlyle, with whom Holmes was well familiar, wrote two articles on Richter in *Miscellanies.* Madeleine B. Stern points out that the London 1867 edition of Thomas De Quincey's *Confessions of an English Opium-Eater* includes *Analects* from John [*sic*] Paul Richter, including one entitled "The Grandeur of Man in His Littleness," the evident source of Holmes's remark.

149 Watson quoted Carlyle in *A Study in Scarlet* (see note 59 to that novel, above), and Holmes feigned complete ignorance of his writings, a pretence he here abandons.

150 Why only two chambers? Robert Keith Leavitt, in "Annie Oakley in Baker Street," concludes that this "indicated confidence rather in Tonga's than in his own accuracy. He knew he would have time for only two shots at best." Roger Johnson, in private correspondence with this editor, makes the more practical suggestion that the other chambers may have already been loaded.

151 Kennington Oval, now officially the Foster's Oval, is the home of Surrey County Cricket Club and was "a cricket-ground second only to Lord's in public favour and in interest" (*Baedeker*).

152 Now Bond Way, according to Bernard Davies. Holmes's route is illustrated in the map reproduced here.

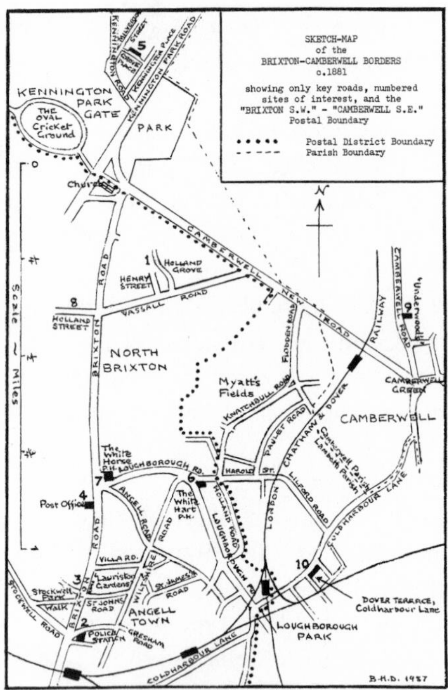

Holmes's route.
Courtesy of Bernard H. Davies

153 Knight's Place was "a terrace of houses in Wandsworth Road, on the left as one emerges from Miles Street, the crumbling remains of which may still be seen," notes Davies.

"We had been following the guidance of Toby."
Richard Gutschmidt, *Das Zeichen der Vier* (Stuttgart: Robert Lutz Verlag, 1902)

to the ground and an occasional eager whine which spoke of a hot scent.

We had traversed Streatham, Brixton, Camberwell, and now found ourselves in Kennington Lane, having borne away through the side-streets to the east of the Oval.[151] The men whom we pursued seemed to have taken a curiously zig-zag road, with the idea probably of escaping observation. They had never kept to the main road if a parallel side-street would serve their turn. At the foot of Kennington Lane they had edged away to the left through Bond Street[152] and Miles Street. Where the latter street turns into Knight's Place,[153] Toby ceased to advance but began to run backward and forward with one ear cocked and the other drooping, the very picture of canine indecision. Then he waddled round in circles, looking up to us from time to time, as if to ask for sympathy in his embarrassment.

"What the deuce is the matter with the dog?" growled Holmes. "They surely would not take a cab or go off in a balloon."

"Perhaps they stood here for some time," I suggested.

"Ah! it's all right. He's off again," said my companion, in a tone of relief.

He was indeed off, for after sniffing round again he suddenly made up his mind and darted away with an energy and determination such as he had not yet shown. The scent appeared to be much hotter than before, for he had not even to put his nose on the ground but tugged at his leash and tried to break into a run. I could see by the gleam in Holmes's eyes that he thought we were nearing the end of our journey.

Our course now ran down Nine Elms until we came to Broderick and Nelson's large timber-yard, just past the White Eagle tavern.[154] Here the dog, frantic with excitement, turned down through the side gate into the enclosure, where the sawyers were already at work. On the dog raced through sawdust and shavings, down an alley, round a passage, between two woodpiles, and finally, with a triumphant yelp, sprang upon a large barrel which still stood upon the hand-trolley on which it had been brought. With lolling tongue and blinking eyes, Toby stood upon the cask, looking from one to the other of us for some sign of appreciation. The staves of the barrel and the wheels of the trolley were smeared with a dark liquid, and the whole air was heavy with the smell of creosote.

Sherlock Holmes and I looked blankly at each other and then burst simultaneously into an uncontrollable fit of laughter.

"Burst into an uncontrollable fit of laughter."
Charles A. Cox, *The Sign of the Four* (Chicago and New York: The Henneberry Company, n.d.)

154 Charles O. Merriman, in "Tar Derivatives Not Wanted," reports on his fruitless reconstruction of Holmes's walk: "I certainly passed the Southampton Arms, the Nine Elms Brewery and other hostelries but of the White Eagle Tavern, there was no sign."

CHAPTER VIII

The Baker Street Irregulars

"What now?" I asked. "Toby has lost his character for infallibility."

"He acted according to his lights," said Holmes, lifting him down from the barrel and walking him out of the timber-yard. "If you consider how much creosote is carted about London in one day, it is no great wonder that our trail should have been crossed. It is much used now, especially for the seasoning of wood. Poor Toby is not to blame."

"We must get on the main scent again, I suppose."

"Yes. And, fortunately, we have no distance to go. Evidently what puzzled the dog at the corner of Knight's Place was that there were two different trails running in opposite directions. We took the wrong one. It only remains to follow the other."

There was no difficulty about this. On leading Toby to the place where he had committed his fault, he cast about in a wide circle and finally dashed off in a fresh direction.

"We must take care that he does not now bring us to the place where the creosote-barrel came from," I observed.

"I had thought of that. But you notice that he keeps on the

pavement, whereas the barrel passed down the roadway. No, we are on the true scent now."

It tended down towards the river-side, running through Belmont Place and Prince's Street. At the end of Broad Street[155] it ran right down to the water's edge, where there was a small wooden wharf. Toby led us to the very edge of this and there stood whining, looking out on the dark current beyond.

"We are out of luck," said Holmes. "They have taken to a boat here."

Several small punts and skiffs were lying about in the water and on the edge of the wharf. We took Toby round to each in turn, but, though he sniffed earnestly, he made no sign.

Close to the rude landing-stage was a small brick house, with a wooden placard slung out through the second window. "Mordecai Smith" was printed across it in large letters, and,

Workers on the "Silent Highway."
Street Life in London (1877)

155 ". . . of Belmont Place, Prince's Street and Broad Street there was no trace," Charles Merriman reports. Prince's Street, explains Bernard Davies, "survives as the eastern half of Black Prince Road, Lambeth, but Belmont Place is, alas, no more. It was, however, a similar row of buildings opposite Knight's Place at the corner of Nine Elms Lane, long since rebuilt." There is a gap in Watson's account, Davies notes, between Belmont Place, which the correct trail evidently passed, and Prince's Street. The actual route may have involved the re-crossing of Kennington Lane and then a detour, "possibly via Tyers Street, until the riverside pier was reached 'at the end of Broad Street' " (which Davies identifies as now Black Prince Road, West).

underneath, "Boats to hire by the hour or day." A second inscription above the door informed us that a steam launch was kept—a statement which was confirmed by a great pile of coke[156] upon the jetty. Sherlock Holmes looked slowly round, and his face assumed an ominous expression.

"This looks bad," said he. "These fellows are sharper than I expected. They seem to have covered their tracks. There has, I fear, been preconcerted management here."

He was approaching the door of the house, when it opened, and a little curly-headed lad of six came running out, followed by a stoutish, red-faced woman with a large sponge in her hand.

"You come back and be washed, Jack," she shouted. "Come back, you young imp; for if your father comes home and finds you like that, he'll let us hear of it."

"Dear little chap!" said Holmes strategically. "What a rosy-cheeked young rascal! Now, Jack, is there anything you would like?"

156 Not a beverage—this is carbonised coal, used as a fuel in furnaces.

"A curly-headed lad rushed out, followed by a stoutish woman, with a sponge in her hand."
Artist unknown, *The Sign of the Four* (New York and Boston: H. M. Caldwell Co., n.d.)

" 'Dear little chap!' said Holmes strategically."
Richard Gutschmidt, *Das Zeichen der Vier* (Stuttgart: Robert Lutz Verlag, 1902)

The youth pondered for a moment.

"I'd like a shillin'," said he.

"Nothing you would like better?"

"I'd like two shillin' better," the prodigy answered, after some thought.

"Here you are, then! Catch!—A fine child, Mrs. Smith!"

"Lor' bless you, sir, he is that, and forward. He gets a'most too much for me to manage, 'specially when my man is away days at a time."

"Away, is he?" said Holmes in a disappointed voice. "I am sorry for that, for I wanted to speak to Mr. Smith."

"He's been away since yesterday mornin', sir, and, truth to tell, I am beginnin' to feel frightened about him. But if it was about a boat, sir, maybe I could serve as well."

"I wanted to hire his steam launch."

"Why, bless you, sir, it is in the steam launch that he has gone. That's what puzzles me; for I know there ain't more coals

" 'Lor' bless you, sir, he is that forward he gets almost too much for me to manage.' "
H. B. Eddy, Sunday *American*, April 28, 1912

in her than would take her to about Woolwich and back. If he'd been away in the barge I'd ha' thought nothin'; for many a time a job has taken him as far as Gravesend, and then if there was much doin' there he might ha' stayed over. But what good is a steam launch without coals?"

"He might have bought some at a wharf down the river."

"He might, sir, but it weren't his way. Many a time I've heard him call out at the prices they charge for a few odd bags. Besides, I don't like that wooden-legged man, wi' his ugly face and outlandish talk. What did he want always knockin' about here for?"

"A wooden-legged man?" said Holmes, with bland surprise.

"Yes, sir, a brown, monkey-faced chap that's called more'n once for my old man. It was him that roused him up yesternight, and, what's more, my man knew he was comin', for he had steam up in the launch. I tell you straight, sir, I don't feel easy in my mind about it."

"But, my dear Mrs. Smith," said Holmes, shrugging his shoulders, "you are frightening yourself about nothing. How could you possibly tell that it was the wooden-legged man who came in the night? I don't quite understand how you can be so sure."

"His voice, sir. I knew his voice, which is kind o' thick and foggy. He tapped at the winder—about three it would be. 'Show a leg, matey,' says he: 'time to turn out guard.' My old man woke up Jim—that's my eldest—and away they went, without so much as a word to me. I could hear the wooden leg clackin' on the stones."

"And was this wooden-legged man alone?"

"Couldn't say, I am sure, sir. I didn't hear no one else."

"I am sorry, Mrs. Smith, for I wanted a steam launch, and I have heard good reports of the—Let me see, what is her name?"

"The *Aurora*, sir."

"Ah! She's not that old green launch with a yellow line, very broad in the beam?"

"No, indeed. She's as trim a little thing as any on the river. She's been fresh painted, black with two red streaks."

"Thanks. I hope that you will hear soon from Mr. Smith. I am going down the river, and if I should see anything of the *Aurora* I shall let him know that you are uneasy. A black funnel, you say?"

"No, sir. Black with a white band."

"Ah, of course. It was the sides which were black. Good morning, Mrs. Smith. There is a boatman here with a wherry,[157] Watson. We shall take it and cross the river."

"The main thing with people of that sort," said Holmes, as we sat in the sheets of the wherry, "is never to let them think that their information can be of the slightest importance to you. If you do they will instantly shut up like an oyster. If you listen to them under protest, as it were, you are very likely to get what you want."

"Our course now seems pretty clear," said I.

"What would you do, then?"

"I would engage a launch and go down the river on the track of the *Aurora*."

"My dear fellow, it would be a colossal task. She may have touched at any wharf on either side of the stream between here and Greenwich.[158] Below the bridge[159] there is a perfect labyrinth of landing-places for miles. It would take you days and days to exhaust them, if you set about it alone."

157 A light row-boat, pointed at both ends.

158 Greenwich is situated on the Thames, about six miles below London Bridge, and was the site of a culinary rite of spring known as the Whitebait Dinner, celebrated by Cabinet Ministers and other Government members on or around Trinity Sunday (a week after Whitsunday, the seventh Sunday or fiftieth day after Easter) at the Ship tavern, the West India Dock Tavern, or the Trafalgar Tavern. Whitebait, a form of herring, is not much more than an inch in length and was considered a great delicacy, to be eaten with cayenne pepper, lemon juice, brown bread and butter, and fine hock (white Rhine wine, or Hochheimer). As the consumption of hock began to overshadow that of whitebait, administrations condemned the dinner's excess, and it was cancelled, sometimes for whole decades, but kept being resumed as the urge arose again. William Gladstone is reputed to have done away with the bacchanalia more than once, and then for good between 1892 and 1894, but ministerial revellers demanded its reinstatement in 1895.

159 Mordecai Smith's house was between Vauxhall Bridge and Lambeth Bridge, and while "below the bridge" seems to refer to the stretch of the river between Lambeth Bridge and Greenwich, in casually referring to "the bridge," Holmes probably meant *London* Bridge, the last bridge in the metropolis (until the Tower Bridge opened in 1894).

160 Wharf owners.

161 After a short delay, Holmes took Watson's suggestion without acknowledging the source. See note 182, below.

162 Millbank Penitentiary stood on seven acres on the north bank of the Thames, near Vauxhall Bridge, between Chelsea and Westminster. Built from designs by philosopher-jurist Jeremy Bentham (1748–1832) and described variously as round, octagonal, and shaped like a six-point star, the building's design grew out of Bentham's invention of the 24-hour Panopticon surveillance system, wherein prisoners would ideally internalise the guards' all-seeing eye as their own private behaviour monitor. Most of the Millbank population, which included women, was destined for Australian deportation. Prisoners observed complete and utter silence and wore strangely designed caps pulled down over half their faces, which prevented them from seeing others or being looked at in the eye. They made shoes and mail bags, a reflection of Bentham's belief that industry led to social rehabilitation. The prison was torn down sometime between 1890 and 1903, and the site now houses the Tate Collection (Tate Britain). Peter Mark Roget, author of the famous *Thesaurus of English Words and Phrases* (1852), was a physician at the Penitentiary in 1823.

163 In the south of Westminster. This seems somewhat out of the way for Holmes and Watson, headed homeward to the north-west, but perhaps traffic considerations made it convenient.

London Bridge (*ca.* 1890).
Victorian and Edwardian London

"Employ the police, then."

"No. I shall probably call Athelney Jones in at the last moment. He is not a bad fellow, and I should not like to do anything which would injure him professionally. But I have a fancy for working it out myself, now that we have gone so far."

"Could we advertise, then, asking for information from wharfingers?"[160]

"Worse and worse! Our men would know that the chase was hot at their heels, and they would be off out of the country. As it is, they are likely enough to leave, but as long as they think they are perfectly safe they will be in no hurry. Jones's energy will be of use to us there, for his view of the case is sure to push itself into the daily press, and the runaways will think that everyone is off on the wrong scent."[161]

"What are we to do, then?" I asked, as we landed near Millbank Penitentiary.[162]

"Take this hansom, drive home, have some breakfast, and get an hour's sleep. It is quite on the cards that we may be afoot to-night again. Stop at a telegraph office, cabby! We will keep Toby, for he may be of use to us yet."

We pulled up at the Great Peter Street[163] Post-Office, and Holmes despatched his wire.

"Whom do you think that is to?" he asked, as we resumed our journey.

"I am sure I don't know."

"You remember the Baker Street division of the detective police force whom I employed in the Jefferson Hope case?"

"Well?" said I, laughing.

"This is just the case where they might be invaluable. If they fail I have other resources; but I shall try them first. That wire was to my dirty little lieutenant, Wiggins,[164] and I expect that he and his gang will be with us before we have finished our breakfast."

It was between eight and nine o'clock now, and I was conscious of a strong reaction after the successive excitements of the night. I was limp and weary, befogged in mind and fatigued in body. I had not the professional enthusiasm which carried my companion on, nor could I look at the matter as a mere abstract intellectual problem. As far as the death of Bartholomew Sholto went, I had heard little good of him and could feel no intense antipathy to his murderers. The treasure, however, was a different matter. That, or part of it, belonged rightfully to Miss Morstan. While there was a chance of recovering it I was ready to devote my life to the one object. True, if I found it, it would probably put her forever beyond my reach. Yet it would be a petty and selfish love which would be influenced by such a thought as that. If Holmes could work to find the criminals, I had a tenfold stronger reason to urge me on to find the treasure.

A bath at Baker Street and a complete change freshened me up wonderfully. When I came down to our room[165] I found the breakfast laid and Holmes pouring out the coffee.

"Here it is," said he, laughing and pointing to an open newspaper. "The energetic Jones and the ubiquitous reporter have fixed it up between them. But you have had enough of the case. Better have your ham and eggs first."

I took the paper from him and read the short notice, which was headed "Mysterious Business at Upper Norwood."

> About twelve o'clock last night [said the *Standard*],[166] Mr. Bartholomew Sholto, of Pondicherry Lodge, Upper Norwood, was found dead in his room under circumstances which point to foul play. As far as we can learn, no actual traces of violence

164 How exactly does one address a telegram to a "street Arab," so as to effect delivery?

165 Christopher Morley notes that this remark suggests that Dr. Watson's bedroom was on an upper floor. Other commentators place Holmes's bed-chamber adjoining the sitting room. Alternatively, the bath could have been on the floor above. See this editor's "Layout of a 'Most Desirable Residence.' "

166 Evidently the *Standard* was taken regularly by the lodgers, for Watson's scrapbooks contained clippings from it (see *A Study in Scarlet*, note 166 and accompanying text).

were found upon Mr. Sholto's person, but a valuable collection of Indian gems which the deceased gentleman had inherited from his father has been carried off. The discovery was first made by Mr. Sherlock Holmes and Dr. Watson, who had called at the house with Mr. Thaddeus Sholto, brother of the deceased. By a singular piece of good fortune, Mr. Athelney Jones, the well-known member of the detective police force, happened to be at the Norwood police station and was on the ground within half an hour of the first alarm. His trained and experienced faculties were at once directed towards the detection of the criminals, with the gratifying result that the brother, Thaddeus Sholto, has already been arrested, together with the housekeeper, Mrs. Bernstone, an Indian butler named Lal Rao, and a porter, or gatekeeper, named McMurdo. It is quite certain that the thief or thieves were well acquainted with the house, for Mr. Jones's well-known technical knowledge and his powers of minute observation have enabled him to prove conclusively that the miscreants could not have entered by the door or by the window but must have made their way across the roof of the building, and so through a trap-door into a room which communicated with that in which the body was found. This fact, which has been very clearly made out, proves conclusively that it was no mere haphazard burglary. The prompt and energetic action of the officers of the law shows the great advantage of the presence on such occasions of a single vigorous and masterful mind. We cannot but think that it supplies an argument to those who would wish to see our detectives more de-centralized,[167] and so brought into closer and more effective touch with the cases which it is their duty to investigate.

"Isn't it gorgeous!" said Holmes, grinning over his coffee cup. "What do you think of it?"

"I think that we have had a close shave ourselves of being arrested for the crime."

"So do I. I wouldn't answer for our safety now, if he should happen to have another of his attacks of energy."

At this moment there was a loud ring at the bell, and I could hear Mrs. Hudson, our landlady, raising her voice in a wail of expostulation and dismay.

167 It is unclear what the author of the comment is addressing. The Detective Department of the Metropolitan Police, founded in 1842, was initially composed of two inspectors and six sergeants, dressed in civilian clothes. When, in 1878, the corruption of its three chief inspectors was exposed, it was reorganised into the "Criminal Investigation Department." (The term "Scotland Yard," the name for police headquarters, is often used when only the CID itself is meant.) For no discernible reason, the police's criminal investigation unit is referred to as the CID only in "The Mazarin Stone," "The Three Garridebs," and here (the former two taking place after the turn of the century). In all other cases, Holmes prefers "the Yard." While the CID had its central office in Scotland Yard, officers of the department were placed in the various divisions of the district, and officers of the detective department travelled everywhere in the performance of their various duties, including to foreign states and the colonies, as needed. Thus it may be said that by 1888, the CID was already "decentralized."

"By heavens, Holmes," said I, half-rising, "I believe that they are really after us."

"No, it's not quite so bad as that. It is the unofficial force—the Baker Street irregulars."[168]

As he spoke, there came a swift pattering of naked feet upon the stairs, a clatter of high voices, and in rushed a dozen dirty and ragged little street Arabs. There was some show of discipline among them, despite their tumultuous entry, for they instantly drew up in line and stood facing us with expectant faces. One of their number, taller and older than the others,[169] stood forward with an air of lounging superiority which was very funny in such a disreputable little scarecrow.

"Got your message, sir," said he, "and brought 'em on sharp. Three bob and a tanner[170] for tickets."

"Here you are," said Holmes, producing some silver. "In future they can report to you, Wiggins, and you to me. I cannot have the house invaded in this way.[171] However, it is just as well that you should all hear the instructions. I want to find the whereabouts of a steam launch called the *Aurora*, owner Mordecai Smith, black with two red streaks, funnel black with a white band. She is down the river somewhere. I want one boy to be at Mordecai Smith's landing-stage opposite Millbank to say if the boat comes back. You must divide it out among yourselves and do both banks thoroughly. Let me know the moment you have news. Is that all clear?"

"Yes, guv'nor," said Wiggins.

"The old scale of pay, and a guinea to the boy who finds the boat. Here's a day in advance. Now, off you go!"

He handed them a shilling each, and away they buzzed down the stairs, and I saw them a moment later streaming down the street.

"If the launch is above water they will find her," said Holmes as he rose from the table and lit his pipe. "They can go everywhere, see everything, overhear everyone. I expect to hear before evening that they have spotted her. In the meanwhile, we can do nothing but await results. We cannot pick up the broken trail until we find either the *Aurora* or Mr. Mordecai Smith."

"Toby could eat these scraps, I dare say. Are you going to bed, Holmes?"

168 The "Baker Street boys," or "Baker Street irregulars," notwithstanding their near-mythic status, are mentioned only in *A Study in Scarlet* (see text accompanying note 179, above), *The Sign of Four*, and "The Crooked Man." Cartwright, who assisted Holmes in *The Hound of the Baskervilles* (see text accompanying note 75, below), was *not* a street Arab but a District Messenger. Those irregulars who are named are Wiggins (*A Study in Scarlet* and here) and Simpson ("The Crooked Man").

169 The irregulars seem to have been in a time warp, for though at least seven years must have passed since *A Study in Scarlet*, Wiggins, the leader then as now, is still a "disreputable little scarecrow." See Mel Hughes's "Wiggin' Out."

170 A "bob" is a shilling and a "tanner" a sixpence. William S. Baring-Gould remarks that "[th]e boys had come from some distance if their tickets by bus or Underground cost threepence each." "Three bob and a tanner" is 42*d.* (pence); for a "dozen" boys, that is $3\frac{1}{2}$*d.* each. *Baedeker* gives the bus fares as 1*d.* to 6*d.*, depending on distance, while the "average" fare on the Underground is 2*d.*

171 Holmes issued the same instructions in *A Study in Scarlet*, but evidently to no effect.

172 Why Watson, who served in India, would identify "Hindoos and Mohammedans" with "savages" using stone-headed maces and blow-pipes is a mystery.

". . . and away they buzzed down the stairs . . ."
Richard Gutschmidt, *Das Zeichen der Vier* (Stuttgart: Robert Lutz Verlag, 1902)

"No; I am not tired. I have a curious constitution. I never remember feeling tired by work, though idleness exhausts me completely. I am going to smoke and to think over this queer business to which my fair client has introduced us. If ever man had an easy task, this of ours ought to be. Wooden-legged men are not so common, but the other man must, I should think, be absolutely unique."

"That other man again!"

"I have no wish to make a mystery of him to you, anyway. But you must have formed your own opinion. Now, do consider the data. Diminutive footmarks, toes never fettered by boots, naked feet, stone-headed wooden mace, great agility, small poisoned darts. What do you make of all this?"

"A savage!"[172] I exclaimed. "Perhaps one of those Indians who were the associates of Jonathan Small."

"Hardly that," said he. "When first I saw signs of strange weapons, I was inclined to think so; but the remarkable character of the footmarks caused me to reconsider my views. Some of the inhabitants of the Indian Peninsula are small men, but none could have left such marks as that. The Hindoo proper has long and thin feet. The sandal-wearing

"They can go everywhere, see everything, overhear everyone."
De Fryas Tecken (Stockholm: Aftonbladets Tryckerj, 1928)

Mohammedan has the great toe well separated from the others, because the thong is commonly passed between. These little darts, too, could only be shot in one way. They are from a blowpipe. Now, then, where are we to find our savage?"

"South America," I hazarded.

He stretched his hand up and took down a bulky volume from the shelf.

"This is the first volume of a gazetteer which is now being published. It may be looked upon as the very latest authority.[173] What have we here? 'Andaman Islands, situated 340 miles to the north of Sumatra, in the Bay of Bengal.' Hum! hum! What's all this? 'Moist climate, coral reefs, sharks, Port Blair,[174] convict barracks, Rutland Island, cottonwoods'—Ah, here we are! 'The aborigines of the Andaman Islands may perhaps claim the distinction of being the smallest race upon this earth, though some anthropologists prefer the Bushmen of Africa, the Digger Indians of America,[175] and the Tierra del Fuegians.[176] The average height is rather below four feet,

173 As will be seen, the gazetteer is so wholly inaccurate that one must question how Holmes obtained it. Julia Carlson Rosenblatt, in "Who Was Tonga? And Why Were They Saying Such Terrible Things about Him?," suggests that "the little affair of Jonathan Small was part of a more elaborate conspiracy, one sufficiently thorough as to have assured the infiltration into Holmes's library of a deliberately misleading work. . . . Doubtless the man who called himself Jonathan Small, like Tonga, had never seen the islands or the Penal Settlement there." Rosenblatt's suspicions come to rest, not surprisingly, on the involvement of Moriarty.

174 See note 45, above.

175 A derogatory and ethnographically meaningless term for many indigenous peoples of North America, particularly Oregon, Idaho, several southwestern states, and parts of California. While the word purports to describe a livelihood of digging roots from the ground for sustenance, it is not based on actual practice.

176 Tierra del Fuego is a large archipelago at the southernmost tip of South America. The *Encyclopædia Britannica* (9th Ed.) describes the true aborigines of the archipelago (there are three tribes) unflatteringly, and with an ethnocentrism common to the period. Charles Darwin famously visited Tierra del Fuego in 1831–1836 and, then only in his early twenties, contributed to the erroneous notion of the indigenous tribes as cannibalistic, reversing his assessment later in his career.

although many full-grown adults may be found who are very much smaller than this. They are a fierce, morose, and intractable people, though capable of forming most devoted friendships when their confidence has once been gained.' Mark that, Watson. Now, then listen to this.

" 'They are naturally hideous, having large, misshapen heads, small, fierce eyes, and distorted features. Their feet and hands, however, are remarkably small. So intractable and fierce are they, that all the efforts of the British officials have failed to win them over in any degree. They have always been a terror to shipwrecked crews, braining the survivors with their stone-headed clubs or shooting them with their poisoned arrows. These massacres are invariably concluded by a cannibal feast.' Nice, amiable people, Watson![177] If this fellow had been left to his own unaided devices, this affair might have taken an even more ghastly turn. I fancy that, even as it is, Jonathan Small would give a good deal not to have employed him."

"But how came he to have so singular a companion?"

"Ah, that is more than I can tell. Since, however, we had already determined that Small had come from the Andamans, it is not so very wonderful that this islander should be with him. No doubt we shall know all about it in time. Look here, Watson; you look regularly done. Lie down there on the sofa, and see if I can put you to sleep."

He took up his violin from the corner, and as I stretched myself out he began to play some low, dreamy, melodious air—his own, no doubt, for he had a remarkable gift for improvisation. I have a vague remembrance of his gaunt limbs, his earnest face, and the rise and fall of his bow. Then I seemed to be floated peacefully away upon a soft sea of sound, until I found myself in dreamland, with the sweet face of Mary Morstan looking down upon me.

177 The Gazetteer's description is surely wrong. *Encyclopædia Britannica* (11th Ed.) notes that the "average height of [native Andaman] males is 4 ft. 10½ in.; of females, 4 ft. 6 in.," and Andrew Lang, writing in *Quarterly Review* (July 1904; quoted in Roger Lancelyn Green's "Dr. Watson's First Critic"), concluded that Tonga was a "purely fictitious little monster," since the Andamanese "have neither the malignant qualities, nor the heads like mops, nor the customs, with which they are credited by Sherlock." To this T. S. Blakeney adds his personal knowledge that Andaman Islanders "(a) are NOT cannibals—I was told in 1936, whilst on a visit to the Andaman Islands, by the Chief Commissioner, that when the aborigines had been questioned about this practice, they expressed horror at the idea; (b) are not naturally hideous . . . ; [and] (c) their average height is more than 4 ft. 9 in. to 5 ft. [rather] than under 4 ft." "A man like Sherlock Holmes," concludes Lang, "who wrote a monograph on over a hundred varieties of tobacco-ash, ought not to have been gulled by a gazetteer."

Julia Carlson Rosenblatt proposes that Tonga was a member of a particular tribe of negrito people (the term "negrito" encompasses some eighteen to nineteen tribes, including the Andamanese) known by anthropologists as the Sakai, the indigenous minority of the Malaysian peninsula. "Sakai," which means "savage," is generally considered to be a disparaging term; the Sakai are also called Sng'oi, *orang asli* (original people), and Mani ("human being"), and are referred to by a host of still other names, variously preferred in greater or lesser degree by ethnologists and the people themselves. The Sakai traditionally used the blow gun and poisoned darts; they are wavy haired, and have been described as dolichocephalic—that is, the

"Miss Morstan."
Artist unknown, *Sherlock Holmes Series*, Vol. I
(New York & London: Harper & Bros., 1904)

skull is much longer than it is wide. In addition, they are somewhat small of stature. Indeed, Tonga—a name for the language of the Mani—is one of the tribal names by which Malay negritos are designated.

CHAPTER IX

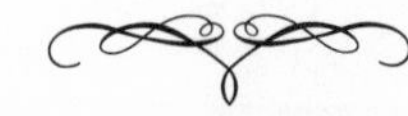

A Break in the Chain

It was late in the afternoon before I woke, strengthened and refreshed. Sherlock Holmes still sat exactly as I had left him, save that he had laid aside his violin and was deep in a book. He looked across at me as I stirred, and I noticed that his face was dark and troubled.

"You have slept soundly," he said. "I feared that our talk would wake you."

"I heard nothing," I answered. "Have you had fresh news, then?"

"Unfortunately, no. I confess that I am surprised and disappointed. I expected something definite by this time. Wiggins has just been up to report. He says that no trace can be found of the launch. It is a provoking check, for every hour is of importance."

"Can I do anything? I am perfectly fresh now, and quite ready for another night's outing."

"No; we can do nothing. We can only wait. If we go ourselves, the message might come in our absence and delay be caused. You can do what you will, but I must remain on guard."

"Then I shall run over to Camberwell and call upon Mrs. Cecil Forrester. She asked me to, yesterday."

"On Mrs. Cecil Forrester?" asked Holmes with the twinkle of a smile in his eyes.

"Well, of course, on Miss Morstan, too. They were anxious to hear what happened."

"I would not tell them too much," said Holmes. "Women are never to be entirely trusted—not the best of them."[178]

I did not pause to argue over this atrocious sentiment.

"I shall be back in an hour or two," I remarked.

"All right! Good luck! But, I say, if you are crossing the water you may as well return Toby, for I don't think it is at all likely that we shall have any use for him now."

I took our mongrel accordingly and left him, together with a half-sovereign, at the old naturalist's in Pinchin Lane. At Camberwell I found Miss Morstan a little weary after her night's adventures but very eager to hear the news. Mrs. Forrester, too, was full of curiosity. I told them all that we had done, suppressing, however, the more dreadful parts of the tragedy. Thus, although I spoke of Mr. Sholto's death, I said nothing of the exact manner and method of it. With all my omissions, however, there was enough to startle and amaze them.

"It is a romance!" cried Mrs. Forrester. "An injured lady, half a million in treasure, a black cannibal, and a wooden-legged ruffian. They take the place of the conventional dragon or wicked earl."

"And two knight-errants to the rescue," added Miss Morstan, with a bright glance at me.

"Why, Mary, your fortune depends upon the issue of this search. I don't think that you are nearly excited enough. Just imagine what it must be to be so rich and to have the world at your feet!"

It sent a little thrill of joy to my heart to notice that she showed no sign of elation at the prospect. On the contrary, she gave a toss of her proud head, as though the matter were one in which she took small interest.

"It is for Mr. Thaddeus Sholto that I am anxious," she said. "Nothing else is of any consequence; but I think that he has behaved most kindly and honourably throughout. It is our duty to clear him of this dreadful and unfounded charge."

178 "I am not a whole-souled admirer of womankind, as you are aware, Watson . . . ," remarks Holmes in *The Valley of Fear*.

It was evening before I left Camberwell, and quite dark by the time I reached home. My companion's book and pipe lay by his chair, but he had disappeared. I looked about in the hope of seeing a note, but there was none.

"I suppose that Mr. Sherlock Holmes has gone out?" I said to Mrs. Hudson as she came up to lower the blinds.

"No, sir. He has gone to his room, sir. Do you know, sir," sinking her voice into an impressive whisper, "I am afraid for his health."

"Why so, Mrs. Hudson?"

"Well, he's that strange, sir. After you was gone he walked and he walked, up and down, and up and down, until I was weary of the sound of his footstep. Then I heard him talking to himself and muttering, and every time the bell rang out he came on the stair-head, with 'What is that, Mrs. Hudson?' And now he has slammed off to his room, but I can hear him walking away the same as ever. I hope he's not going to be ill, sir. I ventured to say something to him about cooling medicine,[179] but he turned on me, sir, with such a look that I don't know how ever I got out of the room."

"I don't think that you have any cause to be uneasy, Mrs. Hudson," I answered. "I have seen him like this before. He has some small matter upon his mind which makes him restless."

I tried to speak lightly to our worthy landlady, but I was myself somewhat uneasy when through the long night I still from time to time heard the dull sound of his tread, and knew how his keen spirit was chafing against this involuntary inaction.

At breakfast-time he looked worn and haggard, with a little fleck of feverish colour upon either cheek.

"You are knocking yourself up, old man," I remarked. "I heard you marching about in the night."

"No, I could not sleep," he answered, "this infernal problem is consuming me. It is too much to be baulked by so petty an obstacle, when all else had been overcome. I know the men, the launch, everything; and yet I can get no news. I have set other agencies[180] at work and used every means at my disposal. The whole river has been searched on either side, but there is no news, nor has Mrs. Smith heard of her husband. I shall come to the conclusion soon that they have scuttled the craft. But there are objections to that."

179 A preparation believed to be capable of lowering the temperature of the blood. Victorians embraced patent medicines, of which there were over 1,500 by 1860. Many were innocuous, but an infants' teething medication made up of treacle mixed with opium caused numerous deaths. Indeed, a number of patent medicines contained alcohol or opiates—otherwise, how would they have "worked"? Hostetter's Celebrated Stomach Bitters, apart from prolonging life, cured depression; and, to purify your blood, you could try Vogeler's Curative Compound—and then administer it to your livestock, too. The advertising claims of many patent medicines defy modern belief.

John Hall, in "The Lady of the House," contends that this remark by Mrs. Hudson supports the view that she was of an older generation—at least, older than Holmes, although there is no direct evidence on the point. "Positively motherly in fact," is Hall's description of the landlady.

Victorian patent medicine (1895). Was this a seven-per-cent solution?
Victorian Advertisments

180 Is this a reference to Holmes's rivals? Or to the Irregulars?

"Or that Mrs. Smith has put us on a wrong scent."

"No, I think that may be dismissed. I had inquiries made, and there is a launch of that description."

"Could it have gone up the river?"

"I have considered that possibility, too, and there is a search-party who will work up as far as Richmond.[181] If no news comes to-day I shall start off myself tomorrow and go for the men rather than the boat. But surely, surely, we shall hear something."

We did not, however. Not a word came to us either from Wiggins or from the other agencies. There were articles in most of the papers upon the Norwood tragedy. They all appeared to be rather hostile to the unfortunate Thaddeus Sholto. No fresh details were to be found, however, in any of them, save that an inquest was to be held upon the following day. I walked over to Camberwell in the evening to report our ill-success to the ladies, and on my return I found Holmes dejected and somewhat morose. He would hardly reply to my questions and busied himself all the evening in an abstruse chemical analysis which involved much heating of retorts and distilling of vapours, ending at last in a smell which fairly drove me out of the apartment. Up to the small hours of the morning I could hear the clinking of his test-tubes, which told me that he was still engaged in his malodorous experiment.

In the early dawn I woke with a start and was surprised to find him standing by my bedside, clad in a rude sailor dress with a pea-jacket and a coarse red scarf round his neck.

"I am off down the river, Watson," said he. "I have been turning it over in my mind, and I can see only one way out of it. It is worth trying, at all events."

"Surely I can come with you, then?" said I.

"No; you can be much more useful if you will remain here as my representative. I am loath to go, for it is quite on the cards that some message may come during the day, though Wiggins was despondent about it last night. I want you to open all notes and telegrams, and to act on your own judgment if any news should come. Can I rely upon you?"

"Most certainly."

"I am afraid that you will not be able to wire to me, for I can hardly tell yet where I may find myself. If I am in luck, however, I may not be gone so very long. I shall have news of some sort or other before I get back."

181 Richmond was a favourite summer-resort of Londoners, and the stretch of the Thames between Richmond and Hampton Court was especially popular for short boating excursions. Extra trains to both destinations ran at reduced fares (and with special extended-return privileges) throughout the season.

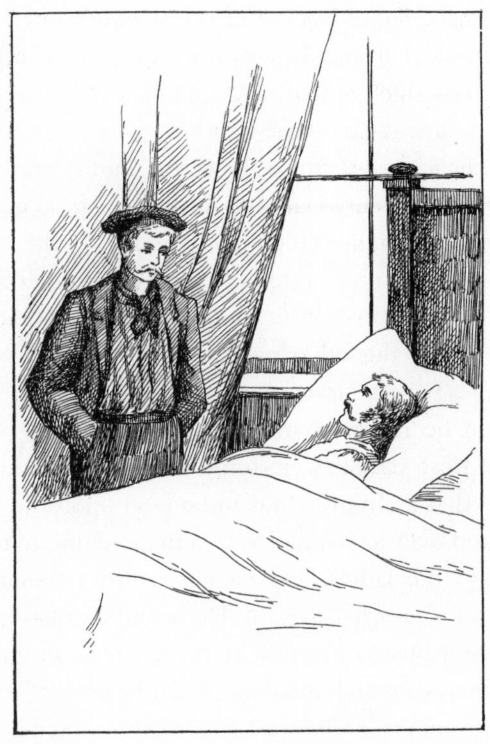

" 'I woke with a start, and was surprised to find him standing by my bedside, clad in a rude sailor dress.' "
Artist unknown, *The Sign of the Four* (New York and Boston: H. M. Caldwell Co., n.d.)

I had heard nothing of him by breakfast time. On opening the *Standard*, however, I found that there was a fresh allusion to the business.

> With reference to the Upper Norwood tragedy we have reason to believe that the matter promises to be even more complex and mysterious than was originally supposed. Fresh evidence has shown that it is quite impossible that Mr. Thaddeus Sholto could have been in any way concerned in the matter. He and the housekeeper, Mrs. Bernstone, were both released yesterday evening. It is believed, however, that the police have a clue as to the real culprits, and that it is being prosecuted by Mr. Athelney Jones, of Scotland Yard, with all his well-known energy and sagacity. Further arrests may be expected at any moment.

"That is satisfactory so far as it goes," thought I. "Friend Sholto is safe, at any rate. I wonder what the fresh clue may be, though it seems to be a stereotyped form whenever the police have made a blunder."

I tossed the paper down upon the table, but at that moment my eye caught an advertisement in the agony column. It ran in this way:

> LOST—Whereas Mordecai Smith, boatman, and his son Jim, left Smith's Wharf at or about three o'clock last Tuesday morning in the steam launch *Aurora*, black with two red stripes, funnel black with a white band, the sum of five pounds will be paid to anyone who can give information to Mrs. Smith, at Smith's Wharf, or at 221B, Baker Street, as to the whereabouts of the said Mordecai Smith and the launch *Aurora*.

" 'I am off down the river, Watson.' "
Richard Gutschmidt, *Das Zeichen der Vier* (Stuttgart: Robert Lutz Verlag, 1902)

This was clearly Holmes's doing. The Baker Street address was enough to prove that. It struck me as rather ingenious, because it might be read by the fugitives without their seeing in it more than the natural anxiety of a wife for her missing husband.[182]

It was a long day. Every time that a knock came to the door or a sharp step passed in the street, I imagined that it was either Holmes returning or an answer to his advertisement. I tried to read, but my thoughts would wander oft to our strange quest and to the ill-assorted and villainous pair whom we were pursuing. Could there be, I wondered, some radical flaw in my companion's reasoning? Might he not be suffering from some huge self-deception? Was it not possible that his nimble and speculative mind had built up this wild theory upon faulty premises? I had never known him to be wrong, and yet the keenest reasoner may occasionally be deceived. He was likely, I thought, to fall into error through the over-refinement of his logic—his preference for a subtle and bizarre explanation when a plainer and more commonplace one lay ready to his

182 Could Holmes actually have intended to solicit information with this advertisement? Charles B. Stephens argues that, having said nothing to Watson to prepare him for visitors and failing to provide Watson with the large reward offered, Holmes must have anticipated no answers to the advertisement. Rather, Stephens believes, Holmes was sure that the appearance of the advertisement, *which included his address*, would alert Small to his involvement in the case and flush the fugitives, whom he could then catch as they emerged from their hiding place.

If Stephens interprets this action correctly, then Holmes's reliance on the address to achieve the desired result indicates that Holmes believed that professional criminals were involved in the affair—perhaps Moriarty and his gang—and that they would know Holmes's address. Certainly neither Small nor Smith would have any knowledge of Sherlock Holmes and his address. It should be kept in mind that at the time of the events recorded here, Watson had only published *A Study in Scarlet* (1887), and so the reading public knew nothing of the later-famous 221B Baker Street lodgings.

Earlier, Watson himself suggested running an advertisement to locate the *Aurora* (see note 161, above, and text accompanying). Holmes rejected the idea, stating that an advertisement would lead "[o]ur men [to] know that the chase was hot at their heels" and flee. On reflection, he evidently realised the merit of Watson's idea and decided that flight was exactly the result he needed. Stephens applauds Holmes's bold gamble and criticises Watson for his lack of similar praise but fails to credit the feelings Watson must have harboured about Holmes's earlier, somewhat churlish dismissal of Watson's suggestion.

hand. Yet, on the other hand, I had myself seen the evidence, and I had heard the reasons for his deductions. When I looked back on the long chain of curious circumstances, many of them trivial in themselves, but all tending in the same direction, I could not disguise from myself that even if Holmes's explanation were incorrect the true theory must be equally outré and startling.

At three o'clock on the afternoon there was a loud peal at the bell, an authoritative voice in the hall, and, to my surprise, no less a person than Mr. Athelney Jones was shown up to me. Very different was he, however, from the brusque and masterful professor of common sense who had taken over the case so confidently at Upper Norwood. His expression was downcast, and his bearing meek and even apologetic.

"Good-day, sir; good-day," said he. "Mr. Sherlock Holmes is out, I understand?"

"Yes, and I cannot be sure when he will be back. But perhaps you would care to wait. Take that chair and try one of these cigars."

"Thank you; I don't mind if I do," said he, mopping his face with a red bandanna handkerchief.

"His expression was downcast and his bearing meek."
W. H. Hyde, *Harper's Weekly*, 1899 (reused from "The Resident Patient" and recaptioned, in *Sherlock Holmes Series*, Vol. I [New York & London: Harper & Bros., 1904])

"And a whisky and soda?"

"Well, half a glass. It is very hot for the time of year; and I have had a good deal to worry and try me. You know my theory about this Norwood case?"

"I remember that you expressed one."

"Well, I have been obliged to reconsider it. I had my net drawn tightly round Mr. Sholto, sir, when pop he went through a hole in the middle of it. He was able to prove an alibi which could not be shaken. From the time that he left his brother's room he was never out of sight of someone or other. So it could not be he who climbed over roofs and through trapdoors. It's a very dark case, and my professional credit is at stake. I should be very glad of a little assistance."

"We all need help sometimes," said I.

"Your friend Mr. Sherlock Holmes is a wonderful man, sir," said he, in a husky and confidential voice. "He's a man who is not to be beat. I have known that young man go into a good many cases, but I never saw the case yet that he could not throw a light upon. He is irregular in his methods and a little quick perhaps in jumping at theories; but, on the whole, I think he would have made a most promising officer, and I don't care who knows it. I have had a wire from him this morning, by which I understand that he has got some clue to this Sholto business. Here is his message."

He took the telegram out of his pocket and handed it to me. It was dated from Poplar[183] at twelve o'clock.

> Go to Baker Street at once. If I have not returned, wait for me. I am close on the track of the Sholto gang. You can come with us to-night if you want to be in at the finish.

"This sounds well. He has evidently picked up the scent again," said I.

"Ah, then he has been at fault too," exclaimed Jones with evident satisfaction. "Even the best of us are thrown off sometimes. Of course this may prove to be a false alarm; but it is my duty as an officer of the law to allow no chance to slip. But there is someone at the door. Perhaps this is he."

A heavy step was heard ascending the stair, with a great wheezing and rattling as from a man who was sorely put to it for breath. Once or twice he stopped, as though the climb were

183 Near the East and West India Docks, Poplar was a borough between Limehouse and West Ham.

The South-West India Dock (*ca.* 1875).
Victorian and Edwardian London

too much for him, but at last he made his way to our door and entered. His appearance corresponded to the sounds which we had heard. He was an aged man, clad in seafaring garb, with an old pea-jacket buttoned up to his throat. His back was bowed, his knees were shaky, and his breathing was painfully asthmatic. As he leaned upon a thick oaken cudgel his shoulders heaved in the effort to draw the air into his lungs. He had a coloured scarf round his chin, and I could see little of his face save a pair of keen dark eyes, overhung by bushy white brows and long grey side-whiskers. Altogether he gave me the impression of a respectable master mariner who had fallen into years and poverty.

"What is it, my man?" I asked.

He looked about him in the slow methodical fashion of old age.

"Is Mr. Sherlock Holmes here?" said he.

"No; but I am acting for him. You can tell me any message you may have for him."

"It was to him himself I was to tell it," said he.

"But I tell you that I am acting for him. Was it about Mordecai Smith's boat?"

"Yes. I knows well where it is. An' I knows where the men he is after are. An' I knows where the treasure is. I knows all about it."

"Then tell me, and I shall let him know."

"It was to him I was to tell it," he repeated, with the petulant obstinacy of a very old man.

"Well, you must wait for him."

"No, no; I ain't goin' to lose a whole day to please no one. If Mr. Holmes ain't here, then Mr. Holmes must find it all out for himself. I don't care about the look of either of you, and I won't tell a word."

He shuffled towards the door, but Athelney Jones got in front of him.

"Wait a bit, my friend," said he. "You have important information, and you must not walk off. We shall keep you, whether you like or not, until our friend returns."

The old man made a little run towards the door, but, as

" 'Pretty sort o' treatment this!' he cried, stamping his stick."
F. H. Townsend, *The Sign of Four* (London: George Newnes, Ltd., 1903)

Athelney Jones put his broad back up against it, he recognized the uselessness of resistance.

"Pretty sort o' treatment this!" he cried, stamping his stick. "I come here to see a gentleman, and you two, who I never saw in my life, seize me and treat me in this fashion!"

"You will be none the worse," I said. "We shall recompense you for the loss of your time. Sit over here on the sofa, and you will not have long to wait."

He came across sullenly enough and seated himself with his face resting on his hands. Jones and I resumed our cigars and our talk. Suddenly, however, Holmes's voice broke in upon us.

"I think that you might offer me a cigar too," he said.

We both started in our chairs. There was Holmes sitting close to us with an air of quiet amusement.

"Holmes!" I exclaimed. "You here! But where is the old man?"

"Here is the old man," said he, holding out a heap of white hair. "Here he is—wig, whiskers, eyebrows, and all. I thought my disguise was pretty good, but I hardly expected that it would stand that test."[184]

" 'Here is the old man,' said he, holding out a heap of white hair."
Richard Gutschmidt, *Das Zeichen der Vier* (Stuttgart: Robert Lutz Verlag, 1902)

184 "It is astonishing," remarks D. Martin Dakin, "that Watson, as on other occasions, failed to recognise at close range a man whom he knew so well, especially as he had actually seen him start out in the same seafaring garb a short while before." Dakin suggests that Watson did in fact see through Holmes's disguises, but pretended to be taken in, in order to spare his feelings.

"Ah, you rogue!" cried Jones, highly delighted. "You would have made an actor and a rare one.[185] You had the proper workhouse cough, and those weak legs of yours are worth ten pound a week. I thought I knew the glint of your eye, though. You didn't get away from us so easily, you see."

"I have been working in that get-up all day," said he, lighting his cigar. "You see, a good many of the criminal classes begin to know me—especially since our friend here took to publishing some of my cases[186]: so I can only go on the warpath under some simple disguise like this. You got my wire?"

"Yes; that was what brought me here."

"How has your case prospered?"

"It has all come to nothing. I have had to release two of my prisoners, and there is no evidence against the other two."

"Never mind. We shall give you two others in the place of them. But you must put yourself under my orders. You are welcome to all the official credit, but you must act on the lines that I point out. Is that agreed?"

"Entirely, if you will help me to the men."

"Well, then, in the first place I shall want a fast police-boat—a steam launch—to be at the Westminster Stairs[187] at seven o'clock."

"That is easily managed. There is always one about there,[188] but I can step across the road and telephone[189] to make sure."

"Then I shall want two staunch men in case of resistance."

"There will be two or three in the boat. What else?"

"When we secure the men we shall get the treasure. I think that it would be a pleasure to my friend here to take the box round to the young lady to whom half of it rightfully belongs. Let her be the first to open it. Eh, Watson?"

"It would be a great pleasure to me."

"Rather an irregular proceeding," said Jones, shaking his head. "However, the whole thing is irregular, and I suppose we must wink at it. The treasure must afterwards be handed over to the authorities until after the official investigation."

"Certainly. That is easily managed. One other point. I should much like to have a few details about this matter from the lips of Jonathan Small himself. You know I like to work the details of my cases out. There is no objection to my having an unofficial interview with him, either here in my rooms or elsewhere, as long as he is efficiently guarded?"

185 Compare Watson's remark from "A Scandal in Bohemia": "The stage lost a fine actor, even as science lost an acute reasoner, when [Holmes] became a specialist in crime." The suggestion that Holmes was an actor in his youth is taken up in detail by William S. Baring-Gould, who proposes that Holmes toured America with the Sasanoff Shakespeare Company from 1879 to 1880. See *Chronological Table* and *Theatrical Mr. Holmes*, by Michael Harrison.

186 Of course, only one case had actually been published before *The Sign of Four*—namely, *A Study in Scarlet* (1887). William S. Baring-Gould comments, "It is possible that Holmes here confused the one published case with the number of cases Watson had undoubtedly *chronicled* by this time." However, H. B. Williams suggests that Holmes must have been referring to some of the cases that may have appeared in small pamphlet form and been lost since. "Whatever the medium," Williams concludes, "its circulation was such that the criminal and lower classes of London were familiar with Holmes and his methods." See also note 182.

187 Probably a reference to Westminster Pier, a public pier located on the Victoria Embankment just below Westminster Bridge. Watson may have misspoken, conflating the Pier with the Whitehall Stairs, which are situated some two hundred yards down the Thames.

188 The Thames Police or, more formally, the Thames Division of the Metropolitan Police, founded in 1839, patrolled the river in a fleet of rowing boats that, by 1898, numbered twenty-eight; the boats were still in use in the 1920s. (The police did not acquire motorboats until 1910.) Under the command of Superintendent George Steed, the force consisted in 1887 of 44 inspectors, 4 sergeants, and 124 constables, according to Charles

Dickens, Jr. (*Dictionary of the Thames*, 1887). These numbers had increased 10 percent by the following year. Descriptions of the uniforms of "Wet Bobs" vary, with all sources agreeing that the men wore a blue reefer coat, or double-breasted jacket—removed for rowing—and loose-fitting trousers. There was a variety of headgear: a hard glazed hat, a peaked yachtsman's cap, or a straw hat. The officers decorated their collars with a nickel anchor. Dickens, Jr., writes: "Both night and day several boats patrol the river in different parts; a fresh boat starting from the station hard every two hours to relieve the one whose watch is up. Each boat contains an inspector and two men, the latter of whom do the rowing, and a careful system of supervision is maintained by which the passing of each boat is checked at varying points. Two steam launches are also employed"; by 1898, eight more steam launches had been added. The work was dangerous, and between 1857 and 1901 at least two officers drowned in the line of duty.

189 Col. E. Ennalls Berl points out the absence of a telephone at 221B Baker Street at this time. Not until the events of "The Retired Colourman" (generally dated 1899—see *Chronological Table*) is there a record of a telephone at the Baker Street lodgings. Although one historian of Scotland Yard records that as late as 1898, neither the Yard nor any of the two hundred Metropolitan Police stations had telephones, one senior Scotland Yard official confirms that the Yard had telephone service from 1887 on.

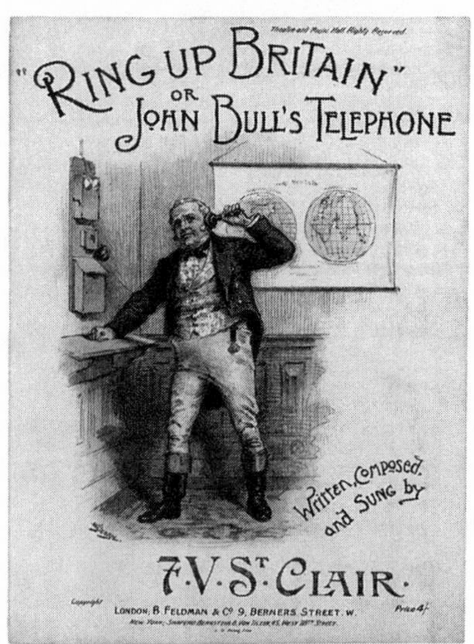

Song sheet for *"Ring Up Britain" or John Bull's Telephone* (*ca.* 1880).

1888 telephone, made by Western Electric and provided in London by the National Telephone Company.

"Well, you are master of the situation. I have had no proof yet of the existence of this Jonathan Small. However, if you can catch him, I don't see how I can refuse you an interview with him."

"That is understood, then?"

"Perfectly. Is there anything else?"

"Only that I insist upon your dining with us. It will be ready in half an hour. I have oysters[190] and a brace of grouse,[191] with something a little choice in white wines.[192] Watson, you have never yet recognized my merits as a housekeeper."

190 Julia Carlson Rosenblatt and Frederic H. Sonnenschmidt, the latter then Culinary Dean of the Culinary Institute of America, write, in *Dining with Sherlock Holmes*, "[T]he cuisine of Victorian England was fairly overrun by this delicious mollusk—but only in season. By law the availability of oysters was restricted to the period of September through April, or, by convenient mnemonic, the months with an 'r' in them."

191 Fletcher Pratt, in "The Gastronomic Holmes," points out that one brace of grouse would be insufficient for three men, one of whom was Watson, "who did nothing to preserve his figure." He concludes that there were three brace, and "they could only have been served in the classic manner prescribed by both Brillat-Savarin and Escoffier—roasted with the breasts only served, accompanied by a bread sauce, potato chips and a gravy made from the unused portions of the birds." A "brace" refers to a pair of grouse, usually 8 to 10 ounces in size.

Rosenblatt and Sonnenschmidt point out that Holmes referred to himself as "housekeeper" and Mrs. Hudson must have had the night off. "But having been occupied with his investigation all day, Holmes could not have done much in advance of his return. . . . Holmes merely stopped at a shop on his way home and purchased the grouse already cooked." Thus, they suggest "Cold Roast Grouse with Cold Cuts."

192 Fletcher Pratt suspects "a Montrachet with a domaine bottling," while Jørgen Cold, in "What Did Sherlock Holmes Drink?," remarks, "There is hardly any doubt that a good white wine in London at that time must have been Rhein wine and supposedly a *Steinberger Kabinett*." Rosenblatt and Sonnenschmidt comment, "With this dish, English gourmets usually prefer a mixture of light and dark beer. A Frenchman would usually accompany it with champagne or chablis. Holmes's choice of white wine on this occasion may reflect his French ancestry."

CHAPTER X

THE END OF THE ISLANDER

OUR MEAL WAS a merry one. Holmes could talk exceedingly well when he chose, and that night he did choose. He appeared to be in a state of nervous exaltation. I have never known him so brilliant. He spoke on a quick succession of subjects—on miracle plays,[193] on mediaeval pottery,[194] on Stradivarius violins,[195] on the Buddhism of Ceylon,[196] and on the warships of the future—handling each as though he had made a special study of it. His bright humour marked the reaction from his black depression of the preceding days. Athelney Jones proved to be a sociable soul in his hours of relaxation and faced his dinner with the air of a *bon vivant.* For myself, I felt elated at the thought that we were nearing the end of our task, and I caught something of Holmes's gaiety. None of us alluded during dinner to the cause which had brought us together.

When the cloth was cleared, Holmes glanced at his watch and filled up three glasses with port.[197]

"One bumper,"[198] said he, "to the success of our little expedition. And now it is high time we were off. Have you a pistol, Watson?"

"I have my old service-revolver in my desk."

193 A miracle play, one of three principal kinds of drama of the Middle Ages (along with the mystery play and the morality play), presents an account, real or fictitious, of the life, miracles, or martyrdom of a saint, and episodes of divine intercession in the lives of humans. Originally in Latin and drawn largely from Scripture, the dramas were enacted in Roman Catholic churches by the clergy, with priests miming and choirs performing antiphonies. By the thirteenth century they had evolved beyond presentation as a part of church services into vernacular, boisterous, sometimes ribald performances at public festivals. These performances were presented by town guild members (who were paid actors), and the sets were erected on special wheeled stages. Scenes from the Bible mixed with secular material. Almost all surviving miracle plays concern either the Virgin Mary or St. Nicholas, with the Virgin Mary frequently appearing as *deus ex machina*. As popular farce was incorporated into the drama, the Church distanced itself, finally suppressing the very plays it had helped to develop. The rich form assumed a life of its own, heavily influencing the course and development of British theatre. In Cornwall, miracle plays were performed at an early date in the Cymric dialect, and this may explain Holmes's interest (see "The Devil's Foot," in which Holmes studies the Cornish language). Other medieval studies of Holmes include palimpsests ("The Golden Pince-Nez"), music ("The Bruce-Partington Plans"), and English charters ("The Three Students").

194 A curious subject for Holmes to discuss: According to the *Encyclopædia Britannica* (9th Ed.), "Though great quantities of pottery for domestic use were made" from the eleventh to fifteenth centuries in England and France, "it was extremely fragile, and, being of very coarse ware, without artistic beauty, few specimens have been preserved to our times."

195 Holmes himself owned one, according to "The Cardboard Box." See *A Study in Scarlet*, note 97.

196 Perhaps Holmes followed the debate that raged during the 1880s concerning the ethnology of Ceylon's minority Muslims, who were struggling to separate themselves socially and politically from another powerful minority, the Tamils, with whom they shared a language but not a religion, as Tamils are Hindu. The majority religion of Ceylon was, of course, Buddhism, in particular the relatively conservative Theravada form.

197 "It is to be noted," observes Fletcher Pratt, "that Holmes poured [the port] himself; another sign of the true gourmet, who would rather let a gorilla handle his sister than a waiter touch his port." An excellent overview of an Englishman's port is given in Patricia Guy's "Consumer Dourobles: A Study of Victorian Port Styles," in her collection *Bacchus in Baker Street*.

198 "[A]ccording to [Samuel] Johnson from 'bump,' but probably from *French* Bon-Pere, the fixed toast in monastic life of old, now used for 'full measure' " (*Slang Dictionary*, 1865).

"You had best take it, then. It is well to be prepared. I see that the cab is at the door. I ordered it for half-past six."

It was a little past seven before we reached the Westminster wharf and found our launch awaiting us. Holmes eyed it critically.

"Is there anything to mark it as a police-boat?"

"Yes; that green lamp at the side."

"Then take it off."

The small change was made, we stepped on board, and the ropes were cast off. Jones, Holmes, and I sat in the stern. There was one man at the rudder, one to tend the engines, and two burly police-inspectors forward.

"Where to?" asked Jones.

"To the Tower. Tell them to stop opposite to Jacobson's Yard."

Our craft was evidently a very fast one. We shot past the long lines of loaded barges as though they were stationary. Holmes smiled with satisfaction as we overhauled a river steamer and left her behind us.

"We ought to be able to catch anything on the river," he said.

"Well, hardly that. But there are not many launches to beat us."

"We shall have to catch the *Aurora*, and she has a name for being a clipper. I will tell you how the land lies, Watson. You recollect how annoyed I was at being baulked by so small a thing?"

"Yes.

"Well, I gave my mind a thorough rest by plunging into a chemical analysis. One of our greatest statesmen has said that a change of work is the best rest.[199] So it is. When I had succeeded in dissolving the hydrocarbon[200] which I was at work at, I came back to our problem of the Sholtos, and thought the whole matter out again. My boys had been up the river and down the river without result. The launch was not at any landing-stage or wharf, nor had it returned. Yet it could hardly have been scuttled to hide their traces, though that always remained as a possible hypothesis if all else failed. I knew that this man Small had a certain degree of low cunning, but I did not think him capable of anything in the nature of delicate finesse. That is usually a product of higher education. I then reflected that since he had certainly been in London some

199 T. S. Blakeney queries, "Presumably Gladstone is meant; can anyone say when and where he made this remark, and quote the authority for it?"

200 "It is inconceivable that dissolving a hydrocarbon should be a problem, even momentarily, to a chemist," Remsen Ten Eyck Schenck writes, in "Baker Street Fables." "Holmes might as well have said 'when I had succeeded in tying my boot-lace,' with the air of having triumphed over great obstacles after days of heroic effort."

Dr. John D. Clark agrees, in "A Chemist's View of Canonical Chemistry": "There is rarely any difficulty in dissolving a hydrocarbon. . . . All you have to do is apply a lighter liquid hydrocarbon, and *voilà*!, you have your solution. If you have ever removed a glob of tar from a fender with a gasoline-soaked rag, you know what I mean."

But Leon S. Holstein (" '7. Knowledge of Chemistry—Profound' ") disagrees: "[I]t is my understanding, from those versed in the art, that one method of examining unknown organic compounds is to first determine physical properties, one of which is the solubility or insolubility in various reagents. The remark in question was made merely to convey that whatever compound or admixture he was working on, Holmes had determined that it was soluble in some standard reagent."

Lee R. Walters, in "The Hydrocarbon Puzzle," asserts that Holmes was working on dissolving carbazol (carbazole) in a new solvent—concentrated sulfuric acid, which was not reported as a solvent system until 1902.

time—as we had evidence that he maintained a continual watch over Pondicherry Lodge—he could hardly leave at a moment's notice, but would need some little time, if it were only a day, to arrange his affairs. That was the balance of probability, at any rate."

"It seems to me to be a little weak," said I; "it is more probable that he had arranged his affairs before ever he set out upon his expedition."

"No, I hardly think so. This lair of his would be too valuable a retreat in case of need for him to give it up until he was sure that he could do without it. But a second consideration struck me. Jonathan Small must have felt that the peculiar appearance of his companion, however much he may have top-coated him, would give rise to gossip, and possibly be associated with this Norwood tragedy. He was quite sharp enough to see that. They had started from their head-quarters under cover of darkness, and he would wish to get back before it was broad light. Now, it was past three o'clock, according to Mrs. Smith, when they got the boat. It would be quite bright, and people would be about in an hour or so. Therefore, I argued, they did not go very far. They paid Smith well to hold his tongue, reserved his launch for the final escape, and hurried to their lodgings with the treasure-box. In a couple of nights, when they had time to see what view the papers took, and whether there was any suspicion, they would make their way under cover of darkness to some ship at Gravesend or in the Downs,[201] where no doubt they had already arranged for passages to America or the Colonies."

"But the launch? They could not have taken that to their lodgings."

"Quite so. I argued that the launch must be no great way off, in spite of its invisibility. I then put myself in the place of Small and looked at it as a man of his capacity would. He would probably consider that to send back the launch or to keep it at a wharf would make pursuit easy if the police did happen to get on his track. How, then, could he conceal the launch and yet have her at hand when wanted? I wondered what I should do myself if I were in his shoes. I could only think of one way of doing it. I might hand the launch over to some boat-builder or repairer, with directions to make a trifling change in her. She would then be removed to his shed or yard, and so be effectu-

201 An anchorage in the English Channel, between the Thames Estuary and the Straits of Dover. Protected to the west by the land mass of Kent and to the east by a line of sandbars and shoals called the Goodwin Sands, it was a holding-over spot for ships.

202 D. Martin Dakin wonders at Holmes's dismissal of this sensible suggestion by Athelney Jones. "I can see no other reason than that he wanted the chase just for the fun of it."

ally concealed, while at the same time I could have her at a few hours' notice."

"That seems simple enough."

"It is just these very simple things which are extremely liable to be overlooked. However, I determined to act on the idea. I started at once in this harmless seaman's rig and inquired at all the yards down the river. I drew blank at fifteen, but at the sixteenth—Jacobson's—I learned that the *Aurora* had been handed over to them two days ago by a wooden-legged man, with some trivial directions as to her rudder. 'There ain't naught amiss with her rudder,' said the foreman. 'There she lies, with the red streaks.' At that moment who should come down but Mordecai Smith, the missing owner! He was rather the worse for liquor. I should not, of course, have known him, but he bellowed out his name and the name of his launch. 'I want her to-night at eight o'clock,' said he—'eight o'clock sharp, mind, for I have two gentlemen who won't be kept waiting.' They had evidently paid him well, for he was very flush of money, chucking shillings about to the men. I followed him some distance, but he subsided into an alehouse; so I went back to the yard, and, happening to pick up one of my boys on the way, I stationed him as a sentry over the launch. He is to stand at the water's edge and wave his handkerchief to us when they start. We shall be lying off in the stream, and it will be a strange thing if we do not take men, treasure, and all."

"You have planned it all very neatly, whether they are the right men or not," said Jones; "but if the affair were in my hands I should have had a body of police in Jacobson's Yard and arrested them when they came down."[202]

"Which would have been never. This man Small is a pretty shrewd fellow. He would send a scout on ahead, and if anything made him suspicious he would lie snug for another week."

"But you might have stuck to Mordecai Smith, and so been led to their hiding-place," said I.

"In that case I should have wasted my day. I think that it is a hundred to one against Smith knowing where they live. As long as he has liquor and good pay, why should he ask questions? They send him messages what to do. No, I thought over every possible course, and this is the best."

While this conversation had been proceeding, we had been

shooting the long series of bridges which span the Thames. As we passed the City the last rays of the sun were gilding the cross upon the summit of St. Paul's. It was twilight before we reached the Tower.

"That is Jacobson's Yard," said Holmes, pointing to a bristle of masts and rigging on the Surrey side.[203] "Cruise gently up and down here under cover of this string of lighters."[204] He took a pair of night-glasses[205] from his pocket and gazed some time at the shore. "I see my sentry at his post," he remarked, "but no sign of a handkerchief."

"Suppose we go downstream a short way and lie in wait for them," said Jones, eagerly.

We were all eager by this time, even the policemen and stokers, who had a very vague idea of what was going forward.

"We have no right to take anything for granted," Holmes answered. "It is certainly ten to one that they go downstream, but we cannot be certain. From this point we can see the entrance of the yard, and they can hardly see us. It will be a clear night and plenty of light. We must stay where we are. See how the folk swarm over yonder in the gaslight."

"They are coming from work in the yard."

"Dirty-looking rascals, but I suppose every one has some little immortal spark concealed about him. You would not think it, to look at them. There is no *a priori*[206] probability about it. A strange enigma is man!"

"Someone calls him a soul concealed in an animal," I suggested.

The Tower of London (1888).

203 "Overlooking the Watson error—he says 'Surrey' here, when he means 'Kent,' " writes Michael Harrison, in *The London of Sherlock Holmes*—"we realise that we are in another world than theirs: a world in which, though steamships with electric light were crossing the Atlantic in under five days, the sailing-ship was still the commoner; not until the next century was steam to overtake sail."

204 Flat-bottomed boats, broad and not entirely unlike barges, commonly used to convey cargo from ship to shore.

205 Binoculars with large objective lenses, for viewing in the dark. In normal daylight, the human eye's diameter is about 4 to 4½ millimetres, whereas at night it can be as large as 7 to 7½ millimetres. To accommodate the larger nighttime diameter, a pair of binoculars with a large field works best to admit more light.

Night glasses.
Victorian Shopping (Harrod's 1895 Catalogue)

206 Deductive; relating to or derived from reasoning by self-evident propositions.

"Winwood Reade is good upon the subject," said Holmes. "He remarks that, while the individual man is an insoluble puzzle, in the aggregate he becomes a mathematical certainty. You can, for example, never foretell what any one man will do, but you can say with precision what an average number will be up to. Individuals vary, but percentages remain constant. So says the statistician.[207] But do I see a handkerchief? Surely there is a white flutter over yonder."[208]

"Yes, it is your boy," I cried. "I can see him plainly."

"And there is the *Aurora*," exclaimed Holmes, "and going like the devil! Full speed ahead, engineer. Make after that launch with the yellow light. By heaven, I shall never forgive myself if she proves to have the heels of us!"

She had slipped unseen through the yard-entrance and passed between two or three small craft, so that she had fairly got her speed up before we saw her. Now she was flying down the stream, near in to the shore, going at a tremendous rate. Jones looked gravely at her and shook his head.

"She is very fast," he said. "I doubt if we shall catch her."

"We must catch her!" cried Holmes between his teeth. "Heap it on, stokers! Make her do all she can! If we burn the boat we must have them!"

We were fairly after her now. The furnaces roared, and the powerful engines whizzed and clanked like a great metallic heart. Her sharp, steep prow cut through the still river-water and sent two rolling waves to right and to left of us. With every throb of the engines she sprang and quivered like a living thing. One great yellow lantern in our bows threw a long, flickering funnel of light in front of us. Right ahead a dark blur upon the water showed where the *Aurora* lay, and the swirl of white foam behind her spoke of the pace at which she was going. We flashed past barges, steamers, merchant-vessels, in and out, behind this one and round the other. Voices hailed us out of the darkness, but still the *Aurora* thundered on, and still we followed close upon her track.

"Pile it on, men, pile it on!" cried Holmes, looking down into the engine-room, while the fierce glow from below beat upon his eager, aquiline face. "Get every pound of steam you can."

"I think we gain a little," said Jones with his eyes on the Aurora.

207 Holmes paraphrases Winwood Reade's *The Martyrdom of Man* (1872):

> All the events which occur upon the earth result from Law: even those actions which are entirely dependent on the caprices of the memory, or the impulse of the passions, are shown by statistics to be, when taken in the gross, entirely independent of the human will. As a single atom, man is an enigma; as a whole, he is a mathematical problem. As an individual, he is a free agent; as a species, the offspring of necessity.

208 D. Martin Dakin humorously points out, "One imagines that few Victorian street urchins were in the habit of carrying handkerchiefs, and if one had done so, it would not have stayed white for long." He concludes that Holmes provided it to him for signalling purposes.

"The furnaces roared, and the powerful engines whizzed and clanked like a great metallic heart."
Richard Gutschmidt, *Das Zeichen der Vier* (Stuttgart: Robert Lutz Verlag, 1902)

"I am sure of it," said I. "We shall be up with her in a very few minutes."

At that moment, however, as our evil fate would have it, a tug with three barges in tow blundered in between us. It was only by putting our helm hard down[209] that we avoided a collision, and before we could round them and recover our way the *Aurora* had gained a good two hundred yards. She was still, however, well in view, and the murky, uncertain twilight was settling into a clear, starlit night. Our boilers were strained to their utmost, and the frail shell vibrated and creaked with the fierce energy which was driving us along. We had shot through the Pool,[210] past the West India Docks, down the long Deptford Reach,[211] and up again after rounding the Isle of Dogs.[212] The dull blur in front of us resolved itself now clearly into the dainty *Aurora*. Jones turned our searchlight upon her, so that we could plainly see the figures upon her deck. One man sat by the stern, with something black between his knees, over

209 Jack Tracy explains, in *Encyclopaedia Sherlockiana*: "[M]eaning that the helm was turned fully to one side . . ."

210 Segment of the Thames, from below London Bridge to a little above Regent's Canal. A centre of trade from the founding of London by the Romans around 33 A.D. through 1950, the Pool saw perhaps its heaviest traffic during the nineteenth century, with the construction of St. Katharine Docks (1824). Among the buildings along this stretch of the river were the Billingsgate Fish Market and the Old Customs House. River transport in the Pool slowed down considerably with the railroad boom of the 1870s.

211 From the end of Limehouse Reach to Greenwich Ferry.

212 The name "Isle of Dogs" dates from at least 1588 and is the title of a lost play by Thomas Nashe and Ben Jonson that was suppressed for sedition almost immediately following its first performance at the Swan Theatre in July 1597. Originally a peninsula jutting out into the river between Limehouse and Blackwall, the Isle of Dogs became an "island" when a canal was built across it in the early nineteenth century. It was subsequently abandoned and incorporated into the West and East India Docks. The Millwall dock followed in mid-century, as well as a town on the south-east tip of the Isle that included sawmills, potteries, brickfields, timber wharves, a cement factory, and a church. The odd name has never been satisfactorily explained.

which he stooped. Beside him lay a dark mass, which looked like a Newfoundland dog. The boy held the tiller, while against the red glare of the furnace I could see old Smith, stripped to the waist, and shovelling coals for dear life. They may have had some doubt at first as to whether we were really pursuing them, but now as we followed every winding and turning which they took there could no longer be any question about it. At Greenwich we were about three hundred paces behind them. At Blackwall we could not have been more than two hundred and fifty. I have coursed many creatures in many countries[213] during my checkered career, but never did sport give me such a wild thrill as this mad, flying man-hunt down the Thames. Steadily we drew in upon them, yard by yard. In the silence of the night we could hear the panting and clanking of their machinery. The man in the stern still crouched upon the deck, and his arms were moving as though he were busy, while every now and then he would look up and measure with a glance the distance which still separated us. Nearer we came and nearer. Jones yelled to them to stop. We were not more than four boat's-lengths behind them, both boats flying at a tremendous pace. It was a clear reach of the river, with Barking Level[214] upon one side and the melancholy Plumstead Marshes[215] upon the other. At our hail the man in the stern sprang up from the deck and shook his two clenched fists at us, cursing the while in a high, cracked voice. He was a good-sized, powerful man, and as he stood poising himself with legs astride I could see that from the thigh downward there was but a wooden stump upon the right side. At the sound of his strident, angry cries, there was movement in the huddled bundle upon the deck. It straightened itself into a little black man—the smallest I have ever seen—with a great, misshapen head and a shock of tangled, dishevelled hair. Holmes had already drawn his revolver, and I whipped out mine at the sight of this savage, distorted creature. He was wrapped in some sort of dark ulster or blanket, which left only his face exposed, but that face was enough to give a man a sleepless night. Never have I seen features so deeply marked with all bestiality and cruelty. His small eyes glowed and burned with a sombre light, and his thick lips were writhed back from his teeth, which grinned and chattered at us with half animal fury.

213 G. W. Welch, in " 'No Mention of That Local Hunt, Watson,' " notes this and numerous other hunting references in the Canon and concludes that Watson, an avid hunter, must have been disabled from hunting by his wound.

214 Barking Reach was the site of the outlets of London's "new and gigantic system of drainage . . ." (so described in *Baedeker*).

215 During the early nineteenth century, Royal Artillery officers used the Plumstead Marshes for live firing practice, but Harold Clunn, in *The Face of London*, presents a grim prognosis for anyone venturing near these foetid "swamps of stagnant water" at mid-century: "no provision whatever had been made for drainage, and many . . . ditches, which were dangerous to health, had not been cleaned out within the memory of living men." Cases of marsh ague were reported. However, the whiff of gentrification was just around the corner. With the growth of the Royal Arsenal at nearby Woolwich creating job opportunities, the separate suburb of Plumstead joined the march of progress, its population spiking to 24,502 in 1861 (from 1,166 in 1801).

"Fire if he raises his hand," said Holmes quietly.

We were within a boat's-length by this time, and almost within touch of our quarry. I can see the two of them now as they stood, the white man with his legs far apart, shrieking out curses, and the unhallowed dwarf with his hideous face, and his strong yellow teeth gnashing at us in the light of our lantern.

It was well that we had so clear a view of him. Even as we looked he plucked out from under his covering a short, round piece of wood, like a school-ruler, and clapped it to his lips. Our pistols rang out together. He whirled round, threw up his arms, and, with a kind of choking cough, fell sideways into the stream. I caught one glimpse of his venomous, menacing eyes amid the white swirl of the waters. At the same moment the wooden-legged man threw himself upon the rudder and put it hard down, so that his boat made straight in for the southern bank, while we shot past her stern, only clearing her by a few feet. We were round after her in an instant, but she was already

"Our pistols rang out together."
Charles A. Cox, *The Sign of the Four* (Chicago and New York: The Henneberry Company, n.d.)

"Our pistols rang out together."
Richard Gutschmidt, *Das Zeichen der Vier* (Stuttgart: Robert Lutz Verlag, 1902)

nearly at the bank. It was a wild and desolate place, where the moon glimmered upon a wide expanse of marsh-land, with pools of stagnant water and beds of decaying vegetation. The launch, with a dull thud, ran up upon the mud-bank, with her bow in the air and her stern flush with the water. The fugitive sprang out, but his stump instantly sank its whole length into the sodden soil. In vain he struggled and writhed. Not one step could he possibly take either forwards or backwards. He yelled in impotent rage and kicked frantically into the mud with his other foot; but his struggles only bored his wooden pin the deeper into the sticky bank. When we brought our launch alongside he was so firmly anchored that it was only by throwing the end of a rope over his shoulders that we were able to haul him out and to drag him, like some evil fish, over our side. The two Smiths, father and son, sat sullenly in their launch but came aboard meekly enough when commanded. The *Aurora* herself we hauled off and made fast to our stern. A solid iron chest of Indian workmanship stood upon the deck. This, there could be no question, was the same that had contained the ill-omened treasure of the Sholtos. There was no key, but it was of considerable weight, so we transferred it carefully to our own little cabin. As we steamed slowly upstream again, we flashed our searchlight in every direction, but there was no sign

"He whirled round, threw up his arms, and with a kind of choking cough, fell sideways into the stream."
Arthur Twidle, *The Sign of Four*, collected in
Works of A. Conan Doyle (New York: D. Appleton and Co., 1903)

"He yelled in impotent rage."
F. H. Townsend, *The Sign of Four* (London: George Newnes, Ltd., 1903)

of the Islander. Somewhere in the dark ooze at the bottom of the Thames lie the bones of that strange visitor to our shores.

"See here," said Holmes, pointing to the wooden hatchway. "We were hardly quick enough with our pistols." There, sure enough, just behind where we had been standing, stuck one of those murderous darts which we knew so well. It must have whizzed between us at the instant we fired. Holmes smiled at it and shrugged his shoulders in his easy fashion, but I confess that it turned me sick to think of the horrible death which had passed so close to us that night.

CHAPTER XI

The Great Agra Treasure

Our captive sat in the cabin opposite to the iron box which he had done so much and waited so long to gain. He was a sunburned reckless-eyed fellow, with a network of lines and wrinkles all over his mahogany features, which told of a hard, open-air life. There was a singular prominence about his bearded chin which marked a man who was not to be easily turned from his purpose. His age may have been fifty or thereabouts, for his black, curly hair was thickly shot with grey. His face in repose was not an unpleasing one, though his heavy brows and aggressive chin gave him, as I had lately seen, a terrible expression when moved to anger. He sat now with his handcuffed hands upon his lap, and his head sunk upon his breast, while he looked with his keen, twinkling eyes at the box which had been the cause of his ill-doings. It seemed to me that there was more sorrow than anger in his rigid and contained countenance. Once he looked up at me with a gleam of something like humour in his eyes.

"Well, Jonathan Small," said Holmes, lighting a cigar, "I am sorry that it has come to this."

"And so am I, sir," he answered frankly. "I don't believe that

216 In American and English law, the acts of one felon in the course of committing the felony are generally attributed to all co-conspirators, and a killing in the course of a robbery is "felony-murder," not merely manslaughter, and hence may be subject to capital punishment. In short, Small's confidence would be misplaced.

"He sat now with his hand-cuffed hands on his lap, and his head sunk on his breast, while he gazed at the box."
Artist unknown, *The Sign of Four* (New York and Boston: H. M. Caldwell Co., n.d.)

I can swing over the job.[216] I give you my word on the Book that I never raised hand against Mr. Sholto. It was that little hell-hound Tonga who shot one of his cursed darts into him. I had no part in it, sir. I was as grieved as if it had been my blood-relation. I welted the little devil with the slack end of the rope for it, but it was done, and I could not undo it again."

"Have a cigar," said Holmes; "and you had best take a pull out of my flask, for you are very wet. How could you expect so small and weak a man as this black fellow to overpower Mr. Sholto and hold him while you were climbing the rope?"

"You seem to know as much about it as if you were there, sir. The truth is that I hoped to find the room clear. I knew the habits of the house pretty well, and it was the time when Mr. Sholto usually went down to his supper. I shall make no secret of the business. The best defence that I can make is just the simple truth. Now, if it had been the old major I would have swung for him with a light heart. I would have thought no more of knifing him than of smoking this cigar. But it's cursed hard that I should be lagged[217] over this young Sholto, with whom I had no quarrel whatever."

"You are under the charge of Mr. Athelney Jones, of Scotland Yard. He is going to bring you up to my rooms, and I shall ask you for a true account of the matter. You must make a clean breast of it, for if you do I hope that I may be of use to you. I think I can prove that the poison acts so quickly that the man was dead before ever you reached the room."

"That he was, sir. I never got such a turn in my life as when I saw him grinning at me with his head on his shoulder as I climbed through the window. It fairly shook me, sir. I'd have half killed Tonga for it if he had not scrambled off. That was how he came to leave his club, and some of his darts too, as he tells me, which I dare say helped to put you on our track; though how you kept on it is more than I can tell. I don't feel no malice against you for it. But it does seem a queer thing," he added, with a bitter smile, "that I, who have a fair claim to half a million of money, should spend the first half of my life

"He sat now with his handcuffed hands upon his lap."
Richard Gutschmidt, *Das Zeichen der Vier* (Stuttgart: Robert Lutz Verlag, 1902)

217 The *Slang Dictionary* (1865) explains: "[I]mprisoned, apprehended, or transported for a crime. From the *Old Norse*, LAGDA, 'laid,' laid by the leg."

218 The infamous prison in Princetown, in the Dartmoor Forest, was built in the early nineteenth century for French prisoners of war, said to have numbered 9,000 in 1811. In the war of 1812–1814, upwards of 2,000 American seamen who refused to serve in the British Navy against their country were also confined there. The prison remains in use and has a reputation for toughness, although a report by H.M. Chief Inspector of Prisons Anne Owers, made public after a visit to Dartmoor in November 2001, shows how much penal thinking has changed: "We discovered a prison which was itself imprisoned in its own past—locked into unsuitable but historic buildings and, more importantly, into an outdated culture of over-control and disrespect for prisoners."

219 The adjective "broad" is inserted in American texts.

Dartmoor Prison (*ca.* 1900).

building a breakwater in the Andamans, and am like to spend the other half digging drains at Dartmoor.[218] It was an evil day for me when first I clapped eyes upon the merchant Achmet and had to do with the Agra treasure, which never brought anything but a curse yet upon the man who owned it. To him, it brought murder, to Major Sholto it brought fear and guilt, to me it has meant slavery for life."

At this moment Athelney Jones thrust his[219] face and heavy shoulders into the tiny cabin.

"Quite a family party," he remarked. "I think I shall have a pull at that flask, Holmes. Well, I think we may all congratulate each other. Pity we didn't take the other alive; but there was no choice. I say, Holmes, you must confess that you cut it rather fine. It was all we could do to overhaul her."

"All is well that ends well," said Holmes. "But I certainly did not know that the *Aurora* was such a clipper."

"Smith says she is one of the fastest launches on the river, and that if he had had another man to help him with the engines we should never have caught her. He swears he knew nothing of this Norwood business."

"Neither he did," cried our prisoner—"not a word. I chose his launch because I heard that she was a flier. We told him nothing; but we paid him well, and he was to get something handsome if we reached our vessel, the *Esmeralda*, at Gravesend, outward bound for the Brazils."[220]

"Well, if he has done no wrong we shall see that no wrong comes to him. If we are pretty quick in catching our men, we are not so quick in condemning them." It was amusing to notice how the consequential Jones was already beginning to give himself airs on the strength of the capture. From the slight smile which played over Sherlock Holmes's face, I could see that the speech had not been lost upon him.

"We will be at Vauxhall Bridge presently," said Jones, "and shall land you, Dr. Watson, with the treasure-box. I need hardly tell you that I am taking a very grave responsibility upon myself in doing this. It is most irregular; but of course an agreement is an agreement. I must, however, as a matter of duty, send an inspector with you, since you have so valuable a charge. You will drive, no doubt?"

"Yes, I shall drive."

"It is a pity there is no key, that we may make an inventory first. You will have to break it open. Where is the key, my man?"

"At the bottom of the river," said Small shortly.

"Hum! There was no use your giving this unnecessary trouble. We have had work enough already through you. However, Doctor, I need not warn you to be careful. Bring the box back with you to the Baker Street rooms. You will find us there, on our way to the station."

They landed me at Vauxhall, with my heavy iron box, and with a bluff, genial inspector as my companion. A quarter of an hour's drive brought us to Mrs. Cecil Forrester's. The servant seemed surprised at so late a visitor. Mrs. Cecil Forrester was out for the evening, she explained, and likely to be very late. Miss Morstan, however, was in the drawing-room; so to the drawing-room I went, box in hand, leaving the obliging inspector[221] in the cab.

She was seated by the open window, dressed in some sort of white diaphanous material, with a little touch of scarlet at the neck and waist. The soft light of a shaded lamp fell upon her as she leaned back in the basket chair, playing over her sweet, grave face, and tinting with a dull, metallic sparkle the rich coils of her luxuriant hair. One white arm and hand drooped over the side of the chair, and her whole pose and figure spoke of an absorbing melancholy. At the sound of my footfall she

220 This was popular usage for the country of Brazil. See, *e.g.*, *Robinson Crusoe* by Daniel Defoe, wherein the hero refers to his plantation "in the Brazils."

221 "An obliging inspector indeed!" Ronald S. Bonn writes, in "The Problem of the Postulated Doctor." "And what must that obliging inspector's feelings have been, some time later—quite a long time later, Watson admits—when the doctor reappeared and coolly showed him an empty box?"

sprang to her feet, however, and a bright flush of surprise and of pleasure coloured her pale cheeks.

"I heard a cab drive up," she said. "I thought that Mrs. Forrester had come back very early, but I never dreamed that it might be you. What news have you brought me?"

"I have brought something better than news," said I, putting down the box upon the table and speaking jovially and boisterously, though my heart was heavy within me. "I have brought you something which is worth all the news in the world. I have brought you a fortune."

She glanced at the iron box.

"Is that the treasure then?" she asked, coolly enough.

"Yes, this is the great Agra treasure. Half of it is yours and half is Thaddeus Sholto's. You will have a couple of hundred thousand each. Think of that! An annuity of ten thousand pounds. There will be few richer young ladies in England. Is it not glorious?"

I think I must have been rather over-acting my delight, and that she detected a hollow ring in my congratulations, for I saw her eyebrows rise a little, and she glanced at me curiously.

"If I have it," said she, "I owe it to you."

"No, no," I answered, "not to me, but to my friend Sherlock Holmes. With all the will in the world, I could never have followed up a clue which has taxed even his analytical genius. As it was, we very nearly lost it at the last moment."

"Pray sit down and tell me all about it, Dr. Watson," said she.

I narrated briefly what had occurred since I had seen her last. Holmes's new method of search, the discovery of the *Aurora*, the appearance of Athelney Jones, our expedition in the evening, and the wild chase down the Thames. She listened with parted lips and shining eyes to my recital of our adventures. When I spoke of the dart which had so narrowly missed us, she turned so white that I feared that she was about to faint.

"It is nothing," she said as I hastened to pour her out some water. "I am all right again. It was a shock to me to hear that I had placed my friends in such horrible peril."

"That is all over," I answered. "It was nothing. I will tell you no more gloomy details. Let us turn to something brighter. There is the treasure. What could be brighter than that? I got leave to bring it with me, thinking that it would interest you to be the first to see it."

"It would be of the greatest interest to me," she said. There was no eagerness in her voice, however. It had struck her, doubtless, that it might seem ungracious upon her part to be indifferent to a prize which had cost so much to win.

"What a pretty box!" she said, stooping over it. "This is Indian work, I suppose?"

"Yes; it is Benares[222] metal-work."

"And so heavy!" she exclaimed, trying to raise it.[223] "The box alone must be of some value. Where is the key?"

"Small threw it into the Thames," I answered. "I must borrow Mrs. Forrester's poker."

There was in the front a thick and broad hasp, wrought in the image of a sitting Buddha. Under this I thrust the end of the poker and twisted it outward as a lever. The hasp sprang open with a loud snap. With trembling fingers I flung back the lid. We both stood gazing in astonishment. The box was empty!

No wonder that it was heavy. The iron-work was two-thirds

" 'Then I say "thank god," too.' "
Richard Gutschmidt, *Das Zeichen der Vier* (Stuttgart: Robert Lutz Verlag, 1902)

222 Benares, then the most populous city in the North-Western Provinces of India (a political division imposed by the British in 1835), was as renowned for its gold filigree work as for its sacred funeral ghats, terraced landings leading down to the Ganges River, where it is considered propitious to die and be cremated. Visitors to Benares bring home an enduring memory of the dense, particulated smoke rising from the ghats.

223 And yet, as Donald A. Redmond points out, in Small's description in Chapter XII, the box is described as in "a bundle in [Achmet's] hand, done up in a shawl."

of an inch thick all round. It was massive, well made, and solid, like a chest constructed to carry things of great price, but not one shred or crumb of metal or jewellery lay within it. It was absolutely and completely empty.

"The treasure is lost," said Miss Morstan, calmly.

As I listened to the words and realized what they meant, a great shadow seemed to pass from my soul. I did not know how this Agra treasure had weighed me down, until now that it was finally removed. It was selfish, no doubt, disloyal, wrong, but I could realize nothing save that the golden barrier was gone from between us.

"Thank God!" I ejaculated from my very heart.

She looked at me with a quick, questioning smile.

"Why do you say that?" she asked.

"Because you are within my reach again," I said, taking her hand. She did not withdraw it. "Because I love you, Mary, as truly as ever a man loved a woman.[224] Because this treasure, these riches, sealed my lips. Now that they are gone I can tell you how I love you. That is why I said, 'Thank God.' "

"Then I say 'Thank God,' too," she whispered, as I drew her to my side.

Whoever had lost a treasure, I knew that night that I had gained one.

224 Nathan Bengis, in "A Scandal in Baker Street, Part II," puts forward the rather far-fetched theory that Mary Morstan was Watson's *second* great love, the first being Helen Stoner, the heroine of "The Speckled Band." To reach this conclusion, he relies on the veracity of the play *The Speckled Band* by Arthur Conan Doyle (first performed in 1910), in which it is disclosed that Dr. Watson knew Enid Stonor (a thinly disguised version of Helen Stoner) in India. The truth of the play, Bengis reasons, is evident from the fact that Watson did nothing to attempt to suppress its performance. (Of course, Watson may have felt that the play was so far from the truth that none of his family or friends would believe it to be anything but a work of fiction.) Bengis draws evidence from the play that Watson and Enid were lovers in India, a fact concealed in Watson's tale of "The Speckled Band," which, Bengis believes, was written to clear her of accusations of complicity in the death of her stepfather.

Bengis worries that Watson does not say to Mary that his love is greater than any other man's, only that it is equal. "It is easy to see now," he concludes, "that [Mary Morstan], jealous as she was, must have felt that in Watson's affections she was always second to 'that other.' "

CHAPTER XII

The Strange Story of Jonathan Small

A VERY PATIENT man was that inspector in the cab, for it was a weary time before I rejoined him. His face clouded over when I showed him the empty box.

"There goes the reward!" said he, gloomily. "Where there is no money there is no pay. This night's work would have been worth a tenner each to Sam Brown and me if the treasure had been there."

"Mr. Thaddeus Sholto is a rich man," I said; "he will see that you are rewarded, treasure or no."

The inspector shook his head despondently, however.

"It's a bad job," he repeated; "and so Mr. Athelney Jones will think."

His forecast proved to be correct for the detective looked blank enough when I got to Baker Street and showed him the empty box. They had only just arrived, Holmes, the prisoner, and he, for they had changed their plans so far as to report themselves at a station upon the way. My companion lounged in his armchair with his usual listless expression, while Small sat stolidly opposite to him with his wooden leg cocked over his sound one. As I exhibited the empty box he leaned back in his chair and laughed aloud.

"This is your doing, Small," said Athelney Jones angrily.

"Yes, I have put it away where you shall never lay hand on it," he cried exultantly. "It is my treasure, and if I can't have the loot I'll take darned good care that no one else does. I tell you that no living man has any right to it, unless it is three men who are in the Andaman convict-barracks and myself. I know now that I cannot have the use of it, and I know that they cannot. I have acted all through for them as much as for myself. It's been the sign of four with us always. Well, I know that they would have had me do just what I have done, and throw the treasure into the Thames rather than let it go to kith or kin of Sholto or Morstan.[225] It was not to make them rich that we did for Achmet. You'll find the treasure where the key is and where little Tonga is. When I saw that your launch must catch us, I put the loot away in a safe place.[226] There are no rupees[227] for you this journey."

"You are deceiving us, Small," said Athelney Jones, sternly; "if you had wished to throw the treasure into the Thames, it would have been easier for you to have thrown box and all."

"Easier for me to throw, and easier for you to recover," he answered, with a shrewd, side-long look. "The man that was clever enough to hunt me down is clever enough to pick an iron box from the bottom of a river. Now that they are scattered over five miles or so, it may be a harder job. It went to my heart to do it, though. I was half mad when you came up with us. However, there's no good grieving over it. I've had ups in my life, and I've had downs, but I've learned not to cry over spilled milk."

"This is a very serious matter, Small," said the detective. "If you had helped justice, instead of thwarting it in this way, you would have had a better chance at your trial."

"Justice!" snarled the ex-convict. "A pretty justice! Whose loot is this, if it is not ours? Where is the justice that I should give it up to those who have never earned it? Look how I have earned it! Twenty long years in that fever-ridden swamp, all day at work under the mangrove-tree, all night chained up in the filthy convict-huts, bitten by mosquitoes, racked with ague, bullied by every cursed black-faced policeman who loved to take it out of a white man. That was how I earned the

225 And yet the Morstan family seems to have stood by Small, according to Small's account.

226 Denise Rogers suggests that it is more likely that Sholto (a) broke up the treasure into small packets and hid them, (b) deposited them *retrievably* in the Thames (in a "safe place"), or (c) only got a part of the treasure (the rest was hidden by Bartholomew Sholto). She also considers the possibility that Watson himself disposed of the treasure. S. E. Dahlinger, in "In Search of the Agra Treasure," has no doubt that Holmes, Watson, and Athelney Jones conspired to keep the treasure for themselves.

227 The coins struck by the British government of East India from 1860 until independence.

Agra treasure, and you talk to me of justice because I cannot bear to feel that I have paid this price only that another may enjoy it! I would rather swing a score of times, or have one of Tonga's darts in my hide, than live in a convict's cell and feel that another man is at his ease in a palace with the money that should be mine."

Small had dropped his mask of stoicism, and all this came out in a wild whirl of words, while his eyes blazed, and the handcuffs clanked together with the impassioned movement of his hands. I could understand, as I saw the fury and the passion of the man, that it was no groundless or unnatural terror which had possessed Major Sholto when he first learned that the injured convict was upon his track.

"You forget that we know nothing of all this," said Holmes, quietly. "We have not heard your story, and we cannot tell how far justice may originally have been on your side."

"Well, sir, you have been very fair-spoken to me, though I can see that I have you to thank that I have these bracelets upon my wrists. Still, I bear no grudge for that. It is all fair and above-board. If you want to hear my story, I have no wish to hold it back. What I say to you is God's truth, every word of it. Thank you, you can put the glass beside me here, and I'll put my lips to it if I am dry.

"I am a Worcestershire man myself, born near Pershore.[228] I dare say you would find a heap of Smalls living there now if you were to look. I have often thought of taking a look round there, but the truth is that I was never much of a credit to the family, and I doubt if they would be so very glad to see me. They were all steady, chapel-going folk, small farmers, well known and respected over the country-side, while I was always a bit of a rover. At last, however, when I was about eighteen, I gave them no more trouble, for I got into a mess over a girl and could only get out of it again by taking the Queen's shilling[229] and joining the Third Buffs,[230] which was just starting for India.

"I wasn't destined to do much soldiering, however. I had just got past the goose-step and learned to handle my musket, when I was fool enough to go swimming in the Ganges. Luckily for me, my company sergeant, John Holder,[231] was in the water at the same time, and he was one of the finest swimmers in the service. A crocodile took me just as I was half-way across

228 A town in the midland county of Worcestershire, England. As farmers, Small's family would have participated in the chief occupation of the region; Pershore is the epicentre of a large agricultural area that still produces quantities of fruit and vegetables today.

229 A shilling was formerly given to a soldier on enlistment. The expression, then, means enlisting in the armed forces.

230 "This is a real and very famous regiment," Mrs. Crighton Sellars records (above, note 46), "officially known as the Buffs (East Kent Regiment) consisting of the Third Foot. It is one of the oldest in the British Army, having its origin at the time of Queen Elizabeth [I]." Sellars questions whether Small belonged to this regiment, which was in the Crimea until after the Indian Mutiny ended. "The Buffs' previous service in India was under General Grey at Punniar against the Mahrattas in 1843, and I doubt if Small went there with them at that date, particularly as they had not been in England before that, but went to India from New South Wales."

231 T. S. Blakeney suggests that Holder was a younger brother of Alexander Holder, the banker in "The Beryl Coronet."

232 A day-labourer. The word derives from the Tamil *kuli*.

Recruiting sergeants at Westminster.
Street Life in London (1877)

and nipped off my right leg as clean as a surgeon could have done it, just above the knee. What with the shock and the loss of blood, I fainted, and should have been drowned if Holder had not caught hold of me and paddled for the bank. I was five months in hospital over it, and when at last I was able to limp out of it with this timber toe strapped to my stump, I found myself invalided out of the Army and unfitted for any active occupation.

"I was, as you can imagine, pretty down on my luck at this time, for I was a useless cripple, though not yet in my twentieth year. However, my misfortune soon proved to be a blessing in disguise. A man named Abel White, who had come out there as an indigo-planter, wanted an overseer to look after his coolies[232] and keep them up to their work. He happened to be a friend of our colonel's, who had taken an interest in me since the accident. To make a long story short, the colonel recommended me strongly for the post, and, as the work was mostly to be done on horseback, my leg was no great obstacle, for I had enough thigh[233] left to keep a good grip on the saddle. What I had to do was to ride over the plantation, to keep an eye on the men as they worked, and to report the idlers. The pay was fair, I had comfortable quarters, and altogether I was content to spend the remainder of my life in indigo-planting. Mr. Abel White was a kind man, and he would often drop into my little shanty and smoke a pipe with me, for white folk out there feel their hearts warm to each other as they never do here at home.

"Well, I was never in luck's way long. Suddenly, without a note of warning, the great mutiny[234] broke upon us. One month India lay as still and peaceful, to all appearance, as Surrey or Kent; the next there were two hundred thousand black devils let loose, and the country was a perfect hell. Of course you know all about it, gentlemen—a deal more than I do, very like, since reading is not in my line. I only know what I saw with my own eyes. Our plantation was at a place called Muttra,[235] near the border of the North-West Provinces.[236] Night after night the whole sky was alight with the burning bungalows, and day after day we had small companies of Europeans passing through our estate with their wives and children, on their way to Agra, where were the nearest troops. Mr. Abel White was an obstinate man. He had it in his head that the affair had been exaggerated, and that it would blow over as suddenly as it had sprung up. There he sat on his veranda, drinking whisky-pegs[237] and smoking cheroots, while the country was in a blaze about him. Of course we stuck by him, I and Dawson, who, with his wife, used to do the book-work and the managing. Well, one fine day the crash came. I had been away on a distant plantation and was riding slowly home in the evening, when my eye fell upon something all huddled together at the bottom of a steep nullah.[238] I rode down to see what it was, and the cold struck through my heart when I found it was Dawson's wife, all cut into ribbons and half-eaten by jackals and native dogs. A little further up the road Dawson himself was lying on his face, quite dead, with an empty revolver in his hand, and four Sepoys[239] lying across each other in front of him. I reined up my horse, wondering which way I

233 The English text has "knee," but this seems consistent with Small's statement that his leg was severed "just above the knee."

234 The Indian Mutiny of 1857–1858, also known as the Sepoy Rebellion ("sepoy" being the term for native soldiers), was the shocking, ultimately unsuccessful uprising that grew out of increasing Indian resentment toward British westernisation. Violence was sparked in early 1857 when sepoys in the Bengal army were issued the new Enfield rifles, whose cartridges, which could only be loaded by biting off one end, were rumoured to be greased with beef tallow and pork fat. Such a situation would have posed a grave religious insult to the army's Hindus and Muslims, and many began to suspect the government of trying to convert them to Christianity.

It was only the latest in a list of grievances against a British government that, under the leadership of governor-general Lord Dalhousie, had reduced troop salaries, taken over property from Indian landowners, and spoken of upending the caste system by recruiting "cheaper," lower-caste soldiers to replace the Brahmins and Rajputs then in service. By the time the governing East India Company ordered the cartridges greased with a more benign substance, it was too late for appeasement. On May 9, 1857, eighty-five sepoys at Meerut refused to use the rifles and were subsequently stripped of their uniforms, shackled, and marched off to prison to serve ten-year sentences. The next day, sepoys from three different units stormed the jail to release the imprisoned soldiers. In the ensuing melee, some fifty British men, women, and children were killed.

From there, the mutineers rode to Delhi. Simon Schama, in the third volume of his magisterial *History of Britain*, describes how in the moments before the violence, Harriet Tytler, the wife of the captain of the 38th

Native Infantry, "could see there was something very wrong. Servants running about in a wild way, guns tearing down the main street. . . . What could it all mean?" Her French maid, Marie, responded, "Madame, this is a revolution." Many European women and children who escaped Delhi were able to do so with the help of sympathetic sepoys, but others were less fortunate. More officers and their families were massacred, seemingly indiscriminately.

Terrible atrocities were committed on both sides. At Kanpur, a local ruler named Nana Sahib—perhaps seeking revenge over rent income that had been taken away from him—promised safe passage down the Ganges to a large group of European women and children. Once on board, the majority were shot, and several of the forty boats were set on fire; two hundred survivors were taken back to a former officer's residence at Kanpur, where they were killed as well. The British desire for vengeance against those they referred to as "niggers" grew to a frenzy. As A. N. Wilson writes, "From the very first, the British decided to meet cruelty with redoubled cruelty, terror with terror, blood with blood." There were reports, recounts Wilson, of Muslims smeared with pork fat before they were killed; Indians lashed to mouths of cannons and blown to pieces by grapeshot; women and children raped and then burnt alive; a bayoneted sepoy being roasted over a fire. Hundreds of Indians were executed by being shot from cannons.

In the end, after a lengthy siege of Lucknow, British troops were able to retake the city and finally bring the hostilities to an end. Peace was declared on July 8, 1858. One immediate result of the mutiny was the elimination of the East India Company, as well as an understanding that governing India effectively would require some consultation with Indians. For the next ninety years, India served under direct British rule, a period of time known as "the Raj."

Less than three decades after the violence, the ninth edition of the *Encyclopædia Britannica* (1875–1889) contemplated the motives for rebellion by musing, "The truth seems to be that native opinion throughout India was in a ferment, predisposing men to believe the wildest stories, and to act precipitately upon their fears. . . . Repeated annexations, the spread of education, the appearance of the steam engine and the telegraph wire, all alike revealed a consistent determination to substitute an English for an Indian civilization. The Bengal sepoys, especially, thought that they could see into the future farther than the rest of their countrymen. . . . They had everything to gain, and nothing to lose, by a revolution."

235 Twenty-five to thirty miles above Agra, this was the administrative headquarters of the district of Muttra in the North-West Provinces of India and is a Hindu holy city, the birthplace of Krishna.

236 In 1853, this province (one of eight) was separated from Bengal, of which it till then formed the north-west portion. In 1876 it was combined with the demesne known as Oudh, a region that had been annexed as a British province in 1856—an event that helped bring about the Indian Mutiny. According to the *Anglo-Indian Dictionary* (1885), "The united province contains an area of over a million square miles, and a population of forty-four million, or nearly equal to that of Germany."

237 A whisky or brandy with soda. Christopher Morley explains that the origin of the name is the witticism that "each drink is a peg in your coffin."

238 A ravine running down to a river.

239 Native Indian soldiers then under British control. In "The Indian Elements in the Holmes Tales: Jewels and Tigers," Paul Beam should turn; but at that moment I saw thick smoke curling up from Abel White's bungalow and the flames beginning to burst through the roof. I knew then that I could do my employer no good, but would only throw my own life away if I meddled in the matter. From where I stood I could see hundreds of the black fiends, with their red coats still on their backs, dancing and howling round the burning house. Some of them pointed at me, and a couple of bullets sang past my head: so I broke away across the paddy-fields, and found myself late at night safely within the walls at Agra.

"As it proved, however, there was no great safety there, either. The whole country was up like a swarm of bees. Wherever the English could collect in little bands, they held just the ground that their guns commanded. Everywhere else they were helpless fugitives. It was a fight of the millions against the hundreds; and the cruellest part of it was that these men that we fought against, foot, horse, and gunners, were our own picked troops, whom we had taught and trained, handling our own weapons and blowing our own bugle-calls. At Agra there were the 3rd Bengal Fusiliers,[240] some Sikhs,[241] two troops of

"I broke away across the paddy-fields."
Richard Gutschmidt, *Das Zeichen der Vier* (Stuttgart: Robert Lutz Verlag, 1902)

describes this passage recounting Dawson's death as "a good microcosm of all the English feared: a man dead in a far land, defending his family from overwhelming numbers of inhuman beasts—futilely, as it transpires, for his wife is cruelly murdered and left for dog-meat."

240 "By which," Mrs. Crighton Sellars writes, "[Small] probably means (or else Watson deliberately misquotes him) the Third Bengal Infantry—the famous *Guttrieka-pultran*—which stood firm and loyal [to the British Empire] during the Mutiny."

241 Sikhism is a monotheistic religion that was founded in Punjab in the late fifteenth or early sixteenth century by Guru Nanak. It has elements of Hinduism and Islam but is significantly different from both of the dominant Indian faiths. Sikhs oppose the caste system and believe in karma and rebirth. Adherence to the notion of nobility of sacrifice, particularly in wartime, was adopted early on by the culture, when Govind Singh (born in 1666), the tenth and last leader of the Sikhs, made every man a soldier, calling them not Sikhs ("disciples") but Singhs ("lions"). Ranjit Singh (1780–1839) consolidated his followers into a kingdom, but the Sikhs lost considerable ground during the Anglo-Sikh wars of 1845–1849, which resulted in the annexation of Punjab to the British dominion of India. The most emblematic and oft-cited Sikh battle in history occurred at Saragarhi, on September 12, 1897. Twenty-one members of the 36th Sikh Regiment of the Bengal Infantry were attacked and killed by 10,000 to 12,000 members of a Pashtun (Pathan) tribe, the Afridi. The battle became an immediate and unqualified symbol of collective bravery and willingness to fight to the death for a cause, in this case the protection of key Sikh forts.

242 The battle of Shahganj, a western suburb of Agra, took place on July 5, 1857.

243 Hartley R. Nathan, in "The Sign of the Four: A Potpourri of Devil Worshippers, Sikh Troopers and More," offers an explanation of the religious festivals of mid-Victorian India and concludes that in terming the faithful "devil-worshippers," it is likely that "Small, an uneducated army grunt, misinterpreted the local religious practices he observed."

horse, and a battery of artillery. A volunteer corps of clerks and merchants had been formed, and this I joined, wooden leg and all. We went out to meet the rebels at Shahgunge[242] early in July, and we beat them back for a time, but our powder gave out, and we had to fall back upon the city.

"Nothing but the worst news came to us from every side—which is not to be wondered at, for if you look at the map you will see that we were right in the heart of it. Lucknow is rather better than a hundred miles to the east, and Cawnpore about as far to the south. From every point on the compass there was nothing but torture and murder and outrage.

"The city of Agra is a great place, swarming with fanatics and fierce devil-worshippers of all sorts.[243] Our handful of men were lost among the narrow, winding streets. Our leader moved across the river, therefore, and took up his position in the old fort of Agra. I don't know if any of you gentlemen have ever read or heard anything of that old fort. It is a very queer place—the queerest that ever I was in, and I have been in some rum corners, too. First of all, it is enormous in size. I should think that the enclosure must be acres and acres. There is a modern part, which took all our garrison, women, children, stores, and everything else, with plenty of room over. But the modern part is nothing like the size of the old quarter, where nobody goes, and which is given over to the scorpions and the centipedes. It is all full of great, deserted halls, and winding passages, and long corridors twisting in and out, so that it is

Charge of the Highlanders before Kawnpore under General Havelock (*ca.* 1857).

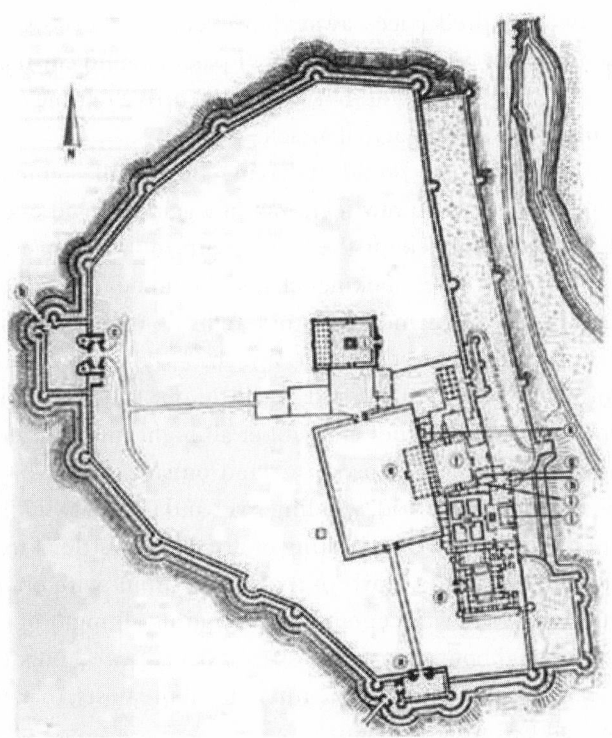

Plan of Agra Fort.

easy enough for folk to get lost in it. For this reason it was seldom that anyone went into it, though now and again a party with torches might go exploring.

"The river washes along the front of the old fort, and so protects it, but on the sides and behind there are many doors, and these had to be guarded, of course, in the old quarter as well as in that which was actually held by our troops. We were short-handed, with hardly men enough to man the angles of the building and to serve the guns. It was impossible for us, therefore, to station a strong guard at every one of the innumerable gates. What we did was to organize a central guard-house in the middle of the fort, and to leave each gate under the charge of one white man and two or three natives. I was selected to take charge during certain hours of the night of a small isolated door upon the south-west side of the building. Two Sikh troopers were placed under my command, and I was instructed if anything went wrong to fire my musket, when I might rely upon help coming at once from the central guard. As the guard was

244 William S. Baring-Gould notes that Small evidently used—and Watson accepted—"Punjaubee" (Punjabi) and "Sikh" as interchangeable terms, which of course they are not.

245 In a battle fought in the village of Chillian Wallah on January 13, 1849, the British won a crucial tactical victory over the Sikhs. It was the penultimate battle of the Anglo-Sikh wars.

246 According to the *Anglo-Indian Dictionary*, "bhang" was a drink prepared from the leaves of the *cannabis sativa* plant, better known as marijuana.

247 A muzzle-loading rifle.

a good two hundred paces away, however, and as the space between was cut up into a labyrinth of passages and corridors, I had great doubts as to whether they could arrive in time to be of any use in case of an actual attack.

"Well, I was pretty proud at having this small command given me, since I was a raw recruit, and a game-legged one at that. For two nights I kept the watch with my Punjabees.[244] They were tall, fierce-looking chaps, Mahomet Singh and Abdullah Khan by name, both old fighting-men, who had borne arms against us at Chilian Wallah.[245] They could talk English pretty well, but I could get little out of them. They preferred to stand together and jabber all night in their queer Sikh lingo. For myself, I used to stand outside the gateway, looking down on the broad, winding river and on the twinkling lights of the great city. The beating of drums, the rattle of tom-toms, and the yells and howls of the rebels, drunk with opium and with bhang,[246] were enough to remind us all night of our dangerous neighbours across the stream. Every two hours the officer of the night used to come round to all the posts, to make sure that all was well.

"The third night of my watch was dark and dirty, with a small driving rain. It was dreary work standing in the gateway hour after hour in such weather. I tried again and again to make my Sikhs talk, but without much success. At two in the morning the rounds passed and broke for a moment the weariness of the night. Finding that my companions would not be led into conversation, I took out my pipe and laid down my musket to strike the match. In an instant the two Sikhs were upon me. One of them snatched my firelock[247] up and levelled it at my head, while the other held a great knife to my throat and swore between his teeth that he would plunge it into me if I moved a step.

"My first thought was that these fellows were in league with the rebels, and that this was the beginning of an assault. If our door were in the hands of the Sepoys the place must fall, and the women and children be treated as they were in Cawnpore. Maybe you gentlemen think that I am just making out a case for myself, but I give you my word that when I thought of that, though I felt the point of the knife at my throat, I opened my mouth with the intention of giving a scream, if it was my last one, which might alarm the main guard. The man who held me

"In an instant the two Sikhs were upon me."
J. Watson Davis, *Tales of Sherlock Holmes* (New York: A. L. Burt Company, 1906)

seemed to know my thoughts; for, even as I braced myself to it, he whispered: 'Don't make a noise. The fort is safe enough. There are no rebel dogs on this side of the river.' There was the ring of truth in what he said, and I knew that if I raised my voice I was a dead man. I could read it in the fellow's brown eyes. I waited, therefore, in silence, to see what it was that they wanted from me.

" 'Listen to me, *sahib*,' said the taller and fiercer of the pair, the one whom they called Abdullah Khan. 'You must either be with us now, or you must be silenced forever. The thing is too great a one for us to hesitate. Either you are heart and soul with us on your oath on the cross of the Christians, or your body this night shall be thrown into the ditch, and we shall pass over to

Firelock.

"In an instant the two sikhs were upon me."
Richard Gutschmidt, *Das Zeichen der Vier* (Stuttgart: Robert Lutz Verlag, 1902)

our brothers in the rebel army. There is no middle way. Which is it to be—death or life? We can only give you three minutes to decide, for the time is passing, and all must be done before the rounds come again.'

" 'How can I decide?' said I. 'You have not told me what you want of me. But I tell you now that if it is anything against the safety of the fort I will have no truck with it, so you can drive home your knife, and welcome.'

" 'It is nothing against the fort,' said he. 'We only ask you to do that which your countrymen come to this land for. We ask you to be rich. If you will be one of us this night, we will swear to you upon the naked knife, and by the threefold oath, which no Sikh was ever known to break, that you shall have your fair share of the loot. A quarter of the treasure shall be yours. We can say no fairer.'

" 'But what is the treasure, then?' I asked. 'I am as ready to be rich as you can be if you will, but show me how it can be done.'

" 'You will swear, then,' said he, 'by the bones of your father, by the honour of your mother, by the cross of your faith, to raise no hand and speak no word against us, either now or afterwards?'

" 'I will swear it,' I answered, 'provided that the fort is not endangered.'

" 'Then my comrade and I will swear that you shall have a quarter of the treasure, which shall be equally divided among the four of us.'

" 'There are but three,' said I.

" 'No; Dost Akbar[248] must have his share. We can tell the tale to you while we wait them. Do you stand at the gate, Mahomet Singh, and give notice of their coming. The thing stands thus, *sahib*, and I tell it to you because I know that an oath is binding upon a Feringhee,[249] and that we may trust you. Had you been a lying Hindoo, though you had sworn by all the gods in their false temples, your blood would have been upon the knife and your body in the water. But the Sikh knows the Englishman, and the Englishman knows the Sikh. Hearken, then, to what I have to say.

" 'There is a rajah in the northern provinces who has much wealth, though his lands are small. Much has come to him from his father, and more still he has set by himself, for he is of a low nature and hoards his gold rather than spend it. When the troubles broke out he would be friends both with the lion and the tiger—with the Sepoy and with the Company's[250] Raj. Soon, however, it seemed to him that the white men's day was come, for through all the land he could hear of nothing but of their death and their overthrow. Yet, being a careful man, he made such plans that, come what might, half at least of his treasure should be left to him. That which was in gold and silver he kept by him in the vaults of his palace; but the most precious stones and the choicest pearls that he had he put in an iron box and sent it by a trusty servant, who, under the guise of a merchant, should take it to the fort at Agra, there to lie until the land is at peace. Thus, if the rebels won he would have his money; but if the Company conquered, his jewels would be saved to him. Having thus divided his hoard, he threw himself into the cause of the Sepoys, since they were strong upon his borders. By his doing this, mark you, *sahib*, his property becomes the due of those who have been true to their salt.

" 'This pretended merchant, who travels under the name of Achmet, is now in the city of Agra and desires to gain his way

248 Several commentators note that, with the exception of "Singh," none of these are Sikh names. Dr. Andrew Boyd, who observes that "[n]o educated man with years of service in the Indian Army could possibly have recorded them, even if he was recording another man's garbled narrative, without comment," concludes that Watson's Indian Army record is fraudulent and that he had a dark and sinister past, as well as a criminal career. D. Martin Dakin expresses more kindly that either the Indians were in fact Muslims, and Small incorrectly assumed they were Sikhs from their fighting qualities and British sympathies, or else they were Sikhs and Small, not really knowing their names, got them muddled up or even invented them.

Rising to the defence of Dr. Watson, Lt. Col. T. F. Foss points out that in the Medical Department, Watson would not have had significant contact with Sikhs and therefore may not have recognised Small's mistake/falsehood. In a similarly forgiving vein, Otis Hearn proposes that Watson unconsciously substituted *Afghan* names for the real names, at least for the first two.

249 A term applied to any European.

250 With the conquest of India, England actively fostered the cultivation and sale of opium through the British East India Company (familiarly known as John Company), which had a government-controlled monopoly on its Indian trade. So important did opium become to the British economy that efforts by China (which had outlawed the drug in 1799) to halt its import led the British to instigate and claim victory in two "Opium Wars," in 1839–1842 (which also resulted in the cession of Hong Kong to England) and 1856–1860, and British importation of opium from India to China increased annually, from 52,925 piculs (of 133⅓ lbs.) in 1850 to 96,839 piculs in 1880. The company did not survive the

Indian Mutiny, after which the British government took direct control of Indian matters.

251 A. Carson Simpson reports that the *moeda d'ouro* (coin of gold, anglica moidore) was first issued in Portugal during the reign of Pedro II (1683–1706) but ceased to be minted in 1732. It is unlikely, he concludes, that Jonathan Small encountered any *Portuguese* moidores. However, Simpson notes, Brazil minted moidores until the early 1830s, and it was undoubtedly these with which Small became familiar in India.

into the fort. He has with him as travelling-companion my foster-brother Dost Akbar, who knows his secret. Dost Akbar has promised this night to lead him to a side-postern of the fort, and has chosen this one for his purpose. Here he will come presently, and here he will find Mahomet Singh and myself awaiting him. The place is lonely, and none shall know of his coming. The world shall know the merchant Achmet no more, but the great treasure of the rajah shall be divided among us. What say you to it, *sahib*?'

"In Worcestershire the life of a man seems a great and a sacred thing; but it is very different when there is fire and blood all round you, and you have been used to meeting death at every turn. Whether Achmet the merchant lived or died was a thing as light as air to me, but at the talk about the treasure my heart turned to it, and I thought of what I might do in the old country with it, and how my folk would stare when they saw their ne'er-do-well coming back with his pockets full of gold moidores.[251] I had, therefore, already made up my mind. Abdullah Khan, however, thinking that I hesitated, pressed the matter more closely.

" 'Consider, *sahib*,' said he, 'that if this man is taken by the commandant he will be hung or shot, and his jewels taken by the Government, so that no man will be a rupee the better for them. Now, since we do the taking of him, why should we not do the rest as well? The jewels will be as well with us as in the Company's coffers. There will be enough to make every one of us rich men and great chiefs. No one can know about the matter, for here we are cut off from all men. What could be better for the purpose? Say again, then, *sahib*, whether you are with us, or if we must look upon you as an enemy.'

" 'I am with you heart and soul,' said I.

" 'It is well,' he answered, handing me back my firelock. 'You see that we trust you, for your word, like ours, is not to be broken. We have now only to wait for my brother and the merchant.'

" 'Does your brother know, then, of what you will do?' I asked.

" 'The plan is his. He has devised it. We will go to the gate and share the watch with Mahomet Singh.'

"The rain was still falling steadily, for it was just the beginning of the wet season. Brown, heavy clouds were drifting across the sky, and it was hard to see more than a stonecast. A deep moat lay in front of our door, but the water was in places nearly dried up, and it could easily be crossed. It was strange to me to be standing there with those two wild Punjabees waiting for the man who was coming to his death.

"Suddenly my eye caught the glint of a shaded lantern at the other side of the moat. It vanished among the mound-heaps, and then appeared again coming slowly in our direction.

" 'Here they are!' I exclaimed.

" 'You will challenge him, *sahib*, as usual,' whispered Abdullah. 'Give him no cause for fear. Send us in with him, and we shall do the rest while you stay here on guard. Have the lantern ready to uncover, that we may be sure that it is indeed the man.'

"The light had flickered onward, now stopping and now advancing, until I could see two dark figures upon the other side of the moat. I let them scramble down the sloping bank, splash through the mire, and climb halfway up to the gate before I challenged them.

" 'Who goes there?' said I in a subdued voice.

" 'Friends,' came the answer. I uncovered my lantern and threw a flood of light upon them. The first was an enormous Sikh with a black beard which swept nearly down to his cummerbund. Outside of a show I have never seen so tall a man. The other was a little, fat, round fellow with a great yellow turban and a bundle in his hand, done up in a shawl. He seemed to be all in a quiver with fear, for his hands twitched as if he had the ague, and his head kept turning to left and right with two bright little twinkling eyes, like a mouse when he ventures out from his hole. It gave me the chills to think of killing him, but I thought of the treasure, and my heart set as hard as a flint within me. When he saw my white face he gave a little chirrup of joy and came running up towards me.

" 'Your protection, *sahib*,' he panted, 'your protection for the unhappy merchant Achmet. I have travelled across Rajpootana[252] that I might seek the shelter of the fort at Agra. I have been robbed and beaten and abused because I have been the friend of the Company. It is a blessed night this when I am once more in safety—I and my poor possessions.'

" 'What have you in the bundle?' I asked.

" 'An iron box,' he answered, 'which contains one or two lit-

252 An immense tract of country in India, consisting of twenty states.

" 'I shall reward you, young Sahib, and your governor also, if he will give me the shelter I ask.' "
Herbert Denman, *Lippincott's Monthly Magazine*, 1890

tle family matters which are of no value to others but which I should be sorry to lose. Yet I am not a beggar; and I shall reward you, young *sahib*, and your governor also if he will give me the shelter I ask.'

"I could not trust myself to speak longer with the man. The more I looked at his fat, frightened face, the harder did it seem that we should slay him in cold blood. It was best to get it over.

" 'Take him to the main guard,' said I. The two Sikhs closed in upon him on each side, and the giant walked behind, while they marched in through the dark gateway. Never was a man so compassed round with death. I remained at the gateway with the lantern.

"I could hear the measured tramp of their footsteps sounding through the lonely corridors. Suddenly it ceased, and I heard voices and a scuffle, with the sound of blows. A moment later there came, to my horror, a rush of footsteps coming in my direction, with a loud breathing of a running man. I turned my lantern down the long straight passage, and there was the fat man, running like the wind, with a smear of blood across his face, and close at his heels, bounding like a tiger, the great, black-bearded Sikh, with a knife flashing in his hand. I have never seen a man run so fast as that little merchant. He was gaining on the Sikh, and I could see that if he once passed me and got to the open air he would save himself yet. My heart softened to him, but again the thought of his treasure turned me hard and bitter. I cast my firelock between his legs as he raced past, and he rolled twice over like a shot rabbit. Ere he could stagger to his feet the Sikh was upon him and buried his knife twice in his side. The man never uttered moan nor moved muscle but lay where he had fallen. I think myself that he may have broken his neck with the fall. You see, gentlemen,

". . . and close at his heels, bounding like a tiger, the great black-bearded sikh, with a knife flashing in his hand."
Richard Gutschmidt, *Das Zeichen der Vier* (Stuttgart: Robert Lutz Verlag, 1902)

"The sikh was upon him."
F. H. Townsend, *The Sign of Four* (London: George Newnes, Ltd., 1903)

that I am keeping my promise. I am telling you every word of the business just exactly as it happened, whether it is in my favour or not."

He stopped and held out his manacled hands for the whisky and water which Holmes had brewed for him. For myself, I confess that I had now conceived the utmost horror of the man not only for this cold-blooded business in which he had been concerned but even more for the somewhat flippant and careless way in which he narrated it. Whatever punishment was in store for him, I felt that he might expect no sympathy from me. Sherlock Holmes and Jones sat with their hands upon their knees, deeply interested in the story but with the same disgust written upon their faces. He may have observed it, for there was a touch of defiance in his voice and manner as he proceeded.

"It was all very bad, no doubt," said he. "I should like to know how many fellows in my shoes would have refused a share of this loot when they knew that they would have their throats cut for their pains. Besides, it was my life or his when once he was in the fort. If he had got out, the whole business would come to light, and I should have been court-martialled and shot as likely as not; for people were not very lenient at a time like that."

"Go on with your story," said Holmes shortly.

"Well, we carried him in, Abdullah, Akbar, and I. A fine weight he was, too, for all that he was so short. Mahomet Singh was left to guard the door. We took him to a place which the Sikhs had already prepared. It was some distance off, where a winding passage leads to a great empty hall, the brick walls of which were all crumbling to pieces. The earth floor had sunk in at one place, making a natural grave, so we left Achmet the merchant there, having first covered him over with loose bricks. This done, we all went back to the treasure.

"It lay where he had dropped it when he was first attacked. The box was the same which now lies open upon your table. A key was hung by a silken cord to that carved handle upon the top. We opened it, and the light of the lantern gleamed upon a collection of gems such as I have read of and thought about when I was a little lad at Pershore. It was blinding to look upon them. When we had feasted our eyes we took them all out and made a list of them. There were one hundred and forty-three diamonds of the first water,[253] including one which has been called, I believe, 'the Great Mogul,'[254] and is said to be the second largest stone in existence. Then there were ninety-seven very fine emeralds, and one hundred and seventy rubies, some of which, however, were small. There were forty carbuncles, two hundred and ten sapphires, sixty-one agates, and a great quantity of beryls, onyxes, cats'-eyes, turquoises, and other stones, the very names of which I did not know at the time, though I have become more familiar with them since.[255] Besides this, there were nearly three hundred very fine pearls, twelve of which were set in a gold coronet. By the way, these last had been taken out of the chest, and were not there when I recovered it.

"After we had counted our treasures we put them back into the chest and carried them to the gateway to show them to Mahomet Singh. Then we solemnly renewed our oath to stand by each other and be true to our secret. We agreed to conceal

253 The phrase "gem of the first Water"—referring to the highest clarity and color in a diamond, and to the excellence of such attributes as pellucidity and limpidity—was coined by the famous seventeenth-century merchant Jean Baptiste Tavernier in his book *Travels in India* (1676; trans. V. Ball and William Crooke).

254 The Great Mogul, discovered by an Indian slave in 1701 and now lost, weighed between 787 and 793 carats in the rough and only about 280 cut; the story goes that the lapidary charged with cutting it botched the job and, rather than receiving payment for his work, was forced to pay a fine to the gem's owner, Sháh Jahán (see note 96, above). However, Nicholas Utechin believes that the reference here is to the Agra Diamond, which belonged to the Duke of Brunswick at the time of the Mutiny. (An 1860 catalogue of the Duke's jewel collection indicates he purchased it on November 22, 1844, probably from George Blogg, a London diamond merchant.) "What happened is clear," writes Nicholas Utechin, in "*The* Treasure," "[T]he valet stole it, along with other stones and somehow sold it off to our Indian rajah, who added it to his own collection and gave it all the name of the 'Agra treasure.' " Utechin suggests that Morstan and Sholto sold it back to the Duke, who kept the transaction a secret in order to save face.

255 Certainly not by handling them (Small was in the company of the treasure for only a few days), but rather in his mind—one imagines Small studying pictures of the jewels he briefly saw in the iron box so many years before.

256 Sir Archdale Wilson (1803–1874), commander of the force that retook Delhi.

257 Sir Colin Campbell (1792–1863), later Lord Clyde. When, in 1857, he was offered the command of the army in India after successful service in the Crimea (1854), his first action was to break the siege of Lucknow.

"We solemnly renewed our oath to be true to our secret."
Harold C. Earnshaw, *The Sign of Four*
(London and Edinburgh: T. Nelson & Sons, n.d.)

our loot in a safe place until the country should be at peace again, and then to divide it equally among ourselves. There was no use dividing it at present, for if gems of such value were found upon us it would cause suspicion, and there was no privacy in the fort nor any place where we could keep them. We carried the box, therefore, into the same hall where we had buried the body, and there, under certain bricks in the best-preserved wall, we made a hollow and put our treasure. We made careful note of the place, and next day I drew four plans, one for each of us, and put the sign of the four of us at the bottom, for we had sworn that we should each always act for all, so that none might take advantage. That is an oath that I can put my hand to my heart and swear that I have never broken.

"Well, there's no use my telling you gentlemen what came of the Indian mutiny. After Wilson[256] took Delhi and Sir Colin[257] relieved Lucknow the back of the business was broken. Fresh troops came pouring in, and Nana Sahib made himsel+f scarce over the frontier. A flying column under Colonel Greathed[258] came round to Agra and cleared the Pandies[259] away from it. Peace seemed to be settling upon the country, and we four were beginning to hope that the time was at hand when we might safely go off with our shares of the plunder. In a moment, however, our hopes were shattered by our being arrested as the murderers of Achmet.

"It came about in this way. When the rajah put his jewels into the hands of Achmet, he did it because he knew that he was a trusty man. They are suspicious folk in the East, however: so what does this rajah do but take a second even more trusty servant and set him to play the spy upon the first. This second man was ordered never to let Achmet out of his sight, and he followed him like his shadow. He went after him that night and saw him pass through the doorway. Of course, he thought he had taken refuge in the fort and applied for admission there himself next day, but could find no trace of Achmet. This seemed to him so strange that he spoke about it to a sergeant of Guides,[260] who brought it to the ears of the commandant. A thorough search was quickly made,[261] and the body was discovered. Thus at the very moment that we thought that all was safe we were all four seized and brought to trial on a charge of murder—three of us because we had held the gate that night, and the fourth because he was known to have been in the company of the murdered man. Not a word about the jewels came out at the trial, for the rajah had been deposed and driven out of India; so no one had any particular interest in them. The murder, however, was clearly made out, and it was certain that we must all have been concerned in it. The three Sikhs got penal servitude for life, and I was condemned to death, though my sentence was afterwards commuted to the same as the others.

"It was rather a queer position that we found ourselves in then. There we were all four tied by the leg and with precious little chance of ever getting out again, while we each held a secret which might have put each of us in a palace if we could only have made use of it. It was enough to make a man eat his heart out to have to stand the kick and the cuff of every petty jack-in-office, to have rice to eat and water to drink, when that gorgeous fortune was ready for him outside, just waiting to be picked up. It might have driven me mad; but I was always a pretty stubborn one, so I just held on and bided my time.

258 Probably Sir Edward Harris Greathed (1812–1881), who commanded the column that relieved Agra.

259 On March 19, 1857, on a parade ground at Barrackpore, near Calcutta, Mangal Pande, of the 34th Bengal Regiment, urged his regimental mates not to load their rifle cartridges (loading required biting off one end), said to have been smeared with beef tallow and pork fat (see note 234, above). Confrontations with an adjutant and a commanding general ensued, in response to which Pande shot himself in the chest. He survived the suicide attempt but was summarily hanged by the British for his act of defiance, which presaged the Indian Mutiny. Thereafter, Indians who fought in the uprising against British rule were called "pandies."

260 The Corps of Guides was a crack Indian regiment raised in 1846 by Lieutenant (later Sir) Harry Lumsden. Said to have been made up variously of electrical and mechanical engineers and Pashtuns, the Guides offered a higher rate of pay than some other regiments, tended to attract a higher calibre of recruit, and quickly established a reputation as an elite corps. Their uniforms also differed from other regiments': Wishing to introduce clothing that was more practical than the traditional heavy red wool of the British army, Lumsden was said to have soaked cotton in muddy water, a process that created the fabric known by the Hindi word "khaki" (meaning "dust-coloured"). In other versions of the story, the fabric existed but Lumsden received credit for outfitting the Guides in it. "Guides" is properly capitalised, although it is not in any known edition of *The Sign of Four*.

261 Not so thorough, however, that the treasure—hidden in the very room in which the body lay covered by "loose bricks"—was found.

"At last it seemed to me to have come. I was changed from Agra to Madras,[262] and from there to Blair Island[263] in the Andamans. There are very few white convicts at this settlement, and, as I had behaved well from the first, I soon found myself a sort of privileged person. I was given a hut in Hope Town, which is a small place on the slopes of Mount Harriet,[264] and I was left pretty much to myself. It is a dreary, fever-stricken place, and all beyond our little clearings was infested with wild cannibal natives, who were ready enough to blow a poisoned dart at us if they saw a chance.[265] There was digging and ditching and yam-planting, and a dozen other things to be done, so we were busy enough all day; though in the evening we had a little time to ourselves. Among other things, I learned to dispense drugs for the surgeon, and picked up a smattering of his knowledge. All the time I was on the lookout for a chance of escape; but it is hundreds of miles from any other land, and there is little or no wind in those seas: so it was a terribly difficult job to get away.

"The surgeon, Dr. Somerton, was a fast, sporting young chap, and the other young officers would meet in his rooms of an evening and play cards. The surgery, where I used to make up my drugs, was next to his sitting-room, with a small window between us. Often, if I felt lonesome, I used to turn out the lamp in the surgery, and then, standing there, I could hear their talk and watch their play. I am fond of a hand at cards myself, and it was almost as good as having one to watch the others. There was Major Sholto, Captain Morstan, and Lieutenant Bromley Brown,[266] who were in command of the native troops, and there was the surgeon himself, and two or three prison-officials, crafty old hands who played a nice, sly, safe game. A very snug little party they used to make.

"Well, there was one thing which very soon struck me, and that was that the soldiers used always to lose and the civilians to win. Mind, I don't say there was anything unfair, but so it was. These prison-chaps had done little else than play cards ever since they had been at the Andamans, and they knew each other's game to a point, while the others just played to pass the time and threw their cards down anyhow. Night after night the soldiers got up poorer men, and the poorer they got the more keen they were to play. Major Sholto was the hardest hit. He used to pay in notes and gold at first, but soon it came

262 The southern area of the Indian peninsula.

263 Blair, or Port Blair, capital of the Andaman Islands, was settled in September 1789, largely through the efforts of Lieutenant Archibald Blair, R.N., acting under the direction of the Bengal government and army Captain Alexander Kyd. Blair, a surveyor and inventor, had undertaken his first voyage to the Andaman Islands in 1788. The port initially did not bear his name; he himself called the settlement Port Cornwallis, after Commodore William Cornwallis, the commander-in-chief of the British-Indian navy. After Blair returned to England in 1795, the settlement changed location at least once before taking hold at the spot he had selected. Of course, it was much later—more than forty years after his death in 1815—that the Andaman penal colony was established there (see note 45, above).

264 At 365 metres, it is the highest point in South Andaman.

265 According to the *Encyclopædia Britannica* (9th Ed.), "[The Andaman natives] were always very hostile to strangers, repulsing all approaches with treachery, or with violence and showers of arrows." No wonder. The British who arrived in 1859 decimated the Andamanese not only with guns and artillery but by introducing bronchitis, syphilis, measles, and smallpox. A pre-1859 population of 3,000 to 3,500 was reduced, by 1895, to approximately 400.

266 Perhaps he wrote the letter to Major Sholto telling of Small's escape (see note 145, above).

to notes of hand and for big sums. He sometimes would win for a few deals, just to give him heart, and then the luck would set in against him worse than ever. All day he would wander about as black as thunder, and he took to drinking a deal more than was good for him.

"One night he lost even more heavily than usual. I was sitting in my hut when he and Captain Morstan came stumbling along on the way to their quarters. They were bosom friends, those two, and never far apart. The major was raving about his losses.

" 'It's all up, Morstan,' he was saying as they passed my hut. 'I shall have to send in my papers. I am a ruined man.'

" 'Nonsense, old chap!' said the other, slapping him upon the shoulder. 'I've had a nasty facer[267] myself, but—' That was all I could hear, but it was enough to set me thinking.

"A couple of days later Major Sholto was strolling on the beach: so I took the chance of speaking to him.

" 'I wish to have your advice, Major,' said I.

" 'Well, Small, what is it?' he asked, taking his cheroot from his lips.

" 'I wanted to ask you, sir,' said I, 'who is the proper person to whom hidden treasure should be handed over. I know where half a million worth lies, and, as I cannot use it myself, I thought perhaps the best thing that I could do would be to hand it over to the proper authorities, and then perhaps they would get my sentence shortened for me.'

" 'Half a million, Small?' he gasped, looking hard at me to see if I was in earnest.

" 'Quite that, sir—in jewels and pearls. It lies there ready for anyone. And the queer thing about it is that the real owner is outlawed and cannot hold property, so that it belongs to the first comer.'

" 'To Government, Small,' he stammered, 'to Government.' But he said it in a halting fashion, and I knew in my heart that I had got him.

" 'You think, then, sir, that I should give the information to the Governor-General?' said I quietly.

" 'Well, well, you must not do anything rash, or that you might repent. Let me hear all about it, Small. Give me the facts.'

"I told him the whole story, with small changes, so that he

267 Slang for a blow or slap to the face; figuratively, a blow to one's fortunes.

could not identify the places. When I had finished he stood stock-still and full of thought. I could see by the twitch of his lip that there was a struggle going on within him.

" 'This is a very important matter, Small,' he said at last. 'You must not say a word to anyone about it, and I shall see you again soon.'

"Two nights later he and his friend, Captain Morstan, came to my hut in the dead of the night with a lantern.

" 'I want you just to let Captain Morstan hear that story from your own lips, Small,' said he.

"I repeated it as I had told it before.

" 'It rings true, eh?' said he. 'It's good enough to act upon?'

"Captain Morstan nodded.

" 'Look here, Small,' said the Major. 'We have been talking it over, my friend here and I, and we have come to the conclusion that this secret of yours is hardly a Government matter, after all, but is a private concern of your own, which, of course, you have the power of disposing of as you think best. Now the

" 'I want you just to let Captain Morstan hear that story from your own lips, Small,' said he."
Richard Gutschmidt, *Das Zeichen der Vier* (Stuttgart: Robert Lutz Verlag, 1902)

question is: What price would you ask for it? We might be inclined to take it up, and at least look into it, if we could agree as to terms.' He tried to speak in a cool, careless way, but his eyes were shining with excitement and greed.

" 'Why, as to that, gentlemen,' I answered, trying also to be cool but feeling as excited as he did, 'there is only one bargain which a man in my position can make. I shall want you to help me to my freedom, and to help my three companions to theirs. We shall then take you into partnership and give you a fifth share to divide between you.'

" 'Hum!' said he. 'A fifth share! That is not very tempting.'

" 'It would come to fifty thousand apiece,' said I.

" 'But how can we gain your freedom? You know very well that you ask an impossibility.'

" 'Nothing of the sort,' I answered. 'I have thought it all out to the last detail. The only bar to our escape is that we can get no boat fit for the voyage, and no provisions to last us for so long a time. There are plenty of little yachts and yawls at Calcutta or Madras which would serve our turn well. Do you bring one over. We shall engage to get aboard her by night, and if you will drop us on any part of the Indian coast you will have done your part of the bargain.'

" 'If there were only one,' he said.

" 'None or all,' I answered. 'We have sworn it. The four of us must always act together.'

" 'You see, Morstan,' said he, 'Small is a man of his word. He does not flinch from his friends. I think we may very well trust him.'

" 'It's a dirty business,' the other answered. 'Yet, as you say, the money will save our commissions handsomely.'

" 'Well, Small,' said the Major, 'we must, I suppose, try and meet you. We must first, of course, test the truth of your story. Tell me where the box is hid, and I shall get leave of absence and go back to India in the monthly relief-boat to inquire into the affair.'

" 'Not so fast,' said I, growing colder as he got hot. 'I must have the consent of my three comrades. I tell you that it is four or none with us.'

" 'Nonsense!' he broke in. 'What have three black fellows to do with our agreement?'

" 'Black or blue,' said I, 'they are in with me, and we all go together.'

"Well, the matter ended by a second meeting, at which Mahomet Singh, Abdullah Khan, and Dost Akbar were all present. We talked the matter over again, and at last we came to an arrangement. We were to provide both the officers with charts of the part of the Agra fort, and mark the place in the wall where the treasure was hid. Major Sholto was to go to India to test our story. If he found the box he was to leave it there, to send out a small yacht provisioned for a voyage, which was to lie off Rutland Island, and to which we were to make our way, and finally to return to his duties. Captain Morstan was then to apply for leave of absence, to meet us at Agra, and there we were to have a final division of the treasure, he taking the Major's share as well as his own. All this we sealed by the most solemn oaths that the mind could think or the lips utter. I sat up all night with paper and ink, and by the morning I had the two charts all ready, signed with the sign of four—that is, of Abdullah, Akbar, Mahomet, and myself.

"Well, gentlemen, I weary you with my long story, and I know that my friend Mr. Jones is impatient to get me safely stowed in chokey.[268] I'll make it as short as I can. The villain Sholto went off to India, but he never came back again. Captain Morstan showed me his name among a list of passengers in one of the mail-boats very shortly afterwards. His uncle had died, leaving him a fortune,[269] and he had left the Army; yet he could stoop to treat five men as he had treated us. Morstan went over to Agra shortly afterwards and found, as we expected, that the treasure was indeed gone. The scoundrel had stolen it all, without carrying out one of the conditions on which we had sold him the secret. From that I lived only for vengeance. I thought of it by day and I nursed it by night. It became an overpowering, absorbing passion with me. I cared nothing for the law—nothing for the gallows. To escape, to track down Sholto, to have my hand upon his throat—that was my one thought. Even the Agra treasure had come to be a smaller thing in my mind than the slaying of Sholto.

"Well, I have set my mind on many things in this life, and never one which I did not carry out. But it was weary years before my time came. I have told you that I had picked up something of medicine. One day when Dr. Somerton was

268 From the Hindi *chauki*, meaning a police station.

269 The "uncle" sounds like a convenient cover-up for the treasure, and Charles A. Meyer speculates that with the assistance of fellow officer Col. Sebastian Moran, Sholto was able to pawn some of it. However, Meyer disregards Small's corroboration of Sholto's declaration, that only the coronet with 12 pearls was missing from the treasure. Even if Small did not have opportunity for a truly detailed inventory of the treasure (notwithstanding his apparent grasp of its contents), one would expect that were a significant portion—reflecting a "considerable sum of money"—missing, he would have noticed. From what source, then, did Sholto accumulate his fortune? Could the "uncle" be real?

down with a fever a little Andaman Islander was picked up by a convict-gang in the woods. He was sick to death and had gone to a lonely place to die. I took him in hand, though he was as venomous as a young snake, and after a couple of months I got him all right and able to walk. He took a kind of fancy to me then, and would hardly go back to his woods, but was always hanging about my hut. I learned a little of his lingo from him, and this made him all the fonder of me.

"Tonga—for that was his name—was a fine boatman and owned a big, roomy canoe of his own. When I found that he was devoted to me and would do anything to serve me, I saw my chance of escape. I talked it over with him. He was to bring his boat round on a certain night to an old wharf which was never guarded, and there he was to pick me up. I gave him directions to have several gourds of water and a lot of yams, coconuts, and sweet potatoes.

"He was stanch and true, was little Tonga. No man ever had a more faithful mate. On the night named he had his boat at the wharf. As it chanced, however, there was one of the convict-guard down there—a vile Pathan[270] who had never missed a chance of insulting and injuring me. I had always vowed vengeance, and now I had my chance. It was as if fate had placed him in my way that I might pay my debt before I left the island. He stood on the bank with his back to me, and his carbine on his shoulder. I looked about for a stone to beat out his brains with, but none could I see.

"Then a queer thought came into my head and showed me where I could lay my hand on a weapon. I sat down in the darkness and unstrapped my wooden leg. With three long hops I was on him. He put his carbine to his shoulder, but I struck him full, and knocked the whole front of his skull in. You can see the split in the wood now where I hit him. We both went down together, for I could not keep my balance; but when I got up I found him still lying quiet enough. I made for the boat, and in an hour we were well out at sea. Tonga had brought all his earthly possessions with him, his arms and his gods. Among other things, he had a long bamboo spear, and some Andaman coconut matting, with which I made a sort of a sail. For ten days we were beating about, trusting to luck, and on the eleventh we were picked up by a trader which was going from Singapore to Jiddah[271] with a cargo of Malay pilgrims. They

270 A Hindi term for Afghans. Perhaps the most useful colonial accounts of the Pashtuns are to be found in the writings of Mountstuart Elphinstone (1779–1859) and Sir Robert Warburton (see *A Study in Scarlet*, note 15).

271 A town in what was to become the Kingdom of Saudi Arabia (which comprised several regions that unified in 1932). Jiddah, on the eastern coast of the Red Sea, was of importance mainly as the principal landing-place of pilgrims to Mecca.

272 "Queer strangers do not hire fast steam launches," Robert R. Pattrick writes, in "Moriarty Was There," "and have them stand in readiness for a day or two, on the basis of a promise. Something more tangible is required, and Small as yet had nothing to prove his story of 'a big sum.' " Pattrick concludes that Professor Moriarty must have assisted Small with planning, advances of funds for expenses, and a hideout, all for a fee.

"With three long hops I was on him."
F. H. Townsend, *The Sign of Four* (London: George Newnes, Ltd., 1903)

were a rum crowd, and Tonga and I soon managed to settle down among them. They had one very good quality: they let you alone and asked no questions.

"Well, if I were to tell you all the adventures that my little chum and I went through, you would not thank me, for I would have you here until the sun was shining. Here and there we drifted about the world, something always turning up to keep us from London. All the time, however, I never lost sight of my purpose. I would dream of Sholto at night. A hundred times I have killed him in my sleep. At last, however, some three or four years ago, we found ourselves in England. I had no great difficulty in finding where Sholto lived, and I set to work to discover whether he had realized on the treasure, or if he still had it. I made friends with someone who could help me[272]—I name no names, for I don't want to get anyone else in a hole—and I soon found that he still had the jewels. Then I tried to get at him in many ways; but he was pretty sly and had always

"With three long hops I was on him."
H. B. Eddy, *San Francisco Call,* October 17, 1907

two prize-fighters, besides his sons and his *khitmutgar*, on guard over him.

"One day, however, I got word that he was dying. I hurried at once to the garden, mad that he should slip out of my clutches like that, and, looking through the window, I saw him lying in his bed, with his sons on each side of him. I'd have come through and taken my chance with the three of them, only even as I looked at him his jaw dropped, and I knew that he was gone. I got into his room that same night, though, and I searched his papers to see if there was any record of where he had hidden our jewels. There was not a line, however, so I came away, bitter and savage as a man could be. Before I left I bethought me that if I ever met my Sikh friends again it would be a satisfaction to know that I had left some mark of our hatred; so I scrawled down the sign of the four of us, as it had been on the chart, and I pinned it on his bosom. It was too much that he should be taken to the grave without some token from the men whom he had robbed and befooled.

"We earned a living at this time by my exhibiting poor Tonga at fairs and other such places as the black cannibal. He would eat raw meat and dance his war-dance: so we always had a hatful of pennies after a day's work. I still heard all the news from Pondicherry Lodge, and for some years there was no news to hear, except that they were hunting for the treasure. At last, however, came what we had waited for so long. The treasure had been found. It was up at the top of the house, in Mr. Bartholomew Sholto's chemical laboratory. I came at once and had a look at the place, but I could not see how, with my wooden leg, I was to make my way up to it, I learned, however, about a trap-door in the roof, and also about Mr. Sholto's supper-hour. It seemed to me that I could manage the thing easily through Tonga. I brought him out with me with a long rope wound round his waist. He could climb like a cat, and he

"Then slid down myself."
F. H. Townsend, *The Sign of Four* (London: George Newnes, Ltd., 1903)

soon made his way through the roof, but, as ill-luck would have it, Bartholomew Sholto was still in the room, to his cost. Tonga thought he had done something very clever in killing him, for when I came up by the rope I found him strutting about as proud as a peacock. Very much surprised was he when I made at him with the rope's end and cursed him for a little bloodthirsty imp. I took the treasure box and let it down, and then slid down myself, having first left the sign of the four upon the table, to show that the jewels had come back at last to those who had most right to them. Tonga then pulled up the rope, closed the window, and made off the way that he had come.

"I don't know that I have anything else to tell you. I had heard a waterman speak of the speed of Smith's launch, the *Aurora*, so I thought she would be a handy craft for our escape. I engaged with old Smith, and was to give him a big sum if he got us safe to our ship. He knew, no doubt that there was some screw loose,[273] but he was not in our secrets. All this is the truth, and if I tell it to you, gentlemen, it is not to amuse you—for you have not done me a very good turn—but it is because I believe the best defence I can make is just to hold back nothing, but let all the world know how badly I have myself been served by Major Sholto, and how innocent I am of the death of his son."

"A very remarkable account," said Sherlock Holmes.[274] "A fitting wind-up to an extremely interesting case. There is nothing at all new to me in the latter part of your narrative, except that you brought your own rope. That I did not know. By the way, I had hoped that Tonga had lost all his darts; yet he managed to shoot one at us in the boat."

"He had lost them all, sir, except the one which was in his blow-pipe at the time."

"Ah, of course," said Holmes. "I had not thought of that."

"Is there any other point which you would like to ask about?" asked the convict affably.

"I think not, thank you," my companion answered.

"Well, Holmes," said Athelney Jones, "you are a man to be humoured, and we all know that you are a connoisseur of crime; but duty is duty, and I have gone rather far in doing what you and your friend asked me. I shall feel more at ease when we have our story-teller here safe under lock and key. The cab still waits, and there are two inspectors downstairs. I

273 According to the *Slang Dictionary*, "[W]hen friends become cold and distant towards each other, it is said there is a SCREW LOOSE betwixt them; the same phrase is also used when anything goes wrong with a person's credit or reputation"—or, more familiarly today, with a person's mind.

274 Remarkable indeed, concludes John Linsenmeyer, in "Further Thoughts on *The Sign of the Four*." Small's account contains an "unacceptable proportion of unexplained mysteries." First, why were two officers in the Bombay Army (Sholto and Morstan, who were with the '34th Bombay Infantry') assigned to guard duty in the Andaman Islands, which was part of the *Bengal* Presidency? (But see note 46, above.) Second, Linsenmeyer notes the preposterous names of the co-conspirators (see note 248, above). Third, why would Sholto, if his history were as Small described it, name his house Pondicherry Lodge, Pondicherry being a *French* enclave on the eastern coast of India? Fourth, why are the descriptions of the Andamanese in general and Tonga in particular so different from the true nature of the Andamanese? Finally, why was one of Small's guards a "Pathan," a member of a group Linsenmeyer describes as "wild, undisciplined, and incredibly violent Moslem hillbillies"? In short, Linsenmeyer concludes that Holmes was "humbugged" by Small.

am much obliged to you both for your assistance. Of course you will be wanted at the trial. Good night to you."

"Good night gentlemen both," said Jonathan Small.

"You first, Small," remarked the wary Jones as they left the room. "I'll take particular care that you don't club me with your wooden leg, whatever you may have done to the gentleman at the Andaman Isles."[275]

"Well, and there is the end of our little drama," I remarked, after we had sat some time smoking in silence. "I fear that it may be the last investigation in which I shall have the chance of studying your methods. Miss Morstan has done me the honour to accept me as a husband in prospective."[276]

He gave a most dismal groan.

"I feared as much," said he. "I really cannot congratulate you."[277]

I was a little hurt.

"Have you any reason to be dissatisfied with my choice?" I asked.

"Not at all. I think she is one of the most charming young

" 'I am much obliged to you both for your assistance.' "
Richard Gutschmidt, *Das Zeichen der Vier* (Stuttgart: Robert Lutz Verlag, 1902)

275 T. S. Blakeney finds some redeeming features in Small. First, he took his defeat by Holmes in sporting fashion. Second, there were extenuating circumstances in his story of Achmet's murder. "In the predicament [Small] was in, it really boiled down to his own life, or Achmet's (and the latter was an emissary of a rebel). Given war conditions, and particularly those obtaining in the Mutiny, where the British were terribly outnumbered and every man's life among them was of value, Small would have been a pedant indeed, as well as a traitor to the interests of the Fort, if he preferred Achmet's life to his own." Blakeney considers him no worse than John Turner ("The Boscombe Valley Mystery"), reformed bushranger and later murderer of an old acquaintance. A similar view is expressed by David Galerstein, in " 'I Have the Right to Private Judgement,' " in which Galerstein considers the "innocence" of men such as Captain Croker ("The Abbey Grange") and Jefferson Hope (*A Study in Scarlet*) compared to the "guilt" of Small. Galerstein questions the soundness of Holmes's "private" judgement.

276 Watson's marriage to Mary Morstan has created nightmares for those attempting to reconcile the date of the events recorded in this case (likely summer 1888—see *Appendix*) with the date of the events recorded in "The Five Orange Pips." In the latter case, explicitly dated by Watson in September 1887, Watson states that "my wife was on a visit to her mother's." If "The Five Orange Pips" occurred before *The Sign of Four*, then the "wife" referred to there could not be Mary Morstan. To add further confusion, while the American edition's version of "The Five Orange Pips" follows the *Strand Magazine* version in using the word "mother," the first English book publication of "The Five Orange Pips" replaces the word "mother" with "aunt." The latter was adopted as the "definitive text" by Edgar W. Smith for the Limited Editions Club publication of the *Adventures* in 1950 and has been widely copied.

Based in part on the reference to Watson's "wife," some chronologists reject dating "The Five Orange Pips" in September 1887 and date the case after *The Sign of Four*. However, this is a shaky foundation, for according to Mary Morstan (see Chapter II, above), her mother died before 1878, and she had no living relatives in England. ("My father was an officer in an Indian regiment, who sent me home when I was quite a child. My mother was dead, and I had no relative in England."). Ian McQueen states: "Let us say here and now that we no more believe in the existence of Mary Watson's aunt than we do in the orphan-girl's mother. Both were figments of Conan Doyle's imagination, erroneously inserted in the manuscript while he was editing Watson's notes for publication." McQueen suggests that Conan Doyle was misled by Watson's notes into assuming that Watson was already married in September 1887 and invented the visit to Mary's mother as the most plausible explanation for his absence from home.

It has been ingeniously suggested that Mary Morstan and Mrs. Cecil Forrester's relationship was practically that of aunt and niece. Philip Weller, in "A Relative Question," suggests that the "mother" is Mary Morstan's stepmother. However, neither argument seems very convincing, and this editor believes that the aunt/wife reference in "The Five Orange Pips" must be to a wife who preceded Mary Morstan and died before 1888 and to whom Watson, out of delicacy for the feelings of his *current* wife, makes little or no reference.

277 J. N. Williamson fancifully excuses Holmes's remark as an honest expression of worry, in light of Holmes's knowledge of Watson's "on-again-off-again relationship with Irene Adler, which resulted, after the death of Godfrey Norton, in the divorce of John and Mary and the marriage of John and Irene." Ebbe Curtis Hoff, however, more reasonably suggests that "Holmes could not congratulate Watson because (1) he lost a potential colleague in Mary; (2) he lost his Boswell; and (3) he saw ahead a tragic bereavement for his friend." The last, Hoff concludes, was based on Holmes's early observations of Mary Morstan's fatal illness. (Hoff suggests that this was likely clubbing of the fingertips, not mentioned in Watson's narrative, obscured by Watson's romantic visions of Mary.)

In "The Empty House," Watson refers to Holmes consoling him for his "sad bereavement." Most scholars accept the conventional view that this refers to the death of Mary Morstan. Others, seeing that Watson rarely discusses his wife in the Canon, take the view that his marriage was an unsuccessful one and that his "bereavement" does *not* refer to grief over his wife's death. Wingate Bett, in "Watson's Second Marriage," advances the hypothesis that "bereavement" there means deprivation, either by estrangement or by mental derangement. C. Alan Bradley and William A. S. Sarjeant note that Watson does not even identify the name of the deceased person; "it could have been Watson's mother, his father or his brother, for all that the chronicle tells us."

278 Esther Longfellow, in "The Distaff Side of Baker Street," argues that one only learns the effect of marriage by *being* married and concludes that Holmes must have wed. If this were so, however, one would have expected Holmes to say, "I should never marry *again*." But Brad Keefauver, in *Sherlock and the Ladies*, reads more into Holmes's unnecessary explanation: "[T]he detective is being both sincere and more emotional than he himself would ever admit. He's disappointed, even a bit bitter over the whole thing." Holmes and Watson both loved Mary Morstan, but "Watson was just the one to make the first move."

" 'I shall never marry myself, lest I bias my judgement.' "
Frederic Dorr Steele, *Collier's*, 1903 (recaptioned and reused with slight alteration in *Adventures of Sherlock Holmes*, Vol. I [New York: Limited Editions Club, 1950]). The astute reader will readily recognize this as the cover drawn by Steele for "The Norwood Builder," *Collier's*, 1903, *sans* hand-print (see *The New Annotated Sherlock Holmes*, Volume II, page 830).

ladies I ever met and might have been most useful in such work as we have been doing. She had a decided genius that way; witness the way in which she preserved that Agra plan from all the other papers of her father. But love is an emotional thing, and whatever is emotional is opposed to that true, cold reason which I place above all things. I should never marry myself, lest I bias my judgment."[278]

"I trust," said I, laughing, "that my judgment may survive the ordeal. But you look weary."

"Yes, the reaction is already upon me. I shall be as limp as a rag for a week."

"Strange," said I, "how terms of what in another man I

should call laziness alternate with your fits of splendid energy and vigour."

"Yes," he answered, "there are in me the makings of a very fine loafer, and also of a pretty spry sort of a fellow. I often think of those lines of old Goethe: '*Schade dass die Natur nur* einen *Mensch aus dir schuf, Denn zum würdigen Mann war und zum Schelmen der Stoff.*'[279] By the way, apropos of this Norwood business, you see that they had, as I surmised, a confederate in the house, who could be none other than Lal Rao, the butler: so Jones actually has the undivided honour of having caught one fish in his great haul."

"The division seems rather unfair," I remarked. "You have done all the work in this business. I get a wife out of it, Jones gets the credit; pray what remains for you?"

"For me," said Sherlock Holmes, "there still remains the cocaine-bottle." And he stretched his long, white hand up for it.[280]

279 Morris Rosenblum attributes the lines to the *Xenien*, a collection written by Goethe and Schiller in 1796. The phrase may be translated, "Nature, alas, made only one being out of you although there was material enough for a good man and a rogue."

C. Alan Bradley and William A. S. Sarjeant offer a fresh interpretation: Holmes is not speaking of himself but instead "lamenting the fact that there were not two Watsons, one to marry Miss Morstan and the other to stay with him in Baker Street."

280 Bradley and Sarjeant write that, though Watson's announcement was a blow to Holmes, the latter's reaching for the drug was less the response of a man in shock than "a gesture of defiance—defiance of the doctor who had been striving to wean his friend from cocaine, but who had now signified that his personal priorities had switched elsewhere."

APPENDIX

The Dating of *The Sign of Four*

The dating of *The Sign of Four* is one of the most vexing problems of chronology, in part because there is a wealth of internal evidence and in part because of its pivotal role in fixing the dates of other Canonical events. The following table summarises the conclusions of the major chronologists, although there are numerous other works worthy of consultation:

Chronology	Date Assigned
Canon	July 7 or Sept. 1888
Bell, H. W. *Sherlock Holmes and Dr. Watson: The Chronology of Their Adventures*	Sept. 7, 1887, Wed.
Blakeney, T. S. *Sherlock Holmes: Fact or Fiction?*	July 1888
Christ, Jay Finley. *An Irregular Chronology of Sherlock Holmes of Baker Street*	Sept. 25, 1888, Tues.
Brend, Gavin. *My Dear Holmes*	July 1887
Baring-Gould, William S., "New Chronology of Sherlock Holmes and Dr. Watson"	Sept. 7, 1888, Fri.
Baring-Gould, William S. *The Chronological Holmes*. Mr. Baring-Gould uses the same dates in *Sherlock Holmes of Baker Street: A Life of the World's First Consulting Detective* and *The Annotated Sherlock Holmes*	Sept. 18, 1888, Tues.
Zeisler, Ernest Bloomfield. *Baker Street Chronology: Commentaries on the Sacred Writings of Dr. John H. Watson*	Apr. 16, 1888, Mon.
Folsom, Henry T. *Through the Years at Baker Street: A Chronology of Sherlock Holmes*	July 17, 1888, Tues.
Folsom, Henry T. *Through the Years at Baker Street: A Chronology of Sherlock Holmes*, Revised Edition	July 17, 1888, Tues.

Dakin, D. Martin. *A Sherlock Holmes Commentary*	Sept. 27, 1888, Thurs.
Cummings, Carey. *The Biorhythmic Holmes: A Chronological Perspective*	Sept. 27, 1888, Thurs.
Butters, Roger. *First Person Singular: A Review of the Life and Work of Mr. Sherlock Holmes, the World's First Consulting Detective, and His Friend and Colleague, Dr. John H. Watson*	July 1887
Bradley, C. Alan, and William A. S. Sarjeant. *Ms. Holmes of Baker Street: The Truth about Sherlock*	Sept. 18, 1888, Tues.
Hall, John. *"I Remember the Date Very Well": A Chronology of the Sherlock Holmes Stories of Arthur Conan Doyle*	July 7 or Sept. 1888
Thomson, June. *Holmes and Watson*	July 7 or Sept. 1888

The Hound of the Baskervilles [1]

1 *The Hound of the Baskervilles* appeared in the *Strand Magazine*, in monthly parts, from August 1901 to April 1902 (vols. 22 and 23). The first book edition was published by George Newnes in 1902, before the final installment appeared in the *Strand*. The first American edition, published by McClure, Phillips & Co., also appeared in 1902. See *Appendix 2* for a discussion of the various acknowledgements.

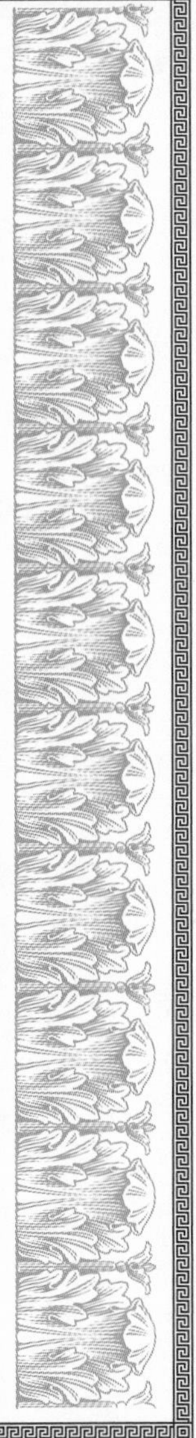

The Hound of the Baskervilles

The immortal words "Mr. Holmes, they were the footprints of a gigantic hound!" conjure fear as few others in the twentieth-century canon. Based on local legends of black dogs and vengeful ghosts, and called the greatest mystery ever penned, The Hound of the Baskervilles *(1902), a tale of Gothic horror set in the fantastic moors of England, enthralled readers of the* Strand Magazine *(in which it was serialised) with its strange warnings and clues and clever host of suspects. Watson shines here, both as the narrator and as the principal investigator until Holmes sweeps down on the scene to ratchet up the drama one more notch. Widely acknowledged to be one of the century's first bestsellers, the novel did little to quell the disappointment of readers who longed for a resolution of the question of whether Holmes—killed off in 1893's "The Final Problem"—had somehow cheated death at the hands of the villainous Professor Moriarty. The novel, the faithful realised unhappily, recounted events which predated Holmes's apparent death. The public had to wait until 1903, when "The Empty House" was published, for news that Holmes was firmly back in the land of the living.*

Twentieth-Century Fox's *The Hound of the Baskervilles.*
San Francisco Chronicle, March 30, 1939

CHAPTER I

Mr. Sherlock Holmes

Mr. Sherlock Holmes, who was usually very late in the mornings, save upon those not infrequent occasions when he stayed up all night, was seated at the breakfast-table.[2] I stood upon the hearth-rug and picked up the stick which our visitor had left behind him the night before.[3] It was a fine, thick piece of wood, bulbous-headed, of the sort which is known as a "Penang lawyer."[4] Just under the head was a broad silver band, nearly an inch across. "To James Mortimer, M.R.C.S.,[5] from his friends of the C.C.H.," was engraved upon it, with the date "1884." It was just such a stick as the old-fashioned family practitioner used to carry—dignified, solid, and reassuring.

"Well, Watson, what do you make of it?"

Holmes was sitting with his back to me, and I had given him no sign of my occupation.

"How did you know what I was doing? I believe you have eyes in the back of your head."

"I have, at least, a well-polished, silver-plated coffee-pot in front of me," said he. "But, tell me, Watson, what do you make of our visitor's stick? Since we have been so unfortunate as to

2 In "The Speckled Band," Watson feels "surprise, and perhaps just a little resentment" when Holmes not only rises first but unceremoniously wakes him up, "for I was myself regular in my habits"—a lofty claim at odds with much of the rest of the Canon, where Holmes is almost always the first one up and out. Here, the implication is that Watson has for once bested his friend, is relaxing after his meal, "and in the warm glow of comfortable satiety he dares to venture some pregnant observations of his own," as Vincent Starrett points out. In *A Study in Scarlet* (see note 53), Watson describes Holmes as having "invariably breakfasted and gone out" before he can even rouse himself from his bed; he refers to his own "late habits" and confesses that "I get up at all sorts of ungodly hours." This was presumably before Watson commenced his practise in Paddington. In "The Engineer's Thumb," after being roused before seven o'clock, Watson expects to discover Holmes taking his breakfast. In "The Speckled Band," however, Watson describes himself as "regular in my habits" and Holmes as a "late riser as a rule."

3 Holmes's clients make a habit of leaving their belongings behind (for example, in "The Yellow Face"). "The result was always highly satisfactory," Gavin Brend writes, "for Holmes invariably made a reconstruction of the missing client from the missing article." In *The Sign of Four*, when Watson challenges Holmes by presenting him with a watch whose provenance he is convinced Holmes can't deduce, Holmes outdoes himself—and insults Watson—by declaring, correctly, that the watch once belonged to Watson's dissolute brother. A little later, Holmes remarks that Dr. Mortimer had waited over an hour for them (a fact obviously imparted by Mrs. Hudson), but curiously, notes Brad Keefauver, in *The Armchair Baskerville Tour*, Holmes voices no criticism of Mrs. Hudson for allowing Mortimer to wait unobserved in their rooms.

4 A cane or walking-stick with a large, irregular head and imported from Penang, an island in Malaysia, off the northwest coast of Malaya. Its uses as a weapon were legion; Fitzroy Simpson of "Silver Blaze" owned one, "weighted with lead."

5 Member of the Royal College of Surgeons. In 1540, Henry VIII created the Company of Barber-Surgeons by joining the Worshipful Company of Barbers (incorporated in 1462) and the Guild of Surgeons. The surgeons broke away from the barbers in 1745 to form the Company of Surgeons. In 1800, the Company received a Royal Charter to become the Royal College of Surgeons in London; the title was changed in 1843, again by Royal Charter, to the Royal College of Surgeons of England. This diploma is now regarded as a specialist higher qualification in surgery,

Dustjacket, *The Hound of the Baskervilles*.
(New York: Grosset & Dunlap, *ca*. 1930)

miss him and have no notion of his errand, this accidental souvenir becomes of importance. Let me hear you reconstruct the man by an examination of it."

"I think," said I, following so far as I could the methods of my companion, "that Dr. Mortimer is a successful elderly medical man, well-esteemed, since those who know him give him this mark of their appreciation."

"Good!" said Holmes. "Excellent!"

"I think also that the probability is in favour of his being a country practitioner who does a great deal of his visiting on foot."

"Why so?"

"Because this stick, though originally a very handsome one, has been so knocked about that I can hardly imagine a town practitioner carrying it. The thick iron ferrule is worn down, so it is evident that he has done a great amount of walking with it."

"Perfectly sound!" said Holmes.

"And then again, there is the 'friends of the C.C.H.' I should guess that to be the Something Hunt, the local hunt to whose members he has possibly given some surgical assistance, and which has made him a small presentation in return."

"Really, Watson, you excel yourself," said Holmes, pushing back his chair and lighting a cigarette. "I am bound to say that in all the accounts which you have been so good as to give of my own small achievements you have habitually underrated your own abilities. It may be that you are not yourself luminous, but you are a conductor of light. Some people without possessing genius have a remarkable power of stimulating it.[6] I confess, my dear fellow, that I am very much in your debt."

He had never said as much before, and I must admit that his words gave me keen pleasure, for I had often been piqued by his indifference to my admiration and to the attempts which I had made to give publicity to his methods. I was proud, too, to think that I had so far mastered his system as to apply it in a way which earned his approval. He now took the stick from my hands and examined it for a few minutes with his naked eyes. Then, with an expression of interest, he laid down his cigarette, and, carrying the cane to the window, he looked over it again with a convex lens.

"Interesting, though elementary," said he, as he returned to his favourite corner of the settee. "There are certainly one or two indications upon the stick. It gives us the basis for several deductions."

"Has anything escaped me?" I asked, with some self-importance. "I trust that there is nothing of consequence which I have overlooked?"

"I am afraid, my dear Watson, that most of your conclusions were erroneous. When I said that you stimulated me I meant, to be frank, that in noting your fallacies I was occasionally guided towards the truth. Not that you are entirely wrong in this instance. The man is certainly a country practitioner."

"Then I was right."

The Royal College of Surgeons.
Queen's London (1897).

awarded to doctors who have already qualified in their profession and have elected to practise in the surgical branch of it, by examination at a middle stage of their junior careers. In Mortimer's day, the M.R.C.S. was the surgical half of the standard qualification to practise, *not* an advanced degree, and surgeons in fact occupied a lower position in the medical hierarchy than physicians, who diagnosed patients and prescribed medication. Surgeons' duties included the treatment of wounds and performance of then-standard surgical procedures, the range of which was smaller than it of course is today. Mortimer apparently did not possess the *medical* half of the qualification to practise medicine, usually a license from the Society of Apothecaries, which conferred the letters L.S.A. (originally for Licentiate of the Society of Apothecaries; the title was changed in 1907 to L.M.S.S.A., indicating that the examination included surgery).

6 Although "double-edged testimony to Watson's assistance is only too typical," as T. S. Blakeney comments, the competition between the two men is perhaps more evident in this novel than elsewhere in the Canon. The foundation is laid in the opening pages, as we have seen, with the unspoken competition over which man breakfasted first, and the demonstrations of Holmes's superiority extend to the final pages, when Holmes criticizes Watson's investigative powers even more mortifyingly than usual, while simultaneously praising his friend's skills as a detective. William Hyder, in "The Rise of the Underdog: Dr. Watson in *The Hound of the Baskervilles*" points out that embarrassingly, several of Holmes's own deductions prove incorrect, while several of Watson's are later verified. Still, "It was a securely-founded friendship," Blakeney continues, "which survived this withering frankness of expression."

7 Charing Cross Hospital was established in 1823 in Villiers Street, London, as a charitable institution known as the West London Infirmary, although it traces its origins to a meeting initiated by Dr. Benjamin Golding in 1818. The infirmary was small, treating twelve patients at a time. It acquired the name Charing Cross Hospital in 1827. Its function as a teaching hospital got fully under way in 1834, when a new building was opened in Agar Street that could accommodate twenty-two students. A separate medical school building was opened in Chandos Place in 1881, and in

Surgeons perform an operation before medical students at Charing Cross Hospital (*ca.* 1890).

"He looked over it again with a convex lens."
Richard Gutschmidt, *Der Hund von Baskerville*
(Stuttgart: Robert Lutz Verlag, 1903)

"To that extent."

"But that was all."

"No, no, my dear Watson, not all—by no means all. I would suggest, for example, that a presentation to a doctor is more likely to come from a hospital than from a hunt, and that when the initials 'C.C.' are placed before that hospital the words 'Charing Cross' very naturally suggest themselves."

"You may be right."

"The probability lies in that direction. And if we take this as a working hypothesis we have a fresh basis from which to start our construction of this unknown visitor."

"Well, then, supposing that 'C.C.H.' does stand for 'Charing Cross Hospital,'[7] what further inferences may we draw?"

"Do none suggest themselves? You know my methods. Apply them!"

"I can only think of the obvious conclusion that the man has practised in town before going to the country."

"I think that we might venture a little farther than this. Look at it in this light. On what occasion would it be most probable that such a presentation would be made? When would his friends unite to give him a pledge of their good will? Obviously at the moment when Dr. Mortimer withdrew from the service of the hospital in order to start in practice for himself. We know there has been a presentation. We believe there has been a change from a town hospital to a country practice. Is it, then, stretching our inference too far to say that the presentation was on the occasion of the change?"

"It certainly seems probable."

"Now, you will observe that he could not have been on the *staff* of the hospital, since only a man well-established in a London practice could hold such a position, and such a one would not drift into the country. What was he, then? If he was in the hospital and yet not on the staff, he could only have been a

"He looked over it again with a convex lens."
Sidney Paget, *Strand Magazine*, 1901

1894 the venerable Charing Cross Theatre (which became Toole's Theatre in 1878 and was the venue in 1892 for the first play of Arthur Conan Doyle's good friend J. M. Barrie) was demolished to make way for the facility's expansion and various improvements, which included the building of additional laboratories. The hospital continues today under the full name Charing Cross and Westminster Medical School, with the school being part of the Imperial College School of Medicine.

house-surgeon or a house-physician—little more than a senior student. And he left five years ago—the date is on the stick. So your grave, middle-aged family practitioner vanishes into thin air, my dear Watson, and there emerges a young fellow under thirty, amiable, unambitious, absent-minded, and the possessor of a favourite dog, which I should describe roughly as being larger than a terrier and smaller than a mastiff."

I laughed incredulously as Sherlock Holmes leaned back in his settee and blew little wavering rings of smoke up to the ceiling.

"As to the latter part, I have no means of checking you," said I, "but at least it is not difficult to find out a few particulars about the man's age[8] and professional career."

From my small medical shelf I took down the Medical Directory[9] and turned up the name. There were several Mortimers, but only one who could be our visitor. I read his record aloud.

> Mortimer, James, M.R.C.S., 1882, Grimpen, Dartmoor,[10] Devon. House-surgeon, from 1882 to 1884, at Charing Cross Hospital. Winner of the Jackson Prize[11] for Comparative Pathology, with essay entitled "Is Disease a Reversion?" Corresponding member of the Swedish Pathological Society. Author of "Some Freaks of Atavism"[12] (*Lancet*, 1882), "Do We Progress?" (*Journal of Psychology*, March, 1883). Medical Officer[13] for the parishes of Grimpen, Thorsley, and High Barrow.

"No mention of that local hunt, Watson," said Holmes, with a mischievous smile, "but a country doctor, as you very astutely observed. I think that I am fairly justified in my inferences. As to the adjectives, I said, if I remember right, amiable, unambitious, and absent-minded. It is my experience that it is only an amiable man in this world who receives testimonials, only an unambitious one who abandons a London career for the country and only an absent-minded one who leaves his stick and not his visiting-card after waiting an hour in your room."

"And the dog?"

"Has been in the habit of carrying this stick behind his master. Being a heavy stick the dog has held it tightly by the middle, and the marks of his teeth are very plainly visible. The dog's jaw, as shown in the space between these marks, is too

8 Actually, Mortimer's age is *not* given in the Medical Directory.

9 The Medical Directory was created under the 1858 Medical Act, through which Parliament sought to regulate both the medical profession and medical education in the United Kingdom. In an age when disputes concerning qualifications were rampant among professionals in London, Edinburgh, and Glasgow, and when anyone could hang out a shingle and collect fees from patients "provided he does not assume misleading titles" (*Encyclopædia Britannica*, 9th Ed.), the 1858 Act, considered draconian by some for its exclusion of Continental practitioners, also aimed to end quackery. A General Medical Council was established to assume oversight of practices and conduct. The directory listed practitioners with a degree in medicine or surgery from a British university; licentiates, members, or fellows of the Royal Colleges of Physicians or Surgeons in London, Dublin, or Edinburgh; licentiates or fellows of the Faculty of Physicians and Surgeons of Glasgow; and licentiates of the Apothecaries' Halls of London and Dublin. Registering—which cost five pounds—conferred certain rights on practitioners, among them the ability to sue patients for nonpayment.

10 Notwithstanding the numerous references to Dartmoor and its locales, real and fictitious, several commentators contend that the events of *The Hound of the Baskervilles* actually take place in Herefordshire. Maurice Campbell, in "The Hound of the Baskervilles: Dartmoor or Herefordshire?," reaches that result on the basis of identification of buildings and heraldic markings. Roger Robinson similarly makes a case for Herefordshire in "The Hound: Dartmoor or Oxfordshire?" Dartmoor, known for the beauty of its heaths and craggy hills, is in the county of Devon, in southwest England, between the Bristol and English

Channels; less rugged Herefordshire borders Wales. However, those who reject Dartmoor as the locale are a distinct minority, and there appears little reason to doubt the majority view holding with the Dartmoor identification.

11 The annual *Jacksonian* Prize was founded in 1800 by Samuel Jackson, F.R.S., M.R.C.S., and £10 was awarded by the Royal College of Surgeons to a Fellow or Member of the College (or Fellow in Dental Surgery) who made a significant contribution to advancement of surgery and authored a dissertation on a practical subject in surgery. In 1967, the prize money was increased to £250, and in 1995 to £2,500. Although there have been several joint winners in the last fifty years, there have been a number of years since 1957 when no award was given. Dr. Mortimer's name does not appear among the prize winners from 1882 through 1888; nor are the titles of the winning dissertations readily available. Nineteenth-century winners of note include Sir Frederick Treves, discoverer of the "Elephant Man," who received the award in 1883 for his paper on obstruction of the intestine in the abdominal cavity. Canonical echoes among other winners include one *John Clay* (1866), William *Watson* Cheyne (1880), John Bland-*Sutton* (1892), and William McAdam *Eccles* (1900).

12 Atavism refers to the recurrence of an ancestral characteristic, particularly after a long period of its absence. It was also a criminological term encouraged by Italian criminologist and physician Cesare Lombroso (1835–1909), who held that individuals engaging in criminal acts did so not by choice but because they were "atavistic" and had never evolved past the uncivilised nature of our primitive forebears.

The ninth edition of the *Encyclopædia Britannica* refers to such individuals as men "who live in the midst of our civilization as mere savages. . . . [T]he existing system of law can scarcely be brought to distinguish them from criminals. Moralists attribute to atavism a large number of offences which lawyers attribute to guilty dispositions." But the *Britannica* editor appears sceptical of this view: "It is not, however, owing to atavism, but to the mere continuance of an old order of things, that so many of our ill-educated classes, shepherds, agricultural labourers, and even factory hands, are as little developed, and live a life as little intellectual as savages. Latent in our small hamlets and large cities there is more savagery than many reformers are aware of, and it needs but little experience to discover something of the old barbarity lurking still in minds and hearts under a thin veil of civilisation."

In his *L'uomo delinquente* (1876; partially translated in 1911 as *The Criminal Man*), Lombroso pointed to certain physical and mental abnormalities of these "born criminals," such as skull size and asymmetries of the face and other parts of the body. His views have since been discredited, but Lombroso's role in bringing science to the study of criminal behaviour is regarded as pivotal.

In the 1880s, the term was associated with Ernst Haeckel (1834–1919), who popularised Darwinism in Germany. Haeckel's "ontogeny recapitulates phylogeny"—the concept, now known to be insupportable, that an embryo in the course of its development goes back to earlier evolutionary stages and finally comes to resemble the latter, more complex organisms from which it evolved—grew out of a nascent but highly imperfect understanding of genetics. During the period between the widespread acceptance of Darwinian evolution and the understanding of the principles of genetics, atavism was invoked frequently to explain why certain people inexplicably exhibited the traits of their ancestors. Mortimer's paper may have explored such "freaks."

broad in my opinion for a terrier and not broad enough for a mastiff. It may have been—yes, by Jove, it *is* a curly-haired spaniel."[14]

He had risen and paced the room as he spoke. Now he halted in the recess of the window. There was such a ring of conviction in his voice that I glanced up in surprise.

"My dear fellow, how can you possibly be so sure of that?"

"For the very simple reason that I see the dog himself on our very doorstep,[15] and there is the ring of its owner. Don't move, I beg you, Watson. He is a professional brother of yours, and your presence may be of assistance to me. Now is the dramatic moment of fate, Watson, when you hear a step upon the stair which is walking into your life, and you know not whether for good or ill. What does Dr. James Mortimer, the man of science, ask of Sherlock Holmes, the specialist in crime? Come in!"

The appearance of our visitor was a surprise to me since I had expected a typical country practitioner. He was a very tall, thin man, with a long nose like a beak, which shot out between two keen, grey eyes,[16] set closely together and sparkling brightly from behind a pair of gold-rimmed glasses. He was clad in a professional but rather slovenly fashion, for his frock-coat was dingy and his trousers frayed. Though young, his long back was already bowed, and he walked with a forward thrust of his head and a general air of peering benevolence. As he entered his eyes fell upon the stick in Holmes's hand, and he ran towards it with an exclamation of joy.

"I am so very glad," said he. "I was not sure whether I had left it here or in the Shipping Office. I would not lose that stick for the world."

"A presentation, I see," said Holmes.

"Yes, sir."

"From Charing Cross Hospital?"

"From one or two friends there on the occasion of my marriage."[17]

"Dear, dear, that's bad!" said Holmes, shaking his head.

Dr. Mortimer blinked through his glasses in mild astonishment.

"Why was it bad?"

"Only that you have disarranged our little deductions. Your marriage, you say?"

"Yes, sir. I married, and so left the hospital, and with it all

13 The duties of the Medical Officer were akin to those of medical examiners in the United States today and included: reporting on death rate and causes of mortality; identifying and dealing with public nuisances and condemning unsafe dwellings; and investigating epidemics and outbreaks of disease and instituting measures to limit contagion, such as quarantine and improved public hygiene.

Most Medical Officers were qualified and registered to practise medicine and perform surgery and usually derived income from house calls, attendance at births, and registration of births. In addition, Medical Officers treated the insane, and, as is evident from Mortimer's treatment of Sir Charles Baskerville, also maintained private practices. If Mortimer were only "a humble M.R.C.S.," he need not have been qualified in medicine. See note 5, above.

14 "Deduction, confirmed almost immediately after by the visible evidence of that deduction's correctness?" ponders Michael Harrison, in *Cynological Mr. Holmes*. "Or no deduction at all, but a simple little joke at Watson's expense . . ."

15 Harrison also wonders how Holmes could have seen the dog "on our very doorstep," for the Baker Street houses, he asserts, all had canopies over their front entrances.

16 Brad Keefauver builds a thesis, based on the physical description of Dr. Mortimer and on his behavioural characteristics, that Mortimer is Holmes's brother. Joy and Vic Holly, in "The Times of Dr. Mortimer," note the similarities of description to Charles Augustus Milverton and suggest that *they* were brothers, while Gordon R. Speck, in "The Hound and the Stalking-horse," reaches the same conclusion about Mortimer and Moriarty. Jerry Neal Williamson carries this hypothesis one step further in "Dr. Mortimer-Moriarty," alleging

"He was clad in a professional but rather slovenly fashion, for his frockcoat was dingy and his trousers frayed."
Richard Gutschmidt, *Der Hund von Baskerville*
(Stuttgart: Robert Lutz Verlag, 1903)

hopes of a consulting practice. It was necessary to make a home of my own."

"Come, come, we are not so far wrong after all," said Holmes. "And now, Dr. James Mortimer—"

"Mister, sir, Mister—a humble M.R.C.S."[18]

"And a man of precise mind, evidently."

"A dabbler in science, Mr. Holmes, a picker-up of shells on the shores of the great unknown ocean.[19] I presume that it is Mr. Sherlock Holmes whom I am addressing and not—"

"No, this is my friend Dr. Watson."

"Glad to meet you, sir. I have heard your name mentioned in connection with that of your friend. You interest me very much, Mr. Holmes. I had hardly expected so dolichocephalic[20] a skull or such well-marked supra-orbital development.[21] Would you have any objection to my running my finger along your parietal fissure?[22] A cast of your skull, sir, until the original is available, would be an ornament to any anthropological

that "Dr. James Mortimer" was, in reality, Colonel James Moriarty, brother of Professor James Moriarty. He points out the great similarities in the physical descriptions of Dr. Mortimer and Professor Moriarty (in "The Final Problem").

17 There is much speculation regarding the character of Mortimer's wife, who never appears in Watson's chronicles: Frederick J. Jaeger and Rose M. Vogel, in *The Hound from Hell*, part-pastiche and part-essay, postulate that she did not exist, and that Mortimer conjured her up to provide a convenient foil for certain actions in connection with his plan to murder the Baskervilles. David Stuart Davies, in "The Strange Case of the Solitary Husband," argues that the marriage was an unhappy one and that Mortimer's wife "was obviously an ogre who dominated the country practitioner." Bruce E. Southworth, in "Mortimer's Motivation," contends that Mortimer suffered a decline in his mental faculties and that his loving wife removed him to the country to ease his life. Auberon Redfearn, in "Mortimer, His Medicine, His Mind, and His Marriage," calls the mystery woman "very remarkable" for putting up with Dr. Mortimer's frequent absences and tireless pursuit of his hobbies.

18 Dr. Mortimer's insistence on "Mister" is strange, for he raises no subsequent objection to being referred to as "Doctor."

19 Mortimer, whose idea of "pure amusement" consists of a visit to the Museum of the College of Surgeons, paraphrases Sir Isaac Newton: ". . . to myself I seem to have been only like a boy playing on the sea-shore and diverting myself in now and then finding a smoother pebble or a prettier shell than ordinary, whilst the great ocean of truth lay all undiscovered before me" (quoted in Sir David Brewster's *Memoirs of the Life, Writings,* *and Discoveries of Sir Isaac Newton* [Edinburgh: Edmonston & Douglas, 2nd edition, 1860], Vol. II, p. 331).

20 Having a relatively long head with cephalic index of less than 75. The cephalic index is arrived at by measuring the cranium at its widest point and dividing that number by the measurement of the cranium at its longest point; that number is then multiplied by 100.

21 Above the socket of the eyes.

22 Presumably Mortimer here refers to the juncture of the skull bones on top of the head, known as the sagittal suture. As a rule, the sagittal suture disappears in adults by the time they are thirty to forty years of age; perhaps the presence of the "fissure," obvious to Dr. Mortimer, made Holmes's skull worthy of study?

23 Mortimer appears here to be a student of phrenology—character assessment through study of the shape of the skull. See *A Study in Scarlet*, note 206. Note that this avocation is one shared by Professor James Moriarty ("The Final Problem").

24 Ian McQueen finds this deduction a bit of a stretch, arguing that a nicotine-stained forefinger would be apparent on any heavy smoker of cigarettes, whether store-bought or hand-rolled. "Was it just a guess, or had Holmes perhaps observed a tobacco pouch rather than a cigarette case sticking out of Mortimer's pocket when he noticed the Baskerville parchment? He might then have referred to [Mortimer's] forefinger in order to make his so-called deduction appear the more impressive."

"His eyes fell upon the stick in Holmes's hand."
Sidney Paget, *Strand Magazine*, 1901

museum. It is not my intention to be fulsome, but I confess that I covet your skull."[23]

Sherlock Holmes waved our strange visitor into a chair.

"You are an enthusiast in your line of thought, I perceive, sir, as I am in mine," said he. "I observe from your forefinger that you make your own cigarettes.[24] Have no hesitation in lighting one."

The man drew out paper and tobacco and twirled the one up in the other with surprising dexterity. He had long, quivering fingers as agile and restless as the antennæ of an insect.

Holmes was silent, but his little darting glances showed me the interest which he took in our curious companion.

"I presume, sir," said he at last, "that it was not merely for the purpose of examining my skull that you have done me the honour to call here last night and again today?"

"No, sir, no; though I am happy to have had the opportunity of doing that as well. I came to you, Mr. Holmes, because I recognise that I am myself an unpractical man, and because I am suddenly confronted with a most serious and extraordinary problem. Recognising, as I do, that you are the second highest expert in Europe—"

"Indeed, sir! May I inquire who has the honour to be the first?" asked Holmes, with some asperity.

"To the man of precisely scientific mind the work of Monsieur Bertillon."[25]

"Then had you not better consult him?"

"I said, sir, to the precisely scientific mind. But as a practical man of affairs it is acknowledged that you stand alone. I trust, sir, that I have not inadvertently—"

"Just a little," said Holmes. "I think, Dr. Mortimer, you would do wisely if without more ado you would kindly tell me plainly what the exact nature of the problem is in which you demand my assistance."

25 Alphonse Bertillon (1853–1914) was chief of criminal identification for the Paris police from 1880. Before fingerprinting, there was *Bertillonage*, or the Bertillon system, which aimed to classify criminals through bodily measurements. Inspired by his anthropologist father, Bertillon reasoned that while a criminal might alter his appearance by wearing a wig, or conceal his identity by using an alias, his physical dimensions were nearly impossible to change.

Under the Bertillon system, officers took two pictures of each suspect, one face-forward and one side view (Bertillon is often credited with popularising both the mug shot and the crime-scene photo), and then carefully noted on an index card the precise dimensions of the suspect's head, various limbs, and appendages; any defining body characteristics; and in particular, the shape of the ear. Eleven different measurements were taken in all.

The Bertillon system was officially adopted in France in 1888, and its use quickly spread to police departments throughout the world. But its imperfections were demonstrated when it was discovered in 1903 that two suspects, a Will West and a William West—though allegedly no relation—possessed almost identical measurements, and thus had been classified as the same person. The two Wests did have different fingerprints. (While there is some dispute over the matter, it seems likely that the Wests were in fact identical twins.) Bertillon reluctantly began including fingerprinting as a supplement to his system, and eventually the practice replaced *Bertillonage* altogether.

For a discussion of Holmes's own scientific technique, see "Sherlock Holmes and Fingerprinting" in *The New Annotated Sherlock Holmes*, Volume II, page 860.

CHAPTER II

The Curse of the Baskervilles

I HAVE IN MY pocket a manuscript," said Dr. James Mortimer.

"I observed it as you entered the room," said Holmes.

"It is an old manuscript."

"Early eighteenth century, unless it is a forgery."

"How can you say that, sir?"

"You have presented an inch or two of it to my examination all the time that you have been talking. It would be a poor expert who could not give the date of a document within a decade or so. You may possibly have read my little monograph upon the subject.[26] I put that at 1730."

"The exact date is 1742." Dr. Mortimer drew it from his breast-pocket. "This family paper was committed to my care by Sir Charles Baskerville, whose sudden and tragic death some three months ago created so much excitement in Devonshire. I may say that I was his personal friend as well as his medical attendant. He was a strong-minded man, sir, shrewd, practical, and as unimaginative as I am myself. Yet he took this document very seriously, and his mind was prepared for just such an end as did eventually overtake him."

26 Because Holmes evidently thinks that Mortimer is likely to have read this paper, it must have been published in a scientific journal that enjoyed wide circulation, reasons Walter Klinefelter, in "The Writings of Sherlock Holmes." On the basis of H. W. Bell's 1886 date for *The Hound of the Baskervilles*, Klinefelter ascribes Holmes's "little monograph" to a period before that year. Tage LaCour, in *Ex Bibliotheca Holmesiana*, assigns it to 1887 and asserts that it is also mentioned in "The Golden Pince-Nez." This latter point is incorrect; Holmes is found engrossed in a palimpsest, but he never mentions his monograph, even though "The Golden Pince-Nez" is unanimously dated long after the events of *The Hound of the Baskervilles*.

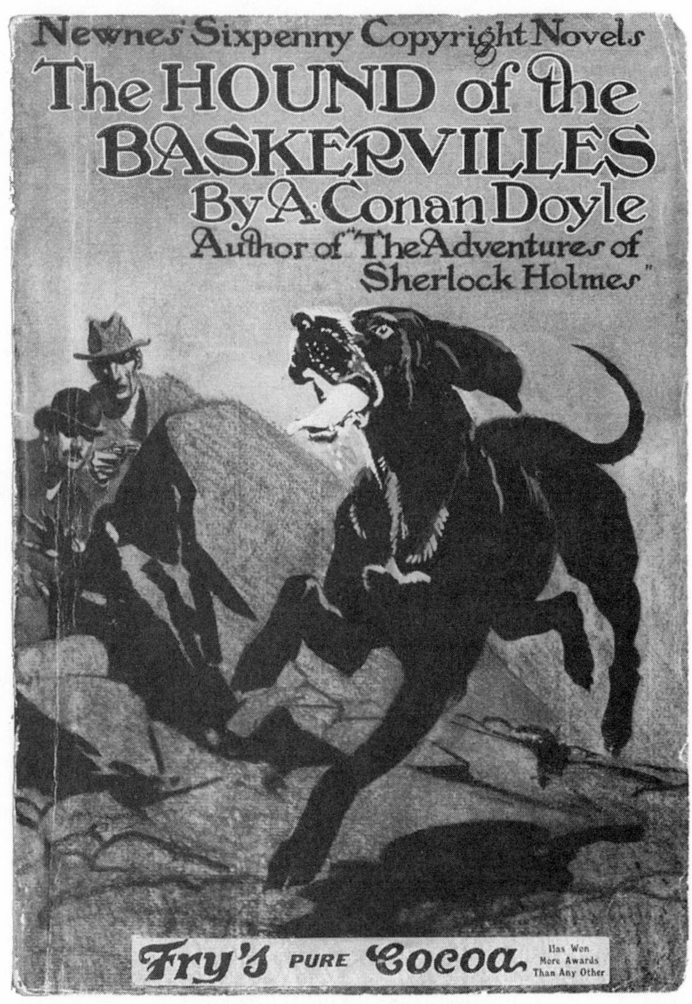

Dustjacket, *The Hound of the Baskervilles.*
Sixpenny Copyright Novels (London: George Newnes, Ltd., 1912)

Holmes stretched out his hand for the manuscript, and flattened it upon his knee.

"You will observe, Watson, the alternative use of the long *s* and the short.[27] It is one of several indications which enabled me to fix the date."

I looked over his shoulder at the yellow paper and the faded script. At the head was written: "Baskerville Hall," and below, in scrawling figures: "1742."[28]

"It appears to be a statement of some sort."

"Yes, it is a statement of a certain legend which runs in the Baskerville family."

27 Arthur Godfrey, Editor of *The Pictou Advocate*, Pictou, Nova Scotia, in a letter to the *Baker Street Journal*, explains the rule for usage of the typographical symbol for a long "s" (*f*): "The long 's' was never used as the initial letter of a word if the capital 'S' was used, nor was it used at the end of a word. It occurred only in the body of a word, and it was there used (properly) exclusively, except where it was doubled, and then the second 's' was a short one. For example, 'mi*f*sed.' " As to the dating of the manuscript, Dr. Lionel K. J. Glassey, tutor in palaeography in the Department of History at the University of Glasgow, points out that the practice of alternately using the long and short "s" in documents is one dating from 1500 and that, by 1780, the practice had come to an end, placing the manuscript well within bounds.

28 If this were the "inch or two" of manuscript protruding from Dr. Mortimer's pocket, it goes a long way toward explaining Holmes's remarkable ability to give the date of the document "within a decade or so."

"Dr. Mortimer turned the manuscript to the light and read."
Richard Gutschmidt, *Der Hund von Baskerville*
(Stuttgart: Robert Lutz Verlag, 1903)

"But I understand that it is something more modern and practical upon which you wish to consult me?"

"Most modern. A most practical, pressing matter, which must be decided within twenty-four hours. But the manuscript is short and is intimately connected with the affair. With your permission I will read it to you."

Holmes leaned back in his chair, placed his finger-tips together, and closed his eyes, with an air of resignation. Dr. Mortimer turned the manuscript to the light, and read in a high, crackling voice the following curious, old-world narrative:

> Of the origin of the Hound of the Baskervilles there have been many statements, yet as I come in a direct line from

Hugo Baskerville, and as I had the story from my father, who also had it from his, I have set it down with all belief that it occurred even as is here set forth. And I would have you believe, my sons, that the same Justice which punishes sin may also most graciously forgive it, and that no band is so heavy but that by prayer and repentance it may be removed. Learn then from this story not to fear the fruits of the past, but rather to be circumspect in the future, that those foul passions whereby our family has suffered so grievously may not again be loosed to our undoing.

Know then that in the time of the Great Rebellion (the history of which by the learned Lord Clarendon[29] I most earnestly commend to your attention) this Manor of

"Dr. Mortimer turned the manuscript to the light and read."
Sidney Paget, *Strand Magazine*, 1901

29 Edward Hyde, first Earl of Clarendon (1609–1674), wrote *History of the Rebellion and Civil Wars in England Begun in the Year 1641* (completed in 1674 but not published until 1702), the book to which the Baskerville manuscript evidently refers. Hyde served as Lord High Chancellor of England under Charles II and as Chancellor of the University of Oxford. In the judgement of the *Encyclopædia Britannica* (9th Ed.), "That he was a historian of wide grasp and deep insight cannot be maintained; his works are professedly pleadings on behalf of the Episcopalian Royalists and himself; but, though it would be too much to allege that his accuracy is never warped by his purpose, we may in general accept his statements of fact as correct." Having survived this slight, *History of the Rebellion* is still in print today, in a multi-volume facsimile of the definitive 1888 edition, edited by W. Dunn Macray.

Baskerville was held by Hugo of that name, nor can it be gainsaid that he was a most wild, profane, and godless man. This, in truth, his neighbours might have pardoned, seeing that saints have never flourished in those parts, but there was in him a certain wanton and cruel humour which made his name a by-word through the West. It chanced that this Hugo came to love (if, indeed, so dark a passion may be known under so bright a name) the daughter of a yeoman who held lands near the Baskerville estate. But the young maiden, being discreet and of good repute, would ever avoid him, for she feared his evil name. So it came to pass that one Michaelmas[30] this Hugo, with five or six of his idle and wicked companions, stole down upon the farm and carried off the maiden, her father and brothers being from home, as he well knew. When they had brought her to the Hall the maiden was placed in an upper chamber, while Hugo and his friends sat down to a long carouse as was their nightly custom. Now, the poor lass upstairs was like to have her wits turned at the singing and shouting and terrible oaths which came up to her from below, for they say that the words used by Hugo Baskerville, when he was in wine, were such as might blast the man who said them. At last in the stress of her fear she did that which might have daunted the bravest or most active man, for by the aid of the growth of ivy which covered (and still covers) the south wall, she came down from under the eaves, and so homeward across the moor, there being three leagues betwixt the Hall and her father's farm.

It chanced that some little time later Hugo left his guests to carry food and drink—with other worse things, perchance—to his captive, and so found the cage empty and the bird escaped. Then, as it would seem, he became as one that hath a devil, for rushing down the stairs into the dining-hall, he sprang upon the great table, flagons and trenchers[31] flying before him, and he cried aloud before all the company that he would that very night render his body and soul to the Powers of Evil if he might but overtake the wench. And while the revellers stood aghast at the fury of the man, one more wicked or, it may be, more drunken than the rest, cried out that they should put the hounds upon her. Whereat Hugo ran from the house, crying to his grooms that they should saddle his mare and unkennel the pack, and giving the hounds a kerchief of

30 September 29, dedicated to the Archangel Michael and all angels.

31 Platters or plates for the service of meat.

the maid's, he swung them to the line,[32] and so off full cry in the moonlight over the moor.

Now, for some space the revellers stood agape, unable to understand all that had been done in such haste. But anon their bemused wits awoke to the nature of the deed which was like to be done upon the moorlands. Everything was now in an uproar, some calling for their pistols, some for their horses, and some for another flask of wine. But at length some sense came back to their crazed minds, and the whole of them, thirteen in number, took horse and started in pursuit. The moon shone clear above them, and they rode swiftly abreast, taking that course which the maid must needs have taken if she were to reach her own home.

They had gone a mile or two when they passed one of the night shepherds upon the moorlands, and they cried to him to know if he had seen the hunt. And the man, as the story goes, was so crazed with fear that he could scarce speak, but at last he said that he had indeed seen the unhappy maiden, with the hounds upon her track. "But I have seen more than that," said he, "for Hugo Baskerville passed me upon his black mare, and there ran mute behind him such a hound of hell as God forbid should ever be at my heels."

So the drunken squires cursed the shepherd and rode onwards. But soon their skins turned cold, for there came a sound of galloping across the moor, and the black mare, dabbled with white froth, went past with trailing bridle and empty saddle. Then the revellers rode close together, for a great fear was on them, but they still followed over the moor, though each, had he been alone, would have been right glad to have turned his horse's head. Riding slowly in this fashion, they came at last upon the hounds. These, though known for their valour and their breed, were whimpering in a cluster at the head of a deep dip or goyal,[33] as we call it, upon the moor, some slinking away and some, with starting hackles and staring eyes, gazing down the narrow valley before them.

The company had come to a halt, more sober men, as you may guess, than when they started. The most of them would by no means advance, but three of them, the boldest, or, it may be the most drunken, rode forward down the goyal. Now it opened into a broad space in which stood two of those great stones, still to be seen there, which were set by certain forgot-

32 In hunting, to cause the hounds to spread out before they are drawn to the "line" of the fox's scent.

33 A gully or ravine.

The Hound of the Baskervilles.
Sidney Paget, *Strand Magazine*, 1901

ten peoples in the days of old. The moon was shining bright upon the clearing, and there in the centre lay the unhappy maid where she had fallen, dead of fear and of fatigue. But it was not the sight of her body, nor yet was it that of the body of Hugo Baskerville lying near her, which raised the hair upon the heads of these three dare-devil roysterers, but it was that, standing over Hugo, and plucking at his throat, there stood a foul thing, a great, black beast, shaped like a hound, yet larger than any hound that ever mortal eye has rested upon. And even as they looked the thing tore the throat out of Hugo Baskerville, on which, as it turned its blazing eyes and dripping jaws upon them, the three shrieked with fear and rode for dear life, still screaming, across the moor. One, it is said, died that very night of what he had seen, and the other twain were but broken men for the rest of their days.

Such is the tale, my sons, of the coming of the hound which is said to have plagued the family so sorely ever since. If I have set it down it is because that which is clearly known hath less terror than that which is but hinted at and guessed. Nor can it be denied that many of the family have been unhappy in their deaths, which have been sudden, bloody, and myste-

Cromlech near Drewsteignton.
An Exploration of Dartmoor, by J. Ll. W. Page (1895)

rious. Yet may we shelter ourselves in the infinite goodness of Providence, which would not for ever punish the innocent beyond that third or fourth generation which is threatened in Holy Writ. To that Providence, my sons, I hereby commend you, and I counsel you by way of caution to forbear from

"There in the centre lay the unhappy maid where she had fallen."
Sidney Paget, *Strand Magazine*, 1901

"It was that, standing over Hugo, and plucking at his throat, there stood a great, black beast."
Richard Gutschmidt, *Der Hund von Baskerville* (Stuttgart: Robert Lutz Verlag, 1903)

crossing the moor in those dark hours when the powers of evil are exalted.[34] [This from Hugo Baskerville[35] to his sons Rodger and John, with instructions that they say nothing thereof to their sister Elizabeth.]

When Dr. Mortimer had finished reading this singular narrative he pushed his spectacles up on his forehead and stared across at Mr. Sherlock Holmes. The latter yawned and tossed the end of his cigarette into the fire.

"Well?" said he.

"Do you not find it interesting?"

"To a collector of fairy-tales."

Dr. Mortimer drew a folded newspaper out of his pocket. "Now, Mr. Holmes, we will give you something a little more recent. This is the *Devon County Chronicle* of June[36] 14th of this year. It is a short account of the facts elicited at the death of Sir Charles Baskerville which occurred a few days before that date."

My friend leaned a little forward and his expression became intent. Our visitor readjusted his glasses and began:

34 See *Appendix 3* for a discussion of the suggestion that Hugo is to be identified as Richard Cabell.

35 This Hugo appears to be the great-grandson of the Hugo of legend. If the events recounted took place at the time of the Great Rebellion (1641–1651) and the scroll, written at a time when writer Hugo had three children presumably old enough to read, is dated 1742, his birthdate would be approximately ninety years after the legendary Hugo's, and thus he would likely be the fourth generation descended from him. We may assume that his son Rodger was an ancestor of the three Baskerville brothers; Charles, the unnamed man who was Henry's father; and Rodger, the father of Vandeleur/Stapleton.

36 Curiously, the version of the newspaper account in the *Strand Magazine* has the date of the paper as *May* 14 and the date of death (later in the account) as *May* 4.

The recent sudden death of Sir Charles Baskerville, whose name has been mentioned as the probable Liberal[37] candidate for Mid-Devon[38] at the next election, has cast a gloom over the county. Though Sir Charles had resided at Baskerville Hall for a comparatively short period his amiability of character and extreme generosity had won the affection and respect of all who had been brought into contact with him. In these days of *nouveaux riches* it is refreshing to find a case where the scion of an old county family which has fallen upon evil days is able to make his own fortune and to bring it back with him to restore the fallen grandeur of his line. Sir Charles, as is well known, made large sums of money in South African speculation. More wise than those who go on until the wheel turns against them, he realized his gains and returned to England with them. It is only two years since he took up his residence at Baskerville Hall, and it is common talk how large were those schemes of reconstruction and improvement which have been interrupted by his death. Being himself childless, it was his openly-expressed desire that the whole countryside should, within his own lifetime, profit by his good fortune, and many will have personal reasons for bewailing his untimely end. His generous donations to local and county charities have been frequently chronicled in these columns.

"The circumstances connected with the death of Sir Charles cannot be said to have been entirely cleared up by the inquest, but at least enough has been done to dispose of those rumours to which local superstition has given rise. There is no reason whatever to suspect foul play, or to imagine that death could be from any but natural causes. Sir Charles was a widower, and a man who may be said to have been in some ways of an eccentric habit of mind. In spite of his considerable wealth he was simple in his personal tastes, and his indoor servants at Baskerville Hall consisted of a married couple named Barrymore, the husband acting as butler and the wife as housekeeper. Their evidence, corroborated by that of several friends, tends to show that Sir Charles's health has for some time has been impaired, and points especially to some affection of the heart, manifesting itself in changes of colour, breathlessness, and acute attacks of nervous depres-

37 William Gladstone, the great Liberal Prime Minister, resumed the office in 1880. It was not until 1885 that Lord Salisbury, a Conservative, became Prime Minister.

38 Prior to the Local Government Act of 1888, "Mid-Devon" (another name for the Ashburton division of the county) was not a parliamentary borough. The date of Royal Assent to the Act was August 13, 1888, to be effective not later than November 8, 1888. How far in advance of August could Sir Charles have been the "probable candidate" for a district not yet officially created? Either the date of Holmes's involvement in *The Hound of the Baskervilles*, discussed in *Appendix 5*, must take this into account, and those chronologies who date the case prior to 1888 must be rejected, or we must conclude that the borough named is Watsonian obfuscation.

sion. Dr. James Mortimer, the friend and medical attendant of the deceased, has given evidence to the same effect.

The facts of the case are simple. Sir Charles Baskerville was in the habit every night before going to bed of walking down the famous Yew Alley of Baskerville Hall. The evidence of the Barrymores shows that this had been his custom. On the 4th of June Sir Charles had declared his intention of starting next day for London, and had ordered Barrymore to prepare his luggage. That night he went out as usual for his nocturnal walk, in the course of which he was in the habit of smoking a cigar. He never returned. At twelve o'clock Barrymore, finding the hall door still open, became alarmed and, lighting a lantern, went in search of his master. The day had been wet, and Sir Charles's footmarks were easily traced down the Alley, and it was at the far end of it that his body was discovered. One fact which has not been explained is the statement of Barrymore that his master's footprints altered their character

"His body was discovered."
Sidney Paget, *Strand Magazine*, 1901

from the time that he passed the moor-gate, and that he appeared from thence onwards to have been walking on his toes. One Murphy, a gipsy horse-dealer, was on the moor at no great distance at the time, but he appears by his own confession to have been the worse for drink. He declares that he heard cries, but is unable to state from what direction they came. No signs of violence were to be discovered upon Sir Charles's person and though the doctor's evidence pointed to an almost incredible facial distortion—so great that Dr. Mortimer refused at first to believe that it was indeed his friend and patient who lay before him—it was explained that this is a symptom which is not unusual in cases of dyspnœa[39] and death from cardiac exhaustion. This explanation was borne out by the post-mortem examination, which showed long standing organic disease, and the coroner's jury returned a verdict in accordance with the medical evidence.[40] It is well that this is so, for it is obviously of the utmost importance that Sir Charles's heir should settle at the Hall, and continue the good work which has been so sadly interrupted. Had the prosaic finding of the coroner not finally put an end to the romantic stories which have been whispered in connection with the affair, it might have been difficult to find a tennant for Baskerville Hall. It is understood that the next-of-kin is Mr. Henry Baskerville, if he be still alive, the son of Sir Charles Baskerville's younger brother. The young man, when last heard of, was in America, and inquiries are being instituted with a view to informing him of his good fortune.

Dr. Mortimer refolded his paper and replaced it in his pocket.

"Those are the public facts, Mr. Holmes, in connection with the death of Sir Charles Baskerville."

"I must thank you," said Sherlock Holmes, "for calling my attention to a case which certainly presents some features of interest. I had observed some newspaper comment at the time, but I was exceedingly preoccupied by that little affair of the Vatican cameos, and in my anxiety to oblige the Pope[41] I lost touch with several interesting English cases. This article, you say, contains all the public facts?"

"It does."

39 Difficult or laboured breathing.

40 Under the English legal system, the coroner, a public appointee, was charged, in the event of a sudden or violent death, to inquire how the decedent came to his or her death. For this purpose, a jury of not fewer than twelve persons was convened and an inquisition held before the coroner and the jury. If a person were found guilty of murder or other homicide by the jury, the coroner committed the alleged criminal to prison for trial, certified the material evidence to the court, and bound over the proper persons to prosecute or give evidence at the trial.

41 Leo XIII was elected to the papacy on February 20, 1878, and held office until his death on July 20, 1903. Viewed as less conservative than his immediate predecessor, Pius IX, he worked to reconcile Victorian religion and science, undoing the damage caused by Pius IX's *Syllabus of Errors*, which had dealt a serious setback to rationalism and secularism. Leo XIII, who had studied law but was best known for his economic teachings, also used his position as head of the Church to expose what he perceived to be the failures of both Marxism and imperial capitalism.

Aside from his work on the Vatican cameos, Holmes investigated the "sudden death of Cardinal Tosca . . . at the express desire of" Leo XIII ("Black Peter"). Perhaps the Master Detective's special allegiance to Leo XIII can be partly explained by the pope's awarding of a gold medal to a popular cocaine-based cocktail, *Vin Mariani*, also enjoyed by Queen Victoria and by Leo's successor, St. Pius X.

"Then let me have the private ones." He leaned back, put his finger-tips together, and assumed his most impassive and judicial expression.

"In doing so," said Dr. Mortimer, who had begun to show signs of strong emotion, "I am telling that which I have not confided to anyone. My motive for withholding it from the coroner's inquiry is that a man of science shrinks from placing himself in the public position of seeming to indorse a popular superstition. I had the further motive that the Baskerville Hall, as the paper says, would certainly remain untenanted if anything were done to increase its already rather grim reputation. For both these reasons I thought that I was justified in telling rather less than I knew, since no practical good could result from it, but with you there is no reason why I should not be perfectly frank.

"The moor is very sparsely inhabited, and those who live near each other are thrown very much together. For this reason I saw a good deal of Sir Charles Baskerville. With the exception of Mr. Frankland, of Lafter Hall, and Mr. Stapleton, the naturalist, there are no other men of education within many miles. Sir Charles was a retiring man, but the chance of his illness brought us together, and a community of interests in science kept us so. He had brought back much scientific information from South Africa, and many a charming evening we have spent together discussing the comparative anatomy of the Bushman and the Hottentot.[42]

"Within the last few months it became increasingly plain to me that Sir Charles's nervous system was strained to breaking point. He had taken this legend which I have read you exceedingly to heart—so much so that, although he would walk in his own grounds, nothing would induce him to go out upon the moor at night. Incredible as it may appear to you, Mr. Holmes, he was honestly convinced that a dreadful fate overhung his family, and certainly the records which he was able to give of his ancestors were not encouraging. The idea of some ghastly presence constantly haunted him, and on more than one occasion he has asked me whether I had on my medical journeys at night ever seen any strange creature or heard the baying of a hound. The latter question he put to me several times, and always with a voice which vibrated with excitement.

"I can well remember driving up to his house in the evening,

42 The San (Bushmen), a shortening of the names Soaqua, Sonqua, and San-qua, live in South Africa. The Khoikhoi, or Khoekhoen, also known by the names Nama and Hottentot, today make up approximately 5 percent of Namibia's population of 1.7 million. Both groups' relatively short stature made them the subject of study by comparative anatomists in the 1880s, although many such investigations were marred and rendered largely irrelevant by ethnocentrist assumptions. In "Anthropology in *The Hound of the Baskervilles*," W. M. Krogman suggests that the particular topic of conversation would have been the development of the buttocks and external genitalia of these two racial groups. This being the age of phrenology (see *A Study in Scarlet*, note 206, above), relative brain size might also have been discussed. The pitfalls of imperial ethnocentricity aside, a rich area of study was shared language derivation: Both the Khoikhoi and the San speak "click" languages, wherein many words are expressed with clicking sounds, rendered with exclamation marks. The beautiful 1984 comedic film *The Gods Must Be Crazy* depicts the San culture and its disruption by a soda bottle.

"I saw his eyes fix themselves over my shoulder."
Sidney Paget, *Strand Magazine*, 1901

some three weeks before the fatal event. He chanced to be at his hall door. I had descended from my gig[43] and was standing in front of him, when I saw his eyes fix themselves over my shoulder, and stare past me with an expression of the most dreadful horror. I whisked round and had just time to catch a glimpse of something which I took to be a large black calf passing at the head of the drive. So excited and alarmed was he that I was compelled to go down to the spot where the animal had been and look around for it. It was gone, however, and the incident appeared to make the worst impression upon his mind. I stayed with him all the evening and it was on that occasion, to explain the emotion which he had shown, that he confided to my keeping that narrative which I read to you when first I came. I mention this small episode because it assumes some importance in view of the tragedy which followed, but I was

43 A light two-wheeled carriage pulled by a single horse.

convinced at the time that the matter was entirely trivial and that his excitement had no justification.

"It was at my advice that Sir Charles was about to go to London. His heart was, I knew, affected, and the constant anxiety in which he lived, however chimerical the cause of it might be, was evidently having a serious effect upon his health. I thought that a few months among the distractions of town would send him back a new man. Mr. Stapleton, a mutual friend, who was much concerned at his state of health, was of the same opinion. At the last instant came this terrible catastrophe.

"On the night of Sir Charles's death Barrymore the butler, who made the discovery, sent Perkins the groom on horseback to me, and as I was sitting up late I was able to reach Baskerville Hall within an hour of the event. I checked and corroborated all the facts which were mentioned at the inquest. I followed the footsteps down the Yew Alley, I saw the spot at

"Sir Charles lay on his face, his arms out,
his fingers dug into the ground . . ."
Richard Gutschmidt, *Der Hund von Baskerville* (Stuttgart: Robert Lutz Verlag, 1903)

the moor-gate where he seemed to have waited, I remarked the change in the shape of the prints after that point, I noted that there were no other footsteps save those of Barrymore on the soft gravel, and finally I carefully examined the body, which had not been touched until my arrival. Sir Charles lay on his face, his arms out, his fingers dug into the ground, and his features convulsed with some strong emotion to such an extent that I could hardly have sworn to his identity. There was certainly no physical injury of any kind. But one false statement was made by Barrymore at the inquest. He said that there were no traces upon the ground round the body. He did not observe any. But I did—some little distance off, but fresh and clear."

"Footprints?"

H. T. Webster, *New York Herald Tribune*, April 16, 1938

"Footprints."

"A man's or a woman's?"

Dr. Mortimer looked strangely at us for an instant, and his voice sank almost to a whisper as he answered:

"Mr. Holmes, they were the footprints of a gigantic hound!"[44]

44 "As any naturalist will assure you, it is not possible to identify the breed of a dog by his footprint any more [than] the hue of a rose from its odour," Professor Remsen Schenck objects, in a letter to the editor of the *Baker Street Journal*. "As Gertrude Stein might put it, when it comes to pawprints 'a dog is a dog is a dog.' " Schenck concedes that the size of the dog could be determined and perhaps whether the dog was shaggy (producing blurred tracks). "But to decide just like that whether a given set of prints were made by a Great Dane, a hound, a Newfoundland, a St. Bernard, or just plain dog? Never!"

Robert Clyne replies in another letter to the editor of the *Journal*: "Technically [Professor Schenck] may be right—but he has not taken into consideration the psychological impact of the Legend. Mortimer was acting quite normally in assuming that the dog was a hound." Edgar W. Smith, editor of the *Journal*, responds: "There is a point here. And there is, in addition to the psychological impact, a poetic one as well. I remember one of my sons, when he was very young, going about the house muttering: "Mr. Holmes, they were the footprints of a gigantic cocker-spaniel!" That, I am sure, would not have had quite the same dramatic effect . . ."

CHAPTER III

The Problem

I CONFESS THAT AT these words a shudder passed through me. There was a thrill in the doctor's voice which showed that he was himself deeply moved by that which he told us. Holmes leaned forward in his excitement, and his eyes had the hard, dry glitter which shot from them when he was keenly interested.

"You saw this?"

"As clearly as I see you."

"And you said nothing?"

"What was the use?"

"How was it that no one else saw it?"

"The marks were some twenty yards from the body, and no one gave them a thought. I don't suppose I should have done so had I not known this legend."

"There are many sheep-dogs on the moor?"

"No doubt, but this was no sheep-dog."

"You say it was large?"

"Enormous."

"But it had not approached the body?"

"No."

Dustjacket, *The Hound of the Baskervilles.*
(London: Evelyn, Nash & Grayson, Ltd., *ca.* 1940)

"What sort of night was it?"

"Damp and raw."

"But not actually raining?"

"No."

"What is the alley like?"

"There are two lines of old yew hedge, twelve feet high and impenetrable. The walk in the centre is about eight feet across."

"Is there anything between the hedges and the walk?"

"Yes, there is a strip of grass about six feet broad on either side."

"I understand that the yew hedge is penetrated at one point by a gate?"

"Yes, the wicket-gate which leads on to the moor."

"Is there any other opening?"

"None."

"So that to reach the Yew Alley one either has to come down it from the house or else to enter it by the moor-gate?"

"There is an exit through a summer-house at the far end."

"Had Sir Charles reached this?"

"No; he lay about fifty yards from it."

"Now, tell me, Dr. Mortimer—and this is important—the marks which you saw were on the path and not on the grass?"

"No marks could show on the grass."

"Were they on the same side of the path as the moor-gate?"

"Yes; they were on the edge of the path on the same side as the moor-gate."

"You interest me exceedingly. Another point. Was the wicket-gate closed?"

"Closed and padlocked."

"How high was it?"

"About four feet high."

"Then anyone could have got over it?"

"Yes."

"And what marks did you see by the wicket-gate?"

"None in particular."

"Good Heaven! Did no one examine?"

"Yes, I examined myself."

"And found nothing?"

"It was all very confused. Sir Charles had evidently stood there for five or ten minutes."

"How do you know that?"

"Because the ash had twice dropped from his cigar."

"Excellent! This is a colleague, Watson, after our own heart. But the marks?"

"He had left his own marks all over that small patch of gravel. I could discern no others."

Sherlock Holmes struck his hand against his knee with an impatient gesture.

"If I had only been there!" he cried. "It is evidently a case of extraordinary interest, and one which presented immense opportunities to the scientific expert. That gravel page upon which I might have read so much has been long ere this smudged by the rain and defaced by the clogs of curious peasants. Oh, Dr. Mortimer, Dr. Mortimer, to think that you should not have called me in! You have indeed much to answer for."

"I could not call you in, Mr. Holmes, without disclosing these facts to the world, and I have already given my reasons for not wishing to do so. Besides, besides—"

"Why do you hesitate?"

"There is a realm in which the most acute and most experienced of detectives is helpless."

"You mean that the thing is supernatural?"

"I did not positively say so."

"No, but you evidently think it."

" 'You have indeed much to answer for.' "
Sidney Paget, *Strand Magazine*, 1901

"Since the tragedy, Mr. Holmes, there have come to my ears several incidents which are hard to reconcile with the settled order of Nature."

"For example?"

"I find that before the terrible event occurred several people had seen a creature upon the moor which corresponds with this Baskerville demon, and which could not possibly be any animal known to science. They all agreed that it was a huge creature, luminous, ghastly, and spectral. I have cross-examined these men, one of them a hard-headed countryman, one a farrier,[45] and one a moorland farmer, who all tell the same story of this dreadful apparition, exactly corresponding to the hell-hound of the legend. I assure you that there is a reign of terror in the district, and that it is a hardy man who will cross the moor at night."

"And you, a trained man of science, believe it to be supernatural?"

"I do not know what to believe."

Holmes shrugged his shoulders. "I have hitherto confined my investigations to this world," said he. "In a modest way I have combatted evil, but to take on the Father of Evil himself would, perhaps, be too ambitious a task. Yet you must admit that the footmark is material."

"The original hound was material enough to tug a man's throat out, and yet he was diabolical as well."

"I see that you have quite gone over to the supernaturalists. But now, Dr. Mortimer, tell me this. If you hold these views, why have you come to consult me at all? You tell me in the same breath that it is useless to investigate Sir Charles's death, and that you desire me to do it."

"I did not say that I desired you to do it."

"Then how can I assist you?"

"By advising me as to what I should do with Sir Henry Baskerville, who arrives at Waterloo Station"—Dr. Mortimer looked at his watch—"in exactly one hour and a quarter."

"He being the heir?"

"Yes. On the death of Sir Charles we inquired for this young gentleman, and found that he had been farming in Canada.[46] From the accounts which have reached us he is an excellent fellow in every way. I speak now not as a medical man but as a trustee and executor of Sir Charles's will."

45 That is, a blacksmith.

46 Peter H. Wood, in "He Has Been Farming in Canada," studies the subject in some detail. Although Wood suggests that Henry Baskerville spent some time in Virginia, the exact place in Western Canada where he farmed remains unknown. Wood traces the history of several Western Canadian farms, including one frequented by the outlaws Robert LeRoy Parker and Harry Alonzo Longabaugh, a k a Butch Cassidy and the Sundance Kid.

"There is no other claimant, I presume?"

"None. The only other kinsman whom we have been able to trace was Rodger Baskerville, the youngest of the three brothers of whom poor Sir Charles was the elder. The second brother, who died young, is the father of this lad Henry. The third, Rodger, was the black sheep of the family. He came of the old masterful Baskerville strain, and was the very image, they tell me, of the family picture of old Hugo. He made England too hot to hold him, fled to Central America, and died there in 1876 of yellow fever. Henry is the last of the Baskervilles. In one hour and five minutes[47] I meet him at Waterloo Station. I have had a wire that he arrived at Southampton this morning. Now, Mr. Holmes, what would you advise me to do with him?"

"Why should he not go to the home of his fathers?"

"It seems natural, does it not? And yet, consider that every Baskerville who goes there meets with an evil fate. I feel sure that if Sir Charles could have spoken with me before his death he would have warned me against bringing this, the last of the old race, and the heir to great wealth, to that deadly place. And yet it cannot be denied that the prosperity of the whole poor, bleak countryside depends upon his presence. All the good work which has been done by Sir Charles will crash to the ground if there is no tenant of the Hall. I fear lest I should be swayed too much by my own obvious interest in the matter, and that is why I bring the case before you and ask for your advice."

Holmes considered for a little time. "Put into plain words, the matter is this," said he. "In your opinion there is a diabolical agency which makes Dartmoor an unsafe abode for a Baskerville—that is your opinion?"

"At least I might go the length of saying that there is some evidence that this may be so."

"Exactly. But surely, if your supernatural theory be correct, it could work the young man evil in London as easily as in Devonshire. A devil with merely local powers like a parish vestry[48] would be too inconceivable a thing."

"You put the matter more flippantly, Mr. Holmes, than you would probably do if you were brought into personal contact with these things. Your advice, then, as I understand it, is that the young man will be as safe in Devonshire as in London. He comes in fifty minutes.[49] What would you recommend?"

47 Note that ten minutes have mysteriously passed.

48 In this context, the administrative body of the local Church of England parish.

49 Another fifteen minutes vanishes. Apparently Watson has omitted much of the actual dialogue.

"I recommend, sir, that you take a cab, call off your spaniel, who is scratching at my front door, and proceed to Waterloo to meet Sir Henry Baskerville."

"And then?"

"And then you will say nothing to him at all until I have made up my mind about the matter."

"How long will it take you to make up your mind?"

"Twenty-four hours. At ten o'clock tomorrow, Dr. Mortimer, I will be much obliged to you if you will call upon me here, and it will be of help to me in my plans for the future if you will bring Sir Henry Baskerville with you."

"I will do so, Mr. Holmes."

He scribbled the appointment on his shirt-cuff and hurried off in his strange, peering, absent-minded fashion. Holmes stopped him at the head of the stair.

"Only one more question, Dr. Mortimer. You say that before

"He scribbled the appointment on his shirt cuff."
Sidney Paget, *Strand Magazine*, 1901

"He scribbled the appointment on his shirt cuff."
Richard Gutschmidt, *Der Hund von Baskerville*
(Stuttgart: Robert Lutz Verlag, 1903)

Sir Charles Baskerville's death several people saw this apparition upon the moor?"

"Three people did."

"Did any see it after?"

"I have not heard of any."

"Thank you. Good morning."

Holmes returned to his seat with that quiet look of inward satisfaction which meant that he had a congenial task before him.

"Going out, Watson?"

"Unless I can help you."

"No, my dear fellow, it is at the hour of action that I turn to you for aid. But this is splendid, really unique from some points of view. When you pass Bradley's would you ask him to send up a pound of the strongest shag tobacco? Thank you. It would be as well if you could make it convenient not to return before evening. Then I should be very glad to compare impressions as to this most interesting problem which has been submitted to us this morning."

I knew that seclusion and solitude were very necessary for my friend in those hours of intense mental concentration during which he weighed every particle of evidence, constructed alternative theories, balanced one against the other, and made up his mind as to which points were essential and which immaterial. I therefore spent the day at my club,[50] and did not return to Baker Street until evening. It was nearly nine o'clock when I found myself in the sitting-room once more.

My first impression as I opened the door was that a fire had broken out, for the room was so filled with smoke that the light of the lamp upon the table was blurred by it. As I entered, however, my fears were set at rest, for it was the acrid fumes of strong, coarse tobacco, which took me by the throat and set me coughing. Through the haze I had a vague vision of Holmes in his dressing-gown coiled up in an arm-chair with his black clay pipe between his lips. Several rolls of paper lay around him.

"Caught cold, Watson?" said he.

"No, it's this poisonous atmosphere."

"I suppose it *is* pretty thick, now that you mention it."

"Thick! It is intolerable."

"Open the window, then! You have been at your club all day, I perceive."

"My dear Holmes!"

"Am I right?"

"Certainly, but how—?"

He laughed at my bewildered expression.

"There is a delightful freshness about you, Watson, which makes it a pleasure to exercise any small powers which I possess at your expense. A gentleman goes forth on a showery and miry day. He returns immaculate in the evening with the gloss still on his hat and his boots. He has been a fixture, therefore, all day. He is not a man with intimate friends. Where, then, could he have been? Is it not obvious?"

"Well, it is rather obvious."

"The world is full of obvious things which nobody by any chance ever observes. Where do you think that I have been?"

"A fixture also."

"On the contrary, I have been to Devonshire."

50 It is tempting to identify this club as the United Service Club, founded in May 1831 as the general military club for naval and military officers. Ralph Nevill, in his *London Clubs, Their History and Treasures*, observes that the club had the nickname "Cripplegate"—"from the prevailing advanced years and infirmity of its members. . . . The United Service contains many interesting pictures, [including a portrait of] Major-General Charles G. Gordon, by Dickinson, from a photograph. . . . In the upper billiard-room is a picture of the Battle of Trafalgar, the frame of which is wood from the timbers of the *Victory*." The United Service Club faces Pall Mall, and Watson must have joined it *after* the events of "The Greek Interpreter," for he would surely otherwise have mentioned the proximity of "his" club to that of Mycroft.

In "The Clubbable Watson," Dean Dickensheet argues that Watson would have been excluded by the cliques as a mere army *doctor* and suggests that Watson was a member of the Savage Club, located at Nos. 6 and 7 Adelphi Terrace, near Cox & Co. (where Watson's tin dispatch-box filled with untold tales was on deposit—see "The Veiled Lodger"), as well as the Author's Club, of which Arthur Conan Doyle was also a member.

"In spirit?"

"Exactly. My body has remained in this arm-chair; and has, I regret to observe, consumed in my absence two large pots of coffee and an incredible amount of tobacco. After you left I sent down to Stamford's[51] for the Ordnance map of this portion of the moor,[52] and my spirit has hovered over it all day. I flatter myself that I could find my way about."

"A large-scale map, I presume?"

"Very large."[53] He unrolled one section and held it over his knee. "Here you have the particular district which concerns us. That is Baskerville Hall in the middle."

"With a wood round it?"

"Exactly. I fancy the Yew Alley, though not marked under that name, must stretch along this line, with the moor, as you perceive, upon the right of it. This small clump of buildings here is the hamlet of Grimpen,[54] where our friend Dr. Mortimer has his headquarters. Within a radius of five miles there are, as you see, only a very few scattered dwellings. Here is

"He unrolled one section and held it over his knee."
Richard Gutschmidt, *Der Hund von Baskerville*
(Stuttgart: Robert Lutz Verlag, 1903)

51 Karl Baedeker's *London and Its Environs: Handbook for Travellers* (1896) gives "E. *Stanford*" of 26 Cockspur Street, Charing Cross, as the agent for the Ordnance Survey Maps.

52 Philip Weller, in "Moor Maps and Mileages," points out that no single Ordnance map of Dartmoor fits the description provided by Watson. Jay Finley Christ, in "A Very Large Scale Map," using such maps, concludes that no place shown on the maps meets all of the necessary determinants. "It is for cartologists, amateur and pro, to determine which places were fictional and which were pure Devon; and [echoing a footnote in Thomas Hardy's *Far from the Madding Crowd*] it is our happy privilege to indicate that some of the distances and places 'do not answer precisely to the [Canonical] description.' And so much the worse for them!"

53 Holmes means "large-scale" in the sense of a map of a small area, showing fine details. In 1801, the first series of 1-inch maps (that is, one inch equalling 63,360 inches [1 mile]) of England were produced. The year 1846 saw the production of larger-scale maps of England (6 inches equalling one mile), and very large-scale maps (25 inches to the mile) were produced in 1855.

The terminology can be confusing: "Large-scale" means smaller numbers if the "representative fraction," or "RF," scale is used. This method gives as the ratio of map distances to actual distance on the surface of the Earth, without indication of units (for example, 1:63,360, 1:10,060). (Note that there are 12 x 5,280, or 63,360, inches to the mile.) According to the *Encyclopædia Britannica* (9th Ed.), the typical Ordnance Survey parish map had a large scale of 1:2500, the typical town map a very large scale of 1:500 (and, of course, consisted of numerous sheets). Thus a map at the normal 1-inch (1:63,360 RF) scale showing a radius of five miles (10 miles wide) would be

10 inches wide, while a 6-inch scale map (1:10,060) would be 5 feet square. At the parish scale of 1:2500, a five-mile radius requires a map over 20 feet square and at the town scale of 1:500 would be over 100 feet square! (Sabine Baring-Gould's fine handbook entitled *Devon* [1907] reproduces the entire area on a map about two feet square, which uses a scale of 4 miles to the inch (that is, 1:253,440), but of course this does not show anything so small as

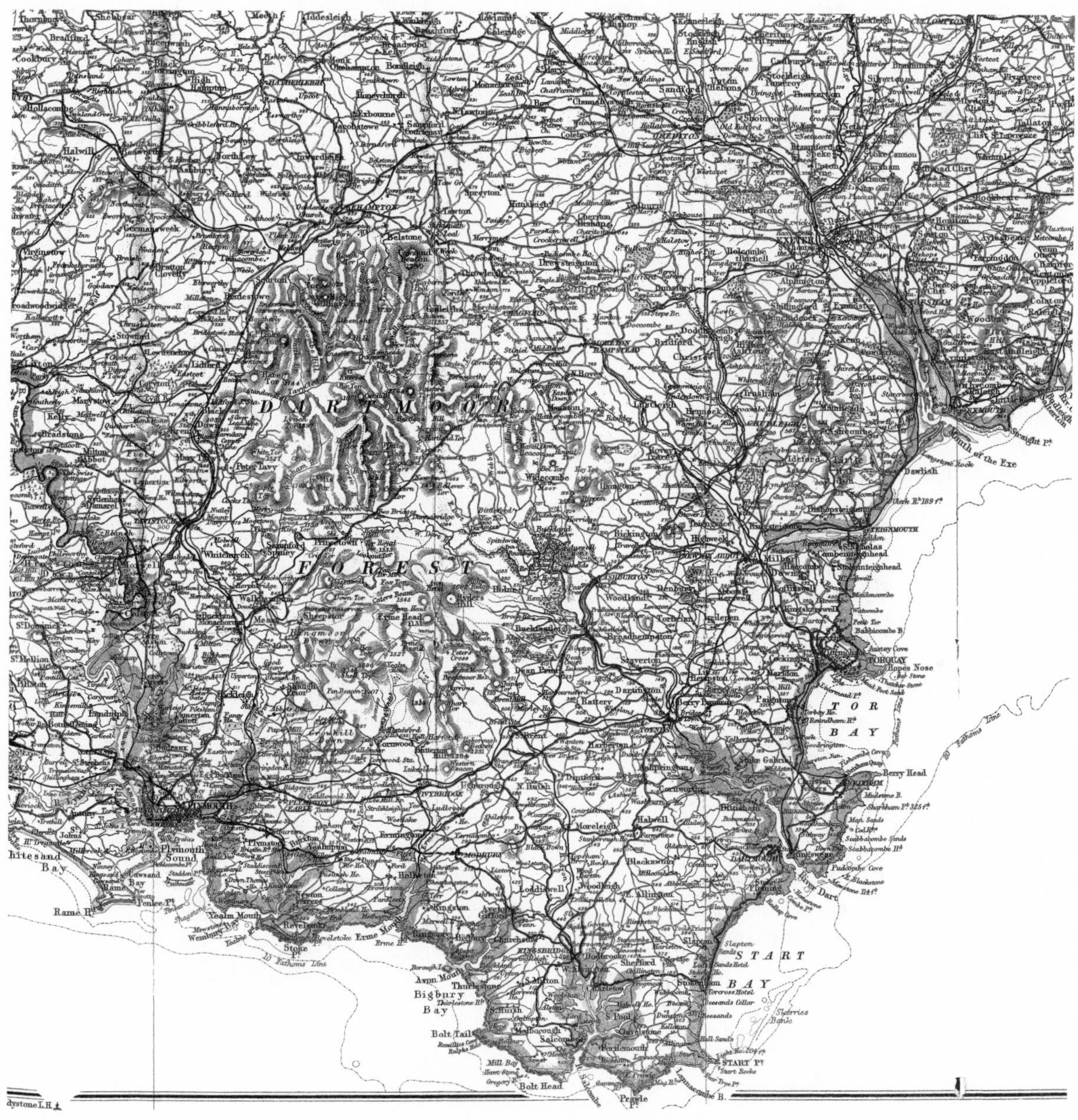

Section of map of Dartmoor (original scale 4 miles to 1 inch, reproduced here at approximately 10 miles to 1 inch).

Sabine Baring-Gould, *Devon*, 1907

a "clump of buildings.") If Holmes had only a single map showing the relevant area, it was likely a 6-inch scale map, which would be convenient to use if folded. Watson states that Holmes "unrolled" a section—rolling such a map would have produced an unwieldy five-foot-long tube!

54 While there is no "Grimpen" listed in either *Beeton's British Gazetteer* or Karl Baedeker's *Great Britain: Handbook for Travellers*, several sources note *Grimspound*, characterised in *Baedeker as* "a curious enclosure, the object of which is uncertain." Sabine Baring-Gould's *Devon* describes it in more detail as "a circular enclosure in singularly perfect condition, with a gateway, paved, to the S.E. It encloses 24 hut circles, of which at least 12 can be proved to have been inhabited. The settlement belongs to the early Bronze Age."

Numerous commentators consider the true identity of "Grimpen" and the "Grimpen Mire." David L. Hammer, in *The Game Is Afoot*, concludes that the village is actually Hexworthy. This is based on his conclusion that Brook Manor is Baskerville Hall (see *Appendix 4*). Bernard Davies, in "Radical Rethinks on Baskervillean Problems—I," points out in admirable detail that the layout of the village of Postbridge and that of Grimpen are virtually identical. He dismisses the absence of a nearby mire by pointing out that the Grimpen Mire had not always been there, and it may just as well have vanished as mysteriously as it appeared. He also identifies Laughter Hole Farm as Lafter Hall and Stannon as Merripit House but offers no identification of Baskerville Hall. The identification of Postbridge as Grimpen is also made by Anthony Howlett, in *Some Observations on the Dartmoor of Sherlock Holmes*.

Philip Weller, in *The Dartmoor of "The Hound of the Baskervilles": A Practical Guide to the Sherlock Holmes Locations*, sums up various candidates: Grimspound (no houses, no mire); Widecombe in the Moor (far from any mires); Postbridge (no mires, no suitable Baskerville Hall), Poundsgate (no suitable mire); Holne (large village, a little too close to a Baskerville Hall candidate); and Hexworthy (meets all requirements, except a post office; mail was delivered to and collected from the Hexworthy pub).

In a subsequent article, entitled "Take Moor Care: Some Considerations of Playing the Game on Dartmoor," Weller rejects Davies's identification of Postbridge (without specifically referring to Davies's article), pointing out that Stannon Mire, near Postbridge, while shown on some maps as a "mire," "even in Victorian times . . . was cultivated, and those who walk across it will find it difficult to find a spot where one can sink more than a foot into the mud, even in the wettest of seasons." He raises other objections to Davies's Merripit House on the basis of its proximity to other residences.

Weller perhaps best sums up the entire quandary when he writes: "It has to be admitted from the outset that, apart from those few locations in the case which are given their real Dartmoor names . . . , none of the Dartmoor locations . . . have been definitively identified."

" 'That is Baskerville Hall in the middle.' "
Sidney Paget, *Strand Magazine*, 1901

Lafter Hall,[55] which was mentioned in the narrative. There is a house indicated here which may be the residence of the naturalist—Stapleton, if I remember right, was his name. Here are two moorland farm-houses, High Tor[56] and Foulmire.[57] Then fourteen miles away[58] the great convict prison of Princetown.[59] Between and around these scattered points extends the desolate, lifeless moor. This, then, is the stage upon which tragedy has been played, and upon which we may help to play it again."

"It must be a wild place."

"Yes, the setting is a worthy one. If the devil did desire to have a hand in the affairs of men—"

"Then you are yourself inclining to the supernatural explanation."

55 If "the narrative" refers to the narration of the legend of the Hound, Holmes is incorrect; Lafter Hall is *not* mentioned there. William S. Baring-Gould writes that there is no Lafter Hall on their map but a Laughter Tor, "and it seems fair to assume that Laughter ('Lafter') Hall stood somewhere in its vicinity." David L. Hammer, in *For the Sake of the Game*, discards that attribution, as there are no halls in the vicinity of the Tor.

Watson, later writing to Holmes from Baskerville Hall, describes "Lafter Hall" as "four miles to the south of us." Philip Weller considers the candidates: Laughter Hole Farm (near a Grimpen candidate but no suitable Baskerville Hall to the north); Hannaford Manor (no suitable Hall to the north); Spitchwick Manor (no Moor views, no suitable Hall to the north); White-Oxen Manor (close to Hall candidates but no Moor views and no views of approaches to stone huts); Leigh Grange (no Moor views); Greendown (no Moor views); and Hayford Hall (ideal in all respects except, unfortunately, it was only a farm and not a "hall" until 1912, long after the events here).

56 Baring-Gould locates a Higher Tor and a Higher White Tor but no High Tor.

57 Presumably this is a place, not the name of a farm house.

58 Pointing out that the moor's south-east corner forms a quadrant from the prison varying in radius from seven to eleven miles, in *The Dartmoor of "The Hound of the Baskervilles,"* Philip Weller calculates that fourteen miles from the prison would be off the moor altogether, and that "fourteen" is possibly a typographical error and should read "four." Weller adds, in "Moor Maps and Mileages," that "fourteen miles" was apparently a colloquialism for any long distance.

59 See note 218 of *The Sign of Four*, above.

"The devil's agents may be of flesh and blood, may they not? There are two questions waiting for us at the outset. The one is whether any crime has been committed at all; the second is, what is the crime and how was it committed? Of course, if Dr. Mortimer's surmise should be correct, and we are dealing with forces outside the ordinary laws of Nature, there is an end of our investigation. But we are bound to exhaust all other hypotheses before falling back upon this one. I think we'll shut that window again, if you don't mind. It is a singular thing, but I find that a concentrated atmosphere helps a concentration of thought.[60] I have not pushed it to the length of getting into a box to think, but that is the logical outcome of my convictions. Have you turned the case over in your mind?"

"Yes, I have thought a good deal of it in the course of the day."

"What do you make of it?"

"It is very bewildering."

"It has certainly a character of its own. There are points of distinction about it. That change in the footprints, for example. What do you make of that?"

"Mortimer said that the man had walked on tiptoe down that portion of the alley."

"He only repeated what some fool had said at the inquest. Why should a man walk on tiptoe down the alley?"

"What then?"

"He was running, Watson—running desperately, running for his life, running until he burst his heart and fell dead upon his face."

"Running from what?"

"There lies our problem. There are indications that the man was crazed with fear before ever he began to run."

"How can you say that?"

"I am presuming that the cause of his fears came to him across the moor. If that were so, and it seems most probable, only a man who had lost his wits would have run *from* the house instead of towards it. If the gipsy's evidence may be taken as true, he ran with the cries for help in the direction where help was least likely to be. Then again, whom was he waiting for that night, and why was he waiting for him in the Yew Alley rather than in his own house?"

"You think that he was waiting for someone?"

60 T. S. Blakeney draws our attention to "The Man with the Twisted Lip," in which Watson shares a room at The Cedars with Holmes. While Watson sleeps, Holmes stays up all night thinking and goes through "an ounce of shag tobacco." "If it is true that the English people enjoy a 'frowst' more than others," Blakeney writes—"frowst" meaning a stuffy or stale odour—"Holmes was, on unimpeachable testimony, English of the English."

"The man was elderly and infirm. We can understand his taking an evening stroll, but the ground was damp and the night inclement. Is it natural that he should stand for five or ten minutes, as Dr. Mortimer, with more practical sense than I should have given him credit for, deduced from the cigar ash?"

"But he went out every evening."

"I think it unlikely that he waited at the moor-gate every evening. On the contrary, the evidence is that he avoided the moor. That night he waited there. It was the night before he was to take his departure for London. The thing takes shape, Watson. It becomes coherent. Might I ask you to hand me my violin, and we will postpone all further thought upon this business until we have had the advantage of meeting Dr. Mortimer and Sir Henry Baskerville in the morning."

CHAPTER IV

Sir Henry Baskerville

61 A British title of hereditary rank, not nobility, introduced in 1611 by James I to raise funds. According to Alfred Miles's *Household Oracle* (1897), the title immediately follows barons' younger sons and precedes Knights of the Thistle (but is below Knights of the Garter). Baronetcies are acceded to by the title holder's eldest legitimate son.

OUR BREAKFAST-TABLE was cleared early, and Holmes waited in his dressing-gown for the promised interview. Our clients were punctual to their appointment, for the clock had just struck ten when Dr. Mortimer was shown up, followed by the young baronet.[61] The latter was a small, alert, dark-eyed man about thirty years of age, very sturdily built, with thick black eyebrows, and a strong, pugnacious face. He wore a ruddy-tinted tweed suit, and had the weather-beaten appearance of one who has spent most of his time in the open air, and yet there was something in his steady eye and the quiet assurance of his bearing which indicated the gentleman.

"This is Sir Henry Baskerville," said Dr. Mortimer.

"Why, yes," said he, "and the strange thing is, Mr. Sherlock Holmes, that if my friend here had not proposed coming round to you this morning I should have come on my own. I understand that you think out little puzzles, and I've had one this morning which wants more thinking out than I am able to give to it."

"Pray take a seat, Sir Henry. Do I understand you to say that

Sir Henry Baskerville.
Sidney Paget, *Strand Magazine*, 1901

you have yourself had some remarkable experience since you arrived in London?"

"Nothing of much importance, Mr. Holmes. Only a joke, as like as not. It was this letter, if you can call it a letter, which reached me this morning."

He laid an envelope upon the table, and we all bent over it. It was of common quality, greyish in colour. The address, "Sir Henry Baskerville, Northumberland Hotel,"[62] was printed in rough characters; the post-mark "Charing Cross,"[63] and the date of posting the preceding evening.

"Who knew that you were going to the Northumberland Hotel?" asked Holmes, glancing keenly across at our visitor.

62 *Baedeker* lists no Northumberland Hotel, and Michael Harrison, in *The London of Sherlock Holmes* and elsewhere, identifies this as the Northumberland Arms, a tavern/inn, which, in a pleasant twist of fate, is now the Sherlock Holmes tavern and restaurant, at No. 11, Northumberland Street. If Sir Henry sought anonymity, this was a sound choice; however, as the heir, he would have been expected to stay in more luxurious lodgings, and some scholars therefore question Harrison's identification. Vernon Goslin, in "Did Baskerville Stay at the Northumberland Hotel?," concludes that three large, well-known hotels—the Métropole, the Victoria, and the Grand, all in Northumberland Avenue (and all owned by the same company)—were far more likely places for Sir Henry to stay. A. Godfrey Hunt dismisses the Grand on the grounds that Stapleton would not take a cab in Trafalgar Square to drive to a hotel that is in fact on Trafalgar Square. Furthermore, Watson probably would not have chosen the Northumberland Hotel alias for a hotel on Trafalgar Square. Catherine Cooke, in "We Found Ourselves at the Northumberland Hotel," points out that the Hotel Victoria was originally planned in the early 1880s as the Northumberland Hotel but ran into financial difficulties and, when opened in 1887, used the other name, presumably in honour of the Queen's Golden Jubilee.

63 A district in central London, it is so named for the stone cross placed there in 1290 by Edward I, marking the final stop of twelve along the route of the funeral procession for his first wife, Eleanor of Castile. (The decaying cross was destroyed in 1643 and replaced with a copy in 1863.) "Charing" is thought by some to be a corruption of *chère reine*, or French for "beloved queen"; others think it a corruption of the village "Cheringe," which stood there in the thirteenth century. It is frequently mentioned in the Canon, and Holmes and Watson regularly used the Charing Cross railway station. In "The Bruce-Partington Plans," a trap for a foreign agent was set at the Charing Cross Hotel. Even a century earlier, Samuel Johnson had remarked, "I think the full tide of human existence is at Charing Cross."

Today Charing Cross Road, long the home of antiquarian booksellers, may be best remembered from the title of Helene Hanff's 1970 *84, Charing Cross Road* (and the subsequent film), a charming record of a New Yorker's tender, sometimes combative correspondence with a bookseller located there.

64 Charles M. Pickard contends that Mortimer himself sent the note, in disregard of Holmes's instructions to remain silent about his suspicions of Stapleton.

Northumberland Avenue from Trafalgar Square (1894). The "Northumberland Hotel"?

"No one could have known. We only decided after I met Dr. Mortimer."

"But Dr. Mortimer was, no doubt, already stopping there?"

"No, I had been staying with a friend," said the doctor. "There was no possible indication that we intended to go to this hotel."

"Hum! Someone seems to be very deeply interested in your movements." Out of the envelope he took a half-sheet of foolscap paper folded into four. This he opened and spread flat upon the table. Across the middle of it a single sentence had been formed by the expedient of pasting printed words upon it. It ran:

AS YOU VALUE YOUR LIFE OR YOUR REASON KEEP AWAY FROM THE MOOR.

The word "moor" only was printed in ink.

"Now," said Sir Henry Baskerville, "perhaps you will tell me Mr. Holmes, what in thunder is the meaning of that, and who is it that takes so much interest in my affairs?"

"What do you make of it, Dr. Mortimer? You must allow that there is nothing supernatural about this, at any rate?"

"No, sir, but it might very well come from someone who was convinced that the business is supernatural."[64]

"What business?" asked Sir Henry, sharply. "It seems to me

that all you gentlemen know a great deal more than I do about my own affairs."

"You shall share our knowledge before you leave this room, Sir Henry. I promise you that," said Sherlock Holmes. "We will confine ourselves for the present, with your permission, to this very interesting document, which must have been put together and posted yesterday evening. Have you yesterday's *Times*, Watson?"

"It is here in the corner."

"Might I trouble you for it—the inside page, please, with the leading articles?"[65] He glanced swiftly over it, running his eyes up and down the columns. "Capital article this on Free Trade.[66] Permit me to give you an extract from it.

> You may be cajoled into imagining that your own special trade or your own industry will be encouraged by a protective tariff,

"He glanced swiftly over it."
Sidney Paget, *Strand Magazine*, 1901

65 The "leading articles" or "leaders" are equivalent to American editorials.

66 Gavin Brend, who dates *The Hound of the Baskervilles* in 1899, argues that although free trade would not then have been written about widely, "presumably somebody at Printing House Square was slightly in advance of his time. An article on Free Trade in 1886 or 1889 would surely be quite out of the question." Nonetheless, the 9th edition of the *Encyclopædia Britannica* (1875–1889) devotes eleven pages to the subject.

67 The curve of the upper jaw-bone.

> but it stands to reason that such legislation must in the long run keep away wealth from the country, diminish the value of our imports, and lower the general conditions of life in this island.

What do you think of that, Watson?" cried Holmes, in high glee, rubbing his hands together with satisfaction. "Don't you think that is an admirable sentiment?"

Dr. Mortimer looked at Holmes with an air of professional interest, and Sir Henry Baskerville turned a pair of puzzled dark eyes upon me.

"I don't know much about the tariff and things of that kind," said he; "but it seems to me we've got a bit off the trail so far as that note is concerned."

"On the contrary, I think we are particularly hot upon the trail, Sir Henry. Watson here knows more about my methods than you do, but I fear that even he has not quite grasped the significance of this sentence."

"No, I confess that I see no connection."

"And yet, my dear Watson, there is so very close a connection that the one is extracted out of the other. 'You,' 'your,' 'your,' 'life,' 'reason,' 'value,' 'keep away,' 'from the.' Don't you see now whence these words have been taken?"

"By thunder, you're right! Well, if that isn't smart!" cried Sir Henry.

"If any possible doubt remained it is settled by the fact that 'keep away' and 'from the' are cut out in one piece."

"Well, now—so it is!"

"Really, Mr. Holmes, this exceeds anything which I could have imagined," said Dr. Mortimer, gazing at my friend in amazement. "I could understand anyone saying that the words were from a newspaper; but that you should name which, and add that it came from the leading article, is really one of the most remarkable things which I have ever known. How did you do it?"

"I presume, doctor, that you could tell the skull of a Negro from that of an Esquimaux?"

"Most certainly."

"But how?"

"Because that is my special hobby. The differences are obvious. The supra-orbital crest, the facial angle, the maxillary curve,[67] the—"

"But this is my special hobby, and the differences are equally obvious. There is as much difference to my eyes between the leaded bourgeois type[68] of a *Times* article and the slovenly print of an evening halfpenny paper as there could be between your Negro and your Esquimaux. The detection of types is one of the most elementary branches of knowledge to the special expert in crime,[69] though I confess that once when I was very young I confused the *Leeds Mercury*[70] with the *Western Morning News*.[71] But a *Times* leader is entirely distinctive, and these words could have been taken from nothing else. As it was done yesterday the strong probability was that we should find the words in yesterday's issue."

"So far as I can follow you, then, Mr. Holmes," said Sir Henry Baskerville, "someone cut out this message with a scissors—"

"Nail-scissors," said Holmes. "You can see that it was a very short-bladed scissors, since the cutter had to take two snips over 'keep away.' "

"That is so. Someone, then, cut out the message with a pair of short-bladed scissors, pasted it with paste—"

"Gum," said Holmes.

"With gum on to the paper. But I want to know why the word 'moor' should have been written?"

"Because he could not find it in print. The other words were all simple, and might be found in any issue, but 'moor' would be less common."

"Why, of course, that would explain it. Have you read anything else in this message, Mr. Holmes?"

"There are one or two indications, and yet the utmost pains have been taken to remove all clues. The address, you observe, is printed in rough characters. But *The Times* is a paper which is seldom found in any hands but those of the highly educated. We may take it, therefore, that the letter was composed by an educated man who wished to pose as an uneducated one, and his effort to conceal his own writing suggests that that writing might be known, or come to be known by you. Again, you will observe, that the words are not gummed on in an accurate line, but that some are much higher than others. 'Life,' for example, is quite out of its proper place. That may point to carelessness or it may point to agitation and hurry upon the part of the cutter. On the whole I incline to the latter view, since the matter

68 Bourgeois (pronounced "ber-joyce" by printers and type founders) is an intermediate size of type, between brevier and long primer. It measures 102½ lines to the foot (pica, for comparison, is 71½ lines to the foot, or about 6 lines to the inch) and approximates 9-point type. Leading is the space between lines of type. According to Peter Calamai, Victorian newspaper scholar, in private correspondence to this editor, the leading in the *Times* "would most likely have been one point, with the result called 9 on 10." Note that bourgeois has no reference to the *font* used, only the size. Of course, different newspapers used different fonts as well, but Holmes does not mention them.

69 Madeleine B. Stern opines that "specimens of Granjon's *civilité*, the Estienne, the Bodoni, Fournier Le Jeune, the great Enschedé type specimen book with its exotic fonts, had all . . . found their way to Holmes's library."

70 The *Mercury* was established in 1718, but not until its purchase in 1801 by Edward Baines (1744–1848) did it begin to exert influence over Liberal politics, becoming the organ of party opinion in Leeds. Before Baines's tenure, the *Mercury*—like most provincial papers—had no significant effect on national politics; reporting was nonexistent or shoddy. Baines's skills as a newspaperman were considerable, and he was passionate in his political beliefs. He pushed for representation of industrial Leeds (and other cities and towns like it) in Parliament and for ending the slave trade in England; on the other hand, he opposed factory legislation, the right of the working class to vote, and universal suffrage. The *Mercury*, which by the late 1800s was one of the most important and widely read papers outside those of the major cities, was published both in a daily and a weekly edition.

71 There were 1,163 provincial newspapers in England and Wales in 1881. In "A History of the *Western Morning News*," Margaret Sutton notes that it was the first paper in England to publish a weather forecast and the first to have its own private wire in Fleet Street.

was evidently important, and it is unlikely that the composer of such a letter would be careless. If he were in a hurry it opens up the interesting question why he should be in a hurry, since any letter posted up to early morning would reach Sir Henry before he would leave his hotel. Did the composer fear an interruption—and from whom?"

"We are coming now rather into the region of guess-work," said Dr. Mortimer.

"Say, rather, into the region where we balance probabilities and choose the most likely. It is the scientific use of the imagination, but we have always some material basis on which to start our speculations. Now, you would call it a guess, no doubt, but I am almost certain that this address has been written in an hotel."

"How in the world can you say that?"

"If you examine it carefully you will see that both the pen and the ink have given the writer trouble. The pen has spluttered twice in a single word, and has run dry three times in a short address, showing that there was very little ink in the bottle. Now, a private pen or ink-bottle is seldom allowed to be in such a state, and the combination of the two must be quite rare. But you know the hotel ink and the hotel pen, where it is rare to get anything else. Yes, I have very little hesitation in saying that could we examine the wastepaper baskets of the hotels round Charing Cross until we found the remains of the mutilated *Times* leader we could lay our hands straight upon the person who sent this singular message. Halloa! Halloa! What's this?"

He was carefully examining the foolscap, upon which the words were pasted, holding it only an inch or two from his eyes.

"Well?"

"Nothing," said he, throwing it down. "It is a blank half-sheet of paper, without even a watermark upon it. I think we have drawn as much as we can from this curious letter; and now, Sir Henry, has anything else of interest happened to you since you have been in London?"

"Why, no, Mr. Holmes. I think not."

"You have not observed anyone follow or watch you?"

"I seem to have walked right into the thick of a dime novel," said our visitor. "Why in thunder should anyone follow or watch me?"

“He was carefully examining the foolscap, upon which the words were pasted, holding it only an inch or two from his eyes.”
Richard Gutschmidt, *Der Hund von Baskerville*
(Stuttgart: Robert Lutz Verlag, 1903)

“We are coming to that. You have nothing else to report to us before we go into this matter?”

“Well, it depends upon what you think worth reporting.”

“I think anything out of the ordinary routine of life well worth reporting.”

Sir Henry smiled. “I don’t know much of British life yet, for I have spent nearly all my time in the States and in Canada. But I hope that to lose one of your boots is not part of the ordinary routine of life over here.”

“You have lost one of your boots?”

“My dear sir,” cried Dr. Mortimer, “it is only mislaid. You will find it when you return to the hotel. What is the use of troubling Mr. Holmes with trifles of this kind?”

“Well, he asked me for anything outside the ordinary routine.”

“Exactly,” said Holmes, “however foolish the incident may seem. You have lost one of your boots, you say?”

72 Polished.

"Holding it only an inch or two from his eyes."
Sidney Paget, *Strand Magazine*, 1901

"Well, mislaid it, anyhow. I put them both outside my door last night, and there was only one in the morning. I could get no sense out of the chap who cleans them. The worst of it is that I only bought the pair last night in the Strand, and I have never had them on."

"If you have never worn them, why did you put them out to be cleaned?"

"They were tan boots, and had never been varnished.[72] That was why I put them out."

"Then I understand that on your arrival in London yesterday you went out at once and bought a pair of boots?"

"I did a good deal of shopping. Dr. Mortimer here went round with me. You see, if I am to be squire down there I must dress the part, and it may be that I have got a little careless in my ways out West. Among other things I bought these brown boots—gave six dollars for them—and had one stolen before ever I had them on my feet."

"It seems a singularly useless thing to steal," said Sherlock

Holmes. "I confess that I share Dr. Mortimer's belief that it will not be long before the missing boot is found."

"And now, gentlemen," said the baronet, with decision, "it seems to me that I have spoken quite enough about the little that I know. It is time that you kept your promise, and gave me a full account of what we are all driving at."

"Your request is a very reasonable one," Holmes answered. "Dr. Mortimer, I think you could not do better than to tell your story as you told it to us."

Thus encouraged, our scientific friend drew his papers from his pocket, and presented the whole case as he had done upon the morning before. Sir Henry Baskerville listened with the deepest attention, and with an occasional exclamation of surprise.

"Well, I seem to have come into an inheritance with a vengeance," said he, when the long narrative was finished. "Of course, I've heard of the hound ever since I was in the nursery. It's the pet story of the family, though I never thought of taking it seriously before.[73] But as to my uncle's death—well, it all seems boiling up in my head, and I can't get it clear yet. You don't seem quite to have made up your mind whether it's a case for a policeman or a clergyman."

"Precisely."

"And now there's this affair of the letter to me at the hotel. I suppose that fits into its place."

"It seems to show that someone knows more than we do about what goes on upon the moor," said Dr. Mortimer.

"And also," said Holmes, "that someone is not ill-disposed towards you, since they warn you of danger."

"Or it may be that they wish for their own purposes to scare me away."

"Well, of course, that is possible also. I am very much indebted to you, Dr. Mortimer, for introducing me to a problem which presents several interesting alternatives. But the practical point which we now have to decide, Sir Henry, is whether it is or is not advisable for you to go to Baskerville Hall."

"Why should I not go?"

"There seems to be danger."

"Do you mean danger from this family fiend or do you mean danger from human beings?"

73 There are many "pet stories" associated with families and locations throughout England and Wales. The tale of the "shadow hound" that haunted the Vaughans of Hergest Court, in Wales, was popularised in the novel *Malvern Chase*, by W. S. Symonds (1881). Theo Brown, in *Devon Ghosts* (1992), tells of receiving, in 1963, a tale of the Baskerville Mynors family of Herefordshire—after cruel treatment of a faithful hound by his master, the death of a head of the family was thereafter always announced by the baying of a hound. "Black Shuck" was another well-known local Norfolk legend, about a black, shaggy dog the size of a small calf, whose fiery gaze caused death. Arthur Conan Doyle may have heard the legend of Black Shuck from his friend Fletcher Robinson (discussed in *Appendix 2*) when they golfed together at Cromer (in Norfolk) in 1901 and passed it on to Dr. Watson, who was then writing up his account of *The Hound of the Baskervilles*.

"Well, that is what we have to find out."

"Whichever it is, my answer is fixed. There is no devil in hell, Mr. Holmes, and there is no man upon earth who can prevent me from going to the home of my own people, and you may take that to be my final answer." His dark brows knitted and his face flushed to a dusky red as he spoke. It was evident that the fiery temper of the Baskervilles was not extinct in this their last representative. "Meanwhile," said he, "I have hardly had time to think over all that you have told me. It's a big thing for a man to have to understand and to decide at one sitting. I should like to have a quiet hour by myself to make up my mind. Now, look here, Mr. Holmes, it's half-past eleven now, and I am going back right away to my hotel. Suppose you and your friend, Dr. Watson, come round and lunch with us at two? I'll be able to tell you more clearly then how this thing strikes me."

"Is that convenient to you, Watson?"

"Perfectly."

"Then you may expect us. Shall I have a cab called?"

"I'd prefer to walk, for this affair has flurried me rather."

"I'll join you in a walk, with pleasure," said his companion.

"Then we meet again at two o'clock. Au revoir, and good morning!"

We heard the steps of our visitors descend the stair and the bang of the front door. In an instant Holmes had changed from the languid dreamer to the man of action.

"Your hat and boots, Watson, quick! Not a moment to lose!" He rushed into his room in his dressing-gown, and was back again in a few seconds in a frock-coat. We hurried together down the stairs and into the street. Dr. Mortimer and Baskerville were still visible about two hundred yards ahead of us in the direction of Oxford Street.

"Shall I run on and stop them?"

"Not for the world, my dear Watson. I am perfectly satisfied with your company, if you will tolerate mine. Our friends are wise, for it is certainly a very fine morning for a walk."

He quickened his pace until we had decreased the distance which divided us by about half. Then, still keeping a hundred yards behind, we followed into Oxford Street and so down Regent Street. Once our friends stopped and stared into a shop window, upon which Holmes did the same. An instant afterwards he gave a little cry of satisfaction, and, following the direction of his eager eyes, I saw that a hansom cab with a man inside which had halted on the other side of the street was now walking slowly onwards again.

"There's our man, Watson! Come along! We'll have a good look at him, if we can do no more."

At that instant I was aware of a bushy black beard and a pair of piercing eyes turned upon us through the side window of the cab. Instantly the trap-door at the top flew up, something was screamed to the driver, and the cab flew madly off down Regent Street. Holmes looked eagerly round for another, but no empty one was in sight. Then he dashed in wild pursuit amid the stream of the traffic, but the start was too great, and already the cab was out of sight.

" 'There's our man, Watson! Come along.' "
Sidney Paget, *Strand Magazine*, 1901

"At that instant I was aware of a bushy black beard and a pair of piercing eyes turned upon us through the side window of the cab."
Richard Gutschmidt, *Der Hund von Baskerville*
(Stuttgart: Robert Lutz Verlag, 1903)

"There now!" said Holmes, bitterly, as he emerged panting and white with vexation from the tide of vehicles. "Was ever such bad luck and such bad management, too? Watson, Watson, if you are an honest man you will record this also and set it against my successes!"

"Who was the man?"

"I have not an idea."

"A spy?"

"Well, it was evident from what we have heard that Baskerville has been very closely shadowed by someone since he has been in town. How else could it be known so quickly that it was the Northumberland Hotel which he had chosen? If they had followed him the first day, I argued that they would follow him also the second. You may have observed that I twice strolled over to the window while Dr. Mortimer was reading his legend."

"Yes, I remember."

"I was looking out for loiterers in the street, but I saw none. We are dealing with a clever man, Watson. This matter cuts very deep, and though I have not finally made up my mind whether it is a benevolent or a malevolent agency which is in touch with us, I am conscious always of power and design. When our friends left I at once followed them in the hopes of marking down their invisible attendant. So wily was he that he had not trusted himself upon foot, but he had availed himself of a cab, so that he could loiter behind or dash past them and so escape their notice. His method had the additional advantage that if they were to take a cab he was all ready to follow them. It has, however, one obvious disadvantage."

"It puts him in the power of the cabman."

"Exactly."

"What a pity we did not get the number!"

"My dear Watson, clumsy as I have been, you surely do not seriously imagine that I neglected to get the number? 2704 is our man. But that is no use to us for the moment."

"I fail to see how you could have done more."

"On observing the cab I should have instantly turned and walked in the other direction. I should then at my leisure have hired a second cab, and followed the first at a respectful distance, or, better still, have driven to the Northumberland Hotel and waited there. When our unknown had followed Baskerville home we should have had the opportunity of playing his own game upon himself, and seeing where he made for. As it is, by an indiscreet eagerness, which was taken advantage of with extraordinary quickness and energy by our opponent, we have betrayed ourselves and lost our man."

We had been sauntering slowly down Regent Street during this conversation, and Dr. Mortimer, with his companion, had long vanished in front of us.

"There is no object in our following them," said Holmes. "The shadow has departed and will not return. We must see what further cards we have in our hands, and play them with decision. Could you swear to that man's face within the cab?"

"I could swear only to the beard."

"And so could I—from which I gather that in all probability it was a false one. A clever man upon so delicate an errand has no use for a beard save to conceal his features. Come in here, Watson!"

He turned into one of the district messenger offices,[74] where he was warmly greeted by the manager.

"Ah, Wilson, I see you have not forgotten the little case in which I had the good fortune to help you?"

"No, sir, indeed I have not. You saved my good name, and perhaps my life."[75]

"My dear fellow, you exaggerate. I have some recollection, Wilson, that you had among your boys a lad named Cartwright, who showed some ability during the investigation."

"Yes, sir, he is still with us."

"Could you ring him up? Thank you! And I should be glad to have change of this five-pound note."

A lad of fourteen, with a bright, keen face, had obeyed the summons of the manager. He stood now gazing with great reverence at the famous detective.

"Let me have the Hotel Directory,"[76] said Holmes. "Thank you! Now, Cartwright, there are the names of twenty-three hotels here, all in the immediate neighbourhood of Charing Cross. Do you see?"

"Yes, sir."

"You will visit each of these in turn."

"Yes, sir."

"You will begin in each case by giving the outside porter one shilling. Here are twenty-three shillings."

"Yes, sir."

"You will tell him that you want to see the waste paper of yesterday. You will say that an important telegram has miscarried, and that you are looking for it. You understand?"

"Yes, sir."

"But what you are really looking for is the centre page of *The Times* with some holes cut in it with scissors. Here is a copy of

74 The District Messenger Service Co. was a private concern with numerous branch offices, which competed with the Post Office. Messengers cost 3*s.* per half-mile, 6*d.* per mile, 8*d.* per hour, fares extra. Holmes also used a district messenger in "The Six Napoleons" and may have used one in "The Illustrious Client" and "The Bruce-Partington Plans" as well.

The district messenger boy was a popular figure in children's literature. James Otis Kaler, author of over 150 children's books published under the name James Otis, including the popular *Toby Tyler* (1880), published a short collection of three tales entitled *A District Messenger Boy and a Necktie Party* (1898), which told in the first story of a persevering lad who, after hard work as a messenger, is rewarded: ". . . and to-day the district messenger boy is in a fair way to become a successful merchant." The Game of the District Messenger Boy, or Merit Rewarded was brought out by McLoughlin Brothers in New York in 1896. Each player pushes a metallic messenger-boy piece along, with punishments meted out for "untidiness," "drowsiness," "loitering," and even "stupidity" and advances earned for "integrity" and "ambition." The point of the board game is to become president of the Telegraph Company.

The Game of District Messenger Boy (1886).

The Times. It is this page. You could easily recognize it, could you not?"

"Yes, sir."

"In each case the outside porter will send for the hall porter, to whom also you will give a shilling. Here are twenty-three shillings. You will then learn in possibly twenty cases out of the twenty-three that the waste of the day before has been burned or removed. In the three other cases you will be shown a heap of paper, and you will look for this page of *The Times* among it. The odds are enormously against your finding it. There are ten shillings over in case of emergencies. Let me have a report by

" 'Here are the names of twenty-three hotels.' "
Sidney Paget, *Strand Magazine*, 1901

75 Brad Keefauver suggests that this is "Wilson, the notorious canary-trainer" of "Black Peter."

76 There were numerous hotel directories; the British Museum Reference Collection lists eight. Depending on the date assigned to *The Hound of the Baskervilles*, Holmes may have had at hand *The Official Hotel Directory and the Official Hotel Tariffs, Etc.* (London: J. P. Segg & Co., 1894, *etc.*) or *The XYZ Through Route Railway Guide and Hotel Directory* (London, 1884–1886), among others.

wire at Baker Street before evening. And now, Watson, it only remains for us to find out by wire the identity of the cabman, No. 2704, and then we will drop into one of the Bond Street[77] picture-galleries and fill in the time until we are due at the hotel."

77 New Bond Street, diverging to the right (south) from Oxford Street, is continued by Old Bond Street to Piccadilly, and it contained, according to *Baedeker*, "numerous attractive and fashionable shops . . . and several picture galleries." Among those listed in the 1896 directory are the Grafton Gallery, Lemercier Gallery (later Doré Gallery), Agnew's, Hanover Gallery, Fine Art Society, Dowdeswell Galleries, Continental Gallery, and (according to Augustus J. C. Hare's *Walks in London* [1884]) Grosvenor Gallery.

CHAPTER V

Three Broken Threads

Sherlock Holmes had, in a very remarkable degree, the power of detaching his mind at will. For two hours the strange business in which we had been involved appeared to be forgotten, and he was entirely absorbed in the pictures of the modern Belgian masters.[78] He would talk of nothing but art, of which he had the crudest ideas, from our leaving the gallery until we found ourselves at the Northumberland Hotel.

"Sir Henry Baskerville is upstairs expecting you," said the clerk. "He asked me to show you up at once when you came."

"Have you any objection to my looking at your register?" said Holmes.

"Not in the least."

The book showed that two names had been added after that of Baskerville. One was Theophilus Johnson and family, of Newcastle; the other Mrs. Oldmore and maid, of High Lodge, Alton.[79]

"Surely that must be the same Johnson whom I used to know," said Holmes, to the porter. "A lawyer, is he not, gray-headed, and walks with a limp?"

78 The modern Belgian school included the painters James Ensor (also a printmaker), Constantin Meunier, and Henry Van De Velde (also an architect). Ensor became a member of the XX group, twenty artists whose show in 1886 in Brussels included Gauguin and Odilon Redon.

The rock group They Might Be Giants recorded a song in 1994 entitled "Meet James Ensor," about the famed artist. In a fine example of cultural feedback, the group was named after the quirky 1971 film *They Might Be Giants*, starring George C. Scott as a delusional judge who believes that he is Sherlock Holmes and co-starring Joanne Woodward as Dr. Mildred Watson, his would-be psychiatrist and love interest; the two team up to track down Moriarty. The film was directed by Anthony Harvey and written by James Goldman, author of the award-winning *The Lion in Winter* (1968), and was based on Goldman's stageplay.

79 Alton is in Hampshire, on the river Wey, 16 miles north-east of Winchester. There are many breweries in the town, and, according to *Baedeker's Great Britain*, "the ale known as 'Alton Ale' is much esteemed." There is also an Alton in Staffordshire, 15 miles north-east of Stafford.

The Glades of the New Forest, a branch of the Franco-Midland Hardware Company, the international Holmesian study group, carried out an expedition to Alton in 1993 to attempt to identify High Lodge. Jane Weller, in "The 'High Lodge' Picnic" and in a private communication to this editor, reports that the 1888 maps of Alton reveal no High Lodge, and that no one was listed in any of the directories or in the 1881 or 1891 Census with the name of Oldmore. In 1889, there was an Alton Lodge, located on High Street, at the highest point in the town, close to the railway station, and the occupants had the same name as a former mayor of Gloucester (but not Oldmore). Of course, there never has been a mayor of Gloucester named Oldmore.

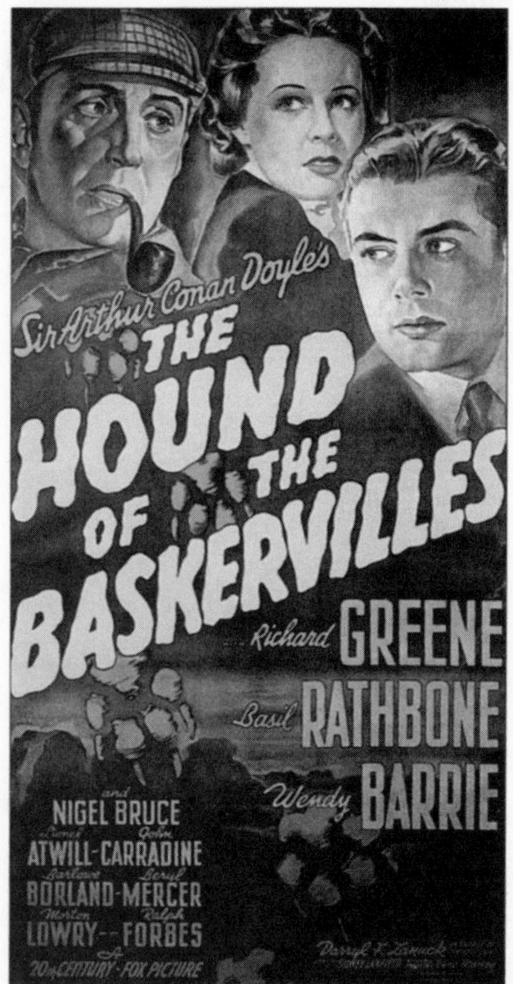

Poster for *The Hound of the Baskervilles* (United States: Twentieth-Century Fox, 1939), starring Basil Rathbone as Sherlock Holmes and Nigel Bruce as Dr. Watson.

"No, sir, this is Mr. Johnson the coal-owner, a very active gentleman, not older than yourself."

"Surely you are mistaken about his trade?"

"No, sir; he has used this hotel for many years, and he is very well known to us."

"Ah, that settles it. Mrs. Oldmore, too; I seem to remember the name. Excuse my curiosity, but often in calling upon one friend one finds another."

"She is an invalid lady, sir. Her husband was once Mayor of Gloucester. She always comes to us when she is in town."

"Thank you; I am afraid I cannot claim her acquaintance. We have established a most important fact by these questions, Watson," he continued, in a low voice, as we went upstairs together. "We know now that the people who are so interested in our friend have not settled down in his own hotel. That means that while they are, as we have seen, very anxious to watch him, they are equally anxious that he should not see them. Now, this is a most suggestive fact."

"What does it suggest?"

"It suggests—halloa, my dear fellow, what on earth is the matter?"

As we came round the top of the stairs we had run up against Sir Henry Baskerville himself. His face was flushed with anger, and he held an old and dusty boot in one of his hands. So furi-

"He held an old and dusty boot in one of his hands."
Sidney Paget, *Strand Magazine*, 1901

"He held an old and dusty boot in one of his hands."
Richard Gutschmidt, *Der Hund von Baskerville*
(Stuttgart: Robert Lutz Verlag, 1903)

ous was he that he was hardly articulate, and when he did speak it was in a much broader and more Western dialect than any which we had heard from him in the morning.

"Seems to me they are playing me for a sucker in this hotel," he cried. "They'll find they've started in to monkey with the wrong man unless they are careful. By thunder, if that chap can't find my missing boot there will be trouble. I can take a joke with the best, Mr. Holmes, but they've got a bit over the mark this time."

"Still looking for your boot?"

"Yes, sir, and mean to find it."

"But surely, you said that it was a new brown boot?"

"So it was, sir. And now it's an old black one."

"What! you don't mean to say—?"

"That's just what I do mean to say. I only had three pairs in the world—the new brown, the old black, and the patent leathers, which I am wearing. Last night they took one of my brown ones, and today they have sneaked one of the black. Well, have you got it? Speak out, man, and don't stand staring!"

An agitated German waiter had appeared upon the scene.

"No, sir; I have made inquiry all over the hotel, but I can hear no word of it."

"Well, either that boot comes back before sundown, or I'll see the manager and tell him that I go right straight out of this hotel."

"It shall be found, sir—I promise you that if you will have a little patience it will be found."

"Mind it is, for it's the last thing of mine that I'll lose in this den of thieves. Well, well, Mr. Holmes, you'll excuse my troubling you about such a trifle—"

"I think it's well worth troubling about."

"Why, you look very serious over it."

"How do you explain it?"

"I just don't attempt to explain it. It seems the very maddest, queerest thing that ever happened to me."

"The queerest, perhaps," said Holmes, thoughtfully.

"What do you make of it yourself?"

"Well, I don't profess to understand it yet. This case of yours is very complex, Sir Henry. When taken in conjunction with your uncle's death I am not sure that of all the five hundred cases of capital importance which I have handled[80] there is one which cuts so deep. But we hold several threads in our hands, and the odds are that one or other of them guides us to the truth. We may waste time in following the wrong one, but sooner or later, we must come upon the right."

We had a pleasant luncheon in which little was said of the business which had brought us together. It was in the private sitting-room to which we afterwards repaired that Holmes asked Baskerville what were his intentions.

"To go to Baskerville Hall."

"And when?"

"At the end of the week."

"On the whole," said Holmes, "I think that your decision is a wise one. I have ample evidence that you are being dogged in London,[81] and amid the millions of this great city it is difficult

80 In "The Final Problem," Holmes speaks of handling "over a thousand cases." Obviously there were many that were *not* of "capital importance," and Watson chose to publish some of them (*e.g.*, "The Yellow Face") for their special features.

81 Of course Sir Henry was "dogged" in Dartmoor, too.

82 Why would Holmes ask about men with beards, when he earlier made it clear that he believed the beard to be false?

to discover who these people are or what their object can be. If their intentions are evil they might do you a mischief, and we should be powerless to prevent it. You did not know, Dr. Mortimer, that you were followed this morning from my house?"

Dr. Mortimer started violently. "Followed! By whom?"

"That, unfortunately, is what I cannot tell you. Have you among your neighbours or acquaintances on Dartmoor any man with a black, full beard?"[82]

"No—or, let me see—why, yes. Barrymore, Sir Charles's butler, is a man with a full, black beard."

"Ha! Where is Barrymore?"

"He is in charge of the Hall."

"We had best ascertain if he is really there, or if by any possibility he might be in London."

"How can you do that?"

"Give me a telegraph form. 'Is all ready for Sir Henry?' That will do. Address to Mr. Barrymore, Baskerville Hall. Which is the nearest telegraph-office? Grimpen. Very good, we will send a second wire to the postmaster, Grimpen: 'Telegram to Mr. Barrymore, to be delivered into his own hand. If absent, please return wire to Sir Henry Baskerville, Northumberland Hotel.' That should let us know before evening whether Barrymore is at his post in Devonshire or not."

"That's so," said Baskerville. "By the way, Dr. Mortimer, who is this Barrymore, anyhow?"

"He is the son of the old caretaker, who is dead. They have looked after the Hall for four generations now. So far as I know, he and his wife are as respectable a couple as any in the county."

"At the same time," said Baskerville, "it's clear enough that so long as there are none of the family at the Hall these people have a mighty fine home and nothing to do."

"That is true."

"Did Barrymore profit at all by Sir Charles's will?" asked Holmes.

"He and his wife had five hundred pounds each."

"Ha! Did they know that they would receive this?"

"Yes; Sir Charles was very fond of talking about the provisions of his will."

"That is very interesting."

"I hope," said Dr. Mortimer, "that you do not look with suspicious eyes upon everyone who received a legacy from Sir Charles, for I also had a thousand pounds left to me."

"Indeed! And anyone else?"

"There were many insignificant sums to individuals and a large number of public charities. The residue all went to Sir Henry."

"And how much was the residue?"

"Seven hundred and forty thousand pounds."[83]

Holmes raised his eyebrows in surprise. "I had no idea that so gigantic a sum was involved," said he.

"Sir Charles had the reputation of being rich, but we did not know how very rich he was until we came to examine his securities. The total value of the estate was close on to a million."

"Dear me! It is a stake for which a man might well play a desperate game. And one more question, Dr. Mortimer. Supposing that anything happened to our young friend here—you will forgive the unpleasant hypothesis!—who would inherit the estate?"

"Since Rodger Baskerville, Sir Charles's younger brother, died unmarried, the estate would descend to the Desmonds, who are distant cousins. James Desmond is an elderly clergyman in Westmorland."

"Thank you. These details are all of great interest. Have you met Mr. James Desmond?"

"Yes; he once came down to visit Sir Charles. He is a man of venerable appearance and of saintly life. I remember that he refused to accept any settlement from Sir Charles, though he pressed it upon him."

"And this man of simple tastes would be the heir to Sir Charles's thousands?"

"He would be the heir to the estate, because that is entailed.[84] He would also be the heir to the money unless it were willed otherwise by the present owner, who can, of course, do what he likes with it."

"And have you made your will, Sir Henry?"

"No, Mr. Holmes, I have not. I've had no time, for it was only yesterday that I learned how matters stood. But in any case I feel that the money should go with the title and estate. That was my poor uncle's idea. How is the owner going to restore the glories of the Baskervilles if he has not money enough to keep up the property? House, land, and dollars must go together."

"Quite so. Well, Sir Henry, I am of one mind with you as to the advisability of your going down to Devonshire without

83 Over $3.7 million in U. S. currency—a vast fortune, over $85 million in today's purchasing power. At least one statistical source estimates that the average net worth of the *top* 1 percent of the English population was about $265,000 in U.S. currency. Sir Henry—meet Lord Mount-James (of "The Missing Three-Quarter"), "one of the richest men in England"!

84 A limit on the right of succession, usually imposed by a testator's will. By the time of *The Hound of the Baskervilles*, however, land in England could no longer be tied up for a greater period than the lives of persons in existence and twenty-one years thereafter. This is the current law of most of the United States as well, called the "rule against perpetuities." The subjects of entail and means by which entail was often broken are considered in "Breaking the Entail," by Robert S. Pasley. See also "The Priory School," where James Wilder sought to have his illegitimate father, the Duke of Holdernesse, break the entail in his favour. In Jane Austen's *Pride and Prejudice* (1813), the Bennet family, consisting of five daughters, must endure the loss of their Hertfordshire estate, Longbourn, to the girls' father's cousin, William Collins, because of the entail.

delay. There is only one provision which I must make. You certainly must not go alone."

"Dr. Mortimer returns with me."

"But Dr. Mortimer has his practice to attend to, and his house is miles away from yours. With all the good will in the world, he may be unable to help you. No, Sir Henry, you must take with you someone, a trusty man, who will be always by your side."

"Is it possible that you could come yourself, Mr. Holmes?"

"If matters came to a crisis I should endeavour to be present in person; but you can understand that, with my extensive consulting practice and with the constant appeals which reach me from many quarters, it is impossible for me to be absent from London for an indefinite time. At the present instant one of the most revered names in England is being besmirched by a blackmailer,[85] and only I can stop a disastrous scandal. You will see how impossible it is for me to go to Dartmoor."

"Whom would you recommend, then?"

Holmes laid his hand upon my arm.

"If my friend would undertake it there is no man who is better worth having at your side when you are in a tight place. No one can say so more confidently than I."

The proposition took me completely by surprise, but before I had time to answer Baskerville seized me by the hand and wrung it heartily.

"Well, now, that is real kind of you, Dr. Watson," said he. "You see how it is with me, and you know just as much about the matter as I do. If you will come down to Baskerville Hall and see me through I'll never forget it."

The promise of adventure had always a fascination for me, and I was complimented by the words of Holmes and by the eagerness with which the baronet hailed me as a companion.

"I will come with pleasure," said I. "I do not know how I could employ my time better."

"And you will report very carefully to me," said Holmes. "When a crisis comes, as it will do, I will direct how you shall act. I suppose that by Saturday all might be ready?"

"Would that suit Dr. Watson?"

"Perfectly."

"Then on Saturday, unless you hear to the contrary, we shall meet at the 10:30 train[86] from Paddington."[87]

We had risen to depart when Baskerville gave a cry of tri-

85 Michael P. Malloy, who dates "Charles Augustus Milverton" after *The Hound of the Baskervilles*, identifies the blackmail victim as Milverton's murderess. Philip Cornell, in a fine piece entitled "Blackmail's Dark Waters," demonstrates that Holmes seems to react particularly strongly to cases of blackmail and to exhibit more sympathy for the victims of blackmail than he does for other victims (see, for example, "The 'Gloria Scott,' " "The Boscombe Valley Mystery," "The Second Stain," and most notably "Charles Augustus Milverton"). Cornell suggests that Holmes may have had an experience, either personally or in his family, that led to this intense aversion. Of course, we learn later that there *was* no blackmail case at hand here, but Cornell finds it noteworthy that when Holmes needs a pretext, it is a case of blackmail that springs to his lips.

86 In "The Railways of Dartmoor in the Days of Sherlock Holmes," B. J. D. Walsh concludes that Watson and company would have taken either the 10:30 or the 10:35 to Exeter, arriving at 2:28 P.M., where they would have had to change for Coombe Tracey (which Walsh identifies with Bovey Tracey) on the Moretonhampstead Branch. Although there was a slower train at 11:45, only by taking the 10:30 or the 10:35 could they have had the chance of obtaining lunch at Exeter. Neither the 10:30 nor the 10:35 train had yet acquired a restaurant car, and they did not do so until July 1899 and October 1899, respectively. From Exeter, Walsh concludes, Watson and his friends would have caught the 4:12 P.M. train and, after changing at Newton Abbot, would have reached Bovey Tracey at 5:40.

Bernard Davies also considers the railway journeys, in "Railways and Roads in the Hound." He identifies Coombe Tracey as Totnes and concludes that Watson and his party travelled not to Bovey but to Hemsworthy Gate, proceeding from there to Wide-

"The proposition took me completely by surprise."
Sidney Paget, *Strand Magazine*, 1901

combe or in the general direction of Postbridge and Bellever.

87 The first Paddington Station was built in 1838, by engineer Isambard Kingdom Brunel, as the London terminus of the Great Western Railway, serving the rural heartlands, the West Country, industrial Bristol, and the South Wales coalfields. It was at this station that Queen Victoria arrived on completing her first railway journey in 1842, on the *Phlegethon*, which travelled at 44 m.p.h. Reportedly, the Prince Consort asked afterward that future trains carrying the Queen travel more slowly. In 1853, Brunel began construction on the permanent terminus, working with eminent architect Matthew Digby Wyatt. Completed in 1855, its ironwork and *art nouveau*–like cement work created a light, elegant, and graceful structure. In 1854, the Great Western Hotel was opened adjacent to the station. Since its original construction, the station has been expanded and rebuilt numerous times.

umph, and diving into one of the corners of the room he drew a brown boot from under a cabinet.

"My missing boot!" he cried.

"May all our difficulties vanish as easily!" said Sherlock Holmes.

"But it is a very singular thing," Dr. Mortimer remarked. "I searched this room carefully before lunch."

"And so did I," said Baskerville. "Every inch of it."

"There was certainly no boot in it then."

"In that case the waiter must have placed it there while we were lunching."

The German was sent for, but professed to know nothing of the matter, nor could any inquiry clear it up. Another item had been added to that constant and apparently purposeless series of small mysteries which had succeeded each other so rapidly. Setting aside the whole grim story of Sir Charles's death, we had a line of inexplicable incidents all within the limits of two days, which included the receipt of the printed letter, the black-bearded spy in the hansom, the loss of the new brown boot, the loss of the old black boot, and now the return of the new brown boot. Holmes sat in silence in the cab as we drove back to Baker Street, and I knew from his drawn brows and keen face that his mind, like my own, was busy in endeavouring to frame some scheme into which all these strange and apparently disconnected episodes could be fitted. All afternoon and late into the evening he sat lost in tobacco and thought.

Just before dinner two telegrams were handed in. The first ran:

> Have just heard that Barrymore is at the Hall.
>
> BASKERVILLE.

The second:

> Visited twenty-three hotels as directed, but sorry to report unable to trace cut sheet of *Times*.
>
> CARTWRIGHT.[88]

"There go two of my threads, Watson. There is nothing more stimulating than a case where everything goes against you. We must cast round for another scent."

"We have still the cabman who drove the spy."

"Exactly. I have wired to get his name and address from the Official Registry.[89] I should not be surprised if this were an answer to my question."

The ring at the bell proved to be something even more satisfactory than an answer, however, for the door opened and a rough-looking fellow entered who was evidently the man himself.

"I got a message from the head office that a gent at this address[90] had been inquiring for 2704," said he. "I've driven my cab this seven years and never a word of complaint. I came here straight from the Yard to ask you to your face what you had against me."[91]

"I have nothing in the world against you, my good man," said Holmes. "On the contrary, I have half a sovereign for you if you will give me a clear answer to my questions."

"Well, I've had a good day and no mistake," said the cabman, with a grin. "What was it you wanted to ask, sir?"

"First of all your name and address, in case I want you again."

"John Clayton, 3, Turpey Street, the Borough.[92] My cab is out of Shipley's Yard,[93] near Waterloo Station."

88 Brad Keefauver finds it far-fetched that a fourteen-year-old wrote this telegram or that he could have accomplished the given task. He raises the possibility that young Cartwright had been waylaid by Stapleton.

89 By the "Registry," Holmes presumably means the registration files of the Public Carriage Office. In 1895, more than 11,000 horse-drawn cabs serviced the streets of London, employing more than 20,000 horses. Regulation of the trade after 1850 was the responsibility of the Metropolitan Police, located in an annex to New Scotland Yard in Whitehall called "the Bungalow." The PCO moved to 109 Lambeth Road in 1919, remaining there until 1966, when it moved to its present home, 15 Penton Street, Islington. On the formation of Transport for London in July 2000, charged with regulation of all surface transportation on behalf of the Greater London Authority, the Public Carriage Office became a part of that body.

90 "Are we to believe," asks Brad Keefauver, "that Holmes wired the Official Registry with just his address?"

91 *Baedeker* cautions the London tourist: "Many of the London cabmen are among the most insolent and extortionate of their fraternity. The traveller, therefore, in his own and the general interest, should resist all attempts at overcharging, and should, in the case of persistency, demand the cabman's number, or order him to drive to the nearest police court or station."

92 Although William S. Baring-Gould concludes that Clayton means the borough of Marylebone, in which Baker Street is located, this is more likely a reference to Southwark, a central metropolitan borough of London on the Surrey side of London Bridge, one of the busiest parts of London and known for more than five hundred years as The Borough.

Sherlock Holmes made a note of it.

"Now, Clayton, tell me all about the fare who came and watched this house at ten o'clock this morning and afterwards followed the two gentlemen down Regent Street."

The man looked surprised and a little embarrassed.

"Why, there's no good my telling you things, for you seem to know as much as I do already," said he. "The truth is that the gentleman told me that he was a detective, and that I was to say nothing about him to anyone."

"My good fellow, this is a very serious business, and you may find yourself in a pretty bad position if you try to hide anything from me. You say that your fare told you that he was a detective?"

"Yes, he did."

"When did he say this?"

"When he left me."

"Did he say anything more?"

"He mentioned his name."

Holmes cast a swift glance of triumph at me.

"Oh, he mentioned his name, did he? That was imprudent. What was the name that he mentioned?"

"His name," said the cabman, "was Mr. Sherlock Holmes."

Never have I seen my friend more completely taken aback than by the cabman's reply. For an instant he sat in silent amazement. Then he burst into a hearty laugh:

"A touch, Watson—an undeniable touch!" said he.[94] "I feel a foil as quick and as supple as my own. He got home upon me very prettily that time. So his name was Sherlock Holmes, was it?"

"Yes, sir, that was the gentleman's name."

"Excellent! Tell me where you picked him up, and all that occurred."

"He hailed me at half-past nine in Trafalgar Square. He said that he was a detective, and he offered me two guineas if I would do exactly what he wanted all day and ask no questions. I was glad

" 'John Clayton, 3, Turpey Street, the Borough.' "
Richard Gutschmidt, *Der Hund von Baskerville* (Stuttgart: Robert Lutz Verlag, 1903)

93 A yard where cabs are kept when off duty.

94 W. W. Robson points out that Holmes here paraphrases Laertes, in *Hamlet*, V, ii: "A touch, a touch, I do confess." Is this further evidence of Holmes's acting career or merely of his knowledge of literature?

" 'His name,' said the cabman, 'was Mr. Sherlock Holmes.' "
Sidney Paget, *Strand Magazine*, 1901

enough to agree. First we drove down to Northumberland Hotel, and waited there until two gentlemen came out and took a cab from the rank. We followed their cab until it pulled up somewhere near here."

"This very door," said Holmes.

"Well, I couldn't be sure of that, but I dare say my fare knew all about it. We pulled up half-way down the street and waited an hour and a half. Then the two gentlemen passed us, walking, and we followed down Baker Street and along—"

"I know," said Holmes.

"Until we got three-quarters down Regent Street. Then my gentleman threw up the trap, and he cried that I should drive right away to Waterloo Station as hard as I could go. I whipped up the mare, and we were there under the ten minutes. Then he paid up his two guineas, like a good one, and away he went into the station. Only just as he was leaving he turned round and said: 'It might interest you to know that you have been driving Mr. Sherlock Holmes.' That's how I came to know the name."

"I see. And you saw no more of him?"

"Not after he went into the station."

"And how would you describe Mr. Sherlock Holmes?"

The cabman scratched his head. "Well, he wasn't altogether such an easy gentleman to describe. I'd put him at forty years of age, and he was of a middle height, two or three inches shorter than you, sir. He was dressed like a toff,[95] and he had a black beard, cut square at the end, and a pale face. I don't know as I could say more than that."

"Colour of his eyes?"

"No, I can't say that."

"Nothing more that you can remember?"

"No, sir; nothing."

"Well, then, here is your half-sovereign. There's another one waiting for you if you can bring any more information. Good night!"

"Good night, sir, and thank you!"

John Clayton departed chuckling, and Holmes turned to me with a shrug of the shoulders and a rueful smile.

"Snap goes our third thread, and we end where we began," said he. "The cunning rascal! He knew our number, knew that Sir Henry Baskerville had consulted me, spotted who I was in Regent Street, conjectured that I had got the number of the cab and would lay my hands on the driver, and so sent back this audacious message. I tell you, Watson, this time we have got a foeman who is worthy of our steel. I've been checkmated in London.[96] I can only wish you better luck in Devonshire. But I'm not easy in my mind about it."

"About what?"

"About sending you. It's an ugly business, Watson, an ugly, dangerous business, and the more I see of it the less I like it. Yes, my dear fellow, you may laugh, but I give you my word that I shall be very glad to have you back safe and sound in Baker Street once more."

95 The word "toff" means a dandy or swell and, according to the 1865 *Slang Dictionary*, derives from the word "tufts," which referred to University students, generally the sons of noblemen, who were distinguished by golden tufts, or tassels, attached to their school caps—a privilege ended in 1870. Other derivations include "toffee-nosed," probably related to the timeless practice of brown-nosing.

96 In "The Retired Colourman," Holmes notes that Josiah Amberley "excelled at chess—one mark, Watson, of a scheming mind." Holmes makes various chess-related remarks in the Canon:

"I must plan some fresh opening move, for this gambit won't work." ("The Illustrious Client")

"Check number one." ("The Priory School")

"It is a provoking check." (*The Sign of Four*)

Of course, the word "check" has long been used to mean a hindrance *outside* the context of chess, and chess metaphors are far less common in Holmes's speech-patterns than card-playing metaphors, which are found in at least five tales (including *The Hound of the Baskervilles*). Nonetheless, Svend Petersen concludes, in "When the Game Was Not Afoot," that "abundant evidence" supports the view that Holmes was a chess devotee.

CHAPTER VI

Baskerville Hall

Sir Henry Baskerville and Dr. Mortimer were ready upon the appointed day, and we started as arranged for Devonshire. Mr. Sherlock Holmes drove with me to the station, and gave me his last parting injunction and advice.

"I will not bias your mind by suggesting theories or suspicions, Watson," said he; "I wish you simply to report facts in the fullest possible manner to me, and you can leave me to do the theorizing."

"What sort of facts?" I asked.

"Anything which may seem to have a bearing, however indirect, upon the case, and especially the relations between young Baskerville and his neighbours, or any fresh particulars concerning the death of Sir Charles. I have made some inquiries myself in the last few days, but the results have, I fear, been negative. One thing only appears to be certain, and that is that Mr. James Desmond, who is the next heir, is an elderly gentleman of a very amiable disposition so that this persecution does not arise from him. I really think that we may eliminate him entirely from our calculations. There remain the people who will actually surround Sir Henry Baskerville upon the moor."

"Would it not be well in the first place to get rid of this Barrymore couple?"

"By no means. You could not make a greater mistake. If they are innocent it would be a cruel injustice, and if they are guilty we should be giving up all chance of bringing it home to them. No, no, we will preserve them upon our list of suspects. Then there is a groom at the Hall, if I remember right. There are two moorland farmers. There is our friend Dr. Mortimer, whom I believe to be entirely honest, and there is his wife, of whom we know nothing. There is this naturalist Stapleton, and there is his sister, who is said to be a young lady of attractions. There is Mr. Frankland, of Lafter Hall, who is also an unknown factor, and there are one or two other neighbours. These are the folk who must be your very special study."

"I will do my best."

"You have arms, I suppose?"

"Yes, I thought it as well to take them."

"Most certainly. Keep your revolver near you night and day, and never relax your precautions."

Our friends had already secured a first-class carriage, and were waiting for us upon the platform.

"No, we have no news of any kind," said Dr. Mortimer, in answer to my friend's questions. "I can swear to one thing, and that is that we have not been shadowed during the last two days. We have never gone out without keeping a sharp watch, and no one could have escaped our notice."

"You have always kept together, I presume?"

"Except yesterday afternoon. I usually give up one day to pure amusement when I come to town, so I spent it at the Museum of the College of Surgeons."[97]

"And I went to look at the folk in the park,"[98] said Baskerville. "But we had no trouble of any kind."

"It was imprudent, all the same," said Holmes, shaking his head and looking very grave. "I beg, Sir Henry, that you will not go about alone. Some great misfortune will befall you if you do. Did you get your other boot?"

"No, sir, it is gone for ever."

"Indeed. That is very interesting. Well, good-bye," he

97 The Museum was the creation of John Hunter, F.R.S. (1728–1793), surgeon, anatomist, and the founder of experimental pathology, whose extraordinary private collection of over 14,000 preparations of human, animal, and plant material was purchased by the British government in 1799 and given over to the care of the Company (later the Royal College) of Surgeons. Hunter, a mechanically minded boy who grew up on a farm near Glasgow and left school at thirteen to roam the fields and teach himself animal economy, first officially took up the scalpel under the guidance of his brother, William Hunter, a London obstetrician and teacher of anatomy and dissection. He displayed an instant talent for the work, and William arranged for him to have surgical training at St. George's, St. Bartholomew's, and Chelsea Hospitals in London, also publishing his younger brother's first paper, "The State of the Testis in the Foetus and on the Hernia Congenita," in *Medical Commentaries* (1762). The perfectly preserved results of the experiments and dissections John Hunter carried out over the ensuing decades—most performed in a succession of homes that were part cadaver storage-place, part menagerie, with live jackals roaming the sitting-rooms and fossils displayed on the shelves of the dens—eventually formed the nucleus of one of the world's greatest museums of comparative anatomy, pathology, osteology, and natural history. Hunter performed many famous, and some infamous, experiments, working on problems as diverse as syphilis and popliteal aneurysm, and never threw anything away. By 1941, when the College of Surgeons suffered extensive bomb damage, the Hunterian Museum held nearly 65,000 specimens. Much of the surviving material, including 3,500 of John Hunter's original eighteenth-century specimens and some spectacular paintings of wild animals by George Stubbs (1724–1806), commissioned by Hunter, is still on display in four museums within the Royal College of Surgeons of England.

Jane Weller offers an overview of the Hunterian Museum in "A Place of Pure Amusement?: The Museum of the Royal College of Surgeons."

98 Presumably Hyde Park, which Dickens's *Dictionary of London* calls "the great fashionable promenade of London." Peter Calamai suggests an alternate interpretation: "[A] drawing from *The Graphic* of Sept. 7, 1887, show[s] St. James's Park dotted with the wrapped bodies of homeless, poor people at mid-day. Such scenes were common in all the public parks for several years toward the end of the 1880s as a depression gripped the country, and many artisans were thrown out of work. It would have been quite a sight for a visitor from Canada."

"Our friends were waiting for us upon the platform."
Sidney Paget, *Strand Magazine*, 1901

added, as the train began to glide down the platform. "Bear in mind, Sir Henry, one of the phrases in that queer old legend which Dr. Mortimer has read to us, and avoid the moor in those hours of darkness when the powers of evil are exalted."

I looked back at the platform when we had left it far behind, and saw the tall, austere figure of Holmes standing motionless and gazing after us.

The journey was a swift and pleasant one, and I spent it in making the more intimate acquaintance of my two companions, and in playing with Dr. Mortimer's spaniel. In a very few hours the brown earth had become ruddy, the brick had changed to granite, and red cows grazed in well-hedged fields where the lush grasses and more luxuriant vegetation spoke of a richer, if a damper, climate. Young Baskerville stared eagerly out of the window, and cried aloud with delight as he recognised the familiar features of the Devon scenery.

"I've been over a good part of the world since I left it, Dr. Watson," said he; "but I have never seen a place to compare with it."

"I never saw a Devonshire man who did not swear by his county," I remarked.

"It depends upon the breed of men quite as much as on the county," said Dr. Mortimer. "A glance at our friend here reveals the rounded head of the Celt, which carries inside it the Celtic enthusiasm and power of attachment. Poor Sir Charles's head was of a very rare type, half Gaelic, half Ivernian[99] in its characteristics. But you were very young when you saw Baskerville Hall, were you not?"

"I was a boy in my teens at the time of my father's death, and had never seen the Hall, for he lived in a little cottage on the south coast. Thence I went straight to a friend in America. I tell you it is all as new to me as it is to Dr. Watson, and I'm as keen as possible to see the moor."

"Are you? Then your wish is easily granted, for there is your

"I looked back at the platform when we had left it far behind, and saw the tall, austere figure of Holmes standing motionless and gazing after us."
Richard Gutschmidt, *Der Hund von Baskerville* (Stuttgart: Robert Lutz Verlag, 1903)

99 A corrupt form of "Hibernian," the Latin term referring to the inhabitants of Ireland.

first sight of the moor," said Dr. Mortimer, pointing out of the carriage window.

Over the green squares of the fields and the low curve of a wood there rose in the distance a grey, melancholy hill, with a strange jagged summit, dim and vague in the distance, like some fantastic landscape in a dream. Baskerville sat for a long time, his eyes fixed upon it, and I read upon his eager face how much it meant to him, this first sight of that strange spot where the men of his blood had held sway so long and left their mark so deep. There he sat, with his tweed suit and his American accent, in the corner of a prosaic railway-carriage, and yet as I looked at his dark and expressive face I felt more than ever how true a descendant he was of that long line of high-blooded, fiery, and masterful men. There were pride, valour and strength in his thick brows, his sensitive nostrils, and his large hazel eyes. If on that forbidding moor a difficult and dangerous quest should lie before us, this was at least a comrade for whom one might venture to take a risk with the certainty that he would bravely share it.

The train pulled up at a small wayside station,[100] and we all descended. Outside, beyond the low, white fence, a wagonette[101] with a pair of cobs[102] was waiting. Our coming was evidently a great event, for station-master and porters clustered round us to carry out our luggage. It was a sweet, simple country spot, but I was surprised to observe that by the gate there stood two soldierly men in dark uniforms, who leaned upon their short rifles and glanced keenly at us as we passed. The coachman, a hard-faced, gnarled little fellow, saluted Sir Henry Baskerville, and in a few minutes we were flying swiftly down the broad white road. Rolling pasture lands curved upwards on either side of us, and old gabled houses peeped out from amid the thick green foliage, but behind the peaceful and sunlit countryside there rose ever, dark against the evening sky, the long, gloomy curve of the moor, broken by the jagged and sinister hills.

The wagonette swung round into a side road, and we curved upwards through deep lanes worn by centuries of wheels, high banks on either side, heavy with dripping moss and fleshy hart's-tongue ferns.[103] Bronzing bracken and mottled bramble gleamed in the light of the sinking sun. Still steadily rising, we passed over a narrow granite bridge, and skirted a noisy stream,

100 In "Always on Sunday, Watson!," William H. Gill suggests that the station was either Brent or Ivybridge, south of the moor. William S. Baring-Gould proposes that Watson and his party continued along the line to Coryton Station. Philip Weller points out that the latter station is "on the wrong side of the Moor for the setting sun to have been seen over the Moor." He considers three other stations as well, Ashburton, Bovey Tracey, and Buckfastleigh, but discards them all as failing in one respect or another to match Watson's description.

101 A four-wheeled carriage, open, or made with a removable cover, with inward-facing benches in addition to the customary front seats or benches.

A wagonette.

102 Short-legged, strong horses, usually used for heavy carriage work.

103 A variety of fern with long, fleshy fronds.

which gushed swiftly down, foaming and roaring amid the grey boulders. Both road and stream wound up through a valley dense with scrub oak and fir. At every turning Baskerville gave an exclamation of delight, looking eagerly about him and asking countless questions. To his eyes all seemed beautiful, but to me a tinge of melancholy lay upon the countryside, which bore so clearly the mark of the waning year. Yellow leaves carpeted the lanes and fluttered down upon us as we passed. The rattle of our wheels died away as we drove through drifts of rotting vegetation—sad gifts, as it seemed to me, for Nature to throw before the carriage of the returning heir of the Baskervilles.

"Halloa!" cried Dr. Mortimer, "what is this?"

A steep curve of heath-clad land, an outlying spur of the moor, lay in front of us. On the summit, hard and clear like an equestrian statue upon its pedestal, was a mounted soldier, dark and stern, his rifle poised ready over his forearm. He was watching the road along which we travelled.

"What is this, Perkins?" asked Dr. Mortimer.

Our driver half turned in his seat.

"There's a convict escaped from Princetown, sir. He's been out three days now, and the warders watch every road and every station, but they've had no sight of him yet. The farmers about here don't like it, sir, and that's a fact."

"Well, I understand that they get five pounds if they can give information."

"Yes, sir, but the chance of five pounds is but a poor thing compared to the chance of having your throat cut. You see, it isn't like any ordinary convict. This is a man that would stick at nothing."

"Who is he, then?"

"It is Selden, the Notting Hill[104] murderer."

I remembered the case well, for it was one in which Holmes had taken an interest on account of the peculiar ferocity of the crime and the wanton brutality which had marked all the actions of the assassin. The commutation of his death sentence had been due to some doubts as to his complete sanity, so atrocious was his conduct. Our wagonette had topped a rise and in front of us rose the huge expanse of the moor, mottled with gnarled and craggy cairns[105] and tors. A cold wind swept down from it and set us shivering. Somewhere there, on that desolate plain, was lurking this fiendish man, hiding in a burrow like a

104 Notting Hill, also known as Kensington Park and, much earlier, as Notting Dale, is characterised by Harold P. Clunn in *The Face of London* as "a handsome quarter of the Royal Borough of Kensington." Although many of the neo-classical homes commissioned by the Ladbroke family and built by high-society architects were impressive in the mid-Victorian era, the area was notorious for its pig-keepers, brickfields, and attendant public-health nuisances, with rubbish and effluent standing in holes where the clay for brickmaking had been dug. Charles Dickens wrote of the neighbourhood's being simultaneously "studded thickly with elegant villas and mansions" and "a plague-spot, scarcely equalled for its insalubrity by any other in London" (*Household Words*, 1850).

105 Its Gaelic predecessor, the term *carn*, meant a "heap of stones."

wild beast, his heart full of malignancy against the whole race which had cast him out. It needed but this to complete the grim suggestiveness of the barren waste, the chilling wind, and the darkling sky. Even Baskerville fell silent and pulled his overcoat more closely around him.

We had left the fertile country behind and beneath us. We looked back on it now, the slanting rays of a low sun turning the streams to threads of gold and glowing on the red earth new turned by the plough and the broad tangle of the woodlands. The road in front of us grew bleaker and wilder over huge russet and olive slopes, sprinkled with giant boulders. Now and then we passed a moorland cottage, walled and roofed with stone, with no creeper to break its harsh outline. Suddenly we looked down into a cup-like depression, patched with stunted oaks and firs which had been twisted and bent by the fury of years of storm. Two high, narrow towers rose over the trees. The driver pointed with his whip."

"Baskerville Hall," said he.

Its master had risen, and was staring with flushed cheeks and shining eyes. A few minutes later we had reached the lodge gates, a maze of fantastic tracery in wrought iron, with weather-bitten pillars on either side, blotched with lichens, and surmounted by the boars' heads of the Baskervilles. The lodge was a ruin of black granite and bared ribs of rafters, but facing it was a new building, half constructed, the first-fruit of Sir Charles's South African gold.

Through the gateway we passed into the avenue, where the wheels were again hushed amid the leaves, and the old trees shot their branches in a sombre tunnel over our heads. Baskerville shuddered as he looked up the long, dark drive to where the house glimmered like a ghost at the farther end.

"Was it here?" he asked, in a low voice.

"No, no, the Yew Alley is on the other side."

The young heir glanced round with a gloomy face.

"It's no wonder my uncle felt as if trouble were coming on him in such a place as this," said he. "It's enough to scare any man. I'll have a row of electric lamps up here inside of six months, and you won't know it again with a thousand-candle power Swan and Edison[106] right here in front of the hall door."

The avenue opened into a broad expanse of turf, and the house lay before us. In the fading light I could see that the cen-

106 Joseph Swan demonstrated a carbon filament lightbulb in Newcastle at least ten months prior to Thomas Alva Edison's announcement of his invention. Swan received a British patent in 1878 for the same bulb that Edison patented in the United States in 1879. Swan filed suit for patent infringement, and as part of the settlement,

Ediswan Electric Lamps.
Victorian Advertisments

Edison was forced to take Swan in as a partner in his British electric works. The company was called the Edison and Swan United Electric Company. The company marketed lightbulbs under the trade name "Ediswan." Eventually, however, Edison acquired all of Swan's interest in the company. William S. Baring-Gould inappropriately corrects Watson's reporting here, claiming that since Edison and Swan marketed two different lightbulbs, Sir Henry must have said "Swan or Edison."

Light bulb by Thomas Edison (*ca.* 1885).

"The driver pointed with his whip—'Baskerville Hall,' said he."
Sidney Paget. *Strand Magazine*, 1901

107 A term describing a building topped with battlements, embrasures, or loopholes (the last being openings through which small arms may be fired or which permit observation).

108 The panes of a mullioned window are divided by a vertical bar. They are found especially in Gothic architecture. Hurlstone, the ancestral home of the Musgraves ("The Musgrave Ritual"), also has mullioned windows.

tre was a heavy block of building from which a porch projected. The whole front was draped in ivy, with a patch clipped bare here and there where a window or a coat-of-arms broke through the dark veil. From this central block rose the twin towers, ancient, crenellated,[107] and pierced with many loopholes. To right and left of the turrets were more modern wings of black granite. A dull light shone through heavy mullioned[108] windows, and from the high chimneys which rose from the steep, high-angled roof there sprang a single black column of smoke.

"Welcome, Sir Henry! Welcome to Baskerville Hall!"

A tall man had stepped from the shadow of the porch to open the door of the wagonette. The figure of a woman was silhouetted against the yellow light of the hall. She came out and helped the man to hand down our bags.

"You don't mind my driving straight home, Sir Henry?" said Dr. Mortimer. "My wife is expecting me."

109 Beams or rafters.

110 Also known as a "cat," a "dog" is a double tripod set before an open fireplace and used as a toasting-stand.

" 'Welcome, Sir Henry.' "
Sidney Paget, *Strand Magazine*, 1901

"Surely you will stay and have some dinner?"

"No, I must go. I shall probably find some work awaiting me. I would stay to show you over the house, but Barrymore will be a better guide than I. Good-bye, and never hesitate night or day to send for me if I can be of service."

The wheels died away down the drive while Sir Henry and I turned into the hall, and the door clanged heavily behind us. It was a fine apartment in which we found ourselves, large, lofty, and heavily raftered with huge balks[109] of age-blackened oak. In the great old-fashioned fireplace behind the high iron dogs[110] a log-fire crackled and snapped. Sir Henry and I held out our hands to it, for we were numb from our long drive. Then we gazed round us at the high, thin window of old stained glass, the oak panelling, the stags' heads, the coat-of-arms upon the walls, all dim and sombre in the subdued light of the central lamp.

"It's just as I imagined it," said Sir Henry. "Is it not the very picture of an old family home? To think that this should be the same hall in which for five hundred years my people have lived! It strikes me solemn to think of it."

I saw his dark face lit up with a boyish enthusiasm as he gazed about him. The light beat upon him where he stood, but long shadows trailed down the walls and hung like a black canopy above him. Barrymore had returned from taking our luggage to our rooms. He stood in front of us now with the subdued manner of a well-trained servant. He was a remarkable-looking man, tall, handsome, with a square black beard and pale distinguished features.

"Would you wish dinner to be served at once, sir?"

"Is it ready?"

"In a very few minutes, sir. You will find hot water in your rooms. My wife and I will be happy, Sir Henry, to stay with you until you have made your fresh arrangements, but you will understand that under the new conditions this house will require a considerable staff."

"What new conditions?"

"I only meant, sir, that Sir Charles led a very retired life, and we were able to look after his wants. You would, naturally, wish to have more company, and so you will need changes in your household."

"Do you mean that your wife and you wish to leave?"

"Only when it is quite convenient to you, sir."

"But your family have been with us for several generations, have they not? I should be sorry to begin my life here by breaking an old family connection."

I seemed to discern some signs of emotion upon the butler's white face.

"I feel that also, sir, and so does my wife. But to tell the truth, sir, we were both very much attached to Sir Charles, and his death gave us a shock and made these sur-

" 'But your family have been with us for several generations, have they not?' "
Richard Gutschmidt, *Der Hund von Baskerville* (Stuttgart: Robert Lutz Verlag, 1903)

roundings very painful to us. I fear that we shall never again be easy in our minds at Baskerville Hall."

"But what do you intend to do?"

"I have no doubt, sir, that we shall succeed in establishing ourselves in some business. Sir Charles's generosity has given us the means to do so. And now, sir, perhaps I had best show you to your rooms."

A square balustraded gallery ran round the top of the old hall, approached by a double stair. From this central point two long corridors extended the whole length of the building, from which all the bedrooms opened. My own was in the same wing as Baskerville's and almost next door to it. These rooms appeared to be much more modern than the central part of the house, and the bright paper and numerous candles did something to remove the sombre impression which our arrival had left upon my mind.

But the dining-room which opened out of the hall was a place of shadow and gloom. It was a long chamber with a step separating the daïs where the family sat from the lower portion reserved for their dependents. At one end a minstrels' gallery overlooked it. Black beams shot across above our heads, with a smoke-darkened ceiling beyond them. With rows of flaring torches to light it up, and the colour and rude hilarity of an old-time banquet, it might have softened; but now, when two black-clothed gentlemen sat in the little circle of light thrown by a shaded lamp, one's voice became hushed and one's spirit subdued. A dim line of ancestors, in every variety of dress, from the Elizabethan knight to the buck of the Regency,[111] stared down upon us and daunted us by their silent company. We talked little, and I for one was glad when the meal was over and we were able to retire into the modern billiard-room and smoke a cigarette.

"My word, it isn't a very cheerful place," said Sir Henry. "I suppose one can tone down to it, but I feel a bit out of the picture at present. I don't wonder that my uncle got a little jumpy if he lived all alone in such a house as this. However, if it suits you, we will retire early tonight, and perhaps things may seem more cheerful in the morning."

I drew aside my curtains before I went to bed and looked out from my window. It opened upon the grassy space which lay in front of the hall door. Beyond, two copses of trees moaned and

111 The period 1811–1820, during which the Prince of Wales was given the powers of regent because of the insanity of George III. While the intellectual life of England flourished, the moral atmosphere of the era was dissolute, and the life of the Regency "buck" was filled with gambling, sport, drink, and flirtation. Conan Doyle captures its flavour in *Rodney Stone* (1896). In the following incident, Stone's uncle explains to the prince why he has given up duelling:

> "A painful incident happened the last time that I was out, and it sickened me of it."
>
> "You killed your man—?"
>
> "No, no, sir, it was worse than that. I had a coat that Weston has never equalled. To say that it fitted me is not to express it. It was me—like the hide on a horse. I've had sixty from him since, but he could never approach it. The sit of the collar brought tears into my eyes, sir, when first I saw it; and as to the waist—"
>
> "But the duel, Tregellis!" cried the Prince.
>
> "Well, sir, I wore it at the duel, like the thoughtless fool that I was. It was Major Hunter, of the Guards, with whom I had had a little *tracasserie*, because I hinted that he should not come into Brookes's smelling of the stables. I fired first, and missed. He fired, and I shrieked in despair. 'He's hit! A surgeon! A surgeon!' they cried. 'A tailor! A tailor!' said I, for there was a double hole through the tails of my masterpiece. No, it was past all repair. You may laugh, sir, but I'll never see the like of it again."

"The dining-room was a place of shadow and gloom."
Sidney Paget, *Strand Magazine*, 1901

swung in a rising wind. A half moon broke through the rifts of racing clouds. In its cold light I saw beyond the trees a broken fringe of rocks and the long, low curve of the melancholy moor. I closed the curtain, feeling that my last impression was in keeping with the rest.

And yet it was not quite the last. I found myself weary and yet wakeful, tossing restlessly from side to side, seeking for the sleep which would not come. Far away a chiming clock struck out the quarters of the hours, but otherwise a deathly silence lay upon the old house. And than suddenly, in the very dead of night, there came a sound to my ears, clear, resonant, and unmistakable. It was the sob of a woman, the muffled, strangling gasp of one who is torn by an uncontrollable sorrow. I sat up in bed and listened intently. The noise could not have been far away, and was certainly in the house. For half an hour I waited with every nerve on the alert, but there came no other sound save the chiming clock and the rustle of the ivy on the wall.

CHAPTER VII

The Stapletons of Merripit House

THE FRESH BEAUTY of the following morning did something to efface from our minds the grim and grey impression which had been left upon both of us by our first experience of Baskerville Hall. As Sir Henry and I sat at breakfast the sunlight flooded in through the high mullioned windows, throwing watery patches of colour from the coats-of-arms which covered them. The dark panelling glowed like bronze in the golden rays, and it was hard to realize that this was indeed the chamber which had struck such a gloom into our souls upon the evening before.

"I guess it is ourselves and not the house that we have to blame!" said the baronet. "We were tired with our journey and chilled by our drive, so we took a grey view of the place. Now we are fresh and well, so it is all cheerful once more."

"And yet it was not entirely a question of imagination," I answered. "Did you, for example, happen to hear someone, a woman I think, sobbing in the night?"

"That is curious, for I did when I was half asleep fancy that I heard something of the sort. I waited quite a time, but there was no more of it, so I concluded that it was all a dream."

"I heard it distinctly, and I am sure that it was really the sob of a woman."

"We must ask about this right away."

He rang the bell and asked Barrymore whether he could account for our experience. It seemed to me that the pallid features of the butler turned a shade paler still as he listened to his master's question.

"There are only two women in the house, Sir Henry," he answered. "One is the scullery-maid, who sleeps in the other wing. The other is my wife, and I can answer for it that the sound could not have come from her."

And yet he lied as he said it, for it chanced that after breakfast I met Mrs. Barrymore in the long corridor with the sun full upon her face. She was a large, impassive, heavy-featured woman with a stern, set expression of mouth. But her tell-tale eyes were red and glanced at me from between swollen lids. It was she, then, who wept in the night, and if she did so her husband must know it. Yet he had taken the obvious risk of discovery in declaring that it was not so. Why had he done this? And why did she weep so bitterly? Already round this pale-faced, handsome, black-bearded man there was gathering an atmosphere of mystery and of gloom. It was he who had been the first to discover the body of Sir Charles, and we had only his word for all the circumstances which led up to the old man's death. Was it possible that it was Barrymore, after all, whom we had seen in the cab in Regent Street? The beard might well have been the same. The cabman had described a somewhat shorter man, but such an impression might easily have been erroneous. How could I settle the point for ever? Obviously the first thing to do was to see the Grimpen postmaster, and find whether the test telegram had really been placed in Barrymore's own hands. Be the answer what it might, I should at least have something to report to Sherlock Holmes.

Sir Henry had numerous papers to examine after breakfast, so that the time was propitious for my excursion. It was a pleasant walk of four miles along the edge of the moor, leading me at last to a small grey hamlet, in which two larger buildings, which proved to be the inn and the house of Dr. Mortimer, stood high above the rest. The postmaster, who was also the village grocer, had a clear recollection of the telegram.

"Certainly, sir," said he, "I had the telegram delivered to Mr. Barrymore exactly as directed."

"Who delivered it?"

"My boy here. James, you delivered that telegram to Mr. Barrymore at the Hall last week, did you not?"

"Yes, father, I delivered it."

"Into his own hands?" I asked.

"Well, he was up in the loft at the time, so that I could not put it into his own hands, but I gave it into Mrs. Barrymore's hands, and she promised to deliver it at once."

"Did you see Mr. Barrymore?"

"No, sir; I tell you he was in the loft."

"If you didn't see him, how do you know he was in the loft?"

"Well, surely his own wife ought to know where he is," said the postmaster, testily. "Didn't he get the telegram? If there is any mistake it is for Mr. Barrymore himself to complain."

It seemed hopeless to pursue the inquiry any farther, but it was clear that in spite of Holmes's ruse we had no proof that Barrymore had not been in London all the time. Suppose that it were so—suppose that the same man had been the last who had seen Sir Charles alive, and the first to dog the new heir when he returned to England. What then? Was he the agent of others, or had he some sinister design of his own? What interest could he have in persecuting the Baskerville family? I thought of the strange warning clipped out of the leading article of *The Times*. Was that his work, or was it possibly the doing of someone who was bent upon counteracting his schemes? The only conceivable motive was that which had been suggested by Sir Henry, that if the family could be scared away a comfortable and permanent home would be secured for the Barrymores. But surely such an explanation as that would be quite inadequate to account for the deep and subtle scheming which seemed to be weaving an invisible net round the young baronet. Holmes himself had said that no more complex case had come to him in all the long series of his sensational investigations. I prayed, as I walked back along the grey, lonely road, that my friend might soon be freed from his preoccupations and able to come down to take this heavy burden of responsibility from my shoulders.

Suddenly my thoughts were interrupted by the sound of running feet behind me and by a voice which called me by

"I turned, expecting to see Dr. Mortimer, but to my surprise it was a stranger who was pursuing me."
Richard Gutschmidt, *Der Hund von Baskerville*
(Stuttgart: Robert Lutz Verlag, 1903)

name. I turned, expecting to see Dr. Mortimer, but to my surprise it was a stranger who was pursuing me. He was a small, slim, clean-shaven, prim-faced man, flaxen-haired and lean-jawed, between thirty and forty years of age, dressed in a grey suit and wearing a straw hat. A tin box for botanical specimens hung over his shoulder, and he carried a green butterfly-net in one of his hands.

"You will, I am sure, excuse my presumption, Dr. Watson," said he, as he came panting up to where I stood. "Here on the moor we are a homely folk, and do not wait for formal introductions. You may possibly have heard my name from our mutual friend, Mortimer. I am Stapleton, of Merripit House."[112]

"Your net and box would have told me as much," said I, "for I knew that Mr. Stapleton was a naturalist. But how did you know me?"

"I have been calling on Mortimer, and he pointed you out to me from the window of his surgery as you passed. As our road

112 Merripit was an ancient tenement in the midst of Dartmoor (later part of Postbridge); the place-name is still in use, to designate a Hill, a House, and other naturally occurring and built locations. David L. Hammer, in *The Game Is Afoot*, identifies Nun's Cross Farm, three-quarters of a mile south-west of the Fox Tor Mire, as Merripit House. Philip Weller agrees that this is the best candidate but points out that the building was a farm throughout its nineteenth-century existence.

"It was a stranger pursuing me."
Sidney Paget, *Strand Magazine*, 1901

lay the same way, I thought that I would overtake you and introduce myself. I trust that Sir Henry is none the worse for his journey?"

"He is very well, thank you."

"We were all rather afraid that after the sad death of Sir Charles the new baronet might refuse to live here. It is asking much of a wealthy man to come down and bury himself in a place of this kind, but I need not tell you that it means a very great deal to the countryside. Sir Henry has, I suppose, no superstitious fears in the matter?"

"I do not think that it is likely."

"Of course you know the legend of the fiend dog which haunts the family?"

"I have heard it."

"It is extraordinary how credulous the peasants are about here! Any number of them are ready to swear that they have seen such a creature upon the moor." He spoke with a smile, but I seemed to read in his eyes that he took the matter more seriously. "The story took a great hold upon the imagination of Sir Charles, and I have no doubt that it led to his tragic end."

"But how?"

"His nerves were so worked up that the appearance of any dog might have had a fatal effect upon his diseased heart. I fancy that he really did see something of the kind upon that last night in the Yew Alley. I feared that some disaster might occur, for I was very fond of the old man, and I knew that his heart was weak."

"How did you know that?"

"My friend Mortimer told me."[113]

"You think, then, that some dog pursued Sir Charles, and that he died of fright in consequence?"

"Have you any better explanation?"

"I have not come to any conclusion."

"Has Mr. Sherlock Holmes?"

The words took away my breath for an instant, but a glance at the placid face and steadfast eyes of my companion showed that no surprise was intended.

"It is useless for us to pretend that we do not know you, Dr. Watson," said he. "The records of your detective have reached us here,[114] and you could not celebrate him without being known yourself. When Mortimer told me your name he could not deny your identity. If you are here, then it follows that Mr. Sherlock Holmes is interesting himself in the matter, and I am naturally curious to know what view he may take."

"I am afraid that I cannot answer that question."

"May I ask if he is going to honour us with a visit himself?"

"He cannot leave town at present. He has other cases which engage his attention."

"What a pity! He might throw some light on that which is so dark to us. But as to your own researches, if there is any possible way in which I can be of service to you, I trust that you will command me. If I had any indication of the nature of your suspicions, or how you propose to investigate the case, I might perhaps even now give you some aid or advice."

"I assure you that I am simply here upon a visit to my friend Sir Henry, and that I need no help of any kind."

"Excellent!" said Stapleton. "You are perfectly right to be wary and discreet. I am justly reproved for what I feel was an

113 Frederick J. Jaeger and Rose M. Vogel, in *The Hound from Hell*, express shock that Dr. Watson is not made suspicious of Dr. Mortimer by this apparent betrayal of patients' confidences.

114 All of the major chronologists, with the exception of H. W. Bell, conclude that in light of Stapleton's clear reference to Watson's published writings, the case must have taken place after 1887 (see *Appendix 5*). But Peter A. Ruber ("On a Defence of H. W. Bell") argues that Stapleton could be referring to newspaper accounts of Holmes's activities: "During these years Holmes surely would have been without problems had it not been for the . . . publicity that spread his fame world-wide." See also Peter Calamai's "A Peek in Mrs. Hudson's Scrapbook: Victorian Newspaper Accounts of Sherlock Holmes," for a collection of hitherto unknown press clippings.

unjustifiable intrusion, and I promise you that I will not mention the matter again."

We had come to a point where a narrow grassy path struck off from the road and wound away across the moor. A steep, boulder-sprinkled hill lay upon the right which had in bygone days been cut into a granite quarry. The face which was turned towards us formed a dark cliff, with ferns and brambles growing in its niches. From over a distant rise there floated a grey plume of smoke.

"A moderate walk along this moor-path brings us to Merripit House," said he. "Perhaps you will spare an hour that I may have the pleasure of introducing you to my sister."

My first thought was that I should be by Sir Henry's side. But then I remembered the pile of papers and bills with which his study table was littered. It was certain that I could not help him with those. And Holmes had expressly said that I should study the neighbours upon the moor. I accepted Stapleton's invitation, and we turned together down the path.

"It is a wonderful place, the moor," said he, looking round over the undulating downs, long green rollers, with crests of jagged granite foaming up into fantastic surges. "You never tire of the moor. You cannot think the wonderful secrets which it contains. It is so vast, and so barren, and so mysterious."

"You know it well, then?"

"I have only been here two years. The residents would call me a new-comer. We came shortly after Sir Charles settled. But my tastes led me to explore every part of the country round, and I should think that there are few men who know it better than I do."

"Is it so hard to know?"

"Very hard. You see, for example, this great plain to the north here, with the queer hills breaking out of it. Do you observe anything remarkable about that?"

"It would be a rare place for a gallop."

"You would naturally think so, and the thought has cost folk their lives before now. You notice those bright green spots scattered thickly over it?"

"Yes, they seem more fertile than the rest."

Stapleton laughed.

"That is the great Grimpen Mire,"[115] said he. "A false step yonder means death to man or beast. Only yesterday I saw one

115 Michael Harrison notes, in *In the Footsteps of Sherlock Holmes*, that Grimpen Mire is Grimspound Bog, "but here I would ask the reader to join with me in praising Watson's sensitive ear. How much more sinister does 'Grimpen Mire' sound?" However, according to David L. Hammer, in *The Game Is Afoot*, Grimspound Bog was never a mire. Philip Weller points out that there is no such location as Grimspound Bog on Dartmoor and that in the small, marshy area on the eastern side of Grimspound one can only sink ankle deep, even though this area has never been artificially drained. Weller also notes that Fletcher Robinson recorded that the mire he visited with Arthur Conan Doyle in 1901 was well to the west of Grimspound, and Robinson's description perfectly matches Fox Tor Mires. Of course, any such visit occurred well after the events of *The Hound of the Baskervilles*. Both Hammer and Weller propose Fox Tor Mires as a more likely candidate, and Anthony Howlett, a founder of the Sherlock Holmes Society of London, calls this proposal "one of the few certain identifications." Weller writes, to this editor, that Grimspound is pronounced, in the Dartmoor dialect, "Grimspun," making the match even closer.

Grimspound.
An Exploration of Dartmoor, by J. Ll. W. Page (1895).

of the moor ponies wander into it. He never came out. I saw his head for quite a long time craning out of the bog-hole, but it sucked him down at last. Even in dry seasons it is a danger to cross it, but after these autumn rains it is an awful place. And yet I can find my way to the very heart of it and return alive. By George, there is another of those miserable ponies!"

Something brown was rolling and tossing among the green sedges. Then a long, agonized, writhing neck shot upwards and a dreadful cry echoed over the moor. It turned me cold with horror, but my companion's nerves seemed to be stronger than mine.

"It's gone!" said he. "The Mire has him. Two in two days, and many more, perhaps, for they get in the way of going there in the dry weather, and never know the difference until the Mire has them in its clutch. It's a bad place, the great Grimpen Mire."

"And you say you can penetrate it?"

"Yes, there are one or two paths which a very active man can take. I have found them out."

"But why should you wish to go into so horrible a place?"

"Well, you see the hills beyond? They are really islands cut off on all sides by the impassable Mire, which has crawled round them in the course of years. That is where the rare plants and the butterflies are, if you have the wit to reach them."

" 'That is the great Grimpen Mire.' "
Sidney Paget, *Strand Magazine*, 1901

"I shall try my luck some day."

He looked at me with a surprised face. "For God's sake put such an idea out of your mind," said he. "Your blood would be upon my head. I assure you that there would not be the least chance of your coming back alive. It is only by remembering certain complex landmarks that I am able to do it."

"Halloa!" I cried. "What is that?"

A long, low moan, indescribably sad, swept over the moor. It filled the whole air, and yet it was impossible to say whence it came. From a dull murmur it swelled into a deep roar and then sank back into a melancholy, throbbing murmur once again. Stapleton looked at me with a curious expression in his face.

"Queer place, the moor!" said he.

"But what is it?"

"The peasants say it is the Hound of the Baskervilles calling for its prey. I've heard it once or twice before, but never quite so loud."

I looked round, with a chill of fear in my heart, at the huge swelling plain, mottled with the green patches of rushes. Nothing stirred over the vast expanse save a pair of ravens, which croaked loudly from a tor behind us.

"You are an educated man. You don't believe such nonsense as that?" said I. "What do you think is the cause of so strange a sound?"

"Bogs make queer noises sometimes. It's the mud settling, or the water rising, or something."

"No, no, that was a living voice."

"Well, perhaps it was. Did you ever hear a bittern[116] booming?"

"No, I never did."

"It's a very rare bird—practically extinct—in England now, but all things are possible upon the moor. Yes, I should not be surprised to learn that what we have heard is the cry of the last of the bitterns."[117]

"It's the weirdest, strangest thing that ever I heard in my life."

"Yes, it's rather an uncanny place altogether. Look at the hillside yonder. What do you make of those?"

The whole steep slope was covered with grey circular rings of stone, a score of them at least.

"What are they? Sheep-pens?"

"No, they are the homes of our worthy ancestors. Prehistoric man lived thickly on the moor,[118] and as no one particular has lived there since, we find all his little arrangements exactly as he left them. These are his wigwams with the roofs off. You can even see his hearth and his couch if you have the curiosity to go inside."

"But it is quite a town. When was it inhabited?"

"Neolithic man—no date."

"What did he do?"

"He grazed his cattle on these slopes, and he learned to dig for tin when the bronze sword began to supersede the stone axe. Look at the great trench in the opposite hill. That is his mark. Yes, you will find some very singular points about the moor, Dr. Watson. Oh, excuse me an instant. It is surely *Cyclopides*."[119]

A small fly or moth had fluttered across our path, and in an instant Stapleton was rushing with extraordinary energy and

116 Bitterns are a member of the subfamily *Botaurinae*, which is made up of small and medium-sized herons. According to The Royal Society for the Protection of Birds, these shy, elusive creatures, which seek their food in twilight, were made nearly extinct by 1886 due to habitat destruction and persecution—as Stapleton indicates presently. They are a wetland species and live in reedbeds. Their foghorn-like call has given rise over the centuries to numerous superstitions.

Bittern.
Bewick's British Birds (1826)

117 Lisa McGaw writes, in "Some Trifling Notes on Sherlock Holmes and Ornithology," that Stapleton identifies the bird once he intuits that Watson was unfamiliar with it—and not before—and that, in any case, it is improbable that a bittern would live anywhere but in a marsh. Walter Shepherd, in *On the Scent with Sherlock Holmes* (1978), also points out that Watson's description of the sound he heard on the moor—"a deep, muttered rumble, musical and yet menacing, rising and falling like the low, constant murmur of the sea"—is totally unlike the authorities' descriptions of a bittern: James Fisher characterises it as a "penetrating *b=wump*," and Peterson, Mountfort and Hollom (*A Field Guide to the Birds of Britain and Europe*) as "beginning with two or three grunts, followed by an audible intake of breath and concluding with a loud, penetrating *woomp*!"

speed in pursuit of it. To my dismay the creature flew straight for the great Mire, but my acquaintance never paused for an instant, bounding from tuft to tuft behind it, his green net waving in the air. His grey clothes and jerky, zigzag, irregular progress made him not unlike some huge moth himself. I was standing watching this pursuit with a mixture of admiration for his extraordinary activity and fear lest he should lose his footing in the treacherous Mire, when I heard the sound of steps, and, turning round, found a woman near me upon the path. She had come from the direction in which the plume of smoke indicated the position of Merripit House, but the dip of the moor had hid her until she was quite close.

I could not doubt that this was the Miss Stapleton of whom I had been told, since ladies of any sort must be few upon the moor, and I remembered that I had heard someone describe her as being a beauty. The woman who approached me was certainly that, and of a most uncommon type. There could not have been a greater contrast between brother and sister, for Stapleton was neutral-tinted, with light hair and grey eyes, while she was darker than any brunette whom I have seen in England—slim, elegant and tall. She had a proud, finely cut face, so regular that it might have seemed impassive were it not for the sensitive mouth and the beautiful dark, eager eyes. With her perfect figure and elegant dress she was, indeed, a strange apparition upon a lonely moorland path. Her eyes were on her brother as I turned, and then she quickened her pace towards me. I had raised my hat, and was about to make some explanatory remark, when her own words turned all my thoughts into a new channel.

"Go back!" she said. "Go straight back to London, instantly."

I could only stare at her in stupid surprise. Her eyes blazed at me, and she tapped the ground impatiently with her foot.

"Why should I go back?" I asked.

"I cannot explain." She spoke in a low, eager voice, with a curious lisp in her utterance. "But for God's sake do what I ask you. Go back, and never set foot upon the moor again."

"But I have only just come."

"Man, man!" she cried. "Can you not tell when a warning is for your own good? Go back to London! Start tonight! Get away from this place at all costs! Hush, my brother is coming! Not a word of what I have said. Would you mind getting that

118 Baedeker's *Great Britain* (1894) characterises the moors as abounding in menhirs, stone circles, and "other relics of the ancient Britons." Michael Harrison notes a stone circle at Grimspound and comments, "Here our Neolithic, Hamitic-speaking ancestors built themselves what may almost be called a New Stone Age metropolis, not far from the curiously—and most suggestively—named Hound Tor."

But Philip Weller, a leading expert on the Dartmoor of Holmes's time, in private correspondence with this editor, responds: "Harrison's comments are, like Watson's deductions about Mortimer's walking stick, almost totally erroneous, in that [Harrison] seems to have uncritically accepted Stapleton's reference to the huts being 'Neolithic' in the same way that Watson subsequently accepted Stapleton's periodisation. The huts at Grimspound are not Neolithic, since they are (like almost all of the prehistoric huts on Dartmoor) from the Bronze Age. There is no New Stone Age metropolis near Hound Tor or anywhere else on Dartmoor. Grimspound is not the most prolific stone hut settlement on Dartmoor, in that it contains only 24 stone hut remains, whereas Ryder's Rings, adjacent to the Houndianly-appropriate Black Tor and Shipley Tor, has more than 50 stone huts and storehouses. The inhabitants of these huts were certainly not Hamitic-speaking."

119 See *Appendix 1* for a discussion of the *Cyclopides*.

" 'Go back!' she said."
Sidney Paget, *Strand Magazine*, 1901

orchid[120] for me among the mare's-tails[121] yonder? We are very rich in orchids on the moor, though, of course, you are rather late to see the beauties of the place."

Stapleton had abandoned the chase, and came back to us breathing hard and flushed with his exertions.

"Halloa, Beryl!" said he, and it seemed to me that the tone of his greeting was not altogether a cordial one.

"Well, Jack, you are very hot."

"Yes, I was chasing a *Cyclopides*. He is very rare, and seldom found in the late autumn. What a pity that I should have missed him!"

He spoke unconcernedly, but his small light eyes glanced incessantly from the girl to me.

"You have introduced yourselves, I can see."

120 See *Appendix 1* for a discussion of the orchid.

121 *Hippuris vulgaris*, a plant resembling a horse's tail. R. F. May points out that mare's-tail is "a plant of ponds, lakes and slow-running water." Instead, he proposes, Mrs. Stapleton likely misidentified the marsh horsetail (*Equisetum palustre*). May's conclusions respecting the orchid are discussed in *Appendix 1*.

122 A farmer who fattens livestock for market.

" 'Go back! Go straight back to London, instantly!' "
Richard Gutschmidt, *Der Hund von Baskerville* (Stuttgart: Robert Lutz Verlag, 1903)

"Yes. I was telling Sir Henry that it was rather late for him to see the true beauties of the moor."

"Why, who do you think this is?"

"I imagine that it must be Sir Henry Baskerville."

"No, no," said I. "Only a humble commoner, but his friend. My name is Dr. Watson."

A flush of vexation passed over her expressive face.

"We have been talking at cross purposes," said she.

"Why, you had not very much time for talk," her brother remarked, with the same questioning eyes.

"I talked as if Dr. Watson were a resident instead of being merely a visitor," said she. "It cannot much matter to him whether it is early or late for the orchids. But you will come on, will you not, and see Merripit House?"

A short walk brought us to it, a bleak moorland house, once the farm of some grazier[122] in the old prosperous days, but now put into repair and turned into a modern dwelling. An orchard surrounded it, but the trees, as is usual upon the moor, were stunted and nipped, and the effect of the whole place was mean and melancholy. We were admitted by a strange, wizened, rusty-coated old manservant, who seemed in keeping with the house. Inside, however, there were large rooms furnished with an elegance in which I seemed to recognize the taste of the lady. As I looked from their windows at the interminable granite-flecked moor rolling unbroken to the farthest horizon I could not but marvel at what could have brought this highly educated man and this beautiful woman to live in such a place.

"Queer spot to choose, is it not?" said he, as if in answer to my thought. "And yet we manage to make ourselves fairly happy, do we not, Beryl?"

"Quite happy," said she, but there was no ring of conviction in her words.

"I had a school," said Stapleton. "It was in the North country. The work to a man of my temperament was mechanical and uninteresting,[123] but the privilege of living with youth, of helping to mould those young minds and of impressing them with one's own character and ideals, was very dear to me. However, the fates were against us. A serious epidemic broke out in the school, and three of the boys died. It never recovered from the blow, and much of my capital was irretrievably swallowed up. And yet, if it were not for the loss of the charming companionship of the boys, I could rejoice over my own misfortune, for, with my strong tastes for botany and zoology, I find an unlimited field of work here, and my sister is as devoted to Nature as I am. All this, Dr. Watson, has been brought upon your head by your expression as you surveyed the moor out of our window."

"It certainly did cross my mind that it might be a little dull—less for you, perhaps than for your sister."

"No, no, I am never dull," said she, quickly.

"We have books, we have our studies, and we have interesting neighbours. Dr. Mortimer is a most learned man in his own line. Poor Sir Charles was also an admirable companion. We knew him well, and miss him more than I can tell. Do you think that I should intrude if I were to call this afternoon and make the acquaintance of Sir Henry?"

"I am sure that he would be delighted."

"Then perhaps you would mention that I propose to do so.

123 In "Sherlockian Schools and Schoolmasters," Frederick Bryan-Brown (himself a respected schoolmaster) calls this statement, "apart from its inherent hypocrisy, . . . nonsensical." He questions how Stapleton could simultaneously feel uninterested and privileged, and suggests that, based on how the reader eventually comes to understand the character, Stapleton's first thought is far truer than the second.

We may in our humble way do something to make things more easy for him until he becomes accustomed to his new surroundings. Will you come upstairs, Dr. Watson, and inspect my collection of *Lepidoptera*?[124] I think it is the most complete one in the south-west of England. By the time that you have looked through them lunch will be almost ready."

But I was eager to get back to my charge. The melancholy of the moor, the death of the unfortunate pony, the weird sound which had been associated with the grim legend of the Baskervilles—all these things tinged my thoughts with sadness. Then on the top of these more or less vague impressions there had come the definite and distinct warning of Miss Stapleton, delivered with such intense earnestness that I could not doubt that some grave and deep reason lay behind it. I resisted all pressure to stay for lunch, and I set off at once upon my return journey, taking the grass-grown path by which we had come.

It seems, however, that there must have been some short cut for those who knew it, for before I had reached the road I was astounded to see Miss Stapleton sitting upon a rock by the side of the track. Her face was beautifully flushed with her exertions, and she held her hand to her side.

"I have run all the way in order to cut you off, Dr. Watson," said she. "I had not even time to put on my hat. I must not stop, or my brother may miss me. I wanted to say to you how sorry I am about the stupid mistake I made in thinking that you were Sir Henry. Please forget the words I said, which have no application whatever to you."

"But I can't forget them, Miss Stapleton," said I. "I am Sir Henry's friend, and his welfare is a very close concern of mine. Tell me why it was that you were so eager that Sir Henry should return to London."

"A woman's whim, Dr. Watson. When you know me better you will understand that I cannot always give reasons for what I say or do."

"No, no. I remember the thrill in your voice. I remember the look in your eyes. Please, please, be frank with me, Miss Stapleton, for ever since I have been here I have been conscious of shadows all round me. Life has become like that great Grimpen Mire, with the little green patches everywhere into which one may sink and with no guide to point the track. Tell me, then, what it was that you meant, and I will promise to convey your warning to Sir Henry."

124 A large order of insects comprising the butterflies, moths, and skippers. The British Broadcasting Company estimates that in the mid-nineteenth century, there were over 3,000 butterfly collectors in England, as compared with a few hundred today. Professional collectors brought exotic specimens from the jungles to the trophy rooms of the wealthy, and high demand supported elaborate public auctions in London. Lionel Walter Rothschild (1868–1937), 3rd baronet and 2nd Baron Rothschild, is probably the best-known amateur butterfly enthusiast of his time. He suffered from a stutter as a child and by seven years of age turned his attention to *Lepidoptera* and *Coleoptera* (beetles), captured on the grounds of the family estate in Hertfordshire and housed in a shed. By his twenty-first birthday he had gone a long way toward amassing what would become the largest such collection obtained by a single individual—2.25 million moths and butterflies (along with thousands of animals and birds). It was bequeathed to the British Museum at his death, and the Walter Rothschild Zoological Museum is now part of the Natural History Museum.

An expression of irresolution passed for an instant over her face, but her eyes had hardened again when she answered me.

"You make too much of it, Dr. Watson," said she. "My brother and I were very much shocked by the death of Sir Charles. We knew him very intimately, for his favourite walk was over the moor to our house. He was deeply impressed with the curse which hung over his family, and when this tragedy came I naturally felt that there must be some grounds for the fears he had expressed. I was distressed, therefore, when another member of the family came down to live here, and I felt that he should be warned of the danger which he will run. That was all which I intended to convey."

"But what is the danger?"

"You know the story of the hound?"

"I do not believe in such nonsense."

"But I do. If you have any influence with Sir Henry, take him away from a place which has always been fatal to his family. The world is wide. Why should he wish to live at the place of danger?"

"Because it *is* the place of danger. That is Sir Henry's nature.

" 'You make too much of it, Dr. Watson,' said she."
Richard Gutschmidt, *Der Hund von Baskerville*
(Stuttgart: Robert Lutz Verlag, 1903)

" 'You know the story of the hound?' "
Sidney Paget. *Strand Magazine*, 1901

I fear that unless you can give me some more definite information than this it would be impossible to get him to move."

"I cannot say anything definite, for I do not know anything definite."

"I would ask you one more question, Miss Stapleton. If you meant no more than this when you first spoke to me, why should you not wish your brother to overhear what you said? There is nothing to which he, or anyone else, could object."

"My brother is very anxious to have the Hall inhabited, for he thinks that it is for the good of the poor folk upon the moor. He would be angry if he knew that I had said anything which might induce Sir Henry to go away. But I have done my duty now, and I will say no more. I must get back, or he will miss me and suspect that I have seen you. Good-bye!"

She turned, and had disappeared in a few minutes among the scattered boulders, while I, with my soul full of vague fears, pursued my way to Baskerville Hall.

CHAPTER VIII

First Report of Dr. Watson

FROM THIS POINT onwards I will follow the course of events by transcribing my own letters to Mr. Sherlock Holmes which lie before me on the table. One page is missing,[125] but otherwise they are exactly as written, and show my feelings and suspicions of the moment more accurately than my memory, clear as it is upon these tragic events, can possibly do.

Baskerville Hall, *Oct. 13th*

My dear Holmes:

My previous letters and telegrams have kept you pretty well up-to-date as to all that has occurred in this most God-forsaken corner of the world. The longer one stays here the more does the spirit of the moor sink into one's soul, its vastness, and also its grim charm. When you are once out upon its bosom you have left all traces of modern England behind you, but on the other hand you are conscious everywhere of the homes and the work of the prehistoric people. On all sides of you as you walk are the houses of these forgotten folk, with their graves and the huge monoliths which are supposed to have marked their temples. As you look at their grey stone huts against the scarred

125 "Why should a page be missing?" asks William S. Baring-Gould. "Holmes was not careless with Watson's correspondence, we may be sure. The statement is particularly curious because the two letters, as reproduced, seem to be complete." An explanation for the missing page is discussed at note 210, below.

hillsides you leave your own age behind you, and if you were to see a skin-clad, hairy man crawl out from the low door, fitting a flint-tipped arrow on to the string of his bow, you would feel that his presence there was more natural than your own. The strange thing is that they should have lived so thickly on what must always have been most unfruitful soil. I am no antiquarian, but I could imagine that they were some unwarlike and harried race who were forced to accept that which none other would occupy.

All this, however, is foreign to the mission on which you sent me, and will probably be very uninteresting to your severely practical mind. I can still remember your complete indifference as to whether the sun moved round the earth or the earth round the sun. Let me, therefore, return to the facts concerning Sir Henry Baskerville.

If you have not had any report within the last few days it is because up till today there was nothing of importance to relate. Then a very surprising circumstance occurred, which I shall tell you in due course. But, first of all, I must keep you in touch with some of the other factors in the situation.

One of these, concerning which I have said little, is the escaped convict upon the moor. There is strong reason now to believe that he has got right away, which is a considerable relief to the lonely householders of this district. A fortnight has passed since his flight, during which he has not been seen and nothing has been heard of him. It is surely inconceivable that he could have held out upon the moor during all that time. Of course, so far as his concealment goes there is no difficulty at all. Any one of these stone huts would give him a hiding-place. But there is nothing to eat unless he were to catch and slaughter one of the moor sheep. We think, therefore, that he has gone, and the outlying farmers sleep the better in consequence.

We are four able-bodied men in this household, so that we could take good care of ourselves, but I confess that I have had uneasy moments when I have thought of the Stapletons. They live miles from any help. There are one maid, an old manservant, the sister and the brother, the latter not a very strong man. They would be helpless in the hands of a desperate fellow like this Notting Hill criminal, if he could once effect an entrance. Both Sir Henry and I were concerned at their situation, and it was suggested that Perkins the groom should go over to sleep there, but Stapleton would not hear of it.

The fact is that our friend the baronet begins to display a considerable interest in our fair neighbour. It is not to be wondered at, for time hangs heavily in this lonely spot to an active man like him, and she is a very fascinating and beautiful woman. There is something tropical and exotic about her which forms a singular contrast to her cool and unemotional brother. Yet he also gives the idea of hidden fires. He has certainly a very marked influence over her, for I have seen her continually glance at him as she talked as if seeking approbation for what she said. I trust that he is kind to her. There is a dry glitter in his eyes, and a firm set of his thin lips, which go with a positive and possibly a harsh nature. You would find him an interesting study.

He came over to call upon Baskerville on that first day, and the very next morning he took us both to show us the spot where the legend of the wicked Hugo is supposed to have had its origin. It was an excursion of some miles across the moor to a place which is so dismal that it might have suggested the

"He took us to show us the spot."
Sidney Paget, *Strand Magazine*, 1901

126 Cotton grass (*Eriophorum angustifolium*) is a plant that at maturity has heads that look like cotton balls. The seed hairs are used to make candle wicks and paper, and for pillow stuffing and tinder.

story. We found a short valley between rugged tors which led to an open, grassy space flecked over with the white cotton grass.[126] In the middle of it rose two great stones, worn and sharpened at the upper end, until they looked like the huge, corroding fangs of some monstrous beast. In every way it corresponded with the scene of the old tragedy. Sir Henry was much interested, and asked Stapleton more than once whether he did really believe in the possibility of the interference of the supernatural in the affairs of men. He spoke lightly, but it was evident that he was very much in earnest. Stapleton was guarded in his replies, but it was easy to see that he said less than he might, and that he would not express his whole opinion out of consideration for the feelings of the baronet. He told us of similar cases, where families had suffered from some evil influence, and he left us with the impression that he shared the popular view upon the matter.

On our way back we stayed for lunch at Merripit House, and it was there that Sir Henry made the acquaintance of Miss Stapleton. From the first moment that he saw her he appeared to be strongly attracted by her, and I am much mistaken if the feeling was not mutual. He referred to her again and again on our walk home, and since then hardly a day has passed that we have not seen something of the brother and sister. They dine here tonight, and there is some talk of our going to them next week. One would imagine that such a match would be very welcome to Stapleton, and yet I have more than once caught a look of the strongest disapprobation in his face when Sir Henry has been paying some attention to his sister. He is much attached to her, no doubt, and would lead a lonely life without her, but it would seem the height of selfishness, if he were to stand in the way of her making so brilliant a marriage. Yet I am certain that he does not wish their intimacy to ripen into love, and I have several times observed that he has taken pains to prevent them from being *tête-à-tête*. By the way, your instructions to me never to allow Sir Henry to go out alone will become very much more onerous if a love-affair were to be added to our other difficulties. My popularity would soon suffer if I were to carry out your orders to the letter.

The other day—Thursday, to be more exact—Dr. Mortimer lunched with us. He has been excavating a barrow at Long Down, and has got a prehistoric skull which fills him with great joy. Never was there such a single-minded enthusiast as he! The Stapletons came in afterwards, and the good doctor took us all to the Yew Alley, at Sir Henry's request, to show us exactly how everything occurred upon that fatal night. It is a long, dismal walk, the Yew Alley, between two high walls of clipped hedge, with a narrow band of grass upon either side. At the far end is an old, tumble-down summer-house. Half-way down is the moor-gate where the old gentleman left his cigar-ash. It is a white wooden gate with a latch. Beyond it lies the wide moor. I remembered your theory of the affair and tried to picture all that had occurred. As the old man stood there he saw something coming across the moor, something which terrified him so that he lost his wits, and ran and ran until he died of sheer horror and exhaustion. There was the long, gloomy tunnel down which he fled. And from what? A sheep-dog of

"The Yew Alley."
Sidney Paget, *Strand Magazine*, 1901

the moor? Or a spectral hound, black, silent, and monstrous? Was there a human agency in the matter? Did the pale, watchful Barrymore know more than he cared to say? It was all dim and vague, but always there is the dark shadow of crime behind it.

One other neighbour I have met since I wrote last. This is Mr. Frankland, of Lafter Hall, who lives some four miles to the south of us. He is an elderly man, red-faced, white-haired, and choleric. His passion is for the British law, and he has spent a large fortune in litigation. He fights for the mere pleasure of fighting, and is equally ready to take up either side of a question, so that it is no wonder that he has found it a costly amusement. Sometimes he will shut up a right of way and defy the parish to make him open it. At others he will with his own hands tear down some other man's gate and declare that a path has existed there from time immemorial, defying the owner to prosecute him for trespass. He is learned in old manorial[127] and communal rights, and he applies his knowledge sometimes in favour of the villagers of Fernworthy[128] and sometimes against them, so that he is periodically either carried in triumph down the village street or else burned in effigy, according to his latest exploit. He is said to have about seven law-suits upon his hands at present, which will probably swallow up the remainder of his fortune, and so draw his sting and leave him harmless for the future. Apart from the law he seems a kindly, good-natured person, and I only mention him because you were particular that I should send some description of the people who surround us. He is curiously employed at present, for, being an amateur astronomer, he has an excellent telescope,[129] with which he lies upon the roof of his own house and sweeps the moor all day in the hope of catching a glimpse of the escaped convict. If he would confine his energies to this all would be well, but there are rumours that he intends to prosecute Dr. Mortimer for opening a grave without the consent of the next-of-kin, because he dug up the neolithic skull in the barrow on Long Down. He helps to keep our lives from being monotonous, and gives a little comic relief where it is badly needed.

And now, having brought you up-to-date in the escaped convict, the Stapletons, Dr. Mortimer, and Frankland, of Lafter Hall, let me end on that which is most important, and tell you

127 In feudal law, a lord exercised jurisdiction over his tenants through the manorial court. As the basis for landlord-tenant relations, the laws still have some applicability.

128 William S. Baring-Gould notes that while there was no *village* of Fernworthy, there was a substantial farming district of that name three miles from Lew House in Dartmoor. David L. Hammer, in *The Game Is Afoot*, identifies Fernworthy as the village of Ponsworthy, in the vicinity of Brook Manor, his candidate for Baskerville Hall. Phillip Weller asserts that there *was* a hamlet of Fernworthy, four miles north-north-east of Postbridge, which was submerged when a reservoir was established in 1936–1942. There is a circle of stones near this Fernworthy (also known as Foggymead Circle), 65 feet across, slightly flattened east to west, which contains twenty-seven stones that are graded in height from north to south, at which position the tallest is about 4 feet. It was excavated in 1897, and charcoal fragments were found throughout the circle, which may complement Frankland's suggestion that the Fernworthy folk might burn him in effigy.

129 Jim Ferreira, in "The Question of the Rooftop Telescope," considers whether this is an astronomical telescope (made for viewing the heavens, usually with a lense which naturally inverts the image) or a terrestrial telescope (made for viewing objects on the land or sea and which therefore includes a special lense to right the otherwise inverted image) and concludes, primarily on the basis of Watson's ease of use and failure to comment on an inverted image, that it is the latter.

"He is curiously employed at present, for, being an amateur astronomer, he has an excellent telescope."
Richard Gutschmidt, *Der Hund von Baskerville*
(Stuttgart: Robert Lutz Verlag, 1903)

more about the Barrymores, and especially about the surprising development of last night.

First of all about the test telegram, which you sent from London in order to make sure that Barrymore was really here. I have already explained that the testimony of the postmaster shows that the test was worthless and that we have no proof one way or the other. I told Sir Henry how the matter stood, and he at once, in his downright fashion, had Barrymore up and asked him whether he had received the telegram himself. Barrymore said that he had.

"Did the boy deliver it into your own hands?" asked Sir Henry.

Barrymore looked surprised, and considered for a little time.

"No," said he, "I was in the box-room at the time, and my wife brought it up to me."

"Did you answer it yourself?"

"No; I told my wife what to answer, and she went down to write it."

In the evening he recurred to the subject of his own accord.

"I could not quite understand the object of your questions this morning, Sir Henry," said he. "I trust that they do not mean that I have done anything to forfeit your confidence?"

Sir Henry had to assure him that it was not so and pacify him by giving him a considerable part of his old wardrobe, the London outfit having now all arrived.

Mrs. Barrymore is of interest to me. She is heavy, solid person, very limited, intensely respectable, and inclined to be puritanical. You could hardly conceive a less emotional subject. Yet I have told you how, on the first night here, I heard her sobbing bitterly, and since then I have more than once observed traces of tears upon her face. Some deep sorrow gnaws ever at her heart. Sometimes I wonder if she has a guilty memory which haunts her, and sometimes I suspect Barrymore of being a domestic tyrant. I have always felt that there was something singular and questionable in this man's character, but the adventure of last night brings all my suspicions to a head.

And yet it may seem a small matter in itself. You are aware that I am not a very sound sleeper, and since I have been on guard in this house my slumbers have been lighter than ever. Last night, about two in the morning, I was aroused by a stealthy step passing my room. I rose, opened my door, and peeped out. A long black shadow was trailing down the corridor. It was thrown by a man who walked softly down the passage with a candle held in his hand. He was in shirt and trousers, with no covering to his feet. I could merely see the outline, but his height told me that it was Barrymore. He walked very slowly and circumspectly, and there was something indescribably guilty and furtive in his whole appearance.

I have told you that the corridor is broken by the balcony which runs round the hall, but that it is resumed upon the farther side. I waited until he had passed out of sight, and then I followed him. When I came round the balcony he had reached the end of the farther corridor, and I could see from the glimmer of light through an open door that he had entered one of the rooms. Now, all these rooms are unfurnished and unoccupied, so that his expedition became more mysterious than ever. The light shone steadily, as if he were standing motionless. I crept down the passage as noiselessly as I could and peeped round the corner of the door.

Barrymore was crouching at the window with the candle

"He stared out into the blackness."
Sidney Paget, *Strand Magazine*, 1901

held against the glass. His profile was half turned towards me, and his face seemed to be rigid with expectation as he stared out into the blackness of the moor. For some minutes he stood watching intently. Then he gave a deep groan, and with an impatient gesture he put out the light. Instantly, I made my way back to my room, and very shortly came the stealthy steps passing once more upon their return journey. Long afterwards when I had fallen into a light sleep I heard a key turn somewhere in a lock, but I could not tell whence the sound came. What it all means I cannot guess, but there is some secret business going on in this house of gloom which sooner or later we shall get to the bottom of. I do not trouble you with my theories, for you asked me to furnish you only with facts. I have had a long talk with Sir Henry this morning, and we have made a plan of campaign founded upon my observations of last night. I will not speak about it just now, but it should make my next report interesting reading.

CHAPTER IX

SECOND REPORT OF DR. WATSON

The Light Upon the Moor

Baskerville Hall, *Oct. 15th*

My dear Holmes,

If I was compelled to leave you without much news during the early days of my mission you must acknowledge that I am making up for lost time, and that events are now crowding thick and fast upon us. In my last report I ended upon my top note with Barrymore at the window, and now I have quite a budget already which will, unless I am much mistaken, considerably surprise you. Things have taken a turn which I could not have anticipated. In some ways they have within the last forty-eight hours become much clearer and in some ways they have become more complicated. But I will tell you all, and you shall judge for yourself.

Before breakfast on the morning following my adventure I went down the corridor and examined the room in which Barrymore had been on the night before. The western window through which he had stared so intently has, I noticed, one peculiarity above all other windows in the house—it commands the nearest outlook on to the moor. There is an opening between two trees which enables one from this point of view to look right down upon it, while from all the other windows it is only a distant glimpse which can be obtained. It follows, therefore, that Barrymore, since only this window would serve his purpose, must have been looking out for something or somebody upon the moor. The night was very dark, so that I can hardly imagine how he could have hoped to see anyone. It had struck me that it was possible that some love intrigue was on foot. That would have accounted for his stealthy movements and also for the uneasiness of his wife. The man is a striking-looking fellow, very well equipped to steal the heart of a country girl, so that this theory seemed to have something to support it. That opening of the door which I had heard after I had returned to my room might mean that he had gone out to keep some clandestine appointment. So I reasoned with myself in the morning, and I tell you the direction of my suspicions, however much the result may have shown that they were unfounded.

But whatever the true explanation of Barrymore's movements might be, I felt that the responsibility of keeping them to myself until I could explain them was more than I could bear. I had an interview with the baronet in his study after breakfast, and I told him all that I had seen. He was less surprised than I had expected.

"I knew that Barrymore walked about nights, and I had a mind to speak to him about it," said he. "Two or three times I have heard his steps in the passage, coming and going, just about the hour you name."

"Perhaps, then, he pays a visit every night to that particular window," I suggested.

"Perhaps he does. If so, we should be able to shadow him, and see what it is that he is after. I wonder what your friend Holmes would do if he were here?"

"I believe that he would do exactly what you now suggest," said I. "He would follow Barrymore and see what he did."

"Then we shall do it together."

"But surely he would hear us."

"The man is rather deaf, and in any case we must take our chance of that. We'll sit up in my room tonight, and wait until he passes." Sir Henry rubbed his hands with pleasure, and it was evident that he hailed the adventure as a relief to his somewhat quiet life upon the moor.

The baronet has been in communication with the architect who prepared the plans for Sir Charles, and with a contractor from London, so that we may expect great changes to begin here soon. There have been decorators and furnishers up from Plymouth, and it is evident that our friend has large ideas, and means to spare no pains or expense to restore the grandeur of his family. When the house is renovated and refurnished, all that he will need will be a wife to make it complete. Between ourselves, there are pretty clear signs that this will not be wanting if the lady is willing, for I have seldom seen a man more infatuated with a woman than he is with our beautiful neighbour, Miss Stapleton. And yet the course of true love does not run quite as smoothly as one would under the circumstances expect. Today, for example, its surface was broken by a very unexpected ripple, which has caused our friend considerable perplexity and annoyance.

After the conversation which I have quoted about Barrymore, Sir Henry put on his hat and prepared to go out. As a matter of course, I did the same.

"What, are *you* coming, Watson?" he asked, looking at me in a curious way. "That depends on whether you are going on the moor," said I.

"Yes, I am."

"Well, you know what my instructions are. I am sorry to intrude, but you heard how earnestly Holmes insisted that I should not leave you, and especially that you should not go alone upon the moor."

Sir Henry put his hand upon my shoulder, with a pleasant smile.

"My dear fellow," said he, "Holmes, with all his wisdom, did not foresee some things which have happened since I have been on the moor. You understand me? I am sure that you are the last man in the world who would wish to be a spoil-sport. I must go out alone."

It put me in a most awkward position. I was at a loss what to say or what to do, and before I had made up my mind he picked up his cane and was gone.

But when I came to think the matter over my conscience reproached me bitterly for having on any pretext allowed him

"Sir Henry put his hand upon my shoulder."
Sidney Paget, *Strand Magazine*, 1901

to go out of my sight. I imagined what my feelings would be if I had to return to you and to confess that some misfortune had occurred through my disregard for your instructions. I assure you my cheeks flushed at the very thought. It might not even now be too late to overtake him, so I set off at once in the direction of Merripit House.

I hurried along the road at the top of my speed without seeing anything of Sir Henry, until I came to the point where the moor-path branches off. There, fearing that perhaps I had come in the wrong direction, after all, I mounted a hill from which I could command a view—the same hill which is cut into the dark quarry. Thence I saw him at once. He was on the moor-path, about a quarter of a mile off, and a lady was by his side who could only be Miss Stapleton. It was clear that there was already an understanding between them and that they had met by appointment. They were walking slowly along in deep conversation, and I saw her making quick little movements of her hands as if she were very earnest in what she was saying, while he listened intently, and once or twice shook his head in strong dissent. I stood among the rocks watching them, very much puzzled as to what I should do next. To follow them and break into their intimate conversation seemed to be an outrage, and yet my clear duty was never for an instant to let him out of my sight. To act the spy upon a friend was a hateful task. Still, I could see no better course than to observe him from the hill, and to clear my conscience by confessing to him afterwards what I had done. It is true that if any sudden danger had threatened him I was too far away to be of use, and yet I am sure that you will agree with me that the position was very difficult, and that there was nothing more which I could do.

Our friend, Sir Henry, and the lady had halted on the path, and were standing deeply absorbed in their conversation, when I was suddenly aware that I was not the only witness of their interview. A wisp of green floating in the air caught my eye, and another glance showed me that it was carried on a stick by a man who was moving among the broken ground. It was Stapleton with his butterfly-net. He was very much closer to the pair than I was, and he appeared to be moving in their direction. At this instant Sir Henry suddenly drew Miss Stapleton to his side. His arm was round her, but it seemed to me that she was straining away from him with her face averted. He stooped his head to hers, and she raised one hand as if in protest. Next moment I saw them spring apart and turn hurriedly round. Stapleton was the cause of the interruption. He was running wildly towards them, his absurd net dangling behind him. He gesticulated and almost danced with excitement in front of the lovers. What the scene meant I could not imagine, but it seemed to me that Stapleton was abusing Sir Henry, who offered explanations, which became more angry as the other refused to accept them. The lady stood by in haughty silence. Finally Stapleton turned upon his heel and beckoned in a peremptory way to his sister, who, after an irresolute glance at Sir Henry, walked off by the side of her brother. The naturalist's angry gestures showed that the lady was included in his displeasure. The baronet stood for a minute looking after them, and then he walked slowly back the way that he had come, his head hanging, the very picture of dejection.

"Sir Henry suddenly drew Miss Stapleton to his side."
Sidney Paget, *Strand Magazine*, 1901

What all this meant I could not imagine, but I was deeply ashamed to have witnessed so intimate a scene without my friend's knowledge. I ran down the hill, therefore, and met the baronet at the bottom. His face was flushed with anger and his brows were wrinkled, like one who is at his wits' ends what to do.

"Halloa, Watson! Where have you dropped from?" said he. "You don't mean to say that you came after me in spite of all?"

I explained everything to him: how I had found it impossible to remain behind, how I had followed him and how I had

"Stapleton was the cause of the interruption."
Richard Gutschmidt, *Der Hund von Baskerville*
(Stuttgart: Robert Lutz Verlag, 1903)

witnessed all that had occurred. For an instant his eyes blazed at me, but my frankness disarmed his anger, and he broke at last into a rather rueful laugh.

"You would have thought the middle of that prairie a fairly safe place for a man to be private," said he, "but, by thunder, the whole countryside seems to have been out to see me do my wooing—and a mighty poor wooing at that! Where had you engaged a seat?"

"I was on that hill."

"Quite in the back row, eh? But her brother was well up to the front. Did you see him come out on us?"

"Yes, I did."

"Did he ever strike you as being crazy—this brother of hers?"

"I can't say that he ever did."

"I dare say not. I always thought him sane enough until today, but you can take it from me that either he or I ought to be in a strait-jacket. What's the matter with me, anyhow? You've lived near me for some weeks, Watson. Tell me straight, now! Is there anything that would prevent me from making a good husband to a woman that I loved?"

"I should say not."

"He can't object to my worldly position, so it must be myself he has this down on. What has he against me? I never hurt man or woman in my life that I know of. And yet he would not so much as let me touch the tips of her fingers."

"Did he say so?"

"That, and a good deal more. I tell you, Watson, I've only known her these few weeks, but from the first I just felt that she was made for me, and she, too—she was happy when she was with me, and that I'll swear. There's a light in a woman's eyes that speaks louder than words. But he has never let us get together, and it was only today for the first time that I saw a chance of having a few words with her alone. She was glad to meet me, but when she did it was not love that she would talk about, and she wouldn't have let me talk about it either if she could have stopped it. She kept coming back to it that this was a place of danger, and that she would never be happy until I had left it. I told her that since I had seen her I was in no hurry to leave it, and that if she really wanted me to go, the only way to work it was for her to arrange to go with me. With that I offered in as many words to marry her, but before she could answer down came this brother of hers, running at us with a face on him like a madman. He was just white with rage, and those light eyes of his were blazing with fury. What was I doing with the lady? How dared I offer her attentions which were distasteful to her? Did I think that because I was a baronet I could do what I liked? If he had not been her brother I should have known better how to answer him. As it was I told him that my feelings towards his sister were such as I was not ashamed of, and that I hoped that she might honour me by becoming my wife. That seemed to make the matter no better, so then I lost my temper, too, and I answered him rather more hotly than I should, perhaps, considering that she was standing by. So it ended by his going off with her, as you saw, and here am I as badly puzzled a man as any in this country. Just tell me what it all means, Watson, and I'll owe you more than ever I can hope to pay."

I tried one or two explanations, but, indeed, I was completely puzzled myself. Our friend's title, his fortune, his age, his character, and his appearance are all in his favour, and I know nothing against him, unless it be this dark fate which runs in his family. That his advances should be rejected so brusquely without any reference to the lady's own wishes, and that the lady should accept the situation without protest, is very amazing. However, our conjectures were set at rest by a visit from Stapleton himself that very afternoon. He had come to offer apologies for his rudeness of the morning, and after a long private interview with Sir Henry in his study the upshot of their conversation was that the breach is quite healed, and that we are to dine at Merripit House next Friday as a sign of it.

"I don't say now that he isn't a crazy man," said Sir Henry; "I can't forget the look in his eyes when he ran at me this morning, but I must allow that no man could make a more handsome apology than he has done."

"Did he give any explanation of his conduct?"

"His sister is everything in his life, he says. That is natural enough, and I am glad that he should understand her value. They have always been together, and according to his account he has been a very lonely man with only her as a companion, so that the thought of losing her was really terrible to him. He had not understood, he said, that I was becoming attached to her, but when he saw with his own eyes that it was really so, and that she might be taken away from him, it gave him such a shock that for a time he was not responsible for what he said or did. He was very sorry for all that had passed, and he recognized how foolish and how selfish it was that he should imagine that he could hold a beautiful woman like his sister to himself for her whole life. If she had to leave him he had rather it was to a neighbour like myself than to anyone else. But in any case it was a blow to him, and it would take him some time before he could prepare himself to meet it. He would withdraw all opposition upon his part if I would promise for three months to let the matter rest, and to be content with cultivating the lady's friendship during that time without claiming her love. This I promised, and so the matter rests."

So there is one of our small mysteries cleared up. It is something to have touched bottom anywhere in this bog in which we are floundering. We know now why Stapleton looked with disfavour upon his sister's suitor—even when that suitor was so eligible a one as Sir Henry. And now I pass on to another thread which I have extricated out of the tangled skein,[130] the mystery of the sobs in the night, of the tear-stained face of Mrs. Barrymore, of the secret journey of the butler to the western lattice-window. Congratulate me, my dear Holmes, and tell me that I have not disappointed you as an agent—that you do not regret the confidence which you showed in me when you sent me down. All these things have by one night's work been thoroughly cleared.

I have said "by one night's work," but, in truth, it was by two nights' work, for on the first we drew entirely blank. I sat up with Sir Henry in his room until nearly three o'clock in the morning, but no sound of any sort did we hear except the chiming clock upon the stairs. It was a most melancholy vigil, and ended by each of us falling asleep in our chairs. Fortunately we were not discouraged, and we determined to try again. The next night we lowered the lamp and sat smoking cigarettes, without making the least sound. It was incredible how slowly the hours crawled by, and yet we were helped through it by the same sort of patient interest which the hunter must feel as he watches the trap into which he hopes the game may wander. One struck, and two, and we had almost for the second time given it up in despair, when in an instant we both sat bolt upright in our chairs, with all our weary senses keenly on the alert once more. We had heard the creak of a step in the passage.

Very stealthily we heard it pass along until it died away in the distance. Then the baronet gently opened his door, and we set out in pursuit. Already our man had gone round the gallery, and the corridor was all in darkness. Softly we stole along until we had come into the other wing. We were just in time to catch a glimpse of the tall, black-bearded figure, his shoulders rounded, as he tiptoed down the passage. Then he passed through the same door as before, and the light of the candle framed it in the darkness and shot one single yellow beam

130 Apparently a favourite phrase of Watson's, for Arthur Conan Doyle's notebooks reveal that Watson gave this as the original title of *A Study in Scarlet.*

across the gloom of the corridor. We shuffled cautiously towards it, trying every plank before we dared to put our whole weight upon it. We had taken the precaution of leaving our boots behind us, but, even so, the old boards snapped and creaked beneath our tread. Sometimes it seemed impossible that he should fail to hear our approach. However, the man is fortunately rather deaf, and he was entirely preoccupied in that which he was doing. When at last we reached the door and peeped through we found him crouching at the window, candle in hand, his white, intent face pressed against the pane, exactly as I had seen him two nights before.

We had arranged no plan of campaign, but the baronet is a man to whom the most direct way is always the most natural. He walked into the room, and as he did so Barrymore sprang up from the window with a sharp hiss of his breath, and stood, livid and trembling, before us. His dark eyes, glaring out of the white mask of his face, were full of horror and astonishment as he gazed from Sir Henry to me.

"What are you doing here, Barrymore?"

"Nothing, sir." His agitation was so great that he could hardly speak, and the shadows sprang up and down from the shaking of his candle. "It was the window, sir. I go round at night to see that they are fastened."

"On the second floor?"

"Yes, sir, all the windows."

"Look here, Barrymore," said Sir Henry, sternly, "we have made up our minds to have the truth out of you, so it will save you trouble to tell it sooner rather than later. Come now! No lies! What were you doing at that window?"

The fellow looked at us in a helpless way, and he wrung his hands together like one who is in the last extremity of doubt and misery.

"I was doing no harm, sir. I was holding a candle to the window."

"And why were you holding a candle to the window?"

"Don't ask me, Sir Henry—don't ask me! I give you my word, sir, that it is not my secret, and that I cannot tell it. If it concerned no one but myself I would not try to keep it from you."

A sudden idea occurred to me, and I took the candle from the window-sill, where the butler had placed it.

" 'What are you doing here, Barrymore?' "
Sidney Paget, *Strand Magazine*, 1901

"He must have been holding it as a signal," said I. "Let us see if there is any answer."

I held it as he had done, and stared out into the darkness of the night. Vaguely I could discern the black bank of the trees and the lighter expanse of the moor, for the moon was behind the clouds. And then I gave a cry of exultation, for a tiny pin-point of yellow light had suddenly transfixed the dark veil, and glowed steadily in the centre of the black square framed by the window.

"There it is!" I cried.

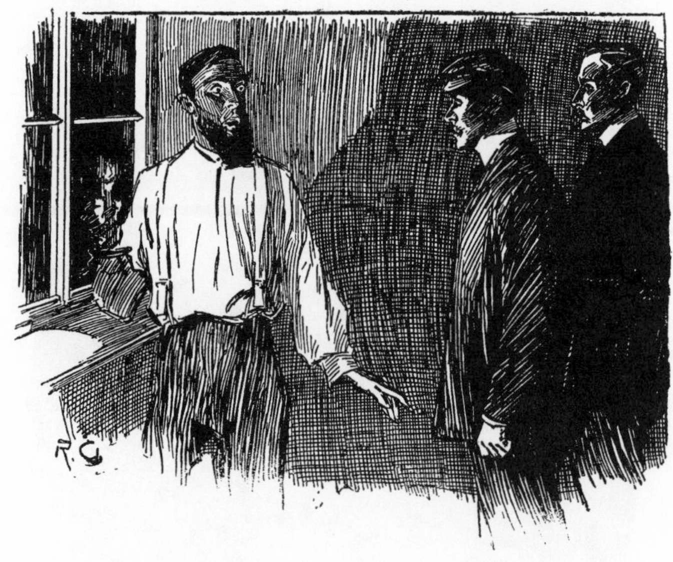

"'What are you doing here, Barrymore?'"
Richard Gutschmidt, *Der Hund von Baskerville*
(Stuttgart: Robert Lutz Verlag, 1903)

"No, no, sir, it is nothing—nothing at all," the butler broke in; "I assure you, sir—"

"Move your light across the window, Watson!" cried the baronet. "See, the other moves also! Now, you rascal, do you deny that it is a signal? Come, speak up! Who is your confederate out yonder, and what is this conspiracy that is going on?"

The man's face became openly defiant. "It is my business, and not yours. I will not tell."

"Then you leave my employment right away."

"Very good, sir. If I must, I must."

"And you go in disgrace. By thunder, you may well be ashamed of yourself. Your family has lived with mine for over a hundred years under this roof, and here I find you deep in some dark plot against me."

"No, no, sir; no, not against you!"

It was a woman's voice, and Mrs. Barrymore, paler and more horror-struck than her husband, was standing at the door. Her bulky figure in a shawl and skirt might have been comic were it not for the intensity of feeling upon her face.

"We have to go, Eliza. This is the end of it. You can pack our things," said the butler.

"Oh, John, John, have I brought you to this? It is my doing, Sir Henry—all mine. He has done nothing except for my sake, and because I asked him."

"Speak out, then! What does it mean?"

"My unhappy brother is starving on the moor. We cannot let him perish at our very gates. The light is a signal to him that food is ready for him, and his light out yonder is to show the spot to which to bring it."

"Then your brother is—"

"The escaped convict, sir—Selden, the criminal."

"That's the truth, sir," said Barrymore. "I said that it was not my secret, and that I could not tell it to you. But now you have heard it, and you will see that if there was a plot it was not against you."

This, then, was the explanation of the stealthy expeditions at night and the light at the window. Sir Henry and I both stared at the woman in amazement. Was it possible that this

" 'The escaped convict, sir.' "
Sidney Paget, *Strand Magazine*, 1901

stolidly respectable person was of the same blood as one of the most notorious criminals in the country?

"Yes, sir, my name was Selden, and he is my younger brother. We humoured him too much when he was a lad, and gave him his own way in everything, until he came to think that the world was made for his pleasure, and that he could do what he liked in it. Then, as he grew older, he met wicked companions, and the devil entered into him, until he broke my mother's heart and dragged our name in the dirt. From crime to crime he sank lower and lower, until it is only the mercy of God which has snatched him from the scaffold; but to me, sir, he was always the little curly-headed boy that I had nursed and played with, as an elder sister would. That was why he broke prison, sir. He knew that I was here, and that we could not refuse to help him. When he dragged himself here one night, weary and starving, with the warders hard at his heels, what could we do? We took him in and fed him and cared for him. Then you returned, sir, and my brother thought he would be safer on the moor than anywhere else until the hue and cry was over, so he lay in hiding there. But every second night we made sure if he was still there by putting a light in the window, and if there was an answer my husband took out some bread and meat to him. Every day we hoped that he was gone, but as long as he was there we could not desert him. That is the whole truth, as I am an honest Christian woman, and you will see that if there is blame in the matter it does not lie with my husband, but with me, for whose sake he has done all that he has."

The woman's words came with an intense earnestness which carried conviction with them.

"Is this true, Barrymore?"

"Yes, Sir Henry. Every word of it."

"Well, I cannot blame you for standing by your own wife. Forget what I have said. Go to your room, you two, and we shall talk further about this matter in the morning."

When they were gone we looked out of the window again. Sir Henry had flung it open, and the cold night wind beat in upon our faces. Far away in the black distance there still glowed that one tiny point of yellow light.

"I wonder he dares," said Sir Henry.

"It may be so placed as to be only visible from here."

"Very likely. How far do you think it is?"

"Out by the Cleft Tor, I think."[131]

"Not more than a mile or two off."

"Hardly that."

"Well, it cannot be far if Barrymore had to carry out the food to it. And he is waiting, this villain, beside that candle. By thunder, Watson, I am going out to take that man!"

The same thought had crossed my own mind. It was not as if the Barrymores had taken us into their confidence. Their secret had been forced from them. The man was a danger to the community, an unmitigated scoundrel for whom there was neither pity nor excuse. We were only doing our duty in taking this chance of putting him back where he could do no harm. With his brutal and violent nature, others would have to pay the price if we held our hands. Any night, for example, our neighbours, the Stapletons, might be attacked by him, and it may have been the thought of this which made Sir Henry so keen upon the adventure.

"I will come," said I.

"Then get your revolver and put on your boots. The sooner we start the better, as the fellow may put out his light and be off."

In five minutes we were outside the door, starting upon our expedition. We hurried though the dark shrubbery, amid the dull moaning of the autumn wind and the rustle of the falling leaves. The night-air was heavy with the smell of damp and decay. Now and again the moon peeped out for an instant, but clouds were driving over the face of the sky, and just as we came out on the moor a thin rain began to fall. The light still burned steadily in front.

"Are you armed?" I asked.

"I have a hunting-crop."[132]

"We must close in on him rapidly, for he is said to be a desperate fellow. We shall take him by surprise and have him at our mercy before he can resist."

"I say, Watson," said the baronet, "what would Holmes say to this? How about that hour of darkness in which the power of evil is exalted?"

As if in answer to his words there rose suddenly out of the vast gloom of the moor that strange cry which I had already heard upon the borders of the great Grimpen Mire. It came with the wind through the silence of the night, a long, deep

131 How did Dr. Watson know this landmark? Had someone pointed it out to him in an unmentioned conversation?

Although all editions of *The Hound of the Baskervilles* capitalise the "C" and "T" in "Cleft Tor," it may well have been a description that Watson later recalled as a place name. William S. Baring-Gould identifies the landmark as the Cleft Rock, a tourist attraction.

132 This was of course Holmes's favourite weapon—he brings his hunting-crop down on John Clay's wrist in "The Red-Headed League" before Clay can produce a revolver; threatens Windibank with it in "A Case of Identity"; and carries the "loaded" variety in "The Six Napoleons."

mutter, then a rising howl, and then the sad moan in which it died away. Again and again it sounded, the whole air throbbing with it, strident, wild, and menacing. The baronet caught my sleeve, and his face glimmered white through the darkness.

"Good heavens, what's that, Watson?"

"I don't know. It's a sound they have on the moor. I heard it once before."

It died away, and an absolute silence closed in upon us. We stood straining our ears, but nothing came.

"Watson," said the baronet, "it was the cry of a hound."

My blood ran cold in my veins, for there was a break in his voice which told of the sudden horror which had seized him.

"What do they call this sound?" he asked.

"Who?"

"The folk on the countryside."

"Oh, they are ignorant people. Why should you mind what they call it?"

"Tell me, Watson. What do they say of it?"

I hesitated, but could not escape the question.

"They say it is the cry of the Hound of the Baskervilles."

He groaned, and was silent for a few moments.

"A hound it was," he said at last, "but it seemed to come from miles away over yonder, I think."

"It was hard to say whence it came."

"It rose and fell with the wind. Isn't that the direction of the great Grimpen Mire?"

"Yes, it is."

"Well, it was up there. Come now, Watson, didn't you think yourself that it was the cry of a hound? I am not a child. You need not fear to speak the truth."

"Stapleton was with me when I heard it last. He said that it might be the calling of a strange bird."

"No, no, it was a hound. My God, can there be some truth in all these stories? Is it possible that I am really in danger from so dark a cause? You don't believe it, do you, Watson?"

"No, no."

"And yet it was one thing to laugh about it in London, and it is another to stand out here in the darkness of the moor and to hear such a cry as that. And my uncle! There was the footprint of the hound beside him as he lay. It all fits together. I don't think that I am a coward, Watson, but that sound seemed to freeze my very blood. Feel my hand!"

It was as cold as a block of marble.

"You'll be all right tomorrow."

"I don't think I'll get that cry out of my head. What to you advise that we do now?"

"Shall we turn back?"

"No, by thunder; we have come out to get our man, and we will do it. We are after the convict and a hell-hound, as likely as not, after us. Come on. We'll see it through if all the fiends of the pit were loose upon the moor."

We stumbled slowly along in the darkness, with the black loom of the craggy hills around us, and the yellow speck of light burning steadily in front. There is nothing so deceptive as the distance of a light upon a pitch-dark night, and sometimes the glimmer seemed to be far away upon the horizon and sometimes it might have been within a few yards of us. But at last we could see whence it came, and then we knew that we were indeed very close. A guttering candle was stuck in a crevice of the rocks which flanked it on each side so as to keep the wind from it, and also to prevent it from being visible, save in the direction of Baskerville Hall. A boulder of granite concealed our approach, and crouching behind it we gazed over it at the signal light. It was strange to see this single candle burning there in the middle of the moor, with no sign of life near it—just the one straight, yellow flame and the gleam of the rock on each side of it.

"What shall we do now?" whispered Sir Henry.

"Wait here. He must be near his light. Let us see if we can get a glimpse of him."

The words were hardly out of my mouth when we both saw him. Over the rocks, in the crevice of which the candle burned, there was thrust out an evil, yellow face, a terrible animal face, all seamed and scored with vile passions.[133] Foul with mire, with a bristling beard, and hung with matted hair, it might well have belonged to one of those old savages who dwelt in the burrows on the hillsides. The light beneath him was reflected in his small, cunning eyes, which peered fiercely to right and left through the darkness, like a crafty and savage animal who has heard the steps of the hunters.

Something had evidently aroused his suspicions. It may

133 Compare the description of the face of the villainous Dr. Grimesby Roylott: "A large face, seared with a thousand wrinkles, burned yellow with the sun and marked with every evil passion . . ." ("The Speckled Band"). Watson seems here and elsewhere to embrace the popular conception, epitomised by the work of criminologist Cesare Lombroso (see note 12, above), that criminals could be identified by certain physical characteristics. In "The Empty House," Watson writes of Colonel Moran: "But one could not look upon his cruel blue eyes, with their drooping, cynical lids, or upon the fierce, aggressive nose and the threatening, deep-lined brow, without reading Nature's plainest danger-signals."

"Over the rocks was thrust out an evil yellow face."
Sidney Paget, *Strand Magazine*, 1901

have been that Barrymore had some private signal which we had neglected to give, or the fellow may have had some other reason for thinking that all was not well, but I could read his fears upon his wicked face. Any instant he might dash out the light and vanish in the darkness. I sprang forward, therefore, and Sir Henry did the same. At the same moment the convict screamed out a curse at us and hurled a rock which splintered up against the boulder which had sheltered us. I caught one glimpse of his short, squat, strongly-built figure as he sprang to his feet and turned to run. At the same moment by a lucky chance the moon broke through the clouds. We rushed over the brow of the hill, and there was our man running with great speed down the other side, springing over the stones in his way with the activity of a mountain goat. A lucky long shot of my revolver might have crippled him, but I had brought it only to

"I sprang forward therefore, and Sir Henry did the same."
Richard Gutschmidt, *Der Hund von Baskerville* (Stuttgart: Robert Lutz Verlag, 1903)

defend myself if attacked, and not to shoot an unarmed man who was running away.

We were both swift runners and in fairly good training,[134] but we soon found that we had no chance of overtaking him. We saw him for a long time in the moonlight until he was only a small speck moving swiftly among the boulders upon the side of a distant hill. We ran and ran until we were completely blown,[135] but the space between us grew ever wider. Finally we stopped and sat panting on two rocks, while we watched him disappearing in the distance.

And it was at this moment that there occurred a most strange and unexpected thing. We had risen from our rocks and were turning to go home, having abandoned the hopeless chase. The moon was low upon the right, and the jagged pinnacle of a granite tor stood up against the lower curve of its silver disc. There, outlined as black as an ebony statue on that shining background, I saw the figure of a man upon the tor. Do not think that it was a delusion, Holmes. I assure you that I have never in my life seen anything more clearly. As far as I could judge, the figure was that of a tall, thin man. He stood with his legs a little separated, his arms folded, his head bowed, as if he were brooding over that enormous wilderness of peat and granite which lay before him. He might have been the very spirit of that terrible place. It was not the convict. This man was far from the place where the latter had disappeared. Besides, he was a much taller man. With a cry of surprise I pointed him out to the baronet, but in the instant during which I had turned to grasp his arm the man was gone. There was the sharp pinnacle of granite still cutting the lower edge of the moon, but its peak bore no trace of that silent and motionless figure.

I wished to go in that direction and to search the tor, but it was some distance away. The baronet's nerves were still quivering from that cry, which recalled the dark story of his family, and he was not in the mood for fresh adventures. He had not seen this lonely man upon the tor, and could not feel the thrill which his strange presence and his commanding attitude had given to me. "A warder, no doubt," said he. "The moor has been thick with them since this fellow escaped." Well, perhaps his explanation may be the right one, but I should like to have some further proof of it. Today we mean to communicate to the Princetown people where they should look for their missing

134 The *Strand Magazine* text (identical to that of the George Newnes edition) reads, "We were both fair runners and in good condition . . ." The text given appears first in the 1902 McClure, Phillips edition of *The Hound of the Baskervilles*.

135 Exhausted, winded.

man, but it is hard lines[136] that we have not actually had the triumph of bringing him back as our own prisoner. Such are the adventures of last night, and you must acknowledge, my dear Holmes, that I have done you very well in the matter of a report. Much of what I tell you is no doubt quite irrelevant, but still I feel that it is best that I should let you have all the facts and leave you to select for yourself those which will be of most service to you in helping you to your conclusions. We are certainly making some progress. So far as the Barrymores go, we have found the motive of their actions, and that has cleared up

"I saw the figure of a man upon the tor."
Sidney Paget, *Strand Magazine*, 1901

136 According to the 1865 *Slang Dictionary*, this is a soldier's term for hardship or difficulty, derived from "hard duty on the *lines* in front of the enemy." Synonymous phrases include "hard lot" and "hard luck."

the situation very much. But the moor with its mysteries and its strange inhabitants remains as inscrutable as ever. Perhaps in my next I may be able to throw some light upon this also. Best of all would it be if you could come down to us. In any case you will hear from me again in the course of the next few days.[137]

137 This sentence is not found in the *Strand Magazine* and various early English book texts (but is included in the 1929 John Murray text).

CHAPTER X

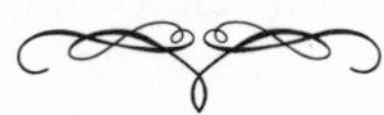

Extract from the Diary of Dr. Watson

So far I have been able to quote from the reports which I have forwarded during these early days to Sherlock Holmes. Now, however, I have arrived at a point in my narrative where I am compelled to abandon this method and to trust once more to my recollections, aided by the diary which I kept at the time.[138] A few extracts from the latter will carry me on to those scenes which are indelibly fixed in every detail upon my memory. I proceed, then, from the morning which followed our abortive chase of the convict and our other strange experiences upon the moor.

October 16th. A dull and foggy day, with a drizzle of rain. The house is banked in with rolling clouds, which rise now and then to show the dreary curves of the moor, with thin, silver veins upon the sides of the hills, and the distant boulders gleaming where the light strikes upon their wet faces. It is melancholy outside and in. The baronet is in a black reaction after the excitements of the night. I am conscious myself of a weight at my heart and a feeling of impending danger—ever-present danger, which is the more terrible because I am unable to define it.

138 Compelled, argues Robert Pattrick, by the missing page—see note 125, above, and note 144, below.

And have I not cause for such a feeling? Consider the long sequence of incidents which have all pointed to some sinister influence which is at work around us. There is the death of the last occupant of the Hall, fulfilling so exactly the conditions of the family legend, and there are the repeated reports from peasants of the appearance of a strange creature upon the moor. Twice I have with my own ears heard the sound which resembled the distant baying of a hound. It is incredible, impossible, that it should really be outside the ordinary laws of Nature. A spectral hound which leaves material footmarks and fills the air with its howling is surely not to be thought of. Stapleton may fall in with such a superstition, and Mortimer also; but if I have one quality upon earth it is common sense, and nothing will persuade me to believe in such a thing. To do so would be to descend to the level of these poor peasants who are not content with a mere fiend-dog, but must needs describe him with hell-fire shooting from his mouth and eyes. Holmes would not listen to such fancies, and I am his agent. But facts are facts, and I have twice heard this crying upon the moor. Suppose that there were really some huge hound loose upon it; that would go far to explain everything. But where could such a hound lie concealed, where did it get its food, where did it come from, how was it that no one saw it by day? It must be confessed that the natural explanation offers almost as many difficulties as the other. And always, apart from the hound, there was the fact of the human agency in London, the man in the cab, and the letter which warned Sir Henry against the moor. This at least was real, but it might have been the work of a protecting friend as easily as an enemy. Where was that friend or enemy now? Had he remained in London, or had he followed us down here? Could he—could he be the stranger whom I had seen upon the tor?

It is true that I have had only the one glance at him, and yet there are some things to which I am ready to swear. He is no one whom I have seen down here, and I have now met all the neighbours. The figure was far taller than that of Stapleton, far thinner than that of Frankland. Barrymore it might possibly have been, but we had left him behind us, and I am certain that he could not have followed us. A stranger, then, is still dogging us, just as a stranger had dogged us in London. We have never shaken him off. If I could lay my hands upon that man, then at last we might find ourselves at the end of all our difficulties. To this one purpose I must now devote all my energies.

My first impulse was to tell Sir Henry all my plans. My second and wisest one is to play my own game and speak as little as possible to anyone. He is silent and distrait. His nerves have been strangely shaken by that sound upon the moor. I will say nothing to add to his anxieties, but I will take my own steps to attain my own end.

We had a small scene this morning after breakfast. Barrymore asked leave to speak with Sir Henry, and they were closeted in his study some little time. Sitting in the billiard-room, I more than once heard the sound of voices raised, and I had a pretty good idea what the point was which was under discussion. After a time the baronet opened his door and called for me.

"Barrymore considers that he has a grievance," he said. "He thinks that it was unfair on our part to hunt his brother-in-law down when he, of his own free will, had told us the secret."

The butler was standing, very pale but very collected, before us.

"I may have spoken too warmly, sir," said he, "and if I have I am sure that I beg your pardon. At the same time, I was very much surprised when I heard you two gentlemen come back this morning and learned that you had been chasing Selden. The poor fellow has enough to fight against without my putting more upon his track."

"If you had told us of you own free will it would have been a different thing." said the baronet. "You only told us, or rather your wife only told us, when it was forced from you and you could not help yourself."

"I didn't think you would have taken advantage of it, Sir Henry—indeed I didn't."

"The man is a public danger. There are lonely houses scattered over the moor, and he is a fellow who would stick at nothing. You only want to get a glimpse of his face to see that. Look at Mr. Stapleton's house, for example, with no one but himself to defend it. There's no safety for anyone until he is under lock and key."

"He'll break into no house, sir. I give you my solemn word upon that. And he will never trouble anyone in this country again. I assure you, Sir Henry, that in a very few days the necessary arrangements will have been made and he will be on his

139 "How are they making arrangements to get their convict relation on board a ship bound for South America?" asks Brad Keefauver. "A pair of country servants do not have the connections to get a wanted criminal to a place half a world away." He proposes that Moriarty employed Selden, engineered the prison break, and arranged the trip to South America.

140 Dr. Watson's attitude is reminiscent of the English penal policy of "transportation," the government program of removal of criminals from England and shipping them to America or the Australian colonies, which ended in England in the late 1860s only when the receiving countries refused to accept any more transportees. Both Dr. Watson and the government seem to believe that so long as a criminal is removed from England, it little matters where he or she goes or whether the convict continues in his or her criminal ways.

"The butler was standing, very pale but very collected, before us."
Sidney Paget, *Strand Magazine*, 1902

way to South America.[139] For God's sake, sir, I beg of you not to let the police know that he is still on the moor. They have given up the chase there, and he can lie quiet until the ship is ready for him. You can't tell on him without getting my wife and me into trouble. I beg you, sir, to say nothing to the police."

"What do you say, Watson?"

I shrugged my shoulders. "If he were safely out of the country[140] it would relieve the taxpayer of a burden."

"But how about the chance of his holding someone up before he goes?"

"He would not do anything so mad, sir. We have provided him with all that he can want. To commit a crime would be to show where he was hiding."

"That is true," said Sir Henry. "Well, Barrymore—"

"God bless you, sir, and thank you from my heart! It would have killed my poor wife had he been taken again."

"I guess we are aiding and abetting a felony, Watson?[141] But, after what we've heard,[142] I don't feel as if I could give the man up, so there is an end of it. All right, Barrymore, you can go."

With a few broken words of gratitude the man turned, but he hesitated and then came back.

"You've been so kind to us, sir, that I should like to do the best I can for you in return. I know something, Sir Henry, and perhaps I should have said it before, but it was long after the inquest that I found it out. I've never breathed a word about it yet to mortal man. It's about poor Sir Charles's death."

The baronet and I were both upon our feet.

"Do you know how he died?"

"No, sir, I don't know that."

"What, then?"

"I know why he was at the gate at that hour. It was to meet a woman."

"The butler was standing, very pale but very collected, before us."
Richard Gutschmidt, *Der Hund von Baskerville*
(Stuttgart: Robert Lutz Verlag, 1903)

141 According to the *Police Code*, "*An accessory before the fact* is one who, directly or indirectly, so counsels, procures, commands, or instigates another, that a crime is committed. . . . A person aiding, abetting, counselling or procuring the commission of an offence punishable on summary conviction is liable to the same punishment as the principal offender (11 & 12 Vict., c. 43, s.5)." But in fact it appears that Holmes, Watson, and indeed Sir Henry are accessories *after* the fact, for, according to the *Police Code*, "*An accessory after the fact* is one (except married women screening their husbands) who, knowing a felony to have been committed, receives, comforts, or assists the felon in such manner as to enable him to escape from punishment." Punishment for an accessory after the fact is universally less stringent than that for the principal offender, except in cases of sedition or treason.

142 What is it that they heard? That the criminal—described earlier as a man who had committed a murder of "peculiar ferocity" and exhibited "wanton brutality"—had a sister? Mrs. Barrymore certainly never suggested that Selden had repented or changed in any way. Sir Henry's condonation here seems incredible.

"To meet a woman? He?"

"Yes, sir."

"And the woman's name?"

"I can't give you the name, sir, but I can give you the initials. Her initials were L.L."

"How do you know this, Barrymore?"

"Well, Sir Henry, your uncle had a letter that morning. He had usually a great many letters, for he was a public man and well known for his kind heart, so that everyone who was in trouble was glad to turn to him. But that morning, as it chanced, there was only this one letter, so I took the more notice of it. It was from Coombe Tracey,[143] and it was addressed in a woman's hand."

"Well?"

"Well, sir, I thought no more of the matter, and never would have done had it not been for my wife. Only a few weeks ago she was cleaning out Sir Charles's study—it had never been touched since his death—and she found the ashes of a burned letter in the back of the grate. The greater part of it was charred to pieces, but one little slip, the end of a page, hung together, and the writing could still be read, though it was grey on a black ground. It seemed to us to be a postscript at the end of the letter, and it said: 'Please, please, as you are a gentleman, burn this letter, and be at the gate by ten o'clock.' Beneath it were signed the initials L.L."

"Have you got that slip?"

"No, sir, it crumbled all to bits after we moved it."

"Had Sir Charles received any other letters in the same writing?"

"Well, sir, I took no particular notice of his letters. I should not have noticed this one only it happened to come alone."

"And you have no idea who L.L. is?"

"No, sir. No more than you have. But I expect if we could lay our hands upon that lady we should know more about Sir Charles's death."

"I cannot understand, Barrymore, how you came to conceal this important information."

"Well, sir, it was immediately after that our own trouble came to us. And then again, sir, we were both of us very fond of Sir Charles, as we well might be considering all that he has done for us. To rake this up couldn't help our poor master, and

143 William S. Baring-Gould suggests that Coombe Tracey is a conflation of Widecombe and Bovey Tracey. The latter village is a station on the Great Western Railway about 6 miles from Newton Abbot and was the demesne of William de Tracey, one of the murderers of St. Thomas à Becket. Philip Weller notes (and rejects) numerous additional candidates, including Combe (no railway station); Ashburton (too close to candidates for Baskerville Hall); Buckfastleigh (not an express station); South Brent (too close to Hall sites); Ivybridge (too far from Moor); Newton Abbot (same); and Totnes (same). See also note 86, above.

it's well to go carefully when there's a lady in the case. Even the best of us—"

"You thought it might injure his reputation?"

"Well, sir, I thought no good could come of it. But now you have been kind to us, and I feel as if it would be treating you unfairly not to tell you all that I know about the matter."

"Very good, Barrymore; you can go."

When the butler had left us, Sir Henry turned to me. "Well, Watson, what do you think of this new light?"

"It seems to leave the darkness rather blacker than before."

"So I think. But if we can only trace L.L. it should clear up the whole business. We have gained that much. We know that there is someone who has the facts if we can only find her. What do you think we should do?"

"Let Holmes know all about it at once. It will give him the clue for which he has been seeking. I am much mistaken if it does not bring him down."

I went at once to my room and drew up my report of the morning's conversation for Holmes.[144] It was evident to me that he had been very busy of late, for the notes which I had from Baker Street were few and short, with no comments upon the information which I had supplied and hardly any reference to my mission. No doubt his blackmailing case is absorbing all his faculties. And yet this new factor must surely arrest his attention and renew his interest. I wish that he were here.

October 17th.—All day today the rain poured down, rustling on the ivy and dripping from the eaves. I thought of the convict out upon the bleak, cold, shelterless moor. Poor fellow! Whatever his crimes,[145] he has suffered something to atone for them. And then I thought of that other one—the face in the cab, the figure against the moon. Was he also out in that deluge—the unseen watcher, the man of darkness? In the evening I put on my waterproof and I walked far upon the sodden moor, full of dark imaginings, the rain beating upon my face and the wind whistling about my ears. God help those who wander into the Great Mire now, for even the firm uplands are becoming a morass. I found the Black Tor[146] upon which I had seen the solitary watcher, and from its craggy summit I looked out myself across the melancholy downs. Rain squalls drifted across their russet face, and the heavy, slate-coloured clouds hung low over the landscape, trailing in grey wreaths down the

144 W. W. Robson suggests that this may be the "missing page" mentioned by Watson (see text accompanying note 125), although an alternate explanation is tendered by Donald Yates (see note 210, below). Robert R. Patrick, in a careful analysis entitled "Watson Writes from Baskerville Hall," concludes that the "missing page" was another letter from Watson largely containing the conversation with Laura Lyons (which Watson ultimately had to quote from his diary) and that the letter was never received by Holmes, because it was either lost by the Post Office or kept by a local resident as a souvenir.

145 See note 142, above.

146 According to Sabine Baring-Gould's *A Book of Dartmoor*, Black Tor lies about one and one-half miles to the south-west of Princetown and has on it a logan stone that can be rocked by means of a natural handle. Philip Weller states that there are at least four Black Tors on Dartmoor, and that a better candidate is the one adjacent to Shipley Tor, just over two miles to the south-south-west of Hayford Hall, a strong candidate for Baskerville Hall (see *Appendix 4*). Again, this may be a description, rather than a place name, which Watson later altered. See note 131, above.

"In the evening I put on my waterproof and I walked far upon the sodden moor."
Richard Gutschmidt, *Der Hund von Baskerville* (Stuttgart: Robert Lutz Verlag, 1903)

sides of the fantastic hills. In the distant hollow on the left, half hidden by the mist, the two thin towers of Baskerville Hall rose above the trees. They were the only signs of human life which I could see, save only those prehistoric huts which lay thickly upon the slopes of the hills. Nowhere was there any trace of that lonely man whom I had seen on the same spot two nights before.

As I walked back I was overtaken by Dr. Mortimer driving his dog-cart over a rough moorland track, which led from the outlying farm-house of Foulmire. He has been very attentive to us, and hardly a day has passed that he has not called at the Hall to see how we were getting on. He insisted upon my climbing into his dog-cart and he gave me a lift homewards. I found him much troubled over the disappearance of his little spaniel. It had wandered on to the moor and had never come back. I gave him such consolation as I might, but I thought of the pony on the Grimpen Mire, and I do not fancy that he will see his little dog again.

"By the way, Mortimer," said I, as we jolted along the rough road, "I suppose there are few people living within driving distance of this whom you do not know?"

"Hardly any, I think."

"Can you, then, tell me the name of any woman whose initials are L.L.?"

He thought for a few minutes. "No," said he. "There are a few gipsies and labouring folk for whom I can't answer, but among the farmers or gentry there is no one whose initials are those. Wait a bit, though," he added, after a pause. "There is Laura Lyons[147]—her initials are L.L.—but she lives in Coombe Tracey."

"Who is she?" I asked.

"She is Frankland's daughter."

"What? Old Frankland the crank?"

"Exactly. She married an artist named Lyons, who came sketching on the moor. He proved to be a blackguard and deserted her. The fault, from what I hear, may not have been

"From its craggy summit I look out myself across the melancholy downs."
Sidney Paget, *Strand Magazine*, 1902

147 It has delighted a generation of Sherlockians that "Laura Lyons" was the Playmate of the Month in the February 1976 issue of *Playboy* magazine. Hugh M. Hefner, publisher of *Playboy*, in an interview with this editor published in the *Baker Street Journal* discussing his long affinity with Sherlock Holmes, stated for the first time that this was her real name, ending years of speculation.

entirely on one side.[148] Her father refused to have anything to do with her, because she had married without his consent, and perhaps for one or two other reasons as well. So, between the old sinner and the young one the girl has had a pretty bad time."

"How does she live?"

"I fancy old Frankland allows her a pittance, but it cannot be more, for his own affairs are considerably involved. Whatever she may have deserved, one could not allow her to go hopelessly to the bad. Her story got about, and several of the people here did something to enable her to earn an honest living. Stapleton did for one, and Sir Charles for another. I gave a trifle myself. It was to set her up in a typewriting business."

He wanted to know the object of my inquiries, but I managed to satisfy his curiosity without telling him too much, for there is no reason why we should take anyone into our confidence. Tomorrow morning I shall find my way to Coombe Tracey, and if I can see this Mrs. Laura Lyons, of equivocal reputation, a long step will have been made towards clearing one incident in this chain of mysteries. I am certainly developing the wisdom of the serpent,[149] for when Mortimer pressed his questions to an inconvenient extent I asked him casually to what type Franklin's skull belonged, and so heard nothing but craniology for the rest of our drive. I have not lived for years with Sherlock Holmes for nothing.

I have only one other incident to record upon this tempestuous and melancholy day. This was my conversation with Barrymore just now, which gives me one more strong card which I can play in due time.

Mortimer had stayed to dinner, and he and the baronet played *écarté*[150] afterwards. The butler brought me my coffee into the library, and I took the chance to ask him a few questions.

"Well," said I, "has this precious relation of yours departed, or is he still lurking out yonder?"

"I don't know, sir. I hope to Heaven that he has gone, for he has brought nothing but trouble here! I've not heard of him since I left out food for him last, and that was three days ago."

"Did you see him then?"

"No, sir; but the food was gone when next I went that way."

"Then he was certainly there?"

"So you would think, sir, unless it was the other man who took it."

148 Is Dr. Mortimer implying that she committed adultery? See note 160, below, for the husband's grounds for divorce.

149 Compare Christ's advice to the apostles in *Matthew* 10:16: "Be ye therefore wise as serpents, and harmless as doves." Watson chooses this phrase (rather than a more colloquial comparison to an owl) to suggest a devious purpose to his "wisdom."

150 A card game for two people, played widely during the first quarter of the nineteenth century in the Paris *salons*, and related to euchre—with both possibly deriving from the Spanish game triumph. The piquet pack of 32 cards is used, made up of the seven through the king of each suit, plus the ace. The value of the cards is almost the same as in whist, except that the king has a ranking higher than that of (in descending order of importance) the jack, ace, and ten; hence the ace can take the ten. As in whist, trumps are the most powerful cards, with a seven of trumps being able to take the king of another suit. Rounds proceed until a player reaches 5 points, and if both players have 5, the goal becomes another 5 points. Points are achieved by winning most or all of the tricks; having the king of trumps, or dealing it as the trump card; and beating an opponent who reaches a state of vulnerability (with that condition having two definitions, depending upon whether one is the dealer or the non-dealer).

I sat with my coffee-cup half-way to my lips, and stared at Barrymore.

"You know that there is another man, then?"

"Yes, sir; there is another man upon the moor."

"Have you seen him?"

"No, sir."

"How do you know of him, then?"

"Selden told me of him, sir, a week ago or more. He's in hiding, too, but he's not a convict, so far as I can make out. I don't like it, Dr. Watson—I tell you straight, sir, that I don't like it." He spoke with a sudden passion of earnestness.

"Now, listen to me, Barrymore! I have no interest in this matter but that of your master. I have come here with no object except to help him. Tell me, frankly, what it is that you don't like."

Barrymore hesitated for a moment, as if he regretted his outburst, or found it difficult to express his own feelings in words.

"It's all these goings-on, sir," he cried, at last, waving his hand towards the rain-lashed window which faced the moor. "There's foul play somewhere, and there's black villainy brewing, to that I'll swear! Very glad I should be, sir, to see Sir Henry on his way back to London again!"

"But what is it that alarms you?"

"Look at Sir Charles's death! That was bad enough, for all that the coroner said. Look at the noises on the moor at night. There's not a man would cross it after sundown if he was paid for it. Look at this stranger hiding out yonder, and watching and waiting! What's he waiting for? What does it mean? It means no good to anyone of the name of Baskerville, and very glad I shall be to be quit of it all on the day that Sir Henry's new servants are ready to take over the Hall."

"But about this stranger," said I. "Can you tell me anything about him? What did Selden say? Did he find out where he hid, or what he was doing?"

"He saw him once or twice, but he is a deep one, and gives nothing away. At first he thought that he was the police, but soon he found that he had some lay[151] of his own. A kind of gentleman he was, as far as he could see, but what he was doing he could not make out."

"And where did he say that he lived?"

"Among the old houses on the hillside—the stone huts where the old folk used to live."

151 Slang for a job, situation, or purpose, also used by Hall Pycroft in "The Stock-Broker's Clerk."

" 'You know that there is another man, then?' "
Sidney Paget, *Strand Magazine*, 1902

"But how about his food?"

"Selden found out that he has got a lad who works for him and brings him all he needs. I dare say he goes to Coombe Tracey for what he wants."

"Very good, Barrymore. We may talk further of this some other time."

When the butler had gone I walked over to the black window, and I looked through a blurred pane at the driving clouds and at the tossing outline of the wind-swept trees. It is a wild night indoors, and what must it be in a stone hut upon the moor? What passion of hatred can it be which leads a man to lurk in such a place at such a time? And what deep and earnest purpose can he have which calls for such a trial? There, in that hut upon the moor, seems to lie the very centre of that problem which has vexed me so sorely. I swear that another day shall not have passed before I have done all that man can do to reach the heart of the mystery.

CHAPTER XI

The Man on the Tor[152]

THE EXTRACT FROM my private diary which forms the last chapter has brought my narrative up to the 18th of October, a time when these strange events began to move swiftly towards their terrible conclusion. The incidents of the next few days are indelibly graven upon my recollection, and I can tell them without reference to the notes made at the time. I start, then, from the day which succeeded that upon which I had established two facts of great importance, the one that Mrs. Laura Lyons of Coombe Tracey[153] had written to Sir Charles Baskerville and made an appointment with him at the very place and hour that he met his death, the other that the lurking man upon the moor was to be found among the stone huts upon the hillside. With these two facts in my possession I felt that either my intelligence or my courage must be deficient if I could not throw some further light upon these dark places.

I had no opportunity to tell the baronet what I had learned about Mrs. Lyons upon the evening before, for Dr. Mortimer remained with him at cards until it was very late. At breakfast, however, I informed him about my discovery, and asked him

152 The manuscript of Chapter XI, which resides in the Berg Collection of the New York Public Library and is the only known portion of the manuscript extant (other than single pages), was published in facsimile by the Baker Street Irregulars in 2001.

153 "Newton Abbot" in numerous places in the manuscript, and one assumes that the balance of the original manuscript must have been consistent. It has been changed to Coombe Tracey in the handwriting of Arthur Conan Doyle. This is an important clue as to location, for Newton Abbot was and remains a real town in Dartmoor. See notes 86 and 143, above. Philip Weller notes, in a private communication to this editor, that "it is located some six miles as the bittern booms from the nearest part of Dartmoor, and it is therefore not on the Moor."

whether he would care to accompany me to Coombe Tracey. At first he was very eager to come, but on second thoughts it seemed to both of us that if I went alone the results might be better. The more formal we made the visit the less information we might obtain. I left Sir Henry behind, therefore, not without some prickings of conscience, and drove off upon my new quest.

When I reached Coombe Tracey I told Perkins to put up the horses, and I made inquiries for the lady whom I had come to interrogate. I had no difficulty in finding her rooms, which were central and well appointed. A maid showed me in without ceremony, and as I entered the sitting-room a lady who was sitting before a Remington typewriter,[154] sprang up with a pleasant smile of welcome. Her face fell, however, when she saw that I was a stranger, and she sat down again and asked me the object of my visit.[155]

The first impression left by Mrs. Lyons was one of extreme beauty. Her eyes and hair were of the same rich hazel colour, and her cheeks, though considerably freckled, were flushed with the exquisite bloom of the brunette, the dainty pink which lurks at the heart of the sulphur rose.[156] Admiration was,

"A lady, who was sitting before a Remington typewriter, sprang up with a pleasant smile of welcome."
Richard Gutschmidt, *Der Hund von Baskerville* (Stuttgart: Robert Lutz Verlag, 1903).

154 E. Remington & Sons, the gun-makers of Ilion, New York, was the first company to put a typewriter on the production line, but, although the Remington name is indelibly associated with the machines, the family's involvement with them was relatively brief. The firearms manufacturing company was founded by Eliphalet Remington, a blacksmith who, as a young man, made his own pocket revolver by fashioning a barrel on his father's forge; he bought the firing mechanism from a dealer. He formed the Remington Typewriter Company as a separate entity in 1873, and worked in cooperation with Christopher Latham Sholes, a Milwaukee newspaperman-printer, poet, and inventor who held the patent on the first usable, efficient typewriter, which Sholes licensed to Remington. Within five years Sholes had arrived at the consummate design—the Remington 2 model, with its famed qwerty keyboard, featuring the shift key, which physically moved the carriage to produce capitals letters. The marketing firm of Wyckoff, Seamans, and Benedict acquired sole distribution rights in 1883 and, in 1886, sole manufacturing rights, buying the typewriter portion of the business from Remington. The Remington brand name remained in place. In the summer of 1894, the Remington Company, as it continued to be called, placed Model No. 6 on the market—by far its most serviceable and popular design—with the slogan "to save time is to lengthen life." All of these early models were of an upstrike, or "blind," design: When the typist hit a key, the type swung up against the platen and made its impression on the paper; the typist (or "typewriter," then the more common term for the individual using the machine) had to lift the carriage in order to determine if the correct key had been struck. A frontstrike ("visible") model was not marketed until 1908. Apart from typewriters, Remington also made sewing machines, and many of the first type-

I repeat, the first impression. But the second was criticism. There was something subtly wrong with the face, some coarseness of expression, some hardness, perhaps, of eye, some looseness of lip which marred its perfect beauty. But these, of course, are afterthoughts. At the moment I was simply conscious that I was in the presence of a very handsome woman, and that she was asking me the reasons for my visit. I had not quite understood until that instant how delicate my mission was.

"I have the pleasure," said I, "of knowing your father."

It was a clumsy introduction, and the lady made me feel it.

"There is nothing in common between my father and me," she said. "I owe him nothing, and his friends are not mine. If it were not for the late Sir Charles Baskerville and some other kind hearts I might have starved for all that my father cared."

"It was about the late Sir Charles Baskerville that I have come here to see you."

The freckles started out on the lady's face.

"What can I tell you about him?" she asked, and her fingers played nervously over the stops[157] of her typewriter.

"You knew him, did you not?"

"I have already said that I owe a great deal to his kindness. If I am able to support myself it is largely due to the interest which he took in my unhappy situation."

"Did you correspond with him?"

The lady looked quickly up, with an angry gleam in her hazel eyes.

"What is the object of these questions?" she asked, sharply.

"The object is to avoid a public scandal. It is better that I should ask them here than that the matter should pass outside our control."

She was silent and her face was very pale. At last she looked up with something reckless and defiant in her manner.

"Well, I'll answer," she said. "What are your questions?"

"Did you correspond with Sir Charles?"

"I certainly wrote to him once or twice to acknowledge his delicacy and his generosity."

"Have you the dates of those letters?"

"No."

"Have you ever met him?"

"Yes, once or twice, when he came into Coombe Tracey. He

Remington typewriter,
Standard Model No. 2 of 1878.

writers, which sold for a hefty $100 and were in fact manufactured by the sewing machine department of the Remington arms company, resembled the beautiful, early machines prized by seamstresses, with their decorative flower panels, mother-of-pearl inlay, and, in some cases, bronze finishes.

155 "[A] somewhat strange reaction to someone who might have been bringing new business," remarks Dorothyanne Evans, in "Laura Lyons."

156 *Rosa Hemisphaerica*, also known as the sulphur rose, is native to Southwest Asia. The bushes grow 5 to 6 feet tall and 4 feet wide and have abundant greyish leaves; the double blooms are a striking yellow, and the scent is musky. Along with the species *Rosa Ecae* and *Rosa Foetida* (the latter found in Persia), *Rosa Hemisphaerica* was imported to Europe, possibly as early as 1625, because there was no yellow rose stock. The three became the progenitors of modern yellow hybrids.

157 This odd usage for "keys" is not to be found in the *Oxford English Dictionary* (2nd Ed.) or in descriptions of contemporary typewriting machines. It may refer to the tab stops, clip-like devices used to set tabs manu-

was a very retiring man, and he preferred to do good by stealth."

"But if you saw him so seldom and wrote so seldom, how did he know enough about your affairs to be able to help you, as you say that he has done?"

She met my difficulty with the utmost readiness.

"There were several gentlemen who knew my sad history and united to help me. One was Mr. Stapleton, a neighbour and intimate friend of Sir Charles. He was exceedingly kind, and it was through him that Sir Charles learned about my affairs."

I knew already that Sir Charles Baskerville had made Stapleton his almoner[158] upon several occasions, so the lady's statement bore the impress of truth upon it.

"Did you ever write to Sir Charles asking him to meet you?" I continued.

Mrs. Lyons flushed with anger again.

"Really, sir, this is a very extraordinary question."

"I am sorry, madam, but I must repeat it."

"Then I answer—certainly not."

"Not on the very day of Sir Charles's death?"

The flush had faded in an instant, and a deathly face was before me. Her dry lips could not speak the "No" which I saw rather than heard.

"Surely your memory deceives you," said I. "I could even quote a passage of your letter. It ran, 'Please, please, as you are a gentleman, burn this letter, and be at the gate by ten o'clock.' "

I thought that she had fainted, but she recovered herself by a supreme effort.

"Is there no such thing as a gentleman?" she gasped.

"You do Sir Charles an injustice. He *did* burn the letter. But sometimes a letter may be legible even when burned. You acknowledge now that you wrote it?"

"Yes, I did write it," she cried, pouring out her soul in a torrent of words. "I did write it. Why should I deny it? I have no reason to be ashamed of it. I wished him to help me. I believed that if I had an interview I could gain his help, so I asked him to meet me."

"But why at such an hour?"

"Because I had only just learned that he was going to London next day and might be away for months. There were reasons why I could not get there earlier."

ally, and although this seems to be an odd part of the machine over which to "play" one's fingers, the Paget illustration of the scene bears out this interpretation. Because Paget was clearly not present, we must take it that he, too, understood Watson's phrase to mean that the lady was manipulating the tab stops. One could actually create tab stops on a typewriter; but this was a technique that was difficult to master—the province of professional typists such as Laura Lyons.

158 One who distributes another's charity.

" 'Really, sir, this is a very extraordinary question.' "
Sidney Paget, *Strand Magazine*, 1902

"But why a rendezvous in the garden instead of a visit to the house?"

"Do you think a woman could go alone at that hour to a bachelor's house?"

"Well, what happened when you did get there?"[159]

"I never went."

"Mrs. Lyons!"

"No, I swear it to you on all I hold sacred. I never went. Something intervened to prevent my going."

"What was that?"

"That is a private matter. I cannot tell it."

"You acknowledge, then, that you made an appointment with Sir Charles at the very hour and place at which he met his death, but you deny that you kept the appointment?"

159 This and the two preceding sentences are an insert to the manuscript, evidently a point recalled later by Watson.

"That is the truth."

Again and again I cross-questioned her, but I could never get past that point.

"Mrs. Lyons," said I, as I rose from this long and inconclusive interview, "you are taking a very great responsibility and putting yourself in a very false position by not making an absolutely clean breast of all that you know. If I have to call in the aid of the police you will find how seriously you are compromised. If your position is innocent, why did you in the first instance deny having written to Sir Charles upon that date?"

"Because I feared that some false conclusion might be drawn from it, and that I might find myself involved in a scandal."

"And why were you so pressing that Sir Charles should destroy your letter?"

"If you have read the letter you will know."

"I did not say that I had read all the letter."

"You quoted some of it."

"I quoted the postscript. The letter had, as I said, been burned, and it was not all legible. I ask you once again why it was that you were so pressing that Sir Charles should destroy this letter which he received on the day of his death."

"The matter is a very private one."

"The more reason why you should avoid a public investigation."

"I will tell you, then. If you have heard anything of my unhappy history you will know that I made a rash marriage and had reason to regret it."

"I have heard so much."

"My life has been one incessant persecution from a husband whom I abhor. The law is upon his side, and every day I am faced by the possibility that he may force me to live with him.[160] At the time that I wrote this letter to Sir Charles I had learned that there was a prospect of my regaining my freedom if certain expenses could be met.[161] It meant everything to me—peace of mind, happiness, self-respect—everything. I knew Sir Charles's generosity, and I thought that if he heard the story from my own lips he would help me."

"Then how is it that you did not go?"

"Because I received help in the interval from another source."

160 Compare the considerably different statement of Dr. Mortimer: "[Lyons] proved to be a blackguard and deserted her." Is Mortimer's version merely the story Laura Lyons put out to spare her own reputation? Victorian society had little regard for divorced (or separated) women.

The laws of England gave Laura Lyons little likelihood of *divorce* but a reasonable prospect of *separation.* According to Judge Albert M. Rosenblatt, now a justice of the New York Court of Appeals, "Under the [laws of England], a judicial separation could be obtained by either the husband or the wife on the ground of adultery, cruelty, or desertion." Under the Divorce Act of 1858, while a husband could seek dissolution of the marriage on the grounds of his wife's adultery, the *wife* could only seek dissolution on the grounds of incestuous adultery; bigamy with adultery; rape; sodomy; bestiality; adultery coupled with sufficient cruelty to serve as grounds for divorce in the ecclesiastical courts; or adultery coupled with desertion without reasonable excuse for two years or more. The *Encyclopædia Britannica* (9th Ed.) concludes, "The reason why the adultery of the husband is considered a less serious offence than the adultery of the wife will be obvious to every one."

By 1895, Parliament had made some reforms to the divorce laws, extending the grounds for a wife seeking divorce to include aggravated assault upon the wife within the Offences Against the Person Act; conviction for an assault on her resulting in a fine of more than £5 or imprisonment for more than two months; desertion; or persistent cruelty to her or wilful neglect to maintain her or her infant children, if by such cruelty or neglect the wife was "caused" to leave and live apart from him. In such circumstances, the wife could apply for an order containing any or all of the following provisions—(1) that the applicant be not forced to cohabit with her husband, (2) that

"Why, then, did you not write to Sir Charles and explain this?"

"So I should have done had I not seen his death in the paper next morning."[162]

The woman's story hung coherently together, and all my questions were unable to shake it. I could only check it by finding if she had, indeed, instituted divorce proceedings against her husband at or about the time of the tragedy.[163]

It was unlikely that she would dare to say that she had not been to Baskerville Hall if she really had been, for a trap would be necessary to take her there, and could not have returned to Coombe Tracey until the early hours of the morning. Such an excursion could not be kept secret. The probability was, therefore, that she was telling the truth, or, at least, a part of the truth. I came away baffled and disheartened.[164] Once again I had reached that dead wall which seemed to be built across every path by which I tried to get at the object of my mission. And yet the more I thought of the lady's face and of her manner the more I felt that something was being held back from me. Why should she turn so pale? Why should she fight against every admission until it was forced from her? Why should she have been so reticent at the time of the tragedy? Surely the explanation of all this could not be as innocent as she would have me believe. For the moment I could proceed no farther in that direction, but must turn back to that other clue which was to be sought for among the stone huts upon the moor.

And that was a most vague direction. I realized it as I drove back and noted how hill after hill showed traces of the ancient people. Barrymore's only indication had been that the stranger lived in one of these abandoned huts, and many hundreds of them are scattered throughout the length and breadth of the moor. But I had my own experience for a guide, since it had shown me the man himself standing upon the summit of the Black Tor. That, then, should be the centre of my search. From there I should explore every hut upon the moor until I lighted upon the right one. If this man were inside it I should find out from his own lips, at the point of my revolver if necessary, who he was and why he had dogged us so long. He might slip away from us in the crowd of Regent Street but it would puzzle him to do so upon the lonely moor. On the other hand, if I should find the hut, and its tenant should not be within it, I must remain there, however long the vigil, until he returned.

the applicant have custody of any children under sixteen years of age, or (3) that the husband pay to her an allowance not exceeding £2 a week.

The harshness of Victorian divorce laws is a theme forming the backdrop for the drama of "The Abbey Grange." Arthur Conan Doyle was a staunch advocate of reform of the laws and served as president of the national Divorce Law Reform Union in 1909.

161 In the manuscript, the phrase is "if a certain sum of money could be found for his expenses my husband was willing to leave the country."

162 "This was quick work," notes William S. Baring-Gould, "as Sir Charles was not discovered until midnight." Peter Calamai dissents. Laura Lyons's account is credible, he asserts in a private communication to this editor, if she is referring to the *Devon County Chronicle*, a morning newspaper, which Calamai indicates would have been in the hands of news agents by 6:00 A.M. Given the importance of Sir Charles to the local community, it is no wonder that someone immediately tipped off the newspaper.

163 In the manuscript, Watson suggests instead that he check Laura Lyons's story by "obtaining the last English address of the husband, and discussing whether he had indeed left England at the date she named."

164 The manuscript contains the following additional observations, which Watson struck subsequently in later versions. "Either she was an accomplished actor and a deep conspirator, or Barrymore had misread the letter, or the letter was a forgery—unless indeed there could by some extraordinary coincidence be a second lady writing from Newton Abbott whose initials were L.L. For the time my clue had come to nothing and I could only turn back to that other one which lay among the stone huts upon the Moor." These are interesting speculations, but with hindsight, perhaps Watson felt that they cast him (and the lady) in a poorer light than either deserved.

Holmes had missed him in London. It would indeed be a triumph for me if I could run him to earth where my master had failed.

Luck had been against us again and again in this inquiry, but now at last it came to my aid. And the messenger of good fortune was none other than Mr. Frankland, who was standing, grey-whiskered and red-faced, outside the gate of his garden, which opened on to the high road along which I travelled.

"Good day, Dr. Watson," cried he, with unwonted good humour, "you must really give your horses a rest, and come in to have a glass of wine and to congratulate me."

" 'Good-day, Dr. Watson,' he cried."
Sidney Paget, *Strand Magazine*, 1902

"'It is a great day for me, sir—one of the red-letter days of my life,' he cried, with many chuckles."
Richard Gutschmidt, *Der Hund von Baskerville*
(Stuttgart: Robert Lutz Verlag, 1903)

My feelings towards him were far from being friendly after what I had heard of his treatment of his daughter, but I was anxious to send Perkins and the wagonette home, and the opportunity was a good one. I alighted and sent a message to Sir Henry that I should walk over in time for dinner. Then I followed Frankland into his dining-room.

"It is a great day for me, sir—one of the red-letter days of my life," he cried, with many chuckles. "I have brought off a double event. I mean to teach them in these parts that law is law, and that there is a man here who does not fear to invoke it. I have established a right of way through the centre of old Middleton's park, slap across it, sir, within a hundred yards of his own front door. What do you think of that? We'll teach these magnates that they cannot ride rough-shod over the rights of the commoners, confound them! And I've closed the wood where the Fernworthy folk used to picnic. These infernal people seem to think that there are no rights of property, and that

165 The manuscript refers instead to "the Mayor of Plymouth." Although Sir John Morland remains unidentified, obviously Watson later recognised that he had failed to cover up the real name of the party.

they can swarm where they like with their papers and their bottles. Both cases decided, Dr. Watson, and both in my favour. I haven't had such a day since I had Sir John Morland for trespass,[165] because he shot in his own warren."

"How on earth did you do that?"

"Look it up in the books, sir. It will repay reading—*Frankland v. Morland*, Court of Queen's Bench. It cost me £200, but I got my verdict."

"Did it do you any good?"

"None, sir, none. I am proud to say that I had no interest in the matter. I act entirely from a sense of public duty. I have no doubt, for example, that the Fernworthy people will burn me in effigy tonight. I told the police last time they did it that they should stop these disgraceful exhibitions. The county constabulary is in a scandalous state, sir, and it has not afforded me the protection to which I am entitled. The case of *Frankland v. Regina* will bring the matter before the attention of the public. I told them that they would have occasion to regret their treatment of me, and already my words have come true."

"How so?" I asked.

The old man put on a very knowing expression.

"Because I could tell them what they are dying to know; but nothing would induce me to help the rascals in any way."

I had been casting round for some excuse by which I could get away from his gossip, but now I began to wish to hear more of it. I had seen enough of the contrary nature of the old sinner to understand that any strong sign of interest would be the surest way to stop his confidences.

"Some poaching case, no doubt?" said I, with an indifferent manner.

"Ha, ha, my boy, a very much more important matter than that! What about the convict on the moor?"

I started. "You don't mean that you know where he is?" said I.

"I may not know exactly where he is, but I am quite sure that I could help the police to lay their hands on him. Has it never struck you that the way to catch that man was to find out where he got his food, and so trace it to him?"

He certainly seemed to be getting uncomfortably near the truth. "No doubt," said I; "but how do you know that he is anywhere upon the moor?"

"I know it because I have seen with my own eyes the messenger who takes him his food."

My heart sank for Barrymore. It was a serious thing to be in the power of this spiteful old busybody. But his next remark took a weight from my mind.

"You'll be surprised to hear that his food is taken to him by a child. I see him every day through my telescope upon the roof. He passes along the same path at the same hour, and to whom should he be going except to the convict?"

Here was luck indeed! And yet I suppressed all appearance of interest. A child! Barrymore had said that our unknown was supplied by a boy. It was on his track, and not upon the convict's, that Frankland had stumbled. If I could get his knowledge it might save me a long and weary hunt. But incredulity and indifference were evidently my strongest cards.

"I should say that it was much more likely that it was the son of one of the moorland shepherds taking out his father's dinner."

The least appearance of opposition struck fire out of the old autocrat. His eyes looked malignantly at me, and his grey whiskers bristled like those of any angry cat.

"Indeed, sir!" said he, pointing out over the wide-stretching moor. "Do you see that Black Tor over yonder? Well, do you see the low hill beyond with the thorn-bush upon it? It is the stoniest part of the whole moor. Is that a place where a shepherd would likely to take his station? Your suggestion, sir, is a most absurd one."

I meekly answered that I had spoken without knowing all the facts. My submission pleased him and led him to further confidences.

"You may be sure, sir, that I have very good grounds before I come to an opinion. I have seen the boy again and again with his bundle.[166] Every day, and sometimes twice a day, I have been able—but wait a moment, Dr. Watson. Do my eyes deceive me, or is there at the present moment something moving upon that hillside?"

It was several miles off, but I could distinctly see a small dark dot against the dull green and grey.

"Come, sir, come!" cried Frankland, rushing upstairs. "You will see with your own eyes and judge for yourself."

The telescope, a formidable instrument mounted upon a tri-

166 The manuscript originally added the remark, "Without my telescope it would of course have been impossible." Watson must have realised later that this was mere talk, for two sentences later, Frankland spots the boy with his unaided eyes.

167 That is, strips of lead used as roofing.

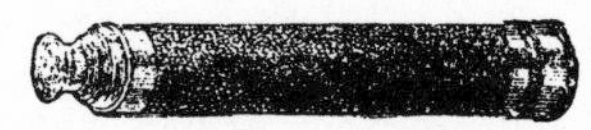

Telescopes.
Victorian Shopping (Harrod's 1895 Catalogue)

pod, stood upon the flat leads[167] of the house. Frankland clapped his eye to it and gave a cry of satisfaction.

"Quick, Dr. Watson, quick, before he passes over the hill!"

There he was, sure enough, a small urchin with a little bundle upon his shoulder, toiling slowly up the hill. When he reached the crest I saw the ragged, uncouth figure outlined for an instant against the cold blue sky. He looked round him, with a furtive and stealthy air, as one who dreads pursuit. Then he vanished over the hill.

"Well! Am I right?"

"Certainly, there is a boy who seems to have some secret errand."

"And what the errand is even a county constable could guess. But not one word shall they have from me, and I bind you to secrecy also, Dr. Watson. Not a word! You understand?"

"Just as you wish."

"They have treated me shamefully—shamefully. When the facts come out in *Frankland v. Regina* I venture to think that a thrill of indignation will run through the country. Nothing would induce me to help the police in any way. For all they cared it might have been me, instead of my effigy, which these rascals burned at the stake. Surely you are not going! You will help me to empty the decanter in honour of this great occasion!"

But I resisted all his solicitations and succeeded in dissuading him from his announced intention of walking home with me. I kept the road as long as his eye was on me, and then I struck off across the moor and made for the stony hill over which the boy had disappeared. Everything was working in my favour, and I swore that it should not be through lack of energy or perseverance that I should miss the chance which Fortune had thrown in my way.

The sun was already sinking when I reached the summit of the hill, and the long slopes beneath me were all golden-green on one side and grey shadow on the other. A haze lay low upon the farthest skyline, out of which jutted the fantastic shapes of Belliver and Vixen Tor.[168] Over the wide expanse there was no sound and no movement. One great grey bird, a gull or curlew, soared aloft in the blue heaven. He and I seemed to be the only living things between the huge arch of the sky and the desert beneath it. The barren scene, the sense of loneliness, and the mystery and urgency of my task all struck a chill into my heart. The boy was nowhere to be seen. But down beneath

"Frankland clapped his eye to it and gave a cry of satisfaction."
Sidney Paget, *Strand Magazine*, 1902

168 Sabine Baring-Gould's *Devon* (1907) describes Vixen Tor as a "castellated Mass" in the Walkham Valley, between Ward Bridge and Merrivale Bridge. There is no mention of Belliver in the book, and again Watson seems to have gained from an unknown source a detailed knowledge of the local names applied to landmarks on the moor.

169 Slang for a small pan.

170 Oddly, originally referred to as "half-empty" in the manuscript. Does this change —which many may regard as reflecting Watson's innate optimism—suggest anything about Watson's propensity to imbibe spirits?

me, in a cleft of the hills, there was a circle of the old stone huts, and in the middle of them there was one which retained sufficient roof to act as a screen against the weather. My heart leaped within me as I saw it. This must be the burrow where the stranger lurked. At last my foot was on the threshold of his hiding-place—his secret was within my grasp.

As I approached the hut, walking as warily as Stapleton would do when with poised net he drew near the settled butterfly, I satisfied myself that the place had indeed been used as a habitation. A vague pathway among the boulders led to the dilapidated opening which served as a door. All was silent within. The unknown might be lurking there, or he might be prowling on the moor. My nerves tingled with the sense of adventure. Throwing aside my cigarette, I closed my hand upon the butt of my revolver, and, walking swiftly up to the door, I looked in. The place was empty.

But there were ample signs that I had not come upon a false scent. This was certainly where the man lived. Some blankets rolled in a waterproof lay upon that very stone slab upon which neolithic man had once slumbered. The ashes of a fire were heaped in a rude grate. Beside it lay some cooking utensils and a bucket half-full of water. A litter of empty tins showed that the place had been occupied for some time, and I saw, as my eyes became accustomed to the chequered light, a pannikin[169] and a half-full[170] bottle of spirits standing in the corner. In the middle of the hut a flat stone served the purpose of a table, and upon this stood a small cloth bundle—the same, no doubt, which I had seen through the telescope upon the shoulder of the boy. It contained a loaf of bread, a tinned tongue, and two tins of preserved peaches. As I set it down again, after having examined it, my heart leaped to see that beneath it there lay a sheet of paper with writing upon it. I raised it, and this was what I read, roughly scrawled in pencil:

> Dr. Watson has gone to Coombe Tracey.

For a minute I stood there with the paper in my hands thinking out the meaning of this curt message. It was I, then, and not Sir Henry, who was being dogged by this secret man. He had not followed me himself, but he had set an agent—the boy, perhaps—upon my track, and this was his report. Possibly

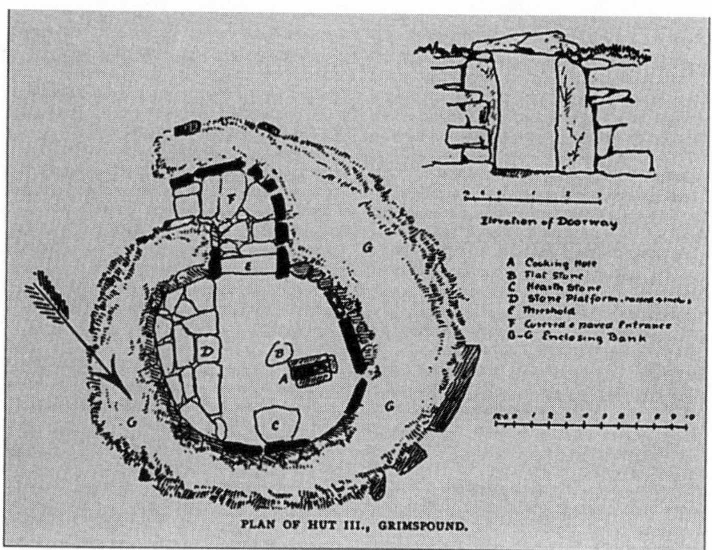

Plan of Grimspound hut, perhaps the very hut in which Holmes stayed.
Sabine Baring-Gould, *A Book of Dartmoor* (London: Methuen and Co., 1900)

I had taken no step since I had been upon the moor which had not been observed and repeated. Always there was this feeling of an unseen force, a fine net drawn round us with infinite skill and delicacy, holding us so lightly that it was only at some supreme moment that one realized that one was indeed entangled in its meshes.

If there was one report there might be others, so I looked round the hut in search of them. There was no trace, however, of anything of the kind, nor could I discover any sign which might indicate the character or intentions of the man who lived in this singular place, save that he must be of Spartan habits, and cared little for the comforts of life. When I thought of the heavy rains and looked at the gaping roof I understood how strong and immutable must be the purpose which had kept him in that inhospitable abode. Was he our malignant enemy, or was he by chance our guardian angel? I swore that I would not leave the hut until I knew.

Outside the sun was sinking low and the west was blazing with scarlet and gold. Its reflection was shot back in ruddy patches by the distant pools which lay amid the great Grimpen Mire. There were there the two towers of Baskerville Hall, and there a distant blur of smoke which marked the village of Grimpen. Between the two, behind the hill, was the house of the Stapletons. All was sweet and mellow and peaceful in the golden evening light, and yet as I looked at them my soul shared none of the peace of Nature, but quivered at the vagueness and the terror of that interview which every instant was bringing nearer.[171] With tingling nerves, but a fixed purpose, I sat in the dark recess of the hut and waited with sombre patience for the coming of its tenant.

And then at last I heard him. Far away came the sharp clink of a boot striking upon a stone. Then another and yet another, coming nearer and nearer. I shrank back into the darkest corner, and cocked the pistol in my pocket, determined not to discover myself until I had an opportunity of seeing something of the stranger. There was a long pause, which showed that he had stopped. Then once more the footsteps approached and a shadow fell across the opening of the hut.

"It is a lovely evening, my dear Watson," said a well-known voice. "I really think that you will be more comfortable outside than in."

171 Watson's original comment in the manuscript was, "and yet here was I waiting for some crisis, waiting with my nerves in a quiver, knowing that . . ."

"With tingling nerves, but a fixed purpose, I sat in the dark recess of the hut."
Richard Gutschmidt, *Der Hund von Baskerville* (Stuttgart: Robert Lutz Verlag, 1903)

The shadow of Sherlock Holmes.
Sidney Paget, *Strand Magazine*, 1902

CHAPTER XII

Death on the Moor

For a moment or two I sat breathless, hardly able to believe my ears. Then my senses and my voice came back to me, while a crushing weight of responsibility seemed in an instant to be lifted from my soul. That cold, incisive, ironical voice could belong to but one man in all the world.

"Holmes!" I cried—"Holmes!"

"Come out," said he, "and please be careful with the revolver."

I stooped under the rude lintel, and there he sat upon a stone outside, his grey eyes dancing with amusement as they fell upon my astonished features. He was thin and worn, but clear and alert, his keen face bronzed by the sun and roughened by the wind. In his tweed suit and cloth cap[172] he looked like any other tourist upon the moor, and he had contrived, with that cat-like love of personal cleanliness which was one of his characteristics, that his chin should be as smooth and his linen as perfect as if he were in Baker Street.[173]

"I never was more glad to see anyone in my life," said I, as I wrung him by the hand.

"Or more astonished, eh?"

172 Sidney Paget does not depict this "cloth cap" as a fore-and-aft, or deerstalker, the iconic hat associated with Holmes and depicted by Paget in "The Boscombe Valley Mystery," but rather as a hat that a modern reader might term a "driving cap." Jay Finley Christ, in "The Pipe and the Cap," states that the typical tourist wore the deerstalker. "It was as distinctive as was the *Baedeker* in his fist. It was by no means a proprietary of Mr. Sherlock Holmes—if, indeed, in those days, he *ever* wore one."

173 Noting the absence of shaving gear, C. Alan Bradley and William A. S. Sarjeant point to this as one of the strongest pieces of evidence for their thesis that Holmes was a woman. But Watson never mentions a Sherlockian beard, and Ron Miller, in "Will the Real Sherlock Holmes Please Stand Up?," suggests that his jaw was hairless, revealing American Indian ancestry.

Scene from *The Hound of the Baskervilles* (Great Britain: Stoll Picture Productions, Ltd., 1921), starring Eille Norwood as Sherlock Holmes and Hubert Willis as Dr. Watson.

"Well, I must confess to it."

"The surprise was not all on one side, I assure you. I had no idea that you had found my occasional retreat, still less that you were inside it, until I was within twenty paces of the door."

"My footprint, I presume?"

"No, Watson; I fear that I could not undertake to recognize your footprint amid all the footprints of the world. If you seriously desire to deceive me you must change your tobacconist; for when I see the stub of a cigarette marked Bradley, Oxford Street,[174] I know that my friend Watson is in the neighbourhood. You will see it there beside the path. You threw it down, no doubt, at that supreme moment when you charged into the empty hut."

"Exactly."

"I thought as much—and knowing your admirable tenacity, I was convinced that you were sitting in ambush, a weapon within reach, waiting for the tenant to return. So you actually thought that I was the criminal?"

"I did not know who you were, but I was determined to find out."

"Excellent, Watson! And how did you localize me? You saw

174 No sign of Bradley has been found, but J. C. Wimbush, in "Watson's Tobacconist," notes R. H. Hoar & Co., Ltd., which (until 1890) occupied the corner of a store at No. 6, Prince's Street—running north from Oxford Street just west of Regent Circus. *Baedeker* lists Amber & Co., at 238 and 536 Oxford Street, and the *London Dictionary and Guidebook for 1879* by Charles Dickens the Younger lists "Benson, W., 135 Oxford-st."

175 The "perhaps" seems to indicate that Holmes had not received Watson's previous letter.

"There he sat upon a stone."
Sidney Paget, *Strand Magazine*, 1902

me perhaps,[175] on the night of the convict hunt, when I was so imprudent as to allow the moon to rise behind me?"

"Yes, I saw you then."

"And have, no doubt, searched all the huts until you came to this one?"

"No, your boy had been observed, and that gave me a guide where to look."

"The old gentleman with the telescope, no doubt. I could not make it out when first I saw the light flashing upon the lens." He rose and peeped into the hut, "Ha, I see that Cartwright has brought up some supplies. What's this paper? So you have been to Coombe Tracey, have you?"

"Yes."

"To see Mrs. Laura Lyons?"

Scene from *The Hound of the Baskervilles* (Great Britain: Stoll Picture Productions, Ltd., 1921), starring Eille Norwood as Sherlock Holmes.

"Exactly."

"Well done! Our researches have evidently been running on parallel lines, and when we unite our results I expect we shall have a fairly full knowledge of the case."

"Well, I am glad from my heart that you are here, for indeed the responsibility and the mystery were both becoming too much for my nerves. But how in the name of wonder did you come here, and what have you been doing? I thought you were in Baker Street working out that case of blackmailing."

"That was what I wished you to think."

"Then you use me, and yet do not trust me!" I cried, with some bitterness. "I think that I have deserved better at your hands, Holmes."

"My dear fellow, you have been invaluable to me in this as in many other cases, and I beg that you will forgive me if I have seemed to play a trick upon you. In truth, it was partly for your own sake that I did it, and it was my appreciation of the danger which you ran which led me to come down and examine the matter for myself. Had I been with Sir Henry and you it is evident[176] that my point of view would have been the same as yours, and my presence would have warned our very formidable opponents to be on their guard. As it is, I have been able to

176 In the Doubleday edition and other American editions, the word is "confident," clearly a typographical error.

get about as I could not possibly have done had I been living at the Hall, and I remain an unknown factor in the business, ready to throw in all my weight at a critical moment."

"But why keep me in the dark?"

"For you to know could not have helped us, and might possibly have led to my discovery. You would have wished to tell me something, or in your kindness you would have brought me out some comfort or other, and so an unnecessary risk would be run. I brought Cartwright down with me—you remember the little chap at the Express office—and he has seen after my simple wants: a loaf of bread[177] and a clean collar. What does man want more? He has given me an extra pair of eyes upon a very active pair of feet, and both have been invaluable."

"Then my reports have all been wasted!" My voice trembled as I recalled the pains and the pride with which I had composed them.

Holmes took a bundle of papers from his pocket.

"Here are your reports, my dear fellow, and very well thumbed, I assure you. I made excellent arrangements, and they are only delayed one day upon their way. I must compliment you exceedingly upon the zeal and the intelligence which you have shown over an extraordinarily difficult case."

I was still rather raw over the deception which had been practised upon me, but the warmth of Holmes's praise drove my anger from my mind. I felt also in my heart that he was right in what he said, and that it was really best for our purpose that I should not have known that he was upon the moor.

"That's better," said he, seeing the shadow rise from my face. "And now tell me the result of your visit to Mrs. Laura Lyons—it was not difficult for me to guess that it was to see her that you had gone, for I am already aware that she is the one person in Coombe Tracey who might be of service to us in the matter. In fact, if you had not gone today it is exceedingly probable that I should have gone tomorrow."

The sun had set and dusk was settling over the moor. The air had turned chill, and we withdrew into the hut for warmth. There, sitting together in the twilight, I told Holmes of my conversation with the lady. So interested was he that I had to repeat some of it twice before he was satisfied.

"This is most important," said he, when I had concluded. "It fills up a gap which I had been unable to bridge in this most

177 Trevor H. Hall, in *The Late Mr. Sherlock Holmes and Other Literary Studies*, points out the deceit practised by Holmes, in perpetuating the myth that "in his more intense moments [Holmes] would permit himself no food" ("The Norwood Builder"): "Watson's inspection of the interior of the hut revealed a good deal more than a loaf of bread. We must presume that only the demands of friendship and the dominating personality of the great detective prevented Watson from succumbing to the extreme temptation of answering Holmes's question with a simple statement of the facts." Hall points out the "pannikin and a half-full bottle of spirits," "a tinned tongue, and two tins of preserved peaches." There was also "a litter of empty tins," which undoubtedly contained other portable comestibles.

complex affair. You are aware, perhaps, that a close intimacy exists between this lady and the man Stapleton?"

"I did not know of a close intimacy."

"There can be no doubt about the matter. They meet, they write, there is a complete understanding between them. Now, this puts a very powerful weapon into our hands. If I could only use it to detach his wife—"

"His wife?"

"I am giving you some information now, in return for all that you have given me. The lady who has passed here as Miss Stapleton is in reality his wife."

"Good heavens, Holmes! Are you sure of what you say? How could he have permitted Sir Henry to fall in love with her?"

"Sir Henry's falling in love could do no harm to anyone except Sir Henry. He took particular care that Sir Henry did not make love to her, as you have yourself observed. I repeat that the lady is his wife and not his sister."

"But why this elaborate deception?"

"Because he foresaw that she would be very much more useful to him in the character of a free woman."

All my unspoken instincts, my vague suspicions, suddenly took shape and centred upon the naturalist. In that impassive, colourless man, with his straw hat and his butterfly-net, I seemed to see something terrible—a creature of infinite patience and craft, with a smiling face and a murderous heart.

"It is he, then, who is our enemy—it is he who dogged us in London?"

"So I read the riddle."

"And the warning—it must have come from her!"

"Exactly."

The shape of some monstrous villainy, half seen, half guessed, loomed though the darkness which had girt me so long.

"But are you sure of this, Holmes? How do you know that the woman is his wife?"

"Because he so far forgot himself as to tell you a true piece of autobiography upon the occasion when he first met you, and I dare say he has many a time regretted it since. He *was* once a schoolmaster in the North of England. Now, there is no one more easy to trace than a schoolmaster. There are scholastic agencies by which one may identify any man who has been in the profession. A little investigation showed me that a school had come to grief under atrocious circumstances, and that the man who had owned it—the name was different—had disappeared with his wife. The descriptions agreed. When I learned that the missing man was devoted to entomology the identification was complete."

The darkness was rising, but much was still hidden by the shadows.

"If this woman is in truth his wife, where does Mrs. Laura Lyons come in?" I asked.

"That is one of the points upon which your own researches have shed a light. Your interview with the lady has cleared the situation very much. I did not know about a projected divorce between herself and her husband. In that case, regarding Stapleton as an unmarried man, she counted no doubt upon becoming his wife."

"And when she is undeceived?"

"Why, then we may find the lady of service.[178] It must be our first duty to see her—both of us—tomorrow. Don't you think, Watson, that you are away from your charge rather long? Your place should be at Baskerville Hall."

The last red streaks had faded away in the west and night had settled upon the moor. A few faint stars were gleaming in a violent sky.

"One last question, Holmes," I said, as I rose. "Surely there is no need of secrecy between you and me. What is the meaning of it all? What is he after?"

Holmes's voice sank as he answered—"It is murder, Watson—refined, cold-blooded, deliberate murder. Do not ask me for particulars. My nets are closing upon him, even as his are upon Sir Henry, and with your help he is already almost at my mercy. There is but one danger which can threaten us. It is that he should strike before we are ready to do so. Another day—two at the most—and I have my case complete, but until then guard your charge as closely as ever a fond mother watched her ailing child. Your mission today has justified itself, and yet I could almost wish that you had not left his side—Hark!"

A terrible scream—a prolonged yell of horror and anguish burst out of the silence of the moor. That frightful cry turned the blood to ice in my veins.

"Oh, my God!" I gasped. "What is it? What does it mean?"

178 "When [Laura Lyons] heard of [Sir Charles's] death, she should have been terribly upset," writes Dorothyanne Evans (see note 155, above). If she had no connection to the death, Evans argues, she could hardly have failed to notice the coincidence of the time set for her meeting with Sir Charles and the time of his death and would have voiced her suspicions. Her silence leads Evans to contend that it was Laura Lyons who suggested to Stapleton the plot with the hound. "Laura realises that Holmes is hot on the trail when he comes to interview her telling her that Stapleton was involved in the murder. She convincingly deceives Holmes into thinking she is the innocent party, at the same time cunningly finding out how much Holmes knows about Stapleton and then admitting that he manipulated her into doing his villainy." While Holmes correctly deduces that Stapleton had an accomplice to help look after the hound, Evans concludes, Holmes was in error in identifying Anthony, Stapleton's butler, as that accomplice—it was in fact Stapleton's mistress Laura Lyons.

"Night had settled upon the moor."
Frederic Dorr Steele, *Later Adventures of Sherlock Holmes*, Vol. II, 1952.
Originally prepared as a publicity drawing for Twentieth-Century Fox's film *The Hound of the Baskervilles* (1939), appearing in trade journals.

Holmes had sprung to his feet, and I saw his dark, athletic outline at the door of the hut, his shoulders stooping, his head thrust forward, his face peering into the darkness.

"Hush!" he whispered. "Hush!"

The cry had been loud on account of its vehemence, but it had pealed out from somewhere far off on the shadowy plain. Now it burst upon our ears, nearer, louder, more urgent than before.

"Where is it?" Holmes whispered; and I knew from the thrill of his voice that he, the man of iron, was shaken to the soul. "Where is it, Watson?"

"There, I think." I pointed into the darkness.

"No, there!"

Again the agonized cry swept through the silent night,

louder and much nearer than ever. And a new sound mingled with it, a deep, muttered rumble, musical and yet menacing, rising and falling like the low, constant murmur of the sea.

"The hound!" cried Holmes. "Come, Watson, come! Great heavens, if we are too late!"

He had started running swiftly over the moor, and I had followed at his heels. But now from somewhere among the broken ground immediately in front of us there came one last despairing yell, and then a dull, heavy thud. We halted and listened. Not another sound broke the heavy silence of the windless night.

I saw Holmes put his hand to his forehead, like a man distracted. He stamped his feet upon the ground.

"He has beaten us, Watson. We are too late."

"No, no, surely not!"

"Fool that I was to hold my hand. And you, Watson, see what comes of abandoning your charge! But, by Heaven, if the worst has happened, we'll avenge him!"

Blindly we ran through the gloom, blundering against boulders, forcing our way through gorse bushes, panting up hills and rushing down slopes, heading always in the direction whence those dreadful sounds had come. At every rise Holmes looked eagerly round him, but the shadows were thick upon the moor and nothing moved upon its dreary face.

"Can you see anything?"

"Nothing."

"But, hark, what is that?"

A low moan had fallen upon our ears. There it was again upon our left! On that side a ridge of rocks ended in a sheer cliff, which overlooked a stone-strewn slope. On its jagged face was spread-eagled some dark, irregular object. As we ran towards it the vague outline hardened into a definite shape. It was a prostrate man face downwards upon the ground, the head doubled under him at a horrible angle, the shoulders rounded and the body hunched together as if in the act of throwing a somersault. So grotesque was the attitude that I could not for the instant realize that that moan had been the passing of his soul. Not a whisper, not a rustle, rose now from the dark figure over which we stooped. Holmes laid his hand upon him, and held it up again, with an exclamation of horror. The gleam of the match which he struck shone upon his clotted fingers and upon the ghastly pool which widened slowly

"It was a prostrate man face downwards upon the ground."
Sidney Paget, *Strand Magazine*, 1902

from the crushed skull of the victim. And it shone upon something else which turned our hearts sick and faint within us—the body of Sir Henry Baskerville!

There was no chance of either of us forgetting that peculiar ruddy tweed suit—the very one which he had worn on the first morning that we had seen him in Baker Street. We caught the one clear glimpse of it, and then the match flickered and went out, even as the hope had gone out of our souls. Holmes groaned, and his face glimmered white through the darkness.

"The brute! the brute!" I cried, with clenched hands. "Oh, Holmes, I shall never forgive myself for having left him to his fate."

"I am more to blame than you, Watson. In order to have my case well rounded and complete, I have thrown away the life of my client. It is the greatest blow which has befallen me in my career. But how *could* I know—how could I know—that he would risk his life alone upon the moor in the face of all my warnings?"

"That we should have heard his screams—my God, those

"It was a prostrate man face downwards upon the ground."
Frederic Dorr Steele, *Later Adventures of Sherlock Holmes*, Vol. II, 1952.
Originally prepared as a publicity drawing for Twentieth-Century Fox's film *The Hound of the Baskervilles* (1939), appearing in trade journals.

screams!—and yet have been unable to save him! Where is this brute of a hound which drove him to his death? It may be lurking among these rocks at this instant. And Stapleton, where is he? He shall answer for this deed."

"He shall. I will see to that. Uncle and nephew have been murdered—the one frightened to death by the very sight of a beast, which he thought to be supernatural, the other driven to his end in his wild flight to escape from it. But now we have to prove the connection between the man and the beast. Save from what we heard, we cannot even swear to the existence of the latter, since Sir Henry has evidently died from the fall. But, by heavens, cunning as he is, the fellow shall be in my power before another day is past!"

We stood with bitter hearts on either side of the mangled body, overwhelmed by this sudden and irrevocable disaster which had brought all our long and weary labours to so piteous an end. Then, as the moon rose, we climbed to the top of the rocks over which our poor friend had fallen, and from the summit we gazed out over the shadowy moor, half silver and half gloom. Far away, miles off, in the direction of Grimpen, a single steady, yellow light was shining. It could only come from the lonely abode of the Stapletons. With a bitter curse I shook my fist at it as I gazed.

"Why should we not seize him at once?"

"Our case is not complete. The fellow is wary and cunning to the last degree. It is not what we know, but what we can prove. If we make one false move the villain may escape us yet."

"What can we do?"

"There will be plenty for us to do tomorrow. Tonight we can only perform the last offices to our poor friend."

Together we made our way down the precipitous slope and approached the body, black and clear against the silvered stones. The agony of those contorted limbs struck me with a spasm of pain and blurred my eyes with tears.

"We must send for help, Holmes! We cannot carry him all the way to the Hall. Good heavens, are you mad?"

He had uttered a cry and bent over the body. Now he was dancing and laughing and wringing my hand. Could this be my stern, self-contained friend? These were hidden fires, indeed!

"A beard! A beard! The man has a beard!"

"It was a prostrate man face downwards upon the ground."
Richard Gutschmidt, *Der Hund von Baskerville*
(Stuttgart: Robert Lutz Verlag, 1903)

"A beard?"

"It is not the baronet—it is—why, it is my neighbour, the convict!"

With feverish haste we had turned the body over, and that dripping beard was pointing up to the cold, clear moon. There could be no doubt about the beetling forehead,[179] the sunken animal eyes. It was, indeed, the same face which had glared upon me in the light of the candle from over the rock—the face of Selden, the criminal. Then in an instant it was all clear to me. I remembered how the baronet had told me that he had handed his old wardrobe to Barrymore. Barrymore had passed it on in order to help Selden in his escape. Boots, shirt, cap—it was all Sir Henry's. The tragedy was still black enough, but this man had at least deserved death by the laws of his country. I told Holmes how the matter stood, my heart bubbling over with thankfulness and joy.

"Then the clothes have been the poor fellow's death," said he. "It is clear enough that the hound has been laid on from some article of Sir Henry's—the boot which was abstracted in the hotel, in all probability—and so ran this man down. There is one very singular thing, however: How came Selden, in the darkness, to know that the hound was on his trail?"

"He heard him."

"To hear a hound upon the moor would not work a hard man like this convict into such a paroxysm of terror that he would risk recapture by screaming wildly for help. By his cries he must have run a long way after he knew the animal was on his track. How did he know?"

"A greater mystery to me is why this hound, presuming that all our conjectures are correct—"

"I presume nothing."

"Well, then, why this hound should be loose tonight. I suppose that it does not always run loose upon the moor. Stapleton would not let it go unless he had reason to think that Sir Henry would be there."[180]

"My difficulty is the more formidable of the two, for I think that we shall very shortly get an explanation of yours, while mine may remain for ever a mystery. The question now is, what shall we do with this poor wretch's body? We cannot leave it here to the foxes and the ravens."

"I suggest that we put it in one of the huts until we can communicate with the police."

179 Another example of the phrenological point of view—see note 23, above.

180 "But what on earth," asks Harald Curjel, in "The Dartmoor Campaign," "[were Stapleton] and the hound doing on Black Tor 'miles off' from Merripit House on the night of Selden's death?" Curjel argues that Stapleton would not loose the hound without reason to think that his intended victim would be present. While Stapleton had *suggested* that Sir Henry visit him, "surely it would have been vain clutching at a straw to hope that his guest would come, unaccompanied and at night, to Merripit House, let alone to the slopes of Black Tor." Notwithstanding Holmes's assurance that an explanation would be forthcoming, the question remains unanswered.

"It was the face of Selden, the criminal."
Sidney Paget, *Strand Magazine*, 1902

"Exactly. I have no doubt that you and I could carry it so far. Halloa, Watson, what's this? It's the man himself, by all that's wonderful and audacious! Not a word to show your suspicions—not a word, or my plans crumble to the ground."

A figure was approaching us over the moor, and I saw the dull red glow of a cigar. The moon shone upon him, and I could distinguish the dapper shape and jaunty walk of the naturalist. He stopped when he saw us, and then came on again.

"Why, Dr. Watson, that's not you, is it? You are the last man that I should have expected to see out on the moor at this time of night. But, dear me, what's this? Somebody hurt? Not—don't tell me that it is our friend Sir Henry!"

He hurried past me and stooped over the dead man. I heard a sharp intake of his breath and the cigar fell from his fingers.

"Who—who's this?" he stammered.

"It is Selden, the man who escaped from Princetown."

Stapleton turned a ghastly face upon us, but by a supreme

"He hurried past me and stooped over the dead man."
Richard Gutschmidt, *Der Hund von Baskerville*
(Stuttgart: Robert Lutz Verlag, 1903)

effort he had overcome his amazement and his disappointment. He looked sharply from Holmes to me.

"Dear me! What a very shocking affair! How did he die?"

"He appears to have broken his neck by falling over these rocks. My friend and I were strolling on the moor when we heard a cry."

"I heard a cry also. That was what brought me out. I was uneasy about Sir Henry."

"Why about Sir Henry in particular?" I could not help asking.

"Because I had suggested that he should come over. When he did not come I was surprised, and I naturally became alarmed for his safety when I heard cries upon the moor. By the way"—his eyes darted again from my face to Holmes's—"did you hear anything else besides a cry?"

"No," said Holmes; "did you?"

"No."

"What do you mean, then?"

"Oh, you know the stories that the peasants tell about a phantom hound, and so on. It is said to be heard at night upon the moor. I was wondering if there were any evidence of such a sound tonight."

"We heard nothing of the kind," said I.

"And what is your theory of this poor fellow's death?"

"I have no doubt that anxiety and exposure have driven him off his head. He has rushed about the moor in a crazy state and eventually fallen over here and broken his neck."

"That seems the most reasonable theory," said Stapleton, and he gave a sigh which I took to indicate his relief. "What do you think about it, Mr. Sherlock Holmes?"

My friend bowed his compliments.

"You are quick at identification," said he.

"We have been expecting you in these parts since Dr. Watson came down. You are in time to see a tragedy."

"Yes, indeed. I have no doubt that my friend's explanation will cover the facts. I will take an unpleasant remembrance back to London with me tomorrow."

"Oh, you return tomorrow?"

"That is my intention."

" 'Who—who's this?' he stammered."
Sidney Paget, *Strand Magazine*, 1902

"I hope your visit has cast some light upon those occurrences which have puzzled us?"

Holmes shrugged his shoulders. "One cannot always have the success for which one hopes. An investigator needs facts, and not legends or rumours. It has not been a satisfactory case."

My friend spoke in his frankest and most unconcerned manner. Stapleton still looked hard at him. Then he turned to me.

"I would suggest carrying this poor fellow to my house, but it would give my sister such a fright that I do not feel justified in doing it. I think that if we put something over his face[181] he will be safe until morning."

And so it was arranged. Resisting Stapleton's offer of hospitality, Holmes and I set off to Baskerville Hall, leaving the naturalist to return alone. Looking back we saw the figure moving slowly away over the broad moor, and behind him that one black smudge on the silvered slope which showed where the man was lying who had come so horribly to his end.[182]

"We're at close grips at last," said Holmes, as we walked together across the moor. "What a nerve the fellow has! How he pulled himself together in the face of what must have been a paralysing shock when he found that the wrong man had fallen a victim to his plot. I told you in London, Watson, and I tell you now again, that we have never had a foeman more worthy of our steel."

"I am sorry that he has seen you."

"And so was I at first. But there was no getting out of it."

"What effect do you think it will have upon his plans, now that he knows you are here?"

"It may cause him to be more cautious, or it may drive him to desperate measures at once. Like most clever criminals, he may be too confident in his own cleverness and imagine that he has completely deceived us."

"Why should we not arrest him at once?"

"My dear Watson, you were born to be a man of action. Your instinct is always to do something energetic. But supposing, for argument's sake, that we had him arrested tonight, what on earth the better off should we be for that? We could prove nothing against him. There's the devilish cunning of it! If he were acting through a human agent we could get some evidence, but if we were to drag this great dog to the light of day it would not help us in putting a rope round the neck of its master."

181 And this will keep away "the foxes and the ravens" about which Holmes worries?

182 The American editions end Chapter XII at this point, and the remaining material appears at the beginning of Chapter XIII.

"Surely we have a case."

"Not a shadow of one—only surmise and conjecture. We should be laughed out of court if we came with such a story and such evidence."

"There is Sir Charles's death."

"Found dead without a mark upon him. You and I know that he died of sheer fright, and we know also what frightened him; but how are we to get twelve stolid jurymen to know it? What signs are there of a hound? Where are the marks of its fangs. Of course, we know that a hound does not bite a dead body, and that Sir Charles was dead before ever the brute overtook him. But we have to *prove* all this, and we are not in a position to do it."

"Well, then, tonight?"

"We are not much better off tonight. Again, there was no direct connection between the hound and the man's death. We never saw the hound. We heard it; but we could not prove that it was running upon this man's trail. There is a complete absence of motive. No, my dear fellow; we must reconcile ourselves to the fact that we have no case at present, and that it is worth our while to run any risk in order to establish one."

"And how do you propose to do so?"

"I have great hopes of what Mrs. Laura Lyons may do for us when the position of affairs is made clear to her. And I have my own plan as well. Sufficient for tomorrow is the evil thereof;[183] but I hope before the day is past to have the upper hand at last."

I could draw nothing further from him, and he walked, lost in thought, as far as the Baskerville gates.

"Are you coming up?"

"Yes; I see no reason for further concealment. But one last word, Watson. Say nothing of the hound to Sir Henry. Let him think that Selden's death was as Stapleton would have us believe. He will have a better nerve for the ordeal which he will have to undergo tomorrow, when he is engaged, if I remember your report aright, to dine with these people."

"And so am I."

"Then you must excuse yourself, and he must go alone. That will be easily arranged. And now, if we are too late for dinner, I think that we are both ready for our suppers."

183 Compare the New Testament: "Sufficient unto the day is the evil thereof" (Matthew, 6:34). In neither context is the speaker really expecting "evil"—the English Standard Version of the Bible renders the full passage as "Therefore do not be anxious about tomorrow, for tomorrow will be anxious for itself. Sufficient for the day is its own trouble."

CHAPTER XIII

Fixing the Nets

Sir Henry was more pleased than surprised to see Sherlock Holmes, for he had for some days been expecting that recent events would bring him down from London. He did raise his eyebrows, however, when he found that my friend had neither any luggage nor any explanations for its absence. Between us we soon supplied his wants, and then over a belated supper we explained to the baronet as much of our experience as it seemed desirable that he should know. But first I had the unpleasant duty of breaking the news of Selden's death to Barrymore and his wife. To him it may have been an unmitigated relief, but she wept bitterly in her apron. To all the world he was the man of violence, half animal and half demon; but to her he always remained the little wilful boy of her own girlhood, the child who had clung to her hand.

Evil indeed is the man who has not one woman to mourn him.

"I've been moping in the house all day since Watson went off in the morning," said the baronet. "I guess I should have some credit, for I have kept my promise. If I hadn't sworn not

Scene from *The Hound of the Baskervilles* (United States: Twentieth-Century Fox, 1939), starring Basil Rathbone as Sherlock Holmes and Nigel Bruce as Dr. Watson.

to go about alone I might have had a more lively evening, for I had a message from Stapleton asking me over there."

"I have no doubt that you would have had a more lively evening," said Holmes, dryly. "By the way, I don't suppose you appreciate that we have been mourning over you as having broken your neck?"

Sir Henry opened his eyes. "How was that?"

"This poor wretch was dressed in your clothes. I fear your servant who gave them to him may get into trouble with the police."

"That is unlikely. There was no mark on any of them, so far as I know."

"That's lucky for him—in fact, it's lucky for all of you, since you are all on the wrong side of the law in this matter. I am not sure that as a conscientious detective my first duty is not to arrest the whole household. Watson's reports are most incriminating documents."

"But how about the case?" asked the baronet. "Have you made anything out of the tangle? I don't know that Watson and I are much the wiser since we came down."

"I think that I shall be in a position to make the situation rather more clear to you before long. It has been an exceedingly difficult and most complicated business. There are several points upon which we still want light—but it is coming, all the same."

"We've had one experience, as Watson has no doubt told you. We heard the hound on the moor, so I can swear that it is not all empty superstition. I had something to do with dogs when I was out West, and I know one when I hear one. If you can muzzle that one and put him on a chain I'll be ready to swear you are the greatest detective of all time."

"I think I will muzzle him and chain him all right if you will give me your help."

"Whatever you tell me to do I will do."

"Very good; and I will ask you also to do it blindly, without always asking the reason."

"Just as you like."

"If you will do this I think the chances are that our little problem will soon be solved. I have no doubt—"

He stopped suddenly and stared fixedly up over my head into the air. The lamp beat upon his face, and so intent was it and so still that it might have been that of a clear-cut classical statue, a personification of alertness and expectation.

"What is it?" we both cried.

I could see as he looked down that he was repressing some internal emotion. His features were still composed, but his eyes shone with amused exultation.

"Excuse the admiration of a connoisseur," said he, as he waved his hand towards the line of portraits which covered the opposite wall. "Watson won't allow that I know anything of art, but that is mere jealousy, because our views upon the subject differ. Now, these are a really very fine series of portraits."

"Well, I'm glad to hear you say so," said Sir Henry, glancing with some surprise at my friend. "I don't pretend to know much about these things, and I'd be a better judge of a horse or steer than of a picture. I didn't know that you found time for such things."

"I know what is good when I see it, and I see it now. That's a Kneller,[184] I'll swear, that lady in the blue silk over yonder, and the stout gentleman with the wig ought to be a Reynolds.[185] They are all family portraits, I presume?"

184 Sir Godfrey Kneller (1648–1723) was a painter of British portraits, including those of Charles II, William III, and George I, each of whom he served as court artist. Born in Lübeck, Germany, he came to England in his late twenties and was renowned almost equally for the superb quality of his pictures—he was unsurpassed until Sir Joshua Reynolds—and for his personal vanity. One of his painterly trademarks was the elongation of the oval of all his heads. Among his most well-known surviving work is the collection of portraits of the Kit-cat Club celebrities, influential Whigs who supported a Protestant monarchy and helped put William III on the throne.

185 Sir Joshua Reynolds (1723–1792), English portrait painter and aesthetician, who was elected the first president of the Royal Academy at its founding in 1768. Before his election, one of his signal contributions to the art world was to arrange for the exhibition of the work of contemporary artists, under the Society of Artists, which he also founded; prior to 1760, there had been no such shows. Among persistent criticisms of his work are that his colours were not permanent and that he compromised his paint surface by adding bitumen and coal materials to his pigments. The oft-repeated rebuttal by his patron Sir George

The Duchess of Devonshire and her daughter.
Sir Joshua Reynolds (1786)

"He stopped suddenly and stared fixedly up over my head into the air."
Sidney Paget, *Strand Magazine*, 1902

"Every one."

"Do you know the names?"

"Barrymore has been coaching me in them, and I think I can say my lessons fairly well."

"Who is the gentleman with the telescope?"

"That is Rear-Admiral Baskerville, who served under Rodney[186] in the West Indies. The man with the blue coat and the roll of paper is Sir William Baskerville, who was Chairman of Committees[187] of the House of Commons under Pitt."[188]

"And this Cavalier[189] opposite to me—the one with the black velvet and the lace?"

"Ah, you have a right to know about him. That is the cause

Beaumont: "Never mind, a faded portrait by Reynolds is better than a fresh one by anybody else." While Sir Joshua's early portraits were celebrated for their spontaneity and the freshness of their backgrounds (he posed at least one subject in front of the seashore), by the time he had reached his late thirties he inclined more to self-consciousness, formality, and the antique. In keeping with this shift in his thinking, from 1769 to 1791 he wrote and delivered an important series of lectures on grandeur in art and the study of the old masters.

186 George Brydges Rodney, first Baron Rodney (1719–1792). While his highest naval rank was rear-admiral of Great Britain, and his fame is far less, nineteenth-century scholars rated him second only to the near-legendary Lord Nelson. Among his accomplishments was the capture of Martinique, in 1762, during the Seven Years' War. He also suffered lifelong debt after being sued by British merchants whose goods he looted during his capture, the previous year, of St. Eustatius. The fact that the merchants had been trading illegally with American revolutionary forces did not take away the sting, or cost, of their lawsuits. Rodney was also the victim, throughout his life, of his own greed and self-serving impulses, including charges of nepotism for awarding his son a highly questionable post-captaincy at the age of only fifteen.

187 The member appointed to preside over a house of Parliament whenever it resolves itself into a committee of the whole, similar to the President *pro tempore* of the U. S. Senate or the Speaker of the U. S. House of Representatives.

188 William Pitt (also known as Pitt the Younger, 1759–1806), who became prime minister of England at twenty-four and served for eighteen years; his father had served as prime minister, off and on, from 1756 to 1768. Pitt the Younger presided over the French Revolutionary and Napoleonic wars but was, ironically, a pacifist by nature. Like many great statesmen, he was a mass of contradictions, failing to champion adequately the civil rights of his own countrymen, for instance, while simultaneously bringing Great Britain back from near-financial ruin following the American Revolution. Public finance was perhaps his area of greatest expertise: He levied new taxes, virtually put an end to smuggling and fraud, and overhauled customs and excise duties. One of his actions with ongoing repercussions was the abolishment of the Irish parliament.

189 In the English Civil Wars (1642–1651), the name was adopted by Charles I's supporters, who contemptuously called their opponents Roundheads; at the Restoration, the court party preserved the name "Cavalier," which survived until the rise of the term "Tory."

190 "It is not known for certain who painted the portrait of Hugo Baskerville," the Marquis of Donegall states, in "Who Painted Hugo Baskerville?" "It is, however, fairly safe to deduce that, as the family portraits at Baskerville Hall included a Reynolds and a Kneller, it was the tradition of the Baskerville family to be painted by the best-known artist of the time." The Marquis speculates that Hugo Baskerville's portrait, likely painted in the 1640s, was by the Dutchman Franz Hals (1582/3–1666), leading portraitist of the day.

191 The description corresponds to that of a Cavalier; Roundheads were far less flamboyant, even severe, in their dress. Love-locks, whether affixed (by hairdresser's glue) to the temple or the space in front of the ear, were curled hairpieces positioned so that they

of all the mischief, the wicked Hugo, who started the Hound of the Baskervilles. We're not likely to forget him."

I gazed with interest and some surprise upon the portrait.[190]

"Dear me!" said Holmes, "He seems a quiet, meek-mannered man enough, but I dare say that there was a lurking devil in his eyes. I had pictured him as a more robust and ruffianly person."

"There's no doubt about the authenticity, for the name and the date, 1647, are on the back of the canvas."

Holmes said little more, but the picture of the old roysterer seemed to have a fascination for him, and his eyes were continually fixed upon it during supper. It was not until later, when Sir Henry had gone to his room, that I was able to follow the trend of his thoughts. He led me back into the banqueting-hall, his bedroom candle in his hand, and he held it up against the time-stained portrait on the wall.

"Do you see anything there?"

I looked at the broad plumed hat, the curling love-locks,[191] the white lace collar, and the straight, severe face which was framed between them. It was not a brutal countenance, but it was prim, hard and stern, with a firm-set, thin-lipped mouth, and a coldly intolerant eye.

"Is it like anyone you know?"

"There is something of Sir Henry about the jaw."

"Just a suggestion, perhaps. But wait an instant!"

He stood upon a chair, and holding up the light in his left hand, he curved his right arm over the broad hat, and round the long ringlets.

"Good heavens!" I cried, in amazement.

The face of Stapleton had sprung out of the canvas.

"Ha, you see it now. My eyes have been trained to examine faces and not their trimmings. It is the first quality of a criminal investigator that he should see through a disguise."

"But this is marvellous. It might be his portrait."

"Yes, it is an interesting instance of a throw-back,[192] which appears to be both physical and spiritual. A study of family portraits is enough to convert a man to the doctrine of reincarnation. The fellow is a Baskerville—that is evident."

"With designs upon the succession."

"Exactly. This chance of the picture has supplied us with one of our most obvious missing links. We have him, Watson,

"He curved his right arm over the broad hat, and round the long ringlets."
Richard Gutschmidt, *Der Hund von Baskerville* (Stuttgart: Robert Lutz Verlag, 1903)

we have him, and I dare swear that before tomorrow night he will be fluttering in our net as helpless as one of his own butterflies. A pin, a cork, and a card, and we add him to the Baker Street collection!"

He burst into one of his rare fits of laughter[193] as he turned away from the picture. I have not heard him laugh often, and it has always boded ill to somebody.

I was up betimes[194] in the morning, but Holmes was afoot earlier still, for I saw him as I dressed coming up the drive.

"Yes, we should have a full day today," he remarked, and he rubbed his hands with the joy of action. "The nets are all in place, and the drag is about to begin. We'll know before the day is out whether we have caught our big, lean-jawed pike, or whether he has got through the meshes."

"Have you been on the moor already?"

"I have sent a report from Grimpen to Princetown as to the

would rest on the shoulder and, ideally, hang in front of it. Usually, they were festooned with bows and ribbons.

192 Why did this escape the notice of Dr. Mortimer? "If he knew enough about atavism to write a book on the subject, he must have been well-versed in it indeed," Charles M. Pickard writes in "The Reticence of Doctor Mortimer." Mortimer must have seen the portrait on his many visits to the Hall and surely would have noticed the resemblance between Stapleton and Hugo. Indeed, he even tells Holmes that Rodger "was the very image, they tell me, of the family picture of old Hugo." Pickard argues that Mortimer must have reasoned that Stapleton was most likely Rodger's son and observed that none of the trouble had arisen until Stapleton moved in. He shared this conclusion with Holmes, but Holmes admonished him to remain silent, to permit Holmes to trap Stapleton.

193 See *A Study in Scarlet*, note 48, above, for a detailed discussion of Holmes's expressions of humour.

194 Timely or seasonably; usually, early.

" 'Good heavens!' I cried, in amazement."
Sidney Paget, *Strand Magazine*, 1902

death of Selden. I think I can promise that none of you will be troubled in the matter. And I have also communicated with my faithful Cartwright, who would certainly have pined away at the door of my hut as a dog does at his master's grave if I had not set his mind at rest about my safety."

"What is the next move?"

"To see Sir Henry. Ah, here he is!"

"Good morning, Holmes," said the baronet. "You look like a general who is planning a battle with his chief of the staff."

"That is the exact situation. Watson was asking for orders."

"And so do I."

"Very good. You are engaged, as I understand, to dine with our friends the Stapletons tonight."

"I hope that you will come also. They are very hospitable people, and I am sure that they would be very glad to see you."

"I fear that Watson and I must go to London."

"To London?"

"Yes, I think that we should be more useful there at the present juncture."

The baronet's face perceptibly lengthened. "I hoped that you were going to see me through this business. The Hall and the moor are not very pleasant places when one is alone."

"My dear fellow, you must trust me implicitly and do exactly what I tell you. You can tell your friends that we should have been happy to have come with you, but that urgent business required us to be in town. We hope very soon to return to Devonshire. Will you remember to give them that message?"

"If you insist upon it."

"There is no alternative, I assure you."

I saw by the baronet's clouded brow that he was deeply hurt by what he regarded as our desertion.

"When do you desire to go?" he asked, coldly.

"Immediately after breakfast. We will drive into Coombe Tracey, but Watson will leave his things as a pledge that he will come back to you. Watson, you will send a note to Stapleton to tell him that you regret that you cannot come."

"I have a good mind to go to London with you," said the baronet. "Why should I stay here alone?"

"Because it is your post of duty. Because you gave me your word that you would do as you were told, and I tell you to stay."

"All right, then, I'll stay."

"One more direction! I wish you to drive to Merripit House. Send back your trap, however, and let them know that you intend to walk home."

"To walk across the moor?"

"Yes."

"But that is the very thing which you have so often cautioned me not to do."

"This time you may do it with safety. If I had not every confidence in your nerve and courage I would not suggest it, but it is essential that you should do it."

"Then I will do it."

"And as you value your life, do not go across the moor in any direction save along the straight path which leads from Merripit House to the Grimpen Road, and is your natural way home."

"I will do just what you say."

"Very good. I should be glad to get away as soon after breakfast as possible, so as to reach London in the afternoon."

I was much astounded by this programme, though I remembered that Holmes had said to Stapleton on the night before that his visit would terminate next day. It had not crossed my mind, however, that he would wish me to go with him, nor could I understand how we could both be absent at a moment which he himself declared to be critical. There was nothing for it, however, but implicit obedience; so we bade good-bye to our rueful friend, and a couple of hours afterwards we were at the station of Coombe Tracey and had dispatched the trap upon its return journey. A small boy was waiting upon the platform.

"Any orders, sir?"

"You will take this train to town, Cartwright. The moment you arrive you will send a wire to Sir Henry Baskerville, in my name, to say that if he finds the pocket-book which I have dropped he is to send it by registered post to Baker Street."

"Yes, sir."

"And ask at the station office if there is a message for me."

The boy returned with a telegram, which Holmes handed to me. It ran—

> Wire received. Coming down with unsigned warrant.[195] Arrive five-forty.
>
> Lestrade.

"That is in answer to mine of this morning. He is the best of the professionals, I think, and we may need his assistance. Now, Watson, I think that we cannot employ our time better than by calling upon your acquaintance, Mrs. Laura Lyons."

His plan of campaign was beginning to be evident. He would use the baronet in order to convince the Stapletons that we were really gone, while we should actually return at the instant when we were likely to be needed. That telegram from London, if mentioned by Sir Henry to the Stapletons, must

195 Ian McQueen ponders why, as must be assumed, Holmes requested an *unsigned* warrant. "Presumably Lestrade meant a warrant for the arrest of Stapleton, but no such authority would be required for an arrest on a serious charge such as murder, and a warrant without signature would have no validity in any case."

remove the last suspicions from their minds. Already I seemed to see our nets drawing closer round that lean-jawed pike.

Mrs. Laura Lyons was in her office, and Sherlock Holmes opened his interview with a frankness and directness which considerably amazed her.

"I am investigating the circumstances which attended the death of the late Sir Charles Baskerville," said he. "My friend here, Dr. Watson, has informed me of what you have communicated, and also of what you have withheld in connection with that matter."

"What have I withheld?" she asked defiantly.

"You have confessed that you asked Sir Charles to be at the gate at ten o'clock. We know that that was the place and hour of his death. You have withheld what the connection is between these events."

"There is no connection."

"In that case the coincidence must indeed be an extraordinary one. But I think that we shall succeed in establishing a connection after all. I wish to be perfectly frank with you, Mrs. Lyons. We regard this case as one of murder, and the evidence may implicate not only your friend, Mr. Stapleton, but his wife as well."

The lady sprang from her chair. "His wife!" she cried.

"The fact is no longer a secret. The person who has passed for his sister is really his wife."

Mrs. Lyons had resumed her seat. Her hands were grasping the arms of her chair, and I saw that the pink nails had turned white with the pressure of her grip.

"His wife!" she said again. "His wife! He was not a married man."

Sherlock Holmes shrugged his shoulders.

"Prove it to me! Prove it to me! And if you can do so—!" The fierce flash of her eyes said more than any words.

"I have come prepared to do so," said Holmes, drawing several papers from his pocket. "Here is a photograph of the couple taken in York four years ago. It is indorsed 'Mr. and Mrs. Vandeleur,' but you will have no difficulty in recognizing him, and her also, if you know her by sight. Here are three written descriptions by trustworthy witnesses of Mr. and Mrs. Vandeleur, who at that time kept St. Oliver's private school. Read them, and see if you can doubt the identity of these people."

"The lady sprang from her chair."
Sidney Paget, *Strand Magazine*, 1902

She glanced at them, and then looked up at us with the set, rigid face of a desperate woman.

"Mr. Holmes," she said, "this man had offered me marriage on condition that I could get a divorce from my husband. He has lied to me, the villain, in every conceivable way. Not one word of truth has he ever told me. And why—why? I imagined that all was for my own sake. But now I see that I was never anything but a tool in his hands. Why should I preserve faith with him who never kept any with me? Why should I try to shield him from the consequences of his own wicked acts? Ask me what you like, and there is nothing which I shall hold back. One thing I swear to you, and that is, that when I wrote the letter I never dreamed of any harm to the old gentleman, who had been my kindest friend."

"I entirely believe you, madam," said Sherlock Holmes. "The recital of these events must be very painful to you, and perhaps it will make it easier if I tell you what occurred, and you can check me if I make any material mistake. The sending of this letter was suggested to you by Stapleton?"

"He dictated it."

"I presume that the reason he gave was that you would receive help from Sir Charles for the legal expenses connected with your divorce?"

"Exactly."

"And then after you had sent the letter he dissuaded you from keeping the appointment?"

"He told me that it would hurt his self-respect that any other man should find the money for such an object, and that though he was a poor man himself he would devote his last penny to removing the obstacles which divided us."

"He appears to be a very consistent character. And then you heard nothing until you read the reports of the death in the paper?"

"No."

"And he made you swear to say nothing about your appointment with Sir Charles?"

"He did. He said that the death was a very mysterious one, and that I should certainly be suspected if the facts came out. He frightened me into remaining silent."

"Quite so. But you had your suspicions?"

She hesitated and looked down. "I knew him," she said. "But if he had kept faith with me I should always have done so with him."

"I think that on the whole you have had a fortunate escape," said Sherlock Holmes. "You have had him in your power and he knew it, and yet you are alive. You have been walking for some months near to the edge of a precipice. We must wish you good morning now, Mrs. Lyons, and it is probable that you will very shortly hear from us again."

"Our case becomes rounded off, and difficulty after difficulty thins away in front of us," said Holmes, as we stood waiting for the arrival of the express from town. "I shall soon be in the position of being able to put into a single connected narrative one of the most singular and sensational crimes of modern times. Students of criminology will remember the analogous incidents in Grodno, in Little Russia,[196] in the year '66, and of course there are the Anderson murders in North Carolina,[197] but this case possesses some features which are entirely its

196 Grodno was a Lithuanian district of western Russia, near St. Petersburg, heavily Jewish, in the area now known as Belorussia; "Little Russia" was the Czarist name for the area now called Ukraine. That is, Grodno was not in Little Russia. In some American editions, the town is given as "Godno," a nonexistent location.

197 Possibly Holmes meant *South* Carolina. In 1866, Lt. Charles Snyder, commander of the military post of Anderson, S.C., reported the fatal shooting by Reuben Golding, a "desperate and ruffianly" white man, of A. Payton, a black man. The murder shocked the community, and other crimes of Golding's may have been brought to light. What possible relevance the case had to the one at hand is unknown. *Fort* Anderson was an important Civil War emplacement in North Carolina, but Anderson County and the town of Anderson were located in South Carolina.

own. Even now we have no clear case against this very wily man. But I shall be very much surprised if it is not clear enough before we go to bed this night."

The London express came roaring into the station, and a small, wiry bulldog of a man had sprung from a first-class carriage. We all three shook hands, and I saw at once from the reverential way in which Lestrade gazed at my companion that he had learned a good deal since the days when they had first worked together. I could well remember the scorn which the theories of the reasoner used then to excite in the practical man.

"Anything good?" he asked.

"The biggest thing for years," said Holmes. "We have two hours before we need think of starting. I think we might employ it in getting some dinner, and then, Lestrade, we will take the London fog out of your throat by giving you a breath of the pure night-air of Dartmoor. Never been there? Ah, well, I don't suppose you will forget your first visit."

"We all three shook hands."
Sidney Paget, *Strand Magazine*, 1902

CHAPTER XIV

THE HOUND OF THE BASKERVILLES

One of Sherlock Holmes's defects—if, indeed, one may call it a defect—was that he was exceedingly loth to communicate his full plans to any other person until the instant of their fulfilment. Partly it came no doubt from his own masterful nature, which loved to dominate and surprise those who were around him. Partly also from his professional caution, which urged him never to take any chances. The result, however, was very trying for those who were acting as his agents and assistants. I had often suffered under it, but never more so than during that long drive in the darkness. The great ordeal was in front of us; at last we were about to make our final effort, and yet Holmes had said nothing, and I could only surmise what his course of action would be. My nerves thrilled with anticipation when at last the cold wind upon our faces and the dark, void spaces on either side of the narrow road told me that we were back upon the moor once again. Every stride of the horses and every turn of the wheels was taking us nearer to our supreme adventure.

Our conversation was hampered by the presence of the driver of the hired wagonette, so that we were forced to talk of

198 But he is apparently not armed, and when Holmes has killed the hound, Lestrade proffers a brandy flask, which must have been in his hip-pocket. See text accompanying note 204, below.

Advertisement for Eille Norwood's *The Hound of the Baskervilles*.
San Francisco Examiner, December 4, 1921

trivial matters when our nerves were tense with emotion and anticipation. It was a relief to me, after that unnatural restraint, when we at last passed Frankland's house and knew that we were drawing near to the Hall and to the scene of action. We did not drive up to the door, but got down near the gate of the avenue. The wagonette was paid off and ordered to return to Coombe Tracey forthwith, while we started to walk to Merripit House.

"Are you armed, Lestrade?"

The little detective smiled. "As long as I have my trousers, I have a hip-pocket, and as long as I have my hip-pocket I have something in it."[198]

"Good! My friend and I are also ready for emergencies."

"You're mighty close about this affair, Mr. Holmes. What's the game now?"

"A waiting game."

"My word, it does not seem a very cheerful place," said the detective, with a shiver, glancing round him at the gloomy slopes of the hill and at the huge lake of fog which lay over the Grimpen Mire. "I see the lights of a house ahead of us."

"That is Merripit House and the end of our journey. I must request you to walk on tiptoe and not to talk above a whisper."

We moved cautiously along the track as if we were bound for the house, but Holmes halted us when we were about two hundred yards from it.

"This will do," said he. "These rocks upon the right make an admirable screen."

"We are to wait here?"

"Yes, we shall make our little ambush here. Get into this hollow, Lestrade. You have been inside the house, have you not, Watson? Can you tell the position of the rooms? What are those latticed windows at this end?"

"I think they are the kitchen windows."

"And the one beyond, which shines so brightly?"

"That is certainly the dining-room."

"The blinds are up. You know the lie of the land best. Creep forward quietly and see what they are doing—but for Heaven's sake don't let them know that they are watched!"

I tiptoed down the path and stooped behind the low wall which surrounded the stunted orchard. Creeping in its shadow, I reached a point whence I could look straight through the uncurtained window.

There were only two men in the room, Sir Henry and Stapleton. They sat with their profiles towards me on either side of the round table. Both of them were smoking cigars, and coffee and wine were in front of them. Stapleton was talking with animation, but the baronet looked pale and distrait. Perhaps the thought of that lonely walk across the ill-omened moor was weighing heavily upon his mind.

As I watched them Stapleton rose and left the room, while Sir Henry filled his glass again and leaned back in his chair, puffing at his cigar. I heard the creak of a door and the crisp sound of boots upon gravel. The steps passed along the path on the other side of the wall under which I crouched. Looking

"I could look straight through the uncurtained window."
Sidney Paget, *Strand Magazine*, 1902

over, I saw the naturalist pause at the door of an out-house in the corner of the orchard. A key turned in a lock, and as he passed in there was a curious scuffling noise from within. He was only a minute or so inside, and then I heard the key turn once more, and he passed me and re-entered the house. I saw him rejoin his guest, and I crept quietly back to where my companions were waiting to tell them what I had seen.

"You say, Watson, that the lady is not there?" Holmes asked, when I had finished my report.

"No."

"Where can she be, then, since there is no light in any other room except the kitchen?"

"I cannot think where she is."

I have said that over the great Grimpen Mire there hung a dense, white fog. It was drifting slowly in our direction, and banked itself up like a wall on that side of us, low, but thick and well defined. The moon shone on it, and it looked like a great shimmering icefield, with the heads of the distant tors as rocks borne upon its surface. Holmes's face was turned towards it, and he muttered impatiently as he watched its sluggish drift.

"It's moving towards us, Watson."

"Is that serious?"

"Very serious, indeed—the one thing upon earth which could have disarranged my plans. He can't be very long now. It is already ten o'clock. Our success and even his life may depend upon his coming out before the fog is over the path."

The night was clear and fine above us. The stars shone cold

"I could look straight through the uncurtained window."
Richard Gutschmidt, *Der Hund von Baskerville*
(Stuttgart: Robert Lutz Verlag, 1903)

and bright, while a half-moon bathed the whole scene in a soft, uncertain light. Before us lay the dark bulk of the house, its serrated roof and bristling chimneys hard outlined against the silver-spangled sky. Broad bars of golden light from the lower windows stretched across the orchard and the moor. One of them was suddenly shut off. The servants had left the kitchen. There only remained the lamp in the dining-room where the two men, the murderous host and the unconscious guest, still chatted over their cigars.

Every minute that white wooly plain which covered one-half of the moor was drifting closer and closer to the house. Already the first thin wisps of it were curling across the golden square of the lighted window. The farther wall of the orchard was already invisible, and the trees were standing out of a swirl of white vapour. As we watched it the fog-wreaths came crawling round both corners of the house and rolled slowly into one dense bank, on which the upper floor and the roof floated like a strange ship upon a shadowy sea. Holmes struck his hand passionately upon the rock in front of us, and stamped his feet in his impatience.

"If he isn't out in a quarter of an hour the path will be covered. In half an hour we won't be able to see our hands in front of us."

"Shall we move farther back upon higher ground?"

"Yes, I think it would be as well."

So as the fog-bank flowed onwards we fell back before it until we were half a mile from the house, and still that dense white sea, with the moon silvering its upper edge, swept slowly and inexorably on.

"We are going too far," said Holmes. "We dare not take the chance of his being overtaken before he can reach us. At all cost, we must hold our ground where we are." He dropped on his knees and clapped his ear to the ground. "Thank heaven, I think that I hear him coming."

A sound of quick steps broke the silence of the moor. Crouching among the stones, we stared intently at the silver-tipped bank in front of us. The steps grew louder, and through the fog, as through a curtain, there stepped the man whom we were awaiting. He looked round him in surprise as he emerged into the clear, starlit night. Then he came swiftly along the path, passed close to where we lay, and went on up the long

"He looked round him in surprise."
Sidney Paget, *Strand Magazine*, 1902

slope behind us. As he walked he glanced continually over either shoulder, like a man who is ill at ease.

"Hist!" cried Holmes, and I heard the sharp click of a cocking pistol. "Look out! It's coming!"

There was a thin, crisp, continuous patter from somewhere in the heart of that crawling bank. The cloud was within fifty yards of where we lay, and we glared at it, all three, uncertain what horror was about to break from the heart of it. I was at Holmes's elbow, and I glanced for an instant at his face. It was pale and exultant, his eyes shining brightly in the moonlight. But suddenly they started forward in a rigid, fixed stare, and his lips parted in amazement. At the same instant Lestrade

199 Elliot Kimball, in "Watson's Neurosis," praises Lestrade's behaviour, maintaining that it is a sign of the intelligence of "the courageous little man" that he "succumbed, momentarily" to the unknown, and that any other response would have been "senseless." The question is how this analysis reflects on Holmes and Watson, who did not flinch.

200 Stephen Farrell, in "It Can't Be Quite a Dead Dog; There's Still More Life to Be Wrung Out of It: A Discourse upon Marksmanship in *The Hound*," wonders why Holmes did not fire again before the animal reached Sir Henry. His delay not only made killing the hound (who, atop Sir Henry, would have been thrashing about) problematic but also risked injuring or killing Sir Henry by mistake.

"The Hound of the Baskervilles."
Sidney Paget, *Strand Magazine*, 1902

gave a yell of terror and threw himself face downwards upon the ground.[199] I sprang to my feet, my inert hand grasping my pistol, my mind paralysed by the dreadful shape which had sprung out upon us from the shadows of the fog. A hound it was, an enormous coal-black hound, but not such a hound as mortal eyes have ever seen. Fire burst from its open mouth, its eyes glowed with a smouldering glare, its muzzle and hackles and dewlap were outlined in flickering flame. Never in the delirious dream of a disordered brain could anything more savage, more appalling, more hellish, be conceived than that dark form and savage face which broke upon us out of the wall of fog.

With long bounds the huge black creature was leaping down the track, following hard upon the footsteps of our friend. So paralysed were we by the apparition that we allowed him to pass before we had recovered our nerve. Then Holmes and I both fired together, and the creature have a hideous howl, which showed that one at least had hit him.[200] He did not pause, however, but bounded onwards. Far away on the path we saw Sir Henry looking back, his face white in the moonlight, his hands raised in horror, glaring helplessly at the frightful thing which was hunting him down.

But that cry of pain from the hound had blown all our fears to the winds. If he was vulnerable he was mortal, and if we could wound him we could kill him. Never have I seen a man run as Holmes ran that night.[201] I am reckoned fleet of foot, but he outpaced me as much as I outpaced the little professional. In front of us as we flew up the track we heard scream after scream from Sir Henry and the deep roar of the hound. I was in time to see the beast spring upon its victim, hurl him to the ground and worry at his throat. But the next instant Holmes had emptied five barrels[202] of his revolver into the creature's flank.[203] With a last howl of agony and a vicious snap in the air it rolled upon its back, four feet pawing furiously, and then fell limp upon its side. I stooped, panting, and pressed my pistol to the dreadful, shimmering head, but it was useless to press the trigger. The giant hound was dead.

Sir Henry lay insensible where he had fallen. We tore away his collar, and Holmes breathed a prayer of gratitude when we saw that there was no sign of a wound and that the rescue had

Scene from *The Hound of the Baskervilles* (Great Britain: Gainsborough Pictures, 1931), starring Robert Rendel as Sherlock Holmes and John Stuart as Sir Henry Baskerville (pictured).

201 Edward J. Van Liere notes, in "Sherlock Holmes and Doctor Watson, Perennial Athletes," that Watson, who "had doubtless seen first-class track men perform," here elevates Holmes above all others in terms of speed and endurance.

202 Philip Weller, in a private communication with this editor, explains Watson's description of "emptied barrels," often criticised because of its implication of a multiple-barrelled weapon. When a bullet was fired, the *casing* remained in the weapon's rotating cartridge chamber, while the *projectile* (bullet) was propelled out of the barrel. The chamber was then rotated, and a fresh bullet lined up with the barrel.

> The barrel would, however, have been filled with the expanding gases from each cartridge in turn as the revolver was fired, as those gases drove the bullet out of the barrel, and the barrel would thus have been emptied of both the bullet and the gases each time that the pistol was fired. Watson might more correctly have said that the barrel was emptied five times, rather than that five barrels were emptied, but the latter turn of phrase was a very commonly used colloquialism which requires no apology.

Of course, Watson is only speaking figuratively. Only the obsolete "pepperpot" pistol would have had five *barrels*—Watson means five *chambers* of a conventional pistol.

203 Robert Keith Leavitt, in "Annie Oakley in Baker Street," notes that this was a poor choice of a target. Flank wounds would not necessarily be lethal and might well have been reflected; in this case, the bullet could have struck Sir Henry.

204 Did this come from Lestrade's "hip-pocket"? See note 198, above. James Edward Holroyd, in *Baker Street By-Ways*, reports that his friend Bill McGowran, of the *London Evening News*, "has a theory that Lestrade was a tippler and that this explains the fact that while we first meet him as an inspector, he is still the same rank twenty years later." There is no real Canonical evidence for this thesis. Only in "The Noble Bachelor" does Holmes offer Lestrade a drink, and even in circumstances where they share cigars (for example, "The Six Napoleons"), there is no mention of alcohol.

"Holmes emptied five barrels of his revolver into the creature's flank."
Sidney Paget. *Strand Magazine*, 1902

been in time. Already our friend's eyelids shivered and he made a feeble effort to move. Lestrade thrust his brandy-flask between the baronet's teeth,[204] and two frightened eyes were looking up at us. "My God!" he whispered. "What was it? What, in Heaven's name, was it?"

"It's dead, whatever it is," said Holmes. "We've laid the family ghost once and for ever."

In mere size and strength it was a terrible creature which was lying stretched before us. It was not a pure bloodhound and it was not a pure mastiff; but it appeared to be a combination of the two[205]—gaunt, savage, and as large as a small lioness. Even now, in the stillness of death, the huge jaws seemed to be dripping with a bluish flame, and the small, deep-set, cruel eyes were ringed with fire. I placed my hand upon the glowing muzzle, and as I held them up my own fingers smouldered and gleamed in the darkness.

"Phosphorus,"[206] I said.

"A cunning preparation of it," said Holmes, sniffing at the dead animal. "There is no smell which might have interfered with his power of scent. We owe you a deep apology, Sir Henry, for having exposed you to this fright. I was prepared for a hound, but not for such a creature as this. And the fog gave us little time to receive him."

"You have saved my life."

"'It's dead, whatever it is,' said Holmes."
Richard Gutschmidt, *Der Hund von Baskerville*
(Stuttgart: Robert Lutz Verlag, 1903)

205 Michael L. Burton, in "On the Hound," carefully reviews all of the evidence and concludes that Watson's description of the breed mix is accurate. Others reach different conclusions:

"From its gigantic size I would hazard that there was more likely some Great Dane or Scottish Wolfhound mixture involved," Stuart Palmer writes, in "Notes on Certain Evidences of Caniphobia in Mr. Sherlock Holmes and His Associates." Owen Frisbie comments, in "On the Origin of the Hound of the Baskervilles," that Watson's contention that the hound is both bloodhound and mastiff cannot be accurate, and that it is instead staghound ("for size and drive") and bloodhound ("for ability and will to take the line of a human").

Shirley Purves argues for a combination of Doberman pinscher and Irish Wolfhound, in "Consider the Hound." She also puts forward the possibility of a Cuban bloodhound crossbred with a Tibetan mastiff. Don Wright, in "The Hound of Hell Is Alive and Well," argues for a pit bull terrier. Philip Weller rises to the support of Watson, specifically rejecting some of the foregoing as well as others in "Barking Up the Wrong Yew Tree."

206 But phosphorus can kill dog or man, comments Stuart Palmer, note 205, above. D. A. Redmond suggests, in "Some Chemical Problems in the Canon," that the substance was not phosphorus but barium sulphide, while Walter Shepherd, in *On the Scent with Sherlock Holmes* (1986), proposes zinc sulphide or calcium sulphide. Frederick J. Jaeger and Rose M. Vogel, in *Hound from Hell*, contend for a bioluminous substance based on the studies of Raphael Dubois published in 1886. Michael Bedford and Bruce Dettman, in " 'A Cunning Preparation,' " sidestep the problem by positing that the substance was on a leather muzzle, not the *dog's* muzzle.

" 'Phosphorus!' I said."
Sidney Paget, *Strand Magazine*, 1902

"Having first endangered it. Are you strong enough to stand?"

"Give me another mouthful of that brandy, and I shall be ready for anything. So! Now, if you will help me up. What do you propose to do?"

"To leave you here. You are not fit for further adventures tonight. If you will wait, one or other of us will go back with you to the Hall."

He tried to stagger to his feet; but he was still ghastly pale and trembling in every limb. We helped him to a rock, where he sat shivering with his face buried in his hands.

"We must leave you now," said Holmes. "The rest of our work must be done, and every moment is of importance. We have our case, and now we only want our man."

"It's a thousand to one against our finding him at the house," he continued, as we retraced our steps swiftly down the path. "Those shots must have told him that the game was up."

"We were some distance off, and this fog may have deadened them."

"He followed the hound to call him off—of that you may be certain. No, no, he's gone by this time! But we'll search the house and make sure."

The front door was open, so we rushed in and hurried from room to room, to the amazement of a doddering old manservant, who met us in the passage. There was no light save in the dining-room, but Holmes caught up the lamp, and left no corner of the house unexplored. No sign could we see of the man whom we were chasing. On the upper floor, however, one of the bedroom doors was locked.

"There's someone in here!" cried Lestrade. "I can hear a movement. Open this door!"

A faint moaning and rustling came from within. Holmes struck the door just over the lock with the flat of his foot, and it flew open. Pistol in hand, we all three rushed into the room.

But there was no sign within it of that desperate and defiant villain whom we expected to see. Instead we were faced by an object so strange and so unexpected that we stood for a moment staring at it in amazement.

The room had been fashioned into a small museum, and the walls were lined by a number of glass-topped cases full of that collection of butterflies and moths the formation of which had been the relaxation of this complex and dangerous man. In the centre of this room there was an upright beam, which had been placed at some period as a support for the old worm-eaten balk of timber which spanned the roof. To this post a figure was tied, so swathed and muffled in the sheets which had been used to secure it that one could not for the moment tell whether it was that of a man or a woman. One towel passed round the throat, and was secured at the back of the pillar. Another covered the lower part of the face and over it two dark eyes—eyes full of grief and shame and a dreadful question-

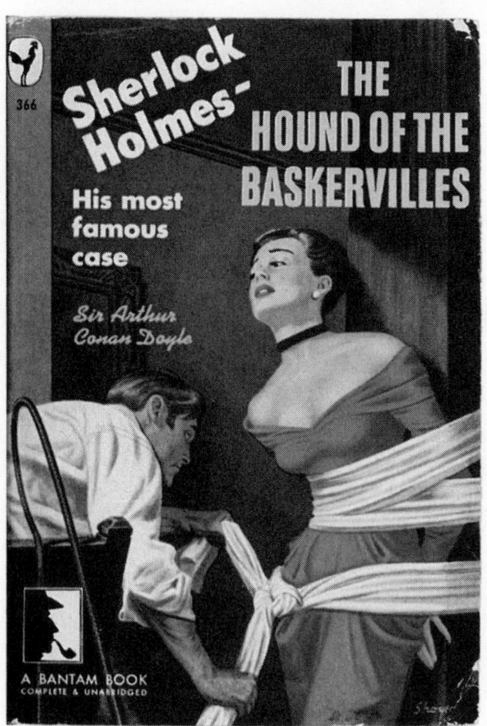

Bill Shoyer, *The Hound of the Baskervilles.* (New York: Bantam Books, 1949)

ing—stared back at us. In a minute we had torn off the gag, unswathed the bonds, and Mrs. Stapleton sank upon the floor in front of us. As her beautiful head fell upon her chest I saw the clear read weal of a whip-lash across her neck.[207]

"The brute!" cried Holmes. "Here, Lestrade, your brandy-bottle! Put her in the chair! She has fainted from ill-usage and exhaustion."

She opened her eyes again. "Is he safe?" she asked. "Has he escaped?"

"He cannot escape us, madam."

"No, no, I did not mean my husband. Sir Henry? Is he safe?"

"Yes."

"And the hound?"

"It is dead."

She gave a long sigh of satisfaction. "Thank God! Thank God! Oh, this villain! See how he has treated me!" She shot her arms out from her sleeves, and we saw with horror that they were all mottled with bruises. "But this is nothing—nothing! It

207 Dean W. Dickensheet, in "Upon the Victorian Reticence of John H. Watson, M.D.," points out that notwithstanding that she is swathed in sheets, Beryl's weal is on her *neck*. The truth, he concludes, is that "[t]he diabolical Stapleton, having bound his recalcitrant wife to the beam, stripped her to the waist (at least) and savagely beat her upon the back and (probably) breasts, exhibiting the diablerie of a man attempting to disfigure those desirable charms which he believes he has lost to another." Dickensheet's more lurid scene is genteelly illustrated in the cover drawn by Bill Shoyer for a 1949 paperback reissue of *The Hound of the Baskervilles*. The inside cover reads, "He had tied her to an upright beam in the centre of the room, her perfect figure and elegant dress swathed in the sheets that dug into her flesh and secured her to the post. She was tall, dark, and slender, with a proud, finely cut face so regular it would have been impassive except for the sensitive mouth and the beautiful, dark, eager eyes. The eyes—full of fear and grief—stared out at her tormentor with a dreadful questioning." *Quelle difference!*

is my mind and soul that he has tortured and defiled. I could endure it all, ill-usage, solitude, a life of deception, everything, as long as I could still cling to the hope that I had his love, but now I know that in this also I have been his dupe and his tool." She broke into passionate sobbing as she spoke.

"You bear him no good-will, madam," said Holmes. "Tell us, then, where we shall find him. If you have ever aided him in evil, help us now and so atone."

"There is but one place where he can have fled," she answered. "There is an old tin mine on an island in the heart of the Mire. It was there that he kept his hound, and there also he had made preparations so that he might have a refuge. That is where he would fly."

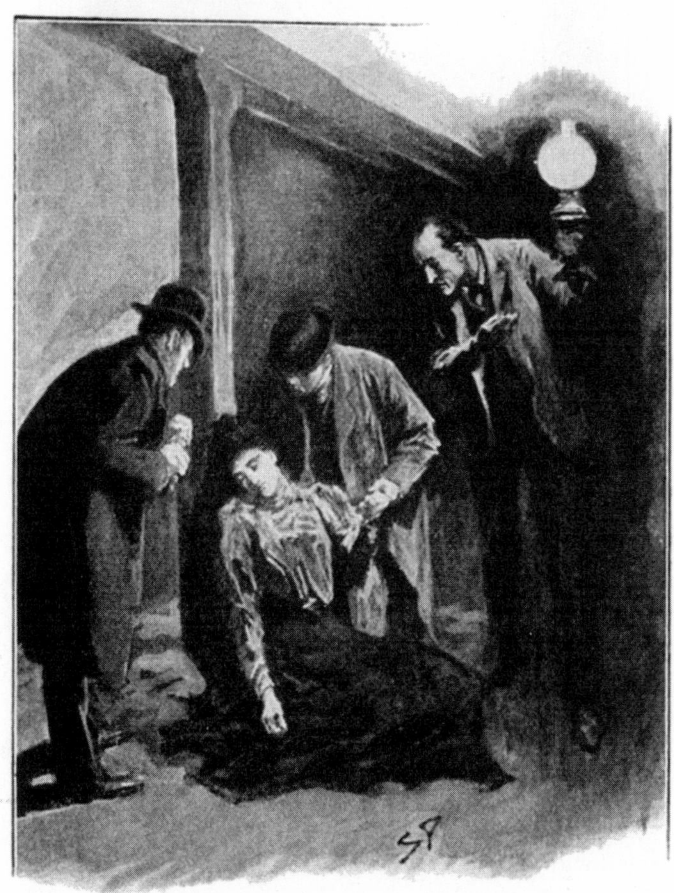

"Mrs. Stapleton sank upon the floor."
Sidney Paget, *Strand Magazine*, 1902

" 'The brute!' cried Holmes. 'Here, Lestrade, your brandy-bottle!' "
Frederic Dorr Steele, *Later Adventures of Sherlock Holmes*, Vol. II, 1952. Although captioned "drawn by Mr. Steele especially for this edition," Andrew Malec shows that the work first illustrated Mary Robert Rinehart's novel *Sight Unseen*, which appeared in *Everybody's Magazine*, August 1916 (note the '16 next to the artist's signature).

The fog-bank lay like white wool against the window. Holmes held the lamp towards it.

"See," said he. "No one could find his way into the Grimpen Mire tonight."

She laughed and clapped her hands. Her eyes and teeth gleamed with fierce merriment.

"He may find his way in, but never out," she cried. "How can he see the guiding wands tonight? We planted them together, he and I, to mark the pathway through the Mire. Oh, if I could only have plucked them out today! Then indeed you would have had him at your mercy."

It was evident to us that all pursuit was in vain until the fog had lifted. Meanwhile we left Lestrade in possession of the house, while Holmes and I went back with the baronet to Baskerville Hall. The story of the Stapletons could no longer be withheld from him, but he took the blow bravely when he learned the truth about the woman whom he had loved. But the shock of the night's adventures had shattered his nerves, and before morning he lay delirious in a high fever,[208] under the care of Dr. Mortimer. The two of them were destined to travel together round the world before Sir Henry had become once more the hale, hearty man that he had been before he became master of the ill-omened estate.

And now I come rapidly to the conclusion of this singular narrative, in which I have tried to make the reader share those dark fears and vague surmises which clouded our lives so long, and ended in so tragic a manner. On the morning after the death of the hound the fog had lifted and we were guided by Mrs. Stapleton to the point where they had found a pathway through the bog. It helped us to realize the horror of this woman's life when we saw the eagerness and joy with which she laid us on her husband's track. We left her standing upon the thin peninsula of firm, peaty soil which tapered out into the widespread bog. From the end of it a small wand planted here and there showed where the path zigzagged from tuft to tuft of rushes among those green-scummed pits and foul quagmires which barred the way to the stranger. Rank reeds and lush, slimy water-plants sent an odour of decay and a heavy miasmatic vapour into our faces, while a false step plunged us more than once thigh-deep into the dark, quivering mire, which shook for yards in soft undulations around our feet. Its tenacious grip plucked at our heels as we walked, and when we sank into it it was as if some malignant hand was tugging us down into those obscene depths, so grim and purposeful was the clutch in which it held us. Once only we saw a trace that someone had passed that perilous way before us. From amid a

208 Undoubtedly another example of the epidemic of brain fever in the Canon. Seven patients in the Canon are mentioned as having the disease "brain fever," which, Alvin E. Rodin and Jack D. Key write in *Medical Casebook of Dr. Arthur Conan Doyle*, "we can characterize . . . as one which follows quickly on a severe emotional shock, which exhibits weight loss, weakness, pallor, and high fever, and which has a protracted course. Most patients recover, but insanity or death is possible." A vague affliction, to be sure, but Watson is in good company: Nineteenth-century fiction is rife with instances of the malady. Rodin and Key note other well-known victims, including Catherine Linton in Emily Brontë's *Wuthering Heights* (1847), Emma Bovary in Gustave Flaubert's *Madame Bovary* (1857), and Lucy Feverel in George Meredith's *The Ordeal of Richard Feverel* (1859). Such prevalence of brain fever in the literature of the day would seem to validate it as a medical diagnosis; Rodin and Key further cite an 1892 medical textbook that lists "fever" as a manifestation of an hysterical reaction, as well as a modern dictionary that equates brain fever with meningitis.

tuft of cotton-grass which bore it up out of the slime some dark thing was projecting. Holmes sank to his waist as he stepped from the path to seize it, and had we not been there to drag him out he could never have set his foot upon firm land again. He held an old black boot in the air. "Meyers,[209] Toronto," was printed on the leather inside.

"It is worth a mud bath," said he. "It is our friend Sir Henry's missing boot."

"Thrown there by Stapleton in his flight."

"Exactly. He retained it in his hand after using it to set the hound upon his track. He fled when he knew the game was up,

"He held an old black boot in the air."
Sidney Paget, *Strand Magazine*, 1902

209 Watson got the name wrong; Joseph *Meier* was a boot and shoe manufacturer located on Queen Street West in Toronto, notes Donald A. Redmond.

still clutching it. And he hurled it away at this point of his flight. We know at least that he came so far in safety."

But more than that we were never destined to know, though there was much which we might surmise.[210] There was no chance of finding footsteps in the mire, for the rising mud oozed swiftly in upon them, but as we at last reached firmer ground beyond the morass we all looked eagerly for them. But no slightest sign of them ever met our eyes. If the earth told a true story, then Stapleton never reached that island of refuge towards which he struggled through the fog upon that last night. Somewhere in the heart of the great Grimpen Mire, down in the foul slime of the huge morass which had sucked him in, this cold and cruel-hearted man is for ever buried.

Many traces we found of him in the bog-girt island where he had hid his savage ally. A huge driving-wheel and a shaft half-filled with rubbish showed the position of an abandoned mine. Beside it were the crumbling remains of the cottages of the miners, driven away, no doubt, by the foul reek of the surrounding swamp. In one of these a staple and chain, with a quantity of gnawed bones, showed where the animal had been confined. A skeleton with a tangle of brown hair adhering to it lay among the *débris*.

"A dog!" said Holmes. "By Jove, a curly-haired spaniel.[211] Poor Mortimer will never see his pet again. Well, I do not know that this place contains any secret which we have not already fathomed. He could hide his hound, but he could not hush its voice, and hence came those cries which even in the daylight were not pleasant to hear. On an emergency he could keep the hound in the out-house at Merripit, but it was always a risk, and it was only on the supreme day, which he regarded as the end of all his efforts, that he dared do it. This paste in the tin is no doubt the luminous mixture with which the creature was daubed. It was suggested, of course, by the story of the family hell-hound, and by the desire to frighten old Sir Charles to death. No wonder the poor devil of a convict ran and screamed, even as our friend did, and as we ourselves might have done, when he saw such a creature bounding through the darkness of the moor upon his track. It was a cunning device, for, apart from the chance of driving your victim to his death, what peasant would venture to inquire too closely into such a creature

210 In a daring work of speculation entitled "A Vindication of Stapleton," Donald Yates reconstructs the missing page from Watson's narrative (see note 125, above) and explains the mystery of Stapleton's disappearance. Sir Henry, Yates concludes, knew of Stapleton's plan to loose the hound and furthermore knew that Holmes, Watson, and Lestrade would be lying in wait to save him. Since Sir Henry could not tolerate Stapleton's mistreatment of Beryl, he urged Beryl, Laura Lyons, and the manservant Antonio, whose sympathies lay with his mistress, to force Stapleton onto the moor in a panic. Antonio had removed the secret wands showing the path to safety, and Stapleton perished immediately. To save face, Holmes, when he became aware of this conspiracy and that his rôle was only that of an actor, removed a page from Watson's correspondence that would have undermined his absolute authority.

211 "Sheer brilliance," sniffs Stuart Palmer, "since the skeletal remains of a spaniel differ slightly if at all from [those of] any other small dog." Benjamin S. Clark sees a more sinister significance in the presence of the bones. He reasons that the spaniel could not have strayed there by itself and finds it unlikely that Stapleton would have risked—unnecessarily, with other plentiful supplies of meat at hand—taking his neighbour's dog (or permitting the hound itself to take the dog) for fodder. Clark reasons that the spaniel could not have "penetrated" the bog without Mortimer, and that the logical conclusion is that Mortimer was colluding with Stapleton, since "even if the doctor had come on the path to the island by chance he would, if he were an honest man, have immediately publicised his discovery of the hound."

should he get sight of it, as many have done, upon the moor! I said it in London, Watson, and I say it again now, that never yet have we helped to hunt down a more dangerous man than he who is lying yonder"—he swept his long arm towards the huge mottled expanse of green-splotched bog which stretched away until it merged into the russet slopes of the moor.[212]

"Where the animal had been confined."
Sidney Paget, *Strand Magazine*, 1902

212 Ian McQueen concludes that it is premature to announce Stapleton's death. "Holmes assumed from the lack of footprints on the 'firmer ground beyond the morass' that Stapleton had perished in the swamp, but this can be neither proved nor disproved." McQueen asks why, if such ground showed footmarks, there were none of Stapleton's from the afternoon before, proving he had left for Merripit House with his dog. Indeed, Emily O'Brien, in "Did Stapleton Escape to Samoa?," finds evidence of Stapleton's escape in *The Beach of Falesa*, a novella by Robert Louis Stevenson, written near the end of his life. The Stevenson novella, originally entitled "Uma," is not to be confused with the narrative screenplay by Dylan Thomas entitled *The Beach at Falesa* (1964), which covers some of the same ground.

CHAPTER XV

A Retrospection

It was the end of November, and Holmes and I sat, upon a raw and foggy night, on either side of a blazing fire in our sitting-room in Baker Street. Since the tragic upshot of our visit to Devonshire he had been engaged in two affairs of the utmost importance, in the first of which he had exposed the atrocious conduct of Colonel Upwood[213] in connection with the famous card scandal of the Nonpareil Club,[214] while in the second he had defended the unfortunate Mme. Montpensier from the charge of murder which hung over her in connection with the death of her step-daughter Mlle. Carère, the young lady who, as it will be remembered, was found six months later alive and married in New York.[215] My friend was in excellent spirits over the success which had attended a succession of difficult and important cases, so that I was able to induce him to discuss the details of the Baskerville mystery. I had waited patiently for the opportunity, for I was aware that he would never permit cases to overlap, and that his clear and logical mind would not be drawn from its present work to dwell upon memories of the past. Sir Henry and Dr. Mortimer were, however, in London, on their way to that long voyage which had

213 Dr. Julian Wolff, in his *Practical Handbook of Sherlockian Heraldry*, identifies Colonel Upwood with Sir William Gordon-Cumming, a lieutenant-colonel in the Scots Guards during the Zulu War (1879). In 1891 Sir William brought an action for slander against a family who had accused him of cheating at the illegal card game baccarat. A long-time friend of Gordon-Cumming's, the Prince of Wales—the future King Edward VII—himself was subpoenaed as a witness; he was the first in the Royal Family ever to give evidence in a civil court action, and had been compelled to appear (by Gordon-Cumming's lawyer, Sir Edward Clarke) on the basis of Article 42 of the Queen's Regulations for the army, which directed that anyone who saw an illegal action being performed by a soldier or officer report it to the appropriate commanding officer. Largely because of the Prince's evidence under vicious cross-examination by Gordon-Cumming's counsel, who delved into the

Prince's personal life, Sir William lost the Baccarat Case, as it became known. The case aroused great interest, with many people convinced of Sir William's innocence; some believed that it was perhaps Edward who had committed some unknown illegal action not revealed in the course of the trial, and that Gordon-Cumming was merely covering for his friend. As a result of the scandal, public opinion turned for a time against the Prince, but ultimately his reputation was undamaged. The effect on Gordon-Cumming's life, on the other hand, was complete and devastating. He was ostracised from society.

214 In "Who Was Cecil Forrester?," Robert Keith Leavitt writes that the Nonpareil must have been "a discreet, footnote kind of club composed of journalists." He hazards this guess on the basis of the fact that Nonpareil was a type-face. Originally, the name signified the type's unsurpassable beauty; in 1886, at the urging of type-foundry inventor Nelson C. Marks, who was working to regularise printers' nomenclature, the word "nonpareil" was adopted by the U.S. Typefounders' Association and other groups as a size designation (6-point).

215 This sentence and the preceding do not appear in the *Strand Magazine* text.

"A retrospection."
Sidney Paget, *Strand Magazine*, 1902

been recommended for the restoration of his shattered nerves. They had called upon us that very afternoon, so that it was natural that the subject should come up for discussion.

"The whole course of events," said Holmes, "from the point of view of the man who called himself Stapleton, was simple and direct, although to us, who had no means in the beginning of knowing the motives of his actions and could only learn part of the facts, it all appeared exceedingly complex. I have had the advantage of two conversations with Mrs. Stapleton, and the case has now been so entirely cleared up that I am not aware that there is anything which has remained a secret to us. You will find a few notes upon the matter under the heading B in my indexed list of cases."

"Perhaps you would kindly give me a sketch of the course of events from memory."

"Certainly, though I cannot guarantee that I carry all the facts in my mind. Intense mental concentration has a curious way of blotting out what has passed. The barrister who has his case at his fingers' end, and is able to argue with an expert upon his own subject, finds that a week or two of the courts will drive it all out of his head once more.[216] So each of my cases displaces the last, and Mlle. Carère has blurred my recollection of Baskerville Hall. Tomorrow some other little problem may be submitted to my notice, which will in turn dispossess the fair French lady and the infamous Upwood. So far as the case of Hound goes, however, I will give you the course of events as nearly as I can, and you will suggest anything which I may have forgotten.

"My inquiries show beyond all question that the family portrait did not lie, and that this fellow was indeed a Baskerville. He was the son of that Rodger Baskerville,[217] the younger brother of Sir Charles, who fled with a sinister reputation to South America, where he was said to have died unmarried. He did, as a matter of fact, marry, and had one child, this fellow, whose real name is the same as his father. He married Beryl Garcia, one of the beauties of Costa Rica, and, having purloined a considerable sum of public money, he changed his name to Vandeleur and fled to England, where he established a school in the east of Yorkshire.[218] His reason for attempting this special line of business was that he had struck up an acquaintance with a consumptive tutor upon the voyage home, and that he had used this man's ability to make the undertaking a success. Fraser, the tutor, died, however, and the school which had begun well, sank from disrepute into infamy. The Vandeleurs found it convenient to change their name to Stapleton, and he brought the remains of his fortune, his schemes for the future, and his taste for entomology to the south of England. I learn at the British Museum that he was a recognized authority upon the subject, and that the name of Vandeleur has been permanently attached to a certain moth which he had, in his Yorkshire days, been the first to describe.[219]

"We now come to that portion of his life which has proved to be of such intense interest to us. The fellow had evidently made inquiry, and found that only two lives intervened

216 This sentence and the next two do not appear in the *Strand Magazine* text.

217 S. Kanto, in "Stapleton no Shoutai" [The true identity of Stapleton], argues that Stapleton could not be Rodger Baskerville Jr. He reconstructs the Baskerville family tree and finds that Rodger Sr. was born in 1842, and Stapleton in 1854, when his supposed father was twelve years old. Kanto concludes that Stapleton was Jack Baskerville, an illegitimate son of the father of Sir Charles Baskerville. He further suggests that Jack and Rodger Jr. co-operated in the crime, with Jack committing the attempted murder and planning that Rodger Jr. would claim the estate.

218 Yorkshire was England's largest county, north of the river Humber and bounded on the east by the North Sea (the "German Ocean"). Divided into areas known as Ridings (derived from the Middle English "thriding" or "thirding," meaning a third part), Yorkshire was largely agricultural, although the West Riding contained the major manufacturing centres of Leeds, Sheffield, Halifax, and Huddersfield and was described by *Beeton's British Gazetteer* as "one of the greatest manufacturing districts in the world." In his "Clinical Notes by a Resident Patient," Christopher Morley expresses the view that Holmes came from Yorkshire.

219 Philip Weller reports, in "Stapleton—An Un-Natural Naturalist," that his examination of the records of the British Museum shows that "the attachment was by no means permanent, and that all reference to the name of Vandeleur has been removed in connection with entomology."

between him and a valuable estate. When he went to Devonshire his plans were, I believe, exceedingly hazy, but that he meant mischief from the first is evident from the way in which he took his wife with him in the character of his sister. The idea of using her as a decoy was clearly already in his mind, though he may not have been certain how the details of his plot were to be arranged. He meant in the end to have the estate, and he was ready to use any tool or run any risk for that end. His first act was to establish himself as near to his ancestral home as he could, and his second was to cultivate a friendship with Sir Charles Baskerville and with the neighbours.[220]

"The baronet himself told him about the family hound, and so prepared the way for his own death. Stapleton, as I will continue to call him, knew that the old man's heart was weak, and that a shock would kill him. So much he had learned from Dr. Mortimer. He had heard also that Sir Charles was superstitious, and had taken this grim legend very seriously. His ingenious mind instantly suggested a way by which the baronet could be done to death, and yet it would be hardly possible to bring home the guilt to the real murderer.

"Having conceived the idea, he proceeded to carry it out with considerable finesse. An ordinary schemer would have been content to work with a savage hound. The use of artificial means to make the creature diabolical was a flash of genius upon his part. The dog he bought in London from Ross and Mangles, the dealers in Fulham Road.[221] It was the strongest and most savage in their possession. He brought it down by the North Devon line,[222] and walked a great distance over the moor, so as to get it home without exciting any remarks. He had already on his insect hunts learned to penetrate the Grimpen Mire, and so had found a safe hiding-place for the creature. Here he kennelled it and waited his chance.

"But it was some time coming. The old gentleman could not be decoyed outside of his grounds at night. Several times Stapleton lurked about with his hound, but without avail. It was during these fruitless quests that he, or rather his ally, was seen by peasants, and that the legend of the demon dog received a new confirmation. He had hoped that his wife might lure Sir Charles to his ruin, but here she proved unexpectedly independent. She would not endeavour to entangle the old gentleman in a sentimental attachment which might deliver him over

220 Benjamin S. Clark suggests that Dr. Mortimer became the confederate of Vandeleur/Stapleton while treating a certain consumptive tutor named Fraser. Clark asserts that when Mortimer came to see Holmes in Baker Street, he was already plotting against Sir Henry Baskerville and *deliberately* left behind his walking stick, to induce Holmes's conclusions regarding Mortimer's character and to establish his complete lack of criminal leanings.

221 A West End thoroughfare extending from Brompton Road, just south of Hyde Park, to Fulham Palace Road, almost to the Thames, in the borough of Fulham; it serves as the dividing line between the boroughs of Chelsea and Kensington.

222 Originally the North Devon Railway, the line became part of the London and South-Western Railway in 1865. B. J. D. Walsh, in "The Railways of Dartmoor in the Days of Sherlock Holmes," notes that Stapleton would have been headed to Yeoford Junction or Okehampton. There were roads from either of those two places to Moretonhampstead, and from Moretonhampstead he could have continued on to Bovey Tracey. See also Philip Weller's "The Railways of the Hound: Platform One."

to his enemy. Threats and even, I am sorry to say, blows failed to move her. She would have nothing to do with it, and for a time Stapleton was at a deadlock.

"He found a way out of his difficulties through the chance that Sir Charles, who had conceived a friendship for him, made him the minister of his charity in the case of this unfortunate woman, Mrs. Laura Lyons. By representing himself as a single man, he acquired complete influence over her, and he gave her to understand that in the event of her obtaining a divorce from her husband he would marry her. His plans were suddenly brought to a head by his knowledge that Sir Charles was about to leave the Hall on the advice of Dr. Mortimer, with whose opinion he himself pretended to coincide. He must act at once, or his victim might get beyond his power. He therefore put pressure upon Mrs. Lyons to write this letter, imploring the old man to give her an interview on the evening before his departure for London. He then, by a specious argument, prevented her from going, and so had the chance for which he had waited.

"Driving back in the evening from Coombe Tracey, he was in time to get his hound, to treat it with his infernal paint, and to bring the beast round to the gate at which he had reason to expect that he would find the old gentleman waiting. The dog, incited by it master, sprang over the wicket-gate and pursued the unfortunate baronet, who fled screaming down the Yew Alley. In that gloomy tunnel it must indeed have been a dreadful sight to see that huge black creature, with its flaming jaws and blazing eyes, bounding after its victim. He fell dead at the end of the alley from heart disease and terror. The hound had kept upon the grassy border while the baronet had run down the path, so that no track but the man's was visible. On seeing him lying still the creature had probably approached to sniff at him, but, finding him dead, had turned away again. It was then that it left the print which was actually observed by Dr. Mortimer. The hound was called off and hurried away to its lair in the Grimpen Mire, and a mystery was left which puzzled the authorities, alarmed the countryside, and finally brought the case within the scope of our observation.

"So much for the death of Sir Charles Baskerville. You perceive the devilish cunning of it, for really it would be almost impossible to make a case against the real murderer. His only accomplice was one who could never give him away,[223] and the

223 But a few paragraphs later, Holmes remarks, "There can be no question that he had a confidant . . ."

H. T. Webster, *New York Herald Tribune*, April 28, 1928.

grotesque, inconceivable nature of the device only served to make it more effective. Both of the women concerned in the case, Mrs. Stapleton and Mrs. Laura Lyons, were left with a strong suspicion against Stapleton. Mrs. Stapleton knew that he had designs upon the old man, and also of the existence of the hound. Mrs. Lyons knew neither of these things, but had been impressed by the death occurring at the time of an uncancelled appointment which was only known to him. However, both of them were under his influence, and he had nothing to fear from them. The first half of his task was successfully accomplished, but the more difficult still remained.

"It is possible that Stapleton did not know of the existence of an heir in Canada. In any case he would very soon learn it from his friend Dr. Mortimer, and he was told by the latter all the details about the arrival of Henry Baskerville. Stapleton's

"—that creature, with its flaming jaws and blazing eyes."
Frederic Dorr Steele, *Later Adventures of Sherlock Holmes*, Vol. II, 1952

first idea was that this young stranger from Canada might possibly be done to death in London without coming down to Devonshire at all. He distrusted his wife ever since she had refused to help him in laying a trap for the old man, and he dared not leave her long out of his sight for fear he should lose his influence over her. It was for this reason that he took her to London with him. They lodged, I find, at the Mexborough Private Hotel, in Craven Street,[224] which was actually one of those called upon by my agent in search of evidence. Here he kept his wife imprisoned in her room while he, disguised in a beard, followed Dr. Mortimer to Baker Street, and afterwards to the station and to the Northumberland Hotel. His wife had some inkling of his plans; but she had such a fear of her husband—a fear founded upon brutal ill-treatment—that she dare not write to warn the man whom she knew to be in danger. If the letter should fall into Stapleton's hands her own life would not be safe. Eventually, as we know, she adopted the expedient of cutting out the words which would form the message, and addressing the letter in a disguised hand. It reached the baronet, and gave him the first warning of his danger.

"It was very essential for Stapleton to get some article of Sir

224 Craven Street is a short street extending from the Strand to the Victoria Embankment, where it meets Northumberland Avenue. The Mexborough Hotel would have been virtually in the shadow of the Northumberland Hotel, at which Sir Henry stayed. See note 62, above.

Henry's attire, so that, in case he was driven to use the dog, he might always have the means of setting him upon his track. With characteristic promptness and audacity he set about this at once, and we cannot doubt that the boots[225] or chambermaid of the hotel was well bribed[226] to help him in his design. By chance, however, the first boot which was procured for him was a new one, and, therefore, useless for his purpose. He then had it returned and obtained another—a most instructive incident, since it proved conclusively to my mind that we were dealing with a real hound, as no other supposition could explain this anxiety to obtain an old boot and this indifference to a new one. The more *outré* and grotesque an incident is the more carefully it deserves to be examined, and the very point which appears to complicate a case is, when duly considered and scientifically handled, the one which is most likely to elucidate it.

"Then we had the visit from our friends next morning, shadowed always by Stapleton in the cab.[227] From his knowledge of our rooms and of my appearance, as well as from his general conduct, I am inclined to think that Stapleton's career of crime has been by no means limited to this single Baskerville affair. It is suggestive that during the last three years there have been four considerable burglaries in the West country, for none of which was any criminal ever arrested. The last of these, at Folkestone Court, in May, was remarkable for the cold-blooded pistolling of the page, who surprised the masked and solitary burglar. I cannot doubt that Stapleton recruited his waning resources in this fashion, and that for years he has been a desperate and dangerous man.

"We had an example of his readiness of resource that morning when he got away from us so successfully, and also of his audacity in sending back my own name to me through the cabman. From that moment he understood that I had taken over the case in London, and that therefore there was no chance for him there. He returned to Dartmoor and awaited the arrival of the baronet."

"One moment!" said I. "You have, no doubt, described the sequence of events correctly, but there is one point which you have left unexplained. What became of the hound when its master was in London?"

"I have given some attention to this matter, and it is undoubtedly of importance. There can be no question that

225 That is, the servant whose tasks included boot-cleaning.

226 Benjamin S. Clark, who maintains that Dr. Mortimer stole the boot, rejects the idea that the hotel's "boots" had been suborned. He reasons that Stapleton, "even disguised," would not have risked stealing the boot from the hotel for so little gain ("a few days") when he could more easily have taken the boot from Baskerville Hall; and he thinks it unlikely that Stapleton, immediately upon arrival in London, could target (and then would be willing to bribe adequately) the right "boots."

227 Why, ponders Clark, did Stapleton follow the pair, when he already had the location of Sir Henry's hotel and had observed the meeting with Holmes? It would not be because he feared that Holmes had advised bringing in Scotland Yard; rather, he wished to draw attention away from Mortimer, who, in order to be of help, had to remain free from suspicion.

Stapleton had a confidant, though it is unlikely that he ever placed himself in his power by sharing all his plans with him. There was an old manservant at Merripit House, whose name was Anthony. His connection with the Stapletons can be traced for several years, as far back as the schoolmastering days, so that he must have been aware that his master and mistress were really husband and wife. This man has disappeared and has escaped from the country. It is suggestive that Anthony is not a common name in England, while Antonio is so in all Spanish or Spanish-American countries. The man, like Mrs. Stapleton herself, spoke good English, but with a curious lisping accent. I have myself seen this old man cross the Grimpen Mire by the path which Stapleton had marked out. It is very probable, therefore, that in the absence of his master it was he who cared for the hound, though he may never have known the purpose for which the beast was used.

"The Stapletons then went down to Devonshire, whither they were soon followed by Sir Henry and you. One word now as to how I stood myself at that time. It may possibly recur to your memory that when I examined the paper upon which the printed words were fastened I made a close inspection for the watermark. In doing so I held it within a few inches of my eyes, and was conscious of a faint smell of the scent known as white jessamine.[228] There are seventy-five perfumes,[229] which it is very necessary that a criminal expert should be able to distinguish from each other, and cases have more than once within my own experience depended upon their prompt recognition. The scent suggested the presence of a lady,[230] and already my thoughts began to turn towards the Stapletons. Thus I had made certain of the hound, and had guessed at the criminal before ever we went to the West country.

"It was my game to watch Stapleton. It was evident, however, that I could not do this if I were with you, since he would be keenly on his guard. I deceived everybody, therefore, yourself included, and I came down secretly when I was supposed to be in London. My hardships were not so great as you imagine, though such trifling details must never interfere with the investigation of a case. I stayed for the most part at Coombe Tracey, and only used the hut upon the moor when it was necessary to be near the scene of action. Cartwright had come down with me, and in his disguise as a country boy he was of

228 Also spelled jasmine. Any member of the genus *Jasminum*, shrubs in the olive family (*Oleaceae*). *Jasminum* contains about 300 tropical and subtropical species; all are fragrant, flowering, and woody. The plants are native to the Old World—that is, not North America.

229 Christopher Morley, in his "Clinical Notes by a Resident Patient," suggests that Holmes may have written a monograph on the subject, accompanied by "a Memorandum by J.H.W. on the Types of Women Likely to Favour the Several Modes of Allure."

230 In "Promise Her Anything, but Give Her Bisulfate of Baryta, Or Sherlock Holmes, Parfumeur," Katherine Karlson argues that Holmes must have made a thorough study of perfumes and their properties at some earlier date, in the course of another investigation. Perhaps Holmes's investigation was even of a personal nature. Karlson writes that a woman who wears perfume tends to find one with properties that suit her nature. From Beryl's choice of white jessamine, she suggests, Holmes would have looked for a non-Englishwoman; tropical scents were not popular among the British. "Despite her sojourn in the harsh clime of East Yorkshire as the sedate and respectable Mrs. Vandeleur," Karlson concludes, Beryl, "one of the beauties of Costa Rica," "could not change her individual fragrance 'signature' any more than she could her native Latin temperament."

231 Ian McQueen chides Holmes for not having anticipated the overwhelming possibility of sudden fog, and for taking his oversight lightly.

great assistance to me. I was dependent upon him for food and clean linen. When I was watching Stapleton, Cartwright was frequently watching you, so that I was able to keep my hand upon all the strings.

"I have already told you that your reports reached me rapidly, being forwarded instantly from Baker Street to Coombe Tracey. They were of great service to me, and especially that one incidentally truthful piece of biography of Stapleton's. I was able to establish the identity of the man and the woman, and knew at last exactly how I stood. The case had been considerably complicated through the incident of the escaped convict and the relations between him and the Barrymores. This also you cleared up in a very effective way, though I had already come to the same conclusions from my own observations.

"By the time that you discovered me upon the moor I had a complete knowledge of the whole business, but I had not a case which could go to a jury. Even Stapleton's attempt upon Sir Henry that night, which ended in the death of the unfortunate convict, did not help us much in proving murder against our man. There seemed to be no alternative but to catch him red-handed, and to do so we had to use Sir Henry, alone and apparently unprotected, as a bait. We did so, and at the cost of a severe shock to our client we succeeded in completing our case and driving Stapleton to his destruction. That Sir Henry should have been exposed to this is, I must confess, a reproach to my management of the case, but we had no means of foreseeing the terrible and paralysing spectacle which the beast presented, nor could we predict the fog which enabled him to burst upon us at such short notice.[231] We succeeded in our object at a cost which both the specialist and Dr. Mortimer assure me will be a temporary one. A long journey may enable our friend to recover not only from his shattered nerves but also from his wounded feelings. His love for the lady was deep and sincere, and to him the saddest part of all this black business was that he should have been deceived by her.

"It only remains to indicate the part which she had played throughout. There can be no doubt that Stapleton exercised an influence over her which may have been love or may have been fear, or very possibly both, since they are by no means incompatible emotions. It was, at least, absolutely effective. At his command she consented to pass as his sister, though he found the limits of his power over her when he endeavoured to make her the direct accessory to murder. She was ready to warn Sir Henry so far as she could without implicating her husband, and again and again she tried to do so. Stapleton himself seems to have been capable of jealousy, and when he saw the baronet paying court to the lady, even though it was part of his own plan, still he could not help interrupting with a passionate outburst which revealed the fiery soul which his self-contained manner so cleverly concealed. By encouraging the intimacy he made it certain that Sir Henry would frequently come to Merripit House, and that he would sooner or later get the opportunity which he desired. On the day of the crisis, however, his wife turned suddenly against him. She had learned something of the death of the convict, and she knew that the hound was being kept in the out-house on the evening that Sir Henry was coming to dinner. She taxed her husband with his intended crime, and a furious scene followed, in which he showed her for the first time that she had a rival in his love.[232] Her fidelity turned in an instant to bitter hatred, and he saw that she would betray him. He tied her up, therefore, that she might have no chance of warning Sir Henry, and he hoped, no doubt, that when the whole countryside put down the baronet's death to the curse of his family, as they certainly would do, he could win his wife back to accept an accomplished fact, and to keep silent upon what she knew. In this I fancy that in any case he made a miscalculation, and that, if we had not been there, his doom would none the less have been sealed. A woman of Spanish blood does not condone such an injury so lightly. And now, my dear Watson, without referring to my notes, I cannot give you a more detailed account of this curious case. I do not know that anything essential has been left unexplained."

"He could not hope to frighten Sir Henry to death, as he had done the old uncle, with his bogy hound."

"The beast was savage and half-starved. If its appearance did not frighten its victim to death, at least it would paralyse the resistance which might be offered."

"No doubt. There only remains one difficulty. If Stapleton came into the succession, how could he explain the fact that he, the heir, had been living unannounced under another name so close to the property? How could he claim it without causing suspicion and inquiry?"

232 This is Victorian euphemism, presumably, for Beryl Stapleton's discovery that her husband had been engaging in sexual relations with Laura Lyons; he clearly did not *love* Laura Lyons and only wished to use her as a tool in his plans.

"It is a formidable difficulty,[233] and I fear that you ask too much when you expect me to solve it. The past and the present are within the field of my inquiry, but what a man may do in the future is a hard question to answer. Mrs. Stapleton has heard her husband discuss the problem on several occasions. There were three possible courses. He might claim the property from South America, establish his identity before the British authorities there, and so obtain the fortune without ever coming to England at all; or he might adopt an elaborate disguise during the short time that he need be in London; or, again, he might furnish an accomplice with the proofs and papers, putting him in as heir, and retaining a claim upon some proportion of his income. We cannot doubt, from what we know of him, that he would have found some way out of the difficulty. And now, my dear Watson, we have had some weeks of severe work, and for one evening, I think, we may turn our thoughts into more pleasant channels. I have a box for *Les Huguenots*.[234] Have you heard the De Reszkes?[235] Might I trouble you then to be ready in half an hour, and we can stop at Marcini's for a little dinner on the way?"[236]

"Be ready in half an hour."
Sidney Paget, *Strand Magazine*, 1902

233 Scholars are deeply troubled by Holmes's dismissal of the task as merely "formidable." The second plan, of disguise, and the third plan, an accomplice, are generally given short shrift. Holmes's first suggestion—that Stapleton might claim the property from South America—has even greater difficulties; it will be recalled that (presumably under the name of Baskerville) Stapleton "purloined a considerable sum of public money" before fleeing to England. Benjamin Clark proposes another possibility: The claim to the estate originates not with Stapleton but with a family friend, who arranges for evidence to be found showing the legitimacy of a previously unknown heir. The friend informs the court and helps to locate the heir. Such a friend, suggests Clark, was the nefarious Dr. Mortimer.

D. Martin Dakin suggests as an alternative: "no doubt some judicious oiling of palms, such as was not unknown in Latin America then, could have kept the authorities quiet and even induced them to support [Stapleton/Baskerville Jr.'s] claim. It would have rubbed some of the gilt off the gingerbread not to be able to enjoy his inheritance in person, but it looks as if Rodger Baskerville junior was more interested in the money than in the estate proper."

In "Stapleton's Solution," Hugh T. Harrington offers the ingenious suggestion that Laura Lyons was a Baskerville, the illegitimate child of Rodger Baskerville and Mrs. Frankland, and that Stapleton proposed to marry her and to claim the estate through her. He bases this surmise on the coincidence of her and Sir Henry's eye colour, stating that they are the only two individuals in the entire Canon with hazel eyes.

234 *Les Huguenots*, first presented in 1836, made Giacomo Meyerbeer (1791–1864) the most successful composer in Europe and helped redefine French grand opera, though the earlier *Robert le Diable* (1831) is arguably his most famous work. A child prodigy on the piano, he was born Yaakov Liebmann Beer and was descended from a long line of prominent rabbis; his own father, however, was a wealthy Berlin sugar refiner.

Les Huguenots commemorates the massacre of Protestants by Catholics on St. Bartholomew's Day in Paris on August 24, 1572, at the same time celebrating the romance and opulence of sixteenth-century France. John Farrell, in "A Fiddle, Opera, and Holmes," notes that performances of the opera were "events of great popular interest and enthusiasm, often the hottest tickets in town. They were called 'The Night of Seven Stars'"—demanding seven major vocal talents—"and were not cheap tickets." Farrell cites a Metropolitan Opera performance on December 26, 1894, starring the de Reszkes, Lillian Nordica, Schalchi, Plançon, Maurel, and Nellie Melba, as "the first time ever that tickets at the Met were raised to the exorbitant price of seven dollars apiece." Farrell suggests that the tickets were a gift from a grateful client and do not reflect an enthusiasm for opera on Holmes's part.

235 Although Holmes probably meant the brothers, who frequently appeared together, there were actually *three* singing de Reszkes, Jean (1850–1925), tenor; Edouard (1853–1917), bass; and Josephine (1855–1891), soprano. According to the *Grove Dictionary of Music Online*, Jean was celebrated for his "beautiful voice, fine musicianship, and handsome appearance," Edouard for his "huge voice and giant stature." Both performed extensively around the world. Josephine had a six-year career in Paris, but was not a success in 1881 when she sang *Aida* at Covent Garden and retired from the stage, except for a few performances in 1884 with her brothers in Paris.

Harold Schonberg disputes the dating (see note 234, above) of the *Les Huguenots* appearance of the de Reszkes at the Met, reporting that they appeared there in the opera once, on November 25, 1896. He is alone in this. William S. Baring-Gould notes that Anthony Boucher, in correspondence with Dr. Charles Goodman, states that the de Reszkes sang the opera together twenty-one times from 1891 to 1901 at the Metropolitan, as well as performing it in London and elsewhere. According to scholar François Nouvion, the de Reszkes performed in *Les Huguenots* at Covent Garden on June 15, 1889, May 20, 1891, July 8, 1893, and June 16, 1899. Patrick Drazen, in "On the de Reszkes," adds July 11, 1887, and Boucher, in "Footnote to a Footnote," adds a performance in 1888. None of these dates coincide with any dates suggested for *The Hound of the Baskervilles* by the major chronologists (see *Appendix 5*), and until 1890, the opera season in London was almost invariably the summer. In fact, only two autumnal performances of *Les Huguenots* were given at Covent Garden, on October 20, 1890, and October 26, 1891, and the de Reszkes appeared in neither. However, as Boucher notes, a careful reading of Holmes's remark reveals that he did *not* state that they were appearing in that evening's performance.

In "The Records of Baker Street," Boucher questions whether the de Reszkes were Holmes's real reason for taking in *Les Huguenots*, proposing instead that Holmes was driven by suppressed romantic longing for Irene Adler, who undoubtedly earlier performed the rôle of the page Urbain. "Irene Adler's spectacular entrance as Urbain must have been unforgettable; and it is more than understandable that a man might haunt later performances of *Les Huguenots*, half in vain hopes of finding a new portrayal to eclipse her memory, half to nurse the pleasant pain of recollection." Guy Warrack conjectures that the de Reszke *Huguenots* may have been the occasion of Holmes's first glimpse of Adler, but this places *The Hound of the Baskervilles* before

"A Scandal in Bohemia," a dating not agreed to by other chronologists.

236 D. Martin Dakin is among those who find the uncertain fate of Beryl Garcia Stapleton less than satisfactory. "Did she return to her native land?" he wonders. "And why was Sir Henry so hurt that he should have been deceived by her? What did he expect the poor girl to do? She tried her best to save him, by every means short of betraying her husband (and risking being murdered by him)." Dakin wishfully suggests that she and Sir Henry might have married after all.

Appendix 1

The Butterfly and the Orchid

The Butterfly. The Editors of the *Catalogue of an Exhibition on Sherlock Holmes held at Abbey House Baker Street London NW1 May–September 1951* dispute Stapleton's identification of the butterfly on the moors as a *Cyclopides.*

> The generic name *Cyclopides* is no longer valid; it was erected in 1819 by Hübner for five species, only one of which was British. This is the butterfly now known as the Chequered Skipper; the name *Cyclopides* for this form lingered on in books on natural history for some years, and its use by Stapleton is quite understandable. However, his statement "He is very rare" is, for Dartmoor, a considerable understatement; for it would have been the first and only record for that part of England.

The Editors then consider alternatives and conclude that the butterfly in question was likely one of the group known as the Skippers (*Hesperiidae*). Skippers share a distinctive darting and rapid flight, and the Editors find Watson's description of "a small fly or moth" "very suggestive, since this group of butterflies is primitive and approaches the moths in a number of respects." Further identification is not practical, although the Editors also point out that October, the apparent month of the events, is far too late for any Skippers.

Walter Shepherd, in *On the Scent with Sherlock Holmes* (1978), makes the clever suggestion that Stapleton confused the name with *Cyclorrhapha*, a sub-order of flies containing several large British species and including the hover-flies, house-flies, blow-flies, and bot-flies.

> A brightly coloured hover-fly might well catch the eye of a naturalist, even when engrossed in a tricky conversation, and its darting, dodging flight, interspersed with brief stationary hovers, would compel a pursuer to make the 'jerky, zig-zag, irregular progress' that Watson records. But the problem of the name remains, for no naturalist, even in the most desper-

ate state, could ever refer to a single insect as a "*Cyclorrhapha.*"

The most likely explanation, Shepherd proposes, is that "Stapleton ejaculated '*Cyclopides*' merely as a means of breaking up the conversation, which had drifted dangerously towards the hound concealed on the moor."

The Orchid. There is also controversy over the identity of the orchid noted by Stapleton. The Editors of the *Catalogue* consider several possibilities. The primary candidate is *Orchis Prætermissa Druce* (the common marsh-orchid). "In many ways this seems the most likely; it is a marsh orchid, and common on Dartmoor. Moreover, it is one of the few orchids that might be found actually growing in amongst the mare's-tails (*Hippuris vulgaris L.*), provided that the water was not deep at that point." However, the dates of the adventure are wrong for this flower, which is very unlikely to appear after mid-August.

Similarly, *Orchis Latifolia L. sec Pugsley* (the early spotted orchid), while growing among *Hippuris*, flowers in early summer (May–June). *Orchis Ericetorum (Linton) E. S. Marshall* (the heath spotted orchid) is common on Dartmoor, where it can be found up to 1,750 feet, but it prefers acid conditions and is unlikely to be growing among *Hippuris*, and it flowers at the wrong time. On the other hand, *Hammarbya Paludosa (L.) O. Kuntze* (the bog orchid) flowers late, and, although it is not very likely to be growing with *Hippuris*, such growth is not impossible. "The difficulty here," note the Editors, "is to imagine why Mrs. Stapleton wanted it, since her interest in orchids seems to have been aesthetic rather than technical; it is an inconspicuous plant, never more than six inches high and often considerably less, and with small greenish flowers."

Weighing the remaining possibilities, the Editors conclude that the most attractive candidate is *Spiranthes Spiralis (L.) Koch* (ladies' tresses). Found on Dartmoor, this striking plant flowers from September to October. Indeed, according to the Editors, "It is probably the only orchid that could have been found in full flower on Dartmoor on the date in question." However, it is not commonly found in wet places, such as Watson described. Perhaps Watson meant that the orchid was *near* the *Hippuris*, on a dry patch. "[I]t must be assumed that Watson and Mrs. Stapleton were not actually *in* the marsh at the time the conversation took place."

On the other hand, R. F. May, taking into consideration the same difficulties in his essay "*Hound of the Baskervilles*: A Botanical Enquiry," suggests that the orchid was the Marsh Spotted Orchid (*Dactylorchis maculata subspecies ericetorum*), which grows in damp acid peaty soil and in spongy marshes and is widely established in suitable places all over Britain. He notes, "This plant has been seen in flower occasionally as late as the second half of September . . ."

APPENDIX 2

The Source of *The Hound of the Baskervilles*

Three different acknowledgements appeared in important editions of *The Hound of the Baskervilles*. In the first part, published in the *Strand Magazine* in August 1901, this footnote follows the title:

> This story owes its inception to my friend, Mr. Fletcher Robinson, who has helped me both in the general plot and in the local details.—A. C. D.

In the first book edition, the acknowledgement reads:

> MY DEAR ROBINSON:
> It was to your account of a West-Country legend that this tale owes its inception. For this and for your help in detail all thanks.
>
> Yours most truly,
> A. CONAN DOYLE
>
> HINDHEAD, HASLEMERE.

In the first American edition, the acknowledgement reads:

> MY DEAR ROBINSON:
> It was your account of a west country legend which first suggested the idea of this little tale to my mind.
>
> For this, and for the help you gave me in its evolution, all thanks.
>
> Yours most truly,
> A. CONAN DOYLE

Philip Weller points out, in "Nightmare on Yew Alley," that this was actually the earliest book acknowledgement of Robinson's involvement, being a reproduction of a letter from Doyle to Robinson dated January 26, 1902. The original letter resides in the Berg Collection of the New York Public Library.

In the Preface to *The Complete Sherlock Holmes Long Stories: A Study in Scarlet, The Sign of Four, The Hound of the Baskervilles,*

The Valley of Fear, published in 1929, Arthur Conan Doyle wrote:

> Then came *The Hound of the Baskervilles.* It arose from a remark by that fine fellow, whose premature death was a loss to the world, Fletcher Robinson, that there was a spectral dog near his home on Dartmoor. That remark was the inception of the book, but I should add that the plot and every word of the actual narrative was my own.

As usual, Conan Doyle makes no mention of Dr. Watson, and so the reader is left to sort out how much of the tale is fiction, how much historical record.

Appendix 3

Was Richard Cabell "Hugo Baskerville"?

James Branch Cabell (1879–1958), the famed writer of medieval romanticism and fantasy, was descended from a venerable Southern family and counted among his ancestors English nobility. In his "Fifteenth Letter: To Richard Cabell of Buckfastleigh, Devon, Armiger, Lord of the Manor of Brooke," Cabell writes to his ancestor:

> It must remain to me always, Sir Richard, a source of regret that by another writer you were high-handedly plucked from my family-tree some while before I myself had the chance to employ you. . . . [W]hen your bond had run out—in the October of 1677—then black hounds came racing over Dartmoor; and toward midnight they gathered around Brooke Manor House, breathing smoke and fire, and howling expectantly. These creatures, having served you for the agreed time, were come now for their agreed payment, the country-side remarked later. And these fire-breathing hounds obtained their earned wages: for at midnight you mounted your black mare, and you rode away, across the dark moor, in the company of these hounds. Your body, when men found it, was badly mangled; it was scorched here and there; and your throat was torn open. . . . Dr. [Watson] . . . left out of his book that which is, to me, the most interesting part of your story. For they record, Sir, that after your burial you did not rest quietly in your grave. . . . It appears enough to say that your corpse was dug up and reburied in the same place, just outside the south porch of the parish church, with all the ceremonies necessitated by your post-mortem restlessness. And besides that, a very special edifice was erected above your grave, to prevent your coming out again to trouble the neighbourhood you had once adorned.

Others confirm the identification of Hugo Baskerville with Richard Cabell (who, notwithstanding Branch Cabell's pretensions, was apparently never knighted). Rev. Sabine Baring-Gould, grandfather of the great Sherlockian scholar William S.

Baring-Gould, recounts the legend in his *Devon*, and the grandson certainly appears to endorse his ancestor's identification. Walter Klinefelter, in his splendid *Ex Libris A. Conan Doyle Sherlock Holmes*, does so as well.

Susan Cabell Djabri, in *The Story of the Sepulchre: The Cabells of Buckfastleigh and the Conan Doyle Connection*, denies that Richard Cabell was actually the man described in the Baskerville legend and says that the legend was about a "composite character," built up out of various elements of the family history. In a fine piece of scholarship entitled *The Curious Incident of the Hound on Dartmoor: A Reconsideration of the Origins of* The Hound of the Baskervilles, Janice McNabb rejects the identification as tenuous at best and concludes that the legend is substantially a work of fiction. May we attribute it to Stapleton?

237 See note 86, above.

Appendix 4

The Search for Baskerville Hall

Philip Weller writes, in "The Mire and the Moor," "Even a cursory investigation of the locations described by Watson . . . will reveal that very few of these can be identified easily, and an extensive investigation will reveal that some of them simply cannot be found. Applying Holmes's infamous maxim that, when the impossible has been eliminated, whatever remains must be the truth, we eliminate the impossibility that these Dartmoor locations do not exist on Dartmoor." In this spirit, numerous scholars assert claims of discovery of the original of Baskerville Hall.

Manaton area residence. Percy Metcalfe, in "In Search of Baskerville Hall," lays out many of the geographical issues and concludes that the Hall is "some miles north-west of Bovey Tracey, probably in the Manaton area." Bernard Davies[237] rejects this as unlikely, on the basis that the train trip he has reconstructed based on Watson's descriptions would make a trip to the outskirts of Manaton "a ridiculously roundabout journey." This is in turn based on his identification of Totnes as Coombe Tracey.

Lew Trenchard House. William S. Baring-Gould writes, "A rather thorough investigation of the halls and houses in the vicinity of Coryton Station has unhappily, to date, revealed none that might be described as having 'twin towers, ancient, crenellated, and pierced with many loopholes . . . ' " He then argues for Lew House (or Hall), at Lew Trenchard, near Lew Down, Devon, as the original Hall. Baring-Gould notes the presence of lodge gates which are "a maze of fantastic tracery in wrought iron with weather-bitten pillars on either side, blotched with lichens . . . ," as well as an avenue opening into a broad expanse of turf. The house, Baring-Gould observes, may be described as "a heavy block of a building from which a porch" projects, "draped in ivy, with a patch clipped bare here and there where a window or a coat-of-arms" appears, "heavy mullioned windows," "high chimneys," and a "steep, high-angled roof." Baring-Gould forgivably omits to mention that Lew House was the family home of the Baring-Goulds for three centuries. Anthony Howlett writes, "If ever a house ought to be Baskerville Hall, this it it. Unfortunately it palpably is not . . ." David Hammer, in *The Game Is Afoot*, points out, "The chief and insurmountable objection is that it is on the wrong side of the moor, and too far from what have been designated [by Hammer] as Grimpen Mire, Grimpen, and Cleft Tor. All of the distances furnished by Watson would have to be in substantial error for Lew Trenchard Manor to be Baskerville Hall." Philip Weller adds that there are no views at all of the Moor from the Manor.

Mount Edgcumbe. On the basis of the boars' heads alone, Dr. Julian Wolff, in his *Practical Handbook of Sherlockian Heraldry*, identifies "Baskerville Hall" as Mount Edgcumbe in Devonshire, the family seat of the Edgcumbes, whose coat of arms is blazoned: "Gules, on a Bend Erminois, between two Cottifes or, three Boars Heads couped, Argent."

Brook Manor. David L. Hammer concludes that Baskerville Hall is Brook Manor, the ancestral home of Richard Cabell.[238] The geographical location is suitable, although Hammer admits that Brook Manor is "smaller than one would imagine Baskerville Hall to be." Furthermore, while its chimneys give a suitable appearance, it does not have "two high, narrow towers," lodge gates, a ruined lodge and new lodge, or a yew alley. Anthony Howlett calls Brook Manor "[o]ne of the more probable locations [of Baskerville Hall]," but Philip Weller criticises this candidate in detail:

> (a) It is not located in a hollow, but in a v-shaped valley. (b) it does not have any towers. (c) It is L-shaped, rather than being a central block with wings. (d) Although there is now a tunnel-like driveway which travels through the trees and opens out in front of the house, one cannot see the gate area from the house, and this was not the driveway in 1889, when the drive travelled along the open bank of the River Marble. (e) There is no gatehouse at the end of the driveway. (f) There are not gateposts at the end of the driveway. (g) There are no crenellations. (h) There are no coats of arms. (i) The walls are not lined with black granite. (j) There is no yew alley. (k) It is located almost two miles from the edge of the Moor. (1) One cannot see a light on the Moor from the west window of the house, since one cannot see the Moor from any window in the house. (m) One would have to travel through

238 See *Appendix 3*.

at least four farms to reach the nearest part of the Moor. (n) The Moon could never be partially obscured by trees to the south of the house, since it would need to be above the higher hills which surround the trees to be seen at all. (o) There are no stunted oaks and firs, since the trees are full-grown and healthy through not being exposed to the winds of the Moor. The three good elements of candidacy which have recommended this building are its age, its occupation by an unpopular squire in the 17th Century, and the hound legend associated with it, although with the last it is a legend involving multiple hounds.

Hayford Hall. Howard Brody, in an award-winning essay entitled "The Location of Baskerville Hall," points out the strengths of the Brook Manor attribution except for its situation (in the middle of woods and streams) and location (a mile or so east of the Moor). Brody notes on his modern map a neighbouring house, Hayford Hall, which is situated in relative isolation directly upon the Moor. "I cannot document that Hayford Hall itself was in existence in 1888," he writes. Philip Weller writes to this editor:

> Although it does not closely resemble the description of Baskerville Hall, [Hayford Hall] is almost perfectly located with reference to the Moor. It is situated in a cup-like depression, surrounded by trees, and there is a yew alley from which one can walk directly onto the Moor. From the house one can see a split outcrop of rock on the Moor upon which a candle could be located to signal to the house. There is a good track leading across the width of the Moor for three leagues to a group of farms. It is within easy walking distance of excellent candidates for the Great Grimpen Mire (Fox Tor Mires), Merripit House (Nun's Cross Farm), Grimpen (a track along the edge of the Moor, exactly as required, to Hexworthy), and Black Tor (Black Tor above the River Aune). It is certainly old enough, in that there has been a house on this site since 1413, and it was in existence in 1889, although it was then a farm and was occupied by Christopher Hawkins. It does have strong connection with Dartmoor hounds, in that it was used as a hunting lodge for the South Devon Hunt, and a 19th Century owner is said to have died in the saddle whilst hunt-

ing on Dartmoor. There is even a solitary hound legend, and there are very few of these on Dartmoor, associated with the stream which rises in the grounds, the Dean Burn, although it bears no resemblance to the legend of *The Hound of the Baskervilles*. The house also has familial connections with the Cabell family of Brook Manor and Cromer.

Lustleigh Hall. Put forth by Roger Lancelyn Green, in "Baskerville Hall," this candidate is three miles north of Bovey Tracey, exactly fourteen miles from Princetown. The main dining room matches Watson's description.[239]

Other Candidates. Philip Weller discusses in detail other candidates:

- Wooder Manor Hotel (does not satisfy any structural requirements or geographical requirements, but is self-promoted as "Baskerville Hall"). Kelvin Jones, in "The Geography of the Hound of the Baskervilles," argues its merits;
- Bagpark (its appropriate physical characteristics did not exist contemporaneously with *The Hound of the Baskervilles*, and there are no reasonably adjacent mires);
- Natsworthy Manor (the house has no clear view of the Moor and no adjacent mires);
- Heatree House (distant from a mire);
- Moretonhampstead Manor House Hotel (used as "Baskerville Hall" in the 1931 filming of *The Hound of the Baskervilles* but not built until 1907);
- Leighon (no suitable mires nearby);
- Lukesland (on the extreme southern edge of the Moor, an unlikely location).

In truth, the game remains afoot in the search for the *real* Baskerville Hall.

239 A photograph of the dining room accompanies the article.

APPENDIX 5

The Dating of *The Hound of the Baskervilles*

There is a fair amount of disagreement among the major chronologists concerning the dating of *The Hound of the Baskervilles*, influenced primarily by the juxtaposition of incongruous characterisations (*e.g.*, the relationship with Lestrade, the absence of mention of Mary Morstan) with explicit dates:[240]

Source	Date Assigned to Beginning of Case
Canon	Oct. 1889
Bell, H. W. *Sherlock Holmes and Dr. Watson: The Chronology of Their Adventures*	Sept. 28, 1886, Tues.
Blakeney, T. S. *Sherlock Holmes: Fact or Fiction?*	Early Oct. 1889
Christ, Jay Finley. *An Irregular Chronology of Sherlock Holmes of Baker Street*	Sept. 28, 1897, Tues.
Brend, Gavin. *My Dear Holmes*	Oct. 1899
Baring-Gould, William S., "New Chronology of Sherlock Holmes and Dr. Watson"	Oct. 1, 1889, Tues.
Baring-Gould, William. *The Chronological Holmes*. Mr. Baring-Gould uses the same dates in *Sherlock Holmes of Baker Street: A Life of the World's First Consulting Detective* and *Annotated Sherlock Holmes*.	Sept. 25, 1888, Tues.
Zeisler, Ernest Bloomfield. *Baker Street Chronology: Commentaries on the Sacred Writings of Dr. John H. Watson*	Sept. 25, 1900, Tues.
Folsom, Henry T. *Through the Years at Baker Street: A Chronology of Sherlock Holmes*	Sept. 25, 1888, Tues.
Folsom, Henry T. *Through the Years at Baker Street: A Chronology of Sherlock Holmes*, Revised Edition	Sept. 25, 1900, Tues.
Dakin, D. Martin. *A Sherlock Holmes Commentary*	Sept. 25, 1900, Tues.

240 Rev. G. Basil Jones, in "The Dog and the Date," neatly argues that the case occurred in 1899 but that Holmes required that Watson conceal the date. See also Alan Howard's "A New Year for the Hound." A number of other scholars assert still different dates; see Andrew Jay Peck and Leslie S. Klinger, *"The Date Being—": A Compendium of Chronological Data*.

Butters, Roger. *First Person Singular: A Review of the Life and Work of Mr. Sherlock Holmes, the World's First Consulting Detective, and His Friend and Colleague, Dr. John H. Watson*	Oct. 1889
Bradley, C. Alan, and William A. S. Sarjeant. *Ms. Holmes of Baker Street: The Truth about Sherlock*	Sept. 26, 1899, Tues.
Hall, John. *"I Remember the Date Very Well": A Chronology of the Sherlock Holmes Stories of Arthur Conan Doyle*	Autumn 1889
Thomson, June. *Holmes and Watson*	Autumn 1888

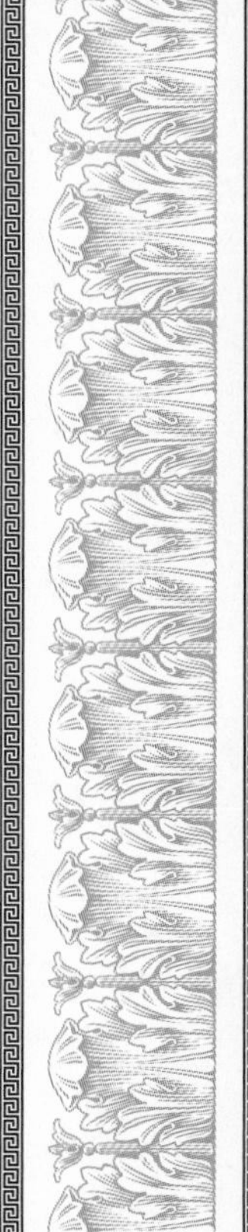

THE VALLEY OF FEAR[1]

1 *The Valley of Fear* was published in serial form in the *Strand Magazine* from Sept. 1914 to May 1915. Uniquely among the serialised long stories, each installment was introduced by text likely prepared by the editors (see notes 42, 64, 70, 82, and 116, below). The first British book edition was published in June 1915 by Smith, Elder & Co.; the first American edition appeared earlier, in Feb. 1915, published by George H. Doran Co. of New York. Many changes occurred between the *Strand Magazine* and American texts, and some are noted specifically below. See generally David A. Randall's "*The Valley of Fear* Bibliographically Considered."

The Valley of Fear

The Valley of Fear, *published at the onset of the Great War and comprising the last long account of Holmes and Watson, combines to near perfection a classic "locked-room" mystery—which comes to Holmes's attention via a tip from a disaffected lieutenant of Professor Moriarty's—and a hard-boiled detective story, set twenty years earlier and featuring the victim in Holmes's case. Modern readers may quickly penetrate the mystery itself, as it features a clever device that has by now been so frequently copied as to become a cliché. For Edwardian readers, however, the story (serialised in the* Strand Magazine*) was enthralling. So, too, was the backstory of the tale, which recounted the violent history of the Molly Maguires, a secret organisation enmeshed in labour unrest in the Pennsylvania coal mines of the 1880s. Drawn from Allan Pinkerton's significantly fictionalised book* The Molly Maguires and the Detectives *(1877), this portion of* The Valley of Fear *takes a critical view, as did most people at the time, of the Irish miners and the violence in which they purportedly engaged. And while modern historians find the Mollies to be less villainous than oppressed, the rôle of the Pinkertons distorted, and the character of the "hero" less than spotless, Watson's version remains a gripping account of courage in the Valley of Fear.*

CONAN DOYLE'S

GREAT NEW

SHERLOCK HOLMES

SERIAL

"The Valley of Fear"

THRILLING WITH INCIDENT AND EXCITEMENT

WILL COMMENCE IN OUR NEXT NUMBER

WHAT SHERLOCK HOLMES FOUND IN THE ENVELOPE.

The Valley of Fear.

Part I

The Manor house of Birlstone

Chap I. The Warning

"I am inclined to think —" said ~~Watson~~ I

"I should do so" Sherlock Holmes ~~interrupted~~ remarked impatiently.

I believe that I am one of ~~Watson was~~ the most long suffering of mortals but I admit ~~a flush~~ that I was annoyed at the sardonic interruption ~~of annoyance came to his cheeks~~.

"Really, Holmes" said I severely ~~said he~~ "You are a little ~~annoying~~ trying at times"

~~Holmes~~ He was too much absorbed with his own thoughts to give any immediate answer to my remonstrance. He leaned upon his hand, with his untasted breakfast before him, and he stared at the slip of paper which he had just drawn from its envelope.

FACSIMILE OF THE MS. OF THE OPENING WORDS OF "THE VALLEY OF FEAR."

Advertisement for *The Valley of Fear* and ms. of the opening words of the manuscript. *Strand Magazine*, 1914

PART I

The Tragedy of Birlstone

CHAPTER I

The Warning

"I AM INCLINED to think—" said I.[2]

"I should do so," Sherlock Holmes remarked, impatiently.

I believe that I am one of the most long-suffering of mortals, but I admit that I was annoyed at the sardonic interruption.

"Really, Holmes," said I, severely, "you are a little trying at times."

He was too much absorbed with his own thoughts to give any immediate answer to my remonstrance. He leaned upon his hand, with his untasted breakfast before him, and he stared at the slip of paper which he had just drawn from its envelope. Then he took the envelope itself, held it up to the light, and very carefully studied both the exterior and the flap.

"It is Porlock's writing," said he, thoughtfully. "I can hardly doubt that it is Porlock's writing, though I have seen it only twice before. The Greek ε with the peculiar top flourish is distinctive.[3] But if it is Porlock, then it must be something of the very first importance."

He was speaking to himself rather than to me; but my vexation disappeared in the interest which the words awakened.

"Who, then, is Porlock?" I asked.

2 Watson was not originally the narrator of this adventure, or so William S. Baring-Gould believes. He explains, "The original manuscript (176 folio pages with many deletions, corrections, and additions in the author's hand) shows that such expressions as 'said Dr. Watson' and 'said he' are crossed out and the direct 'said I' substituted." The manuscript of *The Valley of Fear* is owned by a private collector and has been little studied. Four pages of notes on *The Valley of Fear* are owned by Peter E. Blau, B.S.I. Recently published by the Baker Street Irregulars, in a volume entitled *Murderland* (apparently considered originally as a picturesque name for the setting of the tale), they outline a very different story from that eventually recorded by Dr. Watson. Many of the character names are different. For example, John Douglas seems to have operated under the names John Durant or Durrant and John Desmond; McMurdo's first name is John as well. "Max Mackey" may be another

name for Ted Baldwin. McMurdo kills someone called "Red Mike" (Boss McGinty?). Douglas has a son of seventeen, who appears to be an important character. The "Scowrers" are only referred to as "MM." With the exception of a specific scene reproduced at note 71, below, the notes will not be further considered here.

3 That Porlock would use the Greek ἐ in a note otherwise written in English reveals a bit about his education and background. Owen Dudley Edwards, editor of the Oxford University Press edition of *The Valley of Fear*, observes, "Scholars and aesthetes often used [the Greek ἐ], Oscar Wilde among them." Remarking upon Porlock's use of the character as ostentatious, Edwards suggests that Porlock may have come originally from the world of academia. Conveniently for Holmes, the Greek ἐ also appears as a distinctive characteristic of important handwriting specimens in *The Sign of Four* (Thaddeus Sholto's hand, whose similarities to Oscar Wilde have already been noted) and "The Reigate Squires" (where there is no suggestion, other than ownership of Pope's Homer, that either writer is an aesthete or scholar).

4 Did Holmes's contact consider literary history in choosing Porlock as his assumed name? Samuel Taylor Coleridge wrote "Kubla Khan" in an opium-induced state of inspiration some three or four miles outside the village of Porlock (located across the Bristol Channel from Wales). Before he was able to finish the poem, a man from Porlock stopped by on business, interrupting Coleridge's creative drive and leaving "Kubla Khan" forever unfinished. Anthony Boucher considers the possible connection but reaches no discernible conclusions, writing, " 'A person on business from Porlock' interrupted for ever the highest flight of the genius of Samuel Taylor Coleridge; a letter from Porlock pro-

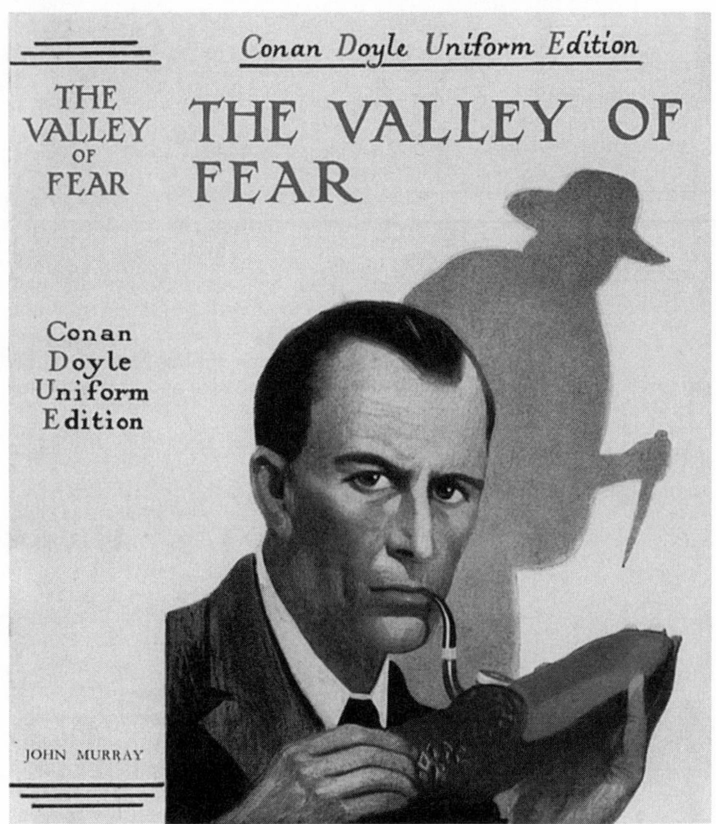

Dustjacket, *The Valley of Fear.* (London: John Murray, 1922)

"Porlock, Watson, is a *nom-de-plume*,[4] a mere identification mark, but behind it lies a shifty and evasive personality.[5] In a former letter he frankly informed me that the name was not his own, and defied me ever to trace him among the teeming millions of this great city. Porlock is important, not for himself, but for the great man with whom he is in touch. Picture to yourself the pilot-fish with the shark, the jackal with the lion—anything that is insignificant in companionship with what is formidable. Not only formidable, Watson, but sinister—in the highest degree sinister. That is where he comes within my purview. You have heard me speak of Professor Moriarty?"[6]

"The famous scientific criminal, as famous among crooks as—"

"My blushes, Watson!" Holmes murmured, in a deprecating voice.

voked one of the greatest displays of the genius of Sherlock Holmes. I feel sure that some deeper meaning is latent here, but cannot define it." Boucher also wonders why "that noblest Holmesian of them all," Vincent Starrett, did not mention the Sherlockian connection in his essay "Persons from Porlock," published in *Bookman's Holiday*, in which he considers the problem of great artists dealing with "persons from Porlock" who intrude on their artistic work (or indeed, as Starrett points out, even marry them). Perhaps "Porlock" chose his or her pseudonym purely for its internal rhyme with "Sherlock"?

5 See *Appendix 1* for a discussion of the candidates for the person behind the mask of "Fred Porlock."

6 In "The Final Problem," which was written and published before *The Valley of Fear*, Watson claims never to have heard of Professor Moriarty, Holmes's cunning nemesis who features prominently in that story. Yet all of the major chronologists except Gavin Brend concur that the events in *The Valley of Fear* occurred *before* those of "The Final Problem" (see *Appendix 3*). Given the conversation between Holmes and Watson here, Watson's later denial in "The Final Problem" seems merely literary license, as John Dardess puts it in "On the Dating of *The Valley of Fear*," "necessary for the properly dramatic introduction of Moriarty to the public." Dardess points out that if, when writing "The Final Problem," Watson had admitted to knowing the professor, the description that followed would have been superfluous. Similar views are expressed by G. B. Newton, in "The Date of *The Valley of Fear*," and James Buchholtz, in "A Tremor at the Edge of the Web." The latter writes that the description of Moriarty, which Watson here assigns to Holmes, had doubtless been made on an earlier occasion, but its transposition becomes *artistically* necessary, as Watson, the practised story-teller, instantly and rightly recognised. D. Martin Dakin, in *A Sherlock Holmes Commentary*, makes the same point, suggesting that Watson took the liberty of telescoping the events and put into Holmes's mouth in 1891 a speech introducing him to Moriarty, which in reality he spoke some years earlier.

But B. M. Castner, in "The Professor and *The Valley of Fear*," argues that the inclusion of Moriarty in *The Valley of Fear* is the fiction, not Watson's ignorance in "The Final Problem." He makes a compelling case for the proposition that Professor Moriarty—that is, the man playing that rôle during the months immediately preceding "The Final Problem"—was Sherlock Holmes, infiltrating the Moriarty gang to gather evidence. The real Moriarty, the theory goes, had perished earlier, probably at Holmes's hands. Not until 1914, when Holmes was reunited with Watson after having been presumed dead, did the detective decide to work with Watson in introducing Moriarty into *The Valley of Fear* (in which Moriarty plays no rôle) and reveal the truth of Moriarty's earlier death. In "On the Track of Moriarty: *The Valley of Fear*," Michael P. Malloy reviews Watson's use of literary devices in other stories and concludes that Watson did not know of the existence of a connection between Moriarty and the murder in *The Valley of Fear* until sometime after 1903.

"I was about to say, as he is unknown to the public."

"A touch! A distinct touch!" cried Holmes. "You are developing a certain un-expected vein of pawky humour, Watson, against which I must learn to guard myself.[7] But in calling Moriarty a criminal you are uttering libel in the eyes of the law, and there lie the glory and the wonder of it! The greatest schemer of all time, the organizer of every devilry, the controlling brain of the underworld, a brain which might have made or marred the destiny of nations. That's the man. But so aloof is he from general suspicion—so immune from criticism—so admirable in his management and self-effacement, that for those very words that you have uttered he could hale you to a court and emerge with your year's pension as a solatium[8] for his wounded character. Is he not the celebrated author of *The Dynamics of an Asteroid*, a book which ascends to such rarefied heights of pure mathematics that it is said that there was no man in the scientific press capable of criticizing it?[9] Is this a man to traduce? Foul-mouthed doctor and slandered professor—such would be your respective rôles! That's genius, Watson. But if I am spared by lesser men our day will surely come."

"May I be there to see!" I exclaimed devoutly. "But you were speaking of this man Porlock."

"Ah, yes—the so-called Porlock is a link in the chain some little way from its great attachment. Porlock is not quite a sound link—between ourselves. He is the only flaw in that chain so far as I have been able to test it."

"But no chain is stronger than its weakest link."

"Exactly, my dear Watson. Hence the extreme importance of Porlock. Led on by some rudimentary aspirations towards right, and encouraged by the judicious stimulation of an occasional ten-pound note sent to him by devious methods, he has once or twice given me advance information which has been of value—that highest value which anticipates and prevents rather than avenges crime. I cannot doubt that, if we had the cipher, we should find that this communication is of the nature that I indicate."[10]

Again Holmes flattened out the paper upon his unused plate. I rose and, leaning over him, stared down at the curious inscription, which ran as follows:[11]

7 In *The Valley of Fear*, Holmes is operating at the peak of his powers, according to Anthony Boucher, and his ease and confidence shine through in Watson's depiction of him. This is a "ripe, mature Holmes," writes Boucher, in his Introduction to *The Final Adventures of Sherlock Holmes*, Volume I, "free from external eccentricities, his hand unburdened by either the cocaine needle or the violin's bow. Here is Holmes as the perfect thinking mind, in cryptanalysis, in observation, in deduction. And here, more than in any other Canonical story that comes to mind, is Holmes at his most completely charming, whether playfully dangling the cryptically obvious before his colleagues (whom for once he respects) or ruefully admitting 'a distinct touch' from Watson's pawky humour."

8 Legal damages for wounded feelings or punishment.

9 Whatever the merits of Moriarty's book, Walter Shepherd gathers that Holmes must have found it incomprehensible, since dynamics is a subject of *applied* mathematics, not *pure* mathematics. We may assume, Shepherd writes in *On the Scent with Sherlock Holmes*, that he at least looked through the book but was completely baffled by it, though he may thus have learned what an asteroid is and so added an iota to his knowledge of astronomy.

The great science/science fiction writer Isaac Asimov points out that *The Dynamics of an Asteroid* is a misleading title, for asteroids behave no differently from other bodies orbiting the sun. Asimov's explanation for the title is that Professor Moriarty wrote on the problematical behaviour of a single fragment following the explosion of a planet, often hypothesised to be the source of the asteroid belt.

10 According to George H. Strum ("Doubleday's Code"), Porlock's cipher is based on the

534	C2	13	127	36	31	4	17	21	41
DOUGLAS		109	293	5	37	BIRLSTONE			
26	BIRLSTONE	9	127	171					

"What do you make of it, Holmes?"

"It is obviously an attempt to convey secret information."

"But what is the use of a cipher message without the cipher?"

"In this instance, none at all."

"Why do you say 'in this instance'?"

"Because there are many ciphers which I would read as easily as I do the apocrypha of the agony column: such crude devices amuse the intelligence without fatiguing it. But this is different. It is clearly a reference to the words in a page of some book. Until I am told which page and which book I am powerless."

"But why 'Douglas' and 'Birlstone'?"[12]

"Clearly because those are words which were not contained in the page in question."

"Then why has he not indicated the book?"

"Your native shrewdness, my dear Watson, that innate cunning which is the delight of your friends, would surely prevent you from enclosing cipher and message in the same envelope. Should it miscarry, you are undone. As it is, both have to go wrong before any harm comes from it. Our second post is now overdue,[13] and I shall be surprised if it does not bring us either a further letter of explanation, or, as is more probable, the very volume to which these figures refer."

Holmes's calculation was fulfilled within a very few minutes by the appearance of Billy, the page,[14] with the very letter which we were expecting.

"The same writing," remarked Holmes, as he opened the envelope, "and actually signed," he added, in an exultant voice, as he unfolded the epistle. "Come, we are getting on, Watson."

His brow clouded, however, as he glanced over the contents.

"Dear me, this is very disappointing! I fear, Watson, that all our expectations come to nothing. I trust that the man Porlock will come to no harm.

system described by Abner Doubleday in his book *Reminiscences of Forts Sumter and Moultrie in 1860–1861*, published in 1876. Strum concludes that Porlock must have read Doubleday's book.

11 Curiously, the American editions have "47" in place of the second "127," and the *Strand Magazine* text has "13." If Holmes's translation is accurate, "127" is the correct cipher.

12 Dr. Karl Krejci-Graf, among others, puzzles over the fact that Porlock codes the irrelevant part of the message while leaving significant information uncoded. "What is the use of a cipher if you give everything away by writing name and locality in open script?" he asks, in "Contracted Stories." "The point seems to be that Porlock had found a way to include the names in the cipher but that Watson, who had to change the names to protect the client, had not the same ingenuity."

13 Mail was collected and delivered from six to eleven times *daily* in the districts of London outside the City (where twelve deliveries were made daily).

14 This marks the first public identification of Billy the page, who appears in ten of the Sherlock Holmes tales but is referred to by name in only three (the other two being "The Mazarin Stone" and "Thor Bridge"). And although *The Valley of Fear* was not published until 1914, Charles Rogers's play *Sherlock Holmes* (1894) and William Gillette's play *Sherlock Holmes* (1899) both feature a page named Billy. Is the name a coincidence? Or did Rogers or Gillette personally visit the Holmes household? For more, see this editor's "Paging Through the Canon."

The cipher—and the man who solved it.
Frank Wiles, *Strand Magazine*, 1914

DEAR MR. HOLMES:

I will go no further in this matter. It is too dangerous. He suspects me. I can see that he suspects me. He came to me quite unexpectedly after I had actually addressed this envelope with the intention of sending you the key to the cipher. I was able to cover it up. If he had seen it, it would have gone hard with me. But I read suspicion in his eyes. Please burn the cipher message, which can now be of no use to you.

FRED PORLOCK.[15]

Holmes sat for some little time twisting this letter between his fingers, and frowning, as he stared into the fire.

"After all," he said at last, "there may be nothing in it. It may be only his guilty conscience. Knowing himself to be a traitor, he may have read the accusation in the other's eyes."

"The other being, I presume, Professor Moriarty."

15 T. F. Foss, in "The Case of the Professor's Ineptitude," wonders at Moriarty's failure to follow up on this patently stealthy concealment and characterises Moriarty as a "slaphappy, irresponsible criminal practitioner." But D. Martin Dakin counters with the thought that Porlock may well have been eliminated, for he is never heard from again. The letter itself seems to be a highly unnecessary risk for Porlock. Sending Holmes a letter asking him to destroy the cipher message was pointless and carried at least as much danger as simply sending the cipher key.

That Porlock did not follow up the cipher with a simple, one-word key seems itself telling. "The clear inference," deduces John Hall, in *Sidelights on Holmes*, "is surely that Porlock sent neither message, or at least not of his free will." Unlike Foss, Hall takes a generous view of Moriarty, believing that the mastermind "persuaded" Porlock to send the messages to Holmes. His curiosity piqued, Holmes would be persuaded to take on the case, and might inadvertently help Moriarty complete his crime.

"No less. When any of that party talk about 'He' you know whom they mean. There is one predominant 'He' for all of them."

"But what can he do?"

"Hum! That's a large question. When you have one of the first brains of Europe up against you, and all the powers of darkness at his back, there are infinite possibilities. Anyhow, Friend Porlock is evidently scared out of his senses. Kindly compare the writing in the note to that upon its envelope; which was done, he tells us, before this ill-omened visit. The one is clear and firm; the other hardly legible."

"Why did he write at all? Why did he not simply drop it?"

"Because he feared I would make some inquiry after him in that case, and possibly bring trouble on him."

"No doubt," said I. "Of course"—I had picked up the original cipher message and was bending my brows over it—"it's pretty maddening to think that an important secret may lie here on this slip of paper, and that it is beyond human power to penetrate it."

Sherlock Holmes had pushed away his untasted breakfast and lit the unsavoury pipe which was the companion of his deepest meditations. "I wonder!" said he, leaning back and staring at the ceiling. "Perhaps there are points which have escaped your Machiavellian intellect. Let us consider the problem in the light of pure reason. This man's reference is to a book. That is our point of departure."

"A somewhat vague one."

"Let us see then if we can narrow it down. As I focus my mind upon it, it seems rather less impenetrable. What indications have we as to this book?"

"None."

"Well, well, it is surely not quite so bad as that. The cipher message begins with a large 534, does it not? We may take it as a working hypothesis that 534 is the particular page to which the cipher refers. So our book has already become a *large* book, which is surely something gained. What other indications have we as to the nature of this large book? The next sign is C2. What do you make of that, Watson?"

"Chapter the second, no doubt."

"Hardly that, Watson. You will, I am sure, agree with me that

16 A sparkling flash of light; figuratively, a brilliant witticism or insight.

" 'Let us consider the problem in the light of pure reason' "
Frederic Dorr Steele, *Final Adventures of Sherlock Holmes*, Vol. I, 1952.
Reuse of a portion of the cover for "Wisteria Lodge," which appeared in *Collier's*, 1908.

if the page be given, the number of the chapter is immaterial. Also that if page 534 finds us only in the second chapter, the length of the first one must have been really intolerable."

"Column!" I cried.

"Brilliant, Watson. You are scintillating this morning. If it is not column, then I am very much deceived. So now, you see, we begin to visualize a large book, printed in double columns, which are each of a considerable length, since one of the words is numbered in the document as the two hundred and ninety-third. Have we reached the limits of what reason can supply?"

"I fear that we have."

"Surely you do yourself an injustice. One more coruscation,[16] my dear Watson—yet another brain-wave! Had the volume been an unusual one, he would have sent it to me. Instead of that he had intended, before his plans were nipped, to send me the clue in this envelope. He says so in his note. This would seem to indicate that the book is one which he thought I would have no difficulty in finding for myself. He had it—and he imagined that I would have it too. In short, Watson, it is a very common book."

"What you say certainly sounds plausible."

"So we have contracted our field of search to a large book, printed in double columns and in common use."

"The Bible!" I cried triumphantly.

"Good, Watson, good! But not, if I may say so, quite good enough! Even if I accepted the compliment for myself, I could hardly name any volume which would be less likely to lie at the elbow of one of Moriarty's associates. Besides, the editions of Holy Writ are so numerous that he could hardly suppose that two copies would have the same pagination. This is clearly a book which is standardized. He knows for certain that his page 534 will exactly agree with my page 534."

"But very few books would correspond with that."

"Exactly. Therein lies our salvation. Our search is narrowed down to standardized books which anyone may be supposed to possess."

"Bradshaw!"[17]

"There are difficulties, Watson. The vocabulary of Bradshaw is nervous and terse, but limited. The selection of words would hardly lend itself to the sending of general messages. We will eliminate Bradshaw. The dictionary is, I fear, inadmissible for the same reason.[18] What then is left?"

"An almanack!"

"Excellent, Watson! I am very much mistaken if you have not touched the spot. An almanack! Let us consider the claims of *Whitaker's Almanack*.[19] It is in common use. It has the requisite number of pages. It is in double column. Though reserved in its earlier vocabulary, it becomes, if I remember right, quite garrulous towards the end." He picked the volume from his desk. "Here is page 534, column two, a substantial block of print dealing, I perceive, with the trade and resources of British India. Jot down the words, Watson! Number thirteen is 'Mahratta.'[20] Not, I fear, a very auspicious beginning. Number one hundred and twenty-seven is 'Government,' which at least makes sense, though somewhat irrelevant to ourselves and Professor Moriarty. Now let us try again. What does the

17 That is, *Bradshaw's General Railway and Steam Navigation Guide for Great Britain and Ireland.* David St. John Thomas, in his introduction to a modern facsimile of the August 1887 guide, calls it

> a British national institution. Its contents—advertisement as well as "editorial"—reflected the prosperity of the times. . . . The man who regularly subscribed to *Bradshaw* had an honoured place in his community; parsons took an especial pride in displaying it on their shelves and understood its intricacies so that they could proffer advice on the best routes. Indeed, plotting the quickest cross-country journey between a West country resort and a Scottish fishing port, or between a Welsh coal-mining valley and the Constable Country, was a frequently-played parlour game in the days that every one and everything going more than a dozen or so miles did so behind a steam engine running on rails to a schedule published in *Bradshaw*.

18 Robert Winthrop Adams proposes, in "John H. Watson, M.D., Characterologist," that the dictionary Holmes considers would have been Watson's copy of the "British Webster"—that is, *The Comprehensive English Dictionary*, by John Ogilvie, LL.D. (London, Edinburgh & Glasgow, 1868), a staple of many libraries at the time.

Howard R. Schorin finds it surprising that Holmes would so quickly proclaim the dictionary inadmissable for purposes of the cipher. In "Cryptography in the Canon," he defends the venerable reference book, reminding us that "it is precisely this book which has been used for such messages since the Revolutionary and Napoleonic wars, when the numbered-source code was most popular and in use."

Roger Johnson, in private correspondence,

disputes these conclusions, pointing out that many dictionaries were available (for example, *Nuttall's Standard Dictionary*, edited by the Rev. James Wood [London and New York: Frederick Warne & Co.] was very popular) and suggests that Holmes discarded a dictionary as the key because of the large variety available. The reason Holmes states is absurd: no dictionary can be termed "limited."

19 Britain's best-known almanac, first published in 1868. A copy of the 1878 edition—along with a Bradshaw's railway guide and twelve pictures of Britain's most attractive women—is buried in a time capsule underneath Cleopatra's Needle, the Egyptian granite obelisk erected on Victoria Embankment in 1878.

20 Mahratta is a variant of Maratha, or the Hindu people from India's Maharashtra region. (Maharashtra's capital is Mumbai, or Bombay.) The article on the Empire of India in the 1900 *Whitaker's Almanac* conveys something of a hostile attitude toward the legacy left by Maratha founder and king Sivaji, who spent most of his life doing battle with the dominant Mughal empire. It states:

> Simultaneously with the decline of the Moguls rose the power of the Mahrattas. They were Hindus, and the country from which they came may be roughly described by drawing two lines from Nagpur to Surat and Goa on the west coast. The founder of their power was Sivaji (1627–1680), a chieftain of the family of Bhonslah. . . . In 1760 Delhi was in their hands, and though they suffered a disastrous defeat at Panipat in 1761, at the hands of Ahmed Shah, the Afghan invader, they remained for some time the first Power in India, and were the most dangerous opponents of the English. Their system, however, was one of organised

Mahratta government do? Alas! the next word is 'pig's-bristles.' We are undone, my good Watson! It is finished!"

He had spoken in jesting vein, but the twitching of his bushy eyebrows[21] bespoke his disappointment and irritation. I sat helpless and unhappy, staring into the fire. A long silence was broken by a sudden exclamation from Holmes, who dashed at a cupboard, from which he emerged with a second yellow-covered volume in his hand.

"We pay the price, Watson, for being too up-to-date!" he cried. "We are before our time, and suffer the usual penalties. Being the seventh of January,[22] we have very properly laid in the new almanack. It is more than likely that Porlock took his message from the old one. No doubt he would have told us so had his letter of explanation been written. Now let us see what page 534 has in store for us. Number thirteen is 'there,' which is much more promising. Number one hundred and twenty-seven is 'is'—'There is' "—Holmes's eyes were gleaming with excitement, and his thin, nervous fingers twitched as he counted the words—" 'danger.' Ha! Ha! Capital! Put that down, Watson. 'There is danger-may-come-very-soon-one.' Then we have the name 'Douglas'—'rich—country—now—at—Birlstone—House—Birlstone—confidence—is—pressing.' There, Watson! What do you think of pure reason and its fruits? If the green-grocer had such a thing as a laurel wreath, I should send Billy round for it."

I was staring at the strange message which I had scrawled, as he deciphered it, upon a sheet of foolscap on my knee.

"What a queer, scrambling way of expressing his meaning!" said I.

"On the contrary, he has done quite remarkably well," said Holmes. "When you search a single column for words with which to express your meaning, you can hardly expect to get everything you want. You are bound to leave something to the intelligence of your correspondent. The purport is perfectly clear. Some devilry is intended against one Douglas, whoever he may be, residing as stated, a rich country gentleman. He is sure—'confidence' was as near as he could get to 'confident'—that it is pressing. There is our result, and a very workmanlike little bit of analysis it was."

Holmes had the impersonal joy of the true artist in his better work, even as he mourned darkly when it fell below the

"Holmes's eyes were gleaming with excitement, and his thin, nervous fingers twitched as he counted the words—'danger.' 'Ha! ha! Capital! Put that down, Watson.' "
Frank Wiles, *Strand Magazine*, 1914

high level to which he aspired. He was still chuckling over his success when Billy swung open the door and Inspector MacDonald of Scotland Yard was ushered into the room.

Those were the early days at the end of the '80's, when Alec MacDonald was far from having attained the national fame which he has now achieved. He was a young but trusted member of the detective force, who had distinguished himself in several cases which had been entrusted to him. His tall, bony figure gave promise of exceptional physical strength, while his great cranium and deep-set, lustrous eyes spoke no less clearly of the keen intelligence which twinkled out from behind his bushy eyebrows. He was a silent, precise man, with a dour nature and a hard Aberdonian[23] accent.

Twice already in his career had Holmes helped him to attain success,[24] his own sole reward being the intellectual joy of the problem.[25] For this reason the affection and respect of the

plunder rather than of settled government. Like the Pindaris, a horde of freebooters who followed in their train, they were a scourge to the country. It was not until both Pindaris and Mahrattas were finally overthrown in 1818, that India enjoyed the blessings of internal peace. The Mahratta empire, containing within itself the seeds of disintegration, was fated to bend before the superior sway of European adventurers, who, either from love of adventure or thoughts of gain, had been attracted in increasing numbers to the shores of India.

Hugo Koch, in a masterful study entitled *Some Observations Upon the Date of the Tragedy of Birlstone: The Evidence of Whitaker's Almanack: 1890*, concludes that the page number "534" is fictionalised and that the cipher was indeed drawn from the same page as the "Mahratta" reference. From a minute examination of the relevant pages for the almanacs from 1881 to 1914, he determines that only two editions contain the cipher clues that Holmes reads out loud: those for 1890 and 1904. The latter may be rejected on the ground of Moriarty's death in 1891.

Jennifer Decker, after consulting page 534 of *Whitaker's* for 1879 to 1912, makes the unconventional assertion (in "Piercing the Veil at Last") that the cipher was based not on *Whitaker's* at all but on Samuel Taylor Coleridge's "Rime of the Ancient Mariner," taking the choice of "Porlock" as the writer's alias as her initial clue (see note 4, above). Frankly, the message she derives from the work, although cleverly explained, seems to this editor to be gibberish.

21 This is the only reference in the Canon to Holmes's eyebrows. Note that Inspector MacDonald's eyebrows are also described as bushy.

22 January 7 is the day after the traditional date of Holmes's birthday. Surely it is clear, chides Nathan Bengis, in a much-repeated analysis in "What Was the Month?" that there had been some small jollification the night before in celebration of the Master's birthday, and that his lack of appetite was the result of a hangover? Bengis also suggests that the events of January 6 were undertaken on that date as a deliberate warning to Holmes. In both "The Empty House" and "The Red Circle," Holmes appears to paraphrase Shakespeare's *Twelfth Night*, lending ammunition to those who believe that Holmes's birthday was "twelfth night," or January 6. That January 6 was both the date of the *Saturday Review* issue in which Christopher Morley (founder of the Baker Street Irregulars) first suggested the birthdate and the birthday of Felix Morley (Christopher's brother), however, sheds some doubt on the issue.

23 The fishing port of Aberdeen was the principal city of northern Scotland, with large factories for the manufacture of cotton, woolen and linen fabrics, whale fisheries, and ship-building establishments. It became a royal burgh (town) in 1176.

24 In fact, MacDonald has not appeared previously in Watson's records, and makes no further appearance after *The Valley of Fear.*

25 John Hall gathers much from Holmes's oblique comment here. "It is clear from the conversation," he declares, in *The Abominable Wife and Other Unrecorded Cases of Mr. Sherlock Holmes*, "that Holmes had attempted to interest MacDonald in the activities of Professor Moriarty prior to *The Valley of Fear* itself, but without much success."

26 Roger Johnson writes, in private correspondence to this editor, "Note that the Scottish-born and raised Conan Doyle calls MacDonald a 'Scotchman,' although we [the English] have been told for decades that the

"The inspector was staring with a look of absolute amazement at a paper upon the table. It was the sheet upon which I had scrawled the enigmatic message."
Frank Wiles, *Strand Magazine*, 1914

Scotchman for his amateur colleague were profound, and he showed them by the frankness with which he consulted Holmes in every difficulty. Mediocrity knows nothing higher than itself, but talent instantly recognizes genius, and MacDonald had talent enough for his profession to enable him to perceive that there was no humiliation in seeking the assistance of one who already stood alone in Europe, both in his gifts and in his experience. Holmes was not prone to friendship, but he was tolerant of the big Scotchman,[26] and smiled at the sight of him.

"You are an early bird, Mr. Mac,"[27] said he. "I wish you luck with your worm. I fear this means that there is some mischief afoot."

"If you said 'hope' instead of 'fear,' it would be nearer the truth, I'm thinking, Mr. Holmes," the inspector answered, with a knowing grin. "Well, maybe a wee nip would keep out the raw morning chill. No, I won't smoke, I thank you. I'll have to be pushing on my way, for the early hours of a case are the precious ones, as no man knows better than your own self. But—but—"

The inspector had stopped suddenly, and was staring with a look of absolute amazement at a paper upon the table. It was the sheet upon which I had scrawled the enigmatic message.

word 'Scotch' is unacceptable and must be replaced by 'Scottish' or 'Scots.' The only exceptions today relate to food and drink: Scotch eggs, Scotch pancakes, and of course Scotch whisky. Needless to say, other Scottish writers of the period, such as Robert Louis Stevenson, unaffectedly called themselves Scotch."

27 "Lestrade," notes Ian McQueen, in *Sherlock Holmes Detected: The Problems of the Long Stories*, "for all his long association with Holmes, was never addressed except with due familiarity."

28 Curiously, the *Strand Magazine* and English editions have "this morning," even though forthcoming witness statements indicate that the body was found the previous evening. The correction of this apparent error by the American editors seems to indicate that the editors and the author (who presumably would have corrected the English editions had the error been pointed out) simply did not communicate with each other after submission of the manuscript.

" 'What's this, Mr. Holmes? Man, it's witchcraft! Where in the name of all that's wonderful did you get those names?' "
Arthur I. Keller, *Associated Sunday Magazines*, 1914

"Douglas!" he stammered. "Birlstone! What's this, Mr. Holmes? Man, it's witchcraft! Where in the name of all that is wonderful did you get those names?"

"It is a cipher that Dr. Watson and I have had occasion to solve. But why—what's amiss with the names?"

The inspector looked from one to the other of us in dazed astonishment. "Just this," said he, "that Mr. Douglas, of Birlstone Manor House, was horribly murdered last night!"[28]

CHAPTER II

Sherlock Holmes Discourses

It was one of those dramatic moments for which my friend existed. It would be an over-statement to say that he was shocked or even excited by the amazing announcement. Without having a tinge of cruelty in his singular composition, he was undoubtedly callous from long over-stimulation. Yet, if his emotions were dulled, his intellectual perceptions were exceedingly active. There was no trace then of the horror which I had myself felt at this curt declaration, but his face showed rather the quiet and interested composure of the chemist who sees the crystals falling into position from his over-saturated solution.

"Remarkable!" said he; "remarkable!"

"You don't seem surprised."

"Interested, Mr. Mac, but hardly surprised. Why should I be surprised? I receive an anonymous communication from a quarter which I know to be important, warning me that danger threatens a certain person. Within an hour I learn that this danger has actually materialized, and that the person is dead. I am interested, but, as you observe, I am not surprised."

In a few short sentences he explained to the inspector the

Dustjacket, *The Valley of Fear.*
(London: George Newnes, Ltd., *ca.* 1920)

facts about the letter and the cipher. MacDonald sat with his chin on his hands, and his great sandy eyebrows bunched into a yellow tangle.

"I was going down to Birlstone this morning," said he. "I had come to ask you if you cared to come with me—you and your friend here. But from what you say we might perhaps be doing better work in London."

"I rather think not," said Holmes.

"Hang it all, Mr. Holmes!" cried the inspector. "The papers will be full of the Birlstone Mystery in a day or two, but where's the mystery if there is a man in London who prophesied the crime before ever it occurred? We have only to lay our hands on that man and the rest will follow."

"No doubt, Mr. Mac. But how do you propose to lay your hands on the so-called Porlock?"

MacDonald turned over the letter which Holmes had handed him. "Posted in Camberwell—that doesn't help us much. Name, you say, is assumed. Not much to go on, certainly. Didn't you say that you have sent him money?"

"Twice."

"And how?"

"In notes to Camberwell post-office."

"Did you ever trouble to see who called for them?"

"No."

The inspector looked surprised and a little shocked. "Why not?"

"Because I always keep faith. I had promised when he first wrote that I would not try to trace him."

"You think there is some one behind him?"

"I *know* there is."

"This Professor that I've heard you mention?"

"Exactly!"

Inspector MacDonald smiled, and his eyelid quivered as he glanced towards me. "I won't conceal from you, Mr. Holmes, that we think in the C.I.D.[29] that you have a wee bit of a bee in your bonnet over this professor. I made some inquiries myself about the matter. He seems to be a very respectable, learned, and talented sort of man."

"I'm glad you've got so far as to recognize the talent."

"Man, you can't but recognize it! After I heard your view I made it my business to see him. I had a chat with him on eclipses. How the talk got that way I canna think; but he had out a reflector lantern and a globe, and made it all clear in a minute. He lent me a book, but I don't mind saying that it was a bit above my head, though I had a good Aberdeen upbringing. He'd have made a grand meenister with his thin face and grey hair and solemn-like way of talking. When he put his hand on my shoulder as we were parting, it was like a father's blessing before you go out into the cold, cruel world."[30]

Holmes chuckled and rubbed his hands. "Great!" he said;

29 See *The Sign of Four*, note 167.

30 The Professor Moriarty described in "The Final Problem" resembles MacDonald's description little if at all; in fact, Ian McQueen observes that the two descriptions "could well have been of two different people." (In "The Final Problem," Holmes speaks of Moriarty thus: "He is extremely tall and thin, his forehead domes out in a white curve, and his two eyes are deeply sunken in his head. He is clean-shaven, pale, and ascetic-looking, retaining something of the professor in his features. His shoulders are rounded from much study, and his face protrudes forward and is for ever slowly oscillating from side to side in a curiously reptilian fashion.") Certainly MacDonald's thin, gray hair, and ministerial comparison are not wholly inconsistent with Holmes's description in "The Final Problem," but MacDonald notably makes no mention of the prominent forehead, sunken eyes, or, most distinctively, the oscillation.

In "The Empty House," Holmes tells Watson of "Professor James Moriarty, who had one of the great brains of the century." McQueen suggests that the Moriarty who met with MacDonald is not that Professor Moriarty but another person who succeeded him, with the name "Moriarty" merely indicating his position as the leader of the "Moriarty gang." McQueen breaks down the line of succession by surmising that the *Colonel* James Moriarty mentioned in "The Final Problem" as the professor's "brother" was in fact Colonel Sebastian Moran, Professor Moriarty's chief lieutenant, revealed in "The Empty House" to have been present at Holmes's confrontation with the professor at the Reichenbach Falls. Colonel Moran, McQueen continues, succeeded to leadership of the Moriarty gang after the professor's death and adopted the name "James Mori-

"great! Tell me, Friend MacDonald; this pleasing and touching interview was, I suppose, in the Professor's study?"

"That's so."

"A fine room, is it not?"

"Very fine—very handsome indeed, Mr. Holmes."

"You sat in front of his writing-desk?"

"Just so."

"Sun in your eyes and his face in the shadow?"

"Well, it was evening; but I mind that the lamp was turned on my face."

"It would be. Did you happen to observe a picture over the Professor's head?"

"I don't miss much, Mr. Holmes. Maybe I learned that from you. Yes, I saw the picture—a young woman with her head on her hands, keeking[31] at you sideways."

"That painting was by Jean Baptiste Greuze."[32]

The inspector endeavoured to look interested.

"Jean Baptiste Greuze," Holmes continued, joining his finger tips and leaning well back in his chair, "was a French artist who flourished between the years 1750 and 1800. I allude, of course, to his working career. Modern criticism has more than endorsed the high opinion formed of him by his contemporaries."

The inspector's eyes grew abstracted.

"Hadn't we better—" he said.

"We are doing so," Holmes interrupted. "All that I am saying has a very direct and vital bearing upon what you have called the Birlstone Mystery. In fact, it may in a sense be called the very centre of it."

MacDonald smiled feebly, and looked appealingly to me. "Your thoughts move a bit too quick for me, Mr. Holmes. You leave out a link or two, and I can't get over the gap. What in the whole wide world can be the connection between this dead painting man and the affair at Birlstone?"

"All knowledge comes useful to the detective," remarked Holmes. "Even the trivial fact that in the year 1865 a picture by Greuze, entitled 'La Jeune Fille à l'Agneau,' fetched one million two hundred thousand francs—more than forty thousand pounds[33]—at the Portalis sale[34] may start a train of reflection in your mind."[35]

arty," combined with his military profession, to solidify his leadership position. After Moran's capture, he was succeeded as the head of the criminal organisation by another professor—probably a former university colleague of the first Professor James Moriarty—who again used the title "James Moriarty," together with his own occupation, to be known (again) as "Professor James Moriarty." (McQueen dates *The Valley of Fear* after "The Empty House," placing him in a distinct minority among chronologists.) It is this new leader that MacDonald has seen, not the original Professor Moriarty with whom Holmes once fought.

31 "Peeping" in the American editions. "Keek" is a distinctively Scottish word, meaning "peek" or "peep." Robert Louis Stevenson used it from time to time.

32 Jean Baptiste Greuze (1725–1805), a French painter of enormous popularity during his lifetime, is now generally thought of as a painter of overly sentimental and melodramatic works, though his technical skills are still highly regarded. His first major success was *The Father Reading the Bible to His Children*, exhibited at the 1755 Salon in Paris. Encouraged by that painting's reception and by the encouragement of Denis Diderot, Greuze continued painting moralistic scenes such as *The Village Betrothal* (1761) and *The Wicked Son Punished* (1778). He hoped to gain recognition as a historical painter, but after his *Septimius Severus Reproaching Caracalla* was humiliatingly rejected by the 1769 Salon, Greuze turned to painting sexually suggestive pictures of seemingly innocent young girls. It is this latter type of painting to which Holmes refers.

With his earlier work no longer in favor, Greuze died in poverty. His paintings are displayed at the Louvre, Versailles, the Wallace

Collection in London, the National Gallery in Edinburgh, and the Metropolitan Museum of Art in New York.

33 The amount of "forty thousand pounds" appears in the manuscript and in the *Strand Magazine* and various American editions, while "four thousand pounds" appears in the first English edition. Forty thousand seems to be correct, as the exchange rate in 1865 was much closer to 30 francs to the pound than 300 francs to the pound.

34 Thomas L. Stix, in "Who's Afraid of the Big Bad Moriarty?," remarks upon the painting's supposed sale at "Portalis" when he writes, "The picture actually was sold to Disraeli for £1,800 at the Portalis sale in 1865. Our authorities are the Parke-Bernet Galleries and Professor Kuhn, Curator of the Fogg Museum at Harvard. The picture proved to be a forgery. Portalis refunded the £1,800 to Disraeli, and the picture 'after Greuze' was subsequently sold 'as is' for £45."

Yet Jack Tracy seems to be in possession of more accurate information, reporting in "The Portalis Sale of 1865" that Holmes (and Stix) confused the French name "Portalis," the surname of a distinguished family of jurists (Jean Étienne Marie Portalis was influential in drawing up the Napoleonic Code), with the Pourtalés Gallery of Art, a private Paris gallery. The collection of James-Alexandre Comte de Pourtalés-Gorgier (1776–1855) was sold at auction in 1865, according to the terms of his will, which directed that it should be liquidated for the benefit of his heirs ten years following his death. While Tracy confirms the price of £4,000 (100,200 francs) for Greuze's *Innocence*, the *Encyclopædia Britannica* (11th Ed.) reported the Pourtalés sale price at 1,000,200 francs, close to the figure mentioned by Holmes. Tracy (now deceased) does not mention which of several sources he relied on, and the correct amount remains in doubt.

35 Note that two different Greuze paintings are actually being referenced here, as Julian Wolff clarifies in an editorial in the *Baker Street Journal*. The first painting is the one seen by Inspector Alec MacDonald in Professor Moriarty's study: "a young woman with her head on her hands, peeping [keeking] at you sideways." "This seems to be the painting in the National Gallery of Scotland (Catalogue No. NG437)," notes Wolff, "described as 'Girl with Arms Folded' and reproduced [here]." Despite numerous attempts by Sherlockians to locate the *latter* painting, *La Jeune Fille à l'Agneau* is not identified as owned by Moriarty, nor does Holmes imply that it is—only that the work owned by Moriarty must have been very expensive.

The National Gallery of Scotland acquired its *Girl with Arms Folded* in 1861 as a bequest from Lady Murray of Henderland, according to museum sources. Where, one wonders, did Moriarty acquire his? Might the Gallery's *Girl* be a copy, substituted by the professor in a daring theft? Or might the professor's be a copy, or a hitherto unknown work by Greuze?

It was clear that it did. The inspector looked honestly interested.

"I may remind you," Holmes continued, "that the Professor's salary can be ascertained in several trustworthy books of reference. It is seven hundred a year."

"Then how could he buy—"[36]

"Quite so! How could he?"

"Ay, that's remarkable," said the inspector thoughtfully. "Talk away, Mr. Holmes. I'm just loving it. It's fine!"

Holmes smiled. He was always warmed by genuine admiration—the characteristic of the real artist. "What about Birlstone?" he asked.

"We've time yet," said the inspector, glancing at his watch. "I've a cab at the door, and it won't take us twenty minutes to Victoria.[37] But about this picture—I thought you told me once, Mr. Holmes, that you had never met Professor Moriarty."

"No, I never have."

"Then how do you know about his rooms?"

"Ah, that's another matter. I have been three times in his rooms, twice waiting for him under different pretexts and leaving before he came. Once—well, I can hardly tell about the once to an official detective. It was on the last occasion that I took the liberty of running over his papers—with the most unexpected results."

"You found something compromising?"

"Absolutely nothing. That was what amazed me. However, you have now seen the point of the picture. It shows him to be a very wealthy man. How did he acquire wealth? He is unmarried. His younger brother is a station-master in the west of England.[38] His chair is worth seven hundred a year. And he owns a Greuze."

"Well?"

"Surely the inference is plain."

"You mean that he has a great income, and that he must earn it in an illegal fashion?"

"Exactly. Of course, I have other reasons for thinking so—dozens of exiguous threads which lead vaguely up towards the centre of the web where the poisonous motionless creature is lurking. I only mention the Greuze because it brings the matter within the range of your own observation."

36 T. F. Foss, continuing in his critical assessment of Moriarty (see note 15, above), argues that in buying such a painting the professor exhibited a "reckless disregard of what people might think. . . . It is not unlikely that some of the Professor's more cultured visitors were [art critics] and they might talk. People do, and these things get about. Before long, an efficient H.M. Inspector of Income Taxes would want an adequate explanation of how a man whose income was only £700 a year could afford to adorn his walls with such expensive works of art." But D. Martin Dakin defends the professor's reputation: "[W]hat was the use of him having a beautiful picture and hiding it away—like keeping a diamond necklace in the bank strong room?"

37 "Birlstone," as we shall see, is near the Weald forest, in the region of the northern borders of Sussex. According to Baedeker's *Great Britain*, there are three rail routes to the area, via the Southern Eastern Railway to Dorking (1¼ to 1½ hours), leaving from Charing Cross, Cannon Street, and London Bridge Stations; via the London, Brighton, and South Coast Railway (1 hour 7 minutes to 1¾ hours), from London Bridge and Victoria Stations; and via the South Western Railway to Guildford (¾ to 1½ hours), from Waterloo Station. The history of Victoria Station is discussed in detail by Catherine Cooke in "A Certain Gracious Railway Station."

38 As noted earlier (see note 30, above), the professor's other brother, also named James, is a colonel. (In "The Final Problem," writing of the deceased Professor Moriarty, Watson makes reference to "recent letters in which Colonel James Moriarty defends the memory of his brother.") In light of the "younger" brother remark here, we may conclude that Col. James Moriarty was Professor James Moriarty's older brother. John Bennett Shaw,

"Well, Mr. Holmes, I admit that what you say is interesting: it's more than interesting—it's just wonderful. But let us have it a little clearer if you can. Is it forgery, coining, burglary—where does the money come from?"

"Have you ever read of Jonathan Wild?"[39]

"Well, the name has a familiar sound. Some one in a novel, was he not? I don't take much stock of detectives in novels—chaps that do things and never let you see how they do them. That's just inspiration: not business."

"Jonathan Wild wasn't a detective, and he wasn't in a novel.[40] He was a master criminal, and he lived last century—1750 or thereabouts."

"Then he's no use to me. I'm a practical man."

"Mr. Mac, the most practical thing that you ever did in your life would be to shut yourself up for three months and read twelve hours a day at the annals of crime. Everything comes in circles—even Professor Moriarty. Jonathan Wild was the hidden force of the London criminals, to whom he sold his brains and his organization on a fifteen per cent. commission. The old wheel turns and the same spoke comes up. It's all been done before, and will be again. I'll tell you one or two things about Moriarty which may interest you."

"You'll interest me, right enough."

"I happen to know who is the first link in his chain—a chain with this Napoleon-gone-wrong at one end, and a hundred broken fighting men, pickpockets, blackmailers, and card-sharpers at the other, with every sort of crime in between. His chief of the staff is Colonel Sebastian Moran, as aloof and guarded and inaccessible to the law as himself. What do you think he pays him?"

"I'd like to hear."

"Six thousand a year. That's paying for brains, you see—the American business principle. I learned that detail quite by chance. It's more than the Prime Minister gets.[41] That gives you an idea of Moriarty's gains and of the scale on which he works. Another point: I made it my business to hunt down some of Moriarty's cheques lately—just common innocent cheques that he pays his household bills with. They were drawn on six different banks. Does that make any impression on your mind?"

the greatest collector of things Sherlockian and a devastating wit, reached the conclusion that all three brothers likely bore the name "James" and founded a society in Moriarty, New Mexico, that celebrated the "Brothers Three."

39 The notorious criminal mastermind Jonathan Wild (*ca.* 1682–1725) ran a vast network of thieves in London for fifteen years. Realising that it was safer, and in most cases more profitable, to return stolen property to its original owners than to sell it on the open market, Wild built up his business by paying generous "commissions" to his employees. Eventually arranging robberies himself, he controlled a huge organisation that dealt severely with criminals who refused to participate; it is said that some 120 criminals were executed based on Wild's testimony against them or leaks as to their activities. In return for his "policing," Wild operated to some extent with the blessing of the authorities. According to the *Encyclopædia Britannica* (11th Ed.), "At last either the authorities became more strict or Wild less cautious. He was arrested, tried at the Old Bailey, and after being acquitted on a charge of stealing lace, found guilty of taking a reward for restoring it to the owner without informing the police." Wild was hanged at Tyburn on May 24, 1725.

40 While Jonathan Wild was not a fictional character, it is possible that MacDonald was confused by Henry Fielding's fictionalised black satire *The Life of Mr. Jonathan Wild the Great* (1743), a novel that portrayed Wild as a sort of criminal superhero. *The Cambridge History of English and American Literature in 18 Volumes* (1907–1921) described the book as follows: "So we have Jonathan Wild, thief, 'fence' and gallows-bird, steadily held up before us throughout fifty-six chapters as a hero, a great man; while Heartfree, the simple, affectionate, open nature—the good man—is treated as 'silly,' 'low' and 'pitiful.' . . . [N]ot even Swift has produced so remarkable a piece of sustained irony, so full of movement, so various, so finely worked in its minutest particulars, or so vivid in its pictures of 'low' life."

41 In 1900, according to *Whitaker's Almanack*, the Prime Minister (the Marquis of Salisbury) and other top ministers were paid £5,000 per year, the modern equivalent of over £330,000, or U.S. $640,000.

"Queer, certainly. But what do you gather from it?"

"That he wanted no gossip about his wealth. No single man should know what he had. I have no doubt that he has twenty banking accounts—the bulk of his fortune abroad in the Deutsche Bank or the Credit Lyonnais as likely as not. Sometime when you have a year or two to spare I commend to you the study of Professor Moriarty."

Inspector MacDonald had grown steadily more impressed as the conversation proceeded. He had lost himself in his interest. Now his practical Scotch intelligence brought him back with a snap to the matter in hand.

"He can keep, anyhow," said he. "You've got us side-tracked with your interesting anecdotes, Mr. Holmes. What really counts is your remark that there is some connection between the professor and the crime. That you get from the warning received through the man Porlock. Can we for our present practical needs get any farther than that?"

"We may form some conception as to the motives of the crime. It is, as I gather from your original remarks, an inexplicable, or at least an unexplained, murder. Now, presuming that the source of the crime is as we suspect it to be, there might be two different motives. In the first place, I may tell you that Moriarty rules with a rod of iron over his people. His discipline is tremendous. There is only one punishment in his code. It is death. Now, we might suppose that this murdered man—this Douglas, whose approaching fate was known by one of the arch-criminal's subordinates—had in some way betrayed the chief. His punishment followed and would be known to all—if only to put the fear of death into them."

"Well, that is one suggestion, Mr. Holmes."

"The other is that it has been engineered by Moriarty in the ordinary course of business. Was there any robbery?"

"I have not heard."

"If so, it would, of course, be against the first hypothesis and in favour of the second. Moriarty may have been engaged to engineer it on a promise of part spoils, or he may have been paid so much down to manage it. Either is possible. But, whichever it may be, or if it is some third combination, it is down at Birlstone that we must seek the solution. I know our man too well to suppose that he has left anything up here which may lead us to him."

"Then to Birlstone we must go!" cried MacDonald, jumping from his chair. "My word! It's later than I thought. I can give you, gentlemen, five minutes for preparation, and that is all."

"And ample for us both," said Holmes, as he sprang up and hastened to change from his dressing gown to his coat. "While we are on our way, Mr. Mac, I will ask you to be good enough to tell me all about it."

"All about it" proved to be disappointingly little, and yet there was enough to assure us that the case before us might well be worthy of the expert's closest attention. He brightened and rubbed his thin hands together as he listened to the meagre but remarkable details. A long series of sterile weeks lay behind us, and here, at last, there was a fitting object for those remarkable powers which, like all special gifts, become irksome to their owner when they are not in use. That razor brain blunted and rusted with inaction.

Sherlock Holmes's eyes glistened, his pale cheeks took a warmer hue, and his whole eager face shone with an inward light when the call for work reached him. Leaning forward in the cab, he listened intently to MacDonald's short sketch of the problem which awaited us in Sussex. The inspector was himself dependent, as he explained to us, upon a scribbled account forwarded to him by the milk train in the early hours of the morning. White Mason, the local officer, was a personal friend, and hence MacDonald had been notified very much more promptly than is usual at Scotland Yard when provincials need their assistance. It is a very cold scent upon which the Metropolitan expert is generally asked to run.

> DEAR INSPECTOR MACDONALD
> [said the letter which he read to us]:
> Official requisition for your services is in separate envelope. This is for your private eye. Wire me what train in the morning you can get for Birlstone, and I will meet it—or have it met if I am too occupied. This case is a snorter. Don't waste a moment in getting started. If you can bring Mr. Holmes, please do so; for he will find something after his own heart. We would think the whole thing had been fixed up for theatrical effect, if there wasn't a dead man in the middle of it. My word, it *is* a snorter!

"Your friend seems to be no fool," remarked Holmes.

"No, sir, White Mason is a very live man, if I am any judge."

"Well, have you anything more?"

"Only that he will give us every detail when we meet."

"Then how did you get at Mr. Douglas and the fact that he had been horribly murdered?"

"That was in the enclosed official report. It didn't say 'horrible.' That's not a recognized official term. It gave the name John Douglas. It mentioned that his injuries had been in the head, from the discharge of a shot-gun. It also mentioned the hour of the alarm, which was close on to midnight last night. It added that the case was undoubtedly one of murder, but that no arrest had been made, and that the case was one which pre-

"Leaning forward in the cab, Holmes listened intently to MacDonald's short sketch of the problem which awaited us in Sussex."
Frank Wiles, *Strand Magazine*, 1914

sented some very perplexing and extraordinary features. That's absolutely all we have at present, Mr. Holmes."

"Then, with your permission, we will leave it at that, Mr. Mac. The temptation to form premature theories upon insufficient data is the bane of our profession. I can see only two things for certain at present: a great brain in London, and a dead man in Sussex. It's the chain between that we are going to trace."

CHAPTER III

The Tragedy of Birlstone[42]

And now for a moment I will ask leave to remove my own insignificant personality and to describe events which occurred before we arrived upon the scene by the light of knowledge which came to us afterwards. Only in this way can I make the reader appreciate the people concerned and the strange setting in which their fate was cast.

The village of Birlstone is a small and very ancient cluster of half-timbered cottages on the northern border of the county of Sussex. For centuries it had remained unchanged; but within the last few years its picturesque appearance and situation have attracted a number of well-to-do residents, whose villas peep out from the woods around. These woods are locally supposed to be the extreme fringe of the great Weald forest,[43] which thins away until it reaches the northern chalk downs.[44] A number of small shops have come into being to meet the wants of the increased population; so there seems some prospect that Birlstone may soon grow from an ancient village into a modern town. It is the centre for a considerable area of country, since Tunbridge Wells,[45] the nearest place of impor-

42 The October 1914 issue of the *Strand Magazine* contained this summary of the prior issue's contents: "The opening chapters of this new and thrilling adventure of Sherlock Holmes, which commenced in our last issue, described the receipt by Holmes of a cipher message, from which he deduces that some devilry is intended against a man named Douglas, a rich country gentleman living at Birlstone in Sussex, and that the danger is a pressing one. Almost as soon as he has deciphered the message he is visited by Inspector MacDonald, of Scotland Yard, who brings the news that Mr. Douglas has been murdered that morning [*sic*—see note 28, above]. He asks Sherlock Holmes and Dr. Watson to accompany him to the scene of the crime, and the three go off together."

43 The ancient stretch of forest known as the Weald (from the Old English *wald*, or *weald*, meaning forest) is nearly forty miles wide and rests between the chalk hills of the North and South Downs. It was once part of the much larger forest of Andredsweald ("the wood or forest without habitations"). As Watson notes in "Black Peter," the Weald was heavily forested and once served as a centre for the iron industry, but the area remains one of England's most densely wooded places. It is now heavily used for agriculture.

44 The treeless range of chalk hills extending from the north of Hampshire through Surrey into Kent.

45 According to *Baedeker's Great Britain*, Tunbridge Wells was "one of the most popular inland watering-places in England . . . and owes its present favour rather to its pretty surroundings and invigorating air than to its somewhat weak chalybeate springs." It became "a favourite resort of the Puritans, who have left traces of their partiality in such names as Mount Ephraim and Mount Zion; and it is still specially affected by adherents of the Evangelical school." Tunbridge Wells was a station on the Hastings branch of the South-Eastern Railway, between Tunbridge Junction and Hastings.

tance, is ten or twelve miles to the eastward, over the borders of Kent.

About half a mile from the town, standing in an old park famous for its huge beech trees, is the ancient Manor House of Birlstone. Part of this venerable building dates back to the time of the First Crusade,[46] when Hugo de Capus[47] built a fortalice[48] in the centre of the estate, which had been granted to him by the Red King. This was destroyed by fire in 1543, and some of its smoke-blackened corner stones were used when, in Jacobean times,[49] a brick country house rose upon the ruins of the feudal castle.[50]

The Manor House, with its many gables and its small diamond-paned windows, was still much as the builder had left it in the early seventeenth century. Of the double moats which had guarded its more warlike predecessor, the outer had been allowed to dry up, and served the humble function of a kitchen garden. The inner one was still there and lay forty feet in breadth, though now only a few feet in depth, round the whole house. A small stream fed it and continued beyond it, so that the sheet of water, though turbid, was never ditch-like or unhealthy. The ground floor windows were within a foot of the surface of the water.

The only approach to the house was over a drawbridge, the chains and windlass of which had long been rusted and broken. The latest tenants of the Manor House had, however, with characteristic energy, set this right, and the drawbridge was not only capable of being raised, but actually was raised every evening and lowered every morning. By thus renewing the custom of the old feudal days the Manor House was converted into an island during the night—a fact which had a very direct bearing upon the mystery which was soon to engage the attention of all England.

The house had been untenanted for some years and was threatening to moulder into a picturesque decay when the Douglases took possession of it. This family consisted of only two individuals, John Douglas and his wife. Douglas was a remarkable man, both in character and in person; in age he may have been about fifty, with a strong-jawed, rugged face, a grizzling moustache, peculiarly keen gray eyes, and a wiry, vigorous figure which had lost nothing of the strength and activity of youth. He was cheery and genial to all, but somewhat off-

46 The First Crusade, in which European Christians marched upon Jerusalem and captured the city, took place from 1095 to 1099. The movement was instigated by Pope Urban II, who called Christians to arms in his speech at the Council of Clermont in 1095; he spoke of the desecration of the holy lands and abuse of pilgrims, encouraging his supporters to rise up as they echoed his cry of "*Deus volt*" ("God wills it"). The ragtag "People's Crusade," led by preachers Walter Sans Avoir (Walter the Penniless) and Peter the Hermit, were defeated by the Turks, but four other armies amassed at Constantinople and besieged Jerusalem in July 1099, massacring the city's Muslims and Jews even after the governor had surrendered.

47 There is no known historical figure named Hugo de Capus. "The name," H. W. Bell writes, in "Three Identifications," "seems not to have existed in England, or indeed anywhere nearer than the province of Carniola in the present kingdom of Yugoslavia." In *Practical Handbook of Sherlockian Heraldry*, Julian Wolff suggests that Holmes was likely referring to "Hugo comes [*sic*]," the name of a nephew and companion of William the Conqueror, whose descent from Hugh Capet, King of France, could account for the "de Capus." "Hugo's father, the half-brother of William," Wolff elaborates, "was awarded seven hundred manors, and it is not unlikely that the Red King, William Rufus, the Conqueror's son, granted Birlstone to Hugo to build a fortalice there."

48 A small fortified building.

49 That is, during the reign of King James I, 1603–1625.

50 H. W. Bell identifies the house as Brambletye Manor, which was twelve miles from Tunbridge Wells and stood next to the ruins of

Brambletye House (immortalised in Horatio Smith's 1826 novel *Brambletye House*). The crest, he states, was that of the last known occupant of Brambletye House, Sir James Richards, Bart., who lived there in the reign of Charles II. Bell also notes that Arthur Conan Doyle lived for some years in the neighbourhood.

A better identification seems to be that of James Montgomery, who, through the efforts of James Keddie, Jr., reproduced a title page of *The Valley of Fear* with the handwritten inscription "With all kind remembrances from Arthur Conan Doyle who hopes you have pleasant memories of Groombridge House which is the old house herein described. June 22/21." Groombridge Place, Montgomery reveals (in his pamphlet entitled *A Case of Identity*), is a manor house about three miles from Tunbridge Wells. The village of Groombridge is actually in two counties, the New Town being in Sussex and the Old Town in Kent. While the Groombridge manor house has many of the characteristics described by Dr. Watson, it is deficient in many respects, including the placement of the windows, the number of moats, and the absence of stone pillars at its gate. David L. Hammer, in *The Game Is Afoot*, accepts the Groombridge identification and ascribes the deviations from Watson's description to "a writer's inspiration seeking to sharpen and heighten."

D. Martin Dakin is not so sanguine about the discrepancy. He calls attention to several architectural impossibilities, including, most tellingly, the drawbridge, which is simply not present at Groombridge (although part of the original castle). Dakin maintains that the theory (advanced by Charles O. Merriman, in "A Case of Identity—No. 2") that Watson "decided to incorporate [the drawbridge] to whet the appetite of his reading public" is insupportable and furthermore

> implies a travesty of the facts by Watson, without any excuse on grounds of discretion, that would be highly damaging to his integrity as an author. . . . [W]e may have to acknowledge sadly that, in spite of the charm of Groombridge Place and the authentic atmosphere it radiates, the true original of Birlstone manor either still awaits discovery, or has suffered the demolition that has overtaken so many fine country houses whose owners cannot afford to keep them up and whose local councils will not accept them as a charge on the rates.

Most recently, Catherine Cooke, in "The Ancient Manor House of Birlstone," carefully weighs Merriman's and Dakin's arguments and concludes that Merriman's points carry the day, explaining away the discrepancy of the drawbridge on the grounds that Watson may have deliberately obfuscated its description at the behest of the actual owner, who wished to remain anonymous. Of course, this argument could be used to undercut *every* aspect of Watson's description and so must be used cautiously. Nevertheless, the weight of modern opinion seems to be on the side of Groombridge.

hand in his manners, giving the impression that he had seen life in social strata on some far lower horizon than the county society of Sussex.

Yet, though looked at with some curiosity and reserve by his more cultivated neighbours, he soon acquired a great popularity among the villagers, subscribing handsomely to all local objects, and attending their smoking concerts[51] and other functions, where, having a remarkably rich tenor voice, he was always ready to oblige with an excellent song. He appeared to have plenty of money, which was said to have been gained in the Californian gold fields, and it was clear from his own talk and that of his wife that he had spent a part of his life in America.

The good impression which had been produced by his generosity and by his democratic manners was increased by a reputation gained for utter indifference to danger. Though a wretched rider, he turned out at every meet, and took the most amazing falls in his determination to hold his own with the best. When the vicarage caught fire he distinguished himself also by the fearlessness with which he reentered the building to save property, after the local fire brigade had given it up as impossible. Thus it came about that John Douglas of the Manor House had within five years won himself quite a reputation in Birlstone.

His wife, too, was popular with those who had made her acquaintance, though, after the English fashion, the callers upon a stranger who settled in the county without introductions were few and far between. This mattered the less to her, as she was retiring by disposition, and very much absorbed, to all appearance, in her husband and her domestic duties. It was known that she was an English lady who had met Mr. Douglas in London, he being at that time a widower. She was a beautiful woman, tall, dark, and slender, some twenty years younger than her husband, a disparity which seemed in no wise to mar the contentment of their family life.

It was remarked sometimes, however, by those who knew them best, that the confidence between the two did not appear to be complete, since the wife was either very reticent about her husband's past life or else, as seemed more likely, was imperfectly informed about it. It had also been noted and commented upon by a few observant people that there were signs sometimes of some nerve-strain upon the part of Mrs. Douglas,

51 That is, a concert at which smoking was permitted. How modern!

and that she would display acute uneasiness if her absent husband should ever be particularly late in his return. On a quiet countryside, where all gossip is welcome, this weakness of the lady of the Manor House did not pass without remark, and it bulked larger upon people's memory when the events arose which gave it a very special significance.

There was yet another individual whose residence under that roof was, it is true, only an intermittent one, but whose presence at the time of the strange happenings which will now be narrated brought his name prominently before the public. This was Cecil James Barker,[52] of Hales Lodge, Hampstead.

Cecil Barker's tall, loose-jointed figure was a familiar one in the main street of Birlstone village; for he was a frequent and welcome visitor at the Manor House. He was the more noticed as being the only friend of the past unknown life of Mr. Douglas who was ever seen in his new English surroundings. Barker was himself an undoubted Englishman; but by his remarks it was clear that he had first known Douglas in America and had there lived on intimate terms with him. He appeared to be a man of considerable wealth, and was reputed to be a bachelor.

In age he was rather younger than Douglas—forty-five at the most—a tall, straight, broad-chested fellow, with a clean-shaved, prize-fighter[53] face, thick, strong, black eyebrows, and a pair of masterful black eyes which might, even without the aid of his very capable hands, clear a way for him through a hostile crowd. He neither rode nor shot, but spent his days in wandering round the old village with his pipe in his mouth, or in driving with his host, or in his absence with his hostess, over the beautiful countryside. "An easy-going, free-handed gentleman," said Ames, the butler. "But, my word! I had rather not be the man that crossed him!" He was cordial and intimate with Douglas, and he was no less friendly with his wife, a friendship which more than once seemed to cause some irritation to the husband, so that even the servants were able to perceive his annoyance. Such was the third person who was one of the family when the catastrophe occurred.

As to the other denizens of the old building, it will suffice out of a large household to mention the prim, respectable, and capable Ames, and Mrs. Allen, a buxom and cheerful person, who relieved the lady of some of her household cares. The

52 In "Barker, the Hated Rival," Darlene Cypser identifies Cecil James Barker as Barker, Holmes's "hated rival" of "The Retired Colourman."

53 Originally, this meant one who fought for a prize, but the word came to mean a professional boxer. Arthur Conan Doyle, as we have seen, was a boxer. He declared himself "well-qualified for the heavy-weight division," and in 1910, he was invited (but declined) to judge the world heavy-weight championship match between James J. Jeffries and Jack Johnson. His splendid novel of the ring, *Rodney Stone* (1896), was ranked by *The Bookman* (January 1897) among his four or five best works. "The Ring is supposed just now to be very wholesome," the reviewer wrote. "At least an admiration for its past is held to check decadence. So be it." Beverly Stark, reviewing Conan Doyle's *Sir Nigel* in *The Bookman* in November 1906, called *Rodney Stone* the best of Conan Doyle's work, and apparently Arthur Bartlett Maurice, the "Junior Editor" of *The Bookman* for many years and an avowed Sherlockian, did as well.

other six servants in the house bear no relation to the events of the night of January 6th.

It was at eleven-forty-five that the first alarm reached the small local police station, in charge of Sergeant Wilson, of the Sussex Constabulary. Mr. Cecil Barker, much excited, had rushed up to the door and pealed furiously upon the bell. A terrible tragedy had occurred at the Manor House, and John Douglas had been murdered. That was the breathless burden of his message. He had hurried back to the house, followed within a few minutes by the police sergeant, who arrived at the scene of the crime a little past twelve o'clock, after taking prompt steps to warn the county authorities that something serious was afoot.

On reaching the Manor House, the sergeant had found the drawbridge down, the windows lighted up, and the whole household in a state of wild confusion and alarm. The white-faced servants were huddling together in the hall, with the frightened butler wringing his hands in the doorway. Only Cecil Barker seemed to be master of himself and his emotions. He had opened the door which was nearest to the entrance, and he had beckoned to the sergeant to follow him. At that moment there arrived Dr. Wood, a brisk and capable general practitioner from the village. The three men entered the fatal room together, while the horror-stricken butler followed at their heels, closing the door behind him to shut out the terrible scene from the maid-servants.

The dead man lay on his back, sprawling with outstretched limbs in the centre of the room. He was clad only in a pink dressing-gown, which covered his night clothes. There were carpet slippers upon his bare feet. The doctor knelt beside him and held down the hand-lamp which had stood on the table. One glance at the victim was enough to show the healer that his presence could be dispensed with. The man had been horribly injured. Lying across his chest was a curious weapon, a shot-gun with the barrel sawed off a foot in front of the triggers. It was clear that this had been fired at close range and that he had received the whole charge in the face, blowing his head almost to pieces. The triggers had been wired together, so as to make the simultaneous discharge more destructive.

The country policeman was unnerved and troubled by the tremendous responsibility which had come so suddenly upon

"The doctor knelt beside him, and held down the hand-lamp. One glance was enough to show the healer that his presence could be dispensed with."
Frank Wiles, *Strand Magazine*, 1914

him. "We will touch nothing until my superiors arrive," he said, in a hushed voice, staring in horror at the dreadful head.

"Nothing has been touched up to now," said Cecil Barker. "I'll answer for that. You see it all exactly as I found it."

"When was that?" The sergeant had drawn out his note-book.

"It was just half-past eleven. I had not begun to undress, and I was sitting by the fire in my bedroom when I heard the report. It was not very loud—it seemed to be muffled. I rushed down. I don't suppose it was thirty seconds before I was in the room."

"Was the door open?"

"Yes, it was open. Poor Douglas was lying as you see him. His bedroom candle was burning on the table. It was I who lit the lamp some minutes afterwards."

"Did you see no one?"

"No. I heard Mrs. Douglas coming down the stair behind me, and I rushed out to prevent her from seeing this dreadful sight. Mrs. Allen, the housekeeper, came and took her away. Ames had arrived, and we ran back into the room once more."

"But surely I have heard that the drawbridge is kept up all night."

"Yes, it was up until I lowered it."

"Then how could any murderer have got away? It is out of the question. Mr. Douglas must have shot himself."

"That was our first idea. But see!" Barker drew aside the curtain, and showed that the long, diamond-paned window was open to its full extent. "And look at this!" He held the lamp down and illuminated a smudge of blood like the mark of a boot-sole upon the wooden sill. "Some one has stood there in getting out."

"You mean that some one waded across the moat?"

"Exactly!"

"Then, if you were in the room within half a minute of the crime, he must have been in the water at that very moment."

"I have not a doubt of it. I wish to heaven that I had rushed to the window! But the curtain screened it, as you can see, and so it never occurred to me. Then I heard the step of Mrs. Douglas, and I could not let her enter the room. It would have been too horrible."

"Horrible enough!" said the doctor, looking at the shattered head and the terrible marks which surrounded it. "I've never seen such injuries since the Birlstone railway smash."

"But, I say," remarked the police-sergeant, whose slow, bucolic common sense was still pondering over the open window. "It's all very well your saying that a man escaped by wading this moat, but what I ask you is—how did he ever get into the house at all if the bridge was up?"

"Ah, that's the question," said Barker.

"At what o'clock was it raised?"

"It was nearly six o'clock," said Ames, the butler.

"I've heard," said the sergeant, "that it was usually raised at sunset. That would be nearer half-past four than six at this time of year."

"Mrs. Douglas had visitors to tea," said Ames. "I couldn't raise it until they went. Then I wound it up myself."

"Then it comes to this," said the sergeant: "If anyone came from outside—*if* they did—they must have got in across the bridge before six and been in hiding ever since, until Mr. Douglas came into the room after eleven."

"That is so. Mr. Douglas went round the house every night the last thing before he turned in to see that the lights were right. That brought him in here. The man was waiting and shot him. Then he got away through the window and left his gun behind him. That's how I read it—for nothing else will fit the facts."

The sergeant picked up a card which lay beside the dead man upon the floor. The initials V. V., and under them the number 341, were rudely scrawled in ink upon it.

"What's this?" he asked, holding it up.

Barker looked at it with curiosity. "I never noticed it before," he said. "The murderer must have left it behind him."

"V. V. 341. I can make no sense of that."

The sergeant kept turning it over in his big fingers. "What's V. V.? Somebody's initials, maybe. What have you got there, Dr. Wood?"

It was a good-sized hammer which had been lying on the rug in front of the fireplace—a substantial, workmanlike hammer. Cecil Barker pointed to a box of brass-headed nails upon the mantelpiece.

"Mr. Douglas was altering the pictures yesterday," he said. "I saw him myself, standing upon that chair and fixing the big picture above it. That accounts for the hammer."

"We'd best put it back on the rug where we found it," said the sergeant, scratching his puzzled head in his perplexity. "It will want the best brains in the force to get to the bottom of this thing. It will be a London job before it is finished." He raised the hand-lamp and walked slowly round the room. "Hullo!" he cried, excitedly, drawing the window curtain to one side. "What o'clock were those curtains drawn?"

"When the lamps were lit," said the butler. "It would be shortly after four."

"Some one had been hiding here, sure enough." He held down the light, and the marks of muddy boots were very visible in the corner. "I'm bound to say this bears out your theory, Mr. Barker. It looks as if the man got into the house after four when the curtains were drawn, and before six, when the bridge was raised. He slipped into this room because it was the first that he saw. There was no other place where he could hide, so he popped in behind this curtain. That all seems clear enough. It is likely that his main idea was to burgle the house, but Mr. Douglas chanced to come upon him, so he murdered him and escaped."

"That's how I read it," said Barker. "But, I say, aren't we wasting precious time? Couldn't we start out and scour the country before the fellow gets away?"

The sergeant considered for a moment.

"There are no trains before six in the morning[54]; so he can't get away by rail. If he goes by road with his legs all dripping, it's odds that some one will notice him. Anyhow, I can't leave here myself until I am relieved. But I think none of you should go until we see more clearly how we all stand."

The doctor had taken the lamp and was narrowly scrutinizing the body. "What's this mark?" he asked. "Could this have any connection with the crime?"

The dead man's right arm was thrust out from his dressing gown and exposed as high as the elbow. About halfway up the forearm was a curious brown design, a triangle inside a circle, standing out in vivid relief upon the lard-coloured skin.

"It's not tattooed," said the doctor, peering through his glasses. "I never saw anything like it. The man has been branded at some time, as they brand cattle. What is the meaning of this?"

"I don't profess to know the meaning of it," said Cecil Barker; "but I have seen the mark on Douglas any time this last ten years."

"And so have I," said the butler. "Many a time when the master has rolled up his sleeves I have noticed that very mark. I've often wondered what it could be."

"Then it has nothing to do with the crime, anyhow," said the sergeant. "But it's a rum[55] thing all the same. Everything about this case is rum. Well, what is it now?"

54 This is plainly and curiously incorrect. As Ian McQueen notes, White Mason was able to send his message to Scotland Yard "by the five-forty train" (see text accompanying note 56, below).

55 John Camden Hotten's *Slang Dictionary* (1865) credits "rum" as originally meaning "fine, good, gallant, or valuable, perhaps in some way connected with Rome. Now-a-days it means indifferent, bad, or questionable, and we often hear even persons in polite society use such a phrase as 'what a rum fellow he is, to be sure,' in speaking of a man of singular habits or appearance."

E. Cobham Brewer's *Dictionary of Phrase and Fable* (1898) has a different slant on it, defining the word to mean "Queer, quaint, old-fashioned. This word was first applied to Roman Catholic priests, and subsequently to other clergymen. Thus Swift speaks of 'a rabble of tenants and rusty dull rums' (country parsons). As these 'rusty dull rums' were old-fashioned and quaint, a 'rum fellow' came to signify one as odd as a 'rusty dull rum.' " Brewer traces a tentative etymology back to booksellers doing business with the West Indies. Rather than money, rum was exchanged for those books that would not sell particularly well in England.

Sergeant Wilson, of course, may have meant to express either meaning in this situation: "bad or questionable," "queer or quaint," or some combination of both.

The butler had given an exclamation of astonishment and was pointing at the dead man's outstretched hand.

"They've taken his wedding-ring!" he gasped.

"What!"

"Yes, indeed. Master always wore his plain gold wedding-ring on the little finger of his left hand. That ring with the rough nugget on it was above it, and the twisted snake-ring on the third finger. There's the nugget and there's the snake, but the wedding-ring is gone."

"He's right," said Barker.

"Do you tell me," said the sergeant, "that the wedding ring was *below* the other?"

"Always!"

"Then the murderer, or whoever it was, first took off this ring you call the nugget-ring, then the wedding-ring, and afterwards put the nugget-ring back again."

"That is so!" The worthy country policeman shook his head. "Seems to me the sooner we get London on to this case the better," said he. "White Mason is a smart man. No local job has ever been too much for White Mason. It won't be long now before he is here to help us. But I expect we'll have to look to London before we are through. Anyhow, I'm not ashamed to say that it is a deal too thick for the likes of me."

CHAPTER IV

DARKNESS

56 This plainly contradicts Sergeant Wilson's earlier assertion that there were no trains before six in the morning. See note 54, above.

57 Newspapermen; reporters. For a remarkable reconstruction of the press accounts of this case, see Peter Calamai's presentation "Pressmen Down Like Flies."

At three in the morning the chief Sussex detective, obeying the urgent call from Sergeant Wilson of Birlstone, arrived from headquarters in a light dog-cart behind a breathless trotter. By the five-forty train in the morning[56] he had sent his message to Scotland Yard, and he was at the Birlstone station at twelve o'clock to welcome us. Mr. White Mason was a quiet, comfortable-looking person, in a loose tweed suit, with a clean-shaven, ruddy face, a stoutish body, and powerful handy legs adorned with gaiters, looking like a small farmer, a retired gamekeeper, or anything upon earth except a very favourable specimen of the provincial criminal officer.

"A real downright snorter, Mr. MacDonald," he kept repeating. "We'll have the pressmen[57] down like flies when they understand it. I'm hoping we will get our work done before they get poking their noses into it and messing up all the trails. There has been nothing like this that I can remember. There are some bits that will come home to you, Mr. Holmes, or I am mistaken. And you also, Dr. Watson, for the medicos will have a word to say before we finish. Your room is at the Westville Arms. There's no other place, but I hear that it is clean and good. The man will carry your bags. This way, gentlemen, if *you* please."

He was a very bustling and genial person, this Sussex detective. In ten minutes we had all found our quarters. In ten more we were seated in the parlour of the inn and being treated to a rapid sketch of those events which have been outlined in the previous chapter. MacDonald made an occasional note, while Holmes sat absorbed with the expression of surprised and reverent admiration with which the botanist surveys the rare and precious bloom.

"Remarkable!" he said, when the story was unfolded. "Most remarkable! I can hardly recall any case where the features have been more peculiar."

"I thought you would say so, Mr. Holmes," said White Mason in great delight. "We're well up with the times in Sussex. I've told you now how matters were, up to the time when I took over from Sergeant Wilson between three and four this morning. My word, I made the old mare go! But I need not have been in such a hurry as it turned out, for there was nothing immediate that I could do. Sergeant Wilson had all the facts. I checked them and considered them and maybe added a few of my own."

"What were they?" asked Holmes, eagerly.

"Well, I first had the hammer examined. There was Dr. Wood there to help me. We found no signs of violence upon it. I was hoping that, if Mr. Douglas defended himself with the hammer, he might have left his mark upon the murderer before he dropped it on the mat. But there was no stain."

"That, of course, proves nothing at all," remarked Inspector MacDonald. "There has been many a hammer murder and no trace on the hammer."

"Quite so. It doesn't prove it wasn't used. But there might have been stains, and that would have helped us. As a matter of fact there were none. Then I examined the gun. They were buck-shot cartridges, and, as Sergeant Wilson pointed out, the triggers were wired together so that if you pulled on the hinder one, both barrels were discharged. Whoever fixed that up had made up his mind that he was going to take no chances of missing his man. The sawn gun was not more than two feet long—one could carry it easily under one's coat. There was no complete maker's name, but the printed letters 'P-E-N' were on the fluting between the barrels, and the rest of the name had been cut off by the saw."

"A big 'P' with a flourish above it, 'E' and 'N' smaller?" asked Holmes.

"Exactly."

"Pennsylvania Small Arm Company—well-known American firm,"[58] said Holmes.

White Mason gazed at my friend as the little village practitioner looks at the Harley Street specialist who by a word can solve the difficulties that perplex him.

"That is very helpful, Mr. Holmes. No doubt you are right. Wonderful! Wonderful! Do you carry the names of all the gun makers in the world in your memory?"

Holmes dismissed the subject with a wave.

"No doubt it is an American shot-gun," White Mason continued. "I seem to have read that a sawed-off shot-gun is a weapon used in some parts of America. Apart from the name upon the barrel, the idea had occurred to me. There is some evidence, then, that this man who entered the house and killed its master was an American."

MacDonald shook his head. "Man, you are surely travelling over-fast," said he. "I have heard no evidence yet that any stranger was ever in the house at all."

"The open window, the blood on the sill, the queer card, the marks of boots in the corner, the gun."

"Nothing there that could not have been arranged. Mr. Douglas was an American, or had lived long in America. So had Mr. Barker. You don't need to import an American from outside in order to account for American doings."

"Ames, the butler—"

"What about him? Is he reliable?"

"Ten years with Sir Charles Chandos[59]—as solid as a rock. He has been with Douglas ever since he took the Manor House five years ago. He has never seen a gun of this sort in the house."

"The gun was made to conceal. That's why the barrels were sawn. It would fit into any box. How could he swear there was no such gun in the house?"

"Well, anyhow, he had never seen one."

MacDonald shook his obstinate Scotch head. "I'm not convinced yet that there was ever anyone in the house," said he.

58 Christopher Morley, in examining the question of "Was Sherlock Holmes an American?," makes much of Holmes's familiarity with matters American in this and other tales. See also note 126, below. He refrains from speculating on the details of the times and places of Holmes's American travels. In "Sherlock Holmes in Gilded Age New York," however, Barrett Potter adopts William S. Baring-Gould's suggestion that Holmes toured America in his youth with the Sassanoff Shakespeare Company (put forward in Baring-Gould's *Sherlock Holmes of Baker Street: A Life of the World's First Consulting Detective*) and further speculates that Holmes was also temporarily engaged in the New York production of Gilbert and Sullivan's *H.M.S. Pinafore* in 1879 and observed the mark on a prop at that time.

59 While Sir Charles has no part in this story, Julian Wolff notes (in *Practical Handbook of Sherlockian Heraldry*) that not only did his ancestor Sir John Chandos appear prominently in chronicles of English chivalry but, more importantly, his squire was one Nigel Loring, whose history is recounted in Arthur Conan Doyle's *The White Company* (1891) and *Sir Nigel* (1906).

"I'm asking you to conseedar"—his accent became more Aberdonian as he lost himself in his argument—"I'm asking you to conseedar what it involves if you suppose that this gun was ever brought into the house and that all these strange things were done by a person from outside. Oh, man, it's just inconceivable! It's clean against common sense! I put it to you, Mr. Holmes, judging it by what we have heard."

"Well, state your case, Mr. Mac," said Holmes, in his most judicial style.

"The man is not a burglar, supposing that he ever existed. The ring business and the card point to premeditated murder for some private reason. Very good. Here is a man who slips into a house with the deliberate intention of committing murder. He knows, if he knows anything, that he will have a deeficulty in making his escape, as the house is surrounded with water. What weapon would he choose? You would say the most silent in the world. Then he could hope when the deed was done to slip quickly from the window, to wade the moat, and to get away at his leisure. That's understandable. But is it understandable that he should go out of his way to bring with him the most noisy weapon he could select, knowing well that it will fetch every human being in the house to the spot as quick as they can run, and that it is all odds that he will be seen before he can get across the moat? Is that credible, Mr. Holmes?"

"Well, you put the case strongly," my friend replied thoughtfully. "It certainly needs a good deal of justification. May I ask, Mr. White Mason, whether you examined the farther side of the moat at once to see if there were any signs of the man having climbed out from the water?"

"There were no signs, Mr. Holmes. But it is a stone ledge, and one could hardly expect them."

"No tracks or marks?"

"None."

"Ha! Would there be any objection, Mr. White Mason, to our going down to the house at once? There may possibly be some small point which might be suggestive."

"I was going to propose it, Mr. Holmes; but I thought it well to put you in touch with all the facts before we go. I suppose if anything should strike you—" White Mason looked doubtfully at the amateur.

60 Elms that have been "pollarded" have had their branches pruned to form a close rounded head.

61 Julian Wolff wonders whether Watson may have confused the "ramping lion of Capus" with the "rampant lion" of the King of Scotland, last seen on the battlefield of Culloden in 1746.

"I have worked with Mr. Holmes before," said Inspector MacDonald. "He plays the game."

"My own idea of the game, at any rate," said Holmes, with a smile. "I go into a case to help the ends of justice and the work of the police. If ever I have separated myself from the official force, it is because they have first separated themselves from me. I have no wish ever to score at their expense. At the same time, Mr. White Mason, I claim the right to work in my own way and give my results at my own time—complete rather than in stages."

"I am sure we are honoured by your presence and to show you all we know," said White Mason, cordially. "Come along, Dr. Watson, and when the time comes we'll all hope for a place in your book."

We walked down the quaint village street with a row of pollarded elms[60] on either side of it. Just beyond were two ancient stone pillars, weather-stained and lichen-blotched, bearing upon their summits a shapeless something which had once been the ramping lion of Capus of Birlstone.[61] A short walk along the winding drive with such sward and oaks around it as one only sees in rural England; then a sudden turn, and the long, low Jacobean house of dingy, liver-coloured brick lay before us, with an old-fashioned garden of cut yews on either side of it. As we approached it, there was the wooden drawbridge and the beautiful broad moat as still and luminous as quicksilver in the cold, winter sunshine.

Three centuries had flowed past the old Manor House, centuries of births and of home-comings, of country dances and of the meetings of fox-hunters. Strange that now in its old age this dark business should have cast its shadow upon the venerable walls. And yet those strange peaked roofs and quaint overhung gables were a fitting covering to grim and terrible intrigue. As I looked at the deep-set windows and the long sweep of the dull-coloured, water-lapped front, I felt that no more fitting scene could be set for such a tragedy.

"That's the window," said White, "that one on the immediate right of the drawbridge. It's open just as it was found last night."

"It looks rather narrow for a man to pass."

"Well, it wasn't a fat man, anyhow. We don't need your

deductions, Mr. Holmes, to tell us that. But you or I could squeeze through all right."

Holmes walked to the edge of the moat and looked across. Then he examined the stone ledge and the grass border beyond it.

"I've had a good look, Mr. Holmes," said White Mason. "There is nothing there; no sign that anyone has landed. But why should he leave any sign?"

"Exactly. Why should he? Is the water always turbid?"

"Generally about this colour. The stream brings down the clay."

"How deep is it?"

"About two feet at each side and three in the middle."

"So we can put aside all idea of the man having been drowned in crossing."

"Holmes examined the stone ledge and the grass border beyond it."
Frank Wiles, *Strand Magazine*, 1914

"No; a child could not be drowned in it."

We walked across the drawbridge, and were admitted by a quaint, gnarled, dried-up person, who was the butler—Ames. The poor old fellow was white and quivering from the shock. The village sergeant, a tall, formal, melancholy man, still held his vigil in the room of fate. The doctor had departed.

"Anything fresh, Sergeant Wilson?" asked White Mason.

"No, sir."

"Then you can go home. You've had enough. We can send for you if we want you. The butler had better wait outside. Tell him to warn Mr. Cecil Barker, Mrs. Douglas, and the housekeeper that we may want a word with them presently. Now, gentlemen, perhaps you will allow me to give you the views I have formed first, and then you will be able to arrive at your own." He impressed me, this country specialist. He had a solid grip of fact and a cool, clear, common-sense brain, which should take him some way in his profession. Holmes listened to him intently, with no sign of that impatience which the official exponent too often produced.

"Is it suicide, or is it murder—that's our first question, gentlemen, is it not? If it were suicide, then we have to believe that this man began by taking off his wedding-ring and concealing it; that he then came down here in his dressing gown, trampled mud into a corner behind the curtain in order to give the idea some one had waited for him, opened the window, put blood on the—"

"We can surely dismiss that," said MacDonald.

"So I think. Suicide is out of the question. Then a murder has been done. What we have to determine is whether it was done by some one outside or inside the house."

"Well, let's hear the argument."

"There are considerable difficulties both ways, and yet one or the other it must be. We will suppose first that some person or persons inside the house did the crime. They got this man down here at a time when everything was still and yet no one was asleep. They then did the deed with the queerest and noisiest weapon in the world so as to tell every one what had happened—a weapon that was never seen in the house before. That does not seem a very likely start, does it?"

"No, it does not."

"Well, then, every one is agreed that after the alarm was

given only a minute at the most had passed before the whole household—not Mr. Cecil Barker alone, though he claims to have been the first, but Ames and all of them—were on the spot. Do you tell me that in that time the guilty person managed to make footmarks in the corner, open the window, mark the sill with blood, take the wedding-ring off the dead man's finger, and all the rest of it? It's impossible!"

"You put it very clearly," said Holmes. "I am inclined to agree with you."

"Well, then, we are driven back to the theory that it was done by some one from outside. We are still faced with some big difficulties; but anyhow they have ceased to be impossibilities. The man got into the house between four-thirty and six—that is to say, between dusk and the time when the bridge was raised. There had been some visitors, and the door was open; so there was nothing to prevent him. He may have been a common burglar, or he may have had some private grudge against Mr. Douglas. Since Mr. Douglas has spent most of his life in America, and this shot-gun seems to be an American weapon, it would seem that the private grudge is the more likely theory. He slipped into this room because it was the first he came to, and he hid behind the curtain. There he remained until past eleven at night. At that time Mr. Douglas entered the room. It was a short interview, if there were any interview at all; for Mrs. Douglas declares that her husband had not left her more than a few minutes when she heard the shot."

"The candle shows that," said Holmes.

"Exactly. The candle, which was a new one, is not burned more than half an inch. He must have placed it on the table before he was attacked; otherwise, of course, it would have fallen when he fell. This shows that he was not attacked the instant that he entered the room. When Mr. Barker arrived the lamp was lit and the candle put out."[62]

"That's all clear enough."

"Well, now, we can reconstruct things on those lines. Mr. Douglas enters the room. He puts down the candle. A man appears from behind the curtain. He is armed with this gun. He demands the wedding-ring—Heaven only knows why, but so it must have been. Mr. Douglas gave it up. Then either in cold blood or in the course of a struggle—Douglas may have gripped the hammer that was found upon the mat—he shot

62 Strangely, the American text has "the candle was lit and the lamp was out," which makes no sense and contradicts Ames's testimony.

" 'Ames, I understand that you have often seen this very unusual mark, a branded triangle inside a circle, upon Mr. Douglas's forearm?' "
Frank Wiles, *Strand Magazine*, 1914

Douglas in this horrible way. He dropped his gun and also it would seem this queer card—V. V. 341, whatever that may mean—and he made his escape through the window and across the moat at the very moment when Cecil Barker was discovering the crime. How's that, Mr. Holmes?"

"Very interesting, but just a little unconvincing."

"Man, it would be absolute nonsense if it wasn't that anything else is even worse!" cried MacDonald. "Somebody killed the man, and whoever it was I could clearly prove to you that

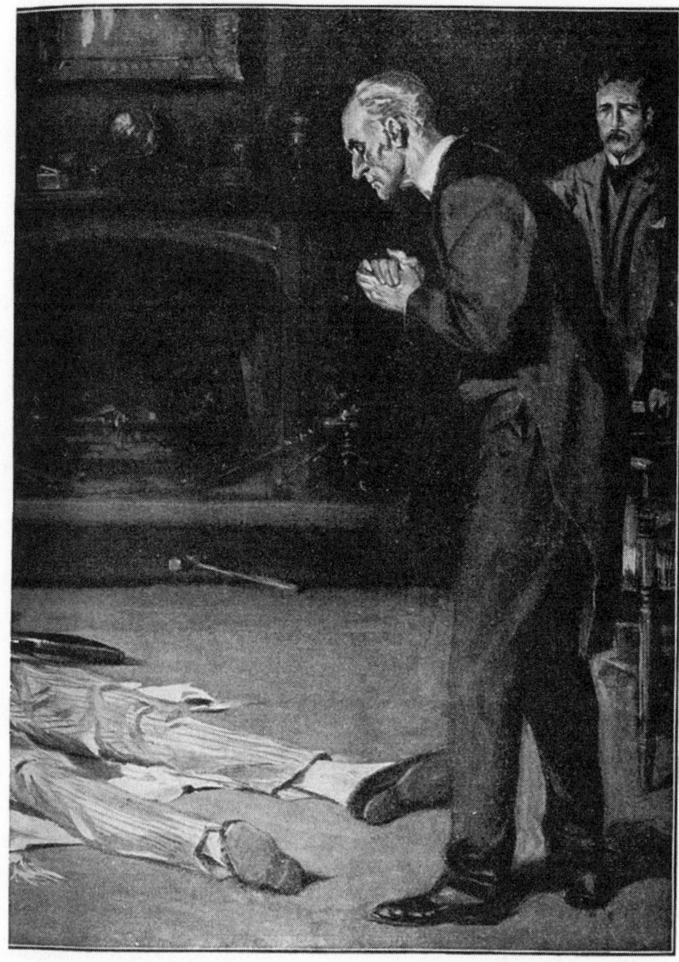

he should have done it some other way. What does he mean by allowing his retreat to be cut off like that? What does he mean by using a shotgun when silence was his one chance of escape? Come, Mr. Holmes, it's up to you to give us a lead, since you say Mr. White Mason's theory is unconvincing."

Holmes had sat intently observant during this long discussion, missing no word that was said, with his keen eyes darting to right and to left, and his forehead wrinkled with speculation.

"I should like a few more facts before I get so far as a theory, Mr. Mac," said he, kneeling down beside the body. "Dear me! these injuries are really appalling. Can we have the butler in for a moment? . . . Ames, I understand that you have often seen this very unusual mark—a branded triangle inside a circle—upon Mr. Douglas's forearm?"

"Frequently, sir."

"You never heard any speculation as to what it meant?"

"No, sir."

"It must have caused great pain when it was inflicted. It is undoubtedly a burn. Now, I observe, Ames, that there is a small piece of plaster at the angle of Mr. Douglas's jaw. Did you observe that in life?"

"Yes, sir, he cut himself in shaving yesterday morning."

"Did you ever know him to cut himself in shaving before?"

"Not for a very long time, sir."

"Suggestive!" said Holmes. "It may, of course, be a mere coincidence, or it may point to some nervousness which would indicate that he had reason to apprehend danger. Had you noticed anything unusual in his conduct, yesterday, Ames?"

"It struck me that he was a little restless and excited, sir."

"Ha! The attack may not have been entirely unexpected. We do seem to make a little progress, do we not? Perhaps you would rather do the questioning, Mr. Mac?"

"No, Mr. Holmes, it's in better hands."

"Well, then, we will pass to this card—V. V. 341. It is rough cardboard. Have you any of the sort in the house?"

"I don't think so."

Holmes walked across to the desk and dabbed a little ink from each bottle on to the blotting-paper. "It was not printed in this room," he said; "this is black ink and the other purplish. It was done by a thick pen, and these are fine. No, it was done elsewhere, I should say. Can you make anything of the inscription, Ames?"

"No, sir, nothing."

"What do you think, Mr. Mac?"

"It gives me the impression of a secret society of some sort; the same with this badge upon the forearm."

"That's my idea, too," said White Mason.

"Well, we can adopt it as a working hypothesis and then see how far our difficulties disappear. An agent from such a society makes his way into the house, waits for Mr. Douglas, blows his head nearly off with this weapon, and escapes by wading the moat, after leaving a card beside the dead man, which will, when mentioned in the papers, tell other members of the society that vengeance has been done. That all hangs together. But why this gun, of all weapons?"

"Holmes had gone to the window and was examining with his lens the blood-mark upon the sill."
Frank Wiles, *Strand Magazine*, 1914

"Exactly."

"And why the missing ring?"

"Quite so."

"And why no arrest? It's past two now. I take it for granted that since dawn every constable within forty miles has been looking out for a wet stranger?"

"That is so, Mr. Holmes."

"Well, unless he has a burrow close by or a change of clothes ready, they can hardly miss him. And yet they have missed him up to now!" Holmes had gone to the window and was examining with his lens the blood mark on the sill. "It is clearly the tread of a shoe. It is remarkably broad; a splayfoot one would say. Curious, because, so far as one can trace any footmark in this mud-stained corner, one would say it was a more shapely sole. However, they are certainly very indistinct. What's this under the side table?"

"Mr. Douglas's dumb-bells," said Ames.

"Dumb-bell—there's only one. Where's the other?"

"I don't know, Mr. Holmes. There may have been only one. I have not noticed them for months."

"One dumb-bell—" Holmes said, seriously, but his remarks were interrupted by a sharp knock at the door.

A tall, sunburned, capable-looking, clean-shaved man looked in at us. I had no difficulty in guessing that it was the Cecil Barker of whom I had heard. His masterful eyes travelled quickly with a questioning glance from face to face.

"Sorry to interrupt your consultation," said he, "but you should hear the latest news."

"An arrest?"

"No such luck. But they've found his bicycle. The fellow left his bicycle behind him. Come and have a look. It is within a hundred yards of the hall door."

We found three or four grooms and idlers standing in the drive inspecting a bicycle which had been drawn out from a clump of evergreens in which it had been concealed. It was a well used Rudge-Whitworth,[63] splashed as from a considerable journey. There was a saddlebag with spanner and oilcan, but no clue as to the owner.

"It would be a grand help to the police," said the inspector, "if these things were numbered and registered. But we must be thankful for what we've got. If we can't find where he went to, at least we are likely to get where he came from. But what in the name of all that is wonderful made the fellow leave it behind? And how in the world has he got away without it? We don't seem to get a gleam of light in the case, Mr. Holmes."

"Don't we?" my friend answered, thoughtfully. "I wonder!"

63 The brand name of the bicycle provides a potentially valuable clue as to the date of this story. The Rudge-Whitworth company was created in 1894, when Whitworth Cycles purchased a bicycle company that had been started in 1868 by Dan Rudge and several friends, including the designer Walter Phillips and Henry Clarke, who supplied wheels. (Rudge himself, a public-house owner and engineer who began by making velocipedes, an early form of bicycle, died of cancer in 1880, at the age of thirty-nine.) By the early part of the twentieth century, Rudge-Whitworth had switched its focus to motorcycles.

Most chronologists generally assign the dates 1887 and 1888 to the events of *The Valley of Fear* (see *Chronological Table*). If Watson's notes are correct, however, the bicycle was either a Rudge or a Whitworth but not a Rudge-Whitworth. Perhaps, when Watson wrote up his notes many years later (recall that *The Valley of Fear* was not published until 1915), he simply translated an insignificant bit of data into a familiar name.

CHAPTER V

The People of the Drama[64]

"Have you seen all you want of the study?" asked White Mason as we re-entered the house.

"For the time," said the inspector; and Holmes nodded.

"Then perhaps you would now like to hear the evidence of some of the people in the house? We could use the dining-room, Ames. Please come yourself first and tell us what you know."

The butler's account was a simple and a clear one, and he gave a convincing impression of sincerity. He had been engaged five years ago, when Douglas first came to Birlstone. He understood that Mr. Douglas was a rich gentleman who had made his money in America. He had been a kind and considerate employer—not quite what Ames was used to, perhaps, but one can't have everything. He never saw any signs of apprehension in Mr. Douglas—on the contrary, he was the most fearless man he had ever known. He ordered the drawbridge to be pulled up every night because it was the ancient custom of the old house, and he liked to keep the old ways up.

Mr. Douglas seldom went to London or left the village, but on the day before the crime he had been shopping at Tun-

64 The *Strand Magazine* for November 1914 contains the following summary:

> The opening chapters of this new and thrilling adventure of Sherlock Holmes described the receipt by Holmes of a cipher message, from which he deduces that some devilry is intended against a man named Douglas, a rich country gentleman living at the Manor House, Birlstone, in Sussex, and that the danger is a pressing one. Almost as soon as he has deciphered the message he is visited by Inspector MacDonald, of Scotland Yard, who brings the news that Mr. Douglas has been murdered that morning [*sic*]. He asks Sherlock Holmes and Dr. Watson to accompany him to Birlstone, where they are met by Mr. White Mason, the chief Sussex detective, from whom they learn the details of the crime. The murdered man had been horribly injured, while lying

across his chest was a curious weapon—a shot-gun with the barrel sawn off a foot in front of the triggers. Near him was found a card with the initials "V. V." and the number "341" scrawled on it in ink, and about half-way up the forearm was a curious design—a branded triangle inside a circle. All four then proceed to the Manor House, and, when the present instalment opens, are examining the room in which the crime occurred, accompanied by Mr. Cecil Barker, a friend of the Douglases, who has been staying with them.

bridge Wells. He, Ames, had observed some restlessness and excitement on the part of Mr. Douglas that day, for he had seemed impatient and irritable, which was unusual with him. He had not gone to bed that night, but was in the pantry at the back of the house, putting away the silver, when he heard the bell ring violently. He heard no shot, but it was hardly possible he should, as the pantry and kitchens were at the very back of the house and there were several closed doors and a long passage between. The housekeeper had come out of her room, attracted by the violent ringing of the bell. They had gone to the front of the house together.

As they reached the bottom of the stair he had seen Mrs. Douglas coming down it. No, she was not hurrying—it did not seem to him that she was particularly agitated. Just as she reached the bottom of the stair Mr. Barker had rushed out of the study. He had stopped Mrs. Douglas and begged her to go back.

"For God's sake, go back to your room!" he cried. "Poor Jack is dead. You can do nothing. For God's sake, go back!"

After some persuasion upon the stairs Mrs. Douglas had gone back. She did not scream. She made no outcry whatever. Mrs. Allen, the housekeeper, had taken her upstairs and stayed with her in the bedroom. Ames and Mr. Barker had then returned to the study, where they had found everything exactly as the police had seen it. The candle was not lit at that time, but the lamp was burning. They had looked out of the window, but the night was very dark and nothing could be seen or heard. They had then rushed out into the hall, where Ames had turned the windlass which lowered the drawbridge. Mr. Barker had then hurried off to get the police.

Such, in its essentials, was the evidence of the butler.

The account of Mrs. Allen, the housekeeper, was, so far as it went, a corroboration of that of her fellow-servant. The housekeeper's room was rather nearer to the front of the house than the pantry in which Ames had been working. She was preparing to go to bed when the loud ringing of the bell had attracted her attention. She was a little hard of hearing. Perhaps that was why she had not heard the sound of the shot; but in any case the study was a long way off. She remembered hearing some sound which she imagined to be the slamming of a door. That was a good deal earlier—half an hour at least before the ring-

" 'For God's sake, go back to your room!' he cried."
Frank Wiles, *Strand Magazine*, 1914

ing of the bell. When Mr. Ames ran to the front she went with him. She saw Mr. Barker, very pale and excited, come out of the study. He intercepted Mrs. Douglas, who was coming down the stairs. He entreated her to go back, and she answered him, but what she said could not be heard.

"Take her up. Stay with her!" he had said to Mrs. Allen.

She had therefore taken her to the bedroom and endeavoured to soothe her. She was greatly excited, trembling all over, but made no other attempt to go downstairs. She just sat in her dressing-gown by her bedroom fire, with her head sunk

65 The American editions inexplicably omit the phrase "from Ireland."

in her hands. Mrs. Allen stayed with her most of the night. As to the other servants, they had all gone to bed, and the alarm did not reach them until just before the police arrived. They slept at the extreme back of the house, and could not possibly have heard anything.

So far the housekeeper—who could add nothing on cross-examination save lamentations and expressions of amazement.

Mr. Cecil Barker succeeded Mrs. Allen as a witness. As to the occurrences of the night before, he had very little to add to what he had already told the police. Personally, he was convinced that the murderer had escaped by the window. The blood-stain was conclusive, in his opinion, on that point. Besides, as the bridge was up, there was no other possible way of escaping. He could not explain what had become of the assassin or why he had not taken his bicycle, if it were indeed his. He could not possibly have been drowned in the moat, which was at no place more than three feet deep.

In his own mind he had a very definite theory about the murder. Douglas was a reticent man, and there were some chapters in his life of which he never spoke. He had emigrated to America from Ireland[65] when he was a very young man. He had prospered well, and Barker had first met him in California, where they had become partners in a successful mining claim at a place called Benito Canyon. They had done very well, but Douglas had suddenly sold out and started for England. He was a widower at that time. Barker had afterwards realized his money and come to live in London. Thus they had renewed their friendship.

Douglas had given him the impression that some danger was hanging over his head, and he had always looked upon his sudden departure from California, and also his renting a house in so quiet a place in England, as being connected with this peril. He imagined that some secret society, some implacable organization, was on Douglas's track, which would never rest until it killed him. Some remarks of his had given him this idea; though he had never told him what the society was, nor how he had come to offend it. He could only suppose that the legend upon the placard had some reference to this secret society.

"How long were you with Douglas in California?" asked Inspector MacDonald.

"Five years altogether."

"He was a bachelor, you say?"

"A widower."

"Have you ever heard where his first wife came from?"

"No, I remember his saying that she was of German extraction,[66] and I have seen her portrait. She was a very beautiful woman. She died of typhoid[67] the year before I met him."

"You don't associate his past with any particular part of America?"

"I have heard him talk of Chicago.[68] He knew that city well and had worked there. I have heard him talk of the coal and iron districts. He had travelled a good deal in his time."

"Was he a politician? Had this secret society to do with politics?"

"No, he cared nothing about politics."

"You have no reason to think it was criminal?"

"On the contrary, I never met a straighter man in my life."

"Was there anything curious about his life in California?"

"He liked best to stay and to work at our claim in the mountains. He would never go where other men were if he could help it. That's why I first thought that some one was after him. Then when he left so suddenly for Europe I made sure that it was so. I believe that he had a warning of some sort. Within a week of his leaving half a dozen men were inquiring for him."

"What sort of men?"

"Well, they were a mighty hard-looking crowd. They came up to the claim and wanted to know where he was. I told them that he was gone to Europe and that I did not know where to find him. They meant him no good—it was easy to see that."

"Were these men Americans—Californians?"

"Well, I don't know about Californians. They were Americans, all right. But they were not miners. I don't know what they were, and was very glad to see their backs."

"That was six years ago?"

"Nearer seven."

"And then you were together five years in California, so that this business dates back not less than eleven years at the least?"

"That is so."

"It must be a very serious feud that would be kept up with such earnestness for as long as that. It would be no light thing that would give rise to it."

66 Here and elsewhere in the English editions, "Swedish" appears in lieu of "German" connections. See note 114, below, for an explanation.

67 Watson himself likely suffered from typhoid fever as a result of his service in the Second Afghan war. See *A Study in Scarlet*, note 18.

68 Douglas must have frequented Chicago in the late 1860s and early 1870s, when it was already the second-largest city in the United States, a transporation hub dominated by stockyards and railroads. The Union Stock Yard, the city's largest (eventually covering one square mile), was constructed by a consortium of nine railroad companies and opened on Christmas Day, 1865. Soon, meatpacking operations, eager to capitalise on the vast quantities of livestock now being brought in, had rushed to open in the stockyard's surrounding neighbourhoods.

The city's economic growth was brought to a grinding halt when Chicago was devastated by the Great Fire of 1871, which one Mrs. O'Leary's cow supposedly started by kicking over a lantern. The disaster rendered 90,000 people homeless and caused $200 million worth of property damage, plunging the city into a morass of poverty, unemployment, and crime. By 1875, Chicago had largely rebuilt itself, attracting a large immigrant population with new industries and changing inexorably the makeup and temperament of the city.

Holmes and Watson encounter a former Chicagoan on at least one other occasion: in "The Dancing Men," when they tangle with Abe Slaney, "the most dangerous crook in Chicago."

"I think it shadowed his whole life. It was never quite out of his mind."

"But if a man had a danger hanging over him, and knew what it was, don't you think he would turn to the police for protection?"

"Maybe it was some danger that he could not be protected against. There's one thing you should know. He always went about armed. His revolver was never out of his pocket. But by bad luck, he was in his dressing gown and had left it in the bedroom last night. Once the bridge was up, I guess he thought he was safe."

"I should like these dates a little clearer," said MacDonald. "It is quite six years since Douglas left California. You followed him next year, did you not?"

"That is so."

"And he had been married five years. You must have returned about the time of his marriage."

"About a month before. I was his best man."

"Did you know Mrs. Douglas before her marriage?"

"No, I did not. I had been away from England for ten years."

"But you have seen a good deal of her since."

Barker looked sternly at the detective. "I have seen a good deal of *him* since," he answered. "If I have seen her, it is because you cannot visit a man without knowing his wife. If you imagine there is any connection—"

"I imagine nothing, Mr. Barker. I am bound to make every inquiry which can bear upon the case. But I mean no offense."

"Some inquiries are offensive," Barker answered angrily.

"It's only the facts that we want. It is in your interest and every one's interest that they should be cleared up. Did Mr. Douglas entirely approve your friendship with his wife?"

Barker grew paler, and his great, strong hands were clasped convulsively together. "You have no right to ask such questions!" he cried. "What has this to do with the matter you are investigating?"

"I must repeat the question."

"Well, I refuse to answer."

"You can refuse to answer, but you must be aware that your refusal is in itself an answer, for you would not refuse if you had not something to conceal."

Barker stood for a moment with his face set grimly and his

strong black eyebrows drawn low in intense thought. Then he looked up with a smile. "Well, I guess you gentlemen are only doing your clear duty after all, and I have no right to stand in the way of it. I'd only ask you not to worry Mrs. Douglas over this matter; for she has enough upon her just now. I may tell you that poor Douglas had just one fault in the world, and that was his jealousy. He was fond of me—no man could be fonder of a friend. And he was devoted to his wife. He loved me to come here, and was for ever sending for me. And yet if his wife and I talked together or there seemed any sympathy between us, a kind of wave of jealousy would pass over him, and he would be off the handle and saying the wildest things in a moment. More than once I've sworn off coming for that reason, and then he would write me such penitent imploring letters that I just had to. But you can take it from me, gentlemen, if it was my last word, that no man ever had a more loving, faithful wife and I can say also no friend could be more loyal than I!"

It was spoken with fervour and feeling, and yet Inspector MacDonald could not dismiss the subject.

"You are aware," said he, "that the dead man's wedding-ring has been taken from his finger?"

"So it appears," said Barker.

"What do you mean by 'appears'? You know it as a fact."

The man seemed confused and undecided. "When I said 'appears' I meant that it was conceivable that he had himself taken off the ring."

"The mere fact that the ring should be absent, whoever may have removed it, would suggest to anyone's mind, would it not, that the marriage and the tragedy were connected?"

Barker shrugged his broad shoulders. "I can't profess to say what it suggests," he answered. "But if you mean to hint that it could reflect in any way upon this lady's honour"—his eyes blazed for an instant, and then with an evident effort he got a grip upon his own emotions—"well, you are on the wrong track, that's all."

"I don't know that I've anything else to ask you at present," said MacDonald, coldly.

"There was one small point," remarked Sherlock Holmes. "When you entered the room there was only a candle lighted on the table, was there not?"

"Yes, that was so."

"By its light you saw that some terrible incident had occurred?"

"Exactly."

"You at once rang for help?"

"Yes."

"And it arrived very speedily?"

"Within a minute or so."

"And yet when they arrived they found that the candle was out and that the lamp had been lighted. That seems very remarkable."

Again Barker showed some signs of indecision. "I don't see that it was remarkable, Mr. Holmes," he answered after a pause. "The candle threw a very bad light. My first thought was to get a better one. The lamp was on the table, so I lit it."

"And blew out the candle?"

"Exactly."

Holmes asked no further question, and Barker, with a deliberate look from one to the other of us, which had, as it seemed to me, something of defiance in it, turned and left the room.

Inspector MacDonald had sent up a note to the effect that he would wait upon Mrs. Douglas in her room, but she had replied that she would meet us in the dining-room. She entered now, a tall and beautiful woman of thirty, reserved and self-possessed to a remarkable degree, very different from the tragic and distracted figure I had pictured. It is true that her face was pale and drawn, like that of one who has endured a great shock, but her manner was composed, and the finely-moulded hand which she rested upon the edge of the table was as steady as my own. Her sad, appealing eyes travelled from one to the other of us with a curiously inquisitive expression. That questioning gaze transformed itself suddenly into abrupt speech.

"Have you found anything out yet?" she asked.

Was it my imagination that there was an undertone of fear rather than of hope in the question?

"We have taken every possible step, Mrs. Douglas," said the inspector. "You may rest assured that nothing will be neglected."

"Spare no money," she said in a dead, even tone. "It is my desire that every possible effort should be made."

"Perhaps you can tell us something which may throw some light upon the matter."

"I fear not; but all I know is at your service."

"We have heard from Mr. Cecil Barker that you did not actually see—that you were never in the room where the tragedy occurred?"

"No, he turned me back upon the stairs. He begged me to return to my room."

"Quite so. You had heard the shot, and you had at once come down."

"I put on my dressing-gown and then came down."

"How long was it after hearing the shot that you were stopped on the stair by Mr. Barker?"

"It may have been a couple of minutes. It is so hard to reckon time at such a moment. He implored me not to go on. He assured me that I could do nothing. Then Mrs. Allen, the housekeeper, led me upstairs again. It was all like some dreadful dream.

"Can you give us any idea how long your husband had been downstairs before you heard the shot?"

"No, I cannot say. He went from his dressing room, and I did not hear him go. He did the round of the house every night, for he was nervous of fire. It is the only thing that I have ever known him nervous of."

"That is just the point which I want to come to, Mrs. Douglas. You have known your husband only in England, have you not?"

"Yes, we have been married five years."

"Have you heard him speak of anything which occurred in America and might bring some danger upon him?"

Mrs. Douglas thought earnestly before she answered. "Yes," she said at last. "I have always felt that there was a danger hanging over him. He refused to discuss it with me. It was not from want of confidence in me—there was the most complete love and confidence between us—but it was out of his desire to keep all alarm away from me. He thought I should brood over it if I knew all, and so he was silent."

"How did you know it, then?"

Mrs. Douglas's face lit with a quick smile. "Can a husband ever carry about a secret all his life and a woman who loves him have no suspicion of it? I knew it by his refusal to talk about some episodes in his American life. I knew it by certain precautions he took. I knew it by certain words he let fall. I knew

" 'Have you found out anything yet?' she asked."
Frank Wiles, *Strand Magazine*, 1914

it by the way he looked at unexpected strangers. I was perfectly certain that he had some powerful enemies, that he believed they were on his track, and that he was always on his guard against them. I was so sure of it that for years I have been terrified if ever he came home later than was expected."

"Might I ask," asked Holmes, "what the words were which attracted your attention?"

"The Valley of Fear," the lady answered. "That was an expression he has used when I questioned him. 'I have been in the Valley of Fear. I am not out of it yet.'—'Are we never to get out of the Valley of Fear?' I have asked him when I have seen

him more serious than usual. 'Sometimes I think that we never shall,' he has answered."

"Surely you asked him what he meant by the Valley of Fear?"

"I did; but his face would become very grave and he would shake his head. 'It is bad enough that one of us should have been in its shadow,' he said. 'Please God it shall never fall upon you!' It was some real valley in which he had lived and in which something terrible had occurred to him, of that I am certain; but I can tell you no more."

"And he never mentioned any names?"

"Yes, he was delirious with fever once when he had his hunting accident three years ago. Then I remember that there was

69 Watson seems to be emphasising this point to remind his readers of the somewhat similar incident in *A Study in Scarlet*, in which Jefferson Hope takes Lucy Ferrier's wedding ring off of her finger after her death, then accidentally leaves it behind when murdering his old enemy.

a name that came continually to his lips. He spoke it with anger and a sort of horror. McGinty was the name—Bodymaster McGinty. I asked him when he recovered who Bodymaster McGinty was, and whose body he was master of. 'Never of mine, thank God!' he answered with a laugh, and that was all I could get from him. But there is a connection between Bodymaster McGinty and the Valley of Fear."

"There is one other point," said Inspector MacDonald. "You met Mr. Douglas in a boarding house in London, did you not, and became engaged to him there? Was there any romance, anything secret or mysterious, about the wedding?"

"There was romance. There is always romance. There was nothing mysterious."

"He had no rival?"

"No, I was quite free."

"You have heard, no doubt, that his wedding-ring has been taken. Does that suggest anything to you? Suppose that some enemy of his old life had tracked him down and committed this crime, what possible reason could he have for taking his wedding-ring?"

For an instant I could have sworn that the faintest shadow of a smile flickered over the woman's lips.

"I really cannot tell," she answered. "It is certainly a most extraordinary thing."[69]

"Well, we will not detain you any longer, and we are sorry to have put you to this trouble at such a time," said the inspector. "There are some other points, no doubt; but we can refer to you as they arise."

She rose, and I was again conscious of that quick, questioning glance with which she had just surveyed us: "What impression has my evidence made upon you?" The question might as well have been spoken. Then, with a bow, she swept from the room.

"She's a beautiful woman—a very beautiful woman," said MacDonald, thoughtfully, after the door had closed behind her. "This man Barker has certainly been down here a good deal. He is a man who might be attractive to a woman. He admits that the dead man was jealous, and maybe he knew best himself what cause he had for jealousy. Then there's that wedding-ring. You can't get past that. The man who tears a

"For an instant I could have sworn that the faintest shadow of a smile flickered over the woman's lips."
Arthur I. Keller, *Associated Sunday Magazines*, 1914

wedding-ring off a dead man's—What do you say to it, Mr. Holmes?"

My friend had sat with his head upon his hands, sunk in the deepest thought. Now he rose and rang the bell. "Ames," he said, when the butler entered, "where is Mr. Cecil Barker now?"

"I'll see, sir."

He came back in a moment to say that Mr. Barker was in the garden.

"Can you remember, Ames, what Mr. Barker had on his feet last night when you joined him in the study?"

"Yes, Mr. Holmes. He had a pair of bedroom slippers. I brought him his boots when he went for the police."

"Where are the slippers now?"

"They are still under the chair in the hall."

"Very good, Ames. It is, of course, important for us to know which tracks may be Mr. Barker's and which from outside."

"Yes, sir. I may say that I noticed that the slippers were stained with blood—so indeed were my own."

"That is natural enough, considering the condition of the room. Very good, Ames. We will ring if we want you."

A few minutes later we were in the study. Holmes had

"A faint shadow of a smile flickered over the woman's lips."
Frederic Dorr Steele, *Final Adventures of Sherlock Holmes*, Vol. I, 1952

brought with him the carpet slippers from the hall. As Ames had observed, the soles of both were dark with blood.

"Strange!" murmured Holmes, as he stood in the light of the window and examined them minutely. "Very strange indeed!"

Stooping with one of his quick feline pounces, he placed the slipper upon the blood mark on the sill. It exactly corresponded. He smiled in silence at his colleagues.

The inspector was transfigured with excitement. His native accent rattled like a stick upon railings.

"Man," he cried, "there's not a doubt of it! Barker has just marked the window himself. It's a good deal broader than any boot-mark. I mind that you said it was a splay foot, and here's the explanation. But what's the game, Mr. Holmes—what's the game?"

"He placed the slipper upon the blood-mark on the sill."
Frank Wiles, *Strand Magazine*, 1914

"Ay, what's the game?" my friend repeated, thoughtfully. White Mason chuckled and rubbed his fat hands together in his professional satisfaction. "I said it was a snorter!" he cried. "And a real snorter it is!"

CHAPTER VI

A Dawning Light[70]

THE THREE DETECTIVES had many matters of detail into which to inquire; so I returned alone to our modest quarters at the village inn; but before doing so I took a stroll in the curious old-world garden which flanked the house. Rows of very ancient yew trees cut into strange designs girded it round. Inside was a beautiful stretch of lawn with an old sundial in the middle, the whole effect so soothing and restful that it was welcome to my somewhat jangled nerves. In that deeply peaceful atmosphere one could forget or remember only as some fantastic nightmare that darkened study with the sprawling, blood-stained figure on the floor. And yet, as I strolled round it and tried to steep my soul in its gentle balm, a strange incident occurred, which brought me back to the tragedy and left a sinister impression in my mind.

I have said that a decoration of yew trees circled the garden. At the end which was farthest from the house they thickened into a continuous hedge. On the other side of this hedge, concealed from the eyes of anyone approaching from the direction of the house, there was a stone seat. As I approached the spot I was aware of voices, some remark in the deep tones of a man,

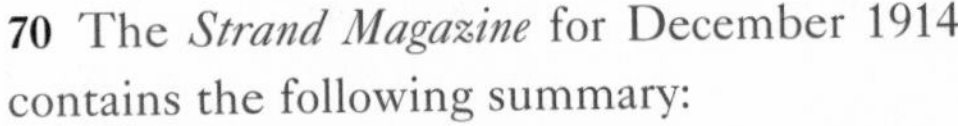

70 The *Strand Magazine* for December 1914 contains the following summary:

> The opening chapters of this new and thrilling adventure of Sherlock Holmes described the receipt by Holmes of a cipher message, from which he deduces that some devilry is intended against a man named Douglas, a rich country gentleman living at the Manor House, Birlstone, in Sussex, and that the danger is a pressing one. Almost as soon as he has deciphered the message he is visited by Inspector MacDonald, of Scotland Yard, who brings the news that Mr. Douglas has been murdered that morning [*sic*].
>
> Holmes, Dr. Watson and the inspector proceed to the scene of the tragedy, where they are met by Mr. White Mason, the chief Sussex detective. The murdered man had been horribly injured, while lying across his chest was a curious weapon—a

shot-gun with the barrel sawn off a foot in front of the triggers. Near him was found a card with the initials "V. V." and the number "341" scrawled on it in ink, and about half-way up the forearm was a curious design—a branded triangle inside a circle. His wedding-ring had been removed and the ring above it replaced.

There is no clue to the murderer except a bloody footprint on the window-sill, and he had apparently made his escape by wading across the moat. Holmes is much struck by the fact that one of Douglas's dumb-bells is missing.

Cecil Barker, Douglas's most intimate friend, is considerably flustered while being cross-examined by the detectives, and confesses that Douglas had been jealous on account of his attentions to Mrs. Douglas. Holmes ascertains from Ames, the butler, that on the previous evening Barker was wearing a pair of bedroom slippers which were stained with blood. The last instalment ends with the following dialogue, which takes place in the study. Holmes, having brought with him the blood-stained slippers from the hall:—

"Strange!" murmured Holmes as he stood in the light of the window and examined them minutely. "Very strange indeed!"

Stooping with one of his quick feline pounces he placed the slipper upon the blood-mark on the sill. It exactly corresponded. He smiled in silence at his colleagues.

The inspector was transfigured with excitement.

"Man!" he cried, "there's not a doubt of it! Barker has just marked the window himself. It's a good deal broader than any boot-mark. I mind that you said it was a splay foot, and here's the explanation. But what's the game, Mr. Holmes—what's the game?"

"Aye, what's the game?" my friend repeated, thoughtfully.

White Mason chuckled and rubbed his fat hands together in his professional satisfaction.

"I said it was a snorter!" he cried. "And a real snorter it is!"

answered by a little ripple of feminine laughter. An instant later I had come round the end of the hedge and my eyes lit upon Mrs. Douglas and the man Barker before they were aware of my presence. Her appearance gave me a shock. In the dining-room she had been demure and discreet. Now all pretense of grief had passed away from her. Her eyes shone with the joy of living, and her face still quivered with amusement at some remark of her companion. He sat forward, his hands clasped and his forearms on his knees, with an answering smile upon his bold, handsome face. In an instant—but it was just one instant too late—they resumed their solemn masks as my figure came into view. A hurried word or two passed between them, and then Barker rose and came towards me.

"Excuse me, sir," said he, "but am I addressing Dr. Watson?"

I bowed with a coldness which showed, I dare say, very plainly the impression which had been produced upon my mind.

"We thought that it was probably you, as your friendship with Mr. Sherlock Holmes is so well known. Would you mind coming over and speaking to Mrs. Douglas for one instant?"

I followed him with a dour face. Very clearly I could see in my mind's eye that shattered figure upon the floor. Here within a few hours of the tragedy were his wife and his nearest friend laughing together behind a bush in the garden which had been his. I greeted the lady with reserve. I had grieved with her grief in the dining-room. Now I met her appealing gaze with an unresponsive eye.

"I fear that you think me callous and hard-hearted," said she.

I shrugged my shoulders.

"It is no business of mine," said I.

"Perhaps some day you will do me justice. If you only realized—"

"There is no need why Dr. Watson should realize," said Barker, quickly. "As he has himself said, it is no possible business of his."

"Exactly," said I, "and so I will beg leave to resume my walk."

"One moment, Dr. Watson," cried the woman, in a pleading voice. "There is one question which you can answer with more authority than anyone else in the world, and it may make a very great difference to me. You know Mr. Holmes and his relations with the police better than anyone else can do. Supposing that a matter were brought confidentially to his knowledge, is it absolutely necessary that he should pass it on to the detectives?"

"Yes, that's it," said Barker, eagerly. "Is he on his own or is he entirely in with them?"

"I really don't know that I should be justified in discussing such a point."

"I beg—I implore that you will, Dr. Watson! I assure you that you will be helping us—helping me greatly if you will guide us on that point."

There was such a ring of sincerity in the woman's voice that for the instant I forgot all about her levity and was moved only to do her will.

"Mr. Holmes is an independent investigator," I said. "He is

"Mr. Holmes is an independent investigator,' I said. 'He is his own master.' "
Frank Wiles, *Strand Magazine*, 1914

his own master, and would act as his own judgment directed. At the same time, he would naturally feel loyalty towards the officials who were working on the same case, and he would not conceal from them anything which would help them in bringing a criminal to justice. Beyond this I can say nothing, and I would refer you to Mr. Holmes himself if you wanted fuller information."

So saying I raised my hat and went upon my way, leaving them still seated behind that concealing hedge. I looked back as I rounded the far end of it, and saw that they were still talking very earnestly together, and, as they were gazing after me, it was clear that it was our interview that was the subject of their debate.

"I wish none of their confidences," said Holmes, when I reported to him what had occurred.[71] He had spent the whole afternoon at the Manor House in consultation with his two colleagues, and returned about five with a ravenous appetite for a high tea which I had ordered for him. "No confidences, Watson; for they are mighty awkward if it comes to an arrest for conspiracy and murder."

"You think it will come to that?"

He was in his most cheerful and *débonnaire* humour. "My dear Watson, when I have exterminated that fourth egg I shall be ready to put you in touch with the whole situation. I don't say that we have fathomed it—far from it—but when we have traced the missing dumb-bell—"

"The dumb-bell!"

"Dear me, Watson, is it possible that you have not penetrated the fact that the case hangs upon the missing dumb-bell? Well, well, you need not be downcast, for between ourselves I don't think that either Inspector Mac or the excellent local practitioner has grasped the overwhelming importance of this incident. One dumb-bell, Watson! Consider an athlete with one dumb-bell, picture to yourself the unilateral development, the imminent danger of a spinal curvature. Shocking, Watson; shocking!"[72]

He sat with his mouth full of toast and his eyes sparkling with mischief, watching my intellectual entanglement. The mere sight of his excellent appetite was an assurance of success, for I had very clear recollections of days and nights without a thought of food, when his baffled mind had chafed before

71 The manuscript of *The Valley of Fear* contains a half-page of dialogue that was omitted from the published version. Its placement is unclear, but it is reproduced here:

> "Mr. Holmes," said Cecil Barker. "Mrs. Douglas and I have determined to put ourselves in your hands and I tell you the exact truth as to what did occur upon the night of January the sixth."
>
> "One moment," said Sherlock Holmes. "You will realise, Mr. Barker, and you also, Mrs. Douglas, that neither Dr. Watson nor I can make any promise as to the use we may make of what you tell us. We ae naturally working with the police and in the interests of Justice."
>
> "We appreciate that, Mr. Holmes. But we have talked it over and we have thought it best to put ourselves in your hands and then you will tell us how we stand with Mr. MacDonald and the police. We will ask no promise from you, and tie your hands in no way."
>
> "Then pray be seated. I should be glad to hear anything that you may have to say. I will not disguise from you

Reproduced in Bruce Kennedy and Robert Watson Douty's *In the Footsteps of Birdy Edwards.*

72 Edward J. Van Liere, in "Sherlock Holmes and Doctor Watson, Perennial Athletes," scoffs at Holmes's conclusion: "The single dumb-bell which worried him could have been used alternately by the right and left hand, and thus unilateral development prevented. Watson, as a medical man, knew this; but like a good soldier he let Holmes have his fun and made no reply."

some problem while his thin, eager features became more attenuated with the asceticism of complete mental concentration. Finally he lit his pipe, and sitting in the ingle-nook[73] of the old village inn, he talked slowly and at random about his case, rather as one who thinks aloud than as one who makes a considered statement.

"A lie, Watson—a great, big, thumping, obtrusive, uncompromising lie—that's what meets us on the threshold! There is our starting point. The whole story told by Barker is a lie. But Barker's story is corroborated by Mrs. Douglas. Therefore she is lying also. They are both lying and in a conspiracy. So now we have the clear problem—why are they lying, and what is the truth which they are trying so hard to conceal? Let us try, Watson, you and I, if we can get behind the lie and reconstruct the truth.

"How do I know that they are lying? Because it is a clumsy fabrication which simply *could* not be true. Consider! According to the story given to us, the assassin had less than a minute after the murder had been committed to take that ring, which was under another ring, from the dead man's finger, to replace the other ring—a thing which he would surely never have done—and to put that singular card beside his victim. I say that this was obviously impossible.

"You may argue—but I have too much respect for your judgment, Watson, to think that you will do so—that the ring may have been taken before the man was killed. The fact that the candle had been lit only a short time shows that there had been no lengthy interview. Was Douglas, from what we hear of his fearless character, a man who would be likely to give up his wedding-ring at such short notice, or could we conceive of his giving it up at all? No, no, Watson, the assassin was alone with the dead man for some time with the lamp lit. Of that I have no doubt at all.

"But the gunshot was apparently the cause of death. Therefore the gunshot must have been fired some time earlier than we are told. But there could be no mistake about such a matter as that. We are in the presence, therefore, of a deliberate conspiracy upon the part of the two people who heard the gunshot—of the man Barker and of the woman Douglas. When on the top of this I am able to show that the blood mark on the windowsill was deliberately placed there by Barker, in order to

73 An alcove next to a large open hearth, usually containing a seat.

74 This is certainly a gentler statement than Holmes's proclamation in *The Sign of Four*: "Woman are never to be entirely trusted—not the best of them."

give a false clue to the police, you will admit that the case grows dark against him.

"Now we have to ask ourselves at what hour the murder actually did occur. Up to half-past ten the servants were moving about the house, so it was certainly not before that time. At a quarter to eleven they had all gone to their rooms with the exception of Ames, who was in the pantry. I have been trying some experiments after you left us this afternoon, and I find that no noise which MacDonald can make in the study can penetrate to me in the pantry when the doors are all shut.

"It is otherwise, however, from the housekeeper's room. It is not so far down the corridor, and from it I could vaguely hear a voice when it was very loudly raised. The sound from a shotgun is to some extent muffled when the discharge is at very close range, as it undoubtedly was in this instance. It would not be very loud, and yet in the silence of the night it should have easily penetrated to Mrs. Allen's room. She is, as she has told us, somewhat deaf; but none the less she mentioned in her evidence that she did hear something like a door slamming half an hour before the alarm was given. Half an hour before the alarm was given would be a quarter to eleven. I have no doubt that what she heard was the report of the gun, and that this was the real instant of the murder.

"If this is so, we have now to determine what Barker and Mrs. Douglas, presuming that they are not the actual murderers, could have been doing from quarter to eleven, when the sound of the shot brought them down, until quarter past eleven, when they rang the bell and summoned the servants. What were they doing, and why did they not instantly give the alarm? That is the question which faces us, and when it has been answered we shall surely have gone some way to solve our problem."

"I am convinced myself," said I, "that there is an understanding between those two people. She must be a heartless creature to sit laughing at some jest within a few hours of her husband's murder."

"Exactly. She does not shine as a wife even in her own account of what occurred. I am not a whole-souled admirer of womankind, as you are aware, Watson,[74] but my experience of life has taught me that there are few wives, having any regard for their husbands, who would let any man's spoken word stand between them and that husband's dead body. Should I ever marry, Watson, I should hope to inspire my wife with some feeling which would prevent her from being walked off by a housekeeper when my corpse was lying within a few yards of her. It was badly stage-managed; for even the rawest investigators must be struck by the absence of the usual feminine ululation. If there had been nothing else, this incident alone would have suggested a prearranged conspiracy to my mind."

"You think then, definitely, that Barker and Mrs. Douglas are guilty of the murder?"

"There is an appalling directness about your questions, Watson," said Holmes, shaking his pipe at me. "They come at me like bullets. If you put it that Mrs. Douglas and Barker know the truth about the murder and are conspiring to conceal it, then I can give you a whole-souled answer. I am sure they do. But your more deadly proposition is not so clear. Let us for a moment consider the difficulties which stand in the way.

"We will suppose that this couple are united by the bonds of a guilty love, and that they have determined to get rid of the man who stands between them. It is a large supposition; for discreet inquiry among servants and others has failed to corroborate it in any way. On the contrary, there is a good deal of evidence that the Douglases were very attached to each other."

"You think, then, definitely, that Barker and Mrs. Douglas are guilty of the murder?' "
Frank Wiles, *Strand Magazine*, 1914

"That, I am sure, cannot be true," said I, thinking of the beautiful smiling face in the garden.

"Well, at least they gave that impression. However, we will suppose that they are an extraordinarily astute couple, who deceive every one upon this point and conspire to murder the husband. He happens to be a man over whose head some danger hangs—"

"We have only their word for that."

Holmes looked thoughtful. "I see, Watson. You are sketching out a theory by which everything they say from the beginning is false. According to your idea, there was never any hidden menace, or secret society, or Valley of Fear, or Boss MacSomebody, or anything else. Well, that is a good sweeping generalization. Let us see what that brings us to. They invent this theory to account for the crime. They then play up to the idea by leaving this bicycle in the park as proof of the existence of some outsider. The stain on the windowsill conveys the same idea. So does the card upon the body, which might have been prepared in the house. That all fits into your hypothesis, Watson. But now we come on the nasty, angular, uncompromising bits which won't slip into their places. Why a cut-off shotgun of all weapons—and an American one at that? How could they be so sure that the sound of it would not bring some one on to them? It's a mere chance, as it is, that Mrs. Allen did not start out to inquire for the slamming door. Why did your guilty couple do all this, Watson?"

"I confess that I can't explain it."

"Then again, if a woman and her lover conspire to murder a husband, are they going to advertise their guilt by ostentatiously removing his wedding-ring after his death? Does that strike you as very probable, Watson?"

"No, it does not."

"And once again, if the thought of leaving a bicycle concealed outside had occurred to you, would it really have seemed worth doing when the dullest detective would naturally say this is an obvious blind, as the bicycle is the first thing which the fugitive needed in order to make his escape."

"I can conceive of no explanation."

"And yet there should be no combination of events for which the wit of man cannot conceive an explanation. Simply as a mental exercise, without any assertion that it is true, let me indicate a possible line of thought. It is, I admit, mere imagination, but how often is imagination the mother of truth?

"We will suppose that there was a guilty secret, a really shameful secret in the life of this man Douglas. This leads to his murder by some one who is, we will suppose, an avenger, some one from outside. This avenger, for some reason which I confess I am still at a loss to explain, took the dead man's wedding ring. The vendetta might conceivably date back to the man's first marriage, and the ring be taken for some such reason.

"Before this avenger got away, Barker and the wife had reached the room. The assassin convinced them that any attempt to arrest him would lead to the publication of some hideous scandal. They were converted to this idea, and preferred to let him go. For this purpose they probably lowered the bridge, which can be done quite noiselessly, and then raised it again. He made his escape, and for some reason thought that he could do so more safely on foot than on the bicycle. He therefore left his machine where it would not be discovered until he had got safely away. So far we are within the bounds of possibility, are we not?"

"Well, it is possible, no doubt," said I, with some reserve.

"We have to remember, Watson, that whatever occurred is certainly something very extraordinary. Well, now, to continue our supposititious case, the couple—not necessarily a guilty couple—realize after the murderer is gone that they have placed themselves in a position in which it may be difficult for them to prove that they did not themselves either do the deed or connive at it. They rapidly and rather clumsily met the situation. The mark was put by Barker's bloodstained slipper upon the window-sill to suggest how the fugitive got away. They obviously were the two who must have heard the sound of the gun, so they gave the alarm exactly as they would have done, but a good half-hour after the event."

"And how do you propose to prove all this?"

"Well, if there were an outsider, he may be traced and taken. That would be the most effective of all proofs. But if not—well, the resources of science are far from being exhausted. I think that an evening alone in that study would help me much."

"An evening alone!"

"I propose to go up there presently. I have arranged it with the estimable Ames, who is by no means whole-hearted about

75 Literally, the "resident spirit" or "spirit of the place." Holmes's attention to the crime scene (about which he jests here) is perhaps his greatest contribution to the forensic sciences.

Barker. I shall sit in that room and see if its atmosphere brings me inspiration. I'm a believer in the *genius loci*.[75] You smile, Friend Watson. Well, we shall see. By the way, you have that big umbrella of yours, have you not?"

"It is here."

"Well, I'll borrow that if I may."

"Certainly—but what a wretched weapon! If there is danger—"

"Nothing serious, my dear Watson, or I should certainly ask for your assistance. But I'll take the umbrella. At present I am only awaiting the return of our colleagues from Tunbridge Wells, where they are at present engaged in trying for a likely owner to the bicycle."

It was nightfall before Inspector MacDonald and White Mason came back from their expedition, and they arrived exultant, reporting a great advance in our investigation.

"Man, I'll admeet that I had my doubts if there was ever an outsider," said MacDonald, "but that's all past now. We've had the bicycle identified, and we have a description of our man; so that's a long step on our journey."

"It sounds to me like the beginning of the end," said Holmes. "I'm sure I congratulate you both with all my heart."

"Well, I started from the fact that Mr. Douglas had seemed disturbed since the day before, when he had been at Tunbridge Wells. It was at Tunbridge Wells then that he had

" 'It sounds to me like the beginning of the end,' said Holmes; 'I'm sure I congratulate you both with all my heart.' "
Frank Wiles, *Strand Magazine*, 1914

become conscious of some danger. It was clear, therefore, that if a man had come over with a bicycle it was from Tunbridge Wells that he might be expected to have come. We took the bicycle over with us and showed it at the hotels. It was identified at once by the manager of the Eagle Commercial as belonging to a man named Hargrave, who had taken a room there two days before. This bicycle and a small valise were his whole belongings. He had registered his name as coming from London, but had given no address. The valise was London-made, and the contents were British, but the man himself was undoubtedly an American."

"Well, well," said Holmes gleefully, "you have indeed done some solid work while I have been sitting spinning theories with my friend! It's a lesson in being practical, Mr. Mac."

"Ay, it's just that, Mr. Holmes," said the inspector with satisfaction.

"But this may all fit in with your theories," I remarked.

"That may or may not be. But let us hear the end, Mr. Mac. Was there nothing to identify this man?"

"So little that it was evident that he had carefully guarded himself against identification. There were no papers or letters, and no marking upon the clothes. A cycle map of the county lay on his bedroom table. He had left the hotel after breakfast yesterday morning on his bicycle, and no more was heard of him until our inquiries."

"That's what puzzles me, Mr. Holmes," said White Mason. "If the fellow did not want the hue and cry raised over him, one would imagine that he would have returned and remained at the hotel as an inoffensive tourist. As it is, he must know that he will be reported to the police by the hotel manager and that his disappearance will be connected with the murder."

"So one would imagine. Still, he has been justified of his wisdom up to date, at any rate, since he has not been taken. But his description—what of that?"

MacDonald referred to his notebook. "Here we have it so far as they could give it. They don't seem to have taken any very particular stock of him; but still the porter, the clerk, and the chambermaid are all agreed that this about covers the points. He was a man about five foot nine in height, fifty or so years of age, his hair slightly grizzled, a grayish moustache, a curved nose, and a face which all of them described as fierce and forbidding."

76 A heavy, double-breasted jacket with a short cut and a close fit. The origin is nautical, as for a garment worn by a midshipman, or one who reefs.

"Well, bar the expression, that might almost be a description of Douglas himself," said Holmes. "He is just over fifty, with grizzled hair and moustache, and about the same height. Did you get anything else?"

"He was dressed in a heavy gray suit with a reefer jacket,[76] and he wore a short yellow overcoat and a soft cap."

"What about the shot-gun?"

"It is less than two feet long. It could very well have fitted into his valise. He could have carried it inside his overcoat without difficulty."

"And how do you consider that all this bears upon the general case?"

"Well, Mr. Holmes," said MacDonald. "when we have got our man—and you may be sure that I had his description on the wires within five minutes of hearing it—we shall be better able to judge. But, even as it stands, we have surely gone a long way. We know that an American calling himself Hargrave came to Tunbridge Wells two days ago with bicycle and valise. In the latter was a sawed-off shot-gun; so he came with the deliberate purpose of crime. Yesterday morning he set off for this place on his bicycle, with his gun concealed in his overcoat. No one saw him arrive, so far as we can learn, but he need not pass through the village to reach the park gates, and there are many cyclists upon the road. Presumably he at once concealed his cycle among the laurels, where it was found, and possibly lurked there himself with his eye on the house, waiting for Mr. Douglas to come out. The shot-gun is a strange weapon to use inside a house; but he had intended to use it outside, and there it has very obvious advantages, as it would be impossible to miss with it, and the sound of shots is so common in an English sporting neighbourhood that no particular notice would be taken."

"That is all very clear," said Holmes.

"Well, Mr. Douglas did not appear. What was he to do next? He left his bicycle and approached the house in the twilight. He found the bridge down and no one about. He took his chance, intending, no doubt, to make some excuse if he met anyone. He met no one. He slipped into the first room that he saw, and concealed himself behind the curtain. Thence he could see the drawbridge go up, and he knew that his only escape was through the moat. He waited until quarter-past eleven, when Mr. Douglas, upon his usual nightly round, came into the room. He shot him and escaped, as arranged. He was aware that the bicycle would be described by the hotel people and be a clue against him, so he left it there and made his way by some other means to London or to some safe hiding place which he had already arranged. How is that, Mr. Holmes?"

"Well, Mr. Mac, it is very good and very clear so far as it goes. That is your end of the story. My end is that the crime was committed half an hour earlier than reported; that Mrs. Douglas and Mr. Barker are both in a conspiracy to conceal something; that they aided the murderer's escape—or at least, that they reached the room before he escaped—and that they fabricated evidence of his escape through the window, whereas in all probability they had themselves let him go by lowering the bridge. That's *my* reading of the first half."

The two detectives shook their heads.

"Well, Mr. Holmes, if this is true, we only tumble out of one mystery into another," said the London inspector.

"And in some ways a worse one," added White Mason. "The lady has never been in America in all her life. What possible connection could she have with an American assassin which would cause her to shelter him?"

"I freely admit the difficulties," said Holmes. "I propose to make a little investigation of my own to-night, and it is just possible that it may contribute something to the common cause."

"Can we help you, Mr. Holmes?"

"No, no! Darkness and Dr. Watson's umbrella—my wants are simple. And Ames—the faithful Ames—no doubt he will stretch a point for me. All my lines of thought lead me back invariably to the one basic question—why should an athletic man develop his frame upon so unnatural an instrument as a single dumb-bell?"

It was late that night when Holmes returned from his solitary excursion. We slept in a double-bedded room, which was the best that the little country inn could do for us. I was already asleep when I was partly awakened by his entrance.

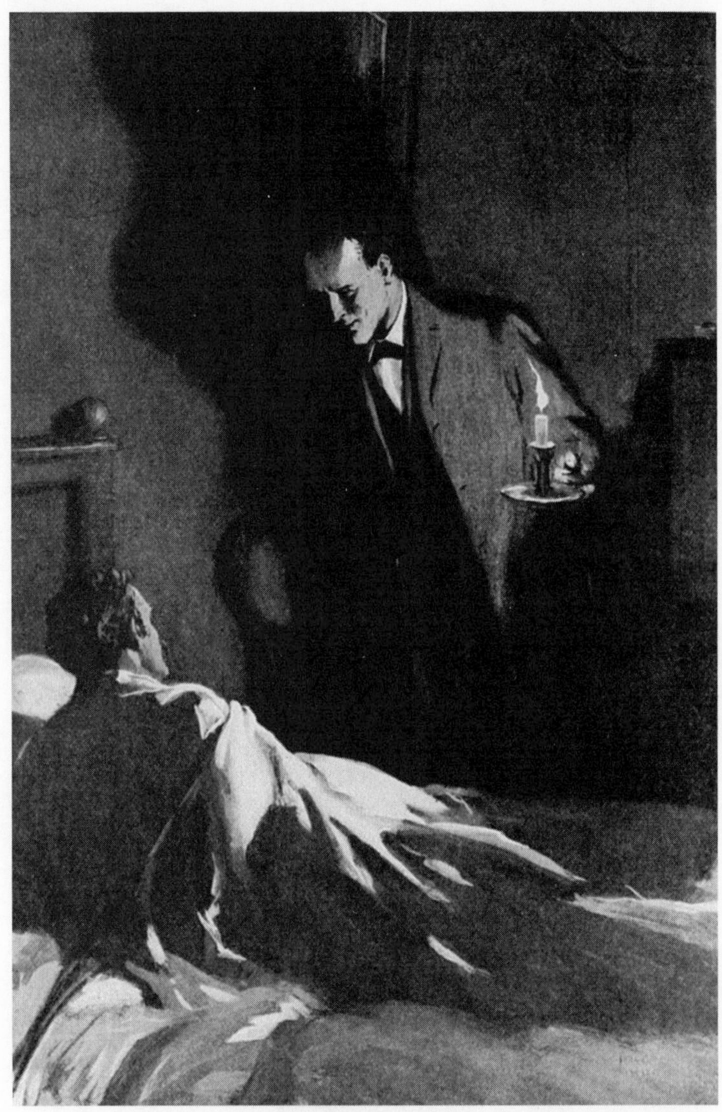

" 'Well, Holmes,' I murmured, 'have you found out anything?' "
Frank Wiles, *Strand Magazine*, 1914

"Well, Holmes," I murmured, "have you found anything out?"

He stood beside me in silence, his candle in his hand. Then the tall, lean figure inclined towards me. "I say, Watson," he whispered, "would you be afraid to sleep in the same room as a lunatic, a man with softening of the brain, an idiot whose mind has lost its grip?"

"Not in the least," I answered in astonishment.

"Ah, that's lucky," he said, and not another word would he utter that night.[77]

" 'Watson, would you be afraid to sleep in the same room with a lunatic?' "
Arthur I. Keller, *Associated Sunday Magazines*, 1914

77 Holmes is here apparently chiding himself, along the lines of his self-chastisement in "The Man with the Twisted Lip." But for what error in judgement?

CHAPTER VII

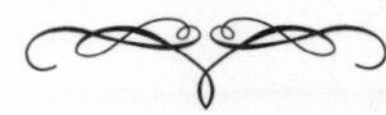

The Solution

NEXT MORNING, AFTER breakfast, we found Inspector MacDonald and Mr. White Mason seated in close consultation in the small parlour of the local police sergeant. On the table in front of them were piled a number of letters and telegrams, which they were carefully sorting and docketing. Three had been placed upon one side.

"Still on the track of the elusive bicyclist?" Holmes asked cheerfully. "What is the latest news of the ruffian?"

MacDonald pointed ruefully to his heap of correspondence.

"He is at present reported from Leicester, Nottingham, Southampton, Derby, East Ham, Richmond, and fourteen other places. In three of them—East Ham, Leicester, and Liverpool—there is a clear case against him, and he has actually been arrested. The country seems to be full of the fugitives with yellow coats."

"Dear me!" said Holmes sympathetically. "Now, Mr. Mac, and you, Mr. White Mason, I wish to give you a very earnest piece of advice. When I went into this case with you I bargained, as you will no doubt remember, that I should not present you with half-proved theories, but that I should retain and work out my own ideas until I had satisfied myself that they were correct. For this reason I am not at the present moment telling you all that is in my mind. On the other hand, I said that I would play the game fairly by you, and I do not think it is a fair game to allow you for one unnecessary moment to waste your energies upon a profitless task. Therefore I am here to advise you this morning, and my advice to you is summed up in three words: Abandon the case."

MacDonald and White Mason stared in amazement at their celebrated colleague.

"You consider it hopeless!" cried the Inspector.

"I consider *your* case to be hopeless. I do not consider that it is hopeless to arrive at the truth."

"But this cyclist. He is not an invention. We have his description, his valise, his bicycle. The fellow must be somewhere. Why should we not get him?"

"Yes, yes; no doubt he is somewhere, and no doubt we shall get him, but I would not have you waste your energies in East Ham or Liverpool. I am sure that we can find some shorter cut to a result."

"You are holding something back. It's hardly fair of you, Mr. Holmes." The Inspector was annoyed.

"You know my methods of work, Mr. Mac. But I will hold it back for the shortest time possible. I only wish to verify my details in one way, which can very readily be done, and then I make my bow and return to London, leaving my results entirely at your service. I owe you too much to act otherwise; for in all my experience I cannot recall any more singular and interesting study."

"This is clean beyond me, Mr. Holmes. We saw you when we returned from Tunbridge Wells last night, and you were in general agreement with our results. What has happened since then to give you a completely new idea of the case?"

"Well, since you ask me, I spent, as I told you that I would, some hours last night at the Manor House."

"Well, what happened?"

"Ah, I can only give you a very general answer to that for the moment. By the way, I have been reading a short but clear and interesting account of the old building, purchasable at the modest sum of one penny from the local tobacconist."

Here Holmes drew a small tract,[78] embellished with a rude

78 James Montgomery, in *A Case of Identity*, identifies the pamphlet as *St. John the Evangelist, Groombridge, Kent*, by B. W. Shepherd-Walwyn, purchasable in 1955 from the local tobacconist for sixpence.

engraving of the ancient Manor House, from his waistcoat pocket.

"It immensely adds to the zest of an investigation, my dear Mr. Mac, when one is in conscious sympathy with the historical atmosphere of one's surroundings. Don't look so impatient, for I assure you that even so bald an account as this raises some sort of picture of the past in one's mind. Permit me to give you a sample. 'Erected in the fifth year of the reign of James I, and standing upon the site of a much older building, the Manor House of Birlstone presents one of the finest surviving examples of the moated Jacobean residence—' "

"You are making fools of us, Mr. Holmes!"

"Tut, tut, Mr. Mac!—the first sign of temper I have detected in you. Well, I won't read it verbatim, since you feel so strongly upon the subject. But when I tell you that there is some account of the taking of the place by a parliamentary colonel in 1644, of the concealment of Charles for several days in the course of the Civil War,[79] and finally of a visit there by the second George,[80] you will admit that there are various associations of interest connected with this ancient house."

"I don't doubt it, Mr. Holmes; but that is no business of ours."

"Is it not? Is it not? Breadth of view, my dear Mr. Mac, is one of the essentials of our profession. The interplay of ideas and the oblique uses of knowledge are often of extraordinary interest.[81] You will excuse these remarks from one who, though a mere connoisseur of crime, is still rather older and perhaps more experienced than yourself."

"I'm the first to admit that," said the detective heartily. "You get to your point, I admit; but you have such a deuced round-the-corner way of doing it."

"Well, well, I'll drop past history and get down to present-day facts. I called last night, as I have already said, at the Manor House. I did not see either Barker or Mrs. Douglas. I saw no necessity to disturb them; but I was pleased to hear that the lady was not visibly pining and that she had partaken of an excellent dinner. My visit was specially made to the good Mr. Ames, with whom I exchanged some amiabilities, which culminated in his allowing me, without reference to anyone else, to sit alone for a time in the study."

"What! With that?" I ejaculated.

79 Charles I's stormy relationship with Parliament led to two civil wars, in 1642–1646 and 1648. In 1644, Charles was soundly defeated by parliamentary forces at Marston Moor, a loss that helped turn the tide of the war against the royalists, undoubtedly leading the "parliamentary colonel" to feel justified in seizing whatever property he may have needed.

Toward the end of his reign, Charles's military and political difficulties gave him plenty of reasons to require protection. He surrendered to the Scots in 1646 and was handed over to Parliament, but escaped in 1647 and took refuge on the Isle of Wight. Re-enlisting the aid of the Scots, Charles returned to battle almost immediately; but his forces were overwhelmed, and the second civil war was quickly over. Charles was beheaded in 1649. See also *A Study in Scarlet*, note 149.

80 George II (1683–1760) was king of Great Britain and Ireland from 1727 to 1760. Passionate about military affairs, he was the last British monarch to appear personally on the battlefield, doing so at Dettingen in 1743 during the War of Austrian Succession.

81 "We see in *The Lion's Mane* an example of how Holmes could bring his out-of-the-way knowledge to bear on a problem," comments T. S. Blakeney, in his seminal work *Sherlock Holmes: Fact or Fiction?* (1932), "and he has a number of interesting remarks on this point in *The Five Orange Pips*." In "The Lion's Mane," Holmes's recollection of a pamphlet on *Cyanea capillata*, a rare form of jellyfish, provides the solution to a mysterious death; in "The Five Orange Pips," Holmes's immediate recognition of "K.K.K." as related to the Ku Klux Klan (no mean feat for an Englishman in 1891, when the story was published) proves critical to finding the culprits.

"No, no, everything is now in order. You gave permission for that, Mr. Mac, as I am informed. The room was in its normal state, and in it I passed an instructive quarter of an hour."

"What were you doing?"

"Well, not to make a mystery of so simple a matter, I was looking for the missing dumb-bell. It has always bulked rather large in my estimate of the case. I ended by finding it."

"Where?"

"Ah, there we come to the edge of the unexplored. Let me go a little further, a very little further, and I will promise that you shall share everything that I know."

"Well, we're bound to take you on your own terms," said the Inspector; "But when it comes to telling us to abandon the case—why in the name of goodness should we abandon the case?"

"For the simple reason, my dear Mr. Mac, that you have not got the first idea what it is that you are investigating."

"We are investigating the murder of Mr. John Douglas, of Birlstone Manor."

"Yes, yes; so you are. But don't trouble to trace the mysterious gentleman upon the bicycle. I assure you that it won't help you."

"Then what do you suggest that we do?"

"I will tell you exactly what to do, if you will do it."

"Well, I'm bound to say I've always found you had reason behind an your queer ways. I'll do what you advise."

"And you, Mr. White Mason?"

The country detective looked helplessly from one to the other. Holmes and his methods were new to him. "Well, if it is good enough for the Inspector, it is good enough for me," he said at last.

"Capital!" said Holmes. "Well, then, I should recommend a nice, cheery country walk for both of you. They tell me that the views from Birlstone Ridge over the Weald are very remarkable. No doubt lunch could be got at some suitable hostelry; though my ignorance of the country prevents me from recommending one. In the evening, tired but happy—"

"Man, this is getting past a joke!" cried MacDonald, rising angrily from his chair.

"Well, well, spend the day as you like," said Holmes, patting him cheerfully upon the shoulder. "Do what you like and go where you will, but meet me here before dusk without fail—without fail, Mr. Mac."

"That sounds more like sanity."

"All of it was excellent advice; but I don't insist, so long as you are here when I need you. But now, before we part, I want you to write a note to Mr. Barker."

"Well?"

"I'll dictate it if you like. Ready?

" 'DEAR SIR,—It has struck me that it is our duty to drain the moat, in the hope that we may find some—' "

"It's impossible," said the Inspector. "I've made inquiry."

"Tut, tut! My dear sir! Do what I ask you."

"Well, go on."

" '—in the hope that we may find something which may bear upon our investigation. I have made arrangements, and the workmen will be at work early to-morrow morning diverting the stream—' "

"Impossible!"

" '—diverting the stream; so I thought it best to explain matters before-hand.' Now sign that, and send it by hand about four o'clock. At that hour we shall meet again in this room. Until then we may each do what we like; for I can assure you that this inquiry has come to a definite pause."[82]

Evening was drawing in when we reassembled. Holmes was very serious in his manner, myself curious, and the detectives obviously critical and annoyed.

"Well, gentlemen," said my friend gravely, "I am asking you now to put everything to the test with me, and you will judge for yourselves whether the observations I have made justify the conclusions to which I have come. It is a chill evening, and I do not know how long our expedition may last; so I beg that you will wear your warmest coats. It is of the first importance that we should be in our places before it grows dark; so with your permission we shall get started at once."

We passed along the outer bounds of the Manor House park until we came to a place where there was a gap in the rails which fenced it. Through this we slipped, and then in the gathering gloom we followed Holmes until we had reached a shrubbery which lies nearly opposite to the main door and the drawbridge. The latter had not been raised. Holmes crouched

82 This ends the portion published in the December 1914 issue of the *Strand Magazine*. The balance of the chapter appeared in the January 1915 issue and was headed by the following summary:

> The opening chapters of this new and thrilling adventure of Sherlock Holmes described the receipt by Holmes of a cipher message, from which he deduces that some devilry is intended against a man named Douglas, a rich country gentleman living at the Manor House, Birlstone, in Sussex, and that the danger is a pressing one. Almost as soon as he has deciphered the message he is visited by Inspector MacDonald, of Scotland Yard, who brings the news that Mr. Douglas has been murdered that morning [*sic*].
>
> Holmes, Dr. Watson, and the inspector proceed to the scene of the tragedy, where they are met by Mr. White Mason, the chief Sussex detective. The murdered man had been horribly injured, while lying across his chest was a curious weapon—a shot-gun with the barrel sawn off a foot in front of the triggers. Near him was found a card with the initials "V. V." and the number "341" scrawled on it in ink, and about half-way up the forearm was a curious design—a branded triangle inside a circle. His wedding-ring had been removed and the ring above it replaced.
>
> There is no clue to the murderer except a bloody footprint on the window-sill, and he had apparently made his escape by wading across the moat. Holmes is much struck by the fact that one of Douglas's dumb-bells is missing.
>
> Cecil Barker, Douglas's most intimate friend, is considerably flustered while being cross-examined by the detectives, and confesses that Douglas had been jealous on account of his attentions to Mrs.

down behind the screen of laurels, and we all three followed his example.

"Well, what are we to do now?" asked MacDonald with some gruffness.

"Possess our souls in patience[83] and make as little noise as possible," Holmes answered.

"What are we here for at all? I really think that you might treat us with more frankness."

Holmes laughed. "Watson insists that I am the dramatist in real life," said he. "Some touch of the artist wells up within me, and calls insistently for a well staged performance.[84] Surely our profession, Mr. Mac, would be a drab and sordid one if we did not sometimes set the scene so as to glorify our results. The blunt accusation, the brutal tap upon the shoulder—what can one make of such a *dénouement*? But the quick inference, the subtle trap, the clever forecast of coming events, the triumphant vindication of bold theories—are these not the pride and the justification of our life's work?[85] At the present moment you thrill with the glamour of the situation and the anticipation of the hunter. Where would be that thrill if I had been as definite as a time-table? I only ask a little patience, Mr. Mac, and all will be clear to you."

"Well, I hope the pride and justification and the rest of it will come before we all get our death of cold," said the London detective with comic resignation.

We all had good reason to join in the aspiration; for our vigil was a long and bitter one. Slowly the shadows darkened over the long, sombre face of the old house. A cold, damp reek from the moat chilled us to the bones and set our teeth chattering. There was a single lamp over the gateway and a steady globe of light in the fatal study. Everything else was dark and still.

"How long is this to last?" asked the Inspector suddenly. "And what is it we are watching for?"

"I have no more notion than you how long it is to last," Holmes answered with some asperity. "If criminals would always schedule their movements like railway trains, it would certainly be more convenient for all of us. As to what it is we—Well, *that's* what we are watching for!"

As he spoke the bright, yellow light in the study was obscured by somebody passing to and fro before it. The laurels

Douglas. Holmes ascertains from Ames, the butler, that on the previous evening Barker was wearing a pair of bedroom slippers which were stained with blood, and on comparing them with the footprints on the window-sill finds that they correspond.

Holmes gives Watson his reasons for believing that Mrs. Douglas and Barker know all about the murder. He advises the other detectives to abandon the case and asks them to meet him that same evening when he promises they shall share everything he knows. The last instalment ends with the dispatch, at Holmes's suggestion, of the following letter to Barker:—

"It has struck me that it is our duty to drain the moat, in the hope that we may find something which may bear upon our investigation. I have made arrangements, and the workmen will be at work early tomorrow morning diverting the stream, so I thought it best to explain matters beforehand."

83 "In your patience possess ye your souls."—Luke, 21:19. Holmes offers the same advice to Watson in "Wisteria Lodge" and "The Three Garridebs." Patience is an important component of Holmes's method: In "The Sussex Vampire," he explains that "[o]ne forms provisional theories and waits for time or fuller knowledge to explode them."

84 This tendency, exhibited in frequent dramatic *denouements* (for example, "The Naval Treaty") and intricate disguises (for example, the Nonconformist clergymen of "A Scandal in Bohemia") may have led Inspector Athelney Jones to remark, in *The Sign of Four* "You would have made an actor and a rare one." Holmes himself notes, in "The Mazarin Stone," that " 'Old Baron Dowson said the night before he was hanged that in my case what the law had gained the stage had lost.' "

85 T. S. Blakeney remarks, "This art was one of Holmes's strongest assets as a detective—[in *The Hound of the Baskervilles*,] he called it the scientific use of the imagination, 'the region where we balance probabilities and choose the most likely.' "

"Then suddenly he hauled something in as a fisherman lands a fish."
Frank Wiles, *Strand Magazine*, 1915

among which we lay were immediately opposite the window and not more than a hundred feet from it. Presently it was thrown open with a whining of hinges, and we could dimly see the dark outline of a man's head and shoulders looking out into the gloom. For some minutes he peered forth in furtive, stealthy fashion, as one who wishes to be assured that he is unobserved. Then he leaned forward, and in the intense silence we were aware of the soft lapping of agitated water. He seemed to be stirring up the moat with something which he had in his hand. Then suddenly he hauled something in as a fisherman lands a fish—some large, round object which obscured the light as it was dragged through the open casement.

"Now!" cried Holmes. "Now!"

We were all upon our feet, staggering after him with our stiffened limbs, while he ran swiftly across the bridge and rang violently at the bell. There was the rasping of bolts from the other side, and the amazed Ames stood in the entrance. Holmes brushed him aside without a word and, followed by all of us, rushed into the room which had been occupied by the man whom we had been watching.

The oil lamp on the table represented the glow which we had seen from outside. It was now in the hand of Cecil Barker, who held it towards us as we entered. Its light shone upon his strong, resolute, clean-shaved face and his menacing eyes.

"What the devil is the meaning of all this?" he cried. "What are you after, anyhow?"

Holmes took a swift glance round, and then pounced upon a sodden bundle tied together with cord which lay where it had been thrust under the writing table.

"This is what we are after, Mr. Barker—this bundle, weighted with a dumb-bell, which you have just raised from the bottom of the moat."

Barker stared at Holmes with amazement in his face. "How in thunder came you to know anything about it?" he asked.

"Simply that I put it there."

"You put it there! You!"

"Perhaps I should have said 'replaced it there,' " said Holmes. "You will remember, Inspector MacDonald, that I was somewhat struck by the absence of a dumb-bell. I drew your attention to it, but with the pressure of other events you had hardly the time to give it the consideration which would have enabled you to draw deductions from it. When water is near and a weight is missing it is not a very far-

Oil lamp.

fetched supposition that something has been sunk in the water. The idea was at least worth testing; so with the help of Ames, who admitted me to the room, and the crook of Dr. Watson's umbrella, I was able last night to fish up and inspect this bundle.

"It was of the first importance, however, that we should be able to prove who placed it there. This we accomplished by the very obvious device of announcing that the moat would be dried to-morrow, which had, of course, the effect that whoever had hidden the bundle would most certainly withdraw it the moment that darkness enabled him to do so. We have no less than four witnesses as to who it was who took advantage of the opportunity, and so, Mr. Barker, I think the word lies now with you."

Sherlock Holmes put the sopping bundle upon the table beside the lamp and undid the cord which bound it. From within he extracted a dumb-bell, which he tossed down to its fellow in the corner. Next he drew forth a pair of boots. "American, as you perceive," he remarked, pointing to the toes. Then he laid upon the table a long, deadly, sheathed knife. Finally he unravelled a bundle of clothing, comprising a complete set of underclothes, socks, a gray tweed suit, and a short yellow overcoat.

"The clothes are commonplace," remarked Holmes, "save only the overcoat which is full of suggestive touches." He held it tenderly towards the light. "Here, as you perceive, is the inner pocket prolonged into the lining in such fashion as to give ample space for the truncated fowling-piece.[86] The tailor's tab is on the neck—'Neal, Outfitter, Vermissa,[87] U.S.A.' I have spent an instructive afternoon in the rector's library, and have enlarged my knowledge by adding the fact that Vermissa is a flourishing little town at the head of one of the best known coal and iron valleys in the United States. I have some recollection, Mr. Barker, that you associated the coal districts with Mr. Douglas's first wife, and it would surely not be too far-fetched an inference that the V. V. upon the card by the dead body might stand for Vermissa Valley,[88] or that this very valley which sends forth emissaries of murder may be that Valley of Fear of which we have heard. So much is fairly clear. And now, Mr. Barker, I seem to be standing rather in the way of your explanation."

It was a sight to see Cecil Barker's expressive face during this exposition of the great detective. Anger, amazement, con-

86 Kelvin Jones identifies this as the shotgun, "so named because these guns were used to shoot wild fowl."

87 "Vermissa" is generally thought to be Pottsville, Pennsylvania, near Schuylkill, where anthracite, or hard coal, was mined. The locations of the events in the "Vermissa Valley" are discussed in detail in Part II, Chapter I.

88 A fictitious name, as will be seen.

sternation, and indecision swept over it in turn. Finally he took refuge in a somewhat acrid irony.

"You know such a lot, Mr. Holmes, perhaps you had better tell us some more," he sneered.

"I have no doubt that I could tell you a great deal more, Mr. Barker; but it would come with a better grace from you."

"Oh, you think so, do you? Well, all I can say is that if there's any secret here it is not my secret, and I am not the man to give it away."

"Well, if you take that line, Mr. Barker," said the inspector quietly, "we must just keep you in sight until we have the warrant and can hold you."

"You can do what you damn please about that," said Barker defiantly.

The proceedings seemed to have come to a definite end so far as he was concerned; for one had only to look at that granite face to realize that no *peine forte et dure*[89] would ever force him to plead against his will. The deadlock was broken, however, by a woman's voice. Mrs. Douglas had been standing listening at the half opened door, and now she entered the room.

"You have done enough for us, Cecil," said she. "Whatever comes of it in the future, you have done enough."

"Enough and more than enough," remarked Sherlock Holmes gravely. "I have every sympathy with you, madam, and I should strongly urge you to have some confidence in the common sense of our jurisdiction and to take the police voluntarily into your complete confidence. It may be that I am myself at fault for not following up the hint which you conveyed to me through my friend, Dr. Watson, but at that time I had every reason to believe that you were directly concerned in the crime. Now I am assured that this is not so. At the same time, there is much that is unexplained, and I should strongly recommend that you ask *Mr. Douglas* to tell us his own story."

Mrs. Douglas gave a cry of astonishment at Holmes's words. The detectives and I must have echoed it when we were aware of a man who seemed to have emerged from the wall, who advanced now from the gloom of the corner in which he had appeared. Mrs. Douglas turned, and in an instant her arms were round him. Barker had seized his outstretched hand.

"It's best this way, Jack," his wife repeated; "I am sure that it is best."

89 French for "intense and severe punishment," or a form of torture used against prisoners, arraigned of felonies, who refused either to enter a plea or to submit testimony (known as "standing mute"). Instituted during the reign of Henry IV (1399–1413), the *peine forte et dure* saw the uncooperative prisoner stretched out upon his back; heavy weights were then placed upon his person until he either entered a plea or died. The practice was often referred to as "pressing."

The Newgate Calendar, Volume I, recounts the death in this manner of one Major George Strangwayes. Accused of killing his brother-in-law, Strangwayes admitted to having orchestrated the murder but not to having committed it. Beyond that, he would not discuss the details of the case, nor would he enter a plea, as he hoped to prevent the seizure of his property by the court. When the entreaties of the court proved useless, the chief justice ordered that Strangwayes be "put into a mean room, where no light can enter; that he be laid upon his back, with his body bare, save something to cover his privy parts; that his arms be stretched forth with a cord, one to one side of the prison, and the other to the other side of the prison, and in like manner his legs shall be used; that upon his body be laid as much iron and stone as he can bear, and more . . . and this shall be his punishment till he dies." His friends were given the task of putting the weights on him, and after seeing "the agonies he was put into, and hear[ing] his loud and doleful groans," they added the weight of their own bodies so as to hasten his death and end his suffering.

The last instance of pressing to death occurred at the Cambridge assizes in 1741, and the torture was abolished in 1772, when a refusal to plead either guilty or not guilty to a felony was deemed equivalent to a conviction. In 1828, that law was changed, with any such refusal being construed to imply a plea of not guilty.

"Mrs. Douglas turned, and in an instant her arms were round him. Barker had seized his outstretched hand."
Frank Wiles, *Strand Magazine*, 1915

"Indeed, yes, Mr. Douglas," said Sherlock Holmes, "I am sure that you will find it best."

The man stood blinking at us with the dazed look of one who comes from the dark into the light. It was a remarkable face, bold gray eyes, a strong, short-clipped, grizzled moustache, a square, projecting chin, and a humorous mouth. He took a good look at us all, and then to my amazement he advanced to me and handed me a bundle of paper.

"I've heard of you," said he in a voice which was not quite English and not quite American, but was altogether mellow and pleasing. "You are the historian of this bunch. Well, Dr. Watson, you've never had such a story as that pass through your hands before, and I'll lay my last dollar on that. Tell it your own way, but there are the facts, and you can't miss the public so long as you have those. I've been cooped up two days, and I've spent the daylight hours—as much daylight as I could get in that rat-trap—in putting the thing into words. You're welcome to them—you and your public. There's the story of the Valley of Fear."

"That's the past, Mr. Douglas," said Sherlock Holmes quietly. "What we desire now is to hear your story of the present."

"You'll have it, sir," said Douglas. "May I smoke as I talk? Well, thank you, Mr. Holmes. You're a smoker yourself, if I remember right, and you'll guess what it is to be sitting for two days with tobacco in your pocket and afraid that the smell will give you away." He leaned against the mantelpiece and sucked at the cigar which Holmes had handed him. "I've heard of you, Mr. Holmes, I never guessed that I should meet you. But before you are through with that," he nodded at my papers, "you will say I've brought you something fresh."

Inspector MacDonald had been staring at the newcomer with the greatest amazement. "Well, this fairly beats me!" he cried at last. "If you are Mr. John Douglas of Birlstone Manor, then whose death have we been investigating for these two days, and where in the world have you sprung from now? You seemed to me to come out of the floor like a Jack-in-a-box."

"Ah, Mr. Mac," said Holmes, shaking a reproving forefinger, "you would not read that excellent local compilation which described the concealment of King Charles. People did not hide in those days without excellent hiding places, and the hiding place that has once been used may be again. I had persuaded myself that we should find Mr. Douglas under this roof."

"And how long have you been playing this trick upon us, Mr. Holmes?" said the inspector angrily. "How long have you allowed us to waste ourselves upon a search that you knew to be an absurd one?"

"Not one instant, my dear Mr. Mac. Only last night did I form my views of the case. As they could not be put to the proof until this evening, I invited you and your colleague to take a holiday for the day. Pray what more could I do? When I found the suit of clothes in the moat, it at once became apparent to me that the body we had found could not have been the body of Mr. John Douglas at all, but must be that of the bicyclist from Tunbridge Wells. No other conclusion was possible. Therefore I had to determine where Mr. John Douglas himself could be, and the balance of probability was that with the connivance of his wife and his friend he was concealed in a house which had such conveniences for a fugitive, and awaiting quieter times when he could make his final escape."

"Well, you figured it out about right," said Douglas approvingly. "I thought I'd dodge your British law; for I was not sure how I stood under it, and also I saw my chance to throw these hounds once for all off my track. Mind you, from first to last I have done nothing to be ashamed of, and nothing that I would not do again; but you'll judge that for yourselves when I tell you my story. Never mind warning me, Inspector: I'm ready to stand pat upon the truth.[90]

"I'm not going to begin at the beginning. That's all there"—he indicated my bundle of papers—"and a mighty queer yarn you'll find it. It all comes down to this: That there are some men that have good cause to hate me and would give their last dollar to know that they had got me. So long as I am alive and they are alive, there is no safety in this world for me. They hunted me from Chicago to California; then they chased me out of America; but when I married and settled down in this quiet spot I thought my last years were going to be peaceable.

"I never explained to my wife how things were. Why should I pull her into it? She would never have a quiet moment again, but would always be imagining trouble. I fancy she knew something, for I may have dropped a word here or a word there—but until yesterday, after you gentlemen had seen her, she never knew the rights of the matter. She told you all she knew, and so did Barker here, for on the night when this thing happened there was mighty little time for explanations. She knows everything now, and I would have been a wiser man if I had told her sooner. But it was a hard question, dear," he took her hand for an instant in his own, "and I acted for the best.

"Well, gentlemen, the day before these happenings I was over in Tunbridge Wells, and I got a glimpse of a man in the street. It was only a glimpse; but I have a quick eye for these things, and I never doubted who it was. It was the worst enemy

90 Douglas refers here to the provisions of British law that have long required the police to warn prisoners, before receiving their confessions, that what they say may be held against them—much as police officers in the United States must issue "Miranda" warnings. See "The Dancing Men" for another example of such warnings being given.

I had among them all—one who has been after me like a hungry wolf after a caribou all these years. I knew there was trouble coming, and I came home and made ready for it. I guessed I'd fight through it all right on my own. There was a time when my luck was the talk of the whole United States. I never doubted that it would be with me still.

"I was on my guard all that next day, and never went out into the park. It's as well, or he'd have had the drop on me with that buckshot gun of his before ever I could draw on him. After the bridge was up—my mind was always more restful when that bridge was up in the evenings—I put the thing clear out of my head. I never dreamed of his getting into the house and waiting for me. But when I made my round in my dressing gown, as my habit was, I had no sooner entered the study than I scented danger. I guess when a man has had dangers in his life—and I've had more than most in my time—there is a kind of sixth sense that waves the red flag. I saw the signal clear enough, and yet I couldn't tell you why. Next instant I spotted a boot under the window curtain, and then I saw why plain enough.

"I'd just the one candle that was in my hand, but there was a good light from the hall lamp through the open door. I put down the candle and jumped for a hammer that I'd left on the mantel. At the same moment he sprang at me. I saw the glint of a knife, and I lashed at him with the hammer. I got him somewhere, for the knife tinkled down on the floor. He dodged round the table as quick as an eel, and a moment later he'd got his gun from under his coat. I heard him cock it, but I had got hold of it before he could fire. I had it by the barrel, and we wrestled for it all ends up for a minute or more. It was death to the man that lost his grip.

"He never lost his grip, but he got it butt downward for a moment too long. Maybe it was I that pulled the trigger. Maybe we just jolted it off between us. Anyhow, he got both barrels in the face, and there I was, staring down at all that was left of Ted Baldwin. I'd recognized him in the township, and again when he sprang for me; but his own mother wouldn't recognize him as I saw him then. I'm used to rough work; but I fairly turned sick at the sight of him.

"I was hanging on the side of the table when Barker came hurrying down. I heard my wife coming, and I ran to the door

91 Douglas's clothes must have been soaked with blood and gore as a result of his dressing the corpse; yet Holmes made no comment, and Watson made no note of it. Ian McQueen offers this explanation: Douglas's clothing remained unsoiled because he committed pre-meditated murder and was not acting in self-defence. After overpowering Baldwin, Douglas saw an opportunity to rid himself of his pursuers. He demanded at gunpoint that Baldwin change clothes with him, and then, with Barker's help, he killed him.

"I heard him cock the gun, but I had got hold of it before he could fire."
Frank Wiles, *Strand Magazine*, 1915

and stopped her. It was no sight for a woman. I promised I'd come to her soon. I said a word or two to Barker—he took it all in at a glance—and we waited for the rest to come along. But there was no sign of them. Then we understood that they could hear nothing, and that all that had happened was known only to ourselves.[91]

"It was at that instant that the idea came to me. I was fairly dazzled by the brilliance of it. The man's sleeve had slipped up and there was the branded mark of the lodge upon his forearm. See here!"

The man whom we had known as Douglas turned up his own coat and cuff to show a brown triangle within a circle exactly like that which we had seen upon the dead man.

"It was the sight of that which started me on it. I seemed to see it all clear at a glance. There were his height and hair and figure, about the same as my own. No one could swear to his face, poor devil! I brought down this suit of clothes, and in a quarter of an hour Barker and I had put my dressing gown on him and he lay as you found him. We tied all his things into a bundle, and I weighted them with the only weight I could find and put them through the window. The card he had meant to lay upon my body was lying beside his own.

"My rings were put on his finger; but when it came to the wedding-ring"—he held out his muscular hand—"you can see for yourselves that, I had struck the limit. I have not moved it since the day I was married, and it would have taken a file to get it off. I don't know, anyhow, that I should have cared to part with it; but if I had wanted to I couldn't. So we just had to leave that detail to take care of itself. On the other hand, I brought a bit of plaster down and put it where I am wearing one myself at this instant. You slipped up there, Mr. Holmes, clever as you are; for if you had chanced to take off that plaster you would have found no cut underneath it.[92]

"Well, that was the situation. If I could lie low for a while and then get away where I could be joined by my wife, we should have a chance at last of living in peace for the rest of our lives. These devils would give me no rest so long as I was above ground, but if they saw in the papers that Baldwin had got his man, there would be an end of all my troubles. I hadn't much time to make it all clear to Barker and to my wife, but they understood enough to be able to help me. I knew all about this hiding place, so did Ames; but it never entered his head to connect it with the matter. I retired into it, and it was up to Barker to do the rest.

"I guess you can fill in for yourselves what he did. He opened the window and made the mark on the sill to give an idea of how the murderer escaped. It was a tall order, that, but as the bridge was up there was no other way. Then, when everything was fixed, he rang the bell for all he was worth. What happened afterward you know. And so, gentlemen, you can do what you please; but I've told you the truth and the whole truth, so help me God! What I ask you now is how do I stand by the English law?"

There was a silence, which was broken by Sherlock Holmes.

92 McQueen also points out that unless Douglas deliberately dirtied the piece of plaster, it should have immediately alerted observers to something amiss. A genuine piece of plaster would have been affected by powder blackening and sprayed wadding resulting from the shotgun blast, as well as considerable bleeding.

"The English law is in the main a just law. You will get no worse than your deserts from it. But I would ask you how did this man know that you lived here, or how to get into your house, or where to hide to get you?"

"I know nothing of this."[93]

Holmes's face was very white and grave. "The story is not over yet, I fear," said he. "You may find worse dangers than the English law, or even than your enemies from America. I see trouble before you, Mr. Douglas. You'll take my advice and still be on your guard."

And now, my long-suffering readers, I will ask you to come away with me for a time, far from the Sussex Manor House of Birlstone, and far also from the year of grace in which we made our eventful journey which ended with the strange story of the man who had been known as John Douglas. I wish you to journey back some twenty years in time,[94] and westward some thousands of miles in space, that I may lay before you a singular and terrible narrative—so singular and so terrible that you may find it hard to believe that even as I tell it, even so did it occur. Do not think that I intrude one story before another is finished. As you read on you will find that this is not so. And when I have detailed those distant events and you have solved this mystery of the past, we shall meet once more in those rooms on Baker Street, where this, like so many other wonderful happenings, will find its end.

93 In "Moriarty and the Molly Maguires," Linda J. Reed argues that Cecil Barker is most likely to have been the source of information, perhaps motivated by his desire for Mrs. Douglas.

94 See *Appendix 3* for a discussion of the chronology of the story.

PART[95] II

The Scowrers[96]

CHAPTER I

THE MAN

IT WAS THE fourth of February in the year 1875.[97] It had been a severe winter, and the snow lay deep in the gorges of the Gilmerton Mountains.[98] The steam ploughs had, however, kept the railroad track open, and the evening train which connects the long line of coal-mining[99] and iron-working settlements was slowly groaning its way up the steep gradients which lead from Stagville on the plain to Vermissa, the central township which lies at the head of Vermissa Valley. From this point the track sweeps downward, to Barton's Crossing, Helmdale, and the purely agricultural county of Merton.[100] It was a single track railroad; but at every siding—and they were numerous—long lines of trucks piled with coal and iron ore told of the hidden wealth which had brought a rude population and a bustling life to this most desolate corner of the United States of America.

For desolate it was. Little could the first pioneer who had traversed it have ever imagined that the fairest prairies and the most lush water pastures were valueless compared to this gloomy land of black crag and tangled forest. Above the dark and often scarcely penetrable woods upon their sides, the high,

95 Who wrote this portion of *The Valley of Fear*? Is this merely a re-telling of the contents of Douglas's "bundle of paper"? "[I]t is practically certain that Part Two of the present form of [*The Valley of Fear*], 'The Scowrers,' is not the work of Watson," writes B. M. Castner. "Its author was a skilled writer of fiction, careful with such details as dates, who, given certain basic matters to be worked into the narrative, has turned out a story complete in itself. Internal evidence suggests that it is by the same hand that wrote 'The Country of the Saints,' for *A Study in Scarlet*; and I have no doubt that the hand is that of Watson's long-time advisor and agent, whose initials are believed to have been A.C.D., and who would have been readily accepted by Holmes and Watson, as by any other Britishers, as an authority upon the American scene." Newt Williams, in "Who Wrote 'The Scowrers?,' " makes a similar case that Arthur Conan Doyle wrote this section. But Colin Prestige, in "A

Study in Fear or the Scarlet Valley," contends that John Douglas wrote Part II, whereas Edgar W. Smith (in "On the Authorship of the Tales-Within-the Tales") argues for Allan Pinkerton himself, premier American detective and author of *The Molly Maguires and the Detectives*. Smith suggests that Pinkerton actually helped Watson with the narrative, but this overlooks that Pinkerton died in 1884, many years before Watson would have been interested in the case.

96 It is generally accepted that the "Scowrers" are a thinly disguised version of the Molly Maguires. The Mollies, as they were known, were a secret organisation of some 3,000 miners—most of them Irish-American and Irish immigrants—working in the anthracite coal region of Schuylkill County, Pennsylvania. From 1862 to 1876, the men were allegedly responsible for scores of brutal acts, including the beatings and murders of several mine owners and managers. According to some sources, the group took its name from an Irish widow who resisted when anti-Catholic authorities attempted to oust her from her cottage—"Take that from a son of Molly Maguire!" was the cry.

The Molly Maguires were brought down in 1876, and nineteen members were hanged as a result. Initially, the breakup of the Molly Maguires was lauded as a case of justice served against a ruthless terrorist organisation. "[T]he Molly Maguires killed men and women with whom they had had no dealings, against whom they had no personal grievances, and from whose death they had nothing to gain, except, perhaps, the price of a few rounds of whiskey," raged Cleveland Moffett, in "The Overthrow of the Molly Maguires: Stories from the Archives of the Pinkterton Detective Agency," published in *McClure's Magazine* in 1894. "They committed murders by the score, stupidly, brutally, as a driven ox turns to left or right at the word of command, without knowing why, and without caring."

Yet history has been kinder to the Mollies, who faced horrendous working conditions and blatant discrimination. Pennsylvania mines in those days were unsanitary and dangerous, and workers were forced to endure low wages, black lung disease, and complete dependence on the local employers. In 1868, 179 miners died when the Avondale mine collapsed and a fire erupted, with no safety exit to allow for the miners' escape. "Such conditions, then as now, tried men's souls," writes Hyman Parker, in "Birdy Edwards and The Scowrers Reconsidered." Irish Catholics in particular had to suffer the indignity of encountering "Help Wanted" signs that added, "Irish need not apply."

Serious questions have been raised about the fairness of the proceedings against Mollies who stood trial: There were no Irish or Catholic jurors, and there was at least one juror who did not understand English. Most of the witnesses were turning state's evidence in return for leniency or freedom, and there was much conflicting testimony. The accused maintained their innocence until the end.

Whatever the Molly Maguires' crimes, the organisation played a pivotal role in the history of the American labor movement—as did its official labour union, the fledgling Workingmen's Benevolent Associatioin (WBA), founded in 1868. Literature on the Molly Maguires is complex and controversial. Certainly the starting place, albeit extremely one-sided, is Allan Pinkerton's *The Molly Maguires and the Detectives* (1877). Anthony Bimba's *The Molly Maguires* (tellingly subtitled "The true story of labor's martyred pioneers in the coalfields") presents a different viewpoint. See also *The Molly Maguires*, by Wayne G. Broehl, Jr., and F. P. Dewees's *The Molly Maguires: The Origin, Growth, and Character of the Organization*. Philadelphia Sherlockian Arthur H.

Lewis's *Lament for the Mollies* is a fine work; most recently, Kevin Kenny's *Making Sense of the Molly Maguires* attempts to bring a historical perspective to the struggle. S. B. Liljegren's pamphlet *The Irish Element in The Valley of Fear* is too accepting of Pinkerton's account to be valuable to historians, but traces the history of the "Irish element" in other literature as well as *The Valley of Fear*. H. T. Crown and Mark T. Major's new *A Guide to the Molly Maguires* provides a helpful compendium of facts.

Kelvin Jones identifies the name "Scowrer" as derived from seventeenth-century slang for wild and boisterous men who roamed the streets, terrorising people.

A table summarising the likely historical counterparts to the places and persons named in *The Valley of Fear* is set forth in *Appendix 2.*

97 At the end of the preceding chapter, Watson invites his readers to "journey back some twenty years in time" (to 1875). This would place the case in 1895, contrary to the date assigned by a majority of the chronologists, who place the events at Birlstone in January 1888 (see *Appendix 3*). However, an 1895 date would square with Watson's claim in "The Final Problem," said to have occurred in 1891, that he had not then heard of Professor Moriarty (see note 6, above).

98 A fictitious name. There is, however, a city of Gilberton in Schuylkill County, Pennsylvania, the heart of Molly Maguire territory.

99 The coal mining business of the Schuylkill anthracite region was centered in Pottsville, Pennsylvania, the seat of the Schuylkill County Court House.

100 A fictional county, replacing the very real Chester County named in the manuscript of *The Valley of Fear*. Yet even that was a deliberate misdirection, as "Merton County" is undoubtedly a stand-in for Carbon County, two-thirds of which is agricultural and one-third devoted to anthracite mining, adjoining Schuylkill County.

Allan Pinkerton.
Harper's Weekly, July 12, 1884

bare crowns of the mountains, white snow, and jagged rock, towered upon each flank, leaving a long, winding, tortuous valley in the centre. Up this the little train was slowly crawling.

The oil lamps had just been lit in the leading passenger-car, a long, bare carriage in which some twenty or thirty people were seated. The greater number of these were workmen returning from their day's toil in the lower portion of the valley. At least a dozen, by their grimed faces and the safety lanterns which they carried, proclaimed themselves as miners. These sat smoking in a group and conversed in low voices, glancing occasionally at two men on the opposite side of the car, whose uniforms and badges showed them to be policemen.

Several women of the labouring class and one or two travellers who might have been small local storekeepers made up the rest of the company, with the exception of one young man in a corner by himself. It is with this man that we are concerned. Take a good look at him, for he is worth it.

He is a fresh-complexioned, middle-sized young man, not far, one would guess, from his thirtieth year. He has large,

James McParlan, who used the alias James McKenna and is disguised in *The Valley of Fear* as John McMurdo.
Scribner's 18 (July 1895)

shrewd, humorous grey eyes which twinkle inquiringly from time to time as he looks round through his spectacles at the people about him. It is easy to see that he is of a sociable and possibly simple disposition, anxious to be friendly to all men. Anyone could pick him at once as gregarious in his habits and communicative in his nature, with a quick wit and a ready smile. And yet the man who studied him more closely might discern a certain firmness of jaw and grim tightness about the lips which would warn him that there were depths beyond, and that this pleasant, brown-haired young Irishman might conceivably leave his mark for good or evil upon any society to which he was introduced.

Having made one or two tentative remarks to the nearest miner, and receiving only short, gruff replies, the traveller resigned himself to uncongenial silence, staring moodily out of the window at the fading landscape.

It was not a cheering prospect. Through the growing gloom there pulsed the red glow of the furnaces on the sides of the hills. Great heaps of slag and dumps of cinders loomed up on each side, with the high shafts of the collieries towering above them. Huddled groups of mean, wooden houses, the windows of which were beginning to outline themselves in light, were scattered here and there along the line, and the frequent halting places were crowded with their swarthy inhabitants.

The iron and coal valleys of the Vermissa district were no resorts for the leisured or the cultured. Everywhere there were stern signs of the crudest battle of life, the rude work to be done, and the rude, strong workers who did it.

The young traveller gazed out into this dismal country with a face of mingled repulsion and interest which showed that the scene was new to him. At intervals he drew from his pocket a bulky letter to which he referred, and on the margins of which he scribbled some notes. Once from the back of his waist he produced something which one would hardly have expected to find in the possession of so mild-mannered a man. It was a navy revolver of the largest size.[101] As he turned it slantwise to the light, the glint upon the rims of the copper shells within the drum showed that it was fully loaded. He quickly restored it to his secret pocket, but not before it had been observed by a working man who had seated himself upon the adjoining bench.

"Hullo, mate!" said he. "You seem heeled[102] and ready."

The young man smiled with an air of embarrassment.

"Yes," said he, "we need them sometimes in the place I come from."

"And where may that be?"

"I'm last from Chicago."

"A stranger in these parts?"

"Yes."

"You may find you need it here," said the workman.

"Ah! Is that so?" The young man seemed interested.

"Have you heard nothing of doings hereabouts?"

"Nothing out of the way."

"Why, I thought the country was full of it. You'll hear quick enough. What made you come here?"

"I heard there was always work for a willing man."

"Are you one of the labour union?"[103]

"Sure."

"Then you'll get your job, I guess. Have you any friends?"

"Not yet; but I have the means of making them."

101 William H. Conway and Lynda L. Conway, in their fine annotation of "The Scowrers" entitled *The Valley of Fear & the Molly Maguires*, conclude that this is probably an 1861 Navy .36-calibre revolver.

102 According to J. S. Farmer and W. E. Henley's *Dictionary of Slang*, the term "heeled" means "armed; from the steel spur used in cock-fighting." The term is also used by Abe Slaney in "The Dancing Men."

103 American editions have the more vernacular phrase, "Are you a member of the union?"

"How's that, then?"

"I am one of the Ancient Order[104] of Freemen.[105] There's no town without a lodge, and where there is a lodge I'll find my friends."

The remark had a singular effect upon his companion. He glanced round suspiciously at the others in the car. The miners were still whispering among themselves. The two police officers were dozing. He came across, seated himself close to the young traveller, and held out his hand.

"Put it there," he said.

A hand-grip passed between the two.

"I see you speak the truth," said the workman. "But it's well to make certain." He raised his right hand to his right eyebrow. The traveller at once raised his left hand to his left eyebrow.

"Dark nights are unpleasant," said the workman.

"Yes, for strangers to travel," the other answered.[106]

"That's good enough. I'm Brother Scanlan, Lodge 341, Vermissa Valley. Glad to see you in these parts."

"Thank you. I'm Brother John McMurdo, Lodge 29, Chicago. Bodymaster,[107] J. H. Scott. But I am in luck to meet a brother so early."

"Well, there are plenty of us about. You won't find the order more flourishing anywhere in the States than right here in Vermissa Valley. But we could do with some lads like you. I can't understand a spry man of the Labour Union finding no work to do in Chicago."

"I found plenty of work to do," said McMurdo.

"Then why did you leave?"

McMurdo nodded towards the policemen and smiled. "I guess those chaps would be glad to know," he said.

Scanlan groaned sympathetically.

"In trouble?" he asked, in a whisper.

"Deep."

"A penitentiary job?"

"And the rest."

"Not a killing!"

"It's early days to talk of such things," said McMurdo, with the air of a man who had been surprised into saying more than he intended. "I've my own good reasons for leaving Chicago, and let that be enough for you. Who are you that you should take it on yourself to ask such things?"

104 The "Eminent Order" in some American editions.

105 Most scholars associate the fictional "Ancient Order of Freemen" with the Ancient Order of Hibernians (AOH), a fraternal organisation of Irish Catholics dating back to 1641; the U.S. chapter was founded in New York in 1836. Most, if not all, members of the Molly Maguires were first members of the AOH, which proved a welcome and needed refuge for Irish and Irish-Americans at a time when bigotry against them was rampant. To some outsiders, the Mollies, the AOH, and the Workingmen's Benevolent Association appeared to be one and the same. But whereas John Siney, the head of the WBA, favored arbitration and pledged to oppose violence, the leaders of the AOH pushed the WBA to strike rather than compromise with the mine owners and accept a wage that would have broken the union's contract. With its bold positions and outspoken leaders, the AOH—and the secret society that it allegedly fostered—earned the fierce loyalty of its followers and raised the alarm of Franklin Gowen, president of the Philadelphia and Reading Railroad (and owner of several mines), who grew determined to suppress this threat to his authority.

106 Secret signs, handshakes, and codewords were a regular part of secret societies, and although the rites of the AOH have not been revealed, it is likely that they were similar to those of the Freemasons. Freemasons were obliged to keep secret the several words and various signs revealed to them, and the motto of the order was "Audi Vide Tace" ("Hear, See, Keep Silent"). It was commonly supposed that Masons would reveal themselves to other members by secret hand grips, signs, and codewords. For example, the "pass-grip" of a Master Mason is known as "Tubalcain" (the password that accompanies it). Malcolm

His grey eyes gleamed with sudden and dangerous anger from behind his glasses.

"All right, mate, no offence meant. The boys will think none the worse of you, whatever you may have done. Where are you bound for now?"

"To Vermissa."

"That's the third halt down the line. Where are you staying?"

McMurdo took out an envelope and held it close to the murky oil lamp. "Here is the address—Jacob Shafter, Sheridan Street. It's a boarding-house that was recommended by a man I knew in Chicago."

"Well, I don't know it, but Vermissa is out of my beat. I live at Hobson's Patch,[108] and that's here where we are drawing up. But, say, there's one bit of advice I'll give you before we part. If you're in trouble in Vermissa, go straight to the Union House and see Boss McGinty. He is the Bodymaster of Vermissa Lodge, and nothing can happen in these parts unless Black Jack McGinty wants it.[109] So long, mate. Maybe we'll meet in lodge one of these evenings. But mind my words: If you are in trouble, go to Boss McGinty."

Scanlan descended, and McMurdo was left once again to his thoughts. Night had now fallen, and the flames of the frequent furnaces were roaring and leaping in the darkness. Against their lurid background dark figures were bending and straining, twisting and turning, with the motion of winch or of windlass, to the rhythm of an eternal clank and roar.

"I guess hell must look something like that," said a voice.

McMurdo turned and saw that one of the policemen had shifted in his seat and was staring out into the fiery waste.

"For that matter," said the other policeman, "I allow that hell must *be* something like that. If there are worse devils down yonder than some we could name, it's more than I'd expect. I guess you are new to this part, young man?"

"Well, what if I am?" McMurdo answered in a surly voice.

"Just this, mister, that I should advise you to be careful in choosing your friends. I don't think I'd begin with Mike Scanlan or his gang if I were you."

"What the hell[110] is it to you who are my friends?" roared McMurdo in a voice which brought every head in the carriage round to witness the altercation. "Did I ask you for your

Duncan's guide to the Freemasons, *Duncan's Masonic Ritual and Monitor* (1866), describes the greeting as follows: "The Mason places his thumb on the space between the second and third knuckles of the fellow Mason's right hand, while the fellow Mason moves his thumb to the corresponding space on the first Mason's hand. The thumb is pressed hard between the second and third knuckles of the hands." For more on the Freemasons, see *A Study in Scarlet*, note 109.

107 "Bodymaster" was, and still is, the title used by the Ancient Order of Hibernians to denote the leader of the local lodge or body. The title carried over to the Molly Maguires: Each division had its own bodymaster, usually an ex-miner who now operated a saloon. This person would recruit members, issue the orders, and do "favors" for bodymasters of other districts (see note 130, below).

108 On August 5, 1952, a dynamite truck exploded in Craig's Patch, Pennsylvania, shattering the entire village. "It does not require a very active imagination to identify Craig's Patch with the 'Hobson's Patch' of the story," writes James Montgomery, in "Paging Birdy Edwards." He concludes that the truck was blown up by descendants of the Scowrers/Mollies, who banded together and revived the organisation more than seventy years later.

109 John "Black Jack" Kehoe, the proprietor of the Hibernian House in Girardville and bodymaster for that town, was a prominent leader of both the AOH and the Molly Maguires. Executed in 1878, he was granted a posthumous pardon in 1979 by the governor of Pennyslvania, thanks to intense and tireless lobbying by Kehoe's great-grandson. To this date, Kehoe is the only Molly to have received a pardon. In the 1970 film *The Molly Maguires*, the tough but sympathetic charac-

advice, or did you think me such a sucker that I couldn't move without it? You speak when you are spoken to, and by the Lord you'd have to wait a long time if it was me!"

He thrust out his face and grinned at the patrolmen like a snarling dog.

The two policemen, heavy, good-natured men, were taken aback by the extraordinary vehemence with which their friendly advances had been rejected.

"No offence, stranger," said one. "It was a warning for your own good, seeing that you are, by your own showing, new to the place."

"I'm new to the place; but I'm not new to you and your kind!" cried McMurdo, in cold fury. "I guess you're the same in all places, shoving your advice in when nobody asks for it."

"Maybe we'll see more of you before very long," said one of the patrolmen, with a grin. "You're a real hand-picked one, if I am a judge."

"I was thinking the same," remarked the other. "I guess we may meet again."

"I'm not afraid of you, and don't you think it!" cried McMurdo. "My name's Jack McMurdo—see? If you want me, you'll find me at Jacob Shafter's on Sheridan Street, Vermissa; so I'm not hiding from you, am I? Day or night I dare to look the like of you in the face—don't make any mistake about that!"

There was a murmur of sympathy and admiration from the miners at the dauntless demeanour of the new-comer, while the two policemen shrugged their shoulders and renewed a conversation between themselves.

A few minutes later the train ran into the ill-lit depôt, and there was a general clearing, for Vermissa was by far the largest town on the line. McMurdo picked up his leather grip-sack[111] and was about to start off into the darkness, when one of the miners accosted him.

"By Gar, mate![112] you know how to speak to the cops," he said in a voice of awe. "It was grand to hear you. Let me carry your grip-sack and show you the road. I'm passing Shafter's on the way to my own shack."

There was a chorus of friendly "Good-nights" from the other miners as they passed from the platform. Before ever he had set foot in it, McMurdo the turbulent had become a character in Vermissa.

ter of Kehoe was played by Scotsman Sean Connery.

110 American editors "spiced up" the text with various phrases that apparently were inappropriate for an English audience, here replacing "in thunder" with "in hell." There are numerous other changes in slang expressions, as the American editors tried to make the narrative—originally penned by John Douglas (an American) but undoubtedly rewritten by Watson for his intended English readers—more understandable to an American audience. The result is a mishmash of Englishisms and Americanisms.

111 A travelling-bag. According to Kelvin Jones, "The 'grip-sack' has long been in use in America as a slang term for a hand satchel . . ."

112 "By gosh!" in the *Strand Magazine* and English book text. Similar changes are too numerous to be further noted.

113 The Union House was in Tamaqua, Pennsylvania, but there was a Sheridan House located on Central Street in Pottsville. William H. Conway and Lynda L. Conway report that the building was part hotel and part private residence. "It was three stories high with a ten-pin alley in the rear of the building. In the basement was the dining-room and kitchen along with the laundry. On the first floor the saloon was in the front and at the end of the bar was a small parlor used for card-playing and bagatelle." The "Union House" of the tale is probably a disguised composite of the Sheridan House, the actual Union House, and Jack Kehoe's Hibernian House in Girardville.

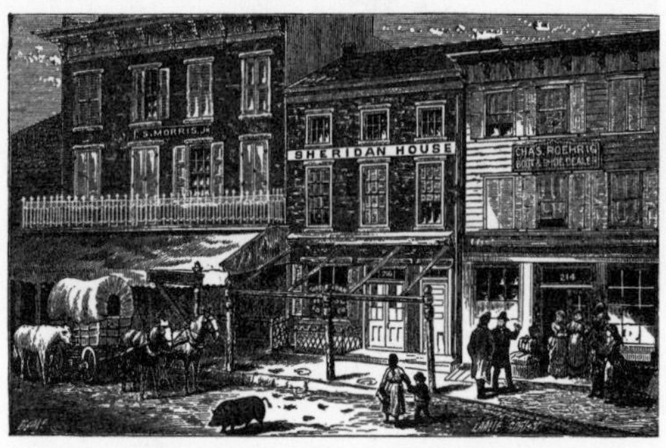

"Dormer calls his hotel the Sheridan House."
The Molly Maguires and the Detectives,
by Allan Pinkerton (1877)

The country had been a place of terror, but the town was in its way even more depressing. Down that long valley there was at least a certain gloomy grandeur in the huge fires and the clouds of drifting smoke, while the strength and industry of man found fitting monuments in the hills which he had spilled by the side of his monstrous excavations. But the town showed a dead level of mean ugliness and squalor. The broad street was churned up by the traffic into a horrible rutted paste of muddy snow. The side-walks were narrow and uneven. The numerous gas-lamps served only to show more clearly a long line of wooden houses, each with its veranda facing the street, unkempt and dirty.

As they approached the centre of the town the scene was brightened by a row of well-lit stores, and even more by a cluster of saloons and gaming-houses, in which the miners spent their hard-earned but generous wages.

"That's the Union House," said the guide, pointing to one saloon which rose almost to the dignity of being an hotel.[113] "Jack McGinty is the boss there."

"What sort of a man is he?" McMurdo asked.

"What! have you never heard of the Boss?"

"How could I have heard of him when you know that I am a stranger in these parts?"

"Well, I thought his name was known right across the Union. It's been in the papers often enough."

"What for?"

"Well"—the miner lowered his voice—"over the affairs."

"What affairs?"

"Good Lord, mister, you are queer goods, if I must say it without offence. There's only one set of affairs that you'll hear of in these parts, and that's the affairs of the Scowrers."

"Why, I seem to have read of the Scowrers in Chicago. A gang of murderers, are they not?"

"Hush, on your life!" cried the miner, standing still in alarm, and gazing in amazement at his companion. "Man, you won't live long in these parts if you speak in the open street like that. Many a man has had the life beaten out of him for less."

"Well, I know nothing about them. It's only what I have read."

"And I'm not saying that you have not read the truth." The man looked nervously round him as he spoke, peering into the

" 'Hush, on your life!' cried the miner, standing still in his alarm, and gazing in amazement at his companion."
Frank Wiles, *Strand Magazine*, 1915

shadows as if he feared to see some lurking danger. "If killing is murder, then God knows there is murder and to spare. But don't you dare to breathe the name of Jack McGinty in connection with it, stranger, for every whisper goes back to him, and he is not one that is likely to let it pass. Now, that's the house you're after—that one standing back from the street. You'll find old Jacob Shafter that runs it as honest a man as lives in this township."

"I thank you," said McMurdo, and shaking hands with his new acquaintance he plodded, his grip-sack in his hand, up the path which led to the dwelling house, at the door of which he gave a resounding knock.

It was opened at once by some one very different from what he had expected. It was a woman, young and singularly beautiful. She was of the German type,[114] blonde and fair-haired, with the piquant contrast of a pair of beautiful dark eyes, with which she surveyed the stranger with surprise and a pleasing embarrassment which brought a wave of colour over her pale face. Framed in the bright light of the open doorway, it seemed

114 As noted earlier (see note 66, above), she is Swedish in the *Strand Magazine* and English texts. David Randall writes, "The story was finished in the summer of 1914 at the latest. We do not know when it was begun. But by the time serialization began in the *Strand Magazine*, World War I had just started and it was patently impossible to have . . . any German depicted as a kindly character in an English publication. This was not vital, however, at the time, in the American editions, so [the] original characterization was not changed." The German identification appears more likely, based on the general population of Pennsylvania.

to McMurdo that he had never seen a more beautiful picture; the more attractive for its contrast with the sordid and gloomy surroundings. A lovely violet growing upon one of those black slag-heaps of the mines would not have seemed more surprising. So entranced was he that he stood staring without a word, and it was she who broke the silence.

"I thought it was father," said she with a pleasing little touch of a German accent. "Did you come to see him? He is down town. I expect him back every minute."

McMurdo continued to gaze at her in open admiration until her eyes dropped in confusion before this masterful visitor.

"No, miss," he said at last, "I'm in no hurry to see him. But your house was recommended to me for board. I thought it might suit me—and now I know it will."

"You are quick to make up your mind," said she, with a smile.

"Anyone but a blind man could do as much," the other answered.

She laughed at the compliment.

"Come right in, sir," she said. "I'm Miss Ettie Shafter, Mr. Shafter's daughter. My mother's dead, and I run the house. You can sit down by the stove in the front room until father comes along—Ah, here he is! So you can fix things with him right away."

A heavy, elderly man came plodding up the path. In a few words McMurdo explained his business. A man of the name of Murphy had given him the address in Chicago. He in turn had had it from some one else. Old Shafter was quite ready. The stranger made no bones about terms, agreed at once to every condition, and was apparently fairly flush of money. For seven dollars[115] a week paid in advance he was to have board and lodging.

So it was that McMurdo, the self-confessed fugitive from justice, took up his abode under the roof of the Shafters, the first step which was to lead to so long and dark a train of events, ending in a far distant land.

115 $12.00 per week in the English editions. According to the Conways, the wages of the local Irish miners were approximately $11.25 per week. In light of the weekly wages, the seven-dollar rent seems more appropriate.

CHAPTER II

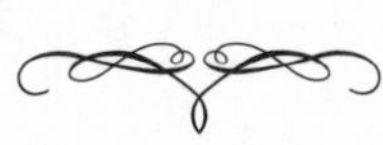

The Bodymaster[116]

McMurdo was a man who made his mark quickly. Wherever he was the folk around soon knew it. Within a week he had become infinitely the most important person at Shafter's. There were ten or a dozen boarders there, but they were honest foremen or commonplace clerks from the stores, of a very different calibre from the young Irishman. Of an evening when they gathered together his joke was always the readiest, his conversation the brightest, and his song the best. He was a born boon companion, with a magnetism which drew good humour from all around him. And yet he showed again and again, as he had shown in the railway-carriage, a capacity for sudden, fierce anger, which compelled the respect and even the fear of those who met him. For the law, too, and all connected with it, he exhibited a bitter contempt which delighted some and alarmed others of his fellow-boarders.

From the first he made it evident, by his open admiration, that the daughter of the house had won his heart from the instant that he had set eyes upon her beauty and her grace. He was no backward suitor. On the second day he told her that he loved her, and from then onwards he repeated the same story

116 The story continued in the February 1915 issue of the *Strand Magazine* with the following summary:

PART I—
THE TRAGEDY OF BIRLSTONE

The opening chapters of this new and thrilling adventure of Sherlock Holmes described the receipt by Holmes of a cipher message, from which he deduces that some devilry is intended against a man named Douglas, a rich country gentleman living at the Manor House, Birlstone, in Sussex, and that the danger is a pressing one. Almost as soon as he has deciphered the message he is visited by Inspector MacDonald, of Scotland Yard, who brings the news that Mr. Douglas has been murdered that morning.

Holmes, Dr. Watson, and the inspector proceed to the scene of the tragedy, where they are met by Mr. White Mason, the chief Sussex detective. The murdered man had been horribly injured, while lying across his chest was a curious weapon—a shot-gun with the barrel sawn off a foot in front of the triggers. Near him was found a card with the initials "V. V." and the number "341" scrawled on it in ink, and about half-way up the forearm was a curious design—a branded triangle inside a circle. His wedding-ring had been removed and the ring above it replaced.

There is no clue to the murderer except a bloody footprint on the window-sill, and he had apparently made his escape by wading across the moat. Holmes is much struck by the fact that one of Douglas's dumb-bells is missing.

Cecil Barker, Douglas's most intimate friend, is considerably flustered while being cross-examined by the detectives, and confesses that Douglas had been jealous on account of his attentions to Mrs. Douglas. Holmes ascertains from Ames, the butler, that on the previous evening Barker was wearing a pair of bedroom slippers which were stained with blood, and on comparing them with the footprints on the window-sill finds that they correspond.

Holmes gives Watson his reasons for believing that Mrs. Douglas and Barker know all about the murder. He advises the other detectives to abandon the case and asks them to meet him that same evening when he promises they shall share everything he knows. Meanwhile the detectives send a note to Barker saying that they intend to drain the moat on the morrow.

On meeting in the evening they hide near the moat, from which they see Barker drag a large bundle. All thereupon rush into the house, and Holmes extracts from the bundle a pair of boots, a knife, and some clothing of American make—and the missing dumb-bell! Holmes's deductions from this discovery cause much astonishment, which is increased when he recommends that *Mr. Douglas* be asked to tell his own story.

At Holmes's words, a man seemed to emerge from the wall. It is Douglas himself, who explains that he has been cooped up since killing, in self-defence, a man who had tried to murder him two days previously. The fact that this man—whom he had known in America, and who had been searching for him for years—was similar in build to himself gave him an idea. He would let it be thought that he (Douglas) had been killed and that the murderer had escaped. The dead man was dressed in Douglas's clothes, and the fact that each bore a similar brand on his arm made the deception easier. Barker then did his best to help his friend by providing misleading clues, with what result we know.

During his enforced hiding Douglas had written an account of the events leading up to the tragedy. This he hands to Dr. Watson, saying, 'There's the story of the Valley of Fear!'

PART II—THE SCOWRERS

The scene now changes to America some twenty years earlier. In a West-bound train from Chicago John McMurdo, a member of the Ancient Order of Freemen, meets Brother Scanlan, a fellow-member of the Order. McMurdo—who, it appears, is fleeing from justice—tells Scanlan he is bound for Vermissa where he intends to put up at a boarding-house kept by Jacob Shafter.

The summary characterises the train on which McMurdo rides at the beginning of Chapter I as "West-bound." This would be so if the train originated in Philadelphia, not Chicago (which is far to the west of the "Gilmerton" mountains). The Philadelphia and Reading

Railroad is the likely line, according to the Conways.

No other summaries appeared in the remaining issues of the *Strand Magazine* in which the tale appeared.

The Valley of Fear.
(New York: Bantam Books, 1950)

with an absolute disregard of what she might say to discourage him.

"Some one else!" he would cry. "Well, the worse luck for some one else! Let him look out for himself! Am I to lose my life's chance and all my heart's desire for some one else? You can keep on saying no, Ettie! The day will come when you will say yes, and I'm young enough to wait."

He was a dangerous suitor, with his glib Irish tongue, and his pretty, coaxing ways. There was about him also that glamour of experience and of mystery which attracts a woman's interest, and finally her love. He could talk of the sweet valleys of County Monaghan from which he came, of the lovely, distant island, the low hills and green meadows of which seemed the more beautiful when imagination viewed them from this place of grime and snow.

Then he was versed in the life of the cities of the North, of Detroit, and the lumber camps of Michigan, and finally of Chicago, where he had worked in a planing mill. And afterwards came the hint of romance, the feeling that strange things had happened to him in that great city, so strange and so intimate that they might not be spoken of. He spoke wistfully of a sudden leaving, a breaking of old ties, a flight into a strange world, ending in this dreary valley, and Ettie listened, her dark eyes gleaming with pity and with sympathy—those two qualities which may turn so rapidly and so naturally to love.

McMurdo had obtained a temporary job as bookkeeper; for he was a well educated man. This kept him out most of the day, and he had not found occasion yet to report himself to the head of the Lodge of the Ancient Order of Freemen. He was reminded of his omission, however, by a visit one evening from Mike Scanlan, the fellow-member whom he had met in the train. Scanlan, the small, sharp-faced, nervous, black-eyed man, seemed glad to see him once more. After a glass or two of whisky he broached the object of his visit.

"Say, McMurdo," said he, "I remembered your address, so I made bold to call. I'm surprised that you've not reported to the Bodymaster. What's amiss that you've not seen Boss McGinty yet?"

"Well, I had to find a job. I have been busy."

"You must find time for him if you have none for anything else. Good Lord, man! you're mad not to have been down to the Union House and registered your name the first morning after you came here! If you fall foul of him—well, you *mustn't*, that's all!"

McMurdo showed mild surprise. "I've been a member of the Lodge for over two years, Scanlan, but I never heard that duties were so pressing as an that."

"Maybe not in Chicago."

"Well, it's the same society here."

"Is it?"

Scanlan looked at him long and fixedly. There was something sinister in his eyes.

"Is it not?"

"You'll tell me that in a month's time. I hear you had a talk with the patrolmen after I left the train."

"How did you know that?"

"Oh, it got about—things do get about for good and for bad in this district."

"Well, yes. I told the hounds what I thought of them."

"By the Lord, you'll be a man after McGinty's heart!"

"What—does he hate the police too?"

Scanlan burst out laughing. "You go and see him, my lad," said he, as he took his leave. "It's not the police, but you, that he'll hate if you don't! Now, take a friend's advice and go at once!"

It chanced that on the same evening McMurdo had another more pressing interview which urged him in the same direction. It may have been that his attentions to Ettie had been more evident than before, or that they had gradually obtruded themselves into the slow mind of his good German host; but, whatever the cause, the boarding-house keeper beckoned the young man into his private room and started onto the subject without any circumlocution.

"It seems to me, mister," said he, "that you are gettin' set on my Ettie. Ain't that so, or am I wrong?"

"Yes, that is so," the young man answered.

"Vell, I vant to tell you right now dat it ain't no manner of use. There's some one slipped in afore you."[117]

"She told me so."

"Vell, you can lay that she told you truth. But did she tell you who it vas?"

"No, I asked her; but she would not tell."

"I dare say not, the leetle baggage! Perhaps she did not vish to vrighten you avay."

"Frighten!" McMurdo was on fire in a moment.

"Ah, yes, my vriend! You need not be ashamed to be vrightened of him. It is Teddy Baldvin."

"And who the devil is he?"

"He is a Boss of Scowrers."

"Scowrers! I've heard of them before. It's Scowrers here and Scowrers there, and always in a whisper! What are you all afraid of? Who *are* the Scowrers?"

117 The accents displayed by old Shafter are unplaceable. Germans pronounce "w" as "v" but the remaining substitutions and mannerisms in Shafter's speech bear no resemblance to either German or Swedish.

The boarding-house keeper instinctively sank his voice, as every one did who talked about that terrible society. "The Scowrers," said he, "are the Ancient Order of Freemen!"

The young man stared. "Why, I am a member of that order myself."

"You! I vould never have had you in my house if I had known it—not if you vere to pay me a hundred dollar a veek."

"What's amiss with the Order? It's for charity and good fellowship. The rules say so."

"Maybe in some places. Not here!"

"What is it here?"

"It's a murder society, that's vat it is."

McMurdo laughed incredulously. "How do you prove that?" he asked.

"Prove it! Are there not vifty murders to prove it? Vat about Milman and Van Shorst, and the Nicholson vamily, and old Mr. Hyam, and little Billy James, and the others? Prove it! Is there a man or a voman in this valley dat does not know it?"

"See here!" said McMurdo, earnestly. "I want you to take back what you've said, or else make it good. One or the other you must do before I quit this room. Put yourself in my place. Here am I, a stranger in the town. I belong to a society that I know only as an innocent one. You'll find it through the length and breadth of the States; but always as an innocent one. Now, when I am counting upon joining it here, you tell me that it is the same as a murder society called the Scowrers, I guess you owe me either an apology or else an explanation, Mr. Shafter."

"I can but tell you vat the whole vorld knows, mister. The bosses of the one are the bosses of the other. If you offend the one, it is the other dat vill strike you. We have proved it too often."

"That's just gossip! I want proof!" said McMurdo.

"If you live here long you vill get your proof. But I forget that you are yourself one of dem. You vill soon be as bad as the rest. But you vill find other lodgings, mister. I cannot have you here. Is it not bad enough dat one of these people come courting my Ettie, and dat I dare not turn him down, but dat I should have another for my boarder? Yes, indeed, you shall not sleep here after to-night!"

So McMurdo found himself under sentence of banishment both from his comfortable quarters and from the girl whom he loved. He found her alone in the sitting-room that same evening, and he poured his troubles into her ear.

"Sure, your father is after giving me notice," he said. "It's little I would care if it was just my room, but indeed, Ettie, though it's only a week that I've known you, you are the very breath of life to me, and I can't live without you!"

"Oh, hush, Mr. McMurdo! Don't speak so!" said the girl. "I have told you, have I not, that you are too late? There is another, and if I have not promised to marry him at once, at least I can promise no one else."

"Suppose I had been first, Ettie, would I have had a chance?"

The girl sank her face into her hands. "I wish to heaven that you *had* been first!" she sobbed.

McMurdo was down on his knees before her in an instant. "For God's sake, Ettie, let it stand at that!" he cried. "Will you ruin your life and my own for the sake of this promise? Follow your heart, acushla![118] 'Tis a safer guide than any promise given before you knew what it was that you were saying."

He had seized Ettie's white hand between his own strong brown ones.

"Say that you will be mine, and we will face it out together!"

"Not here?"

"Yes, here."

"No, no, Jack!" His arms were round her now. "It could not be here. Could you take me away?"

A struggle passed for a moment over McMurdo's face; but it ended by setting like granite. "No, here," he said. "I'll hold you against the world, Ettie, right here where we are!"

"Why should we not leave together?"

"No, Ettie, I can't leave here."

"But why?"

"I'd never hold my head up again if I felt that I had been driven out. Besides, what is there to be afraid of? Are we not free folk in a free country? If you love me, and I you, who will dare to come between?"

"You don't know, Jack. You've been here too short a time. You don't know this Baldwin.[119] You don't know McGinty and his Scowrers."

"No, I don't know them, and I don't fear them, and I don't believe in them!" said McMurdo. "I've lived among rough men, my darling, and instead of fearing them it has always

118 "Acushla" is an Irish term of endearment (usually rendered "darling") that literally means "my pulse" or "my vein" or "pulse (or vein) of my heart."

119 Molly Maguire expert H. T. Crown identifies Ted Baldwin as Tom Hurley, referring to him (in a personal communication to this editor) as "the chief assassin of the Mollies." Cleveland Moffett's article on the Molly Maguires in *McClure's* described how Hurley targeted a bartender named Gomer James in a vengeance killing. Hurley ordered a beer, Moffett wrote, and "James served him promptly, whereupon Hurley threw down a nickel, and lifting the glass in his left hand, pretended to drain it. But he held a pistol, ready cocked, in the right-hand pocket of his sack coat, and while the glass was at his lips, he pulled the trigger. Then, quite unconcerned, he finished his beer, and affected to join in a search for the murderer. At the time he himself was not suspected, there being no evidence of his guilt, except an unobserved hole in his coat."

ended that they have feared me—always, Ettie. It's mad on the face of it! If these men, as your father says, have done crime after crime in the valley, and if every one knows them by name, how comes it that none are brought to justice? You answer me that, Ettie!"

"Because no witness dares to appear against them. He would not live a month if he did. Also because they have always their own men to swear that the accused one was far from the scene of the crime. But surely, Jack, you must have read all this. I had understood that every paper in the States was writing about it."

"Well, I have read something, it is true; but I had thought it was a story. Maybe these men have some reason in what they do. Maybe they are wronged and have no other way to help themselves."

"Oh, Jack, don't let me hear you speak so! That is how he speaks—the other one!"

"Baldwin—he speaks like that, does he?"

"And that is why I loathe him so. Oh, Jack, now I can tell you the truth, I loathe him with all my heart; but I fear him also. I fear him for myself; but above all I fear him for father. I know that some great sorrow would come upon us if I dared to say what I really felt. That is why I have put him off with half-promises. It was in real truth our only hope. But if you would fly with me, Jack, we could take father with us and live for ever far from the power of these wicked men."

Again there was the struggle upon McMurdo's face, and again it set like granite. "No harm shall come to you, Ettie—nor to your father either. As to wicked men, I expect you may find that I am as bad as the worst of them before we're through."

"No, no, Jack! I would trust you anywhere."

McMurdo laughed bitterly. "Good Lord, how little you know of me! Your innocent soul, my darling, could not even guess what is passing in mine. But, halloa, who's the visitor?"

The door had opened suddenly, and a young fellow came swaggering in with the air of one who is the master. He was a handsome, dashing young man of about the same age and build as McMurdo himself. Under his broad-brimmed black felt hat, which he had not troubled to remove, a handsome face with fierce, domineering eyes and a curved hawk-bill of a nose, looked savagely at the pair who sat by the stove.

Ettie had jumped to her feet full of confusion and alarm. "I'm glad to see you, Mr. Baldwin," said she. "You're earlier than I had thought. Come and sit down."

Baldwin stood with his hands on his hips looking at McMurdo. "Who is this?" he asked curtly.

"It's a friend of mine, Mr. Baldwin—a new boarder here. Mr. McMurdo, can I introduce you to Mr. Baldwin?"

The young men nodded in surly fashion to each other.

"Maybe Miss Ettie has told you how it is with us?" said Baldwin.

"I didn't understand that there was any relation between you."

"Did you not? Well, you can understand it now. You can take it from me that this young lady is mine, and you'll find it a very fine evening for a walk."

"Thank you, I am in no humour for a walk."

"Aren't you?" The man's savage eyes were blazing with anger. "Maybe you are in a humour for a fight, Mr. Boarder!"

"That I am," cried McMurdo, springing to his feet. "You never said a more welcome word."

"For God's sake, Jack! Oh, for God's sake!" cried poor, distracted Ettie. "Oh, Jack, Jack, he will do you a mischief!"

"Oh, it's Jack, is it?" said Baldwin with an oath. "You've come to that already, have you?"

"Oh, Ted, be reasonable—be kind! For my sake, Ted, if ever you loved me, be great-hearted and forgiving!"

"I think, Ettie, that if you were to leave us alone we could get this thing settled," said McMurdo quietly. "Or maybe, Mr. Baldwin, you will take a turn down the street with me. It's a fine evening, and there's some open ground beyond the next block."

"I'll get even with you without needing to dirty my hands," said his enemy. "You'll wish you had never set foot in this house before I am through with you!"

"No time like the present," cried McMurdo.

"I'll choose my own time, mister. You can leave the time to me. See here!" He suddenly rolled up his sleeve and showed upon his forearm a peculiar sign which appeared to have been branded there. It was a circle with a triangle within it. "D'you know what that means?"

"I neither know nor care!"

" 'Maybe you are in a humour for a fight, Mr. Boarder?'
" 'That I am,' cried McMurdo, springing to his feet.
'You never said a more welcome word.' "
Frank Wiles, *Strand Magazine*, 1915

"Well, you will know. I'll promise you that. You won't be much older, either. Perhaps Miss Ettie can tell you something about it. As to you, Ettie, you'll come back to me on your knees. D'ye hear, girl? On your knees! And then I'll tell you what your punishment may be. You've sowed—and by the Lord, I'll see that you reap!" He glanced at them both in fury. Then he turned upon his heel, and an instant later the outer door had banged behind him.

For a few moments McMurdo and the girl stood in silence. Then she threw her arms around him.

"Oh, Jack, how brave you were! But it is no use, you must fly! To-night—Jack—to-night! It's your only hope. He will have your life. I read it in his horrible eyes. What chance have you against a dozen of them, with Boss McGinty and all the power of the Lodge behind them?"

McMurdo disengaged her hands, kissed her, and gently pushed her back into a chair.

"There, acushla, there! Don't be disturbed or fear for me. I'm a Freeman myself. I'm after telling your father about it. Maybe I am no better than the others, so don't make a saint of me. Perhaps you hate me too, now that I've told you as much?"

120 The English term "rates" is used in the *Strand Magazine* and English book texts.

"Hate you, Jack? While life lasts I could never do that! I've heard that there is no harm in being a Freeman anywhere but here; so why should I think the worse of you for that? But if you are a Freeman, Jack, why should you not go down and make a friend of Boss McGinty? Oh, hasten, Jack, hasten! Get your word in first, or the hounds will be on your trail."

"I was thinking the same thing," said McMurdo. "I'll go right now and fix it. You can tell your father that I'll sleep here to-night and find some other quarters in the morning."

The bar of McGinty's saloon was crowded as usual, for it was the favourite loafing place of all the rougher elements of the town. The man was popular; for he had a rough, jovial disposition which formed a mask, covering a great deal which lay behind it. But, apart from this popularity, the fear in which he was held through-out the township, and indeed down the whole thirty miles of the valley and past the mountains on each side of it, was enough in itself to fill his bar, for none could afford to neglect his good will.

Besides those secret powers which it was universally believed that he exercised in so pitiless a fashion, he was a high public official, a municipal councillor, and a commissioner of roads, elected to the office through the votes of the ruffians who in turn expected to receive favours at his hands. Assessments[120] and taxes were enormous; the public works were notoriously neglected, the accounts were slurred over by bribed auditors, and the decent citizen was terrorized into paying public blackmail, and holding his tongue lest some worse thing befall him.

Thus it was that, year by year, Boss McGinty's diamond pins became more obtrusive, his gold chains more weighty across a more gorgeous vest, and his saloon stretched farther and farther, until it threatened to absorb one whole side of the Market Square.

McMurdo pushed open the swinging door of the saloon and made his way amid the crowd of men within, through an atmosphere blurred with tobacco smoke and heavy with the smell of spirits. The place was brilliantly lighted, and the huge, heavily gilt mirrors upon every wall reflected and multiplied the garish illumination. There were several bar-tenders in their shirt-sleeves, hard at work mixing drinks for the loungers who fringed the broad, heavily-metalled counter.

At the far end, with his body resting upon the bar and a cigar stuck at an acute angle from the corner of his mouth, there stood a tall, strong, heavily built man who could be none other than the famous McGinty himself. He was a black-maned giant, bearded to the cheek-bones, and with a shock of raven hair which fell to his collar. His complexion was as swarthy as that of an Italian, and his eyes were of a strange dead black, which, combined with a slight squint, gave them a particularly sinister appearance.[121]

All else in the man—his noble proportions, his fine features, and his frank bearing—fitted in with that jovial, man-to-man manner which he affected. Here, one would say, is a bluff, honest fellow, whose heart would be sound however rude his outspoken words might seem. It was only when those dead, dark eyes, deep and remorseless, were turned upon a man that he shrank within himself, feeling that he was face to face with an infinite possibility of latent evil, with a strength and courage and cunning behind it which made it a thousand times more deadly.

Having had a good look at his man, McMurdo elbowed his way forward with his usual careless audacity, and pushed himself through the little group of courtiers who were fawning upon the powerful Boss, laughing uproariously at the smallest of his jokes. The young stranger's bold grey eyes looked back fearlessly through their glasses at the deadly black ones which turned sharply upon him.

"Well, young man, I can't call your face to mind."

"I'm new here, Mr. McGinty."

"You are not so new that you can't give a gentleman his proper title."

"He's Councillor McGinty, young man," said a voice from the group.

"I'm sorry, Councillor. I'm strange to the ways of the place. But I was advised to see you."

"Well, you see me. This is all there is. What d'you think of me?"

"Well, it's early days. If your heart is as big as your body, and your soul as fine as your face, then I'd ask for nothing better," said McMurdo.

"By gosh, you've got an Irish tongue in your head anyhow," cried the saloon-keeper, not quite certain whether to humour this audacious visitor or to stand upon his dignity.

121 As Walter Klinefelter notes, in *Origins of Sherlock Holmes*, this description of McGinty is similar to that of Jack Kehoe given by Allan Pinkerton in *The Molly Maguires and the Detectives*. In particular, Pinkerton notes Kehoe's "plentiful" hair and "dark full whiskers and mustache" and remarks on Kehoe's "cunning" look.

" 'Well, young man, I can't call your face to mind.' "
Frank Wiles, *Strand Magazine*, 1915

"So you are good enough to pass my appearance?"

"Sure," said McMurdo.

"And you were told to see me?"

"I was."

"And who told you?"

"Brother Scanlan, of Lodge 341, Vermissa. I drink your health, Councillor, and to our better acquaintance." He raised a glass with which he had been served to his lips and elevated his little finger as he drank it.

McGinty, who had been watching him narrowly, raised his

thick black eyebrows. "Oh, it's like that, is it?" said he. "I'll have to look a bit closer into this, Mister—"

"McMurdo."

"A bit closer, Mr. McMurdo, for we don't take folk on trust in these parts, nor believe all we're told neither. Come in here for a moment, behind the bar."

There was a small room there, lined with barrels. McGinty carefully closed the door, and then seated himself on one of them, biting thoughtfully on his cigar and surveying his companion with those disquieting eyes. For a couple of minutes he sat in complete silence. McMurdo bore the inspection cheerfully, one hand in his coat-pocket, the other twisting his brown moustache. Suddenly McGinty stooped and produced a wicked-looking revolver.

"See here, my joker," said he. "if I thought you were playing any game on us, it would be short shrift for you."

"This is a strange welcome," McMurdo answered with some dignity, "for the Bodymaster of a Lodge of Freemen to give to a stranger brother."

"Ay, but it's just that same that you have to prove," said

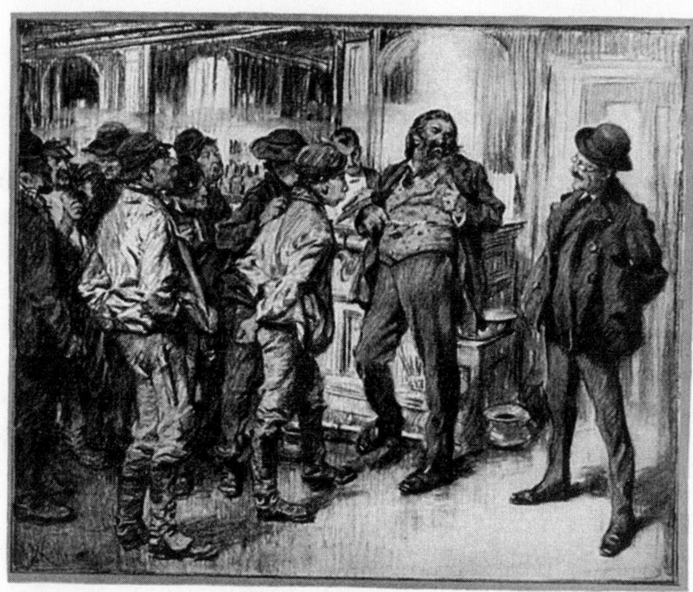

" 'If your heart is as big as your body, and your soul as fine as your face, then I'd ask for nothing better,' said McMurdo."
Arthur I. Keller, *Associated Sunday Magazines*, 1914

"He struck an attitude and without further prelude began his best Irish break-down."
The Molly Maguires and the Detectives, by Allan Pinkerton (1877)

McGinty, "and God help you if you fail. Where were you made?"

"Lodge 29, Chicago."

"When?"

"June 24, 1872."

"What Bodymaster?"

"James H. Scott."

"Who is your district ruler?"

"Bartholomew Wilson."

"Hum! You seem glib enough in your tests. What are you doing here?"

"Working, the same as you, but a poorer job."

"You have your back answer quick enough."

"Yes, I was always quick of speech."

"Are you quick of action?"

"I have had that name among those that knew me best."

"Well, we may try you sooner than you think. Have you heard anything of the Lodge in these parts?"

"I've heard that it takes a man to be a brother."

"True for you, Mr. McMurdo. Why did you leave Chicago?"

"I'm damned if I tell you that!"

McGinty opened his eyes. He was not used to being answered in such fashion, and it amused him. "Why won't you tell me?"

"Because no brother may tell another a lie."

"Then the truth is too bad to tell?"

"You can put it that way if you like."

"See here, mister; you can't expect me, as Bodymaster, to pass into the Lodge a man for whose past he can't answer."

McMurdo looked puzzled. Then he took a worn newspaper-cutting from an inner pocket.

"You wouldn't squeal on a fellow?" said he.

"I'll wipe my hand across your face if you say such words to me!" cried McGinty hotly.

"You are right, Councillor," said McMurdo meekly. "I should apologize. I spoke without thought. Well, I know that I am safe in your hands. Look at that cutting."

McGinty glanced his eyes over the account of the shooting of one Jonas Pinto, in the Lake Saloon, Market Street, Chicago, in the New Year week of '74.

"Your work?" he asked, as he handed back the paper.

McMurdo nodded.

"Why did you shoot him?"

"I was helping Uncle Sam to make dollars. Maybe mine were not as good gold as his, but they looked as well and were cheaper to make. This man Pinto helped me to shove the queer—"[122]

"To do what?"

"Well, it means to pass the dollars out into circulation. Then he said he would split.[123] Maybe he did split. I didn't wait to see. I just killed him and lighted out for the coal country."

"Why the coal country?"

" 'Cause I'd read in the papers that they weren't too particular in those parts."

McGinty laughed. "You were first a coiner and then a murderer, and you came to these parts because you thought you'd be welcome?"

"That's about the size of it," McMurdo answered.

"Well, I guess you'll go far. Say, can you make those dollars yet?"

McMurdo took half a dozen from his pocket. "Those never passed the Washington mint," said he.[124]

"You don't say!" McGinty held them to the light in his enormous hand, which was hairy as a gorilla's. "I can see no difference! Gar! you'll be a mighty useful brother, I'm thinking. We

122 To pass counterfeit money.

123 To inform against one's companions.

124 McMurdo has stated that he was minting gold dollars. These would have been either of the Liberty or Indian head type, both of which were in circulation in 1875. Silver dollars were not then being minted, as Congress had eliminated coinage of the silver dollar in an act commonly referred to as the Crime of 1873. "There have been a great many battles fought against gold," Senator John Sherman told the Ohio Republican Convention in 1895, defending his support of the bill, "but gold has won every time. Gold never has compromised. Gold has made the world respect it all the time. The English people once thought they could get along without gold for a while, but they had to come back to it." The Resumption Act of 1875 (passed in January of that year and backed by President Rutherford Hayes) called for the U.S. treasury to redeem all existing greenback paper money with "hard money" starting in 1879, as well as to reduce the paper money then in circulation. Gold dollars may have seemed like particularly valuable currency when McMurdo was minting them. But the public had faith in the value of greenbacks, and the treasurer accumulated sufficient gold to back them; therefore, when 1879 rolled around, there was no great rush to trade paper money for gold, and greenbacks continued their rise as the popular currency of choice.

Note that McMurdo is speaking figuratively of the "Washington mint." Although the U.S. Mint moved its headquarters to Washington, D.C., in 1873, no coins have ever been produced there.

can do with a bad man or two among us, Friend McMurdo: for there are times when we have to take our own part. We'd soon be against the wall if we didn't shove back at those that were pushing us."

"Well, I guess I'll do my share of shoving with the rest of the boys."

"You seem to have a good nerve. You didn't flinch when I put this pistol on you."

"It was not me that was in danger."

"Who then?"

"It was you, Councillor." McMurdo drew a cocked pistol from the side pocket of his pea-jacket. "I was covering you all the time. I guess my shot would have been as quick as yours."

"By Gar!" McGinty flushed an angry red and then burst into a roar of laughter. "Say, we've had no such holy terror come to hand this many a year. I reckon the Lodge will learn to be proud of you. Well, what the hell do you want? And can't I speak alone with a gentleman for five minutes but you must butt in upon us?"

The bar-tender stood abashed. "I'm sorry, Councillor, but it's Mr. Ted Baldwin. He says he must see you this very minute."

The message was unnecessary, for the set, cruel face of the man himself was looking over the servant's shoulder. He pushed the bartender out and closed the door on him.

"So," said he, with a furious glance at McMurdo. "you got here first, did you? I've a word to say to you, Councillor, about this man."

"Then say it here and now before my face," cried McMurdo.

"I'll say it at my own time, in my own way."

"Tut, tut!" said McGinty, getting off his barrel. "This will never do. We have a new brother here, Baldwin, and it's not for us to greet him in such fashion. Hold out your hand, man, and make it up."

"Never!" cried Baldwin in a fury.

"I've offered to fight him if he thinks I have wronged him," said McMurdo. "I'll fight him with fists, or, if that won't satisfy him, I'll fight him any other way he chooses. Now I'll leave it to you, Councillor, to judge between us as a Bodymaster should."

"What is it, then?"

"A young lady. She's free to choose for herself."

"Is she?" cried Baldwin.

"As between two brothers of the Lodge I should say that she was," said the Boss.

"Oh, that's your ruling, is it?"

"Yes, it is, Ted Baldwin," said McGinty, with a wicked stare. "Is it you that would dispute it?"

"You would throw over one that has stood by you this five years in favour of a man that you never saw before in your life? You're not Bodymaster for life, Jack McGinty, and by God! when next it comes to a vote—"

The Councillor sprang at him like a tiger. His hand closed round the other's neck, and he hurled him back across one of

"His hand closed round the other's neck and he hurled him across one of the barrels."
Frank Wiles, *Strand Magazine*, 1915

the barrels. In his mad fury he would have squeezed the life out of him if McMurdo had not interfered.

"Easy, Councillor! For heaven's sake, go easy!" he cried, as he dragged him back.

McGinty released his hold, and Baldwin, cowed and shaken, gasping for breath, and shivering in every limb, as one who has looked over the very edge of death, sat up on the barrel over which he had been hurled.

"You've been asking for it this many a day, Ted Baldwin. Now you've got it!" cried McGinty, his huge chest rising and falling. "Maybe you think if I were voted down from Bodymaster you would find yourself in my shoes. It's for the Lodge to say that. But so long as I am the chief, I'll have no man lift his voice against me or my rulings."

"I have nothing against you," mumbled Baldwin, feeling his throat.

"Well, then," cried the other, relapsing in a moment into a bluff joviality, "we are all good friends again and there's an end of the matter."

He took a bottle of champagne down from the shelf and twisted out the cork.

"See now," he continued, as he filled three high glasses. "Let us drink the quarrelling toast of the Lodge. After that, as you know, there can be no bad blood between us. Now, then, the left hand on the apple of my throat. I say to you, Ted Baldwin, what is the offense, sir?"

"The clouds are heavy," answered Baldwin.

"But they will for ever brighten."

"And this I swear."

The men drank their glasses, and the same ceremony was performed between Baldwin and McMurdo.

"There!" cried McGinty, rubbing his hands. "That's the end of the black blood. You come under Lodge discipline if it goes further, and that's a heavy hand in these parts, as Brother Baldwin knows—and as you will damn soon find out, Brother McMurdo, if you ask for trouble!"

"Faith, I'd be slow to do that," said McMurdo. He held out his hand to Baldwin. "I'm quick to quarrel and quick to forgive. It's my hot Irish blood, they tell me. But it's over for me, and I bear no grudge."

Baldwin had to take the proffered hand, for the baleful eye

of the terrible Boss was upon him. But his sullen face showed how little the words of the other had moved him.

McGinty clapped them both on the shoulders. "Tut! These girls! These girls!" he cried. "To think that the same petticoats should come between two of my boys! It's the devil's own luck! Well, it's the colleen inside of them that must settle the question; for it's outside the jurisdiction of a Bodymaster—and the Lord be praised for that! We have enough on us, without the women as well. You'll have to be affiliated to Lodge 341, Brother McMurdo. We have our own ways and methods, different to Chicago. Saturday night is our meeting, and if you come then, we'll make you free for ever of the Vermissa Valley."

CHAPTER III

Lodge 341, Vermissa

On the day following the evening which had contained so many exciting events, McMurdo moved his lodgings from old Jacob Shafter's and took up his quarters at the Widow MacNamara's on the extreme outskirts of the town. Scanlan, his original acquaintance aboard the train, had occasion shortly afterwards to move into Vermissa, and the two lodged together. There was no other boarder, and the hostess was an easy-going old Irishwoman who left them to themselves; so that they had a freedom for speech and action welcome to men who had secrets in common.

Shafter had relented to the extent of letting McMurdo come to his meals there when he liked; so that his intercourse with Ettie was by no means broken. On the contrary, it drew closer and more intimate as the weeks went by.

In his bedroom at his new abode McMurdo felt it to be safe to take out the coining moulds, and under many a pledge of secrecy a number of brothers from the Lodge were allowed to come in and see them, each carrying away in his pocket some examples of the false money, so cunningly struck that there was never the slightest difficulty or danger in passing it. Why, with such a wonderful art at his command, McMurdo should condescend to work at all was a perpetual mystery to his companions, though he made it clear to anyone who asked him that if he lived without any visible means it would very quickly bring the police upon his track.

One policeman was indeed after him already; but the incident, as luck would have it, did the adventurer a great deal more good than harm. After the first introduction there were few evenings when he did not find his way to McGinty's saloon, there to make closer acquaintance with "the boys," which was the jovial title by which the dangerous gang who infested the place were known to each other. His dashing manner and fearlessness of speech made him a favourite with them all; while the rapid and scientific way in which he polished off his antagonist in an "all in" bar-room scrap earned the respect of that rough community. Another incident, however, raised him even higher in their estimation.

Just at the crowded hour one night, the door opened and a man entered with the quiet blue uniform and peaked cap of the Coal and Iron Police. This was a special body raised by the railways and colliery owners to supplement the efforts of the ordinary civil police, who were perfectly helpless in the face of the organized ruffianism which terrorized the district.[125] There was a hush as he entered, and many a curious glance was cast at him; but the relations between policemen and criminal are peculiar in the States, and McGinty himself, standing behind his counter, showed no surprise when the inspector enrolled himself among his customers.

"A straight whisky, for the night is bitter," said the police-officer. "I don't think we have met before, Councillor?"

"You'll be the new captain?" said McGinty.

"That's so. We're looking to you, Councillor, and to the other leading citizens, to help us in upholding law and order in this township. Captain Marvin is my name—of the Coal and Iron."

"We'd do better without you, Captain Marvin," said McGinty coldly; "for we have our own police of the township, and no need for any imported goods. What are you but the paid tool of the capitalists, hired by them to club or shoot your poorer fellow-citizen?"

"Well, well, we won't argue about that," said the police offi-

125 In the American editions, they have been disguised as the "mine police." The Conways note, "Coal companies could hire as many policemen as they wished simply by filing an application with the state along with a fee of one dollar. No background checks were conducted. The Coal and Iron Police were the private police force of the Reading Railroad and the colliery owners."

cer good-humouredly. "I expect we all do our duty same as we see it; but we can't all see it the same." He had drunk off his glass and had turned to go, when his eyes fell upon the face of Jack McMurdo, who was scowling at his elbow. "Hullo! Hullo!" he cried, looking him up and down. "Here's an old acquaintance!"

McMurdo shrank away from him. "I was never a friend to you nor any other cursed copper in my life," said he.

"An acquaintance isn't always a friend," said the police-captain, grinning. "You're Jack McMurdo of Chicago, right enough, and don't you deny it!"

McMurdo shrugged his shoulders. "I'm not denying it," said he. "D'ye think I'm ashamed of my own name?"

"You've got good cause to be, anyhow."

"What the devil d'you mean by that?" he roared with his fists clenched.

"No, no, Jack, bluster won't do with me. I was an officer in Chicago before ever I came to this darned coal-bunker, and I know a Chicago crook when I see one."

McMurdo's face fell. "Don't tell me that you're Marvin of the Chicago Central!" he cried.[126]

"Just the same old Teddy Marvin, at your service. We haven't forgotten the shooting of Jonas Pinto up there."

"I never shot him."

"Did you not? That's good impartial evidence, ain't it? Well, his death came in uncommon handy for you, or they would have had you for shoving the queer. Well, we can let that be bygones; for, between you and me—and perhaps I'm going further than my duty in saying it—they could get no clear case against you, and Chicago's open to you to-morrow.

"I'm very well where I am."

"Well, I've given you the office,[127] and you're a sulky dog not to thank me for it."

"Well, I suppose you mean well, and I do thank you," said McMurdo in no very gracious manner.

"It's mum with me so long as I see you living on the straight," said the captain. "But, by the Lord! if you get on the cross after this, it's another story! So good-night to you—and good-night, Councillor."

He left the bar-room, but not before he had created a local hero. McMurdo's deeds in far Chicago had been whispered

126 Robert Linden, the likely historical counterpart of Marvin, was the assistant superintendent of the Chicago office of the Pinkertons until 1875, when he was moved by Pinkerton to Pottsville and formally inducted into Reading's Coal and Iron Police as a captain. In *Lament for the Molly Maguires*, Arthur Lewis reports a similar historical incident in which Captain Linden raided Pat Dormer's Sheridan House in Pottsville. Wayne Melander, in his "The Early American Holmes," adopts the idea that Holmes was Captain Marvin at the close of his American years.

127 Hatton's *Slang Dictionary* (1865) defines this phrase as meaning "[t]o give a hint dishonestly to a confederate, thereby enabling him to win a game or bet, the profits being shared."

" 'I was an officer in Chicago before ever I came to this darned coal-bunker, and I know a Chicago crook when I see one.' "
Frank Wiles, *Strand Magazine*, 1915

before. He had put off all questions with a smile, as one who did not wish to have greatness thrust upon him. But now the thing was officially confirmed. The bar loafers crowded round him and shook him heartily by the hand. He was free of the community from that time on. He could drink hard and show little trace of it; but that evening, had his mate Scanlan not been at hand to lead him home, the feted hero would surely have spent his night under the bar.

On a Saturday night McMurdo was introduced to the Lodge. He had thought to pass in without ceremony as being an initiate of Chicago; but there were particular rites in Vermissa of which they were proud, and these had to be undergone by every postulant.[128] The assembly met in a large room reserved for such purposes at the Union House. Some sixty members

128 This is a sarcastic reference: A postulant is a candidate for admission to holy orders or to a religious community.

assembled at Vermissa; but that by no means represented the full strength of the organization, for there were several other lodges in the valley, and others across the mountains on each side, who exchanged members when any serious business was afoot, so that a crime might be done by men who were strangers to the locality. Altogether there were not less than five hundred scattered over the coal district.

In the bare assembly room the men were gathered round a long table. At the side was a second one laden with bottles and glasses, on which some members of the company were already turning their eyes. McGinty sat at the head with a flat black velvet cap upon his shock of tangled black hair, and a coloured purple stole round his neck, so that he seemed to be a priest presiding over some diabolical ritual. To right and left of him were the higher Lodge officials, the cruel, handsome face of Ted Baldwin among them. Each of these wore some scarf or medallion as emblem of his office.

They were, for the most part, men of mature age; but the rest of the company consisted of young fellows from eighteen to twenty-five, the ready and capable agents who carried out the commands of their seniors. Among the older men were many whose features showed the tigerish, lawless souls within; but looking at the rank and file it was difficult to believe that these eager and open-faced young fellows were in very truth a dangerous gang of murderers, whose minds had suffered such complete moral perversion that they took a horrible pride in their proficiency at the business, and looked with deepest respect at the man who had the reputation for making what they called "a clean job."

To their contorted natures it had become a spirited and chivalrous thing to volunteer for service against some man who had never injured them, and whom in many cases, they had never seen in their lives. The crime committed, they quarrelled as to who had actually struck the fatal blow, and amused each other and the company by describing the cries and contortions of the murdered man.

At first they had shown some secrecy in their arrangements; but at the time which this narrative describes their proceedings were extraordinarily open, for the repeated failures of the law had proved to them that, on the one hand, no one would dare to witness against them, and, on the other, they had an unlimited number of stanch witnesses upon whom they could call, and a well-filled treasure chest from which they could draw the funds to engage the best legal talent in the State. In ten long years of outrage there had been no single conviction, and the only danger that ever threatened the Scowrers lay in the victim himself—who, however outnumbered and taken by surprise, might and occasionally did leave his mark upon his assailants.

McMurdo had been warned that some ordeal lay before him; but no one would tell him in what it consisted. He was led now into an outer room by two solemn brothers. Through the plank partition he could hear the murmur of many voices from the assembly within. Once or twice he caught the sound of his own name, and he knew that they were discussing his candidature. Then there entered an inner guard with a green and gold sash across his chest.

"The Bodymaster orders that he shall he trussed, blinded, and entered," said he.

The three of them then removed his coat, turned up the sleeve of his right arm, and finally passed a rope round above the elbows and made it fast. They next placed a thick black cap right over his head and the upper part of his face, so that he could see nothing. He was then led into the assembly hall.

It was pitch dark and very oppressive under his hood. He heard the rustle and murmur of the people round him, and

"Each Mollie devoutly made the sign of the cross as Monaghan and McKenna entered." [McParlan's (McKenna's) initiation to the Ancient Order of Hibernians.]
The Molly Maguires and the Detectives, by Allan Pinkerton (1877)

then the voice of McGinty sounded, dull and distant through the covering of his ears.

"John McMurdo," said the voice, "are you already a member of the Ancient Order of Freemen?"

He bowed in assent.

"Is your Lodge No. 29, Chicago?"

He bowed again.

"Dark nights are unpleasant," said the voice.

"Yes, for strangers to travel," he answered.

"The clouds are heavy."

"Yes, a storm is approaching."

"Are the brethren satisfied?" asked the Bodymaster.

There was a general murmur of assent.

"We know, Brother, by your sign and by your countersign that you are indeed one of us," said McGinty. "We would have you know, however, that in this county and in other counties of these parts we have certain rites, and also certain duties of our own which call for good men. Are you ready to be tested?"

"I am."

"Are you of stout heart?"

"I am."

"Take a stride forward to prove it."

As the words were said he felt two hard points in front of his eyes, pressing upon them so that it appeared as if he could not move forward without a danger of losing them. None the less, he nerved himself to step resolutely out, and as he did so the pressure melted away. There was a low murmur of applause.

"He is of stout heart," said the voice. "Can you bear pain?"

"As well as another," he answered.

"Test him!"

It was all he could do to keep himself from screaming out, for an agonizing pain shot through his forearm. He nearly fainted at the sudden shock of it; but he bit his lip and clenched his hands to hide his agony.

"I can take more than that," said he.

This time there was loud applause. A finer first appearance had never been made in the Lodge. Hands clapped him on the back, and the hood was plucked from his head. He stood blinking and smiling amid the congratulations of the brothers.

"One last word, Brother McMurdo," said McGinty. "You have already sworn the oath of secrecy and fidelity, and you are

"It was all he could do to keep himself from screaming out."
Arthur I. Keller, *Associated Sunday Magazines*, 1914

aware that the punishment for any breach of it is instant and inevitable death?"

"I am," said McMurdo.

"And you accept the rule of the Bodymaster for the time being under all circumstances?"

"I do."

"Then in the name of Lodge 341, Vermissa, I welcome you to its privileges and debates. You will put the liquor on the table, Brother Scanlan, and we will drink to our worthy brother."

McMurdo's coat had been brought to him; but before putting it on he examined his right arm, which still smarted heavily. There on the flesh of the forearm was a clear-cut circle with a triangle within it, deep and red, as the branding-iron had left it. One or two of his neighbours pulled up their sleeves and showed their own Lodge marks.

"We've all had it," said one; "but not all as brave as you over it."

"Tut! It was nothing," said he; but it burned and ached all the same.

When the drinks which followed the ceremony of initiation had all been disposed of, the business of the Lodge proceeded. McMurdo, accustomed only to the prosaic performances of

129 This is probably a disguised version of the murder of John P. Jones, superintendent of the Lehigh and Wilkes Barre mine at Lansford, who was killed on September 3, 1875, while on his way to work. In the spring of 1876, Michael J. Doyle and Edward Kelly, members of the Ancient Order of Hibernians from Mount Laffee in Schuylkill County, were tried and convicted of first-degree murder in the case.

"He nearly fainted at the sudden shock of it, but he bit his lip and clenched his hands to hide his agony. 'I can take more than that,' said he."
Frank Wiles, *Strand Magazine*, 1915

Chicago, listened with open ears and more surprise than he ventured to show to what followed.

"The first business on the agenda paper," said McGinty, "is to read the following letter from Division Master Windle, of Merton County, Lodge 249. He says:

DEAR SIR:

There is a job to be done on Andrew Rae of Rae & Sturmash, coal-owners near this place.[129] You will remember that your Lodge owes us a return, having had the service of two

130 The protocol of the Molly Maguires said if the bodymaster of one division undertook any action at the request of another, he (in this case, Windle) was entitled to have that "favor" returned at a future date. "The matter of the patrolman last fall" is probably a reference to the highly publicised shooting of police officer Benjamin Yost in Tamaqua on July 6, 1875. Cleveland Moffett reported that James "Powder Keg" Kerrigan, the man who ordered the murder, later claimed that the wrong man had been killed and that his actual target had been another officer who had switched beats with Yost. Kerrigan's wife, Fanny Higgins Kerrigan, testified at the first Yost murder trial in May 1876 that Kerrigan was an informer and a terrible liar. However, a mistrial was declared after a juror died, and a second trial was held in July 1876. Fanny Kerrigan did not testify at that trial, and she moved to Virginia with her husband after charges against him were dropped. In the end, five men were convicted of Yost's murder, four in the second trial and a fifth later; all five were hanged in Pottsville on June 21, 1877, the "Day of the Rope," when five others were also hanged in Schuylkill and Carbon Counties for alleged Molly-related killings.

> brethren in the matter of the patrolman last fall.[130] You will send two good men, they will be taken charge of by Treasurer Higgins of this Lodge, whose address you know. He will show them when to act and where. Yours in freedom,
>
> J.W. Windle, D.M.A.O.F.

"Windle has never refused us when we have had occasion to ask for the loan of a man or two, and it is not for us to refuse him." McGinty paused and looked round the room with his dull, malevolent eyes. "Who will volunteer for the job?"

Several young fellows held up their hands. The Bodymaster looked at them with an approving smile.

"You'll do, Tiger Cormac. If you handle it as well as you did the last, you won't be amiss. And you, Wilson."

131 "Eminent Bodymaster" in the American texts. "Worshipful Master" is a term applied to the head of Masonic lodges and was perhaps deemed too religious-sounding by the American editors.

"I've no pistol," said the volunteer, a mere boy in his teens.

"It's your first, is it not? Well, you have to be blooded some time. It will be a great start for you. As to the pistol, you'll find it waiting for you, or I'm mistaken. If you report yourselves on Monday, it will be time enough. You'll get a great welcome when you return."

"Any reward this time?" asked Cormac, a thick-set, dark-faced, brutal-looking young man, whose ferocity had earned him the nickname of "Tiger."

"Never mind the reward. You just do it for the honour of the thing. Maybe when it is done there will be a few odd dollars at the bottom of the box."

"What has the man done?" asked young Wilson.

"Sure, it's not for the likes of you to ask what the man has done. He has been judged over there. That's no business of ours. All we have to do is to carry it out for them, same as they would for us. Speaking of that, two brothers from the Merton Lodge are coming over to us next week to do some business in this quarter."

"Who are they?" asked some one.

"Faith, it is wiser not to ask. If you know nothing, you can testify nothing, and no trouble can come of it. But they are men who will make a clean job when they are about it."

"And time, too!" cried Ted Baldwin. "Folk are gettin' out of hand in these parts. It was only last week that three of our men were turned off by Foreman Blaker. It's been owing him a long time, and he'll get it full and proper."

"Get what?" McMurdo whispered to his neighbour.

"The business end of a buck-shot cartridge!" cried the man with a loud laugh. "What think you of our ways, Brother?"

McMurdo's criminal soul seemed to have already absorbed the spirit of the vile association of which he was now a member. "I like it well," said he. " 'Tis a proper place for a lad of mettle."

Several of those who sat around heard his words and applauded them.

"What's that?" cried the black-maned Bodymaster from the end of the table.

" 'Tis our new brother, sir, who finds our ways to his taste."

McMurdo rose to his feet for an instant, "I would say, Worshipful Master,[131] that if a man should be wanted I should take it as an honour to be chosen to help the Lodge."

There was great applause at this. It was felt that a new sun was pushing its rim above the horizon. To some of the elders it seemed that the progress was a little too rapid.

"I would move," said the secretary, Harraway, a vulture-faced old graybeard who sat near the chairman, "that Brother McMurdo should wait until it is the good pleasure of the Lodge to employ him."

"Sure, that was what I meant. I'm in your hands," said McMurdo.

"Your time will come, Brother," said the chairman. "We have marked you down as a willing man, and we believe that you will do good work in these parts. There is a small matter to-night in which you may take a hand if it so please you."

"I will wait for something that is worth while."

"You can come to-night, anyhow, and it will help you to know what we stand for in this community. I will make the announcement later. Meanwhile," he glanced at his agenda paper, "I have one or two more points to bring before the meeting. First of all, I will ask the treasurer as to our bank balance. There is the pension to Jim Carnaway's widow. He was struck down doing the work of the Lodge, and it is for us to see that she is not the loser."

"Jim was shot last month when they tried to kill Chester Wilcox of Marley Creek," McMurdo's neighbour informed him.

"The funds are good at the moment," said the treasurer, with the bankbook in front of him. "The firms have been generous of late. Max Linder & Co.[132] paid five hundred to be left alone. Walker Brothers sent in a hundred; but I took it on myself to return it and ask for five. If I do not hear by Wednesday, their winding gear may get out of order. We had to burn their breaker last year before they became reasonable. Then the West Section Coaling Company has paid its annual contribution. We have enough on hand to meet any obligations."

"What about Archie Swindon?" asked a brother.

"He has sold out and left the district. The old devil left a note for us to say that he had rather be a free crossing sweeper in New York than a large mine-owner under the power of a ring of blackmailers. By Gar! it was as well that he made a break for it before the note reached us! I guess he dare not show his face in this valley again."

132 In choosing a disguise for a Vermissa company, Watson may have looked no farther than the newspapers. By 1912, the French comic actor Max Linder (1883–1925) was the highest paid film star in the world. Born Gabriel-Maximilien Leuviefle, he preceded Charlie Chaplin as a recognisable silent-film genius whose slapstick antics captivated audiences. Linder wrote, directed, and starred in all his own early films, which always featured the actor as an upper-class bachelor ("Max") in pursuit of a pretty young woman. His service in the military in World War I was well publicised, as was his suffering from a gas attack and his subsequent breakdown. Commercial failures in the early 1920s may have contributed to his death in a suicide pact with his wife in 1925.

An elderly, clean-shaved man with a kindly face and a good brow rose from the end of the table which faced the chairman. "Mr. Treasurer," he asked, "may I ask who has bought the property of this man that we have driven out of the district?"

"Yes, Brother Morris. It has been bought by the State & Merton County Railroad Company."

"And who bought the mines of Todman and of Lee that came into the market in the same way last year?"

"The same company, Brother Morris."

"And who bought the ironworks of Manson and of Shuman, and of Van Deher and of Atwood, which have all been given up of late?"

"They were all bought by the West Gilmerton General Mining Company."

"I don't see, Brother Morris," said the chairman, "that it matters a nickel to us who buys them, since they can't carry them out of the district."

"With all respect to you, Worshipful Master, I think it may matter very much to us. This process has been going on now for ten long years. We are gradually driving all the small men out of trade. What is the result? We find in their places great companies like the Railroad or the General Iron, who have their directors in New York or Philadelphia, and care nothing for our threats. We can take it out of their local bosses; but it only means that others will be sent in their stead. And we are making it dangerous for ourselves. The small men could not harm us. They had not the money nor the power. So long as we did not squeeze them too dry, they would stay on under our power. But if these big companies find that we stand between them and their profits, they will spare no pains and no expense to hunt us down and bring us to court."

There was a hush at these ominous words, and every face darkened as gloomy looks were exchanged. So omnipotent and unchallenged had they been that the very thought that there was possible retribution in the background had been banished from their minds. And yet the idea struck a chill to the most reckless of them.

"It is my advice," the speaker continued, "that we bear less heavily upon the small men. On the day that they have all been driven out the power of this society will have been broken."

Unwelcome truths are not popular. There were angry cries as the speaker resumed his seat. McGinty rose with gloom upon his brow.

"Brother Morris," said he, "you were always a croaker.[133] So long as the members of this Lodge stand together there is no power in this United States that can touch them. Sure, have we not tried it often enough in the law courts? I expect the big companies will find it easier to pay than to fight, same as the little do. And now, brethren"—McGinty took off his black velvet cap and his stole as he spoke—"this Lodge has finished its business for the evening, save for one small matter which may be mentioned when we are parting. The time has now come for fraternal refreshment and for harmony."

Strange indeed is human nature. Here were these men, to whom murder was familiar, who again and again had struck down the father of the family, some man against whom they had no personal feeling, without one thought of compunction or of compassion for his weeping wife or helpless children, and yet the tender or pathetic in music could move them to tears. McMurdo had a fine tenor voice, and if he had failed to gain the good will of the Lodge before, it could no longer have been withheld after he had thrilled them with "I'm Sitting on the Stile, Mary,"[134] and "On the Banks of Allan Water."[135]

In his very first night the new recruit had made himself one of the most popular of the brethren, marked already for advancement and high office. There were other qualities needed, however, besides those of good fellowship, to make a worthy Freeman, and of these he was given an example before the evening was over. The whisky bottle had passed round many times, and the men were hushed and ripe for mischief when their Bodymaster rose once more to address them.

"Boys," said he, "there's one man in this town that wants trimming up, and it's for you to see that he gets it. I'm speaking of James Stanger, of the *Herald*. You've seen how he's been opening his mouth against us again?"

There was a murmur of assent, with many a muttered oath. McGinty took a slip of paper from his waistcoat pocket.

" 'LAW AND ORDER!' That's how he heads it."

REIGN OF TERROR IN THE
COAL AND IRON DISTRICT

133 Hotten's *Slang Dictionary* (1865) supplies "one who takes a desponding view of everything; an alarmist."

134 Jack Tracy identifies this tune as properly "The Lament of the Irish Emigrant," a ballad composed in 1843 by the Scottish musician William R. Dempster (1808–1871); the words were written by Helen Selina Blackwood, Lady Dufferin (1807–1867). The ballad begins with the line "I'm sitting on the stile, Mary," and conveys the parting thoughts of a man who, in leaving Ireland, must also leave behind the wife he has buried in the nearby graveyard.

135 "On the Banks of Allan Water" is indeed a folk song, believed to have been written by an Englishman, Matthew Lewis (1775–1818), who also wrote the gothic romance *The Monk* (1796). The song concerns a young woman, frequently seen by the river in central Scotland ("On the banks of Allan Water / When the sweet spring-time did fall / Was the miller's lovely daughter / Fairest of them all"), whose heart is broken by a rascal soldier. Bathsheba Everdene sings the song at the harvest supper in Thomas Hardy's novel *Far from the Madding Crowd* (1874).

136 Irish dissatisfaction with English rule dated from the twelfth century, when Henry II traveled to Ireland and declared himself its sovereign. In the centuries that followed, the Irish rebelled constantly against a Protestant government that saw its largely Catholic territory as simultaneously a resource and a threat. Then, from 1845 to 1849, the Irish Potato Famine struck, driving an already struggling population, heavily dependent on potatoes for both sustenance and income, into desperate poverty. One million people died of starvation, typhoid fever, or other diseases related to the famine. Peasants could not pay their rents, and landlords ran out of funds as well, so the British government was relied upon to provide £8,000,000 in relief. But that support was only grudgingly given. Historian Simon Schama, in his masterly *A History of Britain: Volume III: The Fate of Empire 1776–2000*, writes that Sir Charles Trevelyan, assistant secretary of the treasury and the man responsible for relief operations, "believed, without malice yet without sentimentality, that the ordeal had been inflicted by Providence to bring Ireland through pain to a better way of life. His bleak conclusion was that it had all been 'the judgement of God on an indolent and unself-reliant people, and as God had sent the calamity to teach the Irish a lesson, that calamity must not be too much mitigated: the selfish and indolent must learn their lesson so that a new and improved state of affairs must arise.' " Even as the famine raged, Irish farmers were forced to export grains and meats to Britain, since the Irish themselves could not afford to buy them.

Between 1847 and 1854, 1.6 million Irish left their homeland for the United States, and the mass emigration continued for the next few decades. Those who survived the journey were often bitter toward the government they'd left behind. Schama cites John Mitchel, an Irish lawyer and journalist who had been sentenced to Tasmania for printing

"The others withdrawing somewhat from the table, he seated himself upon it and began." [McParlan sings to the crowd.]
The Molly Maguires and the Detectives, by Allan Pinkerton (1877)

Twelve years have now elapsed since the first assassinations which proved the existence of a criminal organization in our midst. From that day these outrages have never ceased, until now they have reached a pitch which makes us the opprobrium of the civilized world. Is it for such results as this that our great country welcomes to its bosom the alien who flies from the despotisms of Europe?[136] Is it that they shall themselves become tyrants over the very men who have given them shelter, and that a state of terrorism and lawlessness should be established under the very shadow of the sacred folds of the starry Flag of Freedom which would raise horror in our minds if we read of it as existing under the most effete monarchy of the East? The men are known. The organization is patent and public. How long are we to endure it? Can we for ever live—

"Sure, I've read enough of the slush!" cried the chairman, tossing the paper down upon the table. "That's what he says of us. The question I'm asking you is what shall we say to him?"

"Kill him!" cried a dozen fierce voices.

"I protest against that," said Brother Morris, the man of the good brow and shaved face. "I tell you, brethren, that our hand is too heavy in this valley, and that there will come a point where in self-defence every man will unite to crush us out.

James Stanger is an old man. He is respected in the township and the district. His paper stands for all that is solid in the valley. If that man is struck down, there will be a stir through this state that will only end with our destruction."

"And how would they bring about our destruction, Mr. Stand-back?" cried McGinty. "Is it by the police? Sure, half of them are in our pay and half of them afraid of us. Or is it by the law courts and the judge? Haven't we tried that before now, and what ever came of it?"

"There is a Judge Lynch that might try the case,"[137] said Brother Morris.

A general shout of anger greeted the suggestion.

"I have but to raise my finger," cried McGinty, "and I could put two hundred men into this town that would clear it out from end to end." Then suddenly raising his voice and bending his huge black brows into a terrible frown, "See here, Brother Morris, I have my eye on you, and have had for some time! You've no heart yourself, and you try to take the heart out of others. It will be an ill day for you, Brother Morris, when your own name comes on our agenda paper, and I'm thinking that it's just there that I ought to place it."

Morris had turned deadly pale, and his knees seemed to give way under him as he fell back into his chair. He raised his glass in his trembling hand and drank before he could answer. "I apologize, Worshipful Master, to you and to every brother in this Lodge if I have said more than I should. I am a faithful member—you all know that—and it is my fear lest evil come to the Lodge which makes me speak in anxious words. But I have greater trust in your judgment than in my own, Worshipful Master, and I promise you that I will not offend again."

The Bodymaster's scowl relaxed as he listened to the humble words. "Very good, Brother Morris. It's myself that would be sorry if it were needful to give you a lesson. But so long as I am in this chair we shall be a united Lodge in word and in deed. And now, boys," he continued, looking round at the company, "I'll say this much, that if Stanger got his full deserts there would be more trouble than we need ask for. These editors hang together, and every journal in the State would be crying out for police and troops. But I guess you can give him a pretty severe warning. Will you fix it, Brother Baldwin?"

"Sure!" said the young man eagerly.

"seditious views" in the *United Irishman*. Escaping to come to America, Mitchel became "the most militant and wrathful of the memorialists of the Great Hunger," and he charged that "The Almighty indeed sent the potato blight, but the English created the famine. . . . A million and a half of men, women and children were carefully, prudently and peacefully slain by the English government." The "Irish problem" continued to be a major issue in British and Irish relations, with the fight for Home Rule figuring prominently in the political battles of the 1870s and 1880s.

By "the alien who flies from the despotisms of Europe," Stanger may have meant more than just the Irish who escaped the Potato Famine. In the same years, German immigrants fled to America to escape armed conflicts with Prussia, Austria, Italy, and the other continental powers, and the coal-mining regions of Pennsylvania had heavy influxes of German and Irish emigrants.

137 While Morris speaks figuratively here, suggesting that the Scowerers risk lynching, there was an actual "Judge Lynch," one Charles Lynch (1737–1796), who was an American Revolutionary soldier and a justice of the peace in Bedford County, Virginia. The terms "lynch law" and "lynching" originate with Lynch's practice of circumventing the colonial justice system and trying Tory conspirators via an extralegal "court."

"How many will you take?"

"Half-a-dozen, and two to guard the door. You'll come, Gower, and you, Mansel, and you, Scanlan, and the two Willabys."

"I promised the new brother he should go," said the chairman.

Ted Baldwin looked at McMurdo with eyes which showed that he had not forgotten nor forgiven. "Well, he can come if he wants," he said in a surly voice. "That's enough. The sooner we get to work the better."

The company broke up with shouts and yells and snatches of drunken song. The bar was still crowded with revellers, and many of the brethren remained there. The little band who had been told off for duty passed out into the street, proceeding in twos and threes along the sidewalk so as not to provoke attention. It was a bitterly cold night, with a half-moon shining brilliantly in a frosty, star-spangled sky. The men stopped and gathered in a yard which faced a high building. The words "Vermissa Herald" were printed in gold lettering between the brightly lit windows. From within came the clanking of the printing press.

"Here, you," said Baldwin to McMurdo, "you can stand below at the door and see that the road is kept open for us. Arthur Willaby can stay with you. You others come with me. Have no fears, boys, for we have a dozen witnesses that we are in the Union Bar at this very moment."

It was nearly midnight, and the street was deserted save for one or two revellers upon their way home. The party crossed the road, and, pushing open the door of the newspaper office, Baldwin and his men rushed in and up the stair which faced them. McMurdo and another remained below. From the room above came a shout, a cry for help, and then the sound of trampling feet and of falling chairs. An instant later a gray-haired man rushed out on the landing.

He was seized before he could get farther, and his spectacles came tinkling down to McMurdo's feet. There was a thud and a groan. He was on his face, and half-a-dozen sticks were clattering together as they fell upon him. He writhed, and his long, thin limbs quivered under the blows. The others ceased at last; but Baldwin, his cruel face set in an infernal smile, was hacking at the man's head, which be vainly endeavoured to defend with his arms. His white hair was dabbled with patches of blood. Baldwin was still stooping over his victim, putting in a short, vicious blow whenever he could see a part exposed, when McMurdo dashed up the stair and pushed him back.

"You'll kill the man," said he. "Drop it!"

Baldwin looked at him in amazement. "Curse you!" he cried. "Who are you to interfere—you that are new to the Lodge? Stand back!" He raised his stick, but McMurdo had whipped his pistol out of his hip pocket.

"Stand back yourself!" he cried. "I'll blow your face in if you lay a hand on me. As to the Lodge, wasn't it the order of the Bodymaster that the man was not to be killed—and what are you doing but killing him?"

"It's truth he says," remarked one of the men.

"By Gar! you'd best hurry yourselves!" cried the man below. "The windows are all lighting up, and you'll have the whole township here inside of five minutes."

There was indeed the sound of shouting in the street, and a little group of compositors and typesetters[138] was forming in

" 'Stand back yourself!' he cried. 'I'll blow your face in if you lay a hand on me.' "
Frank Wiles, *Strand Magazine*, 1915

138 "Pressmen" (reporters) in the American texts.

the hall below and nerving itself to action. Leaving the limp and motionless body of the editor at the head of the stair, the criminals rushed down and made their way swiftly along the street. Having reached the Union House, some of them mixed with the crowd in McGinty's saloon, whispering across the bar to the Boss that the job had been well carried through. Others, and among them McMurdo, broke away into side streets, and so by devious paths to their own homes.[139]

139 The confrontation with Stanger is likely based on an incident involving Thomas Foster, editor of the *Shenandoah Herald*, who was outspoken in his editorials in opposing the Molly Maguires. Arthur Lewis, in *Lament for the Molly Maguires*, reports an occasion on which Foster and reporter Thomas Fielders held off a Molly mob with firearms. Unfortunately, Fielders was extremely nearsighted, could not find his glasses, and was inexperienced with weapons, causing Foster to exclaim, "I'd be safer with the Mollies in here." The Molly mob dispersed before anyone was hurt. Although there were several incidents in which the newspaper suffered property damage, the editor never suffered bodily injury.

CHAPTER IV

The Valley of Fear

When McMurdo awoke next morning he had good reason to remember his initiation into the Lodge. His head ached with the effect of the drink, and his arm, where he had been branded, was hot and swollen. Having his own peculiar source of income, he was irregular in his attendance at his work; so he had a late breakfast and remained at home for the morning writing a long letter to a friend. Afterwards he read the *Daily Herald*. In a special column put in at the last moment he read:

OUTRAGE AT THE HERALD OFFICE—
EDITOR SERIOUSLY INJURED.

It was a short account of the facts with which he was himself more familiar than the writer could have been. It ended with the statement:

> The matter is now in the hands of the police, but it can hardly be hoped that their exertions will be attended by any better results than in the past.

Some of the men were recognized, and there is hope that a conviction may be obtained. The source of the outrage was, it need hardly be said, that infamous society which has held this community in bondage for so long a period, and against which the *Herald* has taken so uncompromising a stand. Mr. Stanger's many friends will rejoice to hear that though he has been cruelly and brutally beaten, and though he has sustained severe injuries about the head, there is no immediate danger to his life.

Below it stated that a guard of Coal and Iron Police, armed with Winchester rifles,[140] had been requisitioned for the defence of the office.

McMurdo had laid down the paper, and was lighting his pipe with a hand which was shaky from the excesses of the previous evening, when there was a knock outside, and his landlady brought to him a note which had just been handed in by a lad. It was unsigned, and ran thus:

I should wish to speak to you; but would rather not do so in your house. You will find me beside the flagstaff upon Miller Hill. If you will come there now, I have something which it is important for you to hear and for me to say.

McMurdo read the note twice with the utmost surprise; for he could not imagine what it meant or who was the author of it. Had it been in a feminine hand, he might have imagined that it was the beginning of one of those adventures which had been familiar enough in his past life. But it was the writing of a man, and of a well-educated one, too. Finally, after some hesitation, he determined to see the matter through.

Miller Hill is an ill-kept public park in the very centre of the town. In summer it is a favourite resort of the people; but in winter it is desolate enough. From the top of it one has a view not only of the whole grimy straggling town, but of the winding valley beneath, with its scattered mines and factories blackening the snow on each side of it, and of the wooded and white-capped ranges which flank it.[141]

McMurdo strolled up the winding path hedged in with evergreens until he reached the deserted restaurant which forms the centre of summer gaiety. Beside it was a bare flagstaff, and

140 In 1848, Oliver Fisher Winchester set up a dress-shirt factory in New Haven, Connecticut, and with the windfall from this business was able to purchase the Volcanic Repeating Arms Company in 1857. Reorganised as the Winchester Repeating Arms Company in 1867, the gun manufacturer made a policy of aggressively acquiring others' designs, including a lever-action repeating rifle designed by B. T. Henry, the Winchester plant manager and chief mechanic. Patented in 1860, it was widely used in the Civil War. Also tremendously popular among Western settlers was the Model 73 (short for The New Model of 1873), favoured by such lawmakers and ruffians as Billy the Kid, Wyatt Earp, and Buffalo Bill Cody. It remained in production for fifty-two years, and 720,610 were manufactured in all. It is likely the Model 73 that the police officers were carrying.

141 Michael Harrison, in *In the Footsteps of Sherlock Holmes*, identifies Miller Hill as the highest point in Tamaqua, behind the railroad station. A modern church, rather than a park, now rests on this site, but a flagpole is still there. The Conways (and David L. Hammer, in *To Play the Game*) are of a different mind, naming the Saint Jerome Cemetery, also in Tamaqua, as "Miller Hill."

underneath it a man, his hat drawn down and the collar of his overcoat raised up. When he turned his face McMurdo saw that it was Brother Morris, he who had incurred the anger of the Bodymaster the night before. The Lodge sign was given and exchanged as they met.

"I wanted to have a word with you, Mr. McMurdo," said the older man, speaking with a hesitation which showed that he was on delicate ground. "It was kind of you to come."

"Why did you not put your name to the note?"

"One has to be cautious, mister. One never knows in times like these how a thing may come back to one. One never knows either who to trust or who not to trust."

"Surely one may trust brothers of the Lodge."

"No, no, not always," cried Morris with vehemence. "Whatever we say, even what we think, seems to go back to that man McGinty."

"Look here," said McMurdo sternly. "It was only last night, as you know well, that I swore good faith to our Bodymaster. Would you be asking me to break my oath?"

"If that is the view you take," said Morris sadly, "I can only say that I am sorry I gave you the trouble to come and meet me. Things have come to a bad pass when two free citizens cannot speak their thoughts to each other."

McMurdo, who had been watching his companion very narrowly, relaxed somewhat in his bearing. "Sure I spoke for myself only," said he. "I am a newcomer, as you know, and I am strange to it all. It is not for me to open my mouth, Mr. Morris, and if you think well to say anything to me I am here to hear it."

"And to take it back to Boss McGinty!" said Morris bitterly.

"Indeed, then, you do me injustice there," cried McMurdo. "For myself I am loyal to the Lodge, and so I tell you straight; but I would be a poor creature if I were to repeat to any other what you might say to me in confidence. It will go no further than me; though I warn you that you may get neither help nor sympathy."

"I have given up looking for either the one or the other," said Morris. "I may be putting my very life in your hands by what I say; but, bad as you are—and it seemed to me last night that you were shaping to be as bad as the worst—still you are new to it, and your conscience cannot yet be as hardened as theirs. That was why I thought to speak with you."

"Well, what have you to say?"

"If you give me away, may a curse be on you!"

"Sure, I said I would not."

"I would ask you, then, when you joined the Freeman's Society in Chicago and swore vows of charity and fidelity, did ever it cross your mind that you might find it would lead you to crime?"

"If you call it crime," McMurdo answered.

"Call it crime!" cried Morris, his voice vibrating with passion. "You have seen little of it if you can call it anything else. Was it crime last night when a man old enough to be your father was beaten till the blood dripped from his white hairs? Was that crime—or what else would you call it?"

"There are some would say it was war," said McMurdo. "A war of two classes with all in, so that each struck as best it could."

"Well, did you think of such a thing when you joined the Freeman's Society at Chicago?"

"No, I'm bound to say I did not."

"Nor did I when I joined it at Philadelphia. It was just a benefit club[142] and a meeting-place for one's fellows. Then I heard of this place—curse the hour that the name first fell upon my ears!—and I came to better myself! My God, to better myself! My wife and three children came with me, I started a drygoods store on Market Square, and I prospered well. The word had gone round that I was a Freeman, and I was forced to join the local Lodge, same as you did last night. I've the badge of shame on my forearm and something worse branded on my heart. I found that I was under the orders of a black villain and caught in a meshwork of crime. What could I do? Every word I said to make things better was taken as treason, same as it was last night. I can't get away; for all I have in the world is in my store. If I leave the society, I know well that it means murder to me, and God knows what to my wife and children. Oh, man, it is awful—awful!" He put his hands to his face, and his body shook with convulsive sobs.

McMurdo shrugged his shoulders. "You were too soft for the job," said he. "You are the wrong sort for such work."

"I had a conscience and a religion; but they made me a criminal among them. I was chosen for a job. If I backed down, I knew well what would come to me. Maybe I'm a coward.

142 That is, one formed to provide health or life insurance for its members and their families. The fraternal insurance movement in America formally began in 1868 when a group of railroad mechanics formed such a group in Readville, Pennsylvania. The insurance industry had previously catered almost exclusively to the rich, but as the middle class grew, demand for insurance grew as well. Fraternal organisations provided members with life insurance, protection against loss of income from sickness or accident, and financial aid when no benefits were otherwise due. Some even arranged for medical care on a fixed-fee basis, through doctors affiliated with the organisation, much in the way that today's HMOs operate. The idea of "fraternal insurance" caught on, particularly in the face of ineffective regulation and poor management among legitimate insurance companies. Leslie Siddeley estimates that by 1920, over 9 million people were insured through fraternal insurance organisations, via over 200 member societies and 120,000 local affiliated lodges. Market forces and regulation, however, led to their decline, and after World War II, they had all but vanished.

Maybe it's the thought of my poor little woman and the children that makes me one. Anyhow I went. I guess it will haunt me for ever.

"It was a lonely house, twenty miles from here, over the range yonder. I was told off for the door, same as you were last night. They could not trust me with the job. The others went in. When they came out their hands were crimson to the wrists. As we turned away a child was screaming out of the house behind us. It was a boy of five who had seen his father murdered. I nearly fainted with the horror of it, and yet I had to keep a bold and smiling face; for well I knew that if I did not it would be out of my house that they would come next with their bloody hands, and it would be my little Fred that would be screaming for his father.

"But I was a criminal then—part sharer in a murder, lost for ever in this world, and lost also in the next. I am a good Catholic, but the priest would have no word with me when he heard I was a Scowrer, and I am excommunicated from my faith.[143] That's how it stands with me. And I see you going down the same road, and I ask you what the end is to be. Are you ready to be a cold-blooded murderer also, or can we do anything to stop it?"

"What would you do?" asked McMurdo abruptly. "You would not inform?"

"God forbid!" cried Morris. "Sure, the very thought would cost me my life."

"That's well," said McMurdo. "I'm thinking that you are a weak man and that you make too much of the matter."

"Too much! Wait till you have lived here longer. Look down the valley! See the cloud of a hundred chimneys that overshadows it! I tell you that the cloud of murder hangs thicker and lower than that over the heads of the people. It is the Valley of Fear—the Valley of Death. The terror is in the hearts of the people from the dusk to the dawn. Wait, young man, and you will learn for yourself."

"Well, I'll let you know what I think when I have seen more," said McMurdo carelessly. "What is very clear is that you are not the man for the place, and that the sooner you sell out—if you only get a dime a dollar for what the business is worth—the better it will be for you. What you have said is safe with me; but by Gar! if I thought you were an informer—"

143 The Catholic church did not relish the adverse publicity incurred by the Molly Maguires' activities. Brother Morris was not alone; miners who were alleged to belong to the organisation were often excommunicated.

"No, no!" cried Morris piteously.

"Well, let it rest at that. I'll bear what you have said in mind, and maybe some day I'll come back to it. I expect you meant kindly by speaking to me like this. Now I'll be getting home."

"One word before you go," said Morris. "We may have been seen together. They may want to know what we have spoken about."

"Ah, that's well thought of."

"I offer you a clerkship in my store."

"And I refuse it. That's our business. Well, so long, Brother Morris, and may you find things go better with you in the future."

That same afternoon, as McMurdo sat smoking, lost in thought, beside the stove of his sitting-room, the door swung open and its framework was filled with the huge figure of Boss McGinty. He passed the sign, and then, seating himself opposite to the young man, he looked at him steadily for some time, a look which was as steadily returned.

"I'm not much of a visitor, Brother McMurdo," he said at last. "I guess I am too busy over the folk that visit me. But I thought I'd stretch a point and drop down to see you in your own house."

"I'm proud to see you here, Councillor," McMurdo answered heartily, bringing his whisky bottle out of the cupboard. "It's an honour that I had not expected."

"How's the arm?" asked the Boss.

McMurdo made a wry face. "Well, I'm not forgetting it," he said; "but it's worth it."

"Yes, it's worth it," the other answered, "To those that are loyal and go through with it and are a help to the Lodge. What were you speaking to Brother Morris about on Miller Hill this morning?"

The question came so suddenly that it was well that he had his answer prepared. He burst into a hearty laugh. "Morris didn't know I could earn a living here at home. He shan't know either; for he has got too much conscience for the likes of me. But he's a good-hearted old chap. It was his idea that I was at a loose end, and that he would do me a good turn by offering me a clerkship in a drygoods store."

"Oh, that was it?"

"Yes, that was it."

"And you refused it?"

"Sure. Couldn't I earn ten times as much in my own bedroom with four hours' work?"

"That's so. But I wouldn't get about too much with Morris."

"Why not?"

"Well, I guess because I tell you not. That's enough for most folk in these parts."

"It may be enough for most folk; but it ain't enough for me, Councillor," said McMurdo boldly. "If you are a judge of men, you'll know that."

The swarthy giant glared at him, and his hairy paw closed for an instant round the glass as though he would hurl it at the head of his companion. Then he laughed in his loud, boisterous, insincere fashion.

"You're a queer card, for sure," said he. "Well, if you want reasons, I'll give them. Did Morris say nothing to you against the Lodge?"

"No."

"Nor against me?"

"No."

"Well, that's because he daren't trust you. But in his heart he is not a loyal brother. We know that well. So we watch him and we wait for the time to admonish him. I'm thinking that the time is drawing near. There's no room for scabby sheep in our pen. But if you keep company with a disloyal man, we might think that you were disloyal, too. See?"

"There's no chance of my keeping company with him; for I dislike the man," McMurdo answered. "As to being disloyal, if it was any man but you he would not use the word to me twice."

"Well, that's enough," said McGinty, draining off his glass. "I came down to give you a word in season, and you've had it."

"I'd like to know," said McMurdo, "how you ever came to learn that I had spoken with Morris at all?"

McGinty laughed. "It's my business to know what goes on in this township," said he. "I guess you'd best reckon on my hearing all that passes. Well, time's up, and I'll just say—"

But his leavetaking was cut short in a very unexpected fashion. With a sudden crash the door flew open, and three frowning, intent faces glared in at them from under the peaks of police caps. McMurdo sprang to his feet and half drew his

"With a crash the door flew open, and three frowning faces glared at them from under the peaks of police caps."
Frank Wiles, *Strand Magazine*, 1915

revolver, but his arm stopped midway as he became conscious that two Winchester rifles were levelled at his head. A man in uniform advanced into the room, a sixshooter in his hand. It was Captain Marvin, once of Chicago, and now of the Coal and Iron Constabulary. He shook his head with a half-smile at McMurdo.

"I thought you'd be getting into trouble, Mr. Crooked McMurdo of Chicago," said he. "Can't keep out of it can you? Take your hat and come along with us."

"I guess you'll pay for this, Captain Marvin," said McGinty. "Who are you, I'd like to know, to break into a house in this fashion and molest honest, law-abiding men?"

"You're standing out in this deal, Councillor McGinty," said the police captain. "We are not out after you, but after this man McMurdo. It is for you to help, not to hinder us in our duty."

"He's a friend of mine, and I'll answer for his conduct" said the Boss.

"By all accounts, Mr. McGinty, you may have to answer for your own conduct some of these days," the captain answered. "This man McMurdo was a crook before ever he came here, and he's a crook still. Cover him, Patrolman, while I disarm him."

"There's my pistol," said McMurdo coolly. "Maybe, Captain Marvin, if you and I were alone and face to face you would not take me so easily."

"Where's your warrant?" asked McGinty. "By Gar! a man might as well live in Russia as in Vermissa while folk like you are running the police. It's a capitalist outrage, and you'll hear more of it I reckon."

"You do what you think is your duty the best way you can, Councillor. We'll look after own."

"What am I accused of?" asked McMurdo.

"Of being concerned in the beating of old Editor Stanger at the *Herald* office. It wasn't your fault that it isn't a murder charge."

"Well, if that's all you have against him," cried McGinty, with a laugh, "you can save yourself a deal of trouble by dropping it right now. This man was with me in my saloon playing poker up to midnight, and I can bring a dozen to prove it."

"That's your affair, and I guess you can settle it in court tomorrow. Meanwhile, come on, McMurdo, and come quietly if you don't want a gun butt across your head. You stand wide, Mr. McGinty, for I warn you I will stand no resistance when I am on duty!"

So determined was the appearance of the captain that both McMurdo and his boss were forced to accept the situation. The latter managed to have a few whispered words with the prisoner before they parted.

"What about—" he jerked his thumb upward to signify the coining plant.

"All right," whispered McMurdo, who had devised a safe hiding place under the floor.

"I'll bid you good-bye," said the Boss, shaking hands. "I'll see Reilly the lawyer and take the defence upon myself. Take my word for it that they won't be able to hold you."

"I wouldn't bet on that. Guard the prisoner, you two, and shoot him if he tries any games. I'll search the house before I leave."

Marvin did so; but apparently found no trace of the concealed plant. When he had descended he and his men escorted McMurdo to headquarters. Darkness had fallen, and a keen blizzard was blowing so that the streets were nearly deserted; but a few loiterers followed the group and, emboldened by invisibility, shouted imprecations at the prisoner.

"Lynch the cursed Scowrer!" they cried. "Lynch him!" They laughed and jeered as he was pushed into the police depôt. After a short formal examination from the inspector in charge he was put into the common cell. Here he found Baldwin and three other criminals of the night before, all arrested that afternoon and waiting their trial next morning.

But even within this inner fortress of the law the long arm of the Freemen was able to extend. Late at night there came a jailer with a straw bundle for their bedding, out of which he extracted two bottles of whisky, some glasses, and a pack of cards. They spent an hilarious night, without an anxious thought as to the ordeal of the morning.

Nor had they cause, as the result was to show. The magistrate could not possibly, on the evidence, have carried the matter to a higher court. On the one hand the compositors and pressmen were forced to admit that the light was uncertain, that they were themselves much perturbed, and that it was difficult for them to swear to the identity of the assailants; although they believed that the accused were among them. Cross examined by the clever attorney who had been engaged by McGinty, they were even more nebulous in their evidence.

The injured man had already deposed that he was so taken by surprise by the suddenness of the attack that he could state nothing beyond the fact that the first man who struck him wore a moustache. He added that he knew them to be Scowrers, since no one else in the community could possibly have any enmity to him, and he had long been threatened on account of his outspoken editorials. On the other hand, it was clearly shown by the united and unfaltering evidence of six citizens, including that high municipal official, Councillor McGinty, that the men had been at a card party at the Union House until an hour very much later than the commission of the outrage.

Needless to say that they were discharged with something very near to an apology from the Bench for the inconvenience to which they had been put, together with an implied censure of Captain Marvin and the police for their officious zeal.

The verdict was greeted with loud applause by a Court in which McMurdo saw many familiar faces. Brothers of the Lodge smiled and waved. But there were others who sat with compressed lips and brooding eyes as the men filed out of the dock. One of them, a little, dark-bearded, resolute fellow, put the thoughts of himself and comrades into words as the ex-prisoners passed him.

"You damned murderers!" he said. "We'll fix you yet!"

CHAPTER V

The Darkest Hour

If anything had been needed to give an impetus to Jack McMurdo's popularity among his fellows it would have been his arrest and acquittal. That a man on the very night of joining the Lodge should have done something which brought him before the magistrate was a new record in the annals of the society. Already he had earned the reputation of a good boon companion, a cheery reveller, and withal a man of high temper, who would not take an insult even from the all-powerful Boss himself. But in addition to this he impressed his comrades with the idea that among them all there was not one whose brain was so ready to devise a bloodthirsty scheme, or whose hand would be more capable of carrying it out. "He'll be the boy for the clean job," said the oldsters to each other, and waited their time until they could set him to his work.

McGinty had instruments enough already, but he recognized that this was a supremely able one. He felt like a man holding a fierce bloodhound in leash. There were curs to do the smaller work, but some day he would slip this creature upon its prey. A few members of the Lodge, Ted Baldwin among them, resented the rapid rise of the stranger and hated him for it, but they kept clear of him, for he was as ready to fight as to laugh.

But if he gained favour with his fellows, there was another quarter, one which had become even more vital to him, in which he lost it. Ettie Shafter's father would have nothing more to do with him, nor would he allow him to enter the house. Ettie herself was too deeply in love to give him up altogether, and yet her own good sense warned her of what would come from a marriage with a man who was regarded as a criminal.

One morning after a sleepless night she determined to see him, possibly for the last time, and make one strong endeavour to draw him from those evil influences which were sucking him down. She went to his house, as he had often begged her to do, and made her way into the room which he used as his sitting-room. He was seated at a table with his back turned and a letter in front of him. A sudden spirit of girlish mischief came over her—she was still only nineteen. He had not heard her when she pushed open the door. Now she tip-toed forward and laid her hand lightly upon his bended shoulders.

If she had expected to startle him, she certainly succeeded; but only in turn to be startled herself. With a tiger spring he turned on her, and his right hand was feeling for her throat. At the same moment with the other hand he crumpled up the paper that lay before him. For an instant he stood glaring. Then astonishment and joy took the place of the ferocity which had convulsed his features—a ferocity which had sent her shrinking back in horror as from something which had never before intruded into her gentle life.

"It's you!" said he, mopping his brow. "And to think that you should come to me, heart of my heart, and I should find nothing better to do than to want to strangle you! Come then, darling," and he held out his arms. "Let me make it up to you."

But she had not recovered from that sudden glimpse of guilty fear which she had read in the man's face. All her woman's instinct told her that it was not the mere fright of a man who is startled. Guilt—that was it—guilt and fear!

"What's come over you, Jack?" she cried. "Why were you so scared of me? Oh, Jack, if your conscience was at ease, you would not have looked at me like that!"

"Sure, I was thinking of other things, and when you came tripping so lightly on those fairy feet of yours—"

"No, no, it was more than that, Jack." Then a sudden suspicion seized her. "Let me see that letter you were writing."

"Ah, Ettie, I couldn't do that."

Her suspicions became certainties. "It's to another woman," she cried. "I know it! Why else should you hold it from me? Was it to your wife that you were writing? How am I to know that you are not a married man—you, a stranger, that nobody knows?"

"I am not married, Ettie. See now, I swear it! You're the only one woman on earth to me. By the cross of Christ I swear it!"

He was so white with passionate earnestness that she could not but believe him.

"Well, then," she cried, "why will you not show me the letter?"

"I'll tell you, acushla," said he. "I'm under oath not to show it, and just as I wouldn't break my word to you so I would keep it to those who hold my promise. It's the business of the Lodge, and even to you it's secret. And if I was scared when a hand fell on me, can't you understand it when it might have been the hand of a detective?"

She felt that he was telling the truth. He gathered her into his arms and kissed away her fears and doubts.

"Sit here by me, then. It's a queer throne for such a queen; but it's the best your poor lover can find. He'll do better for you some of these days, I'm thinking. Now your mind is easy once again, is it not?"

"How can it ever be at ease, Jack, when I know that you are a criminal among criminals, when I never know the day that I may hear you are in dock for murder? 'McMurdo the Scowrer,' that's what one of our boarders called you yesterday. It went through my heart like a knife."

"Sure, hard words break no bones."

"But they were true."

"Well, dear, it's not so bad as you think. We are but poor men that are trying in our own way to get our rights."

Ettie threw her arms round her lover's neck. "Give it up, Jack! For my sake, for God's sake, give it up! It was to ask you that I came here to-day. Oh, Jack, see—I beg it of you on my bended knees! Kneeling here before you I implore you to give it up!"

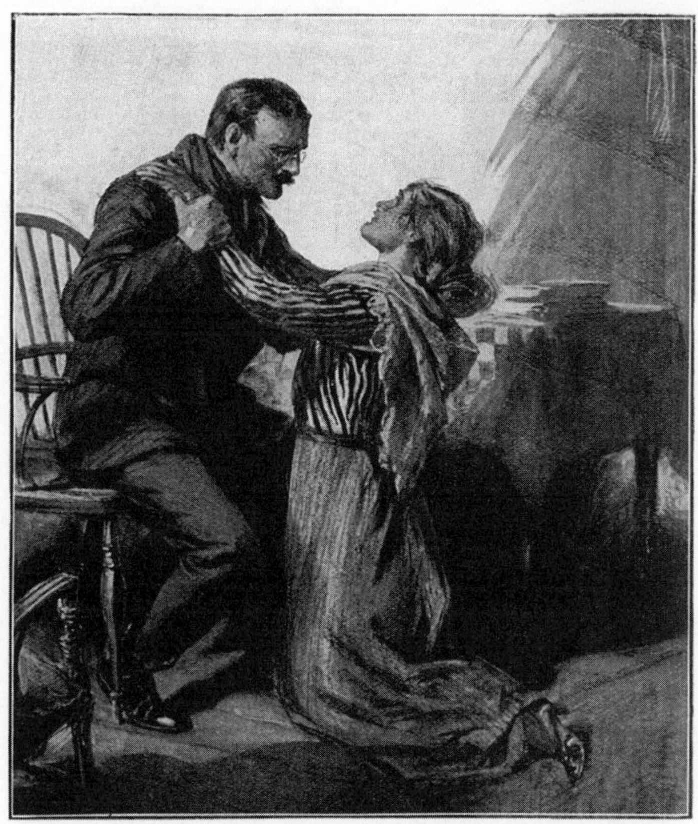

" 'Give it up, Jack! For my sake, for God's sake, give it up!' "
Frank Wiles, *Strand Magazine*, 1915

He raised her and soothed her with her head against his breast.

"Sure, my darlin', you don't know what it is you are asking. How could I give it up when it would be to break my oath and to desert my comrades? If you could see how things stand with me you could never ask it of me. Besides, if I wanted to, how could I do it? You don't suppose that the Lodge would let a man go free with all its secrets?"

"I've thought of that, Jack. I've planned it all. Father has saved some money. He is weary of this place where the fear of these people darkens our lives. He is ready to go. We would fly together to Philadelphia or New York, where we would be safe from them."

" 'Oh, Jack, I implore you to give it up!' "
Arthur I. Keller, *Associated Sunday Magazines*, 1914

McMurdo laughed. "The Lodge has a long arm. Do you think it could not stretch from here to Philadelphia or New York?"

"Well, then, to the West, or to England, or to Germany, where father came from—anywhere to get away from this Valley of Fear!"

McMurdo thought of old Brother Morris. "Sure it is the second time I have heard the valley so named," said he. "The shadow does indeed seem to lie heavy on some of you."

"It darkens every moment of our lives. Do you suppose that Ted Baldwin has ever forgiven us? If it were not that he fears you, what do you suppose our chances would be? If you saw the look in those dark, hungry eyes of his when they fall on me!"

"By Gar! I'd teach him better manners if I caught him at it! But see here, little girl. I can't leave here. I can't. Take that from me once and for all. But if you will leave me to find my own way, I will try to prepare a way of getting honourably out of it."

"There is no honour in such a matter."

"Well, well, it's just how you look at it. But if you'll give me six months, I'll work it so that I can leave without being ashamed to look others in the face."

The girl laughed with joy. "Six months!" she cried. "Is it a promise?"

"Well, it may be seven or eight. But within a year at the furthest we will leave the valley behind us."

It was the most that Ettie could obtain, and yet it was something. There was this distant light to illuminate the gloom of the immediate future. She returned to her father's house more light-hearted than she had ever been since Jack McMurdo had come into her life.

It might be thought that as a member, all the doings of the society would be told to him; but he was soon to discover that the organization was wider and more complex than the simple Lodge. Even Boss McGinty was ignorant as to many things; for there was an official named the County Delegate, living at Hobson's Patch farther down the line, who had power over several different lodges which he wielded in a sudden and arbitrary way. Only once did McMurdo see him, a sly, little gray-haired rat of a man, with a slinking gait and a sidelong glance which was charged with malice. Evans Pott was his name, and even the great Boss of Vermissa felt towards him something of the repulsion and fear which the huge Danton may have felt for the puny but dangerous Robespierre.[144]

One day Scanlan, who was McMurdo's fellow boarder, received a note from McGinty enclosing one from Evans Pott, which informed him that he was sending over two good men, Lawler and Andrews, who had instructions to act in the neighbourhood; though it was best for the cause that no particulars as to their objects should be given. Would the Bodymaster see to it that suitable arrangements be made for their lodgings and comfort until the time for action should arrive? McGinty added that it was impossible for anyone to remain secret at the Union House, and that, therefore, he would be obliged if McMurdo and Scanlan would put the strangers up for a few days in their boarding house.

The same evening the two men arrived, each carrying his

144 Georges-Jacques Danton (1759–1794), one of the two key leaders of the French Revolution, is described by Thomas Carlyle, in his monumental *French Revolution* (1837), as a "huge, brawny figure" with "black brows and rude flattened face," with "lungs of brass." A former head of the Committee of Public Safety (the war dictatorship formed to eliminate counter-revolutionary activity), the moderate Danton became one of the committee's most outspoken critics. During the Reign of Terror, he was charged with conspiring to overthrow the government and guillotined in 1794. The committee at that time was being led by Danton's rival Maximilien Robespierre (1758–1794), whom Carlyle described as an "anxious, slight, ineffectual-looking man." Robespierre had already begun to fall out of favour with the revolutionaries, however, and he was himself guillotined within a few months of Danton. Carlyle deemed Danton and Robespierre the "chief-products of a victorious Revolution," but, he noted, "Two such chief-products are too much for one Revolution!"

gripsack. Lawler was an elderly man, shrewd, silent, and self-contained, clad in an old black frock coat, which with his soft felt hat and ragged, grizzled beard gave him a general resemblance to an itinerant preacher. His companion Andrews was little more than a boy, frank-faced and cheerful, with the breezy manner of one who is out for a holiday and means to enjoy every minute of it. Both men were total abstainers, and behaved in all ways as exemplary members of the society, with the one simple exception that they were assassins who had often proved themselves to be most capable instruments for this association of murder. Lawler had already carried out fourteen commissions of the kind, and Andrews three.

They were, as McMurdo found, quite ready to converse about their deeds in the past, which they recounted with the half-bashful pride of men who had done good and unselfish service for the community. They were reticent, however, as to the immediate job in hand.

"They chose us because neither I nor the boy here drink," Lawler explained. "They can count on us saying no more than we should. You must not take it amiss, but it is the orders of the County Delegate that we obey."

"Sure, we are all in it together," said Scanlan, McMurdo's mate, as the four sat together at supper.

"That's true enough, and we'll talk till the cows come home of the killing of Charlie Williams or of Simon Bird, or any other job in the past. But till the work is done we say nothing."

"There are half a dozen about here that I have a word to say to," said McMurdo, with an oath. "I suppose it isn't Jack Knox of Ironhill that you are after. I'd go some way to see him get his deserts."

"No, it's not him yet."

"Or Herman Strauss?"

"No, nor him either."

"Well, if you won't tell us we can't make you; but I'd be glad to know."

Lawler smiled and shook his head. He was not to be drawn.

In spite of the reticence of their guests, Scanlan and McMurdo were quite determined to be present at what they called "the fun." When, therefore, at an early hour one morning McMurdo heard them creeping down the stairs he awakened Scanlan, and the two hurried on their clothes. When they were dressed they found that the others had stolen out, leaving the door open behind them. It was not yet dawn, and by the light of the lamps they could see the two men some distance down the street. They followed them warily, treading noiselessly in the deep snow.

The boarding house was near the edge of the town, and soon they were at the cross-roads which is beyond its boundary. Here three men were waiting, with whom Lawler and Andrews held a short, eager conversation. Then they all moved on together. It was clearly some notable job which needed numbers. At this point there are several trails which lead to various mines. The strangers took that which led to the Crow Hill, a huge business which was in strong hands which had been able, thanks to their energetic and fearless New England manager, Josiah H. Dunn, to keep some order and discipline during the long reign of terror.

Day was breaking now, and a line of workmen were slowly making their way, singly and in groups, along the blackened path.

McMurdo and Scanlan strolled on with the others, keeping in sight of the men whom they followed. A thick mist lay over them, and from the heart of it there came the sudden scream of a steam whistle. It was the ten-minute signal before the cages descended and the day's labour began.

When they reached the open space round the mine-shaft there were a hundred miners waiting, stamping their feet and blowing on their fingers; for it was bitterly cold. The strangers stood in a little group under the shadow of the engine house. Scanlan and McMurdo climbed a heap of slag from which the whole scene lay before them. They saw the mine engineer, a great bearded Scotchman named Menzies, come out of the engine-house and blow his whistle for the cages to be lowered.

At the same instant a tall, loose-framed young man, with a clean-shaved, earnest face advanced eagerly towards the pit head. As he came forward his eyes fell upon the group, silent and motionless, under the engine house. The men had drawn down their hats and turned up their collars to screen their faces. For a moment the presentiment of Death laid its cold hand upon the manager's heart. At the next he had shaken it off and saw only his duty towards intrusive strangers.

"Who are you?" he asked as he advanced. "What are you loitering there for?"

145 Slag; stony matter fused under heat in a furnace.

146 These were likely the murders of Thomas Sanger, a boss at Heaton & Company, and William Uren, a miner and boarder with Sanger's family. They were gunned down while walking to work on September 1, 1875, at Raven Run, near Girardville.

" 'Who are you?' he asked, as he advanced. 'What are you loitering there for?' "
Frank Wiles, *Strand Magazine*, 1915

There was no answer; but the lad Andrews stepped forward and shot him in the stomach. The hundred waiting miners stood as motionless and helpless as if they were paralysed. The manager clapped his two hands to the wound and doubled himself up. Then he staggered away; but another of the assassins fired, and he went down sidewise, kicking and clawing among a heap of clinkers.[145] Menzies, the Scotchman, gave a roar of rage at the sight and rushed with an iron spanner at the murderers, but was met by two balls in the face which dropped him dead at their very feet.[146]

There was a surge forward of some of the miners, and an inarticulate cry of pity and of anger, but a couple of the strangers emptied their six-shooters over the heads of the

crowd, and they broke and scattered, some of them rushing wildly back to their homes in Vermissa.

When a few of the bravest had rallied, and there was a return to the mine, the murderous gang had vanished in the mists of morning, without a single witness being able to swear to the identity of these men who in front of a hundred spectators had wrought this double crime.

Scanlan and McMurdo made their way back; Scanlan somewhat subdued, for it was the first murder job that he had seen with his own eyes, and it appeared less funny than he had been led to believe. The horrible screams of the dead manager's wife pursued them as they hurried to the town. McMurdo was absorbed and silent; but he showed no sympathy for the weakening of his companion.

"Sure, it is like a war," he repeated. "What is it but a war between us and them, and we hit back where we best can."

There was high revel in the Lodge room at the Union House that night, not only over the killing of the manager and engi-

147 Vic Holly explains that this does not mean "a vain hope" but rather is an English approximation of the Dutch *verloren hoop*, the "lost squad." In British military jargon, this expression means the point of an infantry advance.

"He fired a pistol shot into the left breast of the victim."
The Molly Maguires and the Detectives, by Allan Pinkerton (1877)

neer of the Crow Hill mine, which would bring this organization into line with the other blackmailed and terror-stricken companies of the district, but also over a distant triumph which had been wrought by the hands of the Lodge itself.

It would appear that when the County Delegate had sent over five good men to strike a blow in Vermissa, he had demanded that in return three Vermissa men should be secretly selected and sent across to kill William Hales of Stake Royal, one of the best known and most popular mine owners in the Gilmerton district, a man who was believed not to have an enemy in the world; for he was in all ways a model employer. He had insisted, however, upon efficiency in the work, and had, therefore, paid off certain drunken and idle *employés* who were members of the all-powerful society. Coffin notices hung outside his door had not weakened his resolution, and so in a free, civilized country he found himself condemned to death.

The execution had now been duly carried out. Ted Baldwin, who sprawled now in the seat of honour beside the Bodymaster, had been chief of the party. His flushed face and glazed, bloodshot eyes told of sleeplessness and drink. He and his two comrades had spent the night before among the mountains. They were unkempt and weather-stained. But no heroes, returning from a forlorn hope,[147] could have had a warmer welcome from their comrades.

The story was told and retold amid cries of delight and shouts of laughter. They had waited for their man as he drove home at nightfall, taking their station at the top of a steep hill, where his horse must be at a walk. He was so furred to keep out the cold that he could not lay his hand on his pistol. They had pulled him out and shot him again and again.[148]

None of them knew the man; but there is eternal drama in a killing, and they had shown the Scowrers of Gilmerton that the Vermissa men were to be relied upon. There had been one *contretemps*; for a man and his wife had driven up while they were still emptying their revolvers into the silent body. It had been suggested that they should shoot them both; but they were harmless folk who were not connected with the mines, so they were sternly bidden to drive on and keep silent, lest a worse thing befall them. And so the blood-mottled figure had been left as a warning to all such hard-hearted employers, and the three noble avengers had hurried off into the mountains where unbroken nature comes down to the very edge of the furnaces and the slag heaps. Here they were, safe and sound, their work well done, and the plaudits of their companions in their ears.

It had been a great day for the Scowrers. The shadow had fallen even darker over the valley. But as the wise general chooses the moment of victory in which to redouble his efforts, so that his foes may have no time to steady themselves after disaster, so Boss McGinty, looking out upon the scene of his operations with his brooding and malicious eyes, had devised a new attack upon those who opposed him. That very night, as the half-drunken company broke up, he touched McMurdo on the arm and led him aside into that inner room where they had their first interview.

"See here, my lad," said he. "I've got a job that's worthy of you at last. You'll have the doing of it in your own hands."

"Proud I am to hear it," McMurdo answered.

"You can take two men with you—Manders and Reilly. They have been warned for service. We'll never be right in this district until Chester Wilcox has been settled, and you'll have the thanks of every Lodge in the coal fields if you can down him."

"I'll do my best, anyhow. Who is he, and where shall I find him?"

McGinty took his eternal half-chewed, half-smoked cigar

148 The following was added by bloodthirsty American editors:

> He had screamed for mercy. The screams were repeated for the amusement of the Lodge.
>
> "Let's hear again how he squealed," they cried.

from the corner of his mouth, and proceeded to draw a rough diagram on a page torn from his notebook.

"He's the chief foreman of the Iron Dike Company. He's a hard citizen, an old colour-sergeant[149] of the war, all scars and grizzle. We've had two tries at him; but had no luck, and Jim Carnaway lost his life over it. Now it's for you to take it over. That's the house—all alone at the Iron Dike crossroad, same as you see here on the map—without another within earshot. It's no good by day. He's armed and shoots quick and straight, with no questions asked. But at night—well, there he is with his wife, three children, and a hired help. You can't pick or choose. It's all or none. If you could get a bag of blasting powder at the front door with a slow match to it—"

"What's the man done?"

"Didn't I tell you he shot Jim Carnaway?"

"Why did he shoot him?"

"What in thunder has that to do with you? Carnaway was about his house at night, and he shot him. That's enough for me and you. You've got to settle the thing right."

"There's these two women and the children. Do they go up too?"

"They have to—else how can we get him?"

"It seems hard on them; for they've done nothing."

"What sort of fool's talk is this? Do you back out?"

"Easy, Councillor, easy! What have I ever said or done that you should think I would be after standing back from an order of the Bodymaster of my own Lodge? If it's right or if it's wrong, it's for you to decide."

"You'll do it, then?"

"Of course I will do it."

"When?"

"Well, you had best give me a night or two that I may see the house and make my plans. Then—"

"Very good," said McGinty, shaking him by the hand. "I leave it with you. It will be a great day when you bring us the news. It's just the last stroke that will bring them all to their knees."

McMurdo thought long and deeply over the commission which had been so suddenly placed in his hands. The isolated house in which Chester Wilcox lived was about five miles off in an adjacent valley. That very night he started off all alone to

149 A sergeant responsible for carrying regimental colours in the field. Although it was thought by some scholars to be purely a British rank, there were numerous colour sergeants in the U.S. Army in the Civil War. For example, family records give the rank of one B. F. Shivers as Colour Sergeant of Company K, 17th Regiment, Georgia Volunteer Infantry, Army of Northern Virginia, Confederate States of America, and identify one Andrew Jackson Smith as Colour Sergeant of the 55th Massachusetts Infantry, Army of the Potomac, United States of America.

prepare for the attempt. It was daylight before he returned from his reconnaissance. Next day he interviewed his two subordinates, Manders and Reilly, reckless youngsters who were as elated as if it were a deer-hunt.

Two nights later they met outside the town, all three armed, and one of them carrying a sack stuffed with the powder which was used in the quarries. It was two in the morning before they came to the lonely house. The night was a windy one, with broken clouds drifting swiftly across the face of a three-quarter moon. They had been warned to be on their guard against bloodhounds; so they moved forward cautiously, with their pistols cocked in their hands. But there was no sound save the howling of the wind, and no movement but the swaying branches above them.

McMurdo listened at the door of the lonely house; but all was still within. Then he leaned the powder bag against it, ripped a hole in it with his knife, and attached the fuse. When it was well alight he and his two companions took to their heels, and were some distance off, safe and snug in a sheltering ditch, before the shattering roar of the explosion, with the low, deep rumble of the collapsing building, told them that their work was done. No cleaner job had ever been carried out in the bloodstained annals of the society.

But alas that work so well organized and boldly carried out should all have gone for nothing. Warned by the fate of the various victims, and knowing that he was marked down for destruction, Chester Wilcox had moved himself and his family only the day before to some safer and less known quarters, where a guard of police should watch over them. It was an empty house which had been torn down by the gunpowder, and the grim old colour-sergeant of the war was still teaching discipline to the miners of Iron Dike.

"Leave him to me," said McMurdo. "He's my man, and I'll get him sure if I have to wait a year for him."

A vote of thanks and confidence was passed in full lodge, and so for the time the matter ended. When a few weeks later it was reported in the papers that Wilcox had been shot at from an ambuscade, it was an open secret that McMurdo was still at work upon his unfinished job.

Such were the methods of the Society of Freemen, and such were the deeds of the Scowrers by which they spread their rule of fear over the great and rich district which was for so long a period haunted by their terrible presence. Why should these pages be stained by further crimes? Have I not said enough to show the men and their methods?

These deeds are written in history, and there are records wherein one may read the details of them. There one may learn of the shooting of Policemen Hunt and Evans because they had ventured to arrest two members of the society—a double outrage planned at the Vermissa Lodge and carried out in cold blood upon two helpless and disarmed men. There also one may read of the shooting of Mrs. Larbey when she was nursing her husband, who had been beaten almost to death by orders of Boss McGinty. The killing of the elder Jenkins, shortly followed by that of his brother, the mutilation of James Murdoch, the blowing up of the Staphouse family, and the murder of the Stendals all followed hard upon one another in the same terrible winter.

Darkly the shadow lay upon the Valley of Fear. The spring had come with running brooks and blossoming trees. There was hope for all Nature bound so long in an iron grip; but nowhere was there any hope for the men and women who lived under the yoke of the terror. Never had the cloud above them been so dark and hopeless as in the early summer of the year '75.

CHAPTER VI

Danger

It was the height of the reign of terror. McMurdo, who had already been appointed Inner Deacon, with every prospect of some day succeeding McGinty as Bodymaster, was now so necessary to the councils of his comrades that nothing was done without his help and advice. The more popular he became, however, with the Freemen, the blacker were the scowls which greeted him as he passed along the streets of Vermissa. In spite of their terror the citizens were taking heart to band themselves together against their oppressors. Rumours had reached the Lodge of secret gatherings in the *Herald* office and of distribution of firearms among the law-abiding people. But McGinty and his men were undisturbed by such reports. They were numerous, resolute, and well armed. Their opponents were scattered and powerless. It would all end, as it had done in the past, in aimless talk and possibly in impotent arrests. So said McGinty, McMurdo, and all the bolder spirits.

It was a Saturday evening in May. Saturday was always the Lodge night, and McMurdo was leaving his house to attend it when Morris, the weaker brother of the Order, came to see him. His brow was creased with care, and his kindly face was drawn and haggard.

"Can I speak with you freely, Mr. McMurdo?"

"Sure."

"I can't forget that I spoke my heart to you once, and that you kept it to yourself, even though the Boss himself came to ask you about it."

"What else could I do if you trusted me? It wasn't that I agreed with what you said."

"I know that well. But you are the one that I can speak to and be safe. I've a secret here"—he put his hand to his breast—"and it is just burning the life out of me. I wish it had come to any one of you but me. If I tell it, it will mean murder, for sure. If I don't, it may bring the end of us all. God help me, but I am near out of my wits over it!"

McMurdo looked at the man earnestly. He was trembling in every limb. He poured some whisky into a glass and handed it to him. "That's the physic for the likes of you," said he. "Now let me hear of it."

Morris drank, and his white face took a tinge of colour. "I can tell it you all in one sentence," said he. "There's a detective on our trail."

McMurdo stared at him in astonishment. "Why, man, you're crazy!" he said. "Isn't the place full of police and detectives, and what harm did they ever do us?"

"No, no, it's no man of the district. As you say, we know them, and it is little that they can do. But you've heard of Pinkerton's?"[150]

"I've read of some folk of that name."

"Well, you can take it from me you've no show when they are on your trail. It's not a take-it-or-miss-it Government concern. It's a dead earnest business proposition that's out for results and keeps out till by hook or crook it gets them. If a Pinkerton man is deep in this business, we are all destroyed."

"We must kill him."

"Ah, it's the first thought that came to you! So it will be up at the Lodge. Didn't I say to you that it would end in murder?"

"Sure, what is murder? Isn't it common enough in these parts?"

"It is, indeed; but it's not for me to point out the man that is to be murdered. I'd never rest easy again. And yet it's our own

150 The Pinkerton National Detective Agency was founded by Allan Pinkerton (1819–1884), a Scotsman who emigrated to Illinois in 1842. He settled in West Dundee, near Chicago, and opened up a cooper's shop there. An ardent abolitionist, Pinkerton allowed his shop to serve as one of the many stations on the Underground Railroad.

While chopping wood one day on an uninhabited island in Fox River, Pinkerton stumbled upon evidence that led to the arrest and capture of a gang of counterfeiters. His pivotal role in bringing down the gang resulted in his being named deputy sheriff of Kane County in 1846, then the first city detective of Chicago's police force. But Pinkerton quickly saw that he would never make his fortune as a cop. In 1850, he left the Chicago force to start his own private detective agency, the first of its kind in Chicago and one of only a handful in the country.

The Pinkerton National Detective Agency specialised in train robberies and achieved many spectacular successes, including no less than the thwarting of an 1861 assassination attempt on President-elect Lincoln in Baltimore. During the Civil War, Pinkerton worked for the Union side, heading an organisation that gathered intelligence on Confederate activity. After the war, detectives from the Pinkerton Agency did indeed infiltrate the Molly Maguires. The sign above the door of the agency featured the motto "We Never Sleep" accompanying an illustration of an eye, an indelible image that gave rise to the term "private eye." Among the sixteen books attributed to Pinkerton (as part of "Allan Pinkerton's Detective Stories") are, as we have seen, *The Molly Maguires and the Detectives*, viewed by many historians now as a highly biased work on the labour dispute, and *Criminal Reminiscences and Detective Sketches* (1879).

This is not the Canon's only reference to the famed Pinkerton Agency. A detective

" 'I can tell it you all in one sentence,' said he. 'There's a detective on our trail.' "
Frank Wiles, *Strand Magazine*, 1915

necks that may be at stake. In God's name what shall I do?" He rocked to and fro in his agony of indecision.

But his words had moved McMurdo deeply. It was easy to see that he shared the other's opinion as to the danger, and the need for meeting it. He gripped Morris's shoulder and shook him in his earnestness.

"See here, man," he cried, and he almost screeched the words in his excitement, "you won't gain anything by sitting keening like an old wife at a wake. Let's have the facts. Who is the fellow? Where is he? How did you hear of him? Why did you come to me?"

named "Mr. Leverton, of the Pinkerton's American Agency," provides assistance and vital information to Holmes and Watson in "The Red Circle."

151 "The East" replaces "Philadelphia" in the manuscript. References to "Chicago" are also substituted.

"I came to you, for you are the one man that would advise me. I told you that I had a store in the East[151] before I came here. I left good friends behind me, and one of them is in the telegraph service. Here's a letter that I had from him yesterday. It's this part from the top of the page. You can read it yourself."

This was what McMurdo read:

> How are the Scowrers getting on in your parts? We read plenty of them in the papers. Between you and me I expect to hear news from you before long. Five big corporations and the two railroads have taken the thing up in dead earnest. They mean it, and you can bet they'll get there! They are right deep down into it. Pinkerton has taken hold under their orders, and his best man, Birdy Edwards, is operating. The thing has got to be stopped right now.

"Now read the postscript."

> Of course, what I give you is what I learned in business; so it goes no further. It's a queer cipher that you handle by the yard every day and can get no meaning from.

McMurdo sat in silence for some time, with the letter in his listless hands. The mist had lifted for a moment, and there was the abyss before him.

"Does anyone else know of this?" he asked,

"I have told no one else."

"But this man—your friend—has he any other person that he would be likely to write to?"

"Well, I dare say he knows one or two more."

"Of the Lodge?"

"It's likely enough."

"I was asking because it is likely that he may have given some description of this fellow Birdy Edwards. Then we could get on his trail."

"Well, it's possible. But I should not think he knew him. He is just telling me the news that came to him by way of business. How would he know this Pinkerton man?"

McMurdo gave a violent start.

"By Gar!" he cried, "I've got him. What a fool I was not to know it. Lord! but we're in luck! We will fix him before he can do any harm. See here, Morris, will you leave this thing in my hands?"

"Sure, if you will only take it off mine."

"I'll do that. You can stand right back and let me run it. Even your name need not be mentioned. I'll take it all on myself, as if it were to me that this letter has come. Will that content you?"

"It's just what I would ask."

"Then leave it at that and keep your head shut. Now I'll get down to the Lodge, and we'll soon make old man Pinkerton sorry for himself."

"You wouldn't kill this man?"

"The less you know, Friend Morris, the easier your conscience will be, and the better you will sleep. Ask no questions, and let these things settle themselves. I have hold of it now."

Morris shook his head sadly as he left.

"I feel that his blood is on my hands," he groaned.

"Self-protection is no murder, anyhow," said McMurdo, smiling grimly. "It's him or us. I guess this man would destroy us all if we left him long in the valley. Why, Brother Morris, we'll have to elect you Bodymaster yet; for you've surely saved the Lodge."

And yet it was clear from his actions that he thought more seriously of this new intrusion than his words would show. It may have been his guilty conscience, it may have been the reputation of the Pinkerton organization, it may have been the knowledge that great, rich corporations had set themselves the task of clearing out the Scowrers; but, whatever his reason, his actions were those of a man who is preparing for the worst. Every paper which would incriminate him was destroyed before he left the house. After that he gave a long sigh of satisfaction; for it seemed to him that he was safe; and yet the danger must still have pressed somewhat upon him; for on his way to the Lodge he stopped at old Shafter's. The house was forbidden him; but when he tapped at the window Ettie came out to him. The dancing Irish devilry had gone from her lover's eyes. She read his danger in his earnest face.

"Something has happened!" she cried. "Oh, Jack, you are in danger!"

"Sure, it is not very bad, my sweetheart. And yet it may be wise that we make a move before it is worse."

152 Closely guarded. A "tiler" is the name for the doorkeeper or guard at a Masonic or other fraternal lodge meeting.

"Make a move?"

"I promised you once that I would go some day. I think the time is coming. I had news to-night—bad news—and I see trouble coming."

"The police?"

"Well, a Pinkerton. But, sure, you wouldn't know what that is, acushla, nor what it may mean to the likes of me. I'm too deep in this thing, and I may have to get out of it quick. You said you would come with me if I went."

"Oh, Jack, it would be the saving of you!"

"I'm an honest man in some things, Ettie. I wouldn't hurt a hair of your bonny head for all that the world can give, nor ever pull you down one inch from the golden throne above the clouds where I always see you. Would you trust me?"

She put her hand in his without a word. "Well, then, listen to what I say, and do as I order you; for indeed it's the only way for us. Things are going to happen in this valley, I feel it in my bones. There may be many of us that will have to look out for ourselves. I'm one, anyhow. If I go, by day or night, it's you that must come with me!"

"I'd come after you, Jack."

"No, no, you shall come *with* me. If this valley is closed to me and I can never come back, how can I leave you behind, and me perhaps in hiding from the police with never a chance of a message? It's with me you must come. I know a good woman in the place I come from, and it's there I'd leave you till we can get married. Will you come?"

"Yes, Jack, I will come."

"God bless you for your trust in me. It's a fiend out of hell that I should be if I abused it. Now, mark you, Ettie, it will be just a word to you, and when it reaches you, you will drop everything and come right down to the waiting hall at the depôt and stay there till I come for you."

"Day or night, I'll come at the word, Jack."

Somewhat eased in mind now that his own preparations for escape had been begun, McMurdo went on to the Lodge. It had already assembled, and only by complicated signs and countersigns could he pass through the outer guard and inner guard who close-tiled[152] it. A buzz of pleasure and welcome greeted him as he entered. The long room was crowded, and through the haze of tobacco-smoke he saw the tangled black mane of the Bodymaster, the cruel, unfriendly features of Baldwin, the vulture face of Harraway, the secretary, and a dozen more who were among the leaders of the Lodge. He rejoiced that they should all be there to take counsel over his news.

"Indeed, it's glad we are to see you, Brother!" cried the chairman. "There's business here that wants a Solomon in judgment to set it right."

"It's Lander and Egan," explained his neighbour as he took his seat. "They both claim the head-money given by the Lodge for the shooting of old man Crabbe over at Stylestown, and who's to say which fired the bullet?"

McMurdo rose in his place and raised his hand. The expression of his face froze the attention of the audience. There was a dead bush of expectation.

"Worshipful Master," he said, in a solemn voice, "I claim urgency!"

"Brother McMurdo claims urgency," said McGinty. "It's a claim that by the rules of this Lodge takes precedence. Now, Brother, we attend you."

McMurdo took the letter from his pocket.

"Worshipful Master and Brethren," he said, "I am the bearer of ill news this day; but it is better that it should be known and discussed, than that a blow should fall upon us without warning which would destroy us all. I have information that the most powerful and richest organizations in this State have bound themselves together for our destruction, and that at this very moment there is a Pinkerton detective, one Birdy Edwards, at work in the valley collecting the evidence which may put a rope round the necks of many of us, and send every man in this room into a felon's cell. That is the situation for the discussion of which I have made a claim of urgency."

There was a dead silence in the room. It was broken by the chairman.

"What is your evidence for this, Brother McMurdo?" he asked.

"It is in this letter which has come into my hands," said McMurdo. He read the passage aloud. "It is a matter of honour with me that I can give no further particulars about the letter, nor put it into your hands; but I assure you that there is nothing else in it which can affect the interests of the Lodge. I put the case before you as it has reached me."

"Let me say, Mr. Chairman," said one of the older brethren, "that I have heard of Birdy Edwards, and that he has the name of being the best man in the Pinkerton service."

"Does anyone know him by sight?" asked McGinty.

"Yes," said McMurdo, "I do."

There was a murmur of astonishment through the hall.

"I believe we hold him in the hollow of our hands," he continued, with an exulting smile upon his face. "If we act quickly and wisely, we can cut this thing short. If I have your confidence and your help, it is little that we have to fear."

"What have we to fear, anyhow? What can he know of our affairs?"

"You might say so if all were as staunch as you, Councillor. But this man has all the millions of the capitalists at his back. Do you think there is no weaker brother among all our lodges that could not be bought? He will get at our secrets—maybe has got them already. There's only one sure cure."

"That he never leaves the valley," said Baldwin.

McMurdo nodded. "Good for you, Brother Baldwin," he said. "You and I have had our differences, but you have said the true word to-night."

"Where is he, then? Where shall we know him?"

"Worshipful Master," said McMurdo, earnestly. "I would put it to you that this is too vital a thing for us to discuss in open Lodge. God forbid that I should throw a doubt on anyone here; but if so much as a word of gossip got to the ears of this man, there would be an end of any chance of our getting him. I would ask the Lodge to choose a trusty committee, Mr. Chairman—yourself, if I might suggest it, and Brother Baldwin here, and five more. Then I can talk freely of what I know and of what I advise should be done."

The proposition was at once adopted, and the committee chosen. Besides the chairman and Baldwin, there were the vulture-faced secretary, Harraway; Tiger Cormac, the brutal young assassin; Carter, the treasurer; and the brothers Willaby, fearless and desperate men who would stick at nothing.

The usual revelry of the Lodge was short and subdued: for there was a cloud upon the men's spirits, and many there for the first time began to see the cloud of avenging Law drifting up in that serene sky under which they had dwelt so long. The horrors which they had dealt out to others had been so much a part of their settled lives that the thought of retribution had become a remote one, and so seemed the more startling now that it came so closely upon them. They broke up early and left their leaders to their council.

"Now, McMurdo!" said McGinty when they were alone. The seven men sat frozen in their seats.

"I said just now that I knew Birdy Edwards," McMurdo explained. "I need not tell you that he is not here under that name. He's a brave man, I dare bet, but not a crazy one. He passes under the name of Steve Wilson, and he is lodging at Hobson's Patch."

"How do you know this?"

"Because I fell into talk with him. I thought little of it at the time, nor would have given it a second thought but for this letter; but now I'm sure it's the man. I met him on the cars when I went down the line on Wednesday—a hard case if ever there was one. He said he was a reporter. I believed it for the moment. Wanted to know all he could about the Scowrers and what he called 'the outrages' for a New York paper. Asked me every kind of question so as to get something. You bet I was giving nothing away. 'I'd pay for it and pay well,' said he, 'if I could get some stuff that would suit my editor.' I said what I thought would please him best, and he handed me a twenty-dollar bill for my information. 'There's ten times that for you,' said he, 'if you can find me all that I want.' "

"What did you tell him, then?"

"Any stuff I could make up."

"How do you know he wasn't a newspaper man?"

"I'll tell you. He got out at Hobson's Patch, and so did I. I chanced into the telegraph bureau, and he was leaving it.

" 'See here,' said the operator after he'd gone out, 'I guess we should charge double rates for this.' 'I guess you should,' said I. He had filled the form with stuff that might have been Chinese, for all we could make of it. 'He fires a sheet of this off every day,' said the clerk. 'Yes,' said I; 'it's special news for his paper, and he's scared that the others should tap it.' That was what the operator thought and what I thought at the time; but I think differently now."

"By Gar! I believe you are right," said McGinty. "But what do you allow that we should do about it?"

"Why not go right down now and fix him?" some one suggested.

"Ay, the sooner the better."

"I'd start this next minute if I knew where we could find him," said McMurdo. "He's in Hobson's Patch; but I don't know the house. I've got a plan, though, if you'll only take my advice."

"Well, what is it?"

"I'll go to the Patch to-morrow morning. I'll find him through the operator. He can locate him, I guess. Well, then, I'll tell him that I'm a Freeman myself. I'll offer him all the secrets of the Lodge for a price. You bet he'll tumble to it. I'll tell him the papers are at my house, and that it's as much as my life would be worth to let him come while folk were about. He'll see that that's horse sense. Let him come at ten o'clock at night, and he shall see everything. That will fetch him sure."

"Well?"

"You can plan the rest for yourselves. Widow MacNamara's is a lonely house. She's as true as steel and as deaf as a post. There's only Scanlan and me in the house. If I get his promise—and I'll let you know if I do—I'd have the whole seven of you come to me by nine o'clock. We'll get him in. If ever he gets out alive—well, he can talk of Birdy Edwards' luck for the rest of his days!"

"There's going to be a vacancy at Pinkerton's or I'm mistaken. Leave it at that, McMurdo. At nine to-morrow we'll be with you. You once get the door shut behind him, and you can leave the rest with us."

CHAPTER VII

The Trapping of Birdy Edwards

As McMurdo had said, the house in which he lived was a lonely one and very well suited for such a crime as they had planned. It was on the extreme fringe of the town and stood well back from the road. In any other case the conspirators would have simply called out their man, as they had many a time before, and emptied their pistols into his body; but in this instance it was very necessary to find out how much he knew, how he knew it, and what had been passed on to his employers.

It was possible that they were already too late and that the work had been done. If that was indeed so, they could at least have their revenge upon the man who had done it. But they were hopeful that nothing of great importance had yet come to the detective's knowledge, as otherwise, they argued, he would not have troubled to write down and forward such trivial information as McMurdo claimed to have given him. However, all this they would learn from his own lips. Once in their power, they would find a way to make him speak. It was not the first time that they had handled an unwilling witness.

McMurdo went to Hobson's Patch as agreed. The police

seemed to take particular interest in him that morning, and Captain Marvin—he who had claimed the old acquaintance with him at Chicago—actually addressed him as he waited at the depôt. McMurdo turned away and refused to speak with him. He was back from his mission in the afternoon, and saw McGinty at the Union House.

"He is coming," he said.

"Good!" said McGinty. The giant was in his shirt sleeves, with chains and seals gleaming athwart his ample waistcoat and a diamond twinkling through the fringe of his bristling beard. Drink and politics had made the Boss a very rich as well as powerful man. The more terrible, therefore, seemed that glimpse of the prison or the gallows which had risen before him the night before.

"Do you reckon he knows much?" he asked anxiously.

McMurdo shook his head gloomily. "He's been here some time—six weeks at the least. I guess he didn't come into these parts to look at the prospect. If he has been working among us all that time with the railroad money at his back, I should expect that he has got results, and that he has passed them on."

"There's not a weak man in the Lodge," cried McGinty. "True as steel, every man of them. And yet, by the Lord, there is that skunk Morris. What about him? If any man gives us away, it would be he. I've a mind to send a couple of the boys round before evening to give him a beating up and see what they can get from him."

"Well, there would be no harm in that," McMurdo answered. "I won't deny that I have a liking for Morris and would be sorry to see him come to harm. He has spoken to me once or twice over Lodge matters, and though he may not see them the same as you or I, he never seemed the sort that squeals. But still it is not for me to stand between him and you."

"I'll fix the old devil!" said McGinty with an oath. "I've had my eye on him this year past."

"Well, you know best about that," McMurdo answered. "But whatever you do must be to-morrow, for we must lie low until the Pinkerton affair is settled up. We can't afford to set the police buzzing to-day of all days."

"True for you," said McGinty. "And we'll learn from Birdy

Edwards himself where he got his news if we have to cut his heart out first. Did he seem to scent a trap?"

McMurdo laughed. "I guess I took him on his weak point," he said. "If he could get on a good trail of the Scowrers, he's ready to follow it into hell. I took his money," McMurdo grinned as he produced a wad of dollar notes, "and as much more when he has seen all my papers."

"What papers?"

"Well, there are no papers. But I filled him up about constitutions and books of rules and forms of membership. He expects to get right down to the end of everything before he leaves."

"Faith, he's right there," said McGinty grimly. "Didn't he ask you why you didn't bring him the papers?"

"As if I would carry such things, and me a suspected man, and Captain Marvin after speaking to me this very day at the depot!"

"Ay, I heard of that," said McGinty. "I guess the heavy end of this business is coming on to you. We could put him down an old shaft when we've done with him; but however we work it we can't get past the man living at Hobson's Patch and you being there to-day."

McMurdo shrugged his shoulders. "If we handle it right, they can never prove the killing," said he. "No one can see him come to the house after dark, and I'll lay to it that no one will see him go. Now see here, Councillor, I'll show you my plan and I'll ask you to fit the others into it. You will all come in good time. Very well. He comes at ten. He is to tap three times, and me to open the door for him. Then I'll get behind him and shut it. He's our man then."

"That's all easy and plain."

"Yes; but the next step wants considering. He's a hard proposition. He's heavily armed. I've fooled him proper, and yet he is likely to be on his guard. Suppose I show him right into a room with seven men in it where he expected to find me alone. There is going to be shooting, and somebody is going to be hurt."

"That's so."

"And the noise is going to bring every damned copper in the township on top of it."

"I guess you are right."

"This is how I should work it. You will all be in the big room—same as you saw when you had a chat with me. I'll open the door for him, show him into the parlour beside the door, and leave him there while I get the papers. That will give me the chance of telling you how things are shaping. Then I will go back to him with some faked papers. As he is reading them I will jump for him and get my grip on his pistol arm. You'll hear me call and in you will rush. The quicker the better; for he is as strong a man as I, and I may have more than I can manage. But I allow that I can hold him till you come."

"It's a good plan," said McGinty. "The Lodge will owe you a debt for this. I guess when I move out of the chair I can put a name to the man that's coming after me."

"Sure, Councillor, I am little more than a recruit," said McMurdo, but his face showed what he thought of the great man's compliment.

When he had returned home he made his own preparations for the grim evening in front of him. First he cleaned, oiled, and loaded his Smith & Wesson revolver.[153] Then he surveyed the room in which the detective was to be trapped. It was a large apartment, with a long deal table in the centre, and the big stove at one end. At each of the other sides were windows. There were no shutters on these: only light curtains which drew across. McMurdo examined these attentively. No doubt it must have struck him that the apartment was very exposed for so secret a matter. Yet its distance from the road made it of less consequence. Finally he discussed the matter with his fellow Lodger. Scanlan, though a Scowrer, was an inoffensive little man who was too weak to stand against the opinion of his comrades, but was secretly horrified by the deeds of blood at which he had sometimes been forced to assist. McMurdo told him shortly what was intended.

"And if I were you, Mike Scanlan, I would take a night off and keep clear of it. There will be bloody work here before morning."

"Well, indeed then, Mac," Scanlan answered. "It's not the will but the nerve that is wanting in me. When I saw Manager Dunn go down at the colliery yonder it was just more than I could stand. I'm not made for it same as you or McGinty. If the

153 Horace Smith and Daniel B. Wesson first partnered in 1852 in Norwich, Connecticut, to manufacture a lever-action repeating pistol. Facing financial difficulties, they were forced to sell their enterprise to Oliver Winchester (see note 140, above), who was able to achieve success for his own company using elements of the original design. Undaunted, Smith and Wesson founded their next company in 1856 to manufacture the first revolver with a fully contained cartridge (known as the Model 1). Having obtained patents on both the gun and the cartridge, the partners were the sole producers of that sort of gun until the patent expired in 1872. In 1870 they began selling the Model 3 American, the first large-calibre, or "big-bore," cartridge revolver on the market. This self-ejecting revolver was a favourite among frontiersmen and Western lawmakers—the U.S. cavalry purchased 1,000 of them—and McMurdo was in all likelihood the owner of one of these guns, possibly the popular .45.

Lodge will think none the worse of me, I'll just do as you advise and leave you to yourselves for the evening."

The men came in good time as arranged. They were outwardly respectable citizens, well clad and cleanly; but a judge of faces would have read little hope for Birdy Edwards in those hard mouths and remorseless eyes. There was not a man in the room whose hands had not been reddened a dozen times before. They were as hardened to human murder as a butcher to sheep.

Foremost, of course, both in appearance and in guilt, was the formidable Boss. Harraway, the secretary, was a lean, bitter man with a long, scraggy neck and nervous, jerky limbs—a man of incorruptible fidelity where the finances of the order were concerned,[154] and with no notion of justice or honesty to anyone beyond. The treasurer, Carter, was a middle-aged man with an impassive, rather sulky expression, and a yellow parchment skin. He was a capable organizer, and the actual details of nearly every outrage had sprung from his plotting brain. The two Willabys were men of action, tall, lithe young fellows with determined faces, while their companion, Tiger Cormac, a heavy, dark youth, was feared even by his own comrades for the ferocity of his disposition. These were the men who assembled that night under the roof of McMurdo for the killing of the Pinkerton detective.

Their host had placed whisky upon the table, and they had hastened to prime themselves for the work before them. Baldwin and Cormac were already half-drunk, and the liquor had brought out all their ferocity. Cormac placed his hands on the stove for an instant—it had been lighted, for the nights were still cold.

"That will do," said he, with an oath.

"Ay," said Baldwin, catching his meaning. "If he is strapped to that, we will have the truth out of him."

"We'll have the truth out of him, never fear," said McMurdo. He had nerves of steel, this man; for though the whole weight of the affair was on him his manner was as cool and unconcerned as ever. The others marked it and applauded.

"You are the one to handle him," said the Boss approvingly. "Not a warning will he get till your hand is on his throat. It's a pity there are no shutters to your windows."

154 Colin Prestige points out that the descriptions appear to be wrong here. The remark about "finances" seems applicable to Carter, the treasurer; and one would think that the "capable organiser" would be Harraway, the secretary. The description of Harraway is also inconsistent with earlier depictions of the "vulture-faced old greybeard." In the manuscript of *The Valley of Fear*, Prestige reports, Harraway is originally described as "the secretary treasurer" and the phrase "The treasurer Carter" originally read "The Secretary Stinton." Douglas's notes were evidently confused here.

McMurdo went from one to the other and drew the curtains tighter. "Sure no one can spy upon us now. It's close upon the hour."

"Maybe he won't come. Maybe he'll get a sniff of danger," said the secretary.

"He'll come, never fear," McMurdo answered. "He is as eager to come as you can be to see him. Hark to that!"

They all sat like wax figures, some with their glasses arrested halfway to their lips. Three loud knocks had sounded at the door.

"Hush!" McMurdo raised his hand in caution. An exulting glance went round the circle, and hands were laid upon hidden weapons.

"Not a sound, for your lives!" McMurdo whispered, as he went from the room, closing the door carefully behind him.

With strained ears the murderers waited. They counted the steps of their comrade down the passage. Then they heard him open the outer door. There were a few words as of greeting. Then they were aware of a strange step inside and of an unfamiliar voice. An instant later came the slam of the door and the turning of the key in the lock. Their prey was safe within the trap. Tiger Cormac laughed horribly, and Boss McGinty clapped his great hand across his mouth.

"Be quiet, you fool!" he whispered. "You'll be the undoing of us yet!"

There was a mutter of conversation from the next room. It seemed interminable. Then the door opened, and McMurdo appeared, his finger upon his lip.

He came to the end of the table and looked round at them. A subtle change had come over him. His manner was as of one who has great work to do. His face had set into granite firmness. His eyes shone with a fierce excitement behind his spectacles. He had become a visible leader of men. They stared at him with eager interest; but he said nothing. Still with the same singular gaze he looked from man to man.

"Well!" cried Boss McGinty at last. "Is he here? Is Birdy Edwards here?"

"Yes," McMurdo answered slowly. "Birdy Edwards is here. I am Birdy Edwards!"[155]

There were ten seconds after that brief speech during which the room might have been empty, so profound was the silence.

155 The name "McMurdo" chosen by Edwards as his alias has a fine Irish ring to it. He may have had in mind Lieutenant Archibald McMurdo, an officer on the *Terror*, one of the ships of James Clark Ross used on his expedition to the Antarctic from 1839 to 1843. McMurdo Base is now a permanent land base at the southern end of Ross Island, located on McMurdo Sound at 77°55' S, 166°40' E.

" 'Not a sound, for your lives!' McMurdo whispered."
Arthur I. Keller, *Associated Sunday Magazines*, 1914

The hissing of a kettle upon the stove rose sharp and strident to the ear. Seven white faces, all turned upward to this man who dominated them, were set motionless with utter terror. Then, with a sudden shivering of glass, a bristle of glistening rifle barrels broke through each window, whilst the curtains were torn from their hangings.

At the sight Boss McGinty gave the roar of a wounded bear and plunged for the half-opened door. A levelled revolver met him there with the stern blue eyes of Captain Marvin of the Coal and Iron Police gleaming behind the sights. The Boss recoiled and fell back into his chair.

"You're safer there, Councillor," said the man whom they had known as McMurdo. "And you, Baldwin, if you don't take your hand off your gun, you'll cheat the hangman yet. Pull it out, or by the Lord that made me—there, that will do. There are forty armed men round this house, and you can figure it out for yourself what chance you have. Take their pistols, Marvin!"

There was no possible resistance under the menace of those rifles. The men were disarmed. Sulky, sheepish, and amazed, they still sat round the table.

"I'd like to say a word to you before we separate," said the man who had trapped them. "I guess we may not meet again

"Then with a sudden shivering of glass, a bristle of glistening rifle-barrels broke through each window, whilst the curtains were torn from their hangings."
Frank Wiles, *Strand Magazine*, 1915

until you see me on the stand in the courthouse. I'll give you something to think over between now and then. You know me now for what I am. At last I can put my cards on the table. I am Birdy Edwards of Pinkerton's. I was chosen to break up your gang. I had a hard and dangerous game to play. Not a soul, not one soul, not my nearest and dearest, knew that I was playing it except Captain Marvin here and my employers. But it's over to-night thank God, and I am the winner!"

156 Ian McQueen suggests that Holmes, in joining an Irish secret society in Buffalo to build his "Altamont" reputation (in "His Last Bow"), may have taken a page from McMurdo's book.

The seven pale, rigid faces looked up at him. There was unappeasable hatred in their eyes. He read the relentless threat.

"Maybe you think that the game is not over yet. Well, I take my chance of that. Anyhow, some of you will take no further hand, and there are sixty more besides yourselves that will see a jail this night. I'll tell you this, that when I was put upon this job I never believed there was such a society as yours. I thought it was paper talk, and that I would prove it so. They told me it was to do with the Freemen; so I went to Chicago and was made one.[156] Then I was surer than ever that it was just paper talk; for I found no harm in the society, but a deal of good.

"Still, I had to carry out my job, and I came for the coal val-

157 In America, a slang term for a type of sensational literature, cheaply printed and sold for ten cents or less. Many Sherlock Holmes stories were reprinted in dime novels, and many authors copied the style of Watson's stories. For a brief overview of the Canon in the dime novel format, see J. Randolph Cox's "A. Conan Doyle, Dime Novelist; or, Magnetic Attractions for Bibliophiles." Nils Nordberg's "Sherlock Holmes in the Claws of the Confidence Men; or, The Misadventures of a World Detective," traces the history of Sherlock Holmes as a character in European dime novels.

" 'Halt!' shouted Linden." [The Coal and Iron Police in action.]
The Molly Maguires and the Detectives, by Allan Pinkerton (1877)

leys. When I reached this place I learned that I was wrong and that it wasn't a dime novel[157] after all. So I stayed to look after it. I never killed a man in Chicago. I never minted a dollar in my life. Those I gave you were as good as any others; but I never spent money better. But I knew the way into your good wishes, and so I pretended to you that the law was after me. It all worked just as I thought.

"So I joined your infernal Lodge, and I took my share in your councils. Maybe they will say that I was as bad as you. They can say what they like, so long as I get you. But what is the truth? The night I joined you beat up old man Stanger. I could not warn him, for there was no time, but I held your hand, Baldwin, when you would have killed him. If ever I have suggested things, so as to keep my place among you, they were things which I knew I could prevent. I could not save Dunn and Menzies, for I did not know enough; but I will see that their murderers are hanged. I gave Chester Wilcox warning, so that when I blew his house in he and his folk were in hiding. There was many a crime that I could not stop; but if you look back and think how often your man came home the other road, or was down in town when you went for him, or stayed indoors when you thought he would come out, you'll see my work."

"You blasted traitor!" hissed McGinty through his closed teeth.

"Ay, John McGinty, you may call me that if it eases your

smart. You and your like have been the enemy of God and man in these parts. It took a man to get between you and the poor devils of men and women that you held under your grip. There was just one way of doing it, and I did it. You call me a traitor; but I guess there's many a thousand will call me a deliverer that went down into hell to save them. I've had three months of it. I wouldn't have three such months again if they let me loose in the treasury at Washington for it. I had to stay till I had it all, every man and every secret right here in this hand. I'd have waited a little longer if it hadn't come to my knowledge that my secret was coming out. A letter had come into the town that would have set you wise to it all. Then I had to act and act quickly.

"I've nothing more to say to you, except that when my time comes I'll die the easier when I think of the work I have done in this valley. Now, Marvin, I'll keep you no more. Take them in and get it over."

There is little more to tell. Scanlan had been given a sealed note to be left at the address of Miss Ettie Shafter—a mission which he had accepted with a wink and knowing smile. In the early hours of the morning a beautiful woman and a much-muffled man boarded a special train which had been sent by the railroad company, and made a swift unbroken journey out of the land of danger. It was the last time that ever either Ettie or her lover set foot in the Valley of Fear. Ten days later they were married in Chicago, with old Jacob Shafter as witness of the wedding.

The trial of the Scowrers was held far from the place where their adherents might have terrified the guardians of the law. In vain they struggled. In vain the money of the Lodge—money squeezed by blackmail out of the whole countryside—was spent like water in the attempt to save them. That cold, clear, unimpassioned statement from one who knew every detail of their lives, their organization, and their crimes was unshaken by all the wiles of their defenders. At last after so many years they were broken and scattered. The cloud was lifted for ever from the valley.

McGinty met his fate upon the scaffold, cringing and whining when the last hour came. Eight of his chief followers shared his fate. Fifty-odd had various degrees of imprisonment. The work of Birdy Edwards was complete.

And yet, as he had guessed, the game was not over yet. There was another hand to be played, and yet another and another. Ted Baldwin, for one, had escaped the scaffold; so had the Willabys; so had several others of the fiercest spirits of the gang. For ten years they were out of the world, and then came a day when they were free[158] once more—a day which Edwards, who knew his men, was very sure would be an end of his life of peace. They had sworn an oath on all that they thought holy to have his blood as a vengeance for their comrades. And well they strove to keep their vow!

From Chicago he was chased, after two attempts so near success that it was sure that the third would get him. From Chicago he went, under a changed name, to California, and it was there that the light went for a time out of his life when Ettie Edwards died. Once again he was nearly killed, and once again under the name of Douglas he worked in a lonely canyon, where with an English partner named Barker he amassed a fortune. At last there came a warning to him that the bloodhounds were on his track once more, and he cleared—only just in time—for England.[159] And thence came the John Douglas who for a second time married a worthy mate, and lived for five years as a Sussex country gentleman—a life which ended with the strange happenings of which we have heard.[160]

158 Owen Dudley Edward observes, "[I]t is difficult to see how, since McMurdo had his full account of his murder of Hales of Stake Royal; but presumably the lodge members and the passing couple stayed away." Ian McQueen notes that Douglas "fails to make it clear whether that [ten-year] period was the sentence [Baldwin] served, calculated from the date of conviction, or the total length of his incarceration following his arrest. It is inconceivable that he was ever allowed bail."

159 Dean W. Dickensheet, in " 'Two Good Men,' " presents startling evidence of the avenging presence of the Molly Maguires in Nevada in 1875, evidently on the trail of Edwards, en route from Chicago to California. In "The Birlstone Masquerade," Theodore W. Gibson argues that Allan Pinkerton was protecting the real Birdy Edwards, and that John Douglas was assigned to assume the rôle of Edwards and draw off the avengers.

In a fascinating piece of speculation entitled "The Birlstone Hoax," Charles B. Stephens takes the position that Cecil Barker, not Douglas, was Birdy Edwards. He bases this analysis on Watson's earlier description of Barker as "a tall, straight, broad-chested fellow, with a clean-shaved, prize-fighter face, thick, strong, black eyebrows, and a pair of masterful black eyes which might, even without the aid of his very capable hands, clear a way for him through a hostile crowd." Stephens proposes that Barker came to England to infiltrate Moriarty's gang under the *nom de plume* of "Porlock" and to resume working with Captain Marvin—alias Sherlock Holmes!

160 It is beyond question that the basis for Birdy Edwards (a k a Jack McMurdo, a k a John Douglas) was James McParlan, a detective with the Pinkerton National Detective Agency. In 1873, railroad magnate Franklin Gowen, concerned about the Molly Maguires' power and their ability to undercut his own profits, appealed to Allan Pinkerton to help him bring down the secret society. Pinkerton sent McParlan, a gregarious Irish Catholic immigrant who ingratiated himself with the most influential Mollies and quickly rose through the ranks of the organisation. "James McKenna," as he called himself, spent two years gathering information on the Molly Maguires, learning everything there was to know about how their activities were carried out. Eventually, his cover was blown. After discovering that Jack Kehoe suspected his true identity and planned to murder him, McParlan fled the area and served as the key witness in a series of sensational trials, in which he testified against more than fifty alleged members of the Molly Maguires. Kehoe and eighteen others were convicted and hanged, and Franklin Gowen mysteriously committed suicide in 1889, less than a week before the eleventh anniversary of Kehoe's execution.

Several details in Edwards's tale resonate with events from McParlan's own experience undercover. McParlan claimed to be a counterfeiter, a ruse that explained how he always had enough cash on hand to treat his new friends to another round of drinks. Upon his arrival in town, he immediately impressed the Mollies gathered at the Sheridan House by dancing a hornpipe, singing a song, and then playing a game of euchre in which the local bodymaster served as his partner. Though the story may be apocryphal, Cleveland Moffett wrote that McParlan hotly accused a burly Molly of cheating, then bested him in a fistfight despite being at a significant height and weight disadvantage. "Six times in succession," Moffett wrote, "he [McParlan] floored the bully of Pottsville, and the seventh time Frazer fell heavily on his face and failed to get up again." Like Birdy Edwards, McParlan allowed others to believe that he had once committed murder; and like Edwards, he did what he could to thwart planned attacks, though he was not always successful.

Here, however, the stories of Edwards and McParlan diverge. Modern historians point out that by McParlan's own testimony, he was often on the fine edge of actual participation in the Mollies' violence and speculate that he may well have provoked a portion of it. His testimony in several of the controversial Pennsylvania cases was for the most part unsubstantiated, and in other instances was corroborated only by questionable witnesses who had turned state's evidence. After testifying against the Molly Maguires, McParlan did not go into hiding but became the head of Pinkerton's western division, based in Colorado. In 1906, he was involved in a botched investigation into the murder of Frank Steunenberg, the governor of Idaho, and his questionable exploits and tactics were brought to light by defence attorney Clarence Darrow. After retiring, McParlan died in 1919 in Denver.

EPILOGUE

THE POLICE TRIAL had passed, in which the case of John Douglas was referred to a higher court. So had the Quarter Sessions,[161] at which he was acquitted as having acted in self-defence.

"Get him out of England at any cost," wrote Holmes to the wife. "There are forces here which may be more dangerous than those he has escaped. There is no safety for your husband in England."

Two months had gone by, and the case had to some extent passed from our minds. Then one morning there came an enigmatic note slipped into our letter-box. "Dear me, Mr. Holmes. Dear me!" said this singular epistle. There was neither superscription nor signature. I laughed at the quaint message; but Holmes showed unwonted seriousness.

"Devilry, Watson!" he remarked, and sat long with a clouded brow.[162]

Late last night Mrs. Hudson, our landlady, brought up a message that a gentleman wished to see Holmes, and that the matter was of the utmost importance. Close at the heels of his

161 The English book text refers to the "police court" and the "Assizes."

162 What did Holmes read into this "enigmatic note"? It's possible, muses David Talbott Cox, that the text contained the Greek ε Holmes observed in Porlock's earlier messages, causing Holmes to realise that "Porlock" was Moriarty, bent on exacting retribution for Holmes's interference. Contrarily, Christopher F. Baum reads the situation at its face value, dismissing Professor Moriarty as a candidate for Porlock precisely because Holmes did not (apparently) notice any Greek έs in the note.

" 'I've had bad news—terrible news, Mr. Holmes,' said he."
Frank Wiles, *Strand Magazine*, 1915

messenger came Mr. Cecil Barker, our friend of the moated Manor House. His face was drawn and haggard.

"I've had bad news—terrible news, Mr. Holmes," said he.

"I feared as much," said Holmes.

"You have not had a cable, have you?"

"I have had a note from some one who has."

"It's poor Douglas. They tell me his name is Edwards; but he will always be Jack Douglas of Benito Canyon to me. I told you that they started together for South Africa in the *Palmyra*[163] three weeks ago."

"Exactly."

"The ship reached Cape Town last night. I received this cable from Mrs. Douglas this morning:

163 Donald A. Redmond, in *Sherlock Holmes: A Study in Sources*, notes that "*The Times* for 28 May 1890 records a fire aboard the SS *Palmyra* lying at the Fresh Wharf, Thames-street, struck by a spark from a shovel and extinguished without much damage." If the chronologists are correct (see *Appendix 3*), this would have occurred after the ship's return from Africa. Was there evidence aboard the ship that Moriarty sought to destroy?

Jack has been lost overboard in gale off St. Helena.[164] No one knows how accident occurred.

Ivy Douglas.[165]

"Ha! It came like that, did it?" said Holmes thoughtfully. "Well, I've no doubt it was well stage-managed."[166]

"You mean that you think there was no accident?"

"None in the world."

"He was murdered?"

"Surely!"

"So I think also. These infernal Scowrers, this cursed vindictive nest of criminals—"[167]

"No, no, my good sir," said Holmes. "There is a master hand here. It is no case of sawed-off shot-guns and clumsy six-shooters. You can tell an old master by the sweep of his brush. I can tell a Moriarty when I see one. This crime is from London, not from America."

"But for what motive?"

"Because it is done by a man who cannot afford to fail—one whose whole unique position depends upon the fact that all he does must succeed. A great brain and a huge organization have been turned to the extinction of one man. It is crushing the nut with the triphammer—an absurd extravagance of energy—but the nut is very effectually crushed all the same."

"How came this man to have anything to do with it?"

"I can only say that the first word that ever came to us of the business was from one of his lieutenants.[168] These Americans were well advised. Having an English job to do, they took into partnership, as any foreign criminal could do, this great consultant in crime. From that moment their man was doomed.[169] At first he would content himself by using his machinery in order to find their victim. Then he would indicate how the matter might be treated. Finally, when he read in the reports of the failure of this agent, he would step in himself with a master touch. You heard me warn this man at Birlstone Manor House that the coming danger was greater than the past. Was I right?"[170]

Barker beat his head with his clenched fist in his impotent anger. "Do you tell me that we have to sit down under this? Do you say that no one can ever get level with this king-devil?"

"No, I don't say that," said Holmes, and his eyes seemed to

164 Saint Helena is a lonely island in the Atlantic, 1,200 miles off the west coast of Africa. It became a British colony in 1834 and remains so to this day. After his defeat at Waterloo, Napoleon was exiled to Saint Helena in 1815, living at a farmhouse in Longwood, three miles from the capital of Jamestown, until his death in 1821. Brigadier Étienne Gerard, whose allegedly fictional adventures were also published by Arthur Conan Doyle, visited Saint Helena in an abortive effort to rescue his beloved emperor. "Here, then, was the island of my dreams!" he said, upon seeing its shores. "Here was the cage where our great Eagle of France was confined!"

165 Note that this is the only mention of Mrs. Douglas's first name.

166 Indeed, suggests Theodore W. Gibson, perhaps the "stage management" was the doing of the inventive and resourceful Jack Douglas, who in impersonating Birdy Edwards had attempted earlier to vanish from view, only to be foiled by the inopportune interference of Holmes. See note 170, below.

167 Cornelius Helling, in a letter to the *Sherlock Holmes Journal*, wonders why Holmes, a "walking calendar of crime," needed John Douglas's explanation to recognise the "nest of criminals." Upon observing the sawn shotgun from the Pennsylvania Small Arm Company, the brand on the dead man's forearm, and, above all, the card with the initials V.V. and the number 341 rudely scrawled upon it, why did he not "instantly remember the momentous trial of the infamous Scowrers of Vermissa Valley only fifteen years ago and the remarkable rôle played by the Pinkerton man Birdy Edwards—and so [identify] John Douglas at once with Edwards? Or, perhaps had he his good reasons to keep silent?" (Of course, the initials would have been "M.M." or perhaps "A.O.H.," and it is the name "James McParlan" that Holmes should have recollected.)

168 Alan Olding observes that the following passage "encapsulates the whole tragic history of what was surely Holmes's greatest failure. If we analyse these remarks, we can see at once the frustration of a man who realises that he has been out-manoeuvred from the start; that he has been cheated of his victory, and that, by his unquestioning acceptance at face value of the cipher message from his quondam 'Secret Agent,' he has been used himself, as an unsuspecting tool of the 'controlling brain of the underworld.' "

169 "Is this an admission, or a justification of his failure?" wonders Olding.

170 "Oh, no, Mr. Holmes you were wrong!!" laments Olding, who points to numerous cases ("The Second Stain," "The Boscombe Valley Mystery") in which Holmes, by turning a blind eye, extended his forgiveness and aid toward otherwise worthy people who had confessed to having done wrong. "Why in heaven's name could you not have done the same for this brave man, who had descended into Hell, in his selfless devotion to duty, and to the Law?" D. Martin Dakin raises similar questions: "If Douglas's plan [to disappear] had been allowed to go forward, then indeed, as he said, it might have been assumed that Baldwin had got him, pursuit would have been thrown off and he and his wife could have ended their days in peace. We are driven to the melancholy conclusion that if Holmes had kept his mouth shut (as he did with Captain Croker ["The Abbey Grange"] and Dr. Sterndale ["The Devil's Foot"]) or if he had never been called in at all, the ending would have been a much happier one. Or would the wily Moriarty have found out in any case?"

be looking far into the future. "I don't say that he can't be beat. But you must give me time—you must give me time!"[171]

We all sat in silence for some minutes while those fateful eyes still strained to pierce the veil.

Mr. Sherlock Holmes.
Frederic Dorr Steele, *Final Adventures of Sherlock Holmes*, Vol. I, 1952.
Plainly a reuse of the cover for "The Priory School," *Collier's*, 1904.

171 Why, ponders Michael Waxenberg, in "Organized Thoughts on Organized Labor, or Labour's Libels Lost in The Valley of Fear," did Holmes need time to beat Moriarty? This conversation probably occurred in early 1890 (see *Appendix 3*). Perhaps, Waxenberg argues, Moriarty's gang had close ties to British organised labour, and Holmes did not want to cause unnecessary harm to the labour movement at that time. By 1891, however, certain court cases had given trade unions the right to threaten to strike and picket and the old relationships with organised criminals became obsolete; therefore, Holmes was then free to round up the Moriarty gang without injuring the trade union movement.

APPENDIX 1

"Who, Then, Is Porlock?"

Watson's desire to "pierce the veil" of the identity of "Fred Porlock" is shared by many scholars.

Ronald A. Knox considers at length, in "The Mystery of Mycroft," the position of Holmes's enigmatic brother, Mycroft Holmes, who figures prominently in "The Greek Interpreter" and other stories. Mycroft, Knox argues, was a man of "nefarious associations" who often collaborated with Professor Moriarty and therefore was able to pass along inside information to Holmes. "It is easy to understand," Knox reasons,

> that some of [Holmes's] "most interesting cases" came to him through Mycroft, and that Mycroft was able to supply his brother, perplexed over a difficult problem, with "an explanation which was afterwards proved to be the correct one ['The Greek Interpreter']." Although the thing cannot be proved, I am strongly of the opinion that Mycroft was in fact the "Fred Porlock" who acted as his brother's informer in *The Valley of Fear*. Sherlock—Porlock; there is a subconscious reminiscence in the choice of an alias which suggests a family connection. And who more likely than Mycroft, with his tidy and orderly brain, his great capacity for storing facts, to use *Whitaker's Almanack* as the basis of a cipher message?

But there are other views. David Talbott Cox theorises, in "Poor Sherlock," that Professor Moriarty himself was Porlock, and as such sent Holmes intentionally misleading messages. In this case, he "called in" Holmes to put pressure on the Scowrers to pay his fee. Noah Andre Trudeau, in "Fred Porlock—Probing 'A Link in the Chain,' " agrees with Cox's conclusion but psychoanalyses that "Porlock" was the "good" personality of a schizophrenic Professor Moriarty.[172] In "Porlock—Piercing the Nom de Plume," Paul B. Smedegaard advocates for Colonel Sebastian Moran, Moriarty's chief of staff and "the second most dangerous man in London" ("The Empty House"), who intended to supplant his master. Thomas Andrew, in "The Porlock Puzzle: An Abbreviated Solution," proposes Mrs. Hudson as the agent, while Russell McDermott,

172 See also Gordon R. Speck's "Fred Porlock's Identity," which suggests that Moriarty used the *nom de plume* to hide his duplicity in ridding his organisation of assertive or incompetent members.

in "Porlock, the Professor, and Colonel James," suggests Colonel James Moriarty, who sought to take over his brother's organisation. After considering the suggestions of Knox, Cox, Smedegaard, Dandrew, and McDermott, Christopher F. Baum, in "The Problem of Porlock," also concludes that Porlock was Colonel James Moriarty. Colonel Moran, Baum argues, lacked the necessary intelligence for the role, as evidenced by his foolishly attempting to kill Holmes by using the same air-gun he had used on Ronald Adair ("The Empty House").[173]

Still other candidates abound: In "A Case of Identity," Paul Zens, pointing out that Porlock is a town in the northwest corner of the western county of Somerset, makes a case for the third Moriarty brother, "the station master in the west of England." He traces a career for the young Moriarty, beginning as a station master and ending as "Deputy Chief of Transportation" in the Moriarty organization, eventually relocating to London. Alan Olding, in "The Spy Who Stayed in the Warm," suggests Adolphe Verloc of Joseph Conrad's *The Secret Agent.*

The most compelling summation of the issue is a letter by Donald Alan Webster to the *Baker Street Journal*, which (because it has received so little attention) is quoted here in full. "Ever since *The Valley of Fear*," writes Webster,

> many individuals have asked Watson's question, "Who, then, is Porlock?" Eight contrivers of the Porlock letters have been suggested. These are Mrs. Cecil Forrester, Mycroft Holmes, Sherlock Holmes, Mrs. Hudson, Shinwell Johnson, Sebastian Moran, and all three Jameses Moriarty. Some of these can easily be eliminated. Porlock was "scared out of his senses." Moran would not have been. Colonel James Moriarty's letters to *The Times* indicate that he was no friend of Sherlock Holmes and was presumably not even aware of his brother's criminal activities. The idea that Professor James Moriarty wrote the letters to mislead Holmes is possible but improbable. The professor would not be likely to take the unnecessary risk of accidentally giving Holmes an important clue. The notion that Holmes himself wrote the letters in order to conceal from Watson that his information on Moriarty came from opium-created visions does not deserve a refutation. I feel that important clues have been overlooked.
>
> Clue No. 1—Porlock is close to Moriarty and knows of his

173 Baum's rejection of the candidacy of *Professor* Moriarty is challenged by Donald K. Pollock, Jr., in a letter to the *Baker Street Journal*, in which he points out that Moriarty may well have disguised his handwriting in the Porlock notes. Baum responds in another letter that it is unlikely that one could disguise his hand in the same way three times. He admits, however, the weight of Pollock's argument that Professor and Colonel Moriarty would have had similar handwriting and withdraws his definitive conclusion that Colonel Moriarty was Porlock. Who, then?

criminal activities. Since Holmes emphasises how well-concealed Moriarty was, very few of his gang would know this. Only the well-paid (£6000 a year) inner circle would know (in his gang at least).

Clue No. 2—Porlock is not well paid. Porlock's willingness to sell out to Holmes for a mere £10 reveals that Porlock is desperate and therefore not getting £6000 a year.

Clue No. 3—Porlock is living with Prof. Moriarty. Porlock writes, "He came to me quite unexpectedly after I had actually addressed this envelope with the intention of sending you the key to the cipher. I was able to cover it up." This would not be possible if Porlock and the professor were living in different houses.

Clue No. 4—Porlock was not a member of Moriarty's gang. Every one writing about Porlock till now has assumed that he was a gang member, but our first three clues point against that. The only gang members close to the professor were the highly paid inner circle (clue no. 1), but Porlock could not have been one of them since he was not highly paid (clue no. 2). Furthermore, in order to be well-concealed, the professor would hardly be living with a gang member (clue no. 3). Porlock, therefore, must be someone close to the professor who discovered the criminal connection by chance. Who could he be? Of the suggested Porlocks the only ones likely to be living with the professor were his brothers. We have already eliminated the colonel. The station-master is unlikely. Holmes's image of a spider in the centre of its web indicates that Prof. Moriarty lived in London. A station-master in the west of England must live in the west of England. Moriarty is unmarried, so it is not his wife and not likely a son or daughter. Given the mores of the time, a mistress is not likely. She would not have been living with him.[174] Who is left? Who is there who would always be around? From whom secrets could not be kept? Who would be notoriously underpaid? I think the answer to the question "Who, then, is Porlock?" lies downstairs, not upstairs.

In "Excellent, Watson! . . . An Almanac!," P. H. Wood makes a detailed response to Webster's arguments. Agreeing with his first "clue" but rejecting the rest, Wood deduces that Porlock (1) apparently has a strong motive to prevent the Birlstone

174 P. H. Wood scoffs at this statement as displaying "an amazing lack of acquaintance with the facts of Victorian life." See Christopher Redmond's *In Bed with Sherlock Holmes*, which considers at length Victorian sexual mores and their reflections in the Canon.

murder, risking death; (2) cannot leave Moriarty's employ, because of some hold over him; (3) has not long been with the gang (otherwise, there would have been more occasions of attempts to hinder Moriarty; (4) has a good education; (5) must have come in contact with Moriarty; and (6) must hold a fairly senior position with the gang. Wood concludes that Porlock is a university man with a mathematical background, was tutored or employed by Moriarty when Moriarty was a coach, and was induced into accepting a senior administrative post. His responsibilities would have been communication and security. He speculates that Porlock was the younger brother of Ivy Douglas.

Yet no identification is fully satisfactory, and the truth may remain undiscovered until further information comes to light.

Appendix 2

People, Places, and Incidents in *The Valley of Fear* with Their Pennsylvania Counterparts[175]

Description in The Valley of Fear	Counterpart
The Valley of Fear	The Pennsylvania anthracite region in the 1870s
Vermissa Valley	Panther Valley, Schuylkill Valley, Mahanoy Valley, and Shenandoah Valley
Vermissa	Pottsville, Shenandoah, Tamaqua, and Girardville
Birdy Edwards (a k a Jack McMurdo	James McParlan (a k a James McKenna)
Boss McGinty	Jack Kehoe, Mike (Muff) Lawlor, and Pat Dormer
Union House	Hibernia House (Girardville) and others including Sheridan House (Pottsville)
Scowrers	Molly Maguires
Eminent Order of Freemen	Ancient Order of Hiberni-ans
Captain Teddy Marvin	Captain Robert Linden
Ted Baldwin	Thomas Hurley
Vermissa Herald	*Shenandoah Evening Herald*
James Stanger, Editor, *The Herald*	Thomas Foster, Editor, *The Herald*
Mike Scanlan	Frank McAndrew
Merton County	Carbon County
J. W. Windle	Thomas Fisher and Alexander Campbell
Treasurer Higgins	Jimmy Kerrigan
"the patrolman"	Patrolman Benjamin Yost
Evans Pott	Barney Dolan
Andrews	Thomas Munley
Lawlor	Michael Doyle

175 Compiled by Julia Carson Rosenblatt for her brilliant introduction to *The Valley of Fear*, by Arthur Conan Doyle, edited by Leslie S. Klinger (Indianapolis: Gasogene Books, 2004).

Tiger Cormac	Michael J. Doyle (from Mt. Laffee, PA)
Young Wilson	Edward Kelly (from Mt. Laffee, PA)
Andrew Rae	John P. Jones
Rae and Sturmash Coal Company	Lehigh and Wilkes-Barre Coal Company
Josiah Dunn	Thomas Sanger
Menzies the mine engineer	William Uren
Crow Hill Mine	Heaton's Colliery in Raven's Run
State and Merton County Railroad	Philadelphia and Reading Railroad
Ettie Shafter	Emma Schoeple

APPENDIX 3

The Dating of *The Valley of Fear*

The Valley of Fear is a chronologist's nightmare—largely because Dr. Watson, in "The Final Problem," which plainly occurs in 1891, claims ignorance of Professor Moriarty,[176] whereas here he states that the case occurred at the "end of the 80's."[177]

Chronology	Date Assigned to Beginning of Case
Canon	Jan. 7, late 1880s
Bell, H. W. *Sherlock Holmes and Dr. Watson: The Chronology of Their Adventures*	Jan. 7, 1887, Fri.
Blakeney, T. S. *Sherlock Holmes: Fact or Fiction?*	Jan. 7, 1890, Tues.
Christ, Jay Finley. *An Irregular Chronology of Sherlock Holmes of Baker Street*	Jan. 7, 1889, Mon.
Brend, Gavin. *My Dear Holmes*	Jan. 1900
Baring-Gould, William S., "New Chronology of Sherlock Holmes and Dr. Watson"	Jan. 7, 1888, Sat.
Baring-Gould, William. *The Chronological Holmes*. Mr. Baring-Gould uses the same dates in *Sherlock Holmes of Baker Street: A Life of the World's First Consulting Detective* and *Annotated Sherlock Holmes*	Jan. 7, 1888, Sat.
Zeisler, Ernest Bloomfield. *Baker Street Chronology: Commentaries on the Sacred Writings of Dr. John H. Watson*	Jan. 7, 1888, Sat.
Folsom, Henry T. *Through the Years at Baker Street: A Chronology of Sherlock Holmes*	Jan. 7, 1888, Sat.
Folsom, Henry T. *Through the Years at Baker Street: A Chronology of Sherlock Holmes*. Revised Edition.	Jan. 7, 1888, Sat.
Dakin, D. Martin. *A Sherlock Holmes Commentary*	Jan. 7, 1888, Sat.

176 See note 6, above.

177 For additional chronological material, arguing for dates including Jan. 1891, 1897, and around 1900, see *"The Date Being—?": A Compendium of Chronological Data*, by Andrew Jay Peck and Leslie S. Klinger.

Butters, Roger. *First Person Singular: A Review of the Life and Work of Mr. Sherlock Holmes, the World's First Consulting Detective, and His Friend and Colleague, Dr. John H. Watson*	Jan. 7, 1887, Fri.
Bradley, C. Alan, and William A. S. Sarjeant, *Ms. Holmes of Baker Street: The Truth about Sherlock*	Jan. 7, 1888, Sat.
Hall, John. *"I Remember the Date Very Well": A Chronology of the Sherlock Holmes Stories of Arthur Conan Doyle*	Jan. 7, 1889, Mon.
Thomson, June. *Holmes and Watson*	Jan. 7, 1888, Sat.

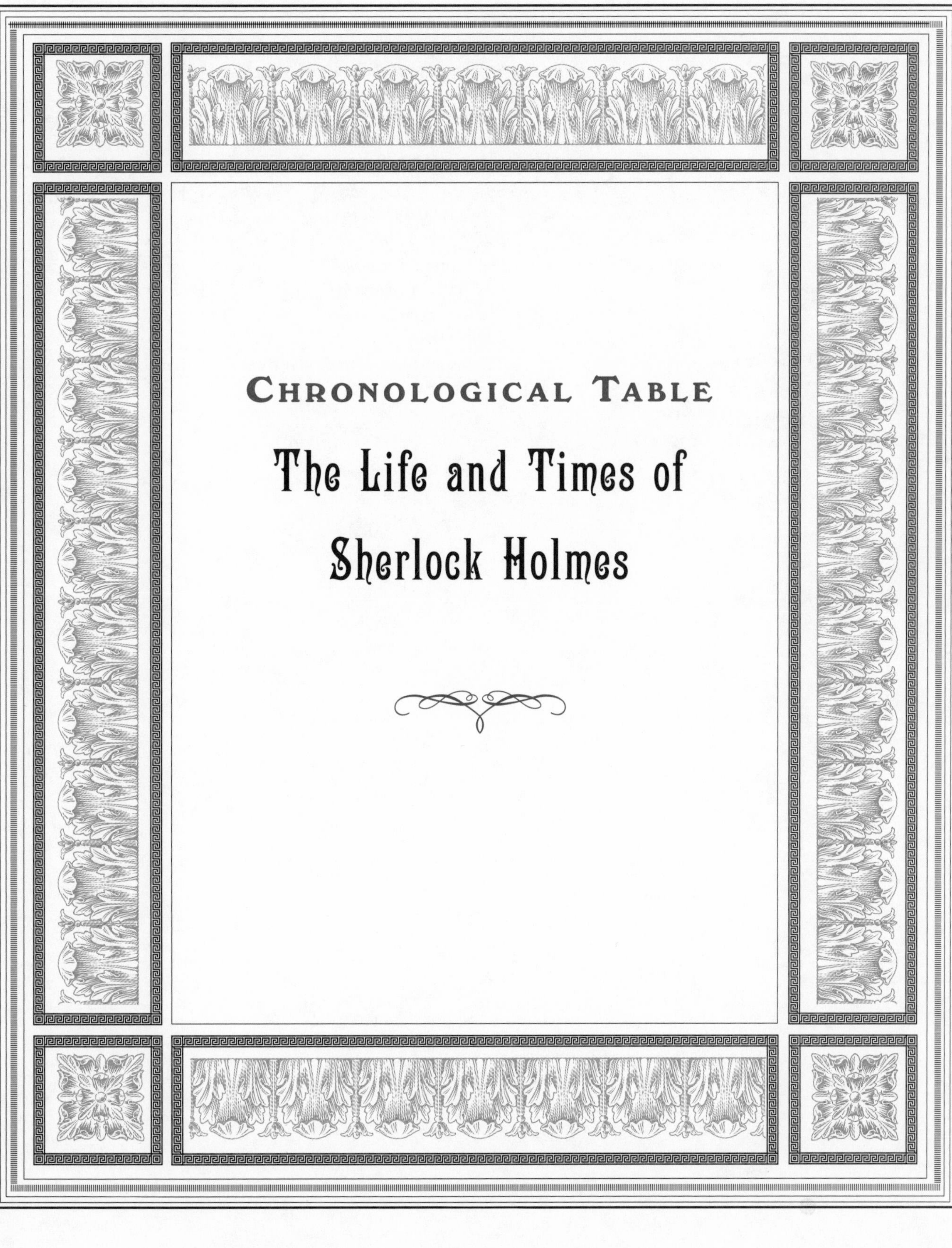

Chronological Table

The Life and Times of Sherlock Holmes

Chronological Table[1]

The Life and Times of Sherlock Holmes

Year	Life of Sherlock Holmes	Life of John H. Watson	Life of Arthur Conan Doyle	Events in England	Events on the Continent	Events in the World
1844	Siger Holmes and Violet Sherrinford marry.			Richard D'Oyly-Carte born.	Charles XIV, King of Sweden and Norway, dies; Oscar I succeeds to throne. Friedrich Nietzsche, Sarah Bernhardt born.	
1845	Sherrinford Holmes born.			Irish potato famine; Anglo-Sikh War begins.	Engels publishes *Condition of the Working Class in England.*	Poe publishes "The Raven." Texas and Florida become states.

[1] The table includes speculations about the lives of Sherlock Holmes and John H. Watson, M.D., drawn from William S. Baring-Gould's *Sherlock Holmes of Baker Street: A Life of the World's First Consulting Detective*, which are not supported by the text of the Canon. The dates given for the Canonical cases represent a "consensus" of the major chronologists compiled in *"The Date Being—?": A Compendium of Chronological Data*, by Andrew Jay Peck and Leslie S. Klinger. (A "consensus" is the choice of a majority of the fifteen chronologists for some cases; for others, the choice of a plurality of the major chronologists.) Those cases for which there is no consensus date are marked "*," and the date given is this editor's choice.

Year	Life of Sherlock Holmes	Life of John H. Watson	Life of Arthur Conan Doyle	Events in England	Events on the Continent	Events in the World
1846	James Moriarty born.			Repeal of Corn Laws. Planet Neptune discovered.	Austrian and Russian troops enter Cracow; Austria annexes Cracow.	Oregon settlement sets U.S. boundary at 49th parallel. Mormons commence move to Utah.
1847	Mycroft Holmes born.			Ten Hours' Act.	Sonderbund War in Switzerland.	Thomas Alva Edison, inventor, born.
1848				W. G. Grace born.	Second French Republic. Birth of painter Paul Gauguin.	Marx and Engels's *Communist Manifesto* published.
1851				Opening of the Crystal Palace.	Foucault demonstrates earth's rotation with huge pendulum.	First Australian gold discoveries. *New York Times* first published.
1852		John Hamish Watson born.		First Derby-Disraeli government.	Louis Napoleon proclaims himself Napoleon III; Second French Empire begins.	Polygamy instituted in Utah.

Year	Life of Sherlock Holmes	Life of John H. Watson	Life of Arthur Conan Doyle	Events in England	Events on the Continent	Events in the World
1853				Lillie Langtry, Cecil Rhodes born.	Tenor Edouard de Reszke born.	Telegraph system established in India.
1854	William Sherlock Scott Holmes born.	Family moves to Australia (date approx.).		Crimean War begins. Birth of Oscar Wilde.	Francis Joseph I, Emperor of Austria, marries Bavarian Princess Elizabeth.	Kansas-Nebraska Act. Sacramento becomes capital of State of California.
1855	Holmes family sails to Bordeaux.			Lord Palmerston becomes Prime Minister. *Daily Telegraph* first published.	Paris World Fair.	Czar Nicholas I of Russia dies.
1856				Treaty of Paris ends Crimean War. "Big Ben" cast.	George Bernard Shaw born in Ireland.	Sigmund Freud born.
1857				Joseph Conrad born.	Publication of Flaubert's *Madame Bovary*.	Indian Mutiny. Transatlantic cable commenced.
1858	Holmes family travels to Montpellier.			Second Derby-Disraeli government.		

Year	Life of Sherlock Holmes	Life of John H. Watson	Life of Arthur Conan Doyle	Events in England	Events on the Continent	Events in the World
1859			Arthur Conan Doyle born May 22 in Edinburgh, 2d child of Charles Doyle and Mary Foley.	Palmerston's second administration; Darwin's *Origin of Species* published.	King Oscar I of Sweden dies; succeeded by Charles XV; German Emperor William II born.	Charles Blondin crosses Niagara Falls on tightrope.
1860	Holmes family returns to England. Violet's father dies; Holmes family sails to Rotterdam, settles in Cologne.			J. M. Barrie born; Wilkie Collins publishes *Woman in White.*	Lenoir constructs first practical internal combustion engine.	Abraham Lincoln elected president.
1861	Holmes family begins Continental tour.	Mary Morstan born.		Mrs. Beeton publishes *Book of Household Management.*	Emancipation of Russian serfs.	Outbreak of American Civil War. Birth of Henry Ford.
1862				Albert Memorial designed.	Sarah Bernhardt debuts in Paris; Bismarck becomes Prussian prime minister.	Henry David Thoreau dies.

Year	Life of Sherlock Holmes	Life of John H. Watson	Life of Arthur Conan Doyle	Events in England	Events on the Continent	Events in the World
1863				Metropolitan Railway (Underground) opens in London.	Civil War breaks out in Afghanistan.	Battle of Gettysburg.
1864	Holmes family returns to England, leases villa in Kennington. Sent to a board school with Mycroft, Sherrinford sent to Oxford.				Prussia and Austria-Hungary defeat Denmark; beginning of Prussian expansion.	Alexander II emancipates the serfs.
1865	Severely ill.	Returns to England, attends Wellington College, Hampshire.		King George V, Rudyard Kipling born.	War breaks out between Boers of Orange Free State and Basutos.	Assassination of Abraham Lincoln. Ku Klux Klan founded.
1866	Taken to Yorkshire, entered as day boy at grammar school near Mycroft.			Herbert George Wells born. Third Derby-Disraeli government formed.	War between Prussia and Austro-Hungarian Empire.	Alfred Nobel invents dynamite.

Year	Life of Sherlock Holmes	Life of John H. Watson	Life of Arthur Conan Doyle	Events in England	Events on the Continent	Events in the World
1867				Extension of suffrage among male workers.	Karl Marx publishes Vol. I of *Das Kapital.*	Canada born through British North America Act. Organisation of Ku Klux Klan.
1868	Sails with parents to St. Malo, travels to Pau; enrolled in fencing salon.		Sent away to Hodder, prep school for Stonyhurst—Jesuit-run public school in Lancashire.	Gladstone (Liberal Party) takes office as prime minister. Publication of Wilkie Collins's *The Moonstone.* Birth of Neville Chamberlain. *Whitaker's Almanack* first appears.		Impeachment of U. S. president Andrew Johnson. Birth of Mahatma Ghandhi.
1869					First performance of Wagner's *Das Rheingold.*	Completion of Suez Canal.
1870			Enters Stonyhurst, remains for 5 years, excelling at cricket and displaying literary talent.	Death of Charles Dickens. Irish land reform.	Franco-Prussian War. Italian troops take Rome.	Birth of Bernard Baruch.

Year	Life of Sherlock Holmes	Life of John H. Watson	Life of Arthur Conan Doyle	Events in England	Events on the Continent	Events in the World
1871	Holmes family returns to England.			Gilbert and Sullivan form partnership. Publication of Darwin's *Descent of Man*. Bank Holidays introduced.	Paris Commune; German Empire proclaimed at Versailles.	U.S. passes Ku Klux Klan Act, banning activities.
1872	Tutored by Professor James Moriarty. Enters Christ Church, Oxford.	Enrolls at University of London; works in surgery at St. Bartholomew's Hospital.		Disraeli's "Crystal Palace" speech.	Civil War in Spain.	U. S. Grant reelected president despite scandals; U. S. General Amnesty Act pardons most ex-Confederates.
1873				Mass production of the typewriter begins.	Cities of Buda and Pesth united.	Gunsmith firm of E. Remington & Sons begins to produce typewriters.
1874	"The 'Gloria Scott' "*; enters Caius College, Cambridge.		Visits London, stays with uncle Richard Doyle, sees Henry Irving in *Hamlet*.	Disraeli (Conservative Party) becomes prime minister. Winston Churchill born.	Harry Houdini (Ehrich Weiss), Marconi born. First Impressionist exhibit.	Herbert Hoover born.

Year	Life of Sherlock Holmes	Life of John H. Watson	Life of Arthur Conan Doyle	Events in England	Events on the Continent	Events in the World
1875			Passes matriculation exam with honors, spends year at Jesuit school at Feldkirch, Austria.	Disraeli acquires the Suez Canal. London main sewage system; first Gilbert and Sullivan operetta performed.	Birth of Albert Schweitzer.	Risings in Bosnia and Herzegovina against Turkish rule.
1876			Decides to become doctor and enrolls at Edinburgh University. Meets Dr. Joseph Bell and Professor Rutherford.	Disraeli becomes Earl of Beaconsfield.	Wagner's "Ring" first performed.	Alexander Graham Bell demonstrates telephone. Serbia and Montenegro declare war on Turkey.
1877	Takes rooms in Montague St. "Months of inaction."			Victoria becomes Empress of India.	Publication of Mozart's complete works begins. Schiaparelli observes canals on Mars.	Death of Brigham Young, leader of the Mormons. Thomas Edison patents phonograph. Publication of Allan Pinkerton's *Molly Maguires and the Detectives*.

Year	Life of Sherlock Holmes	Life of John H. Watson	Life of Arthur Conan Doyle	Events in England	Events on the Continent	Events in the World
1878		Receives degree of doctor of medicine. Attends Netley for army surgeons' course. Sails for India.	Takes part-time doctoring job.	Second Afghan War begins. First performance of *H.M.S. Pinafore.* C.I.D., New Scotland Yard, established.	Congress of Berlin; Austro-German alliance.	Birth of Carl Sandburg.
1879	"The Musgrave Ritual"; appears on London stage in *Hamlet.* Sails for America with Sasanoff Shakespeare Co.		Charles Doyle goes into nursing home. Early stories published anonymously.	Zulu War begins.	Albert Einstein born.	Thomas Edison patents incandescent lamp. Birth of photographer Edward Steichen.
1880	Returns to England from U.S.	Wounded at Battle of Maiwand; escapes to British lines. Suffers enteric fever at Peshawar. Returns to London on *Orontes.* Stays at private hotel in Strand.	Signs on as ship's doctor with Arctic whaler; 7-month voyage. Initial interest in spiritualism, paranormal.	Gladstone takes office again as prime minister. Swan and Edison devise first practical electric lights.		Birth of Douglas MacArthur.

Year	Life of Sherlock Holmes	Life of John H. Watson	Life of Arthur Conan Doyle	Events in England	Events on the Continent	Events in the World
1881	Meets John H. Watson. Takes up residence in Baker Street. *A Study in Scarlet.*	Meets Sherlock Holmes. Moves into Baker Street.	Bachelor of Medicine rec'd. Signs on as ship's doctor with West African steamer. Nearly dies of fever.	Death of Benjamin Disraeli, Thomas Carlyle. Irish Land Act. Flogging abolished in army and navy.	Birth of painter Pablo Picasso.	Tsar Alexander II assassinated; President James Garfield assassinated.
1882			Renounces Catholic faith. Joins George Budd, medical schoolmate, in practice in Plymouth. Becomes concerned about Budd's ethics and sets up own practice in Southsea, Portsmouth.	Death of Charles Darwin.	Triple Alliance between Germany, Austria, and Italy.	Franklin Delano Roosevelt born.
1883	"The Speckled Band."		Publishes first story.		Death of Karl Marx, Richard Wagner.	French in Indochina. Birth of John Maynard Keynes. Mark Twain writes the first book on the typewriter.

Year	Life of Sherlock Holmes	Life of John H. Watson	Life of Arthur Conan Doyle	Events in England	Events on the Continent	Events in the World
1884		Travels to America, woos Lucy Ferrier in San Francisco.[2]	Begins first novel.	First deep tube (underground) railroad; General Gordon reaches Khartoum.	Germans occupy South-West Africa.	Birth of Harry Truman.
1885			Marries Louise Hawkins.	Lord Salisbury (Conservative) becomes prime minister. Death of General Charles George Gordon in Khartoum.	Germany annexes Tanganyika and Zanzibar.	Indian National Congress formed.
1886	"The Beryl Coronet."	Returns to England. Weds Lucy Ferrier, buys practice in Kensington.		Gladstone, Salisbury, serve as prime minister. Irish Home Rule Bill.	Bonaparte and Orléans families banished from France.	Birth of painter Diego Rivera.
1887	"The Resident Patient," "The Reigate Squires."	Publishes *A Study in Scarlet.* 1st wife dies in December.	Publishes *A Study in Scarlet.*	Victoria celebrates golden anniversary of her reign. Field Marshal Montgomery born.	Birth of painter Marc Chagall.	Death of Henry Ward Beecher, Jenny Lind. Birth of artist Georgia O'Keeffe.

[2] Baring-Gould proposed that Watson married one Constance Adams, based on the then-scant information about Arthur Conan Doyle's unpublished play *Angels of Darkness*, which had been suppressed by Sir Arthur's family. The play has subsequently been published, and the woman whom Watson is depicted as wooing is actually Lucy Ferrier, the former wife of Jefferson Hope (of *A Study in Scarlet*). Baring-Gould's thesis has therefore been corrected to refer to the woman actually named in the play. Few scholars today credit the play as a reliable source of historical data about Dr. Watson.

Year	Life of Sherlock Holmes	Life of John H. Watson	Life of Arthur Conan Doyle	Events in England	Events on the Continent	Events in the World
1888	*The Valley of Fear*, "The Noble Bachelor," "The Yellow Face,"* "The Greek Interpreter," *The Sign of Four*, "Silver Blaze," "The Cardboard Box."	Brother Henry dies. Meets and marries Mary Morstan. Buys practice in Paddington.		Jack the Ripper killings begin. T. E. Lawrence born.	Kaiser Wilhelm II takes throne.	Hertz discovers radio waves. Jim Thorpe born.
1889	"A Scandal in Bohemia," "Man with the Twisted Lip," "A Case of Identity," "The Blue Carbuncle," "The Five Orange Pips," "The Boscombe Valley Mystery," "The Stock-Broker's Clerk," "The Naval Treaty," "The Engineer's Thumb," *The Hound of the Baskervilles*,* "The Crooked Man."	Publishes *The Sign of Four* in *Lippincott's Magazine*.	Daughter Mary Louise born. Publishes *Micah Clarke*, *The Sign of Four*.	Cecil Rhodes's British South Africa Company granted royal charter; Barnum & Bailey's Circus appears in London.	Birth of Adolf Hitler. Paris Exhibition and opening of Eiffel Tower.	Second International Franco-Russian alliance. Strowger patents direct-dial telephone.

Year	Life of Sherlock Holmes	Life of John H. Watson	Life of Arthur Conan Doyle	Events in England	Events on the Continent	Events in the World
1890	"The Red-Headed League," "The Copper Beeches," "The Dying Detective."*	Publishes book edition of *The Sign of Four.*	Publishes *White Company.*	Oscar Wilde publishes *Picture of Dorian Gray.*	Suicide of Vincent Van Gogh.	Birth of Dwight D. Eisenhower. Utah legislature bans polygamy. Global influenza epidemics.
1891	"The Final Problem"; travels as "Sigerson."	Sells Paddington practice, returns to Kensington. Arranges for publication of "A Scandal in Bohemia," "The Red- Headed League," "A Case of Identity," "The Boscombe Valley Mystery," "The Five Orange Pips," "The Man with the Twisted Lip" in *Strand.* Mary Morstan dies, possibly in early 1892.	Abandons Southsea practice, writes *Doings of Raffles Haw.* Returns to London and opens practice in Devonshire Place. Soon decides to give up medicine. First stories of *The Adventures of Sherlock Holmes* begin to appear in *Strand Magazine.*	Thomas Hardy publishes *Tess of the d'Urbervilles.*	Triple Alliance (Germany-Italy-Austria) renewed.	Zipper invented. Widespread famine in Russia. Earthquake in Japan kills 10,000 people.

Year	Life of Sherlock Holmes	Life of John H. Watson	Life of Arthur Conan Doyle	Events in England	Events on the Continent	Events in the World
1892	Continues to travel.	"The Blue Carbuncle," "The Speckled Band," "The Engineer's Thumb," "The Noble Bachelor," "The Beryl Coronet," "The Copper Beeches," "Silver Blaze" published in *Strand.*	Takes up skiing. Son Kingsley born.	Gladstone again becomes prime minister. Death of Alfred, Lord Tennyson. Kipling writes of "white man's burden."	Invention of diesel engine by Rudolf Diesel.	Birth of John Paul Getty.
1893	Settles in Montpellier to conduct coal-tar derivatives research.	"The Cardboard Box," "The Yellow Face," "The Stock-Broker's Clerk," "The 'Gloria Scott'," "The Musgrave Ritual," "The Reigate Squires," "The Crooked Man," "The Resident Patient," "The Greek Interpreter," "The Naval Treaty," "The Final Problem" published in *Strand.*	Charles Doyle dies. Louise diagnosed with TB. Remainder of *The Adventures of Sherlock Holmes* and *The Memoirs of Sherlock Holmes* stories published in *Strand.*	Premiere of *Under the Clock*, an "extravaganza" in one act starring Charles H. E. Brookfield as Sherlock Holmes.	Franco-Russian alliance signed.	Chicago World's Fair (Columbian Exposition).

Year	Life of Sherlock Holmes	Life of John H. Watson	Life of Arthur Conan Doyle	Events in England	Events on the Continent	Events in the World
1894	Returns to London. "The Empty House," "The Second Stain,"*[3] "The Golden Pince-Nez," "The Nor-wood Builder."	Sells practice, returns to Baker Street.	Successful lecture tour in America. Play *Waterloo* per-formed.	Gladstone dies in office; Lord Rosebery becomes prime minister.	Dreyfus case begins in France.	1st steel-framed sky-scraper built in Chicago. Nicholas II becomes czar.
1895	"Wisteria Lodge,"* "The Three Students," "The Solitary Cyclist," "Black Peter," "The Bruce-Part-ington Plans."		Buys land in Hindhead for home; travels to Egypt. Publishes *Stark Munro Letters*.	Salisbury regains office of prime minister. Death of Lord Ran-dolph Churchill. H.G. Wells pub-lishes *The Time Machine*.	Lumiere brothers hold public film exhibitions in Paris. Death of Parnell, leader of Irish Home Rule.	Röntgen dis-covers X-rays. Gillette invents safety razor. Sino-Japanese War. Babe Ruth, Jack Dempsey born.

[3] Some chronologists place this case before 1892.

Year	Life of Sherlock Holmes	Life of John H. Watson	Life of Arthur Conan Doyle	Events in England	Events on the Continent	Events in the World
1896	"The Veiled Lodger," "The Sussex Vampire," "The Missing Three-Quarter."		Travels up Nile. Serves as war correspondent for British/Dervish fighting. Publishes *Brigadier Gerard* and *Rodney Stone.*	Czar Nicholas II visits London.	New evidence in Dreyfus case suppressed. Alfred Nobel dies, Nobel prizes created.	First modern Olympics held in Athens. Cracker Jacks, Tootsie Rolls, and S&H Green Stamps introduced.
1897	"The Abbey Grange," "The Devil's Foot."		Meets and falls in love with Jean Leckie. Publishes *Uncle Bernac.*	Queen Victoria's Diamond Jubilee. Publication of Bram Stoker's *Dracula.*	First World Zionist Congress.	Klondike gold rush begins.
1898	"The Dancing Men."			Death of Lewis Carroll. H. G. Wells publishes *War of the Worlds.* Lord Kitchener defeats Dervishes at Omdurman.	German naval race with England. Death of Otto von Bismarck.	Fashoda crisis, Spanish-American War.

Year	Life of Sherlock Holmes	Life of John H. Watson	Life of Arthur Conan Doyle	Events in England	Events on the Continent	Events in the World
1899	"The Retired Colourman," "Charles Augustus Milverton."		Volunteers for army, rejected. *A Duet* published.	Second Boer War begins. Winston Churchill goes to South Africa as war correspondent. Emperor William II visits England.	First magnetic recording of sound.	William Gillette produces and stars in *Sherlock Holmes*, in Syracuse, NY.
1900	"The Six Napoleons."		Serves in hospital unit in South Africa. Writes *The Great Boer War; The War in South Africa: Its Causes and Conduct*. Stands as Unionist candidate in Edinburgh, loses.	Death of Sir Arthur Sullivan, Oscar Wilde.	Paris Metro opens. Death of Friedrich Nietzsche. Publication of Freud's *Interpretation of Dreams*.	Davis Cup tennis matches inaugurated. First Sherlock Holmes film, *Sherlock Holmes Baffled*, appears.

Year	Life of Sherlock Holmes	Life of John H. Watson	Life of Arthur Conan Doyle	Events in England	Events on the Continent	Events in the World
1901	"The Priory School," "Disappearance of Lady Frances Carfax,"* "Thor Bridge."	*The Hound of the Baskervilles* published in *Strand.*	Publishes *The Hound of the Baskervilles.*	Death of Queen Victoria. Edward VII ("Bertie") ascends to throne. First British submarine launched. Boxing recognized as legal sport.	Negotiations for Anglo-German alliance end without agreement.	Assassination of William McKinley; Theodore Roosevelt becomes U.S. president. Australia becomes a Commonwealth. Birth of Walt Disney.
1902	"Shoscombe Old Place," "The Three Garridebs," "The Three Gables,"* "The Illustrious Client," "The Red Circle."*	Moves to rooms in Queen Anne Street. Remarries, returns to practice.	Knighted.	Lord Salisbury retires as prime minister; Arthur Balfour takes office. England signs peace treaty with Boers.	Triple Alliance renewed for six years.	Anglo-Japanese alliance. 1st recording of Enrico Caruso. Death of Levi Strauss.
1903	"The Blanched Soldier," "The Mazarin Stone," "The Creeping Man"; Holmes retires.	Publishes "The Empty House," "The Norwood Builder," "The Dancing Men," "The Solitary Cyclist."	First stories of *The Return of Sherlock Holmes* appear in *Strand.* Publishes *Adventures of Gerard.*	First motor taxis appear in London.	First Tour de France (bicycle race).	Henry Ford founds Ford Motor Co.

Year	Life of Sherlock Holmes	Life of John H. Watson	Life of Arthur Conan Doyle	Events in England	Events on the Continent	Events in the World
1904		Publishes "The Priory School," "Black Peter," "Charles Augustus Milverton," "The Six Napoleons," "The Three Students," "The Golden Pince-Nez," "The Missing Three-Quarter," "The Abbey Grange."		First concert of London Symphony Orchestra.	Anglo-French Entente. Paris Conference on white slave trade.	Russo-Japanese war. Panama Canal started.
1905		Publishes "The Second Stain."		Sir Henry Campbell-Bannerman (L) becomes prime minister. Actor Henry Irving dies.	Tangier crisis precipitated by Kaiser's visit.	Publication of Einstein's relativity theory.

Year	Life of Sherlock Holmes	Life of John H. Watson	Life of Arthur Conan Doyle	Events in England	Events on the Continent	Events in the World
1906			Runs again as Unionist candidate, loses. George Edalji case. Becomes involved in Divorce Law Reform Movement. Louise Doyle dies. Publishes *Sir Nigel*.	Social insurance and parliamentary reform commence.	Franco becomes prime minister of Spain.	International ban on women working night shifts.
1907	"The Lion's Mane."		Marries Jean Leckie. George Edalji released. *Through the Magic Door* published.	Baden-Powell founds Boy Scouts.	Triple Entente. 1st Cubist show in Paris. Oscar II, King of Sweden, dies.	Immigration to U.S. restricted by law.
1908		Publishes "Wisteria Lodge," "The Bruce-Partington Plans."		Herbert H. Asquith becomes prime minister as Liberal. *Strand Magazine* publishes *My African Journey* by Winston Churchill.	Bosnian crisis.	Jack Johnson becomes first black world heavyweight boxing champion.

Year	Life of Sherlock Holmes	Life of John H. Watson	Life of Arthur Conan Doyle	Events in England	Events on the Continent	Events in the World
1909			Writes *Crime of the Congo*. Son Denis born.	Girl Guides established.	First cross-Channel airplane flight.	Admiral Peary reaches North Pole.
1910		Publishes "The Devil's Foot."	Case of Oscar Slater taken up. Son Adrian born. Play *Speckled Band* first produced in London.	Death of King Edward VII ("Bertie"). George V takes throne.	Revolution in Portugal.	Death of Mark Twain, Florence Nightingale. Union of South Africa formed.
1911		Publishes "The Red Circle," "Disappearance of Lady Frances Carfax."		Death of Sir William Gilbert.	Inauguration of air mail service.	Chinese Revolution.
1912	Leaves for America to infiltrate Irish secret society; travels to Chicago.		Publishes *Case of Oscar Slater*, *Lost World*. Daughter Lena Jean born.	Royal Flying Corps established.	Balkan crisis.	Sinking of *Titanic*.
1913		Publishes "The Dying Detective."	Publishes *Poison Belt*.	Suffragette demonstrations.	Balkan War ends.	Modern brassière invented.

Year	Life of Sherlock Holmes	Life of John H. Watson	Life of Arthur Conan Doyle	Events in England	Events on the Continent	Events in the World
1914	Returns to England. "His Last Bow."	Assists Holmes in "His Last Bow."	Forms local volunteer force. Writes *To Arms!*	Ulster Crisis; World War I commences.	Assassination of Archduke Ferdinand; World War I commences.	World War I commences.
1915		Publishes *The Valley of Fear.*	Begins 6-vol. history of *British Campaign in France and Flanders*. Publishes *The Valley of Fear*.	Herbert Asquith remains Prime Minister for Coalition.	Poison gas first used in war.	Ford sells millionth car. Gallipoli campaign begins.
1916			Visits fronts. Announces conversion to spiritualism.	Battle of Jutland; Irish troubles. David Lloyd George (Coalition) becomes prime minister.	Bloody battles at Verdun and the Somme.	Assassination of Rasputin.
1917		Publishes "His Last Bow."	Publishes "His Last Bow."		U.S. enters the Great War. First large-scale use of tanks. Mata Hari executed as spy.	Russian Revolution. John Fitzgerald Kennedy born. "Buffalo Bill" Cody dies.

Year	Life of Sherlock Holmes	Life of John H. Watson	Life of Arthur Conan Doyle	Events in England	Events on the Continent	Events in the World
1918			Son Kingsley dies from pneumonia. Publishes *New Revelation*.	Women over 30 allowed to vote.	Armistice. Kaiser Wilhelm abdicates.	Knute Rockne becomes coach of University of Notre Dame.
1919			Brother Innes dies. Publishes *Vital Message*.	Government of India Act.	Peace of Versailles. Weimar Republic established in Germany. Death of Pierre-Auguste Renoir.	Peace of Versailles. Death of Andrew Carnegie.
1920			Travels to Australia to promote spiritualism.	First Agatha Christie mystery novel published.	Clemenceau resigns; Millerand takes over as premier of France.	U.S. adopts women's suffrage.
1921		Publishes "The Mazarin Stone."	Mother dies. *Wanderings of a Spiritualist* published.	Irish Free State. BBC founded.	Einstein wins Nobel Prize.	First Indian Parliament meets.

Year	Life of Sherlock Holmes	Life of John H. Watson	Life of Arthur Conan Doyle	Events in England	Events on the Continent	Events in the World
1922		Publishes "Thor Bridge."	Lecture tour of America. Announces belief in fairies, publishes *Coming of the Fairies.*	Lloyd George resigns. Bonar Law becomes prime minister, first to come from an overseas possession.	Mussolini becomes prime minister of Italy.	Washington disarmament conference.
1923		Publishes "The Creeping Man."	Returns to America and Canada. Publishes *Our American Adventure.*	Stanley Baldwin becomes prime minister.	Hitler's "Beer Hall Putsch" fails.	Paavo Nurmi runs a near-four-minute mile.
1924		Publishes "The Sussex Vampire," "The Three Garridebs."	Publishes *Our Second American Adventure; Memories and Adventures.*	J. Ramsay MacDonald becomes prime minister, heads first Labor government; succeeded by Baldwin.	Hitler imprisoned.	Leopold and Loeb sentenced for kidnap-slaying of Bobby Franks. J. Edgar Hoover becomes director of F.B.I.
1925		Publishes "The Illustrious Client."	Presides over International Spiritualistic Congress in Paris.	Austen Chamberlain wins Nobel Peace Prize.	Hitler reorganizes Nazi Party, publishes first volume of *Mein Kampf.*	Harold Vanderbilt invents contract bridge.

Year	Life of Sherlock Holmes	Life of John H. Watson	Life of Arthur Conan Doyle	Events in England	Events on the Continent	Events in the World
1926	Publishes "The Blanched Soldier," "The Lion's Mane."	Publishes "The Three Gables," "The Retired Colourman."	Publishes *History of Spiritualism; Land of Mist.*	Queen Elizabeth II born.	Germany admitted to League of Nations.	Harry Houdini dies.
1927		Publishes "The Veiled Lodger," "Shoscombe Old Place."	Oscar Slater freed. *The Case-Book of Sherlock Holmes* and *Pheneas Speaks* published.	Parliament House opens in Canberra, Australia.	First television broadcast. "Black Friday" in Germany, economy collapses.	*The Jazz Singer* (first "talkie") appears. Academy Awards inaugurated; Babe Ruth hits sixty home runs. Lindbergh flies *Spirit of St. Louis* from New York to Paris.
1928			Travels to South Africa.	H. H. Asquith, actress Ellen Terry die.	Kellogg-Briand pact, outlawing war, signed in Paris by 65 states.	Alexander Fleming discovers penicillin.

Year	Life of Sherlock Holmes	Life of John H. Watson	Life of Arthur Conan Doyle	Events in England	Events on the Continent	Events in the World
1929		Dies under circumstances unknown.	Visits Scandinavia, Holland, returns exhausted, has heart attack. Publishes *Maracot Deep, Our African Winter.*	Baldwin again becomes prime minister. Lillie Langtry dies.	Yugoslavia created as dictatorship.	Ernest Hemingway publishes *Farewell to Arms*. "Black Friday" in New York, world economic crisis begins.
1930			Publishes *Edge of the Unknown*; dies July 7.	Britain, U.S., Japan, and Italy sign naval disarmament treaty.	Last Allied troops leave the Saar.	First Sherlock Holmes radio show broadcast in U.S., starring William Gillette.

SELECTED SOURCES

GENERAL

Ackroyd, Peter. LONDON: THE BIOGRAPHY. London: Chatto & Windus, 2000; New York: Doubleday, 2001; Anchor Books, 2003.

Asher, Richard. "Holmes and the Fair Sex." *Sherlock Holmes Journal* 2, No. 3 (Summer 1955): 15–22.

Baedeker, Karl. *Great Britain: Handbook for Travellers.* Leipsic: Karl Baedeker, Publishers, 1894.

———. LONDON AND ITS ENVIRONS. Leipsic: Karl Baedeker, Publisher, 1896.

Baring-Gould, William S. "New Chronology of Sherlock Holmes and Dr. Watson." *Baker Street Journal* [O. S.] 3, No. 2 (Apr. 1948): 107–125, and 3, No. 3 (July 1948): 238–251.

———. ANNOTATED SHERLOCK HOLMES. New York: Clarkson N. Potter, 1967. 2 vols.

———. THE CHRONOLOGICAL HOLMES. New York: Privately printed, 1955.

———. SHERLOCK HOLMES OF BAKER STREET: A LIFE OF THE WORLD'S FIRST CONSULTING DETECTIVE. New York: Clarkson N. Potter, 1962.

Bell, H. W. SHERLOCK HOLMES AND DR. WATSON: THE CHRONOLOGY OF THEIR ADVENTURES. London: Constable & Co., 1932.

Bigelow, S. Tupper. AN IRREGULAR ANGLO-AMERICAN GLOSSARY OF MORE OR LESS UNFAMILIAR WORDS, TERMS AND PHRASES IN THE SHERLOCK HOLMES SAGA. Toronto: Castalotte & Zamba, 1959.

Blakeney, T. S. SHERLOCK HOLMES: FACT OR FICTION? London: John Murray, 1932.

Bradley, C. Alan, and William A. S. Sarjeant. MS. HOLMES OF BAKER STREET: THE TRUTH ABOUT SHERLOCK. Dubuque, Iowa: Gasogene Press, Ltd., 1989.

Brend, Gavin. MY DEAR HOLMES. London: George Allen & Unwin, Ltd., 1951.

Brewer, E. Cobham. DICTIONARY OF PHRASE AND FABLE. Philadelphia: Henry Altemus, 1898.

Butters, Roger. FIRST PERSON SINGULAR: A REVIEW OF THE LIFE AND WORK OF MR. SHERLOCK HOLMES, THE WORLD'S FIRST CONSULTING DETECTIVE, AND

HIS FRIEND AND COLLEAGUE, DR. JOHN H. WATSON. New York: Vantage Press, 1984.

Campbell, Maurice, O.B.E., D.M., F.R.C.P. SHERLOCK HOLMES AND DR. WATSON: A MEDICAL DIGRESSION. London: Ash & Co., 1951.

Christ, Jay Finley. AN IRREGULAR CHRONOLOGY OF SHERLOCK HOLMES OF BAKER STREET. Ann Arbor, Mich.: The Fanlight House, 1947.

Clunn, Harold P. THE FACE OF LONDON. New York: E. P. Dutton & Company, Inc., 1937.

COLLIER'S CYCLOPEDIA OF COMMERCIAL AND SOCIAL INFORMATION AND TREASURY OF USEFUL AND ENTERTAINING KNOWLEDGE, compiled by Nugent Robinson. New York: P. F. Collier, Publisher, 1890.

Cummings, Carey. THE BIORHYTHMICAL HOLMES: A CHRONOLOGICAL PERSPECTIVE. [Albany, N.Y.]: Altamont's Agents' Press, 1980.

Dakin, D. Martin. A SHERLOCK HOLMES COMMENTARY. Newton Abbot: David & Charles, 1972.

ENCYCLOPÆDIA BRITANNICA: A DICTIONARY OF ARTS, SCIENCES AND GENERAL LITERATURE. The R. S. Peale Reprint (9th Ed.). Chicago: The Werner Company, 1893.

ENCYCLOPÆDIA BRITANNICA: A DICTIONARY OF ARTS, SCIENCES, LITERATURE AND GENERAL INFORMATION (11th Ed.). New York: The Encyclopædia Britannica Company, 1911.

ENCYCLOPÆDIA BRITANNICA CD. Version 97. Encyclopædia Britannica, Inc., 1997.

Folsom, Henry T. THROUGH THE YEARS AT BAKER STREET: A CHRONOLOGY OF SHERLOCK HOLMES. Washington, N.J.: Privately printed, 1963.

———. THROUGH THE YEARS AT BAKER STREET: A CHRONOLOGY OF SHERLOCK HOLMES. Revised Edition. Washington, N.J.: Privately printed, 1964.

Gascoigne, Bamber. ENCYCLOPEDIA OF BRITAIN. London: Macmillan, 1994.

Gill, William H. "Some Notable Sherlockian Buildings." *Sherlock Holmes Journal* 4, No. 4 (Apr. 1952): 124–126.

Hall, John. "I REMEMBER THE DATE VERY WELL": A CHRONOLOGY OF THE SHERLOCK HOLMES STORIES OF ARTHUR CONAN DOYLE. Essex, England: Ian Henry Publications, 1993.

———. SIDELIGHTS ON HOLMES. Ashcroft, British Columbia: Calabash Press, 1998.

Hare, Augustus J. C. WALKS IN LONDON. New York: George Routledge and Sons, 1884. 2 vols. in one.

Harrison, Michael. IN THE FOOTSTEPS OF SHERLOCK HOLMES. Newton Abbot: David & Charles, 1971.

———. THE LONDON OF SHERLOCK HOLMES. Newton Abbot: David & Charles, 1972.

———. THE WORLD OF SHERLOCK HOLMES. Plymouth, England: Frederick Muller Limited, 1973.

Hotten, John Camden. THE SLANG DICTIONARY, OR, THE VULGAR WORDS, STREET PHRASES, AND "FAST EXPRESSIONS" OF HIGH AND LOW SOCIETY. London: John Camden Hotten, Piccadilly, 1865.

Hughes, Thomas. TOM BROWN'S SCHOOL DAYS. 1857. 1905 Thomas Nelson edition by Gil Jaysmith.

Jones, Kelvin I. A SHERLOCK HOLMES DICTIONARY. New York: Magico Magazine, 1988.

Klinefelter, Walter. "The Writings of Mr. Sherlock Holmes." *Baker Street Journal* [O. S.] 1, No. 4 (1946): 409–416.

Klinger, Leslie S. "On Sherlock Holmes's Money." *New Baker Street Pillar Box 22* (Spring 1995): 26–28.

La Cour, Tage. EX BIBLIOTHECA HOLMESIANA: THE FIRST EDITIONS OF THE WRITINGS OF SHERLOCK HOLMES. Copenhagen: The Danish Baker Street Irregulars, 1951.

Malec, Andrew. "Frederic Dorr Steele and the Limited Editions Club Edition of the Canon: Six Elusive Original Drawings Rediscovered." THE NORWEGIAN EXPLORERS OF MINNESOTA CHRISTMAS ANNUAL 2003, edited by John Bergquist, 7–42. Minneapolis, Minn.: The Norwegian Explorers of Minnesota, 2003.

McQueen, Ian. SHERLOCK HOLMES DETECTED: THE PROBLEMS OF THE LONG STORIES. Newton Abbot, London, and Vancouver: David & Charles, 1974.

Miles, Alfred H. THE HOUSEHOLD ORACLE. London: Hutchinson & Co., 1897.

Morley, Christopher. SHERLOCK HOLMES AND DR. WATSON: A TEXTBOOK OF FRIENDSHIP. New York: Harcourt, Brace and Company, 1944.

Park, Orlando. SHERLOCK HOLMES, ESQ. AND JOHN H. WATSON, M.D.: AN ENCYCLOPÆDIA OF THEIR AFFAIRS. Evanston, Ill.: Northwestern University Press, 1962.

Peck, Andrew Jay, and Leslie S. Klinger. "THE DATE BEING—?": A COMPENDIUM OF CHRONOLOGICAL DATA. New York: Magico Magazine, 1996.

Porter, Roy. LONDON: A SOCIAL HISTORY. Cambridge, Mass.: Harvard University Press, 2001.

Redmond, Christopher. IN BED WITH SHERLOCK HOLMES: SEXUAL ELEMENTS OF ARTHUR CONAN DOYLE'S STORIES OF THE GREAT DETECTIVE. Toronto: Simon & Pierre, 1984.

Redmond, Donald A. SHERLOCK HOLMES, A STUDY IN SOURCES. Kingston and Montreal: McGill-Queen's University Press, 1982.

Rodin, Alvin E., and Jack D. Key. THE MEDICAL CASEBOOK OF DR. ARTHUR CONAN DOYLE. Malabar, Fla.: Robert E. Krieger Publishing Co., 1984.

Schama, Simon. A HISTORY OF BRITAIN: THE FATE OF EMPIRE, 1776–2000. New York: Hyperion, 2002.

SHERLOCK HOLMES: CATALOGUE OF AN EXHIBITION HELD AT ABBEY HOUSE, BAKER STREET, LONDON, MAY–SEPTEMBER 1951. Presented for the Festival of Britain by the Public Libraries Committee of the Borough of St. Marylebone.

Starrett, Vincent. THE PRIVATE LIFE OF SHERLOCK HOLMES. New York: The Macmillan Company, 1933.

Stern, Madeleine B. SHERLOCK HOLMES: RARE BOOK COLLECTOR. Rockville Centre, N.Y.: Paulette Greene, 1981.

Strachey, Lytton. EMINENT VICTORIANS. New York: G. P. Putnam, 1918; Bartleby.com, 2000.

Symons, Julian. PORTRAIT OF AN ARTIST: CONAN DOYLE. London: Whizzard Press, 1979.

Thomson, June. HOLMES AND WATSON. London: Constable & Company Ltd., 1995.

Tracy, Jack, compiler and editor. THE ENCYCLOPAEDIA SHERLOCKIANA, OR A UNIVERSAL DICTIONARY OF SHERLOCK HOLMES AND HIS BIOGRAPHER JOHN H. WATSON, M.D. New York: Avon Books, 1979. Revised and expanded.

Vincent, Col. Sir Howard. POLICE CODE AND GENERAL MANUAL OF THE CRIMINAL LAW. PRECEDED BY AN ADDRESS TO THE POLICE ON THEIR DUTIES BY THE LORD BRAMPTON (SIR HENRY HAWKINS). London: Francis Edwards and Simpkin, Marshall, Hamilton, Kent & Co. Ltd. 12th Edition, 1904.

Warrack, Guy. SHERLOCK HOLMES AND MUSIC. London: Faber and Faber Ltd., 1947.

Williams, Newt and Lillian. Unpublished handwritten clarifications, comments, and footnotes to Baring-Gould's THE ANNOTATED SHERLOCK HOLMES (*supra*), known as the ANNOTATED "ANNOTATED," now in the library of the Occupants of the Empty House, DuQuoin, Ill., made available to the editor.

Wilson, A. N. THE VICTORIANS. London: Hutchinson, 2002; New York: W. W. Norton, 2003.

Zeisler, Ernest Bloomfield. BAKER STREET CHRONOLOGY: COMMENTARIES ON THE SACRED WRITINGS OF DR. JOHN H. WATSON. Chicago: Alexander J. Isaacs, 1953.

A STUDY IN SCARLET

Adams, Stephen. "Holmes: A Student of London?" *Sherlock Holmes Journal* 2, No. 4 (Winter 1955): 17–18.

Allen, F. A. "Devilish Drugs, Part One." *Sherlock Holmes Journal* 3, No. 3 (Autumn 1957): 12–14.

Andrew, Clifton. "That Scotland Yarder, Gregson—What a Help (?) He Was." In

THE ILLUSTRIOUS CLIENT'S SECOND CASE-BOOK, edited by J. N. Williamson, 35–39. Indianapolis, Ind.: The Illustrious Clients, 1949.

Ashton, Ralph A. "The Secret Weapons of 221B Baker Street." *Baker Street Journal* 9, No. 2 (1959): 99–102.

Austin, Bliss. BAKER STREET CHRISTMAS STOCKING. Pittsburgh, Pa.: Hydraulic Press, 1962.

Axelrad, Arthur M. "Dr. Watson's Bull Pup: A Psycholinguistic Solution." *Dispatch Box* 3 (Oct. 13, 1982): 10–11.

Ball, John, Jr. "Early Days in Baker Street." *Baker Street Journal* 5, No. 4 (Oct. 1955): 211–219.

Ball, John. "The Second Collaboration." *Baker Street Journal* 4, No. 2 (Apr. 1954): 69–74.

Barzun, Jacques. SIMPLE & DIRECT: A RHETORIC FOR WRITERS. New York: Harper & Row, 1975.

Bates, Hampton R. "Dr. Watson and the Jezail Bullet." *Virginia Medical Bulletin*, Nov. 1976, reprinted in *Buffalo Chips* 9, No. 1 (Feb. 1992): 6–7.

———. "Sherlock Holmes and Syphilis." *Canadian Medical Association Journal* 113 (1975): 815.

Belford, Barbara. BRAM STOKER: A BIOGRAPHY OF THE AUTHOR OF DRACULA. New York: Alfred A. Knopf, 1996.

Bell, H. W. "Three Identifications: Lauriston Gardens, Upper Swandam Lane, Saxe-Coburg Square." In 221B: STUDIES IN SHERLOCK HOLMES, edited by Vincent Starrett, 59–67. New York: The Macmillan Co., 1940.

Bell, Whitfield J., Jr. "Holmes and History." *Baker Street Journal* [O.S.] 2, No. 4 (Oct. 1947): 447–456.

Bengis, Nathan. "Sherlock Stays After School." In THE ILLUSTRIOUS CLIENT'S SECOND CASE-BOOK, edited by J. N. Williamson, 72–78. Indianapolis, Ind.: The Illustrious Clients, 1949.

Benton, John L. "Who Was Dr. Watson's 'Good Authority?,' " *Sherlockian Meddler* 9, No. 4 (Dec. 1981): 23–24.

Berg, Emanuel. "For It's Greatly to Their Credit." *Baker Street Journal* 9, No. 2 (Apr. 1959): 90–98.

Black, Stephen M. "Was Watson, Watson?" *Baker Street Journal* 30, No. 2 (June 1980): 86–93.

Blakeney, T. S. "The Location of 'The Three Students.' " *Sherlock Holmes Journal* 4, No. 1 (Winter 1958): 14.

Blaustein, Albert P. "Sherlock Holmes as a Lawyer." *Baker Street Journal* [O.S.] 3, No. 3 (July 1948): 306–308.

Blegen, Theodore C. "These Were Hidden Fires, Indeed!" In EXPLORING SHERLOCK HOLMES, edited by E. W. McDiarmid and Theodore C. Blegen, 9–26. La Crosse, Wisc.: Sumac Press, 1957.

Bleiler, E. F. "Marmelahd or Marmelade." *Armchair Detective* 13, No. 4 (Fall 1980): 334–335.

Bolitho, Hector, and Derek Peel. Without the City Wall: An Adventure in London Street-names North of the River. London: John Murray, 1952.

Boswell, Rolfe. "Quick, Watson, the Fiddle!" *Baker Street Journal* [O.S.] 3, No. 4 (Oct. 1948): 435–440.

Boucher, Anthony. "The Records of Baker Street." *Baker Street Journal* [O.S.] 4, No. 1 (Jan. 1949): 97–104.

Brain, Peter. "Dr. Watson's War Wounds." *The Lancet*, No. 7634 (Dec. 20, 1969): 1354–1355.

Brend, Gavin. "Was Sherlock Holmes at Westminster?" *Sherlock Holmes Journal* 2, No. 1 (July 1954): 39–41.

Bristowe, W. S. "Oxford or Cambridge?" *Sherlock Holmes Journal* 4, No. 2 (Spring 1959): 75–76.

Bryan-Brown, Freddy. "The Influence of Edgar Allan Poe on Doyle and Holmes." *Sherlock Holmes Journal* 20, No. 4 (Summer 1992): 124–127.

Carey, Eugene F. "Holmes, Watson and Cocaine." *Baker Street Journal* 13, No. 3 (Sept. 1963): 176–181, 195.

Christ, Jay Finley. "An Adventure in the Lower Criticism, Part II: Dr. Watson and the Moon." *Baker Street Gasogene*, No. 4 (April 1962): 13–19.

———. "Sherlock and the Canons." *Baker Street Journal* 3, No. 1 (Jan. 1953): 5–12.

Clarkson, Paul S. "'In the Beginning . . .' " *Baker Street Journal* 8, No. 4 (Oct. 1958): 197–209.

Clarkson, Steve. "Another Case of Identity." *Baker Street Journal* 22, No. 2 (June 1972): 84–86.

Cochran, Leonard. "Sherlock Holmes and Logic: The Education of a Genius." *Baker Street Journal* 17, No. 1 (Mar. 1967): 15–19.

Cole, James. "The Curious Incident of Holmes's Doing Little in the Daytime." *Baker Street Journal* 30, No. 3 (Sept. 1980): 170–173.

Connors, Joseph B. "Holmes and the Oxford Manner." In Cultivating Sherlock Holmes, edited by Bryce L. Crawford, Jr., and Joseph B. Connors, 39–47. La Crosse, Wisc.: Published by the Sumac Press for the Norwegian Explorers, 1978.

Cooperman, E. M. "Marfan's Syndrome and Sherlock Holmes." *Canadian Medical Association Journal* 112 (1975): 483.

Cross, Melvin. "The Lantern of Sherlock Holmes." *Baker Street Journal* [O. S.] 1, No. 4 (1946): 433–442.

Curjel, Harald. "Some Further Thoughts on Canonical Weaponry." *Sherlock Holmes Journal* 15, No. 3 (Winter 1981): 82–85.

Curjel, H. E. B. "Young Doctor Stamford of Barts." *Sherlock Holmes Journal* 11, No. 4 (Autumn 1974): 131–133.

Cutter, Robert A. "The Underground." In The Illustrious Client's Second

Case-Book, edited by J. N. Williamson, 83–87. Indianapolis, Ind.: The Illustrious Clients, 1949.

Davies, Bernard, "The Book of Genesis." *Sherlock Holmes Journal,* Centenary Special (1987): 9–37.

Dean, May. "A Demographic Portrait of the Mormons, 1830–1980." In After 150 Years: The Latter-Day Saints in Sesquicentennial Perspective, edited by Thomas G. Alexander and Jessie L. Embry. Provo, Utah: Charles Rudd Center for Western Studies, 1983.

Dickensheet, Dean W. "Sherlock Holmes—Linguist." *Baker Street Journal* 10, No. 3 (July 1960): 133–142.

Dickman, Marshall Shaw. "On Matters Surrounding the Case of the Purloined Letter." *Baker Street Miscellanea*, No. 34 (Summer 1983): 23–31.

Dorwart, Thomas H. "Thoughts Concerning Certain Infamous Conclusions: Being a Reply to Mr. Jason Rouby." *Baker Street Journal* 16, No. 4 (Dec. 1966): 216–218.

Doyle, Arthur Conan. A Study in Scarlet, edited by Owen Dudley Edwards. Oxford and New York: Oxford University Press, 1993.

Drazen, Patrick. "An Etude in Scarlet." *Beeman's Christmas Annual* (1987): 7–10.

Dudley, W. E. "Dr. Holmes, I Presume." *Baker Street Journal* 24, No. 4 (Dec. 1974): 218–220.

Eaton, Herb. "The H.M.S. Troopship 'Orontes,' " *Vermissa Daily Herald* 6, No. 1 (Jan. 1972): 2–6, 8.

Elwin, Verrier. "College Life of Sherlock Holmes." *Motley*. Bombay: Orient Longmans Ltd. (Nov. 1954): 157–163.

Fletcher, George. "Sighting-in on Watson's Bull Pup." *Baker Street Journal* 21, No. 3 (Sept. 1971): 156–157.

Friesland, D. S. *Baker Street Journal* 31, No. 2 (June 1981): 118 (Letters to Baker Street).

Fusco, Andrew G. "The Case Against Mr. Holmes." In Beyond Baker Street: A Sherlockian Anthology, edited by Michael Harrison, 95–108. Indianapolis and New York: The Bobbs-Merrill Co., 1976.

———. "The Final Outrage of Enoch Drebber." *Baker Street Journal* 20, No. 3 (Sept. 1970), 150–153.

Goodman, Charles. "The Dental Holmes." *Baker Street Journal* [O.S.] 2, No. 4 (Oct. 1947): 381–393.

Grazebrook, O. F. Oxford or Cambridge. London: Privately printed, 1949.

Green, Richard Lancelyn. "The Evolution of Sherlock Holmes." *Baker Street Miscellanea*, No. 49 (Spring 1987): 2–9.

Green, Roger Lancelyn. " 'At the University': Some Thoughts on the Academic Experience of Mr. Sherlock Holmes." *Sherlock Holmes Journal* 9, No. 4 (Summer 1970): 123–125.

Griffith, Adrian. "Some Observations on Sherlock Holmes and Dr. Watson at Barts." *St. Bartholomew's Hospital Journal* 55, No. 12 (Dec. 1951): 270–275.

Grosbayne, Bernard. "Sherlock Holmes—Musician." *Baker Street Journal* [O. S.] 3, No. 1 (1948): 47–57.

Hall, Trevor H. "A Note on Sherlock Holmes's Schooling." In SHERLOCK HOLMES: TEN LITERARY STUDIES, edited by Trevor H. Hall, 36–43. London: Gerald Duckworth & Co., 1969.

———. "Sherlock Holmes's University and College," In SHERLOCK HOLMES: TEN LITERARY STUDIES, edited by Trevor H. Hall, 56–85, London: Gerald Duckworth & Co., 1969.

Hendrickson, J. Raymond. "De Re Pharmaca," In LEAVES FROM THE COPPER BEECHES, edited by Ames Johnston, Thomas Hart, Henry A. Shalet, and H. W. Starr, 11–14. Philadelphia, Pa.: Sons of The Copper Beeches, 1959.

Hepburn, W. B. "The Jezail Bullet." *The Practitioner* 19 (July 1966): 100–101, reprinted in *Sherlock Holmes Journal* 8, No. 1 (Winter 1966): 18–19.

Hershey, Dave M. "The True York College." *Sherlock Holmes Review* 2, No. 3 (1990): 123–124.

Holroyd, James E. "Dr. Watson at the Criterion." *Sherlock Holmes Journal* 2, No. 2 (Dec. 1954): 26.

Holstein, L. S. "Bull Pups and Literary Agents." *Baker Street Journal,* Christmas Annual (1958): 54–57.

———. "Inspector G. Lestrade," *Baker Street Journal* 8, No. 2 (Apr. 1958): 78–84.

———. "7. Knowledge of Chemistry—Profound," *Baker Street Journal* 4, No. 1 (Jan. 1954): 44–49.

Horrocks, Peter. "Saints and Sinners: An Appraisal of 'The Country of the Saints.' " *Sherlock Holmes Journal,* Centenary Special (1987): 38–41.

Hoskison, Peter. "Delicate Case of Mr. S. Holmes and His University Home." *Cambridge Evening News*, Jan. 5, 1974.

Howard, Samuel F. "More About Maiwand." *Baker Street Journal* 7, No. 1 (Jan. 1957): 20–25.

Huber, Christine L. "The Sherlock Holmes Blood Test: The Solution to a Century-Old Mystery." *Baker Street Journal* 37, No. 4 (Dec. 1987): 215–220.

Hyder, William. "The Martha Myth." *Baker Street Journal* 41, No. 1 (Mar. 1991): 9–19.

Iraldi, James C. "The Victorian Gondola." *Baker Street Journal* 1, No. 3 (July 1951): 99–103.

James, Garry. "Shooting the Guns of Sherlock Holmes." *Handguns for Sport and Defense* 5, No. 10 (Oct. 1991), 70–75.

Jenkins, William D. "Letters to Baker Street." *Baker Street Journal* 26, No. 1 (March 1976): 46.

Jones, Kelvin I. THE SHERLOCK HOLMES MURDER FILE. New York: Magico Magazine, 1985.

KANSAS: A CYCLOPEDIA OF STATE HISTORY, EMBRACING EVENTS, INSTITUTIONS, INDUSTRIES, COUNTIES, CITIES, TOWNS, PROMINENT PERSONS, ETC. Chicago: Standard Pub. Co., 1912.

Katz, Robert S. "Doctor Watson—A Physician of Mediocre Qualifications?" In A TOUCH OF THE CLASS, edited by Michael H. Kean, 37–42. Wilmette, Ill.: Pondicherry Press, 1981.

Keefauver, Brad. "The Hundred-Year-Old Mystery of Mrs. Sawyer Solved." *WheelWrightings* 10, No. 3 (Jan. 1988): 18–20.

———. "Oxford, Cambridge or . . . ? The Final Answer." *Afghanistanzas* 6, No. 5 (Nov. 1982): 8–10; *Afghanistanzas* 6, No. 6 (Dec. 1982): 11–13.

Keen, Sherry. "Ship's or 'ship's?': That is the Question." *Baker Street Journal* 3, No. 4 (1953): 234–235.

Kennedy, Bruce. "Alma Mater, or Two Unexplained Years." *Baker Street Journal* 19, No. 3 (Sept. 1969): 158–160.

———. "The Victorian Flashlight: Sherlock Holmes and Dark Lanterns." *Baker Street Journal* 30, No. 3 (Sept. 1980): 141–143.

———. "What Bull Pup?" *Baker Street Journal* 16, No. 4 (Dec. 1966): 215.

Kimball, Elliot. DR. JOHN H. WATSON AT NETLEY. Privately printed, 1962; reprinted, New York: Magico Magazine, 1985.

———. "Origin and Evolution of G. Lestrade: 1. Onomatological Considerations." *Sherlock Holmes Journal* 6, No. 1 (Winter 1962): 4–5.

———. "Origin and Evolution of G. Lestrade: 2. A Matter of Mancinism." *Sherlock Holmes Journal* 6, No. 2 (Spring 1963): 43–45.

Klinger, Leslie S. "Art in Whose Blood?" *The Ritual* 21 (Spring 1998): 3–7.

———. "Layout of a 'Most Desirable Residence.' " *Shoso-In Bulletin* 6 (1996): 78–81.

———. "What Do We Really Know About Sherlock Holmes and John H. Watson?" *Baker Street Journal* 54, No. 3 (Autumn 2004): 6–15.

———. "The Writings of Sherlock Holmes," *Baker Street West 1* 3, No. 1 (Jan. 1997), 23–26.

Koelle, George B. "The Poisons of the Canon." In LEAVES FROM THE COPPER BEECHES, edited by Ames Johnston, Thomas Hart, Henry A. Shalet, and H. W. Starr, 91–96. Narbeth, Pa.: Livingston Publishing Company, 1959.

Lai, Rick. "The Hansoms of John Clay." *WheelWrightings* 6, No. 3 (Jan. 1984): 5–8.

Lauterbach, Charles E., and Edward S. Lauterbach. "The Man Who Seldom Laughed." *Baker Street Journal*, Christmas Annual, (1960): 265–271.

Leavitt, Robert Keith. "Annie Oakley in Baker Street: A Note on the Lamentable Limitations of Mr. Sherlock Holmes's Pistol Marksmanship." In PROFILE BY

GASLIGHT: AN IRREGULAR READER ABOUT THE PRIVATE LIFE OF SHERLOCK HOLMES, edited by Edgar W. Smith, 230–242. New York: Simon & Schuster, 1944.

———. "Nummi in Arca or The Fiscal Holmes." In 221B: STUDIES IN SHERLOCK HOLMES, edited by Vincent Starrett, 16–36. New York: The Macmillan Co., 1940.

Linsenmeyer, John. "Sherlock Holmes's University—Oxford or Cambridge?" *Baker Street Journal* 39, No. 2 (June 1989): 71–74.

Mackay, Thomas W. "Mormon as Editor: A Study in Colophons, Headers, and Source Indicators." *Journal of Book of Mormon Studies* 2, No. 1 (Fall 1993): 90–109.

Mackenzie, J. B. "Sherlock Holmes' Plots and Strategy." *Baker Street Journal*, Christmas Annual (1956): 56–61, reprinted from *The Green Bag* 14 (Sept. 1902): 407–411.

MacNaghten, Sir H. "The Education of Holmes." *Sunday Times*, Aug. 26, 1934. Reproduced in SHERLOCK HOLMES SCRAPBOOK, edited by Peter Haining, 42. New York: Clarkson N. Potter, 1974.

Malloy, Michael P. "Tobacco Amblyopia and Holmes." *Baker Street Journal* 26, No. 2 (June 1976): 94–95, 98, 117.

McCleary, George F. "Was Sherlock Holmes a Drug Addict?" In PROFILE BY GASLIGHT: AN IRREGULAR READER ABOUT THE PRIVATE LIFE OF SHERLOCK HOLMES, edited by Edgar W. Smith, 40–45. New York: Simon & Schuster, 1944.

McDiarmid, E. W. "Professor Sherlock Holmes, Ph. D." In EXPLORING SHERLOCK HOLMES, edited by E. W. McDiarmid and Theodore C. Blegen, 27–41. La Crosse, Wisc.: Sumac Press, 1957.

McGowan, Raymond J. "A Chemist's Evaluation of Sherlock Holmes's Monograph on Tobacco." *Sherlock Holmes Journal* 19, No. 3 (Winter 1989): 86–88.

McMillan, Scott, and Garry James. "The Guns of Sherlock Holmes." *Guns & Ammo* 19, No. 4 (Apr. 1975): 51–53, 83.

Melander, Wayne. "Sierra Blanco—Found(?)." *Baker Street Journal* 31, No. 2 (June 1981): 83–89.

Mendelson, Ralph. "Hero Neglected, A True Account." *Baker Street Journal* 19, No. 3 (Sept. 1969): 166–171.

Metcalfe, N. P. "Oxford or Cambridge or Both?" *Baker Street Journal*, Christmas Annual (1956): 7–14.

Meyer, Charles A. "A Computer Analysis of Authorship in *A Study in Scarlet*." *Naval Signals,* No. 16 (Sept. 28, 1983): 3–6.

Michaud, Rosemary. "Another Case of Identity." *Plugs & Dottles*, No. 144 (Sept. 1990): 3, 7.

Montgomery, James. "A Hearty Sea-Story." In SHOTS FROM THE CANON, 24. Philadephia, Pa.: Privately printed, 1953.

———. "Chopin in Baker Street." In Sidelights on Sherlock, n.p. Philadelphia, Pa.: Privately printed, 1951.

Morgan, Robert S. "The Puzzle of the Bull Pup." *Baker Street Journal*, Christmas Annual (1956): 35–40.

———. Spotlight on a Simple Case, or Wiggins, Who Was That Horse I Saw with You Last Night. Wilmington, Del.: Privately printed, 1959.

Morley, Christopher. "Sherlock Holmes Returns." *The Courier* 39, No. 5 (Dec. 1962): 66–67.

———. "Sherlock Holmes Revisits Cambridge." *Baker Street Journal* [O.S.] 3, No. 3 (July 1948): 295–299 (Clinical Notes by a Resident Patient).

———. "Was Sherlock Holmes an American?" In Streamlines, 54–65. Garden City, N.Y.: Doubleday, Doran & Co., Inc., 1936.

Morley, Christopher, writing as Jane Nightwork. "Watson à la Mode." *Baker Street Journal* [O.S.] 1, No. 1 (Jan. 1946): 15–20.

Mortimore, Roger. "That Is to Say, Mr. Holmes." *Baker Street Pillar Box*, No. 13 (1993): 13–16.

Moss, Robert A. "Sherlock Holmes's College at Oxford." *Baker Street Journal* 29, No. 1 (March 1979): 25–27.

Mullen, Robert. The Latter-Day Saints: The Mormons Yesterday and Today. Garden City, N.Y.: Doubleday & Company, 1966.

Murdock, Karen. " 'Columbine's New-fangled Banner' Identified." *Baker Street Journal* 52, No. 1 (Spring 2002): 14–23.

Nathan, Hartley R., and Clifford S. Goldfarb. "Watson: Treason in the Blood?" *Baker Street Journal* 34, No. 4 (Dec. 1984): 234–243.

Newnham-Davis, Lt.-Col. Nathaniel. Dinners and Diners: Where and How to Dine in London. London: Grant Richards, 1899.

Officer, Harvey. "Sherlock Holmes and Music." In 221b: Studies in Baker Street, edited by Vincent Starrett, 71–73. New York: The Macmillan Co., 1940.

Olding, Alan C. "Murder Most Foul." *News from the Diggings* 12, No. 3 (Sept. 1991): 1.

Olney, Clarke. "The Literacy of Sherlock Holmes." *Sherlock Holmes Journal* 2, No. 4 (Winter 1955): 9–15.

Pattrick, Robert R. "Moriarty Was There." *Baker Street Journal,* Christmas Annual (1958): 45–53.

Pennell, Vernon. "Resumé of the Medical Life of John H. Watson, Late of the Army Medical Department, with an Appendix of the London University Regulations for Medical Degrees for the Year 1875." *Sherlock Holmes Journal* 3, No. 2 (Winter 1956): 6–11.

Pforr, John, and Philip Weller. Sherlock Holmes and Scotland Yard: A Love-Hate Relationship? Fareham, Hampshire, England: Franco-Midland Hardware Company, 1992.

Pratt, Fletcher. "Very Little Murder." *Baker Street Journal* 5, No. 2 (Apr. 1955): 69–76.

Prestige, Colin. "South London Adventures." *Sherlock Holmes Journal* 3, No. 3 (Aug. 1957): 5–8.

Redmond, D. A. "Marfan's Syndrome and Sherlock Holmes." *Canadian Medical Association Journal* 113 (1975): 19.

———. "The Masons and the Mormons." *Baker Street Journal* 18, No. 4 (Dec. 1968), 229–231.

Rice, Rev. Otis R. "Clergymen in the Canon." *Baker Street Journal* 4, No. 3 (July 1954): 133–143.

Richards, Walter. Her Majesty's Army, Indian and Colonial Forces: A Descriptive Account of the Various Regiments Now Comprising the Queen's Forces in India and the Colonies. London: J. S. Virtue, 1891.

Roberts, S. C. Doctor Watson. London: Faber & Faber, 1931.

———. "The Personality of Sherlock Holmes." *Sherlock Holmes Journal* 1, No. 1 (May 1952): 2–7.

Robinson, Robert E. "Tra-la-la-lira-lira-lay." *Baker Street Miscellanea* 30 (Summer 1982): 15–16, inside back cover.

Rosenblum, Morris. "Foreign Language Quotations in the Canon." *Baker Street Journal* [O. S.] 3, No. 4 (1948): 425–434.

———. "Hafiz and Horace, Huxtable and Holmes." *Baker Street Journal* [O. S.] 1, No. 3 (1946): 261–269.

———. "Some Latin Byways in the Canon." *Baker Street Journal* [O. S.] 3, No. 1 (1948): 15–20.

Rouby, Jason. "The Adventure of the Bluish Carbuncle." *Baker Street Journal* 16, No. 2 (June 1966): 70–73.

Rybrant, Gosta. "Fallet tra-la-la-lira-lira-lay." *Aftonbladet*, Dec. 26, 1953.

Ryder, Cecil A., Jr. "A Study in Masonry." *Sherlock Holmes Journal* 11, No. 3 (Winter 1973): 86–88.

Sayers, Dorothy L. "Holmes' College Career." In Baker Street Studies, edited by H. W. Bell, 1–34. London: Constable & Co., 1934.

Schenck, Remsen Ten Eyck. "Baker Street Fables." *Baker Street Journal* 2, No. 2 (1952): 85–93.

Schonberg, Harold C. "Tra-la-la-lira-lira-lay." *New York Times*, March 7, 1965, II, 11.

Schutz, Robert H. A Bibliography of the Identification of Holmes's College and University. Pittsburgh, Pa.: Arnsworth Castle Business Index, June 1961.

Scrow, William J. "The Pick of a Bad Lot." *Holmesian Observer Annual*, No. 2 (1975): 2–8.

Shanks, John. "You Have Been to University I Perceive." *Three Pipe Problem* 2 (Aug. 11, 1979): 10–16.

Shannon, D.C. "Poor Devil." *The Pharos* [Alpha Omega Alpha—Honor Medical Society, Palo Alto, Calif.] 41, No. 4 (Oct. 1978): 5–9.

Simpson, A. Carson. "Full Thirty Thousand Marks of English Coin." NUMISMATICS IN THE CANON, PART I. Philadelphia, Pa.: Privately printed, 1957.

———. "A Very Treasury of Coin of Divers Realms." NUMISMATICS IN THE CANON, PART. II. Philadelphia, Pa.: Privately printed, 1958.

Simpson, Helen. "Medical Career and Capacities of Dr. J. H. Watson." *Baker Street Studies*, edited by H. W. Bell, 35–62. London: Constable & Co., 1934.

Skornickel, Jr., George R. "Who Was the Mysterious Mrs. Sawyer?" *Subjoined Paper* 1, No. 1 (Oct. 1978): 5–6.

Smith, Edgar W. BAKER STREET INVENTORY. Summit, N.J.: Pamphlet House, 1943.

———. "A Bibliographical Note." *Baker Street Journal* 9, No. 1 (Jan. 1959): 3–4.

———. "Long Road from Maiwand." In PROFILE BY GASLIGHT: AN IRREGULAR READER ABOUT THE PRIVATE LIFE OF SHERLOCK HOLMES, edited by Edgar W. Smith, 195–201. New York: Simon & Schuster, 1944.

———. "Up from the Needle." *Baker Street Journal* [O.S.] 2, No. 1 (Jan. 1947): 85–88.

Smith, William. "That Little Thing of Chopin's: The Laying of the Ghost." *Baker Street Journal* 13, No. 1 (March 1963): 24–30.

Sovine, J. W. "The Singular Bullet." *Baker Street Journal* 9, No. 1 (Jan. 1959): 28–32.

Starrett, Vincent. "The Singular Adventures of Martha Hudson." In BAKER STREET STUDIES, edited by H. W. Bell, 85–130. London: Constable & Co., 1934.

Stavert, Geoffrey S. "Case of the Straw Basher's Hatband." *Sherlock Holmes Journal* 13, No. 4 (Autumn 1978): 122–123.

Steinbrunner, Chris, Charles Shibuk, Otto Penzler, Marvin Lachman, and Francis M. Nevins, Jr. DETECTIONARY. Lockhaven, Pa.: Hammermill Paper Company, 1972.

Stetak, Ruthann, H. "Jefferson Hope: A Fairly Good Dispenser." *Baker Street Journal* 39, No. 3 (Sept. 1989): 144–147.

Stockler, J. R., and R. N. Brodie. "The Problem of the Dog That Wasn't." *Sherlock Holmes Journal* 9, No. 2 (Summer 1969): 61–62.

Stone, P. M. "The Other Friendship: A Speculation." In PROFILE BY GASLIGHT: AN IRREGULAR READER ABOUT THE PRIVATE LIFE OF SHERLOCK HOLMES, edited by Edgar W. Smith, 97–103. New York: Simon & Schuster, 1944.

Thiman, Eric H., MUS. D. "Tra-la-la-lira-lira-lay." *Sherlock Holmes Journal* 4 (Winter 1959): 105 (Letter to the Editor).

Thurbon, William T. "Education of Sherlock Holmes—A Footnote." *Baker Street Miscellanea*, No. 7 (Sept. 1976): 11–12.

Torrese, Dante M. "Firearms in the Canon: The Guns of Sherlock Holmes and John H. Watson." *Baker Street Journal* 42, No. 3 (Sept. 1992): 154–157.

Tracy, Jack. CONAN DOYLE AND THE LATTER-DAY SAINTS. Bloomington, Ind.: Gaslight Publications, 1979 (revised and expanded edition of version privately printed in 1971).

———. " 'Old Woman Be Damned!' A Partial Identification of Jefferson Hope's Accomplice." *Baker Street Journal* 24, No. 2 (June 1974): 105–108.

Tracy, Jack, with Jim Berkey. SUBCUTANEOUSLY, MY DEAR WATSON: SHERLOCK HOLMES AND THE COCAINE HABIT. Bloomington, Ind.: James A. Rock & Company, 1978.

Tully, Thomas. "Bull Pup." *Baker Street Dispatch* 2, No. 6 (Nov.–Dec. 1992): 3–6.

Umansky, Harlan L. "An Adventure in 'Wild Surmise,' " *Baker Street Journal* 32, No. 1 (March 1982): 25–29.

Utechin, Nicholas. SHERLOCK HOLMES AT OXFORD. Oxford: Robert Dugdale, 1977.

———. " 'This Charming Town.' " *Baker Street Journal* 26, No. 3 (Sept. 1976): 135–140.

Vaill, C. B. H. "A Study in Intellects." *Baker Street Journal* [O. S.] 3 , No. 3 (July 1948): 278–282.

Van Liere, Edward J. "Dr. John Watson and the Subclavian Steal." *Archives of Internal Medicine* 118, No. 3 (Sept. 1966): 245–248.

Vaught, Richard L. "Now See Here, Holmes!" *Baker Street Journal* 25, No. 1 (March 1975): 47–54.

Visozkie, Ben. "Who Wrote the American Chapters of *A Study in Scarlet*?" *Baker Street Journal* 50, No. 2 (Summer 2000): 29–36.

Wagley, Philip Franklin. "A Reconsideration of Dr. John H. Watson's Encounter with a Jezail Bullet." *Maryland State Medical Journal* 25, No. 12 (Dec. 1976): 35–37.

Webster, H. T. "Observations of Sherlock Holmes as an Athlete and Sportsman." *Baker Street Journal* [O.S.] 3, No. 1 (1948): 24–31.

Weller, Philip. "On Jezails and Things Afghan." *New Baker Street Pillar Box* 31 (Feb. 1998): 40–41.

Wellman, Manley Wade. "The Great Man's Great Son: An Inquiry into the Most Private Live of Mr. Sherlock Holmes." *Baker Street Journal* [O. S.] 1, No. 3 (July 1946): 326–336.

White, William Braid. "From the Editor's Commonplace Book." *Baker Street Journal* [O.S.] 2, No. 4 (1947): 436 (Letter to the Editor).

———. "Sherlock Holmes and the Equal Temperament." *Baker Street Journal* [O.S.] 1, No. 1 (Jan. 1946): 39–43.

Williams, Theodore. "Lestradean Orthography." *Baker Street Miscellanea*, No. 44 (Winter 1985): 37–38.

Williamson, Jerry N. " 'And Especially Your Eyes.' " *Sherlock Holmes Journal* 3, No. 3 (Autumn 1957): 17–19.

———. "The Sad Case of Young Stamford." *Baker Street Journal* [O.S.] 3, No. 4 (Oct. 1948): 449–451.

———. "Sherlock's Murder Bag." In ILLUSTRIOUS CLIENT'S THIRD CASE-BOOK, edited by J. N. Williamson and H. B. Williams, 84–88. Indianapolis, Ind.: The Illustrious Clients, 1953.

Wolff, Julian. "Just What Was That Little Thing of Chopin's?" *Baker Street Journal* 13, No. 1 (March 1963): 3–4.

———. "That Was No Lady. A Reply to Mr. Stout in Which are Included Some Observations Upon the Nature of Dr. Watson's Wounds." *American Journal of Surgery* 58, No. 2 (Nov. 1942): 310–312. Reprinted in PROFILE BY GASLIGHT: AN IRREGULAR READER ABOUT THE PRIVATE LIFE OF SHERLOCK HOLMES, edited by Edgar W. Smith, 166–172. New York: Simon & Schuster, 1944.

Wood, Cal. "Stamford: A Closer Look." *Baker Street Pages,* No. 32 (Feb. 1968): 1–2.

Woodruff, Wilfrid. JOURNAL. Cited in B. H. Roberts, A COMPREHENSIVE HISTORY OF THE CHURCH OF JESUS CHRIST OF LATTER-DAY SAINTS, 185. Salt Lake City: Church of Jesus Christ of Latter-Day Saints, 1930. 6 vols.

Woods, Carol P. "A Curtailed Report on a Dogged Investigation." *Baker Street Journal* 30, No. 1 (March 1980): 36–38.

Zeisler, Ernest B. "Tra-La-La-Lira-Lira-Lay." *Sherlock Holmes Journal* 4, No. 1 (Winter 1958): 11–12.

THE SIGN OF FOUR

Allen, F. A., M.P.S. "Devilish Drugs, Part One." *May and Baker "Pharmaceutical Bulletin,"* December 1956. Reprinted in *Sherlock Holmes Journal* 3, No. 3 (Autumn 1957): 12–14.

Anderson, Poul. "Art in the Blood." *Baker Street Journal* 6, No. 3 (July 1956): 133–137.

Beam, Paul. "The Indian Elements in the Holmes Tales: Jewels and Tigers." *Canadian Holmes* 5, No. 4 (St. Jean Baptiste Day 1982): 3–11. Reprinted in CANADIAN HOLMES: THE FIRST TWENTY-FIVE YEARS, edited by Christopher Redmond, 185–192. Ashcroft, British Columbia: Calabash Press, 1997.

Bengis, Nathan. "A Scandal in Baker Street, Part II." *Baker Street Journal* [O. S.] 2, No. 3 (July 1947): 311–321.

Berl, Col. E. Ennalls. "Sherlock Holmes and the Telephone." *Baker Street Journal* 3, No. 4 (Oct. 1953): 197–210.

Blakeney, T. S. "Thoughts on *The Sign of the Four.*" *Sherlock Holmes Journal* 3, No. 4 (Summer 1958): 6–8.

Bonn, Ronald S. "The Problem of the Postulated Doctor." *Baker Street Journal* 14, No. 1 (March 1964): 14–21.

Bousquet, Robert J. "Mary Morstan: Clothed in Euphemism." *New Baker Street Pillar Box* 32 (Aug. 1998): 29–31.

Boyd, Dr. Andrew. "Dr. Watson's Dupe." *Encounter* 14, No. 3 (March 1960). Reprinted in *Sherlock Holmes Journal* 5, No. 2 (Spring 1961): 42–44.

Brown, John W. SHERLOCK HOLMES IN STREATHAM. Streatham, London: Local History Publications, 1993.

Clark, John D., PH.D. "A Chemist's View of Canonical Chemistry." *Baker Street Journal* 14, No. 2 (Sept. 1964): 153–155.

Cold, Jørgen. "What Did Sherlock Holmes Drink?" In ILLUSTRIOUS CLIENT'S THIRD CASE-BOOK, edited by J. N. Williamson and H. B. Williams, 110–118. Indianapolis, Ind.: The Illustrious Clients, 1953. Reprinted in SHERLOCK HOLMES: VINTAGE AND SPIRITED, edited by Michael H. Kean, 28–33. New York: Magico Magazine, 1994.

Cooper, Peter. "Holmesian Chemistry." In BEYOND BAKER STREET: A SHERLOCKIAN ANTHOLOGY, edited by Michael Harrison, 67–74. Indianapolis and New York: The Bobbs-Merrill Company, 1976.

Crocker, Stephen F. "Sherlock Holmes Recommends Winwood Reade." *Baker Street Journal* 14, No. 3 (Sept. 1964): 142–144.

Curjel, Harald. "The *Aurora* and the Police Launch." *Baker Street Journal* 31, No. 2 (June 1981): 70–74.

Dahlinger, S. E. "In Search of the Agra Treasure." *Baker Street Journal* 36, No. 4 (Dec. 1986): 217–221.

Davies, Bernard. "Dr. Watson's Deuteronomy." *Sherlock Holmes Journal* 19, No. 4, Pt. I (Summer 1990): 101–121, and 20, No. 1, Pt. II (Winter 1990): 6–23.

———. "Was Holmes a Londoner?" *Sherlock Holmes Journal* 4, No. 2 (Spring 1959): 42–47.

Dickens, Charles. DICKENS'S DICTIONARY OF THE THAMES, FROM ITS SOURCE TO THE NORE. London: J. Smith, 1894.

Donnelson, Gar. " 'PLEASE GIVE THE YARD A CALL, WATSON.' " Lincoln, Neb.: Privately printed, 1986.

Douglass, Ruth. "The Camberwell Poisoner." *Ellery Queen's Mystery Magazine* 9, No. 39 (Feb. 1947): 57–63.

Doyle, Arthur Conan. THE SIGN OF THE FOUR, edited by Christopher Roden. Oxford and New York: Oxford University Press, 1993.

———. UNCOLLECTED SHERLOCK HOLMES, compiled by Richard Lancelyn Green. Hammondsworth, Middlesex, England: Penguin Books, 1963.

Durgin, Cyrus. "The Speckled Band." In THE THIRD CAB, 12–16. Boston: Privately printed, 1960.

Fink, Joseph J. "The Marital Hoax of John H. Watson." *Baker Street Journal* 42, No. 2 (June 1992): 102–105.

Foss, Lt. Col. T. F. "Regina *v.* Holmes and Another." *Baker Street Journal* 18, No. 1 (March 1968): 22–31.

Galerstein, David. " 'I Have the Right to Private Judgement.' " *Baker Street Journal* 24, No.2 (Sept. 1974): 168–173.

Goodman, Charles, D.D.S. "The Dental Holmes." In PROFILE BY GASLIGHT: AN IRREGULAR READER ABOUT THE PRIVATE LIFE OF SHERLOCK HOLMES, edited by Edgar W. Smith, 85–96. New York: Simon & Schuster, 1944.

Green, Roger Lancelyn. "Dr. Watson's First Critic." *Sherlock Holmes Journal* 3, No. 4 (Summer 1958): 8–9.

Grilly, D. M. "A Reply to Miller's 'The Habit of Sherlock Holmes.' " *Trans. Stud.*

Coll. Physicians Phila., Series V, 1 (1979): 324–327. Reprinted as Grilly, David M., "Sherlock Holmes and Cocaine: Fact and Fiction." *Sherlock Holmes Journal* 15, No. 1 (Winter 1980): 11–13.

Guy, Patricia. BACCHUS IN BAKER STREET. Romford, Essex, England: Ian Henry Publications, 1995.

Hall, John. "And Now?—Ballarat." In INTERIM REPORT 1993: THE BOSCOMBE VALLEY CONTRACT REVISITED, 17–19. Hampshire, England: Franco-Midland Hardware Co., 1993.

———. "The Lady of the House: Part Two, Women Are Never to Be Entirely Trusted." *Sherlock* 58 (2003): 29.

Hammer, David L. THE WORTH OF THE GAME. Dubuque, Iowa: Gasogene Press, Ltd., 1993.

Harrison, Michael. THEATRICAL MR. HOLMES. London: Covent Garden Press, 1974.

Hart, Archibald. "The Effects of Trades Upon Hands." *Baker Street Journal* [O. S.] 3, No. 4 (Oct. 1948): 418–420.

Haynes, George Cleve. "Who's Pulling My Leg? A Re-Examination of the Evidence Concerning Dr. Watson's Wounds." *Sherlock Holmes Journal* 23, No. 2 (Summer 1997): 48–49.

Hearn, Otis. "Marginalia to *The Sign of Four.*" *Baker Street Journal* 22, No. 1 (March 1972): 24–25.

Hoff, Ebbe Curtis. "The Adventure of John and Mary." *Baker Street Journal* 9, No. 3 (July 1959): 136–152.

Holly, Raymond. "Dubious and Questionable." *Camden House Journal* 1, No. 3 (March 1979): 2–3.

Holstein, Leon S. "7. Knowledge of Chemistry—Profound." *Baker Street Journal* 4, No. 1 (Jan. 1954): 44–49.

Hughes, Mel. "Wiggin' Out." *Wigmore Street Post Office Journal* 12 (Summer 1998): 21–23.

Hughes, Robert. THE FATAL SHORE. New York: Random House, 1986.

Hyder, William. "Watson's Education and Medical Career." In FROM BALTIMORE TO BAKER STREET, 46–65. Toronto: Metropolitan Toronto Reference Library, 1995.

Jewell, Donald Girard. A CANONICAL DOG'S LIFE: A MONOGRAPH ON CANINES IN THE TIME OF SHERLOCK HOLMES. Westminster: Pinchin Lane Press, 1993 (Sherlock Holmes Natural History Series, Vol. 5).

Jones, Kelvin I. THE CARFAX SYNDROME: BEING A STUDY IN VAMPIRISM IN THE CANON. New York: Magico Magazine, 1984.

Keefauver, Brad. "Clayton's Cabstand Commentary." *Wheelwrightings* 8, No. 2 (Sept. 1985): 29–33.

———. SHERLOCK AND THE LADIES. New York: Magico Magazine, 1988.

Klinger, Leslie S. "The Dating of *The Five Orange Pips.*" *Baker Street Journal* 45, No. 2 (Jun. 1995): 70–79.

———. "Layout of a 'Most Desirable Residence.' " *Shoso-In Bulletin*, No. 6 (1996): 78–81.

———. "The Writings of Sherlock Holmes." *Baker Street West 1* 3, No. 1 (Jan. 1997): 23–26.

Koelle, George B. "The Poisons of the Canon." In Leaves from the Copper Beeches, edited by Ames Johnson, Thomas Hart, Henry A. Shalet, and H. W. Starr, 91–96. Narbeth, Pa.: Livingston Publishing Company, 1959.

Kramer, Matt. Making Sense of Burgundy. New York: William Morrow and Company, 1990.

Laubach, Deborah. "A Study in Number Three." *Calabash* 1 (March 1982): 3–7.

Leavitt, Robert Keith. "Annie Oakley in Baker Street." In Profile by Gaslight: An Irregular Reader about the Private Life of Sherlock Holmes, edited by Vincent Starrett, 230–242. New York: Simon & Schuster, 1944.

———. "Who Was Cecil Forrester?" *Baker Street Journal* [O. S.] 1, No. 2 (Apr. 1946): 201–204.

Leonard, Patrick J., Sr. "Sherlock Holmes, World Champion!" *Baker Street Journal* 29, No. 1 (March 1979): 27–29.

Longfellow, Esther. "The Distaff Side of Baker Street." *Baker Street Journal* [O. S.] 1, No. 1 (Jan. 1946): 9–13.

Merriman, Charles O. "Tar Derivatives Not Wanted." *Sherlock Holmes Journal* 6, No. 1 (Winter 1962): 33 (Wigmore Street Post-Bag).

Metcalfe, Percy. "Reflections on the Sign of Four or Oreamnosis Once Removed," Pt. II. *Sherlock Holmes Journal* 9, No. 1 (Winter 1968): 14–20.

Meyer, Charles A. "The Remarkable Forrester Case." *Canadian Holmes* 13, No. 4 (Summer 1990): 26–27.

———. "The Sign of the Three Golden Balls: Fencing the Agra Treasure." *Sherlock Holmes Journal* 19, No. 4 (Summer 1990): 122–123.

Michell, Humfrey. "The Palace Clock." *Baker Street Journal* 1, No. 1 (Jan. 1946): 89 (Letters to Baker Street).

Miller, W. H. "Some Observations on the Alleged Use of Cocaine by Mr. Sherlock Holmes." *Baker Street Journal* 19, No. 3 (Sept. 1969): 161–165. Reprinted as "The Habit of Sherlock Holmes." *Trans. Stud. Coll. Physicians Phila.*, Series IV, 45 (1978): 252–257.

Montgomery, James. A Study in Pictures. Philadelphia, Pa.: International Printing Co., 1954.

Moriarty, Daniel L. "The Woman Who Beat Sherlock Holmes." *Baker Street Journal* 9, No. 2 (Apr. 1959): 69–82.

Morley, Christopher. "Was Sherlock Holmes an American?" In 221B: Studies in Sherlock Holmes, edited by Vincent Starrett, 5–15. New York: The Macmillan Company, 1940.

Morley, Christopher, writing as Jane Nightwork. "Dr. Watson's Secret." In 221B:

STUDIES IN SHERLOCK HOLMES, edited by Vincent Starrett, 46–53. New York: The Macmillan Company, 1940.

Morton, Humphrey. Entry, "Photographic Competition, 'Holmes's World in 1963.'" *Sherlock Holmes Journal* 6, No. 4 (Spring 1964): 126.

Nathan, Hartley R. "The Sign of the Four: A Potpourri of Devil Worshippers, Sikh Troopers and More." *Baker Street Miscellanea*, No. 66 (Summer 1991): 26–35.

Palmer, Stuart. "Notes on Certain Evidence of Caniphobia in Mr. Sherlock Holmes and His Associates." *Baker Street Journal* 5 No. 4 (Oct. 1955): 197–204.

Pattrick, Robert R. "Moriarty Was There." *Baker Street Journal*, Christmas Annual (1958): 45–53.

———. " 'The Oasis in the Howling Desert.' " *Sherlock Holmes Journal* 4, No. 4 (Spring 1960): 126–128.

Redmond, Christopher. "Art in the Blood: Two Canonical Relatives. II. 'The History of My Unhappy Brother.' " *Baker Street Journal* 15, No. 2 (June 1965): 87–89.

Redmond, Donald A. SHERLOCK HOLMES AMONG THE PIRATES: COPYRIGHT AND CONAN DOYLE IN AMERICA 1890–1930. New York, Westport, Conn., and London: Greenwood Press, 1990 (Contributions to the Study of World Literature, No. 36).

———. SHERLOCK HOLMES: A STUDY IN SOURCES. Kingston and Montreal: McGill-Queen's University Press, 1982.

———. "The Oasis in the Howling Desert." *Baker Street Journal* 27, No. 1 (March 1977): 17–21.

———. "Stop Changing Your Mind, Watson!" *Canadian Holmes* 13, No. 3 (Spring 1990): 28.

Rendall, Vernon. "The Limitations of Sherlock Holmes." In BAKER STREET STUDIES, edited by H. W. Bell, 63–84. London: Constable & Co. Ltd., 1934.

Roberts, Randy. "Dr. Watson's Warning." *Baker Street Journal* 31, No. 2 (June 1981): 80–82.

Roberts, S. C. "The Personality of Sherlock Holmes." *Sherlock Holmes Journal* 1, No. 1 (May 1952): 2–7.

Rosenblatt, Julia C. "Who Was Tonga? And Why Were They Saying Such Terrible Things about Him?" *Baker Street Journal* 25, No. 3 (Sept. 1975): 140–41.

Rosenblatt, Julia Carlson, and Frederic H. Sonnenschmidt. DINING WITH SHERLOCK HOLMES: A BAKER STREET COOKBOOK. Indianapolis, Ind., and New York: The Bobbs-Merrill Company, 1976.

Rosenblum, Morris. "Foreign Language Quotations in the Canon." *Baker Street Journal* [O. S.] 3, No. 4 (Oct. 1948): 425–434.

Sayers, Dorothy L. UNPOPULAR OPINIONS. London: Victor Gollancz Ltd., 1947.

Schenck, Remsen Ten Eyck. "Baker Street Fables." *Baker Street Journal* 2, No. 2 (Apr. 1952): 85–92.

———. "The Effect of Trades Upon the Body." *Baker Street Journal* 3, No. 1 (Jan. 1953): 31–36.

Schweickert, William P. "The Palace Clock." *Varieties of Ash* 1, No. 2 (Jan. 1992): 49–51, 54.

Sellars, Mrs. Crighton. "Dr. Watson and the British Army." *Baker Street Journal* [O. S.] 2, No. 3 (July 1947): 332–341.

Simon, André L., ed. WINES OF THE WORLD. New York, Toronto, London, and Sydney: McGraw-Hill Book Company, 1967.

Simpson, A. Carson. NUMISMATICS IN THE CANON. PART II: A VERY TREASURE OF COIN OF DIVERS REALMS. Philadelphia, Pa.: International Printing Company, 1958.

Stephens, Charles B. "Holmes's Longest Shot?" *Baker Street Journal* [O. S.] 3, No. 1 (Jan. 1948): 44–46.

Tracy, Jack, with Jim Berkey. SUBCUTANEOUSLY, MY DEAR WATSON: SHERLOCK HOLMES AND THE COCAINE HABIT. Bloomington, Ind.: James A. Rock & Company, Publishers, 1978.

Umansky, Harlan L. "An Adventure in 'Wild Surmise.' " *Baker Street Journal* 32, No. 1 (March 1982): 25–29.

Utechin, Nicholas. "*The* Treasure." *Sherlock Holmes Journal* 20, No. 1 (Winter 1990): 1–2.

Webster, H. T. "Observations on Sherlock Holmes as an Athlete and Sportsman." *Baker Street Journal* [O. S.] 3, No. 1 (Jan. 1948): 24–31.

Weller, Philip. "A Relative Question." In FRANCO-MIDLAND HARDWARE COMPANY INTERIM REPORT 1991: THE FINAL PROBLEM CONTRACT REVIEWED, edited by Philip Weller, 33–34. Hornsea, England.: Franco-Midland Hardware Company, 1991.

———. "On Jezails and Things Afghan." *New Baker Street Pillar Box* 31 (Feb. 1998): 40–41.

Whitworth, George Clifford. AN ANGLO-INDIAN DICTIONARY: A GLOSSARY OF INDIAN TERMS USED IN ENGLISH AND OF SUCH ENGLISH OR OTHER NON-INDIAN TERMS AS HAVE OBTAINED SPECIAL MEANING IN INDIA. London: Kegan Paul, Trench & Co., 1885.

Williams, H. B. "The Unknown Watson." *Baker Street Journal* 13, No. 1 (March 1963): 43–45.

Williams, Molly Gabriel. "What Watson Did Not Know." *Baker Street Journal* 29, No. 3 (Sept. 1979): 150–51.

Williamson, J. N. "Sherlock Holmes and Boxing." In ILLUSTRIOUS CLIENT'S CASE-BOOK, edited by J. N. Williamson and H. B. Williams, 55–56. Indianapolis, Ind., The Illustrious Clients, 1948.

———. " 'The Latest Treatise Upon Pathology.' " *Baker Street Journal* 6, No. 4 (Oct. 1956): 208–214.

Wolf, Ben. "Zero Wolf Meets Sherlock Holmes." *Baker Street Journal* 14, No. 2 (June 1964): 108–117.

Wolff, Julian. "A Narcotic Monograph." *Baker Street Journal* 13, No. 3 (Sept. 1963): 182–183.

———. PRACTICAL HANDBOOK OF SHERLOCKIAN HERALDRY. New York: Privately printed, 1955.

Zeisler, Ernest Bloomfield. "A Chronological *Study in Scarlet*." *Baker Street Journal* 7, No. 3 (July 1957): 133–140.

THE HOUND OF THE BASKERVILLES

Austin, Bliss. "Dartmoor Revisited, or Discoveries in Devonshire." A BAKER STREET CHRISTMAS STOCKING. Pittsburgh, Pa.: The Hydraulic Press, 1964.

Baring-Gould, Sabine. A BOOK OF DARTMOOR. London: Wildwood House, 1982, reissuing the 1900 Methuen & Co. edition.

———. DEVON. London: Methuen & Co., 1907.

Bedford, Michael, and Bruce Dettman. " 'A Cunning Preparation.' " *Baker Street Journal* 16, No. 4 (Dec. 1966): 231–233.

Beeching, Wilfrid A. CENTURY OF THE TYPEWRITER. Bournemouth, Dorset, England: British Typewriter Museum Publishing, 1990.

Boucher, Anthony. "Footnote to a Footnote." *Baker Street Journal* 18, No. 2 (June 1968): 100–101.

———. "The Records of Baker Street." *Baker Street Journal* [O. S.] 4, No. 1 (Jan. 1949): 97–104.

Brody, Howard. "The Location of Baskerville Hall." *Baker Street Journal* 29, No. 4 (Dec. 1979): 229–234, 247.

Bryan-Brown, Frederick. "Sherlockian Schools and Schoolmasters." *Sherlock Holmes Journal* 3, No. 1 (Summer 1956): 2–7.

Burton, Michael L. "On the Hound." *Baker Street Journal* 25, No. 3 (Sept. 1975): 154–158.

Cabell, Branch. "Fifteenth Letter: To Richard Cabell of Buckfastleigh, Devon, Armiger, Lord of the Manor of Brooke." In LADIES AND GENTLEMEN, 195–210. New York: Robert M. McBride & Company.

Calamai, Peter. "A Peek in Mrs. Hudson's Scrapbook: Victorian Newspaper Accounts of Sherlock Holmes." *Canadian Holmes* 23, No. 3 (Spring 2000): 4–17.

Campbell, Maurice. "The Hound of the Baskervilles—Dartmoor or Herefordshire?" *Guy's Hospital Gazette* 67 (May 30, 1953): 196–204. Reprinted, New York: Magico Magazine, n.d.

Christ, Jay Finley. "The Pipe and the Cap." *Baker Street Journal* 9, No. 1 (Jan. 1959): 43–45.

———. "A Very Large Scale Map." *Sherlock Holmes Journal* 6, No. 3 (Winter 1963): 72–74.

Clark, Benjamin S. "Dr. Mortimer Before the Bar." In BEST OF THE PIPS, 97–106. New York: Five Orange Pips, 1955.

Clyne, Robert. *Baker Street Journal* 3, No. 1 (Jan. 1953): 60, 62 (Baker Street Mailbag).

Cooke, Catherine. "We Found Ourselves at the Northumberland Hotel." In HOUND AND HORSE, A DARTMOOR COMMONPLACE BOOK, edited by Shirley Purves, 10–13. London: Sherlock Holmes Society of London, 1992.

Cooper, A. G. "Holmesian Humour." *Sherlock Holmes Journal* 6, No. 4 (Spring 1964): 109–113.

Cornell, Philip. "Blackmail's Dark Waters." *Passengers' Log* 7, No. 2 (Jan. 2004): 11–14.

Curjel, Harald. "The Dartmoor Campaign." *Sherlock Holmes Journal* 12, No. 2 (Winter 1975): 41–46.

Davies, Bernard. "Radical Rethinks on Baskervillean Problems—I." In HOUND AND HORSE, A DARTMOOR COMMONPLACE BOOK, edited by Shirley Purves, 28–34. London: Sherlock Holmes Society of London, 1992.

———. "Railways and Roads in 'The Hound.' " *Sherlock Holmes Journal* 14, No. 2 (Winter 1979): 52–56 (Part One), and 14, Nos. 3 & 4 (Summer 1980): 93–98, 109 (Part Two).

Davies, David Stuart. "The Strange Case of the Solitary Husband." *Baker Street Miscellanea* 60 (Winter 1989): 30–31.

Dickensheet, Dean W. "The Clubbable Watson." In A CURIOUS COLLECTION, edited by William J. Walsh, 6–11. Suffern, N.Y.: The Musgrave Ritualists Beta, 1971.

———. "Upon the Victorian Reticence of John H. Watson, M.D." *Baker Street Miscellanea* 22 (Summer 1980): 17–19, 38.

Djabri, Susan Cabell. THE STORY OF THE SEPULCHRE: THE CABELLS OF BUCKFASTLEIGH AND THE CONAN DOYLE CONNECTION. Wimbledon: Shamrock Press Ltd., 1990.

Donegall, Marquis of. "Who Painted Hugo Baskerville?" *Sherlock Holmes Journal* 3, No. 3 (Autumn 1957): 23, 24 (Wigmore Street Post-Bag).

Doyle, Arthur Conan. THE HOUND OF THE BASKERVILLES, edited, with an introduction, by W. W. Robson. Oxford and New York: Oxford University Press, 1993.

———. THE HOUND OF THE BASKERVILLES. New York: Bantam Books, 1949.

———. THE HOUND OF THE BASKERVILLES, Chapter XI. A Facsimile of the Original Manuscript and Commentary. New York: The Baker Street Irregulars, 2001.

Drazen, Patrick. "On the de Reszkes." *Camden House Journal* 4, No. 6 (June 1982): 2–4.

Evans, Dorothyanne. "Laura Lyons." In HOUND AND HORSE, A DARTMOOR COMMONPLACE BOOK, edited by Shirley Purves, 36–37. London: Sherlock Holmes Society of London, 1992.

Ewen, David. Home Book of Musical Knowledge. New York: Grolier, 1954.

Farrell, John. "A Fiddle, Opera, and Holmes." *Cormorant's Ring* 6, No. 2 (Fall 1999): 27–30.

Farrell, Stephen. "It Can't Be Quite a Dead Dog; There's Still More Life to Be Wrung Out of It: A Discourse upon Marksmanship in *The Hound*." In Hound and Horse, A Dartmoor Commonplace Book, edited by Shirley Purves, 46–47. London: Sherlock Holmes Society of London, 1992.

Ferreira, Jim. "The Question of the Rooftop Telescope." *The Hound* 5 (1996): 21–24.

Frisbie, Owen. "On the Origin of the Hound of the Baskervilles." In Best of the Pips, 51–55. New York: Five Orange Pips, 1955.

Gill, William H. "Always on Sunday, Watson!" *Sherlock Holmes Journal* 5, No. 2 (Spring 1961): 62, 64.

Goslin, Vernon. "Did Baskerville Stay at the Northumberland Hotel?" *Sherlock Holmes Journal* 18, No. 1 (Winter 1986): 7–8.

Green, Roger Lancelyn. "Baskerville Hall." *Sherlock Holmes Journal* 8, No. 2 (Spring 1967): 61.

Hare, Augustus J. C. Walks in London. New York: George Routledge and Sons, 1884. 2 vols. in one.

Harrington, Hugh T. "Stapleton's Solution." *Sherlock Holmes Journal* 21, No. 2 (Summer 1993): 50–51.

Harrison, Michael. Cynological Mr. Holmes: Conanical Canines Considered: Dog-lore and Dog-love in the Sherlockian Saga. New York: Magico Magazine, 1985.

Holly, Joy, and Vic Holly. "The Times of Dr. Mortimer." *Camden House Journal* 1, No. 6 (June 1979): 2–3.

Howard, Alan. "A New Year for the Hound." *Sherlock Holmes Journal* 2, No. 3 (Summer 1955): 3–6.

Howlett, Anthony D. Some Observations on the Dartmoor of Sherlock Holmes. London: Sherlock Holmes Society of London, 1979.

Hunt, A. Godfrey. "An Identification of the Northumberland Hotel." *Sherlock Holmes Journal* 18, No. 1 (Winter 1986): 8–9.

Hyder, William. "The Rise of the Underdog: Dr. Watson in *The Hound of the Baskervilles*." In From Baltimore to Baker Street, 66–76. Toronto: Metropolitan Toronto Reference Library, 1995.

Jackson, Steven. "Holmes and Bertillonage." *Sherlock Holmes Journal* 23, No. 1 (Winter 1996): 17–20.

Jaeger, Frederick J., and Rose M. Vogel. The Hound from Hell. Privately printed, 1972.

Jones, Rev. G. Basil. "The Dog and the Date." *Sherlock Holmes Journal* 2, No. 2 (Dec. 1954): 11–13.

Jones, Kelvin I. "The Geography of *The Hound of the Baskervilles*." *Sherlock Holmes Journal* 7, No. 3 (Winter 1965): 84–86, 96.

Kanto, S. "Stapleton no Shoutai" [The True Identity of Stapleton]. In THE WORLD OF SHERLOCK HOLMES, 1986. Summarised by Hirayama Yuichi in "Some Hound Scholarship from Japan." *The Hound* 1 (1992): 34–35. Reprinted in SHERLOCK HOLMES AND JAPAN, edited by Mitch Higurashi and Hirayama Yuichi, 79–84. New York: The Baker Street Irregulars, 2004.

Karlson, Katherine. "Promise Her Anything, But Give Her Bisulfate of Baryta Or Sherlock Holmes, Parfumeur." *Baker Street Journal* 28, No. 4 (Dec. 1978): 218–219.

Keefauver, Brad. ARMCHAIR BASKERVILLE TOUR. New York: Magico Magazine, 1995.

Kimball, Elliott. "Watson's Neurosis." In WATSONIANA, First Series, 33–49. Clinton, Conn.: Toille Press, 1962.

Klinefelter, Walter. EX LIBRIS A. CONAN DOYLE SHERLOCK HOLMES. Chicago: Black Cat Press, 1938.

Klinger, Leslie S. "What Kind of Person Reads *Playboy*? Sherlock Holmes!: An Interview with Hugh M. Hefner." *Baker Street Journal* 50, No. 2 (Summer 2000): 18–25.

Krogman, W. M. "Anthropology in *The Hound of the Baskervilles*." *Baker Street Journal* 20, No. 3 (Sept. 1970): 132–136.

Leavitt, Robert Keith. "Annie Oakley in Baker Street." In PROFILE BY GASLIGHT, AN IRREGULAR READER ABOUT THE PRIVATE LIFE OF SHERLOCK HOLMES, edited by Edgar W. Smith, 230–242. New York: Simon & Schuster, 1944.

———. "Who Was Cecil Forrester?" *Baker Street Journal* [O. S.] 1, No. 2 (Apr. 1946): 201–204.

Malloy, Michael P. "Notes on the Identity of Milverton's Murderer." *Baker Street Journal* 27, No. 4 (Dec. 1977): 198–200.

May, R. F. "*Hound of the Baskervilles*: A Botanical Enquiry." *Sherlock Holmes Journal* 6, No. 1 (Winter 1962): 26.

McGaw, Lisa. "Some Trifling Notes on Sherlock Holmes and Ornithology." *Baker Street Journal* 10, No. 4 (Oct. 1960): 231–234.

McNabb, Janice. THE CURIOUS INCIDENT OF THE HOUND ON DARTMOOR: A RECONSIDERATION OF THE ORIGINS OF *THE HOUND OF THE BASKERVILLES*. Toronto: Bootmakers of Toronto, 1984 (Occasional Papers, No. 1).

Miller, Ron. "Will the Real Sherlock Holmes Please Stand Up?" *Baker Street Journal* 22, No. 4 (Dec. 1972): 232–236.

Morley, Christopher. "Clinical Notes by a Resident Patient." *Baker Street Journal* [O. S.] 2, No. 2 (Apr. 1947): 138–143.

———. "Clinical Notes by a Resident Patient." *Baker Street Journal* [O. S.] 3, No. 1 (Jan. 1948): 32–43.

———. "Clinical Notes by a Resident Patient." *Baker Street Journal* [O. S.] 4, No. 1 (Jan. 1949): 39–46.

O'Brien, Emily. "Did Stapleton Escape to Samoa?" *Baker Street Journal* 27, No. 4 (Dec. 1977): 206–208.

Paget, Winifred. "Full Circle." *Sherlock Holmes Journal* 1, No. 1 (May 1952): 27–28.

Palmer, Stuart. "Notes on Certain Evidences of Caniphobia in Mr. Sherlock Holmes and His Associates." *Baker Street Journal* 5, No. 4 (Oct. 1955): 197–204.

Pasley, Robert S. "Breaking the Entail." *Baker Street Journal* 39, No. 2 (June 1989): 96–98.

Pattrick, Robert R. "Watson Writes from Baskerville Hall." *Baker Street Journal*, Christmas Annual (1960): 293–296.

Petersen, Svend. "When the Game Was Not Afoot." *Baker Street Journal* [O. S.] 4, No. 1 (Jan. 1949): 59–71.

Pickard, Charles M. "The Reticence of Doctor Mortimer." *Baker Street Journal* 7, No. 3 (July 1957): 153–155.

Purves, Shirley. "Consider the Hound." In Hound and Horse, A Dartmoor Commonplace Book, edited by Shirley Purves, 44. London: Sherlock Holmes Society of London, 1992.

Redfearn, Auberon. "Mortimer: His Medicine, His Mind, and His Marriage," In Hound and Horse, A Dartmoor Commonplace Book, edited by Shirley Purves, 40–42. London: Sherlock Holmes Society of London, 1992.

Redmond, D. A. "Some Chemical Problems in the Canon." *Baker Street Journal* 14, No. 3 (Sept. 1964): 145–152.

Robinson, Roger. "The Hound: Dartmoor or Oxfordshire?" *Sherlock Holmes Journal* 13, No. 2 (Summer 1977): 40–41.

Rosenblatt, Albert M. "Divorce, Canonical Style: Checkmate." *Baker Street Journal* 35, No. 1 (March 1985): 15–18.

Ruber, Peter A. "On a Defense of H. W. Bell." *Baker Street Gasogene* 3, No. 3 (1961): 15–17.

Schenck, Remsen Ten Eyck. *Baker Street Journal* 2, No. 4 (Oct. 1952): 232–233 (Baker Street Mailbag).

Schonberg, Harold. "Yet Another Case of Identity." *Sherlock Holmes Journal* 6, No. 4 (Spring 1964): 115–117.

Shepherd, Walter. On the Scent with Sherlock Holmes. London: Arthur Barker Limited, 1978.

———. On the Scent with Sherlock Holmes. Bloomington, Ind.: Gaslight Publications, 1987.

Southworth, Bruce E. "Mortimer's Motivation." *Baker Street Journal* 43, No. 1 (March 1993): 27–30.

Speck, Gordon R. "The Hound and the Stalking-horse." *Wheelwrightings* 9, No. 2 (Sept. 1986): 18–20.

Stern, Madeleine B. The Game's a Head. Rockville Centre, N.Y.: Paulette Greene, 1983.

Sutton, Margaret. "A History of the *Western Morning News*." *The Hound*, No. 3 (1994): 23–27.

Van Liere, Edward, M.D. "Sherlock Holmes and Doctor Watson, Perennial Athletes." *Baker Street Journal* 6, No. 3 (July 1956): 155–164.

Walsh, B. J. D. "The Railways of Dartmoor in the Days of Sherlock Holmes." In HOUND AND HORSE, A DARTMOOR COMMONPLACE BOOK, edited by Shirley Purves, 23–26. London: Sherlock Holmes Society of London, 1992.

Weller, Jane. "The 'High Lodge' Picnic." *New Baker Street Pillar Box*, No. 16 (Oct. 1993): 11, and private communication of July 19, 2000, with the editor.

———. "A Place of Pure Amusement?: The Museum of the Royal College of Surgeons." *The Hound* 2 (1993): 16–18.

Weller, Philip. "Barking Up the Wrong Yew Tree." *Shoso-In Bulletin*, No. 9 (1999): 175–192.

———. THE DARTMOOR OF "THE HOUND OF THE BASKERVILLES": A PRACTICAL GUIDE TO THE SHERLOCK HOLMES LOCATIONS. Bournemouth, England: Sherlock Publications, 1991.

———. THE HOUND OF THE BASKERVILLES: HUNTING THE DARTMOOR LEGEND. Tiverton, Devon, England: Devon Books, 2001.

———. "Moor Maps and Mileages." *The Hound* 4 (1995): 3–6.

———. "The Mire and the Moor." *The Hound* 4 (1995): 26–29.

———. "Nightmare on Yew Alley." *The Hound* 6 (1997): 24–34.

———. "The Railways of the Hound: Platform One." *The Hound* 5 (1996): 4–7.

———. "Stapleton—An Un-Natural Naturalist." *The Hound* 1 (1992): 32–33.

———. "Take Moor Care: Some Considerations of Playing the Game on Dartmoor." *The Hound* 3 (1994): 4–8.

Wills-Wood, Chris. "A Humble MRCS: James Mortimer, Practitioner of Medicine." *The Hound* 2 (1993): 12–14.

Wimbush, J. C. "Watson's Tobacconist." *Sherlock Holmes Journal* 1, No. 2 (Sept. 1952): 35–36.

Wolff, Julian. PRACTICAL HANDBOOK OF SHERLOCKIAN HERALDRY. New York: Privately printed, 1955.

Wood, Peter H. "He Has Been Farming in Canada." *Canadian Holmes* 22, No. 3 (Spring 1999): 3–11.

Wright, Don. "The Hound of Hell Is Alive and Well." *Shoso-In Bulletin*, No. 8 (1998): 105–108.

Yates, Donald. "A Vindication of Stapleton." *Baker Street Journal* 52, No. 2 (Summer 2002): 40–46.

THE VALLEY OF FEAR

Adams, Robert Winthrop. "John H. Watson, M.D., Characterologist." *Baker Street Journal* 4, No. 2 (Apr. 1954): 81–92.

Asimov, Isaac. "The Ultimate Crime." More Tales of the Black Widowers. New York: Doubleday, 1976.

Baum, Christopher F. Letter. *Baker Street Journal* 29, No. 4 (Dec. 1979): 238.

———. "The Problem of Porlock." *Baker Street Journal* 28, No. 4 (Dec. 1978): 220–21.

Bell, H. W. "Three Identifications." In Profile by Gaslight: An Irregular Reader about the Private Life of Sherlock Holmes, edited by Edgar W. Smith, 283–289. New York: Simon & Schuster, 1944.

Bengis, Nathan. "What Was the Month?" *Baker Street Journal* 7, No. 4 (Oct. 1957): 204–214.

Bimba, Anthony. The Molly Maguires. New York: International Publishers, 1932.

Boucher, Anthony. Introduction to The Final Adventures of Sherlock Holmes, by Arthur Conan Doyle. Vol. 1, v–xviii. New York: Limited Editions Club, 1952.

———. "On 'Scowrer.' " In West by One and by One, edited by Poul Anderson, 3–4. San Francisco: Scowrers and Molly Maguires of San Francisco and the Trained Cormorants of Los Angeles County, 1965.

Broehl, Wayne G., Jr. The Molly Maguires. New York: Chelsea House, 1983.

Buchholtz, James. "A Tremor at the Edge of the Web." *Baker Street Journal* 8, No. 1 (Jan. 1958): 5–9.

Calamai, Peter. "Pressmen Down Like Flies." In Bimetallic Question. Montreal: Bimetallic Question, 2000, n.p.

Castner, B. M. "The Professor and *The Valley of Fear*." In West by One and by One, edited by Poul Anderson, 67–81. San Francisco: Scowrers and Molly Maguires of San Francisco and the Trained Cormorants of Los Angeles County, 1965.

Conway, William H., and Lynda L. Conway. Valley of Fear & The Molly Maguires. Cincinnati, Ohio: Classic Specialties Books, 1996.

Cooke, Catherine. "The Ancient Manor House of Birlstone." In Murderland: A Companion Volume to The Baker Street Irregulars' Expedition to The Valley of Fear, edited by Steven T. Doyle, 71–82. New York: The Baker Street Irregulars, 2004.

———. "A Certain Gracious Railway Station." *Sherlock Holmes Railway Journal* 2 (1994): 37–42.

Cox, David Talbott. "Poor Sherlock." *Baker Street Journal* 24, No. 4 (Dec. 1974): 210–213.

Cox, J. Randolph. "A. Conan Doyle, Dime Novelist; or, Magnetic Attractions for Bibliophiles." *Baker Street Miscellanea*, No. 42 (Summer 1985): 32–33.

Crown, H. T., and Mark T. Major. A Guide to the Molly Maguires. Frackville, Pa.: Broad Mountain Publishing Company, 2003.

Cypser, Darlene. "Barker, The Hated Rival." *Baker Street Journal* 35, No. 4 (Dec. 1985): 211–212.

Dandrew, Thomas. "The Porlock Puzzle: An Abbreviated Solution." *Baker Street Journal* 26, No. 1 (March 1976): 6–8.

Dardess, John, M.D. "On the Dating of *The Valley of Fear*." *Baker Street Journal* [O. S.] 3, No. 4 (Oct. 1948): 481–482 (Letters to Baker Street).

Decker, Jennifer. "Piercing the Veil at Last." *Sherlock Holmes Journal* 19, No. 3 (Winter 1989): 88–91.

Dewees, F. P. THE MOLLY MAGUIRES: THE ORIGIN, GROWTH, AND CHARACTER OF THE ORGANIZATION. New York: B. Franklin, 1969 (reprint of 1877 edition).

Dickensheet, Dean W. " 'Two Good Men.' " In WEST BY ONE AND BY ONE, edited by Poul Anderson, 145–151. San Francisco: Scowrers and Molly Maguires of San Francisco and the Trained Cormorants of Los Angeles County, 1965.

Doyle, Arthur Conan. RODNEY STONE. London: Smith, Elder & Co. and New York: D. Appleton & Co., 1896. Reviewed in *The Bookman*, Jan. 1897, 473–474.

———. THE VALLEY OF FEAR, edited, with an introduction, by Owen Dudley Edwards. Oxford and New York: Oxford University Press, 1993.

Doyle, Steven T., ed. MURDERLAND: A COMPANION VOLUME TO THE BAKER STREET IRREGULARS' EXPEDITION TO THE VALLEY OF FEAR. New York: The Baker Street Irregulars, 2004.

Foss, T. F. "The Case of the Professor's Ineptitude." *Sherlock Holmes Journal* 8, No. 4 (Summer 1968): 125–126.

Gibson, Theodore W. "The Birlstone Masquerade." *Baker Street Journal* 6, No. 3 (July 1956): 168–169.

Hammer, David L. TO PLAY THE GAME: BEING A TRAVEL GUIDE TO THE NORTH AMERICA OF SHERLOCK HOLMES. Dubuque, Iowa: Gasogene Press, Ltd., 1991.

Helling, Cornelius. "Secret Societies." *Sherlock Holmes Journal* 5, No. 1 (Winter 1960): 29 (Wigmore Street Post-Bag).

Kennedy, Bruce, and Robert Watson Douty. IN THE FOOTSTEPS OF BIRDY EDWARDS. Privately printed, 1980.

Kenny, Kevin. MAKING SENSE OF THE MOLLY MAGUIRES. London: Oxford University Press, 1998.

Klinefelter, Walter. ORIGINS OF SHERLOCK HOLMES. Bloomington, Ind.: Gaslight Publications, 1983.

Klinger, Leslie S. "Paging Through the Canon." *Wigmore Street Post Office Journal* 12 (Summer 1998): 12–14.

Knox, Ronald A. "The Mystery of Mycroft." In BAKER STREET STUDIES, edited by H. W. Bell, 131–157. London: Constable & Co., 1934.

Koch, Hugo. SOME OBSERVATIONS UPON THE DATE OF THE TRAGEDY OF BIRLSTONE: THE EVIDENCE OF WHITAKER'S ALMANACK: 1890. New York: Privately printed, 1999.

Krejci-Graf, Dr. Karl. "Contracted Stories." *Baker Street Journal* 16, No. 3 (Sept. 1966): 150–157.

Lellenberg, Jon. " 'Miss Porlock, I Presume?' " In Murderland: A Companion Volume to The Baker Street Irregulars' Expedition to The Valley of Fear, edited by Steven T. Doyle, 91–93. New York: The Baker Street Irregulars, 2004.

Lewis, Arthur H. Lament for the Molly Maguires. New York: Harcourt, Brace & World, 1964.

Liljegren, S. B. Irish Element in The Valley of Fear. Uppsala: A.-B. Lundequistska Bokhandeln, and Copenhagen: Ejnar Munksgaard, 1964 (Irish Essay and Studies, No. 7).

Malloy, Michael P. "On the Track of Moriarty: The Valley of Fear." *Baker Street Journal* 27, No. 1, (March 1977): 24–26.

McDermott, Russell. "Porlock, the Professor, and Colonel James." *Baker Street Journal* 27, No. 1 (March 1977): 43.

Melander, Wayne. "The Early American Holmes." *Baker Street Journal* 29, No. 4 (Dec. 1979): 221–228.

Merriman, Charles O. "A Case of Identity—No. 2." *Sherlock Holmes Journal* 5, No. 3 (Winter 1961): 83–86.

Montgomery, James. A Case of Identity. Philadelphia, Pa.: International Printing Company, 1955.

———. "Paging Birdy Edwards." Shots from the Canon. Philadelphia, Pa.: International Printing Company, 1953. (Montgomery's Christmas Annual.)

Morley, Christopher. "Was Sherlock Holmes an American?" In 221b: Studies in Sherlock Holmes, edited by Vincent Starrett, 5–15. New York: The Macmillan Company, 1940.

Newton, G. B. "The Date of *The Valley of Fear*." *Sherlock Holmes Journal* 2, No. 4 (Winter 1955): 38–42.

Nordberg, Nils. "Sherlock Holmes in the Claws of the Confidence Men; or, The Misadventures of a World Detective." *Dime Novel Round-Up* 69, No. 5 (Oct. 2000): 147–159.

Olding, Alan. "The Spy Who Stayed in the Warm." *News from the Diggings*, Christmas Edition (1981): 3–4. Reprinted in *Sherlock Holmes Journal* 16, No. 2 (Summer 1983): 42–43.

Parker, Hyman. "Birdy Edwards and the Scowrers Reconsidered." *Baker Street Journal* 14, No. 1 (March 1964): 3–7.

Pinkerton, Allan. The Molly Maguires and the Detectives. New York: G. W. Gillingham Co., 1897 (New and Enlarged Edition).

Pollock, Donald K., Jr. Letter. *Baker Street Journal* 29, No. 2 (June 1979): 110.

Potter, Barrett. "Sherlock Holmes in Gilded Age New York." *Baker Street Journal* 30, No. 4 (Dec. 1980): 235–242.

Prestige, Colin. "A Study in Fear or the Scarlet Valley." *Sherlock Holmes Journal* 9, No. 2 (Summer 1969): 63–64; Addendum, 9, No. 4 (Summer 1970): 142–143.

Randall, David A. "The Valley of Fear Bibliographically Considered." *Baker Street Journal* [O. S] 1, No. 2 (Apr. 1946): 232–237.

Reed, Linda J. "Moriarty and the Molly Maguires." *Wheelwrightings* 13, No. 2 (Sept. 1990): 26–28.

Schorin, Howard R. "Cryptography in the Canon." *Baker Street Journal* 13, No. 4 (Dec. 1963): 214–216.

Siddeley, Leslie. "The Rise and Fall of Fraternal Insurance Organizations." *Humane Studies Review* 7, No. 2 (Spring 1992).

Smedegaard, Paul B. "Porlock—Piercing the Nom De Plume." *Baker Street Journal* 25, No. 3 (Sept. 1975): 164–165, 176.

Smith, Edgar W. "On the Authorship of the Tales-Within-the Tales." In THE THIRD CAB, 42–47. Boston: Privately printed, 1960.

Speck, Gordon R. "Fred Porlock's Identity." *Columbine's New-Fangled Banner*, No. 9 (Aug. 1986): 7–8.

Stephens, Charles B. "The Birlstone Hoax." *Baker Street Journal* [O. S.] 4, No. 1 (Jan. 1949): 5–11.

Stix, Thomas L. "Who's Afraid of the Big Bad Moriarty?" *Baker Street Journal* 12, No. 4 (Dec. 1962): 200, 243.

Strum, George H. "Doubleday's Code." *Baker Street Journal* 43, No. 2 (June 1993): 115–117.

Thomas, David St. John. Introduction to BRADSHAW'S GENERAL RAILWAY AND STEAM NAVIGATION GUIDE FOR GREAT BRITAIN AND IRELAND for August 1887. Reprint. Newton Abbot, England: David & Charles, 1968.

Tracy, Jack. "The Portalis Sale of 1865." *Baker Street Journal* 26, No. 1 (March 1976): 29–33.

Trudeau, Noah Andre. "Fred Porlock—Probing 'A Link in the Chain.' " *Baker Street Journal* 26, No. 1 (March 1976): 9–10, 22.

Van Liere, Edward J. "Sherlock Holmes and Doctor Watson, Perennial Athletes." In A DOCTOR ENJOYS SHERLOCK HOLMES, 117–126. New York, Washington, and Hollywood: Vanguard Press, 1959.

Waxenberg, Michael. "Organized Thoughts on Organized Labor, or Labour's Libels Lost in *The Valley of Fear*." *Baker Street Journal* 43, No. 2 (June 1993): 86–90.

Webster, Donald Alan. Letter. *Baker Street Journal* 30, No. 3 (Sept. 1980): 179–180.

Wolff, Julian. PRACTICAL GUIDE TO SHERLOCKIAN HERALDRY. New York: Privately printed, 1955.

———. "Re: Greuze." *Baker Street Journal* 12, No. 4 (Dec. 1962): 195–197 ("The Editor's Gas-lamp").

Wood, P. H. "Excellent, Watson! . . . An Almanac!" *Baker Street Journal* 44, No. 1 (March 1994): 34–39.

Zens, Paul. "A Case of Identity." *Baker Street Journal* 25, No. 2 (June 1975): 91–93.

Notes for Scholars

There are significant differences between this edition and Baring-Gould's classic *Annotated Sherlock Holmes*. Baring-Gould emphasised the "chronology" of the stories—the dates on which the events recounted in the stories actually occurred—and devoted a significant portion of his notes to that topic. Sherlockian "chronologisation" is a complex science, and I have not intended to belittle the efforts of the chronologists by summarising and relegating their work to an appendix following the text. However, to point out all of the "clues" used by various chronologists in reaching their conclusions would have multiplied the notes exceedingly. Students of the techniques of devising a chronology are advised to read Andrew Jay Peck's introduction to *"The Date Being—?": A Compendium of Chronological Data*, available in an expanded and revised edition by Judge Peck and this editor.

There are at least three starting points for a modern textual analysis of each story: the *Strand Magazine* version, the original English book version, and the original American book version, which have surprising differences. Also important to any student of the text are the *Oxford Sherlock Holmes*, edited generally by Owen Dudley Edwards, and the Heritage (Limited Editions Club) edition of the Canon, edited by Edgar W. Smith. Both purport to present "definitive" text, the former with notes. My own version of the text relies most heavily on the English book text of the stories, under the theory that these versions received the most careful review from the author. However, "careful" review is a relative term, and numerous textual problems exist. In my notes, I have indicated significant variations among the sources.

While an examination of the original manuscript of the story, to review changes made by the author before submission for publication, would be very valuable, of the 56 stories, only 37 manuscripts are extant, and all but 13 are in the hands of private collectors, unavailable to students. Five of the manuscripts have been published in facsimile, "The Priory School," "The Dying Detective," "The Lion's Mane," "Shoscombe Old Place," and "The Six Napoleons." Scholars have examined a few manuscripts *in situ* and published their notes, and I have taken advantage of those available resources. In an apparent scholarly "first," I was also able to compare a typescript of the author's manuscript of "The Six Napoleons" to the published version and note significant changes made *after* submission of the manuscript.

Acknowledgements

The evolution of the volumes has been a long one, and there are many who helped me along the way. My patient friends Alan Olding, Roger Johnson, Philip Weller, and Bill Hyder spent a great deal of time under very short deadlines correcting errors in the manuscript, but they are blameless for those that remain! Christopher Roden provided early discouraging words that led me to the right path, and he has been a friend ever since. Steven Doyle and Mark Gagen edited and published the *Sherlock Holmes Reference Library*, from which these volumes grew, and invested in the results when no one else was interested. Michael Dirda introduced me to my publisher and was "midwife" to these volumes—I hope that his hopes have been fulfilled.

My Sherlockian mentors Otto Penzler, Peter Blau, Don Pollock, Nicholas Meyer, David Stuart Davies, Julie Rosenblatt, Chris Redmond, and Bernard Davies helped me in countless ways. Jerry Wachs, Al Rosenblatt, Catherine Cooke, Dick Sveum, Peter Calamai, Hirayama Yuichi, Bill Barnes, Dan Stashower, Costa Rossakis, and Bob Katz, to mention only a few, have been generous with their friendship. Nicholas Utechin and especially Steve Rothman, editors of the world's leading Sherlockian journals, have been immensely supportive of my work from the beginning. Kinsprit Susan Dahlinger kindly read parts of this book in draft and gave me critical insights. Jerry Margolin, the world's greatest collector of original Sherlock Holmes art, was a great help with the illustrations, including loans of precious items. Mike Whelan generously took vacation time to read and correct the introduction and was always available for wise counsel and friendship. George Vanderburgh helped me get started with scans of relevant text, and Bill Cochran kindly made the work of Newt and Lillian Williams available to me. John Sohl and John Farrell, fellow members of the Goose Club of the Alpha Inn of Santa Monica first pointed me in scholarly directions. Countless other Sherlockians made contributions on research topics, which I have attempted to acknowledge *in situ*. My dear friend and occasional co-author Andy Peck gave general and constant support as well as specific suggestions.

This edition could not have been produced without the help of Ronald L. De Waal's *Universal Sherlock Holmes*, Jack Tracy's *Encyclopaedia Sherlockiana*, Steve

Clarkson's *Canonical Compendium*, and scores of other handbooks, reference works, indexes, and collections. Each of those essential reference works is the product of many, many hours of patient research and labour by pioneers who went largely unrewarded. My own work on the Holmes canon has made me bow down in admiration to those scholars who came before me, especially those who laboured before computers and such specialised reference works existed. This work is an attempt to stand on the shoulders of those giants.

The W. W. Norton team has been incredible. My editor Robert Weil's immediate enthusiasm for the project, thoughtful criticisms, careful pruning, and constant cheerleading gave the work its present shape. It was a delight (and relief) to find that Bob so closely shared my vision for these volumes. Janet Byrne and Patricia Chui got down into the trenches of the notes and made an enormous contribution, constantly suggesting new topics to annotate and then doing the initial spade work. Other Norton colleagues—Brendan Curry and Tom Mayer, who shepherded the materials through publication; Julia Druskin, production manager, who unblinkingly handled the daunting task of reproducing hundreds of illustrations; Jo Anne Metsch, who created the stunning design of both volumes; Chin-Yee Lai, who brilliantly designed the cover; Eleen Cheungy, who painstakingly oversaw the design of the jackets; Nancy Palmquist, managing editor; Bill Rusin, sales director—all earned my immense gratitude and admiration. Louise Brockett and Rachel Salzman brought unbounded energy to the publicity and promotion of the project. Special thanks to Drake McFeely, president, and Jeannie Luciano, publisher, whose belief in the project made it all possible.

Megan Underwood Beatie, Camille McDuffie, and Lynn Goldberg, at Goldberg McDuffie & Co., put immense effort and great inspiration into finding ways to bring this work to the attention of readers and reviewers and made the publicity process memorable, enjoyable, and rewarding for a first-timer.

My law partner, Bob Kopple, has been an unstinting cheerleader for the entire project from the beginning. My agent, Don Maass, was tireless and undaunted by numerous obstacles. My friend and attorney Jonathan Kirsch, who combines a brilliant law career with an astonishing quantity of biblical scholarship, not only provided essential help but is my constant rôle model.

My dear friend Barbara Roisman Cooper put in countless hours checking and correcting countless footnotes, and she has earned my deepest gratitude. Her husband, Marty, also contributed sage advice about publicity and put up with numerous Sherlockian events. Bob and Mallory Kroner, and Mike and Donna Sedgwick all warmed me with their friendship and smiled tolerantly at my constant ramblings on Sherlock Holmes.

My family has been understanding to a fault, and my children, Matt, Wendy, Stacy, Evan, and Amanda, have given me uncritical love. My parents, Jack and

Lenore, taught me to love books and people; sadly, neither survived to see this work published.

Lastly, and most of all, *the* woman, my beloved wife, Sharon: She gave me the impetus to begin this work; she gave me her own time, listening, reading, collating, checking, proofreading, and commenting; she allowed me to steal hundreds of weekend and evening hours from her and our family; and she gave me her unstinting friendship and love throughout. Without her, this work would not exist.